東吳

EASTERN WU
~ REALM OF THE SUN CLAN ~

BY T. P. M. THORNE

COVER ART BY T. P. M. THORNE

Cover art: *an artistic representation of China during the Han Dynasty. The region that is consistently controlled by the Sun clan is shaded in light green (it is an approximate representation); the region is known interchangeably as southern Yang Province or as Jiangdong ('River East', or 'East of the River') for its location relative to the Yangtze River. The grey area represents Jing Province and, to the far south, Jiaozhi Province and other remote areas; the Jing portion is fought over throughout this work (the Suns fight Jing's Governor, Liu Biao, initially and the Han Chancellor Cao Cao later on). The remaining area is either controlled by the Han government or is nominally loyal to it.*

TABLE OF CONTENTS

FOREWORD

This is my sixth historical novel taking place in the era that is known popularly as the time of the 'Three Kingdoms': it follows on directly from 'East of the River: Home of the Sun Clan' (though there is no obligation to read that prior work – this has been designed, like all of my work, to work in isolation) and aims to tell the story of that same family as they live through the rise of the warlord Cao Cao and the continuing decline of the Han Dynasty that has ruled China for hundreds of years. This novel is, in fact, set during the period prior to the actual Three Kingdoms (3K) era, better termed 'the last years of the Eastern Han' (the novel ends a whole decade before the last Han emperor abdicated), although that was when most of the more famous figures – Cao Cao, Guan Yu, Lü Bu, Yuan Shao, Zhou Yu, and, of course, Sun Jian and Sun Ce – were active: all of the aforementioned were actually dead by the time that the 3K era started, and many more – Liu Bei, Zhuge Liang and Cao Pi to name just three – did not live for long thereafter. Sun Quan was one of the few men that lived for decades after the fall of the Han – he outlived the Han by 32 years – and this novel is, in one sense, a telling of the story of how he rose from the position of brother and son of famous heroes to becoming a powerful warlord in his own right.

To tell the story of Sun Quan is to also tell the story of 'Bofu' (to use Sun Ce's style/courtesy name) during his last eventful years: it took me close to a fifth of the book to cover Bofu's last battles with the remnants of his former lord Yuan Shu's following and the subsequent clashes – political and military – with the Han emperor's ambitious 'guardian', Cao Cao. The remaining time is, by circumstance, the story of the last years of Bofu's close friend, 'sworn brother' and strategist, 'Gongjin' (as Zhou Yu is known throughout the main text, for it is his style name): it is impossible to tell the story of Sun Quan's rise without emphasising the integral part that Gongjin played, not least for his most famous exploit, namely the destruction of the Han navy at the 'Battle of Red Cliffs'.

But revisiting the years after the strategist Zhuge Liang first began his career has not been without its problems for this author: a fair few scenes in my first work, 'Crouching Dragon: The Journey of Zhuge Liang' were seen from the point of view of Sun Quan's court (despite the novel's 'protagonist' being a vassal of Sun Quan's rival Liu Bei), and yet those scenes (and the perspective that they were shown from) are also important to the story that I have to tell in this work. I therefore made a compromise: there are a small number of scenes in the last three acts (Zhuge Liang meeting Sun Quan's court for the first time, Sun Quan's 'slicing of the table to demonstrate his authority' and some of the 'war room' scenes during the Battle of Red Cliffs are the most obvious examples) that draw upon existing scenarios and reuse *dialogue* from 'Crouching Dragon' – *all narrative is rewritten* – though, where possible, those 'shared scenes' are extended or shortened to better focus on the Sun clan. The overwhelming majority of the content of those last three acts is, like the entirety of the preceding acts, newly-presented work by its very nature: different focal points include Sun Quan's cousin Ben's loyalty dilemma, the loss of loved ones after various political and tactical missteps and the resulting internal strife that Quan was desperate to conceal from allies, rivals and enemies alike.

The relatively plentiful historical documents that survive are my main source of inspiration, although there are moments when 'information gaps', inconsistencies between sources or the need for strong characterisation – my main focus - mean that I must be inventive: I shall let my audience be the judge of what resulted (as usual) and hope that you enjoy it.

T. P. M. Thorne, the author

PROLOGUE: A WORD BEFORE PARTING

Two men in plain robes and simple black caps left the grand audience hall of their lord and moved to the treasury offices nearby; their short walk through the streets of the southern city of Chaisang was deliberately slow despite the general mood being one of great urgency. One of the men turned to the other upon reaching the building and said, "After you."

"No, after you," the other man replied mechanically.

"Not much interested in etiquette today, Gongjin...?" the first man asked dryly.

The second man – Zhou Yu of Lujiang, whose courtesy name was 'Gongjin' – smiled slightly and said, "Have we not both had enough of 'etiquette' today, Ziheng...?"

The first man – Lü Fan of Xi, whose courtesy name was 'Ziheng' – sighed and replied, "I won't disagree. But please, go ahead anyway, and I will have tea brought for us."

Zhou Yu nodded silently and passed his friend and colleague, who then turned to a junior official and said, "Have a servant bring us tea, please."

Zhou Yu and Lü Fan were sat together in the meeting room of the treasury office within minutes, with Lü as host and Zhou as guest. Lü Fan sipped his tea from a dish and stared at Zhou Yu, who had opted to sit with an empty dish and stare at it blankly: the two were uncharacteristically silent for several minutes before Lü said, "You're absolutely committed to this plan of yours, then."

"What other choice have I...?" Zhou Yu retorted as his eyes turned from the dish to his friend. "In some ways, Ziheng, nothing has changed: Jing is a problem just as it always has been, and ever since those first heady days when Bofu, you and I were first able to lead the people of Jiangdong into battle against Liu Biao and Huang Zu in an effort to avenge the death of Bofu's father, I-!"

"But that's not what 'has not changed', is it...?" Lü Fan asked.

"...No," Zhou Yu sighed. "No, it isn't."

"Bofu" was the courtesy name of Sun Ce, whose birth age was similar to Zhou Yu and Lü Fan and whose charisma, strength and courage had taken the grieving Sun clan forward and elevated them from leaders of a vassal militia to rulers of a quarter of Han Dynasty China.

"What do you hope to achieve...?" Lü Fan asked.

"...Is that not obvious...?" Zhou Yu chortled. "I thought that you and I agreed on everything of this nature, Ziheng! I thought-!"

Zhou Yu suddenly paused.

"...Are you alright...?" Lü Fan prompted.

"Yes, yes, of course," Zhou Yu insisted. "I was just thinking and became distracted, that's all."

"...Alright," Lü Fan said cautiously. "To answer your question, Gongjin, I do, of course, agree with you on the 'Liu' matter and always did: the sudden improvement of the man's fortunes – and in no other way more than his acquisition of an army of tens of thousands that includes bandits and Yuan Shu's former- ...What's so funny?"

"Nothing," Zhou Yu insisted, despite the fact that he was smiling inexplicably; he gestured slightly and said, "Please, go on."

"...Alright," Lü Fan replied. "As I was saying, I- ...Oh, I see why you laugh: yes, that took me a moment... it is the same things, over and over... but I must continue. Yes, I want to see Liu's threat eliminated and will resort to any scheme to achieve it because I see in him the greatest threat at present."

"So why do you ask why I employ controversial schemes, make strange alliances and whatnot?" Zhou Yu asked. "Is there some other way to end the threat and work toward our other goals – the removal of Liu Zhang of Yi Province as a threat, confronting the ever-present Cao Cao, and the founding of a strong southern state that can grow and prosper under the benevolent rule of the Sun clan of Fuchun...?"

"...Not, I admit, that I can see," Lü Fan replied. "Perhaps I just wondered whether this latest excursion was another great adventure, and that maybe you hoped to find yourself another beauty like Lady Qiao...?"

Zhou Yu – whose epithets included 'Handsome Zhou' in reference to his appearance – smiled and said, "My lady is enough for me, Ziheng, and I think that you are being flippant now. What is it that you fear?"

"...You are an irreplaceable foundation stone, Gongjin," Lü Fan replied. "Your genius far exceeds mine; the army admire you as much as Bofu; you will one day be a great patron of the arts as well as our finest field officer and Chief Commander. Don't take risks that-"

"I have heard this twice from Lu Su," Zhou Yu interrupted. "I do what I must."

"...Please promise me that you haven't got grander things in mind for Lu Su," Lü Fan said suddenly. "I know that you owe him for his generosity, but-"

"If – as you ever-so-slightly hint – the worst occurred, then I must think of the need for diplomacy while the state recovers its wits, after which I would hope that you would take my place," Zhou Yu replied. "I think that Bofu would prefer that in the long term, and it is for him that I do all this, because the vision of a powerful, independent south is our shared dream."

"It's why we're both doing all this in a way, isn't it...?" Lü Fan said wistfully. "I wonder when we shall see our dream truly realised..."

"The sooner I leave, the sooner that question will be answered," Zhou Yu replied.

"...Then I shall say 'good luck', Gongjin, and see you to your carriage," Lü Fan said. "We shall not speak again for a while, quite possibly, while you proceed with your efforts, and..."

"...Perhaps," Gongjin replied: he was smiling sadly as he spoke, because he understood his friend's fears and shared them. The future of the southern region of Jiangdong rested in Zhou Yu's hands, and the next steps taken, if he faltered, might cause yet more upheaval in a vast and eroded empire that was already on the verge of collapse.

****

ACT I: THE LITTLE CONQUEROR

1

Han Dynasty China was vast, but the politics of the north – where the imperial capital was always based, regardless of the exact location – was far-reaching, as it was, above all, an empire. But one place seemed to be gradually slipping free of the bonds: that place was the harsh, sparsely-populated southern part of Yang Province in the southwest, which was physically divided from the north by the Yangtze River and known colloquially as Jiangdong – 'East of the River'. Han influence had always been weak due to lack of commercial interest, since industry and agriculture were lacking and the main trade routes went north, toward the Middle East and Rome, rather than south, which simply led to tribal territories and the vast southern seas. That lack of influence was not always disadvantageous: the Han Empire had been subject to a number of mostly self-inflicted crises in recent times, and being unaffected by all but the worst of them was highly desirable.

Nowhere in the world was devoid of chaos: the Roman emperor Septimius Severus was busy trying to restore order in the wake of a damaging civil war, and that would mostly involve more resource-draining campaigns against foreign powers that were subject to Roman rule. For once, there was some similarity in situations: the Han Dynasty court was now trying to restore order in the wake of what had become known as the 'Dong Zhuo Crisis', the 'Yuan Brothers Feud', and, most recently, the 'Pretender Crisis' to name but three of the many disasters that had scarred the nation. But the people of the south had their own problems – some of them quite avoidable – and cared nothing for the political wrangling that was taking place beyond the north bank of the snaking Yangtze River.

Life in the Jiangdong region was tough: heavy rain, humidity, river pirates, marshlands and diseases and were a fact of life, as was the knowledge that a person was far less likely to be recognised for achievements by the history books. But once in a while, a person appeared that made the entire nation sit up and take notice: and at the heights of the so-called 'Yellow Turban Rebellion' – a million-man, Taoist-cult-instigated peasant uprising that brought the corrupt Han Dynasty to its knees 15 years earlier – a talented man appeared that outperformed most of the heroes of the north and quickly earned the moniker 'Tiger of Jiangdong'. His name was Sun Jian.

"…Do you think I'll be remembered in the same way as my father…? Do you think that people will say, 'Sun Ce was a great man, like Sun Jian'…?"
The eldest son of Sun Jian asked the question as he moved his eyes back and forth between two of his most trusted advisers and friends – the famously handsome and clever Zhou Yu and the quiet, unassuming genius Lü Fan.
"…Why wouldn't they, Bofu?" Lü Fan replied, deliberately using Sun Ce's 'courtesy name' as a sign of their strong friendship.
"I dunno, Ziheng… I suppose that I just worry that I'll be remembered as a madman," Bofu chuckled. "I know that Old Cheng and the rest say that Dad was 'reckless' – well, I know that

well enough, 'cause I saw it with my own eyes, but... he'll be remembered for his loyalty to the Han, no matter what, but me, I'm... well, aren't I risking being labelled a traitor...?"

Zhou Yu – whose courtesy name was 'Gongjin' – laughed and said, "Nonsense, Bofu, nonsense: what's going on in Lujiang right now is what's defined as 'treachery', 'treason' and 'madness', not what we're doing."

"And us taking a piece of Guangling Prefecture...?" Bofu asked.

"Taking *back* a piece of Guangling Prefecture," Gongjin retorted. "That place is no more a part of Xu Province than Danyang was."

"Then there's me exploding at Wei Teng last week," Bofu said. "I saw you and that rude little friend of yours, 'Lu Su', sneaking off to discuss it, Gongjin: I'm sure that Ziheng probably took a few people off to one side for a chat, and Mother did too, probably."

"Lady Wu and I took Wei Teng 'off to one side' to tell him how lucky he was, and to please not rile you up any more, because she nearly did fall in that well," Lü Fan replied dryly.

"*Aiee*... she scared me, mainly 'cause I know she'd have done it," Bofu said. "That's what I mean! Even as 'unpredictable' as Dad was sometimes, did Mother ever threaten to throw herself down a well for anything *he* did...?"

"If I might just return to my 'sneaking off' with Lu Su for a minute...?" Gongjin asked. "Yes, I wanted to discuss your outburst with him, because yes, you're right, we do risk a bad reputation by your doing such things. Lu Su's not as useless as you insist, Bofu: in fact, I see him as a future visionary."

"If he ever learns to watch his tongue and not say stupid things," Bofu chortled; but after a pause, he sighed and added, "I... I suppose I shouldn't criticise him for that. Me and my brother have a worse problem, one that we inherited from Dad... *doing* stupid things. Dad did things that had a price... and that's what you were discussing with Lu Su, am I right...?"

Gongjin did not reply to the question, but his sombre expression betrayed his thoughts.

Sun Jian's greatest quality – and his greatest weakness – was his fearlessness. The 'Tiger of Jiangdong' was willing to take risks that made his contemporaries balk, and his first famous act – repelling a small band of pirates single-handedly with a bluff – actually preceded his military career; it came as no surprise, therefore, when he showed similar 'recklessness' during the Yellow Turban campaign. Sun Jian and his initial allies – of whom the most notable were the noble Huang Gai, the cautious Cheng Pu, the plain-speaking Han Dang and Sun's self-appointed bodyguard, Zu Mao – relieved the Yellow Turbans' siege of Wan City in Jing Province in such a short time that people wondered whether Sun Jian – who breached the city alone and at night to open the gates – was sent by the heavens. The victories continued, but the rewards were slow to materialise: 'The men of the north', Cheng Pu often remarked, 'look down on the south, so we should not hope for much'. Sun Jian was given other pacification assignments in the wake of the Yellow Turban Rebellion, however, and gained his first dedicated adviser in the wise Zhu Zhi as he travelled. It seemed to be inevitable that Sun Jian would one day become a national icon – but then the Liang Province Rebellion began.

The Imperial court had long been controlled by a small clique of elevated eunuch servants that were known as the 'Ten Attendants': they were corrupt and endlessly ambitious, and they had ensured that most senior roles were occupied by an ally or a person that was willing to pay their bribes. As a consequence, the rebellion in the northwest – which had, itself, resulted from local government corruption – was 'managed' by sending a succession of corrupt, inept or underqualified administrators and military leaders to confront the mixture of Qiang tribespeople and disaffected Han Chinese peasants. Sun Jian should have been called upon to lead an army, but he was made a military consultant and assigned to a contemptuous Han official that ignored all of his advice. To make matters worse, Sun Jian was fighting alongside a Liang Province general that had full autonomy and was playing both sides for personal gain: his name was Dong Zhuo, and within three years he would be the self-appointed Chancellor of State and an infamous tyrant that wielded the powerless boy emperor as a puppet and a tool.

"What worries me now is 'Excellency of Works' Cao Cao's future intent," Lü Fan admitted. "Is he the new Dong Zhuo, or is he simply misunderstood...?"
"Maybe we shouldn't worry too much about Cao," Bofu suggested. "After all, isn't Yuan Shao going to challenge him...? With an army that size, Cao's a dead man... in which case, we'd be better off worrying about what kind of man Yuan Shao is, and after being a slave to his brother for most of my life, I can't say I'm hopeful."
"Yuan Shao and Yuan Shu are as different as they are similar," Gongjin said. "I do not think that Yuan Shao would dare to risk his inherited place in society. But I also start to seriously doubt his ability to defeat Cao Cao, since he was none too effective against Dong Zhuo."
"True enough," Bofu sighed.

The Liang Province Rebellion was damaging to Sun Jian's reputation, but it wrongly cemented Dong Zhuo's reputation as a man of action and ensured him undeserved promotions. Sun Jian returned to Jiangdong with a label of a failure, while Dong continued the fight with the veteran general Huangfu Song; their assured victory against the weakened rebels was snatched away from them by the death of Emperor Ling, but Dong would enjoy another stroke of luck as an unforeseen opportunity allowed him to exploit the power vacuum that had been created in the aftermath of Ling's death.

The new Empress Dowager and her brother, Commander-in-Chief Hè Jin, immediately seized power for Ling's eldest son, but the surviving 'Ten Attendants' – who had been critically divided over who should inherit the throne – were keen to exert their authority over the Dowager and her son, now created Emperor Shao; the resulting feud led to the death of Hè Jin, the last of the 'Ten' and most of the palace eunuchs. Dong Zhuo – who had been invited to the capital Luoyang as additional military muscle by Hè Jin and his deputy Yuan Shao – used his newfound position as the highest-ranking military officer in the city to seize power, grant himself the highest civilian rank and establish his own followers as the new guardians of the young emperor. What followed was almost impossible to believe: Dong Zhuo deposed and quietly murdered Emperor Shao and the Dowager, and then he installed the deposed sovereign's younger half-brother, Prince Liu Xie, as Emperor Xian.

In reaction to the regicide and a subsequent violent purge of disaffected courtiers, Yuan Shao – who was, in addition to being the late Hè Jin's most trusted ally, the chieftain of one of the wealthiest and most influential clans in the empire – immediately called upon his fellow warlords to join his fight against Dong Zhuo. Sun Jian was one of the first to lend his might to the 'Eastern Pass Coalition' that hoped to defy the tyrant chancellor, but Jian's place in society affected his role from the first moment: despite his considerable achievements and a recently-awarded title of 'lesser marquis', Sun could not lead his own militia, since he was not a landowner or high-ranking administrator. The only option was to pledge his allegiance to a man that had the rights that he lacked, and his choice of 'master' – a choice that would affect the rest of his life – was Yuan Shu, the embittered, jealous brother of Coalition Commander Yuan Shao. Yuan Shu eagerly accepted the service of such a famous hero, but his plans extended beyond Sun's temporary servitude or his own place as the brother of his clan's chieftain: he had the intention of challenging Shao for the clan chieftainship and command of the Eastern Pass Coalition, and Shao unwittingly gave Shu the chance to do so when his orders amounted to little more than 'blockade the capital'. Dong Zhuo was barely challenged, and he continued to do as he pleased, including torturing and slaughtering anyone in Luoyang that was in any way related to the coalition members.

"...As we've said before, it's really Yuan Shao's fault that our clan's suffered in the way that it has," Bofu grumbled. "If he'd kept his brother in check, or done a better job against Dong Zhuo, maybe backed up Dad and Cao Cao instead of just *sitting there*..."
"And at the same time, he'd be to blame for the whole country suffering," Lü Fan suggested. "In his case, it is 'that one commits as great an evil as an evil man by doing nothing to stop him'. Dong Zhuo might have been stopped in two years, and the peace restored in three. Instead, it has been fifteen years since the Yellow Turban Rebellion, and they still ravage Yu Province; it has been fourteen years since the Liang Province Rebellion, and now the Qiang tribes rule the region unopposed and kill each other over it; it has been ten years since Dong Zhuo murdered Shaodi and seized the capital, and the wounds are still open... because it has been eight years since the greedy, childish Yuan brothers began their all-consuming feud, which ended only because of the death of one of them."
"And a gross miscalculation of their own power in the case of the one that died," Gongjin said. "I imagine that Yuan Shao will also overestimate his strength..."
"But will a Yuan's greed kill another Sun...?" Bofu murmured.

The inactivity of the Eastern Pass Coalition drove two of its lower-ranking volunteers close to madness: Sun Jian was one, and Yuan

Shao's best friend Cao Cao was the other. Both men decided that they would defy orders and act: Cao's efforts ended with a humiliating defeat, but while Sun Jian's began in much the same way, they ended with a crushing direct attack on Dong Zhuo's forces as the tyrant looted and burned Luoyang and began a westward retreat to the former Han capital Chang'an.

To the disgust of all, Dong Zhuo escaped, partly because Sun Jian's men were under-resourced and exhausted but mainly because Yuan Shao did nothing once again: Yuan Shu took credit for his vassals' successes and openly challenged his brother with a letter that denounced Shao's illegitimate birth and apparent incompetence. Yuan Shao's reaction was to order an attack on Sun Jian as he retreated from the gutted capital, which provoked a military retaliation from Yuan Shu: the Yuan feud had begun, and there was more fighting in the first few months than the coalition had seen in the years since it challenged Dong Zhuo.

The other leading coalition members were forced to take sides, despite their influence, because the Yuan clan outranked them all: the majority of the lesser members could go home or follow the warlord of their choice, but for Sun Jian – who just wanted to return to his hometown of Fuchun and never see a Yuan clansman again – a horrible truth awaited. Yuan Shu had, by the nature of the pledge that Sun Jian had made, seized full control of Jian's army and, somehow, Sun Jian himself: the hero and his clan now 'belonged' to Yuan Shu and had to follow his every selfish command. The first of those commands – which should have been to pursue Dong Zhuo and rescue the abducted imperial court – was to attack Yuan Shao's perceived ally Liu Biao, who was the Governor of Jing Province. Sun Jian was inwardly heartbroken as he returned to a place that he had once liberated from the Yellow Turbans, since his job was now to siege the same cities that he had once freed from sieges and attack the same people that he had so recently defended.

"...By your last statement, Bofu, I presume you mean 'Will adding your sword to the cause fought by Yuan Shao lead to your own demise'," Gongjin said. "It does not have to be the case: after all, you're an independent warlord now, appointed by the court as 'Marquis of Wu' and 'Rebellion-supressing General', with a region the size of Yuan's own four provinces under your control, even if you lack the population or resources to match. But why would we join Yuan anyway? What mandate for attacking the imperial capital does the man have...?"
"...True," Bofu replied. "Cao Cao could surprise us all and be a benevolent guardian for the emperor."
Lü Fan smiled and said, "Perhaps."
"...But all this talk about Yuan Shao just makes me think about Yuan Shu more and more, and about Father, and... and what happened to him," Bofu admitted. "And when I do that, I think about *Liu Biao*... and how I hate his kinsman Liu *Xun* for dragging me away from Jing, where I was so *close* to avenging Dad...!"

Sun Jian's Jing Province campaign was not a personal one: he had no quarrel with Liu Biao, but orders were orders. Sun did as he was told, and Liu Biao was soon placed under such pressure that there was only one solution if he did not want to cede the province to Yuan Shu: he ordered his followers to find a way to rid Jing of Sun Jian, even if that meant killing him by underhanded means. Liu Biao's powerful ally, Huang Zu, lured Sun Jian into an ambush and killed him; that ended Yuan Shu's Jing campaign and placed the role of Sun clan patriarch in the hands of Bofu's cousin Sun Ben, since Bofu was considered to be too young and inexperienced. The Sun clan's militia retreated to Yang Province, but the unsympathetic Yuan Shu was only interested in what service his human 'property' could still provide; in addition to that, Liu Biao's unapologetic stance left Bofu and his allies embittered and determined that Liu – and, if at all possible, Yuan Shu – would suffer for their attitudes somehow in the years to come.

"...The feud with Liu Biao will have to wait," Lü Fan insisted. "Right now, we-"
"Yeah, yeah, I know... we have to focus on Liu Xun, and what's left of Yuan Shu's following," Bofu grumbled. "...I still can't believe that Zhang Xun let himself be talked into going to Lujiang! Why didn't he come *here*...?"
"Who knows," Gongjin replied. "If he survives this, we'll ask him."
"He was always loyal to Yuan Shu... even after 'that'," Bofu sighed. "In a way, I shouldn't forgive him, but..."

When Bofu came of age, he demanded that Sun Ben – whose late father was Sun Jian's twin brother – relinquish control of the clan to him; regardless of whether Ben was glad to be relieved of the burden of dealing with Yuan Shu or it was genuine willingness to see Bofu inherit his father's role, the wish was granted. Bofu then confronted Yuan Shu and demanded the return of his father's men, to which the response was ridicule: the young, untested Bofu would need to prove his worth first by showing that he could raise an army of his own, a task which Yuan Shu dismissed as impossible. Bofu so impressed his father's surviving allies – Cheng Pu, Huang Gai, Han Dang and Zhu Zhi – that they joined his cause: Bofu had started to gather his own allies as well, including Gongjin, Lü Fan and a number of enthusiastic relatives. The new militia's first battle was with the local bandit king Zu Lang, who almost killed Bofu before retreating: the outcome impressed Yuan Shu enough to consider giving 'the boy' assignments, although the ambitious Shu continued to seek greater service from Sun Ben and Sun Jian's brother-in-law Wu Jing.

The first of Bofu's campaigns would be to seize Lujiang Prefecture in northern Yang Province from its Han-appointed Administrator, Lu Kang: the elderly Kang had rebuked Sun Jian and his son for taking orders from Yuan Shu, and a 'past offence' – Lu Kang having refused to see Bofu as he returned from Jing with his father's coffin – gave Bofu the 'reason' that he needed in order to carry out his mission. Lu Kang perished, and Lujiang became Yuan Shu's: the hungry warlord then ordered Bofu to seize the adjacent Jiujiang Prefecture, and then the prefectures in southern Yang, and Bofu complied. The appointed governor, Liu Yao, the tribes of Wu Prefecture, the powerful Buddhist cultist Ze Rong, the bandit king Zu Lang and the infamous wandering mercenary Taishi Ci were all pitted against Bofu, and one-by-one they were defeated, killed or compelled to join him.

The Sun clan's victories contrasted greatly with the losses that Yuan Shu was experiencing against his brother Shao and Cao Cao in the north, but hubris and insanity were driving Shu's actions by this point, and when Cao Cao – who had risen, four years into the Yuan feud, from Yuan Shao's vassal to imperial guardian by pure circumstance – suffered a disastrous self-inflicted loss whilst uprooting one of Dong Zhuo's former vassals from Wan City in Jing Province, Yuan Shu declared himself as the First Emperor of the Zhong Dynasty, an act that made him an isolated heretic and traitor at a single stroke. Thousands deserted Yuan Shu, and the Sun clan – who, by then, controlled most of Jiangdong – seized the opportunity and broke ties with Yuan Shu, removing his main military arsenal and exposing him to a coalition of warlords that eventually forced him to burn his capital to the ground and consider seeking refuge with, of all people, Yuan Shao. The Yuan brothers were reconciled at a distance, but Yuan Shu died on a dirt road with nothing to show for all of his efforts.

That should have been the end of it: Bofu was now free to take his revenge on Liu Biao, and he wasted no time in mobilising an army and a navy to advance to southern Jing and conquer it. But fate had been cruel: Yuan Shu's last surviving loyalists took his coffin to Lujiang Prefecture to seek refuge with Yuan Shu's chosen Administrator Liu Xun, but Liu betrayed them and declared as an independent warlord. The replacement of the divisive Yuan with imperial relative Liu Xun acted as an attractive and cohesive force for Yuan Shu's men, whether they were former loyalists or former deserters; they journeyed to Lujiang in their thousands, giving Liu Xun an army but providing him with a supply problem that he remedied by invading Jiangdong, attacking the rural farming region of Haihun County and assuming control of food production that was fuelling Bofu's campaign against Huang Zu. The threat forced Bofu to withdraw from Jing, as Liu Xun – who had a lot of new mouths to feed, and was hungry in other ways – had set his sights on the rest of Yang Province, and that meant Jiangdong.

"…I swear that I'll kill Liu Xun for this," Bofu growled.
"Please, Bofu, stick to the plan!" Gongjin said. "We-!"
"I meant 'after the plan', Gongjin," Bofu insisted. "I know the plan… I hate it, but I know it, understand it and intend to follow it, like it or not."
"…I hope so," Gongjin said. "Our success depends on it."
"…I'm going riding… maybe I might go hunting," Bofu decided.
"Alright," Gongjin said. "Are you going 'alone'…?"
"If you want to come along, you're welcome to," Bofu replied. "As you say, I won't be alone, will I…? I'll have a load of guards to protect me."
"I think that I shall go back to the chancellery," Lü Fan said. "Enjoy your hunt."
Bofu smiled and said, "I'll try to. You'll get a share of what I catch, Ziheng, so hope that I get lucky!"

Bofu left his home with Gongjin and his bodyguards and walked to the barracks stables: he was greeted by smiles and respectful bows at every stage of the journey.

"You promise that you'll stick to the plan...?" Gongjin said.

"Yes!" Bofu replied.

"And you promise that you'll let us keep up...?" Bofu's chief bodyguard – his distant cousin Sun Hè – asked bluntly.

"...We'll see," Bofu replied.

"*Aiee...* he's unbelievable," Sun Hè said to his colleague Song Qian. "We have to get ourselves fast horses or he'll be off on his own again."

Bofu entered the stables and slapped the chief stable-keeper's arm, saying, "Hey, Old Yin! Is he ready to go?"

'Old Yin' laughed and said, "Of course, Lord Sun!"

"Then let's not waste any more time!" Bofu said.

"Can you not give us those nags you gave us last time, Yin?" Sun Hè implored. "We want to be able to keep up with him!"

Bofu grinned and looked at Old Yin, who said, "I shall do my best."

Bofu led his bodyguards and Gongjin out of Qu'e City and onto the path that led to the hunting grounds: once again, Bofu was greeted by smiles, bows and calls by people of every age, class and profession.

"Perhaps he doesn't need us: the most that anyone might want to do is invite him to dinner," Sun Hè joked.

Bofu was grinning as he kept his horse at a steady trot; once he felt that he had fooled his guards for long enough, he urged his horse to a gallop and shouted, "**Race you!**"

"**AAAAAGH! Stop! Come back! I'll give up being a 'Sun' and go back to being 'Yu Hè' if you keep doing this to me!**" Sun Hè cried.

"**We have to catch up!**" Song Qian urged. "**Everyone hurry!**"

Gongjin laughed, stirred his horse and sped after Bofu, who was cackling maniacally and whooping with excitement. People were forced to move out of Bofu's way as he sped toward them, but most just laughed and waved him off: to some, it seemed that the Sun clan were Jiangdong, and Jiangdong was the Sun clan.

Hours later, Bofu led Gongjin and his exhausted bodyguards back to the city: they had caught a lot of game, and spirits were generally high.

"We'll let some of the men have some meat," Bofu said as he travelled. "Is there anyone I promised some meat to that I didn't already keep my promise...?"

"...Were we supposed to keep a list...?" Sun Hè asked.

Bofu laughed at the notion.

"...Do you think that you can stick to the plan now...?" Gongjin asked knowingly.

"Yeah," Bofu replied. "It'll hurt, pretending to be a toady... especially after Yuan Shu... but yeah."

****

2

The busy court of Lujiang Prefecture's Administrator, Liu Xun, had suddenly become a place where the future was completely uncertain. The administrator's chief adviser, Liu Yè, shook his head and said, "I am at a total loss, my lord, as to where we go from here. We're both distant relatives of His Majesty, so what we do now makes even less sense to me. We're independent, but from what...?"

"You're one of the many people in this room that told me to capture Yuan Shu's remaining vassals!" Liu Xun retorted. "We're independent from Yuan Shu's defunct regime and the web of control that is being weaved by Sun Ce! And we're also independent of the rest of Yang Province, which is controlled by *who* right now...?"

The officials exchanged nervous glances as Liu Yè replied, "The government: the *Han* government in Xuchang. Yuan Shu's appointed provincial inspector, Hui Qu, is a rebel with nowhere to run, if he is even still alive..."

Liu Xun waved his hand and said, "The Han government has no jurisdiction in Yang Province! The place is lawless! The Qian Hill Bandits, tribes, pirates and Sun Ce control the province now: I cannot hope to survive, and Lujiang cannot hope to remain out of Sun Ce's grip, if we do not act independently. The court's choice of governor, Liu Yao, is dead, so I shall act as a 'governor in waiting' might do and pacify the region myself. By capturing Yuan Shu's heir and minions, we prove to the court that we are not their enemy: that leaves us free to attack Jiangdong and start to take the region back – for the Han, of course – from that thief Sun Ce!"

"For the Han, 'of course'," Liu Yè snickered. "But will Sun Ce just let you do as you intend...? He also claims to be taking over Jiangdong 'for the Han', and he has titles from the court."

"But Sun Ce is not, as you have pointed out, an imperial relative, as I am," Liu Xun retorted. "He'll defer to my newfound might or fall by my sword!"

"...He's unlikely to 'defer', and he defeated us very easily last time, when he had far more distractions," Liu Yè noted. "We should not be so overconfident."

"On the contrary, I say to you that you should not underestimate what we can achieve," Liu Xun said. "Yuan Shu's army was divided by his last treacherous proclamation, but now that he is dead they seek a new man to follow, one that will not alienate them from the rest of the world. I am that man, Mister Liu Yè: already – just two weeks after Yuan Yao and the rest came into my possession – men have started to come here, turning over wanted Yuan family members and conspirators to us and asking if they can be part of what is to come! Thousands of men are already here, and thousands, maybe many *tens* of thousands more will follow!"

The officials murmured optimistically.

"...Sun Ce's actions will dictate the ease with which your plan will work, and the Han court's opinion is not yet known," Liu Yè suggested. "Your 'newfound might' mainly consists of locals and deserters, and we don't know if we can control them."

Liu Xun flicked his baggy sleeve as a sign of the highest contempt and said, "Stop demoralising my court! The Han's Excellency of Works, Cao Cao, is an old friend, and Sun Ce is an excitable pirate whose days of acting freely are at an end!"

One of Yuan Shu's loyalists – the adviser Yan Xiang – had been moving backwards and forwards between his lord's various domains in the months leading up to the inevitable end; he had at one point been feared missing, perhaps dead, only to reappear with some hired men to assist his lord's crossing into Xu Province. When that crossing failed, Yan Xiang left his lord once again and tried to secure an alternative escape route from a base near the Yang-Yu provincial border; he reacted anxiously at the news that Liu Xun was being self-servingly cautious, but the news that his lord was dead and that all of his efforts had been for nothing left him silent for some time.

"What will we do now, Mister Yan?" one mercenary asked.

"…I… I don't know," the thin, weary Yan Xiang admitted. "I'd planned for this moment from the second that he insisted that he would become… what he said that he had become. But now the moment is finally here, I'm strangely numb: I am not sure whether I should now honour my lord's memory, or think of the populace, or…"

"No offence, but we only want to know if we'll be paid," the mercenary said. "If Yuan is dead, then–"

"You'll be paid," Yan Xiang promised. "And I've decided: the best thing to do now is go into Yu Province, try and gather more forces, and then return to Yang and restore order, perhaps with Yuan Yin or the late lord's son as an untainted new ruler. That new order will need men like you, so expect to be paid extremely well, better than Cao Cao would pay you."

The mercenary smiled and said, "Well put, Mister Yan. It isn't that I was considering turning you over, necessarily, but there are other men that would."

"I know that very well," Yan Xiang replied as he examined a tear in the left sleeve of his weathered state robes. "Shall we go northward, then…?"

"Lead the way!" the mercenary said through laughter.

Bofu's cousin Sun Ben was based in a fenced military camp close to the Lujiang-Jiujiang prefectural border; Ben's younger brother, Sun Fu, had joined him once again so that they could plan their part of removing Liu Xun from Lujiang Prefecture.

"…Is Zhou Yu really serious about grovelling to Liu Xun?" Sun Fu asked of the reflective Sun Ben.

"Completely," Sun Ben replied. "My only worry is that it will be an obvious ruse: when has Bofu ever grovelled to anyone?"

"…Liu Xun is arrogant, and quite stupid too," Sun Fu suggested.

"I agree, but he has counsel that may see through it and warn him," Sun Ben replied.

"…We're throwing everything at Liu Xun, are we…?" Sun Fu asked.

"I'm not sure," Sun Ben admitted. "We were forced to abandon a campaign against Huang Zu in order to do this, and that will arouse suspicions that we might be vulnerable, so we have to leave good people in northwest Yuzhang to guard against Huang and Liu Biao."

"What I don't get is why Liu Xun attacked Haihun County if he's on the Han side now: so are we!" Sun Fu said. "He's abducted Yuan Shu's heir, Yuan Shu's coffin and whatever money and people he had left. What's he up to...?"

"Liu Xun isn't loyal to Yuan Shu's cause now, but he's determined to destroy us and be lord of something more than Lujiang, whether that's the court's will or not," Sun Ben replied. "Now that Xun's got a growing army, he's been sending scouts to places that we haven't taken yet and envoys to our enemies throughout Jiangdong: that indicates that he's planning more raids to gather food and stage a 'pacification operation', whether it is of his own design or on behalf of the Han or Cao Cao, and that's bad. We need to take Lujiang, turn his new army's thinking to our way of thinking, and then show Cao Cao that we're loyal to the Han; if Liu Xun achieves too much, he'll fully inherit Yuan Shu's army, say we're rebels and eliminate us."

"...I really cannot be bothered with any of this anymore," Sun Fu said. "We never get a moment's rest!"

"Don't worry, it all changes after Liu Xun and Liu Biao are defeated," Sun Ben replied. "We'll get recognition from the Han government for our efforts, and then we can start to enjoy life a little more."

"...I hope so," Sun Fu sighed.

Liu Xun was determined that he would secure the allegiance of all of Yuan Shu's former officials; he had already coerced an oath of allegiance out of Yuan Shu's cousin and former adviser Yuan Yin, but General Zhang Xun and the adviser Yang Hong – both of whom were part of Yuan Shu's retinue when he attempted an escape to Xu Province – were proving to be more difficult. Liu Xun had each of the two men brought to him individually so that he could reason with them.

"I don't understand," Liu Xun chortled theatrically. "If Yuan Shu is dead, then who is it that you follow now, Zhang Xun...? If Yuan Shu's blood cousin can forget a dead past and look to a living future, why can't you...?"

Zhang Xun looked around Liu Xun's private study and asked, "What part of this room – the room itself, or what is in it – came into your possession without Lord Yuan's having willed it so...?"

Liu Xun sneered and replied, "Your attempts at turning my arguments against me will not work, General! I am nobility, unlike you, little shopkeeper's boy! I watched you crawl up from the rank of private to where you are now, fighting and grovelling for every promotion! I am Administrator of Lujiang Prefecture because I am *entitled*, as a scion of the royal house, to a position of high status! Yuan Shu *gave* me this place after Sun Ce took it from Lu Kang, because Sun was a rustic soldier, while I am an educated official! I have what I have not because of Yuan Shu, but because status is my birth-right! I would be an administrator or governor anyway! Where would *you* be, though...? That's why you are loyal: I see that. But he's dead. Not only that, General, but he died a beggar after betraying the Son of Heaven, by having the audacity to announce to the world that His Majesty was no longer mandated, and that the sun now rose for him!"

"Yet you remained loyal, despite that announcement reducing the status of you and your clan," Zhang Xun retorted. "*Why*, Administrator Liu...?"

Liu Xun stifled rage and said, "Because, little soldier, I valued the bond of lord and vassal, as you do... but when the lord is no more, the vassal must be open-minded."

"I have a lord," Zhang Xun replied. "Lord Yuan Yao, son of-"

"No, no," Liu Xun said disparagingly. "Yuan Yao is not your lord, General Zhang. Heaven has struck Yuan Shu's clan down for its treachery: when, exactly, did Yuan Yao rebuke his father...? Did he not accept the title 'Crown Prince' willingly...? That makes him a traitor to the Han as well, and I intend to turn him over to Cao Cao at some point."

"But you want my service," Zhang Xun prompted.

"I know that you ultimately planned to go southward, to Sun Ce," Liu Xun said. "I know that this was a short stop for you... but Sun Ce is a rebel, General Zhang, a rebel bent on conquering Jiangdong and then northern Yang. I must do as Governor Liu Yao and Administrator Wang Lang once tried to do, and oppose him."

"Bofu is not a hankerer," Zhang Xun insisted. "He only wants-"

"Where is his tribute to the Han?" Liu Xun asked. "He has sent an empty pledge, nothing more, a promise that he is not Yuan Shu's vassal anymore. But when the province cried out for stability after Yuan's death, what did he do...? He annexed southern Guangling and attacked Jiangxia!"

Zhang Xun lowered his head and sighed.

"You see Sun Ce as a friend, and that is very nice and all, but it isn't practical," Liu Xun continued. "You have always known that, General Zhang, else you would have betrayed Yuan Shu when he did: you like the man at a social level, but when it comes to your politics, you are completely polarised."

"...I must concede that you are right," Zhang Xun said. "Bofu is a friend that is always 'just out of reach', because he and I differ in our attitude to loyalty, and that puts a chasm between us. But that chasm exists between you and me as well, Administrator, because I owe the Yuans a debt that I must pay in full."

"... ... ...You are unbelievably stubborn," Liu Xun complained. "Can you not see that you have repaid the debt already...? You stayed with him until his last breath! Look at how many other men did not do that, men that owe him as much, like his senior adviser, Yan Xiang, and General Chen Lan!"

"Yan Xiang did not betray Lord Yuan," Zhang Xun insisted.

"Then why is he not with you...?" Liu Xun heckled.

"...You know that he is alive," Zhang Xun realised.

"Of course!" Liu Xun chuckled. "He was securing military reinforcement for Yuan Shu after the loss of Ji Ling; he then joined you for the failed river crossing, whereupon he fled westward yet again in order to try and secure a different escape route: I am right, am I not...?"

"...You are," Zhang Xun admitted. "You were approached...?"

"He sent a man to request reinforcements," Liu Xun replied nonchalantly. "But what could I do to help? I had Sun Ben and Li Shu to worry about. That isn't the point, though: the point, General Zhang, is where he is *now*."

"...You insinuate that Mister Yan has abandoned our cause," Zhang Xun prompted.

"What 'cause'?" Liu Xun scoffed. "Yuan Shu is a corpse! His capital, Shouchun, is a pile of rubble! His money is spent, his army is scattered, and his name is forever tarnished as a heretic! What will it take, Zhang Xun, to make you see that Yuan Shu is no more and that you must now see things differently???"

Zhang Xun was silent.

"...Fine," Liu Xun conceded. "Go back to your quarters and rot, then. **GUARDS!**"

"...Wait."

Liu Xun was forced to gesture to his newly-arrived guards in order to stop them from taking hold of Zhang Xun.

"If, by aiding you militarily, I guarantee the life of Lord Yuan's son, then the debt is repaid," Zhang Xun suggested. "I will do nothing that threatens Lord Yuan's family or provokes needless hostility between you and Sun Bofu... but in all other things, I will support your army."

"...Very good," Liu Xun said. "You may retire to your quarters to collect your family and belongings, whereupon you shall go to the barracks. You will be a consultant for now."

Zhang Xun clasped his hands together and said, "As you wish, Administrator Liu."

"*Aiee...* what a difficult man," Liu Xun muttered as he watched Zhang Xun and his guards depart. "I hope that Yang Hong is more immediately receptive."

"**You hankerer, traitor and wretch!**" Yang Hong screamed at Liu Xun within minutes of his arrival at the private study. "**After all that Lord Yuan did for you, you kidnap his family, his coffin and his loyal subjects! You'll die a thousand deaths!**"

"...I'm sensing that you will not be as flexible as Zhang Xun," Liu Xun retorted. "I despair, Mister Yang: you are an adviser by profession, and yet you are even more stubborn in clinging to the will of a treasonous corpse! What has Yuan Shu – a man that was rude, condescending and aggressive to even his staunchest loyalists and most prestigious allies – done to deserve such loyalty from smart men...?"

Yang Hong flicked his sleeve and said, "Liar! Traitor! Thief and fiend! Stealer of coffins, keeper of land and kidnapper of your dead lord's army and children!"

"...Still, at least you do not call him 'His Majesty' anymore, which is a start," Liu Xun sighed.

"Only because it was his will in his last days!" Yang Hong protested. "The Han's mandate *has* been exhausted! Yuan Shao or Cao Cao will be the instrument of the Han's end now, and if not them, their progeny! And they are each of them only half the man that Lord Yuan was!"

"I admit that Yuan Shu was a hero once, but I've had my eyes opened," Liu Xun countered. "The bumbling Yuan Shao is an unfit chieftain, and the devious, licentious Cao Cao is a madman that will probably have to be replaced as Excellency of Works – preferably by a member of the Liu clan – when his usefulness has ended; but in his last days, Yuan Shu was both mad *and* unfit for purpose! And now he is *dead*, so *please*... see *sense*...?"

"Your 'sense' consists of seizing Lujiang, befriending the 'defiler of aunts' in exchange for recognised authority – which will, no doubt, involve harming Lord Yuan's family – and luring your lord's lonely vassals to you with promises of wealth, no doubt with a view to building a kingdom of your own and supplanting Cao Cao as the operator of the imperial puppet in Xuchang," Yang Hong heckled. "Look for another man to help your wicked plan: I would sooner die than betray my lord's last wish that I protect his children."

"...Fine," Liu Xun said. "You will be glad to hear that I have no intention of harming Yuan's children *or* you, despite your needlessly offending me: you'll be returned to your quarters, where I hope that you'll do some thinking. **GUARDS!**"

"**I think only of what might have been!**" Yang Hong said as he was led away. "**Enjoy your brief grip on power, Liu Xun: your own arrogance will soon rob you of it!**"

"...*Demented imbecile*," Liu Xun grumbled. "...Still, I have Zhang Xun: what, then, does Sun Ce intend to do, I wonder...?"

Yuan Shu's former adviser, Yan Xiang, was intercepted in Yu Province as he travelled along a quiet road with his small retinue: he was taken to a nearby military camp and eventually brought before Cao Cao's adviser Xun Yòu, who had hurried to the camp from the Han capital Xuchang to learn of Yan's intentions.

"Well, well," Xun Yòu chuckled. "Who'd have thought that the devious Yan Xiang would end up being captured so easily...? Have you come to donate your head to His Excellency, as Mister Han Yin did before you, or join him as Yuan Huan has done...?"

"People speak of 'wise Xun Gongda'," Yan Xiang said politely. "I hope that I have heard correctly."

"I don't know which people you refer to," Xun Yòu retorted. "Why were you aimlessly wandering, Mister Yan...? Your master is dead, so what is your plan?"

"...I'm not sure," Yan Xiang replied. "He passed away as I was on my way here... I learned of it as I crossed the border. I had hoped to find friends among the men that he inspired, I suppose..."

"The Yellow Turbans of Runan...?" Xun Yòu prompted.

"Liu Pi, leader of the *former* Yellow Turbans of Runan," Yan Xiang replied. "My lord was not inclined to ally himself with cultists."

"But he was inclined to declaring himself as an alternative sovereign," Xun Yòu challenged. "And you, Mister Yan, were happy to serve him regardless."

"I remonstrated, Mister Xun," Yan Xiang insisted. "Time and time again, I remonstrated, but he had astrologers that observed celestial changes, political analysts that saw enduring weakness in the successive Han courts that spanned many decades, and his own personal belief that the Han were doomed."

"...And you did not entirely agree with him...?" Xun Yòu prompted.

"The Han is weak, but the question is whether the answer is to kill the patient to 'end their suffering' or give them medicine in order to help them recover," Yan Xiang replied carefully. "I have always been an advocate of trying medicine before resorting to other things. Lord Yuan was being guided by the wrong voices, many of them in his own head, and that is very sad, since he was once a valiant hero that rode into the imperial palace, side-by-side with his brother, to slaughter the 'Ten' and save the same dynasty that he later came to torment."

Xun Yòu smirked and said, "I suspect that you are bargaining for your life."

"If you want to kill me, kill me," Yan Xiang retorted. "If my life had been paramount, Mister Xun, I would have deserted Lord Yuan, not do everything I could to preserve him *and* the stable, prosperous state that he had built... a state that now teeters at a precipice as villains vie for it. Sometimes a much-needed 'balancing force' can take an unusual form, and it must not be dismissed for being imperfect."

"...I am inclined to agree," Xun Yòu said as he thought of his own lord Cao Cao, whose more questionable actions included two successive genocidal rampages in Xu Province and forcing his affections on the aunt of a recently-surrendered general.

"I do not deny that Lord Yuan strayed from the path in later years, but he was once a man that wanted to maintain the order we cherish," Yan Xiang continued. "I believe that he still wanted order, Mister Xun, but that hubris and desperation clouded his judgement and caused him to mistake chaos for order. But the fact is that he is dead: right now, I am more concerned for northern Yang, for Yang Province as a whole in fact, and also for Yu Province, both of which suffer without a single point of light to look to."

Xun Yòu hummed thoughtfully and said, "Answer honestly, Mister Yan: would you say that you were widely respected...?"

"I was able to find men to aid Lord Yuan when his capital still visibly burned and his head carried a high price: I appealed to their need for stability as well as their love of money," Yan Xiang replied. "I survived a meeting with Chen Lan, and angry men in Yu let me leave their company despite disliking my words... I suppose that is because I am respected, yes."

"...And I find your having survived to be an impressive feat in itself," Xun Yòu admitted. "I think that you can yet be of use to the Han Dynasty; would you like to be of use to the Han Dynasty, Mister Yan...?"

"A man of talent wants nothing more than to be useful," Yan Xiang replied. "I will serve the Han directly as I once did, Mister Xun: loyally, and without rest. I erred in allowing Lord Yuan's dreams to draw me away from the light, and even he saw, in the end, that he should have me call him 'lord' and not 'majesty'. Now I am offered a chance to redeem myself fully, and I would be a fool to refuse it."

"...Then you shall accompany me to Xuchang," Xun Yòu declared. "I cannot guarantee that you will meet His Excellency, but you will, at least, meet my colleagues and face their scrutiny: if you are deemed sincere, then you will soon have your chance to restore stability in the south..."

"And if I am not, I join Han Yin in the afterlife," Yan Xiang said with a smile.

Xun Yòu reciprocated the smile and said, "I'm glad that we understand each other."

Days passed. Bofu sat in front of the desk in his private study and stared at a half-finished letter to his enemy Liu Xun; he grimaced at every ingratiating character that he had scrawled and fought the urge to say what he actually felt.

"...This is *ridiculous*," Bofu whispered as he stared at the flickering fires that lit the room; it was night, and he had been trying to pen the letter for hours. "This is *ridiculous*... I'm the son of the 'Tiger of Jiangdong', not a... a...!"

Bofu's beautiful young wife – who, because she was the elder of the two Qiao sisters, was known as Daqiao – shuffled into the room and giggled, saying, "You're still trying to be a toady!"

"Yes, and it's *killing me*," Bofu groaned. "I want to tell him that I want to-! ...Well, you know... something *violent*... but *instead*, I have to...!"

"Just think of it as something that has something good happen after you do it," Daqiao suggested. "Like... like maybe when our children are born. Giving birth is very painful, but I don't mind, because then we'll have our own children!"

Bofu smiled, turned around fully and placed his hand on Daqiao's swollen stomach.

"I sound silly explaining it the way that I am, I know that, but I'm tired," Daqiao explained. "But you know what I mean."

"Yes, I do," Bofu replied. "I'll write this piece of grovelling rubbish and send it... because it's just as you say... at the end of it, I can deal with him properly. I was worried that it might tarnish my reputation, but it won't."

"Everybody knows that you're a hero," Daqiao insisted.

"...Including Liu Xun," Bofu noted. "He surely won't believe that I mean this load of... ... ...but I have to hope that he *does* believe it, or we've got a worse war on our hands. I'd better be sure and make it sound convincing, not too grovelling but more 'I'm scared of Liu Xun's potential'... which I suppose I *should be*, really..."

"Whatever you write, I'm sure that he's stupid enough to fall for it," Daqiao replied. "Anyhow... I just wanted see if you were going to try and get some sleep or not."

"I'll be a few minutes more," Bofu promised. "I can do this now."

Daqiao smiled and retreated to the sleeping quarters.

"...For everyone that's depending on me, Liu Xun, I'll kiss your behind for now, just this *once*," Bofu said as he started to write again. "It'll only make kicking it that much more of a pleasure."

But Bofu would have to do more than write one letter, and he knew it: wooing Liu Xun's court and fooling them into thinking that the famous Sun Ce had suddenly lost his nerve would be a long, emotionally-taxing process. But the future was at stake: a quick victory would allow the Sun clan to take full control of Lujiang and return their focus to destroying the rulers of Jing Province, while a single misstep could lead to anything, such as a Lujiang-Jing pincer or an admonishment by the imperial court.

The initial signs were good: to the dismay of many of the more cynical minds in Lujiang's capital Huancheng, Bofu's flattery worked and Liu Xun entertained the idea that the 'son of the tiger' might be a future ally, or even a vassal. The Administrator of Lujiang was succumbing to hubris once again.

****

3

"...All is ready."

Gongjin was stood on his porch and watching the night sky as he spoke; his wife – who was the younger of the Qiao sisters, and known as Xiaoqiao – frowned and asked, "What is ready...?"

"The pieces on the board are all placed correctly," Gongjin replied. "Liu Xun responds as I had hoped he would, readily accepting the gifts that Bofu sends him and grinning like a fool at every flattering word. Sun Ben and Sun Fu have relocated their forces in a show of weakness, but they are poised. And I am ready to set sail at a moment's notice. All that is left to do now is plant the false suggestion..."

"And then you will take Lujiang back," Xiaoqiao supposed.

"Bloodlessly, hopefully," Gongjin said. "As well as selfishly worrying for our clans' home regions, the people have suffered enough, and our reputation must be a good one; Bofu was forced to terrorise the place four years ago at Yuan Shu's command, so I'd prefer that we weren't seen to be doing so again."

"I should quite like to visit Wan County when it is liberated," Xiaoqiao said.

"We'll both visit our home counties," Gongjin replied. "We'll go together, all of us if possible... ... ...mm. I don't know if we should send an envoy or not."

"Don't send Lu Su!" Xiaoqiao giggled.

Gongjin laughed and replied, "I wouldn't dare! He's the right man for that kind of thing when the mission is at least a little sincere, but not a complete falsehood like this one. I wondered if should maybe go myself..."

"Don't," Xiaoqiao pleaded. "Our child will need a father."

"I'll need to place myself in danger from time to time, but you shouldn't worry, I'm quite smart you know," Gongjin chuckled. "I'll be fine if I do go... though this might be better suited to Ziheng, Quan Rou, or one of the Zhang brothers..."

"I'll leave you to think," Xiaoqiao said. "You need to be right."

"...I do," Gongjin murmured as Xiaoqiao walked away; he turned to face the night sky and placed his full attention on Lujiang.

The communications between Bofu and Liu Xun continued. Liu Xun's adviser Liu Yè was alarmed when the flattery changed to suggestions about mutual interests and possible targets for military action: Xun allowed a private meeting in his study to discuss it, but he was already blind to reason.

"My lord, this is quite obviously a ruse," Liu Yè protested. "Why, you must ask, would Sun Ce *want* you to march an army into Jiangdong to 'assist him in taking Shangliao County'? This mighty tiger that sends navies to Jiangxia to fight Huang Zu suddenly can't handle a tiny pocket of civilian resistance that's right under his nose...?"

"As he says, this 'tiny pocket of resistance', as you so quaintly put it, is led by a man that is every bit another Taishi Ci or Zu Lang," Liu Xun retorted.

"So he should send one of those two men to take the place, then, since he now owns both of them," Liu Yè countered.

"...And I'm supposed to feed the tens of thousands of Yuan Shu's former soldiers that are now descending upon this prefecture to join us with *what*...?" Liu Xun asked. "Northern Haihun only has so much: if I go further south and take Shangliao, I also seize control of the crops and food stores that are the main reason why that 'tiny pocket of resistance' has held out for so long. And there's something else that your poor estimation of my ability prevents you from thinking."

"I... I don't estimate you poorly," Liu Yè insisted. "Nonetheless, I don't know what you mean, so please enlighten me."

Liu Xun smirked and said, "He asks if I would join him because he knows that I will surely march into Shangliao and take it sooner or later anyway, since I already sail southward and raid Haihun with what you would call 'impunity'. Nothing inspires a hungry man more than a guaranteed meal at the end of a long march, so I'll have thousands – close to *thirty-thousand* now, I believe – of Yuan Shu's men at my command, hungry for food and territory. It is better to ask me to share, I think, rather than waiting for me to take. And perhaps I will still *take*..."

"A battle between the two of you would be as between two tigers: both are bound to be hurt!" Liu Yè protested. "Don't risk such a thing, or an ambush, or being cut off from Huancheng, or-!"

"You are still in the past, and are therefore of no use to me," Liu Xun scoffed. "You grade me as the humble administrator with a few thousand men at my command, that you had to save from Zhen Bao; I am a very powerful warlord now, a man with in excess of thirty-thousand men at my command, just like Sun Ce, only mine are trained soldiers and not a bunch of fickle, shabby pirates. I was a Liu Bei, but now I am a Liu Biao, and just as capable of dealing with the likes of Sun Ce. He knows that, which is why he is humble: that is all there is to it."

"...*Ayah*... you are not to be made to see sense," Liu Yè realised. "Fine: I will remonstrate no further."

"Good!" Liu Xun said condescendingly. "I would rather have you at my side, Mister Liu, than at the back of the room. I shall respond positively to this suggestion and ready my men for the journey: a journey that, at the end of it, will have delivered us our first proper foothold in Jiangdong... and once we have that foothold, the rest can only follow."

Liu Xun and his reluctant consultant Zhang Xun led a force of thousands toward the Yangtze River, intent on travelling southward – past the long-suffering peoples of northern Haihun – and seizing Shangliao; as soon as the move was confirmed, Bofu and Gongjin left their base at the city of Qu'e in Danyang Prefecture and sailed down the Yangtze toward Lujiang with one army while Sun Ben and Sun Fu pursued Liu Xun and blockaded the route that led back to his base. With Liu Xun trapped in Jiangdong, the Lujiang defence forces were generally disorganised and confused: Bofu and Gongjin had a clear route to Lujiang's capital, Huancheng, and they quickly surrounded it.

"...Wasn't this going to happen...?" Yuan Yin sighed as he peered over the battlements of Huancheng and shuddered at the thousands of Jiangdong soldiers.

"So what happens now, Mister Yuan...?" an officer asked.

"...In a way, I want to laugh!" Yuan Yin replied. "I brought my lord's remains here, along with his family, so that he should have a dignified end, and Liu Xun took me as a hostage! I surrendered to Liu Xun, only because I thought that it would, perhaps, provide a new opportunity to save my lord's progeny and ensure his proper burial, and now I have Sun Ce – the one man that hates Liu Xun and my lord more than any other – standing at the gates now, demanding that we capitulate! Can I surrender twice in a row to despicable types without laughing or crying...?"

"Lord Liu has treated you graciously," the officer growled.

"Oh, yes, he has," Yuan Yin replied sarcastically. "He has indeed...! My lord is still unburied, and my lord's children are still quartered in lodgings that one would think twice before offering to Shanyue pelt traders. Yang Hong is obviously a rotting prisoner, and-!"

"Lord Liu left you here with rank as a consultant for moments such as these," the officer interrupted. "What do we do, Mister Yuan? Either offer advice or be thrown over the wall!"

"...I will personally accompany the lord's coffin from this place while another man feigns negotiations," Yuan Yin ordered. "Once my lord's remains are removed from Huancheng, my suggestion is that you find a way to escape with your loyal men and let Sun Ce take the city."

"You advocate running away???" the officer exclaimed.

"...Perhaps you don't remember how this city came to be occupied by your lord, Major, but I do," Yuan Yin retorted. "That man below, Sun Ce, on the orders of my – *our* – late lord, Yuan Shu, drove its previous master, old Lu Kang, to his grave with a relentless siege, and many a good man probably accompanied Lu's miserable descent into the netherworld. There will be people in this city that remember it all too well... what do you think they'll do if you order them to stand firm...?"

"...Your... your point is noted," the officer said. "So you intend to secure your lord's remains and flee northward, then?"

"If Sun Ce gets his hands on Lord Yuan's coffin or any of his vassals or children, I cannot say what he will do to them," Yuan Yin insisted. "I will risk the journey to the north: it would be better to do that than let the Suns have a victory."

"And what of Yuan's children, and Yang Hong...?" the officer asked.

"If it is permitted, free Yang Hong and allow the young lord and ladies to follow me," Yuan Yin replied. "I shall get going now."

The officer nodded, and Yuan Yin retreated from the wall.

"...What's taking so long?" Bofu muttered as he stared at Huancheng with an uncomfortable sense of déjà vu. "Please, gods, they don't intend to say that they're going to hold out...!"

"Stay calm," Gongjin pleaded. "Liu Xun's got a lot of good men to fight through before he stands a chance of getting back here."

As soon as night fell, Yuan Yin used a skirmish at the eastern gates of Huancheng to cover his escape from the city: he and six other men carried no passengers on their ox-drawn cart, only pieces of valuable cargo, namely the lifeless corpse of Yuan Shu and most of Yuan's remaining treasures. Two riders were sent after the cart, but when four of Yuan Yin's men blocked the way and delayed the riders, any hope of capturing the convoy disappeared. The incident was immediately reported to Bofu's command tent, and he was less than pleased.

"…Why didn't we pursue?" Bofu asked of his officer Chen Wu.

"There was a risk of harming the troublemakers at the east gates," the tall, charismatic Chen Wu replied. "I was most concerned with our actions being bloodless, as you ordered."

"…Yeah, that's right," Bofu realised. "Sorry, Zilie, I'm having a go at you when you were doing what was right. It's just that… well…"

"It might have been someone important," Gongjin supposed. "It was a cart with some boxes on it, Bofu: that'll be Yuan Shu's coffin and some of his money at worst, and that wouldn't get far, not with all the bandits."

"…So who do we have in the city now…?" Bofu wondered.

"From the people that were staging that fight at the east gates, I've learned that Yuan Yin, Yang Hong, Zhang Xun and Yuan Shu's children are 'guests' at Liu Xun's pleasure," Chen Wu reported. "It seems that Zhang Xun surrendered to Liu Xun and has accompanied him to Shangliao willingly, and-"

"What???" Bofu exclaimed. "He… *why*…?"

"Let him finish, Bofu," Gongjin said. "Carry on, Zilie."

"…Yang Hong is probably locked away, under some form of house arrest," Chen Wu continued. "The young Yuans are alive and well, under a lesser form of house arrest; Yuan Yin also surrendered, but the people seemed to be hinting that he might have been one of the escapees…"

"…So we probably lost Yuan Yin," Bofu sighed. "That's… not so bad. And it sounds as though you've made friends with those troublemakers, Zilie."

"They were asking what we intended," Chen Wu explained. "I've reassured them that we mean no harm, and they've taken me at my word after a tour of our camp: they've agreed to assist us in taking the city peacefully."

"Excellent, Zilie," Gongjin said. "Once again, you're the man that wins people around. Go and rest now, you've earned it."

Chen Wu bowed to Bofu and Gongjin in turn before he retreated; Bofu then turned to Gongjin and asked, "Would I be mad if I said that I wanted to give amnesty to the Yuans…?"

Gongjin smiled and replied, "I was hoping that you would say that. The answer is 'Not at all', of course; such a benevolent act can only aid our cause."

"Good… I thought I was losing my mind," Bofu chuckled. "Thing is, I have no quarrel with Yuan Yao… so why harm him…?"

"…You truly are a hero of the age, Bofu," Gongjin said. "Let no one tell you otherwise."

The situation inside Huancheng City was gradually deteriorating as fears of another siege wore away the nerves of the potential defenders: Yuan Shu's imprisoned adviser Yang Hong killed himself with a concealed dagger when he learned that Bofu was at the gates, and Shu's heir, Yuan Yao, feared the worst.

"Must we fight…?" Yuan Yao asked of his few remaining courtiers and officers.

"I wouldn't do it," one adviser replied. "It is better to surrender or die by our own hands, Lord Yuan."

Yuan Yao turned to look at his terrified sister and said, "I cannot bring myself to harm her, nor can I let anyone else do it. But won't she be poorly treated by Sun Ce and his barbarians...?"

"I will face whatever they inflict upon me as a Yuan, dear brother!" Lady Yuan insisted, although her voice was noticeably cracking. "No... no slight tarnishing of my person can take away from me the prestige of our clan!"

"...But I can't let them harm you, dear sister: I'd only be half a man," Yuan Yao sighed. "Perhaps... perhaps it is better to-"

Yuan Yao's speech was interrupted by a terrified local official that ran into the room and cried, "**The city gates are breached!**"

The sounds of approaching soldiers shook every person present to their core.

"Then... there is no time for an honourable end!" Yuan Yao said.

Seconds later, Bofu and Gongjin entered the room: they were conspicuous for not bearing their weapons, although the same could not be said of the guards that surrounded them.

"...Son of Sun Jian, I shan't let you defile my sister!" Yuan Yao declared as he lunged at Bofu with a sword; Bofu's lead bodyguards – Sun Hè and Song Qian – stepped forward to parry the attack and prevent another.

"**No bloodshed!**" Bofu cried as Yuan Yao backed away and joined his terrified courtiers and sister. "...Look, Yao... Lady Yuan... I didn't come here to hurt either of you."

"...You... didn't...?" Lady Yuan prompted.

"Not at all," Bofu promised. "I know what you've probably heard, but... I don't have anything against any of you, okay...? Yeah, I didn't get on very well with your father, and I have to be honest, that encounter might have been different; but all I want to offer to you is somewhere to be, which is all that *I* ever wanted."

Yuan Yao looked at Lady Yuan, who smiled and said, "I think that we can trust him, Brother."

"...Yes," Yuan Yao said as he sheathed his sword. "I think so too. Regardless, Mister Sun, we're now at your mercy: where would you have us be...?"

"Jiangdong," Bofu replied. "In fact, I want to take as many as we can support."

"...Very well," Yuan Yao said. "Unfortunately, our cousin, Yuan Yin, stole away with our father's coffin. Something tells me that you might have let us give him a proper funeral, which is something that Liu Xun appeared hesitant to do."

"I wouldn't have been crying for him, but yeah, I'd have given you that," Bofu replied. "Who knows...? Perhaps we'll find him. Now, though, we should hurry and evacuate this place."

"If there is anything that I can do to help, just ask," Yuan Yao said. "The people... have suffered enough."

While Bofu and Gongjin completed their near-bloodless seizure of Huancheng and the surrounding Wan County, the oblivious Liu Xun was awaiting word of a second raid on Haihun's supplies to provide resources for his newest expedition.

"...What's taking so long...?" Liu Xun complained. "Those fool peasants haven't tried to hide the grain from me, have they...?"

"I only wish it were that," Liu Yè sighed. "My thought is that-"

"**I need none of your pessimism, Mister Liu Yè!**" Liu Xun barked. "**General Zhang Xun!**"

Zhang Xun saluted unenthusiastically and said, "What is your command, Lord Liu?"

"Send a small detachment to find out what's delaying the Haihun operation," Liu Xun ordered. "This is intolerable! I-!"

"**REPORT!**"

All eyes turned to a dishevelled, hysterical messenger, who continued by saying, "**The Haihun force has been routed by an army led by a 'Huang Gai' and a 'Cheng Pu'! The road to the river is blocked by an army led by a 'Sun Ben' and a 'Sun Fu'! The road to the east is blocked by a 'Zu Lang'! The-!**"

"**No more!**" Liu Xun cried. "No more, no...! ...No...! Sun Ce, you larcenous wretch, you... you *tricked me*...!"

Liu Yè sighed and muttered, "You tricked *yourself*, you fool."

"...How can I feed my men without grain from Haihun...?" Liu Xun whimpered. "How can I keep the loyalty of my new army, trapped as we are across the river, when we are surrounded on all sides by Sun Ce's leering pirate friends...? And Huancheng... no... he... he cannot have... he cannot have led me here so that he could...!"

"...I'd say that it's likely," Liu Yè replied.

"Ziyang, you're my wits and sense where I lack them within my own skull," Liu Xun said as he stared at Liu Yè. "Ziyang, I-!"

"So now I am 'Ziyang'...?" Liu Yè snickered as he glared at Liu Xun with contempt. "Now that we are in this near-inescapable fix, I am 'Ziyang', the man entrusted with saving us."

"I was wrong to rebuke you, I see that now," Liu Xun said. "I beseech you, Ziyang, to use those great wits of yours to give us a way out of Jiangdong!"

"...We'll lose most of your new recruits, that much is certain," Liu Yè replied. "We must conserve our resources for the loyal men that have always followed you."

"Yes, yes!" Liu Xun said. "I'll do all that you say!"

"General Zhang, I must ask for your total support," Liu Yè said.

"You'll have it," Zhang Xun promised. "I do not intend to defect to Sun Bofu's forces, as much as I would perhaps like to... the bond between lord and vassal must always transcend one's own wishes. Lord Liu is a representative of Lord Yuan Shu's legacy, and the young lord relies on-"

"Forgive my interrupting you, but the moment is upon us," Liu Yè said. "General Zhang, we will need to smash through the northern blockade and somehow get to the Great River. From there, we can sail westward, hopefully to a secure Huancheng; if, as I suspect, Sun Ce has seized the place while we've been here on this fool's errand, we'll send an envoy to Jing – I'll go myself, if needs be – to request assistance from Liu Biao."

"He and I, we're distant kin, Liu Biao and I, just as you and I are, Ziyang," Liu Xun rambled. "Yes, he's bound to help if... if... oh, can I have lost Huancheng...?"

"Who better to lose it to, Lord Liu, than the man that won it for you all those years ago...?" Liu Yè chortled. "Now, let us get ready for what is ahead of us."

Liu Xun's forces began a hasty retreat along the path that they had taken: many men quietly broke away from the march as the desperate situation became clear, and many more were of a mind to desert when the rear of the force was struck by a gang of riders that were led by the former bandit king Zu Lang.

"**Another mouldy branch off the royal tree comes here to thrash our hairy arses, but all you'll get is being snapped in two!**" Zu Lang heckled as he personally led the attacks on Liu Xun's rear guard.

When Zu Lang's attack was reported to Liu Xun, he grimaced and said, "I won't be made a corpse in a place like this, and not by trash like *Zu Lang*! Somebody chase him away!"

"I'll go," Zhang Xun suggested.

"We can't afford to lose you," Liu Yè said. "I'll send some of the newer men."

"**They'll defect and join our pursuers!**" Liu Xun cried.

"So be it if they do," Liu Yè retorted. "We cannot afford to have anything but unreliable men at the front."

"...Fine!" Liu Xun whined. "Whatever it takes!"

Within a short time, Zu Lang withdrew; the problem that now faced the dwindling army of invaders was a force led by Sun Ben and Sun Fu. The Jiangdong army had completely blockaded the road to the Yangtze River, leaving Liu's forces with no choice but to fight.

"...**How dare those fools challenge me again, Ziyang!**" Liu Xun exclaimed. "**Even with all of the desertions, I still outnumber them!**"

"*Please*, **Lord Liu, no more baseless arrogance!**" Liu Yè complained. "**Where are Cheng Pu, Huang Gai, Dong Xi, Chen Wu, Zhou Yu, or *Taishi Ci*...?**"

"*Ayah*... I forgot that Sun Ce had *Taishi Ci*," Liu Xun murmured.

"**And I'm but one able mind, up against perhaps three or four,**" Liu Yè continued. "**Sun Ce has Cheng Pu, Zhou Yu, Lü Fan and Zhu Zhi... maybe more. Our only hope is to throw caution to the wind and break through with an unexpected show of desperate force while we still have the numbers!**"

Liu Xun nodded slowly and said, "**Whatever it takes.**"

Liu Yè ordered a full charge: there were still several thousand men on the march, and none of Bofu's officers had more than a few hundred soldiers. Without the benefits of a military array, the Jiangdong forces temporarily crumpled in the face of a concentrated strike by the better-trained men from Lujiang; the situation changed, however, when forces led by Huang Gai and Cheng Pu arrived from the northeast, the famous Taishi Ci led a force from the southwest and Zu Lang returned with an even larger army of former bandits.

"**These wretched vermin are everywhere, on all sides!**" Liu Xun cried as panic enveloped him. "**I don't want to die in this awful place, Ziyang!**"

Liu Yè gave orders to Zhang Xun via a series of hand signals, as verbal instructions were unlikely to be heard above the noise of the battle; Zhang Xun led Yuan Shu's former soldiers and a small band of Liu Xun's loyal men against the Jiangdong forces while Liu Yè guided his lord through the mayhem with the aid of the rest of the loyalists. Liu Xun and his adviser would reach the river, as would Zhang Xun; the entire mission had been very costly, however, as Liu Xun had lost not only the vast majority of his new army but his base in northern Yang Province.

Bofu and Gongjin, meanwhile, were preparing to leave Lujiang Prefecture in the capable hands of General Li Shu; the Jiangdong forces were now gathered at the Yangtze River as overseers of a mass exodus of people, animals and materiel.

"I won't fail you again, Lord Sun," Li Shu promised.

"How did you fail me...?" Bofu chuckled. "Honestly, you need to be a little less serious. Now, Gongjin, are we sure that-?"

"General Li Shu has enough men," Gongjin insisted. "Chen Wu's incredible way of genuinely winning people around has ensured that we're taking most of Yuan's troops back with us as friends... we didn't even need Yuan Yao to help us in the end."

"Zilie could charm the birds and beasts to join us," Bofu joked. "Anyhow, we should be off if all's in order here. Where do you reckon Liu Xun is...?"

Gongjin coaxed Bofu away from the penitent Li Shu and toward the docks as he replied, "Hopefully, dead... but he's shifty, self-serving and aided by Liu Yè, who's easily one of the future threats if he's ever counsel to a dangerous enemy of ours. That being the case, Xun's probably on his way back to Huancheng with whatever is left of his army... which will not be much."

"...He'll try and get help from Liu Biao, won't he...?" Bofu said.

"Oh, I imagine that it's crossed his mind," Gongjin replied. "If he does, that's perfect: it gives us the excuse that we need to eliminate Liu Xun and transition straight back to dealing with our enemies in Jing Province."

A thought suddenly occurred to Bofu: he looked at the tens of thousands of people that were waiting to cross the Yangtze and asked, "How are we going to feed all of these people, Gongjin...? Where will they live...?"

"Jiangdong is a big, sparsely-populated place with vast areas of untilled land, just waiting for a new generation of ambitious people to cultivate it," Gongjin replied. "We won't need to feed them: they'll feed themselves. They'll be free of all of the politics and strife of the north, and they'll have us to thank for it."

Bofu grinned and said, "You always know what to say. I'm resolved, Gongjin: we just made a fool of Liu Xun and stole everything back that he took from the Yuans and from me, and next, we'll deal with Liu Biao. We're almost there... we've almost built a place that's truly ours."

Bofu and Gongjin had arrived at Huancheng with 20,000 of their 50,000 men: they returned to Jiangdong with close to 30,000 extra soldiers that had once belonged to Yuan Shu, although some were actually men that had been recruited by Sun Jian, Sun Ben or Sun Ce and stolen by Yuan Shu in days long gone. In addition to that, Bofu had invited the soldiers' families and much of Lujiang's civilian population, which numbered beyond 100,000, to cross the river as well: when Liu Xun finally learned of it, he knew that there was only one place left to turn if he hoped to regain any of what he had lost.

★★★★★★★★★★★★

4

Jing Province Governor Liu Biao rubbed his grey beard and stared at his assembled courtiers with tired eyes.

"...As if I don't have enough problems as it is," Liu Biao grumbled. "Liu Xun has just shown himself to be more unlucky – or maybe incompetent – than my other distant relation, Liu Bei: Bei, at least, can argue that he started life a sandal weaver and knew nothing of civil administration. What's Liu Xun's excuse...?"

The politician Huan Jie – whose previous lord was Bofu's father Sun Jian – frowned and said, "You do not intend to help him then, Lord Liu...?"

"Of course I'm going to help him!" Liu Biao snapped. "Do I have a choice...? Sun Ce just lured Liu Xun into a child's trap and stole what Xun's envoy estimates to be in excess of twenty-thousand men – I suspect more, but he pares it down to avoid further humiliation – and Xun's prefectural domain. I... I cannot imagine ever making such a mistake myself. I have to help him, to somehow see if we cannot coax some of those thousands of defectors 'back to the light', else Sun Ce's got what, sixty, *eighty*-thousand men to throw at me when he comes back here...? But can I trust such a stupid man not to lose things of mine as well...?"

The adviser Kuai Liang – who was noticeably more frail than usual – coughed uncomfortably and said, "My lord, I suggest that you leave this to Huang Zu initially. As you say, we have to be concerned about the current row that's brewing between Cao Cao and Yuan Shao, and also our squatters in Nan County."

"...And at what point might I get involved...?" Liu Biao asked.

"Hopefully, never," Kuai Liang replied. "Huang Zu's got a lot of capable men. But if Huang were to lose any encounter – no matter how small – we would probably have to launch everything that we have at Sun Ce in a show of strength."

Liu Biao turned to Admiral Cai Mao and said, "I'm sure that I don't need to tell you this, but... ready your men to go north or south."

Cai Mao bowed silently.

"...Mister Kuai, tell Mister Huang Zu to take this absolutely seriously and send only his best," Liu Biao continued. "Liu Xun must regain what he has lost, and Sun Ce must be smashed."

Kuai Liang bowed slightly and said, "I shall send word at once."

Huang Zu's court in the southern prefecture of Jiangxia was quite different to his lord's courts in Jiangling and Xiangyang: many of the attendees were former pirates and hired mercenaries, and the tone was far more informal. The ageing magnate laughed as he read the instruction letter from Liu Biao and said, "He must be so embarrassed, that Liu Xun! Sun Ce's robbed him of everything!"

Many of the courtiers laughed derisively.

"...But I suppose that I shouldn't be laughing," Huang Zu sighed. "Sun Ce's growing stronger... stronger than the father... but can he beat the great son of a better man...?"

Huang Zu turned his gaze to his son Huang Shè, who said, "I would willingly take the fight to Sun Ce, Father."

"You are best placed to lead this of all my sons and kin," Huang Zu suggested. "You'll take five-thousand men and as many hundreds of ships and boats as are needed. General Han Xi will accompany you, and the lord's nephew Liu Hu will provide support. The lord's other esteemed nephew, Liu Pan, and I will become personally involved should the need arise."

"I will not be bested by Sun Jian's runt of a cub," Huang Shè promised. "I shall make you proud, Father."

"No heroics," Huang Zu insisted. "Don't let Sun Ce goad you into anything. Keep it simple: smash him, and then come home. The amazing Liu Xun is currently headquartered along the flats near Mount Xisai: go and rendezvous with him at once."

Huang Shè and Han Xi bowed respectfully and left the court with their retinues; Huang Zu noticed that a scruffy man in his twenties was staring at him and asked, "Something to say, Gan Ning...?"

"I jus' wondered why you never asked me or none o' me lads t'go along... s'all, boss," Gan Ning replied. "I thought that we might be kinda useful, y'know, wi-"

"I'm not so desperate as to need *you* at this moment in time," Huang Zu said. "In fact, you shouldn't even be here! **Su Fei!**"

The world-weary officer Su Fei exhaled loudly and replied, "My lord, Gan Ning is-"

"**Don't make me tell you again!**" Huang Zu barked.

Su Fei looked at Gan Ning, who shrugged indifferently and left the hall with his allies.

"...My lord, Gan is a future talent," Su Fei pleaded. "He's an expert shot, a master of scare tactics, a-"

"He's a faithless cutthroat!" Huang Zu said.

"Yes, my lord, he *was*, but not anymore!" Su Fei protested. "He's learning the classics! He's-!"

"He's *what*...?" Huang Zu chortled. "Gan Ning, *reading books*???"

Su Fei shook his head sadly; he was forced to shout over the mocking laughter, saying, "**He'd be an asset!**"

"...Don't be *ridiculous*," Huang Zu scoffed. "Your role in this campaign – and I don't want to hear that you used Gan Ning to fulfil it – is to prevent any pincer attacks by watching at Wulin and Red Cliffs, just as you have done before. Go at once."

Su Fei bowed humbly and left Huang Zu's court.

"What is my role, my lord...?" a brawny officer asked.

"You will remain here, Zhang Shuo," Huang Zu replied. "Your role is to continue recruiting and training; the same goes for Chen Jiu."

Zhang Shuo turned to his colleague Chen Jiu, who looked to his lord Huang Zu and said, "As you command."

Huang Zu lowered his head and muttered, "This won't end well."

"...Am I comin' with you or what...?" Gan Ning asked as Su Fei passed him on his way out of Huang Zu's mansion.

"Not officially," Su Fei replied.

Gan Ning laughed and said, "He really don't like me, does he? What is it that I've did that makes me so diff'rent to all the other 'cutthroats' he has workin' f'r'im...?"

"...I honestly don't know," Su Fei replied. "But I'll win him around, Xingba: it'll take time, but I swear that I'll get you employed."

"I know you're tryin' mate, an' I 'preciate it," Gan Ning said. "So what is it, Wulin again...?"

Su Fei nodded and said, "Wulin and Red Cliffs."

"S'go, then!" Gan Ning chuckled.

Liu Xun had retreated to the region around Mount Xisai – which was in the west of Lujiang – after his humiliating and simultaneous defeats at Shangliao, Haihun and Huancheng. He now had around 4,000 men, since most of his recruits from Yuan Shu's armies had deserted; he looked around him at the defensive position that his loyalists – led by the reluctant defector Zhang Xun – had constructed and said to his adviser Liu Yè, "Will it be enough to repel Sun Ce…?"

"We're not looking to 'repel Sun Ce' from this camp," Liu Yè replied. "This is a ring of wooden beams, some tents and some lookout towers. We're entirely dependent on Liu Biao's assistance now. If Sun Ce ever got here, he'd destroy us."

"…Do I not know that?" Liu Xun heckled.

"If you know, then why ask?" Liu Yè retorted.

A soldier approached and said, "Lord Liu, a General Huang Shè will arrive shortly with five-thousand men and fifteen-hundred boats."

"Aha! So Liu Biao has kept his word!" Liu Xun said excitedly. "With a fleet of that size on its way, Sun Ce is doomed!"

"Sun Ce's defeated Huang Zu a few times now," Liu Yè noted. "We should have a backup plan."

Liu Biao frowned and said, "I shan't rebuke you again, Ziyang, for you have been right too many times. What would we do if…?"

"Go to Xuchang," Liu Yè replied. "There's no other option."

Liu Xun nodded slowly and said, "Yes… Mengde would surely ensure a decent role at the court for me, so it… it wouldn't be as good as what I have known, but it would be something."

Liu Yè looked at Zhang Xun – who was visibly irritated at Liu Xun's lack of interest in any other person's wellbeing but his own – as he replied, "We'll be able to negotiate for our *families* at that point, Lord Liu."

"…Mm…? …Oh, yes, our families," Liu Xun said. "Sun Ce has not hurt them thus far, so I am unconcerned. He has gained at least a little understanding of 'the way of things'."

Bofu was the lord of a vast dominion, and for that dominion's administration to function effectively, he had to report to his court in Qu'e when he was not present. Bofu had left his younger brother Sun Yi – whose appearance and countenance were eerily similar to Bofu's – as the main military guardian, while state affairs were managed by his maternal uncle Wu Jing, his mother, Lady Wu – whose role as a woman with authority was not unique, but it was certainly unusual at the time – and a small group of trusted officials that Bofu had taken time to gather and build bonds of trust with.

"My nephew says that he has received word of a mighty fleet approaching Lujiang," Wu Jing said to the packed court. "We are deploying more men and vessels to 'even the odds', so to speak. Dong Xi is moving up from Yuzhang, and-"

"But my brother might need my help," Sun Yi prompted.

"*Ayah*… Stop trying to run at swords!" Wu Jing pleaded. "Your father and eldest brother are stress enough for my ageing bones!"

Lady Wu laughed and said, "My Yi is just worried. Now, Mister Zhang: how goes the 'pacification' of Gan Ji's followers?"

"We're showing restraint, Lady Wu, as requested," the politician and adviser Zhang Zhao replied. "It would, however, be a lie to say that there have not been serious incidents."

Lady Wu sighed woefully and said, "My son should have shown more care. Gan Ji harmed not a soul... but what's done is done. What word from Wu Prefecture, Mister Quan...?"

The statesman Quan Rou coughed deliberately and replied, "Administrator Zhu Zhi reports no signs of activity from the pirates, bandits or 'White Tiger' Yan's Shanyue followers. I should also like to report our cordial relations with the imperial court's new Administrator of Guangling, Chen Deng, who has made no challenge to our reclamation of southern Guangling thus far."

"That's something," Lady Wu said. "Mister Gu Yong, how goes the redistribution of food to account for all of our new residents, and indeed the redistribution of the residents themselves...?"

"It will take time," the politician Gu Yong replied.

"...Quan should take some people," Lady Wu mused.

"Begging your pardon, Lady Wu...?" Zhang Zhao prompted.

"Mm...? ...Oh, uh, my apologies, gentlemen, for thinking aloud of things that should be discussed," Lady Wu said. "My second son Quan should be here, really... or perhaps not. But he must take some of the poor people that have found themselves here in Jiangdong at such short notice. Everyone must do their part."

"Better he isn't here, Mother," Sun Yi suggested. "He might-"

"He's... not here," Lady Wu interrupted; Sun Yi was about to mention that his older brother Sun Quan – who was going through an emotional crisis – had recently stolen money from the state treasury to pay for vices, and that would not be received well by a court founded on honesty and fairness, and not least by Sun Quan's new father-in-law, Magistrate Xie Jiong, who was in Jiangdong as a guest.

"...Oh, right, of course, Mother," Sun Yi said as he realised his error. "Should I visit him personally and relay your suggestion...?"

"No, I'll write," Lady Wu insisted. "What else have we to worry about...? ... ...Oh, yes. Hua Xin's behaving... but are the tribes in Kuaiji and Yuzhang behaving...?"

"So far, General Hè Qi's work in the south has quelled a lot of the unrest, although we may need to post him back there once we know that the Shanyue are dealt with," Gu Yong explained.

"...Hè Qi is the shiny man that likes to wear expensive clothes and armour, isn't he...?" Lady Wu said. "You'll have to excuse me, but I'm having to remember rather a lot, as all of you do, all whilst managing a rowdy den of tigers."

Some of the officials laughed.

"...Dong Xi is moving to aid Ce, you said...?" Lady Wu prompted.

"He is," Wu Jing replied.

"...He seemed like a very honest sort," Lady Wu recalled. "My son's has him, and young Gongjin and Ziheng, and my husband's friends to help him. It's all... going to be *fine*."

Lady Wu winced as she spoke; Sun Yi sensed that there was something wrong, but he was not going to ask.

"We're going to discuss banal matters now," Wu Jing said. "Did you wish to retire, dear sister...?"

"...I'll stay," Lady Wu replied. "If Ce, impatient type that he is, can sit through an hour of talk about crops and tax, then so can I; I can see that Yi is anxious to get back to barracks, though, and I won't keep him."

"Thank you, Mother," Sun Yi said as he backed away from the host seats and retreated from the courtroom.

"...What a bother it is, gentlemen, having to keep worrying about all of these greedy, self-destructive fools like Yuan Shu and Liu Xun," Lady Wu continued.

"I quite agree, Lady Wu," Xie Jiong said. "I welcome the day when we can just live our lives without constant talk of rebellions, tribal uprisings and pointless wars."

"...That, sadly, is a day that may never come," Wu Jing murmured.

Word of Liu Xun's expulsion from Lujiang reached Wu Prefecture in eastern Yang Province, which included the vast estate of retired general Xu Zhao; that estate was currently home to the supplanted Administrator of Wu Prefecture, Sheng Xian, who was in self-imposed exile after losing his seal of office to the popular local agitator Xu Gong. Sheng had lost his popularity by being seen as ineffectual against corruption, raids by local Shanyue tribespeople and economic woes, but he had his followers; some chose to join him in exile and were willing to die for him.

Xu Gong had subsequently been overthrown by Sun clan forces: he allied with the same Shanyue tribes that had made his predecessor unpopular and started a guerrilla war against the Suns that ended in defeat. Xu Gong and a Shanyue chieftain, 'White Tiger' Yan, were then forced to hide on Xu Zhao's estate as well; Gong eventually found an opportunity to work with the Sun clan, despite still being openly hostile to their annexation of the region, while White Tiger – who remained on the estate as a guest – continued to work against the Suns through his network of tribal followers. Sheng Xian was offered no such chance to return to the fold; his followers were understandably resentful, but Sheng Xian was as stoic and optimistic as always.

"I say to you yet *again*, gentlemen," Sheng Xian declared, "that I will one day be returned to office. Cao Cao is a true hero of the age: Lü Bu is gone, Yuan Shu is gone, and he will deal with this mess as soon as all of the other, more important troubles are dealt with, such as the Qiang warlords and Zhang Lu!"

One of Sheng Xian's long-time vassals – a man named Dai Yuan – shook his fist and said, "We're left to *rot*, Administrator Sheng! Cao Cao will *never* help us, no matter how often you say it!"

A second man, Gui Lan, nodded and said, "Mister Dai is right. Look at the fate of Liu Xun, who had turned back to the light! The Suns are only going to be removed by intriguing against them!"

"I'm not interested in all that 'plotting' nonsense, gentlemen," Sheng Xian insisted. "I've always been a simple man, devoted to serving the Han loyally and doing my job as best I can. I haven't the ability to scheme as some men do."

"Then let us scheme for you!" Dai Yuan pleaded. "We cannot bear to see you trapped while villains like Xu Gong enjoy rank and-!"

"The matter will resolve itself in good time," Sheng Xian insisted. "Let the court deal with these things, gentlemen, and keep your hearts free of the darkness that comes with all of that plotting."

Gui Lan sighed and said, "You are as stubborn as ever, Administrator, but you are right, so I cannot criticise you."

"...All will be well," Sheng Xian chuckled. "You wait and see..."

The man that had usurped Sheng Xian, only to be usurped himself – Xu Gong – pondered Liu Xun's defeat as he sat in the court of Bofu's appointed 'Acting Administrator of Wu Prefecture', Zhu Zhi. Xu Gong was normally known for his defiant tone and conviction that he was still the rightful Administrator in the region, but his perceived 'submission' to the Suns and actions against his former ally 'White Tiger' Yan had started to damage him, and the loss of a potential ally for future reclamation campaigns had left him speechless, a fact which was not lost on the observant Zhu Zhi.

Xu Gong retreated to his home after the meeting; he passed two of his dwindling collection of trusted aides and entered his living quarters, where his son Lang was waiting for him.

"*Damn* Sun Ce… damn his *clan* and *all that follow them*!" Xu Gong muttered as he passed his son and went into his private study.

"…Please do not write again," Xu Lang sighed. "Heng only just avoided being caught the last time and-!"

"**Then I'll send Yan this time!**" Xu Gong retorted. "I must make the court see sense, before Sun Ce conquers everything!"

Xu Lang shook his head and watched as his father started to pen another letter to Cao Cao's office in Xuchang; the consequences of such a letter being intercepted were obvious, but Xu Gong was a man driven by desperation, and no-one would stop him now.

Guangling Prefecture was situated to the northeast of Bofu's capital Qu'e, and was separated from the rest of Jiangdong – and northern Yang Province as well – by the Yangtze River; for that reason – and the fact that it was connected to the same land mass as Xu Province at its northern tip – the proper jurisdiction of the area was contested continually, and it was, at present, divided between the Han's appointed Administrator of Guangling, Chen Deng – who answered to the governor of Xu Province – and the Sun clan. Cao Cao had never defined Chen Deng's remit clearly, but there were some that thought that he should 'take the southern region back' once the pirates in the northern region were properly dealt with. The pirate king Xue Zhou had been humbled repeatedly in recent times, and so Chen Deng was petitioned by several officials and forced to give a response to his court.

"I cannot justify attempting to seize southern Guangling at this moment," Chen Deng insisted. "Xue Zhou is not completely defeated, and Sun Ce is very, very dangerous. Neither Governor Che nor Excellency Cao has issued the appropriate orders and I would prefer to do such a thing only when I am told to."

"But Sun Ce is a traitor, and inaction makes us look weak!" one official heckled. "What's stopping him from deciding he wants the rest of Guangling if we don't act…?"

"Sense," Chen Deng replied. "I am not helpless, gentlemen, and Sun Ce knows that. Let him have southern Guangling for now: I'm sure that the court has a plan for the future."

Chen Deng was considered a hero by many, so his stance, while unpopular, was accepted; the Guangling administration would do nothing until an opportunity and an order told them otherwise.

****

5

Huang Shè and Han Xi's fleet carpeted the waters of the Yangtze River as it moved eastward: the fishermen and other civilian users of the waterways were quick to abandon their positions and seek cover inland. Most if not all of the Jing men were adept at the fine art of river combat: men had to be able to live, eat, sleep and even fight on the unwieldy vessels, which varied in size from small boats or rafts with sails to large battleships with thousands of crewmen. The training was intense and necessary, as one wrong step or moment of giddiness could result in a fall into the cold, treacherous waters and almost certain death in combat conditions; southern Jing men were some of the finest river-warriors, able to engage in archery or close-quarters combat with single and two-handed weapons like spears, swords and pikes, and all taking place on floating, wobbling water vehicles that they might have to leap between as they advanced or retreated.

Bofu's navy was almost as well trained, and his fleet was quickly growing in size as his allies gathered around him for what was looking to be a very important battle for supremacy in the region. The prodigious martial artist Dong Xi and two former pirates – the unyielding Zhou Tai and the humble Jiang Qin – had now added their forces to Bofu's: they would soon be joined by Bofu's cousin Xu Kun, the irrepressible Ling Cao, the unbelievably impulsive and reckless Lü Meng and the veteran Han Dang, who had travelled from Wu Prefecture in the east to join his old colleagues Cheng Pu and Huang Gai. There were now two parts of the Yangtze River that looked to be made of more wood and men than water, and it was highly likely that the battle would cost a lot of lives if it was not brought to a swift end through an act of morale-breaking heroism by one side or the other.

"…So many men and boats," Bofu said as he marvelled at the sight of the two large navies. "I doubt that we'll see this again in our lifetime, Gongjin."

"We might, we might not," Gongjin replied. "That depends, as it always does, on the state of the northern court."

The grey-haired Cheng Pu harrumphed and said, "The sooner we're free of their foolishness, the better, Zhou Gongjin. What's the plan…?"

"What plan can one have when the situation is as simple as this, Demou…?" the veteran Huang Gai asked. "I would have thought that the answer here is 'sail toward them and break them as quickly as possible'."

"And you'd be right, Mister Huang," Gongjin said. "Lü Fan and I have discussed it at great length, and we both decided the same thing: the great 'Tiger of Jiangdong' is the man that we must look to for inspiration."

"Suits me!" Bofu cackled. "I-!"

"No heroics, Bofu!" Sun Hè pleaded. "We've done this too many times already, and I can't guarantee that I can watch your back during a river fight!"

"*Bah…* don't fret so much, Bohai!" Bofu insisted. "I've been practicing this stuff endlessly in the last two years, which you know well enough."

"…Well I'm not so nimble these days, not since my leg got hurt, so I'll manage things from the command ship," Cheng Pu grumbled. "Remember that your leg is not so trustworthy since you were shot by Ze Rong's men, Lord Sun."
"It's fine now," Bofu insisted. "Let's get this over with! Taishi Ziyi! Let's you and I show these men what true heroes look like!"
The brawny Taishi Ci smirked and said, "I'm already there in spirit, Lord Sun: my body won't take long to catch up!"
"And you're lucky I didn't charge already!" Ling Cao cried.
"…*Aiee*… such recklessness," Huang Gai muttered.

Huang Shè and Han Xi watched with horror as Bofu, Sun Hè, Gongjin, Taishi Ci and Ling Cao led a force of several hundred highly-trained men toward his fleet at great speed: they were already hopping onto the Jing vessels and engaging the front lines before their craft had even slowed. At first, their tactics – which involved moving past the front lines of boats – seemed to be suicide, as they risked being surrounded, but it quickly became clear that something more was happening.
"At that speed, they'll be at the main ships in no time at all!" Huang Shè exclaimed. "We'll have to be ready with archers!"
"That's the least of our worries!" Han Xi noted. "Their smaller craft are parting… and their larger ships are moving to ram into our small boats as their leaders pass them!"
As Han Xi spoke the words, the actions that they described came to pass: many of Huang Zu's vanguard boats were being capsized and smashed by the larger Jiangdong vessels, and the men that were thrown overboard were being shot and stabbed as they tried to swim toward land.
"This is a *rout*!" Huang Shè gasped. "How can this be???"
"**RETREAT!**" Han Xi ordered. "**RETREAT AND REGROUP!**"
The rear forces abandoned their doomed colleagues and moved to the west in order to regain some momentum: Bofu and his allies pressed their attack, dancing from boat to boat and engaging in duels that almost always ended with the demoralised Jing men falling into the icy waters.
"**It's Taishi Ci!**" one Jing sailor sobbed as Taishi leapt onto the adjacent boat, fended off two men's attacks simultaneously and knocked a third into the water with a swift, powerful kick; the famous hero from the northern frontier town of Donglai followed the feat by defeating both of his remaining assailants and dispatching the terrified man that had uttered his name.
"**Where's Liu Xun?**" Bofu cried. "**Where's that Liu Xun???**"
But Bofu knew that Liu Xun was not present: he knew that there was a second army on the land, and there was a force to meet that threat as well.

Sun Ben, Dong Xi, Lü Meng and Xu Kun had brought a force of 20,000 to meet Liu Xun's 10,000 men, many of whom were borrowed from Huang Zu: Sun Ben laughed and shouted, "**WHOSE MEN DO YOU STEAL NOW, LIU XUN?**"
"**I hate every last member of that accursed Sun clan!**" Liu Xun whined.
"**We'll win,**" Huang Zu's son Yi promised.
"**We're outnumbered two-to-one at the least!**" Liu Xun noted.

"**We'll try a small array,**" Liu Yè suggested. "**I am familiarising myself with the better ones, but a simple one should be enough to make corpses of them!**"

Zhang Xun nodded and turned to one of Huang Yi's captains: an order was carried down the ranks, and the men started to form lines or circles.

"...An array!" Sun Ben's strategist for the mission, Lü Fan, said with amusement. "So Liu Xun's counsel is not completely useless... we should- ...Oh, not again! **Lü Meng, you fool! Come back!**"

The reckless young officer Lü Meng had decided to charge at the array without waiting for orders: Xu Kun was determined to ride after him, but Sun Ben ordered him to hold firm.

"**How sad that I share ancestry with *Lü Bu* and *Lü Meng*, two of the most stupid men that ever dwelled upon this world!**" Lü Fan lamented. "**Soon they'll *both* be dead!**"

But Lü Meng stopped short of entering the enticing openings in the walls of men, as something within him – a spark of something that would one day come to define him – told him that it might be a bad idea, and he retreated. At that moment, Huang Yi mistakenly sensed weakness and bellowed, "**Two detachments should charge at once!**"

"*Ayah*! **No, General Huang, they should *not*!**" Liu Yè protested, but he was not deemed important enough for Huang Zu's men to heed him: dozens of riders and hundreds of infantrymen rushed forward, whereupon they met with arrows and a retaliatory charge by Xu Kun and Dong Xi.

"**They've turned it to their advantage!**" Huang Yi exclaimed.

"**Our morale is shattered now, you...!**" Liu Yè cried. "**...We *had them*! If you had only waited, listened, then we *had them*! But we can turn it around! Reorganise your archery division and shoot at them!**"

But the second phase of Lü Fan's straightforward plan was already being put into motion: Sun Fu and Chen Wu brought new forces to the battle, trapping Liu Xun and Huang Yi in a three-way pincer.

"**We have to get away!**" Liu Xun screamed as he watched Huang Yi's position become hopelessly overwhelmed by Dong Xi's militia; Liu Yè's pointless array disintegrated, and the soldiers scattered in all directions.

"**This did not have to end like this!**" Liu Yè complained. "**One day, I want to serve a lord that *listens*!**"

Huang Yi's subsequent retreat ensured the collapse of the Jing contingent of the invading forces; Liu Xun and what was left of his loyalists fled to the northwest to join an emergency force led by Liu Biao's nephew Liu Hu.

"Victory is ours," Lü Fan said as he looked at Lü Meng, who was visibly embarrassed.

"...Strange, though, that an act of unbridled idiocy might have sped up the conclusion," Sun Ben said.

"Only because Huang Yi and Liu Xun were more stupid than Lü Meng," Lü Fan retorted. "Mister Lü, *please*, be an ambassador for our shared – *distantly* shared – bloodline in future... *please*...? Heaven gave you brains, so *use them*, man, instead of trying to pointlessly dash them on the ground at every opportunity!"

"I am entirely at fault, and I will try to be more thoughtful and less foolish in the future," Lü Meng promised.

"...I won't hold my breath," Lü Fan muttered.

"We should pursue Liu Xun at once," Sun Ben suggested.

"We should," Lü Fan replied. "**ADVANCE!**"

While Liu Xun struggled to find a safe place to regroup, Huang Shè and Han Xi's efforts to do the same had ended in failure: Bofu's fleet pursued them relentlessly and decimated the fleet of smaller boats that had survived the first encounter.

"**We should retreat, young lord!**" Han Xi urged. "**We cannot win here!**"

"**...This goes against everything I believe, but alright!**" Huang Shè replied. "**All forces withdraw to Jiangxia! Liu Xun is on his own!**"

The Jing naval forces fled westward: Bofu wanted to pursue, but Gongjin restrained him and said, "**We must ensure that Liu Xun is routed first! We can finish what we started against Liu Biao's minions soon enough!**"

Bofu nodded agreeably and lowered his sword; he was surrounded by screaming, drowning Jing sailors, capsized boats and floating corpses, and the enormity of the battle was now starting to impact on him emotionally.

"**We'll certainly need to pursue,**" Gongjin continued. "**Huang Zu will not flee: he's invested too much in this mission. We must chase him back to Jiangxia at the very least.**"

Bofu nodded for a second time and began a slow, meandering journey across a sea of boats, bodies and debris that would bring him back to his command ship.

"Reports tell us that Liu Xun has regrouped near his Mount Xisai base," Cheng Pu said once the officers were gathered in the command room of the lead ship. "We cannot allow him to reorganise and try another attack. We must chase him and be rid of him."

"He'll flee," Gongjin suggested. "He'll go north now, to Xuchang."

Everybody expected Cheng Pu to heckle Gongjin, as he had done so often in the past: instead, the older man smiled and said, "You're probably right."

And Gongjin was correct: as soon as Liu Xun realised that Huang Zu's forces had been routed on the river as well as on land, he abandoned his base and fled northward to Yu Province with Liu Yè and Zhang Xun. Sun Fu was then tasked with restoring Huancheng City while General Li Shu managed the stabilisation of the region generally, and the majority returned to Jiangdong proper. Huang Zu learned of the losses and shuddered; he knew that Bofu would now advance on Jiangxia once again, and that he would probably emerge as the victor.

****

6

The Han Dynasty's Excellency of Works, Cao Cao, retired to his private study and studied a series of reports from his agents in Yang Province; what he read caused him to frown thoughtfully and sigh. His sickly aide, Guo Jia, noted his mood and asked, "What concerns you specifically...?"

"...Sun Ce becomes ever more of a formidable force," Cao Cao replied. "Such a man must be dealt with correctly."

"You want to destroy him...?" Guo Jia asked.

"Not if I don't have to," Cao Cao insisted. "I have genuine respect for his father, for he and I were the only ones that challenged Dong Zhuo at Luoyang. If there were more Sun Jians, the nation would have been at peace a long time ago... what I must learn is whether Sun Ce is his father's son or something else."

"And what you're reading leaves you divided," Guo Jia prompted.

"Naturally," Cao Cao said. "On the one hand, he rightly betrayed Yuan Shu; on the other, he annexes all of Jiangdong – and part of Guangling – to form some sort of personal kingdom, chases away loyal, honest Han officials like Liu Yao and Wang Lang, and fraternises with criminals like Zu Lang. His earlier actions – such as driving poor old Lu Kang to despair and death, or harassing Liu Yao – are forgivable because he did those things as Yuan Shu's vassal. Everything that he does now is of his own free will, and is less forgivable."

"...What will you do with Yan Xiang and Liu Xun...?" Guo Jia asked.

Cao Cao smirked and said, "You are being clever again, Fengxiao! I know that I would seem to be somewhat hypocritical if I forgave those two and condemned Sun Ce, but the world is not simple, is it...? Those two come to me separately as men that have gambled and lost, men that now want to be forgiven and allowed to serve the Han government; I shall make use of them both in different ways. Sun Ce is unapologetic, aggressive and free-spirited, which might not be compatible with what I'm trying to do... namely, reunifying the empire."

"Can he not be a vassal king...?" Guo Jia asked semi-seriously.

"He'll be a vassal, plain and simple," Cao Cao chuckled. "We're none of us meant to be kings, Fengxiao. If the Son of Heaven desired such an elevation, then so be it, but I doubt that Sun Ce would be given such an honour! No, he's being an upstart; on the other hand, he might be useful if he'd agree to be a friend..."

"...Which, I suspect, involves a marriage alliance between his clan and yours," Guo Jia prompted.

"My youngest brother has a daughter that is yet to be betrothed to anyone, and I know that Ce has three brothers of about the right age to be a match," Cao Cao replied. "I know that Sun Ce's only recently married and his beautiful young wife – one of the famous Qiao sisters, whose beauty has long piqued my curiosity – is only recently with child, but I imagine that one of Sun Ce's high-ranking relations has daughters, though... now that I think of it, his cousin Sun Ben has a daughter, actually."

"Are you hoping to marry one of these young 'tiger daughters' yourself, Lord Cao...?" Guo Jia teased.

"No, no!" Cao Cao chuckled. "I'm thinking more about my sons, specifically my 'Yellow-beard', Zhang: he's a lot like Sun Ce, and so he'll be a match for the fiery Sun women. After an alliance like that – Cao and Sun, bloodlines intertwined – we can be sure that Sun Ce will behave a little better, and perhaps be more like his famous father."

"Your plan to make Yan Xiang 'Inspector of Yang Province' might undo any good work," Guo Jia suggested.

"Reports indicate that Sun Ce has given a new home to Liu Yao's son, Yuan Shu's son and daughter, and some of Liu Xun's kin that disapproved of his seizing Lujiang," Cao Cao retorted. "If Yan Xiang were a vassal of Liu Biao, I would worry; Sun Ce will not act against Yan Xiang, not when he sees that he is back in the region to restore order for the Han. I'm not sending Liu Xun back, of course: he needs to be kept on a tight leash, and I want his adviser Liu Yè to join me."

"I shall not disagree with that last point," Guo Jia said. "Liu Yè would be a magnificent addition to our growing pool of talent, as Liu Fu was."

"...So all that remains is to put this proposal to Sun Ce once he's finished playing 'pirates' with Huang Zu," Cao Cao continued. "I hope, for his sake, that he agrees."

Jing Governor Liu Biao was startled when he finally learned of the extent of Huang Zu and Liu Xun's defeat: he summoned most of his senior advisers, administrators and politicians to his northern capital Xiangyang and said, "Men are here that I normally leave to run the various parts of my domain, but now is not the time: Sun Ce is preparing to attack Jiangxia again. It won't be straight away, but we will most likely hear of his sailing from Qu'e in a matter of weeks. Gentlemen, I am perturbed: what must I do...?"

The adviser Kuai Liang coughed uncomfortably and replied, "You have too many problems to focus on Jiangxia alone: that's why you've given such autonomy to Huang Zu."

"That's not a helpful response," Liu Biao said when he realised that Kuai Liang had nothing more to say. "Do the Pang brothers, or your brother Yue, or maybe Wang Can, Fu Xun, Han Song... has *anyone* got a useful word for me...?"

The politician Han Song smiled and said, "Perhaps we might ask the Han court to do something about Sun Ce...?"

"Mister Han Song, that is *absurd*: the Han court – Cao Cao, in truth – has branded us as rebels for 'sheltering' Zhang Xiu," the young adviser Wang Can said.

"How dare you call my suggestion 'absurd', Wang Can!" Han Song retorted. "How dare you call *anything* absurd, when-!"

"When I find the sounds and faces of donkeys to be a comfort," Wang Can sighed. "I can little hope to reach the heights of fame for anything else, can I...? I can little hope to have my very sound advice taken seriously when men like you can simply throw that irrelevant fact at me! I had only expected my young age to be an obstacle, but now I am twenty-two, and I am still heckled when I try to make a valid point. I am trying to keep the discussion within a sensible boundary: your suggestion *was* absurd, Mister Han Song, because Cao Cao feels that we did nothing to expel Zhang Xiu – a man that he deeply hates for the personal losses that Zhang inflicted upon him – and no amount of cheap jokes at my expense will change that fact into a fiction."

The politician Fu Xun smiled and said, "My last heckles happened yesterday, and risk of shame will keep them there."

Han Song laughed and said, "I am rightly humbled, Mister Wang. Like the lord, I am reaching for hopes. Cao Cao would never help us… and no, I won't suggest Liu Zhang. What about calling upon men from the 'four semi-autonomous prefectures'…?"

The politician Huan Jie nodded and said, "That might be an idea: if we were to 'suggest' to them – and let's be realistic, gentlemen, and say that it would be less a lie and more a prophecy – that Sun Ce will turn his attentions to Lingling, Changsha, Guiyang and maybe even Wuling when he is finished with Jiangxia… then we might solicit offers of military aid."

"Unfortunately, Mister Huan, those regions lack real generals or militias," the adviser Kuai Yue said.

"…Sadly correct," Liu Biao agreed. "And besides, I get enough regular reports from those regions to know that they're under constant pressure from tribal activity."

There was a short silence, after which Kuai Yue said, "I think that we are wasting time by looking for allies. Yuan Shao is the only man that has the resources to aid our fight with Sun Ce, and everybody knows that he is planning to attack Xuchang and secure His Majesty."

"…Lord and brother-in-law, we should just remain as we are, and hope that Huang Zu recovers some of the spirit that made him a valuable ally in years past," Cai Mao suggested. "It has to be said that he excels at defence, so we will not lose Jiangxia."

Liu Biao smiled and said, "That's the first useful words! I should be telling Huang Zu to get every last man that he has harassing Yuzhang to withdraw to Jiangxia and aid the fortification of the place. I'll write at once…"

Huang Zu, meanwhile, had decided that there was an opportunity to strike at Bofu's westernmost holdings while the latter was in his capital Qu'e, which was situated at the eastern end of Jiangdong; he summoned his demoralised son Huang Shè to his private study and said, "I need you to try one last effort to give us a foothold in Jiangdong and ruin Sun Ce's chances of an easy path to Xiakou. The fortress city of Chaisang is on our side of Po County Lake, and if we take it we can feel safer. Can you do that for me?"

Huang Shè averted his gaze.

"Sun Ce is in Qu'e, and cannot possibly hope to get here to relieve the city if we act quickly," Huang Zu continued. "Our spies tell us that Ce's left about two-hundred men in Chaisang, and that the appointed commander is a recent recruit named Xu Sheng, a nobleman from Jiujiang who is famed for his arrogance and lack of respect for those he deems as below him. Such a man cannot possibly hope to hold a city for Sun Ce when it is staffed by two-hundred ruffians and you'll have two-*thousand* men."

"…I will do it, Father," Huang Shè replied at last. "I am your son, and must not allow one serious defeat to destroy me."

"I have every faith in you," Huang Zu insisted.

Chaisang's affluent, ostentatious guardian, Xu Sheng, was being visited by the adviser Qin Song at the time that Huang Shè brought his small fleet down the river network and prepared to attack the isolated city: Qin met with Xu on the battlements and said, "Every man, woman and child is safely within the walls now. What will you do to save this place, Mister Xu...?"

"I am 'Major' Xu, Mister Qin," Xu Shèng replied. "As for what I intend to do...? I am sick of this now. Time and again, my family have been forced to move from here to there, avoiding the pointless bickering between ignorant warlords of dubious breeding. Langya in Qing Province became a den of iniquity for the dregs of humanity, so our clan moved to Lu County in Yu Province, where we have endured Yuan Shu's ridiculous self-elevation to an emperor and the nationwide consequences of that pig-herder Dong Zhuo being created the Chancellor of State. Now I am in Jiangdong – a place that, I was promised, offers sanctuary to the weary traveller, and Huang Zu sends his pup here to drive me away before I've even unpacked. I'm not running again, Mister Qin, certainly not from ill-bred creatures like Huang Shè."

"That's a nice speech for your 'well-bred' friends to applaud, but it won't get rid of Huang Shè and it won't endear you to the men," Qin Song scolded. "Your pretty robes and armour might have paid for a larger militia or-"

"It isn't the *quantity* of men, Mister Qin, but the *quality* that matters," Xu Sheng sighed condescendingly. "I have a number of men in my service that are brought with me, and they are *very* well trained, as you – and Huang Shè – shall soon see."

Qin Song looked at the seemingly overconfident soldiers at the walls and muttered, "What fool is this that Lord Sun has left here to lose us Chaisang...?"

Huang Shè led the majority of his men to the walls of Chaisang and prepared for a siege: he expected that the usual cycle of sending men with ladders to scale the walls and whittle away the resources of the occupants was about to begin, and his confidence started to return.

"When we have Chaisang," Huang Shè said to his aides, "Father can begin the great mission to push Sun Ce and his pirates back to their caves and hills!"

"Don't be too overconfident," an adviser suggested. "The speed with which this Xu Sheng recognised the threat and withdrew the populace from the surrounding area gives the impression that-"

"**Chaisang is ours!**" Huang She cried. "**It *has* to be so! BEGIN THE ATTACK!**"

Qin Song observed the first wave of Jing soldiers approaching the walls and said, "**If your intention is to buy your way out of this, Major Xu, then do it now!**"

Xu Sheng smirked and said, "I do not simply *think* that I am their superior. **ARCHERS... AT THE READY...! ...FIRE AT WILL!**"

The row of soldiers that lined the western battlements raised their bows with grace and precision and started a mechanical, obviously oft-practiced process of nocking and firing arrows at frightening speed; Qin Song smiled as he suddenly realised that, despite his countenance, Xu Sheng knew exactly what he was doing. Huang Shè's men fell one after the other as arrows struck them with chilling accuracy, and all of the young commander's re-established confidence disappeared once again.

"**The-! ...Heaven, *why*???**" Huang Shè cried as the number of casualties climbed into the hundreds before his disbelieving eyes.

"**We must withdraw!**" an officer pleaded. "**Withdraw at once, General Huang!**"

"**How can I show my face???**" Huang Shè retorted. "How... can I... face *Father*...?"

Qin Song was laughing as he watched Xu Sheng's elite archers pick off the last of Huang She's first wave of besiegers; Xu then turned to Qin and said, "We've softened them up: now I shall go and deal with him *personally*."

"I'm sure that you can!" Qin Song replied.

Xu Sheng left the battlements and led his small force of elite infantrymen and cavalry out of the western gates of the city with an expensively-decorated spear in hand; Xu proved to be as good a fighter as he boasted, taking several lives personally and managing to kill some of Huang Shè's elite bodyguards. The Jing commander fled the field in tears, his spirit broken, while Xu – who even had the begrudging respect of men that knew that he did not reciprocate – raised his weapon in triumph and enjoyed the glory of a victory that had cost Huang Zu the lives of over a thousand men.

"Another hero," Qin Song declared as he watched the celebrations from atop the battlements of Chaisang.

When Liu Biao's correspondence finally reached Jiangxia, it was belated and unnecessary: Huang Zu was already moving all of his forces out of western Jiangdong and fortifying a defensive position at Shaxian, which was to the east of his prefectural capital.

The former Administrator of Wu Prefecture, Xu Gong, pondered Liu Xun's latest defeat as he sat in the court of his successor Zhu Zhi once again.

"This brings us one step closer to order," Zhu Zhi suggested. "If we can just rout the Shanyue once and for all...!"

"You want to try and track down White Tiger's old allies in their elevated strongholds...?" Xu Gong asked. "That will be no easy feat, and White Tiger certainly won't stick his head out of the undergrowth for you again."

Zhu Zhi's adopted son Zhu Ran scowled and said, "Are *you* still his ally, I wonder...?"

Xu Gong flicked his sleeve as a sign of the highest contempt.

"**You...!**" Zhu Ran cried; he lunged at Xu Gong, but Zhu Zhi grabbed his arm and forced him to sit down again.

"What a lack of temper!" Xu Gong said nervously. "I-!"

"You're being far too *confrontational*, Xu Gong," Zhu Zhi suggested. "My son asked you the question because your tone appeared to be mocking our efforts to end the threat of the Shanyue... which you really shouldn't be doing."

"I... apologise, Administrator," Xu Gong replied. "My nerves are frayed, especially after hearing of the battles around Lujiang. With trust being a rare commodity these days, and seeing what happens to those that lose it..."

"Liu Xun had no trust, and lost only what was wrongfully taken from others," Zhu Zhi said. "Lujiang is now garrisoned by General Li Shu, who serves Lord Sun, who in turn serves the Han; Liu Xun has fled to Cao Cao, who really should make an example of him.

As for what we were originally discussing... I should like to ask Xu Zhao to put aside his eccentric beliefs about charity and stop giving asylum to White Tiger, who is almost certainly coordinating the problems that we still have."

"He won't agree," Xu Gong replied. "Xu Zhao is very stubborn and determined: I should know, since I failed to have him hand over Sheng Xian to me, and then rejoiced when he then went on to ensure my own safety when relations between your lord and me were not so good."

"...Still, Xu Gong, you refer to Lord Sun as 'our lord' as though he not also yours!" Zhu Ran growled.

"And still, Mister Zhu, I insist that he is not," Xu Gong retorted. "I am a subject of the Han directly, as made clear when I received the right to hold the Administrator's seal of office from the imperial court."

"From Chang'an, from the 'regents'!" Zhu Ran heckled. "You-!"

"Let it be," Zhu Zhi ordered. "Xu Gong, your help is requested, on behalf of the Han, and it would be better if we all helped each other, yes...?"

Xu Gong clasped his hands together, bowed and said, "Of course."

When the court session in Wu Prefecture's capital ended, two men went back to their homes with the intention of writing letters to acquaintances: one was Zhu Ran, who was keen to find out what his childhood friend Sun Quan thought of the current situation, while the other was Xu Gong, who wrote another letter to the office of the Excellency of Works, Cao Cao, in the imperial capital Xuchang.

Bofu's 17-year-old younger brother Sun Quan – who was the Magistrate of Yangxian County in the western part of Wu Prefecture – received the letter from his friend Zhu Ran several days later, whereupon he invited his aide Pan Zhang to his private study so that they could discuss it.

"It is truly a wonderful moment, Wengui," Sun Quan began.

"You're still insistent on calling me by my courtesy name, Lord Sun...?" Pan Zhang exclaimed.

"My brother will come to understand that men are men, and that everyone has different flaws and talents," Sun Quan replied confidently. "Some people are harder to fathom than others; I can see the potential in you."

The charismatic Pan Zhang smiled: he knew how lucky he was to have the county magistrate and the brother of the province's ruler as a patron. Pan had once been little more than an infamous borrower of money, gambler, hustler, mercenary and lover of vice, but when a young, impressionable Sun Quan took a liking to his carefree approach to life and sensed a wasted pool of talents, all of Pan's detractors were silenced and several military and administrative roles followed. Bofu disliked Pan intensely, since he blamed the man for his brother's brief descent into vice and petty theft, but Sun Quan was now behaving as a statesman should – despite the continued presence of Pan Zhang – and so there was little point to saying anything further.

"If my brother has defeated Liu Xun, that can mean only one thing: he can turn his attentions back to Liu Biao!" Sun Quan continued. "If only I could be in the vanguard, Wengui, and destroy Huang Zu and Liu Biao with my own two hands! But I am not like Ce and Yi; I am not as weak and sickly as Kuang, but even my sister Shangxiang has more warrior bones in her than I do, so I must leave the fighting to others... ... ...I wonder if Zhou Tai will be the one to kill Huang Zu."

"You're too self-critical," Pan Zhang suggested. "You-"

"I pine for the comfort of the jar, but wine will not solve my problems, no matter how well it is brewed, and no matter how fine the rice it was made with," Sun Quan said. "I must remain sober, continue to try and impress my brother with how well I manage this county, and hope that I will be truly, completely forgiven for my... 'mistake'."

"I'm blamed for that, Lord Sun," Pan Zhang replied.

"What you amongst others taught me, Wengui, was the breadth and scale of the world: I am my own man, and chose to be a fool in that world," Sun Quan insisted. "I now choose to be a statesman. I can never be what Father was... which used to bother me, but now it does not. Now, I aspire to be something else... but again, I digress!

"Once Liu Biao is defeated, there will be no more enemies, no more grudges and blood feuds: at that moment, the Han court must decide whether it will accept what my brother is doing... which he knows. There's a chance that Cao Cao – who is, some say, the embodiment of the court now, and 'Chancellor of State in all but name' – might insist that my brother submit, yield Jiangdong to northern bureaucrats, and give us some paltry reward for all of our efforts. What, I wonder, would my brother do if he was confronted with such a challenge...?"

"...You've thought about this a lot, I see," Pan Zhang noted.

"Were such a thing to happen, I would lose this county," Sun Quan said. "It would be just as it was when Father returned from fighting the Yellow Turbans: Ce would receive some sort of reward – perhaps a higher form of marquisate – and perhaps a handful of taxable households, while everyone else received meaningless rhetoric and pitiful, low-ranking positions in a northern-dominated government. Men just like Wang Lang, Tao Qian and Liu Yao would be sent here... and all that we have achieved would be undone. I only hope that Zhou Yu, Lü Fan, Zhang Zhao, Qin Song and the rest of them are sure to tell my brother to stand firm."

"I doubt that he needs them to tell him," Pan Zhang suggested. "Lord Sun Ce is a hero of the era."

"...He is," Sun Quan replied. "I am... *lucky*... to be a son and brother to such men."

"And I am lucky to have you as lords and masters," Pan Zhang said. "It has not gone unnoticed that you have become a great statesman, and *I* have now started to learn from *you* and become a better man myself. My debts are repaid, my subordinates are happy, and your other officials no longer have cause to complain. Now there is nothing that cannot be accomplished."

Sun Quan smiled and said, "I hope so."

****

7

A week passed. Word reached Zhu Zhi that Bofu was preparing for a more decisive attack on Huang Zu than was previously planned, and within a few days, another pressing letter was urging aggressive action against Bofu: it had been sent by the Wu Prefecture official Xu Gong, and it was being read by its recipient Cao Cao, the Han's Excellency of Works, who had summoned his most trusted aides to discuss it.
"...This man Xu Gong is becoming more and more insistent... and more and more *careless*," the adviser Guo Jia sighed.
"One can understand the reasoning behind his words, Fengxiao," Cao Cao said. "He again calls Sun Ce 'another Xiang Yu', and 'warns me' that I should consider the lad to be the greatest threat to the Han that we have faced thus far. I just don't know whether I should heed him or not."
A tall, middle-aged adviser with a sour expression waved his hand and said, "Ignore him."
"Can we afford to, Elder Cheng...?" Xun Yòu asked.
"Xu Gong is a troublemaker that benefitted from the regency of Li Jue and Guo Si, else he'd be rotting in a cell or worse," Cheng Yu retorted. "How the man that overthrew Sheng Xian can have the nerve to say 'punish the violent hankerer' is beyond me; and, furthermore, I think that his constant slander is more about hypocritical revenge than concern for the Han Dynasty."
Cao Cao laughed and said, "Your point is valid, Elder Cheng. He threatens to 'go above my authority' if I do not heed him, but I don't think that he'd dare write directly to His Majesty and draw more attention to himself. No, our main concern is not Sun Ce of Fuchun: it is *Liu Bei*..."

Liu Bei was the descendant of a disinherited prince of the realm who began life as a weaver of straw mats and shoes: financial aid from a relative elevated him to a private school student, and the Yellow Turban Rebellion gave him his first opportunity to be noticed by the Han court. Bei - along with his equally famous allies Zhang Fei and Guan Yu – quelled several small Yellow Turban uprisings in the northern frontier region of Yòu Province, for which Bei was made a county magistrate; he surrendered the title involuntarily at a later date and led a private militia against rebellions for Xu Province Governor Tao Qian.
Several relocations, promotions, resignations and misfortunes followed, but fate returned Bei and his small army to Xu Province when Cao Cao invaded it for personal reasons; a local magnate, Mi Zhu, pushed for Bei to inherit the province from the ailing Tao Qian, but he quickly lost it when disaffected officials – who included the future Administrator of Guangling, Chen Deng – colluded with the renegade warlord Lü Bu and expelled Bei from his office while he was on campaign against the Sun clan's then-master Yuan Shu. The usurped governor then endured a year-long siege and finally yielded to Lü Bu, who assigned Bei to a western defensive position in order to guard – and act as an expendable buffer – against whomever the inconstant Bu was currently fighting. Lü Bu finally decided to ally with Yuan Shu, who had

declared himself as the First Emperor of the Zhong Dynasty: Liu Bei was routed by the untrusting Bu and chased into Yan Province, which was now home to the temporary imperial capital Xuchang. Cao Cao – who was now Emperor Xian's guardian – allied with his old enemy Liu Bei and marched into Xu Province, this time as a protector; a long, costly siege finally ended with the death of Lü Bu, but it also ended the brief peace between Cao Cao and Xu's former governor Liu Bei.

Cao Cao assigned one of his own followers, Che Zhou, as the governor of Xu Province in the wake of defeating Lü Bu, rather than reinstating Liu Bei: this very public act left Bei resentful, and as soon as an opportunity arose – and that opportunity came in the form of a commission to block Yuan Shu's passage to Ji Province – Bei left Cao's service and returned to his base in western Xu Province. Liu Bei's time in Xuchang had introduced him to a small clique of officials that hated Cao Cao and intended to stage a coup with the aid of a secret document; Bei readily joined the plot and intended to aid it with a military campaign in Xu Province that would, it was hoped, inspire the procrastinating Yuan Shao to finally act. Cao Cao rightly suspected that Liu Bei's next move was imminent, and so Xu Gong's protestations would go unanswered while proven threats were dealt with.

Another week passed: the reports of Huang Shè's latest defeat reached Wu County City and provoked minor celebration in Zhu Zhi's court.

"Huang Zu's forces have been routed *again*!" Zhu Zhi said. "This latest victory, though relatively minor, shows that we're gaining new talent all of the time."

"Yes, Mister Zhu," Xu Gong said. "Xu Sheng sounds like a man of great talent, and I am honoured to share lineage with him, no matter how distant."

"...The Shanyue raided a village that's not more than a day's ride from here," Zhu Ran noted. "They're becoming brazen again, and that always escalates. Have any of your people heard anything, Mister Xu...?"

"Nothing," Xu Gong replied coldly. "I have nothing more to do with the Shanyue. And 'my people' consists of a handful of old allies."

"All proven facts," Zhu Zhi said with a smile. "My son merely asks, since the Shanyue are none too bright and some of them might not know that you have severed your ties with White Tiger."

Xu Gong bowed silently.

"Mister Lü, it is nice to have you here," Zhu Zhi said as he turned to the quiet, observant Lü Dai. "You, of course, are here to offer 'local advice'."

"I am," Lü Dai replied.

"...'Local advice'...?" Xu Gong murmured; the officer-official Lü Dai was, in fact, a native of neighbouring Guangling Prefecture.

"We look forward to your contributions, Mister Lü," Zhu Zhi said.

The discussions shifted to other matters; at the end of the meeting, Zhu Zhi invited his adopted son Ran to his private study and said, "Don't press Xu Gong too often, son, else he might be less careless."

"He could hardly be more careful," Zhu Ran replied. "He's

obviously up to something, though... that he cannot hide."
"Yes, but his correspondence disappears, despite our putting a ring of surveillance around Xu Zhao," Zhu Zhi mused. "Perhaps... perhaps we are wrong to assume that he contacts White Tiger now. Perhaps we must consider other recipients."
"Chen Deng in northern Guangling, the pirate king Xue Zhou on the Guangling waterways, Cao Cao in Xuchang, Yuan Shao in Ji Province, Liu Biao in Jing Province, Liu Bei in Xu Province; is there anyone else...?" Zhu Ran asked.
"...Chen Deng is a possibility; Xue Zhou is an unlikely ally," Zhu Zhi replied. "Cao Cao is as likely as Chen Deng; Yuan Shao might want to avenge his brother, but there are others that would suffer first. Liu Biao is certainly a possibility, since he might appreciate warnings about our movements; Liu Bei, not at all likely. Chen Deng, Cao Cao, and Liu Biao... are the most likely contacts for a Xu Gong that looks to lose his head."
"Lü Dai's been sent here because of worries about Chen Deng facilitating recapture of southern Guangling by attacking Wu Prefecture by circling around from the east, so Lord Sun Ce's advisers are thinking as you do, Father," Zhu Ran supposed. "But Chen wouldn't dare act against Lord Sun without permission from Cao Cao..."
"...Which is why we must be careful and miss nothing," Zhu Zhi said. "Cao Cao fears Lord Sun, but we know that he prefers diplomacy over action, especially with the threat of a war with Yuan Shao looming. We can convince Cao Cao of our benevolent intent if we are not contradicted, but Xu Gong is just the sort of man that might create enough tension to force Cao's hand..."
"...Then we must find out what he's doing, if anything, and quickly," Zhu Ran prompted.
"Indeed, yes," Zhu Zhi replied. "Hopefully, he's harmless, but something tells me that he means only the worst for us..."

"...Weeks... and he does *nothing*."
Jing Governor Liu Biao was confused; Huang Zu's letters spoke of a readiness for an attack, but the Sun clan were apparently unmoving. Liu's Xiangyang court was divided on the meaning of the inaction, but Liu Biao wanted some clarity.
"One cannot ask for the impossible and be surprised when he receives nothing," Kuai Yue insisted. "Does anything happening in the *north* make any sense...? Cao Cao is actually *courting* Zhang Xiu now, while continuing to label us as criminals for 'protecting' Zhang! Liu Bei betraying Cao Cao's trust and now poised to take Xu Province for himself for a second time! Yuan Shao is rumoured to be forging alliances with the *Qiang*, *Gong Du* and the *Yellow Turbans*! And all this tavern talk about 'secret edicts'..."
"I'll believe it all when I see it," Liu Biao said dismissively. "But... but then perhaps Sun Ce is delaying while he waits to see what happens in the north... for if Yuan Shao does as we suspect, he'll demand my support, at which point Cao Cao will want Sun Ce's help to keep me busy, and Sun will effectively be receiving a mandate from the Han government to seize my province!"
"...Unlikely," the politician Fu Xun said. "Cao Cao knows that Sun Ce would be impossible to remove once he was rooted here. And if the 'secret edict' rumours prove true, it might be the case that Liu

and Sun would fight side-by-side against Cao Cao…"

Liu Biao laughed disdainfully and said, "Nonsense! There can be no peace between Jing and Jiangdong as long as a Sun or Liu is left alive! He's made that very clear!"

"An edict would change that," the politician Huan Jie said. "A genuine edict would force all of the warlords to put aside their differences and ally against Cao Cao, which would end his threat to you and-"

"Do you remember what happened when the warlords were called upon to unite against a tyrant last time?" Liu Biao heckled.

"There was no edict last time," Wang Can noted. "Yuan Shao was the highest authority, and we none of us knew his intentions."

"And in that respect, nothing's changed," Liu Biao said. "If Liu Bei really intends to seize Xu Province *again* and be soundly beaten and chased out of the place *again*… which is what will surely happen… then I am speechless. And as for any edict that ever appears, it would probably be the work of Yuan Shao's cronies or Cao's detractors in the capital, most certainly, and even if it wasn't, it would still be labelled as such."

"But it would save you," Fu Xun said. "Isn't that reason enough to hope for such an edict and to support it if it materialised…?"

"Of course," Liu Biao replied. "It would be the end to one of my problems, at least…"

More time passed, and it became obvious to the increasingly fearful Xu Gong that Cao Cao had no intention of acting against the Sun clan in Jiangdong.

"…Fools… *fools*…!" Xu Gong hissed as he penned another letter: this one would go to Emperor Xian directly, and it would make every one of the points that Xu had already put to the Excellency of Works.

"Reconsider!" Xu Gong's son Lang pleaded.

"I cannot reconsider!" Xu Gong insisted. "Sun Ce will only tolerate us while he has to: if I do not do this, our deaths will come sooner rather than later!"

"You've said so before, Father," Xu Lang said, "but-!"

"Never has it been so urgent, son," Xu Gong interrupted. "Who's left, mm…? Wang Lang, Liu Yao, Zu Lang, Taishi Ci, Liu Xun, Yuan Shu, White Tiger, Haixi Chen… they're either dead, put to flight or serving him now. My influence has gone, my support collapsed, all because I was fool enough to work with the Suns! Liu Biao is the last obstacle, and once Sun Ce seizes Jing Province – and for all of Cao's dismissive words, he surely knows that to be Ce's true intent – there can be only one fate for Xu Gong… death, death to the third degree, which means everyone close to me – including *you* – dies as well!"

"We cannot be sure that he'd do that, Father, not if you just accepted his rule, which seems benevolent," Xu Lang protested. "It is by your current actions that-"

"You're young, and idealistic: I'm older, and know men's minds," Xu Gong retorted. "Sun Ce is no better than his former master Yuan Shu: the servant has learned from the master, and now he is intent on turning Jing and Yang Provinces into a kingdom. He'll use men while he has to, but I assure you that Zu Lang, Taishi Ci and I will pay for our earlier 'crimes' as soon as he is enthroned."

"...I cannot sway you," Xu Lang said.

"What I do, I do because I must," Xu Gong replied. "I will send this to His Majesty – and another letter to that fool Cao Cao, just to let him know what I have done – and then, perhaps, when my words are read to the Imperial court as a whole, we will see an end to this madness."

Xu Gong's letters would not go to Xuchang straight away, as he had to minimise the risk of them being intercepted; they would begin their journey as Sun Ce began his next campaign against the lord of Jiangxia Prefecture, Huang Zu.

****

8

More weeks passed, wherein Bofu's wife Daqiao gave birth to two healthy girls just as the next military confrontation with Huang Zu loomed: he invited his closest relatives and friends to celebrate the occasion with a banquet, but the mood was not as jovial as it should have been.

"You're painfully silent, Boyang," Bofu said to his cousin Sun Ben.

"…I was wondering which of Cao's kin it is that *your* daughters will be betrothed to, Cousin," Sun Ben replied.

Bofu's mother, Lady Wu, stared at her volatile son and hoped that she could diffuse the situation if it became violent; she then looked to her former love rival – Sun Jian's consort, Lady Chen – and nodded purposefully.

"…You're not being fair," Bofu retorted after a short silence.

"Please let's not argue!" Wu Jing cried. "Nephew, I have worked alongside Boyang many a time, and-!"

"It really doesn't matter how many times 'who has worked with who', Uncle," Bofu interrupted. "Boyang is being unfair. I have not answered Cao Cao's letter yet, so what reason do you have, Cousin, for ruining this banquet with icy challenges…?"

Sun Ben noticed that most of the guests – who included Sun Quan, Sun Yi, Sun Kuang, Wu Jing, Xu Kun, Gongjin, Lü Fan and Ben's own brother Fu – were in agreement with Bofu; he smiled awkwardly, bowed and said, "I am being unfair, Bofu, as you say. If there has been no presumption, there has been no offence."

"I intended to discuss it after the banquet," Bofu explained. "I wouldn't just go ahead and betroth your daughter to Cao Zhang, even though I have a right to as head of the clan. Dad wouldn't have, and neither would I."

Bofu's tomboyish sister, Shangxiang – who was attending the banquet in martial arts training clothes instead of a robe – laughed and asked, "Is Cao Zhang a hero? We Suns should only marry other heroes."

"*Ayah*… I knew you'd have something to say," Bofu groaned.

Sun Ben – who was grateful for Shangxiang's mood-lightening interjection – smiled at her and said, "Perhaps *you* would like to marry Cao Zhang."

"She'd beat him up, and Cao Cao'd send her back," Sun Yi joked.

After a brief period of laughter that Shangxiang enjoyed more than anyone, Lady Wu waved her hand and said, "Let's talk no more of marriage alliances now. What matters to me at this moment are my two beautiful granddaughters."

"Well said, dear sister," Wu Jing said. "Let us forget all of our worries for a few hours and be merry! Music! Let us rejoice!"

Bofu nodded at Sun Ben, who reciprocated the gesture.

The banquet continued for another hour, at which point the event started to scale down and some people started to leave. Gongjin went to the home of his friend and former benefactor Lu Su, whose proponents did not extend far past Gongjin at that point in time because of his perceived tactlessness.

"I hope that I am not visiting too late…?" Gongjin said.

"Not at all, not at all!" the short, thin Lu Su replied as he escorted

Gongjin into his living quarters. "How did the banquet go?"

"One or two awkward moments," Gongjin replied as he sat opposite Lu Su and took up a tea dish. "Bofu's getting better at controlling his temper, though, so there were no fights."

"The marriage alliances were the cause, I'm guessing," Lu Su said.

"Right again, Zijing," Gongjin replied. "First a second marquisate, then *this*: Cao Cao's *scared* of Bofu, which scares *me*."

"You fear an assassination attempt," Lu Su prompted.

"...It... it isn't impossible, but it's unlikely," Gongjin replied. "It might be beneficial if Sun Kuang and Sun Ben accept the proposals that have been offered... but this isn't the north. Cao Cao expects Sun Ben to willingly give his daughter over, just as Yuan Shao has merrily wed his vassals' daughters to Wuhuan chieftains, or how successive emperors have given their lower-ranking daughters to Xiongnu and Xianbei chieftains to keep the peace. Sun Kuang, that's different; Cao Cao's brother won't question protocol, and Kuang, who is training to be an official, will be glad of a pretty wife with some good connections in the capital. Sun Ben might worry that Cao Zhang will mistreat his daughter, or that she will be lost amid a sea of consorts as Zhang comes to emulate his father. I must be honest and say that the alliances do smooth relations, but I entirely understand if any party says 'no'."

"...That's their decision, though, and a poor use of our time," Lu Su said frankly.

Gongjin laughed and replied, "I suppose it is!"

"Oh! I, uh... that was a poor choice of words," Lu Su realised.

"You sold half of your material possessions to fund my militia, Zijing, and followed me here to Jiangdong as a trusted friend," Gongjin replied. "I know your ways and don't mind them. What *is* a better use of our time is to use it to discuss the possible outcomes of the upcoming battle with Huang Zu."

Lu Su sipped tea from his dish and said, "You're not suggesting that we have another morbid conversation about 'worst case scenarios', are you...?"

"Bofu entrusts his legacy to his brothers, Lü Fan and me," Gongjin explained. "He knows that stray arrows and missteps are a fact of life, and even a hero such as he is not infallible."

"...It would be a shame, what with him having a little family now," Lu Su sighed.

"Sun Jian lived and died, and so will Bofu," Gongjin said. "My own wife will soon be blessing me with a child, but I know that I might not see them grow to adulthood and have planned for it. Now, Zijing, let us discuss the various alternatives that-"

"Forgive me for asking, Gongjin, but why...?" Lu Su asked. "I am unpopular. Lord Sun's mother dislikes me, Lord Sun dislikes me, and most of the lord's vassals, inherited and earned, have little to say to me."

"I'm always fighting to change that," Gongjin promised. "Now, please, let us talk of our options..."

While Gongjin and Lu Su had their conversation, the banquet ended and Bofu began his own discussions with his family regarding Cao Cao's letter.

"Being a son-in-law to the brother of the Han's Excellency of Works might be a good thing," the sickly Sun Kuang suggested.

"I'm sure that Lady Cao will be pretty, since the Caos are marrying most of the most beautiful women in the land."

"You sound like you don't mind going ahead, 'Little Marquis'," Bofu noted. "Boyang, I know that you're not sure, but-"

"It wasn't the case that I was – or am – against it," Sun Ben insisted. "You've made it my choice, which you didn't have to do as the head of our clan."

"Is that a slight?" Xu Kun asked. "If it is, Ben, then-!"

"It wasn't, I assure you," Sun Ben replied. "I yielded the chieftainship willingly, and I have never openly or privately contested Bofu as our lord. I truly gave way to a worthier man."

Sun Quan looked at Sun Ben and studied his expression for signs of dishonesty.

"...I don't think that you're somehow 'less worthy' than I am," Bofu said. "Your father and my father were twins, you're older than me... you'd be right to wonder why, given what a great job you did as clan chieftain, that you-"

"I am not unhappy," Sun Ben insisted. "Now, returning to the matter of my daughter marrying Cao Zhang: what word is there about his nature...?"

"Is he a pig?" Shangxiang asked.

"...You shouldn't even be here!" Bofu complained. "Go and-!"

"I do have a right to be here," Shangxiang retorted. "If Mother can be here, and Lady Chen, then why not me...?"

"It's more about *age*, sister, and *experience*," Sun Yi suggested. "You're twelve, and never leave the confines of the estate, so what do you know about the world...?"

"Whose fault's that, though?" Shangxiang retorted. "I want to go out and talk to people!"

"...And after the one time you did, I'm not keen for you to do so again," Bofu admitted. "Honestly, that market trader didn't know what to do after you had a go at him."

Lady Wu smiled and said, "Shangxiang, please retire. This is a discussion between people that understand all of the politics. I'll be sure and tell you all about it when we're done."

Shangxiang bowed slightly and retreated.

"...*Aiee*... Thank you, Mother," Bofu sighed.

"You're all a handful, each and every one of you," Lady Wu replied. "But you and Yi are right: we have little time, and we must consider everything carefully. Shangxiang will only prolong the conversation with her antics. Now, please continue: we were querying Cao Zhang's character."

"Cao Cao's a very private man, but rumours get out from time to time," Wu Jing said. "Cao Cao's eldest surviving son, Cao Pi, is said to be a fairly scholarly type, but also adept at poetry, martial arts and so-forth, like his father. Zhang is the second son, but is said to be 'unenthusiastic about the pen', believing that 'real men' prove their worth on the battlefield."

"...I can't say anything, can I...?" Bofu chuckled. "Yi and I are much the same." Sun Quan scowled at the implied suggestion that he was not a 'real man'; Bofu noticed Quan's expression and Kuang's sadness in turn, forcing him to add, "Not that I mean that I don't respect scholars and officials, I just meant the 'not having an interest in it myself' part, okay...?"

Sun Yi nudged Sun Quan playfully and said, "You're our brother.

Kuang too. We're the ones at fault for not being smart enough to do what you do."

"…I know that you meant no offence," Sun Quan replied. "I am at fault in this matter, just as I am very often the one at fault."

"Let's not revisit 'that' now," Lady Wu pleaded. "If Cao Zhang is militarily minded, so be it: as Ce has noted, he and Yi are not fond of scholarly things but they are both good men nonetheless. If you need more time to ponder, Ben, then take that time."

Sun Ben nodded silently.

"…I need to organise the defences so that they're up to the job while we're away," Bofu realised. "Yi's coming with me this time, and Ziheng and Gongjin say that I need to fortify our positions in case of Huang Zu trying to go around us."

"Then we should say no more for now," Sun Ben suggested. "Cao Cao can wait a little bit longer for an answer, I think: we need to do all that we can to fortify Jiangdong and deal with Huang Zu and his master once and for all. Who's going to guard Chaisang?"

"Leave that Xu Sheng fellow there," Wu Jing suggested. "If reports of his victory against Huang Shè's surprise attack are correct – and I have no reason to doubt Qin Song's eyes and words – then Xu's just the man we need there."

"…He's obnoxious, but alright," Bofu agreed. "Gongjin did say the man would 'surprise me', and he has."

"This is a discussion that you should be having with your advisers and generals," Lady Wu said. "But before you do so, visit your wife and children."

"I will," Bofu replied. "We'll all meet again here in the hall in an hour, okay…? And somebody tell Old Cheng and the rest that I'd like them there as well."

"Should I wait here…?" Sun Hè asked.

"The likelihood of assassins in my bedchambers is low, Bohai, so yes!" Bofu chuckled as he left the meeting. "Enjoy a night away from guarding me from myself, Cousin, and spend some time with *your* family!"

Sun Hè laughed and said, "I shall."

Xu Kun, Wu Jing and the other men that intended to be at the military meeting bowed respectfully and left within minutes of Bofu's departure; Sun Kuang, Sun Quan, Lady Wu and Lady Chen were the only ones that remained.

"I must return to Yangxian," Sun Quan said. "My brother has no need of me at the meeting."

"…Nor me," Sun Kuang said.

"You should neither of you be so bitter," Lady Chen suggested. "In so many ways, your contributions as statesmen will matter more, and your brother Lord Sun is all too aware of that."

"I know, Lady Chen, but can I help wishing that I was a hero like Ce?" Sun Quan replied honestly. "Everything that I have said before, it still stands."

Lady Chen nodded respectfully.

"…I must retire," Lady Wu said. "I am weary… even the joy can drain the spirit."

"Farewell for now, Mother, Lady Chen, Brother," Sun Quan said as he got to his feet and bowed to each person in turn. "I hope that we will soon have those peaceful times that we so often allude to, so that we can be together like this always."

Lady Wu smiled, and Sun Quan retreated.

"…I need to retire as well," Sun Kuang sighed. "Everything feels like a chore for me nowadays."

"Save your strength, 'Little Marquis'," Lady Wu replied gently. "The best days are yet to come."

Sun Kuang paid respects and retreated; Lady Chen then turned to Lady Wu and said, "Are you not feeling well again…?"

"People get sick, dear sister," Lady Wu replied. "The entire nation is sick: my sons will be the ones to make everything better."

Bofu went to Daqiao, who was being attended to by her sister Xiaoqiao, a doctor and two maidservants.

"…Lord Sun," Xiaoqiao hailed.

"No need for formalities," Bofu replied warmly. "How're my wife and the little tigresses…?"

"Mother and children are strong," the doctor said.

"Just what I wanted to hear!" Bofu replied as he knelt by Daqiao, who was cradling her daughters protectively. "I just hope that I don't end up with two little Shangxiangs, because the one we have is enough!"

The room was filled with smiles.

"…As pretty as their mother, as strong as their father," Bofu whispered as he touched the hand of one of his daughters. "Will there be more…?"

"Heaven willing, a million," Daqiao replied.

"…We'll do our best…!" Bofu chuckled softly.

Within an hour, Bofu was overseeing another meeting, this time with his senior officials – Lü Fan, Sun Ben, Sun Fu, Sun Yi, Cheng Pu, Huang Gai, Gu Yong, Zhang Zhao, Zhang Hong, Wu Jing and Xu Kun.

"We should speak quickly and return to work," Cheng Pu said.

"Where's Gongjin…?" Bofu asked.

"He's on his way," Lü Fan replied. "No Sun Hè…?"

"The poor man needs a rest," Bofu said. "Yes, I know that applies to us all, but-"

"We should really be back at our posts, Lord Sun," Cheng Pu said.

"And you will be soon enough," Bofu insisted. "For a grey-haired old man, you really do have a lot of enthusiasm."

Cheng Pu smiled and said, "I'm not rising to it."

Bofu grinned and turned to the serious Lü Fan, who said, "We'll throw everything we have at Huang Zu, as we've discussed before: Cao Cao's being cautious, which means that we have nothing to fear from the north, and Liu Xun is no longer a threat. Hua Xin's being uppity, but-"

"Hua Xin?" Cheng Pu exclaimed. "Has that soft-headed fool forgotten that he's not got any support and yielded to us for that very reason…?"

"Times change," Lü Fan replied. "Hua Xin's a Han loyalist, and as the situation in the north continues to evolve, and as we continue to quarrel with enemies within and without, men like Hua embody the ideals of a peaceful Han Empire. Liu Ji painted a disparaging picture of Hua, as did Taishi Ci, but desperation can make a decent man appear to be something else entirely."

"So he's alright then, is that what you're telling me…?" Bofu asked desperately. "He's alright, but he doesn't like me."

"He's frightened of our possible intentions," Lü Fan replied.

"So was Lu Kang," Bofu noted. "I mean, he was a hero, wasn't he, that brought peace to places he governed... and I killed him."

"He was needlessly defiant and too concerned with doing his job, and suffered an unfortunate price for it," Cheng Pu said. "In that respect, he was like your father. If Hua Xin can be reasoned with, and he is a good man that we can work with, then fine; if not, then we must accept it to be his choice and act accordingly. We cannot jeopardise our great design for the sake of appeasing one neurotic man."

"...We'll leave him until I've defeated Huang Zu," Bofu decided.

"If someone might have let me finish, I might have said that very thing," Lü Fan said. "The plan is simple enough: we push Huang Zu deep into his territory and start to annex southern Jiangxia into Yuzhang, just as Zu tried to annex lands east of Po County Lake into Jiangxia. We then placate Hua Xin, and then we return to Xiakou to defeat Huang Zu definitively."

"Why not just push into Jiangxia and smash Huang Zu outright in one go...?" Xu Kun asked. "Why go, win, leave, wait and go back when we can go once and be done with it...?"

Gongjin finally arrived at the meeting: he began his contribution by saying, "To do that would leave us exposed to any possible action by Chen Deng, the Shanyue, or Cao Cao himself, should there be a sudden 'change of heart'."

"Agreed," Cheng Pu said. "We must take no risks."

"And I am travelling to Xuchang to join the court, so the truth of the situation will be much clearer," Zhang Hong said. "I expect to find Cao to be agreeable, but we'll know soon enough if he is not."

"...I've dragged you all here to discuss things that are already in motion, haven't I...?" Bofu realised.

"Dong Xi, Zhou Tai, Jiang Qin, Taishi Ci, Chen Wu and Ling Cao are readying the army and navy, Zu Lang has moved his people into Po County, Hè Qi and Han Dang are providing support, and as soon as we're done here I intend to join them," Cheng Pu replied. "We have but two worries: being noticed, and being too slow."

"Then we sail on the first clear morning," Bofu declared.

Two days passed where the weather – the direction of the wind in particular – was not considered to be favourable for setting sail; Bofu spent the days with his family and at the hunting grounds near the city as he tried to deal with his frustration at having to wait. But on the third day, Bofu's court was startled by the arrival of a hysterical messenger from Zhu Zhi's court in Wu Prefecture, and many expected an unwanted campaign against the Shanyue to be the outcome.

"**I'll put White Tiger's head on a spike!**" Bofu cried as he stormed into the court and glared at the handful of nervous officials that had been invited to the reduced session. "**Time and again, I'm prevented from-!**"

"**It isn't the Shanyue!**" Gongjin interrupted.

Bofu's eyes wandered as he took his host seat.

"It's *Xu Gong*... he's been writing to Xuchang," Lü Fan explained.

"...Xu Gong...? ...To the capital...?" Bofu murmured.

"This might have been potentially worse than the Shanyue... no, being honest, it definitely would have been worse," Lü Fan continued. "He's chosen to speak of you in very unhelpful terms."

"…What exactly do you mean by 'unhelpful'…?" Bofu asked. "Stop coating it in honey and just say it."

Lü Fan turned to his colleague Gu Yong, who said, "My lord, he has obviously been petitioning Cao Cao repeatedly but getting nowhere, so he has tried to petition the throne… to petition *His Majesty*, asking that you be forced to relocate to Xuchang and-"

"He wrote to the *Son of Heaven*…?" Bofu exclaimed. "…'Relocate'…? B-but I forgave the man, and gave him a job! What the hell else did he say? Do we know?"

"Fortunately, yes, we know, and even more fortunately, His Majesty never will, unless Xu Gong sent multiple couriers, which is unlikely," Gu Yong replied. "He compared you to *Xiang Yu*, the-"

"The founder of the Chu State, who's usually blamed for the collapse of the Qin Dynasty, and the Han founder's nemesis," Bofu said. "It's one of the things that I *do* remember…"

"He's compared you to a man like that…?" Sun Yi exclaimed. "That means he's accusing you of…!"

"Cheng Pu's aware of it, and he's saying the same thing as Zhu Zhi, which happens to be my own thinking and Ziheng's as well," Gongjin said. "Xu Gong will have to be silenced. That carries its own risks, most obviously that Cao Cao will learn of it and may then think worse of us and better of him, but we can't risk this kind of correspondence getting through to-"

"I want to read it for myself," Bofu growled.

Lü Fan sighed miserably and passed the intercepted letter to Bofu.

"…This… … …*this*…!" Bofu whined angrily. "I… was so… patient, so… and when I wanted to kill the man… and he sends this… to Xuchang… this would have meant my death for *treason*, the bastard! This would have meant death to me, my family, my children, my brothers, my mother, perhaps my whole *clan*!"

"So he'll need to die, then," Sun Ben said.

"If I could fly to his house, kill him and fly back here in the space of one night, I'd do it myself!" Bofu replied. "My only regret is that others will get the pleasure of it… no, this is too much… and I want him dead as soon as it is possible. Speed a man back, tell Zhu Zhi-"

"It shall be done at once," Lü Fan said as he retreated from the meeting hall.

"…*Bastard*…!" Bofu whimpered.

"The damage has almost certainly been contained," Gu Yong said.

"I'll be in Xuchang soon, my lord, and I will vouch for you!" Zhang Hong insisted.

"We should think no more of it and press on with our plan to eliminate Huang Zu," Gongjin implored.

"Oh, don't worry, I intend to," Bofu chortled. "He isn't going to demoralise or halt me… all he's done is remind me that problems need dealing with. Xu Gong is as good as dealt with now… and Huang Zu's next."

＊＊＊＊＊＊＊＊＊＊＊＊

9

Two days after the interception of Xu Gong's letter to Emperor Xian, Xu's family was awoken in the middle of the night by the sound of intruders that were attempting to breach the front door of his home; Xu knew immediately that his actions had been exposed and that his clan was doomed.

"We'll defend you to our deaths, Lord Xu!" an armed attendant promised.

"Send word to my son!" Xu Gong screamed at a young servant. **"Someone must survive this!"**

The servant fled the house through the kitchen.

"What's happening???" Xu Gong's wife wailed; Xu's two consorts were also crying hysterically.

"This is Heaven's will, but I know not why!" Xu Gong replied as the intruders – who were members of Administrator Zhu Zhi's private militia – finally defeated and killed his loyal servants and entered his home.

"Xu Gong, you are guilty of betraying your lord Sun Ce," the group captain announced. "Surrender at once."

Xu Gong brandished a sword and smiled, saying, "Not to the likes of Sun Ce."

"Fine," the captain retorted. "The outcome will be the same."

Xu Gong's son Lang hurried to his father's home, despite his father having ordered the servant to keep him away; his father's aides Heng and Yan accompanied him, and both men were as carelessly anxious to rescue their lord. But it was too late, even if there had been a chance to stage a rescue: the three horrified men were forced to hide and watch at a distance as soldiers removed the corpses of Xu Gong and his wife from the house.

"...Father... Mother...!" Xu Lang whispered.

The group captain was dropping Xu Gong's severed head into a sack for presentation to Zhu Zhi: Heng noted it and said, "Young lord, they must pay... the Suns, they must all answer for this...!"

Xu Lang was too distressed to answer, but that emotion would soon be replaced by rage; Heng and Yan escorted their new lord from the scene and prepared for a life as fugitives with nothing left to achieve but some sort of revenge.

Zhu Zhi was initially elated when he learned that Xu Gong was dead; but when he then learned of his failure to capture Xu Lang, he summoned his aides and said, "We'll have to find him, gentlemen. As we know from our own Lord Sun Ce, there is no more dangerous force than a son with nothing in his heart but vengeance against the murderer of his father."

"There are not many that follow Xu," General Yuan Xiong said.

"Even one is one too many," Zhu Zhi replied.

"We'll do everything we can," Lü Dai said.

"Please do," Zhu Zhi replied. "The son of Xu Gong *must* be found!"

****

10

The lord of Jiangxia, Huang Zu, balked at the first reports from his base at Shaxian; the defences were at breaking point, and Jing's navy was being humiliated by the Jiangdong invaders.

"**Must I do everything myself???**" Huang Zu cried. "**Must I really go to the front at my age???**"

"Lord Huang, I again ask that you consider using Gan Ning!" the officer Su Fei protested.

"Not your pirate friend again…!" Huang Zu said as he got to his feet and took up his Administrator's sword of authority from its pedestal. "*You*, yes, are coming with me to Shaxian! But your friend can stay clear of me!"

"…As you wish," Su Fei groaned.

Huang Zu arrived at his Shaxian base as Bofu's generals Ling Cao and Zhou Tai were about to breach the eastern gates of the military camp that kept Bofu's forces from seizing the main civilian settlement nearby; the sudden arrival of extra land and river forces led Lü Fan to signal a retreat as a precaution.

"**Lord Huang!**" General Han Xi exclaimed.

"Father…?" Huang Shè murmured.

"**No more faffing about!**" Huang Zu said. "**We need to push these fools back!**"

"**You brought Chen Jiu and Zhang Shuo…? Then who guards the capital?**" Huang Shè asked.

"**Keep your mind here!**" Huang Zu retorted. "**I have left Pan Jun and Deng Long in charge of the capital, but if we cannot hold Sun Ce here, what good is that? Get yourselves together and fight, *now*, or everything is lost!**"

Huang Zu's presence and words inspired the Jing forces; they fought with renewed vigour, which prompted Bofu to hold an emergency meeting on the Jiangdong command ship.

"I'm not worried that we'll lose, but I don't want to lose lots of men," Bofu explained. "How do we do this?"

"I say that we just charge, like Huang Zu did, and throw them off!" Ling Cao declared.

"…We must be aware of traps," Lü Fan suggested. "Huang Zu is a bit better at that sort of thing than the other men are."

Cheng Pu and Huang Gai lowered their heads in sombre reflection as Bofu replied, "I know that, Ziheng. Huang Zu's had enough of our scalps as it is, so *no*, Ling Cao, I'm not charging blindly, because Huang Zu's entirely the wrong man to do that to."

Ling Cao bowed low and said, "I apologise, Lord Sun, for my foolish suggestion and for harming our morale by-"

"You didn't harm our morale," Cheng Pu insisted. "You just reminded us of what we're dealing with a little too much. We're tougher than that, else we'd none of us be here."

"So what about traps…?" Bofu prompted.

"…Huang Zu lacks the heroes that we have," Gongjin said. "He relies entirely on mediocrities and overrated family members. His traps would involve pursuits into dangerous territory, and this is no place for such things if my topography is right. If we challenge and break his navy, smash his camp, and surround Shaxian

simultaneously, we'll crush their morale and likely force a retreat. If he follows certain routes, we chase and break them; if he follows others, we do nothing."
Cheng Pu nodded slowly and said, "Very sound."
"And to truly break them, we must, sadly, be merciless," Lü Fan suggested. "We must not look to take famous prisoners and collect meek men; we must, in fact, do the opposite, or at worst kill every man we face."
"Huang Zu's a villain to his core, rotten right down to his humours, and he means to destroy us all, like Xu Gong, so I have no problem with destroying his clan," Bofu admitted. "If that's what we should do, it suits me fine."

Huang Zu was divided on whether he should be spearheading his navy or overseeing operations from within the military camp on land; his son Shè approached him and said, "Father, you should remain in the camp. I've failed before, but that will lower Sun Ce's estimation of me and make him overconfident."
Huang Zu smiled and said, "A valid point. I'd also like to try sailing a small detachment past his main fleet and either attacking from the rear of striking into the heart of Yuzhang, where support for the Suns is dwindling and Hua Xin, the court's appointed Administrator, is said to be wavering again."
Liu Biao's nephew Liu Hu bowed and said, "I would like the honour of leading that stealth attack."
Another of Liu Biao's nephews, Liu Pan, said, "I will go with you."
"No, no," Huang Zu insisted. "You must stay, Liu Pan! I need you here in the camp as land forces co-commander and for general support; Chen Jiu can accompany Liu Hu."
"As you command," Chen Jiu said.
"...So it is decided," Huang Zu said after a short pause for thought. "General Zhang Shuo, Liu Pan and I will hold the base and lead armies to attack Sun Ce on the land. My sons and Han Xi will lead the main naval force, and Chen Jiu and Liu Hu will attempt a flanking operation or, if the 'reconnaissance at point' deems that to be impossible, an attack on a target in Yuzhang that weakens support for our enemy and opens the way for a possible pincer. Let us begin."

The Jing and Jiangdong navies were fairly evenly matched in terms of boats and men; the Sun clan benefitted from more individual commanders with charisma, and that would be one of the deciding factors. Bofu, Gongjin, Sun Hè, Song Qian, Taishi Ci, Ling Cao, Zhou Tai and Jiang Qin led their men personally and engaged the smaller boat crews once again.
"Are we just going to let Sun Ce rout us again?" Han Xi complained as he watched his enemies' approach from the Jing command ship.
"Of course not," Huang Shè replied. **"ARCHERS...!"**
The officers carried their lord's command to the individual boats, and archers readied their bows for a missile attack against the Jiangdong forces.
"ARCHERS!" a Jiangdong scout warned.
"Huang Shè's been talking to his father," Cheng Pu said as he observed the developing battle from a medium-sized boat in the

centre of the Jiangdong fleet.

"Let this better Huang from a better line do something, Cheng Demou!" Huang Gai replied. **"Archery Captain Fu, follow me!"**

Huang Gai led a small detachment of boats along the southern side of the main fleet and prepared to combat the Jing archers with archers of his own; Bofu, meanwhile, was forced to fall back as he narrowly avoided coming into range of the enemy arrow attack. His fearless general Ling Cao did not stop, however, and Zhou Tai was forced to retrieve him before he was struck.

"For goodness' sakes, man, show some sense!" Jiang Qin said as Ling Cao returned to the 'safety point'. **"If you have to charge a hail of arrows, at least have a plan first!"**

Huang Shè laughed as he watched his enemies' desperate attempts to dodge his archers' attacks and said, **"See, Han Xi, how we can still show these ignorant men our superiority!"**

"You won't get me as you got my father, Huang Zu!" Bofu screamed. **"Your head will be mine to sacrifice to his altar!"**

Taishi Ci crouched low and braved the arrows in order to advance on the nearest level archery position; he and his men hopped from boat to boat, dodging the strikes of the Jing swordsmen and pike-men until they were close enough to cut down the bowmen and end their assault.

"Why has the archery support thinned???" Huang Shè cried.

Huang Gai's men reached the front and started to fire at the Jing ships: many of the archers were forced to take cover, and that reduced the Jing defences further.

"I'll confront them personally!" Han Xi suggested as he fled the deck of the command ship. **"Consider a strategic retreat!"**

Huang Shè's brother Yi was leading the vanguard, and the loss of the archery divisions left him exposed: he tried to stage a fighting retreat, but Bofu, Sun Yi, Sun Hè, Song Qian and Zhou Tai surrounded his position.

"...Jiangdong scum!" Huang Yi cried as he tried one last futile attack on Bofu; Sun Hè advanced and cut him down.

"Huang Yi is dead!" Bofu said. **"Huang Shè, you're next!"**

Huang Shè could sense that something had happened to his brother, and that the battle might be lost after all: he lowered his head and said, "Death to you, Sun Ce! If Yi is dead... then I *can't* let *you* live now!"

Han Xi led a group of his elite men onto the maze of small boats in order to confront Bofu; he screamed when he learned that his lord's son had already been killed and charged blindly, shouting, **"We'll have our revenge, Sun Ce!"**

"Not before I have mine!" Bofu retorted as he shoved Sun Hè aside and engaged Han Xi directly. The bobbing vessels proved to be hazardous duelling ground, but Bofu and his allies had no choice but to meet the swords and pikes of Han Xi's men with their own.

"...I have to fight!" Huang Shè decided. "I-! ...**What???**"

Cheng Pu and Lü Fan had ordered the Jiangdong ships to close in on the Jing ships: in addition to that, Gongjin, Jiang Qin and Ling Cao had approached the Jing ships from all sides during the chaos and were overseeing the boarding of the medium-sized vessels, which left the command ship dangerously isolated.

70

"...**Han Xi, Brother, I shall soon join you!**" Huang Shè cried as he prepared to join the battle on the smaller boats.

"**Dogs of Jiangdong!**" Han Xi heckled as he pressed an attack on Bofu, who had momentarily lost his footing; Bofu recovered and slashed at Han Xi's midriff with his sword, wounding him fatally.

"D-*dogs*...!" Han Xi gasped as he collapsed and fell into the water. Huang Shè might have stood a chance if Han Xi had still been alive to provide support: his command ship was now under attack from all sides, and with his cause lost, he tried to retreat on a small boat.

"**Where are you running to?**" Taishi Ci shouted as he and his men pursued and cut down two of Huang Shè's bodyguards.

"**Faster!**" Huang Shè screamed. "**FASTER, DAMN YOU!**"

"**Jiang Qin, Zhou Tai, Ling Cao: pursue!**" Gongjin ordered.

"**I have to be the one to kill Huang Shè!**" Bofu insisted. "**I have to-!**"

"**Did Huang Zu's arrow kill your father?**" Gongjin asked.

"It-! ...No," Bofu replied. "But the order was enough."

"Right," Gongjin said. "Huang Zu might be worth the risk, but not his son. He isn't a hero like you: it doesn't take a tiger to kill a mouse, any cat or dog will do."

"I was going to chase him too, but I won't now you've said that, Gongjin," Sun Yi chuckled.

"...**Seize the boats and ships, and kill any men that don't surrender straight away,**" Bofu ordered. "**We have to cripple Huang Zu so that he can't bother us again... and then, when the time's right, we come back and finish him off.**"

On the land, the battle against Huang Zu's forces was being led by Sun Ben, Sun Fu, Dong Xi and Lü Meng, with Qin Song providing what little advice was required.

"**If Lü Meng wants to live to see grandchildren, he needs to learn some sense,**" Qin Song complained.

Dong Xi nodded and said, "**He does need to learn some restraint. But then so do the lord and Ling Cao.**"

There was no doubting Lü Meng's talent on the battlefield, however: he was getting the better of every man that challenged him and had already defeated two of Huang Zu's better majors.

"**Commander Huang, we may be forced to withdraw to the camp!**" Liu Pan said fearfully.

"**Against reckless idiots such as this...?**" Huang Zu scoffed. "**This 'Lü Meng' is another Sun Jian, begging for arrows to end his career early!**"

Huang Zu signalled to his archers, and a small volley of missiles was fired at the Jiangdong infantry; Zhang Shuo led an infantry charge moments later.

"Has he any other tricks, or is that it...?" Qin Song sighed.

"**It isn't the trap; it's the man that it's set for that decides its effectiveness,**" Dong Xi retorted. "**Lü Meng and Sun Fu are not withdrawing!**"

"**My fool brother is letting Lü Meng rob him of his sense!**" Sun Ben fretted.

"**But the arrows are being fired upward, and your brother advances under the arc... so perhaps he is not so much of a fool,**" Qin Song said.

"**But a line of infantry protects the archers!**" Sun Ben cried.
"**And they're flinching!**" Dong Xi noted. "**It's time for me to go and add my own spear to the fray!**"
Huang Zu fumed as his men buckled under the series of unexpected attacks: he punched the air and said, "**My sons have the better men: all I am left with is fools and cowards!**"
Liu Pan realised that Dong Xi was quickly carving his way through the Jing front lines, and his approach was only moments away.
"**We have to retreat!**" Liu Pan suggested.
"**I know, I know, I...! ...Damn them all!**" Huang Zu replied as he signalled to his men and turned his horse to flee the field.
"**Come back, Huang Zu!**" Dong Xi shouted through laughter. "**When will we know your face?**"
Zhang Shuo was the last to realise that his lord had fled: he fought his way out of the pincer that he was now trapped within and returned to the camp.
"**Now we destroy his camp!**" Sun Ben declared.

The demoralising effect of Huang Zu's retreat was compounded further by two pieces of news from the river. Firstly, Huang Zu's sons were dead and his naval fleet had been decimated; secondly – and no less serious militarily – Liu Hu's attempts to sneak around the Jiangdong fleet had been foiled by Han Dang and Hè Qi, and Hu had been killed as well.
"White clothes, white clothes," Huang Zu mumbled as Liu Pan tried to rouse a more useful response from him. "White clothes... we'll both need... white... to mourn... but what do I tell my wife...? What do I tell the lord...? **How do I face my ancestors???**"
"You must evacuate your family from Shaxian at once," Liu Pan implored. "I will get the white clothes, just-!"
"It's not your place to do such mundane things," Huang Zu said. "Is there not a man that can do it for you...?"
"**That's what I meant!**" Liu Pan cried desperately.
The sudden outburst broke Huang Zu out of his semi-trance: he shook his head briefly and said, "You... yes, yes, I know. Forget white clothes: if we all don't want to end up in coffins, then I need to be the man that I am! Who is in command of the defences? Where is Sun Ce? Any word from Lord Liu...?"
"Su Fei commands our forces while I am here," Liu Pan replied. "Sun Ce has come here personally, bringing with him most of his forces. The rivers are blockaded, and we have yet to receive word from Uncle."
"...But can he spare Cai Mao when Cao Cao looms large...?" Huang Zu said. "It... it is simply the case that in my complacency I have not acquired any heroes lately, while Sun Ce has them by the bushel. But I still have Zhang Shuo, Chen Jiu, Su Fei, tens of thousands of men and my own wits, and that is enough."
"...Su Fei continually speaks well of Gan Ning," Liu Pan said apprehensively. "Perhaps he-"
"Gan Ning is a cutthroat, a man that cannot be trusted," Huang Zu insisted. "He'd sell my head to Sun Ce for a jar of cheap wine."
"...Perhaps it is as you say," Liu Pan replied. "I'll go and reassume command and try to calm the men."
"I shall join you shortly," Huang Zu promised.

In nearby Yuzhang Prefecture in southwest Yang Province, the reappointed Administrator, Hua Xin, observed the reports on the battles between Liu Biao and the Sun clan with contempt.

"I was made to surrender, but I don't see why I should have," Hua Xin said to his court, which now largely agreed with him. "Sun Ce and Huang Zu are surely the enemies of Heaven, with all of their pointless wrangling for things that aren't theirs!"

"We should watch our words," one official suggested.

"I'll be silent no more!" Hua Xin replied. "Any sane man can now see that Sun Ce is a violent hegemon, and Liu Biao is little better."

"What can we do...?" a second official asked.

"My only thought now is to appeal to the Han court," Hua Xin said. "I intend to write to His Excellency Cao Cao, stressing that the madness in this region has gone on long enough! And if that doesn't work, I'll write to His Majesty!"

The majority of the officials voiced their agreement with the decision: one of the few men that did not agree was anxious to leave the meeting and report Hua Xin's intentions to Bofu as soon as possible.

"...*Aiee*... All is lost."

Huang Zu let his weathered battle helmet fall from his hand: Bofu's forces had surrounded Shaxian's main settlements, blockaded every road and water supply and started to pressurise the gates of the camp.

"Then aren't we fools to stay here...?" Liu Pan asked.

"My men cannot hold for much longer, so yes, we'd be fools to stay here," Huang Zu replied. "We must sacrifice more men to provide distractions for our retreat, which upsets me, but what choice do I have...?"

"I'll do what I can to hold them at bay," Su Fei promised.

"You'll do no such thing," Huang Zu replied. "I need both of you alive, you and Liu Pan: place others in that suicidal role... perhaps this finally a use for your friend Gan Ning."

"...Perhaps," Su Fei sighed.

"We'll flee via the west gate while others are making noise at the eastern and southern gates and a decoy flees through the northern gates," Huang Zu continued. "We can commandeer fishing boats to go back to Northern Xiakou if needs be."

"It shall be as you say," Liu Pan replied.

Bofu received word of Hua Xin's intentions at around the same time that Huang Zu was staging his retreat; Bofu stamped his foot and screamed, **"Another one that wants to label me as 'another Xiang Yu'! I am not another Xiang Yu!"**

"And Hua Xin is not another Xu Gong," Lü Fan suggested. "Hua Xin's regained a lot of popular support in recent times: he must therefore be treated differently to Xu Gong, or we will lose Yuzhang Prefecture."

"...So what must I do...?" Bofu asked. "I have an old man that wants to pick a fight that's creeping up behind me, and another old man that's running away in front of me that I want to catch. What do I do...?"

"Let Huang Zu flee," Gongjin replied. "As for Hua Xin... I suggest that we send Zhou Tai and Yu Fan to Yuzhang to appeal for calm and peace."

"A good idea," Lü Fan said.

"*Why*...?" Bofu asked as he turned to look at Cheng Pu.

"Because Zhou Tai's reputation is very good in Yuzhang, and because Yu Fan was a subordinate of Wang Lang that can help Hua Xin to see that he is mistaking one situation for another," Cheng Pu replied.

"...Alright, I get it, we want to preserve Hua Xin," Bofu said. "But can I really let Huang Zu go now...?"

Jiang Qin's pursuing, but I've given him orders to withdraw if the lay of the land is at all treacherous," Lü Fan explained. "We've captured Huang Zu's family, thousands of Huang Zu's boats and ships, killed or captured tens of thousands of Huang Zu's men, and completely broken his hold on the region to the west of Po County Lake; he's got to go and hide in his capital now and request reinforcements from Liu Biao that Biao daren't send if he wants to leave his back exposed to Cao Cao."

"...Write to Yu Fan, and have him speak to Hua Xin as you suggest," Bofu replied sombrely. "I'll go to talk with Hua Xin personally once Yu Zhongxiang's talked him around, and then I'll rendezvous with everyone at Chaisang."

"It shall all be done," Lü Fan said.

Jiang Qin and his men pursued Huang Zu's small defence force relentlessly: Huang's vassal Su Fei had quietly assigned his friend Gan Ning as a part of the rear guard, hoping that the young prodigy would gain some merit for it. Gan Ning's unit was adept at scare tactics and feints, and Gan himself was a gifted archer, even on horseback: the small gang employed all of those talents to keep the pursuers at bay.

"**These men that Huang Zu has guarding the rear are quite good!**" Jiang Qin realised. "**SHOW CARE, EVERYONE!**"

Gan Ning was able to wound one of Jiang Qin's riders, but his own men were proving to be difficult targets due to their constantly-shifting movements. It then started to rain, and the impending marshlands were treacherous enough when they were dry, so Jiang Qin ordered his men to halt.

"Are we not going to go any further...?" a captain asked.

"No," Jiang Qin replied sternly. "I won't risk losing a single one of you men to one of Huang Zu's ambushes."

"But it's to avenge the lord's father!" the captain exclaimed. "We'd gladly give our lives to-!"

"To what...? To die needlessly and probably lose sight of him anyway...?" Jiang Qin insisted. "There will be other times."

Gan Ning had a scout report Jiang Qin's retreat to Huang Zu, who exhaled loudly and said, "Perhaps this is a trial, after which- ...Wait... Messenger, did you say that you were sent by...! ...*Su Fei*...!"

Su Fei guessed the reason for his lord's change of tone: he laughed nervously and said, "My lord, Gan has-"

"**You put a faithless murderer in the rear guard???**" Huang Zu shrieked. "**What if he had been *bought*, fool??? I said that Gan Ning will *never serve me*! Do not use him again!**"

Liu Pan looked at Su Fei, who sighed and said, "He has served you well today."

74

"I don't care!" Huang Zu retorted. **"Today he 'serves me well', but tomorrow he'll take my head to Sun Ce! Don't make me tell you again!"**
Su Fei left his lord and rode to the rear guard to notify Gan Ning that his services would not be required for the rest of the journey.
"…I must be frank and say that we are running out of options," Liu Pan said. "Mister Huang, we may need men like Gan Ning, and if he has a price – just as many others do in your employ – then find it and offer something that no man can match."
Huang Zu grunted angrily and rode on; Liu Pan and the rest of his entourage followed, including Gan Ning, who was certain that he could gain some trust. Huang Zu's force eventually reached a military garrison and commandeered the few boats that were there: they crossed the Yangtze River and took shelter in the fortress city of Northern Xiakou, where they would remain until Jiangxia's capital was better fortified and the demoralised Liu Biao had a better idea.

****

11

It took two days for Bofu's ally Yu Fan to receive word of his mission and travel to Yuzhang Prefecture's capital Nanchang in order to convince Administrator Hua Xin to abandon his plans to 'rebel': Yu was not greeted warmly, especially after it was announced that Zhou Tai had brought an army into the region and set up a base and that Jiang Qin was about to do the same.

"You mean to conquer us violently this time?" Hua Xin asked.

Yu Fan looked around the court and said, "I can see that there are many men here that once disapproved of you and understood my lord Sun Ce; now the situation is reversed, which is unfortunate."

"You have not answered my question," Hua Xin countered.

"...No, because I was distracted by the change of mood," Yu Fan replied. "What has Lord Sun Ce done to deserve this? Haven't Taishi Ci and Zhou Tai, amongst others, been defending this region against Liu Pan and Huang Zu for the last few months at least...? The people cheer and offer food to Zhou Tai's men, so why is Zhou Tai's lord – in whose name he does these things – suddenly a villain...?"

Some of the officials murmured as they pondered the point.

"**We are fed up of the violence!**" Hua Xin cried.

"And Lord Sun is not...?" Yu Fan retorted. "I assure you that he is, Administrator. You *are* the Administrator, aren't you...?"

Hua Xin took the question as a threat and said, "At present, yes."

"And it is my lord's hope that you *continue* to be the Administrator here," Yu Fan continued. "We mean you and the people of Yuzhang no harm. And now that Huang Zu is repelled, there should be no more violence."

"...Perhaps I have been wrong," Hua Xin said.

"It would be easy enough to look at every influential man at the moment and see something that you should not be seeing," Yu Fan suggested. "What does Cao Cao intend...? What does Liu Biao intend...? What does Yuan Shao intend...? My lord is also an influential man, so your question is justified."

Hua Xin lowered his head and said, "I know that you are here because my militia's movements have been reported to your lord, and perhaps my intention to write to the capital is known as well. What happens now...?"

"Nothing, if that's what you want," Yu Fan replied. "If you intend nothing, then my lord can intend nothing as well."

"...Which is, in effect, a choice on my part to surrender again, for my intent was to fight, as ridiculous as that now seems!" Hua Xin chuckled. "I surrender...!"

"And Lord Sun will arrive shortly to speak with you, allay your fears, thank you for your work here and ask you to continue to aid us in the future," Yu Fan said.

"I... am grateful," Hua Xin replied, "and I shall not err again."

Liu Biao read the report from Jiangxia and threw it to the floor, screaming like a wild animal as he did so; his adviser Kuai Yue shook his head and said, "This will, admittedly, be difficult to recover from, my lord."

"Difficult...?" Liu Biao chortled. "It will be *impossible*!"

"Nothing is impossible," Wang Can suggested. "With proper advice, the-"

"My nephew is *dead*," Liu Biao said with tears in his eyes. "I must wear white and apologise to my kin for robbing them of a son! Huang Zu's lost his *entire family*! All this for *one man's father*! It's Cao Cao and Xu Province all over again!"

"There must be some way to end this madness... there *must be*," Kuai Yue murmured.

"The only path is to kill them all, or die trying to!" Liu Biao cried. **"Sun Ce will not rest until we are all bleached bones! If we kill him, then another Sun will come, and then another! Hoping for peace is *futile*! And I do not *want* peace now! It is mutually personal!"**

"Then I will travel to Jiangxia and give counsel to Huang Zu," Kuai Yue said. "We do not know when Sun Ce will be back, but we must be ready at all times for him and all of our other worries."

Liu Biao nodded and said, "Leave at once."

Bofu was relieved when Yu Fan sent word that Hua Xin would capitulate for a second time: as soon as the messenger had left his command tent Bofu lowered his head, cupped his hands over his face and said, "If I'd had to kill another stubborn old man that misunderstood me, I... ... ...Gongjin, I'm weary. I'm twenty-four, but inside I'm older than Dad was when he... ... ...Will this ever end...? Will it...?"

Gongjin – who was Bofu's only company – shook his head and replied, "I honestly don't know. These are volatile times, and-"

"I have so much blood on my hands," Bofu continued. "I killed Lu Kang, I killed Liu Yao, I-"

"Don't do it, Bofu," Gongjin interrupted. "You're tired, and you're angry that Huang Zu has escaped again. Every man that you've killed was unfortunate, yes, but when and where were you offered a choice beyond dying yourself...?"

Bofu snorted miserably.

"Lu Kang was a 'stubborn old man' that refused to yield to your lord and treat your indentured father kindly, even after your father was dead, and even Lu's closest kin acknowledge that you were left with no choice but to starve him out when he refused to surrender Huancheng to you," Gongjin continued. "In fact, his son Ji and nephew Xun live here in Jiangdong now and respect you for what you've achieved, and although Kang's elder son Jun serves in the Han court he has stated that he bears us no malice either in his correspondence with Ji. And look at who else you have serving in your court: Liu Ji, son of the governor Liu Yao that you 'killed', but he too acknowledges that you are blameless and hurries here to assist us in placating Hua Xin. Yuan Yao, son of our lord-turned-enemy Yuan Shu, is now a willing courtier, and his sister seeks a husband among our nobles; Taishi Ci, who was once our fiercest enemy, is now one of our most trustworthy friends. I could go on. Every man that truly knows you can see that you are a good man and that you only do what must be done: it's time that you tried to understand that yourself."

"...Thank you, Gongjin," Bofu said. "You always know exactly the right thing to say."

"When I always know the right thing to *do*, I'll be truly happy,"

Gongjin chuckled.

Hua Xin greeted Bofu at the gates of Nanchang with his Administrator's seal in his hands: Bofu placed a hand on the silk-wrapped stamp and shook his head, saying, "I want to be clear, esteemed Mister Hua, that you earned this post and that I have no right to take it from you."
Hua Xin examined Bofu's face with weary eyes and asked, "Do you find your life to be a difficult one?"
"Of course," Bofu replied. "But I believe that I can make Jiangdong a great place, and I'll do anything to make that happen. The Han's neglected the south for far too long: even you have to admit that."
"I do," Hua Xin said, "but everything to the south of the Great River is considered to be low-priority: all wealthy eyes point to the north. Perhaps, when peace is restored, we will see more development in the south..."
"There's no harm in doing some of that ourselves," Bofu retorted. "If only you'd see the good we've achieved, Mister Hua! If only you'd see how we're turning dead ground into fields, towns into cities, filling the treasury and improving people's lives! Yeah, I know that we-"
"Let us continue this conversation in my office," Hua Xin suggested. "I think that I owe you a banquet, at the very least."
"You are too kind," Bofu replied.

Hua Xin had his servants prepare a banquet in Bofu's honour, but Bofu defied the protocol and insisted that he would serve Hua Xin as though he were an honoured guest.
"I have wronged you!" Hua Xin cried. "You should not be serving me tea!"
"On the contrary, I made you worry, and I must atone for that," Bofu retorted. "In addition, you are a wise man and my elder, and so I should acknowledge your greater standing."
"*Aiee*... you are no monster!" Hua Xin said. "I'll never speak ill of you again!"
Bofu smiled gratefully, but some damage had already been done; a number of Yuzhang officials had been too eager to support Hua Xin's denunciation of the Sun clan and had already sent their own petitions to the court in Xuchang.

"...I must decide what must be done about Sun Ce."
The Han's Excellency of Works, Cao Cao, tapped his desk with a knife and turned to face the five advisers that he had invited to his private study.
"He has provisionally accepted both of the marriage proposals," Xun Yòu noted.
"But he conquers Yang Province with impunity," Cao Cao retorted.
"He yielded to the Han court using very humble terms, Excellency," Chen Qun said.
"But he confidently leads massive war fleets to the west to try and take Jiangxia from Huang Zu," Cao Cao retorted.
"He has the same enemies as you, Excellency," Xun Yòu's uncle, Xun Yu, suggested.
"Liu Biao is a shared enemy, but he has no quarrel with Yuan Shao or Liu Bei, and our reasons for despising Liu Biao could not

be more different," Cao Cao retorted.

"Xun Wenruo is partly right, since Yuan Shao attacked Sun Ce's father, and that was the act that began the Yuan feud," Guo Jia noted. "And Liu Bei served Yuan Shao and harboured Lü Bu: Bu was a hated enemy of his father."

"But yet I am only partly right," Xun Yu chuckled. "How am I wrong, Fengxiao?"

"Yuan Shao attacked Yuan Shu in the only way that was available to him at that moment, and Sun Ce knows that very well," Guo Jia replied. "Liu Bei was an ally of Lü Bu purely by way of circumstance, and Sun Ce knows that as well. Never rule out an alliance, no matter how bizarre; do we not court *Zhang Xiu…*?"

"True enough," Xun Yu conceded.

"And let's not forget that we now have a very different Liu Bei," Guo Jia continued.

"…I should have smashed him when he was there in front of me!" Cao Cao lamented. "Damn you, Liu Bei! **Damn you!**"

Liu Bei's followers had just seized Xu Province's capital, Xiapi, and killed Cao Cao's selected governor Che Zhou; the act was arousing suspicion that the normally cautious Liu Bei expected some sort of support, most likely political, and the probable source of that support was the General of Chariots and Cavalry, Dong Cheng, who was long known to hate Cao Cao.

"Sun Ce has been repeatedly denounced by Xu Gong, as we know, but we have also received similar words of condemnation from mid-ranking officials in Yuzhang in the last few days," Guo Jia said. "Sun Ce is deemed to be a minor hegemon, a reincarnation of Xiang Yu… or, as Xu Gong put it once, a 'Little Conqueror' that has lofty plans for turning Jiangdong – and, it seems, the rest of Yang Province, Guangling, and Jiangxia as well – into 'a reborn State of Chu' that he can rule as he pleases."

"I have my old friend Benchu threatening me, the Qiang causing chaos in the northwest, more Yellow Turbans in Runan, Liu Bei taking over Xiapi… and now I am expected to worry about Sun Ce!" Cao Cao complained. "What do I do, gentlemen? Do I ignore the petitions, trust this young tiger and keep my eyes turned northward, or do I add him to my list of issues that must be dealt with at once…?"

"Now is the time to appoint an Inspector of Yang Province, in order to stamp your authority on the region and make Sun Ce understand that he is master of what the Han gives him to rule and nothing more," Xun Yu said. "We must appoint a man that will placate the men that once followed Yuan Shu; men like Chen Lan, who now terrorises the region as one of the leaders of the Qian Hill Bandits. We must choose a man that has dealt with Sun Ce before if we can, someone that can anticipate his every move and keep us well informed."

"…I know that I will probably regret this, but I have no man that fits that description and also has my full confidence," Cao Cao sighed. "Liu Xun is an arrogant hankerer that must be kept at court; Zhang Xun is like a loyal dog that barks about the well-being of his dead master's children and has no will of his own; Liu Yè, I admit, is a smart man, but he's wrongly blamed for Liu Xun's bad decisions and will, by his own confession, have little sway with most of Liu Xun's defected soldiers. That leaves one man, but... but what do I unleash by sending him...?"

"You must take the risk," Xun Yòu insisted. "We have too many other problems to worry about."

Cao Cao turned to the fifth adviser, who had remained silent throughout: it was Yuan Huan, a former adviser to Yuan Shu that had defected in the wake of Shu's decision to declare as an emperor and risen up the ranks upon reaching Xuchang.

"The man that you refer to is a former colleague, and I must admit that he is competent," Yuan Huan said. "Our options are, as you say, limited: he at least knows the region well."

"...Fine," Cao Cao grumbled. "Heaven mocks me once again: send *Yan Xiang*."

Guo Jia laughed and said, "If nothing else, it will be amusing."

And so Yan Xiang began the journey from Xuchang to Shouchun, where he was expected to take up the post of Inspector of Yang Province: the former adviser to Yuan Shu would have the full support of the Han government, though that would not be in the form of any sort of standing army. It would not take long for word of Yan's appointment to reach Jiangdong – not least because it would be announced to Bofu's court by an imperial messenger – and it would cause as much anger as Cao Cao had guessed.

But the Excellency of Works was a desperate man that was resorting to desperate measures: within days, he was supressing an imminent coup within the capital and vehemently denying the authenticity of a secret imperial decree – dubbed the 'Girdle Edict' in reference to how it was supposedly smuggled out of the palace – that denounced Cao as a traitor and a tyrant and called upon the warlords to unite and destroy him. Word of that edict – and the potentially more damaging fact that he had ordered the death of Imperial Consort Dong, the pregnant daughter of the conspirator Dong Cheng and a favourite of Emperor Xian – would take time to circulate, but the challenge to Cao Cao's court in Xuchang would be a divisive and agenda-changing issue that threatened to bring about more chaos than anything that had come before.

****

12

Bofu's fleet began a swift withdrawal from the Shaxian region after having left troops to contain Huang Zu. Bofu – who had returned to Shaxian after placating Hua Xin – turned to Gongjin and asked, "Why am I going back to Qu'e…?"

"Matters of state," Gongjin replied. "Firstly, we must discuss the potential consequences of our own actions: Xuchang is bound to have found out that Xu Gong is dead by now, and our continued attacks on Jing Province might be sending out erroneous messages that tally well with the slander."

"…And secondly…?" Bofu prompted.

"Secondly," Gongjin said, "we must reassure Cao Cao of our goodwill… though that might be difficult if he's done what I understand him to have done."

"…To us…?" Bofu asked apprehensively.

"In a sense, yes," Gongjin replied. "He's… … …Bofu, Wu Jing has sent word that he's appointed a new Inspector of Yang Province."

"Not Liu Xun," Bofu groaned.

"No," Gongjin said. "…In a way, *better*, but in another way, *worse*… he's appointed *Yan Xiang*."

Bofu laughed ironically and said, "Please tell me that you're playing some sort of prank. I didn't even know he was alive; that's a shock enough! But Cao Cao's…?"

"I know, I wondered if there's been some sort of mistake, or that it is another Yan Xiang," Gongjin replied. "But it's him. Somehow, he survived everything and now he works for Cao Cao."

Bofu was numbed by the revelation and stared blankly.

"That's not all," Gongjin continued. "The intelligence that we were getting before we departed was right: Liu Bei's done as some suspected he would and attacked Xiapi, killing the governor and–"

"Liu Bei's governing Xu Province again?" Bofu exclaimed.

"It didn't last long," Gongjin explained. "Cao's advisers must have recommended a swift march that took Bei by surprise, that or Xu's people betrayed him again. He's fled to Yuan Shao, who's–"

"Liu Bei and Yuan Shao are allies against Cao Cao now?" Bofu chuckled. "That lot are completely mad. Yuan Shao was Cao's best friend, and both he and Cao hated Liu Bei, and then Cao sided with Bei to kill Lü Bu, and now *this*…?"

"If I may…?" Gongjin said. "Yuan Shao's distributing abusive literature about Cao Cao, accusing him of all manner of things. Cao's supposed to have murdered a pregnant Imperial consort that was related to one of the conspirators, and–"

"Cao's committed *regicide*…?" Bofu exclaimed.

"*Supposedly*," Gongjin said. "And a 'secret' Imperial edict's *supposedly* surfaced that labels Cao as 'another Dong Zhuo' and–"

"Wait, wait, but that means we're marrying our kin to a tyrant," Bofu realised. "How far have we gone with the responses?"

"Thankfully, not far beyond acknowledging his letter," Gongjin said. "We can still get out of it, I think, *if we must*: I recall an unpleasant rumour about a great hero that supposedly stole the Imperial Seal, so I tend to be cautious."

Bofu nodded soberly at the reference to an infamous story about his own father.

"Huang Zu's a broken man: he can wait," Gongjin continued. "We must ascertain the situation in the north before we do any more."
"The north always has to be more important than the south, doesn't it," Bofu muttered.

Within days, Bofu was back in Qu'e, capital of his vast homeland of Jiangdong; the capital was now considered to be in Wu Prefecture – rather than neighbouring Danyang – after a boundary change to evenly divide responsibility, but Danyang's Administrator, Wu Jing, was still based in Qu'e while suitable arrangements were made further west. The officials gathered, with the senior military officials taking seats to Bofu's right and senior civilian officials taking seats to his left; the remainder occupied rows at the back of the long hall. Once every man was seated – and Lady Wu had taken her special place to the left of her brother Wu Jing – Bofu awaited the words of his aide Gu Yong.
"Firstly, we have some new faces," Gu Yong said. "There is Xu Sheng, whose brave actions in Chaisang are well known."
Xu Sheng smiled boldly.
Gu Yong gestured toward a boy of 12 years of age that sat at the far end of the row of courtiers and said, "Amongst our junior officials, Lu Ji, the cousin of Lu Xun."
"...*Lu Ji*...?" Cheng Pu whispered. "Lu Kang's *son*...?"
Huang Gai nodded silently.
Gu Yong gestured toward a miserable, thin-faced official at the rear of the hall and said, "And newly installed in a civil service role, Mister Zhuge Jin."
"Donkey Face is still here, then," Zhang Zhao muttered.
"We can also welcome Magistrate Sun Quan from Yangxian County, and Mister Sun Jing from his base at Kuaiji Prefecture," Gu Yong concluded.
"Good to see you, Uncle," Bofu hailed.
"I am glad to be here, lord and nephew," Sun Jing replied.
"And Quan, of course, is always a heart-warming sight," Bofu said as he looked at Sun Quan and smiled.
"I am glad to be back again so soon, Brother," Sun Quan replied.
"...Everyone knows the latest news," Bofu said. "Any ideas...?"
"Cao Cao is His Majesty's guardian," Zhang Zhao replied. "When Yuan was 'too busy' to save the Son of Heaven from the bandits, Cao Cao did so. And yet we are now told that Cao is the villain!"
Cheng Pu snorted angrily.
"And by *whom*...?" Zhang Zhao asked theatrically. "...By Dong Cheng, Liu Bei, and Yuan Shao! Dong Cheng is a former ally of Dong Zhuo that used an army of criminals to prise His Majesty from the Regents' grip and then betrayed them; Liu Bei is a habitual thief that has twice tried to steal Xu Province from dead men and failed; and Yuan Shao has the dubious honours of firstly being Commander-in-Chief of a silent human wall while Dong Zhuo pillaged towns and murdered sovereigns, secondly a shameless land-grabber that attacked the lord's esteemed father when his crimes were exposed by another, and, thirdly, being the brother of that aforementioned 'other' – a demented heretic that treated heroes as possessions and dared to emulate Wang Mang!"
"...A rousing condemnation," Gongjin chuckled. "You excel yourself again, Zibu."

"Am I wrong...?" Zhang Zhao asked.

"We cannot be entirely sure, but you're probably very right," Gongjin replied.

"Since Cao Cao rescued the Son of Heaven, he has built a temporary capital, reorganised the Imperial army, destroyed the Yellow Turbans, pacified the Xiongnu, removed the stain of Lü Bu's presence from the world and started the expensive process of restoring the sacked ruins of Luoyang to their former glory," Zhang Zhao said. "I find it difficult to believe that such a man is now murdering innocent pregnant consorts and making the Son of Heaven so frightened for his life that he resorts to soliciting aid from his former captors and giving them secret edicts."

"So what do you make of Cao appointing *Yan Xiang* as the new provincial inspector...?" Bofu asked pointedly.

All eyes turned to Zhang Zhao, who laughed awkwardly and replied, "It is an odd move, but it can be explained!"

"Go on then," the veteran Han Dang chuckled. "Explain."

Zhang Zhao looked to his colleagues for support.

"I might do an equally competent job, and therefore save Mister Zhang his voice, which appears to be faltering," Lü Fan said. "Cao Cao looked at our dominance in Jiangdong and thought little of it; nobody cares about the south. But now Li Shu guards Lujiang, and we have parts of Guangling and Jiujiang as well: they're all to the north of the Great River, and that makes Cao worry. Most of the inhabitants of Lujiang and Jiujiang liked Yuan Shu, because he typically governed with a firm but generous hand; they only turned on him when he made his audacious claim to the throne."

"And...?" Sun Yi prompted. "Didn't Yan Xiang serve Yuan Shu loyally...? He used to heckle Father and Bofu as well, and he was a toady that stayed with Shu after that 'claim' you mentioned."

"He was a toady to an extent, but he had his limits," Lü Fan replied. "Yan Xiang remonstrated when Yuan Shu raised the subject of thrones, so I understand: yes, Yan aided Yuan thereafter, as a vassal should, since the bond between lord and vassal is like that of a father and son and should only be violated when the lord has truly lost all of their humanity."

Lü Fan paused; Sun Quan was glaring at him, and he could not be sure whether the intensity was due to interest in his words or a desire to one day have revenge for Lü Fan having exposed and reported his thefts from the treasury.

"...'Lord and vassal', 'bond'; right," Sun Yi prompted. "And...?"

"He'll get to it, Yi!" Bofu replied.

"Yi, you're so much like Lord Sun," Lü Fan said. "I'll get to the point: Cao Cao wants Yuan Shu's supporters in Lujiang to join him. Yuan Shu's followers are torn between serving Lord Sun, following the 'unambitious' Yuan Yao – who now lives here in Jiangdong as a nobleman – and remaining in Lujiang, quietly hoping that someone might offer them a livelihood. Some have formed the Qian Hill Bandits, but most want normality. Yan Xiang is, they hope, the best of old and new; to Cao, Yan's return to Jiujiang is a chance to grow his army and match the quarter-of-a-million men that Yuan Shao's supporters boast of."

"...Have we had any defections...?" Wu Jing asked.

"A few, a very small number, hundreds at the most, almost entirely peasant farmers and low-level soldiers," the politician

Quan Rou said. "Most have stayed with Li Shu."

"But the intention is to siphon away our support in Lujiang and Jiujiang, and I can't let that happen," Bofu said. "Cao's about to be attacked by Yuan Shao and Liu Bei, perhaps Liu Biao as well; if he took Yu and northern Yang and lost them again, I'd have to go and pacify northern Yang again! What if *Liu Biao* seized the region...? Hasn't Cao Cao been looking at Liu Bei while he fights him...? Cao shouldn't be taking what he can't keep!"

"And his actions are a direct violation of our implied closeness," Qin Song suggested. "He proposes marriage alliances on the one hand, and then he sends a loyal vassal of an old enemy of your clan to steal people from you on the other."

"That too," Bofu replied. "I see what Lü Ziheng and others are saying, but Cao knows what Yuan Shu and his cronies did to us. Was there no other man...?"

"Show caution!" Zhang Zhao pleaded. "My brother reports nothing untoward! And Cao Cao is the *Excellency of Works*!"

"Yeah, and *Dong Zhuo* was the *Chancellor of State*," Han Dang heckled. "We kicked his arse all the same, 'cause the rotten beggar had it coming!"

"The 'Two Zhangs' are not veterans of the Yuan years as we are," Cheng Pu said. "Huang Gongfu, Han Yigong, Zhu Junli and I were there at the beginning, with Lord Sun's father, and we remember Yan Xiang: he is a repulsive dog that mocked Lord Sun Jian and Lord Sun Ce with equal relish. If such a man is now the provincial inspector, then that tells me only one thing: Cao Cao isn't preparing for a future peace with Lord Sun Ce, he's preparing for a future *war*."

"It is probably just a precaution," Zhang Zhao suggested. "He doesn't know Lord Sun as we all do."

"There's word from Wu Prefecture that other correspondence between Xu Gong and the capital has been found," Qin Song said. "Xu Gong was writing to Cao Cao before he tried to petition the Son of Heaven, and he appears to have been an unofficial spy that Cao Cao never really turned away. We only have one half of the correspondence, but one can guess a few things from the half that we have."

"Be *restrained*, Lord Sun!" Zhang Zhao cried.

"No," Bofu chortled. "He's planning on taking something from me...? Fine: then I'll take something from him!"

"It's probably an error of communications!" Zhang Zhao said.

"He *was* behind that second attack by Haixi Chen," Bofu retorted. "We all wondered at the time, but this proves it. And he won't get another chance to attack me."

"What about Sheng Xian and White Tiger?" Cheng Pu asked. "Can we just leave either of them be after what Xu Gong tried to do...?"

Gu Yong shook his head; Lü Fan noticed the action and said, "Mister Gu Yuantan, you should speak if you have something to say: your words will enlighten us."

"Raiding Xu Zhao's estate and capturing the two of them has been raised, mused and rejected on a number of occasions," Gu Yong replied. "Sheng Xian's 'crime' was ineffectiveness, and 'White Tiger' Yan gives the impression of having no claws or teeth of his own, so attacking him risks increasing sympathy for him. Xu Gong was Cao's contact: there's no connection between Sheng and Cao,

and no connection between the Shanyue and Cao either."
"It might be better to be *safe* than *sorry*," Cheng Pu retorted.
Bofu lowered his head and muttered, "Must I kill *everyone*...?"
Lady Wu heard her son's quiet lament and sighed sadly.
"Hè Qi has returned to Wu Prefecture, and Han Dang can return there shortly as well, so the Shanyue will be contained," Qin Song continued. "If we reinforced Li Shu and assumed an aggressive stance, Yan Xiang might think twice before trying to harm us. That way, we can return our attentions to completing our campaign against Huang Zu."
"I agree," Lü Fan said. "We shouldn't be attacking Yan Xiang unless he gives us serious cause to."
"...Alright," Bofu conceded.

When the meeting ended, Bofu approached his brother Sun Quan and grasped his arms tightly.
"You intend to crush me...?" Sun Quan asked tonelessly.
"Don't be daft," Bofu chuckled as he hugged his brother properly. "Every time I see you, you're more impressive! You're making a good husband to Lady Xie. And your friend, Pan Zhang-"
Sun Quan pushed Bofu away and said, "Are you going to start attacking him again, Brother? He has done nothing wrong!"
"...I know that," Bofu replied. "I was going to say that the officials are being very courteous and telling me what great work he's doing; you're a good judge of men and saw talents in Pan that I missed. Well done, Brother, for finding us another hero. Oh, and Zhou Tai sends his regards."
Sun Quan smiled gratefully and asked, "Where is he...?"
"He is stationed in Yuzhang at present, since I'm going back there to smash Huang Zu once and for all and need his help for that," Bofu explained. "I was considering bringing you along, if-"
"I am a man of the pen, not the sword," Sun Quan said. "I'm not a fighter like Yi, and I'm not sagacious like Zhou Gongjin. I'm fine to go back to Yangxian, where my lack of military insight cannot harm our cause."
"...You're the future, Quan," Bofu replied. "When there's no need for swords and intrigue, you'll be the man that builds the new world. May it happen soon."
Sun Quan touched Bofu's arm and said, "So long as the sword is unharmed at that point, I hope for that time too."

The timid, long-faced Zhuge Jin was shuffling out of the great entrance to Bofu's mansion when he met upon the young talent Lu Ji, who was smiling.
"...Get it over with," Zhuge Jin sighed.
"Your brother Liang is a friend of Pang Tong," Lu Ji said.
Zhuge Jin was startled by the question; he laughed and replied, "I thought that you intended to tell me that I look like a donkey."
Lu Ji frowned; Ji's cousin Lu Xun - who was only 4 years older than Ji - approached the two and said, "It's not often that I see Cousin Gongji looking so perplexed! Did you ask him a particularly profound question, Mister Zhuge...?"
"No," Zhuge Jin replied. "I-"
"People can be very cruel, Mister Zhuge," Lu Ji said. "Your appearance is entirely irrelevant: Pang Tong, some say, is

'hideous', but he has a mind that defines intellectual beauty."
Zhuge Jin sighed and replied, "You sound like Liang. He always had a million more things going on in his head than the sum of all of the men he was surrounded by."
"Your brother is nicknamed 'Crouching Dragon'," Lu Ji noted. "And Pang Tong is known as 'Young Phoenix'. I look forward to meeting them both and spending hours discussing the world."
"If I can ever convince my brother to come to Jiangdong, I will introduce you to him, young sir," Zhuge Jin promised. "As for Pang Tong... well, I hear that he is considering travelling to Jiangdong or may already be here."
"If Lord Sun Ce had Pang Tong and Zhuge Liang, he'd be the lord of the entire world if that was Heaven's will," Lu Xun said.
"You're both very gracious," Zhuge Jin said pointedly.
"How so...? ...Because Lord Sun 'indirectly killed my father'...?" Lu Ji chuckled. "Father regretted having to view the Suns as an enemy; I am not burdened by that."
"Perhaps I should have one of you write to my brother," Zhuge Jin said. "He's obsessed with serving *Liu Bei*."
"That's unfortunate," Lu Xun replied. "Liu Bei is at best a well-meaning mediocrity with poor judgement, at worst an incompetent hankerer that undoes his own schemes."
"...I'll refrain from passing that on," Zhuge Jin sighed. "Good day to you both."
The three officials exchanged bows, and Zhuge Jin retreated.
"He is a very miserable man," Lu Ji noted.
"He fears that he will never be trusted," Lu Xun said. "He is obviously loyal and sincere, so that's a pity."

Qin Song and Jiang Qin were walking along the path that led to the outer gates of Bofu's mansion when they met upon Xu Sheng, who bowed and said, "Hello again, Mister Qin; oh, and my sincere condolences, Mister Jiang."
"...For what?" Jiang Qin asked.
"For the financial misfortune that you obviously suffer," Xu Sheng replied. "Why else would you be dressed like a pauper...?"
Qin Song covered his face with his sleeve; Jiang Qin frowned and said, "I just don't like to waste money on fancy robes when plain ones'll do: s'pose it comes from living day to day as a lad."
"Ah, I see," Xu Sheng sighed condescendingly.
"Your defence of Chaisang was a brilliant effort, Mister Xu," Jiang Qin continued. "P'raps we can sit and enjoy a dish of tea one day, and you can tell me a bit about your fighting style and your training methods."
"Maybe," Xu Sheng replied indifferently. "Good day, gentlemen."
"Same to you," Jiang Qin said, and Xu Sheng walked away with a sneer on his face.
"*Aiee*...! On the battlefield he's a hero, but otherwise, he's a pompous buffoon!" Qin Song said.
"...Such a shame," Jiang Qin sighed.

Bofu staged a grand banquet to celebrate the reunion of his family; Bofu's uncle Sun Jing was treated as a guest of honour since he rarely returned to Qu'e.
"Once Huang Zu's defeated, we can reorganise," Bofu explained.

"I have lots of trustworthy men now; I want us to be together."

"You want to recall me from Kuaiji indefinitely, Nephew...?" Sun Jing exclaimed.

"...And I must leave Yangxian...?" Sun Quan asked.

"Kuaiji and Yangxian are very different, Brother," Bofu replied. "Uncle's serving as a gate guard against any problems that we might have from Jiaozhi, which some of my politicians say might have to be our next target for pacification."

"Politicians are always looking for fights," Xu Kun complained. "Aren't they supposed to do the opposite...?"

"They're right, though, Nephew," Wu Jing said. "When we've dealt with Liu Biao and Huang Zu – and, maybe, Cao Cao as well – we still need to worry about the Shanyue in Wu, the–"

"The point of this conversation isn't discussing how much more fighting we have to do, Uncle," Bofu pleaded. "I want us all to be closer. I want to see you all, and I want to see my children grow, and... ... ...what's so funny, Mother...?"

All eyes turned to the smiling Lady Wu, who said, "You raised the subject without needing to be reminded; you are a family man now, and their safety worries you. You're just like your father, Ce. And you, Quan, happily wed to the daughter of wise Xie Jiong... and Yi, to Lady Xū! It's magnificent! Your father would be so proud if... well, he *is* proud, looking down as he does!"

"...I need to talk to him," Bofu declared. "I need to go to Dad's altar, pay my respects, and tell him that I finally intend to honour the promise that I made six years ago. This time, I'm going to smash Huang Zu once and for all: and then, after that, when the time's right, I'm going into northern Jing, and there will be nowhere for Liu Biao to run to, no one for him to hide behind..."

Sun Ben coughed deliberately and asked, "What would you do if Cao Cao was to ask for our help?"

"...I don't know," Bofu replied. "It depends on whether the 'Girdle Edict' is real or not... or rather, whether certain people decide that it's real. If a lot of good men rise up against him, I'll join Yuan Shao or remain neutral; if the good refused to challenge him, then I would leave the matter to Cao and Yuan or aid the Han in any way that I can. I can't be fairer than that."

"...And what about Yan Xiang...?" Sun Ben asked further.

"I can't agree with the advisers," Bofu admitted. "I'm going to write to Li Shu and ask him to act."

"That's too risky!" Wu Jing complained. "Cao Cao will retaliate!"

Bofu smiled and said, "I intend to explain...!"

The next morning saw two plans put into motion: firstly, Bofu left Qu'e and sailed westward yet again, intent on destroying Huang Zu. At the same time, a messenger sped ahead of General Li Shu's reinforcements and took a letter to his camp in southern Lujiang: it contained instructions to take decisive action against Inspector Yan Xiang, who had wasted no time in recruiting men and ordering the reconstruction of Shouchun City in neighbouring Jiujiang Prefecture.

****

13

Bofu prepared for his next attack on Jiangxia by training his forces on the Po County Lake in secret and stockpiling supplies in Chaisang; they then advanced by land and river, blockading the waterways and building several camps along the roads to southern Xiakou. Huang Zu was horrified when he learned that the Jiangdong forces had returned so quickly and that they were so well prepared: his composure failed him, and his remaining allies – the adviser Kuai Yue, Pan Jun, and Generals Zhang Shuo, Chen Jiu and Su Fei – struggled in their efforts to stabilise him.

"Is that all the respite I get...? *Two months*???" Huang Zu exclaimed. "I have barely started mourning my dead sons, and Liu Pan has left us, and...!"

Kuai Yue shook his head and said, "It is as I have already said: I am not surprised, Lord Huang, but I am not prepared either."

"And as I have already said, I haven't had time to rebuild my fleet!" Huang Zu complained. "The most that I can do is defend myself! But for how long???"

"My lord," Su Fei began, "the-"

"**No Gan Ning! No Gan Ning!**" Huang Zu shrieked. "**Don't you *dare* mention Gan Ning!**"

"...Lord Huang, you've mentioned him three times more than I intended to," Su Fei replied. "I was going to say that the reinforcements from Xiangyang are here and that we've completed the construction of two hundred boats and recruited four thousand new men. All in all, we can commit eight thousand men and three hundred vessels if we have to."

"It will have to do," Huang Zu said. "Just don't let that river rat get to Xiakou!"

While Bofu casually surrounded Huang Zu, his general in Lujiang Prefecture, Li Shu, had marched eastward from his base in Wan County to Inspector Yan Xiang's temporary capital – the walled city of Liyang – in the south of Jiujiang Prefecture, where he was trying to recruit soldiers. Yan Xiang was taken completely by surprise, and he did not have the resources to repel an army of 5,000 men.

"**Somebody notify His Excellency!**" Yan Xiang shouted at one of his aides. "**Get somebody out of the camp and away from here! Get them to Xuchang and warn His Excellency!**"

"What will you do...?" the aide asked.

"I died here once before and didn't realise it," Yan Xiang replied. "This time I'll be sure. Now *go*, man, and get word to the capital!"

Li Shu's army was not being especially careful, so Yan Xiang's aides were able to smuggle a messenger out of the besieged city; a desperate civilian mob opened the gates to the city a few days later, and Inspector Yan Xiang was captured within an hour of that.

"Well, well," Yan Xiang chuckled as Li Shu paced back and forth in front of him. "I get a *general*, do I...? Have we met...?"

"You were always arrogant," Li Shu said. "But you're brave too, which truly surprises me. It won't save you though."

"I know," Yan Xiang replied. "Come to think of it, I've probably died twice before. A man only has so much luck."

"...Your head will go to my lord," Li Shu said.

"Ah, but who will your lord's head go to...?" Yan Xiang retorted. "I'm the Han court's appointed Inspector, General: your acts will not go unpunished."

"It isn't your problem, Yan Xiang, so why worry...?" Li Shu said. "**Guards**: take him away."

Yan Xiang smiled as he was escorted from Li Shu's command tent: his face still carried part of that smile when his severed head was returned to Li Shu a few minutes later.

Two days passed; word of Yan Xiang's death reached the Qian Hills, where Chen Lan and Lei Bo – two of the leaders of the confederacy of bandits that were named for the place and both of them former officers under Yuan Shu – addressed their subordinates with glee.

"Yan Xiang's dead now, which means we can get back to what we were doing," Chen Lan said. "Sun Ce doesn't seem to care about us: all the same, we'll team up with Mei Qian's lot. There's still a lot of rewards to be had around the river, and we don't want to miss out!"

The bandits cheered at the news.

"...What if Cao sends someone else...?" Lei Bo asked.

"Liu Xun...?" Chen Lan retorted.

Lei Bo laughed and said, "You're right! Who can he send...?"

"...This is intolerable," Cao Cao growled as he absorbed the news that Yan Xiang was dead and that any semblance of order in northern Lujiang and northern Jiujiang was on the verge of collapsing altogether. The news could not have come at a worse time, as Yuan Shao was advancing southward and Cao Cao was looking to check his advance at the Yellow River; Cao slammed his palm against his leg and cried, "Sun Ce didn't even give me the chance to negotiate...!"

"You may go," the adviser Xun Yu said to the messenger, who retreated immediately.

"...But it makes clearer the meaning of a letter that was brought here just a few hours ago," Guo Jia said. "The letter – from Sun Ce, supposedly – says that he 'apologises' for the actions of his general, but that it is his understanding that Li Shu acted correctly when he followed the discretional notion that 'an officer in the field should not always wait for approval, and act in a timely manner' if he is faced with a need to 'quell a perceived threat'. He hopes that you understand."

"Oh, I understand," Cao Cao muttered.

"Are we certain that Yan Xiang didn't provoke this...?" the adviser Chen Qun asked. "As a veteran of dealing with Yuan Shu's advisers, I know what Yan Xiang can be like."

"Sun Ce's in Jiangxia, fighting Huang Zu, and has had no time to 'react to anything'," Xun Yu scoffed. "This was planned."

"I agree, Uncle," Xun Yòu said. "And it has to be said that some interpret Sun Ce's 'requests' – made in his own petition to His Majesty, which includes the suggestion that his friend Lü Fan should be or is in his opinion already appointed as *Administrator of Guiyang* – as belligerent, arrogant and, indicative of an ambition to rule the south."

"*Guiyang*...?" Chen Qun exclaimed. "I didn't know about that. Guiyang's one of Liu Biao's semi-autonomous prefectures in southern Jing."

"Sun Ce's famous father, Sun Jian, pacified a rebellion there twenty years ago or thereabouts," Guo Jia noted. "And Sun Jian was also made the Administrator of neighbouring Changsha for a short time, so I suspect some further 'claim of rights' here."

"The weight of evidence is considerable," Xun Yòu said. "What, then, do we do...?"

"Li Shu isn't the only general that can 'act in a timely manner'," Cao Cao replied. "I had pondered this course, but now I am pushed to it..."

"I suspect that I know what you're going to do, Excellency, but that's not going to help us restore order in northern Yang," Xun Yòu said. "Who can we send now...? Who can be the Inspector of Yang Province and survive...?"

"I will send Liu Fu," Cao Cao replied. "This time, I am confident: send *Liu Fu*."

Huang Zu's reorganised and reinforced army and navy were providing a formidable challenge for Bofu's reduced retinue: Dong Xi, Hè Qi, Han Dang, Jiang Qin, Chen Wu and Ling Cao had all been allocated to other regions, partly because they were needed to quell uprisings but mainly because the general expectation had been that the resistance in Jiangxia would be feeble.

"I've underestimated Huang Zu, and after I said that I wouldn't," Bofu grumbled.

"We all did," Lü Fan replied. "We won't break him quickly."

"...No," Bofu murmured.

"Worried that your 'other front' might land you in trouble...?" Gongjin asked.

"...What 'other front'...?" Cheng Pu prompted.

"I, uh... I ordered Li Shu to attack Yan Xiang," Bofu admitted. "Yan was moving to Liyang! How could I ignore that?"

"...So Cao will probably want to retaliate," Cheng Pu said. "That's not helpful."

"We won't be here *that long*...!" Bofu chuckled.

But Huang Zu's defences held up, and plans for a swift campaign turned to thoughts of a siege or retreat; at the same time, the Administrator of Guangling Prefecture, Chen Deng, received a letter from Cao Cao and retreated to his study to ponder it further. His brother, Chen Ying, asked, "What bothers you...?"

"His Excellency asks that I do something quite absurd," Chen Deng replied. "He asks – and by 'asks', I mean 'orders' – that I launch an immediate, 'pre-emptive' attack on Sun-controlled southern Guangling and, if possible, the eastern part of Wu Prefecture, for the purpose of 'territorial reclamation'."

Chen Ying laughed and said, "It's a joke, surely!"

"...This is a proper order," Chen Deng replied. "I've a mind to ask Father's advice. He was able to outthink Lü Bu and the whole of Yuan Shu's counsel. But this says 'immediately', and Father's in Pei County on the other side of the province..."

"What will you do...?" Chen Ying asked.

"I have to obey!" Chen Deng replied. "As insane as it is, I must obey: I must attack a neighbouring province without provocation, for despite His Excellency's use of the words 'pre-emptive' and 'reclamation', there is no immediate cause for such a provocative act that I can see. And then I must face the wrath of the son of the 'Tiger of Jiangdong'. I will be honest, Brother, and say that I do not disagree with the order, just the timing and circumstances. If I was doing this with an army of fifty-thousand, I would be happy... but what can I do with what I actually have...? And what if Liu Bei returns, or Zang Ba rebels again, or Yuan Shao sends an army down from Qing...?"

"...So who can you turn to...?" Chen Ying asked.

"Sad to say," Chen Deng replied, "there is only one person that I can turn to..."

A week passed.

Bofu's nerves were frayed once again: Huang Zu was proving to be as formidable as he had been 8 years previously, and that meant a cautious approach when time was not on his side. Matters were made worse still when a messenger brought word of an alliance and an invasion that was scarcely believable.

"**REPORT!**" the messenger began. "**The acting Administrator of Wu Prefecture, Zhu Zhi, requests immediate aid! The Administrator of Northern Guangling, Chen Deng, has seized Southern Guangling and launched an attack on Wu with the aid of the Shanyue!**"

Bofu choked and tried not to scream.

"...You may go, and get some refreshment and rest," Gongjin said to the messenger, who retreated at once.

"The *Shanyue*...?" Cheng Pu exclaimed. "*Chen Deng*... allied to the *Shanyue tribes*...?"

The messenger had left a written account that Lü Fan was now reading; he sighed and said, "It's White Tiger: he's left Xu Zhao's estate and he's commanding the Shanyue again."

"**I *knew* that we should have just raided that fool's lands and got rid of his guests before they harmed us!**" Cheng Pu cried. "**Once this is over, we should burn that idiot's estate to the ground!**"

"I caused this," Bofu said. "By attacking Yan Xiang-"

"As you said, Yan Xiang had moved down to Liyang, and that meant encroaching on us sooner or later," Gongjin insisted. "You – we – had no choice. For whatever mad reason he had, Cao Cao left us with no choice."

"But we have to leave here *again*!" Bofu complained. "Huang Zu will survive *again*! I have to come back here *again*! I don't *want* to come here *again*! I wanted this to be the last time that I had to fight him!"

"Heaven's will is unfathomable," Gongjin said. "Let's press our enemy one last time and then go."

"This is becoming monotonous," Huang Zu complained as he watched the swift approach of Bofu's navy. "How many times must we do this...?"

"To answer your question, 'As many times as it is necessary',"

Kuai Yue replied. "But if we want to win, we must be the aggressors. We must meet him on the river if we don't want him to attack Xiakou."

"I'll lead the navy," General Chen Jiu said.

"Zhang Shuo and I will be ready to support you if you fail," Huang Zu replied.

Chen Jiu's navy advanced to meet Bofu's vanguard; an additional force led by Liu Biao's deputy naval commander Zhang Yun was also approaching the Jiangdong navy, and that was a cause for concern.

"Has Liu Biao diverted all of his forces here...?" Lü Fan wondered. "Have Cao Cao and Liu Biao made peace, and...?"

"I doubt it," Gongjin replied. "That's not Cai Mao we're dealing with, so Liu Biao is keeping his best naval general close to him."

"Cai Mao might be on his way," Bofu suggested. "We want to retreat now, so that's not a good thing: we'll have to be quick."

"**Leave it to me!**" Lü Meng cried.

"For once I won't try to stop you!" Lü Fan said to Lü Meng, who advanced immediately.

"**I'll have to do my bit!**" Bofu cackled. "**Let's make them glad that we're leaving!**"

"**I'm with you, Brother!**" Sun Yi said.

"*Aiee...* here we go again," Sun Hè complained.

"Only now there's *two of them*," Song Qian muttered.

"I'll be there to help you," Gongjin said.

Sun Hè and Song Qian led their bodyguard forces after Bofu, Gongjin and Sun Yi, who led the charge; Lü Fan turned to Taishi Ci and asked, "What do you plan to do...?"

"Why are you not just ordering Taishi to advance, Mister Lü?" Xu Kun said.

"He needs no orders," Lü Fan replied.

Taishi Ci smiled and said, "I'm best placed as reinforcements this time, I think. That's why General Xu Kun and I were not asked to join the charge."

"So there's some plan amid all this...?" Xu Kun exclaimed.

Lü Fan nodded silently.

Bofu's charge was blunted by Zhang Yun, whose forces overtook Chen Jiu's and surged forward; the men from northern Jing were no less competent as river fighters, and they suddenly had a numerical advantage.

"**PRESS FORWARD!**" Chen Jiu bellowed. "**AID ZHANG YUN!**"

The Jing men leapt from boat to boat and engaged Bofu's small militia: men fell in all directions as the Jiangdong men defended their isolated position, but their skills would not be enough. It was then that Taishi Ci advanced: he led his elite men toward Zhang Yun and turned the battle around. Within minutes of that, Zhou Tai sailed a line of boats along the southern bank of the river and split Chen Jiu's and Zhang Yun's forces; Sun Ben, Cheng Pu and Sun Fu had the medium-sized vessels close in on the battle and provide archer support to Bofu, who now had an advantage over Zhang Yun. The chaos worsened when Huang Zu – who had noted Lü Meng's northern approach – advanced out of Xiakou with Zhang Shuo, personally ordered archers to fire volleys from the riverbank and sent Su Fei's naval militia to intercept Lü Meng.

It was a battle that might have gone either way: the outcome of the main river battle was decided by Taishi Ci, Bofu, Gongjin, Sun Yi and Zhou Tai, who charged wildly and struck fear into the Jing sailors, while Lü Meng's refusal to withdraw gave him an unexpected victory over the unprepared Su Fei. Huang Zu retreated to Xiakou, and the expectation was that the Jiangdong forces would now surround and siege the walled port city: none was more surprised than Huang Zu when it was announced that the enemy had withdrawn completely.

"...He... he came all this way to...?" Huang Zu exclaimed as he paced back and forth across his grand meeting hall. "...We must do this *again*...?"

"He can't have planned a retreat," Chen Jiu said. "He stocked Chaisang far too well, and his men were prepared for a siege. Something's happened."

"Such as...?" Zhang Shuo asked.

"...Take your pick," Kuai Yue replied. "Cao Cao has diverted his forces to Guandu; Yuan Shao is courting rebel factions in Yu Province; Zhang Xiu has made peace with Cao Cao, and now acts as a buffer between our lord and Yuan Shao..."

"None of that would concern Sun Ce," Huang Zu suggested.

"Not directly," Kuai Yue retorted. "But there are rumours of a disagreement between Han officials in Lujiang and Sun Ce's garrison in Wan County, and that might have led to conflict. Messengers and travellers can get through from the east now, so we're bound to find out quite soon."

"If only I had the strength to pursue," Huang Zu lamented. "I hate the Suns, and I will never be able to rest until they are all as dead as my family...!"

Bofu and Gongjin stood on the deck of the Jiangdong navy command ship and watched the world sail by.

"It'll be morning soon," Gongjin said. "We'll be back in Qu'e before you know it."

"And from there...?" Bofu asked.

"We *rest* before we do anything," Gongjin insisted. "Li Shu has withdrawn to Wan County, and Xuchang has yet to visibly respond, though I doubt that they can with Yuan Shao about to attempt an invasion; Chen Deng and White Tiger – a pair that I never imagined describing as allies – have been halted by Zhu Zhi's militia, and the defences in and around all of the county cities are adequate to survive any siege."

"Yeah, but can we afford to rest anyway...?" Bofu asked. "The-"

"Forgive my interrupting, but you, your brother Yi, your cousins, me, Zhou Tai, Lü Meng, we're all coming back from a heated naval battle in Jiangxia," Gongjin noted. "We must move slowly, cautiously, and be measured: Chen Deng is one of the men that outmanoeuvred Liu Bei, Yuan Shu's best thinkers and then Lü Bu's adviser Chen Gong, all before leading a victorious army against the pirate king Xue Zhou and frightening Lü Bu's men with tales of his valour. He's no fool, and he's no coward either."

"You make him sound more dangerous than Huang Zu," Bofu said.

"He might well be," Gongjin replied. "He's as shifty as Xu Gong, as crafty as Wang Lang, as bold as Zu Lang and as popular with the people of northern Guangling as Liu Yao was in Danyang. And don't forget that he doesn't attack alone: if White Tiger has returned, the Shanyue tribes have fully regrouped and will tax us to the limit."

Bofu nodded seriously and said, "We'll definitely need rest, then. We'll probably be in Wu and Guangling for months."

"We must certainly be prepared for that," Gongjin replied. "When we get to Qu'e, you rest, you spend time with Daqiao and your children, you hunt, you do whatever it takes to be ready for what is to come."

The situation was, after many months, as similar as it was different: Liu Biao and Huang Zu had repeatedly escaped the full brunt of the Sun clan's wrath, saved at critical moments by events beyond anyone's control. To the wider nation, the Sun-Liu feud was an irrelevance: it was the fate of the Han Empire that mattered, and its fate now seemed to depend upon the outcome of the battle between Excellency of Works Cao Cao and Commander-in-Chief Yuan Shao. That battle would take place in the north, more specifically the region around the city of Guandu, to the north of the capital Xuchang: the Sun clan and the rulers of Jing Province would be drawn into the Yuan-Cao war by the gravity of politics whilst still being embroiled in personal struggles, and at the end of it all, everything would be changed once again.

****

ACT II: AN UNSEEN THREAT

14

Han Dynasty China was at breaking point once again, and despite their best efforts to make Jiangdong a place where the 'politics of the north' did not affect them, the Sun clan and their followers were as affected by state matters as they had always been. In the past, it had been the threat of the cultist army known as the Yellow Turbans that had forced Sun Jian to leave his family and travel north as a militia commander; after the Yellow Turbans, the tyrant Dong Zhuo had given Sun Jian cause to pledge temporary allegiance to the nobleman Yuan Shu and unwittingly become Yuan's lifetime servant. That lifetime debt had not lasted for very long, as Sun Jian had been assassinated while he led an invasion of Jing Province for his overly ambitious master; Jian's eldest son Sun Ce – or 'Bofu', as he preferred to be known – eventually inherited the chieftainship of the clan and the shackles of indenture that Yuan Shu had placed on them.

Bofu conquered the Jiangdong region in the name of his lord, but he always hoped that he would one day govern alone: when Yuan Shu declared as an alternative emperor – and was then branded as a heretic-traitor by all – Shu effectively severed the lord-vassal ties that Bofu could not cut, and the Sun clan were free. That freedom meant that Jiangdong was also free, and it also meant that an old score could finally be settled: Bofu could journey westward and destroy Liu Biao and Huang Zu, the rulers of Jing Province and the men that killed his father.

Bofu's first Jing campaign ended with a forced retreat in order to deal with Yuan Shu's appointed Administrator of Lujiang, Liu Xun; that unwanted distraction yielded benefits in the form of 30,000 defected soldiers and a foothold in northern Yang Province. The second campaign was halted as a precaution, since there were still potential enemies in the form of the Shanyue tribes and Cao Cao's appointed Administrator of Guangling Prefecture, Chen Deng; the short-lived mission coincided with the birth of Bofu's daughters, but it also coincided with several unwanted events. Firstly, Yuzhang's Administrator, Hua Xin, expressed a desire to rebel; secondly, a long-time detractor – a former Administrator of Wu Prefecture named Xu Gong – attempted to petition Emperor Xian and labelled Bofu as a future nemesis to the Han Dynasty itself. Hua Xin was spared, but Xu Gong and his family were not: Xu Gong's son and aides had escaped the purge, and Wu Prefecture's Administrator, Zhu Zhi, was striving to locate them before they could do harm to the Sun clan. The third and most recent campaign ended with a third victory over Huang Zu, but they had to withdraw and turn their attentions to Wu Prefecture, where two unlikely allies – Chen Deng and the Shanyue – were now staging an invasion after having seized southern Guangling. This was all happening against the backdrop of another state emergency, as the nobleman Yuan Shao – the brother of Bofu's late master – and the Han Emperor's senior minister Cao Cao were about to do battle for the future of the Han Dynasty: Bofu knew that he might be asked to contribute somehow, but the matter was complex, and a wrong decision could be costly.

Bofu stopped in his capital Qu'e, intent on spending some time with his family before he embarked on what would doubtless be a long campaign against the formidable Chen Deng and the Sun clan's old enemy 'White Tiger' Yan, the 'king' of the Wu Shanyue tribes. Questions about the future plagued him: Bofu could see a time when the warlords were finally brought under control, but the Shanyue, Qiang, Di, Wuhuan, Nanman and other non-Han tribes were always rebelling against what they saw as occupiers and enemies, and Bofu had tired of them.

"I *have* to do something about the tribes," Bofu said to a group of officials that included Lü Fan, Gongjin, Zhang Zhao, Gu Yong, Qin Song, Quan Rou, his uncle Wu Jing and the young scholars Lu Xun and Lu Ji.

"By 'something', Nephew, you mean what...?" Wu Jing asked.

"Sooner or later, everyone's got to do something about them," Bofu retorted. "Take Liang Province: the whole mess there was started by the Qiang and the Di, and the Qiang are still the cause of chaos there now. The Xiongnu that live in Bing Province might supply troops to the Han from time to time, but they're mostly raiders that-"

"To be entirely fair, Bofu, the Southern Xiongnu are mostly benevolent," Gongjin said. "All of the trouble was caused by rebel splinter factions led by Yufuluo – who is now dead – and his son Liu Bao, who has been very quiet since his uncle Huchuquan became chieftain."

"...A fair point," Bofu replied. "But the Shanyue here in Yang are just a pain. All of them are. And the Nanman people always make trouble. And then there's the people of Jiaozhi: yeah, they make no trouble at the moment, while that old fellow Shi Xie is ruling them and spreading that Buddhist stuff that be believes in, but what happens when he dies, or if he or his successor suddenly decides to be another Ze Rong and turn the whole 'Buddha' thing into an excuse to invade...?"

"Ze Rong wasn't a Buddhist," Lü Fan said. "He said that he was, and he used a lot of the mantras and slogans, but in the end he was a cultist that had distorted the faith into an excuse to steal and kill, just as Zhang Jue did when he distorted Taoism into his ironically-named 'Way of Peace'."

"And that felon Zhang Lu that rules Hanzhong, who dared to rename the birthplace of the Han Dynasty and practice that abomination of a 'faith' that he calls the 'Way of Five Pecks of Rice'!" Zhang Zhao cried.

"Yes, Zhang Lu is also a good example," Lü Fan said. "Shi Xie practices the Buddhist faith as it was meant to be, which is why his people are so quiet. You cannot despise every man of faith because of a few bad examples, Lord Sun."

"...I'd prefer that you called me 'Bofu'," Bofu replied. "And I'd prefer that we spent less time on the ones that don't make trouble and focus on the ones that do. Are the Shanyue in any way peaceful or harmless...?"

"They are a constant source of worry," Qin Song admitted.

"And they're making trouble right now, *again*, just when I had hoped that I would finally be rid of Huang Zu!" Bofu said. "The only reason that Chen Deng is able to cheerfully invade Wu Prefecture is because he has White Tiger's help! The only reason that Xu Gong was able to cause me trouble was because he had help from White Tiger! I have resisted the call by Old Cheng and others that urged me to attack Elder Xu Zhao's estate and kill all of his fugitive guests, but this latest insult is one too many. Xu will take White Tiger back under his protection if we win; he'd take Chen Deng, too, and he'd have taken Yuan Shu, I think, if he'd asked humbly enough!"

"Probably," Zhang Zhao muttered. "That old fool Xu Zhao is a nuisance, hero of old or not... perhaps the time has come for decisive action."

"We have to accept that military force is the only thing that some – most – people understand," Bofu declared. "When that greedy what's-his-name in Liang Province was stealing the money, the people's words were ignored: they only got rid of him by killing his toadies and chasing him out. Dong Zhuo had to be met with violence; Yuan Shu was never going to be fair while men fought with words."

Lu Ji shook his head and sighed quietly.

"And those men were like us... Han people, I mean," Bofu continued. "These other people, like the Qiang and Di, their tribal brains are simple and they don't grasp our way of life, and they twist minds: when Han men marry their women, they become like them and their children come out like Ma Chao or Lü Bu. Dong Zhuo started out courting them, and ended up a sadist that burned people alive and watched them scream for fun."

"To be fair, his 'parties' were his conceit, and had nothing to do with tribes," Lü Fan suggested. "Dong Zhuo was not turned into a sadist, he always was one."

Cheng Pu entered the meeting hall at that moment and said, "Sorry I'm late, Lord Sun."

"No problem," Bofu replied. "You can give your opinion on the Shanyue now."

"Kill the entire lot of them," Cheng Pu grumbled as he took a seat to Bofu's right that made him the only representative of the military. "The late lord and I spent... oh, I forget how long it was, maybe three years, in Changsha, Guiyang and whatnot, fighting those wretched barbarians, and then we went to fight the Qiang, who were no better. The Shanyue are scum that will never learn to live alongside us."

"...Or, more precisely, *beneath us*," Lu Ji murmured; Lu Xun heard the words and frowned.

"I don't want to annihilate them, but I do want to make them stop attacking us, and the way I see it, the only way to do that is to smash them so badly that they crawl into their holes and never come out again," Bofu said. "You officials know that most of your problems are about raids by tribes, tribes fighting each other and direct attempts to take over regions: if we got rid of them, that would leave pirates and bandits, and although they only understand violence, they're smarter and-"

"Wait, wait," Lü Fan said. "I heard a voice from the end of our line, and I believe that it was young Lu Ji that spoke."

Bofu looked at Lu Ji – who was at the very end of the row of officials – and asked, "What did you want to say?"

"...Watch your words, cousin," Lu Xun whispered.

Lu Ji smiled sadly and said, "Long ago, Guan Yiwu served Duke

Huan of the state of Qi as his chancellor. Isn't it true, gentlemen, that Duke Huan was able to unite the lords and pacify the people without resorting to violence...?"

"What do *you* know?" Zhang Zhao scoffed.

"Let him speak," Bofu insisted.

"Do not let baseless guilt force you to waste time listening to a puppy!" Zhang Zhao protested. "He is too young, too ignorant of the ways of the world to contribute to this discussion, and should not even be here!"

"Nonetheless, he was invited, because wisdom can sometimes gift itself to men that have yet to see a grey hair," Gongjin said. "Please, Lu Ji, continue."

Lu Ji bowed slightly and said, "A wise man once said, 'If the peoples in far-flung places are not submissive, then all of the facets of our culture – civility, virtue, respect and so forth – are to be extolled to them in order to win their hearts and minds and lead them to emulate us'."

Gongjin smiled and said, "Confucius."

"Indeed," Lu Ji replied. "The vast majority of those present speak only of the use of violence, but say nothing about sharing our values and virtues with them and reasoning with them. I, Ji, might – as some say – be 'young' and 'ignorant', but I think and I feel, and I am unsettled by what I have heard today... it saddens me."

Zhang Zhao pointed at Lu Ji and hissed, "You...!"

"...Life is burdensome, and it is rare that one can take actions that are based upon his ideals," Gongjin suggested. "It is, however, quite right that we have allowed ourselves to become so incensed at the actions of the Shanyue that we risked resorting to violence without properly considering the alternatives."

Bofu nodded slowly and lowered his eyes.

"...We should really worry about 'dealing with the tribes once and for all' when Liu Biao, Huang Zu and Chen Deng are no longer problems," Lü Fan suggested. "For now, we should be resting or preparing for battle."

"I'll go on to Dantu," Cheng Pu said. "Lord Sun and the rest of you can rendezvous with me there."

"Yeah," Bofu replied. "See you then."

The officials paid their respects and left the hall; once Bofu, Gongjin and Lü Fan were the only ones present, Lü Fan said, "Lu Ji's left you haunted, hasn't he...?"

"It wasn't his intention," Bofu replied. "Lu Ji was right to remind us that violence isn't the answer to everything. It's the answer to *almost* everything, sad to say... but his father made his name by trying alternatives that actually worked. Lu Kang was Magistrate of Gaocheng, Administrator of Wuling and then Administrator of Guiyang: every place that he went, he made a difference."

"You're allowing your decisions during the siege of Huancheng to shape your moods, Bofu, but you must not," Gongjin insisted. "You did what was necessary."

"...Perhaps," Bofu said, "but if I had spared Lu Kang and killed Wang Lang, instead of the other way around... I mean, look at that boy Ji. Thank goodness he didn't die in that siege: he's a genius, and a kind one at that."

"There's a story – I don't know if it's true – about Lu Ji... one day I may ask him," Gongjin said. "His father took him to Yuan Shu's estate – perhaps a few months before you were sent to attack Huancheng – so that Ji would have his first taste of mingling with noble lords in court. Sadly, that's probably the meeting where Yuan asked Lu Kang for support and was refused, triggering the attacks… but I digress. Yuan Shu decided to distribute oranges as treats for his guests, and Ji – it is said – took several and hid them in his sleeve."

"Was he caught?" Bofu asked. "I mean, I presume he was if the story's known…"

"He was," Gongjin said, "and when Yuan Shu confronted the boy – who was five or six at the time – he replied, 'They are for my mother'. Yuan Shu was left feeling amused and awkward, so I understand, and merely commended the boy for his filial devotion and let the matter rest."

"…I hope he let him keep the oranges," Bofu grumbled. "He wouldn't have if it was one of *us*, I know *that*."

"Yuan ordered you to siege Lu's home city and starve the people to death a few months later," Lü Fan noted. "A few oranges mean little either way."

"…No, they don't," Bofu replied. "Anyhow… we've got to focus on Chen Deng now, haven't we…? I'll spend a bit of time in Qu'e, and then I'll advance to Dantu. Gongjin, you should stay here: I'll have Ziheng and Old Cheng for this one, and we need someone to react quickly if Cao Cao does anything else while I'm away."

"There are others that can react to Cao Cao," Gongjin said. "I'm going to Ba Qiu – near Luling – to train the new naval recruits and oversee the expansion of our fleet."

"Alright," Bofu replied.

"…And if I might ask about Cao Cao…?" Lü Fan said. "The 'Girdle Edict' is certainly a magnificent inspiration that, it's currently rumoured, has led to Liu Biao pledging allegiance to Yuan Shao, and Liu Bei is rallying in Yu Province."

"…Yeah, Gongjin mentioned it," Bofu replied. "I'm divided: any friend of Liu Biao should really be my enemy, but Cao Cao's a special case. The Yuans feuded while the people suffered, and I don't want my feud with Liu Biao to be written about in the same way. If that edict's real – and with Cao all but admitting to killing Consort Dong, and remembering what he did in Xu Province a few years back, and thinking about that stuff about Zhang Xiu's aunt and getting his own son killed, the edict probably *is* real – then my duty is to rescue the Son of Heaven, like Dad tried to do."

Gongjin smiled and said, "So you're mulling the idea of…?"

"…Beating Chen Deng… taking all of Guangling, not just the south… and then launching a pincer attack on Cao… Li Shu from Lujiang, us from Guangling…? …Yeah, I am," Bofu admitted. "I'm tempted. I really am. I know what history books might say, but it would be to honour the Girdle Edict, wouldn't it…? If Liu Biao, Yuan Shao, Liu Bei and me all attacked Cao from all sides, he couldn't win, and then we're the ones writing the history books, aren't we…? …But…"

"…But what if Cao wins somehow, or if the edict's proven to be a counterfeit and a rescue isn't what the Son of Heaven wants…?" Lü Fan prompted.

"Exactly," Bofu replied. "Can we be sure…? Yuan Shao's the head of the coalition again, and he's not only a proven incompetent, he's Yuan Shu's brother, and we can't be sure that a desire to be emperor doesn't run in their blood. I could be helping one Wang Mang to defeat another."

"Liu Bei's not much better," Gongjin said. "He's said to dream not only of having his disinheritance rescinded, but that he might one day be the Son of Heaven."

"The bumbling mat weaver, an emperor...?" Lü Fan chortled. "The only people that would want Liu Bei as the Han Emperor are the Yellow Turbans! He'd be overthrown before he'd chaired his first court session, he's so inept."

"That too," Bofu said. "*Liu Biao* and *Liu Bei* are the western arms of the pincer...? Liu Biao's a redundant old corpse with maybe three good generals, and Liu Bei is Liu Bei. Add Commander Do-nothing to the north, and it's the Eastern Pass Coalition all over again: we'd end up doing everything and watching Yuan Shao get all the praise if we won, or getting blamed for it all if we lost, I know it."

"...Think it over," Gongjin said. "We've plenty of time."

Bofu retired to his bedchambers and sat next to his wife Daqiao, who asked, "What concerns you, Husband...?"

"...Can't you call me 'Bofu', like my friends do...?" Bofu said miserably. "Calling me 'Husband' makes me feel... I dunno... old."

"You call me 'Lady Qiao', which makes me sound 'old'," Daqiao retorted. "And don't dodge my question! You're upset about something serious."

"...That old man I starved out at Huancheng a few years back... Lu Kang," Bofu replied. "His son and nephew are in my court now."

"I know," Daqiao said.

"...Yeah, well... I probably ramble about it all the time, don't I," Bofu sighed.

"You were having a meeting about the future," Daqiao said. "You were going to talk to the advisers about what happens after you've beaten Chen Deng."

"Yeah, and Kang's son made us all feel like villains!" Bofu replied. "He said that we made him feel 'uneasy' with all our talk about dealing with the tribes using force! Zhang Zhao was right, though... what he muttered as he was leaving the meeting... that we can't be soft with them, because they always rise up again later rather than sooner. Kindness never worked, or they'd not be like they are now. But all the same, I'm tired... *really* tired..."

Daqiao smiled and said, "Forget about it all, just for tonight. Say goodnight to our daughters, and then come to bed."

Bofu laughed and said, "You're right. It's like Gongjin said: we have plenty of time."

Bofu's brother Sun Quan was ensuring that he knew everything that was going on in Qu'e: his father-in-law Xie Jiong was visiting Yangxian County, so he was forced to explain – and justify – the current situation.

"My brother inherited a great burden," Sun Quan protested. "The villain Yuan Shu had made a slave of our father, in fact he made slaves of the entire clan and all that chose to follow us, and we were treated poorly."

"I am aware of what Yuan Shu became, so that is quite

believable," Xie Jiong said. "But it has little bearing on the present, does it, my son-in-law...?"

"You currently serve the Han government as Magistrate of Xu County: before that, you served the Department of the Imperial Secretariat in a consultant role," Sun Quan replied. "You've seen what the tyrant Dong Zhuo's actions have done, and how those actions still reverberate years after his death."

"They do," Xie Jiong admitted.

"Yuan Shu was, in some ways, worse, because he went as far as Wang Mang of old times, and claimed a right to the throne," Sun Quan continued. "But before that, he started a needless feud with his brother at a critical moment, and my father suffered first when Yuan Shu sent a crony to attack him at Yang City. After that, my father was ordered to attack Liu Biao, and Huang Zu killed him. The offence is not necessarily the kill – although that is considered as treacherous, sneaky and wholly unnecessary – but rather the contempt that was shown in the aftermath. Our father was a hero that had once saved Jing Province from the Yellow Turbans and fought Dong Zhuo's minions around the tombs of the sovereigns: he deserved better."

"...And Sun Jian was bound by an oath to serve his lord that he could not break without good reason," Xie Jiong mused.

"Father's actions in Jing were not personal," Sun Quan insisted. "Liu Biao made it personal. And after his death, my cousin Sun Ben took charge of the clan while we mourned: he quickly found that Yuan Shu showed no regret and simply wished that we would continue to serve him properly and not 'mope': that was echoed by the majority of his officials, including Yan Xiang."

Xie Jiong nodded silently.

"My brother took control of the clan after he had concluded his mourning, and quickly showed that he is as great a man as Father," Sun Quan continued. "He's made Jiangdong a place to live rather than exist. He's pacified the tribes, tamed the bandits and pirates, and brought order to the local government: the biggest obstacles were, sad to say, the men that the government sent here, like Liu Yao, who allied with the cult leader Ze Rong, and Wang Lang, who colluded with crime lords to keep his grip on Kuaiji. Nothing is clear, Father-in-law."

"No, no, that's right," Xie Jiong admitted.

"Liu Biao has done nothing but harass Yuzhang Prefecture since Yuan Shu was toppled," Sun Quan continued. "Liu fears our righteous desire for revenge, for reparation, and provokes us further with incursions that we must respond to. Cao Cao fears my brother wrongly, and remedies his fears with callous and foolish acts, like making Yan Xiang the Inspector of Yang and failing to reprimand and withdraw his appointed Administrator of Guangling, Chen Deng, who right now attacks Wu Prefecture with the aid of the Shanyue."

"All quite visible," Xie Jiong admitted.

"So my brother is forced to play the part of 'villain', when he is really a hero," Sun Quan insisted. "The 'Girdle Edict' proves that Cao Cao has ill intent; Liu Biao might side with Yuan Shao, as we will, but he gives refuge to Dong Zhuo's vassals and has a crime lord, Huang Zu, as his gate guard in Jiangxia. What villains have you seen in Jiangdong's courts...?"

"...None," Xie Jiong replied. "And to be honest, I am here to stay. I've witnessed the changes from my place on the outer fringes of the Imperial Secretariat's office: having narrowly avoided the 'two terrible journeys' – the one from Luoyang to Chang'an, and the one that eventually brought the court to Xuchang – I've watched as the 'Ten' made way for Dong Zhuo, who then made way for Wang Yun, who quickly fell and made way for the 'regents', who then made way for Cao Cao. There can never be a reason for killing a pregnant consort of the Son of Heaven, not even the allegation that her father plotted against the Excellency of Works; the 'Girdle Edict', though suspect, has some ring of truth to it that Cao Cao himself provides. I am here in Jiangdong because this is where sanity still reigns. I cannot serve the Han court in its current form, so I shall stay here and do what I can to aid Lord Sun's administration until such time that a stable, incorrupt, benevolent government exists in the north, and I shall call upon the rest of our clan to do the same. I can only hope that Yuan Shao or Cao Cao – whichever one of them 'wins' – chooses to build that stable government, and does not prolong the cycle of madness instead."

"It is what we all hope," Sun Quan said.

Bofu decided to go hunting to calm his nerves before he departed for Dantu: his bodyguards followed him to the stables as usual, and, as always, he was greeted by Old Yin and the other stable keepers when he arrived.

"Off on campaign again soon, Lord Sun?" Old Yin asked.

"I will be, yeah," Bofu replied. "I-"

"You will be punished, unbeliever! Master Gan Ji's blood is on your hands!"

Bofu turned in time to see two soldiers dragging away a young man that had tried to approach his entourage; the man's cry was met with little heckling by the onlookers, and that unnerved Bofu and his loyalists.

"Pay them no mind, Lord Sun," Old Yin said. "They're getting to be more vocal since the crackdowns, but there aren't many of them, really. A few thousand, perhaps... some folk say 'tens of thousands', but..."

Bofu noticed that one of the young stable hands was frowning miserably and staring at the ground: he turned to Old Yin and asked, "Was Gan Ji really that popular...?"

"There are *hundreds* of thousands of people in Jiangdong," Sun Hè noted. "And Gan Ji was making trouble."

"...Was he...?" Bofu retorted. "Or was he just spreading peaceful religion, like Shi Xie's doing in Jiaozhi...? People weren't shouting at me like that man was before I had Gan Ji executed. People weren't being aggressive, they weren't staring at me with lifeless faces, they weren't-!"

"Bofu, just forget it," Sun Hè implored. "One angry acolyte and a couple of miserable people are going to suddenly represent everyone in Jiangdong...?"

"...We probably shouldn't go hunting," Song Qian suggested.

"For one noisy fool...?" Sun Hè chortled. "Lord Sun needs to relax, and he relaxes by hunting. Gan Ji was dealt with months ago, and this is-"

"It isn't new, no, but that 'noisy fool' got quite close," Song Qian retorted. "We-"

"*Aiee*... I should not have killed that man!" Bofu lamented. "He-!"

"We're going hunting, and you're going to enjoy yourself for a while," Sun Hè said sternly. "Please fetch Lord Sun's saddle."

"Yes, Mister Sun," Old Yin replied.

Bofu was not approached or heckled as he rode to the gates of Qu'e, but he was suddenly aware of everything around him in a way that he had not been before: the smiling faces and the respectful bows of the majority were suddenly less important than the scowls, turning of backs, lowered gazes and emotionless stares of the minority that had always been there as well. Some were disgruntled followers of past governors like Liu Yao; others were unavenged victims of attacks by Shanyue raiders; there were some that were victims of pirates or bandits, some of whom were now in Bofu's employ; some were, of course, followers of Gan Ji, the Taoist 'saint' that Bofu had executed upon learning of his own mother's devotion to the man.

Once Bofu was outside the gates, he urged his horse and galloped away at great speed without giving his bodyguards any warning: he was anxious to be alone and enjoy the adrenalin of the run and the chase.

"**Wait, Bofu!**" Sun Hè cried. "...He was worried about his safety not two minutes ago! Now he...!"

"We must pursue!" Song Qian said.

The small army of bodyguards followed their haunted lord, who went on to hunt in silence and returned to the city without a smile on his face or a word to say. Bofu did regain some composure later on, but his behaviour worried his allies, who sensed that the pressures of his status were starting to take their toll at last.

✳✳✳✳✳✳✳✳✳✳✳✳

15

Bofu's forces began their march eastward to reinforce Wu Prefecture, but they briefly stopped in Dantu, a region to the east of Qu'e that was also on the southern bank of the Yangtze River.

"How goes things, Old Cheng?" Bofu asked as he met Cheng Pu at the gates of the Dantu military camp.

"Zhu Zhi's managing, especially now that Ling Cao's got his act together," Cheng Pu replied. "It's becoming clearer now: Hè Qi had just left to go back to Kuaiji, and Deng Dang's recently died, so parts of the army weren't quite in order. We hadn't been keeping watch on White Tiger, who left Xu Zhao's estate and met up with Chen Deng's envoy. It isn't our finest hour: Xu Gong's people are probably hiding on that estate as well, Lord Sun, and-"

"We'll get to dealing with all of that when Chen Deng's pushed out of our territory," Bofu interrupted.

"...Of course," Cheng Pu sighed.

"And have word sent to Kuaiji and Yuzhang that I want Hè Gongmiao to get any help that he needs," Bofu added. "I want the rebellions crushed and Gongmiao back where we want him."

"It shall be as you order," Lü Fan promised.

"So, Demou... Ling Cao is gaining ground...?" Bofu prompted.

"You know Ling Cao!" Cheng Pu replied. "His rush tactics are risky against the likes of Huang Zu but perfect against the Shanyue. He's honest as well, so he's doing something about the local criminals as well, which means that we've got the people with us."

"That's what it's all about in the end!" Bofu said. "How long before the supplies are ready...?"

"A few hours, and then we can continue," Cheng Pu reported.

"...Good," Bofu said. "I don't want to be here too long: Huang Zu's getting time to recover, and Cao's sent another man to Lujiang."

"Liu Fu," Cheng Pu replied. "I'm getting my own reports. Liu Fu is, unsurprisingly, another 'scion of the imperial house', but unlike most he's competent, generous, cautious, honest and deep-thinking. I'm hoping that he'll come to understand that he should be helping us, not Cao, but if he doesn't then we have another dangerous enemy on our hands."

"*Ayah*... you describe a friend and then call him an enemy: what does that make *me*...?" Bofu complained.

"It makes you trapped in a difficult situation, Bofu, like all men are right now," Lü Fan insisted. "But Demou is right: Liu Fu persuaded two of Yuan Shu's generals to defect to Cao Cao before Yuan had even declared as an emperor, so Liu Fu is very persuasive. That's not ideal at all."

"...What happens when they learn that I'm here?" Bofu asked.

"We've taken every measure possible to feign your continued presence in Yuzhang," Lü Fan replied. "Your uncle Sun Jing's sons are posing as you and Ben, and some of the men are pretending to be your bodyguard force."

Bofu turned to Sun Hè and said, "Hear that, Bohai? You're as famous as me and have your own decoy as well!"

Sun Hè smiled.

"We'll advance, defeat Chen Deng, come back here and resupply, and then get right back to finishing off Huang Zu," Bofu continued.

"With any luck, that'll all take less than a month."
"And that's if 'Inspector Liu Fu' doesn't distract us first, of course," Cheng Pu grumbled.
"I'm losing my patience, so he really shouldn't," Bofu said. "I refuse to live another year under the same sun and moon as Liu Biao and Huang Zu."

The Han court's newly appointed Inspector of Yang Province, Liu Fu, arrived in Jiujiang Prefecture and immediately travelled to his predecessor's base in the Liyang region; he stopped short of visiting the actual city, as that was still being monitored by agents of Bofu's general Li Shu.
"…This is not the place to build defences against the southerners," Liu Fu said as he looked at the landscape. "We need somewhere better placed."
Cao Cao's official Han Hao – who had escorted Liu Fu to the hazardous region – asked, "Where would you suggest?"
"…We want to be far enough from Lake Chao that they can't sail right up to us, close enough to the Huai River to receive support by river or land, and we want somewhere that isn't too well developed already, which will make it easier for us to build the defences that we need," Liu Fu replied. "Fortunately, before I began this journey I spoke with Man Chong, a man with divinely-gifted genius that has answered all questions and avoided the need to use my meagre talent. Mister Jiang…?"
Liu Fu's 12-year-old assistant, Jiang Ji, bowed slightly and said, "I await your instructions, Inspector Liu."
"We passed Hefei on the way here," Liu Fu noted. "That region is perfect: begin plans for everything to be centred there."
"As you command," Jiang Ji replied.
"What do you intend to do about the Qian Hill Bandits, Inspector?" Han Hao asked.
"Some problems need to be solved with compromise," Liu Fu replied. "The men that have turned to banditry are mostly poorly-educated and are all of them disenfranchised. We need to reach out to them with the promise of a reinvigorated Lujiang: opportunity for all, a new start. I guarantee that many of them will react positively."
"Forgive my tone, but… how can you guarantee something…?" Han Hao asked.
"I know Chen Lan and Lei Bo," Liu Fu replied. "I served Yuan Shu's local government in a minor capacity and met them as I met Qi Ji and Qin Yi. The current intelligence that I have suggests that Chen and Lei deserted when Yuan Shu made his outrageous claim: furthermore, I now understand that the two are recently estranged, with Chen having joined a like-minded fellow by the name of Mei Qian by the Huai River, while Lei Bo has taken his own followers – mostly fellow deserters that served under him in the days of Yuan Shu – and retreated to the area around Mount Song. They're both of them like Zang Ba – men that have turned to banditry because of a rooted belief that they have no other options. I can reach out to Chen and Lei, offer them the opportunities they want, and rehabilitate them, and with them come their followers, many of whom have military training that would be wasted on coffins."

Han Hao smiled and said, "I quite agree. Will you need me here once your 'evacuation' is complete, or can I return to the north...?"
"By all means do what you can to aid Excellency Cao," Liu Fu replied. "Jiang Ji and I will be fine: I am not a man with a shared history of antagonism with the Suns like Yan Xiang. If Li Shu wants to talk to me, he'll find me to be quite agreeable! Furthermore, I am not going to be here in Liyang, but further north, in Hefei, which will be interpreted as a 'lessening of hostilities' until my plans become impossible to obfuscate. I think that would be wise, especially since we cannot spare the resources to fight right now."
Han Hao bowed and said, "You are a very clever man, Mister Liu. If anyone can pacify Yang Province, it is surely you."

Within a day, General Li Shu's spies reported Liu Fu's swift arrival and subsequent departure from Liyang; Li Shu frowned and said, "Strange... and he's left people to dismantle everything in Liyang and relocate...?"
"Yes, General," the messenger replied eagerly.
"...I'll notify Zhou Yu," Li Shu continued. "Lord Sun will doubtless be as glad as I am that this new inspector is not looking to attack us at present."

Chen Deng's forces had been pushed back into southern Guangling by the time that Bofu completed his march, so Bofu crossed the river and began a march northward. Lü Dai, Han Dang and Ling Cao – who had crossed the river already to retake southern Guangling – arrayed their forces in lines and prepared for another attack by Chen Deng's unruly Shanyue warrior allies. The din created by the Shanyue and the reciprocal taunts of the Jiangdong soldiers rendered all but the loudest shouts inaudible, and the atmosphere was practically tangible.
"Lü Fan sends word that Lord Sun will be here soon," Zhu Ran reported.
"Excellent!" Lü Dai said. **"Lord Sun still frightens them – especially White Tiger, after the way that Lord Sun personally slayed his brother."**
"And once Lord Sun's scared the tribes off, Chen Deng'll run off like the slimy coward that he is!" Han Dang said.
"Why wait for Lord Sun?" Ling Cao asked. **"We're all great men! I'll lead another charge straight at their leader!"**
Han Dang looked at Lü Dai, who laughed and replied, **"Go ahead, Mister Ling!"**
"I'll back you up, Ling!" Han Dang promised. **"Zong'er, you'll be my second!"**
Han Dang's young son Zong smiled and said, **"Gladly, Father!"**
        Chen Deng grimaced when he realised that Ling Cao was leading a spirited charge against his central positions: White Tiger had been forced to move to the front to inspire actions from the chieftains that no longer had full respect for him, so he was exposed and vulnerable.
"We have to be seen to have some sort of response to this!" Chen Deng said to his aide Chen Jiao. **"Archers at the ready!"**
Ling Cao's men reached White Tiger, who cried, **"You again???"**
"Waste no more of Lord Sun's time!" Ling Cao bellowed. **"Go

back to your hiding places, you barbarian scum!"

The clash was brief but critical: White Tiger sustained an injury to his arm and was forced to fight his way to the rear lines of his army, and Ling Cao retreated to his own battle lines before he could be struck by arrows. Many of the smaller tribes were panicking and either charging or fleeing: Han Dang met those who charged while Lü Dai and Zhu Ran coordinated archery attacks of their own to support their vanguard. Two of Han Dang's deputies led forces to attack the left and right wings of Chen Deng's rear lines, and with the archers distracted, Ling Cao was free to charge again: his militia penetrated the front lines of disorderly Shanyue infantry and attacked White Tiger's new position.

"**This man is a demon!**" White Tiger cried as he fled from Ling Cao for a second time: more of the Shanyue alliance fragmented and scattered.

"**Where are you going, White Tiger?**" Ling Cao taunted. "**Where are your teeth and claws?**"

"**We'll retreat northward!**" Chen Deng ordered. "**We'll retreat and then we'll regroup! I won't let these southerners make us look like fools!**"

"**As you command!**" Chen Jiao replied.

Lü Dai noticed that Chen Deng was ordering a retreat and signalled to the generals in the field.

"**…That was not as bad… as the old days,**" Han Dang wheezed as he rode back to Zhu Zhi. "**Which is a good thing, 'cause… I'm not as young.**"

"**Are you alright, Father…?**" Han Zong asked.

"…Yeah… **fine, son,**" Han Dang insisted. "**I'm just getting old!**"

"**Ling Cao's pursuing them,**" Lü Dai noted.

"**Let him,**" Han Dang said. "**For once, it… it's the right thing.**"

Chen Deng and White Tiger were able to chase Ling Cao away and regroup by the riverbank to the north of the battlefield.

"What now?" White Tiger asked.

"**You're weak, Yan!**" one chieftain heckled. "**Twice you ran from the Han people! Where is the spirit that you had?**"

White Tiger scowled and said, "**I ran because I was attacked and had no help! Your men just stood there! We had a plan, and you did not follow it!**"

The chieftain spat on the ground at White Tiger's feet and replied, "**You and your Han plans! They are Han plans! All they ever want to do is make stupid plans! If you want to win, you fight! If you won't fight, you don't lead!**"

"**…Next time will be different!**" White Tiger insisted. "**I am ready for their man that takes risks now!**"

"*Aiee*…! O Heaven, why do you make me work with these thugs…?" Chen Deng lamented quietly. "What can I achieve with allies such as these…?"

"Perhaps we should withdraw to northern Guangling," Chen Jiao said. "The-"

"**You!** Chen Deng! I want to go back and fight them now!" White Tiger announced.

"…We were just defeated," Chen Deng retorted. "My men are demoralised: they will not go back without some guarantee that-"

"**They are your men!**" White Tiger barked. "**They should do as**

they are told!"
"...There's an answer I could give to that, but I need your help,"
Chen Deng replied. "I will do as you wish, Mister Yan, but please, I
need your people to act as one!"
"They will!" White Tiger said. "And our enemies will die!"

Ling Cao's forces responded ably to White Tiger's second attack,
but it still left the Jiangdong defenders startled and disoriented.
"A few hours, and back they come again," Lü Dai complained.
"I'm worried that they'll wear us down!"
Han Dang rubbed his grey beard and said, **"Maybe we should let
them have this one. After all, Lord Sun's almost here!"**
"...Alright, retreat to the camp!" Lü Dai ordered.
         All but Ling Cao obeyed the order to withdraw: Ling tried
and failed to reach White Tiger again, but the veteran Shanyue
king was surrounded by bodyguards, better armed and brimming
with newfound confidence.
"...NEXT TIME, WHITE TIGER!" Ling Cao screamed as he began
a reluctant retreat.
"Better!" White Tiger cackled. **"Men who like surprise do not
like surprise now, eh...? They run like deer!"**
A chieftain raised his arm and shouted, **"This place is ours!"**
Chen Deng sensed the growing hubris amongst the Shanyue
chieftains and said, **"I fear that we may be being led into a
trap, Mister Chen Jiao, and that our allies are too arrogant
and stupid to avoid it as we will."**
"But we still need to pursue," Chen Jiao supposed.
"Unfortunately, yes," Chen Deng replied.

White Tiger led his men to the Jiangdong forces' fenced military
camp and surrounded it: Chen Deng followed and set up a
temporary bivouac camp for his own men. Zhu Ran, Ling Cao and
Lü Dai ascended a watchtower and observed the sea of campfires
and tribesmen with a growing sense of unease.
"...So now we wait for Lord Sun," Zhu Ran declared.
"I hope he brought a lot of help," Lü Dai said.
"We didn't need to retreat," Ling Cao suggested. "I-!"
"We have to be realistic," Lü Dai scolded. "Every time we have a
small victory, they fragment, regroup and come back: we need a
big victory that smashes so many of them that they will slither
away and not trouble us like this again in the near future, so that
Lord Sun can complete the task of routing Liu Biao. You'll get your
moment, Mister Ling, and you'll get it soon enough."

"...I'm telling you that a night attack is suicide!" Chen Deng
protested; he was surrounded by a group of Shanyue chieftains
that were determined to end the battle quickly.
"Han plans use night attacks!" White Tiger retorted. "Why can't we
use them?"
"Every path to every gate has been lined with 'wooden phalanxes'
– barriers dressed with wooden stakes – that will prevent your
cavalry charges, slow your infantry, and they, combined with the
tent layout, will turn the base into a maze!" Chen Deng insisted.
"They have watchtowers with archers in them, and you won't
know whether a tent contains the sick, the dead, the sleeping or a

regiment of pike-men or archers until you pass it! Fire will be your only light, and they will be in control of those fires!"

"We will burn their things!" White Tiger retorted. "We'll burn their wooden spikes and their tents and their towers, and use our own fires to guide us!"

"You'll be surrounded by uncontrollable fires," Chen Deng explained desperately. "Even if you won, what would you lose...?"

"So what do you want to do?" White Tiger heckled.

"In the morning, we'll have the light of the sun, and we'll still surround them," Chen Deng replied. "We'll lure the vanguard out with taunts and overwhelm the base and the vanguard in separate yet linked attacks. Their vanguard officer is brave but reckless, and he will not be able to stomach taunts, so the plan will work."

"Alright," White Tiger agreed.

The morning arrived, and the Shanyue began a campaign of sustained heckling and chanting: Ling Cao ran into the command tent and cried, "**They mock us, Mister Lü! They curse us and our families!**"

"The Shanyue curses are nothing to worry about," Lü Dai chuckled. "Their gods have done very little for them up to now, so why would they curse your family if they didn't help the Shanyue keep their lands...?"

"They're trying to bait you, Ling," Han Dang said. "Calm down."

"...It's *unbearable*!" Ling Cao whined as he retreated.

"He'll charge," Han Dang said. "You can see it: Ling's not going to obey sense forever."

"I'm aware of that," Lü Dai replied. "But we've won anyway."

Han Dang smiled and laughed as Lü Dai held up a cloth letter that had been sent by Bofu.

"We'll play along with Chen Deng," Lü Dai continued. "It's as good as over."

Ling Cao finally tired of enduring the chanting after an hour: he put his helmet on, leapt onto his horse and ordered the gatekeepers to open the way.

"**But we're supposed to ignore them!**" one of Ling's infantrymen protested.

"**Men don't hide while other men curse their children to early graves!**" Ling Cao retorted. "**Open the gates!**"

"**You cannot pass!**" a gatekeeper replied. "**The-!**"

"**Do as he says,**" Lü Dai ordered as he approached the gates with Han Dang.

"...**There's a plan,**" Ling Cao realised.

"**Go and do what you do best,**" Lü Dai said. "**All is ready.**"

Ling Cao laughed, raised his spear and shouted, "**For Jiangdong, and for Lord Sun!**"

Ling Cao now enjoyed full support from his militia, since the attack was sanctioned: a dozen riders and over 100 infantrymen followed Ling Cao's charge.

"**Aha! Here comes their brave fool!**" White Tiger cackled. "**SMASH THEM!**"

The Shanyue charged at Ling Cao, who did not flinch: he passed straight through the warriors' attacks – which were all designed to anticipate survivalist reactions that were never manifested – and moved toward White Tiger at speed.

"**You want to die!**" White Tiger bellowed as he met Ling Cao's strike and began a duel with him; his bodyguards did what they could to repel Ling Cao's riders.

While the Shanyue engaged the Jiangdong troops outside their own base, a scout ran to Chen Deng – who was barely prepared for his allies' actions – and screamed, "**REPORT! Enemy forces are reported to the north, west and south!**"

"...**We've been fooled!**" Chen Deng exclaimed. "**Sun Ce himself has probably come here!**"

"**But he's in Jiangxia!**" Chen Jiao said.

Bofu's forces moved at great speed: Bofu was riding at the front of his own army with his brother Yi at his side and a banner hoisted behind him by a flagbearer that read, 'Sun Ce, Marquis of Wu, Rebellion-supressing General'.

"**Sun Ce???**" a Shanyue chieftain screeched. "**Sun Ce is here?!**"

Word travelled quickly that Bofu was riding northward: within minutes of that, it was commonly known that Sun Ben and Sun Fu were leading another force from the north – having sailed up the river in secret – and that Huang Gai and Xu Kun were leading another force from the west.

"**You've made me come back here again! This time I'll not show mercy!**" Bofu declared as he charged headlong into the Shanyue lines: his ferocity was equal to his opponents', and he and his entourage quickly dispatched two lesser chieftains as they moved toward White Tiger.

"It's certainly over now," Chen Deng murmured. "But was I ever likely to succeed...?"

"...**Administrator...?**" Chen Jiao prompted.

Chen Deng's composure returned – at least in part – and he shouted, "**RETREAT! RETREAT AT ONCE!**"

The Northern Guangling forces abandoned their Shanyue allies and fled the battlefield: White Tiger was isolated and was still being relentlessly attacked by Ling Cao, so he could not rally his subordinates. Sun Ben and Sun Fu concentrated on chasing Chen Deng to the north-south border while Bofu, Huang Gai, Han Dang, Lü Dai, Xu Kun and Ling Cao focussed on delivering a powerful message to the Shanyue; bodies were strewn across the ground as the Jiangdong army met the tribal advance with unbridled violence. White Tiger's support collapsed, his allies started to scatter, and the tribal overlord retreated to Wu Prefecture with little to show for his efforts.

"**WE'LL PURSUE!**" Bofu cried. "**We shouldn't stop until-!**"

"**Until *what*...?**" Lü Fan asked. "**Until *what*, Lord Sun...?**"

Bofu turned to look at his friend and adviser; the smile that greeted him reminded him of his need to show restraint, and his bloodlust waned.

"...**Order a withdrawal to the camp,**" Bofu said.

Sun Ben and Sun Fu were late in returning to the Jiangdong camp: Bofu greeted them at the gates and asked, "What happened to you?"

"Chen Deng's a pedantic professional," Sun Ben replied. "He crossed the north-south border and sent a man to say that he'd prefer that we ceased hostilities."

"I'm sure he would," Han Dang chuckled. "We killed at least a hundred of his men and a lot more Shanyue."

"Cao sent word that he 'was aware of Chen Deng's incursion' and can only say that he was 'unable to prevent a general acting in the field according to circumstances'," Lü Fan said. "We can only say, 'Well met', and hope that Cao Cao will consider us even now. His new Inspector of Yang is basing himself in Hefei, not Liyang, so-"

"*Hefei...*?" Bofu exclaimed. "That's further north by a ways, isn't it? ...And it's also a bit sparse..."

"It's an encouraging sign that Cao Cao might be looking for peace in the future," Lü Fan said. "Of course, it depends on why Liu Fu's picked such a rustic place as Hefei when he has so many grander places to choose from. But Liu Fu's left himself completely open by settling there, perhaps to make any attack on him look especially vile, which might also be why..."

"...But I don't care," Bofu admitted. "Ling Cao can go to southern Wu Prefecture and keep the Shanyue down there busy, and Li Shu can watch Liu Fu for us. I'm going back to Yuzhang to get ready for another Jiangxia campaign. Gongjin's at Ba Qiu, and-"

"Straight away...?" Lü Dai exclaimed. "*Rest* first, young lord!"

"Can't afford to," Bofu replied. "Huang Zu's face... I see him laughing at us, laughing at how he keeps being saved by fools like Chen Deng and Liu Xun. No, this is it this time: I'm going back to Jiangxia to finish what *he* started."

"Cheng Demou's in Dantu," Han Dang noted. "Go back to Dantu, get fresh supplies for your men, and *rest for a few days...* don't overstretch yourselves *or* them."

"I talk to the men all the time, Yigong, and they tell me that my fight is their fight," Bofu replied. "They want to go back and fight Huang Zu for the men that have died fighting the man before."

Han Dang bowed and said, "You're like your father, Lord Sun: your heart burns with a tiger's fire, and I'm proud to serve you."

Bofu reciprocated the bow and turned to Han Zong, saying, "You did well out there. Looks like I'm not the only one that's striving to be as good as his father!"

"I hope to serve you as Father has, Lord Sun," Han Zong replied.

"...I'll go back to Dantu," Bofu said thoughtfully. "Han Yigong, it's been good to see you again: you remind me of the days when Dad was... here."

Han Dang smiled sadly.

"...Huang Gongfu, you'll accompany me to Dantu," Bofu said as he turned to Huang Gai. "I'd like you to be with me when we go back to Jiangxia."

Huang Gai bowed humbly and said, "You couldn't keep me away, Lord Sun Ce."

"Lü Dai, you will stay here and keep an eye on Chen Deng for now," Bofu said.

"He won't flinch without me knowing, Lord Sun," Lü Dai promised.

Bofu looked at the faces of his subordinates and smiled, saying, "We're almost there, now. On to Dantu, and then back to Jiangxia: victory awaits us!"

****

16

Bofu's return to Dantu was intended to be a brief affair: he was visibly infuriated when Cheng Pu reported a delay in the arrival of the supplies.

"Who is it...?" Bofu asked. "Danyang Shanyue raiders attacked my supply train I suppose, in support of their brethren in Wu!"

"...We have a lot of new civilians to feed, and yes, the Shanyue and other tribes in every region are making trouble as they always do," Cheng Pu replied.

"Why are they trying to push me further???" Bofu cried. **"I am not a murderer at heart, Demou! I don't want to keep having to go to this place and that place, spilling blood and dashing brains! These people, they keep pushing me to it!"**

"...Calm down, Bofu," Lü Fan pleaded.

Bofu cupped his head in his hands and groaned miserably.

"...I'll go and see what I can do to hurry things up," Cheng Pu said.

"We don't expect miracles, Mister Cheng," Lü Fan replied. "Lord Sun knows that you're doing everything that you can."

"Ziheng's right," Bofu said. "I'm not angry at *you*, Demou."

Cheng Pu bowed slightly and left the command tent.

"...You're not yourself," Lü Fan suggested.

Bofu lifted his head and laughed desperately, saying, "What can I do to keep hold of what and who I am, Ziheng, when everyone's always forcing my hand...? From the day I inherited my father's chieftainship of our clan, I was a slave to Yuan Shu that was measured by my efforts to avenge my father's murder! I'm free of Yuan Shu now, but am I free of Liu Biao...?"

"...Or your conscience," Lü Fan prompted.

"That too," Bofu admitted. "I know it's been obvious, Ziheng, but I can't hide it anymore. I starved Lu Kang to death in Huancheng; I drove Liu Yao to despair and death in Yuzhang; I ordered an innocent Taoist preacher's death because I compared him to Ze Rong and Zhang Jue without thinking. I'm seeing Gan Ji's face every night now, on top of already seeing Liu Yao, Lu Kang-"

"You're tired," Lü Fan suggested. "Yes, Gongjin's told me that you keep reflecting, lamenting... and it isn't healthy. Cao Cao's got the blood of a lot more people on his hands than you have, Bofu, and they really didn't deserve what he did to them."

"That doesn't help me, Ziheng!" Bofu chortled.

"...I know," Lü Fan said, "but-"

"It isn't just the three I mentioned, is it...?" Bofu continued. "Every tribesman, pirate, bandit, cultist, soldier and yes, every civilian that I am somehow responsible for killing in some way is blood on my hands! And no, they didn't all of them deserve it! Was every tribesman another White Tiger...? And did I kill other Zhou Tais, Jiang Qins and Zu Langs at any point...? Was one of those soldiers a future Lü Meng or Chen Wu...?"

Lü Fan coughed deliberately and said, "Nobody ponders that for long, else they'd go mad. Every doctor would stop practising when they lost a patient; every magistrate would flee to the hills when they wrongly adjudicated; every soldier fighting a just cause would let evil triumph because they unintentionally killed a good man on the field. Life is full of difficult choices: that was part of my 'chess lesson', if you recall."

"...I recall, Ziheng," Bofu replied. "I just... don't know what I can do to stop being upset about all of those 'expendable pieces'. I'm even concerned about Huang Zu's family, Xu Gong, Yan Xiang-"

"And that's ridiculous," Lü Fan insisted. "Xu Gong tried to have you arrested and your entire clan put to the sword for a fabricated treason; Huang Zu had his men jeer your father's coffin as you retreated from Jing; Yan Xiang offended your clan repeatedly and never once remonstrated about Yuan Shu's repeated use of improper tactics, including using a hero that had once saved Jing in order to conquer it. Yes, there might be people that have died because of your actions that didn't deserve it: I'm an adviser, and I gave you a lot of the advice that led to a lot of those deaths. In a lot of cases, I see the same faces that you do. But our alternatives were few: you yourself keep saying that people keep 'forcing your hand', so you know that you were left with little or no choice. In many cases, your opponents and enemies had more choices than you, and they lived – and died – by those choices."

"...Yeah, you're right," Bofu said. "Perhaps I need to unwind."

"So long as you're careful, enjoy the forced rest," Lü Fan replied. "There may be moments in the months and years to come when you are not able to rest when you need to; rest now, Bofu, while you can."

"...Bohai suggested going to Qu'e, but if I leave the men here in this dingy camp and go home to my mansion, I'll look like another Yuan Shu," Bofu said. "I'll stay here, stage a few parties for the men to keep them happy, maybe go hunting... there's good hunting grounds near here, right...?"

"There are," Lü Fan replied.

"Then I'll try and look a little more like the man that everyone chose to follow," Bofu declared. "Thanks for the advice, Ziheng."

Lü Fan bowed and said, "That's what I'm here for."

Bofu laughed and replied, "So you are!"

In the meantime, Bofu's orders were sped to all counties in Kuaiji and Yuzhang Prefectures, but not all of the officials were willing to comply with them.

"No, I won't 'gather troops for Hè Qi'!" Yan County Magistrate Tang said to Lü Fan's robed messenger. "Yes, I am well aware that Hè Qi was Magistrate of Yan before I was, but on what grounds...? He's a peasant thug from Shanyin that might try to impress everyone with his fancy clothes and shiny armour, but it merely hides his true nature! And you can *tell him that*!"

The messenger-official smiled knowingly, bowed and replied, "I certainly shall."

Bofu spent the following days entertaining his men and going hunting; morale remained high, and the thought of one last campaign against Huang Zu was a driving motivational factor. Bofu received news that his wife Daqiao was showing signs of being pregnant again, which lifted Bofu's spirits even further.

Meanwhile, Hè Qi had learned of Magistrate Tang's declaration and journeyed to Yan County to respond to him in person.

"Ah, so you've come here, Hè Qi!" Magistrate Tang taunted as Hè

Qi entered his audience hall in full battle dress. "I see that you're still spending your soldiers' wages on yourself!"

The officials murmured uneasily.

"You know very well that I always ensure that everyone receives their pay, Mister Tang," Hè Qi retorted. "What I spend *my* pay on is *my business*."

"But it is also a sign of your poor breeding," Magistrate Tang said. "You dress like a prince to hide the fact that you're anything but. And now your lord Sun Ce writes to me to demand that I furnish you with a militia...? You obviously have money to waste, so buy your own men: I need mine to deal with the problems here!"

"Money buys men's service, yes, but it cannot create them where they do not exist: I need 'your men' to deal with all of the problems at once," Hè Qi replied. "I'm here to end the rebellions against Lord Sun... *all of them*. So I'll ask one last time: will you aid me as Lord Sun has requested...?"

Magistrate Tang flicked his sleeve and said, "No. I won't take orders from men with lower social standing than me: what would my ancestors say...? Now go away."

Hè Qi smiled strangely and looked at the ground for a few moments; and then, in a flash, he advanced on Magistrate Tang and cut him down in a single strike. The entire court started to panic, but Hè Qi cried, "**His is the only head that needed to go in a sack. A new magistrate will be appointed before I leave, and I will personally oversee the recruitment of men here. Lord Sun Ce's bidding can, must and *will be done*.**"

There was no more dissent among the officials in Yan or, indeed, any other county: Hè Qi gathered his army and began the task of dealing with the rebels with equal determination and efficiency.

A week passed: the supplies started to arrive in Dantu, but it was clear that it was going to take several days before the army could start moving again.

"Your face says it all, Lord Sun," Cheng Pu sighed, "but we are–"

"I know, I know," Bofu growled. "I'm going hunting."

"That's probably for the best, Lord Sun," Cheng Pu suggested. "I'll join you this time if you don't mind."

"I'd like to go as well, Lord Sun," Huang Gai said. "I used to enjoy hunting regularly."

"And you couldn't keep me away!" Sun Yi said.

"We should have brought Old Yin," Sun Hè joked. "It'd be like being in Qu'e!"

Bofu smiled forcefully and said, "Let's go get horses, then."

The Dantu stable was busy with soldiers going about their daily training and guarding routines; Bofu was surrounded by smiling, happy faces that made him feel a little better.

"Lord Sun!" the stable keeper hailed. "Hunting again...?"

"Yep," Bofu replied. "I'll get you a piece of meat today, since I didn't have enough to give you yesterday."

"You don't need to, Lord Sun!" the stable keeper replied. "**Fetch the lord's horse!**"

Two stable lads went to collect Bofu's horse.

"...Have you any better horses for us...?" Sun Hè asked.

"My answer is the same as it has been, I'm afraid: a lot of the horses were injured, including your usual steed," the stable keeper replied. "We have what we have, Mister Sun."

"...Fine," Sun Hè sighed. "I won't pester you about it again."

The stable keeper bowed and said, "I am always trying to source new horses."

"Yes, and like everyone else, you're stuck with what fate gives you," Bofu chuckled as the stable lads brought his horse to him. "Don't lose sleep over it."

"Enjoy your hunt, Lord Sun," the stable keeper said.

"I will!" Bofu replied with false cheer.

Bofu rode ahead of his bodyguards and generals, as his horse was considerably better than theirs; Cheng Pu turned to Huang Gai and said, "I know the young lord too well... for he is too much like Wentai. He's plagued by demoralising thoughts."

"He's young, and that wild way he has will pass when he realises that he isn't a god," Huang Gai replied. "Responsibility weighs on us all at first, but-"

"LORD SUN! LORD SUN, COME BACK!"

Bofu had galloped away again: Song Qian and Sun Hè roused the bodyguards to begin their usual pursuit, and Sun Yi joined them.

"...We'll follow!" Cheng Pu said.

"Of course," Huang Gai replied. "Why let these younger men make us both look old?"

Cheng Pu and Huang Gai urged their horses to gallop after the anxious pack of bodyguards.

Bofu laughed as he rode at speed toward the now familiar sight of the Dantu hunting grounds; adrenalin became a false euphoria that temporarily freed him of any cares. But Bofu's euphoria made him oblivious to his surroundings, and so he was totally unprepared when three horsemen appeared in front of him.

"For my father!"

Bofu was shocked at the barely-audible cry, and he could not stop his horse in time: he continued toward the three men, who were not, he now realised, members of his bodyguard force. A sudden force threw Bofu's head back, and a sharp pain robbed him of much of his senses: he could not see the face of the man that had fired the arrow at his head, but he instinctively knew that he had to try and escape. He turned his horse in a random direction and did what he could to maintain speed, but his strength was ebbing away, and he started to slump.

"After him, everyone!" Xu Lang cried. **"We must make sure that he's dead!"**

Xu Gong's three surviving loyalists sped after Bofu's horse, which was now running without guidance: the horse moved in an arc, which brought Bofu and his pursuers into contact with Cheng Pu, Huang Gai and the bodyguards, who immediately understood what was going on.

"BASTARDS!" Cheng Pu screamed. **"YOU'LL DIE BY MY HAND!"**

"Go, go!" Xu Lang ordered.

Xu Gong's loyalists turned their horses and tried to escape Cheng Pu, Huang Gai and the majority of Bofu's bodyguard force, all of whom were now angrily chasing the assailants down like prey; Sun Hè and Sun Yi remained to check Bofu's motionless body for signs of life.

"...*Bofu*...!" Sun Hè said with tears in his eyes. "I...! *Bofu*...!"

Sun Yi was silent, but his eyes were pools of tears.

Cheng Pu was the first to catch up to Xu Lang: Cheng unseated Xu from his horse with a powerful swipe of his hunting spear and leapt from his own horse to complete the kill.

"**BASTARDS...!**" Cheng Pu cried as he slashed at Xu Lang with his hunting knife.

Huang Gai, Song Qian and the rest of the bodyguards hurried after the other two men, who had hesitated when their lord had fallen; they were wrestled to the ground and hacked to death with unrestrained ferocity.

"*Bastards...!*" Cheng Pu whined as he knelt over Xu Lang's mutilated corpse: the thought of burying his former lord's son – a boy that had inspired him as much as Sun Jian had done years before – was too much to bear. It was an emotion shared by Huang Gai, who was crying uncontrollably as he tore at the body of one of Xu Lang's men with his knife; the majority of the bodyguards were confused and unsure of whether they should continue to vent their frustration on the would-be assassins or return to their lord's side.

"Lord Sun...!" Song Qian sobbed. "If he's... I *swear that*...!

"We... we should have caught one," Huang Gai said as his composure started to return. "We don't know who they are, who-"

"*Bastards...!*" Cheng Pu cried as he resumed his frenzied attack on Xu Lang's body: Huang Gai ran to Cheng and pulled him to his feet with all of his might.

"*Stop*, **Demou!**" Huang Gai pleaded. "**No more...!**"

Cheng Pu dropped his knife and exhaled loudly.

"We have to go back to Lord Sun," Huang Gai continued. "He needs us."

Cheng Pu nodded slowly, and the two veterans left Song Qian with the task of recovering the bodies of the assailants.

A number of courtiers abandoned their duties and hurried to Dantu or Qu'e when they learned of the attack: none travelled faster than Gongjin. The atmosphere amongst the informed in Jiangdong was tense and urgent, as Bofu was deemed unlikely to recover fully or, perhaps, at all. None were sure how to proceed, as one sign of exploitable weakness – no matter how slight – might mean more problems than the rattled administration could hope to handle.

****

17

"I don't understand," Gongjin said as he paced back and forth across the command tent at Dantu. "What... what happened...? Who was it...?"

Lü Fan wiped a tear from his eye and said, "It was... it was Xu Gong's people."

"Anyone to do with Xu Gong has to *die*, Ziheng," Sun Yi growled. "Anyone to do with the men that-!"

"They're being dealt with," Lü Fan promised.

"...How do we know that it's Xu Gong's people...?" Gongjin asked. "Didn't Demou and the others cut them to pieces without-?"

Cheng Pu lunged at Gongjin, screaming, **"He's your brother-in-law and your *friend*, you smug-!"**

"Wait, no!" Huang Gai pleaded as he did his best to restrain Cheng Pu.

Gongjin bowed and said, "I meant no offence... please, Demou, I meant no offence. I would have done as you did... or worse."

Huang Gai released Cheng Pu, who hung his head low and sobbed.

"...They were asking questions around the region," Lü Fan explained. "They learned that Lord- ...that Bofu was in Wu, and they started asking around then, and Xu Lang and his friends were recognised... but by the time that Zhu Zhi learned of it, they'd crossed the river to Dantu."

"They ambushed him like cowards, and shot him in the face!" Sun Yi complained. "My brother is a hero that always fought fairly, but they waited for him, three of them, for when he was unarmed and unready, and...!"

"Bofu wrote as best he could on a piece of paper," Lü Fan continued. "He wrote that someone said 'For my father'."

"...Of everyone, I did not expect it to be Xu Gong," Gongjin admitted. "Of all the men that wrongly seek to harm Bofu, I did not expect a worm like Xu Gong to be the one to do the deed from beyond the grave."

Cheng Pu looked up at Gongjin and said, "How can you be so *calm*...? I'd actually started to *like* you! But when I see you, so calm, while your *friend*, your *sworn brother*, your *lord*, your *brother-in-law*-"

"I... I am a strategist, Demou," Gongjin replied miserably. "I have seen this a million times in my nightmares and in my waking thoughts. I have cried countless times and had my wife asking me what's happened, and I had to answer, 'the future'. That sounds theatrical, I know, but I mean it."

Cheng Pu's head fell forward again as he replied, "I know, so have I, but... but now it's happened, and...!"

"We... we're talking like he's dead, and he isn't going to die!" Sun Yi protested.

"Even if he lives, he'll be changed," Gongjin replied. "The damage that's been done, it's... it's serious."

Sun Yi got to his feet, snorted loudly and left the tent.

"...*Xu Gong*...!" Cheng Pu chuckled miserably. "Bloody *Xu Gong*...!"

"All of the great heroes that Lord Sun has matched blades and fists with... all of the bandits, pirates, cultists, strategists and connivers... and he's bested by a reckless, untalented dead man

with three followers," Huang Gai lamented. "What cruelty."
"It's Wentai all over again!" Cheng Pu complained. "He rescued cities by himself! He fought Lü Bu! And he died in a cowardly ambush in a valley! Now *this*!"
"He... Bofu isn't dead," Lü Fan said. "My friend isn't dead."
"No, no, he... he isn't, no," Cheng Pu replied tonelessly.
"...Does Lady Wu come here...?" Huang Gai asked.
"...No," Gongjin replied as his false composure finally started to fail. "The... the doctors say that we have to try and get him back to Qu'e. He... he really shouldn't be moved, but... but he can't stay here. He needs to be with... with his *family*...!"
Gongjin covered his face with his sleeve and fled the tent.
"I owe him an apology," Cheng Pu sighed.
"...Oh, Bofu...!" Sun Hè whimpered; many of the others had forgotten that Bofu's chief bodyguard was even present, and all eyes turned to him as he added, "I have no right to be called a 'Sun'! I am Yu Hè, a useless distant cousin that failed to protect him when he needed me! His father brought me into his home, gave me his name, and treated me like a *son*, and-!"
"Enough, Bohai," Lü Fan pleaded.
"I let him ride ahead!" Sun Hè cried. **"I always let him ride ahead! He needed us, and we let him ride ahead of us, alone, and-!"**
"*Enough*, Bohai!" Lü Fan snapped. **"There's no *point*!** He... he was reckless, and this is just... something that happened. He knew that this might happen."
"Then *why*...?" Sun Hè sobbed.
"...Great men are unfathomable," Lü Fan replied. "That's why they're great men. 'The faster and fiercer the arrow is fired, the less time it spends in flight'. That... is the way of things. Now I must retire from this place, gentlemen... for I can feel my own resolve failing, and I refuse to be forced to run."
"Go on," Sun Hè said, and Lü Fan departed.
"...Is there any way that he can survive, Demou...?" Huang Gai asked suddenly.
"Only through those that inherit his legacy," Cheng Pu replied. "Like... like father, like son, Gongfu... I had just hoped that I wouldn't live to see it again."

Bofu was placed on a cart and transported back to Qu'e, where a silent, sombre populace awaited: Zhang Zhao had redoubled his efforts to round up those that might heckle the fallen hero as he passed through the streets, so the event was largely uncomplicated. Bofu was settled in his own bed within the vast governor's mansion, and all of his family and senior vassals gathered in various rooms to wait for what many supposed to be an inevitable outcome.
"My brother *can't* die!" Sun Quan cried. "This isn't what's supposed to happen!"
"...He won't die, Quan," Lady Wu replied numbly. "He is a tiger, like... like his silly father, who was always worrying us like this...!"
Lady Wu covered her face with her sleeve, and her 'sister', Lady Chen, did her best to comfort her; the tomboyish Shangxiang was unusually silent as she watched the rest of her family with wet eyes and a quivering lip.

"...We have to be pragmatic," Sun Ben suggested. "Liu Biao will learn of this, Chen Deng will learn of it, so will Liu Fu, and Cao Cao too: we need to somehow-"
"Isn't this a bit of a bad time to be putting your name down as a candidate to succeed him...?" Xu Kun said.
"That isn't what I meant!" Sun Ben replied. "Look, Kun, this isn't like when Uncle was shot by Liu Biao! Back then, we were deep in enemy territory and subjects to Yuan Shu! We didn't have the whole of Jiangdong and half of Northern Yang under our control, and we certainly weren't surrounded by enemies!"
"Sadly, Boyang is right," Wu Jing said. "My nephew... ... ...will take time to get better, I think. Until then... *until then*, we need to be strong. Jing and his sons abandoned the Jiangxia front and are on their way here, which will be noticed by Huang Zu. Li Shu left a deputy in charge and is on his way to Qu'e from Lujiang, which will be noticed by Liu Fu. Chen Deng will wonder why Zhu Zhi and Han Dang have left subordinates in charge of their duties and come here so soon after a Shanyue uprising. Cao Cao will learn of it too. So will Yuan Shao. So will they all."
"Zhang Zhao says that we'll need a new 'foreign policy'," Sun Yi muttered. "Am I not here? Is Ben not Ben? Isn't Xu Kun still Xu Kun, and aren't Taishi Ci and the rest still who they are...?"
"Many of the men only follow your brother," Sun Ben admitted. "If it was anyone else, even temporarily, we risk losing a lot of Yuan Shu's men, Zu Lang's bandits, the Yuzhang and Kuaiji 'families', and a lot more besides. Individual men are good to have, but wars are fought and territories defended by armies, not lone heroes."
Xu Kun laughed derisively and said, "So we risk Jiangdong fragmenting if-"
"If *what*...?" Lady Wu asked cuttingly.
"...I meant nothing, dear aunt," Xu Kun pleaded.
"...I know," Lady Wu sighed. "Sorry."
"Why are Gongjin or Ziheng not here...?" Sun Kuang asked. "They're family, aren't they, Mother...?"
"They... they have to plan things, Little Marquis," Lady Wu replied.
Sun Kuang guessed the meaning of his mother's words and said, "Oh... right..."
"...Poor Daqiao," Shangxiang said quietly.
"Indeed," Sun Ben said. "That poor woman's with child again, and already has two daughters to raise: she'll need our help."
"And I should be there, with her, with my son," Lady Wu said as she got to her feet and staggered out of the hall; Lady Chen, Sun Kuang and Sun Quan followed her.

Daqiao was keeping a silent vigil over her husband Bofu, who was generally unresponsive: the surgical removal of the arrow had left its own marks, he was in constant agony, and he was unable to take solid foods.
"...Dear daughter-in-law," Lady Wu said as she entered the bedchambers. "Go and get rest and food: you must think of your unborn child."
"O-of course, yes," Daqiao replied; she touched Bofu's forehead, whispered, "I'll be back soon, Bofu," and departed for the kitchen.
"...Your friends are all here!" Lady Wu whispered as she took Daqiao's place by Bofu's side. "Your uncle Jing and his boys are

coming back here, and Dong Xi, and that shiny man Hè Qi, and your friend Taishi Ci...!"
Bofu exhaled feebly.
"...Your face is... is going to be fine," Lady Wu said with difficulty. "It's all going fine... everyone's fine, the officials and the army are all doing their bit... so when you're better, you can get on with all of those things that you want to do!"
Bofu whined quietly.
"Don't... don't try to speak," Lady Wu pleaded. "You just need to rest, let the cuts heal, and then you can have more food... and then you'll be fine...!"
Bofu snorted softly and sadly.
"But... but I know you," Lady Wu whispered as she took Bofu's hand in her own. "You... you're like your father, and you want to know that everything will be fine, if... if you can't be here. It's all arranged, Bofu... so if you can't be here... we'll be fine. But you *will* be here, so... so rest."
Bofu turned his working eye to face his mother and exhaled slightly to show that he understood; a slight smile appeared at the corner of the undamaged side of his mouth, and he suddenly seemed to be more at ease.
"...My boy...!" Lady Wu whimpered. "Hold on, my dear boy...!"

But Bofu – who was also known as the son of Sun Jian, titled 'Marquis of Wu' and 'Rebellion-supressing General' by the court, branded the 'Little Conqueror' by his detractors, or known simply as Sun Ce – only survived for a few more days before finally expiring at the age of 25, leaving behind a list of achievements that were the envy of his allies and opponents alike. The suddenness of the event was only overshadowed by the potential consequences: for the first time in 5 incredible and eventful years, the future of the Sun clan and its growing legacy was again uncertain, and grief would have to make way for pragmatism if there was any hope of continuing to build on Bofu's success.

✳✳✳✳✳✳✳✳✳✳✳✳

18

There were discussions about the public reaction to the passing of the famous southern hero Sun Ce: some suggested that the news of his death should be kept from the wider world until the Sun clan's worst enemies – Liu Biao and Huang Zu of Jing Province, to name two – were dealt with, but it was quickly decided that hiding the demise of a man that was as sociable, ubiquitous and proactive as Sun Ce was would be impossible. A grand funeral was therefore decided upon, with a period of mourning to precede and follow the event: defences were strengthened at the prefectural border between Yuzhang and Jiangxia, and notification was sent to the Han Imperial capital Xuchang.

People that were normally deemed to be without morals or etiquette, such as the bandit king Zu Lang, wore white clothes and mourned respectfully; the Jiangdong population was almost unanimously sad to see the unifier and protector of the region gone at such a young age and with so much left to do. Qu'e was a sea of white unmarked flags, white clothing and the sounds of mourning, and Sun Ce's mansion residence became the site of his decorated coffin, which received a multitude of visitors and saw a constant vigil by dozens of family members and vassals. But while the public grieving honoured Sun Ce as a son, husband, friend and lord, private negotiations continued that would decide the next clan chieftain and ruler of Jiangdong.

"The situation is simple," Lü Fan said to a small gathering of white-garbed politicians and advisers. "We have two choices: restore Sun Ben as the clan chieftain – a role that he performed admirably before Lord Sun Ce followed his esteemed father – or the role passes to Sun Quan as the-"

"Do we really only have those two choices...?" Zhang Zhao challenged. "I am often viewed as a pompous, inflated pedant that worries about his own well-being, but I care only about the state. I did not always agree with Lord Sun Ce, and he certainly didn't always agree with me, but he provided stability through strength, and that appears to be the only way to do things at present. The army wants a man that inspires them, and many look to *Sun Yi* as the true heir to Lord Sun Ce's legacy."

Some of the officials murmured agreeably.

"...I'm aware of that," Lü Fan replied.

"Sun Yi followed Lord Sun Ce on some of his missions, and his nature is almost identical," Zhang Zhao said. "In fact, he is almost a reincarnation of Lord Sun Ce in likeness and personality!"

"That's what's perceived by some to be the problem," Lü Fan retorted. "Lady Wu would prefer a more cautious and less proactive member of the clan to take us forward... she has suffered the loss of a husband and son, and cannot bear to see another of her sons in a coffin in the next five years."

"I agree with Lü Fan," Officer of Merit Wei Teng said. "I say it because of personal and state reasons: I was almost the victim of a violent outburst by our passionate Lord Sun Ce, but my only crime was raising a point; and with regard to the state, a single act of recklessness has left us without a head, and we cannot suffer such a sudden loss of continuity in the future, not if we're building a state."

Lü Fan turned to Gongjin – who had been sitting silently and observing the discussion without intending to contribute – and asked, "What say you…?"

"…Everyone is right, and everyone is wrong," Gongjin replied. "We need another Lord Sun Ce to control the Shanyue, the pirates and the bandits, but at the same time we need a man that does not 'run at swords', as Mister Wu Jing has said before."

"Yi is reckless," Wu Jing said sadly. "We'll lose him too if we make him the lord, and my poor sister's suffered enough already."

"But to consider *Sun Quan*…?" Zhang Zhao chortled. "Didn't he steal from the state treasury to pay for women and wine…?"

"…That was not a recent offence," Lü Fan insisted.

"It's recent enough, sad to say!" Quan Rou said. "He's not popular with many officials, not least the population of Xuan City and the surrounding county that remember his dismissive and costly attitude to security."

"He would need to be far more mature and responsible for him to be a great leader, and his achievements would have to be many and good to erase the memory of his more costly mistakes," Qin Song suggested.

"If we are so determined that we are not to have Sun Yi, then Sun Ben should be our choice," Zhang Zhao said. "He is the eldest son of Lord Sun Jian's twin brother, brought into the Sun household and all but adopted by Lord Sun Jian, which makes him, technically, the eldest and therefore the rightful heir over Sun Quan. In addition to that, he has served as chieftain before, has the respect of the military and officials alike, knows the problems that we face, and has been shown to be deep-thinking and conscientious: that is all good for the state."

"In the end, Lady Wu will have the final say," Lü Fan replied.

"Forgive me, gentlemen – and most of all, Administrator Wu Jing – but we should not be letting the late lord's mother decide these things," Zhang Zhao said. "This is not a decision that can be made using only passionate arguments: we must be pragmatic and we must be *rational*!"

"…I agree," Gongjin admitted. "But like it or not, Zibu, this is a state built on passions. If the people do not like or love our choice, we will lose everything."

"Which is *precisely* why I advocate Sun Yi!" Zhang Zhao said desperately. "By being Lord Sun Ce reborn, he has the respect of the criminals, the love of the civilian populace, the awe of the army and the deference of the barbarians!"

"…Let us see what Lady Wu decides," Gongjin replied. "I will and have put the very points to her and those around her, but in the end… let us see."

Lady Wu stroked the wooden coffin that housed her son's remains and exhaled loudly; Sun Jian's consort Lady Chen was sobbing for Lady Wu's son as if he were her own, which stirred newfound respect for her in the observant Quan, Yi, Kuang and Shangxiang. The officer Dong Xi entered the room and said, "You asked to speak with me, Lady Wu…?"

Lady Wu turned to the white-robed Dong Xi and smiled, saying, "I

did, Yuanshi. You don't mind if I call you that, I hope…?"
"I am honoured, Lady Wu," Dong Xi replied.
"We'll talk elsewhere," Lady Wu said. "Please follow me."
"But aren't we supposed to remain with Bofu…?" Sun Quan asked.
"It is for him that I go," Lady Wu replied. "My sister cries for us both while I try to make sure that there is no more sadness."
Sun Quan nodded and turned to face the coffin once again.
Lady Wu and Dong Xi retired to the mansion's private study: many of Sun Ce's personal belongings were scattered about the room, and that made both of them even more emotional as they prepared to discuss a future without him.
"Oh, bless him, the messy boy…!" Lady Wu chuckled as she gently moved some bamboo books in order to give Dong Xi somewhere to sit.
"…I can do that," Dong Xi pleaded.
"No, I… I need to be the one to organise the clutter, Yuanshi," Lady Wu insisted. "Now then… I understand that you're quite a smart man."
Dong Xi bowed low and said, "Not at all, Lady Wu! Zhang Zhao, Quan Rou, Lü Fan-"
"They're clever, yes, but I've heard all about you: you're brave, loyal, intelligent and cautious," Lady Wu replied. "You're as skilled as my Bofu was in combat, and as clever as Gongjin. I want your opinion on who should succeed my son."
"I cannot decide such a thing!" Dong Xi retorted.
"I want your opinion, nothing more," Lady Wu insisted.
"…I must be honest and say that the next lord should command from a seat in his capital, not from the saddle of a horse in the vanguard," Dong Xi said. "Brave and charismatic leaders are good for building militias and small states, but when a future nation is at stake, a leader that promises long-term stability is needed."
"That is exactly what I feel," Lady Wu replied. "And you are not the only one. I have spoken to many of the officials and officers, and many of them see a different Jiangdong in the future: in fact, many predict a 'Jiangnan' – the whole of the south – or a 'Wu' – named for my son's marquisate – that will need a wise ruler."
"I will support you and the chosen heir to Lord Sun Ce's legacy, Lady Wu: you have my word," Dong Xi said.
"I wish that I could be as certain of the loyalty of others," Lady Wu replied. "Thank you, Yuanshi… thank you."

Cheng Pu, Huang Gai, Han Dang and Zhu Zhi gathered in one of the guest rooms to discuss their own fairly unique perspective as men that were burying a second courageous lord and hero.
"I can't do this again," Cheng Pu admitted.
"…Will you retire…?" Han Dang asked.
"Don't be ridiculous!" Cheng Pu retorted. "I'm grey, yes, but am I yet sixty…?"
"You nearly are," Han Dang said. "We all of us are getting old. But you know what I meant, Demou."
"…Yes, I know," Cheng Pu replied. "But I won't abandon the Sun clan, no matter who Lady Wu chooses to succeed Lord Sun Ce."
"It warms my heart to hear that," Zhu Zhi said.
"There's a lot of talk about Sun Quan inheriting the role now," Han Dang noted. "That'd be different… too different, maybe, for some."

"So you want to retire then...?" Huang Gai prompted.

"I... I dunno," Han Dang confessed. "I don't like Sun Quan, never have. And he stole money as well, I hear."

"He's improved his attitude in the last few months," Cheng Pu insisted. "I didn't like him either, but seeing him now, his eyes no longer sunken and his brow no longer beaded in sickly sweat from careless living, I can see potential."

"But at the same time, most of the lads want Sun Yi or, at a push, Ben to take over," Han Dang said. "They want a 'real man', not an irresponsible weakling. Some are threatening to leave the Sun clan's service if Quan's made the next lord."

"They should reconsider that," Cheng Pu replied ominously.

"And then there's Zu Lang and the rest," Han Dang said. "And there's all of Yuzhang's lot that we didn't get around to pacifying properly yet, like-"

"**Bloody bandits!**" Cheng Pu cried. "**What good is a failed state to anyone???**"

"...Calm down, Demou," Zhu Zhi said. "All looked bleak after Lord Sun Jian passed away, but-"

"But Wentai didn't 'pass away', did he...?" Cheng Pu retorted. "He was *murdered*, shot down by a cowardly dog called *Huang Zu* that still laughs at us now! What's being done about *him* while we sit around here...?"

"Taishi Ci paid swift respects and hurried back to Yuzhang to be ready for anything that Huang Zu might do," Zhu Zhi said. "Furthermore, we intend to have Xu Sheng and Ling Cao join Taishi in harassing Jiangxia in the very near future. Huang Zu will not know peace, Demou."

Huang Zu's spirits had been lifted by the news that Sun Ce was dead: his lord's nephew Liu Pan had recently returned to Jiangxia after a short period of mourning for his relative Liu Hu, so the navy had one more commander. Liu Pan had immediately set sail for western Yuzhang and started to harass the region once again to relieve the pressure on Jiangxia, but with Sun Ce gone, that was not now the end of Huang Zu's ambitions.

"This is the time to strike," Huang Zu said. "Liu Pan is making gains in Yuzhang while Sun Ce's best men are all crying and screaming over his coffin in Qu'e. There is no Taishi Ci, no Zhou Tai, no Jiang Qin! We shall prepare for an attack on Chaisang and advance eastward from there!"

"We should wait and see who the Sun clan appoints as their ruler," General Chen Jiu suggested. "Remember too, Lord Huang, that Lord Liu is currently advancing on Xuchang as part of an alliance with Yuan Shao that, technically, Sun Ce was a part of. Lord Liu is yet to learn of Sun Ce's demise, and he might not want to-"

"The Suns are the enemy of the Lius and the Huangs," Huang Zu retorted. "There will never be a time when we will fight under one banner! And I will not miss an opportunity to crush the Suns and take Jiangdong! Jiangxia would become 'Jiangnan' – the whole region under the Great River – all of it under my jurisdiction in Lord Liu Biao's name! We'll continue our preparations and add our own strength to Liu Pan's efforts! Soon Jiangdong will belong to the Han once again!"

Word of Sun Ce's death unsettled the Han government's appointed Inspector of Yang Province, Liu Fu, who was busy overseeing the reorganisation of the infrastructure across Lujiang and Jiujiang Prefectures from his base in Hefei County.

"…This is an uncertain time," Liu Fu said soberly.

"You sound concerned, Inspector," the official Jiang Ji said.

"My concerns are rooted in the Sun clan's choice of successor," Liu Fu explained. "I have been asking about the Sun clan: from what I can see, we may get Sun Jian's nephew Sun Ben – who has led the clan before, and would be a less aggressive ruler – or Sun Yi, Sun Jian's third son, who is another Sun Ce that will have additional grudges to settle. Who will ultimately be blamed for Ce's death…? We are not entirely sure who did the deed, but what if the Suns blame His Excellency…?"

"…I see your concern," Jiang Ji replied.

"His Excellency will doubtless be unsure as to whether he should grimace or rejoice," Liu Fu continued. "It removes the threat of the Suns attacking Xuchang – which was always a possibility, no matter how slight – and it might remove Liu Biao as a threat to the west, which gives His Excellency the freedom to concentrate on Liu Bei in Runan and Yuan Shao at Guandu. But as for the future… who can say…?"

Excellency of Works Cao Cao learned of Sun Ce's death a few days later, and he was as emotionally divided as Liu Fu had predicted. It would take time for the identities of the assassins to filter out of Jiangdong, but one thing was clear: things were going to change. For Cao Cao, that was a discussion that would have to be postponed: Yuan Shao was increasing his grip on the land to the south of the ferocious Yellow River, and his staggering numerical advantages – some suggested that his men and horses outnumbered Cao's by as much as 4 to 1 – led many to predict a Yuan victory within weeks, with or without help from the Sun clan. The warlord Liu Bei – who had been given troops by Yuan Shao and despatched to Runan Prefecture in Yu Province – was doing what he could to harass Cao Cao from the west, but the success of his actions was seen as being dependent on the actions of Jing Province Governor Liu Biao, who had vaguely promised military support. What happened next in Jiangdong would decide the extent of Liu Biao's contribution to the coalition against Cao Cao and, perhaps, the outcome of the campaign as a whole.

****

19

Lady Wu continued her efforts to secure an heir to Bofu's legacy by inviting her eldest surviving son, Quan, to speak privately.

"I want to stay with Ce," Sun Quan said tonelessly. "I want to stay with Bofu."

"You must sound like the eighteen-year-old man that you are," Lady Wu replied. "I want to be with my dear son, but the world outside this place still advances, and we must advance with it. An heir is needed."

"Ben, or Yi," Sun Quan said.

"No," Lady Wu replied. "*You*. Bofu wanted it to be *you*."

Sun Quan's eyes filled with new tears as he said, "That's ridiculous! How can he have wanted me to...! ...He...! ...Bofu, I won't leave your side!"

Sun Quan tried to leave the room, but Lady Wu grabbed his arm and said, "No, Quan. You must not run from this responsibility."

"I'm not running!" Sun Quan retorted. "I *wronged him*, Mother! He fought to make Jiangdong great, and I let the Shanyue sack Xuan! He brought prosperity to the region, and I stole the money for drink! I was *rude*, I was *ignorant*, I neglected my duties, I *moped* when I should have *helped*, and even after *all that*, he...! I must go and *apologise*, Mother! **Let me go!**"

"No!" Lady Wu said. "Not until you promise to fulfil his wishes!"

Sun Quan stopped struggling and fell to his knees, whimpering, "Bofu... Bofu, I *can't*...!"

"You *can*: you know your true potential," Lady Wu replied. "You're grieving, like the rest of us, but when you are fully yourself again, you'll take this region to new heights: Bofu could see it, and so do all the men of vision."

Sun Quan shook his head and said, "But Zhang Zhao and the rest of them, they want Yi, and-!"

"They're scared," Lady Wu replied. "You must reassure them."

"How...?" Sun Quan protested. "How can I reassure them...?"

"Be the leader they need," Lady Wu replied. "Yi will support you, and so will Ben. Everything will be fine."

"...If I am chosen, I'll do it," Sun Quan said half-heartedly. "May I go back and mourn my brother...?"

"...Yes," Lady Wu replied weakly.

Sun Quan left his mother and returned to his brother's coffin, where he cried tears of distress, self-loathing and anger; Lady Wu sat and wondered who she had to speak with next, as she knew that she needed allies for the days ahead.

Liu Biao's nephew, Liu Pan, had led another army into Yuzhang in an attempt to exploit the instability in Jiangdong and reverse the fortunes of the Jing forces; the prodigy Taishi Ci was tasked with repelling Liu Pan once again.

"For my friend Bofu, I will put an end to Liu Pan's incursions once and for all!" Taishi Ci said to his subordinate officers.

"But what then...?" an official asked.

"...I honestly don't know," Taishi Ci admitted. "There is a genuine effort underway to choose Lord Sun Ce's heir, and their policy might be different. Bofu would order a full attack on Jiangxia – he was on his way back here to lead that attack when he was murdered – but his successor, be it Sun Ben, or Sun Yi, or someone else… may want to do something else. But that doesn't matter! We have to drive Liu Pan out and stabilise the area before we get other problems."

Lady Wu visited Wu Jing's office in Qu'e and said, "I'm so tired."
"I will go and mourn soon, dear sister," Wu Jing promised.
"I'm not here to prompt you, brother," Lady Wu insisted. "I… I need to talk about-"
"Wait a moment," Wu Jing asked.
Wu Jing guided Lady Wu to his private study and had her sit as the host.
"…This isn't where I should be sitting," Lady Wu complained.
"You were my protector as a child, dear sister," Wu Jing replied. "I honour you now for the strength that you showed then."
Lady Wu smiled and said, "So much has happened since. Our clan was appalled when I announced my desire to marry Jian… but I got my wish. Now I am keeper of a clan of tigers… and it…"
Lady Wu's smile vanished.
"It's a burden," Wu Jing said. "I know it is. But I don't know how I can help."
"They want Yi!" Lady Wu cried. "They want Yi! They want my reckless, silly Yi to take his father and brother's place and 'run at swords' for them!"
"It isn't 'for them', it's for the state," Wu Jing replied. "I don't want to lose Yi the way I lost Wentai and Bofu, of *course I don't*, but apart from Ben – who is seen by some, and wrongly I say, as a mediocre hankerer that will serve bad masters – who else is there, dear sister…?"
"…Quan," Lady Wu said.
Wu Jing exhaled deeply and replied, "I know that you have this strange notion, and yes, it isn't the first time that it's been suggested, but-"
"Bofu *wanted it to be Quan*," Lady Wu said.
"…Bofu did ask me what I thought about the idea once or twice, I admit," Wu Jing replied. "I said to him what I now say to you: 'The idea has its advantages and disadvantages, and I need not relay them'."
Lady Wu nodded sombrely and conceded that she would not get the encouraging words that she wanted from her brother.

Liu Pan had divided his army in order to attack every major settlement in every county along the Jiangxia-Yuzhang prefectural border simultaneously: Taishi Ci divided his forces similarly and countered his opponent at every point. The unwelcome news was sped back to Liu Pan's main camp, where it was met with understandable alarm.
"That's impossible!" Liu Pan exclaimed. "How can every attack be neatly repulsed like this…? Has Taishi divided *himself*…?"
"He's got well-trained men," an adviser said.
"So where is Taishi now…?" Liu Pan wondered.
"…Here," an officer said.
"**What?!**" Liu Pan cried. "**Since when???**"
"Since about an hour ago," the officer replied. "He's arraying men

to the east of us."

"He can only have about a thousand men!" Liu Pan complained. **"How can he counter and attack me at the same time???"**

The answer to Liu Pan's question was that Taishi Ci had ensured that every settlement had a defence force that only required a few soldiers as support; that left Taishi with 600 men that he had now brought to Liu Pan's camp with the intention of removing it from Yuzhang completely. Zhou Tai had sailed to the north to launch an attack on Liu's reserve fleet as well: Liu Pan received that news and fell into a deep depression.

"I've failed repeatedly against them... how can I face my uncle...?" Liu Pan sobbed.

"Forgive my frankness, Lord Liu, but you need to decide what you're going to do," a major said. "I can't control my men if I can't tell them that we have a plan."

"...We'll need to break out of the camp and try and retreat to Jiangxia," Liu Pan replied. "We-"

An excited messenger suddenly ran into the command tent and cried, **"REPORT...!"**

"...Speak," Liu Pan sighed.

"Taishi Ci has begun an attack on the camp!" the messenger reported. **"The east and west gates are breached! The north gates are likely to be breached! The-!"**

"Prepare for a fighting retreat at once!" Liu Pan ordered.

Every man in Liu Pan's disorganised and confused army was forced to try and fight its way out of the nearest gate: Taishi Ci's men were attacking from all directions, and Liu's men were repeatedly retaliating against their own allies. Taishi Ci learned Liu Pan's location and chased after him personally: Liu Pan's bodyguards did what they could to protect their lord, but Taishi was able to pass several of them and swipe at Liu Pan, knocking him from his horse.

"I'm going to die here!" Liu Pan cried, but his bodyguards were finally able to repel Taishi – who had approached Liu virtually alone – before he could do any more harm. Liu Pan was helped to his horse and fled to the riverbank, where his ship awaited; many of the smaller vessels had been damaged while his men repelled an attack by Zhou Tai a short while earlier, so there would not be a large escort.

"Come back here, Liu Pan!" Taishi Ci screamed. **"Come back here and give your head as sacrifice to my lord!"**

"Hurry, and let's be gone!" Liu Pan pleaded. **"For Heaven's sake, HURRY!"**

Liu Pan's ship left the riverbank and began the journey back to a safe port in Huang Zu's territory; Zhou Tai met with Taishi Ci and asked, "Do we pursue...?"

"I was hoping that you could tell me that, Youping," Taishi Ci replied. "I hope that we can learn the name of our next lord soon, find out their intentions, and get back to dealing with Huang Zu."

"*If* that's their intentions," Zhou Tai suggested.

"...It has to be," Taishi Ci replied. "Regardless of which Sun leads us, Huang Zu's end is a matter of 'when' and 'how', not 'if'... it has to be."

Liu Pan's retreat would be his last: he fled Jiangxia and refused further commissions from his uncle Liu Biao. Huang Zu fortified his defences in Jiangxia once again and sent word to his lord Liu Biao, who was advancing eastward to the Imperial capital Xuchang at the time: Huang's letter implied that an attack was already underway, so Liu Biao withdrew his forces to Xiangyang and readied his army for a concerted attack by the Sun clan.

Lady Wu had her late husband's nephew Sun Ben come to her late son's study to speak to her privately; Ben expected her to name him as temporary chieftain at the very least, so he was surprised when she began the conversation with, "I want your promise that you will support my son."
"...'Your son'...? Sun Ben prompted.
"Please promise me that you will help, Boyang," Lady Wu said.
"...I owe my late uncle and you, gracious aunt, for my upbringing, and I would never betray you," Sun Ben replied. "Now, if I may ask... who do you mean when you say 'your son'...?"
"Quan," Lady Wu said.
Sun Ben laughed involuntarily and said, "*Quan*...?"
"Yes, *Quan*," Lady Wu insisted.
"...The officials all think that you're pondering *Yi*!" Sun Ben chuckled. "*Quan*...?"
"What is there to laugh about?" Lady Wu asked angrily.
"I laugh only because I don't know what else to do!" Sun Ben replied. "I've cried *blood* for Bofu! I am *heartbroken*!"
Tears formed in the corners of Lady Wu's eyes as she said, "I know, Boyang."
"Of course I am upset," Sun Ben insisted. "But all the same, you want to appoint *Quan* as Bofu's heir, and then you expect me to react rationally...?"
"Quan has matured into a husband, father and statesman," Lady Wu said.
"But not a warrior," Sun Ben retorted. "Dearest aunt, Jiangdong needs a warrior. Could you imagine Quan racing back and forth fighting barbarians, pirates and fleets of trained sailors...?"
"He would command from a seat, as a governor does," Lady Wu said. "Does Liu Biao do his own dirty work...?"
"Cao Cao does take the field, and so do Liu Bei and Yuan Shao," Sun Ben replied. "Liu Biao used to fight, but he is sixty and in poor health. Quan is younger than Bofu was: do you think that braggarts like Xu Sheng, waverers like Zu Lang and enemies like White Tiger will respect or fear a hidden lord...?"
"...He can lead on the field, but he doesn't have to be in the vanguard!" Lady Wu said desperately. "My silly husband and my poor boy were both reckless, and it cost them both. Quan wouldn't make mistakes like that."
"No, you're right, he wouldn't, because – forgive me for my honesty – he is selfish and cowardly," Sun Ben replied. "I read the reports on what happened in Xuan City. And I know about the money as well, of course."
"How *dare you*...!" Lady Wu hissed.
"I 'dare', dear aunt, because I care about what happens to the state, not me alone," Sun Ben replied. "I can see that I won't be entrusted with leadership again, but I don't care about that: I'd follow anyone if they were going the right way, just as I followed Bofu. Which way is Quan going...?"

Lady Wu scowled and said, "My son is flawed, just as every man is flawed: he made mistakes, but is he pasty and thin now...? Has he stolen anything else...? And Xuan was his first assignment!"

"Yes, and he deliberately left the city gates open and spent his nights having lavish banquets," Sun Ben retorted. "Zhou Tai was nearly killed whilst rescuing him; many others *did* die, and I can tell you that it isn't just Xuan's populace and former employees of his office in Yangxian that would react badly to his appointment."

Lady Wu lowered her head and said, "I know that Zhang Zhao wants Yi, but...!"

"Zhang Zhao isn't the only one, and I can see the reasoning," Sun Ben admitted. "I can't sway you, dear aunt, so I will settle for a polite warning: yes, I'll support whoever succeeds Bofu in any way that I can, but whether others do is dependent upon who is chosen. Choose Yi, and we can progress from the exact point that we were cruelly halted; choose Quan, and we risk civil war."

"...Thank you for your time," Lady Wu said.

Sun Ben got to his feet, bowed humbly and retreated.

"...But I don't want to lose Yi...!" Lady Wu sobbed.

Lady Wu summoned her son Yi an hour later.

"I don't want to be clan chieftain," Sun Yi said before his mother could speak. "I know that almost everybody wants me, but I'm too stupid for that! Can't Ben-?"

"I don't want him as the chieftain again," Lady Wu interrupted. "There aren't many that do: if he'd stayed in the role, he'd never have left Yuan Shu's employ, and we'd have achieved nothing."

"But what can *I* do...?" Sun Yi protested. "My wife's a thousand times smarter than me, Mother; let *her* be chieftain then! Or *Shangxiang*! She'd beat up Huang Zu!"

Lady Wu shook her head and giggled, "*No, Yi!*"

"...I know that he's done a few stupid things, but what about *Quan*...?" Sun Yi proposed. "Bofu said that he's really sensible now, and that his friend Pan Zhang's not a fool anymore, and I've seen for myself that Quan's a real man now."

Lady Wu smiled gratefully and said, "That's exactly what I'd hoped that you'd say."

"...So you weren't going to harass me like Zhang Zhao and the others, then...?" Sun Yi realised.

"It'll be a struggle to contain the likes of Mister Zhang, but he's a smart man, and I think that he can be forced to come up with ways to accommodate the decision," Lady Wu replied. "My only worry was that he would not have the support of his family."

"We Suns are a proper family," Sun Yi said. "We're not like those other clans that kill each other over titles, like the Yuans. Of course we're all behind him!"

Lady Wu thought of Sun Ben's attitude and replied, "I hope so."

"Well I'm with Quan, and so's Kuang," Sun Yi promised. "I'll do whatever I'm asked and go wherever I'm sent: you have my word, Mother."

"...Then all that's left is to announce it," Lady Wu said.

Sun Yi returned to his home and asked his radiant wife, Lady Xū, to sit with him in their living quarters; he was silent for several minutes before he said, "I've just spoken with Mother."

"It was about you ascending to the role of clan chieftain," Lady Xū replied calmly.

"…You knew…?" Sun Yi exclaimed. "Well… no… it was obvious in a way, and you're a diviner as well, so how could you not know…?"

Lady Xū smiled silently.

"…I know that I shouldn't ask, because Bofu really didn't believe or like all that, but… I wonder if you could divine for me…?" Sun Yi said. "I believe… sorry to my brother, but I believe, and I must know whether I should have… have…"

Lady Xū waited until she was sure that her husband had no more to say before she replied, "I anticipated your request and looked to all of the 'methods and ways' for answers to your problems."

"What did you learn?" Sun Yi asked excitedly.

"There is much light around your star, but in other readings your path is clouded and leads to darkness," Lady Xū replied. "The star that represents your brother, Sun Quan, is dimmer but still bright, and it grows in brightness; the other signs point to his having a clearer path… one that leads to less darkness."

"Then my decision was right," Sun Yi said gratefully. "I… I wondered if I should just accept what some of the old men want, and be Bofu's heir, and spare Quan the burden, but… but after what you've just told me… I was right. Thank you."

"You need not thank me, Husband," Lady Xū insisted. "I only tell you what I see, and therefore it is the generosity of Heaven that we must thank."

Sun Yi smiled and said, "For sparing us more pain… I do."

Sun Quan was entranced by the sight of his late father's consort, Lady Chen, weeping for his brother; his three half-siblings – the 10-year-old Sun Lang, and two young girls – clung to Lady Chen's clothes whether they were her children or not, and cried for their own reasons. Lady Chen was now responsible for much of the upbringing of her own offspring and those of Lady Wu and a second, deceased consort that Sun Jian had taken just before his death; some already called Lady Chen 'Aunt' or even 'Second Mother', but Quan had been defiantly resistant to the idea. But Quan was slowly changing his mind: Lady Chen had been very supportive, regardless of his attitude, and she had offered comforting words when his theft of treasury monies was exposed. Now Quan watched Lady Chen mourning a child that was not hers with the same sincerity that she had shown when she mourned his father: if he had not been crying already, it would have moved him to tears. After a final moment of conflict with his own personal principles, Sun Quan walked to Lady Chen, knelt beside her and whispered, "Second Mother."

Lady Chen cried with even greater ferocity, but some of the tears were tears of guiltless joy; a barrier had been broken down, and Sun Quan had accepted her at last. Lady Wu learned of it within hours and decided that it was yet another sign that her son was fit to take the clan forward: it had not been the deciding factor, but it reassured her that her coming announcement – regardless of the consequences – would be the right one.

****

20

Lady Wu had Gongjin order the officials to attend court and await the announcement of their new lord; the apprehensive officials did as they were told, but rumours had worn their nerves ragged and their fear was tangible. Lady Wu knew that many of the men in the court would object to her making the announcement, so she left it to her brother, Danyang Administrator Wu Jing. Sun Quan had been asked to sit by his mother and uncle, as had Sun Yi, Sun Ben and Gongjin: the seating confused the audience and led to anxious behaviour, which only made Wu Jing's task more difficult.

"If we could have *silence*, please...!" Wu Jing asked.

The court fell silent.

"...I shall get to the point, since we've wasted enough time as it is," Wu Jing continued. "It was my nephew's wish that his legacy be continued by someone that would consider every aspect of running a state, not just the expansion and defence of it."

"Sun Ben, then," Cheng Pu murmured.

Wu Jing looked around the court as he added, "It has therefore been decided that the next chieftain of the Sun clan... and... and the next defender of the Jiangdong region... will be Ce's brother..."

"...Yi...?" Huang Gai exclaimed quietly.

"...No... no, it's...!" Cheng Pu whispered.

Wu Jing had paused to gather his composure; Zhang Zhao harrumphed and said, "I apologise for my impatience, but you yourself have said that enough time has been wasted, Administrator Wu."

Wu Jing took a deep breath and said, "The next lord will be *Sun Quan*, the-"

"*Sun Quan*???" one official exclaimed. **"Our 'defender'...? He let Xuan City fall!"**

Sun Quan lowered his head and sighed.

"Forgive my bluntness, but right now we need a 'defender' that can *attack* as well," Zhang Zhao suggested. "Sun *Yi* is better placed as the successor to Lord Sun Ce, and we had all of us expected that-"

"No, no, old man, don't drag me into this," Sun Yi said casually. "I'm fine with Quan. He's much smarter than me."

"But is he capable of 'defending' us, as his role explicitly states...?" Quan Rou asked. "I have no personal grudge against the young master, I merely ask a question: if I had been tasked with this burden, I would admit that I was not capable of it."

"I'm not standing in my brother's way!" Sun Yi said. "I mean both of them when I say that, actually: I won't prevent Quan being our leader, and I won't stand against what was Bofu's last wish."

"*Was it now...?*" Zhang Zhao wondered quietly.

"You ask too much," a junior treasury official heckled. **"Sun Quan is-!"**

"Whatever you were about to say, *don't*," Lü Fan said. **"That's an order from your immediate superior."**

The treasury official flicked his sleeve discreetly and harrumphed.

"This was Lord Sun Ce's last instruction," Cheng Pu said. **"Who is it that defies Lord Sun's will...?"**

"So you're happy with this, General Cheng...?" a major under

Li Shu asked.

"...**Lord Sun Quan will be** *fine*," Cheng Pu said coldly. "**Where is your superior, Major...?**"

"**General Li Shu has returned to Lujiang: he did not want to leave the region undermanned just to stay and hear delayed proclamations,**" the major replied.

"...I hope that's the only reason why he left," Huang Gai muttered.

Zhang Zhao turned to Lady Wu and said, "I appreciate that you have given this thought, Lady Wu, but Quan is eighteen and knows little of the affairs of state beyond what school has taught him. There is more to the court than what one learns in class, and furthermore, he lacks skills with the sword that Lord Sun Ce has used to great effect in the past to save us from calamity. Sun Yi is, by his own tongue, 'not as smart as Quan', but he has fought with the courage of Lord Sun Ce; Sun Ben has already been the clan chieftain during times of strife, and-"

"**Sun Ben led the clan when it was little more than a pack of attack dogs serving Yuan Shu,**" Cheng Pu heckled. "**Lord Sun Ce just about made the transition to leader of a young nation, and now we need to have more stability!**"

Sun Ben scowled at Cheng Pu's apparent belittling of his efforts and ability.

"And can a young magistrate from Yangxian County achieve what Lord Sun Ce has achieved...?" Zhang Zhao asked.

"**Hypocritical pedant!**" Cheng Pu retorted. "**You accuse Quan of being too young when Lord Sun Ce was not much older, and then you recommend Sun Yi when he's younger still! Yi has accepted the decision, so stop making trouble!**"

Sun Quan looked at Lady Wu and whispered, "I want to go back to Bofu now."

"...**Wait!**" Lady Wu shouted.

Wu Jing got to his feet and bellowed, "**Please be silent...!**"

The court fell silent once again.

"...Mister Dong Xi, we have heard a lot of arguments," Lady Wu said as she looked at the trusted officer. "I know you to be a clever man, and when we spoke before you were a great comfort. Now I am confronted by a number of valid reservations and have lost any certainty."

Dong Xi smiled and replied, "Jiangdong is a natural fortress that enjoys the Great River as a barrier to the north and many mountains and smaller rivers elsewhere. Lord Sun Ce governed as wisely and kindly as he fought justly and decently, so the hearts of the people have been won: one need only look to the streets today for proof of that. The young lord Sun Quan can build on that foundation of loyalty, respect and love to become a wise and long-term ruler in future times of peace and prosperity. And there is no shortage of wise heads to call upon to keep the state safe and stable: Zhang Zhao is the man to look to for internal affairs, while others, like me, will gladly serve as the 'claws and teeth' when nature's defences are not enough. We have the support of the vast majority, talents by the bushel and a land that guards itself: with such advantages, why do we worry so...?"

Dong Xi's speech was met by many enthusiastic responses; Zhang Zhao smiled confidently and said, "Put like that, Mister Dong Xi, why indeed...?"

Li Shu's major was one of a minority that did not join in the acclaim for Dong Xi's appraisal: some sat in silence, others muttered or flicked their sleeves, and one man got to his feet and left the hall.

"...We will have to fight for this decision," Cheng Pu said, "but so be it: we must."

Huang Gai and Han Dang nodded agreeably.

Sun Quan turned to Lady Wu and asked, "Can we go back to Bofu now, Mother...?"

"You must first be received as our new leader," Lady Wu replied.

"But I can't think straight!" Sun Quan whispered. "I-!"

"You will have all of the help you need," Lady Wu promised.

"That's right," Sun Yi said. "Don't be afraid, Quan: remember that it's what Bofu wanted!"

"Remember: *they're* afraid," Lady Wu said. "Reassure them."

Sun Quan looked at the mass of expectant officials – many of whom had now fallen silent – and exhaled nervously; after a few moments of contemplation, Sun Quan got to his feet and said, "I accept this heavy burden only because it has been given to me. My brother has placed a great trust in my hands... and with Heaven as my witness, I vow that will do all that I can to prove him right."

"You have everyone here to support you, young lord," Cheng Pu replied.

"We will work as tirelessly for you, young lord, as we did for Lord Sun Ce," Huang Gai promised.

"If Lord Sun Ce could see greatness in you, then it is there," Han Dang said. "I, Dang, will serve you as I did your father and brother."

"As Commandant of Wu Prefecture and Acting Administrator of the same, I, Zhi, will work unyieldingly to restore order," Zhu Zhi declared.

Sun Ben bowed slightly and said, "I, Ben... will support you fully, Lord Sun."

Lady Wu noted Sun Ben's hesitation with a heavy heart.

"I, Zhao, will be your left arm that carries the pen, while Zhou Yu shall be your right arm that carries the sword," Zhang Zhao said.

"It would be an honour," Gongjin said. "I, Yu, want to be as devoted a vassal to Lord Sun Quan as I was a sworn brother to Bofu."

"I gladly accept your help," Sun Quan replied enthusiastically.

"I will lead the internal administration alongside my brother Hong, Lü Fan, Quan Rou, Qin Song, Gu Yong and the countless other talents in the region; Zhou Yu will lead the military against our external concerns alongside Cheng Pu, Dong Xi, Hè Qi, Taishi Ci and the other great heroes that have made this place what it is," Zhang Zhao reiterated confidently. "With the right words and the proper actions, there is nothing that we cannot achieve as a nation: if you lead as one that knows that one man alone cannot walk the ruler's path, then nothing is impossible."

"It shall be as you say," Sun Quan promised.

Wu Jing gestured toward the empty host seat and said, "Take your rightful place, Lord Sun Quan."

Sun Quan got to his feet and moved the short distance to his new seat. Quan caught sight of his friend Zhu Ran, who smiled encouragingly; Quan nodded toward Ran as a sign of gratitude and respect, and then he took his seat. Wu Jing bowed low and announced, "Today we pledge our allegiance, Lord Sun Quan."

The majority of the officials echoed Wu Jing's words and actions.

"Now we must hear your first instructions," Zhang Zhao said. "There are two outstanding issues: firstly, General Taishi requests guidance on what to do next in our on-going feud with Liu Biao and Huang Zu; secondly, we require a stance on the on-going conflict between the Xuchang court and Yuan Shao's 'Girdle Edict Coalition', for want of a better description of it."

"Mock the followers of the edict if you will, Zhang Zhao, but Cao Cao has proved that he is a villain, just as the appraiser Xu Shao prophesied all those years ago," Cheng Pu retorted. "Did he not dam the Si River with the corpses of a hundred thousand innocents? Did he not defile a surrendered warlord's widowed aunt? Did he not kill a pregnant consort? Did he not send a pretender's former adviser – our evil master's right-hand man – to govern over us as an insult? And then, most recently, did he not order Chen Deng to attack Wu Prefecture as 'retaliation' for our reaction to his earlier offence? Does he not criticise our lords for wanting to avenge their father – my dear friend Wentai – when he tore Xu Province apart for his own father?"

Sun Quan stared at his officials and whined quietly as the enormity and complexity of his new role became suddenly and painfully evident.

"*And*," Cheng Pu continued, "is it not the case, Mister Zhang Zhao, that Lord Sun Ce's absence from this world is due to the actions of the son of Xu Gong, a man that was in close contact with Cao Cao and whose suggestions for 'dealing with Lord Sun Ce' included his total removal...?"

"Removal *to the capital*," Zhang Zhao retorted. "Cao Cao has always been fair: he promised rewards for cooperation, and he actually turns a blind eye to the Liu-Sun feud. And, is it not the case, General Cheng Pu, that Chen Deng's actions were reactionary, entirely due to Li Shu's attack on Yan Xiang that Lord Sun Ce may or may not have explicitly ordered, and-"

"**You'd have us ally ourselves to the new Dong Zhuo?**" Cheng Pu heckled.

"No, I'd have us maintain cordial relations with the Han's appointed Excellency of Works, and through him, the Son of Heaven," Zhang Zhao retorted. "Yuan Shao is a famous mediocrity that often mistakes bluster for proper action; Lord Sun Ce has already – in addition to expressing regret for the way that Yan Xiang was dealt with – said that Yuan Shao will likely do nothing again, leaving Jiangdong to be the bearers of responsibility whether Excellency Cao wins or loses. And Yuan is allied to Liu Biao... ponder *that*."

Cheng Pu turned to Sun Quan and cried, "**Lord Sun...!**"

Sun Quan was silent.

"...**Lord Sun Quan, we need your words as guidance!**" Zhang Zhao said.

"*Speak*, for goodness' sake," Sun Ben muttered.

Sun Quan looked up and said, "I, Quan, a-am only recently given this role. I will decide on our future course later, a-after seeking private counsel, but... but at present I am *mourning*. We... we will continue to dissuade Liu Biao and Huang Zu from attacking us, and… and we'll… … …we'll wait before we…"

"Wait before we *what*…?" Sun Ben muttered.

"…**That's all,**" Sun Quan declared: he meant the words to be an order, but they sounded more like a request to surrender. The young heir to the Sun clan and unofficial ruler of the Jiangdong region turned and left the hall via a side door; the officials were left feeling uncomfortable or angry, and they made no secret of it.

"…Oh dear," Lady Wu murmured.

Sun Ben was suddenly disturbed by what he had seen and heard as he began the journey back to his room in the Sun mansion: his brother Fu noticed but waited until the two were seated before he asked, "What is it…?"

"…'Claws and teeth'…?" Sun Ben murmured.

"Yes," Sun Fu replied. "A show of strength to keep Liu Biao and Huang Zu from the door and then maybe get southern Jing from them one day… as reparation for Uncle."

"…I hope that's all it is," Sun Ben muttered.

"What else could it be…?" Sun Fu asked.

"…Dangerous ambition," Sun Ben replied. "Dangerous ambition that we're not supposed to have… that we supposedly didn't have… that supposedly cost us wrongly, but… was it 'supposed'…?"

Sun Fu did not answer.

Within the next days and weeks, word that Sun Quan was the new Sun clan chieftain reached every part of Jiangdong; the reactions were as varied and troublesome as everyone expected. Any hope of a swift return to Jiangxia to defeat Huang Zu was immediately crushed as stories poured into Qu'e that told of tribal uprisings, insurrections and bandit rampages. Sun Quan's first task would be to prove that he could keep what had been bequeathed, and the initial signs were far from good.

****

ACT III: A TIME OF UNCERTAINTY

21

The death of the popular warlord Sun Ce left an immediate power vacuum in the vast region of Han Dynasty China that was known as Southern Yang Province or Jiangdong – 'East of the River'. It was the second time in a decade that a Sun patriarch had fallen to an assassin's arrow: Sun Ce's father, the famous hero Sun Jian, had previously died in an ambush set by Huang Zu, an ally of the Governor of Jing Province, Liu Biao. The Sun clan had thereafter been defined by their feud with Liu Biao and Huang Zu, even when they were still unwilling serf-vassals under the magnate-warlord Yuan Shu, but it was the clan's main focus after gaining their freedom from indenture; time and again, Sun Ce had tried to launch an attack against Liu and Huang once he had stabilised Jiangdong, only to be dragged away by an uprising or some other calamity. The last of those distractions was an invasion of Wu Prefecture – a region to the east of his domain – by the Administrator of neighbouring Guangling Prefecture, Chen Deng: the man behind that invasion could only have been, to most minds, the Han government's Excellency of Works, Cao Cao, and some dared to suggest that the assassin that subsequently killed Sun Ce while he was out hunting – the son of the agitator Xu Gong – might have been supported in some way by Cao, even if it was just by bringing Sun Ce to a place where they could more easily approach him. Nothing could be proved, but nothing could be disproved either, so tensions between the unsanctioned Jiangdong regime and the Han court were at an all-time high.

Cao Cao had more than the suspicions of some of the Sun clan's allies to worry about: he was engaged in a success-or-ruin standoff with his former childhood friend Yuan Shao, who was the brother of the Sun clan's former master and a rich, powerful warlord in his own right. Yuan Shao had once been an antagonist to the Sun clan, having attacked Sun Jian at the start of a 7-year-long feud with his ambitious brother Yuan Shu: since then, Shu had declared as an alternative emperor, lost everything – including the service of the Sun clan – and died a pitiful fugitive, while Cao Cao had risen, by pure chance, from Shao's vassal to the protector of Emperor Xian and the most important minister in the government. Yuan Shao resented the power going to a man that he now perceived as unworthy, and after a series of self-serving campaigns that placed four adjacent provinces under his control, Shao challenged Cao Cao's right to harbour the sovereign in his newly-constructed capital Xuchang.

Cao Cao subsequently became the subject of the slanderous 'Girdle Edict' – a document claimed, by its supporters, to be written by the emperor himself – that condemned him as a tyrant and called for a coalition to remove him from office. Yuan Shao gleefully accepted the edict as genuine and declared war on Cao; Liu Biao reluctantly followed, since he was already on bad terms with Cao, and Sun Ce had been expected to decide who he would support before he was assassinated. It was expected by many that the Sun clan would have postponed its feud with Liu Biao in order to fight Cao Cao, but Sun Ce's heir – his 18-year-old brother Sun Quan – was a completely different personality and even more divisive. The survival of the redeveloped and newly-thriving Jiangdong was at stake, and some wondered if war was the right way to preserve it.

Sun Quan was forced to attend several meetings in the days after his appointment; he watched helplessly as his officials bickered over what his next choice should be.

"**I won't condone a proposal to get into a fight with the Han's Excellency of Works!**" Chief Clerk Zhang Zhao shouted angrily. "**I respect you, Elder Cheng, but that does not mean that I must accept your more ludicrous ideas!**"

"So you want to just *grovel* to Cao Cao, do you, Zhang Zhao...?" Cheng Pu heckled.

"There is a difference between grovelling and showing proper deference!" Zhang Zhao retorted. "He's the appointed guardian of the Son of Heaven!"

"I thought you wanted Sun Yi to inherit the mantle of ruler," Cheng Pu said. "Yi's a brave lad that would have told you what to do with your plan."

"I...! ...Sun Yi is not our lord, Sun *Quan* is our lord, and I won't be dragged into arguments like that," Zhang Zhao replied. "I advocate aggression against Liu Biao because the man craves our lands and committed a grave crime against the lord's family. I cannot recommend aggression against the Han court."

Sun Ce's closest ally Zhou Yu – who was still better known by his courtesy name 'Gongjin' – smiled and said, "There are some that might suggest that Cao Cao is no more the 'Han court' or the 'guardian of the Son of Heaven' than Dong Zhuo was."

"There is no comparison!" Zhang Zhao insisted.

"Not in your eyes, no," Cheng Pu heckled. "Dong Zhuo's dead, Cao Cao's alive, and live men might want to shorten your life for 'advocating aggression'."

"How dare you!" Zhang Zhao retorted. "I am not a coward! Give me a sword and I'll fight at the front! I don't suggest some feeble 'capitulation' out of a sense of self-preservation! The 'Girdle Edict' is a fraud, as much a falsehood as the tale of Sun Jian purloining the Imperial Seal! It's an invention of Yuan Shao and a handful of hankerers that want Cao's power for themselves! If we fight in the name of that spurious document, we'll place our necks under swords and our heads into sacks!"

Some of the officials murmured agreeably.

"Even if one were to disregard the edict, we cannot disregard the acts of war that Cao Cao has been guilty of," Gongjin suggested. "He appointed our former slave-master's adviser, Yan Xiang, as Inspector of Yang Province, which gave him authority over us; and then, when we objected, he ordered Chen Deng to-"

"'Objected'...?" Zhang Zhao scoffed. "Is that what sending Li Shu to murder the man is called now...? 'Objecting'...?"

"...Cao ordered Chen Deng to attack Wu Prefecture," Gongjin continued. "And the more I think about it, the more I wonder if-"

"Not the 'Xu Gong and Cao Cao' conspiracy again," Zhang Zhao heckled. "I respect you too, Zhou Gongjin, but what a fanciful idea! How could Cao Cao know that Chen Deng's incursion – done entirely as a pre-emptive reaction to our own attack on Yan Xiang – would draw Lord Sun Ce back to the east...? How could His

140

Excellency know that our late lord would then go hunting in Dantu...? We don't even have enough clear evidence of who did do it, because the perpetrators were all of them killed and then mutilated beyond recognition!"

"You dog, Zhang Zhao!" Cheng Pu bellowed. **"You dare criticise our reaction to finding that...! ...He is not long gone, and we still wear mourning robes for him!"**

The hall was, as Cheng Pu stated, a sea of white and colourless clothing, and the whole of the region was still conducting daily mourning rituals for the fallen Sun Ce.

"...How dare *you*, Mister Cheng, how dare *you*!" Zhang Zhao said. "How dare you accuse me of being insensitive!"

Cheng Pu scowled and replied, **"Why shouldn't I, when you accuse Sun Hè, Song Qian, Huang Gongfu, me and the entire group of men that dedicated their lives to protecting Lord Sun of-!"**

"I can hear no more!" Sun Quan pleaded. **"This session is ended, gentlemen!"**

The officials watched as Sun Quan fled the hall; his mother, Lady Wu, coughed deliberately and said, "Show more consideration, gentlemen. Your arguments should be more carefully put."

"...I apologise for my part in this," Cheng Pu replied.

"I, Zhao, also apologise for allowing debate to descend into a mindless slandering match," Zhang Zhao said. "Will we continue?"

"Please do," Lady Wu replied as she got to her feet. "I will leave as well, and return to my eldest son's side... I suspect that is where I shall find our new lord."

Lady Wu left the hall; Cheng Pu turned to Zhang Zhao and said, "I vow to you that our anger was our only motivation for our actions on that awful day. Had we been more mindful of the need to know who did the deed..."

"And I vow to you, Cheng Demou, that I meant no accusation when I spoke," Zhang Zhao replied. "Your anger was an anger that any of us would have felt in that place and at that time. I simply rue the fact, as you do, that we cannot be sure of the identities of the agents or all of the external factors involved... but I stress that I believe that Cao Cao was not behind it. He wanted – and wants – to join the houses of Sun and Cao in marriage. He created our late lord a marquis. He is, like us, unsure of who to trust and misrepresents himself at times."

"...You may be right," Cheng Pu admitted.

"I don't agree, but we should try and be constructive now," Gongjin said. "All that matters now is our outward appearance, and it must be strong. Weakness – even the perception of it – will be the end of us."

Sun Quan's cousin Sun Ben snorted irritably; he then turned to his brother Fu and muttered, "With Quan at the helm, we are already at an end."

Sun Fu nodded silently.

Sun Quan had gone back to his brother's elevated coffin, just as Lady Wu had guessed: she placed a reassuring hand on her son's shoulder and said, "You struggle now, but you will find the strength that you need to have."

"I *won't*!" Sun Quan sobbed. "I-I *can't*, Mother! I can't do what...

what I've been asked to do, been *forced* to do!"

"I'm sorry that you see it that way, I truly am," Lady Wu replied. "He's up there now, listening to our pleas for him to return, but... he won't... he *truly can't*."

"**He HAS TO!**" Sun Quan cried as he fell forward and repeatedly slapped the side of the casket with his hand. "**Come back, Bofu...! I can't do what you ask! You must come back and... and...! BOFU...!**"

Lady Wu was too overcome with grief to force her son to be stronger; she fell to her knees and started a lament of her own instead. Lady Chen and Quan's younger siblings were already crying out, and the new voices only made them double their efforts: the Suns screamed as one, imploring Sun Ce to return while knowing that he never would.

Gongjin knew that he would soon be playing the part of Sun Quan's 'sword' in battles against former colleagues; he left the meeting, located his benefactor Lu Su and asked that they retreat to Lu Su's home in the city to talk about the times ahead.

"This is where your role begins," Gongjin said once the two were properly seated as host and guest. "It is your time now."

Lu Su laughed and said, "Don't be ridiculous! Lady Wu's in charge now, Gongjin, and she doesn't like me at all!"

"...No, Zijing, it is the young lord Sun Quan that governs now," Gongjin insisted. "It might not seem so, but he will soon overcome the grief and fear that he feels and start looking for more talents to grow the state. I intend to recommend *you*."

Lu Su's eyes wandered, and he said, "That would allow me to propose my-"

"No, no, not that 'tripod' idea of yours, Zijing," Gongjin pleaded. "Just keep your suggestions to things like military reform, grain harvesting and storage, that sort of thing."

"Oh... alright," Lu Su murmured.

"I know how you treasure that notion of yours, but it places Liu Biao in a very powerful position, and we want him dead," Gongjin continued. "Anyhow... I am keen for Lord Sun to have as many people around him as possible. The-"

"Why do you not call him by his courtesy name, if you don't mind me asking...?" Lu Su said suddenly.

"...My relationship with Lord Sun Quan was, is and always will be different to my relationship with Bofu," Gongjin explained. "Bofu and I were classmates, friends, and our wives are sisters. Bofu and I were very different men, yes, but we shared a vision: Lord Sun Quan is just different. He's of a different generation; we don't share memories of campaigns; he is not my friend. He's family, and he's my lord, but he is not my friend. Bofu was my friend."

"...I see," Lu Su replied. "What about your other friend, 'Ziheng'?"

"That's... difficult," Gongjin admitted. "Lü Fan's refraining from appearing at court where possible, and it's because he fears Lord Sun Quan."

"He really worries that he'll be harmed for 'tattling on Lord Sun'...?" Lu Su asked.

"Yes," Gongjin replied frankly. "And I cannot reassure him."

"...So you don't fully trust Lord Sun Quan to do the right thing, then...?" Lu Su prompted.

"He… he's always had a 'weak side' to his nature," Gongjin replied. "That's why I must surround Lord Sun with the very best men. I've been researching and asking around, and I intend to recommend several people: I intend to begin with recommending positions for Bu Zhi and Zhu Huan and promotions for Lü Dai, Zhuge Jin and you."

"I will gladly do whatever I can to help with- …Well, to help," Lu Su said meekly.

"…'Help with what', you wonder," Gongjin prompted.

"…For what do we strive now…?" Lu Su asked honestly.

"Until this… the creation of a prosperous south and nothing more," Gongjin replied. "But now that Bofu is gone – not just the fact, but why it is so – I must perhaps accept that we have had our hands forced and fulfil the prophecy that has been thrust upon us, intentionally or accidentally, by our enemies; not a 'Chu' but a 'Wu', born of their idiocy, weaned on their mistrust, nurtured to adulthood by their contempt and named by them in the days when their fear took a more constructive form."

"Uh… pardon…?" Lu Su prompted.

"A conversation for another time," Gongjin insisted. "For now, we have too much to do…"

Lu Su hummed thoughtfully and wondered whether he should admit that his own ideas about 'the future of the Empire' were similar to Gongjin's, even if their methods were radically different; Lu instead settled for giving the impression that he did not understand what Gongjin had in mind when he understood all too well and intended to broach the controversial subject with Sun Quan at the first available opportunity.

∗∗∗∗∗∗∗∗∗∗∗∗

22

Days passed, and every attempt at a meeting ended with Sun Quan terminating the session or failing to announce any policies of his own. Cheng Pu met with Gongjin, Huang Gai, Lü Fan, Gu Yong and Zhu Zhi and said, "This can't go on. Gongjin, Ziheng, you were the late Sun Ce's friends and closest counsel; can you not-?"

"I cannot help," Lü Fan replied.

"...And I am finding that I am limited in my influence at present," Gongjin admitted. "The lord is wracked by grief that has made him completely irrational."

"My son is doing what he can to reach him," Zhu Zhi promised.

"...Oh, of course, they're good friends, aren't they, Lord Sun and Zhu Ran," Cheng Pu recalled. "I suppose that's how it works: he'll want that 'Pan Zhang' fellow given a lot of power as well, won't he, now that he rules...?"

"Fortunately, Demou, Pan has become a better person," Gongjin said. "We don't have to worry that the 'grand project' is under threat of implosion."

"We do, even if it isn't from Lord Sun recruiting fools," Cheng Pu insisted. "If he doesn't present himself in armour before the men – which he has not done even once – and provide some sort of solid stance on how we liaise with Cao Cao-"

"There's... been a decision made about that," Gongjin said. "Lord Sun desires a 'smoothing of relations' with Xuchang. He wants to focus on dealing with our internal problems and then ending our long feud with Liu Biao once and for all."

"That's Zhang Zhao's idea," Cheng Pu grumbled. "That pedant is *wrong*, though!"

"...He isn't the only one that advocates this," Lü Fan said. "Most of the 'nobility' – those that were born into families with money, such as Liu Ji and Xu Sheng – want to have cordial relations with the capital and keep away from Yuan Shao's 'dubious' coalition."

"They would say that, Ziheng, because they are self-serving northern aristocrats that crave positions in the imperial court!" Cheng Pu retorted.

"Nonetheless, we cannot have eyes and swords pointed in every direction," Gongjin suggested. "We must seek temporary non-military solutions to problems until we deal with the many, many rebellions that are springing up, at the very least. Cao Cao may or may not beat Yuan Shao, so remaining neutral might be sensible. And we are not 'submitting to Cao Cao': we are pledging our allegiance to the Son of Heaven."

Cheng Pu looked at Gu Yong and said, "And you think what...?"

"I am only interested in maintaining the stability of the region," Gu Yong replied. "If we try to fight Cao Cao, Liu Biao, the Shanyue, tens of thousands of bandits, rebellious officers and pirates at the same time, we can only lose. The first of those is the only one that is actually an optional opponent."

"...Alright," Cheng Pu conceded. "Someone can write to Liu Fu, 'our provincial Inspector', and let him know."

"Lord Sun will do so personally," Gongjin replied.

Yang Province Inspector Liu Fu received Sun Quan's letter within a few days and smiled gratefully.

"His Excellency will be glad of this," Liu Fu said to his aide Jiang Ji. "I know that I certainly am: now that I am getting somewhere with the Qian Hill Bandits and the Huai River Bandits, I don't need the Sun clan sending their man Li Shu to attack me and destabilise the region again. Already, Mister Jiang, I am seeing a more amiable and sensible ruler in Sun Quan. Perhaps he might be someone that His Excellency can do business with, rather than seeking his removal."

"Perhaps, Inspector," Jiang Ji replied. "Speaking of the bandits, Chen Lan and Lei Xu have arrived to see you."

Jiang Ji turned to face the end of the audience hall and nodded to two of the many guards that Liu Fu had surrounded himself with in recent days; Chen Lan and Lei Xu entered the hall moments later and bowed slightly as a sign of respect.

"It is good to see you both," Liu Fu said. "As you can see, I have not invited other officials to join us for this meeting: it will be Jiang Ji, me, and you two."

"So what did you want to talk to us about...?" Lei Xu asked. "Or is this a 'Hongmen'...?"

Liu Fu laughed and replied, "Every armed man in this room is visible, Mister Lei."

"You left Yuan Shu before I did, Mister Liu, and stole two of his generals," Chen Lan noted. "Did you know that he was going to do what he did...?"

"I suspected that he was unstable," Liu Fu replied. "He was bad for Jiujiang, for Lujiang, for the whole province; I relish the chance to undo the damage, correct the mistakes and build a new, more prosperous south."

"...Prosperous...?" Lei Xu prompted.

"Yes, for all," Liu Fu replied. "I know, I know: that sounds like the Yellow Turban mantra! But even the maddest of men sometimes makes a little sense. The problems in the south – even this region above the Great River – stem from social underdevelopment, disrespect, overwhelming economic disparity, lack of opportunity, and making poor use of the resources and people: I intend to reinvent this region and bring an end to its decline."

"...That's an ambitious plan," Chen Lan suggested.

"That's why I need help, gentlemen," Liu Fu replied. "I cannot do what I want to do alone: I'm offering you both a chance to be a part of my project."

Chen Lan laughed and said, "We're bandits!"

"By choice...?" Liu Fu countered.

"...In my case, no," Chen Lan replied. "Cao never wanted us, I don't think, and there's not much to do in this place. We just did what put food in our bellies."

"And you were not the least bit ashamed because the system is corrupt and broken," Liu Fu suggested. "But if everyone had work, education opportunities, food and clean water, honest government, fair taxation, a promise of aid when famines and plagues struck, and a sense of being a part of something bigger... would that make a difference...?"

"Not to 'everyone', Inspector, but... yeah, to most," Lei Xu admitted. "But we thought you were just building a fortress here at Hefei."

"I'm building a walled sanctuary for the people," Liu Fu replied. "I'm building a defensive position against those that want to perpetuate the chaos. But within those walls and the walls of other cities in Yang Province, I want more than a garrison for troops: I want schools, universities, thriving trade hubs, places where scholars, merchants and farmers feel as much at home as the soldiers."

Chen Lan hummed thoughtfully and said, "I'm for that."

"Me n'all," Lei Xu said. "And we'll talk to Mei Qian. He thought this was going to be one of those 'stop or else' conversations that we usually hear: he'll prob'ly wonder if we've gone mad when we tell him what you've said!"

"There is no madness in this room, gentlemen," Liu Fu replied. "I want to be the antidote for the sickness, the calming force that quells the madness."

Chen Lan bowed low and said, "You're a long overdue blessing, Inspector Liu."

Lei Xu echoed Chen Lan's respectful gesture and said, "If you keep your promises, then you're looking at a man that will never stop praising you."

"I don't want praise," Liu Fu insisted. "I just want to heal old wounds. And that starts today, gentlemen, here in Hefei!"

Liu Fu's diplomatic efforts ended the vast majority of the bandit activity in Lujiang and Jiujiang Prefectures and added vast numbers of eager recruits to his ambitious redevelopment project. The beginnings of a fortress city were already starting to appear in Hefei, which worried the Sun clan loyalist Li Shu; Sun Quan showed no sign of reacting, however, as his mind was elsewhere. The Shanyue tribes and armies of bandits were causing chaos throughout the Jiangdong region, and Huang Zu of Jiangxia still loomed like a dark cloud; Liu Fu was seen to be the least of Sun Quan's worries. At the same time, Liu Fu sent Sun Quan's messenger on to Xuchang to convey the young warlord's desire for peace; Cao Cao was more than happy, as that removed all threats from the south and allowed him to concentrate his limited resources on fighting Yuan Shao to the north and Liu Bei to the west. The brief period of southern embroilment in northern politics had ended, and a long period of localised pacification campaigns had begun; the outcome of the famous 'Battle of Guandu' would be decided by the warlords of the north, and the south would only know its long-reaching consequences.

∗∗∗∗∗∗∗∗∗∗∗∗

23

Sun Quan was glad of the company of his friend Zhu Ran: the two sat and talked about their years at school initially, but Ran had always intended to broach the subject of Quan's behaviour since he had become the lord of Jiangdong.

"Forgive me, lord and friend," Zhu Ran said after a conspicuous pause, "but you have not been yourself. There are many of your subjects that worry about you."

"…'Lord and friend'," Sun Quan sighed. "I suppose that is the way it must be from now on, Yifeng."

"It doesn't have to be, Zhongmou, but I refer to you in that way to frame my conversation appropriately," Zhu Ran said. "You're very, very important now, and thousands are relying on you."

Sun Quan exhaled loudly and replied, "I know, Yifeng, but… … …I actually craved this kind of power. But not as a result of what happened, I swear."

"…Of course not," Zhu Ran said.

"I craved it, so badly… and now I have it, it's like some sort of poison chalice," Sun Quan continued. "I don't know where to start, what to do…"

"Nonetheless, you're the lord of this region," Zhu Ran said. "There are officials and generals that are waiting for you to tell them what you're doing."

"And I can't answer them," Sun Quan admitted. "It's strange, but… I'm not afraid. I know that people probably think I'm trying to avoid making decisions because I'm scared, but that's not it. I'm just not ready yet. Bofu took years to get ready to be the clan chieftain, and he was older than I am, and yet I'm supposed to forget how I'm feeling and just pick up where he left off. It's not the same as when Father died: I have so much more to think about than Bofu did…"

"Everyone knows that, but they can only be so accommodating," Zhu Ran replied. "Like it or not, all your enemies are waiting for the right moment, and every hesitation is a signal to them."

Sun Quan nodded thoughtfully and said, "I'll ask Pan Wengui to come to Qu'e. And… and I'll get Zhou Gongjin to come here. I'll ask him about recruiting some more talented men to my court. Maybe they'll let me move at my own pace if there are more talents available to aid the decision-making process."

"…Perhaps," Zhu Ran replied. "What about Lü Fan…?"

Sun Quan sighed and said, "He does not seem to be very keen to assist me. He loiters at the rear of the officials at many of the meetings that he actually attends and proffers no advice; he obviously continues to hold a poor opinion of me."

Zhu Ran laughed disbelievingly and replied, "You really don't…? Zhongmou, he's *scared*!"

Sun Quan frowned and said, "*Scared*…? …Oh, I…! …I've been foolish and blind. I thought that he still… but all along, it is an error of communication."

"There will be many of them, Zhongmou, just as there always have been such errors, but don't let this one rob you of a great talent," Zhu Ran pleaded.

"I shall rectify that at once," Sun Quan promised. "I will visit him this very day and put his mind at ease."

Lü Fan was distressed when his servants announced Sun Quan's arrival at his home: he dressed in his best robes and greeted his lord – who was surrounded by a small entourage of armed bodyguards – with a kowtow.
"There's no need for that, Lü Ziheng," Sun Quan pleaded. "Rise, and think no more of showing such exaggerated deference. You are family, Ziheng, just as you always have been."
"...You forgive me...?" Lü Fan prompted.
"Forgive you for what...?" Sun Quan asked. "You rightly corrected me, Ziheng. If you had not done the proper thing, I would have wasted my life and disgraced my clan. Could I have the right to weep before my brother's coffin if not for you...? I can only *thank you*, Ziheng. And when the time is right, I will let the world know what I nearly became and your place in preventing it."
Lü Fan bowed low and said, "You are truly worthy of your place, Lord Sun!"
"And you, Ziheng, are truly worthy of yours as a trusted confidante," Sun Quan replied. "I want you to assist me as you assisted Bofu; I know that we are not friends as you and Bofu were, but I hope that our family bond will keep us close and allow us to work together to finish what my father and brother started."
"That is all I ask!" Lü Fan said. "It shall be as it always has been, Lord Sun!"
"Excellent," Sun Quan replied. "I shall leave you now... for I'm sure that you were probably busy."
Lü Fan bowed repeatedly as Sun Quan retreated; Fan turned to his relieved family and staff and said, "We have another worthy lord: we shouldn't worry anymore."

Sun Quan returned to his mansion home, where he was greeted by his mother Lady Wu.
"You are already showing that you are a great man, my dear son," Lady Wu said.
"I still can't face the military," Sun Quan admitted. "So many are resentful because they remember Xuan City, but... perhaps I'll find the strength to do that soon."
"...You do not have Bohai among your guards," Lady Wu noted.
"He refuses to serve in that role after... after what happened," Sun Quan replied. "I cannot convince Song Qian to join my guards either. I will ask them to reconsider, but I also intend to request Zhou Tai's service as soon as the moment is right."
"Perhaps that is for the best," Lady Wu said sadly.
"Now I must return to my brother," Sun Quan continued. "Talking to Ziheng has made me emotional."
Sun Quan and Lady Wu returned to the room that housed Sun Ce's decorated funeral casket: Lady Chen, Sun Yi, Sun Kuang, Sun Hè, Quan's uncle Sun Jing and Jing's five sons were all assembled in the room and making traditional lamentations.
"...Lord Sun," Sun Hè said penitently.
"You're family," Sun Quan replied. "Nothing's changed, Bohai."
"But I *failed*!" Sun Hè cried. "I *should have been there*! I-!"
"No more of that!" Lady Wu snapped. "Bofu, like his father, made his own choices. Weep all you want, but don't blame yourself."

148

"...*Bofu*...!" Sun Hè sobbed.

Sun Quan knelt at Sun Hè's side and joined in the lamentations. Lady Wu was visibly unsteady as she knelt next to Sun Quan and joined the chorus minutes later; it was obvious that the grief was taking its toll on her health and that of her frail fourth son Kuang.

The death of Sun Ce had served as a catalyst for more rebellions in every part of Jiangdong: that was not good news for his trusted officer Hè Qi, who had been tasked with pacifying an army of rebels and bandits in Kuaiji Prefecture. Yu Fan – who was a former subordinate of Kuaiji's deposed Administrator, Wang Lang – returned to the region to aid Hè Qi after paying respects to the Sun clan in Qu'e.

"We're seeing more and more fools joining this 'rebellion' now," Hè Qi complained. "What do I do, Zhongxiang...? Must I kill them all, or is there some other way that I cannot see right now...?"

"You're the definition of a professional... and a very ostentatious-looking one at that, Gongmiao," Yu Fan replied. "You are not one for panicking, so what you ask is born of genuine anger that I can't help with."

Hè Qi smiled and said, "No, I suppose not. I'm sick of staring at the inside of tents and colourless rooms lined with battle maps and weapons."

"And I'm here to speed up the process in any way that I can," Yu Fan replied. "I'll liaise with the magistrates and administrators for you so that you can get on with the business of killing the rebels instead of them."

Hè Qi laughed and said, "I'll probably become infamous for that now, won't I...? ...I'm worried, though, Zhongxiang. I support Lord Sun Quan fully, but he's perceived as weak, so I can do nothing to inspire the rebels to surrender to him."

"He'll find strength in time," Yu Fan replied. "Lord Sun Ce was-"

"**R-REPORT...!**"

Hè Qi and Yu Fan turned to the screaming soldier that had scrabbled into the command tent and fallen to his knees: the young man wheezed, looked up and added, "The rebels have mounted an attack on the camp!"

"...Brazen," Hè Qi murmured as Yu Fan dismissed the messenger with a polite wave of his hand.

"But not a concern, correct...?" Yu Fan prompted.

"Not at all," Hè Qi replied. "Their true leaders – scum like Pan Lin – are elsewhere, so this will be some small insects: let's go and swat them away."

Hè Qi dressed in his polished armour, took up an expensive spear and rode to the southern gates of the camp with Yu Fan, who settled for a sword and wore no armour over his official's robes.

"There are about a thousand of them!" a captain reported.

"...There will be far less at the end of the day," Hè Qi said. "**Open the gates.**"

The southern gates of the circular camp were opened, and Hè Qi led 100 cavalrymen and 500 infantrymen onto the field to meet the rebel attackers; Qi always ensured that his men were as well-nourished, well-trained, well-equipped and intimidating as he was, and many of the scruffy, poorly-armed and disorganised rebels

reacted to the advance by falling silent and trying to retreat.
"You've almost halved their numbers without doing anything, Gongmiao!" Yu Fan chuckled.
The front line of the remaining rebels were hollering and gesturing in order to provoke a charge: Hè Qi smiled and said, **"This is nothing that a few arrows and the usual follow-up won't counter. READY...!"**
The Jiangdong forces fired on the rebels and scattered the front lines: Hè Qi then led a cavalry charge into the centre of the rebels to break them utterly. Little was left for the infantry to do; less than 200 of the rebels tried to stand their ground, and they were quickly overwhelmed by the infantry's superior weaponry.
"Magnificent!" Yu Fan cried as Hè Qi returned to his line.
"Not at all," Hè Qi replied. **"When they learn strategy, match us in skill and competence and provide a serious challenge, and I still win, then I'll praise myself."**

Hè Qi and Yu Fan returned to the command tent, at which point Hè Qi laughed and said, "Where were we...?"
"I was saying that our young lord Sun Quan will grow with time," Yu Fan replied.
"...Hopefully, he'll find some strength soon," He Qi said. "I do not mean to be insensitive; I am being pragmatic. These rebels and bandits care nothing for a grieving brother: they care for their own situation, and I must admit that I understand the problems that they face. Even the most honest magistrate or administrator can't truly watch over counties as big as these: the Han system for prefectures and counties has left us with isolated rural communities, all of them dotted about in large, sparse regions, and when those regions are riddled with antagonistic tribespeople and opportunistic criminals, another answer must be found."
Yu Fan nodded agreeably and said, "I hope that the time will come when we can discuss that issue with Lord Sun."
"A better local government structure would prevent nonsense like this escalating as quickly as it does," Hè Qi replied. "Medicine works best when the disease is caught early: could one doctor be expected to practise in such a large place as this county, and if a single doctor could not manage alone, how can a single ruler...?"
"Lord Sun will recover his senses soon," Yu Fan insisted.

But as the days passed, frustration at Sun Quan's lack of presence was expressed more openly across the south.

"...I know that we can't go on like this," Sun Quan's cousin Ben said to a gathering of officers and officials. "I have remonstrated with Lord Sun Quan, because I am aware that every moment of inaction gives strength to our rivals and enemies."
"It isn't insensitivity," Qin Song insisted. "Li Shu, Zhou Tai, Jiang Qin, Taishi Ci... the list goes on: they all need more clarity on our position, or troops, or-"
"They need *leadership*," Sun Ben interrupted. "They need *strong* leadership... I see it, I understand it. But beyond bringing more talented men to the court to bolster the administration, I would not expect to see much activity. He certainly won't be addressing the troops."
"Thank goodness that we chose peace with Cao Cao," Zhang Zhao

150

sighed. "How could we oppose the Imperial court when we're struggling with controlling a few ruffians and barbarians and keeping the army in line...?"

"I'm sure that Gongjin and Ziheng can sway him," Sun Ben replied. "They are not as close to him as they were to Bofu, but he'll listen to them... if Heaven has pity, he'll listen to them."

Sun Quan concluded another session of mourning, invited Gongjin to his private study and said, "You wanted to recommend some talented people to me, Zhou Gongjin, and I am ready to listen: what names did you have in mind...?"

Gongjin bowed low and replied, "There are a few men – not as many as I would like – that will be invaluable in the months and years to come, especially since we will probably be leaving Zhang Hong in Xuchang for the moment."

"He learns the state of the Han court for us," Sun Quan prompted.

"If he is not 'swayed' over time, as Huan Jie was," Gongjin replied.

"...Huan Jie is before my time, but I understand that he is an ungrateful, self-serving wretch that negotiated with Liu Biao for Father's body and joined Liu Biao immediately thereafter," Sun Quan said. "Is Zhang Hong a similar person...?"

"I don't think so," Gongjin replied. "We have our disagreements, but he is, like his brother Zibu, loyal to the south and unlikely to betray us. But he may not be given a choice to remain loyal: in that case, he might withdraw from service and retire, or break contact with us."

Sun Quan nodded thoughtfully.

"...I should like to recommend that Zhuge Jin be promoted from his current low rank," Gongjin continued. "Bofu was concerned about his loyalty, but I always disagreed: he is extremely conscientious, and he might, in fact, be able to sway the intelligentsia in northern Jing to our cause – including his brother Liang, the so-called 'Crouching Dragon', and the 'Young Phoenix' Pang Tong – and hence rob Liu Biao of men to replace the ageing Kuais and Pangs that he relies upon now."

"That would be marvellous!" Sun Quan replied. "I shall speak with the man, and if I like him I shall bring him into my inner circle and prove my worthiness as a lord to him, so that he can act as an ambassador and recruit others."

"I should also like to recommend Bu Zhi of Wu," Gongjin continued. "He's known for his ability to endure difficult situations stoically and adapt with great speed and shrewdness. He's skilled with the pen and the sword, so he could operate as an envoy or general with equal competence."

"I like the sound of him," Sun Quan replied. "Have him come to Qu'e as soon as possible."

"Thirdly, we should bring Lü Dai back to Qu'e in the future, though we should leave him in Guangling for now," Gongjin continued. "He's got a smart head on his shoulders, and at nearly forty years of age he brings a good combination of strength yet to peak and good military experience."

"I agree with your suggestion," Sun Quan replied.

"Next, Lu Ji and Lu Xun must be made more use of," Gongjin said. "Lu Ji is, at the tender age of twelve, a magnificent genius whose intellect is, enviably, far beyond my own; Lu Xun is only a few years older but his potential is obvious."

"I shall not let their ages impede their careers, else I would be a hypocrite," Sun Quan replied. "They shall be made better use of, Zhou Gongjin."

"Lastly – for now, at least – I want to recommend that we invite Wu Can and Zhu Huan, both of Wu County, to the court," Gongjin said. "Wu Can is a hard-working scholar-official that is wasted on small roles; and at twenty-three, Zhu Huan has proven an able official that has earned the praise of Zhu Zhi, who calls him 'a man that I am proud to share ancestry with'."

"It shall be so," Sun Quan replied. "One more thing, Gongjin, before you go... I understand that I am probably seen as 'weak', but I am still in mourning."

"That is understood by the overwhelming majority... where that's possible, Lord Sun," Gongjin said.

"Furthermore, I lack the experience that Bofu had," Sun Quan continued. "Yes, I've been a county magistrate, but I have not commanded armies or shadowed a great commander. That's my own fault, in a way."

"Bofu always intended that you learn more, and plans were in motion, but... nobody expected this to happen when it did," Gongjin suggested.

"No... everyone expected it, but not 'where' and 'when'," Sun Quan replied. "Bofu was never going to enjoy old age, was he...?"

Gongjin lowered his head and exhaled fiercely.

"...I miss him so badly," Sun Quan said.

"...So do I," Gongjin replied.

Sun Quan returned to his brother's coffin after his meeting with Gongjin: the latter joined him within a short time, and they both mourned a beloved brother and friend. But at the same time, discontent was continuing to grow across the land, and there was a genuine fear that Sun Quan might never become the man and lord that the people needed him to be.

****

24

Cao Cao might have been happy that Sun Quan had submitted to Emperor Xian, but that meant that he could not make personal use of Sun's generals for his primarily personal battle with his former friend Yuan Shao: he therefore decided that he would make direct requests for service to specific Sun clan vassals, and one of them was the famous Taishi Ci.

"…What will you do, Commander…?" a major asked as Taishi Ci paced back and forth across his command tent.

"I won't 'submit', as Cao Cao wants," Taishi Ci replied. "I don't ponder my response, Major Zhang; I ponder the tone and wording. Cao Cao is a notoriously vindictive man. I've travelled through Ji'nan – where he is hated – and Xu Province – where his vile sadistic streak left tens of thousands dead – and I've not dismissed the idea that he was behind more than Chen Deng's invasion of Wu Prefecture."

The major, Zhang Yi, nodded seriously.

"…I shall settle for a polite note that my lord Sun Quan has already pledged allegiance to the Son of Heaven, and that means that Cao Cao should not be addressing me directly," Taishi Ci decided. "He talks of my past as a 'vagabond' and 'exile', and implies that I need to 'atone': that is offensive to me, since he's done far worse things than I have ever done or would ever do. I would only travel to Xuchang or Guandu if it gave me a guaranteed opportunity to rid the world of him."

"Do you think that Cao Cao has approached anyone else…?" Zhang Yi asked.

"…Sun Ben, perhaps, and Li Shu must have received a letter, since he's camped next to Liu Fu and has Yan Xiang's blood on his hands already," Taishi Ci replied. "Li Shu is obviously unhappy at Lord Sun Quan's appointment, so… so I can't guarantee what he'd do. Sun Ben… should really refuse, as should anyone."

Li Shu received a more subtle request to surrender from Excellency Cao Cao, and the wording left his blood running cold.

"…What will Lord Sun Quan do…?" Li Shu said to himself.

The letter made it clear that Sun Quan was making overtures to Emperor Xian, and that left Li Shu wondering if he was being issued with an ultimatum: if he capitulated to Cao Cao, then he would be expected to hand his 30,000-strong army over to Cao and face an uncertain fate; if he refused, then Cao Cao might ask Sun Quan to turn Li over to be punished for his part in the death of Inspector Yan Xiang and holding territory illegally in Lujiang.

"…That boy cannot be trusted," Li Shu muttered.

Li Shu had made a decision: he would not submit to Cao Cao, but he would not pledge allegiance to Sun Quan either. Li Shu knew that many of his men were unsure of Sun Quan's credentials as a warlord, while Li had proven his ability by holding Lujiang's southern region for Sun Ce; he concluded that he would put his proposal to them and let them decide what to do.

Sun Quan asked for a private audience with the official Zhuge Jin, who was understandably apprehensive.

"...I am not sure why I am here," Zhuge Jin bleated.
"You really do have such a miserable expression on your face, Mister Zhuge," Sun Quan said.
"I am naturally long-faced: I look like a donkey; that's what everyone says," Zhuge Jin sighed.
"You don't look that much like a donkey... but you are quite glum," Sun Quan said. "You must learn to appear to be less dejected and more stern-faced."
"...I know," Zhuge Jin replied.
"Have you any military training...?" Sun Quan asked.
"I've received a full civil education, horse-riding lessons, and yes, I have learned the basics of sword-fighting," Zhuge Jin replied. "I wouldn't best a proper general, but I can swing a sword about from on top of a horse, I've read the appropriate texts for civil administration and military encounters, and-"
"Excellent!" Sun Quan exclaimed. "You're unbelievably modest and yet you are hugely talented; you're the right man. You'll be my personal secretary, then."
"Thank you, Lord Sun!" Zhuge Jin cried as he started to kowtow repeatedly. "I am unworthy but I will do my very best!"
"There's no need for that," Sun Quan pleaded.
Zhuge Jin stopped kowtowing and said, "You... you do not fret that I am a spy for Liu Biao...?"
"Zhou Gongjin would never recommend a spy to me as a close aide," Sun Quan replied. "Now, tell me... is it true that your brother is a future genius...?"
"Some say that he is, but he lives on a farm in Longzhong and knows nothing of the wider world, so what can he know...?" Zhuge Jin said. "He knows a lot of the local intelligentsia, such as Pang Tong – whose cousin has married my sister – and-"
"Is it true that another sister of yours is married to a Kuai...?" Sun Quan asked.
"*Aiee*... yes, it's true," Zhuge Jin replied.
"It has no impact on you," Sun Quan promised. "Is it also true that your uncle once served as Administrator of Yuzhang...?"
"Before Father died, yes," Zhuge Jin replied.
"It is a shame that he did not remain in the post, else we might have had a better time dealing with Liu Yao," Sun Quan suggested. "Hua Xin caused a lot of trouble."
"I can't say that Uncle would have been any better," Zhuge Jin admitted. "I can see that the Sun clan are making the south into a better place, but Uncle might have mistaken you for something else, as Hua Xin has done."
"...A good answer," Sun Quan said. "I think that we shall get on very well, Mister Zhuge. You'll be entitled to leave to see family, of course... even distant family... so feel free to visit Longzhong."
Zhuge Jin bowed and replied, "I shall do my utmost to aid your quest to build a great nation in the south, Lord Sun."
Sun Quan smiled and said, "Another good answer, Mister Zhuge. We shall get on very well indeed!"

Days passed: Taishi Ci forwarded Cao Cao's submission request to Qu'e, where it was received with alarm by Sun Quan's court.
"We submitted to His Majesty!" the politician Quan Rou said. "Why does His Excellency now demand submission from our generals...?"

"He wanted to poach Taishi, of course," Cheng Pu replied. "Thank the Heavens that he is the hero that Lord Sun Ce always knew him to be... especially since we'll need him to help us quell another problem. Li Shu's rebelled."

"*What???*" Sun Ben exclaimed.

The gasps of stunned officials were followed by a groan from Wu Jing, who said, "He commands *thirty-thousand men*! Has he gone over to Cao...? How many stayed loyal to my nephew...?"

"We don't know the answers to any of the questions... yet," Cheng Pu replied. "Whatever the reasons behind it, he's got to be dealt with and the men recouped."

Sun Quan looked to his mother, Lady Wu, who sighed sadly.

"...He has betrayed my nephew by doing this," Wu Jing said angrily. "This takes priority over the rebellions: who will go and deal with this wicked traitor...?"

"He must be dealt with quickly, before he seeks an alliance with Liu Fu or, worse yet, Liu Biao, as the last man there did," Sun Ben said sadly. "I, Ben, volunteer to go and confront Li Shu: I spent a lot of time in Lujiang and have a good chance of making some of the men see sense. My brother can be my second."

"I approve it," Sun Quan said. "I should like to add that – sad as I shall be to not see him – Uncle Wu Jing should certainly advance the timetable for his move to Danyang's new capital, so that threats there are can be dealt with quickly."

"That was my intention, Nephew," Wu Jing promised.

Sun Quan nodded and said, "And from now on, my mother will be known as 'State Mother Wu' and contribute to all court matters."

"...She contributes already, Lord Sun," Sun Ben replied. "But the title solidifies the role, Lord Sun, and so it is noted."

"And I should like to 'solidify my role' further by saying that I wonder if *Chen Wu* should also go to Lujiang," Lady Wu declared. "Bofu told me that he was instrumental in recruiting a lot of those men that Li Shu now commands."

"That's a valid point, State Mother," Zhang Zhao said. "We want to get as many of those men back as possible, don't we, so an ambassador is more use than a spear, Lord Sun Quan. I second the suggestion."

"It shall be so," Sun Quan replied.

"It's settled, then," Cheng Pu said. "I suggest that Han Dang should return to Wu to aid Zhu Zhi and Ling Cao's pacification of the rebellions there, and additionally support Lü Dai's efforts to dissuade Chen Deng from making further incursions; Huang Gai should join me in acting as support to the force that will meet Li Shu's rebellion. Dong Xi should bolster Yuzhang in case of exploitative action by Huang Zu and to aid Jiang Qin's pacification attempts; Sun Jing should return to Kuaiji for now to aid Hè Qi's pacification campaign."

"I second all of that," Zhang Zhao said.

"I cannot argue," Sun Ben conceded.

"I am happy to return to Kuaiji, lord and nephew," Sun Jing said.

"Then I shall issue orders as I am advised," Sun Quan replied.

There was no official procedure in place for assigning orders, as there was in the north: Sun Quan simply recited the names and assignments with as much sternness as he could muster, and each officer accepted his order and left the Qu'e court to prepare his men. Once the last of the officers had departed, Lü Fan said, "I will aid the Lujiang campaign if it pleases you, Lord Sun."

"I would rather you stayed, Ziheng, but I know that your advice was invaluable to my brother and that victory can only come quicker with your guidance," Sun Quan replied. "I have Zhou Gongjin, Zhang Zhao, Qin Song, Quan Rou and many other talents to rely upon for advice."

"And you have me and Xu Kun to look after the military side of things," Sun Yi suggested. "Bohai too, and Song Qian... all of us."

Sun Quan nodded appreciatively and prepared to retire from the emptied courtroom.

"...I'm really starting to dislike Sun Ben," Cheng Pu admitted as he walked to the main city barracks with Huang Gai and Han Dang. "Every word is deliberately filled with arrogant pettiness."

"He wants to be chieftain again, you can see it," Han Dang replied.

"He won't do anything to oppose the decision," Huang Gai suggested. "He's not got that kind of courage."

"But he might have that kind of courage if a certain general with thirty-thousand stolen troops was prepared to do a deal," Cheng Pu said. "Is that why Ben volunteered to go so quickly...?"

"He wouldn't join forces with Li Shu," Huang Gai replied. "He'd gain an army and lose the people."

"Agreed," Han Dang said. "Even if Quan's as popular as a foot disease in some places, he's got all of the other Suns behind him."

"...My main worry isn't Liu Biao for once," Cheng Pu admitted. "It's Cao Cao: there are two marriage alliance proposals – one of them linking Cao with *Sun Ben* – that have been left unresolved, and two henchmen – Chen Deng in Guangling, and Liu Fu in Lujiang – that could add their own swords to our existing problems, even with Cao distracted at Guandu. And if he wins, and Yuan Shao is defeated, and he can turn and look in this direction... we'll have more difficult decisions to make."

"Once we've defeated Li Shu and got our troops back, it'll all get easier," Han Dang replied. "Focus on that for now, Demou, and stop making more white hairs for your head."

Lü Fan and Gongjin met privately before they left Qu'e to undertake their missions.

"I suppose you know that Lord Sun wants to talk to you about recruits again," Lü Fan prompted.

"Now is not the time for that," Gongjin said. "I must train and deploy the navy from Ba Qiu, you must go to Lujiang and destroy Li Shu before Cao Cao defeats Yuan Shao."

"...So you suspect that to be the only outcome of that conflict as well," Lü Fan prompted.

"Yuan Shao is incapable of winning," Gongjin replied. "His only victories of any note are the palace assault that destroyed the eunuchs – an instinctive, impulsive act, born of a yearning to survive, that was unexpected from a hereditary nobleman – and his victories over Gongsun Zan at Jie Bridge and Yijing, which were entirely due to his opponent's stupidity. Yuan Shao is surrounded by mediocre officials that connive against each other and officers that win merit for poor service and suffer mistrust and slander for scoring victories. He could have a million men, and he'd lose them, somehow, in a battle with a man like Cao Cao."

"…Which means that we must entertain the horrible idea of forging greater ties with Cao Cao in the coming years," Lü Fan prompted.

"And those ties might – most likely *will* – further complicate the relationship between our lord and his kin," Gongjin replied. "We're both of us likely to see things that we don't want to see, Ziheng."

Lü Fan nodded and said, "I am resigned to it."

Guangling Administrator Chen Deng learned of the uprising in Lujiang and the increased military presence in Wu Prefecture at around the same time: he summoned his officials to the command tent of his base near the prefectural border so that he could relay his future intentions.

"There will be no second Southern Guangling campaign," Chen Deng explained. "We will, however, be wary of the obvious threat to our own borders."

"But Sun Quan is not like Sun Ce," the official Chen Jiao said.

"No, he is not," Chen Deng replied, "but Li Shu acts on his own, and we do not know who else might break away; might Wu Prefecture's leadership tire of Sun Quan and hope to expand into Guangling…? We can't be sure of anything."

"The Shanyue keep them busy enough," Chen Jiao suggested.

"Yes, they do, even without White Tiger," Chen Deng replied. "Hopefully, that's enough to mean that we won't be bothered. Zang Ba's remained faithful, Xue Zhou's been broken and Liu Bei's loyalists are purged, so there's no reason to add our forces to the campaign against Yuan Shao: I'm going to stay here and keep an eye on the Suns for His Excellency."

"You can rely on us, Lord Chen!" a major cried.

The officers echoed their comrade's support of Chen Deng, whose popularity ensured that uprooting him from Guangling would be difficult: Chen gratefully accepted the encouraging words.

The first months of Sun Quan's tenure as lord of Southern Yang were dogged by a number of concurrent military campaigns. Li Shu's uprising in Lujiang Prefecture took a large part of Sun Quan's remaining army – around two thirds of it – away from Jiangdong and across the Yangtze River, which left the region poorly defended. The majority of the 15,000 men that were left were divided and allocated to battles with the Shanyue tribes, rebels, bandits and river pirates that were causing trouble in all of the prefectures; Liu Biao might have exploited it had he not been worried about the possibility of attacks from the north, and Huang Zu was too shaken to move beyond his capital.

Liu Fu and Chen Deng watched and waited for the results of the two massive military campaigns that they were trapped between: the Sun clan's battle with their own renegade soldiers in Lujiang was eclipsed by the war between Cao Cao and Yuan Shao that was taking place to the north. That second, larger campaign was about to reach a sudden and devastating conclusion, and the Han Empire's social order would be changed forever.

****

25

"**REPORT!**"
Sun Quan's court in Qu'e was startled by the arrival of a soldier from Lujiang: Zhang Zhao expected the worst as he said, "**Speak plainly, messenger.**"
"**Cao Cao has attained a victory over Yuan Shao at Guandu!**" the messenger reported. "**The-!**"
"**So *soon*?!**" Qin Song exclaimed.
"...It would seem so," Lady Wu said.
Zhang Zhao took the written report from the messenger and politely dismissed him.
"Is it from your brother...?" Quan Rou asked of Zhang Zhao.
"...By way of Lü Fan," Zhang Zhao replied as he studied the letter. "There are additional words from Mister Lü about Lujiang; all is as it was."
"At least the Lujiang situation has not worsened," Lady Wu said with relief. "So how did Cao Cao manage such a swift victory over his rival...?"
"I would like to know that for the future," Sun Quan agreed.
"...It seems that he was lucky," Zhang Zhao said as he continued to read. "The information is patchy, but... ... ...it seems that Yuan Shao lost two of his best generals in quick succession at the early stages, both in battles involving Liu Bei and Bei's famous subordinate Guan Yu, who... ... ...mm. This makes little sense."
"In what way...?" Sun Quan asked.
"It seems that Guan was fighting for *Cao Cao* on at least one occasion," Zhang Zhao replied. "That would have pitted him against his own lord, unless Liu Bei was 'playing both sides'."
"That would make Bei a very treacherous individual, which does – and doesn't – make a lot of sense either," Qin Song suggested.
"Oh, it gets better!" Zhang Zhao chuckled. "Bei was allied to *Yellow Turbans* for part of his campaign in Runan, and attacked Xuchang with them!"
Sun Quan waited for a chorus of gasps to subside before he asked, "How can that be so, Mister Zhang...?"
"Liu Bei is either stupid or mad," Zhang Zhao replied. "Him and Yuan Shao both, since that would have required Yuan's approval: I told you that the 'Girdle Edict' was nonsense!"
"...It seems that you were right to question it," Sun Quan said. "I'm now glad that Bofu did not throw himself into the conflict when he was invited to."
"We should all be," Zhang Zhao replied. "But I am not done! In addition to somehow having Liu Bei fighting for and against him simultaneously, and as well as recruiting Yellow Turbans and criminal gangs to reinforce his western pincer, Yuan Shao also employed Liu Biao, who turned tail and fled before he'd got halfway across Yu Province! That left Yuan Shao with but one effective front along the Yellow River, which – robbed of his best officers – was bound to end badly. This report strongly suggests that he allowed discord between his own advisers to rob him of the talents that he had left... a lesson to us all, Lord Sun."
Sun Quan shook his head and said, "Elaborate, Mister Zhang. Your brother's words are confusing at best."

"He only says what he has seen and heard, and I know him to be reliable," Zhang Zhao insisted. "Yuan Shao lost his momentum and resorted to his usual procrastinating, at which point his advisers started looking to blame and slander each other for the losses, and Yuan lost a man named 'Xu Yòu' to Cao Cao. This Xu fellow fled one night, told Cao Cao where all of Yuan Shao's most important military installations were located – including his main supply depot – and Cao Cao simply exploited the poor security and burned the depot to ashes."

Sun Quan waited for another chorus of gasps and mutterings to end before he asked, "And what happened to Yuan Shao...?"

"His supply depot gone, his best officers and advisers captured, killed or defected, he fled northward, across the Yellow River, and returned to his capital," Zhang Zhao replied. "Cao Cao is now preoccupied with routing Liu Bei's ragtag army in Yu Province."

"...And after that, he'll look southward," Qin Song suggested.

"There is a possibility that he might," Quan Rou agreed.

Sun Quan noticed that Gu Yong was frowning and said, "I know you to be a man that is silent when you question the common thinking. Please, Mister Gu, speak."

"Cao Cao won't look southward," Gu Yong said. "Not yet, at least: Yuan Shao might have lost a depot, but he won't have lost the whole of his two-to-three-hundred-thousand men. He'll regroup for certain, and Cao Cao will want to halt any of his attempts to return to Guandu. Yuan Shao controls four resource-rich provinces, and he can recruit new talents to replace those lost: even if Cao is destined to win in the end, Yuan Shao and his clan are far from finished."

"I don't disagree entirely, but Cao is a man that exploits brief breaks and makes good use of them," Qin Song retorted. "Yuan Shao will dither for months before he'll try to return to Guandu: in the meantime, Cao will try and pacify Yu Province, destroy Liu Bei and change the situations in Jing and Yang Provinces."

"We can expect a formal address from the Imperial court," Quan Rou suggested.

"Oh, undoubtedly," Zhang Zhao said. "And yes, Mister Qin, we can expect Cao Cao to renew calls for the marriage alliances to go ahead at the very least, and we should be cooperative."

"...Is that wise...?" Quan Rou asked.

"The 'Girdle Edict Coalition' is broken, and Cao Cao has emerged as the great statesman of our era," Zhang Zhao replied. "This is the time to reinforce the Sun clan's standing: if we go ahead and have Lady Cao come to Jiangdong to wed Marquis Sun Kuang, and Sun Ben accompanies his daughter to Xuchang to wed her to Cao Zhang, then Lord Sun will be tied to the house of the Excellency of Works, and the stability and security of this region is assured!"

"...Perhaps," Gu Yong said.

"His Excellency Cao Cao will not move against a relation!" Zhang Zhao snapped.

"...He's just defeated his best friend, a man that was probably his sworn brother," Xu Kun suggested. "And that's after he killed that other man that was his good friend, that Zhang Mao."

"Zhang *Miao*," Qin Song said. "But to be fair, Cao was given little choice in either case: Yuan Shao attacked him first, after all, and Zhang Miao was allied to Lü Bu."

"...But can Cao Cao be trusted...?" Lady Wu asked. "I've heard a lot of unpleasant things about his conduct, especially towards women. I don't want to show deference to a man that might try to take advantage of my daughters or, by all accounts, a widow, like me or Lady Chen, or even Daqiao."

"Cao Cao is a flawed man that has changed, reformed and become a hero of the age," Zhang Zhao insisted. "He has made peace with enemies, apologised to the people of Xu Province, rebuilt the Imperial army and rescued His Majesty. We must embrace opportunities to establish greater ties to the Caos."

"...I shall abide by your words if that is Cao Cao's intent," Sun Quan declared. "I agree that a man can correct his ways and become great: if Cao Cao is the hero that will stabilise the empire, then I should be his ally, not his enemy."

"Then let us wait for a messenger from Xuchang," Qin Song said. "We will quickly learn of Cao Cao's intent when that arrives."

Sun Quan's aide Pan Zhang had been asked to travel to Qu'e, but Quan's absence from Yangxian County had left a local government power vacuum that criminals were keen to exploit. A small bandit army formed, and Pan Zhang was best placed to deal with it.

"...I want this dealt with quickly," Pan Zhang said to his subordinate captains. "Lord Sun wants me in the capital, and these fools are distracting me."

The officers reacted enthusiastically, and Pan Zhang led them from his command tent with a decorated spear in hand.

"Here he is! 'Mister Honest'!" the bandits' leader heckled as Pan Zhang rode to the front line of his small militia: Pan was dressed in an expensive suit of armour that only partially hid his colourful patterned robes, and the sight of him led to a chorus of jeers from the enemy side.

"...**They won't be laughing when I take their heads for Lord Sun!**" Pan Zhang shouted angrily. "**Everyone follow my lead!**"

"**Wait, Mister Pan, you're not-!**" an official exclaimed; Pan Zhang ignored all pleas for restraint and charged the bandits on his expensive foreign steed. The bandits scattered as Pan Zhang and his small cavalry and infantry met their disorganised lines; Pan was deliberately targeting men that were wearing valuable items, and some were startled at his obvious interest in taking those valuables for himself. Regardless of the purposes behind Pan Zhang's charge, the bravery and prowess that he showed ensured that the outcome was a complete victory.

"...Those items probably belong to notable persons," an official said as Pan Zhang returned to his command tent with his battle spoils.

"I doubt there's a way to prove who owned what," Pan Zhang replied casually.

"...Will they or their sale value be divided among your officers...?" the official asked snidely.

"No," Pan Zhang replied. "I pay them well enough. Did you secure a meeting with the Ji clan chieftain like I asked you to...?"

"He was as stubborn as you thought he would be, so he was brought here by force," the official replied. "Am I to show him in to see you, then...?"

"Give me a few minutes," Pan Zhang said.

Pan Zhang waited until he was alone and started to place the confiscated trinkets in a box: he hummed a tune as he cleaned each item and dropped it into the container, and he laughed when the task was complete.

"You have a nerve, Pan Zhang!" 'Chief Ji' barked as he was led into Pan Zhang's command tent by two guards. **"I remember when you were a beggar-gambler, and you've owed me money before when-!"**

"That was then, this is now," Pan Zhang replied as he turned to face Chief Ji. "Now listen: your clan runs part of this county's 'underworld', and has connections to Fei Zhan in Danyang, and that's tolerated, because crime's a fact of life... but when you start 'inspiring' bandit gangs to start harassing villages, Ji, that's a step too far."

"Hark at you, hypocritical bastard!" Chief Ji retorted. "You're a famous bad debtor! How many times have you needed to be threatened with death before you paid what you owed? You're a bandit, just a different kind! They're laughing at you out there, about how you picked at the corpses for treasures like a crow!"

"...You really are failing to see the changes, aren't you?" Pan Zhang said. "Ask around: I have no old debts now, and I'm not creating any more. Now I'm going to ask once more, and remember that it's just you here."

"You kill me, Pan Zhang, and my clan will never leave you alone!" Chief Ji heckled.

"...I doubt that, since I won't stop with you," Pan Zhang retorted. "What's it to be...? Either you stick to gambling, women and that kind of thing, and you get to keep your head, or you keep trying to be another Zang Ba and I have to destroy you."

"...I don't have the backing to be Zang Ba," Chief Ji conceded. "But if I did, I'd-!"

"I can imagine," Pan Zhang chuckled.

"But I don't have the people, so I won't 'inspire' anything else," Chief Ji continued. "Can I go now?"

Pan Zhang nodded to the cynical guards, who escorted Chief Ji from the tent.

"...You should have arrested him!" the official hissed.

"There're too many men that'll just take his place," Pan Zhang insisted. "When the hardships are fewer, then we can deal with them properly. Remember that I lived in that world for a time, so I know how it works."

The official nodded soberly.

"Ji'll make no more trouble, and he's the only one that we had to worry about unless Fei Zhan decides to cross the border, so now I can go to Qu'e," Pan Zhang continued. "I'll leave tonight: I've left Lord Sun waiting for long enough. And I'll find out who the new Magistrate's going to be while I'm there, of course... I know you're all sick of taking orders from me."

The official smirked and said, "I don't know what you mean."

Sun Quan left his mansion home and walked the streets of his capital with an entourage; he was unnerved by the lack of deference or delight that his people showed at the sight of him.

"I know what you're thinking, Cousin, but times are tough," Xu Kun suggested. "Their smiles will return when the Shanyue aren't tearing the region apart."

"...I believe it to be more than that," Sun Quan replied.

"Where are we actually going, Brother?" Sun Yi asked.

"To the barracks," Sun Quan replied.

"Are you going to talk to the men?" Xu Kun asked.

"...I just want to see them for now, and let them see me," Sun Quan replied. "I... I know that I do not inspire them as I am, and I cannot be someone else, so I want to see if I can understand how to inspire them in my own way."

"We'll help if we can," Sun Yi promised.

But the reactions of the soldiers were conspicuously muted and, in some cases, irreverent: Sun Quan was not enjoying the trust and favour of his army, and that – coupled with their obvious respect for his younger brother Yi – worried him greatly.

Pan Zhang arrived within days, and Sun Quan eagerly invited him to a private meeting in his study.

"Your recent exploits in Yangxian are known to me, Wengui!" Sun Quan said.

"...Are they...?" Pan Zhang asked defensively.

"The officials are speaking well of you," Sun Quan insisted. "You understand the fine balance between respecting the law and knowing people. Now I must ask that you use that talent for assessing situations to aid me with a dilemma."

"...Dilemma...?" Pan Zhang exclaimed.

"I am lord of Jiangdong, but I do not command respect," Sun Quan explained. "I am always able to rely on the advice of Mother, of Uncle Wu Jing, of men like Zhang Zhao and Qin Song, of familiar friends like Gongjin and Ziheng... but they all say that I must do more, and I cannot see what more I can do at present."

"You were mourning when I arrived," Pan Zhang noted. "Do you mourn a lot...?"

"At every free moment," Sun Quan replied. "I must do, to atone at the very least, to demand forgiveness for my past actions and earn my brother's trust and support."

"He left you the chieftainship," Pan Zhang said. "He must have trusted you."

"...He was wrong to do so, but I must change that," Sun Quan replied. "But the men like my brother Yi and still want him to be clan chieftain. I was not the popular choice, Wengui, and I truly fear a coup."

"So you worry that your brother Yi will usurp you soon?" Pan Zhang exclaimed.

"No, no... Yi is supporting me fully," Sun Quan replied. "I'm worried that a growing number of military figures want him and will put him in the role regardless of whether he wants it or not. And that might mean my being exiled or worse."

"...I can find out some things for you," Pan Zhang suggested.

"No, no, I want you to be of more use to the state," Sun Quan replied. "I want you to go back to Yangxian County for now and do what you can to completely stabilise the place; and when that is done, I want you to go to Yuzhang Prefecture and bolster the defence forces there."

"...Yuzhang?" Pan Zhang exclaimed. "Isn't Taishi Ci in Yuzhang?"

"And Zhou Tai as well, but I want Zhou to come to Qu'e and be

the leader of my bodyguards," Sun Quan explained. "I'll be blunt:
Liu Biao's crony Huang Zu is liaising with criminal elements in
Yuzhang, like Yòu Tu, and getting them to harass us on his behalf.
Taishi Ci is an amazing warrior, and he does make a difference,
but he's not capable of dealing with the entire problem."
"...And I am," Pan Zhang chuckled.
"You can deal with the part that he cannot resolve," Sun Quan
replied. "I have enough loyalists here in Qu'e to defend me."
"Alright," Pan Zhang said. "I shall, as they say, 'go where I am
sent and do what I am told'... but what a world, eh, that we're sat
here having this conversation...?"
"I am having trouble adjusting," Sun Quan replied. "I look at the
map and groan when I consider the size of my domains, the
vastness of the responsibility..."
"You'll get the hang of it, young lord," Pan Zhang insisted. "Just
make sure that you don't lose sight of who you are."
"I won't," Sun Quan replied.
"...Oh, right!" Pan Zhang chuckled. "I forgot to ask you: who's my
new boss?"
"...Mm...? ...What do you mean...?" Sun Quan asked.
"My new boss in Yangxian County," Pan Zhang prompted. "You
must have decided by now: who's the Magistrate...?"
"...*You* are," Sun Quan replied. "Sorry, Wengui, I thought you'd
understood me fully."
"...Me?" Pan Zhang exclaimed. "I'm the Magistrate of Yangxian???"
"You are, and a fine magistrate you'll make," Sun Quan said.
Pan Zhang kowtowed and cried, "I'll work twice as hard, Lord Sun!
I won't disappoint you!"
"Stop it, Wengui," Sun Quan pleaded.
"Me... the magistrate...!" Pan Zhang said soberly. "I swear that I
will toil like a-"
"'Like a horse or dog would'... yes I know," Sun Quan chuckled.
"Make me proud."

****

26

Days and weeks went by: Sun Quan recruited more officials and officers, but he refrained from leaving Qu'e City or spending long periods away from his brother's shrine. Excellency of Works Cao Cao finished his Yu Province campaign against Liu Bei and, as expected, he sent a letter requesting action regarding the Cao-Sun marriage alliance proposals that Zhang Zhao demanded a court session to discuss.

"I will accede to Cao Cao's requests," Sun Quan announced. "Ben has said that he has no problem with his daughter marrying Cao Zhang, and my brother is happy to marry Cao Cao's niece."

Lady Wu was noticeably hesitant, but she offered no words.

"It's settled, then," Qin Song said. "Cao Cao will doubtless want both weddings to be held in Xuchang, but it is better that we negotiate for Lady Cao to journey here."

"Excellency Cao does indeed want both weddings to take place either in Pei County, where his family came from, or Xuchang, where they now reside," Zhang Zhao said. "We should agree, because the capital will be safer than Jiangdong."

Lady Wu hummed thoughtfully and said, "I dislike the idea of my Little Marquis- …I mean Kuang… travelling to Xuchang, especially since I, as his mother, am matchmaker and should not be expected to travel through Jiujiang at such a time as this. Aren't there bandits operating in the Huai River region…?"

"Until recently, that was the case," Zhang Zhao replied. "Chen Lan, Lei Bo and Mei Qian were the leaders, and I am told that they have all surrendered to Liu Fu. The bandit activity is reduced to almost nothing now."

"Liu Fu's managed such stability in only a few months…?" Quan Rou exclaimed.

"…That's very impressive," Sun Quan admitted. "Perhaps we might learn something from Liu Fu and solve our own internal problems just as quickly."

"The problems in Jiujiang are different to ours, Lord Sun," Zhang Zhao insisted.

Sun Quan turned to one of his new recruits – the smartly-dressed, affable Zhu Huan – and said, "You, Mister Zhu, are an advocate of similar methods to Liu Fu."

"I am," Zhu Huan replied. "The problems are and have always been caused by widespread corruption and incompetence. Liu Fu offers stability and improved conditions, and so his problems have faded. Mister Zhang is right to say that it has no impact on areas that have large tribal populations, but where the problem is mainly bandits and pirates, solutions are simpler and less likely to involve violence."

"…We will need to discuss that further," Sun Quan said. "For now, though, the main matter is where my brother is to be wed: I should like to attend my own brother's wedding, and it should be put to Cao Cao that it would be more appropriate for his brother to escort his daughter to Jiangdong, especially now that the Huai River region has been pacified by his subordinates."

Lady Wu smiled and said, "I agree, lord and son."

"…I'm sure that there will be a compromise, especially since it is a lower brother's daughter that weds, and not a son, and the daughter in question will live here in Jiangdong afterwards," Zhang Zhao replied. "But in the case of Lady Sun, she will have to travel to Xuchang, because Cao Zhang will not, of course, be relocating to Qu'e."

Qin Song smiled and said, "That is quite right, Mister Zhao. Cao Cao might fear his son becoming a hostage."

Some of the officials snickered at the barbed comment.

"...Yes, well, I am aware that there were fears about Sun Kuang going to Xuchang," Zhang Zhao said. "But Sun Ben will be placed in a similar predicament."

"We will worry about that if the signs are bad," Lady Wu replied. "We should reply at once, and let us get this matter resolved."

"I agree," Sun Quan said. "Reply at once."

Sun Ben was still based in Lujiang as part of the ongoing struggle to contain Li Shu's rebellion: several thousand men had defected back to the Sun clan when the charismatic Chen Wu reached out to them for a second time, but Li still had over 25,000 on his side and there was no sign of a swift victory.

Zhang Zhao sent a letter to Sun Ben that informed him of the plan to go ahead with the marriage alliances: Ben summoned his brother Fu to his personal tent and said, "We need to go back to Qu'e at once."

"We're being recalled...?" Sun Fu exclaimed.

"We're finally going ahead with the marriage alliances," Sun Ben explained. "You and I will be going to Xuchang to see my daughter wed to Cao Zhang."

"What about the front here?" Sun Fu asked.

"We're not needed here," Sun Ben replied. "Chen Wu, Lü Fan and the rest can cope without us. I wanted to let you know before I announced our departure to them."

"Alright," Sun Fu said.

An assault on the Jiangdong forces' main camp interrupted Sun Ben's announcement: Li Shu had brought 10,000 of his followers and intended to smash the camp before they received another supply delivery.

"...We're cut off and surrounded," Lü Fan reported. "Li Shu has come here personally, so he obviously hopes that he might get a few important scalps and chase us back to Jiangdong."

The command tent resonated with anxious murmurings.

"So how do we get out of this, Ziheng?" Sun Ben asked.

"Cheng Pu sailed downriver to intercept a naval battalion: that was obviously a diversion," Lü Fan replied. "Huang Gai remained, however; I hope to sneak a man out with a plan that should turn this around."

"Fortunately, Li Shu has no decent advisers," Chen Wu said. "His tactics are good, but they are nothing that another half-decent officer couldn't match."

"We'll have plenty of time to outwit him when we're the ones with the geographical advantage," Lü Fan replied. "For now, we must untangle ourselves. Get your men ready, everyone, and I'll brief you when I know what we can do."

The officers and officials retreated save for Chen Wu, Sun Ben and

Sun Fu.

"...Is there something else...?" Lü Fan prompted.

"Chen Wu can speak first," Sun Ben said.

"I wanted to propose using the defectors as our front line when we attack," Chen Wu said. "Normally that would be risky, but I truly feel that they're won around enough to actually harm the enemy instead."

"We'll do that," Lü Fan replied. "Now, Boyang, what did you want to say...?"

Sun Ben nodded and said, "I will be leaving soon."

Chen Wu bowed and departed as Lü Fan replied to Sun Ben by saying, "I am aware of it, of course. You're not uncomfortable with the idea of being tied to Cao Cao...?"

"I objected initially, but recent events have changed everything," Sun Ben said. "Excellency Cao established his position as a great hero and statesman when he defeated Yuan Shao and Liu Bei, proved the 'Girdle Edict' to be a worthless forgery and repelled a Yellow Turban attack on the capital."

"They are but a few of the recent events that you mention, of course, but they are notable ones," Lü Fan replied. "You shall not have to wait long, hopefully: Li Shu is a poor thinker, and so we're likely to break free of this feeble trap soon enough."

"I shall depart now to prepare my men," Sun Ben said. "I have full faith in you, Ziheng, and so it a case of 'As long as it takes'."

Lü Fan bowed politely; Sun Ben and Sun Fu reciprocated the gesture and retreated from the command tent, passing the returning Chen Wu on the way.

"Back so soon...?" Lü Fan prompted.

"I wanted to know if your plan would be one that tried to spare lives," Chen Wu replied. "Your answer affects how I explain our tactics to my captains."

"Naturally," Lü Fan said. "I want to spare lives: every man under Li Shu's command once served Lord Sun, and I want that to be the case again. You overheard my conversation with Sun Ben...?"

Chen Wu bowed slightly and replied, "It is none of my business."

"You'll inherit his responsibilities here, so I argue that it is very much your business," Lü Fan said. "Is the loss of the Sun brothers an impediment...? And I insist that you are completely honest, Zilie: we are both highly-regarded 'extended family' to our lord, and the Suns have always demanded our honesty."

"...To be honest, no," Chen Wu replied. "Ben's divisive, like Lord Sun. He's seen by some – quite a few – as too willing to obey Yuan Shu in our servitude days. I'm told that there are some that might be more likely to join us if he were not here."

"I thought as much," Lü Fan said. "My thanks, Zilie."

Chen Wu bowed and departed for a second time; Lü Fan turned to his battle map and hummed thoughtfully as his attention turned to repelling Li Shu.

The evening came, and Li Shu ordered a change of personnel around the Jiangdong base and retreated to his own camp. After a light meal, the renegade general retired to his personal tent and took up a bamboo book to read; he slowly started to fall asleep, but he was startled by the sound of battle preparations outside. Li Shu got to his feet, stumbled toward the tent entrance and

shouted, "**What's going on???**"
"**Reports of a small unit attacking the camp, Commander!**" a captain replied.
"...A 'small unit'...?" Li Shu exclaimed. "Why do they waste energy on that?"
"It's nothing, Lord Li," an adviser said as he approached the tent. "Rest, and we'll deal with it."
"...Be sure and tell me if anything happens, Mister Shen," Li Shu replied. "I don't pay you to put me in danger."
"I joined you willingly, Lord Li, and toil for more than pay," Mister Shen said as he departed. "I won't let you down."
Li Shu nodded respectfully and returned to his bed: the disturbance ended, and the camp quietened once again.

For a few hours, there was calm: but then, just as Li Shu was in the midst of much-needed sleep, a second small unit attacked the camp and forced Mister Shen to wake Li Shu.
"**I'll tear Lü Fan's throat out!**" Li Shu shrieked as he got to his feet and started to put his armour on. "**He intends to do this to me all night, but I will have the last laugh!**"
"Don't do anything rash," Mister Shen pleaded.
"What do you want me to do? Sit up all night playing weiqi and laughing merrily?" Li Shu retorted. "If he wants to fight at night, *fine*, then I'll fight at night!"
"And won't his camp be prepared for it?" Mister Shen suggested.
"...It will," Li Shu replied.
"Relax and try to ignore the raids," Mister Shen said. "I've posted archers everywhere, so if they stray too close to a light source they'll lose men."
"...Alright," Li Shu conceded. "But I want to attack them early tomorrow morning."
"So do I!" Mister Shen chortled as he departed once again.

The agitated Li Shu readied his men for an attack on the Jiangdong camp shortly after dawn; Lü Fan laughed and said, "We provoked him, I think!"
"So now what...?" Sun Ben asked.
"So now we teach our treacherous friend a couple of lessons," Lü Fan replied. "The first lesson is 'Be sure that you are the readiest at sunrise'..."
"...I won't ask," Sun Ben muttered.
"It'll make sense soon enough," Lü Fan promised.

Li Shu ordered his ground forces to surround the camp and had his navy split into two to block Cheng Pu's return and intercept possible reinforcements from a known camp on the southern bank of the Yangtze River; but just as Li started to suppose that he had the upper hand, Mister Shen was approached by an anxious soldier from Li's own camp.
"**They tricked us,**" Mister Shen groaned. "**Chen Wu's surrounded our camp!**"
"**That's *impossible*!**" Li Shu cried.
Seconds later, a second messenger arrived; Li Shu bit his hand and whined as the youth said, "**REPORT! Huang Gai has countered our naval blockade!**"
"**We've walked into a trap!**" Mister Shen exclaimed. "**We have to retreat and rescue our camp at once!**"

Lü Fan ordered Sun Ben and Sun Fu to charge before Li Shu could respond; the Jiangdong forces had placed recent defectors among the front lines, so Li Shu's men were divided as to whether they should fight, defect or flee. There was a noticeable restraint by the attackers: Sun Ben's cavalry was trying to knock men down with the butts of their spears and swords rather than strike with the blades, and Sun Fu's spear-carrying infantry unit was trying to separate or herd groups of men rather than overwhelm them.

"...**Retreat!**" Li Shu ordered.

The rebels fled as quickly as they could; the Jiangdong forces declined to pursue, which only confused the defectors more. Hundreds of Li Shu's soldiers threw down their arms and fell to their knees in penitence, and they were warmly received for it; others quickly realised that they could peacefully surrender and did so gladly.

"**How will Chen Wu fare, I wonder...?**" Sun Ben said to the triumphant Lü Fan.

"**About the same, I'd say!**" Lü Fan replied.

Li Shu returned to his camp and chased Chen Wu's besiegers away: the defenders reported nothing but calls to surrender and offers of amnesty, and that – along with the demoralising way that they had been encircled in the first place – had driven many men to consider returning to the Sun clan. Li Shu noted the change of mood, so he assembled his officers and said, "Remember why we left the service of that boy! He is cruel, incompetent, spiteful, untrustworthy and cowardly! Where is he now? His brother Yi would be here, were it his responsibility! Sun Ben is here, but where is Sun Quan? I'll tell you: he's in Qu'e, listening to his mother and that pedant toady Zhang Zhao, and planning to turn me – and, I would say, many of *you* – over to Cao Cao!"

The officers mumbled incoherently.

"You have to speak to the men, and make them understand!" Li Shu implored. "If they do not understand that Chen Wu and Sun Ben have been sent here to confuse them, they will go back to Jiangdong! Make them understand that it is not the officers that lead soldiers that are to be noted: it is the men that lead the officers! And above them all, it is *Sun Quan*, a selfish, drunken fool that threw the gates of Xuan open to the Shanyue!"

"...We'll do what we can, Commander," a major said, "but Chen Wu is very persuasive."

"Be *more* persuasive, man, or all is lost!" Li Shu retorted. "The only way that we can return to the fold is if they get rid of that idiot Sun Quan! Give us Sun Yi, or Sun Ben... give us Sun Fu or Sun Jing if they must, but not Sun Quan!"

"General Li is right," Mister Shen said. "Do and say whatever it takes, short of threats... or the worthless Sun Quan will remain the lord of Jiangdong, and Jiangdong will become a distant memory!"

Li Shu's officers – and, after a short rest, Li Shu himself – did all that they could to convince their subordinates to remain as rebels, and they were relatively successful. The entire encounter resulted in fewer than 3,000 defections, so Li Shu still had a large number of supporters. The Lujiang campaign would be a long one, so Sun

Ben was glad to be taking a rest and going to Xuchang, where he would be meeting Cao Cao – who would soon be his daughter's father-in-law – and, he hoped, Emperor Xian, although the latter was unlikely.

"...What would you say to Cao Cao...?" Sun Fu asked of his brother as they shared a pot of tea in Sun Ben's personal tent.

"I'm not sure at present," Sun Ben replied. "It depends on what *he* says, I suppose."

"...There're a lot of things that he might say," Sun Fu said.

Sun Ben smiled dryly and replied, "I know, Guoyi... so there's a lot of things that I might say as well. We'll see."

Sun Fu snorted loudly and said, "We will be accused of all sorts, I just know it."

"I did not propose this, Guoyi," Sun Ben retorted. "Cao Cao proposed it. I did not agree to it either: Bofu made it clear that it was my choice, but in doing so he hinted that it would be preferable if I accepted. The boy's going along with Bofu's conclusions because Zhang Zhao says that's the right course, and... well... being pragmatic, why would I oppose being related to the Excellency of Works...?"

"You really shouldn't call Quan 'the boy'," Sun Fu suggested.

"I know... but he frustrates me," Sun Ben replied. "We're here in Lujiang, fighting our own men, purely because he is so divisive. This should have been done in the same way as before: I serve as Acting Chieftain – or, if they resent me so much, then have Uncle Jing serve – until such time as Sun Quan is properly assessed or Sun Yi can be convinced that he would be better suited. I ask you, Guoyi... was I so incompetent...? Was I so useless that *Quan* is somehow an improvement...?"

"I admit that I don't understand what's going on," Sun Fu said.

"...*Power games*," Sun Ben replied bitterly. "Nobody cared who led the clan when we were Yuan Shu's slaves... but now there's *power* to be had..."

"Perhaps we're better off out of it all, Boyang," Sun Fu suggested.

"...If that's what it takes," Sun Ben replied tonelessly.

****

27

Cao Cao's brother escorted his daughter and bride-to-be, Lady Cao, to Jiangdong so that she could be married to Sun Kuang in Qu'e; Sun Ben and Sun Fu returned to the city before the Caos arrived in order to collect Ben's daughter, Lady Sun, so that they could accompany her to Xuchang and oversee her wedding to Cao Zhang. Sun Ben and Sun Fu were greeted at the gates by Sun Quan, who said, "It is good to have you back here, Boyang."
"I am glad to be back," Sun Ben replied casually. "I am honoured that you should greet me at the gates, Lord Sun, given the situation at present."
Sun Yi – who was part of Sun Quan's entourage – frowned and said, "Are you suggesting that Zhongmou can't even go to his own capital's gates, Boyang…?"
"I meant no misstating of the national situation or our personal one," Sun Ben insisted. "I know that Lord Sun still mourns regularly for Bofu and that there is a need to be near the court in case urgent news comes from one of the many fronts that-"
"There are, indeed, many fronts for me to keep abreast of," Sun Quan interrupted. "Welcome home, Boyang, and Guoyi too."
Sun Fu bowed silently.
"…I want to mourn Bofu, now that I have returned," Sun Ben said.
"By all means," Sun Quan replied.

Sun Quan led Sun Ben and Sun Fu to his brother's temple in the city. Ce's widow, Daqiao, was knelt by the altar with her sister Xiaoqiao: Sun Ben was startled by the size of Daqiao's stomach.
"It will be soon, then!" Sun Ben exclaimed.
Daqiao nodded and said, "Very soon indeed."
"Bofu left one last gift… or rather *two, at least*," Lady Wu sighed.
"I will treasure them as I treasure all that he has left for us."
"Your daughters are well, Lady Qiao…?" Sun Ben asked.
"They are, Boyang," Daqiao replied.
Sun Ben turned to Xiaoqiao and said, "You, too, have been blessed with child, and yet I always forget to ask… forgive me. How is your son…?"
"He is well," Xiaoqiao replied.
Sun Ben turned to Sun Kuang and said, "You're looking well today, Jizuo. How go the preparations…?"
"I am as ready as I will ever be," Sun Kuang replied. "And you…?"
"…My daughter is nervous at the prospect of a life in the capital, but she will be fine," Sun Ben insisted. "After all, she will be the daughter-in-law of-!"
Sun Ben suddenly noticed that Sun Yi, Lady Wu and some of Sun Quan's guards were staring at him with irritated or bitter expressions; he bowed slightly and said, "I am prattling inappropriately in a place of mourning."
"Bofu was fond of you, Boyang, and he always wanted people to feel at ease," Daqiao said as she touched her swollen stomach. "He would not be offended."
Sun Ben walked to the altar and knelt next to Daqiao.
"…I should like to stay, but I must hear from Yuzhang," Sun Quan said. "We will speak later, Boyang, if we have time."

"...Of course, Lord Sun," Sun Ben replied.
Sun Ben turned and bowed very slightly; Sun Quan nodded and retreated with Sun Yi, leaving Sun Ben surrounded by people that were displeased at his conduct.

"He's *bragging*!" Sun Yi said to Sun Quan once the two were in the latter's private study. "He's bragging about being tied to Cao!"
"...It is more excitement than bragging, Shubi," Sun Quan replied. "We've nothing to fear from Boyang: he's always been loyal."
Sun Yi shook his head and said, "But Cao might have been responsible for-!"
"We... we have no proof of who was responsible," Sun Quan interrupted. "We should be glad that the Excellency of Works still wants to be civil."
Lady Wu entered the room and sighed miserably.
"...Why such a sigh, Mother...?" Sun Quan asked.
"Boyang disappoints me," Lady Wu replied. "Secondly, I worry for his daughter, and for Kuang, who will also be tied to Cao Cao."
"...Kuang will be staying here in Jiangdong, and his children will be Suns, not Caos," Sun Quan said. "Boyang's daughter will be married to Cao Zhang, who is supposed to be a future hero."
"But her children will be Caos, not Suns," Lady Wu retorted. "Will blood be forced to fight blood in the years to come...? We have always prided ourselves on our togetherness, our solidarity as a clan! The thought of...!"
Lady Wu sank to her knees and groaned.
"Please be calm, Mother," Sun Quan said. "The Sun clan will not be forced to fight itself. All this constant talk of Boyang being a problem, and risks of in-fighting... it's all wrong, so there's no sense in making yourself ill over it all!"
"...Yes," Lady Wu replied. "There's no sense in my being ill."
"Little Kuang'll be married soon, and then he'll have a family," Sun Yi said. "It's strange, us all being husbands and fathers now, isn't it, Zhongmou...?"
"It is," Sun Quan replied. "It's almost as difficult to get used to as being the lord of Jiangdong... but at least my son is not rising up in rebellion against me. He's too young for that at the moment."
"...I wonder if one of them will be a boy," Lady Wu murmured.
Sun Quan flinched; he knew that his mother was referring to Daqiao's unborn children, and their genders might have a future impact on his own position.
"If so, I wonder if he'll grow up to be like Bofu," Sun Yi said.
"Oh, certainly," Lady Wu chuckled. "That boy had a fire in him that will burn through the generations and the ages."
Sun Quan hummed thoughtfully.

Sun Ben, Ben's daughter and Sun Fu enjoyed a banquet in their honour before they departed for Xuchang; the atmosphere was far from ideal at times, but the attendees managed to make the event a happy one. The trio and their small entourage then began the long journey to Yan Province, which would involve crossing the Yangtze, moving northward through Jiujiang Prefecture and crossing the Huai River; two more rivers and a carriage ride through part of Yu Province then separated them from the temporary capital of the Han Dynasty. The Suns arrived in

Xuchang within days of Lady Cao and her father reaching Qu'e: Cao Cao was aware of his kin's safe arrival in Jiangdong when he greeted the carriage hosting his future daughter-in-law's entourage at the city gates.

"This is a meeting that should be in the history books!" Cao Cao chuckled as he placed his hands on Sun Ben's shoulders.

"Alas, Excellency, I am unimportant, and historians do not keep records of heroes meeting unimportant men," Sun Ben replied.

"That may change," Cao Cao said; he then turned to look at Lady Sun and added, "Boyang, your daughter... is truly beautiful."

Lady Sun smiled and lowered her eyes.

"My son is very fortunate," Cao Cao continued.

"I am looking forward to meeting him," Sun Ben said.

"And so you shall!" Cao Cao replied. "My 'Yellow-beard', as I call him, is a fiery character, much like the Suns... I should say, while I remember, that I wore a white garment for Sun Ce for a time, since I knew and respected his father."

"I shall be sure and pass that on to Lord Sun Quan," Sun Ben said as he looked at the silent, unreadable Zhang Hong, who was part of Cao's greeting party.

"...Yes, that's right, your cousin's younger brother is now the chieftain of your clan," Cao Cao said with false ignorance. "You are particularly different in ages...?"

"I am close to thirty, he is close to twenty," Sun Ben replied.

"...Ah, but where are my manners?" Cao Cao chuckled. "We must go to my mansion, you and your brother and I, and you must meet your future kin! Your daughter will be fine with her attendants and Mister Zhang Hong for company, will she not...?"

"She will, Excellency," Sun Ben replied.

"...You truly have the proper understanding of things, Boyang," Cao Cao said. "But I am not such a stickler for the rules! I insist that you call me 'Mengde'."

Sun Ben bowed low and said, "But surely that would not be proper, Your Excellency!"

"It would be once you are family, and that will be soon, so what do a few days matter...?" Cao Cao retorted. "I always prefer that friends and kin call me 'Mengde'... or 'A'Man', my birth name, if I have been especially stupid."

Sun Fu smiled and stifled laughter.

"Come, follow me to my home!" Cao Cao continued.

Cao Cao's adviser Xun Yòu bowed to Sun Ben, who reciprocated the gesture and started to feel that he had met with a greater change in fortunes than he had originally expected.

Lady Sun was left in the temporary care of her attendants and the loyalist Zhang Hong, and Sun Ben and Sun Fu were escorted to the mansion home of Excellency Cao Cao: Cao's many wives, consorts, sons and daughters greeted the guests, as did the many relations that Cao had brought into his home to live as part of his inner circle.

"This is almost like being at home," Sun Ben admitted. "My uncle, Sun Jian, was very much the same, Excellency, when he-"

"Aha-ha-ha! I said that you should call me 'Mengde', did I not, Boyang...?" Cao Cao chuckled; he then turned to one of his sons – a brawny, stern-faced youth with a yellowish beard – and said, "Greet your future father-in-law properly, Zhang."

Cao Zhang bowed humbly and said, "Sincerest greetings."

"You… are like Bofu," Sun Ben murmured.

"Do you think so…?" Cao Cao exclaimed. "Zhang'er, your future father-in-law pays you an enormous compliment! Sun Ce was one of his generation's finest! Now, Boyang, we shall have a banquet in your honour. I don't care if we're adhering to protocol or not."

"I am truly humbled, Exce- …*Mengde*," Sun Ben replied.

Cao Cao smiled and said, "That's better."

Cao Cao banqueted the Sun brothers in his large audience hall later that night: among the guests were his eldest son and heir Cao Pi, his second son Zhi, the groom-to-be Zhang, his one-eyed 'cousin' Xiahou Dun, his adopted sons Qin Lang and Hè Yan, his rowdy cousin Hong, his quiet cousin Xiu, his unusually obese cousin Zhen, his advisers Xun Yu, Xun Yòu, Jia Xu and Guo Jia, his friend Xu Yòu, and his beautiful principal spouse – and mother of his eldest living sons – Lady Bian. The atmosphere was relaxed and jovial, and Sun Ben was compelled to note, "This is like being at home, when… when Uncle was alive."

"So your household was as informal as rumours told, then…?" Guo Jia asked.

"Oh, yes," Sun Ben replied. "Uncle was a charitable man: so is his widow, my dear aunt Lady Wu, who raised her own brother through tough times and raised me as though… as though I were her own son."

Sun Ben was suddenly forced to reflect on times gone by.

"I have two fine adopted sons in Lang and Yan," Cao Cao said as he gestured toward Qin Lang and Hè Yan. "Hè Yan's grandfather, the valiant Hè Jin, is a hero of mine and it is therefore an honour to protect his son's widow and the heir to his grand legacy; Lang's father, Qin Yilu, met with an early death, and I took his mother, Lady Du, into my household. Now both are my sons in all but name, which was a conscious choice in order to preserve *their* family names. But you will never see lads treated more like sons!"

"…Yu Hè came into our home in much the same way, only Bohai was given the 'Sun' name and continues it," Sun Ben explained. "It is at moments like this, when I view a great family from outside, that I realise a great many things about my own. Uncle – whose appearance is near identical to Father's, so much so that the change was not so drastic – raised me as his own, leaving me to act as a patriarch when he went on campaign in the early days and taking me on campaign in later times."

"…You served under Sun Jian in Jing…?" Xiahou Dun asked.

"I did, and in the campaign against Dong Zhuo as well," Sun Ben replied. "My role was inconsequential, but I saw fighting."

"Like you, my role was minor in that campaign," Cao Xiu said. "How lucky we both were to be standing with heroes, though!"

"Indeed," Sun Ben replied. "Cao and Sun were the only clans that did anything."

"…Which forces me to raise a point, Boyang, and to offer an apology… no, in fact, two apologies," Cao Cao said. "That great dream of ours became a nightmare, and Dong Zhuo escaped, taking the court and His Majesty as hostages and fleeing to Chang'an, leaving behind a smouldering, looted ruin where Luoyang once stood. My first apology is for not serving as reinforcement to your clan's incredible actions against Dong Zhuo, and my second is for allowing that hankering, deluded fool Yuan Shao to set his cronies on you at Yang City."

"I must insist that you retract those apologies, Mengde," Sun Ben replied. "Firstly, I am well informed enough to know that your own army had been compromised, your authority undermined, and your efforts disrespected and dismissed: you were in no position to aid us, thanks to Yuan Shao and Liu Dai. Secondly, I – and the Suns as a whole – cannot hold you, unwilling vassal that you were then, responsible for Yuan Shao's cowardly acts, any more than we Suns can be held responsible for Yuan Shu's despicable behaviour in that same time."

Xiahou Dun bowed slightly and said, "You are a good and sensible man, Sun Boyang. We're going to get along very well."

"...Our clans have much in common," Cao Pi noted.

"Indeed they have, son," Cao Cao said. "We both quelled the Yellow Turbans for the Han, and in the wake of that disastrous campaign against Dong Zhuo, both of our clans were forced to serve the Yuans as they bickered over things that were not theirs. Sun Jian, the 'Tiger of Jiangdong', was cruelly snuffed by Liu Biao and Huang Zu, and Sun Boyang forced to inherit the mantle of leadership and seek vengeance against the will of his lord; I cried with horror as my father was ambushed and killed on a road in Xu Province, and Yuan Shao stood in the way of my gaining righteous revenge against the villain Tao Qian, governor of Xu and friend of deviants and hankerers."

"So many speak well of Tao Qian, but our own experience of the man, like yours, was very poor," Sun Ben replied. "He made a demi-god out of the Buddhist cultist Ze Rong, who did awful things as he migrated across our region, and our Chief Clerk, Zhang Zhao, was once held hostage by him, as were Lü Fan and some distant parts of our clan. He took Danyang to be his stable and stole many able cavalrymen and horses from the place."

Cao Cao smiled and said, "It is nice to meet a man that sees my 'Xu Province dilemma': so many have no comprehension."

"When a man acts, he does not act alone," Sun Ben suggested. "Liu Biao and Tao Qian, like-minded villains that they are, did not slay our kin and our soldiers as lone demons of the battlefield: even Lü Bu, prodigy that he was, was reliant upon support. Even sovereigns need support, do they not, in the form of loyal subjects...? The people of Xu and Jing collaborated in their masters' crimes and were equally unapologetic. It was not Liu Biao that laughed in our faces as we took Uncle's coffin back to Qu'e: it was the common men of Jing."

"...And that makes your Jing campaign a matter of reparation," Xun Yòu prompted.

"Absolutely," Sun Ben replied. "Much of Jiangxia is naturally better suited as a part of the southern region, and for the blood spilled by Liu and Huang – not just the blood of the Suns, but all those that they disrespected – we shall demand justice."

"...My first father, Qin Yilu, probably fought your uncle, Mister Sun," Qin Lang noted.

"General Qin Yilu was one of Lü Bu's most trusted officers, so quite possibly, yes," Sun Ben replied. "Do you have ambition to follow in his footsteps militarily...?"

174

"Not at all," Qin Lang said. "I would rather be an official."

"Whereas my 'Yellow-beard' desires nothing more than the heat of battle," Cao Cao sighed. "Boyang, I hope that you will make him understand the importance of refraining from 'running at swords'."

Sun Ben turned to Cao Zhang and said, "I would prefer not to see my daughter made an early widow. Bofu and his famous father are both proof that heroes are not made of stone: protect your precious life."

Cao Zhang clasped his hands together and bowed silently.

"To see Sun Jian's nephew here and now brings back memories," Cao Cao said. "Your father and uncle were twins, you said...?"

"They were," Sun Ben replied.

"You look a little like Sun Jian yourself," Cao Cao suggested. "I never had the pleasure of meeting Bofu, but Wang Lang tells me that he was as ferocious and magnificent as his father."

"...Our experience of Wang was a poor one," Sun Ben admitted.

"Wang Lang acted according to circumstances," Xun Yu insisted. "He is my friend, and he is truly not a bad man, Mister Sun. You were still in Yuan Shu's service, and the rules were not clear; he solicited the aid of villains out of lack of choice."

"I cannot criticise," Sun Ben conceded. "Our own regrettable exploits include the deaths – direct and indirect – of Liu Yao and Lu Kang, and recruiting the bandit king Zu Lang, whose crimes make him very unpopular in some parts of Danyang."

"Liu Yao was naïve, and Lu Kang too idealistic," Cao Cao replied. "Neither man made the right choices, and what happened is what happened. I am as guilty of poor choices: my Lady Ding refuses to have anything to do with me after my famous catalogue of errors at Wan City."

"Don't raise that matter, Mengde!" Xiahou Dun whined.

"I must, Yuanrang," Cao Cao insisted. "Boyang, you will soon be kin, so have a right to hear the truth. I was a villain on that campaign... just as I was crossing moral boundaries in Xu Province. Yes, I had a right to punish Tao Qian, but I did not have a right to wipe entire villages off of the map."

Sun Ben nodded silently; Sun Fu's gaze wandered.

"And at Wan, I had learned little of treating men kindly," Cao Cao continued. "I allowed my irrational anger at the surrendered Zhang Xiu – who was, like Qin Lang, a relation of one of Dong Zhuo's former henchmen – to guide my actions, and I took Zhang's aunt, the famous beauty Lady Zou, as my concubine without 'adhering to protocol'. I learned that Zhang was angry, and planned to kill him; he learned of my plans and struck first, killing my heir, Ang, my beloved nephew Anmin and my bodyguard Dian Wei. But lo, the man that formulated the plan that destroyed my army and robbed me so severely is now part of my counsel, and I truly bear no grudge."

All eyes turned to the adviser Jia Xu, who bowed nervously.

"You are truly as magnificent a mind as people say, Mengde," Sun Ben replied. "It has to be said that we Suns try to be as 'open-minded': though not the same, we have Yuan Yao and Lady Yuan – Yuan Shu's children – and Liu Ji, son of Liu Yao, living among us as citizens, and we recently promoted Zhuge Jin – whose clan is tied to the Kuais and Pangs of Jing Province – and Lu Ji and Lu Xun – both close relations of Lu Kang – to the upper court. 'Stable states are built on wisdom and benevolence': so say Lü Fan, Gu Yong, Zhou Yu and Zhang Zhao."

"Zhang Zhao's brother Hong has been a great contributor to the court," Cao Cao said. "He defends the Suns' actions robustly."

"...What actions does Mister Zhang need to defend...?" Sun Ben asked carefully.

"Not many, Boyang," Cao Cao chuckled as he looked at Xun Yòu.

"...There are two matters of minor concern," Xun Yòu suggested. "Firstly, there is the death of Yan Xiang, the Han's appointed Inspector of Yang Province."

"The man was a wretch," Sun Ben replied. "Forgive my honesty, Mister Xun, but you could not possibly know how frustrating it was for a snooty, arrogant fool like Yuan Shu to be able to talk down to us while his court – which included Yan Xiang – leered and heckled us, and then to find that Yan had been made Inspector after all that he'd done. He moved his court to Liyang and started to build an army while making no attempt to liaise with us: Li Shu acted as any general would when faced with such an untrustworthy neighbour."

"...But now Li Shu rebels against Sun Quan," Guo Jia noted.

"...That's an entirely different matter," Sun Ben insisted. "What is the second offence...?"

"It is less an offence, rather a 'concern'," Xun Yòu said. "Chen Deng moved his forces into lower Guangling to reclaim lands that shouldn't have been annexed when Danyang and Wu were properly returned to Yang Province... need I go on...?"

"Again, I must protest," Sun Ben retorted. "Chen Deng waited until Bofu was on the other side of the province before attacking without warning, and he employed the services of the Shanyue barbarians in order to do so. And after 'reclaiming' Southern Guangling – right or wrong – he then advanced into Wu Prefecture, which is on the southern side of a natural river boundary: how is *that* part of Xu...?"

"...I think that our subordinates have been making too many decisions about how they carry out our orders," Cao Cao suggested. "Let us drop both matters, especially since the latter is a precursor to the loss of a great hero."

Sun Ben sighed miserably and said, "It is."

"I should like to broach the subject of Sun Ce's legacy at a later date, but for now, let us rejoice the good things that are happening right now!" Cao Cao continued. "To the uniting of our clans... and their future cooperation."

"Indeed, yes," Sun Ben said enthusiastically.

The banquet continued: Cao Cao dismissed his advisers once he was satisfied that they had spoken to the Sun brothers enough to have educated opinions of them, and the event continued as a purely family affair. The Sun brothers retired with a belief that the Caos were flawed but magnificent, like the Sun clan, and that their union could only lead to more stable times; Cao Cao retired with a newfound understanding of the changed situation in the south and a new plan for the months and years ahead.

****

28

The two weddings that joined the houses of Sun and Cao would take place within days of each other: both followed the same general pattern. The theme was red, in stark contrast to the mourning white that had been decorating Qu'e since the death of Sun Ce: the matchmakers – Lady Wu and Cao Cao's brother, in the case of Sun Kuang's marriage, and Cao Cao and Sun Ben in the case of Cao Zhang's – would sit at the guest seats at the upper end of the hall, and the guests, divided by clan, would sit facing the host seats along each side of the hall, much like a regular meeting.

A Taoist priest would conduct the wedding ceremony, wherein the groom – dressed in elaborate red robes and a mortarboard hat – and the bride – who would wear a full-length red dress and veiled headdress – would advance toward the host seats and face each other while a priest spoke traditional words that honoured the matchmakers and declared them as wed. Celebrations followed: they were muted in the case of both weddings, since Xuchang was still concerned about attacks by Yuan Shao and Danyang Prefecture – where Qu'e City was located – was still suffering attacks by Shanyue tribespeople.

"So now we are tied to the Caos," Sun Quan said as he returned to his private study after a lavish banquet for the newlyweds.

"Are you worried, Lord Sun…?" Gongjin asked as he followed Sun Quan and took a seat facing him.

"Less about Kuang, save for 'potential intelligence leaks'… more about Ben," Sun Quan admitted. "Mother's health worries me, so I try to reassure her, but… but she frets about Ben's loyalty, and I am sometimes doubtful of it."

"On an intelligence note, Kuang is kept ignorant of the most important matters and so Lady Cao will have little to report to her uncle," Gongjin replied. "As for Ben… well, yes, he sometimes shows resentment at his place in the grand scheme of things. But would he betray us…? …No, I don't think so."

Sun Quan smirked and said, "You hesitated."

"…Alright, I am not completely sure, but if he did, it would be through being cruelly misguided," Gongjin replied.

"And he is now in the lair of the wolf," Sun Quan suggested. "Cao Cao himself is crafty, and that's without giving consideration to his famous advisers."

"Sun Ben is not part of the 'upper circle' any longer, and his daughter will be in Xuchang," Gongjin replied. "We should focus on worrying about 'normality' – which is what we will now have to return to – rather than the extraordinary. When Cao's brother goes back to Xuchang, he will be reporting a south that has changed: where there were marshes, there are fields, and where there were collections of hovels and shacks, there are towns and cities. Cao Cao should be excited and pleased about the strength that we've brought to the south, but he is just as likely to feel threatened. And when Sun Ben returns, he'll be worrying about his daughter as he returns to the front in Lujiang: his opinions of the capital and the Caos will dictate his actions from there."

"Then let us all hope, sad to say, that Cao Cao is unimpressed," Sun Quan sighed.

Cao Cao held another banquet for Sun Ben and Sun Fu before they returned to Lujiang; it ended on an upbeat note, and Sun Ben said, "I leave here knowing that my daughter is marrying the son of a hero and a hero in his own right."
"You are too kind, Father-in-law," Cao Zhang replied. "I will always treat Lady Sun with the respect that she deserves."
"Retire, Zhang'er," Cao Cao said. "I should like to speak with your father-in-law."
Cao Zhang retreated, which left Cao Cao and Sun Ben alone save for Cao's towering, ever-present bodyguard Xu Chu.
"...The Caos are a clan made up of tigers and tigresses, just like the Suns," Sun Ben said. "As I said, I leave here a content father."
"So there is nothing that you wish to discuss...?" Cao Cao said as he dismissed Xu Chu with a wave of his hand.
"...Not really," Sun Ben replied uneasily.
"Come now, be honest!" Cao Cao insisted. "You do not wonder if I had a hand in your cousin's death, for example...?"
Sun Ben exhaled miserably and said, "Why ruin the moment now...? If I harboured such ideas, Mengde, I'd never have agreed to this!"
"...So who do you consider to be responsible...?" Cao Cao asked.
"Xu Gong's followers," Sun Ben replied. "They were the perpetrators. It is their corpses that were made that day."
"...And Xu Gong's correspondence with me does not concern you?" Cao Cao prompted.
"He was trying to cause the utter destruction of my clan by slandering us," Sun Ben replied. "I had concerns about Bofu's ambitions from time to time, but he was always surrounded by men that made sure that he always remembered where the lines were drawn. The idea that he was 'the new Xiang Yu' and looking to oppose the authority of the Han is ridiculous!"
"But he will be remembered by many as the 'Little Conqueror' regardless, Boyang, because his exploits in the south are breath-taking," Cao Cao suggested. "He's united the region, tamed the criminals and tribes..."
"...Some of that is being undone of late," Sun Ben admitted.
"...Because his brother and successor, Sun Quan, is not universally popular," Cao Cao prompted.
"Loyalty to the Suns was so much a given that this took us all by surprise," Sun Ben confessed. "Li Shu is perhaps the worst of all... but Quan is divisive, he always has been, even if it is only because he is 'not Sun Ce'."
"...Forgive me for raising this, but I've heard some nasty rumours coming out of Guangling that Sun Quan might have had some hand in Sun Ce's death," Cao Cao said carefully.
"I... have heard as much myself," Sun Ben admitted. "But it's quite ridiculous so far as I am concerned: he knew that he was unlikely to be chosen as Bofu's successor, and he'd have had to know where and when Bofu would be at a given point, that his bodyguards would fall behind at that critical point, that the first arrow would find its mark, that the perpetrators would be butchered before they could be made to speak and tell of their

sponsors... I have heard rumours that *I* had a hand in it that rely on the same 'unknowable information'. The simple truth of it is that Xu Gong's men bore a grudge and got lucky, and that's that."

"...But the fact that they were in the right place at the right time is suspicious, is it not...?" Cao Cao suggested.

"His being in Dantu at all was a result of Chen Deng's actions," Sun Ben retorted.

"...Indeed," Cao Cao sighed.

"There are lots of wild theories," Sun Ben continued. "The 'saint' Gan Ji's vengeful spirit is mentioned in one story that I've heard, another says that old Cheng Pu was behind it, another that the officials were perturbed by Bofu's temper after he nearly executed Wei Teng for questioning him, and that they might be behind it. I don't like Cheng Pu or Zhang Zhao, but I respect them: they're not responsible for what happened and I wouldn't try to say that either of them was."

"But the outcome is not ideal, is it...?" Cao Cao said.

"...Bofu's death was not ideal," Sun Ben replied.

"You're not a fool, Boyang... you know what I meant," Cao Cao continued. "You were appointed as acting chieftain of the clan when Sun Jian died, and now you are a mere underling. Does that not rile you...?"

Sun Ben smiled dryly and said, "I stepped aside when Bofu was ready, and I did so gladly, because he was the better man."

"That sounds rehearsed," Cao Cao replied. "And besides, that was for Sun Ce: what about Sun Quan...? Do you 'stand aside for the better man' this time, Boyang...?"

"I could not stand aside, Mengde, for I was never appointed as acting chieftain after Bofu's passing," Sun Ben retorted. "The decision to appoint Quan was made in order to take the state administration in a new direction."

"...That doesn't appear to be a direction that the majority wants to follow," Cao Cao prompted.

"Li Shu has rebelled: there is no sense denying that, because it is as clear as fresh water, but to say 'the majority' are disaffected would be wrong," Sun Ben said. "We're always getting problems with the Shanyue and bandits in the south, but Li Shu draws resources away from our normal pacification efforts. Huang Zu was humbled sufficiently, but we are unable to finish what we started. Aside from that, Lord Sun Quan enjoys a stable government and near-total support in his court."

"...But there is no denying that Sun Quan is perceived as weak by a lot of your officers, and not just by Li Shu," Cao Cao suggested.

"He's mourning," Sun Ben retorted. "Bofu mourned for three years, which is why I had to be the acting chieftain: my only regret is that I was not given the opportunity to do the same for Quan and give him the proper time to gather his thoughts."

"...But there is a clear understanding of the difference between his being a clan chieftain and, as he seems to claim rather a lot, 'Lord of Jiangdong'," Cao Cao said. "I have appointed Liu Fu as Inspector of Yang Province: the 'six prefectures' that your clan chieftain claims to be his domain are, in fact, parts of Yang Province, and Liu Fu is the appointed inspector, not Sun Quan."

"I understand that," Sun Ben replied.

"But does Sun Quan...?" Cao Cao asked. "Li Shu and Sun Quan

appear to be fighting over Lujiang, but neither governs nor owns Lujiang! It is Han territory!"

"I shall ensure that Lord Sun is aware of your concerns when I return to Qu'e," Sun Ben promised.

"...Please do, Boyang," Cao Cao said. "I can see that you are trying to be loyal to Sun Quan, and I hope for your sake that he is worthy of your loyalty."

"Above all, Mengde, I am loyal to the Han," Sun Ben replied. "I will do nothing that compromises the rule of law... Han law."

"...That is something, certainly," Cao Cao said. "I should like to remain in correspondence with you from hereon in. Is that acceptable to you...?"

"Your son is married to my daughter," Sun Ben replied. "There is nothing unacceptable about two fathers maintaining good relations for the sake of their children."

Cao Cao smiled and said, "Very good."

Sun Ben returned to his lavish guest quarters, whereupon he was confronted by Zhang Hong and Sun Fu.

"...Make your accusations and be done with it," Sun Ben sighed as he sat at his host seat.

"I ask for an account of your discussions, nothing more," Zhang Hong said.

"He did what you'd expect," Sun Ben replied. "He posed a few ideas about who might have been responsible for Bofu's death, tried to coax me into saying that I was unhappy at Lord Sun Quan's appointment as clan chieftain, enquired into the state of the Jiangdong region in general, and suggested that we remember that we're masters of nothing but ourselves and that Jiangdong is part of Yang Province."

"...None of that is ideal," Zhang Hong murmured.

"He never broached the subject of his feud with Yuan Shao," Sun Ben continued. "If he had, I might have said that the Yuans tore themselves apart by forgetting the importance of blood ties, and that I will not be another Yuan Shu."

"...Lord Sun Quan would need to be 'another Yuan Shao' for that to be the case, and he is not," Zhang Hong retorted. "His legitimacy is unquestionable."

"I think that I know that, Mister Zhang," Sun Ben sighed.

"What will you do now...?" Zhang Hong asked.

"We are both needed in Lujiang or some other troubled place, so I intend to go back to my lord as soon as possible," Sun Ben replied. "My daughter is part of the Cao household now, and that is that."

Zhang Hong bowed and said, "I will be on hand to wish you both a safe journey."

"My thanks," Sun Ben replied, and Zhang Hong departed.

"...Why are you staring at me like that...?" Sun Ben asked of his younger brother.

"Zhang Hong doesn't trust us," Sun Fu replied. "I don't know who to trust anymore. I don't know if we'll be harmed for this and-"

"*Harmed*???" Sun Ben chortled. "We were instructed to do this!"

"That hardly ever matters, does it...?" Sun Fu retorted. "Men are often told to do things and then admonished – or worse – by the very men that gave the orders. Isn't that why Li Shu's rebelled...?

...Because he fears that doing as he was told to by Bofu will now lead to his death because Quan might want a sacrificial offering – a scapegoat for past disagreements – to smooth his relations with Cao Cao...?"

"...Say no more," Sun Ben insisted. "We've done as we were 'asked', and now we're going back to Lujiang to fight Li Shu. I admit that I now don't know what I'm actually fighting for – the men, the land that isn't actually ours, or both – but Lord Sun Quan asked us to do it, and I want to comply."

"...But your new son-in-law's father, Excellency of Works Cao Cao, thinks differently," Sun Fu suggested.

"...Let's go home," Sun Ben replied miserably.

Sun Ben and Sun Fu returned to Lujiang and the ongoing campaign against Li Shu instead of continuing on to Qu'e to report to Sun Quan; Lü Fan was surprised at the arrival of the Sun brothers, so he invited Sun Ben to the command tent and asked, "Why did you come back here...?"

"Are we not missed, then...?" Sun Ben retorted.

"...We have been managing, Boyang, but of course your safe return is welcomed," Lü Fan replied. "We've gained another thousand or so from Li Shu, and Chen Zilie has even managed to recruit some local men that stayed here after our last campaign against Liu Xun."

"Zilie is an invaluable asset," Sun Ben said. "How can I help, now that I am back?"

"...Well, we're contemplating bringing Ling Cao, Lü Meng and Taishi Ci here to finish this once and for all," Lü Fan explained. "Lord Sun has promoted his ally Pan Zhang to Magistrate of Yangxian, and once that place is pacified, Zhou Tai can go to Qu'e to be the new head of security and Taishi can make way for-"

"This... all sounds like nonsense to me," Sun Ben chuckled disparagingly. "Lord Sun wants to take Zhou Tai off of the front lines to use him as a bodyguard, put his corrupt friend Pan in Yuzhang to be our gate guard against Huang Zu, and move Taishi Ci to Lujiang, when he is not needed here...?"

Lü Fan was silent.

"And moving Ling Cao and Lü Meng here to 'finish this once and for all' can 'finish' in two ways, can it not...?" Sun Ben continued. "Those two are a pair of reckless idiots! They're good for riding at the enemy and smashing heads, not winning hearts! Who is Lord Sun listening to...?"

"...Me," Lü Fan replied. "I want Ling Cao and Lü Meng here because they are popular, and their role will be to target the irredeemable officers that are loyal to Li Shu, not the men that we want to regain. Taishi Ci is a hero that is so needed that we wish we had at least ten of him: how is he 'not needed here'...?"

Sun Ben bowed and said, "I am humbled, Ziheng. Forgive me for my poor insight, which is truly no match for yours."

"I hope, then, that you will not mind my posting you and Fu elsewhere," Lü Fan said calmly.

"I will do as I am told," Sun Ben replied, "and I will-"

"Good," Lü Fan said. "Forgive my terseness, Boyang, but I don't want to waste any more time. Would you and your brother prepare to relocate to Yuzhang...?"

"...Yuzhang...?" Sun Ben exclaimed.

"Li Shu won't be a concern forever, and we still have Huang Zu and Liu Biao to worry about," Lü Fan explained. "I estimate that Li Shu will be routed within a year, and we will want to resume our Jiangxia campaign immediately thereafter; it would make sense, then, for you – as one of our vanguard on that campaign – to be where you will be needed, providing a stable base camp and aiding others against the constant harassment that the area suffers from Liu Biao, the Shanyue and the numerous bandit and pirate gangs. And, of course, if you still have your doubts about Mister Pan Zhang, you can watch him as well. Zhou Gongjin goes back and forth to his training facility in Ba Qiu, in Luling, not far from your brother's previous posting, and I am sure that he will be glad of your presence."

Sun Ben bowed once again and said, "I shall prepare at once."

Sun Fu noted his brother's anger as soon as he returned from the command tent; he sighed and said, "We are now classed as a concern, I suppose."

"...Maybe," Sun Ben replied. "I am now in close personal contact with the *Excellency of Works*, the most important minister in the land, whose second son is married to my daughter, and where am I sent...? *Yuzhang!*"

"...Yuzhang...?" Sun Fu exclaimed.

"Both of us, at once, Yuzhang," Sun Ben explained angrily. "I wanted to stay here and wipe the smirk off of Li Shu's face... but we are to go to Yuzhang and prepare for the next encounter with Huang Zu. Oh, but we'll have good company, Guoyi: Zhou Tai and Taishi Ci are being reassigned, to be replaced by *Pan Zhang*! Oh, and then there's that arrogant 'Xu Sheng' fellow that's guarding Chaisang; mind you, he'll probably fawn on me in the hope of getting closer to the Han court."

"...I really, truly do not understand what is going on anymore, Boyang," Sun Fu complained. "I've spent time in Yuzhang already! I don't want to go back there!"

"...This is a long-term assignment, so we'll have to decide whether our families will go with us," Sun Ben said. "Between us, we have eight sons, four each, and that's eight future tiger generals that will need to start learning their roles."

"I'd rather not leave them in Qu'e," Sun Fu admitted.

"We think alike, then," Sun Ben chortled. "I'll write home at once."

Sun Ben and Sun Fu left Lujiang and travelled to Yuzhang: they were the first of many that would see changes in their roles and fortunes over the coming months. Li Shu continued to suffer a gradual reduction in supporters, with hundreds or thousands defecting or deserting on a monthly basis; Lü Fan was not alone in thinking that the rebellion would be over within two years at the most, and then the focus could turn, at last to Sun Quan's first attempt at avenging his father's death at the hands of the lord of Jiangxia, Huang Zu.

✴✴✴✴✴✴✴✴✴✴✴✴

29

Months passed: Daqiao finally gave birth to not one but two children, and feelings were mixed when one child was found to be a boy, and therefore a posthumous heir to his father Sun Ce.

"…This complicates things," Cheng Pu said to his old friend Huang Gai; the two were sat in the command room of Huang's command ship on the Yangtze River, having just enjoyed a small victory over Li Shu's navy.

"How so?" Huang Gai asked. "State Mother Wu has made it clear that she will allow Lord Sun Quan to continue in his role, and that a posthumous son – a baby that may not see adulthood, and will not see it for close to twenty years if it did – is not the same as a fully grown heir."

"Those that despise Lord Sun Quan will rally around this child," Cheng Pu retorted.

"…So what is it that you advocate…?" Huang Gai asked.

"Nothing!" Cheng Pu chortled. "I am not suggesting anything! I merely state a fact!"

"…I admit that I worry about the same," Huang Gai said. "I think that Lü Fan does as well: he shuddered at the announcement, as though he worried that some ugly thing might happen."

"…It will tell the doubters once and for all, will it not," Cheng Pu replied. "Lord Sun Quan will show the world that he is a benevolent ruler…"

Sun Quan gathered his bodyguards and visited Daqiao, who was quietly concerned about the attitude that would be shown to her male offspring. Sun Quan felt that the meeting was a strange and uncomfortable one; he returned to his home an hour later and invited his friend Zhu Ran to his study.

"…Lady Qiao was behaving most unfortunately," Sun Quan said. "Am I seen as being so untrustworthy? She acted as if…! …But then, I suppose that the world sets no good examples."

"She is most likely tired," Zhu Ran insisted. "My wife was very tired after her first child, and behaved most oddly; Lady Qiao has three girls and a boy to raise, Zhongmou, and with no husband to support her. People might say cruel things in her presence, and she is confused already… so…"

"…True," Sun Quan sighed. "I have been chieftain now for quite a while… half a year, in fact… and the south is still in a constant state of unrest."

"But there is some good news, though, isn't there…?" Zhu Ran suggested. "Li Shu's supporters have halved, Kuang is looking more healthy, and his wife is expecting, and Yi has had a son…"

"…But what is to be done with Shangxiang…?" Sun Quan asked. "She…! …*Aiee*. I am being too soft with her, maybe, because I remember the beatings she gave me and- …Are you laughing?"

"…No," Zhu Ran said with difficulty.

Sun Quan laughed and said, "I suppose it is foolish. But she did hit me quite a bit, and she's the same now… dressing in trousers, wanting to learn to fight… she wants a 'training place' now, somewhere that she can encourage other girls to be like her. Can I allow something like that and not be ridiculed for it…?"

"I admit, I don't envy you having to make such a decision," Zhu Ran replied. "On the other hand, if enemy warlords came here and tried to ravage the women, they'd be beaten up instead."
Sun Quan cackled at the idea and said, "You've convinced me! I'll let her do it!"
"*Ayah*... I don't want the blame for it!" Zhu Ran complained.
"Don't worry, I was going to let her have her way in the end," Sun Quan replied. "I am being soft, maybe... but she's my sister."
"...Forgive my changing the subject, but what do you make of the northern situation...?" Zhu Ran asked.
"There's only one situation in the north?" Sun Quan replied. "From where I'm sitting, there are so many: the Qiang warlords are tamed, Yuan Shao is on the run, Liu Bei has fled to Jing, and there are bandits at every turn. Cao Cao is humbling everybody he faces... and I just hope that he is satisfied with humbling his northern neighbours."
"Yuan Shao's defeat is still proving difficult for me to understand," Zhu Ran admitted. "I understand the nature of war, but he had such advantages! He still has a numerical advantage, even after Guandu! How is it that he just sits there...?"
"That's all that he's ever done," Sun Quan replied. "His legs must be permanently numbed... and that's me, a man that's accused of 'just sitting there', saying that."
"...You seem to be building up to something," Zhu Ran prompted.
"I am finding calm now, and I know that I cannot sit in Qu'e forever," Sun Quan said. "I must start to live up to the Sun name, like the father of that boy I just visited. Zhang Zhao has been persistently cajoling me into touring the state... and although that places me in danger, I will do it, for I can see that my presence might bring some of the unrest to an end."
"...That would probably be beneficial, but be careful," Zhu Ran replied. "In fact, I should like to come with you and-"
"I... wanted to talk to you about that," Sun Quan said. "I have a problem: the magistrate position in Yuyao has become vacant, and I want to you to take up the role, just for now, until-"
"But I haven't been a magistrate before!" Zhu Ran exclaimed. "I'm too young! How can I-?"
"I was capable of ruling Yangxian at eighteen, and I haven't half of the brains that you have," Sun Quan insisted. "I know that Yuyao can be rough, but you're the right man to make it a better place. I want to have you move closer to Qu'e in the future, I promise you: this is just for now."
"Send me to *Longxi* for all I care, if it means helping you, Zhongmou," Zhu Ran replied. "When do I leave...?"

Once Zhu Ran had departed for his home, Sun Quan invited Gongjin to his private study once again and asked, "You have repeatedly mentioned talented men to me. I want to give greater responsibility to Zhu Yifeng, and also to my aide Pan Wengui. What other names do you have for me...?"
"I'm glad that I am being asked once again," Gongjin replied. "Firstly, I would like for you to speak to my friend Lu Zijing."
"...Mother expressed a concern about Lu Su," Sun Quan noted.
"He's commonly perceived as tactless, Lord Sun, but it is more the case that he is honest," Gongjin insisted. "He'll tell you only the

truth, my lord, and help you gain greater clarity for the months and years ahead."

Sun Quan nodded and said, "That's what I need. By all means have the man come to the banquet that I intend to hold for Zhu Ran before he goes to Yuyao."

Gongjin bowed and replied, "I shall, Lord Sun."

Sun Quan's officer Dong Xi was reviewing the events in the rest of Jiangdong from his base in southern Yuzhang Prefecture; his words had been some of the most influential with regards to what support Sun Quan had, but the young lord was still failing to show the necessary presence across his domains, and Dong Xi was as aware as anyone that Quan's continued 'invisibility' was damaging the pacification efforts.

"What a mess," Dong Xi sighed as he prepared to fight yet another small army of bandits with his colleague Jiang Qin.

"The young lord's tryin', Yuanshi, but he isn't a general," Jiang Qin replied. "The lads'll have to learn to take orders from a more refined fellow that don't want to muck in, an' that's that."

"...Is it ever going to be that easy, Gongyi...?" Dong Xi asked.

"You're the smart one, an' you don't seem t'reckon so, so probably not," Jiang Qin replied. "I suppose that I just cling to little hopes."

"...But if the road is not safe, is it right to expect the lord to travel upon it...?" Dong Xi asked suddenly. "I must remember that he is not a general, as you say, and that our role is to get rid of the bandits so that he can pacify the rebels and tribes, since they are distinct issues... isn't that right...?"

"They all blur into one problem for me as well, sometimes," Jiang Qin replied. "But yeah, they're different. How do we do this...?"

"Xu Sheng says he's busy with some rebels around Chaisang, so we have to do this with what men we have," Dong Xi said. "We need to recruit more."

"When we've got rid o' the bandit chiefs like Yòu Tu, some will join us, and so will some o' the locals," Jiang Qin suggested. "Sooner we win, sooner we grow."

Dong Xi led his own militia out of the camp and toward the hillside base of the bandits, who were celebrating a recent raid on a settlement; the senior chief of the bandits, Yòu Tu, laughed when he heard of Dong Xi's arrival and said, **"This one wants to charge uphill! Let's make his trip more fun!"**

The bandits jovially assembled materials – primarily logs and stones – to roll down the hillside, but Dong Xi's men camped at the base of the hill and seemed to be unafraid.

"...**WELL COME ON THEN!**" a lesser bandit chief screamed pointlessly; even if his words had been heard, Dong Xi had no intention of responding to them. At the end of the day, the Jiangdong soldiers packed up and started to return to their base without making a single attempt to storm the hill.

"...Madness," one bandit muttered.

"Cowardice, more like!" a lesser chief said. **"We should just break them!"**

Yòu Tu sensed the mood and said, **"We'll vote."**

The bandits were filled with false pride and started to discuss their next move: the most popular suggestion was launching a direct assault on Dong Xi's base. The majority won the debate, and on the very next morning, the bandits advanced toward the fenced camp.

"They're here, Commander!" Jiang Qin's son Yi reported to the command tent.

"...Predictable," Dong Xi chuckled. "These tactics really shouldn't work anymore, but Heaven keeps allowing fools to be born, so what can I do...? Alright: prepare your father's men."

"As you command!" Jiang Yi replied.

Dong Xi led his men out of the camp and arrayed them in lines; the bandits tried to form orderly lines of their own, but the lesser chiefs were looking to improve their standing with Yòu Tu and others, and small skirmishes and general disorder resulted within minutes.

"...Such a waste of time," Dong Xi sighed.

"**What should I do?**" Jiang Yi asked.

"**Your role is to represent your father,**" Dong Xi replied. "**He's doing his part: now I shall do mine!**"

Dong Xi signalled to his cavalry and infantry forces and led them in a spirited charge that caught the bandits by surprise.

"**He's mad!**" Yòu Tu exclaimed.

"**HERE IS DONG XI OF YUYAO!**" Dong Xi screamed as he reached the enemy front lines. "**WHO HAS COME HERE TO DIE AT MY HANDS?**"

The front line parted as men instinctively retreated: Dong Xi dodged several attempts to unseat him and killed two men in quick succession with his tempered spear. Dong Xi's feats in Shanyin years earlier were still famous: he had personally taken the heads of the bandit kings Huang Longluo and Zhou Bo, and once his self-announcement reached the right ears, panic ensued.

"**Dong Xi of Yuyao???**" Yòu Tu exclaimed. "**We're fighting *Dong Xi of Yuyao*???**"

Dong Xi's victory was assured: the bandits were now a disorderly rabble, and the path to the senior chief was clear. While his elite riders provided cover, Dong Xi repeated his earlier feat, killing two of Yòu Tu's senior subordinates in quick succession; Yòu Tu and the other bandits scattered to avoid a similar fate.

"**What a sight!**" Jiang Yi said as Dong Xi returned. "**Your name will be etched on the minds of these types forever, Commander Dong Xi!**"

"**Your father is waiting for them at their camp, so they'll soon know his name as well,**" Dong Xi replied. "**Now let's try and round a few of them up!**"

Dong Xi and Jiang Yi pursued some of the bandits while the rest returned to their hillside base; Jiang Qin's militia had already slayed the guards and destroyed most of the coverage, and they were ready for another battle. Yòu Tu fled, and the individual bandits that were unable to join his retreat were forced to choose to surrender or die; within an hour, another small problem had been solved.

Cao Cao was travelling back and forth between the Han capital Xuchang, his base at Guandu and a military base at a place called Anmin as he prepared for another confrontation with Yuan Shao at Cangting: he was still concerned about the Sun clan, however, so he asked his adviser Xun Yòu for suggestions.

"You've established marriage alliances," Xun Yòu said. "What else is there but a title of some kind to appease Sun Quan directly...?"

"...What is best...?" Cao Cao asked. "He will not settle for some trifling appointment, and my choice must be the right one. I don't want to give him too many ideas about having a legitimised stake in southern Yang, but I don't want to give him too much military credibility at the same time."

"Wait a while," Xun Yòu suggested. "If the Heavens favour a swift outcome, he'll be defeated by his own generals in the months to come: yes, the signs are that the rebellion by 'Li Shu' will fail, but he will not be the only one. If Sun Quan starts to take root, make him a Han general, who will then answer to you: better yet, secure a hostage from him."

"Others have had that idea as well," Cao Cao admitted. "But yes... I'll wait."

Zhu Ran notified his adoptive father, Zhu Zhi, of his move to Yuyao County in northeast Kuaiji Prefecture: Wu Prefecture was suffering from the usual Shanyue tribal uprisings, so Zhu Zhi – who was stationed in a military camp with Ling Cao, Lü Meng and Han Dang – was compelled to say, "Where could my son go that isn't dangerous...?"

"My eldest son Tong will be old enough to join me on the battlefield in two years," Ling Cao noted. "I wonder if that's what I want... he's smart, or smarter than me, at least."

"How smart's that?" Han Dang joked. "You and A'Meng seem to be vying for some sort of 'biggest fool in the south' title with your mad, blind charges!"

Lü Meng – the "A'Meng" that Han Dang referred to – lowered his head and sighed.

"My son's a thinker," Ling Cao retorted. "I wonder if I'd prefer him to be an official, since I don't really want him to die fighting like I know I will."

"...And while we're on the subject of 'foolishness', can I address Lü Meng *again*...?" Zhu Zhi said. "You received Deng Dang's men because he was your relative and it seemed right. But you lost twenty men unnecessarily in that last debacle: the biggest idiots on the battlefield are supposed to be the Shanyue, not us."

"I shall strive to be less foolish," Lü Meng replied.

"*Ayah*...! Stop saying that! You're always saying that! You don't mean it!" Zhu Zhi complained.

"Really, Junli... that's why he's known as 'A'Meng'," Han Dang chuckled. "He's got the few wits he was born with and not much else. Oh, and don't get mad and try and kill me like you did that official, A'Meng."

Lü Meng bowed slightly and replied, "I killed him in a rage, and also because he was a useless man that had no right to judge me, whereas you and Commandant Zhu are both heroes that I must try to learn from."

"...Not the answer I was expecting," Han Dang admitted. "You're not entirely dim, not like Ling Cao."

Ling Cao smiled and said, "I am still feared by the enemy. That's all that matters when we're dealing with the Shanyue."

"And, unfortunately, it's time for 'dealing with the Shanyue' yet again," Han Dang said. "They're close by, so what do we do...?"

"Are we goading them again...?" Ling Cao asked.

"If we keep goading them, we'll keep losing men, and delaying your move to Lujiang, where you are needed to defeat Li Shu," Zhu Zhi suggested. "I need to be back in the prefectural capital, so I'll leave the Shanyue to the three of you."

"You can trust us, Commandant," Ling Cao promised.

"I'll go and pack, then," Zhu Zhi continued. "Gentlemen..."

The four men exchanged respectful bows, and Zhu Zhi left the command tent.

"Leave the Shanyue to me," Ling Cao said.

"Do you not need a second?" Lü Meng asked.

"By all means!" Ling Cao replied. "We two 'fools' will soon chase them off!"

"I'll stay and guard the camp with my son," Han Dang said. "Have fun, lads."

The Shanyue were not surprised when Ling Cao charged out of the camp to challenge them, but they were no more prepared for the battle that followed: Ling was still as capable as ever, and his hand-picked elite men were like a family that functioned as one, despite the apparent recklessness of their behaviour, so the battle ended quickly.

The Shanyue tribes of Wu Prefecture had mostly chosen to ignore the battle tactics that the Han Chinese forces employed, and their athleticism and skill could only compensate so much: that almost always put them at a disadvantage against opponents that relied on strategy. But Ling Cao presented a dilemma: he gave the Shanyue the straightforward battles that they preferred, but his bravery and fearlessness earned him respect and caused apprehension, much as Sun Ce had done in previous years. Ling Cao had claimed the heads of several low-to-mid-ranking Shanyue chieftains and warrior champions, and that added to his reputation: some tribal chieftains withdrew without fighting when he appeared, and some even considered peace talks that were always rejected because of the perception of weakness and inevitable increase in the hostility of other tribes that followed. What was achieved, however, was a temporary reduction in Shanyue activity that allowed Ling Cao and Lü Meng to relocate to Lujiang Prefecture and add their formidable swords to the fight against Li Shu.

****

30

Days passed in the city of Qu'e, where white cloth still dominated the skyline as a sign of loss. Gongjin brought Lu Su to Zhu Ran's farewell banquet as requested: some of the other guests were obviously upset at the idea, but everybody decided to let the outspoken former magnate ruin his own reputation.

"It is nice to see so many faces, old and new," Sun Quan said. "Mister Bu Zhi and Mister Zhu Huan, this is the second month in my service for both of you: I hope that you will both continue to serve for many years!"

The thin, stony-faced Bu Zhi bowed and replied, "It is also my wish, Lord Sun."

"I will still be serving you in sixty years' time if I can be, Lord Sun," Zhu Huan said.

"...And you, Mister Lu, are a man that has long dwelled at the back of the court, despite, I understand, being a benefactor to my brother-in-law Zhou Gongjin," Sun Quan said as he turned to look at Lu Su.

"And with good reason, Lord Sun!" Zhang Zhao snapped. "The man is tactless, rude, devoid of-!"

"Please, Zibu, let my friend prove his worth," Gongjin said.

Lady Wu looked at Sun Quan – who had turned his head to face her – and smiled slightly.

"...I should like to see whether Mister Lu is worthy of promotion," Sun Quan declared as he turned to face his guests once again. "Mister Lu, you are observant: tell me of the world at present."

Lu Su smiled and said, "At present, the greater world – that which lies beyond the borders of the Empire – is distant and almost inaccessible, and has been so since the Yellow Turban Rebellion sixteen years ago. The Empire, Lord Sun, is still in decline, and one can expect that decline to continue for at least the next twenty years. In that time, one cannot expect places that have always been neglected to enjoy improvement: they will, in fact, see worse conditions as the prosperous regions race to become just as bad by way of administrative incompetence."

"...That I agree with," Zhang Zhao admitted. "But it is nothing that has not been said a thousand times before!"

"Nonetheless, Mister Lu concurs with a wise view," Sun Quan retorted. "I should like to hear more."

"Then I shall continue," Lu Su said. "At present, Lord Sun, the Empire is divided into various 'territories': to the south, Jiangdong and Jiangxia; to the west, Yi Province and Hanzhong suffer a strange union by way of their rulers, the inept Liu Zhang and the Taoist cultist Zhang Lu; in the northwest, the government vies for control of the lands around Chang'an with the Qiang and their rebel allies; to the north, the Southern Xiongnu and Black Mountain Bandits sit poised to increase their control of Bing Province as Yuan Shao's dominance falters; to the northeast, the frontier and trouble spots that are known as Yòu and Qing Provinces are falling further and further under the control of criminals and tribes; lastly, in the centre, Cao Cao, Liu Biao and Yuan Shao continue their selfish quest for dominance, although one of those men will shortly stumble and fall. Heroes are in short supply, and great opportunities abound for those that exist: act for the south now, Lord Sun, and there is no end to what you can achieve in a new 'world' that will be shaped by heroes."

Lu Su's appraisal was met by a brief silence; Lady Wu and Sun Yi exchanged glances that betrayed their appreciation of Lu's words and meaning.

"...We should certainly talk further, Mister Lu," Sun Quan suggested. "For now, however, I want to say again that I will dearly miss the company of my good friend Zhu Yifeng! I know that I shall continue to enjoy the company of many fine scholars and debaters, but he is an old friend, and they are always irreplaceable for any amount of time."

"...Indeed," Gongjin sighed quietly.

"We'll meet again soon, Yifeng, I promise you," Sun Quan continued. "I will find the right man to permanently manage Yuyao soon, I'm sure of it."

"Until then, you can place full trust in me," Zhu Ran replied.

"Perhaps Lu Su should go," Zhang Zhao chuckled. "Oh, wait, I forgot: we're trying to bring *peace* to Yuyao, aren't we...?"

Gongjin grunted disapprovingly.

Once the banquet had ended, Sun Quan asked Lu Su to join him in his study for a private discussion. Once both men were seated, Lu Su bowed humbly and said, "I am truly honoured to be here, Lord Sun."

"You're here with good recommendations, Mister Lu," Sun Quan said. "But at the same time I have men like Zhang Zhao saying that you are a fool. I should like to hear you say more and make up my own mind."

"...And I should like to present to you an idea that I have been told to never utter in your presence," Lu Su replied.

"Oh...?" Sun Quan chuckled. "What idea is that...?"

"An idea that would see you establish 'Jiangnan' as a permanent southern power, initially equal to the north but one day to surpass it," Lu Su explained. "I think of the necessary initial phase as a 'tripod of power'."

Sun Quan leant forward and said, "Tell me more."

"I believe that there will be no revival of the Han Dynasty now, and that several states will form from the divided land," Lu Su explained. "I say this only because that is what is seen when one looks. There can be one winner in the battle between Cao Cao and Yuan Shao, and most believe that the only winner can be Cao Cao. At that point, Cao Cao will try to pacify the north, west and south: power blocs will form initially, but certain warlords can and will rise above the others and become kings. At present, there are only three men that can rise to such heights: Cao Cao, of course, is one of them; Liu Biao of Jing is the second, but only because of his advantageous position at the centre of the Empire; and then, Lord Sun, there is you."

Sun Quan smiled and asked, "You truly believe this to be the case, Mister Lu...?"

"I do," Lu Su replied. "The northwest will either remain a chaotic, ungovernable place, or it will be pacified by Cao Cao; Liu Zhang of Yi and Zhang Lu of Hanzhong will continue to argue until they exhaust each other, and they'll either be absorbed into Cao or

190

Liu's domains or one will consume the other and then be consumed by Cao, Liu, or – should the opportunity arrive – you, Lord Sun."

Sun Quan clapped his hands together and said, "This is magnificent! I have long wanted to have a clear vision for the future, even before I was burdened with the mantle of leadership; I often wondered where my brother's efforts would lead, and now here you are, Lu Zijing, speaking of the future of the nation with such sagacity and such clarity that I now wonder why it was not more obvious to me!"

Lu Su bowed humbly and said, "I am a mediocrity in comparison to others."

"Nonsense!" Sun Quan replied. "You are a great talent. But I require more elaboration: you speak of an intermediate tripartite state, but it places mortal enemies – Liu Biao and I – as kings among men. How will that lead to peace for Jiangdong...?"

"The land will not remain divided as it does, and my plan, as I have hinted, is only describing a 'transitional phase' before the land reunites," Lu Su explained. "It is inevitable now that Huang Zu will be defeated and yield all of the lands below the Great River to you: Jiangdong – and, later, the four 'independent southern counties of Nan Prefecture', Guiyang, Lingling, Wuling and Changsha as well – will become 'Jiangnan', and Liu Biao will doubtless try to seize Yu Province, Yi Province and Hanzhong as compensation for his irretrievable losses. If Liu Biao controlled – albeit temporarily – northern Jing, Yi Province, Hanzhong and, perhaps, some or all of Yu or northern Yang, while Cao Cao controlled the north, and you, Lord Sun, controlled the entire south, the tripartite nation would come into being."

"But I am committed to Liu Biao's destruction, and he to mine," Sun Quan noted. "What is preventing those two allying to rid themselves of us...?"

"Liu Biao is old and weary, Cao Cao is old and weary, while you, Lord Sun, are not even twenty and yet to reach your finest hour," Lu Su replied. "You will outlive them both, and their sons are mediocrities: Liu Biao and Cao Cao have their own feud that puts them beyond reconciliation, so any alliance between the two to destroy us is inconceivable, but they might both look to – and benefit – us, or be further divided and tricked into exhausting each other. Furthermore, either would need a vast navy to invade the south, and such an expedition would take years of planning and be very expensive: all the while, we would be growing our state and our army and navy, and they would be, as the military texts say, 'an exhausted foe' when they arrived, fighting a ready opponent. But they won't get that far: by playing them against each other for total control of the north, we can have them destroy themselves, and then... well, that's up to you and Heaven, Lord Sun."

Sun Quan laughed and said, "Magnificent! Absolutely magnificent! Your words are the words that I needed to hear to clear away the clouds of doubt! We have a vision and a path now! You shall have a high place in my administration from now on, Lu Zijing! There are no limits to what we can achieve!"

"...I am truly honoured, Lord Sun!" Lu Su replied meekly.

The next morning, Gongjin met with Lu Su to discuss his meeting with Sun Quan.

"*Ayah*... you told him about your 'plan'...?" Gongjin despaired.

"Don't be angry, Gongjin," Lu Su pleaded. "He liked it!"

"He would do, since you advocate a three-way war between Sun, Liu and Cao that tacitly promises the imperial throne at the end of it!" Gongjin retorted.

"And your overall plan does not somehow involve Lord Sun reaching greater heights...?" Lu Su asked without thinking. "What matters the method when the desired outcome is reached...?"

Gongjin pointed at Lu Su and hissed, "*You*...!"

"Alright, alright, perhaps I am wrong," Lu Su sighed. "Perhaps I forget that Liu Biao is the one man that must not benefit, not even for a minute..."

"...But then, does it matter...?" Gongjin said as his anger passed. "I am commander of the armed forces, so I will dictate our strategy according to circumstances... even if they somehow lead to us needing to use your ridiculous plan. The point was to get you employed properly, and that goal has been reached. Now we continue to work towards the stabilisation of the south: the most important step is defeating Li Shu, and that is only half done."

Lu Su smiled sheepishly.

"Cao Cao and Liu Biao have both of them made it clear that we will not be allowed to thrive, and by doing so they leave us with no choice but to reciprocate, to plan for our own success at their expense," Gongjin continued. "That I shall do... that *we* shall do... until my dying day, I will fight... for our *survival*."

"But... what if we read Cao Cao wrongly...?" Lu Su asked suddenly. "*Ayah*! Maybe you were right that I should not have-!"

"He will provide us with further proof of his intent over time," Gongjin replied. "I want his intent to be benevolent, more now than ever... but I fear... maybe even *know* that he means us ill... and I vow to you, Zijing, that with one more affront, I will go as far as to risk our own reputation if I must, fulfil the prophecy he forces upon us in its entirety..."

"*Again*, you're on about 'prophecy'," Lu Su complained. "We-!"

"*Not now*," Gongjin said. "You obviously understand the situation, but... not now. When Cao errs again... *then* we'll speak of it."

Lu Su nodded slowly and sighed.

A week later, Chen Wu entered the command tent of the main Jiangdong army camp in Lujiang and said, "A messenger brings word of the imminent arrival of Ling Cao and Lü Meng."

"...That's either a blessing or a curse," Cheng Pu replied.

"It's a *blessing*, Elder Cheng," Lü Fan insisted.

"...Sorry, Ziheng," Cheng Pu replied. "You've proven that you're one of the greatest minds alive enough times for me to not doubt you on this."

"I think that you overpraise me!" Lü Fan chuckled.

"You proved your worth from the first moment, Ziheng, with your 'lessons taught through chess'," Cheng Pu said. "Lord Sun Ce – and all of us, in fact – mostly owe the creation of what we now defend to you."

"...As I said, you overpraise me," Lü Fan replied. "Say no more, Elder Cheng, or I'll start to wonder if my decision to bring Ling and

A'Meng here is actually-"
Huang Gai and Cheng Pu started to laugh uncontrollably.
"...I shouldn't call him that, should I...?" Lü Fan said.
"He deserves it," Chen Wu suggested. "Lü Meng is worse than Ling Cao by far when it comes to thoughtless, impulsive behaviour."
"Better known as 'idiocy'," Cheng Pu said.
"...He disgraces my family name with that idiocy," Lü Fan complained. "People ask if he and I are closely linked, and I am driven to reinforce the fact that many, many branches separate us. Who'd listen to me if they met him first...?"
Cheng Pu took control of his laughter and said, "We'll be fine! We had Ling Cao's recklessness to deal with, and... well, I'm sure he'll forgive me for being jovial if he's looking down, but Lord Sun Ce's recklessness as well, and his brother Yi too, sometimes. We'll be fine. I'm resolved."
"...Ling Cao has the respect of the men, and Lü Meng... well, he's brave," Chen Wu said. "Those two can scare Li Shu and hasten our victory."
"And hasten it we must," Lü Fan suggested. "Cao Cao's tightening his grip on Yu Province, and I suspect that another fight with Yuan Shao might be imminent; that old turtle Huang Zu will poke his head out of his shell eventually, and we must be there to lop it off when he does, else he'll take the initiative and add to our woes; and every week that we're stuck here in Lujiang, another army of rebels or bandits appears in Yuzhang, Kuaiji, Wu or Danyang. We must retake the men that Li Shu has stolen from us, pacify the troublemakers and start preparing for the battles that are ahead of us, and we must do so soon."

Weeks passed: Li Shu's rebel army continued to shrink, but there was no sign of a swift end to the general chaos in Jiangdong. In the north, Cao Cao dealt Yuan Shao another massive blow when he attacked Yuan's last remaining base to the south of the Yellow River and drove his army back to Ji Province; that left most observers with the belief that Cao Cao was not going to be defeated, including the Qiang warlords in Liang Province, and it further reinforced Sun Quan's faith in his new adviser Lu Su. In the meantime, Liu Bei had completed a humiliating retreat into Jing Province, where he was now the guest of Governor Liu Biao: that would not be the amiable meeting of distant relations that Bei hoped for, as Lady Cai – Liu Biao's principal spouse – and her brother, Chief Commander Cai Mao, suspected that he might repeat his previous pattern and try to seize Jing for himself. Liu Biao quietly heeded the advice of his wife, brother-in-law and a growing number of officials and officers, and had Liu Bei travel to the northern tip of his domain to act as a guard against incursions. New power blocs were already being formed, and the following year was predicted, quite rightly, to be a momentous and turbulent one.

****

31

Military and civil affairs were often clouded by personal ones. Sun Quan had finally begun the promised tour of his domains: he wore armour to address the various militias that he met, and he won some respect for his efforts despite his small, scrawny frame failing to match his athletic predecessor. But Quan had barely reached southern Danyang Prefecture when news from his capital Qu'e shook him and forced him to announce an early return.

"…M-my brother is ill," Sun Quan said to his travelling court.

"Which one?" the bandit king Zu Lang asked.

"…Kuang," Sun Quan replied.

"That's not the right reason for going back," Zhang Zhao insisted. "Loss is a terrible thing, Lord Sun, but you cannot – *must not* – be seen to be weak!"

"So you suggest that I wait until he is dead?" Sun Quan snapped. Zhang Zhao groaned disparagingly.

"Look, Lord Sun, I don't normally agree with pedants like Zhang, but you're not doing too well right now," Zu Lang said. "A lot o' my boys want to walk away and form new gangs or join Fei Zhan's lot 'cause they see me as stupid for following you. Now you being here's changed that for some o' them, so-"

"I… I see that, Mister Zu, but I know that my- …I know that *State Mother Wu* would not have this message sent unless the situation was dire," Sun Quan replied. "This message is to say that Kuang has limited time. I cannot miss my brother's last moments under Heaven to appease a few rebels."

"…There will be no remonstrating with you, I can see that," Zhang Zhao said. "I shall assist your swift return to Qu'e, since that will hasten the return to the tour."

"And if my brother dies…?" Sun Quan asked.

"Lord Sun Kuang would have his wife Lady Cao to mourn for him, and State Mother Wu will doubtless insist that you return to your duties and mourn at intervals, as you now do for Lord Sun Ce," Zhang Zhao replied. "We once mocked Yuan Shao for failing to join the coalition against the Yellow Turbans because he was mourning his father: we should not be hypocrites."

"…Alright," Sun Quan conceded. "Dismissed."

Zu Lang shook his head as he turned to leave the tent.

"Not considering betraying us, I hope…?" Qin Song heckled.

"No… I respect the Suns," Zu Lang replied tonelessly. "It isn't me that you all should be worrying about."

Sun Quan returned to Qu'e and rushed to his brother's bedside, where many familiar faces were already in attendance.

"Lord Sun," Sun Hè hailed.

"I'm glad to see that you returned, Brother," Sun Yi said.

"…Quan…!" Sun Kuang wheezed.

"Oh, my poor, fragile Little Marquis…!" Lady Wu whimpered. "Not you as well…!"

"Has his condition worsened…?" Zhang Zhao asked.

"No offence, Zibu, but can this be restricted to the family…?" Gongjin said.

Zhang Zhao bowed humbly and withdrew.

"Oh, my dear, sweet Little Marquis...!" Lady Wu cried. "Not you... not you as well...!"

"Mother... please calm down," Sun Quan said.

"But Heaven is being cruel again, Quan!" Lady Wu retorted. "First my husband, then Bofu... and now this poor boy that never *once* put his life in danger!"

"Perhaps you should rest," Lady Chen suggested. "You've been trying to attend court and rush back and forth..."

"...Perhaps I should, Sister," Lady Wu sighed. "But if anything-"

"I promise that I will call for you," Lady Chen insisted.

"I'll help you," Sun Shangxiang said.

"Good girl," Lady Wu replied as she got to her feet with Shangxiang's help and staggered out of the room.

"...Mother is making herself ill with worry again," Sun Yi noted. "We're not done mourning Bofu yet: she doesn't need this!"

"I'm... sorry," Sun Kuang wheezed.

"That's not what I meant, honestly," Sun Yi said.

"I... know," Sun Kuang replied.

"Save your strength, Husband," Lady Cao pleaded.

Sun Quan looked to Lady Chen, who guessed his unspoken question and said, "Lady Cao has been the most attentive of us, Lord Sun Quan."

"I am a 'Sun' now," Lady Cao insisted. "Our son is a 'Sun'... I am a 'Sun'. My heart is here with everything else."

Sun Quan knelt by his brother's withered body and said, "You must recover soon, Jizuo. I want to give you somewhere to rule for me."

Sun Kuang smiled sadly.

"I'll stay with you for as long as I can," Sun Quan continued. "I'll be here, because family is the most important thing... it always has been."

Sun Kuang survived for three more days before he expired, leaving a single child – a son – to inherit the marquisate that Sun Jian had been awarded by a grateful state and Sun Ce had passed to Kuang as an act of generosity. The news was passed to his father-in-law, who, in turn, passed the news on to his brother, Excelency of Works Cao Cao.

"...So young to have died," Cao Cao said to his adviser Guo Jia.

"You are talking to the wrong man if you want lamentations," Guo Jia chuckled. "As far as I'm concerned, Lord Cao, he's the lucky one: I'm having to deliberately waste myself away with vice to get out of this tedious world."

"...I shall have to let my brother attend the funeral," Cao Cao said.

"Naturally," Guo Jia replied.

"...And he will not be the only one to die this year, will he...?" Cao Cao said.

"No," Guo Jia replied.

"...What a nonsense," Cao Cao muttered. "All of it... a nonsense."

Lü Fan received word of Sun Kuang's passing and said, "I should go back."

"We can manage until you return," Ling Cao promised. "Me, Chen Wu, Old Cheng, Lü Meng, Old Huang-"

Cheng Pu coughed purposely and said, "To keep it short, we'll manage well enough."

Every man in the command tent was wearing at least two articles of white clothing now: Lü Fan sighed and said, "Why do the Suns now suffer such loss...?"

"It puzzles me as well," Cheng Pu admitted.

"...As inappropriate as it might seem, we should turn this into a small advantage," Lü Fan suggested. "If my absence is made known at the right moment..."

"I understand," Cheng Pu replied. "You'll be returning to at least one victory."

Li Shu was easily prevented from learning of Lü Fan's departure from Lujiang, as the additional mourning was barely distinguishable from the old; Fan was welcomed at the gates of Qu'e by Sun Quan, who said, "Ziheng, I have so much to thank you for."

"I am your vassal," Lü Fan replied. "I do what is expected."

"Boyang and Guoyi arrived yesterday," Sun Quan continued. "Uncle Sun Jing and his sons are on the way... Mother is distraught, and I worry for her."

"Is there anything that Ziheng could say to her...?" Sun Yi asked.

"I wish that I could think of something, but what else can I do but repeat things that I have said before?" Lü Fan said. "Is her brother Wu Jing here...?"

"He is, but he is as distressed as Mother," Sun Yi replied. "I keep trying to find something to say to them, but then I end up crying as well."

"But Mother and Uncle Wu will still be glad to see you," Sun Quan insisted. "Even if you cannot find the words to comfort them... it is good to have you here."

"I only wish it were in happier circumstances," Lü Fan replied.

Sun Quan led Lü Fan and his entourage to Sun Kuang's home, where Kuang's widow, Lady Cao, was leading the traditional laments.

"Ziheng!" Gongjin exclaimed.

"We are reunited," Lü Fan replied. "Has Cao Cao been notified...?"

"My father is on his way here, and with Uncle's permission," Lady Cao explained.

"...I see," Lü Fan murmured. "Thank you, Lady Cao, and my condolences to you for your loss, which is also mine. Jizuo was my brother and my friend."

Lady Cao smiled sadly and returned to her mourning rituals.

"Ziheng, my... my Little Marquis...!" Lady Wu whimpered as she approached Lü Fan and embraced him. "Why my Little Marquis...?"

Lü Fan backed away and said, "State Mother, I am humbled by your show of affection, and I do consider you as-"

"You are family, Ziheng, like Gongjin, Bohai, Boyang and Guoyi," Lady Wu insisted. "We all lived as one happy family, but... but first my husband, then Bofu, and now my Little Marquis...!"

"...I know," Lü Fan sighed.

"Did he 'run at swords'...?" Lady Wu asked pointedly.

"No... no, he did not," Lü Fan replied.

"Oh, my poor nephews," Wu Jing croaked. "Whether they fight or not, are their lives cursed to be short...?"

"I hope not," Sun Yi muttered.

"Oh, no, no, Yi, I…! Forgive me!" Wu Jing pleaded.

"I know that you meant no harm, Uncle," Sun Yi replied.

"…I wish I could stay longer, but I have to go back to Lujiang in a few days," Lü Fan said. "I know that Lord Sun can overrule me on that, but-"

"You would rather that he did not," Lady Wu supposed.

"Victory over Li Shu would be a better way to honour Jizuo than prolonging that campaign would be," Lü Fan suggested.

Sun Ben and Sun Fu arrived with their children; the exchange of respectful bows was noticeably frosty, as Lady Wu was still irritated at Sun Ben for his attitude toward Sun Quan's appointment as clan chieftain.

"Does all go well at Lujiang…?" Sun Ben asked.

"It does," Lü Fan replied.

Lady Wu turned to Sun Kuang's coffin and let out a shrill wail: Sun Quan was shaken to the core by the noise, but it did as it was intended and prompted the gathering to kneel and cry out to Sun Kuang's wandering spirit.

The renegade general Li Shu learned of Lü Fan's departure days later, when Fan was already on his way back to Lujiang Prefecture: he gathered his senior officials and said, "This could be a chance to turn our fortunes around. The Suns are cursed by their second grave loss in two years, and the chief strategist has gone back to Qu'e!"

"We should be cautious nonetheless," Mister Shen said. "Lü Fan is very cunning."

"The dead man is like a brother to him, so his wits will be beyond him," Li Shu retorted. "By attacking now, we might get rid of a few of their officers and clear a path to Jiangdong!"

"I still say that we should seek an alliance with Liu Fu," a second adviser said.

"And I still say that no official alliance will be made while I live and breathe!" Li Shu replied. "Cao's after my head in a sack for killing his man Yan Xiang! We're rebels that 'challenged the Han', and he'll kill us all! Don't be fooled by the marriage alliances that he forged with our former lord: did being married to Cao's niece do Sun Kuang any good…?"

The officials mumbled thoughtfully.

"Not from where I'm standing, it didn't," Li Shu continued. "Cao's niece probably poisoned the poor fool. Cao is untrustworthy! And Liu Fu is his man in Lujiang, so we can't trust Liu Fu either!"

"…So when should we march?" a major asked.

"I suggest that we advance quickly if we're doing this," Mister Shen said.

"And I agree," Li Shu replied. "In fact, we shall prepare to march at once! Mister Shen, you will guard Huancheng: I will march in person and bring an end to this!"

Lü Fan returned to the Lujiang camp as Li Shu's army and navy completed their approaches; he met with Cheng Pu at the gates and asked, "Has the fish taken the bait, Elder Cheng…?"

"Like the fool that he is, yes," Cheng Pu replied. "He's failed to see our manoeuvres, so this will be a fine victory to add to the small one we had after you left."

"Then let's pull him in!" Lü Fan chuckled.

Li Shu assembled his 10,000-strong army in front of the four gates of the Jiangdong camp.

"**WHERE IS CHENG PU?**" Li Shu barked. "**WHERE ARE CHEN WU, LING CAO, AND THE OTHER 'HEROES OF JIANGDONG'?**" Li Shu's soldiers started to heckle their enemies; Ling Cao laughed and said, "**When compared to the Shanyue's taunts, they are not bothering me!**"

"**Ling Cao, Chen Wu, Lü Meng: go and show him your faces,**" Cheng Pu said.

Ling Cao led a charge out of the western gates and made for Li Shu's front lines: Lü Meng struck out of the northern gates, and Chen Wu advanced from the south gates. The eastern gate was left closed; a scout reported it to Li Shu, who said, "What kind of trap do they set...? Or... or are they baiting us to leave no men at that gate...? ...**Double the men at the east gate!**"

"**What about the enemy attacks?**" a captain asked.

"**Meet them with arrows!**" Li Shu replied.

Li Shu's forces began an archery assault on the charging militias: the infantry defenders scattered or raised shields to avoid the hail of arrows, but the mood was still optimistic. Lü Meng ignored the danger that he faced and continued his attack: an arrow felled his horse, so he continued his advance on foot, killing two of Li Shu's vanguard infantry captains in brief duels. Ling Cao avoided being struck and tried to attack Li Shu directly: Li's bodyguards repelled him at the loss of two good riders, and morale started to plummet. Chen Wu's chosen tactic – using only the defected men – caused greater division in Li Shu's lines, and many waverers either switched sides or fled the field, just as they had done in previous encounters.

"**We must retreat and secure Huancheng!**" one of Li Shu's advisers suggested.

"**I can't run again!**" Li Shu retorted. "**You're an adviser: turn this around!**"

Cheng Pu led a fourth force out of the western gate: there had still been no march out of the eastern gates, so the army there – which had just been reinforced at the expense of the others – was just sitting there. But that situation quickly changed: most of Chen Wu's regular army had been despatched over the previous days in order to ambush the eastern battalions, and the surprise attack caused Li Shu's men to scatter in all directions. And within minutes of that, a messenger brought Li Shu more bad news: Huang Gai's river forces had sailed downriver without warning and routed Li's navy.

"...**We'll need to retreat!**" Li Shu conceded. "**We-!**"

"**REPORT!**" a second messenger said. "**Taishi Ci has secured Huancheng and blocked all roads to the city! Mister Shen requests immediate-!**"

"*Taishi Ci*???" Li Shu exclaimed. "*How???*"

"**Retreat now, or lose everything!**" an adviser shrieked.

"**We have no choice!**" a second adviser insisted.

Li Shu looked at the shattered remnants of his army and wondered how it could have ended so badly: he silently agreed to his advisers' suggestions and ordered a full retreat from the battlefield. Ling Cao and the other officers had shown extraordinary discipline and singled out the defected officers for their attacks, so the vast majority of the regular soldiers had been spared; many surrendered when no pursuit was ordered, as they could see that they would be forgiven and permitted to serve Sun Quan once again.

Li Shu would survive for a few more weeks and months before his rebellion was completely quelled by Lü Fan and Cheng Pu: it ended with a siege battle against a small walled city in southern Lujiang Prefecture, where most of the surviving officers decided to surrender. At its conclusion, the campaign benefitted Sun Quan by returning over 20,000 of the defectors to his ranks, although the vast majority of the soldiers would need to be reorganised, redistributed and confined to training barracks in Jiangdong until they could be better trusted.

And while that long battle was still being fought, another reached its end: the northern nobleman-warlord Yuan Shao fell ill as the first anniversary of his final, crushing defeat at Cangting loomed, and he did not recover. His death divided his titles, wealth and power between his three sons, Yuan Tan, Yuan Xi and Yuan Shang: it would, to the surprise of all observers, be the youngest – Yuan Shang – that would, as a result of his mother's careful scheming, become the recognised chieftain of the Yuan clan at the expense of his older half-siblings. Cao Cao knew that such a move would inevitably lead to in-fighting amongst the Yuan brothers, and that the death of such a powerful man would leave his vast domain temporarily fragmented, just as Sun Ce's death had done in the south: he was therefore able to focus on other matters, and one chosen aim was to seek greater control over the lord of Jiangdong, Sun Quan.

****

32

"**How dare he!**"
Sun Yi voiced what many others were thinking: Cao Cao's latest –
and, some said, most treacherous – act was to demand that Sun
Quan send his eldest son – who was still an infant – to the capital
to act as, in all but name, a hostage. Several members of the Sun
family – Lady Wu, Lady Chen, Sun Yi, Sun Shangxiang, Wu Jing,
Xu Kun, Sun Ben, Sun Fu, Sun Jing and his sons, Sun Hè and Sun
Quan himself – gathered in Quan's vast audience hall with the
intention of discussing the matter rationally, but that quickly
proved to be impossible.
"He's just a little boy!" Lady Wu sobbed. "How can that vile man
do this to us?"
"That's the point," Wu Jing said. "By requesting the child, Lady Xie
has to go as well, at the very least... if not my nephew, which
removes him from Jiangdong and effectively ends the Sun clan's
dominance here."
"**Cao Cao should *die* for this!**" Sun Yi barked. "**And Kuang's
widow, she-!**"
"Leave that poor girl be," Lady Wu insisted. "She's a 'Sun' now,
just as I am."
Sun Yi exhaled loudly and said, "Alright, Mother... alright."
"...How can we talk freely with those two here...?" Xu Kun asked as
he glared at Sun Ben and Sun Fu. "Ben's daughter is a 'Cao' now!"
"*We're* still Suns," Sun Fu insisted.
"So answer this, then, 'Boyang'," Xu Kun said as he continued to
glare at Sun Ben. "If you'd not married your daughter off to Cao's
son, and we'd made you the clan chieftain again as you wanted,
and if Cao had-!"
"That's enough!" Lady Wu pleaded.
"I'd be angry... I am angry, and I've said as much to Mengde in a
letter," Sun Ben replied. "This probably an adviser's idea, a-"
"*Mengde*???" Sun Yi exclaimed. "**You call the bastard by his
courtesy name after what he's just-!**"
"Please don't start shouting!" Lady Wu said. "It serves no point!"
Sun Yi flicked his sleeve and turned his gaze away from Sun Ben,
who added, "I don't want any more of us to be hostages. We
endured that under Yuan Shu. I know how it feels to be prevented
from seeing my family... I have written, and if our ties mean
anything, he'll reconsider."
"Don't let him have my nephew!" Sun Shangxiang said to her
silent brother Sun Quan. "Are you listening...? Quan, you-!"
"I... I'm listening," Sun Quan promised. "But I've asked Gongjin
and Ziheng to give me their views and-"
"No offence to them, but this is a family decision, *blood family*,"
Xu Kun interrupted. "As your blood cousin, I say that we shouldn't
be doing this, Quan."
"...What does Zhang Zhao suggest...?" Wu Jing asked.
"What do you expect...?" Sun Yi scoffed. "He recommends doing as
Cao asks, of course, him and most of the other toadies as well!"
"And won't 'Ziheng' and 'Gongjin' say the same as well?" Xu Kun
suggested. "Why wouldn't they...?"
"...Where are they...?" Lady Wu asked.

"Ziheng is still in Lujiang, reorganising the army there so Liu Fu can't take advantage of the chaos after Li Shu's rebellion," Sun Quan explained. "Gongjin's at home now."
Xu Kun turned to Sun Jing and said, "Uncle, what do you think...?"
"Isn't it obvious...?" Sun Jing replied. "But this is the Han's Excellency of Works that makes this request, so refusal to comply is practically a declaration of war."
"...I think that we should consult Gongjin," Lady Wu said. "I think that he should attend a private meeting with Quan and me, and that we three should decide this."
Sun Quan nodded and said, "I'll summon him here at once."

Gongjin was warmly received and asked to take a seat as a guest in Sun Quan's private study: once he, Quan and Lady Wu were seated, he said, "Why was I asked to come here, Lord Sun...?
"I have received a 'hostage request'," Sun Quan replied.
"...I see," Gongjin said numbly.
"What should we do...?" Lady Wu asked. "I am weary, Gongjin! In these last two years, I've lost Bofu and my Little Marquis, and I am permanently grieving! I should be rejoicing at my beautiful grandchildren, but when I see the five that have no fathers, I...!"
Gongjin looked at the prematurely frail Lady Wu and asked, "Are you eating properly...?"
"...I... I would be lying if I said that I have an appetite," Lady Wu replied. "But that is not why you are here, Gongjin. Read the request, please."
Gongjin took Cao Cao's letter from Lady Wu and started to read.
"Others flounder, but I know you to be a decisive man," Sun Quan said. "My family hate the idea, but my statesmen are divided. What should I do...? Should I do as the Qiang have done and give Cao Cao what he wants...?"
"...Ma Teng and Han Sui are rebels-turned-barbarians that have done something entirely different: they proffer troops, not hostages... not yet, anyway," Gongjin replied as he threw the letter to one side. "I would not compare you to them."
"But what do I do...?" Sun Quan pleaded.
Gongjin smiled and said, "Long ago, when the state of Chu was born, it covered an area around Mount Jing that amounted to little. But as the years passed – and due entirely to the competency of its government – that little state grew and built a strong foundation at Ying, and then it conquered Jing and Yang Provinces to grow even further. Its legacy has lasted more than nine-hundred years!"
Sun Quan nodded thoughtfully.
"Now, Lord Sun, you've inherited the legacy of your father and elder brother," Gongjin continued. "You control six prefectures, you have tens of thousands of troops, resources and plentiful, and your men are willing to fight and, if necessary, die for you. When we need copper for coins, we get it from our own mountains; when we need salt, we get it from the seawater to the east. Jiangdong is naturally prosperous and – with the exception of problems that everyone faces - its people enjoy relative peace. Our troubles are many but remedied with ease: Li Shu is defeated now, and the others will yield in good time."
Sun Quan hummed agreeably.

"When our fishermen venture out, they leave in the morning and return only in the evening, their boats laden," Gongjin said. "The army is well fed, has excellent training and high morale, so it can never be truly defeated. So why should you send a hostage to Xuchang…? …Because you've received a single unwarranted threat from Cao Cao…?"

"It is not a threat as such," Sun Quan suggested.

"The wording is strict enough to consider it as such," Gongjin replied. "But once you send the hostage that Cao Cao – not His Majesty – 'politely demands' of you, you will have established a connection between you and the Caos that will be much like that which Yuan Shu created with your father… a bond of *indenture*."

Lady Wu snorted irritably.

"And when the Cao clan – for do not think that it would stop with the death of that one man – use His Majesty's authority to command you and your progeny, there will be no choice but to follow their orders, for their orders will be relayed as the will of the Son of Heaven," Gongjin continued. "You would become a vassal lord, bound to the Caos: your multitude of soldiers would be their barracks, your dozens of carriages and ships their fleet and your hundreds of horses their stable… and is that somehow better than being a major independent power in the south…?"

"…No," Sun Quan replied.

"I suggest that you politely refuse to send – or rather delay sending – a hostage for now, Lord Sun, and see what happens over the course of time," Gongjin said. "If my analysis of the Caos is wrong, and they really are destined to reunify the empire by just means, then it will not be too late for you to submit to the Han when the Caos have proved that they truly represent the Han and not themselves. If the Caos decide to employ violence as a persuasive tool, they will only destroy themselves, as Cao has already done once at Wan, because starting a war with Jiangdong is like lighting a fire that will consume everything. For now, feign meekness but resist their aggressive tactics, and wait until your destiny is clear: why should you send a hostage now…?"

Lady Wu smiled and said, "Even I am resolved."

"…I cannot deny that I still have reservations, but you are most persuasive," Sun Quan declared.

"What Gongjin says is entirely right, my son," Lady Wu insisted. "And hearing and seeing him now… it all becomes clearer. I remember when Bofu first introduced Gongjin to us all those years ago in Shu City: the two were obviously going to be such mighty heroes, with their good looks and strong characters. He is a month younger then Bofu, and when he is here, Bofu is here. To me, Gongjin is a son: to you, Quan, he should be your elder brother. Always treat him so."

Sun Quan bowed to Gongjin and said, "That has always been so."

"But you should not bow to me, Lord Sun!" Gongjin protested.

"I shall do as I please," Sun Quan replied, "and by that I mean that I shall show you respect if I choose and refuse Cao's request if I choose. I am the son of the 'Tiger of Jiangdong' and brother of the 'Marquis of Wu'! Cao Cao will not have my son!"

"Nor anything else, Lord Sun, if I have any say in it," Gongjin said.

Gongjin visited Lu Su after leaving the Sun residence: after explaining the latest development to his dumbstruck friend, Gongjin added, "Lady Wu says that she is resolved, and she is not the only one... this is the affront that I was reluctantly waiting for."

"...So now we must discuss this 'prophecy'," Lu Su replied numbly. "I already understand, but... elaborate anyway while I think."

"...We'll be guilty of it ourselves from time to time, of course... that creation of 'destinies' and 'unintended foreshadowing'," Gongjin said wistfully. "A seed of mistrust... should it be planted and watered...? Is it even what it seems...? Sometimes, Zijing, that mistrust is 'misappropriated with intent' – a devious adviser or hankering toady might sow that seed to reach some 'necessary goal' of theirs... Yuan Shao's advisers excelled at it... and right now I believe that we are the victim of such a thing."

Lu Su hummed thoughtfully.

"Xu Gong was not the first man to sow suspicion about our long-term ambitions, but he gave it greater tangibility when he compared Bofu to Xiang Yu, founder of the Chu Empire," Gongjin continued. "From the moment that Cao and his advisers had that foundation, we were condemned to do one of two things... maybe three. We could continue as we were, pleading our innocence, and be picked off one-by-one, condemned anyway; we could yield everything, allow the south to return to its squalid state and disgrace ourselves in the process, disproving the accusation but ultimately doing no good at the same time; or we could do as I have decided to do... as I have already set in motion... we can concede that we must become what has been prophesied."

"...I understand," Lu Su said. "While I went ahead blindly and spoke of what I believed to be necessity, you realised that we had to be cautious: you were waiting for Cao Cao to force our hand."

"I knew that he would," Gongjin replied. "Yes, I've already begun: I have told my lord Sun Quan that he must be the 'new Xiang Yu' that Bofu was not, that he must plan for a future where he is at the very least a king... for Cao Cao has dictated that he has no other choices save for becoming a slave or a corpse."

"...It must be born of mistrust, and not at all deliberate: you'd think that Cao wouldn't force such a destiny on a powerful man that poses such a credible threat to him," Lu Su suggested. "Cao's own 'destiny' as a 'Crafty Villain' was 'forced on him' by Xu Shao's appraisal, and it's made a minor god of him. Why plant such a seed if it yields such a strong tree...?"

"Perhaps he relishes the challenge of felling it," Gongjin replied. "But he'll have a hard time finding an axe that's sharp enough."

Cao Cao was disappointed to learn that his attempts to gain swift control of the Sun clan of Jiangdong had failed, but he had always considered Sun Quan's submission to be an unlikely outcome; he continued to correspond with Sun Ben and turned his attentions back to the humbled Liu Bei, Bei's protector Liu Biao and the untested Yuan brothers. More weeks and months passed, and more pain was to come for the Sun clan as Sun Quan resumed his tour of the lands that he governed.

****

Sun Quan continued his previously-aborted tour of Danyang Prefecture and travelled eastward to Wu Prefecture; he was greeted at the gates of Wu County City, the prefectural capital, by its current custodian, his late father's aide Zhu Zhi, and the military officers Ling Cao and Lü Meng, who had just returned from the campaign against Li Shu in Lujiang Prefecture.

"...You look so frail, Mister Zhu!" Sun Quan exclaimed. "Must I tell Yifeng that you are poorly and have him visit you...?"

"I am not yet fifty," Zhu Zhi replied. "I have just been ill a few times and had a lot to worry about, that's all. I correspond with Ran all the time, Lord Sun, and he knows how I am."

"...All the same, I have no desire to lose you to 'death by worry'," Sun Quan said. "I have recently decided that I must start behaving like the lord of an independent south, and so I no longer acknowledge the slow processes of the Cao-run Han court. You have been acting as Wu Prefecture's Administrator for far too long without ever being properly appointed: I now correct that error and additionally create you 'Righteousness-supporting General', which will carry additional taxable households as well as military resources that I know you need."

"Do not bestow such things upon me!" Zhu Zhi pleaded.

"In addition, Junli," Sun Quan continued, "I grant you the right to semi-retire."

"...Semi-retire...?" Zhu Zhi exclaimed.

"By that, I mean that you will be able to delegate more of your responsibilities to others and have more time to rest," Sun Quan said. "Yifeng is my friend as well as your son, and I can do this small thing for him; you were a friend and confidante of my father and guide to my brother, so I can do this small thing for you."

"...I can never repay your kindness, Lord Sun!" Zhu Zhi sobbed.

"Repay it by living for a long time, Junli," Sun Quan replied.

"...So what do *I* get...?" Han Dang joked.

"You're entitled to higher rank, some more men and many more resources, Mister Han!" Sun Quan replied. "I intend to reward all four of you – Cheng, Huang, Zhu, Han – for your service to three generations of my clan."

"...Let me show you the city, Lord Sun!" Zhu Zhi said. "See what great progress we are making in these better times that the Suns have brought!"

Gu Yong turned to Zhang Zhao and said, "I studied here in Wu, under Cai Yong, when he was hiding from the 'Ten'... it all seems like such a long time ago, Zibu... so much has changed."

"Now we are a great nation that future Cai Yongs will live in, not hide in," Zhang Zhao replied. "You're right, Yuantan: so much has changed, and for the better."

"Will you be staying long, Lord Sun...?" Zhu Zhi asked.

"A few days... but before I go, I am looking to restructure the army, and want to start here," Sun Quan said. "I have received a lot of information and advice, and one thing that has occurred to me is the need to merge some smaller regiments into larger ones, placing the men under more competent commanders."

"I think that is a fine idea," Zhu Zhi replied.

Lü Meng – who had recently inherited his relatively small militia from his brother-in-law Deng Dang – suspected that he would be one of the men that Sun Quan would strip of his subordinates, and he started to ponder a way to avoid it.

Ling Cao was surprised when Lü Meng visited his home at the end of the day and said, "I feel wretched doing this, Colonel Ling, but... might I borrow some money...?"
"Why...? Have you got a gambling problem now, A'Meng?" Ling Cao asked rudely.
"No, Colonel, no!" Lü Meng insisted. "I was lucky enough to be invited to serve in Lujiang, and I believe that I did well enough."
"Of course," Ling Cao replied. "If you'd performed badly I'd have reported it. But you still haven't explained why you want me to lend you money... or how much."
"...My men are scruffy," Lü Meng said, "and-"
Ling Cao and his son Ling Tong started to laugh.
"It is a matter of honouring my late brother-in-law!" Lü Meng protested. "When my men have problems, I often lend them money to help them, but then I cannot afford to outfit them properly! And Lord Sun values officers that ensure that their soldiers are outfitted grandly, so I want to have a militia that Lord Sun will rate highly and allow me to continue the Deng Dang's work! How can I face my sister and say, 'I am now just a plain captain – or even a soldier – with few or no men, and the reason was that they were scruffy'...?"
Ling Cao and Ling Tong had both stopped laughing as Lü Meng spoke: Ling Tong hummed thoughtfully and said, "I would hate to be placed in such a predicament, Father."
"...As would I," Ling Cao admitted. "You're observant, Lü Meng: I hadn't really given it thought, but yes, Lord Sun does heap praise upon men that decorate their men handsomely. It would be a shame if you lost your men after being so useful, so I'll help you... but I want the money back soon, though."
"You won't regret it, I promise," Lü Meng replied gratefully. "Now I must go to others, like General Yuan, and humble myself further... I have little time. I shall return for the loan later."
Ling Cao and Ling Tong bowed to Lü Meng, who returned the gesture and left the house at speed.
"...He's right: Heaven forgive me for my short-sightedness!" Ling Cao muttered.
"I hope that Mister Lü manages to rescue his commission," Ling Tong said.

Sun Quan stayed in Wu Prefecture and toured the eastern counties for a week, ending his tour where it began – at Wu County City – before a planned move southward to Kuaiji: when he finally returned to the gates of the prefectural capital, he was greeted by Zhu Zhi once again, who said, "Stay a night at least, Lord Sun. You must be exhausted."
"I will," Sun Quan replied, "but I will not go without restructuring the army: I didn't do it before I left here before, but I shall do so now with your guidance."
"...I must confess that I expect the restructuring to be rather different to what might have been the case a few days ago," Zhu

Zhi sighed.

Sun Quan had the various colonels, majors and captains array their men so that he could inspect them: he frowned and mumbled when he passed regiments that were unkempt or dressed poorly and smiled and hawed when he found a man that ensured that his men looked, as he termed it, 'magnificent'. There were few that could match Lü Meng, who had borrowed money from family, friends and superiors and used it to purchase impressive field armour and weapons for every man in his unit: Sun Quan laughed and said, "This is a truly shining example!"

"…Yes, Lord Sun," Zhu Zhi grumbled.

"Such care and attention… such well-fed, happy men with such fine armour!" Sun Quan continued. "You served in Lujiang, I understand, Mister Lü."

"I live to serve you, Lord Sun," Lü Meng replied. "Show me your enemies and I will destroy them."

"…And you only have these few men…?" Sun Quan said with disbelief. "Such a handsome, courageous, virtuous, talented officer needs to have a lot more men, Administrator Zhu!"

"*Aiee*… I-I mean *yes*, Lord Sun Quan, yes, perhaps he does," Zhu Zhi replied.

"Some of these other men could learn something from Lü Meng!" Sun Quan continued. "You'll see to it that their regiments are merged into his and that he receives the necessary funds to equip them: I won't have it coming from his own pocket. Give him a bonus for his work in Lujiang as well."

"…As you command," Zhu Zhi murmured.

"But I understand that you're a bit… 'reckless', Lü Meng," Sun Quan continued as he turned his gaze to the young officer. "I appreciate that you want to make a name for yourself, but I want my officers to be as smart as they're brave."

"I have been enlightened," Lü Meng replied. "My head will be a fuller place from now on, Lord Sun Quan, and my brains will one day match my strength."

"…Magnificent!" Sun Quan said as he moved on to the next man. "Lü Meng is truly magnificent!"

Lü Meng lowered his head and smiled; Zhu Zhi glared at him briefly before he followed Sun Quan.

Sun Quan left Wu County City on the following morning and began the journey to Kuaiji in the southeast. Lü Meng used the bonus to repay all of the men that he had borrowed funds from: his last stop was to the home of Ling Cao, who said, "Congratulations, thank you for keeping your word… and 'well played', Lü Meng… 'well played' indeed."

"Zhu Zhi wants to kill me, I think," Lü Meng chuckled. "He was obviously hoping that I would lose my men."

"Only because he thinks that you're reckless and stupid," Ling Cao replied. "But I wouldn't worry… he thinks the same of me, but I'm still here!"

"I'm trying to learn to think before I act," Lü Meng said. "The most important thing was that I saved Deng Dang's legacy for my sister… and, of course, for myself. Now I must build on it. It was my wits that saved my regiment from disappearing, not my prowess in battle, and Lord Sun's knowledge of my 'reputation for

idiocy' shames me; from this day on, I'm going to read and become a smarter man so that I can outwit my enemies when I can't outfight them."
"I wish I could say the same!" Ling Cao chuckled. "But if you manage it, I commend you."

Lü Meng kept his word and began a quest to become a man of learning: he started to source classic texts from bemused scholars and officials and began to read them intently, studying every word and trying to make sense of their meaning with even more care than the average scholar did. Lü Meng would have Jiang Qin – who had already started to read more expansively – as a peer in that endeavour, and although the two would rarely have the chance to meet in person they kept in communication and shared ideas by way of letters. Zhu Zhi, Lü Fan and others heard of it and scoffed at the notion: their faith in Lü Meng's intellect was non-existent, although that would change in the coming years.

****

34

Lady Wu and Lady Chen worked tirelessly to support Sun Quan and the Sun clan. Sun Jian's widows acted as intermediaries between clan and court whilst providing time to mourn for Sun Ce and Sun Kuang with their respective widows and care for the young children when those widows wanted to mourn; the grief-stricken Lady Wu was taking little time to rest, however, and her health was failing. As the days and weeks went by and Sun Quan obliviously continued his tour in northern Kuaiji, Lady Wu devoted more and more time to court affairs and weeping for her lost sons, and on one foggy, wet morning, her energy was finally spent.

"**Uncle! Uncle!**" Sun Shangxiang cried as she ran into the audience hall of Sun Quan's estate and fell to her knees.

"...What's the matter...?" Wu Jing asked.

"M-Mother... she...she...!" Shangxiang said with teary eyes.

"My sister...!" Wu Jing said as he got to his feet and stumbled out of the hall like a man lost in a haze. "She *cannot*...!"

Lady Wu had fallen to her knees in the courtyard of the mansion, and Lady Chen was unable to help her to her feet; Wu Jing rushed to her side and helped her to her room, where she laid motionless and stared at the ceiling.

"...Sister, why wouldn't you *rest*...?" Wu Jing sobbed. "Must I recall Quan to the capital for-!?"

"Recall him, yes... and... and Ziheng, and Gongjin, and that nice Dong Xi as well," Lady Wu said softly. "He was the one that helped me choose... call them all, brother dear, so that I can hear them promise me."

Wu Jing's head fell forward limply.

"...Please hurry," Lady Wu said. "I must hear them promise."

Wu Jing nodded obediently – as though he was the boy that Lady Wu had supported once again – and fled the room in tears.

"You speak as though your time is running out," Lady Chen noted. "Why...? All you need is food, and rest, and-"

"I... no, Sister, no, my soul is tired, and there is no nourishment for that," Lady Wu replied sadly. "My husband and two of my dear sons have gone now... and I cannot bear to lose anymore. I... it sounds... selfish, I suppose, but... I have been ill for a long time, and I have held on for as long as I can, but I can do no more."

"We all need you!" Lady Chen pleaded.

Lady Wu smiled and said, "I hated you once."

Lady Chen was stunned by Lady Wu's frankness.

"...I hated you, because you were more beautiful and younger than me, and you'd taken my place in my husband's bed," Lady Wu continued. "But... but you loved him as I did, silly man that he was, and you love my children as much as your own: I can see you as a sister, a true sister, and a second mother to my children... to carry on now that I can't do any more."

"Recover your strength, sister!" Lady Chen pleaded.

"I can't, I can't," Lady Wu sobbed. "I... I miss my husband, I miss Bofu, and I miss my Little Marquis; Quan has so many left to help him, but who do my husband and sons have in the afterlife...?"

"Won't you miss us as you miss them...?" Lady Chen asked.

"Of course, but... but I'm dying inside," Lady Wu replied. "I'll go eventually... we all do."

"But it doesn't have to be now!" Lady Chen retorted.

"...It can be," Lady Wu said. "I told you, I've been ill for a long time now, but there was so much that couldn't be resolved. But it will be fine now: you will be 'State Mother Wu' in my place, and see the rest of my tigers grow... I'll be looking down, I promise you that. You won't be alone."

Lady Chen took Lady Wu's hand and wept pitifully.

"...I hope that they don't take long," Lady Wu said. "I'm... so very, very... tired."

Sun Quan bit his hand and yelped when he was told of his mother's sudden deterioration: he and his entourage – which included Zhu Ran, who wanted to provide support – left Kuaiji Prefecture and hurried to Qu'e City, where Lü Fan, Gongjin and the other grief-weary members of the Sun clan and its extended family were waiting.

"She will be fine!" Sun Quan insisted as he strode through his capital's streets with vigour that he did not normally show; he entered his mansion, went to his bedridden mother – who, at her request, had been moved to the hall so that she could accommodate the large audience that she had requested – and knelt beside her.

"Ah, Quan... you're here," Lady Wu said. "I always wonder if I should call you 'Zhongmou'; that always seemed to be 'inappropriate', though I don't know why. Perhaps it's because you're going to be a king one day."

"Mother, why are you acting like this???" Sun Quan pleaded.

"I'm spent," Lady Wu said. "I can take no more grief, Quan: perhaps I'm just weak."

"Say no such thing, Sister!" Wu Jing snapped. "You raised me as though you were my mother! I owe everything to you!"

"...That would be why," Lady Wu sighed. "I've been working for such a long time... not that I wouldn't do it all again. I love you all too much."

Wu Jing covered his face with his sleeve and shuddered violently.

"...Where are all of the men that I asked to see...?" Lady Wu said.

"They're... they're here," Sun Quan replied. "D-Dong Xi, Ziheng, Gongjin, Zibu, Elder Cheng, all of them... they're all here."

Lady Wu turned her eyes to Sun Ben and smiled dryly, saying, "You're here too, then... good."

"You are a mother to me, not just an aunt," Sun Ben insisted through tears.

"...Then you'll do as I say," Lady Wu replied. "...See, there's another one... I feel like I have been mother to the world... it's certainly been quite a few, anyway."

"Why are you doing this???" Sun Shangxiang cried. **"Why are you dying???"**

"...I don't know," Lady Wu replied. "But it is my time... and that is that. You'll all be fine, as long as you listen to me and answer... as I wish you to."

"Let us know your will and we will heed it," Zhang Zhao said.

"...Good," Lady Wu said. "I haven't much to say: I just want you all to promise me that you will help my son to govern Jiangnan. That's all."

"Jiang*nan*...?" Qin Song prompted.

"The south... will be independent now," Gongjin said with difficulty. "All the lands... under the Great River will belong to Lord Sun."

"...Promise me that you will help him... all of you," Lady Wu said as she turned her gaze to Sun Ben once again.

"...I... I promise, dear aunt," Sun Ben sobbed. "I promise you."

Every man present – with the exception of Sun Ben, whose pledge had been made to Lady Wu – turned to Sun Quan and gave their word that they would serve him unyieldingly. Many then started to cry: Lady Wu was a woman that had come to dominate the court as a true matriarch and earn the love of the officials in addition to their respect.

"I... I suppose you could say that I lied!" Lady Wu giggled feebly. "I... I have one more wish: I want you to honour Lady Chen as 'State Mother Wu' when I am gone."

Sun Quan turned to the mortified Lady Chen and whispered, "It shall be so."

"But you are just unwell, Mother!" Sun Yi protested. "Not after Dad, and Bofu, and Kuang... Mother, *please*...!"

"You boys, you're all men now, and Shangxiang is old enough to marry... so I have been there for you when you needed me, no matter how many times I nearly couldn't be," Lady Wu said. "I am choosing... so many times, it was nearly forced on me... and now I choose. You can all go now, gentlemen... I'd like to spend some time as a family now. That would be... so very, very nice."

The emotional officials withdrew one by one: Lü Fan and Gongjin were among them, but Lady Wu said, "Where are you two silly boys off to...?"

Lü Fan fell to his knees and cried, "Lady Wu...!"

Gongjin covered his mouth and sobbed openly.

"...I shall miss you all," Lady Wu sighed. "But to see Wentai again... and Bofu... and my Little Marquis...!"

Lady Wu passed away after many days that were spent in the company of the extended family that she had fought to keep together for more than 30 years. Wu Jing – who was, in many ways, still emotionally dependent upon his sister – lost much of his composure and started to decline as well. The loss of such a strong matriarchal figure was always going to be difficult, but such was the extent of Lady Wu's contribution that it was as though the beating heart had been ripped out of the family unit and the court. Lü Fan and Gongjin – who viewed Lady Wu as a second mother – were both like ghosts for days afterwards, and for the four surviving veterans of the days of Sun Jian, Lady Wu had been a vital connection to those fondly-remembered days, and it was truly like the end of an era. They were not wrong: Sun Quan would never rely on Lady Chen as he had done with his biological mother. The young lord of Jiangdong was now 20 years old, and he would now be taking advice from officials before he consulted blood relatives. A new era had truly begun in the south, and it would not begin auspiciously.

****

35

Cheng Pu and Zhu Zhi remained in close contact generally, but they had one specific concern in the current climate, namely the fugitive residents of the retired general Xu Zhao's estate. Cheng Pu had tried, unsuccessfully, on a number of occasions to convince Sun Ce that attacking the estate was the proper course of action; the argument that always ended the conversation was that Xu Zhao was a respected man and that his only known 'guest' at present, Sheng Xian – the former Administrator of Wu Prefecture – was not a threat. Lady Wu's death had altered the mood at court and opened Sun Quan's mind to new approaches to his problems, and Cheng Pu sought a private audience as soon as the initial mourning period ended.

"...I shall try and listen, Elder Cheng, but please understand that I am very distracted," Sun Quan began. "As you know, I am trying to show my strength as a lord, and I am currently exercising my authority and position by making new laws, reviewing the structure of the armed forces, and... well, you know all this. What can I do for you...?"

"...I believe that we must strike at once, Lord Sun, and eliminate a silent threat," Cheng Pu said. "The rebels and bandits are visible; the tribes are visible; but the arrow that struck your brother down came from a hidden threat, the threat of Xu Gong's surviving acolytes. We hoped that we got them all, but he once enthralled the masses in Wu, so could there be just three...?"

Sun Quan hummed thoughtfully.

"And then, Lord Sun, there is Sheng Xian," Cheng Pu continued. "He's an old friend of Wang Lang, who once menaced your brother in Kuaiji, and Cao will doubtless try to reinstate him as Administrator of Wu as a further affront."

"I have given that role to Elder Zhu Junli," Sun Quan replied. "I don't want to reinstate Sheng Xian."

"Will you have any say in it...?" Cheng Pu asked. "Lord Sun, Cao Cao means us no good. Even if we can trust those that defend him and say that the deaths of Lord Sun Ce, Marquis Sun Kuang and First State Mother Wu were in no way 'foul play', we know that he wants the Suns to be stripped of their power and the south restored to the neglected, boggy swamp that it has always been. Liu Fu undertakes some scheme in Hefei that is starting to look more and more like the constructing of a fortress; Chen Deng sits in Northern Guangling like a roosting carrion bird, waiting for an ally to aid his attacks on Wu from within..."

"...Xu Zhao is highly respected," Sun Quan said. "Mother always avoided saying it in court, but Xu Zhao is a retired general, a state hero like Father, and to attack Xu would therefore be like Yuan Shao's men attacking Father at Yang City."

"I was in Yang City, and I don't agree with that analysis," Cheng Pu retorted. "Wentai never harboured villains as fugitives: I would not be here now if he had. Wentai – your father – fought villains, as all true heroes should. If Dong Zhuo or Lü Bu had need of a place of refuge, they would not have found it in Jiangdong. And if Xu Zhao gave refuge to Xu Gong and White Tiger, he could one day offer refuge to other villains, like Huang Zu, or Liu Biao."

"…So what would you have me do…?" Sun Quan asked plainly.
"Xu Zhao would not be harmed, merely warned," Cheng Pu replied. "What I suggest, Lord Sun, is that we enter the estate and remove Sheng Xian."
"…I would agree to such a proposal if we were giving Xu Zhao an opportunity to turn Sheng Xian over to us first," Sun Quan said.
"With all due respect, my lord, we have tried that before, and our requests are ignored," Cheng Pu replied.
"Try one last time," Sun Quan said. "If Xu Zhao does not comply, then you should do whatever is necessary to remove Sheng Xian as a threat. But please remember, Elder Cheng, that Xu is a respected man, and we risk being branded as villains."
"…Then we will be more discreet," Cheng Pu replied.

Excellency of Works Cao Cao was surprised when his office received a visit by the scholar-official Kong Rong – a descendant of Confucius that had long been a critic of Cao – and Wang Lang, the former Administrator of Kuaiji Prefecture and a recent re-addition to the Han court. Cao Cao dismissed all but his adviser Guo Jia and had the visitors enter his study and sit as guests.
"I have just returned from Cangting, so forgive me if I am slightly weary," Cao Cao said. "What can I do for you, gentlemen…?"
"I should like to begin by saying that I am grateful to you, Excellency, for saving my family from Yuan Tan and giving me a governmental post," Kong Rong said.
"…You have already said these things," Cao Cao noted. "Why must you say them again, Mister Kong…?"
"Because I then recommended my friend Mi Heng to you, and that did not end well," Kong Rong replied.
"…I was intending to apologise to you about that, Wenju," Cao Cao said. "Yes, he upset me and a few of my acquaintances with his unguarded comments, but he was a genius that little deserved what happened to him in Jiangxia. I expected better of Liu Biao, sending Mi Heng to Huang Zu's court as he did when Huang is known for his rough nature, short temper and poor sense of humour. Northern Jing is known for its pool of intelligentsia, so I expected better things."
"…What's done is done," Kong Rong replied half-heartedly; he blamed Cao for what he perceived to be a deliberate effort to shorten Mi Heng's life, but he intended to make a request that could not be hampered by bad feeling.
"So… why have you both come here, then…?" Cao Cao prompted.
"We appreciate that you are a busy man, Excellency," Wang Lang said. "Wenju and I are here to beg for the life of another dear friend and great talent whose very existence hangs in the balance: he might soon be going to the first level of Hell if we do not act quickly to save him from the wicked man that torments him."
"Oh…?" Cao Cao exclaimed. "What wicked man is it that you speak of…? Is he known to me…?"
"He is known to you, as is the imperilled one, Excellency," Wang Lang replied. "The endangered man that I refer to is Sheng Xian, cruelly deposed Administrator of Wu Prefecture in Yang Province, who at this very moment hides within the vast estate of the eccentric retired general Xu Zhao, and, of course, his nemesis is Sun Quan, self-proclaimed lord of the south."

Cao Cao smiled and said, "Wang Jingxing, we're not so far removed age-wise, and we're old hands at the games played in the Han court. You were the student of a man that I respected greatly, Chief of Staff Yang Si, and then you went to serve the wretched Tao Qian as an adviser that was not listened to when it mattered. From there, you went to Kuaiji, where you matched wits and swords with Sun Ce and had to concede defeat, fleeing south to Jiaozhi and seeking refuge with kindly Shi Xie before retiring as a broken man, doomed to be forgotten until I had Kong Wenju and Xun Wenruo ask you to come here."
Wang Lang was morbidly silent.
"And Mister Kong Rong, you enjoy being the descendant of Confucius, but have suffered some poor luck," Cao Cao continued. "Your tenure in Qing Province was plagued by the criminals and cultists that I myself faced when I was exiled to Ji'nan by the 'Ten Attendants' for punishing Jian Shuo's uncle. The hero Taishi Ci – who I have not yet been fortunate enough to meet nor recruit – saved you from the Yellow Turbans, and then I, as you point out, saved you from Yuan Tan when he stripped you of your governor's seal, a privilege awarded to you on the recommendation of Tao Qian's successor as Governor of Xu Province, your friend Liu Bei."
Wang Lang and Kong Rong exchanged nervous glances.
"My point is, you wonder…?" Cao Cao chuckled.
"…Well, yes," Kong Rong replied.
"You were both worth my efforts: Sheng Xian is typically perceived as a mediocrity, and the Yuan clan, though weakened by the death of Yuan Shao, still preoccupies me," Cao Cao said. "Why, then, should I leave my back exposed to the Yuans in order to rescue a man that was deposed by popular uprising and replaced with the late Xu Gong…?"
"The situation in Wu was misunderstood by the people," Wang Lang retorted. "Wu Prefecture was caught up in a power struggle between Tao Qian and the various inspectors and governors of Yang Province: Danyang and Guangling became part of Xu Province, and-"
"And, I argue, that in the case of Guangling it is geographically proper for it to be part of Xu Province," Cao Cao interrupted.
"…It is as you say, Excellency," Wang Lang continued. "But at the time, rightly or wrongly, it was not, and then it was, along with Danyang; Wu was next as Tao sought greater influence, and Sheng Xian could do little without the military support of his superior. And then, Excellency, there were the Yellow Turban Rebellion and the Eastern Pass Coalition against Dong Zhuo: the provincial governor – and, out of obedience, the Administrators, including Sheng Xian – did not participate, which made Sheng unpopular as well. But to his credit, he gave sanctuary to many fine scholars, such as Cai Yong, that the 'Ten' and Dong Zhuo threatened, just as you did when you sheltered the Partisans."
Cao Cao hummed thoughtfully and said, "That is to his credit."
"Xu Gong was an opportunist," Kong Rong suggested. "He exploited people's dissatisfaction and, like any demagogue, cajoled people into ousting a kind, decent man by threatening worse calamities if they left him in place. I confess that he even fooled me, for a time… that is regrettable."
"But now Xu Gong is dead, and Sheng Xian will be next," Wang

Lang said. "He will not be safe on Xu Zhao's estate forever: the Lujiang insurrection is over, and when Sun Quan completes his campaign to pacify his ill-gotten territories, he'll want to destroy Sheng Xian in order to remove potential rivals. Sun makes repeated threats, demanding that Sheng be handed over."

"...But he's hardly a threat to the Suns, is he?" Cao Cao chuckled.

"Sheng Xiaozhang is the rightful Administrator of Wu Prefecture and he is a strong candidate for the role of provincial governor should 'ill fortune' befall Liu Fu as it did Yan Xiang," Kong Rong suggested. "How can he be safe...?"

"...So what do you want me to do...?" Cao Cao asked.

"Give him a government post and guarantee safe passage," Kong Rong pleaded. "If it could be done for me to save me from Yuan Tan, Excellency, then do it for noble Sheng Xiaozhang!"

"...I have no desire to see another good man die," Cao Cao replied. "I could not save Liu Yao or Lu Kang from Sun Ce: I shall do what I can to avoid losing Sheng as well. I have not found my relationship with Sun Quan to be ideal of late, but I will secure the safe passage that you suggest and award Sheng with a suitable post. Was that all...?"

"It was, Excellency," Kong Rong said.

Cao Cao and Guo Jia exchanged bows with the visiting officials before they departed; once Cao and Guo were alone, Cao asked, "What should I do...?"

"Do as you promised," Guo Jia replied. "Sheng Xian is a good man, and saving him will only bolster your reputation and give you someone to put in Wu Prefecture when the Suns are routed."

"...I'll appoint him as a 'Commandant of Cavalry'," Cao Cao decided. "He can be on the front line when we begin our campaign to reclaim the south from the Suns."

"That would be best," Guo Jia replied. "But hurry: he might well have less time than I do."

Pan Zhang had been Magistrate of Yangxian County for many months, in which time he had pacified the bandits and brought more stability to the troubled region. Sun Quan summoned him to Qu'e, brought him to his private study and said, "It is time to start giving you more responsibility, Wengui."

"I'm a county magistrate," Pan Zhang retorted. "What are you making me now...?"

"I'm not promoting you – not yet, anyway," Sun Quan said. "I want you to be a part of my future campaign against Huang Zu."

"...You're preparing to resume the grand campaign against Jing," Pan Zhang realised.

"I am the lord of Jiangdong, yet my father and brother are unavenged," Sun Quan said. "Huang Zu is still alive, and that won't do. I want him dead within the year, and Liu Biao dead within a year of that."

"...And I am to be part of the campaign," Pan Zhang supposed.

"I am creating you 'Magistrate of Xi'an County', Wengui, and stationing you there," Sun Quan explained.

"...Forgive me for asking, but I noticed a lot of activity as I travelled," Pan Zhang said. "Are you making a lot of changes...?"

Sun Quan smiled and replied, "I want a new start now. I want it to be clear that I am my own man, and that I am building a future state. I am marrying Xu Kun's daughter, Lady Xu, and Yuan Shu's daughter, Lady Yuan, in order to-"

"*Lucky so and so*," Pan Zhang muttered involuntarily; he immediately realised his error and kowtowed repeatedly, saying, "I spoke poorly! I am-!"

Sun Quan smiled and said, "I am not offended. Both women will be well treated, for I am not Cao Cao, and it is my duty to give my state more tigers, more leaders for future times. My principal wife Lady Xie remonstrates, and my eldest sister Shangxiang gives me unwanted criticism, but Father had two consorts in his later years, and Bofu would not have been satisfied with Lady Qiao as his status grew: I do nothing that others do not do. And the timing is hardly inappropriate: I must be seen as strong, virile, manly."

"As a lord of a state, that's quite true," Pan Zhang replied. "Did you want me to move to Xi'an at once, Lord Sun?"

"My campaign against Huang Zu begins in the next six to nine months," Sun Quan explained. "I want everything and everyone ready before then, naturally, so yes, I want you settled there in the next two months."

"I'm pretty organised now, so that won't be a problem," Pan Zhang replied.

"...I shall succeed where others have failed," Sun Quan declared. "Huang Zu's death is foretold!"

The former Wu Administrator Sheng Xian's small following received word of Cao Cao's intention to save him by way of a letter from Kong Rong, but the threats still concerned them.

"We must not wait for Cao Cao's official seal of appointment to arrive!" the official Dai Yuan pleaded. "We have to escort you away from here, Commandant Sheng!"

"...'Commandant Sheng'," Sheng Xian chuckled. "Do I really look like a commandant?"

"It saves your precious life from Sun Quan's swords," the official Gui Lan retorted. "Mister Dai is right: we must leave Xu Zhao's estate at once."

"I have been safe here for years!" Sheng Xian said. "What has changed? Yes, I know that Sun Quan now rules, but-"

"Sun Quan is entirely different to Sun Ce," Gui Lan replied.

"Xu Gong's error was leaving the safety of this place," Sheng Xian insisted. "And once I am in possession of a commandant's seal, dare he touch me...?"

"Xu Gong had an administrator's seal, and he still died a wretched death," Dai Yuan said. "Yes, it was initially snatched from your hands, but the Han Regency court ratified his position later."

"Ah, but the 'Regents' were not a legitimate authority, whereas Cao Cao acts for His Majesty!" Sheng Xian insisted. "I will be safe for a while longer, gentlemen. Stop fretting! I said that I would be saved sooner or later, and now it comes to pass!"

"...*Aiee*... But will you live long enough to receive the award when its existence is known...?" Dai Yuan murmured.

Sun Quan's appointed Administrator of Wu Prefecture, Zhu Zhi, learned of Cao Cao's messenger from his agents in southern Guangling and had the man delayed while he consulted his old friend Cheng Pu; Cheng wasted no time responding, and Zhu Zhi summoned another old friend, Han Dang, to discuss it.

"Let me guess," Han Dang sighed. "...'Act quickly'."

Zhu Zhi nodded silently.

"...This isn't ideal," Han Dang said. "Is Demou really sure that this is the right way to go...? I mean, if we never attacked Xu Zhao when he was hiding Xu Gong and White Tiger, won't this look really bad for us...?"

"I admit that I don't like it," Zhu Zhi replied. "I am not attacking that estate... it would cause too much unrest. What I'll do instead, then, is something underhanded but necessary if we are to 'act quickly'. They'll guess that it's us, and it will leave Sheng's allies alive to pose a future threat, but... we have no choice."

"...An assassin," Han Dang guessed; Zhu Zhi nodded silently.

Within a week, Sheng Xian was dead: the suddenness of it shocked Dai Yuan, Gui Lan and the rest of Sheng's loyal subordinates, but deliberately-sown gossip left them unable to ascertain whether the assassin had been sent by Sun Quan – who had the most to gain from it at face value – or Cao Cao, who was famous for doing things that prepared the way for future schemes. Sun Quan confused the situation further when he allowed Sheng's allies and family to leave the estate, granted the officials amnesty and offered them roles in the Wu Prefectural government; Cao Cao then failed to demand an inquiry into the murder, which did little to support Dai Yuan and Gui Lan's firm and shared belief that the Suns were responsible. The majority of Sheng's retinue resisted calls to re-join the Wu administration and fled into the hills; Zhu Zhi kept them under surveillance as best he could, but he was able to do little else without proof as the people of Wu openly showed sympathy for Sheng Xian's fate.

"We're safe," Dai Yuan said to Gui Lan as the two sat together in a makeshift hilltop camp, surrounded by allies; many weeks had now passed since Sheng Xian's death.

"For how long...?" Gui Lan asked.

"For as long as we do nothing," Dai Yuan replied.

"And for how long do we 'do nothing'...?" Gui Lan asked.

"...Until we can do something meaningful," Dai Yuan replied. "Until then, Mister Gui... we wait."

Cheng Pu was reluctantly satisfied with the outcome of his plan: attentions could now turn fully toward Sun Quan's first campaign against Huang Zu. Many wondered if a politically divisive, physically unimpressive young man that intended to command from a distance could possibly succeed where an athletic, charismatic 'born hero' like Sun Ce had failed, but nothing had transpired as anyone had supposed it would thus far, and so no one presumed the outcome as Jiangdong and Jiangxia's armies and navies prepared to meet in battle for the first time in nearly 3 years. The battleground would be Xiakou, where Huang Zu adopted a defensive posture and hoped to salvage victory after a string of humiliating defeats.

****

ACT IV: A STRUGGLE FOR ORDER

36

The unrest in the southeast 'Jiangdong' region of Han Dynasty China was not entirely quelled, but the majority of the bandit gangs, deserter armies, rebels and tribal uprisings had been dealt with, and the way was clear for the 20-year-old lord of Jiangdong, Sun Quan, to resume his clan's long-running feud with the Governor of neighbouring Jing Province, Liu Biao, and his ally Huang Zu, the Administrator of Jiangxia in southeast Jing. It was a popular move: Sun Quan's father – the 'Tiger of Jiangdong', Sun Jian – had been dead for over a decade, and his death at Huang Zu's hands was still unavenged despite repeated attempts by Sun Quan's elder brother and predecessor, Sun Ce.

For some, killing Huang Zu and annexing Jiangxia was reparation for the deaths of Sun Jian and Sun Ce, despite the latter being killed by an unconnected group that was looking to avenge the death of their lord, Xu Gong; the creation of 'Jiangnan' – a strong, economically and militarily independent southern state that encompassed all of the lands to the south of the Yangtze River – would realise a grand dream that Sun Ce and his sworn brother Zhou Yu – who was also known by his courtesy name, 'Gongjin' – had fought for in the 5 years that followed Sun Ce's inheritance of his clan's chieftainship. In those 5 years, Sun Ce – who preferred to be known by his courtesy name, 'Bofu' – took a militia of mere hundreds and built an army and state that covered over a quarter of the empire; it was all for his father's lord – the 'Runan Yuan' clan nobleman, Yuan Shu – in the beginning, but when Yuan Shu fell victim to his own hubris and claimed divine right to the imperial throne, Sun Ce was one of the first to break away and forge his own destiny.

When he died at the age of 25, Sun Ce left no male heir, so his mother, Lady Wu, had argued for her more cautious second son, Sun Quan, to succeed him. Sun Ce's wife, Daqiao, later gave birth to a son, but the decision had been made: Quan was now the one that would continue the story of the Sun clan. That decision was far from universally popular, and it even caused a senior general – the guardian of Lujiang Prefecture, Li Shu – to defy the administration. Sun Ben – who had been temporarily awarded the chieftainship after Sun Jian's death – was now linked to the Han Empire's controversial Excellency of Works, Cao Cao, through the marriage of his daughter to Cao's second son, Cao Zhang; he was additionally known to oppose Sun Quan's appointment, so he was quietly monitored. Cao Cao had been linked to Xu Gong, whose acolytes had assassinated Sun Ce, so he was not trusted at all; Cao was not a man to be crossed, however, since he now controlled the imperial capital, Xuchang, surrounded the young Emperor Xian with his own loyalists and revelled in the recent destruction of his former friend and rival, the powerful 'Runan Yuan' clan chieftain Yuan Shao. Shao's death allowed Cao Cao to begin a long-planned reunification of the fractured empire, starting with the Yuan clan's holdings in the northeast: everybody knew that Cao Cao would one day turn southward, but until then, the Sun clan was free to grow in strength and prepare for war.

Sun Quan summoned his officials to his audience hall and asked, "How go the plans for the final confrontation with Huang Zu...?"

"...They go well, Lord Sun, but there are some reservations about selected personnel," the Chief Clerk, Zhang Zhao, said plainly.

"Oh...?" Sun Quan exclaimed. "Who...?"

"Put simply, Ling Cao is not considered to be the right man for this," the politician Quan Rou said. "He is needed in Wu Prefecture, where he battles the Shanyue to great effect."

"So who should I send, then...?" Sun Quan retorted. "Taishi Ci is very ill, Chen Wu was wounded during the last battle with Li Shu, and Hè Qi, Dong Xi and Jiang Qin are hopelessly preoccupied with bandits and rebels; Ling Cao has chased those accursed barbarians back into the hills, and his name strikes fear into the wretched! How is he not the man to lead the vanguard...?"

"...By all means let him lead the vanguard, Lord Sun, but must he be allocated no cautious second, and must there be a two-stage approach...?" Zhang Zhao asked. "What about Zhou Tai, the-"

"Zhou Tai will be part of the main fleet, as will any other man that is well enough to fight," Sun Quan insisted. "The point here is to shock Huang Zu with the unexpectedly swift approach of the vanguard! His navy will be demoralised!"

"Huang Zu will expect this attack," the official Qin Song suggested. "He knows that we've been moving personnel and materiel into Yuzhang, and he knows that we've defeated Li Shu. Why haven't Lü Ziheng and Zhou Gongjin remonstrated?"

Lü Fan and Gongjin were both present; Gongjin smiled and said, "Ling Cao will just frighten them and then withdraw, Mister Qin. He won't have the men or boats to do much else."

"The moment is here and we must seize it," Lü Fan said. "Cao Cao makes peace with the Qiang warlords and with his son's killer, Zhang Xiu of Wan City: the Yuan brothers are newly burdened with a vast domain, great wealth and a horde of disorganised, selfish, bickering toadies that will do little to help their young masters govern or manage their formidable but headless army. The ever-amusing Liu Bei is in the north of Jing, where Liu Biao uses him to defend against an attack, and that attack can only come from one of two antagonists: Cao Cao, or the Qiang, who would be acting in Cao's name."

"Cao intends to attack Liu Biao...?" the official Xie Jiong exclaimed.

"He seems to be intending it, father-in-law," Sun Quan replied.

"So if we want to take Jiangxia, it must be now," Gongjin said. "The navy is ready, men and ships both; our ground forces are ready as well."

"But *Ling Cao*...?" Qin Song protested.

"He will make an appearance to scare them and then withdraw to join the main fleet," Sun Quan said. "What's wrong with that...?"

There were no more challenges: Sun Quan smiled as the discussions turned to other civil matters and the court session concluded on a cautiously optimistic note.

When Sun Quan retired from the meeting and returned to his main quarters, he was confronted by his principal wife, Lady Xie.

"You can't treat me like this, Lord Sun," Lady Xie said angrily. "I have been a faithful, doting wife, and I have given you an heir. But I hear that you 'consider elevating others if they please you'.

How can you now 'elevate others' when I-!"

"I am, as you have said, your *lord* and husband," Sun Quan interrupted. "Don't vex me, my lady; I am lord of Jiangdong, and as my wife and vassal, your role is to *honour* and *obey me*."

Lady Xie snorted irritably and retreated to the bedroom, where Lady Yuan and Lady Xu were sat quietly.

"...I suppose I will have to start kowtowing to one of you," Lady Xie sobbed.

"It is not our decision to make," Lady Yuan replied. "We are all of us as important as we are told we are."

"...And yet 'Shangxiang' does as she pleases," Lady Xie complained. "The south is riddled with *hypocrisy*."

Gongjin visited his friend Lu Su and said, "It is so very nice to see you, Zijing."

"*Ayah*...! That tone!" Lu Su cried as he ushered Gongjin into his living quarters.

"You've enchanted the young lord with your grand ideas," Gongjin continued. "I've wanted to seize Jing Province – all of it – since I realised that the Han Dynasty was beyond salvation, and that we face a divided empire... but I could never truly convince Bofu that it was viable. Yet you, my friend, have succeeded where I failed. We will soon be launching a massive attack on Jiangxia that is intended as more than revenge."

"I am now to blame for the whole thing, then," Lu Su sighed.

"Lady Wu passed away a few months ago now... I still miss her," Gongjin said suddenly. "She began to see the merits of a 'Jiangnan' state as well. She could see that Lord Sun will one day be a feudal king if we did the right things."

"But 'Jiangnan' isn't 'all of Jing', is it...?" Lu Su noted. "My suggestion – my 'tripod theory' – calls for an intermediate stage where Liu, Sun and Cao are-"

"Here's how it will go," Gongjin interrupted. "Cao Cao may or may not get Northern Jing; we will certainly get the whole of the south, including Nan Prefecture and the four 'independent counties', and we want the north as well. Liu Biao will die, and then we will contend with Cao for Yi and Hanzhong. There will be no 'tripod', Zijing. There will be no Liu Biao. Liu Biao will be a corpse."

"Jing's people will be hostile to the Suns," Lu Su suggested.

"Cao Cao governs Xu Province through his cronies, and he twice laid waste to it," Gongjin retorted. "We'll reason with the people, make them see that we only wanted to have righteous vengeance against Liu Biao and Huang Zu. It's us or Cao Cao, and that's surely reason enough to concede to us."

"...Am I joining this voyage...?" Lu Su asked.

"I'm not sure," Gongjin replied. "I expect so, since you're very much in favour and this is seen by Lord Sun as *your* concept being made real."

"I'd better prepare, then," Lu Su said.

Gongjin left Lu Su's home and returned to his Qu'e residence, where his wife, Xiaoqiao, was waiting.

"I... I don't know what I'm doing," Gongjin said as he sat in his host seat in the living quarters and pulled his *qin* – a seven-stringed zither – toward him so that he could start to play it.

"In what way...?" Xiaoqiao asked.

"...I am agreeing to a plan that is quite possibly lunacy," Gongjin replied as he stared at the *qin*. "I am agreeing to a full-scale naval attack on Xiakou when the tribes, rebels and bandits are far from dealt with. And then there is Cao Cao, who looms in the north like a plague of locusts in human form, intent on gobbling up all of the lands that we've worked so hard to improve... but Liu Biao and Huang Zu *must* be eliminated."

"...So why do you agree to it, if it is 'lunacy'...?" Xiaoqiao asked.

"Because... because I am not in full control right now," Gongjin admitted. "I am still inwardly grieving the loss of Lady Wu, and for a host of reasons beside that I truly loved her as a second mother. She prevented Bofu from killing Wei Teng, and she subtly swayed him from attacking Xu Zhao's estate... we've now done the latter, albeit covertly, and assassinated the fugitive Sheng Xian, whether it was necessary or not. She 'calmed the waters', so to speak, and kept Lord Sun from making a lot of bad decisions... unpopular decisions... that he is now free to make."

"Such as...?" Xiaoqiao prompted.

"He's taken Lady Yuan, Yuan Shu's daughter, as a consort, and that sends dangerous messages to Cao Cao and anyone in our faction that still hates the Yuans," Gongjin explained. "He's taken Xu Kun's daughter as a consort as well, which didn't surprise me, since he's long fancied her; the problem is that he obviously tires of his principal wife, Lady Xie, who is not as desirable to him as Lady Xu, and that probably means that he'll demote her in favour of Lady Xu, which is something that he would not have dared to do while Lady Wu lived because she made the match and rightly admired the Xie family. If Lord Sun demoted Lady Xie, that might upset the Xie clan, and we need their support. But he has no interest in the importance of political marriages. Neither do I, of course, but... but I am not the lord of a third of the empire."

Xiaoqiao nodded silently; Gongjin finally found a place to begin within his vast and imaginative mind, and he started to play a tune on the *qin* that implied optimism and resolved calmness.

"...I will say no more," Gongjin declared. "Lord Sun is flawed, yes, but a greater man than most. Lady Wu ensured his appointment for that very reason: she saw in him a different kind of hero, one that could steer the ship through the storms and take us to the safest port of all... freedom to choose our own fate."

The preparations for the battle with Huang Zu were briefly interrupted by the startling news that Cao Cao's attempts at invading Jing Province had been halted before they had barely started: Cao's army had been lured into an ambush and routed by Liu Bei's militia at Bowang Slope, despite being led by three of Cao's best generals. The Jiangdong officials knew that such a victory – especially one that could be had by a perceived mediocrity like Liu Bei – would embolden the Jing army and give them hope of victory over the Suns as well. The preparations continued regardless.

****

37

Months passed, and the Jiangdong forces began the final preparations for war with the Administrator of Jiangxia, Huang Zu: Huang was startled at the size of the fleet that Sun Quan was sending against him and summoned his officials to his court.

"I thought he had internal worries!" Huang Zu cried.

"He does, but they are apparently less important than coming here," the officer Zhang Shuo said. "It appears that the young, untested Quan – who, I understand, is nothing like Sun Ce in physique or temperament – wants to prove that he outclasses his brother by destroying you."

"I've heard that Sun Quan looks strange," the official Pan Jun said. "I've heard that his legs are short and slightly bowed, and his arms are long and thin; I've heard that his head is abnormally large, his body elongated, and-"

"I don't care," Huang Zu interrupted. "He brings a large naval fleet and anywhere up to sixty-thousand men here, gentlemen, so he can look any way that he pleases. How do I kill him and turn his fleet away?"

The officials looked at one-another but did not answer.

"...Must I ask Kuai Yue to come back here...?" Huang Zu complained. "Liu Bei just repelled three of Cao Cao's generals from Bowang with a bit of kindling; am I now to look stupid and be unable to turn these fools back...?"

"...Whether it is due to arrogance or not, Sun Quan is not rushing," the officer Deng Long said. "We might meet them instead of waiting for them to get here."

"I suppose that I ask because that's what I wanted to hear," Huang Zu replied. "I will move everything we have to the waters to the east of Xiakou and blockade the river; the sight of thirty-thousand men and a host of large and small vessels might bluff them into thinking that I have even more to throw at them later, and that might delay or demoralise them at the least."

"A sound idea, Lord Huang," the officer Su Fei said.

"...No *Gan Ning* today, Mister Su...?" Huang Zu asked snidely.

"You forbade his presence, my lord, and I heeded your command," Su Fei replied.

"Right, well... let's get moving," Huang Zu ordered.

Sun Quan was greeted upon his arrival in Chaisang City in Yuzhang Province by Sun Ben, Sun Fu, Zhou Tai, Xu Sheng and a recovering Taishi Ci.

"You've lost a lot of weight, Ziyi," Gongjin said as he looked at the gaunt, miserable Taishi Ci. "Why do you not stay at home and rest if you are so poorly...?"

"I refuse to leave this world without achieving greatness," Taishi Ci replied.

"You're a legend throughout the Empire, Ziyi," Gongjin noted. "What else do you want to do...?"

"I want to make the south a great nation," Taishi Ci replied. "I want to elevate Lord Sun Quan to the greatest of heights and honour Bofu's friendship."

"There will be other times," Sun Quan insisted. "Do not overexert yourself for the likes of Huang Zu, Mister Taishi Ziyi. Colonel Ling will be the vanguard."

Ling Cao bowed humbly and said, "I can only dream of being the famous hero that Taishi Ziyi is, Lord Sun Quan."

"...Don't take risks," Taishi Ci replied knowingly.

"My son Tong is here, Ziyi, and I intend to show him what a colonel looks like," Ling Cao said as he gestured toward a tall youth with similar features. "At fourteen, he is ready to begin his career, and-"

"And he shall be part of the main fleet," Gongjin chuckled. "I know you, Ling, and you're bound to trip up while you prove yourself to your son if he is with you."

"I know you're a great hero, Father," Ling Tong said. "I have been with you in your recent battles against the tribes and-"

"The Shanyue are not the same as Huang Zu," Ling Cao retorted.

"No, they're not," Lü Fan said. "I hope you remember that at the critical moment, Colonel Ling."

Sun Quan turned to face Xu Sheng and said, "My, what a fearsome, impressive general you always are, Mister Xu Sheng! You are always dressed impeccably, and your men are always so well organised."

"I am a man of fine breeding, Lord Sun, trained in the art of managing men and states," Xu Sheng replied. "I would be a disgrace to my clan if I was nothing less than exemplary."

Gongjin and Lü Fan exchanged weary glances.

"Such confidence," Sun Quan sighed. "How can a man lose when he is so confident...?"

"Easily," Cheng Pu muttered.

Sun Quan turned to Zhou Tai and said, "We have been separated for far too long, Youping. I want you as my head of security."

Zhou Tai bowed slightly and replied, "Allow me to second Colonel Ling in this battle, Lord Sun, and prove my worth as a vanguard officer before I-"

"No offence to you, Youping, but I need no second for this campaign," Ling Cao interrupted.

"And you need prove *nothing*, Youping," Sun Quan insisted. "When you took the Shanyue's arrows and blades that were meant for my flesh at Xuan City, you proved that you are a man that truly understands the role of lord and vassal and does what he must to preserve the state. Like it or not, my life must be preserved for the sake of the state, and you are the only man capable of that feat."

Sun Quan's cousin, Sun Hè – who truly believed that he had failed to protect Sun Ce from 'arrows and blades' when he was the head of security – lowered his head and sighed miserably; the nobleman Xu Sheng was less impressed and scoffed at the notion that Zhou Tai was anything more than a self-serving pirate.

"...I see that you have brought Mister Zhuge and Mister Lu with you as support and counsel, Lord Sun," Sun Ben said as he looked at Zhuge Jin and Lu Su.

"Mister Zhuge is my secretary, and Mister Lu Zijing is a genius that has been long neglected," Sun Quan replied. "Why shouldn't they be here...?"

Sun Ben bowed and said, "I meant that I am glad to see them here, Lord Sun, as I am glad to see all of the men that accompany you. How is Uncle Wu…?"

"…Still poorly," Sun Quan replied.

"I'm sure that he will recover," Sun Ben said. "Cousin Kun, how are you…?"

Xu Kun smiled falsely and replied, "As well as can be expected, Cousin Boyang."

"…Let us dally no more," Sun Quan insisted. "Pan Zhang, Jiang Qin and Dong Xi are on their way with additional forces. Ling Cao will proceed as planned, and the main fleet will follow."

As the gathering started to break up, Sun Fu approached Xu Kun and said, "Did you want to talk, Cousin…?"

"Not to you," Xu Kun replied icily. "Not when you intend to question Lord Sun."

"I wasn't going to 'question Lord Sun'," Sun Ben insisted. "I know what this is about: it is my daughter that is married to Cao Zhang, not me."

Xu Kun grunted irritably and walked away.

"He doesn't trust us, does he," Sun Fu sighed.

"No, Brother, I don't think that he does," Sun Ben replied. "It's up to us to prove that we're trustworthy in this next battle with Huang Zu, which must surely – *surely* – be the last time that we do this…"

Ling Cao's naval vanguard force – which amounted to little more than some small boats and around 2,000 men, many of whom were new to Ling – started down the river from Chaisang, moving north and west toward the region around Jiangxia's current capital city, which was named for the place. The plan was to surprise Huang Zu – who was expected to take a defensive stance – by sailing a fleet to Jiangxia City and threatening it before Huang Zu could mobilise, but what greeted Ling Cao's advance force was enough to turn stomachs: the river to the east of Xiakou was blocked by a seemingly impenetrable fleet of ships and boats, and Huang Zu himself was on the command ship of that fleet and confidently making it known. The attacking vanguard halted, and many men were left dumbstruck and fearful.

"**Dear gods!**" one major exclaimed. "**Where did Huang Zu get all that???**"

"**…He must have moved his entire fleet here,**" Ling Cao said.

"**Or is this just part of it…?**" the major retorted.

"**…Don't demoralise the men with such talk, Major Zhang!**" Ling Cao snapped.

Major Zhang Yi sighed and said, "**Sorry, Colonel. But what do we do…?**"

Ling Cao scowled and said, "**We'll have to attack!**"

"**How can we fight that???**" Zhang Yi exclaimed.

"**I promised my lord that I would clear a path to Jiangxia!**" Ling Cao insisted.

"**We're not even an egg against a boulder of that size!**" Zhang Yi protested.

"**But I promised my lord Sun Quan that I would clear a path to Jiangxia!**" Ling Cao insisted yet again.

"**That was the order if Huang Zu was in Jiangxia!**" Zhang Yi said. "**But he isn't, he's here in Xiakou, on his flagship, commanding an army that must be at least twenty**

thousand, and we're unable to proceed now!"

"...I *will not turn back*," Ling Cao muttered.

What Ling Cao did next was a surprise to both armies, even with his famous reputation going before him: he ordered his men to cut through the enemy forces and led that reckless attack personally.

"What mad foolishness is this???" Huang Zu cried as he watched Ling Cao's small boats advancing toward his flagship at speed; the smaller boats were being capsized and outran with ease as Ling Cao – who apparently knew no fear – closed in on the command ship with the intention of trying to board it.

"...This... this man of Jiangdong is a lunatic!" Zhang Shuo said.

"He's coming for me," Huang Zu fretted as his composure left him. "He's going to get here... **he's going to get here!"**

Ling Cao's actions had completely thrown the Jiangxia navy into disarray; some boats were even attacking each other as orders became confused and the location of Ling's men became harder and harder to ascertain. Ling Cao reached the command ship while his brave elite men provided cover and the rest looked on with disbelief.

"He's a bloody madman," one Jiangdong captain muttered.

"Fire arrows at them!" Zhang Yi ordered. **"Give Colonel Ling some cover!"**

"This man is another Sun Jian!" Huang Zu screamed. **"He will send me to join my sons in the netherworld... but I am not ready yet!"**

Huang Zu moved with speed that defied his age as an instinctive urge to survive took over; he shoved his men aside as he moved to the side of the command ship and lowered himself down to the nearest boat.

"Wait, Lord Huang, stay where you are!" Zhang Shuo protested. **"Don't leave yourself isolated! That's how we lost your son!"**

But Huang Zu was irrational, and he did not listen; he pushed one of the sailors overboard and ordered the remaining crew to take him back to Jiangxia.

"Lord Huang Zu is fleeing!" a nearby captain said. **"We must have been routed!"**

The news spread throughout the fleet like a disease; men abandoned their vessels and turned their boats to flee from a threat that was almost entirely imagined.

"It... it's incredible!" Zhang Yi exclaimed. **"We've won! We beat them!"**

"Ling Cao is the greatest of all of Jiangdong's generals!" a captain cried. **"Ling Cao will deliver all of Jing to Lord Sun!"**

Ling Cao, however, was barely aware of the victory that he had gained via his reckless tactics: he was single-mindedly seeking out Huang Zu, and when he realised that Huang was fleeing aboard a small boat, Ling ordered his men to pursue and claim the ageing warlord's head.

"DON'T LET HIM CATCH ME!" Huang Zu screamed. **"I AM LORD OF JIANGXIA! I AM LORD LIU BIAO'S SWORD AND SHIELD! DO NOT LET HIM CATCH ME!"**

For a time, it seemed that Ling Cao would be the man to finally capture the wily Administrator of Jiangxia and deliver his head to the Sun clan, but fate had other ideas. Su Fei's controversial friend Gan Ning – whose forces had been placed at the rear of Huang Zu's fleet so that they would not be noticed by Huang himself – was placed to aid Huang Zu as he fled from Ling Cao, and despite all of the contempt that Huang Zu had shown him, Gan did just that. Huang Zu was too frightened to realise that he had passed a man that he had banned from being part of his navy; Gan Ning moved his boat to a good position, and as Ling Cao approached, Gan took up his bow, nocked an arrow, and at the proper moment – despite the bobbing of the boat being an obvious impediment – he released his arrow and pierced Ling Cao's skull with chilling accuracy.

"…*Done*," Gan Ning said as Ling Cao's lifeless body fell backwards and hit the water. The effect was immediate; the men that accompanied Ling Cao stared at him motionlessly, as though they depended on him to do anything at all, and Huang Zu's forces were able to regain some momentum.

"**Withdraw!**" Zhang Yi said when he realised that something must have happened to reverse the situation. "**Withdraw, withdraw at once!**"

Ling Cao's crewmen finally regained some sense of urgency, whereupon they pulled his body onto the boat and began a retreat. The Jiangxia navy had not recovered enough to pursue the Jiangdong vanguard, but they provided a shield of vessels to facilitate Huang Zu's retreat. Both sides limped back to their bases, but this time it was the Sun clan that had come out of the battle with the worst losses.

"**Father!**" Ling Tong screamed as Ling Cao's coffin was brought onto the command ship of Sun Quan's fleet; the majority of the officials were silent, as they knew that they might have avoided this likely outcome and spared the young Ling Tong the same fate as the Suns.

"…What happened…?" Sun Quan asked numbly.

"What do you *think* happened, Lord Sun?" Sun Ben retorted. "He decided to charge, like he always did! He charged at Huang Zu's arrow, just like Uncle did!"

"…I've erred," Sun Quan said as he covered his face with his sleeve to hide his shame.

"…This is a disaster," Cheng Pu admitted. "Ling Cao is a beacon of hope, idolised by many of the men… and feared by the tribes."

"But we cannot afford to retreat now," Gongjin said. "We've brought everything we have, and-"

"But the reports indicate that Huang Zu might have a lot more!" Sun Ben said.

"He's blocked the river with thousands of ships, and tens of thousands of men!" Major Zhang Yi said. "We thought we were facing a withered, cowering turtle, Lord Sun, and instead we faced a mighty dragon!"

"*Shut up*," Cheng Pu heckled. "Go and get some rest and stop ruining morale."

"…Sorry, General Cheng," Zhang Yi replied. "I'll go away."

"I have made a mistake," Sun Quan murmured.

"This was our shared plan and our shared responsibility, my lord," Gongjin insisted.

"I am ashamed of myself," Lü Fan admitted. "I should have seen this coming."

"We're all tired from months of relentless mourning," Cheng Pu said. "Don't blame yourself alone, Ziheng."

Sun Quan walked to Ling Tong – who was knelt beside his father's coffin and screaming maniacally – and crouched beside him, saying, "I understand."

"...*Father*...!" Ling Tong sobbed.

Gongjin organised a private meeting for the senior officials and asked, "So do we proceed or not...?"

"And achieve what now...?" Sun Ben retorted. "The navy is completely demoralised."

"We can't let Huang Zu think that we only had Ling Cao," Chen Wu suggested.

"But you're not at your best, and neither is Taishi Ci," Lü Fan said. "We could use Dong Xi, or summon Hè Qi..."

"Hè Qi must stay where he is," Gongjin insisted.

"I will advance," Xu Sheng said. "I defeated Huang Zu's rabble at Chaisang with ease, Lord Sun, and can surely succeed where Ling Cao has failed."

"He didn't 'fail'," Cheng Pu said angrily. "We now know the facts! He chased away an entire fleet with a handful of men! He was another Wentai, another Bofu!"

"...Yes, he was," Sun Quan murmured. "His end was the same as theirs as well."

"The man that shot Ling will become known to us eventually," Cheng Pu said. "When we have his name, we'll find him, punish him and give his severed head to Ling's family as a sacrifice."

"So we must proceed, then," Gongjin suggested.

"Yes," Cheng Pu replied. "We must attack Jiangxia and try to lure Huang Zu out so that we can finish him off. We want him and we want Ling Cao's assassin."

"...Then we are resolved," Sun Quan said. "We advance."

Huang Zu laughed when he finally learned that the man that had 'broken the back' of his naval fleet had died.

"Another 'hero' is denied to them, then!" Huang Zu cackled. "Perhaps my time is not yet done!"

"They're on their way here to the capital," Deng Long reported.

"Let them come," Huang Zu scoffed. "What can they do...? My navy is slowly reforming, and when it does, they will be surrounded. In the meantime, they're demoralised, their vanguard general is dead, and something must have happened to Taishi Ci and the rest of the 'great talents' for Sun to not immediately use them instead of the reckless Ling Cao."

"Don't you want to know who saved you...?" Su Fei asked.

"...Don't you *dare*," Huang Zu growled.

"Is it that you want me to lie?" Su Fei retorted. "Lord Huang, the man that saved you by shooting Ling Cao dead with a single arrow is none other than *Gan Ning*, the man that you so despised and tried to-"

"**Not Gan Ning! Not Gan Ning!**" Huang Zu screamed. "***Again, Su Fei, you employ that faithless creature against my will, and even after you told me here, in this court, that you had 'heeded my command'!***"

"He *saved you*!" Su Fei protested.

"And won't he then sell his services to the Sun clan...?" Huang Zu heckled. "Won't he now go to them and say 'I am the marksman that took your Ling Cao: how much will you pay me?' ...This is the last time, Su Fei, and I mean it! He shot Ling Cao – *if* he shot Ling Cao – because he wants a reputation! He's worked for men and then betrayed them before! I should really have him executed, but I am too soft! **No Gan Ning, you hear...? No more Gan Ning!**"

"If he saved your life, Lord Huang, then he should be honoured," Pan Jun said.

"Not if it was for entirely selfish motives," Huang Zu retorted. "He's a cutthroat to the core, and he'll be my death if I keep him now. Su Fei, heed me: *no Gan Ning*."

"...As you command," Su Fei sighed.

Su Fei reported Huang Zu's words to Gan Ning, who said, "What else can I do? He's sent people to try an' get me mates t'leave me service now. I tell you, I have half a mind t'do what he keeps assumin' and bloody join Sun Quan... as if I could. They'd slice me up as soon as I arrived."

"...I don't know why I say this, my friend... perhaps I have lost my wits as my lord has done," Su Fei replied. "My suggestion is that you do no more for Huang Zu from now on... you leave here now, go somewhere and do something else, and-"

"So I'm 'out', then...?" Gan Ning scoffed.

"...I'll recommend that you're promoted to 'Magistrate of Zhu County' for your efforts: Huang'll agree to that 'cause it puts you a way away from him," Su Fei continued. "Zhu County's close to the border with Yuzhang: go to Jiangdong and offer your services to the Suns. They'll have you for certain."

"Yeah, I'm sure they *would* have me," Gan Ning chortled. "Dead or alive, though...?"

"The Suns will take you," Su Fei replied. "They'll employ you for what you know... and perhaps, one day, they'll employ me as well... who knows...?"

"...So this is it, then," Gan Ning said. "You're stayin' here, an' I'm goin' t'some other place."

"We'll meet again, Xingba," Su Fei promised. "Now go, before Huang Zu's gratitude compels him to order your arrest. I'll petition him tomorrow."

Gan Ning patted Su Fei's arm and said, "You're a real mate."

Within a day, Gan Ning had finally retreated from Jiangxia's capital with his men, just as Huang Zu had long wanted: Gan was on his way to Zhu County, and from there, he would go on to Jiangdong when the moment was right.

Sun Quan's army and navy surrounded Jiangxia City and started to besiege it; the Jiangdong men were badly demoralised after the death of Ling Cao, however, and their efforts were half-hearted. Several attempts were made to goad Huang Zu into fighting outside the walls, but Huang – who had stocked the large walled city properly, and therefore had ample food and weapons – refused all challenges and allowed the Jiangdong forces to exhaust themselves pointlessly. That continued for a week, until a messenger brought a letter from Wu Prefectural Administrator Zhu

Zhi that depressed everybody in the command tent.

"...Junli says that the Shanyue are back again," Cheng Pu said despondently. "He... he asks that we might spare Ling Cao."

"...Of course, he cannot know, Ling Cao's coffin is probably still in Chaisang," Gongjin said. "This will be a terrible way to have to inform him."

"The Shanyue are almost supernatural," Xu Kun complained. "It's like they knew he was dead! They've been starting up in Danyang as well, haven't they?"

"Yes... and poor Uncle Wu is barely coping," Sun Quan replied.

Lü Fan hummed thoughtfully and said, "We're getting nowhere here... so perhaps... we should withdraw."

Cheng Pu nodded agreeably.

"...This is a disappointing start to realising our plan, Zijing," Gongjin said as he looked at the miserable Lu Su.

"It cannot be helped," Lu Su replied. "We can go back, rebuild the army and return when Huang Zu is older, weaker and least expects it."

"What choice do we have...?" Gongjin wondered.

"Then we shall withdraw," Sun Quan said. "Inform the other officers at once."

And so another attempt at destroying Huang Zu had been forced to end abruptly: this time it was for the loss of a valued officer, Ling Cao, as much as it was because of the unwanted activities of the Shanyue tribes and other troublesome factions. Sun Quan's forces quietly sailed back to Jiangdong, leaving the defence of the western borders in the hands of Pan Zhang, Jiang Qin, Xu Sheng, Sun Ben, Zhou Tai and the weakened Taishi Ci; every man knew that it would be some time before they would be able to go to Jing Province again, and that they now had a rival claimant in the form of the Han's Excellency of Works, Cao Cao.

****

38

Liu Biao was elated when he heard that both of his enemies – Cao Cao and Sun Quan – had been thwarted in their attempts to invade Jing Province.

"I survive," Liu Biao chuckled. "I am still here."

"But by attacking Bowang, Cao Cao shows that he intends to relieve you of your role as Governor of Jing Province," the adviser Kuai Yue said. "The Suns attacking Jiangxia are no surprise."

"But their incompetence is," the adviser Wang Can suggested. "They put a man called Ling Cao in the vanguard… a man with a reputation for fearless stupidity."

"So Sun Quan is not the hero that his brother was," Liu Biao said. "Perhaps the time has come to turn that situation around, then!"

"We can certainly try," Kuai Yue replied. "At the worst, we'll be repelled, but there's certainly no harm in trying. Ask Huang Zu to start pressurising Chaisang City and other key places in Yuzhang Prefecture, and we'll see what happens."

"…And Cao Cao…?" the politician Huan Jie prompted.

"That's more worrisome," Kuai Yue replied. "He intends a proper invasion when the Yuan brothers are defeated; there's no doubt about that."

"What should I do…?" Liu Biao asked.

Many of the politicians and advisers exchanged glances; there was a growing belief that surrendering to Cao Cao's regime in Xuchang was the only way forward, but most supposed that Liu Biao would never willingly cede Jing Province. Some hoped that he could be compelled to do so; others hoped that his age and poor health might ensure that it would be left to others to decide.

Another man whose health and age were starting to take their toll – Sun Quan's maternal uncle, Wu Jing – retired to his bed as a broken man whenever a day of fighting the Shanyue tribes of Danyang Prefecture had finally come to an end. He was forced to fight battles with Shanyue on an almost daily basis, and as Administrator of Danyang, he often had to take to the field personally as a sign of strength; he had been able to do that until his sister, Lady Wu, passed away, but now it was too much for his weary soul to manage. His visible weakness quickly led to more problems, which in turn led to an accelerated deterioration of his health, and before long, Danyang Prefecture was enduring worse problems than Wu, Kuaiji or Yuzhang.

"My brother would often complain that the constant interruptions that prevented his destruction of Huang Zu would one day drive him insane, and now I truly understand what he meant," Sun Quan said to his packed Qu'e court. "What is the quickest way to resume our conflict with the masters of Jing Province?"

"We must defeat the Shanyue yet again, and we must put an end to the rebellions," Zhang Zhao replied. "We must defeat the bandits, and-"

"Forgive me, Mister Zhang, but I tire of this repetition," Sun Quan said. "Every single day I hear these words! How do we defeat them *properly*?"

"That's like asking for it to rain when it suits us," the official Zhu

Huan suggested. "There will always be men that oppose the regime, so there will always be rebels; there will always be men that prefer to take instead of earn, so there will always be bandits; some of these lands once belonged to others and so long as those others are plentiful in number, embittered and free to act, there will be tribal uprisings and raids. In every case, Lord Sun, there is a way to reduce the frequency or severity, but that is as good as it gets."

"...So what do we do to 'reduce the frequency and severity'...?" Sun Quan asked.

"To dilute rebellions, have good government and eliminate corruption, and also reduce tribal raids and banditry," Zhang Zhao said. "To reduce the numbers of people that resort to banditry, ensure that everyone has what they need and reduce the number of tribal raids. To reduce the tribal raids, bring the wrath of Heaven down upon the wretches and chase them back into their hillside lairs!"

The vast majority of the officials murmured agreeably.

"Is there not something that we can offer to the tribes in order to win their trust and 'bring them into the fold'...?" the young scholar Lu Ji asked.

"You depressed Lord Sun Ce with your whimsical lamentations and twisting of the words of Confucius to create false sympathy for the barbarians, Lu Ji, but no more, you hear...?" Zhang Zhao heckled. "Time and again, we extend the hand of friendship, and in exchange they raid our villages to steal women and food! The only thing that they understand is *violence*! It even determines their choice of leaders, rather than intellect or-!"

"Let's keep to the point," Qin Song suggested. "And the point, gentlemen, is that the same old problems plague us and we have too many other worries. I can see no other solution but the one we have always resorted to, however: we must send our best officers to the trouble spots and smash the troublemakers."

"I should go back to Shicheng, but I'm needed in Lujiang, to bolster the defences, and then I want to go to Haihun and oversee restoration of the supply chain," Cheng Pu said thoughtfully. "Shicheng's really lost discipline since I left, sad to say..."

"Administrator Wu Jing reports a growing problem there, and with all three maladies," Zhang Zhao noted.

"I volunteer to go to Shicheng County in Danyang," Huang Gai said. "I have a similar disciplinary system to Cheng Demou and can replace him effectively."

"A sound idea," Sun Quan replied.

"And there are enough men in Yuzhang that we don't need to worry about one or two going elsewhere," Zhang Zhao said. "Wuhu, also in Danyang, is also problematic: if Taishi Ci – who once used the hills of Wuhu as his base – were well enough, I'd say that he should go, but it will need to be another exemplary figure, or maybe two that, when combining their efforts, match Taishi's common appeal."

"Send Xu Sheng and Jiang Qin," Zhu Huan suggested. "Xu Sheng has a fine team of disciplined archers and a noble air that will reassure the populace of our seriousness, and Jiang Qin is a former pirate that can reach out to the people that Xu Sheng will naturally offend. Mister Wu Can should accompany them and provide additional administrative support."

"I agree to it," Sun Quan said. "Send them at once."

"But what about the problems in Wu...?" Qin Song asked. "We can't ignore them."

"I, Tong, want to confront this threat for you, Lord Sun."

All eyes turned to the white-robed Ling Tong.

"You haven't got the experience that your father had," Cheng Pu suggested. "It would truly be fitting, but how can you take on such a burden...?"

"I used to follow him secretly, Elder Cheng," Ling Tong replied. "I have seen how Father fought the Shanyue."

"Then you'll know not to do the same, young man," Zhang Zhao said. "We must end this unfortunate tradition of losing men that run at swords!"

"There's no need to be heartless," Sun Quan said. "I believe that young men like Ling Tong, Lu Ji and Lu Xun should be given a chance to show what they can do."

"But he can't lead the fight against the Shanyue of Wu!" Zhang Zhao protested.

"I'll assign some of his father's men to him, and make him 'Senior Major'," Sun Quan replied. "Zhu Zhi, Han Dang and Lü Meng will be there to support him as he grows into the role."

Ling Tong bowed low and said, "Thank you, Lord Sun!"

Zhang Zhao looked to Lü Fan, who smiled and said, "I cannot see a problem with that idea, Mister Zhang Zibu."

"I'm sure that the Shanyue won't either!" Zhang Zhao snapped.

"I will match them as Father did, Mister Zhang," Ling Tong said. "You have my word."

"...You are quite serious," Cheng Pu noted. "I think that you may surprise us all, Major Ling."

"What about relieving Uncle Wu...?" Xu Kun asked.

"Go and see him," Sun Quan replied. "Act as his second, Cousin Kun, and do what you can to improve his morale. We're doing everything that we can to help him... make him understand that so that we don't lose him as well."

Ling Tong escorted his father's coffin back to his birthplace – Yuhang County in Wu Prefecture – and mourned the loss of Ling Cao with his family and several guests, which briefly included Sun Quan. Ling Tong then travelled to the prefectural capital, Wu County City, where he was warmly received by Administrator Zhu Zhi, Han Dang and Dang's son Zong.

"We all wear white articles for your father," Zhu Zhi said.

"I am honoured and touched, Administrator," Ling Tong replied.

"Huang Zu'll answer for the death of your father, just like he'll answer for killing Sun Wentai," Han Dang promised. "You'll have your moment."

"Until that day, I want to do my father's work in his stead," Ling Tong replied. "I am here as a senior major, tasked with aiding your pacification of the Shanyue. I will do as I am asked as I learn my role properly and earn the right to one day be a colonel."

"The fact that you are aware that you are not born an officer is the best start that you can have," Zhu Zhi said. "You will have our full support."

Sun Quan's cousin Xu Kun finally travelled to Wu Jing's home in Danyang's prefectural capital, where he was gratefully received by the ailing administrator.

"My sons, Fen and Qi, are taking some of the work on my behalf, even though they are neither of them born governors," Wu Jing explained. "So there was no need for you to come here, Nephew."

"I want to help you somehow," Xu Kun protested. "You look so frail, Uncle!"

"...I see what ailed my poor, dear sister now," Wu Jing replied. "She was so overcome with grief at the loss of so many loved ones. When Wentai died, I felt so guilty... time and again, Nephew, I remonstrated with that difficult man, begged him to be more careful, to preserve his life and spare my sister the heartache of being a widow and having to raise a family alone... I wondered, time and again, if she should remarry, as so many widows do, but she fought on alone, relying on the loyalty of Wentai's allies, and Bofu's great promise, and I confess that I was so... angry... at Wentai for forcing that poor woman, after all of her early woes, to go through all that. In a way, I'm still angry."

Xu Kun frowned and said, "I don't understand."

"...I suppose it sounds like I am rambling," Wu Jing replied. "But Wentai created the path that led to Bofu being forced to become the chieftain of a clan with growing prospects; that boy's skill took us from slaves to masters in five years. Cao Cao was right to fear him! ...But then... was Cao also right to want my nephew dead...?"

"You suspect that Cao Cao was behind Bofu's assassination...?" Xu Kun said.

"It wouldn't surprise me," Wu Jing replied. "I often wonder if Kuang's sudden deterioration and death, and perhaps my dear sister's malady were the work of cruel outsiders... and then I think again and decide that it is simply Heaven's will, and that the whys and wherefores don't really matter in the end. What matters is the outcome, the consequences of the event, and the deaths of Wentai, Bofu and poor Kuang in fairly quick succession were more than my poor sister could stand. She was ultimately killed by grief... and I am being killed by the same."

"Don't talk like that!" Xu Kun pleaded.

"...She often spoke of being 'tired'... *I* am 'tired', Nephew," Wu Jing admitted. "I have had enough of it all... all of the intrigue, the wars, the suffering, the deaths of loved ones... the latest news is something that I am glad my sister was spared."

"What news...?" Xu Kun asked.

"...A messenger sped here ahead of you, to say that Lord Sun Quan's – my nephew's – little boy, his heir, has suddenly died," Wu Jing replied.

"What???" Xu Kun exclaimed. "*When? How*??? But I only just left Qu'e, and-!"

"I lost a few children when they were young; even my dear sister, for all of her healthy offspring, had losses that she deliberately withheld from Wentai because she knew that it would harm him," Wu Jing confessed. "Is that not why we try not to properly name our new-borns or become too attached to them...? There are a lot of things out there to kill a child besides famine and war, Kun..."

"...I've lost one myself, so I know that, Uncle," Xu Kun replied. "I just... I just supposed that Lord Sun Quan – my cousin – is the son

of Sun Jian, and the brother of Bofu, and the lord of Jiangdong, with access to the best doctors, and that he would somehow..."
"...Be above such things...?" Wu Jing chuckled miserably. "His flesh is as fragile as anyone else's: even His Majesty is not invincible, and he is the Son of Heaven! Quan has lost his father, mother and two brothers in the space of eight years... just as I have lost a brother-in-law, a sister and two nephews... and now *this*... I can bear to lose no more, Nephew... I really can't see any more suffering, caused or not."
"You want to retire...?" Xu Kun asked.
"...But I cannot, not while my nephew, Lord Sun Quan, needs me," Wu Jing replied. "I must toil as my sister did, until I can toil no more... that's the way of things. I must go back to Qu'e now to grieve for my nephew's heir. You must go as well."
Xu Kun nodded soberly.

But while the Sun clan mourned the loss of a child, Liu Biao and Huang Zu exploited the continued fragility of Sun Quan's regime and attacked the settlements in Yuzhang Prefecture that were closest to the border with Jiangxia. That, in turn, led to a rebellion by the frustrated populace that Yuzhang's Administrator, Hua Xin, and the existing defenders could not deal with alone. An urgent request was sent to Qu'e, and the exhausted court had no choice but to respond at once.

****

39

It was left to Sun Quan's Chief Clerk, Zhang Zhao, to announce the latest calamity to befall the region.

"A pair of bandits that are going by the names 'Chaisang Qin' and 'Demon Lü' have stirred up a rebellion in several counties across Yuzhang Prefecture," Zhang Zhao explained. "Once again, Hua Xin's leadership has proven to be ineffective: I wonder what might have happened if there weren't so many of our officers there!"

"We have to kill these idiots," Xu Kun said.

"It would be better to capture them," the official Zhu Huan suggested. "Killing bandit leaders for egregious banditry is one thing; when they are masquerading as rebel leaders and playing on the oft-justified frustrations of the common people, they should be shown mercy."

"I agree," Zhang Zhao said. "We must send a man that can reach out to them, an exemplary officer that-"

"But I am running out of such people to send, even with all of my talents!" Sun Quan despaired. "Taishi Ci is still ill, Chen Wu is still far from ready to manage such a great task, Zhou Tai, Dong Xi and Hè Qi are all preoccupied, Ling Cao is *dead*, and I've just had to reassign Xu Sheng and Jiang Qin to Wuhu!"

"It's the last of those men, Jiang Qin, that is the man to use," Zhu Huan suggested. "A kind, frugal former pirate will soon show the rebels that they have misplaced their faith."

"Zhu Huan is right, Nephew," Wu Jing said.

"But you're ill and need great assistance to pacify Danyang!" Sun Quan cried. "How can I protect your precious life and spare us more pain when...!"

Sun Quan's voice failed; Sun Yi smiled at Wu Jing and said, "It's been a difficult few weeks, has it not, Uncle...?"

"I will be fine," Wu Jing insisted. "Send Jiang Qin to deal with the rebellion in Yuzhang."

"I must concur," Zhang Zhao said.

"As do I," Gu Yong said. "Xu Sheng can manage at Wuhu."

"...If Gu Yong is compelled to speak without prompting, then it must be the right course," Sun Quan noted. "Very well: have Jiang Qin go back to Yuzhang."

"The order shall be sent at once," Zhang Zhao promised.

Sun Quan retired to his main quarters, where one of his servants awaited him.

"...How is my lady wife...?" Sun Quan asked tonelessly.

"Which of your wives do you mean...?" the servant replied.

"The...! ...The one that has just *lost a child*, of course!" Sun Quan said angrily.

"We have all lost the child," the servant suggested. "It is a shared pain, Lord Sun."

Sun Quan's eyes wandered as he considered the point; he could hear a chorus of sobbing emanating from the bedchambers, and he realised that Lady Xu and Lady Yuan were expressing as much grief for his lost child as its mother Lady Xie.

"...Who else might I have meant...?" Sun Quan asked as he returned his gaze to his fearless servant.

"Your lordship currently favours Lady Xu, so it might be expected that she would be enquired after first," the servant replied.

"It is that obvious...?" Sun Quan asked pointedly.

"Your lordship is a man that shows his emotions," the servant replied. "Lady Xie has quite obviously fallen from favour, and so it was not my first thought that you would ask her well-being. I enquired nonetheless."

Sun Quan's eyes steeled, and he said, "Do you feel that you address me inappropriately when you speak to me thus...?"

"I am only stating the facts," the servant replied. "If the facts are uncomfortable things, then as a servant I should be instructed by my superiors as to what I must not say."

Sun Quan's eyes wandered for a second time.

"If it is preferred that the household makes no mention of Lady Xie's demotion, I shall speak no more of it," the servant continued. "The most important thing, Lord Sun, is that your will is known, understood and obeyed."

"You... are perhaps wasted as a low-level servant," Sun Quan said.

The servant bowed and said, "I seek nothing else but to serve you, Lord Sun, in whatever capacity you see fit."

"...Your name is Gu Li, is it not...?" Sun Quan prompted.

"It is," the servant Gu Li replied.

"You are not closely related to Gu Yong, a famous official in my service...?" Sun Quan asked.

"Alas, no," Gu Li replied. "His path and mine diverged long ago... so although we share distant ancestry, we share little else. I would give anything for half of the wits in such a man's head, but I must make do with my own."

"...You're now my Senior Attendant," Sun Quan declared.

Gu Li fell to his knees and kowtowed, saying, "Honesty alone cannot warrant such an honour, Your Lordship! Find another man for such a place!"

"My word is final," Sun Quan replied. "Your first task is to find another good man to take your current role. I must have good men with brains in their heads around me, so that I can survive and finish what my brother started."

Gu Li bowed humbly and left the room; Sun Quan went to the bedchambers, looked at his grieving wives and said, "You are all doing my son and the clan a great service; were it that I could cry, but... my eyes have run dry from so much previous misery. Thank you for doing what I want to but cannot do."

"...We need no thanks," Lady Xie insisted. "But Husband... *lord*... why has Heaven punished us so...?"

"All men and women know suffering, be they righteous or otherwise," Sun Quan retorted. "It is not 'punishment', Lady Xie... it is a *test*, and we shall pass it. There will be other heirs in time... and this state will continue."

Lady Xie turned her gaze away from her husband; she knew that the future heirs that her husband spoke of were unlikely to be born to her and that her status was likely to lower further in the coming years, despite her noble roots. The fact only compounded her grief, and she cried for herself as well as her lost son.

Jiang Qin received his orders to relocate to Yuzhang and said to his colleague Xu Sheng, "You'll be alright, o' course, but I just

wanted to say, before I left, that it's been an education workin'
with you, and that I hope to be back soon so's we can get
Danyang back to normal."
"You are most gracious," Xu Sheng replied falsely.
"...I try to be," Jiang Qin said miserably. "I'm going to go and
prepare for my departure now."
"Don't let anything keep you," Xu Sheng replied.
          Jiang Qin retreated to his personal tent in the battle
camp and started to pack; the official Wu Can entered the tent as
he worked and said, "The way that Xu Sheng treats you is most
unpleasant, I must say."
"Ah, don't fuss about it," Jiang Qin replied. "He's like that to
everyone that wasn't born above him; he'll change with time."
"Will he...?" Wu Can chortled. "How long must we wait...?"
"He's a hero, so we'll wait as long as we must," Jiang Qin replied.
"...You're a hero as well, Mister Jiang," Wu Can suggested. "Look
at how you live so frugally despite all of the wealth that Lord Sun
Quan grants you! Look at how you're packing your own things
even though you have servants to do it for you! Look at how you
still know the minds of the people and have lost no sense of
reality as Xu Sheng has!"
"He's lost nothing," Jiang Qin replied. "He was born into a world
that he still lives in, inside, in his soul, even though he's here in
the south. But one day, something'll happen that'll make him open
his eyes properly. Until then, I'll just carry on being me and
talking to him respectfully, as he deserves."
"...Will your entire staff be going...?" Wu Can asked.
"Not everyone," Jiang Qin replied. "I intend to come back here
soon, so-"
"*Soon*...?" Wu Can exclaimed. "Those bandits have riled up four or
five counties, Mister Jiang! How can you hope to be back 'soon'...?"
"...I can hope!" Jiang Qin said. "But I'll leave the officials where I
can and take the officers, so Xu Wenxiang has more help to-"
"*Ayah*... I can't believe it!" Wu Can cried. "You even refer to Xu
Sheng by his courtesy name! Does he extend the same politeness
to you...?"
"Not yet," Jiang Qin replied. "But things change. Once, Mister Wu,
I was a pirate, a worthless, evil dog of a man, but now I have
talented, respectable men like you calling me a hero for thoughts
and actions that require no effort, and I'm merrily going about and
making bad men rethink themselves. Never underestimate a
man's ability to change."
"In the case of that obnoxious man, I hope you're right, Mister
Jiang," Wu Can said.

The veteran Huang Gai arrived in his new office in Shicheng
County City, where he was greeted by a group of nervous civilian
officials that expected the worst.
"I didn't get much of a greeting at the gates," Huang Gai said to
the man that he knew to be his future deputy. "An infantry captain
and a large group of soldiers is no way to greet the acting
magistrate, Mister Bi."
"We were busy trying to get affairs in order after the last Shanyue
attack!" Mister Bi replied. "They attacked Wide Hill Village, and-!"
"But the soldiers should then be patrolling, and not greeting me in

large numbers," Huang Gai retorted. "And what was the Shanyue's impact on civil order…?"
The officials looked at one-another nervously.
"You all know who I am," Huang Gai continued. "I'm very well known, I think; so you knew that my coming here was ominous for anyone that hadn't been doing their jobs properly."
"I assure you that everybody works *very hard*!" Mister Bi replied emphatically. "I ensure discipline, and any man that does not do his fair share does not keep his job!"
"…So what is the cause of the administrative work being left undone?" Huang Gai asked for a second time.
"The… the need to manage the damage done by the Shanyue!" Mister Bi insisted. "I had to allocate men to the affected places, and there were no others that could do their work for them!"
"But if nobody ensures that taxes are collected, work completed, workers paid, crimes punished and food properly distributed, how can we avoid other problems arising…?" Huang Gai asked.
"The problems are temporary," Mister Bi protested.
"I shall ensure that they are, and that there are contingency plans in future," Huang Gai replied. "It isn't the case that the Shanyue or Fei Zhan's bandits just appeared a few days ago, is it…?"
Mister Bi lowered his head and closed his eyes.
"…Mister Gan, Mister Teng, you will now be in charge of improving efficiency," Huang Gai said as he looked at two smartly-dressed men that stood to Mister Bi's left. "Whatever needs to be done to ensure that other things are done, do them."
Mister Gan and Mister Teng bowed humbly.
"…I will be organising my temporary residence: I want a full report on *all matters* by the end of today," Huang Gai continued. "There will be a positive outcome: I won't let the region succumb to incompetence, corruption or wilful neglect."
Huang Gai turned and walked away without bowing; Mister Bi turned to Mister Teng, who said, "We'd better make sure everybody gets their act together, or Old Huang will probably torture us."
"…I'd hoped that we'd seen the last of all this when Old Cheng went," Mister Gan muttered.
"Give him his report," Mister Bi ordered. "I'll do what I can to convince him that we're trying."

When Huang Gai reached his appointed residence, his eldest son Bing said, "Why did you appoint those two local men as the managers…?"
"A man must sometimes make a strong statement, or he will not be heeded," Huang Gai replied. "I know those men are little better than the rest… but I am giving them one last chance. If they do not use that chance to do better, I will make memorable examples of them."

Days later, Sun Quan read the initial reports from Danyang and sighed, saying, "No wonder Uncle is ill. The counties are managed by idiots."
"Xu Sheng and Huang Gai will sort out Wuhu and Shicheng," Zhang Zhao replied. "We can then replace the incompetent and corrupt people in other counties and start rebuilding confidence in our ability to govern."

238

"...I should have made Uncle rest before he returned to his work," Sun Quan fretted.

"Wu Jing is a stubborn man that wants to do his part for the state," Qin Song said. "I honestly don't believe that he could be kept from returning to his post, Lord Sun."

"...I know that I shall lose him soon," Sun Quan murmured. "I... I know it."

"...Lord Sun, I didn't want to raise the matter of eastern Kuaiji, but I must," Zhang Zhao said. "That region – Shanyin in particular – cannot hope to recover from the problems that it suffers without sending more capable men to the region."

"...But who can I send...?" Sun Quan chuckled desperately. "Who have I got to send anywhere...?"

"Forgive my impertinence, Lord Sun, but I request that I be sent to be the Magistrate of Yuyao," the official Zhu Huan said. "It will then be possible for Mister Zhu Ran – whose natural talent makes me proud to share ancestry with him – to become Magistrate of Shanyin and deal with the problems there."

"...You're a clever man," Sun Quan said. "With Gongjin newly returned to Ba Qiu to train our navy and Ziheng inspecting the barracks in Lujiang, I have need of you here, Mister Zhu Xiumu."

"Zhang Zhao, Qin Song, Lu Su, Quan Rou and Gu Yong are here, as each man has at least as much in his head as I have in mine," Zhu Huan replied. "You should also look to Lu Ji, Bu Zhi and Lu Xun in future times, to name but two: I assure you that I will not be missed for long."

"...I reluctantly accede," Sun Quan said. "Mister Zhu Huan, you are now appointed Magistrate of Yuyao County. I will have Zhuge Jin give you the proper documents for you to claim the seal from Zhu Ran and for he, in turn, to receive the seal of office for Shanyin County. I entrust to you the right to act in my stead without first consulting me, since you would be advising me were you here: do whatever is necessary to restore order, but keep me informed of your actions."

"I, Huan, will do as you command," Zhu Huan replied.

Sun Quan turned to Bu Zhi and Lu Su and said, "You two will have to speak more often now: I have need of your wits."

Bu Zhi and Lu Su replied humbly and vowed to do all that they could; Zhu Huan was on his way to Yuyao County by the end of the day, and another problem was halfway to being resolved.

****

40

Jiang Qin's arrival in Yuzhang Prefecture's capital Nanchang was met with relief by the defenders and indifference by the bandit leaders that had forced his return.

"So where are 'Chaisang Qin' and 'Demon Lü' now…?" Jiang Qin asked of the weary prefectural administrator, Hua Xin.

"Goodness knows, Mister Jiang," Hua Xin replied. "But they heard that you were coming and had a man come here to say 'Our reinforcements are welcomed'."

Jiang Qin smiled and said, "Nice taunt. But I won't be going back to my old ways, and neither will my men. And if these two rascals 'Qin' and 'Lü' don't repent, they'll die."

"They're popular," Hua Xin noted. "Time and again, I've been heckled, told that I am a mediocrity that 'failed to pacify the tribes' and so on and so on. I feel useless."

"Don't," Jiang Qin said. "We'll turn this around. My job's to deal with the rebels while Mister Pan Zhang deals with its cause."

"Yes… Liu Biao and Huang Zu's attacks on Xi'an," Hua Xin replied. "The last campaign seems to have emboldened that vile pair."

"Let them enjoy their little victories," Jiang Qin said. "We still have a few surprises left for them. Ling Cao will be avenged, and then Lord Sun's father: Heaven demands it."

Sun Ben left his post and travelled to Xi'an County to see how Pan Zhang was faring against the raiding parties that Liu Biao was sending to the area.

"Keeping an eye on me, are you…?" Pan Zhang joked as he greeted Sun Ben at the city gates.

"You're a favoured man, Mister Pan," Sun Ben replied. "I imagine that you're more likely to be asked to keep an eye on me."

"To what do I owe the honour of your visit…?" Pan Zhang asked as he led Sun Ben through the city.

"I just defeated a small bandit army and thought that I might be of use here rather than go back to my base," Sun Ben explained.

"My thanks, but I won't need any help," Pan Zhang insisted. "Liu Biao's relying on people that I know just as well as he does."

"…How so…?" Sun Ben asked.

"Men are the same all over the world," Pan Zhang replied. "When Liu Biao and Huang Zu look to make trouble, they look for allies of sorts in bandits, crime lords, disaffected 'good people' and thrill-seekers. I'm making deals with and suggestions to the right people, Mister Sun, and that should 'dampen the fire'."

"…I understand, Mister Pan," Sun Ben said.

"I just returned from fighting, as a matter of fact," Pan Zhang continued. "I'd not worry too much about Liu Biao; I gained some men as I fought, since they could see that I knew what I was doing. As soon as the locals start defending themselves as soon as the raids start, the raids will stop."

"…You really are an asset," Sun Ben said.

"Don't praise me yet," Pan Zhang chuckled. "When it's over, though, you can praise me all you want!"

The former northern nobleman Xu Sheng was determined to show that he was the only man that was needed in Wuhu County: he petitioned Sun Quan with a request to be made the Magistrate of Wuhu, and the request was granted. But Xu was still deeply contemptuous of his colleague Jiang Qin, and he objected to the presence of Jiang's men within the civil administration.

"I am Magistrate: I am the law," Xu Sheng said to the assembled officials. "I will have no common *trash* in my government."

Wu Can shook his head and muttered, "This is not the right path."

"I can see that the problem is that there are too many elevated men in this county government," Xu Sheng continued. "The concept of 'class' exists for a reason: it ensures that the wheat is separated from the chaff."

"But does it ensure that the fools are separated from the talented...?" an official asked plainly.

"...I'll ignore that," Xu Sheng retorted. "I'll ignore it because it is a statement born of ignorance. The nobility are schooled as leaders from the time that they learn to walk: how can they not know the proper way of doing things, and the low-born somehow know better...? I will be reassigning a lot of people, I assure you, as I restructure this government into something credible."

"Is it not the case that you're just removing anyone that was appointed by Colonel Jiang...?" one man asked.

Xu Sheng pointed at the man – a civil clerk that worked in Jiang Qin's office – and hissed, "*You...!*"

"Even if it isn't, how is purging the 'common people' going to improve things?" the clerk continued. "The people are annoyed enough without a statement like that!"

Some of the other 'low-born' officials voiced their agreement.

"...**GUARDS!**" Xu Sheng bellowed. "**How dare that man question me! Guards, arrest that wretch at once!**"

Two of Xu Sheng's soldiers took hold of the civil clerk's arms and started to escort him from the hall.

"**Bring his head back to me!**" Xu Sheng barked; the words caused immediate offence and led to a chorus of demands for Xu Sheng to relent. The soldiers stopped moving, as they suspected that they would soon be given different orders.

"**I am Colonel Jiang's clerk!**" the clerk protested. "**You abuse your authority, Xu Sheng!**"

"**I am 'Magistrate Xu' to you!**" Xu Sheng shrieked.

"**You cannot kill that man without seeking Colonel Jiang's approval, Mister Xu!**" Wu Can protested.

"**It's 'Magistrate Xu', and I don't need to ask that old pirate's permission to do anything!**" Xu Sheng retorted.

"**Lord Sun Quan should be informed, then!**" Wu Can said. "**Do this without following proper protocol, *Magistrate*, and you make a mockery of your status!**"

Xu Sheng stared at the mass of officials, who were mostly in opposition to his actions, regardless of their social standing; he turned to the soldiers that held the civil clerk and said, "**Take him to the prison. I'll deal with him later.**"

"**You will regret this, Xu Sheng!**" the clerk screamed as he was dragged from the hall.

"...I will write to Lord Sun at once," Xu Sheng muttered. "I shall not tolerate such *nonsense*!"

Sun Quan received Xu Sheng's request and groaned miserably.

"This arrogant fool cannot be left in Wuhu," Qin Song said. "He's offended Colonel Jiang and guaranteed more in-fighting; that's without the damage he's doing with his behaviour in general!"

"Can I disagree...?" Sun Quan asked. "Gongjin: aid my decision!"

"We cannot afford to lose Jiang Qin *or* Xu Sheng right now," Gongjin said. "I'll write to Xu and 'explain things': he respects me as the son of a former Magistrate of Luoyang, so he'll listen."

"He should listen to any man that has proved himself," Sun Quan suggested. "Does he look down on *me* as 'low-born', Gongjin...?"

"...I shall tell him that he needs to start thinking differently," Gongjin promised. "His defence of Chaisang gave us an important victory, so he really is an asset."

"Provided we can rid him of his obnoxious attitude, else he's a menace," Zhang Zhao said. "This is a state built on rewarding *merit*, not *birth*. Left to him, Wuhu will be governed by pompous northern-born noblemen's sons that will most of them neglect their duties because they 'should not worry too much about properly governing a southern backwater'. That must not happen."

"I'll talk to him!" Gongjin insisted. "In the meantime, Lord Sun, you must-"

"I know what I must do," Sun Quan interrupted. "I must refuse this ludicrous request and remind him that it is Jiang Qin that disciplines Jiang Qin's men."

"...And I shall journey to Yuzhang and inform Colonel Jiang," Qin Song said. "He won't like it, but he's a stoic man, luckily for Xu Sheng. I shall see if I am needed and return only if I am not."

"...Agreed," Sun Quan said miserably.

"Jiang Qin's more noble and dignified than that pompous imbecile Xu Sheng could ever hope to be for all his breeding," Zhang Zhao said. "And I'm from such a 'noble clan' myself, so I say that because it is true. Men must be assessed by their *character*!"

"...I'll write," Gongjin sighed.

Xu Sheng read Sun Quan's response and shuddered; he then read Gongjin's letter and wondered whether he had seriously erred.

"You were too quick to behave in such a conceited way, Magistrate Xu," Wu Can suggested. "Halt the restructuring of the civil administration until you have a proper system in place – I suggest hiring character appraisers – and set that poor clerk free at once."

"...I'll heed your first suggestion because it is in accord with my own thinking and that of Zhou Gongjin," Xu Sheng replied icily. "But that pirate's clerk can stay where he is."

Jiang Qin was having a lot of success in his battles with the rebels in Yuzhang, but the news from Wuhu harmed his morale.

"Why's he done this?" Jiang Qin asked of Qin Song, who had arrived a day earlier.

"Xu Sheng's decided that he doesn't like you," Qin Song replied frankly. "He was asked to write to you, but he has refused."

"But... but I've done nothing to offend him!" Jiang Qin said.

"He's a fool," Qin Song replied. "He dislikes anyone that he considers to be of poor breeding or low character, and he's decided that you're both of those things."

"...I didn't ask to be born," Jiang Qin said. "Alright, nobody forced

me to be a pirate, but I changed! I'm fighting the problems instead of adding to them! Doesn't that mean anything...?"
"Not to Xu Sheng," Qin Song replied.
"...I won't let him change what I've become," Jiang Qin declared. "I'm a better man and intend to stay a better man. Xu prob'ly expects that I'm going to go back to Wuhu and pick a fight, but I have work to do here that I intend to finish. When I'm done I'll go back, hear what my man's s'posed to have done and decide if he needs to be punished. I'll prove I'm not what Xu thinks I am."
"Don't waste your energy, Mister Jiang," Qin Song replied. "Everyone else can see who you are."

Huang Gai was preoccupied with dealing with the bandits and tribes that plagued Shicheng County, so he was often outside the county capital and made few visits to the administrative offices. Huang's chosen managers, Mister Gan and Mister Teng, and their superior Mister Bi started to realise that they were not being pressured for progress reports and supposed that there were no attempts being made to monitor their efforts. The officials quickly started to relax their discipline and revert to what had been normality until Huang Gai's arrival; Gan and Teng allowed officials to come and go freely, took no notice of financial record-keeping and enjoyed banquets when they were supposed to be working. That went on for some time, but Huang Gai had placed a spy in the administration that would make secret reports and send them to his disappointed master.

One day, Huang Gai summoned the court to his audience hall and said, "I have been far too busy to see you all regularly, gentlemen, but I am now able to. Mister Bi, how are you...?"
Mister Bi laughed nervously and replied, "I am fine. How are *you*, Magistrate Huang...?"
"...To be honest, I am weary," Huang Gai said. "Day after day, I go out and fight, and when I return, I return to a city and a county that still has a lot of problems."
The officials exchanged worried glances; Huang Gai was dressed in official's robes and did not appear to be carrying a weapon, but he was accompanied by six soldiers in full armour.
"I'll give you an example," Huang Gai continued. "I was asked to go to Wide Hill Village, because a backlog of civil cases had built up. One woman had been trying to get a stolen donkey from her neighbour for half a year. I'm sure that would probably make some of you laugh, but she is a widow that relies on the animal to transport goods to and from the market in this city. Her husband was a soldier that died fighting the Shanyue, but the monies that he was owed for services rendered was unpaid, and he was not the only one. The village chief had a very nice house, though..."
"Chief Song is not at fault!" Mister Bi protested. "He is careful with his pay, and his fine work warranted a-!"
"I don't like seeing people in power rewarding themselves at the expense of others," Huang Gai said. "If there was unallocated money, it should have gone to those that need it first."
"...So you want to prioritise dealing with the civil cases in Wide Hill...?" Mister Gan asked.
"*Aiee*... you are all the epitome of why the nation is broken," Huang Gai despaired. "No, I do not want that work 'prioritised',

Mister Gan, I want that work *done*, as I want *everything* done!"

"We haven't the resources!" Mister Teng protested.

"A miserable lie," Huang Gai retorted. "I managed a third of the cases myself, personally, and then I instructed Chief Song to do his job and clear the backlog before I relieve him of duty."

"...Ah," Mister Gan said. "M-Magistrate Huang, we-!"

"And now I'm back here to pass judgement once again," Huang Gai continued. "I know that you gentlemen thought that I was either too preoccupied with the unresolved chaos or not the man that I had professed to be, and so you thought that you could 'be as you were'. You were *wrong*."

Huang Gai raised his right hand: four of his soldiers advanced on Mister Teng and Mister Gan and took firm hold of their arms.

"Take them out," Huang Gai ordered. "*Death*."

"*Death*?!" Mister Bi exclaimed; the other officials that had been performing poorly were suddenly terrified.

"**We're not the only ones at fault!**" Mister Gan protested.

"**Spare us!**" Mister Teng pleaded. "**Spare us, Magistrate, or kill every man here, because they're all of them guilty of-!**"

"I won't lie, gentlemen," Huang Gai said sadly. "You've all of you disappointed me, not just Gan and Teng, but they were entrusted with enforcing discipline, and they did not do so. **Death!**"

"**Ayah! Have *mercy*, Magistrate!**" Mister Gan cried.

"**I'm guilty of laziness at worst, Magistrate!**" Mister Teng sobbed. "**Don't take my life for that!**"

"Inaction is as bad as wrongdoing when it has consequences," Huang Gai retorted. "You lived like a pig: show some late dignity and die like a man."

"**Help us, someone!**" Mister Gan screeched. "*PLEASE...!*"

"**SAVE US...!**" Mister Teng cried as he disappeared from view.

"...I trust that this will serve as a lesson," Huang Gai said.

The room was painfully silent: the only sounds were the cries of the two officials, but they were quickly silenced as the soldiers carried out their work. Many men started to sob or cover their faces with their baggy sleeves when the soldiers returned with the heads of Mister Gan and Mister Teng; Mister Bi turned to Huang Gai and said, "I vow to you, on the lives of my family, that I will toil like a *stable full of horses* from now on, Magistrate."

"It should not have taken *this* to make you earn the money that you are paid to do your job," Huang Gai replied. "I'm putting you back in charge of discipline, and I will hold you to your word: if I see any other signs of 'laziness', I will have the head of every man accused and your family will suffer with you."

Mister Bi nodded and kowtowed frantically.

"...Now I can get back to my own urgent work, I hope," Huang Gai continued. "Don't make me invite you here again, gentlemen."

The room was filled with the sound of a fearful chorus of wailing and pleading; Shicheng County saw a great improvement in civil order within days as word quickly spread of Huang Gai's response to anything but the most honest and professional conduct.

∗∗∗∗∗∗∗∗∗∗∗∗

41

Major Ling Tong had been given Ling Cao's army and thrown into battle with the Shanyue tribes of Wu Prefecture without any form of genuine preparation, so it was a great surprise to all – including the overconfident Shanyue chieftains – that Tong was a natural leader and almost as fearsome as his father had been.

"**Cease this pointlessness!**" Ling Tong cried as he led a group of riders in a spirited charge. "**You wasted years of my father's life, but you won't waste mine!**"

"**For Lord Sun and the Han!**" Lü Meng bellowed as he galloped toward the chieftains at speed and without fear.

"**The boy's inviting disaster!**" Zhu Zhi complained.

"I don't think so," Han Dang replied. "**Lü Meng's still worse.**"

"**I'm talking about Lü Meng!**" Zhu Zhi retorted. "**Ling Tong is nowhere near as reckless as his father!**"

Ling Tong was, as Zhu Zhi had observed, a far more reserved character and less prone to taking extreme risks; he allowed Lü Meng to charge at the chieftains and kept his attentions focussed on the warriors on the enemy's front line.

"**I miss being the one to go out first,**" Han Dang admitted.

"**…Idiot! A'Meng, you idiot!**" Zhu Zhi screamed as he watched Lü Meng make risky move after risky move; the young officer was as lucky as he was skilled as Shanyue spears and swords failed to strike him or his steed.

"**Kill them!**" one of the chieftains screeched. "**Kill them all!**"

Ling Tong realised that Lü Meng was actually obstructing the formulated plan with his actions, so he had a subordinate 'retrieve' the carefree officer and force him to withdraw to the front line.

"**…Now there's something that Ling Cao would never have done!**" Han Dang chuckled.

"**The Han men flee!**" a lesser chieftain cried. "**CHARGE!**"

Ling Tong and Lü Meng returned to their front line and turned to face the baying Shanyue warriors, who were starting to advance in disorderly packs of riders and men on foot.

"**Aaaaand we have them!**" Han Dang said with a smile.

"**ARCHERS AT THE READY!**" Zhu Zhi ordered. "**FIRE AT WILL!**"

The Shanyue were forced to retreat by the arrows that rained down upon them; Zhu Zhi nodded at Ling Tong, who raised his spear and said, "**Counterattack at once!**"

"**Charge, brothers, for the glory of Lord Sun Quan!**" Lü Meng declared as he charged at the Shanyue leaders once again; he was virtually unobstructed as the entire Shanyue front line had charged and then scattered.

"***Aiee…! You blasted fool, A'Meng! FOOL!***" Zhu Zhi cried.

"**We've won,**" Han Dang said. "**Don't fret!**"

The three chieftains that had attacked Wu County as a fragile coalition were becoming increasingly worried by Lü Meng's repeated attempts to attack them, and one decided to retreat; another pursued and attacked the first for his show of cowardice, and the Shanyue army as a whole started to fragment and suffer from in-fighting. Ling Tong used the enemy's complete loss of organisation as momentum to finally launch his own attack on the bickering leaders: the chieftain that had fled was cut down by one of Ling's men, and the chieftain that had pursued and attacked his former colleague fled at the sight of it.

"**I'll lend my own sword to it now!**" Han Dang suggested. "**Zong'er, you're my second as always!**"

Han Zong followed his father into battle, although their contribution would be small: Ling Tong and Lü Meng had scattered the remainder of the enemy between them, and Ling Cao's former followers cheered for the son of their fallen leader.

"...**That seemed almost too easy!**" Han Dang joked as he returned to Zhu Zhi's side. "**I have to hand it to Ling Tong: he's won 'em over completely already.**"

"**Lord Sun will be glad,**" Zhu Zhi said. "**He has another hero.**"

"**Yes,**" Han Dang wheezed. "**And a smarter one, too: I don't think that we'll lose this one as quickly.**"

Ling Tong returned to the front line and bowed from atop his horse, saying, "The enemy are routed, Administrator."

"And you, Major Ling Tong, are to be commended for your caution, valour and leadership," Zhu Zhi replied. "I had worried that your first foray a few days ago was a singular case of excellence, but you are obviously a hero in the making. I will be writing to Lord Sun to recommend that you are given your father's rank and full responsibilities."

"I am not yet proven worthy!" Ling Tong protested.

"You are," Zhu Zhi insisted. "Now go back to your duties, and when the day is truly over you should reward your men for a job well done."

"I shall, Administrator," Ling Tong promised.

When Lü Meng returned, Zhu Zhi grunted and said, "Well...?"

"I was following Sun Tzu's instruction that, once the enemy is lured and vulnerable, one should 'set out after them but arrive before them'," Lü Meng explained. "I wanted to repeatedly charge the enemy and overwhelm their own positions, making it so that I was 'arriving before them'."

"...An odd interpretation," Zhu Zhi said.

"It was my own fault, for I was trying to justify my usual urges to charge into battle, forgetting that 'The fray brings danger as well as promise of success' and that 'throwing the full force into that fray promises success and threatens failure'," Lü Meng continued. "In a way, I also breach the rule of 'awaiting the general's assessment of likelihood of victory' by letting anger guide me, so-"

"Alright, alright," Zhu Zhi interrupted. "You're obviously trying to understand what it is to be a thinker... but you must work on that temper, else it will one day be as you were about to say..."

"...That 'the outcome will be collapse'," Lü Meng said. "I will continue to learn, Commander Zhu... I promise."

Zhu Zhi grunted again, but he said no more: he sensed that Lü Meng was fighting a battle within himself in order to become a better man, and there was a genuine chance that he might one day succeed.

Sun Quan was elated when Zhu Zhi's report on Ling Tong's work reached his court in Qu'e City.

"Elder Zhu Junli recommends that I promote Ling to his father's rank, and I certainly shall," Sun Quan declared. "From now on,

that fine man shall be known as 'Colonel Who Routs The Barbarians', and I shall ensure that he has enough taxable households to live a comfortable life in later years."
"If it is truly Zhu Zhi's view that Ling Tong is worthy, then I shall ensure that the proper seal is forwarded to him at once," Zhang Zhao said. "But what do we do about our own growing problems with the Shanyue...?"
"I want to go and deal with them," Sun Yi said. "I'm bored of being stuck in Qu'e."
"You're part of the city's defence forces, *Lieutenant-General Sun*," Zhang Zhao replied. "You should delegate such responsibility to-"
"They're trying to get to Qu'e," Sun Yi retorted. "Attacking them before they get here is the best way to defend the city."
"...That's a valid argument," Zhang Zhao conceded. "I merely worry that-"
"I, too, worry about you risking your life, Shubi," Sun Quan said.
"Life is never without risk," Sun Yi replied. "I can be like Bofu or like Jizuo."
Sun Quan sighed as he accepted the valid argument that had been made before: Sun Ce and Sun Kuang had been very different men but both died young and under very different circumstances.
"If I go, it might stop worse things happening," Sun Yi continued.
"I'll take your place and guard the city, Shubi," Sun Hè said.
"And I'll join you in battle," Xu Kun said. "Uncle wouldn't let me stay and help in Danyang, but damned if I'll sit back and let Shubi fight and-!"
"Your point is taken," Sun Quan chuckled. "You will fight at Shubi's side."
"But be *careful*," Zhang Zhao insisted.

Jing Province Governor Liu Biao received a report from his agitators in Xi'an County and sighed miserably.
"Bad news...?" the politician Huan Jie asked.
"Sun Quan's general, Pan Zhang, has done the impossible and repelled us," Liu Biao complained. "The Suns have yet another man like Taishi Ci."
"Pan Zhang is no Taishi Ci," the adviser Kuai Yue insisted. "He's corrupt, greedy, too fond of pretty trinkets and drink for his own good and notorious for a history as a bad debtor."
"Regardless of all that you say, he has outwitted us!" Liu Biao retorted. "Pan Zhang has 'bought' the local criminals, placated the disaffected and turned the civilian populace into a defence force that can actually delay our actions for long enough for the real soldiers to arrive! That is what Taishi is famous for, isn't it...?"
"...Pan Zhang is obviously a changed man," Kuai Yue said. "Taishi either advises him from the shadows or he has learned tactics from that troublesome man before taking the assignment. Either way, it is as you surmise, Governor: we cannot exploit Taishi Ci's obvious lack of presence – which can only be due to his being injured or sick – if Pan Zhang is just as effective."
"So we're ending the wasteful exercise, then," the adviser Wang Can said.
"What choice is there...?" Liu Biao replied. "We can't afford to waste resources now... not when we have such powerful enemies."

Sun Yi and Xu Kun left Qu'e City and led their forces southward to impede the approach of a large coalition of Shanyue tribes; the enemy was as disorderly and intimidating as always, but neither of the Sun clan scions was worried.

"...**What will we do?**" Xu Kun asked.

"**This is the Shanyue!**" Sun Yi replied. "**There's two real tactics at this point: charge and smash them, or lure them into charging at our spears and arrows!**"

"...**I'm for charging!**" Xu Kun decided.

"**Me too!**" Sun Yi cackled.

"**Be more cautious, General!**" a major pleaded. "**Lord Sun-**"

"**I must look strong, Major Fu Ying!**" Sun Yi retorted. "**I must look invincible! That's how Bofu won the battles, and that's how I'll win them!**"

"**That isn't necessarily so!**" Fu Ying protested. "**Lord Sun-!**"

"**Is not here,**" Sun Yi interrupted. "**But we are: Fu Ying, Sun Gao, you will cover my charge.**"

Xu Kun turned to his officers and said, "**Major Zhang, Major Teng, you'll cover *my* charge.**"

The cousins charged the advancing Shanyue together, and the combined force of their infantries and cavalries ripped through the complacent, unprepared front lines and left the horrified chieftains – regardless of whether they led from the rear or by example – isolated and vulnerable. The tribal coalition collapsed and the men scattered in all directions; the defenders cheered and yelped as they chased down the retreating tribesman and ensured that they were too humiliated to return quickly.

"**And tonight, we go after their camps!**" Sun Yi announced. "**We'll chase them back to the hills!**"

Many men chanted Sun Yi's name: Xu Kun smiled and whispered, "*There*, Heaven, is another Bofu."

Sun Quan's secretary, Zhuge Jin, brought the news of Sun Yi's victory to Sun Quan as he enjoyed a small banquet with Lu Su.

"Shubi is... magnificent," Sun Quan said as he read the report.

"...Your hesitation suggests that something's wrong," Lu Su noted.

"No... no, no, nothing is wrong, Zijing," Sun Quan insisted. "I was just left slightly 'disturbed' by the adulation that my brother enjoys; he is too much like Bofu, and he might demand more commissions and take more risks."

"...You worry for his safety," Lu Su said.

"Naturally," Sun Quan replied. "I... ... ...well, it doesn't matter. He is victorious within a few days, and soon he will be back here, where he is safe."

"All in all, we are winning," Lu Su suggested. "The tribes are unable to gain ground, the rebellions falter, the bandits are on the run, Liu Biao's incursions have been thwarted..."

"And 'peace' – or whatever can be called such – cannot occur quickly enough, Lu Zijing," Sun Quan said. "If your plan is to be realised, then our realm must be stable. Your vision of an intermediate tripartite state is obviously going to happen, and I want us to be ready for that coming storm and what lies beyond it... a state that will surpass and outlast the ailing Han Dynasty, a state that will prove that the men of the south are as great as those in the north... our state, built here and now."

"Forgive my interjection, Lord Sun, but what preparations should be made for Lieutenant-General Sun Yi's return...?" Zhuge Jin asked humbly.

"A banquet, naturally," Sun Quan replied. "A grand banquet for Shubi and Xu Kun... to celebrate their safe return."

Sun Yi and Xu Kun invited their subordinate officers to the command tent for a celebratory banquet before they returned to Qu'e: Xu Kun raised his wine dish and said, **"To the Sun clan, the state of Jiangdong, and the Han."**

Sun Yi and the officers echoed his toast.

"...**I also commend Lieutenant-General Sun Yi,**" Xu Kun added. **"He is the sharpened sword of the Sun clan: let all the barbarians fear his name!"**

Sun Yi's officers – from the lowest captains to his senior majors – cheered and chanted their commander's name. Sun Yi waited for the officers to begin their own private conversations before he turned to Xu Kun and said, "You seem different."

"Don't misunderstand me," Xu Kun replied. "I accept everything. I might not agree with everything that I accept, but that doesn't matter, really, does it...?"

Sun Yi nodded slowly and said, "You are worried about Zhongmou's treatment of your daughter."

"She's treated very well... too well," Xu Kun replied. "She is set to replace Lady Xie as Lord Sun's principal wife. I... well, Lü Fan put it best when I asked his advice: I 'worry that any merits or demotions that I might incur will be entirely due to that union'."

"Zhongmou will be fair," Sun Yi insisted. "He's not perfect, but he's a good man."

"...I know," Xu Kun replied tonelessly. "I know."

Sun Yi's victory was celebrated by Sun Quan, but news from the north distracted the wiser minds in the court: the Yuan brothers had lost their six-month-long battle with the Han army without actually engaging their enemy. Cao Cao had travelled to the Yellow River and begun the battle within months of Yuan Shao's death, but Shao's eldest son Yuan Tan and Shao's chosen heir – his third son, Yuan Shang – had proved to be competent military leaders, and progress was slow; Cao's adviser, Guo Jia, had then proposed leaving the Yuans and attacking Liu Biao, since that might cause the Yuans to start fighting amongst themselves. Cao Cao's efforts to seize northern Jing had faltered at Bowang Slope, but the main purpose had been achieved: the Yuans had started to argue before Cao's retreat had even finished, and in the weeks that followed, Yuan Tan sieged Yè City and was soundly defeated by his younger half-brother Yuan Shang.

The whole debacle was a timely reminder of the importance of family unity: the Sun clan could fall just as easily if there were exploitable divisions, and there was a general keenness to avoid a similar ruse leading to a premature end to the state-building project in Jiangdong.

****

42

Huang Gai and Xu Sheng's efforts were improving two particularly troublesome parts of Danyang Prefecture, but that would do nothing to preserve the life of the world-weary prefectural administrator, Wu Jing; his health failed him, and he finally succumbed. The loss of a beloved maternal uncle affected Sun Quan, Sun Yi and Shangxiang, who were the oldest and had the fondest memories of the highly-strung, slightly pedantic man that had always been there to scold Sun patriarchs for their reckless behaviour; the death also left Danyang without an administrator, and there were few suitable Sun clan family members left to take up a role that was seen as theirs to fill.

"...This feels wrong," Sun Quan said to Lady Chen as he prepared to enter his court and debate the appointment of a new Administrator of Danyang.

"Wu Jing felt like a brother to me once Lady Wu accepted me as her sister, lord and son," Lady Chen replied. "I would lead the mourning if I could."

"Mother would be honoured if you did," Sun Quan said. "I shall leave it to Uncle Wu's sons to decide, but I'm sure that you will be welcome, Second Mother."

"...Who would you appoint in the role...?" Lady Chen asked.

"There really aren't that many men left to take the role," Sun Quan replied. "I can think of only two or three... and I already know the reaction that I'll get."

"I do not envy your responsibility, and I lament the poor intellect that I possess in comparison to Lady Wu," Lady Chen said sadly. "I want to help you, but I can't."

Sun Quan turned to Senior Attendant Gu Li and asked, "What do you think...?"

"I am a mere household servant, not a strategist, adviser or general," Gu Li replied.

"You're observant, and I truly respect your opinion, else I would not ask," Sun Quan insisted.

"...If I regret it later, so be it," Gu Li said with a sigh. "Lord Sun, you will be expected to appoint a trusted relation due to the proximity of Danyang to the capital and its geographical importance to the overall stability of Jiangdong. You will no doubt be asked to choose between your brother Sun Yi, your uncle Sun Jing, one of Sun Jing's older sons, your cousin Xu Kun or one of your other cousins, Sun Ben or Sun Fu. Wu Jing has sons, but I have heard him remark that they cannot succeed him effectively, and your advisers will no doubt say the same."

"...You speak as eloquently as any of my politicians," Sun Quan said with surprise. "Please, Li, go on."

"...If I must," Gu Li replied. "Xu Kun is going to be disregarded as too impetuous, and Sun Jing's sons will probably be ignored on account of their ages, despite Sun Yi being around the same age. Sun Jing will be labelled as mediocre; Sun Yi will be seen as a pacifier that will achieve great things; Sun Ben and Sun Fu will be seen as potentially divisive. The court will probably say that they would prefer Sun Yi to take the role."

Sun Quan smiled and said, "I think that you will be proven

correct, Li, and I shall be very impressed if you are."

Many officials had returned to Qu'e to take part in Wu Jing's funeral services and stayed to discuss his successor; the court was full and the atmosphere was tense. The discussions reached their conclusion as the sun started to set, but some were insistent that further talks were needed.
"...So it comes down to Sun Ben, Sun Jing, Sun Fu or Sun Yi," Zhang Zhao said. "We are in the midst of relocating the state capital, so this comes at an unfortunate time... every man is needed for such a great upheaval, and now we must find a man that can face the Shanyue, Fei Zhan and any rebel armies that appear, all while tackling corruption, incompetence and, if the signs are right, drought and disease."
Sun Quan lowered his head and groaned.
"Sad to say, there are signs of a plague outbreak," Zhang Zhao continued. "At the moment, the problem appears to be confined to eastern Kuaiji, but it only takes a few infected refugees to start a nationwide epidemic."
"The Kuaiji administration is very capable," Zhu Zhi suggested.
"That man we appointed to be the Administrator of Kuaiji, Chunyu Shi, is a blame-fearing toady," Cheng Pu complained. "How will he manage such chaos if he balks at the daily monotonies...?"
"My son and Mister Zhu Huan are very capable, Demou," Zhu Zhi said. "And Chunyu is a bit of a pedant, yes, but he is not a fool."
"I really think that we should make your son the administrator, Junli," Cheng Pu replied.
"No, no," Zhu Zhi protested. "Trust Chunyu Shi! My son is not yet ready to take on a place like Kuaiji. An experienced general would be the right man if Chunyu is not. And we're supposed to be talking about Danyang, not Kuaiji."
"I still say that we're disregarding other choices," Cheng Pu said. "Sun Jing is a very nice man and hard-working in addition, but by his own confession he is not a tiger like Wentai, nor is he a born administrator. Sun Ben is ill-equipped, and–"
"I was chieftain of the clan for three years!" Sun Ben snapped.
"...Indeed you were," Cheng Pu said with a smirk. "But is leading a pack of attack dogs the same as administrating a prefecture...?"
Sun Ben scowled and said, "I was appointed as *Administrator of Yuzhang* by...!"
"...By...?" Cheng Pu sniggered.
"...By Yuan Shu," Sun Ben sighed.
"Who also appointed you as 'Inspector of Yu Province', initially, but were you ever anything but another of his dogs, like the rest of us...?" Cheng Pu taunted. "You're a fine officer, Ben, but you're not an administrator."
"...Who, then...?" Sun Ben asked. "Who will inherit the burden...?"
"Xu Kun is not an administrator," Zhang Zhao insisted. "Sun Jing is not of the right temperament; Sun Jing's sons are sadly inexperienced; Wu Jing's sons, Wu Fen and Wu Qi, are, by their own admission, unfit for the role."
"But Sun Ben and Sun Fu are not the proper choices, and Sun Hè is – wrongly – seen by some as not being a full-blooded 'Sun'," Cheng Pu said. "That leaves Sun Yi, Lord Sun's brother, who is popular, charismatic, inspiring and as loyal as they get."

"And my brother and I are not *any* of those things, then, Cheng Pu...?" Sun Ben heckled.

"...Let's just say that you're 'divisive'," Lü Fan said reluctantly. "Please understand that the following are others' words that I have heard: your marriage alliance to Cao Cao – which would have ruled Kuang out, had he lived – is one concern, and the continued belief that you were too quick to obey Yuan Shu is another among many."

Sun Ben was going to note that Wu Jing had 'been even quicker to obey Yuan Shu' if he himself was guilty, but he quickly remembered that such an observation about a recently-deceased relation would tarnish his reputation, so he bowed slightly and said, "I understand, Ziheng."

Sun Quan smiled; his senior attendant Gu Li had been consistently right in his observations.

"...So we're basically whittled down to appointing Sun Yi," Zhang Zhao said as his gaze – and many others – turned to Sun Quan's younger brother.

"Every day, more and more, Yi resembles Bofu," Gongjin sighed.

"I can't run Danyang!" Sun Yi chuckled nervously.

"There's nobody else," Sun Quan retorted. "Please, do it for me."

"...For you, yeah, of course, but I don't know where to start," Sun Yi said.

"You will have help," Zhang Zhao promised.

"...It's decided then," Sun Quan said.

Sun Yi left the court in a daze; he was greeted upon his return by his principal wife, Lady Xū, and two of his consorts.

"Something concerns you, Husband," Lady Xū said as Sun Yi sat at his host seat and gestured that he would like some wine.

"...Have you, by chance, done any divining...?" Sun Yi asked.

"I often divine instinctively," Lady Xū replied. "I was confused by the readings and chose not to divulge them."

"...Did these 'readings' involve my gaining power unexpectedly...?" Sun Yi asked.

"They... they could be interpreted as such, I suppose," Lady Xū replied. "I saw a conflicted path, one fraught with difficulty, great fortune and great *misfortune*."

"...That's about right," Sun Yi sighed.

"What has happened...?" Lady Xū asked.

"I am to ready the household at once and travel to Wanling County, where I will be taking up the role of 'Administrator of Danyang'," Sun Yi replied.

Lady Xū stifled a gasp; she was worldly enough to know that Yi's appointment carried a very large number of risks.

"...I never expected this," Sun Yi continued. "I'm not sure that I can do this."

"But we must go regardless: that much is clear," Lady Xū said. "I shall assist the servants in any way that I can, Husband."

Sun Yi nodded slowly; the enormity of the role was difficult to understand but easy to estimate, while the external risks – such as becoming a greater target for Sun Quan's enemies – mostly eluded him. The 19-year-old Administrator prepared to leave Qu'e and begin a new chapter in his life.

Lü Fan met with Gongjin at the latter's Qu'e residence and asked, "How goes the naval training...?"

"Fine," Gongjin replied. "I... I cannot help thinking that it's a pity that there was nothing that could be done to 'save' Wu Jing."

"...The Suns are losing a lot of their guiding lights," Lü Fan said. "I know that the likes of Sun Yi are still heroes, but..."

"I wanted your opinion on his appointment," Gongjin said.

"Who else is there...?" Lü Fan asked. "I agree with the decision that was made, even if it places Sun Yi in great danger."

"I'm not alone in thinking that, then," Gongjin replied. "There will be men that will try to use Sun Yi's record in Danyang in order to suggest that he would be better placed as the lord of Jiangdong; there will be men that will pledge allegiance to him and claim to fight in his name, and-"

"There *might* be," Lü Fan interrupted. "Lord Sun Quan has been in the role for three years, and there has been no mention of usurping him since Li Shu's defeat. The failure at Xiakou was the possible turning point, and nobody advocated removing him from office. I don't think that anyone will start rallying behind Sun Yi now, so unless someone is somehow able to convince Sun Quan that his brother is conspiring or, more ridiculous still, if someone actually convinces Sun Yi to conspire, we have nothing to worry about there. I'm more worried about him being killed by others."

"...You're right," Gongjin conceded. "I hope that he survives, Ziheng... because I cannot see the state surviving if it keeps suffering such losses."

Sun Quan organised a farewell banquet for Sun Yi; the two brothers were quickly left dispirited when they reviewed the attendees, since it reminded them just how many of their relations were no longer around.

"...In better times, the atmosphere was so... vibrant," Sun Quan said as he looked at Sun Yi, Gongjin, Lü Fan, his uncle Sun Jing, his cousin Xu Kun and his distant cousin Sun Hè. "All of you have always attended such gatherings..."

"...But now, Lord Sun, it is the turn of others to sit in your presence, like my brother's fine son," Sun Hè declared as he gestured toward his teenaged nephew Sun Shao; he then gestured toward his two eldest sons and added, "My own boys are promising officers too. It is sad that so many have gone so early, but this is a moment for optimism."

"I'm glad to hear you saying such things," Sun Quan replied. "I have missed your strong presence, Bohai, and would dearly love you to be part of my inner circle of trusted guards."

"I cannot, Lord Sun," Sun Hè pleaded. "Let me guard a city, by all means, but not your life. I could not bear to fail again."

"...I reluctantly accept your stance, Bohai," Sun Quan sighed.

"But let's not forget the optimistic part of what Bohai said," Xu Kun suggested.

"I quite agree," Gongjin said. "It is good to see Sun Jing's sons here today; Hao and Yu have served for a while already, and here they are now, joined by Jiao, who reminds me so much of Bofu."

Sun Jiao had been drinking wine since the start of the banquet, and he was now intoxicated; he laughed at Gongjin's comment and said, "I don't look or act like Bofu at all, Gongjin. What made

you say such a silly thing?"
"**Watch your tongue!**" Sun Jing barked. "You may be my son, but you cannot-!"
"I'm not offended," Gongjin insisted.
"No, but I am," Sun Jing replied as he glared at his embarrassed son Jiao. "I did not raise you to be a fool, so don't act like one!"
"My comment was nonsense," Gongjin said. "His resemblance to Bofu is not so great compared to any of your other sons or, indeed, Bofu's brother Yi."
Sun Quan turned to Sun Yi and said, "Heaven forgive me, I cannot spare any men to shield you from the worst of what you face… and… and the fact that I've had to curse you with this burden is because of the same situation."
"I'll have Uncle Wu's advisers and sons to help me," Sun Yi replied. "I have our distant cousin Sun Gao and a Major Fu Ying in my militia too, and they're both very reliable. I'll be fine, Zhongmou."
Wu Jing's son Fen smiled and said, "We'll be the same close family that we've always been, Lord Sun. Qi and I will be Yi's eyes and ears when we can."
"And don't let him do anything reckless," Sun Quan replied.
"I'll be careful," Sun Yi promised.

When the banquet ended, Sun Yi went for a walk through the grounds of Sun Quan's vast estate; it was dark, so he was accidentally startled by the approach of his tomboy younger sister, Sun Shangxiang.
"I saw the trousers, and…!" Sun Yi chuckled. "Where have you been…? I've not seen you!"
"…You're going to write all the time, right…?" Shangxiang asked.
"You almost sound… like a girl," Sun Yi said soberly. "Are you worried for me?"
"Danyang's very dangerous," Shangxiang replied. "I know that from listening."
"You could have been at the banquet," Sun Yi suggested.
"Brother said that he would prefer that I didn't 'get up to mischief', so I stayed away," Shangxiang said. "That's why I'm here now. I wanted to see you and say 'goodbye' properly."
"…The place feels lonely these days," Sun Yi admitted.
"Since Mum died," Shangxiang agreed. "Sometimes, this doesn't feel like a home at all anymore. It's just a house with people in it that I know."
"…Get married, have children," Sun Yi retorted. "You can't just-"
"Where are the heroes…?" Shangxiang asked. "Taishi Ci's alright, but he's nearly forty, and he'd be too scared to suggest marrying me, especially since he has a wife already and she'd have to let me be the principal wife and that wouldn't be fair. Apart from him, who is there…?"
"*Aiee*… I don't know!" Sun Yi replied. "I… I suppose this isn't really a time that has a lot of heroes."
"Only us Suns are heroes," Shangxiang said proudly. "But… but then I won't get a husband if you're right, will I…? I can't marry an ordinary man."
"…I was going to ask how we got to this, but I just realised that it's my own fault," Sun Yi said. "Shangxiang, I… … …*aiee*. Just do

254

what your heart tells you. I just hope that our children will grow up together, like we did."

Shangxiang hugged Sun Yi tightly and whispered, "Promise me that you'll write."

"...I promise," Sun Yi replied as he held his sister and smiled.

When morning arrived, Sun Yi was escorted to the gates of Qu'e by Sun Quan and many of his relations.

"...So the whole administration is moving to Wucheng, then," Sun Yi sighed.

"You knew that," Sun Quan said bemusedly.

"...Yeah, but I suppose that it just sank in," Sun Yi replied. "Qu'e has been home for a long while... I've almost forgotten what Fuchun looks like. Why not move the capital to there...?"

"That place should look the same forever, to remind us of Father and where we came from," Sun Quan insisted.

"...You're right," Sun Yi conceded. "I... I just realised that I'd like to see Fuchun again."

"I promise that I will get you out of Danyang as soon as there's a man to take your place," Sun Quan replied. "I don't want this, Shubi: I want us all to be together. I want our family to be together, and I want Gongjin, Ziheng and Yifeng to be close as well. And when the state is stabilised, I swear that we'll all be together again."

"...But until then, I promise that I'll work as hard as anyone else to finish what we've started," Sun Yi said. "You can trust me, Zhongmou... always."

Sun Quan took Sun Yi's hands in his own and smiled gratefully. A minute passed; Zhang Zhao broke the uncomfortable silence by saying, "Lord Sun, we have much urgent business to discuss."

"...Of course," Sun Quan replied as he released Sun Yi's hands and stepped back.

Sun Yi bowed and said, "Zhongmou... farewell, for now."

Sun Quan was rendered speechless as he watched Sun Yi's carriage depart the city minutes later; Gongjin sighed and said, "Now we must return to our work."

"...Of course," Sun Quan said as he watched his brother Sun Yi leave Qu'e City and begin the journey to Wanling County in Danyang Prefecture. Sun Jian had five living children by Lady Wu when he died: Sun Ce, Sun Quan, Sun Yi, Sun Kuang and Sun Shangxiang. Sun Jian had three surviving children by his consorts, but for Quan, his four full siblings were his 'true family'; but in the last three years, he had lost his two of those siblings, and many suspected that he was gripped by the fear – or even the certainty – of losing another. The lord of Jiangdong was morbidly silent as he left the gates and returned to his home to begin a day or discussions about the state that seemed to be becoming harder to manage with every passing moment.

****

43

Zhuge Jin and Bu Zhi were surprised when a man that was familiar to both of them appeared in Jiangdong's capital and enquired about a place to live; Zhuge Jin finally located the man in a tavern and said, "Yan Jun...! Yan Mancai...!"

"...Ziyu! Zhuge Ziyu!" Yan Jun exclaimed. "My goodness... how long has it been? I thought that you were in Jing Province!"

"Most of my family still is," Zhuge Jin replied.

"You work here...?" Yan Jun prompted.

"I do," Zhuge Jin replied. "I... ... ...I serve in the local government."

"Aha, so you've gained the favour of Lord Sun Quan!" Yan Jun chuckled. "You've done well!"

"Am I transparent...?" Zhuge Jin complained.

"You hesitated," Yan Jun said. "Anyhow... Bu Zishan contacted me and said that he's been employed by Sun Quan, so I decided to come here, see if there was any work to be had in the south. I've been moving around quite a bit – I stayed with Liu Ying in Guangling for a spell, as a matter of fact – and now I've finally had the courage to come to the capital!"

"Liu Ying...?" Zhuge Jin exclaimed. "I'd forgotten about him, I'm so overwhelmed by all the chaos in this region! He's very clever..."

"...And keen to remain neutral," Yan Jun replied pointedly. "Please say no more of him to anyone."

"...So you kept in touch with Bu Zhi...?" Zhuge Jin realised. "I wondered how he had learned that you were here... he must want you to serve Lord Sun as we do."

"He was very, very vague," Yan Jun said. "I can see why: you're originally from Langya, he's from Huaiyin, and I am from the old Xu Province capital Peng, and northern men don't always get a good greeting or deserve one."

"...Peng... oh, of course, I forgot that you're from Peng!" Zhuge Jin exclaimed. "That means that you... saw..."

"I did," Yan Jun replied soberly. "Cao Cao is a demon from the lowest depths of Hell, Ziyu. So many died there... so many... and now that monster is the Excellency of Works. How can the sovereign or the nation be safe with such a wicked man as the senior minister...?"

"...You sound like my brother Liang," Zhuge Jin said.

"The 'Crouching Dragon' of Longzhong," Yan Jun noted. "His views are a little naïve for my tastes, though: the Han Dynasty cannot hope to survive now. Even if it is one day to be restored, it must first fall, as it did in the days of Wang Mang."

"That's the general view in Lord Sun's court," Zhuge Jin said. "It is also my own view. But Liang refuses to be told! He ignores the 'Ten' and their hold over Huandi and Lingdi, and instead focusses on the 'Dong Zhuo crisis' and the years beyond. The rot started long before that sadist came to power!"

"But his debating skills are exemplary, I hear," Yan Jun prompted. "I wanted to go to Jing myself and challenge him, and would have if not for all this ridiculous bickering between all of these warlords that pick at the Empire's bones."

"Men supposedly travel from all around to challenge him, and he always has the last word, even when he is wrong," Zhuge Jin replied. "It pains me to say it, but I worry that his stubborn devotion to the Han will ruin him one day."

"...Meanwhile, Ziyu, you have gained favour!" Yan Jun said.

"Even with Pangs and Kuais for brothers-in-law," Zhuge Jin replied. "Lord Sun Quan, Zhou Yu, Lü Fan, Lu Su and the rest are truly brilliant men. But there are so many problems, Mancai, that Lord Sun is running out of capable talents to manage them all."

"...That's a very important fact to entrust to me, Ziyu," Yan Jun suggested. "Why...?"

"You're needed," Zhuge Jin replied. "I'll speak with Zhang Zhao, the Chief Clerk – with whom I have slightly better relations now – and ask him to recommend you for an important post."

Yan Jun bowed and said, "I would be indebted to you forever for such an opportunity, Ziyu."

"Bu Zhi is the one that lured you here," Zhuge Jin replied, "and it's your own talent that will get you the job. Don't thank me."

Yan Jun was employed by Sun Quan at Zhang Zhao's suggestion within a week of his arrival in the capital; he received a middle-level role based on the references that he received from Bu Zhi and Zhuge Jin and quickly earned promotions. Yan Jun had joined the administration at a busy time: Sun Quan was having the entire court relocated to the city of Wucheng, which was to the southwest of Qu'e.

Wucheng was to the north of the Sun clan's ancestral village of Fuchun, and unlike the river port of Qu'e, it was inland, more or less midway between the south and east sea coasts and the Yangtze River: some perceived that to be a sign of weakness, others as a sign of understandable caution as tensions grew between the Suns, Liu Biao and the Imperial court. There was, however, the oft-forgotten fact that Sun Quan's father, Sun Jian, had been created 'Marquis of Wucheng' by Emperor Ling's Han court after the Yellow Turban Rebellion, and there was also the better-known fact that Sun Ce was created 'Marquis of Wu' by the current administration: there were only a few that connected these facts to the move and Sun Quan's general ambitions, and they were probably correct. Regardless of the actual reasons for the move to Wucheng, preparations were being made, but it would be some time before the idea would become a reality.

****

44

Sun Yi's first impression of the situation in Danyang Prefecture was that he was not going to be able to change anything.

"There's a load of crime lords, bandits, pirates and tribes running large parts of this place!" Sun Yi said to his court. "What should I do...? What *can* I do...?"

"With all due respect, 'Administrator Sun', that's *your* decision," an official replied.

Sun Yi exhaled loudly and said, "I know it is, Mister...?"

"Wang," the official replied.

"...I know it is, Mister Wang, but I'm new here and to this kind of responsibility in general and will need some support," Sun Yi continued. "All I want to know is where I should start."

"What you do first depends on the problems you want to solve, Administrator," Mister Wang retorted. "And, of course, the problems that you're *capable* of solving."

"...I can see that I'll get no help," Sun Yi sighed.

Administrator Sun Yi turned and left his audience hall, ignoring the pleas and heckles of his disaffected courtiers.

"Lord Sun!"

Sun Yi had retired to his private study, where a team of aides and servants – some of them new to him – awaited his instructions: he turned and looked around when his new 'senior attendant' spoke, and it then took Yi a moment to realise that he was the 'lord' that the attendant referred to.

"...I suppose that I *am* 'Lord Sun' here in Danyang," Sun Yi said. "You're... no wait... Bian Hong, wasn't it...?"

The senior attendant nodded silently.

"I'll try and remember names," Sun Yi promised.

"We await your orders," Bian Hong said.

"...I want to get drunk, but that won't solve anything," Sun Yi replied miserably. "I'd go hunting, but I'd probably be 'accidentally shot'; I want to go home, but I'd be letting my brother down."

The servants stared at one-another nervously.

"...None of you really want to be my trusted confidantes, do you...?" Sun Yi said as his principal wife, Lady Xū, entered the room and sat at his side.

"It isn't their place," Lady Xū said.

"No... no, it isn't," Sun Yi murmured. "You may all go."

The attendants and servants withdrew.

"I need help," Sun Yi admitted. "I need good men to help me run my court... but where will I find them...? Must I get Wu Qi and Wu Fen to come back here...?"

"Ask Lord Sun Quan," Lady Xū suggested.

"I can't," Sun Yi replied. "I need to show initiative... I need to think of a way to recruit the right men to form a proper government, but the only people that I have to rely on are the old government, who won't want to help me replace them."

"...It is a dilemma," Lady Xū sighed.

"And I have men like Fei Zhan – who's another Xu Gong – hovering and lurking, waiting for an excuse to trigger a rebellion," Sun Yi continued. "I...! ...Wait... wait. That's it... that's the answer!"

"…You have found a solution," Lady Xū prompted.

"My brother will say that it's madness, so I won't tell him until I've seen if the idea works," Sun Yi continued. "Yes… *they* are the men that I need to help me run this place!"

"…Who are 'they'…?" Lady Xū asked.

Sun Yi smiled and replied, "The men from Wu. The men that helped Sheng Xian, the old man that used to run Wu Prefecture; I don't know their names, but they were honest men that Xu Gong threw out of office. I know that Sheng Xian was killed, and that there are rumours that we sent a man to do it, but we killed Xu Gong, the man that harmed Sheng Xian, so they can surely see that we just want to put things right!"

"…Perhaps you should seek guidance on this idea," Lady Xū said.

"I know it sounds daft, and if they're petty, it won't work, but these men hid on that estate with Sheng Xian for years and refused to serve Xu Gong, so they're really serious," Sun Yi replied. "If I ask, they'll refuse if they hate us, won't they…?"

"…If one were to assume that they are consistent," Lady Xū said.

"I'll put the word out in Wu Prefecture," Sun Yi continued. "I'm sure that they will see that I'm not another Xu Gong, and that they can work with the Suns to stabilise Danyang and then the whole region. I'll start right away!"

Lady Xū briefly considered protesting, but there was no point to it: Sun Yi had set his sights on recruiting Sheng Xian's officials, and no person alive could talk him out of it.

Gongjin visited Qu'e and met with his old friend Lu Su to discuss the latest developments in the north.

"The Yuans are now at each other's throats," Gongjin said.

"Cao Cao's played them perfectly," Lu Su replied. "It seemed that he had grossly mishandled his invasion of northern Jing, when all along it was just a ruse to get the Yuan brothers to relax and inevitably turn on each other."

"*Perhaps*," Gongjin said. "It may still be that the 'ruse' was a genuine invasion attempt that faltered, but… yes, I am forced to admit that it still means that his advisers were able to salvage a great victory from a serious setback."

"And there is no limit to the duplicity, it seems," Lu Su suggested. "Now there are rumours that Cao intends to work with Yuan Tan…"

"Cao's counsel is truly incredible," Gongjin admitted. "It's been said before, but it needs to be said again: we'll have a lot of trouble if we have to fight them."

"And we will, unless we abandon all plans for an independent state," Lu Su suggested. "Such a state will be an impossible dream if Cao cannot be beaten or at the very least humbled."

"…We must hope that Heaven favours us," Gongjin replied.

Sun Yi's request travelled across Wu Prefecture and found the fugitive officials that had once served the deposed Administrator of Wu, Sheng Xian; among them were Dai Yuan and Gui Lan, who had been sheltering with bandits in the northern hills and had lost a lot of their humanity in the process.

"…Go to Danyang… and work for *Sun Yi*…?" Dai Yuan exclaimed.

"That's the suggestion," Gui Lan said. "You want to go…?"

"Of course not!" Dai Yuan replied angrily. "The Suns killed Mister

Sheng! Why would I-!?"

"But that's precisely why we should agree," Gui Lan said. "You were the one that said that we should wait until we could do something meaningful."

"I meant 'raise a militia to attack them', or something!" Dai Yuan retorted. "Not-!"

"You must be tired," Gui Lan chuckled. "You're missing the beauty of this."

Dai Yuan pondered the point for a few moments and smiled.

"...We work for Sun Yi, right under Sun Quan's nose," Gui Lan continued. "He won't have told Quan about this: it's written that we should travel to Danyang, rather than surrender to Zhu Zhi locally. He's trying to impress his brother, and so we'll be going to Danyang secretly, surrounded by potential friends and much, much closer to Liu Fu, the provincial Inspector, whom we could contact... and if we're clever, we'll get such important posts that removing us will be very difficult."

"...This is perfect," Dai Yuan decided. "This is better than anything that I've thought of! O Heaven, thank you for giving us Sun Yi!"

"And to properly show our thanks, we'll give Sun Yi back to Heaven," Gui Lan said. "The Suns have enjoyed a lot of unjustified success in Wu, but when the moment is right... *we'll* take something from *them* for a change."

Jing Governor Liu Biao had been liaising with Yuan Tan and Yuan Shang in an effort to gain their support against Cao Cao: his efforts had failed, and now Cao Cao was sending more soldiers to the Jing-Yu border to harass the ageing warlord.

"I did all I could," the adviser Wang Can said.

"You are not to blame," Liu Biao insisted. "I approved those letters, Mister Wang, and never have I read such beautiful, eloquent words that got to the point most succinctly. But Yuan Tan is too brutish to appreciate sound arguments, and Yuan Shang is surrounded by people that will ultimately destroy him. The recipients were entirely at fault."

"You are most gracious, Lord Liu," Wang Can replied.

"...But now I am in trouble," Liu Biao continued. "Yuan Tan is now allied to Cao, Ma Teng and Han Sui both provide men and horses to Cao, and even *Zhang Xiu* is Cao's friend! Yuan Shang ignores pleas for an alliance, arrogantly thinking that he can resist the might of Cao's army alone, and Yuan Xi cowers in Yòu Province, hoping that he and his do-gooder wife can somehow survive this. I have a large force on my eastern border to guard against Cao, and my brother-in-law, Cai Mao, awaits a call to defend the northern border should Zhang Yun and Liu Bei need the help, but I am most bothered by my southern border: Huang Zu is losing his nerve, and the Suns are bound to try to take Jiangxia again."

"What do you ponder...?" the adviser Kuai Yue asked.

"I wonder if I might send my son Qi to support – or maybe *replace* – Huang Zu," Liu Biao prompted.

"I wouldn't advise it," Kuai Yue said. "If you try and replace Huang now, he might turn against you, and his support in Jiangxia is so great that – and you must forgive my frankness – he really runs the region entirely, while you, Lord Liu, only rule the region through him. He will see your sending your heir to oversee his

work as a sign that you intend to replace him, so I wouldn't-"
"I... I understand," Liu Biao insisted. "I must hope that Heaven favours me."

Days passed: Sun Yi entered his administrative office, grabbed Mister Wang's arm and asked, "Any news at all...? Mister Wang, is there any-?"
"There has been a response," Mister Wang replied as he tugged his arm free of Sun Yi's grip. "A 'Dai Yuan' and a 'Gui Lan' – both of whom claim to have been close to Sheng Xian and served in high offices – are on their way here."
"...That's perfect," Sun Yi said.
"Forgive me, my lord, but I disagree," the officer Fu Ying protested. "These former followers of Sheng Xian might intend to harm you, and-"
"Sheng Xian was surrounded by men that were pure of heart and stubbornly loyal," Sun Yi said. "They preferred exile or death to serving Xu Gong, but now they come here to serve in Danyang. That means that they have understood my sincere motives and want to help me do good!"
Mister Wang glared at Sun Yi and said, "What do you want done in the way of greetings and appropriate security for those greetings, Administrator Sun...?"
"I always carry a sword!" Sun Yi chuckled as he patted the *dao* that hung at his side. "I'm very good with this, so if they really have taken leave of their wits and attack me, they'll take leave of their heads soon after!"
"You should have bodyguards, as Lord Sun Quan does," Fu Ying protested. "Let Sun Gao or me serve as-"
"I don't need more bodyguards!" Sun Yi insisted. "I'm a prefectural administrator! Uncle Wu didn't have loads of bodyguards, did he...?"
Mister Wang snorted irritably and said, "No, Administrator Sun... he did not."
"So I won't have any either," Sun Yi continued. "I'm going to look around the city now: let me know if I'm needed for anything."
"...As you command," Mister Wang replied.
Sun Yi patted Mister Wang's arm and said, "Great. Oh, and a quick point: every man'll need to do some fighting at some point, including you, so, uh... put some meat on those arms! I don't want to look I lead a load of weakling toadies."
"...As you *command*, Administrator," Mister Wang replied bitterly; Senior Attendant Bian Hong – who was being forced to follow Sun Yi almost everywhere that he went and act in multiple capacities – silently shared Wang's frustration.
"Don't be upset," Sun Yi continued. "I'm just stating a fact: I don't think you're a 'weakling toady', but people will be people, yeah...? I'm popular with the fighting men 'cause they respect me for getting in the thick of it with them, and all of my brother's problems stem from him not doing that. That's one thing that I *do* know: fighting men respect strength and don't follow or fear weak men. You can have all the brains in the empire, but that won't matter one bit to soldiers, barbarians or bandits."
"...I understand, Administrator," Mister Wang replied.
"Great!" Sun Yi said. "See you later."

Sun Yi left the office with the visibly irritated Bian Hong at his side, and Fu Ying followed them shortly afterward; Mister Wang then turned to a colleague and said, "Wu Jing was, at least, competent and likeable; the 'fighting men' might like this oafish braggart, but I, my friend, do *not*."
The other official nodded agreeably.

"You really must be more careful in how you speak to the officials here, General Sun!" Fu Ying pleaded. "Your frankness could be misconstrued for-!"
"They're not fools," Sun Yi said as he entered his audience hall. "They're a whole lot smarter than me, anyway: why would they not understand what I'm saying when everyone in Wu, Kuaiji and just about everywhere else that I've ever been to understands me well enough...?"
"...Just be careful, General," Fu Ying replied.
"Everything will be fine when Dai Yuan and Gui Lan get here," Sun Yi insisted. "When I have those two men on my team... what can I *not* do...?"

Sun Quan, meanwhile, was continuing his efforts to improve his physical strength and the opinions that his officers held: he travelled to the Qu'e stables, where the frail keeper, 'Old Yin', still held sway, and prepared to go hunting as Sun Ce once did.
"We have a fine new horse for you, Lord Sun, procured by General Hè Qi on his travels," Old Yin said. "It will be far faster than the one that you've been using."
"Oh...? That's splendid!" Sun Quan replied.
"You don't intend to go racing off and leaving your guards behind as Lord Sun Ce used to, I hope...?" Song Qian prompted.
"That... led to something unfortunate," Sun Quan replied. "I will keep you all close, I assure you. Besides, I am not the great hunter and fierce fighter that Bofu was."
"Your arms are looking far thicker for your training, Lord Sun," Old Yin noted. "You are becoming quite the shot, I hear."
"I... I am becoming a better archer, yes," Sun Quan replied. "I have decided that it will be my specialty: as I lead from afar, so I shall be deadly to my enemies from afar... and the animals that I hunt too, of course...!"
Sun Quan's comment led to a mixture of forced and natural laughter from those present.
"Let us be off, then," Sun Quan said. "I want to be able to tell Shubi that I am a stronger when he returns from Danyang."
Song Qian frowned and asked, "Why, Lord Sun...?"
"It's... a personal complexity," Sun Quan replied. "I know that Shubi impresses all that he meets, just as Bofu did... he shows the way, and I must follow in the only way that I can. Let's go!"
Sun Quan's hunting party would be successful, and the day ended optimistically: Quan's reputation as an archer would grow, and his newfound strength would one day allow him to win an important argument and challenge a formidable enemy.

****

45

When the bandit armies of Danyang learned of Sun Yi's appointment, they collectively assumed that Sun Quan had either lost his mind or run out of appropriate candidates for the role; Sun Yi was known as a brave subordinate officer, but the notion that the impulsive 19-year-old could be a Lieutenant-General and Administrator was beyond credibility. The bandit chieftains quickly decided to put their new overlord to the test and launch an attack on Wanling County: Sun Yi was quick to respond, as fighting was something that he was very familiar with, and, within a day, he had assembled a militia at the gates of the threatened city.

"I said that we'd have to do a lot of fighting, didn't I, Mister Bian?" Sun Yi said.

"…You did, Administrator," Bian Hong replied.

"But you'll need to stay here this time, alright, and keep the office running as usual," Sun Yi continued.

"…As you wish, Administrator," Bian Hong replied.

"Mister Wang: you're in charge of rallying the people," Sun Yi said. Mister Wang bowed silently.

"…I wish Xu Kun was here!" Sun Yi cackled. "We made fools of the Shanyue that tried to attack Qu'e before I came here, and-!"

"You cannot just charge blindly!" Mister Wang protested. "The-!"

"Bandits and tribes are the same," Sun Yi said. "They're *stupid*: every time, all it takes is the same old tried-and-tested ways of chasing them off. I don't like indirectly praising Lü Bu, but his 'camp smashing general'… Gao something… *Gao Shun*! Gao Shun, that was it… pretty much 'wrote the book' on getting rid of bandits like these."

"The Black Mountain Bandits still exist," Mister Wang retorted.

"…Yeah, I know, but he didn't get to finish the job," Sun Yi said. "I won't either; I'll chase them off, and then my new aides will-"

"Oh, yes… *Dai Yuan* and *Gui Lan*," Mister Wang grumbled.

"They'll be here soon," Sun Yi continued. "They'll have loads of ideas! And we should be ready to hear them out! Sun Gao, you'll guard the city; Fu Ying, you'll be my second!"

"*Aiee*… **you're being impetuous, and that is not the proper conduct of an Administrator!**" Mister Wang cried as Sun Yi led his men through the city gates.

"General Sun will be back soon enough," Sun Gao insisted.

Sun Yi made short work of the bandits' vanguard by attacking their forward camps with such ferocity that the leaders started to bicker and contemplate retreat; the demoralising effect of being attacked before they had even started spread like rot through the rest of the coalition, and most of the armies turned back.

"Without Fei Zhan's support, there are now less than a thousand," Sun Yi said as he looked at his battle maps in his command tent. "That's good, because that's pretty much all that *I* have."

"So what will you do next…?" Fu Ying asked.

"…Smash them in battle," Sun Yi replied. "That's not very 'elegant', but what else can I do? They're just bandits and I can't be bothered with all that 'mind games' stuff that people like Gongjin and Ziheng are so good at."

"Smash them we will, then," Fu Ying sighed.

More days passed: Dai Yuan and Gui Lan arrived in Wanling County and were approaching the capital as Sun Yi returned from his victory over the bandits. The former fugitives were immediately invited to Sun Yi's home, where the host had them sit before him and plied them with food and tea.
"You are most gracious, Administrator," Dai Yuan said.
"Call me 'Shubi'," Sun Yi insisted.
"…Your famous brother, Sun Ce, was in the habit of asking men to call him by his courtesy name, but we are your newly-employed vassals, so that would not be proper," Dai Yuan replied.
"…If you say so," Sun Yi sighed. "You know best, after all."
Dai Yuan and Gui Lan exchanged bemused glances.
"…I really need your help, and I hope that I can one day refer to you as friends," Sun Yi continued. "Mister Dai, Mister Gui, the prefecture is overwhelmed with problems that I can't solve alone. Your former lord, Sheng Xian, was an upright man that always did what was right, and it is unfortunate that he was overthrown by that bastard Xu Gong, who later plotted to kill my brother and somehow did so from beyond the grave."
"It is also 'unfortunate' that Sheng Xian was murdered," Gui Lan replied. "He might have been invaluable to the region."
"I honestly know nothing of it," Sun Yi protested. "I have been my brother's sword in battle, and before that I was Bofu's shadow in a few battles. I'm not smart enough for intrigue: if I had met Sheng Xian I would have asked him to join our cause."
"…And what *is* your cause, General Sun…?" Gui Lan asked.
"We're tied by marriage to Excellency Cao," Sun Yi replied. "That makes us vassals of the Han: in fact, my brother's envoy to Xuchang is lobbying for my brother to be made a senior Han general. We're just trying to stabilise and rebuild Jiangdong and make it a great place to be."
"But your brother ignored our lord Sheng Xian and employed Xu Gong instead," Dai Yuan said. "Was that proper…?"
"In hindsight, no, else Bofu would live and Sheng Xian would be Administrator of Wu," Sun Yi replied. "Bofu did as he was advised, based on the things that were known or assumed at the time."
"In what way had Sheng Xian acted to deserve such cruel treatment…?" Dai Yuan asked.
"…Look, I'm trying not to get angry, because I want your help," Sun Yi replied. "Bofu wasn't the only one to miss Sheng Xian's worth: did Liu Yao work with him at all…?"
"…No, he worked with Xu Gong as well," Dai Yuan conceded.
"When we asked around, Sheng was described as weak and useless, and Xu Gong was popular," Sun Yi continued. "If the people of Wu hadn't followed Xu Gong…"
"…So we must disregard the past and look to the future," Gui Lan said tonelessly. "What roles did you have in mind for us…?"
"What roles did you want…?" Sun Yi retorted.
"…We *choose our own roles*…?" Dai Yuan said with disbelief.
"I brought you here to help me stabilise Danyang, just as I said in my letter," Sun Yi insisted. "What roles should you both assume to be of the most help to me…?"
"…I… I would suggest makng me 'Civil Assistant', Administrator

Sun," Dai Yuan said.

"I held the role 'Chief Controller', along with another man, but we always quarrelled, wasting valuable time," Gui Lan recalled.

Sun Yi frowned and said, "Well then you should be… I dunno… how about 'Supreme Chief Controller', so you're not having to argue with people…?"

"…A sound idea that can only work well," Gui Lan replied. "We will serve you loyally, Lord Sun."

Dai Yuan and Gui Lan kowtowed, and Sun Yi said, "No-no-no! Don't do that! There's no need for that! I am quite happy for you to bow a little bit! And call me 'Mister Sun', or 'Administrator'; call me 'General' if you must, but not 'Lord Sun'."

"As you command, Administrator!" Dai Yuan replied.

"We will work tirelessly!" Gui Lan cried.

"Just help me sort out Danyang," Sun Yi said. "That's all I ask."

Dai Yuan and Gui Lan left the meeting and retired to the grand house that Sun Yi had allocated to Gui; the two sat facing each other and smiled.

"And now, we wait," Dai Yuan chuckled.

"This has been so easy," Gui Lan said. "Our roles give us the power to do pretty much what we want at a civil level, and the military must kowtow to us as well."

"Never has a man so readily handed a knife to his killer," Dai Yuan suggested. "But he has it coming to him: he pleads ignorance, but the Suns are fond of doing so. Sun Ce killed Liu Yao and Lu Kang and then he said 'I did not mean to'; Sun Quan destroyed our lord and feigned sincerity afterwards. But this fool Sun Yi has no brain: we have seals of office, and real power, and yet we have been here less than a day! We shall reshape the administration for our own purposes, and then, when the moment is right… we'll forge the right alliances and take this region back for the Han."

"…And make a name – and place – for ourselves," Gui Lan said. "I have hid on estates and in the hills for too long: it is time that life was good, for Heaven knows, Mister Dai, we deserve it."

"So long as we do not fail to live up to Sheng Xian's principles, such rewards are not outside of our reach," Dai Yuan insisted.

"…You said that we should 'wait', but now you want us to be the ones that kill him," Gui Lan noted. "Is that the right course…?"

Dai Yuan smiled and said, "Actually, I think that you and I might agree on something without realising it: we're dead afterwards, and what's the point of that?"

"Exactly," Gui Lan replied. "The military men love him, the fools – but the civil administrators are obviously divided."

"…I will use my role to pry," Dai Yuan said. "Leave it with me… if there's a man that we can manipulate, I will find him."

The court in Qu'e City was less than pleased when the news of Sun Yi's appointments arrived a few days later.

"*Dai Yuan*… and *Gui Lan*???" Lü Fan exclaimed. "**What a fool! Why has Shubi employed those two and made them so important??? Does he willingly invite disaster???**"

"…You're family, Ziheng, but all the same I'd prefer that you didn't call my brother a fool in front of the court," Sun Quan said.

"Sorry, Lord Sun," Lü Fan replied. "But I have just got back from stabilising southern Lujiang, and this wasn't what I wanted to find... I spoke too frankly."

"So go and replace them or him," Xu Kun suggested.

"That wouldn't be proper," Lü Fan replied. "Danyang must be... ruled by a Sun... but... but why has he employed those two? They're Sheng Xian's closest aides!"

"General – or rather *Administrator* – Sun Yi obviously trusts them because of their record for honesty, loyalty and working hard," the politician Quan Rou suggested.

"...They blame us for the death of Sheng Xian," Lü Fan said. "This can only end badly, Lord Sun!"

"Shubi insists that he's spoken to them and explained that he had nothing to do with what happened to Sheng Xian," Sun Quan replied. "They refused to work for me, which surely gave them better opportunities for 'revenge'...?"

"...Alright, that's a fair point," Lü Fan said. "But they should be monitored closely: we don't want to make the same mistakes that we made with Xu Gong."

"I'll write to someone appropriate," Zhang Zhao promised.

Dai Yuan and Gui Lan were outwardly eager to assist Sun Yi in his stabilisation efforts, so much so that Sun Yi trusted them completely and often left them to manage the prefecture while he led armies to deal with bandits and the Shanyue. The two men were quick to ingratiate themselves with the Danyang officials and intelligentsia; their tales of woe and reminiscences about the noble Sheng Xian stirred many to feel pity for Dai and Gui and agree that they just wanted to do good.

Weeks passed: in the north, Cao Cao completely abandoned his campaign against Liu Biao, forged an alliance with Yuan Shao's eldest son Yuan Tan and attacked the fortified city of Yè, the capital of the Yuan's 'empire', with the aim of expelling or killing its lord, Yuan Shao's third son and chosen heir Yuan Shang. The battle for Yè City would see Yuan Shang's Han Chinese soldiers and Wuhuan tribal allies pitted against Cao Cao's Han Chinese soldiers, Qiang tribal militias and Southern Xiongnu conscripts, Yuan Tan's Han Chinese soldiers and the few Wuhuan tribesmen that still followed Tan; victory would mean the end of the Yuan clan's command of Ji Province, but Yuan Tan, like his famous uncle Yuan Shu, was blinded to the threats to his own security by hubris and the need for revenge against the brother that had, in his mind, stolen his birth-right.

In the south, the situation was about to deteriorate further. The bandits of Wu Prefecture had formed a mighty alliance and decided that they would challenge their new ruler; in addition to that, famine was gripping some parts of the region and plague was destroying others. Sun Quan was about to be put under immense pressure that would force him to personally oversee the rescue of his state, and his lack of presence in his capital would, once again, be costly.

＊＊＊＊＊＊＊＊＊＊＊＊

46

Sun Quan stared at the sea of miserable faces in his court and said, "We are at breaking point, then...?"

"My lord, this is ridiculous now," Zhang Zhao admitted. "Zhu Huan is having to have his men run around Yuyao and the surrounding areas, gathering up people that are fleeing the plague and resettling them; Dong Xi is just about able to quell one rebel militia as another appears; Jiang Qin is close to defeating the two troublemakers that he was sent to deal with, but 'close is still too far away'; and now, on top of the existing Shanyue problems in Wu, we have this huge army of criminals to deal with!"

"Can Zhu Zhi manage...?" Sun Quan asked.

"I doubt it," Zhang Zhao replied. "We need to make a great show of force."

"...Xu Kun: you will lead a force of men to support Zhu Zhi," Sun Quan ordered. "Zhou Tai and Chen Wu will provide further reinforcement shortly; Bu Zhi, you will accompany Xu Kun's vanguard force."

"As you command," Bu Zhi replied.

"Lord Sun, you must consider venturing out yourself," Cheng Pu suggested. "We could reach out to these men as much as we could beat them into submission."

"I intend to add my own presence to the battle, but I must first prepare," Sun Quan replied. "Sun Hè will have to stay here as the city's guardian when I leave, and there will need to be replacement administrators if Zhang Zhao is not here."

"Such preparations will take a week, while procuring the provisions for the larger army will take longer," Zhang Zhao said. "We must prepare for this properly, Mister Cheng!"

"I do know that, Mister Zhang," Cheng Pu retorted. "I used to do those things myself."

"Stop bickering!" Sun Quan ordered. "We must all do our part!"

Sun Quan retreated to his study, where he was visited by Sun Hè.

"I wish that you'd return to my bodyguard force, Bohai," Sun Quan said. "I'd rather leave the defence of the city to others and have a familiar face at my side."

"You have Song Qian, and you could take my nephew Shao on campaign if you wanted," Sun Hè replied. "I'd like to keep him with me as a second, though, if I am honest."

"Shao is very reliable," Sun Quan said thoughtfully. "Even at his young age, he shows caution and works diligently. He'll be a future hero. You may keep him here, Bohai, unless I am forced to utilise him for some reason."

"Any more correspondence from Shubi...?" Sun Hè asked.

"Not yet," Sun Quan replied. "He'll be overwhelmed, like I am. Oh, Bohai, I yearn for an end to this..."

While Sun Quan prepared for a long campaign against the bandits of Wu Prefecture, Dai Yuan and Gui Lan were exploiting Sun Yi's latest excursion outside his capital and seeking an audience with Yi's aide Bian Hong; they invited him to Gui Lan's office and had him sit as a guest.

"Is there something that you wanted forwarded to Lord Sun...?"
Bian Hong asked.
"No, Mister Bian," Dai Yuan replied.
"...Then why am I here...?" Bian Hong asked worriedly.
"It... it pains me to say this, but we have all been deceived," Dai
Yuan said. "The Suns are wicked thieves, Mister Bian, that His
Majesty wants purged."
Bian Hong's eyes wandered.
"Your expected reaction was to try to leave, but you obviously
have existing doubts," Gui Lan chuckled.
"...Sun Yi is a liability," Bian Hong said. "He shirks civil duties,
often delegating them to others, including me and your good
selves, and he enjoys drinking and banqueting his officers to
enjoy their adulation and nurture their devotion to him. It cannot
be denied that he is a great warrior, but that is all."
"...Go on," Gui Lan insisted. "You are obviously keen to speak."
"I do not hate him, but I despise his flippant attitude to civil
matters and obvious contempt for the 'men of the pen'," Bian
Hong continued. "His love of drink makes him quite obnoxious at
times, as he becomes very boisterous and tries to spar with his
servants and with me; I know that he is being playful, but not
everybody enjoys such nonsense, and I worry that he will make
mistakes and bring more problems upon us than he solves."
"...I'm afraid that our own opinion is far worse," Dai Yuan said.
"You know, of course, that Sun Ce was responsible for the deaths
of Governor Liu Yao and the noble Lu Kang."
"Lu Xun and Lu Ji have both visited Danyang and made it clear
that they hold no grudge!" Bian Hong retorted. "Liu Ji shows no
animosity either, despite his father's death being more
ignominious and technically the greater offence!"
"...Lu Ji is young, Lu Xun is ambitious but naïve, and Liu Ji has
been tricked into thinking that he is without options," Dai Yuan
suggested. "Liu Ji's uncle, Liu Dai, was once Cao Cao's master,
and the two did not get on: Sun Quan's advisers have said to him,
'That being the case, would he enjoy favour in a court where Cao
is Excellency of Works...?' ...But Excellency Cao is magnanimous."
"He was not 'magnanimous' to Sheng Xian!" Bian Yong retorted.
"Just days – days – before our lord Sheng Xian was murdered, His
Excellency had despatched a seal and intended to order Sun Quan
to allow Shang free passage to Xuchang," Gui Lan recalled. "The
messenger was delayed, and the death soon followed: does that
tell you anything...?"
"...But might Cao Cao have feigned benevolence and killed Sheng
to either frame the Suns or eliminate Sheng so that he could put
his own man in Wu...?" Bian Hong protested. "Cao is the 'Crafty
Villain'! Cao laid waste to Xu Province! Cao-!"
"Put 'Cao' to one side for a moment," Gui Lan said. "Think,
instead, about the Suns. Sun Jian was a hero – that much is
known. But Sun Ce – the 'Little Conqueror' – killed Lu Kang to
take Lujiang for Yuan Shu, and then he took Jiangdong from Wang
Lang and Liu Yao for that same greedy master, a man that then
used the Sun clan's ill-gotten spoils as an excuse to claim that he
was an emperor. Yes, Sun Ce left Yuan Shu's service at that point,
but did he return any of what he had taken in Yuan Shu's name...?
No: he kept Jiangdong, and then he wrested Lujiang from Liu Xun,

the man that Yuan Shu had entrusted it to!"

"...The south has grown and prospered under their supervision!" Bian Hong protested.

"For what purpose...?" Dai Yuan asked. "When Xiang Yu turned the south into the Chu kingdom, he did so to become an emperor; he did just that and then contended with the future Han for the nation. When the Han won, what happened to the south...? Did any of the power that it had as 'Chu' remain, or was it perhaps punished to prevent later rebellions...? What will happen to Sun Quan's south when he confronts His Majesty and loses...?"

"The Suns don't intend to challenge the Han!" Bian Hong insisted. "Sun Ben's daughter is married to Cao Zhang! Sun Kuang's widow is Cao Cao's niece! Why would those houses unite if one suspected the other of plotting sedition...?"

"...Han emperors have married their daughters to Xiongnu and Xianbei chieftains for some time now, in the name of 'keeping the peace', but no 'kept peace' exists regardless," Dai Yuan said. "In the end, marriage alliances mean very little: when two men swear a brotherhood, that's supposed to mean something, but to Yuan Shao, it meant nothing."

"Mister Bian, we have not come to our conclusions lightly," Gui Lan insisted. "We wanted to believe that the Suns were Han loyalists, like us, and that they intended to stabilise the south for the good of the Empire and then ensure a peaceful transition of authority when their work was done, but now there's talk of 'independent states' and references to Sun Quan being a 'feudal king in all but name'.

"Liu Fu, the Inspector of this province, is building a fortress city at Hefei because he fears that the Suns will soon try to take the rest of Jiujiang and Lujiang prefectures; Sun Ce tried to have his mastermind Lü Fan created the Administrator of Guiyang – which is in *Jing* – and tried to invade Guangling, which is in *Xu*; Liu Fu's predecessor, Yan Xiang, was murdered by Sun's enforcer Li Shu, who then rebelled when he realised the error; and who is Administrator of Wu Prefecture now...? Under the legitimate Han government, it was Sheng Xian; under the criminal reign of the 'Regents', it was Xu Gong, and that persisted under the Suns; and then, within no time at all after our lord's demise, Zhu Zhi was announced as Administrator... but was he ever appointed by the court...? No, the court wanted Sheng Xian, but now that can never be!"

"...But the south has improved so much... and Wu Jing was a good man...!" Bian Hong croaked. "I... am torn...!"

"Wu Jing was a kind man, but soft too, and if he were not Sun Jian's brother-in-law, I don't believe that he would have been allied to Sun Ce or Sun Quan," Dai Yuan suggested. "And we have no guarantees that the many, many deaths of late are not the result of in-fighting."

"...'In-fighting'...?" Bian Hong exclaimed.

Gui Lan smiled and said, "Consider this: one day, while he was busy 'pacifying' the ruins of Luoyang, Sun Jian is said to have come across the Imperial Seal... and kept it, for he saw it as a sign that his clan was destined for greatness at the Han's expense. After that, he was happy to serve a rebellious Yuan Shu and invade Jing, which once formed part of the Chu kingdom: he died, passing power to his nephew Sun Ben, who had no ambition. Sun Ce then wrested power from Sun Ben and started to conquer the south, ostensibly for Yuan Shu... but rumours abound of his trading the Imperial Seal for his first army, and that possession of the Seal corrupted Yuan Shu's already shattered mind further, prompting him to do what he did..."

"...It is a dismissed theory!" Bian Hong cried.

"Here in the Sun-devoted south, yes," Dai Yuan replied. "Elsewhere, it is considered."

"...But what has the Imperial Seal to do with 'in-fighting'...?" Bian Hong asked.

"Once the loss of the Seal to Yuan Shu became an issue, Sun Ce wanted to realise the prophecy regardless," Gui Lan suggested. "He conquered Jiangdong, gaining the support of cutthroats and mercenaries like Zu Lang and Taishi Ci as he went... but then his brother Quan met Pan Zhang, the famous bad debtor, and he was consumed by vice and ambition. So now there are three Suns: one that had power wrongly taken, one that took, and one that wants to take. Sun Ben quietly fades into the background, but Sun Quan tries to secure his own allies... and then, in Dantu, he struck, removing Sun Ce and-"

"Ridiculous!" Bian Hong heckled. "Ridiculous! Foolishness!"

"To some, perhaps," Dai Yuan said. "But Sheng Xian was never harmed so long as Lady Wu – who respected heroes and honest gentlemen – was alive. Lady Wu once saved Officer of Merit Wei Teng from Sun Ce's wrath – wrath ignited by an *offhand remark* – by threatening to throw herself down a well: Sun Ce relented, but he had been seen for the unstable, reckless psychotic that he really was under that affable exterior. His officials were scared... truly frightened. And it's said that Sun Yi is 'just like his famous brother'... who wanted to behead an Officer of Merit in the street for a *remark*, and succeeded in killing the Taoist saint Gan Ji for the crime of spreading peace and love amongst the people of Wu... or, to be more precise, taking the love and devotion of the people *away from Sun Ce*... and Sun Yi is said by all to be the *same*."

Bian Hong shuddered.

"And then, in a turn of events that still makes no sense, Sun Ce died, and his emotionally unstable, morally weak younger brother succeeded him, rather than Sun Ben, who was tested, proven and whose daughter was, at the time, betrothed to Cao Zhang," Dai Yuan continued. "They say that the orchestrator of that plan was Lady Wu, who desired 'more stability'... it pains me to think what it took to get to that point, but she got what she wanted. Sun Quan became the lord of Jiangdong... and since then, it's been like watching a tragic stage play. Sun Kuang, Marquis of Wucheng, died suddenly after marrying Lady Cao; Lady Wu suddenly died not long after that; Wu Jing now follows her to the netherworld, and between them came the death of Sheng Xian, a man that lived on Xu Zhao's estate... and Lady Wu is said to have preferred that there was no assault on that estate."

"...All that you say makes sense to me," Bian Hong admitted. "The Suns are tearing themselves apart over the power that the region brings to them."

"Sun Yi has been sent here to replace Wu Jing, rather than Sun Ben, who has been assigned to Yuzhang and made poor use of,"

Gui Lan said. "I predict two scenarios: Sun Yi will be loyal as Sun Quan expects, and Danyang will become a barracks for a future war with Liu Fu for control of the province... or Sun Yi will become increasingly intoxicated with his newfound power as a prefectural administrator and try to contend with Sun Quan using whatever allies he can muster. I now go further and predict two outcomes: regardless of what Sun Yi's actual intent is, Sun and his schemers will assume what they want to assume, and this province will either be a barracks for a future war with Liu Fu... or it will be surrounded and purged by a jealous, untrusting Sun Quan in the months to come. Either way, Mister Bian, the Suns are a poisonous miasma that has lingered over the south for too long, and if it is not cleared soon, it will spread across the Empire. We must act soon."

Bian Hong was already convinced: he bowed and said, "I, Hong, am yours to command. If there is any way that I can save the region and the Han from the Suns, then I will do whatever I am asked to do, regardless of the threat to my own life."

"Your actions will be recorded in history, Bian Hong," Dai Yuan promised. "Today we have made a pact that will purge Yang Province of those wretched Suns and bring everlasting peace back to the Empire!"

"Resume your duties until the right moment arrives," Gui Lan ordered. "We'll act according to circumstances: that way, we cannot be discovered and thwarted."

"As you command," Bian Hong replied.

More time passed. In the north, Yuan Shao's heir Yuan Shang was chased out of Yè City by Cao Cao and his own elder brother Yuan Tan: the humiliated clan chieftain was forced to flee northward to the estate of his brother Yuan Xi in Yòu Province, while Yuan Tan – who took great pleasure in the victory – was sure that Cao Cao would allow him to inherit the Yuan legacy. But Cao Cao intended to 'tie up loose ends', and the first was dealt with almost immediately: Cao paid his respects to his former friend Yuan Shao when he entered Yè, but Xu Yòu – the man that had betrayed Yuan Shao to Cao Cao at Guandu – showed what his lifelong friend Cao claimed to be 'offensive contempt' toward Shao's temple, whereupon Cao's chief bodyguard 'executed' the unprepared Xu Yòu on the spot. Yuan Tan would be next, but Cao Cao would show his usual patience as the complacent Tan reorganised his forces in and around the city of Nanpi.

Sun Quan's advisers were watching Cao Cao's manoeuvres with growing concern: his actions were chillingly precise and seemingly guaranteed to give the warlord the outcomes that he wanted. The defeat of Yuan Shang had taken mere months, where most had predicted years: that meant that a southern campaign could be one or two years away, and that would not end well for the embattled Sun clan, which needed at least that long to restore basic order.

****

47

Colonel Ling Tong was forced to act as the principal military figure in Wu Prefecture as the war with the 'Wu Hills Bandits' confederacy intensified; he defied his 15 years of age and scored early victories against the smaller armies that attacked villages in the capital region, but there was far more work to do.

"We can chase them out of Wu County, but they're everywhere, and we haven't the resources to do much more than delay the inevitable," Ling Tong said in an address to Wu Prefecture Administrator Zhu Zhi and his court in Wu County City. "Once Lord Sun's reinforcements arrive, we can do more."

"You've already achieved far more than anyone expected, Colonel Ling," Zhu Zhi replied. "I trust your judgement: proceed as you have done, and I will ensure that you have the necessary food and other provisions."

"As you command," Ling Tong replied.

Ling Tong bowed to the court and withdrew to prepare his men for another march; Zhu Zhi then turned to Han Dang and said, "Old friend, we have a crisis, but at least we have a new hero to match it. Ling Tong is marvellous."

"I wish that I could help him, but I'm stuck fighting the Shanyue," Han Dang complained. "Still, at least the tribes haven't joined up with the bandits properly, else we'd probably have to evacuate the prefecture and-"

"I won't let Wu fall to anyone," Zhu Zhi replied.

"Me neither," Han Dang said. "But we'd need to relocate the civilians, wouldn't we...?"

"Kuaiji has a plague outbreak," Zhu Zhi replied. "And Danyang is overrun with a host of problems. We *must* sort this region out."

Sun Quan finally completed his preparations for departure from Qu'e, although it was to pacify Wu Prefecture rather than establish a new capital in Wucheng as he had hoped: Sun Hè led his own men to the city gates in order to see his lord's army off.

"You look resplendent in your armour, Lord Sun," Sun Hè said. "I'm sure that your presence will inspire fear and loyalty where they are appropriate."

"...Maintain communications, Bohai," Sun Quan ordered. "Don't be complacent or feel that you are being soft by contacting me or Mister Zhang."

"You can trust that I will act properly, Lord Sun," Sun Hè replied.

"...And watch Shangxiang for me," Sun Quan whispered. "Don't let her make too much trouble."

Sun Hè smiled and said, "I will do as you ask."

"And maintain communications with Shubi," Sun Quan pleaded. "Don't let my brother's impetuous nature get the better of him, especially now that he has those two men working for him."

"I shall do as you command," Sun Hè replied.

"Gu Yong, Yan Jun and Quan Rou are in charge of the court," Zhang Zhao said. "Lu Xun, Lu Ji, Xie Jiong and others are supporting them. We should hurry, Lord Sun."

"...Farewell for now, Cousin Bohai," Sun Quan said. "Stay well."

Sun Hè bowed humbly, and Sun Quan ordered his men to begin

their march. The army of thousands was very conspicuous as it moved, and the standard bearers made it clear that Sun Quan was leading them personally: it would therefore not take long for others to learn of the lord of Jiangdong's absence from his capital, and the cautious Sun Hè knew that it could lead to anything.

Ling Tong and Lü Meng led their forces southward to the Wu County outskirts and prepared to do battle with the Wu Hills Bandits: the senior leaders had retreated to their camps in neighbouring counties, so the bandits' organisation was poor. The first three skirmishes ended with the bandits retreating, but they suddenly regrouped at the border: Ling Tong noticed that the bandits' front lines were chanting abuse in a regimented fashion and advocated caution, but Lü Meng wanted to charge.
"…**Lü Meng, stay your horse,**" Ling Tong pleaded.
"**Forgive me, but you are ten years younger than me, and do not understand bandits,**" Lü Meng retorted. "**We must smash them quickly, Colonel Ling!**"
"**They're up to something,**" Ling Tong insisted.
"**Smashed heads don't think!**" Lü Meng replied as he carried on with his charge.
"…No, they don't, theirs or ours," Ling Tong murmured. "What might they… … …ah! The *baggage train*…!"
Ling Tong turned his horse and retreated; Lü Meng noticed and cried, "**He shows cowardice at this late stage??? …No matter: I shall win the day!**"
The bandits allowed Lü Meng's forces to repeatedly attack their front line and made no attempt to counter and encircle them; he finally realised this and started to think as he withdrew to his own front line.
"…**I'm a fool!**" Lü Meng cried. "**The *baggage train*!**"
Lü Meng contemplated what he should do, but word was quickly spreading that the baggage train was under threat, and the Wu forces were starting to panic; the bandit commanders saw this as their moment and ordered a full charge.
"**Keep calm!**" Lü Meng screamed as he rode back and forth along the front lines, deflecting enemy attacks and trying to keep his own men in line.
"**We have 'em surrounded!**" a bandit chief said. "**Finish 'em off, lads!**"
The bandits' small cavalry converged on Lü Meng, who fought them off bravely; Ling Tong then returned with his team of elite riders and struck at the bandits' rear while his subordinates spread the word that the baggage train was safe. The defenders' morale was restored, and they achieved another victory over the frustrated bandits.
"…You're ten years younger but a hundred years ahead of me in wits, even with all of my reading," Lü Meng said as he approached the weary Ling Tong. "They goaded us into thinning our lines and leaving our baggage train behind… that should have been obvious – for 'without its provisions, an army will lose' – but it took me a while to figure it out, whereas you realised straight away."
"If it was obvious to everyone, the great Sun Tzu would not have needed to include it in his military text," Ling Tong replied. "And it is not so much that it's 'obvious', Colonel Lü: the trick was to

make us forget that it was possible."

"…That's very true," Lü Meng sighed. "I'm really stupid."

"You're too quick to act, but you realised in the end," Ling Tong replied. "My father was the same. 'Recklessness leads to destruction': so simply said, so serious if ignored. We owe it to ourselves and our lord to think first and preserve our lives so that we can fight in the future."

"…Still, we won," Lü Meng sighed.

"Alas, no," Ling Tong said. "They are more organised than the average horde of bandits: they have attacked the county again from the north and east, and General Han Dang and Administrator Zhu need us to aid them."

"You go, Colonel," Lü Meng replied. "I'll make sure they don't come back here."

Ling Tong bowed respectfully and withdrew to organise his men once again.

Time passed: Sun Quan's reinforcements added 15,000 to Zhu Zhi's pacification force, but the number of bandits had climbed to over 50,000, so the war was far from won.

"We'll need to divide initially, tackle each individual army and then gradually coalesce as we score victories," Lü Fan said. "Lord Sun, Zhang Zhao and Zhuge Jin will fight in the east with Zhou Tai, Chen Wu and Song Qian as the main officers; Bu Zhi and I will take a force northward with Han Dang, Ling Tong and Zhang Yi as the main officers; Zhou Gongjin, Lu Su, Cheng Pu and Xu Kun will advance southward and rendezvous with Lü Meng; Zhu Zhi will continue to provide logistics support and liaise with Gu Yong, Yan Jun and Lu Xun in the capital. With this strategy, we hope to defeat this confederacy in a matter of months if not weeks."

"Time is against us," Gongjin suggested. "We should work quickly, Lord Sun: more signs of weakness will lead to more insurrections."

"Then let us march," Sun Quan sighed.

****

48

The south and east of Wu Prefecture became a giant battleground: but in neighbouring Danyang, Sun Yi was starting to gain ground against the bandits and tribes that he faced. Dai Yuan and Gui Lan were perturbed by the successes, since they increased Sun Yi's popularity with the army and civilians alike, which would, in turn, make their chances of 'victory' less likely; they were therefore elated when news reached them of Sun Quan's mobilisation and subsequent departure from Qu'e City with most of the region's armed forces.

"It is now or never," Dai Yuan said.

Gui Lan looked around his finely-furnished home and smiled, saying, "I shall enjoy living in the governor's mansion."

"As I've said, I couldn't care less what you want out of this," Dai Yuan replied. "I want – need – to avenge Sheng Xian and repay his faith in us."

"We can both of us benefit beyond simple revenge," Gui Lan suggested. "We can both of us have his home, his money, his servants, his women..."

"Perhaps," Dai Yuan replied. "But right now, I just want to see justice done. Are we acting or not...?"

"Of course," Gui Lan said. "I'll brief our 'sword' while you make the necessary suggestions to our target..."

Dai Yuan asked to speak with Sun Yi as soon as the latter returned from an exhausting battle with bandits: Yi had taken his aide Bian Hong, who was now more committed than ever to ridding Jiangdong of the Sun clan.

"I'm tired, Mister Dai, so please make this quick," Sun Yi said. "I don't mean to be rude, but... well, I can't be doing with pedantry at the best of times, which is why I employed you."

"You have made significant gains, but Wu is now riddled with bandits, and that might give men in Danyang ideas, so we must pre-empt," Dai Yuan explained. "You must invite the magistrates and nobles to a banquet so that we can broach the subject of a decisive joint effort against the bandits and Shanyue chieftains."

"...Okay, fine," Sun Yi replied cautiously. "Why didn't you suggest this before, though, when Wu wasn't such a mess...?"

"This is a desperate act," Dai Yuan admitted. "We shouldn't be taking the magistrates away from their work locally, but we need a joint strategy, and we shouldn't be sending our plans as written letters that can go astray."

"...I'll write at once," Sun Yi replied.

At around the same time, Gui Lan had travelled to Bian Hong's home and asked for a private audience.

"He is so obnoxious!" Bian Hong complained. "Time and again, he got drunk with his officers and subjected me and others to humiliating 'tests of strength' that-!"

"You'll now have your moment," Gui Lan promised.

"...We are going to act?" Bian Hong exclaimed.

"In a few days' time, there will be an emergency meeting in the guise of a banquet," Gui Lan explained. "The minutes after the end of the banquet will be your moments, Mister Bian... and then,

when the deed is done, you will flee to the hills with your proof, where we will lead our followers to meet you; and then, after contacting Liu Fu, we can act against the Suns as one."
"You can rely on me, Chief Controller," Bian Hong promised.

The magistrates arrived within days, but Sun Yi was unexpectedly distracted by another bandit attack to the east of the city; he was greeted upon his return by an irritated and nervous Gui Lan, who said, "They await you, Administrator Sun, and they are very, very annoyed at being kept waiting."
"Was I at fault...?" Sun Yi huffed. "...I'll go home and prepare."
Gui Lan stared at Bian Hong, who smiled icily.
        Sun Yi entered his home and threw his battle helmet to the floor, saying, "**I am so, so sick of being an Administrator! It was supposed to be a change from being a general, an 'instead of', but all it is to me is more work on top of what I was doing already!**"
A servant hurried to pick up the helmet and return it to its stand while Bian Hong looked on; Sun Yi's principal wife, Lady Xū, entered the room and said, "You are going to rest, I hope."
"Fat chance of that," Sun Yi scoffed. "I have to entertain tonight: all of the magistrates are in the city, and we have important things to discuss."
"...I see," Lady Xū murmured.
"I really can't be doing with it," Sun Yi continued. "I... ... ...My lady, I have a request. Something tells me that I should ask... what can you tell me...?"
"I heard of your return and divined for you," Lady Xū replied. "The signs are muddled, clouded..."
"That'll be because I intend to get very, very drunk after the business is discussed," Sun Yi grumbled as he threw his armour to the floor; another weary servant rushed to retrieve the expensive armour and set it on its mount.
"No... no, I mean that there is hidden danger," Lady Xū said. "You must postpone the meeting and review your security."
Bian Hong shuddered nervously.
"Oh, for-! **I *can't*!**" Sun Yi chortled. "Do you not understand that I *can't*, woman...?"
Lady Xū turned her gaze away.
"I... I apologise," Sun Yi pleaded.
Lady Xū returned her gaze to her husband and smiled, saying, "There is no need. You are a passionate man and speak as you find. I do understand that you cannot easily postpone this meeting, but if there were a way..."
"There... there isn't," Sun Yi sighed.
"Then be cautious," Lady Xū pleaded.
"...Huang Gai and Xu Sheng are two of the guests, and they're both as loyal as it gets," Sun Yi replied. "I have a sword at my side at all times, and even drunk, I can... ... ...well, anyway, I have to get ready."
"I shall leave you then," Lady Xū said as she turned and retreated to the sleeping quarters.
"...Alright, Mister Bian, let's prepare," Sun Yi said.

Sun Yi's banquet was a success in every respect: he provided fine food, finer wine and managed to discuss a military strategy with his impatient magistrates. But as soon as the business had been conducted, Sun Yi started to drink heavily; Huang Gai decided that Sun Yi was being far too careless and said, "Lord Sun Ce was fond of a drink, Lord Sun Yi, but he showed caution."

"Ah, look, Old Huang, I'm in the company of friends, am I not...?" Sun Yi asked.

Dai Yuan and Gui Lan smiled.

"...I am merely showing concern for your welfare, Lord Sun Yi," Huang Gai replied.

"The food was surprisingly good considering the current difficulties," Xu Sheng suggested. "Did you select the very best for us, Lord Sun Yi...?"

"I did, Mister Xu, 'cause you're my friends and guests and whatnot," Sun Yi replied. "Anyhow... some o' you look like you have fleas. Can you not relax...?"

"We're anxious to get back to our counties," Huang Gai said. "In fact, we have collectively agreed that we should leave at once."

"Oh... well, I s'pose you should go if you think you have to," Sun Yi replied. "It was nice t'see you anyways, Gongfu... seeing you reminds me o' Dad."

Huang Gai bowed and said, "As you remind me, Lord Sun: a very good night to you."

The other magistrates took Huang Gai's words as their cue to start getting to their feet and bowing respectfully; Sun Yi laughed and said, "I guess the wine's all mine, then!"

"I shall see you to the city gates, gentlemen," Dai Yuan said.

"I'll come an' all!" Sun Yi protested; he tried to rise, but his sword had gotten caught between the legs of his short table and his seat cushion. Sun Yi was unable to think clearly, so he removed his sword belt instead of freeing the sword and got to his feet, grumbling, "Can't understand what's going on there..."

"You should stay here," Huang Gai suggested. "Don't come to the gates in that condition, Lord Sun Yi."

"Let me at least see you to the door, gentlemen!" Sun Yi chuckled.

Bian Hong smiled as he turned to the servants and said, "All of you to the kitchen: remain there until told otherwise."

The servants retreated immediately, leaving the front of the house emptied of people.

The ensemble of officials moved to the gates of the outer wall of Sun Yi's mansion; Sun Yi bowed as best he could to each of the disappointed magistrates and thanked them for attending, and then Dai Yuan and Gui Lan led the guests out of the mansion and toward the city gates.

"...That went alright," Sun Yi mumbled as he turned to go back into the house; he reached the porch, turned to look at the gates again and said, "Yeah... it went fine."

Sun Yi suddenly felt a sharp pain in his lower back: he groaned weakly as his legs started to fail him. A second sharp pain in his upper back made him yelp as he fell to his knees; he tried to turn, and as he twisted his upper body he gasped with shock.

"Y-you...!" Sun Yi croaked. "W-why...?"

Bian Hong did not answer; he crouched over his fallen master, delivered one last stab to his chest and started to cut his throat as he writhed and struggled. The whole encounter was over in less than two minutes, and within five minutes of that, Bian Hong was leaving the mansion with Sun Yi's severed head in a sack.

Dai Yuan and Gui Lan were the first to return to Sun Yi's mansion; there was already a gathering, and they guessed from the wailing and shouting that their plan had succeeded.

"**Mister Dai! Mister Gui!**" the officer Fu Ying cried. "**It's terrible! *Lord Sun*, he...!**"

"...What has happened?" Dai Yuan asked with feigned concern.

"He's been *killed*, *decapitated*!" the officer Sun Gao replied. "My cousin, he...! ...**The man that did this he... he shall die a thousand deaths!**"

"Where is Bian Hong?" Gui Lan asked. "He's supposed to have checked the security!"

"...He was... not with you at the gates...?" Sun Gao said.

"No, he remained here," Dai Yuan replied.

"The official Mister Wang shook his head and asked, "How did nobody see anything...?"

The lead servant coughed deliberately and said, "Mister Bian ordered us all to the kitchen, every one of us, after the banquet."

"...Then... then it *must* be him!" Fu Ying realised. "That bastard! After all the faith that Lord Sun Yi placed in...!"

"No, that's... that's impossible," Gui Lan said. "Bian Hong is an upright man, a-"

"**Who else is there???**" Sun Gao screamed. "**He stayed here to kill my cousin while he was drunk and defenceless!**"

"There was no fight...?" Dai Yuan exclaimed.

"**No!**" Sun Gao sobbed. "He... his sword is by his seat...!"

"*Aiee*... the one time that he shows trust," Dai Yuan sighed.

"Bian Hong – or whoever did this – must be found at once," Gui Lan said. "He cannot have gotten far... but where does an obvious murderer go, possessed of the head of his victim...?"

Lady Xū came to the door of the mansion and watched the discussion with bitter, teary eyes; she could sense that Dai Yuan and Gui Lan were acting, but everyone else was apparently fooled by their show of sadness.

"...There is only one place that he could go: Hefei, to Liu Fu," Fu Ying said. "He will try and get to the river."

"He will flee to the hills and slowly make his way to the river from there," Dai Yuan suggested. "We will intercept and destroy him."

"Surely we should capture this man and learn whether he had *allies*...?" Lady Xū said cuttingly.

"...With all due respect, Lady Xū, we must act according to circumstances," Gui Lan replied. "If we can catch him, we will, but we must end the threat that he poses first and foremost, and retrieve your husband's head for proper burial."

Lady Xū was overcome with emotion: she covered her face with her sleeve and retreated into the mansion.

"I... did not mean to cause the lady further distress, but we have no time for talk," Gui Lan continued. "Mister Dai, Major Sun, Major Fu: let's hurry and catch this monster before he flees; Mister Wang, please notify the capital."

Dai Yuan and Gui Lan led the search for Bian Hong, and their efforts led them to Bian's trail as he moved toward the hills; they ordered Sun Gao and Fu Ying to search for Bian Hong elsewhere, but Sun Gao refused to separate from the two conspirators as his suspicions grew.

"**THERE!**" Dai Yuan shrieked. "**I SEE HIM!**"

Dai Yuan, Gui Lan, Sun Gao and their soldiers advanced on the unmoving Bian Hong, who expected them to be coming to escort him across the river.

"**I thought I'd have regrets, but I don't!**" Bian Hong cackled as his pursuers approached him; he brandished the gory sack and added, "**Death to all of the Suns! Death to them all!**"

"**BASTARD!**" Gui Lan screamed as he lunged forward and ran Bian Hong through with his sword.

"Wh-what...?" Bian Hong gasped. "You-!"

"You'll say no more," Gui Lan whispered as he forced his sword downward, destroying Bian Hong's intestines.

"Y-you...!" Bian Hong rasped as he dropped the sack and fell to his knees; Sun Gao tried to intervene, but Gui Lan brought his sword down on Bian Hong's head to finish him off.

"...**You could have arrested him!**" Sun Gao screamed.

"I... I could not control my rage," Gui Lan sobbed as he dropped his sword and looked at his shaking hands. "Lord Sun... trusted me... and... I could not save him...! **Why did we not see Bian Hong for what he was???**"

"It's our greatest failure," Dai Yuan sighed. "Lord Sheng Xian, and now Lord Sun Yi... we don't deserve to live!"

"You've avenged Lord Sun," a captain suggested. "Don't sacrifice yourselves needlessly!"

"...Poor Lady Xū," Gui Lan said as he picked up the sack. "We... we must return his head at once, so that she can grieve him whole..."

Sun Gao viewed Dai Yuan and Gui Lan with a newfound sense of anger; he was sure that they had played a part in Sun Yi's death, but many of the local officers were not to be convinced of their treachery. Fu Ying later agreed with Sun Gao's assessment, but the two were powerless: until a successor was appointed, Sun Yi's authority passed to Dai Yuan and Gui Lan, and so the two officers now answered to the very men that they blamed for orchestrating their lord's demise. The men that were loyal to Sun Yi pinned all of their hopes on the reaction in Qu'e: Dai Yuan and Gui Lan, meanwhile, awaited that reaction with inevitable concern.

****

49

The battle against the Wu Hills Bandits was reaching a point where the Sun loyalists were starting to gain the upper hand; Lü Fan's northern armies managed to liaise with Lü Dai's forces in southern Guangling and push the bandits southward, while Gongjin's armies liaised with the Kuaiji administration and prevented the Wu bandits from joining forces with the Kuaiji bandit king Pan Lin. Once the threat of the Wu Hills Bandits was contained in Wu Prefecture, the various armies could start to consolidate and begin the work of relieving captured cities and destroying the enemy encampments; there was a clear path to success, but another piece of terrible news had arrived to harm morale.

"I… am sorry…!" the messenger sobbed as he knelt before Wu Prefecture Administrator Zhu Zhi, who had taken the letter from him without requesting a spoken account. "I… Administrator, I-!"

"You have hurried here to deliver this news," Zhu Zhi said. "Go and rest, young man… and do not apologise for being the bearer of bad news."

The distressed messenger got to his feet, bit his hand and fled the hall in tears.

"How am I supposed to tell Lord Sun *this*…?" Zhu Zhi bleated.

The adviser Bu Zhi – who had come to Wu County City to request resources – frowned and asked, "Tell Lord Sun what, Administrator Zhu…?"

"…Sun Yi has been murdered by his own aide!" Zhu Zhi replied.

The hall was filled with gasps and sobs.

"By his own aide…?" Bu Zhi exclaimed.

Zhu Zhi nodded and said, "This… this could never have come at a good time, but now… when all is bleak…"

"I will notify Lord Sun for you," Bu Zhi suggested.

"…That might be preferable," Zhu Zhi replied. "I should stay and pre-empt any possible consequences, such as a boost in morale amongst the wretched, such as Fei Zhan of Danyang, who might seek an alliance with his ilk here, or the Shanyue. Leave your provision request with me, Mister Bu, and I will deal with it."

"I shall hurry," Bu Zhi promised.

Sun Quan fell to his knees and cried out like a wounded animal when Bu Zhi reported Sun Yi's death to him a day later; Zhuge Jin did what he could to comfort the young lord while Zhang Zhao turned to Bu Zhi and said, "This must be avenged. Dai Yuan and Gui Lan must-"

"There is no proof that they are involved, as the letter states," Bu Zhi interrupted. "I have my own doubts, Mister Zhang, but if we attack them while they have the respect of the officials and some of the officers, we risk another insurrection like the one we suffered in Lujiang."

"…That's quite right," Zhang Zhao realised.

Bu Zhi nodded and said, "In fact, we must assume – no matter how ridiculous it may seem – that the two are innocent bystanders to a lone agent, and this 'Bian Hong' was just aggrieved over some petty matter and-"

"'Petty matter'…?" Sun Quan growled. "…What… what 'petty

matter' warranted *this*...?"

"As I said, we must assume so until we have evidence to the contrary," Bu Zhi replied. "Like it or not, Dai and Gui have ingratiated themselves with your late brother and earned the trust and allegiance of many a man in Danyang. They now administrate the prefecture until a suitable replacement is found."

"I won't have Dai Yuan and Gui Lan running Danyang, not after this!" Sun Quan cried. **"I want them both arrested, Mister Bu, and-!"**

"Arrested for what...?" Bu Zhi asked. "They found and killed Bian Hong in front of others, and then they wept before Sun Yi's coffin. Their reputations are impeccable, just as they were under Sheng Xian in this very province."

"...That's true, Lord Sun," Zhang Zhao confessed. "There are a lot of officials here, in Wu Prefecture, that consider Dai Yuan and Gui Lan to be unfortunate victims of power games and dirty politics."

"...So I must endure these two men...?" Sun Quan asked. "I... I wonder, I wonder if... if they are perhaps innocent. Perhaps... perhaps they are..."

"It might be so," Bu Zhi replied. "At present, to condemn them for their handling of the matter would be the same as condemning the men that killed Xu Gong's followers."

"The comparison has not been lost on me," Sun Quan admitted. "I must go back to the capital at once... I-"

"We cannot do that," Zhang Zhao protested. "In the field, a man must use discretion. We cannot abandon a military campaign to mourn Sun Yi, as much as that might seem disrespectful; Sun Hè will have to travel to Danyang and represent us all, and-"

"He can take over as Administrator while he's there," Sun Quan said. "To any that say 'But Yu Hè is a distant cousin if he is a cousin at all', I say that Yu Hè was brought into our family home by my father, given the name 'Sun', and from that moment he became as close, if not closer, than Boyang and Guoyi. He defended my brother from swords and arrows, just as Zhou Tai once defended me: there are few men that compare to Sun Hè – Sun *Bohai* – in terms of loyalty and piety."

"I quite agree," Zhang Zhao replied. "I will write and-"

"No, Mister Zhang, it should be me," Sun Quan insisted. "I now pass that great burden to Bohai in a moment of shared tragedy; how can I do that via a letter in another man's hand...?"

"That is quite true," Zhang Zhao replied.

"...The truth will come out," Sun Quan said numbly. "Bohai must discover the truth of this... and then I will act upon it."

Sun Hè received Sun Quan's order to travel to Danyang and assembled his family to inform them of his intentions.

"Take me with you, Father!" Sun Hè's eldest son, Sun Zhu, pleaded as his mother started to weep.

"You're barely a man," Sun Hè replied. "I can see that your mother has grasped the seriousness of this... and, in a way, so have you. But you have no place in Danyang: you must stay here and care for your mother and your brothers and sisters."

"Then take me, Uncle," Sun Shao protested. "I am sixteen, and I have had some professional military and civil training, so I can help you. You are practically a father to me now, and-"

"You must stay here as well, to defend the city in my place," Sun Hè said. "I... I don't doubt that I shall be gone for a while."

"That is why I weep!" Sun Hè's wife retorted. "We should all be going with you!"

"Danyang is too dangerous for me to risk that," Sun Hè insisted. "I'll hear no more protests: I leave tonight."

"...Then I shall do as you say, Uncle," Sun Shao replied. "Good luck, and be careful."

Sun Hè hurried to Wanling County City with a small retinue of junior officials and soldiers; he was greeted at the gates by Dai Yuan and Gui Lan, who were both dressed in white garments, and the men exchanged customary bows.

"Welcome, Mister Sun," Dai Yuan said.

"...I wish that we were meeting under better circumstances," Sun Hè replied.

"We've done what we can to stabilise the city and the surrounding county," Gui Lan said. "Magistrate Huang Gai volunteered to come here, but we sent every man back to their own county to ensure that they don't fall to bandits or tribes."

"...That's sensible," Sun Hè replied.

"Lord Sun Yi's subordinates are in a barracks outside the city, where they watch for signs of potential unrest," Gui Lan continued. "I take it that you are here to assume the role of prefectural administrator...?"

"A successor hasn't been decided upon," Sun Hè replied cautiously. "As you know, the suitable personnel are scattered throughout Jiangdong: I'm a soldier, so I doubt that I'd be able to take on such a burden."

"If we can help, we will," Dai Yuan said. "We can hire some more Officers of Merit to properly vet the officials and ensure that we get no more Bian Hongs."

"That sounds like the right course," Sun Hè replied. "I'll go and talk to Sun Gao and the other men before I tour the city: I'll meet you later."

"...That is the proper course," Dai Yuan said.

Sun Hè bowed to Dai and Gui and retreated with his staff; Dai Yuan then turned to Gui Lan and asked, "Do you think that he trusts us...?"

"...Difficult to fathom," Gui Lan replied. "He's smarter than Sun Yi was, and much, much harder to read..."

Sun Hè entered the external barracks and met with Sun Gao and Fu Ying in the command tent.

"We're acting as joint commanders," Sun Gao explained. "We're neither of us qualified to lead, though... the men don't really follow us, in all honesty."

"I did notice that the discipline was poor," Sun Hè admitted. "It isn't your fault, friends; this is a difficult time. I'll be honest and say that I probably won't do much better than either of you: I'm a bodyguard, and I'm an 'honorary Sun'."

"You *are* a 'Sun'," Sun Gao said.

"...What do you think of Dai Yuan and Gui Lan...?" Sun Hè asked.

"...We don't trust them," Fu Ying replied.

"They killed Bian Hong without necessity, since the man wasn't

armed with anything when we found him," Sun Gao explained. "It took us time to fathom it, but it's obvious: Bian greeted Dai and Gui with a vague statement, and then they killed him without a struggle. He expected them, but not as enemies: they used him to kill Lord Sun Yi and then killed him to save their own hides."
Sun Hè's eyes wandered.
"Gui Lan has been looking at Lady Xū in an inappropriate manner," Sun Gao continued. "Dai Yuan is always the model official, but Gui... Gui is no gentleman."
"Can... can you prove anything...?" Sun Hè asked weakly.
"Nothing," Sun Gao sighed.
"They are both of them very cunning," Fu Ying said. "They've promoted officials and officers that are willing to work for them, and rewarded men that are cynical: they rewarded us, and we gave the money to the men, but when Dai and Gui got word of it they made sure the men knew where the money was from."
"*Aiee*... villains... hidden in plain sight!" Sun Hè said. "I have no choice... I must trust in the will of Heaven and confront them."
"No, you mustn't!" Fu Ying pleaded. "They'll kill you! Send word to Magistrates Huang Gai and Xu Sheng, and Commander-in-Chief Zhou, and-!"
"Dai and Gui are cowards, like the 'Ten Attendants' of old," Sun Hè said. "The 'Ten' always got others to do their dirty work... but when confronted, they cried and pleaded for mercy. But I shall show none... that I promise you. Stay here and do what you can to rally the men and follow me."
Sun Gao groaned miserably as Sun Hè retreated; Fu Ying shook his head and said, "We must at least try to do as he has asked."

Sun Hè strode through the city with an obvious scowl on his face; he entered the audience hall of the governor's mansion and stood before Dai Yuan and Gui Lan, who were waiting for him with a small group of officials and officers.
"...You seem agitated, Acting Administrator," Dai Yuan said.
"This ends now, gentlemen," Sun Hè declared. "I've heard enough to know what really happened here."
"What are you saying...?" Mister Wang asked.
"Shubi never was very tactful, so I imagine that he had no fun conversing with some of the pedants in this city," Sun Hè continued. "He was never as good a judge of men as Bofu, sadly, so I can see how he ended up with Bian Hong for an aide and Dai and Gui for ministers."
"Are you accusing us of something, *Acting Administrator*...?" Gui Lan asked.
"I'm the Administrator, plain and simple," Sun Hè replied. "I was sent here to restore order and discover the truth... and the truth is easy enough to fathom. You two came here looking for revenge on the Suns for the death of your master, Sheng Xian, but unlike Xu Gong's men – who at least had the courage to act personally and die afterwards like men – you employed Bian Hong to do the deed and then you silenced him."
"Preposterous!" Dai Yuan chortled.
"You slander us falsely!" Gui Lan snapped.
"No, this is simple enough," Sun Hè retorted. "You're villains, both of you, and you'll both answer for what you've done."

"Us and anyone else that's implicated, of course," Dai Yuan suggested calmly.

"*Yes*, and...!" Sun Hè replied without thinking; his voice trailed when he realised that he had now raised the possibility of other officials – including the other men that were present – suffering for Dai Yuan and Gui Lan's actions.

"Your paranoia will lead to the deaths of dozens of good men," Dai Yuan continued. "Yet again, the Suns prove that they are little more than thugs that rule with clubs and swords. Sun Yi claimed that Sheng Xian would have been spared 'had the truth been known', but you prove that he was either wrong or a liar."

Sun Hè pointed at Dai Yuan and said, "When I report to Lord Sun Quan, you-!"

Gui Lan screamed like an animal and surged forward with his sword drawn; Sun Hè was unprepared for such a desperate act, so he was cut down before he could lower his pointing hand and reach for his sword. The officials gasped and yelped as Gui Lan ended Sun Hè's life with a second slash that split his skull; Gui Lan stared at the corpse and breathed erratically as Dai Yuan got to his feet and walked to his side.

"...I had... no choice," Gui Lan said.

"I know," Dai Yuan replied nervously.

"When Sun Quan learns of this, we're all of us dead men," Mister Wang said. "Our families will be killed as well, to the third degree or worse...!"

"...Then we must do what we can to ensure that he does not learn of it until we have adequately prepared," Dai Yuan replied.

"*You* killed him!" another official cried. "*You-!*"

"**Shut up, you fool!**" Gui Lan screamed as he turned and pointed his bloodied sword at the terrified official. "**He was going to go to Sun Quan and tell him that we all of us murdered Sun Yi! We were all of us dead men!**"

The majority of the officials murmured agreeably.

"**I had no choice!**" Gui Lan continued. "There's only one way to go forward now... we contact Inspector Liu Fu, tell him what we've done – maybe send what's left of this man's head as well – and pledge allegiance."

"Inspector Liu Fu speaks for the Han," Dai Yuan said. "So we'll be 'returning home' if we go to Liu Fu."

"...That's right," Mister Wang said. "The-"

At that moment, Sun Gao and Fu Ying arrived with a small group of soldiers; Dai Yuan and Gui Lan turned and faced them with their swords drawn.

"**You... you bastards!**" Fu Ying cried. "**You murderers!**"

"You misunderstand," Dai Yuan replied. "Sun Hè intended to blame every man here for the actions of one man – Bian Hong – and have us all executed by Sun Quan. He blamed us *all* for the death of Sun Yi."

The majority of the officials drew their swords and stood with Dai Yuan and Gui Lan; Fu Ying laughed incredulously and asked, "What are you all doing???"

"Stand down, gentlemen," a colonel ordered. "I am your superior, so disobeying me is punishable with death."

"Don't do this, Colonel Yin!" Fu Ying pleaded. "They-!"

"**Weapons down!**" Colonel Yin barked. "**Do it or die!**"

The terrified soldiers started to throw their weapons down; Sun Gao and Fu Ying were the last to do so, and they awaited their deaths stoically.

"You're both loyal to Sun Yi, and that's commendable," Dai Yuan said. "Sun Gao, Fu Ying: you're to return to your barracks with Colonel Yin, where you will begin the process of dismantling the facility and moving back into the city, where you can both be clearly seen. Two of the rest of you should remove Sun Hè's body and have it placed in a coffin until suitable burial arrangements are made. From this point forward, Gui Lan and I will assume control of the prefecture until Inspector Liu Fu – not Sun Quan – appoints a new Administrator. We want no more thugs and fools leading us."

Two men hurried to Sun Hè's corpse and carried it away while Colonel Yin ushered Sun Gao, Fu Ying and the rest of the soldiers out of the hall.

"...You're all dismissed, gentlemen," Dai Yuan said to the remainder of the officials. "We must now arrange for alternate accommodation for Sun Yi's family and any household staff that he brought with him."

The officials departed slowly and ponderously.

"...Our path is now straight and devoid of turnings," Dai Yuan said. "We can only go in two directions: back to the life of fugitives, or forward to the life of-"

"You're not addressing doubting officials anymore, Dai," Gui Lan interrupted. "I'm as dead as you if Sun Quan learns of this. I intend to enjoy life from now on... starting right now."

"...Don't molest Lady Xū," Dai Yuan pleaded. "That wouldn't-"

"I'll have my way with the others now, but I intend to marry Lady Xū," Gui Lan said. "The future sons of Gui Lan will benefit... I might even adopt Sun Yi's son as my own if he doesn't make too much trouble."

"...Just be sure and show some sense," Dai Yuan pleaded. "We want to be likened to Ding Yuan and Hè Jin, remember... not Li Jue and Guo Si."

Gui Lan laughed dismissively and began the journey to Sun Yi's sleeping quarters.

When the disarmed Sun Gao and Fu Ying reached their barracks outside the city, Colonel Yin smirked and said, "I shall now address your men and make them aware of the need to look to me before you. Guards... take them to the command tent."

"Is there nothing we can do...?" Sun Gao whispered.

"Hush," Fu Ying replied. "It's Heaven's choice now."

Lady Xū had been momentarily alarmed when Gui Lan entered the sleeping quarters and announced that he would now be the lord of house, but she quickly regained her composure and said, "If that is the decision that has been properly reached, but I do not understand what your seizing of this house has to do with the occupants of this room, Mister Gui Lan."

Sun Yi's consorts looked at Lady Xū and wondered what would happen to her.

"...You're as witty as you're beautiful, Lady Xū," Gui Lan chuckled. "You will make a fine wife."

"I have already been a 'fine wife'," Lady Xū retorted. "Now I am a widow, and my son is without a father."

"I intend to make you my wife and adopt your son," Gui Lan announced. "He will be 'Gui Song', and-"

"That is not proper," Lady Xū said. "I refuse to comply."

"...You might not have noticed, but I am now lord of this prefecture," Gui Lan retorted. "Sun Yi's consorts are now without a master, and I can and will remedy that now. I am offering you the opportunity to be my wife – my principal wife – and yet you 'refuse to comply'...? I offer your son a worthy new father, and-!"

"You misunderstand," Lady Xū said. "I must refuse to comply, Mister Gui Lan, because my husband has only been dead for a few days; when has it ever been proper for a widow to remarry within days of her husband's murder...? People might 'jump to incorrect conclusions' about the widow *and* her new husband."

Gui Lan hummed thoughtfully.

"My son must be able to choose whether he is a 'Sun' or a 'Gui', although I am sure that he will choose wisely," Lady Xū continued. "But now is not the time for such discussions: if it your will that I remain here, then I shall, but I must not be touched. Let us have this discussion again in a month, Mister Gui, when sufficient time has passed."

"...A month...?" Gui Lan said. "...A month... alright... I can wait for a month. It isn't as though I don't have the others to amuse me until then."

Lady Xū smiled and replied, "No, Mister Gui, it is not."

"...You and your son shall be moved to another room and allocated your trusted maids, so that you can see that I am sincere," Gui Lan continued. "The others are mine to do as I like with from this moment on, though."

Lady Xū looked at the nervous consorts and said, "That is out of my hands."

"That's settled, then!" Gui Lan chuckled. "I'll go now... your maids can move you now, so that this room is mine when I return."

"It shall be done," Lady Xū replied.

Gui Lan retreated happily; one of the consorts turned to Lady Xū and said, "You'd *marry him*...? You'd really...? And *we* must...!"

Lady Xū smiled sadly and said, "Endure... for all is not lost yet."

∗∗∗∗∗∗∗∗∗∗∗∗

50

Sun Quan was distracted by the recent loss of his brother Yi, and so the business of addressing troops and issuing commands was often left entirely to Zhang Zhao and Zhuge Jin.

"We will be joined by Bu Zhi, Ling Tong and Zhang Yi shortly," Zhang Zhao said to the officers that filled the eastern force's command tent. "We shall then seize the larger of the two enemy bases here, at Bao."

"...How is Lord Sun...?" Zhou Tai asked.

"Lord Sun Quan is understandably very upset, but he will be ready to address the officers soon," Zhuge Jin replied. "Mister Zhang, please continue."

Zhang Zhao coughed deliberately and said, "Once we have secured Bao, we will separate again, leaving a force to attack the smaller base at Ma while the main army moves southwest to crush their bases there. That is all for now... dismissed."

The officers left the tent in an orderly fashion; Zhang Zhao then turned to Zhuge Jin and said, "You're Lord Sun Quan's personal secretary, Zhuge, so do your job! Or maybe you can't do your job, try as hard as you might, given that you are supposed to lift Lord Sun's flagging spirits and get him back here but can hardly hope to do so with that miserable donkey face of yours!"

"*Aiee*... I didn't ask for my face!" Zhuge Jin retorted. "I didn't ask to be Lord Sun's personal secretary either! And what do I say, mm...? He's lost his mother, three brothers, an uncle and a son in less than two years! It is taking its toll! He drinks to forget and broods unhealthily when he is sober, and so all I can do is minimise that drinking to save his future sanity!"

"...I apologise," Zhang Zhao said. "I..."

"I understand," Zhuge Jin insisted. "You want what is best for the state. But forcing Lord Sun to address his troops in his current condition is unwise and counter-productive. We won't lose their loyalty: Zhou Tai would gladly die for Lord Sun – and has nearly done so once already – while Chen Wu and the rest have already fought Li Shu instead of joining him."

"...You're quite astute behind that face of yours," Zhang Zhao said. "I shall harass you no further; do what you can for Lord Sun, and I'll do everything else."

Bu Zhi, Ling Tong and Zhang Yi reached Sun Quan's camp within a few days, and the final preparations for another fierce battle began. The army – which numbered close to 30,000 – descended on the large Wu Hills Bandit garrison that sat beneath the hills of Bao within two more days, catching the defenders by surprise.

"How the bloody hell did they get all these men 'ere so quick???" the garrison commander exclaimed. **"Get to your posts! Defend the place wi' your lives!"**

Hordes of bandits surged out of the camp and the neighbouring hills in an effort to defend their position; the two vast forces clashed mindlessly while Sun Quan, Zhang Zhao, Zhuge Jin and Bu Zhi looked on.

"What is there for clever men to do?" Zhang Zhao complained. **"Fight,"** Bu Zhi replied. **"Have we no swords?"**

"**We should stay close to Lord Sun!**" Zhang Zhao protested.

"**…But 'Lord Sun' should be close to his men,**" Sun Quan decided. "**I will go and be seen, as Shubi or Bofu would!**"

Zhang Zhao remonstrated, but Sun Quan would not be swayed; he urged his steed forward and advanced to the front lines. A bandit captain noticed the move very quickly and shouted, "**Sun Quan's here! We can get him!**"

Zhou Tai, Ling Tong, Chen Wu and Zhang Yi were leading the forces around the battlefield, with Zhou Tai being the closest to Sun Quan's position; he learned of his lord's decision to be dangerously visible and left command to a subordinate so that he could defend his lord in person. A small group of bandits had tried to attack Sun Quan, but they had already been repelled by Sun's bodyguards by the time that Zhou Tai reached his lord.

"**Get back to the battle, Zhou Tai!**" Zhang Zhao snapped.

"**I will stay and guard Lord Sun!**" Zhou Tai insisted.

"**I can do that!**" Song Qian said. "**That's why I'm here!**"

"**Win for me, Zhou Youping!**" Sun Quan said. "**That's the best way to serve me!**"

Zhou Tai bowed and returned to the battle.

"**I apologise for shouting at your favourite officer, Lord Sun,**" Zhang Zhao said. "**But I-**"

"**REPORT!**" a messenger cried. "**Ling Tong and Chen Wu have breached the camp and started to set it alight!**"

"**The day will be ours!**" Sun Quan cackled.

The bandits were shocked at the news that their camp had been breached, but it did little to affect their morale; they slightly outnumbered the Jiangdong army, and Chen Wu and Ling Tong were forced to abort their raids when a large defensive force repelled them with arrows and stones.

"**We'll retreat to our camp!**" Zhang Zhao suggested. "**They'll probably try to attack us during the night, but we'll be ready for them!**"

"**I disagree,**" Bu Zhi said. "**We must press them until they yield the camp, or we'll be here for days. One decisive second push will break their camp!**"

"**We shall act as Bu Zhi suggests!**" Sun Quan decided. "**No more retreats: smash them utterly!**"

Zhang Zhao reluctantly issued the order to continue fighting, and the officers complied: the exhausted soldiers maintained pressure on the bandits, who were equally tired but considerably more desperate. Chen Wu, Zhou Tai and Ling Tong managed to breach the camp for a second time, despite losses to the arrows that were being fired from guard towers around the perimeter; the remainder of the camp was destroyed, and the bandits abandoned the camp in favour of the nearby walled city of Bao and their familiar hillside camps.

Sun Quan gathered his officials in the command tent and listened patiently as Bu Zhi and Zhang Zhao made proposals for how to move forward.

"…So now we must siege the city," Sun Quan sighed.

"And we must attack the hills as well, and give these creatures no more hiding places," Zhang Zhao said.

"…Attacking hills is risky," Chen Wu suggested. "Nobody should attack uphill if they can avoid it."

"I'm versed in the Art of War, Mister Chen," Zhang Zhao retorted. "I do know that high ground is usually advantageous! That's why they live in the hills! But there are ways to make those hills uninhabitable!"

"...The Shanyue also live in the hills," Zhuge Jin noted.

"Then it deals with two problems at once!" Zhang Zhao retorted.

"Or brings both down on us at once," Bu Zhi said. "We'll siege the city and lure the bandits down with a show of abandoning the ruins of their camp and leaving our own undermanned. No fish can resist such tempting bait."

"We'll do as you say," Sun Quan declared.

In the western prefecture of Yuzhang, Colonel Jiang Qin was reaching the end of a long campaign against the rebellion led by 'Chaisang Qin' and 'Demon Lü': the two bandit kings had lost much of their support as Jiang Qin moved from place to place with a strategy that combined mercy, amnesty and economic relief with brute force and savage intolerance of refusal to surrender. Restoration of ample food supplies, management of disease and provision of work to the able had raised confidence in Sun Quan's government and brought many village chiefs, landowners, vigilante militias and a lot of smaller bandit groups to the negotiating table and left the rebellion with less than a tenth of its initial backing.

"The tribes are staying out of this, thankfully," the adviser Qin Song said. "They're busy harassing Dong Xi and fighting each other. Qin and Lü are floundering: let's act now before disease, famine or another famous death sets us back again."

"...Then let's be done with them," Jiang Qin replied.

"You're worried about returning to Wuhu," Qin Song guessed.

"Xu Sheng has a man answering my letters on his behalf," Jiang Qin complained. "I don't know how to deal with him!"

"It will be made clear when the time is right," Qin Song promised. "Until then, worry about 'Chaisang Qin' and 'Demon Lü'."

"This is their last chance to surrender," Jiang Qin replied. "If they refuse me again, then they're dead men."

"I think that the world can see that you've given them enough chances," Qin Song said. "You let them retreat three times... Heaven won't scold you for denying them a fourth."

Chaisang Qin and Demon Lü were hiding in a walled city: they both insisted on manning the battlements personally and confiscated all of the city's resources for their army's use, which did nothing to endear them to the populace.

"**COME OUT!**" Jiang Qin bellowed. "**S'OVER, YOU TWO!**"

"**DROP DEAD!**" Chaisang Qin retorted.

"...Can they even hear each other...?" one bandit archer asked of a colleague who shrugged in response.

"...I guess we'll have to start sieging the city," Jiang Qin sighed as he looked at the city battlements from the ground below.

"Don't be hasty," Qin Song suggested. "Let's wait..."

"...And let the people decide what they want to do," Jiang Qin supposed. "Alright, we'll wait: we have enough food, after all...!"

Jiang Qin's men camped at a distance that avoided arrow attacks and made a show of eating, drinking and paying little attention to their presumed duties: Chaisang Qin noted it and said, "They're losing order."

"No, they're goading us," Demon Lü replied. "Jiang's clever... he knows we're holding this city with fear. We mustn't let the people know what they're doing."

"But keeping the gates shut is pissing everyone off something terrible!" Chaisang Qin protested.

Demon Lü shook his head and said, "It's that or they'll flee with the food!"

The two bandits argued for several minutes, in which time a representative of the citizens came to the battlements to request more food: he caught sight of the sieging army and realised what was going on immediately.

"What do you want?" Demon Lü asked angrily.

"...The people are hungry," the townsman replied.

"Aren't we all...?" Chaisang Qin heckled. "Get off the wall! Or do you want to volunteer to help us...?"

"...I'll say no more," the townsman replied as he retreated.

"Idiot," Chaisang Qin grumbled. "We had the world in our hands, Lü, until... until these idiots started to ignore us!"

"Two days, then we'll sneak out," Demon Lü said.

But within a day, the people of the city had thrown the gates open to Jiang Qin's forces: Chaisang Qin was caught and Demon Lü fled to the hills, where he defied the authorities for a few days more before his own followers killed him and took his head to Jiang Qin.

"All's well!" Jiang Qin said once he and Qin Song were alone in the command tent. "I'm so glad that this is over that I almost don't mind having to go back to Wuhu. But do I go back now, or...?"

"Report to Lord Sun and remain here until we know that we're not needed in Yuzhang anymore," Qin Song suggested.

"Good idea," Jiang Qin said.

Cao Cao's appointed Inspector of Yang Province, Liu Fu, was disturbed by the correspondence that he was receiving from Dai Yuan and Gui Lan's regime in Danyang Prefecture.

"This is not ideal at all," Liu Fu said to his aide Jiang Ji. "These two misguided men have murdered Sun Yi and Sun Hè in quick succession and now they court me as an ally. I want no part in their self-serving escapade."

"But if we help Dai and Gui, we get a chance to seize Danyang," Jiang Ji suggested.

"We'll never get Danyang this way," Liu Fu replied. "Dai Yuan and Gui Lan are doomed: one way or another, the Suns will discover their treachery, avenge their fallen and get that prefecture back, at which point they'll be more popular than ever: if I'm seen to be liaising with them, I'll be implicated in the murders, and that won't look any better for me in Xuchang than it will in Jiangdong."

"But if we ignore these desperate men, won't they react spitefully...?" Jiang Ji asked.

"I shall reply vaguely, as I have done with others," Liu Fu replied. "Their inevitable destruction will do us no harm."

∗∗∗∗∗∗∗∗∗∗∗∗

51

In Wu Prefecture, the situation was improving for Sun Quan's forces: the siege of Bao had ended with a similar yielding of the city by the people, and the bandits in the hills around Bao had been chased away, caught or killed.

"We now move forward," Sun Quan said to his officers. "I'm going southward to assist the efforts there. Ling Tong, Zhang Yi: you're in charge of seizing the smaller base at Ma."

"As you command," Ling Tong replied.

"I shall not fail you, Lord Sun," Zhang Yi promised.

"...Let's proceed then," Sun Quan said.

The meeting started to break up; Ling Tong was stopped on one of the dirt roads in the camp by Zhang Yi, who said, "You're every bit the hero that your father was, Colonel Ling."

Ling Tong smiled and replied, "Your words mean much to me, Colonel Zhang."

"We'll banquet our subordinate officers tonight and march in the morning," Zhang Yi suggested. "It should boost morale a bit."

"A sound idea," Ling Tong replied.

Ling Tong and Zhang Yi entrusted the banquet arrangements to a local official called Chen Qin, whose name was far from famous: there were few men to choose from, however, so the two colonels hoped that Chen would do a good job. The two officers were horrified when they discovered that the preparations were substandard in every way: many officers were seated inappropriately for their ranks, with some majors seated further from the host than their subordinate captains, and the food and wine were of a grade that did not match the funds that had been allocated to procure them.

"...This is awful," one major said.

"You organise the bloody thing, then, you brainless thug!" Chen Qin retorted.

"What did you say???" the major screamed.

"This is my fault," Ling Tong said, "so I'll deal with it: Mister Chen, you were trusted as master of ceremonies, but you have not performed adequately."

"Oh...?" Chen Qin replied. "What's not done? There's food, drink, guests and seats. What's missing, mm...?"

"...Mister Chen, you seem to have strange ideas about your role," Ling Tong said.

"And what's yours, boy...?" Chen Qin heckled. "Who made *you* a colonel, boy...? You probably don't have any hair where it matters to be a *man*, let alone a *colonel*!"

"Wha-!? ...Stay your tongue!" Zhang Yi ordered.

"I don't have to obey you," Chen Qin retorted. "I'm important too. **I'm important!**"

"...Don't resort to this, Mister Chen," Ling Tong said as politely as he could. "We all make mistakes: I now see that your breath smells of alcohol, and-"

"You're a *boy*... a stupid little *boy*... that owes everything he has to his father's death," Chen Qin taunted. "What would you have if-?"

"You...!" Zhang Yi exclaimed.

"Don't 'You!' me, you useless man," Chen Qin said. "The only person more useless than you is that boy! I ask the rest of you: how can you win a battle with thousands an' thousands of bandits when the officers in charge are *these two*...?"
"Don't make me kill you," a captain growled.
"Oh, really...?" Chen Qin heckled. "You're all stupid: everything's just 'I will kill you!' isn't it...? That's all that any of you know how to do... kill people. You're lucky I didn't feed you what they give the pigs... it's all that you deserve."
"Stop this at once!" Ling Tong pleaded. "What suicidal madness possesses you...?"
"Whatever 'suicidal madness' it is that you reckon I suffer from isn't as bad as what your family suffers from," Chen Qin retorted. "Your father was a bloody fool. Lord Sun had Jiangxia in the palm of his hand, and then your idiot father charged at arrows and ruined the entire campaign: and he spent how many years here in Wu...? Horse piss and scraps, that's all you deserve, you and your useless father; I've half a mind to visit his temple and have a crap in front of it."
"That's it, you're leaving," Zhang Yi said as Ling Tong's face hardened with rage and distress. "You're despicable, Chen Qin, and you're lucky to still be alive."
"Swords and arrows!" Chen Qin cackled as two captains grabbed his arms and led him out of the tent. "Swords and arrows, helmets and boots... you're all the masters, but *why*...? *Colonel* Ling...? Look at him! He's a bloody standard bearer!"
"**Get him out!**" Zhang Yi barked.
Ling Tong was trying to keep his composure, but his face was wet with tears and his lip was quivering.
"...Are you alright...?" Zhang Yi asked once Chen Qin was gone.
"I... am a... soldier," Ling Tong replied. "I... disgrace myself."
"The only disgrace was Chen Qin," Zhang Yi insisted. "Let's leave this and get some rest."
Ling Tong nodded agreeably, and the banquet ended.

Ling Tong was haunted by thoughts of his famous father and did not get much sleep: he joined Zhang Yi at the front of the army as it prepared to march on the following morning and said, "Let us waste no more time."
"You look like a reanimated corpse," Zhang Yi said.
"I feel terrible," Ling Tong admitted. "I'm Ling Tong, son of Ling Cao: am I supposed to be reckless, cautious, or-?"
"Just do as you've done," Zhang Yi suggested. "Let's advance."
The army moved toward Ma at a reasonable pace: the mood was generally fair, but that was at risk of being ruined when the drunken Chen Qin – who had pursued the army – reached the vanguard and said, "There they are... the *colonels*."
"Don't do this," Zhang Yi pleaded.
"Whiny, aren't you...?" Chen Qin heckled. "Hopeless... I ask again: what chance do we have of winning anything if the army's fronted up by you two...?"
"**Go away before I arrest you!**" Zhang Yi screamed.
"For what...?" Chen Qin giggled. "I'm not one of your soldiers: you have no juris... jurisdiction over me, an' I can say what I like! I'm important! I should be leading this, since I'm smarter than you!"

"What you are is drunk, and what you should be is 'somewhere else'," Ling Tong said. "Please, Mister Chen, don't-"

"Stupid little boy, clinging to his father's name," Chen Qin sniggered. "Look at you, spineless arsehole... whining and bleating... y'know'what I reckon? I reckon you're a bastard, maybe a servant's child or something. Yeah, Ling Cao was stupid, but he was *brave*: you, though, you're a bloody-!"

Ling Tong lost control of his emotions as Chen Qin's words struck a nerve: Ling screamed maniacally, leapt from his horse and cut Chen down with a single swipe of his sword.

"...Oh, Heaven help you, Colonel Ling," Zhang Yi murmured.

"I... I couldn't listen anymore," Ling Tong said as he stood over the wounded Chen Qin, who was gasping and pleading for mercy with what strength he had left.

"I'll... I'll put in a good word," Zhang Yi promised. "I-"

"No," Ling Tong insisted. "Don't risk your own job for me. All I ask is that this isn't reported until after the battle."

"...Alright," Zhang Yi said. "Someone pick up this obnoxious man so we can get moving again."

Four soldiers collected Chen Qin and carried him to the supply train; his abusive nature was now very well known, so a lot of the soldiers heckled him as he was carried past them.

"I'll surrender to Discipline Officer Pang after the battle," Ling Tong promised.

"Make the battle count," Zhang Yi said. "You can always atone with good service."

"...I'll admit that it's my intention," Ling Tong replied.

"Ma's bandits are on a hill," Zhang Yi continued. "We'll lose men..."

"...We surely will," Ling Tong replied tonelessly.

The 10,000-strong army reached Ma within a few hours and immediately surrounded the bandits' hilltop encampment; Ling Tong and Zhang Yi seized opposing sides of the hill and made separate preparations to advance while the bandits heckled and started to roll rocks and boulders downhill.

"**We're all going to die!**" one soldier cried.

Ling Tong looked at the enemy base and wondered how many of his men would die trying to scale the hill; he suddenly thought of his father's last valiant efforts against Huang Zu, Chen Qin's taunts and the punishment that he would surely face for killing an unarmed official.

"...**Only through death can I atone!**" Ling Tong bellowed. "**I will lead the charge: let me be your shield and your sword!**"

The other officers and soldiers were dumbfounded: Ling Tong raised his sword and shouted, "**WE MOVE AT ONCE!**"

"...**We're with you!**" a major replied.

Ling Tong charged uphill, dodging the rocks, boulders and arrows with dexterity that matched or even outclassed his father: his men followed at a similar pace, and they reached the summit with surprisingly few losses. The unexpected arrival of thousands of men caused morale within the camp to plummet: the defences were minimal, since the camp was not designed for repelling close-range attackers, and Ling Tong's force quickly demolished the fences and barriers. The news of the surprise victory quickly spread to the other units of the Jiangdong army, and every officer ordered a spirited charge: the bandits started to panic, and as order in the ranks collapsed, the number of launched projectiles decreased, which gave the other forces an even easier ascent. The entire battle was over with an hour, and although the losses were severe, they were nowhere near as bad as had been expected. Ling Tong was hailed for his bravery by one and all, and word was sent to Sun Quan.

"…Magnificent!" Sun Quan said. "Ling Tong's service is truly magnificent, is it not…?"

"There is the matter of his prior offence," Zhang Zhao noted.

"…Prior offence…?" Sun Quan prompted.

"Read for yourself, Lord Sun," Zhang Zhao said as he passed a letter to Sun Quan.

"… … …This is a serious offence, yes," Sun Quan said. "But… but did this 'Chen Qin' really say what is reported here…? If he did, then he was inviting some form of attack, I think, especially when one looks at the behaviour that provoked the rebuke."

"So what will you do…?" Zhang Zhao asked.

"Chen Qin sounds like a complete imbecile, and I'm surprised that he was even serving me in any capacity," Sun Quan replied. "I commend Ling Tong for resisting his first bout of abuse, and although he did not react well in the end, he performed admirably in battle and then he surrendered to the discipline officer… other men might have joined the bandits to escape punishment."

"He obviously charged like a madman in the hope of dying a hero's death instead of facing imprisonment," Zhang Zhao scoffed.

"That charge gave us a victory with minimal casualties," Sun Quan retorted. "We were expecting a lot more deaths, were we not…? Is that not why we gave Ling and Zhang ten-thousand men, in the hope that they'd maybe only lose three or four thousands over a campaign lasting what, two, three, ten days…?"

"…That was always the most likely outcome," Bu Zhi said.

"Instead, he gives us a victory in one day – one day – that allows us to end this campaign more quickly," Sun Quan continued. "He should be promoted for his military accomplishments and imprisoned for his offence; I shall compromise and issue neither promotion nor punishment."

"That's the proper way to approach it," Zhuge Jin agreed.

"…And as for Jiang Qin… his handling of the two rebel-rousers in Yuzhang deserves a promotion for certain," Sun Quan suggested.

"I quite agree," Zhang Zhao said.

"He shall be promoted to a general for his efforts," Sun Quan continued. "It's overdue: after all, he's served the Suns since my brother's first days as clan chieftain and never done less than his best. Qin Song is being humble and says that he 'did not do much compared to Jiang' but I will still ensure that he's given a few more taxable households. How much longer will this campaign go on for, I wonder…?"

"We're probably going to be here for a few weeks at the most, Lord Sun," Bu Zhi replied. "They're faltering now, and the latest victory will rattle them."

"We'll capitalise on it," Zhang Zhao said. "We'll definitely win."

"…And then I can return to the capital," Sun Quan replied. "And… and then I can mourn my brother properly… and, if needs be, avenge him as well."

"Nothing has been heard from Sun Hè beyond an official note that he will be busy for some time," Zhuge Jin reported. "Perhaps we will be able to send reinforcements once Wu is pacified, Lord Sun."

"Oh, yes, certainly," Sun Quan said. "Danyang must be pacified as soon as possible. It *must*."

Weeks passed, and the Wu Hills Bandits confederacy continued to shrink in size and lose the ground that it had gained. And just as those weeks passed in Wu Prefecture, they passed in Danyang Prefecture's capital, where they formed part of a month of patient waiting that would soon come to a painful end.

****

"You're a fool, you know that...? You're a fool."
Dai Yuan's words were directed toward his long-time colleague Gui Lan, who was dressed in elaborate robes and smiling unintelligently. For a month, the two men had been power absolute in Danyang Prefecture by using a combination of secrecy and fear: the magistrates were kept in their counties by prevailing orders, and all of the men that might threaten Dai and Gui had been imprisoned or confined to the city while their fates were decided. During that time, Dai Yuan had concentrated on making changes to the structure of the army to have it better serve them, while Gui Lan had enacted personnel changes in the administration and moved into the governor's mansion; Dai Yuan was happy with those measures, but Gui had gone one step further, taking control of Sun Yi's household staff and sleeping with Sun's consorts.

The two men still enjoyed a good working relationship, but that was becoming increasingly strained as time passed: Inspector Liu Fu was being deliberately distant and vague in his correspondence, various campaigns were coming to an end that gave the Suns more time and resources, and Gui Lan was still intent on wooing Sun Yi's widow, Lady Xū.
"I despair," Dai Yuan said. "I really do despair, Gui Lan."
"You're just jealous!" Gui Lan chuckled.
"It's not funny," Dai Yuan said. "She's Sun Yi's widow!"
"And she'll soon be my wife," Gui Lan retorted. "What can I say...? I have made no move toward her; I have not threatened her; all I have done, Mister Dai, is wait patiently, and she didn't even wait until the full month expired!"
"And you don't worry about the consequences...?" Dai Yuan asked.
"She's truly beautiful," Gui Lan continued. "Her skin, so perfect... her lips, so-"
"Are you even listening to me...?" Dai Yuan asked irritably.
"There will be no consequences!" Gui Lan snapped. "We run Danyang! Sun Yi and Sun Hè are dead, and the rest of the Suns will soon be as dead as they are! Cao Cao's attacked and destroyed the Yuan clan in the north, and Liu Fu's our ally, so-"
"The Yuans haven't been destroyed," Dai Yuan scoffed. "And Liu Fu is either obtuse or self-servingly cunning. He-"
"She wears her best robes, and she scents her body with fine perfumes," Gui Lan said suddenly. "How is she not eager for our future union...?"
"...You're besotted," Dai Yuan said disparagingly. "His consorts are beautiful enough for most men, but you'd really risk this."
"This is auspicious," Gui Lan insisted. "So say no more."
"...Alright, well, enjoy your meeting," Dai Yuan grumbled. "And please, Gui, don't molest her! This is part of courtship, not-!"
"I know, I know!" Gui Lan said as he left Dai Yuan's office.
"...Fool," Dai Yuan sighed.

Gui Lan returned to the governor's mansion and went to Lady Xū's personal quarters; she was sat on a cushion in the centre of the large room, and a pot of tea had been made ready.

"...You're like something that fell from the Heavens," Gui Lan said.
"Please sit," Lady Xū replied politely.
"Of course, of course!" Gui Lan cackled as he passed Lady Xū's maids – who were stood at the side of the room with their heads lowered – and took a seat opposite his future bride.
"...Tea...?" Lady Xū asked.
"I... I am truly captivated by your beauty, Lady Xū," Gui Lan replied. "I... I know that it is not customary for a couple to 'consummate a marriage before it has happened', but nobody need know."
"We should adhere to protocol," Lady Xū said.
"...You divine, do you not...?" Gui Lan recalled. "You've agreed to this because the fates have decreed it, haven't you...?"
"Heaven has decreed what happens here today, yes," Lady Xū said as her eyes moved from Gui Lan to the two maids that stood behind Gui. The besotted Gui Lan did not immediately notice that Lady Xū was looking at something beside him, and he frowned when he finally did; he was dead within seconds of that as one of the maids – the officer Sun Gao in disguise – grabbed Gui and covered his mouth so that the other 'maid' – the officer Fu Ying – could kill him without making too much noise.
"Sorry, my lady, that you had to see that," Sun Gao panted as Gui Lan's body fell backward lifelessly.
"On the contrary, I enjoyed it very much," Lady Xū replied. "I only wish that I could see the other one die as well."
"...He should be dead by now," Fu Ying supposed.
"Their heads will be offered to my husband's altar," Lady Xū said as she got to her feet. "I can now return to wearing my mourning garb: thank you, gentlemen... thank you."
"Thank *you*, my lady, for your brilliance," Sun Gao replied.

Sun Quan had only been back in his capital for a few days when a letter arrived from Danyang Prefecture that stunned and mortified the entire court yet again.
"My cousin...!" Sun Quan gasped. "They killed my cousin too...!"
Sun Hè's sons and nephew were sat by Sun Quan's host seat in white clothes: they hugged each other and sobbed at what was devastating news.
"Those *bastards*," Cheng Pu growled. "**How did nobody act???**"
"They were very clever," Zhang Zhao replied. "Thankfully, in the end, Sun Yi's widow, Lady Xū, was smarter still."
"My court is my family," Sun Quan said. "Inform us all of my sister-in-law's brave and sensible actions."
"She politely rejected Gui Lan's advances, even after they had murdered Sun Hè," Zhang Zhao explained. "She asked Gui to wait for a month, in which time she had her maids make regular shopping trips in the city market that brought them into contact with men that were secretly loyal to the Suns. Through them, she managed to make contact with Sun Gao and Fu Ying, and a plan was hatched: on the appointed day, the maids went out as usual, and Sun Gao and Fu Ying – who, by Heaven's kind will, are both young, small of stature and lacking facial hair – wore suitable disguises and took their places. Gui Lan was so besotted with Lady Xū and sure of her piety that he overlooked security, hence the plan worked.

"That took care of Gui Lan: when he came to meet what he believed to be a willing and ready Lady Xū, Sun Gao and Fu Ying killed him. Dai Yuan's leading general had been asked to visit the barracks, which kept him away from Dai's office: Sun and Fu's subordinates entered the office disguised as low-ranking officials and killed Dai Yuan where he sat."

"A marvellous woman," Cheng Pu said. "What about the villains' allies, external and internal...?"

"Liu Fu was in correspondence with them, but he seems to have been humouring them," Zhang Zhao replied. "There were others within the city: many of them protest that they helped because they were afraid, either of Dai and Gui's power or, once Sun Yi was dead, of Lord Sun's wrath, believing that they would be blamed for their failure to prevent that first wrong. Some continue to insist that they consider Sun Yi's death a separate matter, but most agree that the deaths are connected."

"...I must go to Danyang at once, and oversee this matter in person," Sun Quan declared. "Sun Shao will travel with me."

"We must go too!" Sun Hè's eldest son, Sun Zhu, protested.

"When the initial matters are dealt with, there will be a proper funeral for your father," Sun Quan promised. "Your cousin and I must first destroy those who aided the villains and restore order."

"When Father left here to do that, he himself was the one that was destroyed!" Sun Zhu retorted. "Take care, Lord Sun Quan! Take care!"

"Danyang is now under the control of friends," Sun Quan said. "I have nothing to fear. Zhang Zhao: you will remain here."

"As you command," Zhang Zhao replied.

Sun Quan and his entourage were greeted at the gates of Wanling County City by Huang Gai, Sun Gao and Fu Ying.

"I should have done more," Huang Gai lamented. "I was close to the city! I-!"

"It isn't your fault," Cheng Pu interrupted.

"Your contributions are many and good, Gongfu," Sun Quan insisted. "The villains Dai and Gui fooled everybody... but they only did that with the help of others. Have all of the conspirators been rounded up...?"

"They await you in the governor's hall," Huang Gai replied.

"There is no need for you to remain in the city any longer, Gongfu," Sun Quan said. "Elder Cheng, Song Qian, Sun Shao and a multitude of others surround me, and the worst men are gone or soon to be disposed of. Return to Shicheng and finish your magnificent work, which should hopefully be easier now."

Huang Gai bowed silently.

"...I must see Lady Xū," Sun Quan continued. "That woman is a tigress, a woman whose loyalty to her husband, even after his death, is an example that should be followed. She raises my nephew, and she does so alone... but like Lady Qiao, she will have whatever she needs."

"Lady Xū is in the hall," Fu Ying reported. "She wants to see the men that aided Dai and Gui meet their ends."

"And she shall have her wish," Sun Quan promised. "To the hall, then, gentlemen."

"**MERCY, Lord Sun!**" the official Mister Wang cried as

Sun Quan entered the governor's hall and took his seat as the host; General – formerly Colonel – Yin and a number of other officials were sat close to Mister Wang awaiting their fates.

"Mercy...?" Sun Quan snickered angrily. "Why...?"

"We were fooled!" General Yin pleaded. "Dai and Gui fooled us all! Ask anybody! Anybody! We few were not alone in our ignorance!"

"But you were alone in your complicity, 'General' Yin," Sun Quan retorted. "Yes, the city was fooled by Dai and Gui's clever manipulation of Bian Hong, but you were present when they killed my cousin."

"...They deceived us!" Mister Wang protested. "They convinced us that you were at odds with Inspector Liu Fu and the Han government, and that-!"

"That you would be blamed for my brother's death," Sun Quan interrupted. "But since when does being complicit to a second crime prove your innocence with regard to the first...? How did you come to such a conclusion...?"

"Let us atone with our service from this moment, Lord Sun," General Yin implored.

"Your only service now will be to offer your heads to my fallen relations," Sun Quan retorted. "**Guards: *death*. Each and every one of them.**"

The small group of officials and officers made simultaneous pleas that melded into an incoherent wailing noise, but no individual argument would have been enough to save its maker. Sun Quan, Lady Xū and Sun Shao smiled as each head was returned to the court by a soldier and placed on the floor in front of them; the other city officials grimaced and shrank back in their seats as they quietly thanked the heavens that they had not been implicated in any of the crimes.

"Sun Shao will now be the Commander of Danyang's military," Sun Quan announced. "His young age should fool nobody: Ling Tong, one of my finest officers, is a year younger, and he has just aided my pacification of Wu Prefecture by taking down an entire hilltop garrison in an hour. Lady Xū and the rest of my brother's family will return to the capital with me. And remember what I said, gentlemen: when it comes to military matters, Sun Shao is always to be obeyed and never to be underestimated."

The officials murmured deferentially.

"...What has happened here in Danyang is truly horrible," Sun Quan continued. "To lose my brother, my cousin and my trust in the officials that once surrounded my late uncle, Wu Jing... calling into question the nature of his unexpected passing. I do not know who I intend to appoint as the Administrator as yet... I see that I must choose carefully. You are all on final warning, gentlemen: no more failures."

The fearful officials kowtowed and made pleas for forgiveness.

"I must now bury my poor brother properly, and then my poor cousin," Sun Quan said. "And then we must move on... for there is much left to do."

✱✱✱✱✱✱✱✱✱✱✱✱

53

Weeks passed in the wake of the 'Danyang Incident' and the costly campaign against the Wu Hills Bandits: the lost were mourned and buried properly, and the capital returned to its normal business. Sun Quan insisted on receiving regular word from Danyang Prefecture and its new military commandant, Sun Shao, but there were many – Sun Quan included – that wondered if Shao's appointment was improperly given in a moment of sentimental weakness.

"...Can such a young man hope to control the armies of such a large region, faced with the likes of the bandit king Fei Zhan and looking every day at men that, at the least, stood by while his uncle was cut down...?" Zhang Zhao asked.

"I share your worry," Sun Quan replied. "I must test his ability."

"How so...?" Zhuge Jin asked.

"...Contact Huang Gai," Sun Quan said. "Tell him this..."

Danyang Commandant Sun Shao had constructed a large military camp outside the prefectural capital; he consulted others at every turn, including Lü Fan and Gongjin, so that he could be certain that he was fulfilling his role effectively. One night, as he finished addressing his subordinates and prepared to settle down for rest, a messenger ran into the command tent and shouted, "**ENEMY ATTACKING THE CITY!**"

"...At this late hour...?" Sun Shao exclaimed. "I will deal with this matter personally."

Sun Shao put his armour on and met with his deputy Gao Shou, who said, "This is bad, Commandant. We're surrounded."

"But we're ready, are we not...?" Sun Shao asked.

"Every man is alert and doing his job, and every position is properly manned," Gao Shou replied. "The city is ready as well."

"...Then I must meet this enemy in person!" Sun Shao decided.

But when Sun Shao rode out of the gates of his camp, he was not greeted by bandits or tribes: he was met instead by Huang Gai, who said, "I apologise for the deception, Commandant Sun, but it was Lord Sun Quan's personal order."

"...Lord Sun...?" Sun Shao exclaimed.

"He is on his way here," Huang Gai explained. "He will surely be pleased: had I been a real attacker, I would have certainly suffered terrible losses."

"...I shall take comfort in the fact that I have performed well," Sun Shao said.

Sun Shao greeted Sun Quan at the gates of his camp a day later and said, "That was a very convincing trick that you played on me, Lord Sun."

"Forgive me, cousin, but there can be no more mistakes," Sun Quan replied. "I had to be sure that you were the right man: I am now certain of it and can reassure others as well. You'll receive all of your father's men and resources, the rank of colonel outside of Danyang, and command of Qu'e and Dantu Counties in addition to your responsibilities here."

"But can I manage such responsibility...?" Sun Shao asked.

"You are a natural," Sun Quan replied. "And you are a 'Sun', just like your uncle was... not at birth, perhaps, but in your heart. I only give you what you deserve."
Sun Shao clasped his hands together and bowed humbly, saying, "I will never forget your kindness!"
"Danyang will be safe now, and Wu is as it was," Sun Quan decided. "Maybe... maybe we can finally consider another campaign against our clan's enemies at long, long last..."

The Han's appointed Inspector of Yang Province, Liu Fu, observed the work on Hefei Fortress with a strange smile on his gaunt face: the outer structure of the walled super-city was almost complete after countless delays and good relations between the government and the regional rebel groups were at an all-time high.
"You seem to be very pleased about our situation, Inspector Liu," Assistant Jiang Ji noted.
"...Yes and no," Liu Fu replied. "The stress is making an ill man of me, there's no doubt of that: that last mess – the 'Dai Yuan and Gui Lan situation' – was starting to look like the precursor to a large-scale encounter with the Suns when we are not quite ready yet. But the Danyang matter is resolved, this fortress is taking shape at last, and Liu Biao and Huang Zu are bound to bear more of the brunt of Sun Quan's anger and embarrassment than us."
"...'Embarrassment'...?" Jiang Ji prompted.
"He was unable to protect Sun Yi and Sun Hè and prevent their destruction at the hands of two deranged and somewhat obvious assassins," Liu Fu replied. "Such inability can be seen as weakness... for if the closest members of the clan to the lord are that vulnerable, is Sun Quan so invincible...?"
"...'Deranged'...?" Jiang Ji prompted.
"Dai and Gui had been trapped on that estate alongside Sheng Xian for a long time, and it is now my understanding – having now spoken to a man that met one of their peers shortly after Sheng's assassination – that they had become, oddly enough, 'acolytes' of Sheng Xian, and entirely unsolicited ones at that," Liu Fu explained. "Being trapped with him, listening to him day after day, sharing his fate... it made them increasingly look to him, almost as if he were a Taoist sage or cult leader, even though he had no profound words or ultimate plan for them to follow."
"...I confess to finding that to be pathetic if it is true," Jiang Ji said.
Liu Fu smiled and replied, "I'd be kinder in my phrasing, but... yes. But then we must consider that they were removed from their civil posts by force, suddenly at that, by baying mobs of disaffected people that Xu Gong had convinced that Sheng was the source of all of their problems, and forced to flee for their lives, and we must remember also that their saviour, Xu Zhao, then allowed that same Xu Gong to live next to them after he in turn was ousted by Sun Ce. Add the subsequent decision to let 'White Tiger' Yan – a constant source of misery for Wu – enjoy sanctuary as well, and throw in the freedom with which Xu Gong and White Tiger came and went while they were perpetually trapped – despite having done *nothing wrong at all* – and you have a recipe for slow erosion of sanity at the very least."
"...And then they spent all that time in the hills with bandits afterward," Jiang Ji noted.

"After years of being trapped on Xu Zhao's estate as living martyrs to piousness with each other and some of their family for comfort and Sheng Xian as an unwitting beacon of hope, living on a hillside with the dregs of society and observing their carefree ways must have damaged something," Liu Fu suggested. "To go from passive victims to cunning murderers that then molested Sun Yi's consorts and slept in his bed... such a change takes more than revenge to fuel it. But what's done is done: Sun Yi cannot be brought back, and he was the Sun clansman that many feared most... Sun Quan most of all, if truth be told, since Yi was the 'second Sun Ce' that so many in Jiangdong wanted as chieftain and that so many must now consign to memory."
"...Indeed, yes," Jiang Ji said. "Like it or not, Sun Quan is their ruler now."
"There is always Sun Ben, divisive though he is," Liu Fu replied. "And if Sun Quan makes too many mistakes, then Sun Ben – a man that enjoys His Excellency's respect and favour – might be the only choice left for the followers of that severely weakened clan if it is to endure... and Sun Ben is exactly the man we want, for he will end the violence and 'return the south to the fold'."
"...We might not need the fortress, then...?" Jiang Ji said.
"Hopefully not," Liu Fu replied as he gazed at the walls of Hefei. "My colleague and friend, Man P'oning – whose idea this was, in truth – would be as glad as I if the defences provided by this place were never needed... let it then stand as a memorial to a threat that removed itself, a place of trade and learning, like a flower guarded by thorns. But, sad to say, I think that it will find full use: somehow, sometime... it will be needed."
Jiang Ji turned to look at Hefei City and sighed with resignation.

Gongjin visited the home of his friend and colleague Lü Fan before he made the return trip to the Ba Qiu training facility: he waited until they were seated before he said, "We've not really spoken properly about any of it, have we...?"
"...We've lacked the time, and perhaps the inclination," Lü Fan replied as he examined the sleeve of his white robes. "Do you still discuss state matters with Lu Zijing...?"
"...I do," Gongjin admitted.
"He's a fine man, honest and loyal, and he saved your regiment from destruction, so your trust is understandable and well-placed," Lü Fan said. "But enough of that: what are we discussing and how...?"
Gongjin smiled sadly and replied, "You frame the issue well. This is all so personal, but we've got to treat it like work..."
Lü Fan waited for a few moments before he coughed deliberately.
"Sorry," Gongjin said. "I am, like you, planning for the next campaign against Huang Zu, but... what happened to Shubi and Bohai still haunts me, and I'm unhappy with the last Wu campaign as well."
"We're both moving around constantly these days: you're off again, and so am I soon enough," Lü Fan noted. "When a man is so busy, he gets little time to think about things... but like you, I'm unable to shake what happened from my thoughts. They're in my mind's eye all the time... like Bofu, Wu Jing, Jizuo, Lady Wu and even Ling Cao, because... because... because I still believe that

their deaths were all of them unavoidable if only something –
though I don't know exactly what – had been done differently."

"I feel as though I've failed," Gongjin admitted. "Bofu was my
lord, my friend and my brother-in-law: yes, he was reckless and
yes, I was on the other side of the province, but he and I were
sworn brothers! I...! ...*Aiee*. I am not saying that the other deaths
aren't tragic: I love and miss Shubi and Jizuo as brothers too, and
Lady Wu and her brother were a second mother and esteemed
uncle to me, but... I suppose I wonder whether it's Bofu's death
that began a-"

Gongjin suddenly halted and sighed miserably.

"...'Began a run of bad luck'...?" Lü Fan prompted. "Or 'began a
decline', perhaps...? ...Or... or 'began a new era of destructive in-
fighting, like the last two generations of Yuans have suffered, that
has yet to claim all of its victims'...?"

"Let it be the first of those," Gongjin pleaded. "I don't know what I
truly meant to say, Ziheng, but let's just hope it's the first of
those and that the 'run of bad luck' is now over."

"But... say that it were the second, as some might suppose... what
then...?" Lü Fan asked. "We've turned our backs on the Han
because they're doomed to ruin: even if we continue to support
Lord Sun Quan, if only out of loyalty to Bofu, we're surrounded by
men that respected Bofu for his strength and charisma and have
no such respect for Lord Sun Quan. Shubi was, to some, a future
light to follow, and now he is snuffed, and there are some ugly
rumours floating around regarding his untimely demise, as you
well know... rumours that suggest the third option."

"...I refuse to believe that Lord Sun Quan had any part in Shubi's
death, no more than I accept the wicked rumours that he plotted
the death of Bofu, his mother, Wu Jing or Kuang," Gongjin
insisted. "He can be selfish, yes... he can be ruthless, yes... but he
would not commit fratricide, matricide or in any other way go
against the family ideals that his parents instilled in every one of
them and a lot of others besides."

"...And what about Sun Ben...?" Lü Fan prompted. "He was raised
in that same household: do you consider him to be as far removed
from such things...?"

"... ... ...Like you, I cannot call him 'Boyang' anymore, not without
great effort," Gongjin admitted. "Ben's aloofness at Shubi and
Bohai's funerals was obnoxious: petty griping about his being
posted to Yuzhang is inappropriate at the best of times, but Shubi
and Bohai treated him like a brother!"

"But could he be somehow part of a very successful plot to
remove alternative leaders and figures of importance...?" Lü Fan
asked. "Taishi Ci is ill; Bofu, Shubi, Jizuo, Wu Jing, Lady Wu, all
dead; say – just say – that Huang Zu is more prepared for our
arrival than-"

"No," Gongjin interrupted. "Sun Ben might conspire with Cao Cao,
but not Liu Biao and Huang Zu."

"I at least coaxed that tangible doubt out of you," Lü Fan said.
"What might Sun Ben 'conspire with Cao Cao' to do, do you
think...? How far would he go...?"

"... ... ...It's a difficult matter to discuss," Gongjin pleaded.

"Yet it is *you* that visited *me*," Lü Fan retorted.

"...It is so," Gongjin said with a sigh. "I... I have truly started to wonder whether Ben had any part in Shubi's death. Bofu's death, that's more difficult... perhaps because I would have to get even angrier, because that makes him responsible for Lady Wu, Wu Jing and Jizuo, even if all he did was hasten their decline..."

"...And put Sun Quan in the ruler's seat, intended or otherwise," Lü Fan prompted.

"...But when I speak like this, I think of that oft-repeated mistake, another of the 'old mistakes' that seem to recur and bring down states from within," Gongjin countered. "Sowing the seed of doubt has consequences: if Cheng Demou had not convinced Lord Sun that Sheng Xian was a threat, would Shubi be dead now...?"

"Or would Cao Cao's letter, sent to Sheng to 'rescue him at last' and give him a military commission – a proposal that could not have been anything but coincidental – have begun a war between Sheng and the Suns for control of Wu...?" Lü Fan asked. "Sun Ben knew nothing of Demou's meetings with Lord Sun, and Demou is no traitor: he is, perhaps, insightful and correctly deduced that Sheng would be used to get at us, willingly or not, by Cao Cao. And as we've discussed before, Jizuo's death might have been at the hands of one of Lady Cao's handmaidens wielding poison, Lady Wu and Wu Jing might have been poisoned also, and Chen Deng, Cao's agent, lured Bofu to Dantu, where he died at the hands of the son of Xu Gong, a man that was corresponding with Cao Cao... not Sun Ben or Lord Sun Quan."

"...Cao Cao has much to answer for," Gongjin replied bitterly. "I believe it will eventually come down to a military confrontation if we survive all of the more underhanded attempts to destroy us."

"So do I, and I relish the opportunity to fight the old villain," Lü Fan said. "But we have two other 'old villains' to deal with first, do we not...?"

"...Yes," Gongjin replied. "Let us hurry and dispose of those two, so that we can be ready for the third."

The news of the short-lived coup in Danyang and the scalps that it had claimed did not take long to reach other parts of Jiangdong. In some places, the deaths of two promising young heroes garnered sympathy and won the populace back to the side of the Sun clan; in others, the reports were seen as further proof that the Suns were vulnerable and led to more uprisings or raids. But Wu and Danyang Prefectures had been stabilised, and Kuaiji was seeing improvements thanks to good government and the efforts of Hè Qi's pacification force. The main problem now was Yuzhang Prefecture, where its administrator, Hua Xin, was starting to wonder where his loyalties should be and its main protector, Taishi Ci, was slowly running out of strength: its main problem – Huang Zu, the lord of neighbouring Jiangxia – was waiting for an opportune moment to do damage to the Sun clan, and thoughts increasingly turned to ending that feud once and for all.

****

ACT V: THE JIANGXIA CAMPAIGN

54

A time of great intrigue, misery and loss had left the rulers of the southeast region of the Han Empire known as Jiangdong – 'East of the River' – with a sense that something extremely positive had to happen in order to prevent the collapse of the regime. It had been 13 years since the indentured minor warlord Sun Jian – a famous hero known to many as the 'Tiger of Jiangdong' – had been struck down while fighting the lord Jing Province, Liu Biao, for his lord, and it had now been 4 years since Sun Jian's son Sun Ce – known to his many friends as 'Bofu', but whose independent efforts to pacify and unite the southeast earned him the nickname 'Little Conqueror' amongst his rivals and enemies – had been murdered by the followers of the assassinated agitator Xu Gong whilst out hunting, and much had changed.

Sun Jian's death had passed the mantle of clan chieftain to Sun Ce – after a brief tenure by Ce's older cousin Sun Ben – at a time when that responsibility was marred by thankless service to the ambitious nobleman Yuan Shu, but when Shu committed high treason and heresy by declaring that he was 'First Emperor of the Zhong Dynasty', Sun Ce broke free of the relationship that his father had unwittingly agreed to when he had marched northward to fight the tyrant chancellor Dong Zhuo years before. Now the title 'Chieftain of the Sun clan of Fuchun' brought genuine power and command of a quarter of Han China with it, so when Ce died relatively unexpectedly, there was much discussion about who should follow that charismatic and affable young hero: the choice – championed mainly by Ce's mother, Lady Wu, but otherwise divisive – was to instate Sun Quan, Sun Jian's physically unimpressive and notoriously undisciplined second son.

The army – and those civil officials who fretted that the bandits and tribes only kowtowed to strong leaders – wanted Sun Jian's third son, Sun Yi – whose appearance and personality were eerily similar to Sun Ce's – to rule Jiangdong, while the voices of discontent regarding Sun Quan – who had once battled alcoholism, stolen treasury funds and caused suffering to the citizens of Xuan City when he deliberately neglected its security – were many and diverse in their reasons for wanting somebody else, and one man, General Li Shu, rebelled almost immediately and forced Sun Quan's loyalists to fight a civil war to reclaim Lujiang Prefecture and the 30,000 men that had defected with Li Shu. The Han's 'Excellency of Works', Cao Cao, then forged marriage ties with the Suns, but that did not stop critics accusing him of having a hand in Sun Ce's assassination and, later, the series of sudden deaths that followed the two marriages: Sun Jian's frail fourth son, Kuang – who had married one of Cao Cao's nieces – died within a short time, followed by Sun Jian's widow, Lady Wu, who finally lost the strength to cope with illness and the unbearable personal losses. Li Shu's rebellion was later quelled and the army restored to full strength, but the victory could not be celebrated, as many still resented or even abhorred the idea of Sun Quan governing the south.

A subsequent failure to defeat Liu Biao's ally Huang Zu – which led, through perceived mismanagement on Sun Quan's part, to the death of the reckless but valiant officer Ling Cao in a naval engagement – led to more rebellions and general anarchy, and when illness and emotional exhaustion claimed the life of Quan's maternal uncle, Danyang Prefectural Administrator Wu Jing, Sun Yi was sent to Danyang to restore order. A rebellion in Wu Prefecture then took Sun Quan out of his capital, at which point two men in Sun Yi's administration – who were, in fact, known followers of an assassinated official that blamed the Suns for their lord's death – orchestrated Yi's murder and briefly seized control of Danyang: they were eventually defeated by a scheme and murdered, but not before claiming another important scalp, that of Sun Quan's trusted cousin and security chief, Sun Hè. The losses meant that a lot of posts were now being filled by young and at times untested relations of the embattled lord of Jiangdong, and that did nothing to end the murmurs of discontent or the ambitions of neighbouring warlords, not least the Sun clan's nemesis Liu Biao: an end to that conflict was demanded and greatly sought, if only to secure Sun Quan's place and finally stabilise the south, although others – such as the late Sun Ce's brother-in-law and closest friend and adviser, Zhou Yu, whom most still knew as 'Gongjin' – now saw Quan as having some greater destiny – even, perhaps, the Imperial throne.

As the weeks and months went by, the efforts to pacify the vast Jiangdong region continued: Sun Quan was glad of the news that his reliable officer Hè Qi had finally defeated the rebels in western Kuaiji Prefecture, and the officer Dong Xi reported that the bandit armies in southern Yuzhang Prefecture had lost control of some of the villages that they had captured.

"...I wonder if I should heed Hè Qi's advice to enact boundary changes," Sun Quan said to his assembled advisers.

"I am not a believer in 'leaving things as they are because they are'," Zhang Zhao replied. "We are sick of dealing with criminals and barbarians in Kuaiji, are we not...? If Hè Qi – who knows that region very well – believes that changes are needed, I think that we should listen to him."

"...Very good: we'll do as he suggests, then," Sun Quan said. "What's the news from Yuzhang...?"

"Taishi Ci was forced to repel a group of bandit mercenaries that were obviously working for Huang Zu," Bu Zhi reported. "I wonder if Huang is trying to wear Taishi down... Pan Zhang has made more gains in Xi'an, and Dong Xi is advancing northward to respond to rumours that the agitator Peng Hu is up to something. Sun Ben and Sun Fu each report that their designated regions are stabilising, but that there is still a lot of work to do."

"...That is sadly very true," Sun Quan said. "There is so much that I have not done."

"There is so much that you *have yet to do*," Gongjin insisted. "But at the same time, Lord Sun, you have restored a lot of order."

"But will I be allowed to finish what I have started, I wonder...?" Sun Quan asked.

"...This must not be allowed to go on."

The Administrator of Yuzhang Prefecture, Hua Xin, was addressing a small group of loyal officials in a private room within his mansion: he was obviously preparing to flee, so the audience was tense and fearful.

"I can do no more here in this place," Hua Xin continued. "The region is not really mine to govern, and has not been for some time: Taishi Ci, Sun Ben, Pan Zhang and so forth, they are your lords now, and I am just a relic of Liu Yao's days as the true Governor of Yang Province. I am better off serving the court in a different capacity, and I therefore take my leave to seek that new role in Xuchang."

"We will come with you, or better yet, let us fight to restore your authority, Administrator!" one man cried. "If we cannot, then-!"

"You'd be another Dai Yuan or Gui Lan...?" Hua Xin chuckled. "I refuse to be another Sheng Xian for you to martyr yourselves pointlessly. By all means leave of your own accords, gentlemen, but we will not leave together: this is a personal decision, not a call to arms or an attempt to poach officials for His Excellency. Do as your hearts tell you."

The room was silent: Hua Xin then bowed slightly and retreated to his inner quarters, where his wife and consorts were waiting.

"...That look you give me," Hua Xin said as he glared at his younger wife. "Have I somehow wronged you...?"

"Can we not go to Kuaiji, or at least wait until I have notified our son...?" Hua Xin's wife pleaded.

"Luo Tong made it perfectly clear that he 'is Luo Jun's son, not mine'," Hua Xin retorted. "I have avoided discussing it until now, but we must have closure if this next step is to be a secure one: Tong treated me as though I were his father's killer, but why...?"

"He... is headstrong, husband!" Hua Xin's wife sobbed.

"Stubborn for no reason, angry for no reason, vindictive for no reason," Hua Xin complained. "Yuan Shu killed his father when he conquered Chen County: I served Liu Yao, who was dedicated to thwarting the efforts of Yuan Shu and his minions – including the Suns – to seize power here in Yang! Your son is another one of these fool youths that seems to think that the Suns are noble heroes, but they are wicked, greedy villains! Like Liu Ji, Yuan Yao, Lu Kang and Lu Ji before him, Luo Tong seems to want to embrace the blade that kills his kin!"

Hua Xin's wife sobbed miserably and did not answer.

"I married you, gave you and that ungrateful boy a good home, good food, servants and respect, and if he had shown some of the sense that he seemed, at first, to have, then he would now be in my administration and coming with us to Xuchang to work for His Excellency: instead he has shown contempt for me and 'gone home', fled to Kuaiji to live under the Suns, and that's his fool choice. He walked out of here without even looking back to show respect to *you*, woman, and that should be enough for you to understand that he has cut all ties with us both and forget him! You speak of 'writing to him', but has he written to you...?"

Hua Xin's wife was silent.

"You are *my* wife now, not Luo Jun's," Hua Xin continued, "and if Luo Tong wants to be the son of a corpse and the vassal of a gangster then leave him be! ...Or do you want to leave my side and join him in Kuaiji...?"

"I... will accompany you to Xuchang, Husband, and allow my son to choose his own path," Hua Xin's wife replied.

"...I worry about my choice as much as any of you, but I have no choice," Hua Xin insisted. "Sun Ben – the last of them to have a genuine claim to the Sun clan chieftainship – is here in Yuzhang and desperately hankering for a seat of power; Sun Yi, Sun Kuang and Wu Jing have all died miserable deaths, the first of those at the hands of Sheng Xian's idiot followers. If I stay, I risk more suspicion that I plot against the Suns as Xu Gong did and as Sheng Xian may or may not have done, for all the good that the uncertainty did him. If I stay, I risk Sun Ben seizing power if he suddenly falls from favour and requires a fortress as Li Shu did. To protect not just myself but my family, I must go northward and seek employment with His Excellency Cao Cao: perhaps my knowledge of this region will prove invaluable in the future."

"...We are ready to depart," a servant declared.

"Then let's be gone before some idiot tells the Suns or their many, many thugs in this region," Hua Xin said. "I want my whole body and my soul to reach Xuchang, not my head alone, so that I might do some good."

Hua Xin left his seal of office and fled Yuzhang Prefecture under the cover of night in a carriage bound for the Yangtze River: his 'escape' ended years of service in the region but preceded many years of service as one of Cao Cao's senior advisers.

Two days passed.

"...So Hua Xin's gone, then," Sun Ben chuckled.

"That laugh was like something supernatural," Sun Ben's brother Fu complained.

"I laugh strangely because this is strangely funny and yet it is frightening too," Sun Ben replied. "Now a new Administrator must be appointed: will 'Lord Sun Quan' trust 'good old Cousin Boyang' and give me the role, or will he find someone else... his friend Pan Zhang, perhaps...?"

"He can't make that shameless criminal the Administrator, surely...?" Sun Fu said.

"Is he any more likely to give the role to me...?" Sun Ben chortled.

"...We're on the outside now, aren't we...?" Sun Fu said.

"I don't know... I really don't know," Sun Ben replied. "This might give us a good indication: I saw the looks at Shubi's funeral, but then again that's because I wasn't being as cordial as I might have been."

"...And that's because you don't know whether you can be sure that Quan didn't have a hand in Shubi's death," Sun Fu suggested.

"I... have deliberately avoided the conversation," Sun Ben admitted. "But yes, brother, I do wonder: I therefore wonder if I might suffer a similar fate now. Is Hua Xin's departure a precursor to another ludicrous 'vengeful vassals of the wronged administrator' scheme, like the ones that claimed Bofu and Shubi...? And are they the work of nobody but the loyal vassals in question, or are they down to Quan, or are they down to my daughter's father-in-law Cao Cao, as so many in Quan's court – such as my eternal critic Cheng Pu – now believe...?"

"...Yet you're still maintaining close communications with Cao Cao, aren't you...?" Sun Fu prompted.

"He's my daughter's father-in-law!" Sun Ben protested. "He writes with cheerful anecdotes about my grandchildren, little poems and invitations to banquets, and I reply as best I can, given my limited writing talent, to wish our united families well! Not one word has come here or left there that-!"

"I believe you," Sun Fu interrupted.

"But does *anyone else*...?" Sun Ben whined.

"...So you really believe that Hua Xin's departure will set things in motion...?" Sun Fu prompted.

"Taishi Ziyi is ill enough as it is," Sun Ben replied. "The prefectural administrator fleeing in the middle of the night with all of his worldly goods and leaving the civil offices without a head is hardly going to inspire the people or maintain stability, is it...?"

"We're not done quelling the chaos," Sun Fu said. "And now things might get *worse*."

"Things could get *better* with the right Administrator," Sun Ben suggested. "But that, like all matters, is down to Lord Sun Quan... *Heaven help us*."

Days later, Sun Quan assembled his upper court and said, "Hua Xin has fled: what now...?"

"*Aiee*... we do not need this right now," Zhang Zhao complained.

"I have learned his location, by the way, or rather a significant part of his route," Lü Fan reported. "He stopped in *Hefei* and was warmly received by *Liu Fu* before crossing into *Yan Province*."

"He's going to Cao Cao," the politician Quan Rou supposed.

"...Elder Cheng suggested to me that Hua Xin might still intend us harm, and this proves that there might have been truth in that," Sun Quan decided. "He might flee now because he feared that we were about to uncover his involvement in plots past and present... after all, why would he run when we are achieving victories against the bandits and turning Liu Biao's saboteurs away but stay during the worst...?"

"...What say you, Mister Zhou Yu...?" Zhang Zhao asked as he turned to glare at Gongjin.

"Indeed, yes," Sun Quan said excitedly. "Speak, Gongjin: share your sagely wisdom with us."

"Hua Xin might simply feel that he will become suspected," Gongjin suggested. "I know that Mister Zhang Zhao is expecting me to start heckling Cao Cao, but my focus at the moment is Liu Biao: yes, Hua Xin might be part of some scheme, but it's unlikely, I think, given that Liu Ji, his late lord's son, knows the man well and considers him to be 'capable of intrigue but not appropriately surrounded'."

"What *nonsense*," Lü Fan scoffed. "A master of intrigue could scheme in the company of nothing but his worst enemies, else he'd not be of much use. If he's capable, then-"

"If he's capable, then we're looking at him scheming for His Excellency Cao Cao, are we not!" Zhang Zhao snapped. "I'll have no part in such slander! The-!"

"**Can we-!** ...Can we please, please, *please* discuss the most important aspect of this...?" Sun Quan asked despairingly. "Who will take the man's place...?"

"Not Sun Ben," Xu Kun muttered.

"He's done nothing wrong, cousin," Sun Quan insisted.

"He's done nothing *proven*," Xu Kun retorted. "There's a difference. His daughter is married to one of Cao Cao's sons, he's a former clan chieftain that feels that he was cheated, and let's not forget that Yuan Shu gave him Yuzhang to run years back, in addition to making him Inspector of Yu Province when he was chieftain, so if we start giving him titles that Yuan Shu gave him then we might as well say that he-!"

"Enough," Sun Quan ordered. "Boyang's no traitor."

"So you're going to appoint him as the Administrator, then, Lord Sun...?" Zhang Zhao prompted.

"I will, Zibu, yes... if there are no serious objections that are *based on fact*," Sun Quan replied uneasily.

No serious objections were raised: Sun Ben received instruction that he was to travel to the prefectural capital Nanchang and receive the Administrator's seal. Sun Ben would continue to be scrutinised, but it was an important first step toward repairing the damage to the relationship between the remaining members of Sun Quan's close family and an even more important first step toward restoring order in the region that would serve as headquarters to the upcoming campaign against Huang Zu.

✸✸✸✸✸✸✸✸✸✸✸✸

55

In the north, Cao Cao was completing his takeover of Ji Province, which had been the southern quarter of the Yuan clan's vast domains: the eldest of the Yuan brothers, Yuan Tan, was still enjoying his victory over his younger brother and demanding that Cao Cao help him to finish what they had started. Cao Cao's answer came as a surprise to the young warlord, but not, perhaps, to the more astute: Cao declared Yuan Tan an untrustworthy ally and turned his attentions to attacking Tan's base at Nanpi. Yuan Tan was killed, and Cao Cao merged Tan's army with his own.

"...That leaves Yuan Xi and Yuan Shang," Zhang Zhao reported to a sober Sun Quan. "It was a masterstroke."

"It is also worrying," Sun Quan replied; he then looked at the small group of trusted officials that he had invited to his private meeting room and asked, "When can I expect Cao Cao's deadly gaze to turn toward me...?"

"My lord, I will say that obvious thing yet again and will continue to do so until it is acknowledged by all: His Excellency Cao is connected to your clan by marriage now!" Zhang Zhao protested. "And would he be allowing my brother to send these reports if his intentions were bad...?"

"Of course he would, Mister Zhang!" Gongjin heckled. "Is there any sense in not telling your potential targets of your courage, cunning and might...?"

"I do not believe that His Excellency Cao is intending to 'break the peace' and attack us," Zhang Zhao retorted. "The Yuan brothers wronged the Han; have *we*...?"

"It depends on what you classify as treason," Gongjin suggested. "Or rather, what Cao classifies as treason: to his mind, treason is defying *him*. We've refused to send a hostage and killed one of his appointed Inspectors; he ordered that same Inspector, Yan Xiang – and, later on, Chen Deng – to attack us. What 'peace'...?"

"Cao Cao feigned an alliance with Yuan Tan to seize Ji Province and then reneged," Lü Fan noted. "That is not the action of a benevolent man."

"We cannot be sure of Yuan Tan's intent!" Zhang Zhao protested. "Was he an innocent fawn...? Did he not attack Qing Province and hold Kong Rong's family as hostages when Kong was appointed by the court...? Did he not send an army to rescue our former master, Yuan Shu, on his father's behalf...?"

"...Your point is noted," Gongjin replied.

"The points that we must focus on are Cao's actions thus far," Lü Fan suggested. "He used his old friend Xu Yòu to defeat Yuan Shao and then he killed Xu Yòu; he used Yuan Tan to defeat Yuan Shang and then he killed Yuan Tan."

"...That is true," Sun Quan said. "He uses men and then discards or kills them."

"*Ayah*...! Xu Yòu was corrupt, and Yuan Tan a belligerent hankerer!" Zhang Zhao protested. "We've done nothing to deserve similar treatment!"

"Let us hope that Cao Cao agrees," Gongjin replied.

As the weeks went by, the suspicions about the Po County agitator Peng Hu were proved correct: Peng rallied thousands in rebellion as food stocks dwindled, and Sun Quan's court was once again forced to meet to discuss how they would pacify the disaffected.

"Can Ben not cope with this without further draining national resources...?" Xu Kun complained. "Didn't we just make him Administrator of Yuzhang so that-!"

"I did, indeed, make him Administrator so that there would be stability," Sun Quan interrupted. "But we do not know what is 'his fault' and what is due to the mismanagement – accidental, or even deliberate – of the region by his predecessor."

"I quite agree," the politician Quan Rou said. "Food stocks in Po County are not something that Administrator Sun has had time to look into, I imagine, not when he had the restructuring of the central office to deal with."

"Nonetheless, gentlemen, we are now dealing with an angry mob – which is slowly growing into a small army – in Po County," Sun Quan complained. "They are right to be angry if they have nothing to eat."

"But do these people not realise that forcing us to raise an army to subdue them – an army that must be *fed* – will only exacerbate the problem...?" Zhang Zhao said.

"They are desperate," the young official Lu Xun suggested. "Liu Biao's incursions, the bandits and tribes' constant pillaging and a poor harvest have driven them to breaking point again, and we are seen as not doing enough about it."

"My cousin is right," Lu Ji said. "We must be compassionate and win their hearts back, Lord Sun."

"That is my wish," Sun Quan replied.

"At least it's only Po County this time," Quan Rou said. "It should only take a single officer a few months to supress them."

"No, Mister Quan," Bu Zhi said. "We must act as we did against the Wu Hills Bandits."

"You mean 'smash the egg with a rock'...?" Zhang Zhao asked.

"No, I mean 'meet the egg with a boulder'," Bu Zhi replied. "If it is possible, send a mountain down to meet them."

"Won't that be seen as extreme...?" Lu Ji asked. "Won't that do little to win their hearts...? Doesn't such a reaction usually harden hearts, Mister Bu...?"

"I don't suggest killing everything that moves," Bu Zhi retorted. "I said 'meet', not 'smash'."

"Mister Bu is correct," Lü Fan said. "We must make a show of sending an army so large that it frightens Peng Hu; we will then implement the necessary measures and show that we are doing our best to help the people."

"I will go," Bu Zhi volunteered. "If I have the assistance of Jiang Qin, Dong Xi and Ling Tong, I can break this rebellion in a matter of weeks."

"...I agree to it," Sun Quan declared. "Issue summonses to the officers at once."

"And what of the droughts that are starting to hit large parts of Wu, Kuaiji and Danyang...?" Lu Xun asked. "I don't think that we're likely to see those regions remaining stable if something isn't done."

"So what should be done, in your opinion...?" Sun Quan said.

"We should be opening granaries," Lu Xun replied, "and-"
"But food is scarce!" Zhang Zhao protested. "If there was an abundance of food, young man, would there be riots in Po County? You speak as though you are a wise elder, but-!"
"Those areas can be developed," Lu Xun insisted. "The water sources are fewer, yes, but we can channel clean water from rivers and encourage agricultural development in order to ensure that the food is replenished and future disasters are better prepared for. If we distribute supplies to the needy then the people will be relieved of some of their suffering, and they won't turn to crime, and we can maintain order."
"Very good: such things can be your responsibility, Lu Xun, as Agricultural Commandant," Sun Quan declared. "Begin at once."
"I will not fail you, Lord Sun," Lu Xun promised.

Within days, Jiang Qin and Dong Xi met and combined their forces in the south of Po County in Yuzhang Prefecture while the adviser Qin Song left Dong Xi's side and moved to Xi'an to provide support to Pan Zhang.
"S'actually good that I have to stay here," Jiang Qin admitted. "Xu Sheng still won't talk to me, so going back to Wuhu County weren't my idea of fun."
"Oh...? He won't talk to you...? What, not at all...?" Dong Xi exclaimed. "How odd..."
"He hates me, *really* hates me, but I don't even know what for!" Jiang Qin complained.
"...A strange man," Dong Xi said. "He seems to be another Hè Qi when you see him, or, at worst, another Pan Zhang; but then he speaks, and he's pompous and petty, with no regard for any but his 'fellow nobles'."
"I swore that I'd win him around, but that seems unlikely now," Jiang Qin replied. "I've been promoted to a general, and Xu Sheng certainly don't like that."
"Well, he hasn't been invited here, which is good," Dong Xi said.
"No, but we have Bu Zhi, who seriously gives me the creeps," Jiang Qin admitted. "I look into his eyes and they're *cold*..."
"He's one of those men that strives to be unreadable," Dong Xi replied. "Lü Fan and Zhou Yu have that same look in their eyes when they are meeting certain people."
"...Ah, you're right; s'me being silly!" Jiang Qin chuckled. "I just want done with Peng Hu quickly."
"And we will be," Dong Xi replied.

When Bu Zhi and Ling Tong reached Po County, they divided their forces equally and targeted the four largest armies in the region simultaneously; Ling Tong was fighting with a heavy heart, since he knew that many of the rebels were ordinary villagers that had been pushed too far by circumstance.
"**Don't be fools!**" Ling Tong said as he rode around the battlefield and felled men with the butt of his spear. "**Go home and spare us all this business!**"
A hardened group of bandits had joined the rebel militia; they saw that Ling Tong was trying to avoid bloodshed and tried to surround him as he moved further and further from his main infantry force.

"Look at this boy!" the bandits' leader heckled. **"We've nothing to fear if Sun Quan's using *children* to attack us now!"**

Ling Tong's eyes steeled; he and his riders made an example of the bandits – whose dress and demeanour separated them from the villagers that were fighting – by killing their leader and chasing most of them away. Ling Tong then started to dash around the field, looking for others that might make good examples, but he halted when he realised that at least one of the villagers was a young woman armed with a farming tool.

"...This is wrong! Don't make me harm anyone else!" Ling Tong pleaded.

The rebels were mostly unmoved, so it was deemed necessary to use greater force to win the battle; Ling Tong would retreat from that first day of fighting as a man haunted by what he had seen.

Gongjin approached Sun Quan after an exhausting day of court deliberations and said, "My lord, Ziheng and I must speak with you privately."

"...At once," Sun Quan replied.

Once Gongjin and Lü Fan were seated facing their lord Sun Quan in the latter's private study, Lü Fan said, "A peculiar ally comes to us."

"Oh...?" Sun Quan exclaimed. "Who...?"

"...A pirate by the name of Gan Ning, styled 'Xingba'," Gongjin replied. "He originally hails from Linjiang in Yi Province."

"Gan Ning...?" Sun Quan said.

"He is a former subordinate of Huang Zu," Lü Fan explained. "He brings with him details of personnel, drilling routines, resource depots, training facility locations... he is to us what Xu Yòu was to Cao Cao at Guandu."

"And he can definitely be trusted...?" Sun Quan asked excitedly.

"That's... tough to answer," Gongjin replied.

Sun Quan frowned and asked, "Why? If he is not trustworthy, why are we talking?"

"He is surprisingly honest," Lü Fan chuckled.

"Self-destructively honest," Gongjin said.

"Stop being cryptic," Sun Quan pleaded.

"He admits to being a former 'cutthroat-for-hire', a 'wretched dog' that would kill anyone for the right – often very low – price," Lü Fan explained. "He says that he became enlightened one day, and started to read the classics and whatnot."

"Zhou Tai and Jiang Qin tell a similar story," Sun Quan suggested. "But by trusting them, we have gained great assets."

"Huang Zu was not so accommodating," Gongjin said. "Instead of embracing Gan as we have embraced Zhou Tai and Jiang Qin, he continually rebuked Gan, which led to Gan trying ever harder to impress Huang and secure a proper role. And impress him he should have, since he is a very talented man..."

"...What is it that you are trying to tell me...?" Sun Quan prompted.

"He's very cunning, witty, flexible in his thinking, and an expert river warrior, adept at all the skills," Lü Fan said. "Swordplay... boat-crossing... *archery*..."

Sun Quan did not take long to guess the meaning of Lü Fan's tone: he groaned miserably and said, "He is the man that killed Ling Cao, isn't he...?"

"He confesses to it and apologises for the offence," Gongjin replied. "He insists that he would like to atone for-"

"*Ayah*... I can't employ the man that killed my vanguard general and ruined my campaign!" Sun Quan cried. "I must offer his head to Ling Tong for Ling Cao's temple and punish him for thwarting my plans!"

"That is the proper course," Lü Fan replied.

"...But then we lose the information that this man has, and we cannot make use of his fine skills for our cause," Sun Quan continued. "That's your thought, isn't it...?"

"You can't recruit him without the risk of losing Ling Tong," Gongjin suggested. "The information – if he is not lying or bluffing – can be obtained through other means."

Sun Quan smiled and said, "Within your words I sense 'But if he is skilled, why not use him'... am I right...?'"

"You cannot expect peace between a man and the one that murdered his father," Lü Fan replied purposefully.

"This is not the same as Huang Zu and my father, as you seem to be implying," Sun Quan retorted. "Gan Ning acted impersonally for his lord, a lord that was ungrateful and failed to acknowledge a debt. Huang Zu is an old villain that governs Jiangxia as an independent territory, only nominally answering to Liu Biao; he had the choice to spare Father and did not do so out of spite and jealousy of Father's talent. Furthermore, neither Huang Zu nor Liu Biao is actually sorry, whereas this Gan Ning fellow comes into our midst, admits to his error, apologises and pleads for a chance to atone. Where is the similarity...?"

Gongjin shook his head and said, "There are at least two: a grieving son that requires closure and an unpunished murderer that deserves justice."

"He could atone with good service," Sun Quan replied. "What about the example of Cao Cao and Zhang Xiu, or of Yuan Shao sparing Guan Yu after he killed his champion Yan Liang...?"

"...We can only advise you," Gongjin said. "In the end, Lord Sun, the decision is yours."

"Keep this man's presence a secret for as long as possible," Sun Quan ordered. "We can use the knowledge that he possesses to do damage to Huang Zu's military infrastructure in southern Jiangxia; when he can be kept a secret no longer, I will personally intervene and ask – or, if necessary, order – that Ling Tong put the state before a personal grudge."

"...Alright," Lü Fan replied.

"As you wish, Lord Sun," Gongjin said tonelessly.

"Might I speak with this man...?" Sun Quan asked.

"He... desires a meeting," Lü Fan admitted.

"As quickly as possible!" Sun Quan cried. "Bring him to me!"

As Lü Fan and Gongjin left their lord to fetch Gan Ning, they looked at each other silently; they were both aware that they could have swayed Sun Quan in one direction or another with greater effort, but they were both of two minds about whether they should recruit or destroy Gan Ning. The decision had now been made, and time would tell as to whether it was the right one.

"...Gan Xingba," Sun Quan hailed as Gan Ning was brought before him in the grand meeting hall; there was a small army of guards led by Chen Wu and Song Qian, since there was no desire to take any more chances after what had happened to Sun Yi and Sun Hè several months before.

"Your lordship," Gan Ning replied humbly. "S'good that you agreed t'meet me... you shouldn't o' called me 'Xingba', though, since I ain't done nothing t'earn your trust yet."

"But you're here to do me such a service, are you not...?" Sun Quan asked.

"...I am," Gan Ning replied. "I can tell you anythin' an' ev'rythin' y'need t'know t'get your army into Jiangxia and kick a dozen shades o' sh- ...I, uh, I mean, y'know, uh, than you can-"

"Defeat my enemy Huang Zu," Sun Quan said with a smile. "And defeat him completely. But that's a bold claim, Gan Xingba."

"I'm a man o' me word... these days, at least," Gan Ning replied. "Yeah, I admit, I was a proper little 'orrible beggar when I was younger... but that was then, Your Lordship, and this is now. Only Huang Zu never trusted me, even after I saved 'im."

"Yes, by *killing Ling Cao*," Zhang Zhao heckled.

"Didn't anyone else here ever kill a man an' then wish he hadn't...?" Gan Ning retorted.

"...My brother did... more than once," Sun Quan replied. "I will not judge you as Huang Zu did, Gan Xingba."

"...Su Fei was right: you're the man I was s'posed to follow after all," Gan Ning said. "I only hope he survives so's he can join you as well."

"So what do you know...?" Gongjin asked.

"Naval training stuff, where 'is depots are, where he gets the wood for 'is ships, what men do what, the lot," Gan Ning replied. "I was liked by ev'ryone but Huang, so I'd get answers to whatever I asked, and I asked about a lot 'fore I left."

"...Magnificent," Sun Quan said. "You will be rewarded well for this, Gan Xingba."

"Whatever you reckon is proper, Your Lordship," Gan Ning replied. "I jus' wanna do good."

Sun Quan nodded at Gan Ning, who bowed respectfully and withdrew with Song Qian and six armed men as escorts; Sun Quan then turned to Gongjin and said, "We must delay Ling Tong's learning of Gan's presence or somehow persuade Gan to stop admitting to what he has done. I will not be Cao Cao to Gan's Xu Yòu."

"Colonel Ling will be kept ignorant for as long as possible," Gongjin promised.

"And that, 'Gongjin', is really best described as, 'As long as Huang Zu is unaware of his presence here', is it not...?" Zhang Zhao asked cuttingly.

"...Yes, Mister Zhang, that's right," Gongjin replied. "Let us hope that Huang Zu is very, very disorganised and unpopular, as Gan Ning suggests and even more so, and that he does not find the notion that Gan Ning could be here to be anything other than ridiculous for as long as possible – until Huang's death, preferably – and does not react too soon... because the news will be divisive when it breaks."

Sun Quan hummed ominously but said nothing.

****

56

The battle for Po County entered its seventh day with no sign of Peng Hu admitting defeat. Ling Tong and Jiang Qin defeated the armies that they had intercepted, and Bu Zhi was on the verge of winning a siege against a captured village; Ling Tong joined Dong Xi's march against a larger force that Peng Hu now led in person.

"What will you do to end this, Colonel…?" Ling Tong asked of Dong Xi as the two sat together in their camp's command tent.

"You can call me 'Yuanshi', Ling Gongji," Dong Xi replied. "We're colleagues of the same rank, and I respect you as much as I respected your father."

"You're wrong to do so," Ling Tong pleaded. "I've proved nothing!"

"Your work in Wu is beyond any expectations," Dong Xi insisted.

"I've still got a lot more to do in Wu," Ling Tong said. "I don't know if many others agree with me – I hear that Lu Ji has a similar view – but I want to reach out to the Shanyue instead of constantly warring with them. I believe that they can be won over somehow, just like the people that we're fighting now."

"…I admit that I believe that we're only dooming ourselves to unending conflict by refusing to find some way to live alongside them," Dong Xi replied. "It's their land as much as it's ours, after all. But now I shall answer your question, though you've answered it for me: I intend to reach out, but only after I've scared the ones that cannot be reasoned with."

"…I had to 'scare' some of them when I liberated the west region," Ling Tong said. "It's like the Yellow Turban Rebellion, Colonel: boys and women fight amongst their number and-!"

"I insist that you call me 'Yuanshi'," Dong Xi said, "and yes, I know, I see the boys and women that are fighting us too. But we must not allow that to crush us."

"…I shall heed your words, Dong Yuanshi," Ling Tong replied.

Dong Xi and Ling Tong led their forces out of his camp on the following morning and marched northward to meet Peng Hu's thousands-strong rebel army: Ling Tong noticed that Dong Xi had ordered his standard-bearers to keep the banners lowered and asked, "Why do you not announce yourself…?"

"I have taken great pains not to do so," Dong Xi replied. "When a man establishes a fearsome reputation, that becomes his greatest weapon; Ling Gongji, I understand that Peng has sent a small detachment eastward to pincer Jiang Qin. Could you hurry and intercept it…?"

"Willingly," Ling Tong replied. "But won't you be outnumbered…?"

"I have a hidden army," Dong Xi said with a smile.

Ling Tong took his own force and moved eastward to aid Jiang Qin: Dong Xi continued his march toward Peng Hu's vanguard, and when he was within the right distance to stop and array his men, he suddenly charged.

"**Aiee! This man that we face is insane!**" the rebels' vanguard commander exclaimed. "**Who is he???**"

Dong Xi brandished his spear and used its blunt end to topple countless men as he advanced; when he reached the vanguard commander, Dong Xi twirled his spear and ran the commander through with it before he continued his advance through the astonished rebel ranks.

"Who in the…!" Peng Hu muttered as Dong Xi's riders approached; and then, suddenly, a captain in Dong's ranks issued the order to raise the banners.

"**THIS MAN IS DONG XI???**" a rebel captain screeched. "**IT'S DONG XI OF YUYAO!**"

Many of the rebels started to retreat when they realised that Dong Xi was their opponent; Peng Hu noticed the disarray and advanced to confront his enemy in person, but when Peng finally spotted one of Dong Xi's banners he turned and fled at speed. Peng Hu's retreat ensured that the day was won: Dong Xi killed three of Peng Hu's appointed officers to reinforce his reputation and allowed the rest to surrender or flee.

"…Dong Xi must be Heaven-sent," Sun Quan declared as a beaming Zhang Zhao finished reading the reports from Po County. "Ten days… *ten days*, gentlemen, was all it took to end that rebellion, with mere hundreds killed or injured and order restored! Dong Xi shines most brightly, scaring Peng Hu away as he did with a banner! A *banner*! His feats against the bandits in Shanyin County still chill the bones of wrongdoers after ten years, so much so that the sight of his name is enough to defeat them!"

"His wisdom helped to guide Lady Wu to our present course, Lord Sun, while his incredible talent on the battlefield has won us countless victories over bandits and rebels from eastern Kuaiji to western Yuzhang," Zhang Zhao said. "He must surely be made a general for his efforts."

"He shall be when the moment is right," Sun Quan replied. "For now, appoint him 'Colonel of Surpassing Might' and reward him handsomely. Reward Ling Tong, Jiang Qin and Bu Zhi handsomely as well: to have done this much in *ten days*…!"

"Yuzhang is calmed again," Gongjin said. "I can go back to my work at Ba Qiu, and Lü Ziheng can get back to Lujiang."

"Yes… and plan for our future campaign in Jiangxia," Sun Quan replied. "This time will be different… it must be, and it will be."

Sun Quan's words were met with cautious murmurings: this would be the fifth major campaign against Huang Zu, and few expected it to be any more successful.

Sun Ben sat in his Administrator's office in Nanchang and studied Dong Xi's accounts of the battles against the bandit Peng Hu with a pained expression.

"You… seem to be distressed at the outcome, Father," Ben's eldest son, Sun Lin, said as he entered the private study.

"…I was expecting my brother!" Sun Ben chuckled. "And for a moment there, my son, seeing you in official's robes, you were easy to mistake."

"Uncle is inspecting the troops," Sun Lin replied. "He sent me here to enquire your state of mind… he saw that you were troubled."

"…It should be me that inspects the capital's militia," Sun Ben murmured. "I am not being seen as a competent administrator."

"So that's it," Sun Lin sighed.

"So that's what…?" Sun Ben asked.

"You're completely distracted by the thought that you're not seen as fit to hold the post, but you are, Father," Sun Lin replied. "I'm a man now, not a boy, and I see what you see: we're trusted by Lord Sun Quan in every sense, else he'd not have given you this important strategic position to govern."

"That's quite right," Sun Ben said. "That's... quite right."

"So why are you so miserable...?" Sun Lin asked.

"Po County was an avoidable mess that drew resources away from our mission, and... and Taishi Ci – the man that would usually deal with such things, and, perhaps, the man that should really be sat here – is very ill," Sun Ben replied. "I should have been able to send or create a militia to pacify Po County: when Taishi Ci is relieved of his duties by Lord Sun Quan or by Heaven's will, the instability will reach a point where that uprising in Po County will be seen as nothing. If I could not cope with Po while Taishi lives, then... what of beyond...?"

"I... wish I could help," Sun Lin sighed.

"In years to come, you will be invaluable to me," Sun Ben replied. "But this is my problem, my responsibility, and my... well... 'failing'. I failed to deal with Po County without begging help from Lord Sun Quan. That will not impress my critics. It does not impress anyone... least of all me."

Sun Lin turned to leave, saying, "I am proud to call you 'Father'."

"...My thanks," Sun Ben said with a smile. "Please tell my brother that I will be along shortly to inspect the troops at his side."

"I shall," Sun Lin promised.

Sun Ben waited until he was alone before he threw the reports to one side and muttered, "Who am I now...? Who *should I be*...?"

Huang Zu had asked to be kept informed of all events in Yuzhang Prefecture, so when the adviser Kuai Yue asked for a private audience Huang naturally expected the rumoured loss of Peng Hu's rebellion as a distraction to be the main discussion topic.

"No, Lord Huang, I am here to discuss something else entirely," Kuai Yue said.

"...Your face betrays concern," Huang Zu noted.

"It... is not really 'concern' as such," Kuai Yue replied. "I shall get to the point: Gan Ning has left his post and disappeared: I strongly suspect that he has gone to join the Suns."

Huang Zu laughed disbelievingly and said, "That's bloody ridiculous! He killed their best naval officer, which was harmful enough when Taishi Ci wasn't at death's door! Normally I'd worry, but why would they employ the man that killed Ling Cao, ruined a carefully planned and expensive expedition and caused our feud to go on for three more years...?"

"Where else would he go?" Kuai Yue asked.

"...You really think he's gone to the Suns...?" Huang Zu exclaimed.

Kuai Yue shook his head and said, "I ask again, Lord Huang, 'Where else would he go?' Yes, it might seem to be suicide, but-!"

"I always got angry and snapped at Su Fei, saying that I believed the man to be a heartless 'blade for hire' – and I did – but the Suns are vindictive, small-minded gangsters that don't have the sense to know that you don't 'punish the sword for what the executioner did', else they'd have realised how stupid our feud was and allied against Cao Cao six years ago," Huang Zu retorted. "Why should I now believe that Sun Quan would hire Ling Cao's assassin when he increasingly relies on Ling Tong, Ling Cao's heir, as a senior field officer...?"

"I... I try to avoid this conversation, Lord Huang, but I am starting to wonder if avoiding 'difficult subjects' is one of the worst mistakes of all," Kuai Yue said carefully. "The Suns do not persecute the Jing Province administration as easily and with as much support as they do without good reason: your orders were that Sun Jian – the 'Tiger of Jiangdong' and a hero that confronted Dong Zhuo at Luoyang, duelled Lü Bu to preserve the Imperial tombs and saved numerous cities in this very province years before that – be assassinated, and-"

"He was a demon of the battlefield!" Huang Zu barked. "He scaled the walls of Wan City *on his own* and opened the city, freeing it from an army of Yellow Turbans from right under their noses, and then he, as you say, fought a duel with Lü Bu and lived to talk of it! He was close to unstoppable when understaffed and even when he was *alone*: what were we to do when he turned up here with orders to seize Jing and a large, well-financed army to do it...?"

"...I don't try to justify Sun Jian or suggest that Governor Liu should have yielded to him, for Sun Jian did what he did – reluctantly, admittedly, but obediently – for his rebellious, seditious lord Yuan Shu, who was building his own empire," Kuai Yue replied calmly. "What I am saying is that when the moment came to return the body to his son, you ordered the men to return him in the same mangled condition that he was recovered and in a plain wooden box, just like everyone else."

"He was a man of the people," Huang Zu said with a smirk. "I thought that was what he would have wanted."

"Yes, and that unashamed attitude is why we have a feud fifteen years later," Kuai Yue retorted: Huang Zu's face fell as Kuai continued by saying, "They may have ambitions that go beyond and even replace reparation, but to the wider world it is still reparation that they seek... and it might just have been remedied with an apology or, better yet, avoided altogether by giving Sun Jian back to his men in a slightly more expensive coffin, his body properly treated and not looted for valuables, and the men instructed to do so respectfully, penitently, honouring his days as a national hero. Instead, Lord Huang, they handed him back like a sack of grain and heckled the Sun navy as they retreated: that was a mistake."

"...It's done now, and no, I am not sorry, especially not now that they have taken my sons from me and hounded me until my body has prematurely aged," Huang Zu insisted. "My argument is that they came to Jing to seize it and didn't care who they hurt or what it took, so whichever he was – 'sword' or 'executioner' – Sun Jian got what he deserved for what he was doing. We're supposed to apologise for killing a rebel general that was trying to seize Jing for his rebel master...?"

"The matter is complicated, so I shall say no more of it and return us to the matter at hand," Kuai Yue said.

"Which is ridiculous, Mister Kuai, and I refuse to believe it!" Huang Zu replied. "Unless Gan's taken leave of his senses, he'd never dare go to Jiangdong, and I may say a lot of things about him but not that he's that stupid!"

"But he might be that *desperate*," Kuai Yue retorted. "You owe him a life debt for killing Ling Cao, but instead of rewarding him with high military rank, you posted him to a backwater village and ignored him for two years."

Huang Zu grunted irritably.

"He's popular and respected, so he might have been enjoying favour and receiving a lot of intelligence that the Suns could make good use of," Kuai Yue warned. "We must take steps to limit the potential damage."

"If – *if* – he is in Jiangdong, then this is easily remedied," Huang Zu replied. "All that we have to do is make sure that the world – and most importantly of all, Ling Tong – learns of Gan Ning's part in sabotaging the campaign three years ago… and let the Suns and their cronies do our work for us. In the meantime, I want a search carried out here in Jiangxia in the event that he is not, as I suggest, that stupid, and that he is just neglecting his duties, for which he does deserve fitting punishment that my 'life debt', as you put it, will allow me to commute the sentence to a few lashes and the removal of his magistrate's seal."

"*Aiee*…! If he's still in Jiangxia then you should be promoting and making better use of him, Lord Huang, not driving him further away!" Kuai Yue pleaded. "Do you not remember how he ended up here in Jing…? Do you not remember his role in the uprisings in Yi Province that, had they been successful, would have-?"

"I'll never use a man like Gan Ning," Huang Zu insisted. "I'll warn you as I warned Su Fei: say no more of it! He's another Lü Bu! If I embrace him as a son then he'll betray me later on!"

"…Perhaps," Kuai Yue conceded. "I will ensure that the appropriate rumours are circulated and additionally begin to change procedure and relocate key installations so that any information that Gan Ning's passed to them-"

"*If* he's in Jiangdong!" Huang Zu snapped.

"…That any information that Gan Ning's passed to them *if he's in Jiangdong* is of no use," Kuai Yue continued. "I shall take my leave now and act immediately."

"He cannot be in Jiangdong," Huang Zu muttered as Kuai Yue departed. "He… that…! …No. He won't, *can't* aid the Suns to destroy me now, not after he tried to *save me*… because that… would be *ridiculous*…!"

Huang Zu's orders were distributed quickly: the news of Gan Ning's involvement in Ling Cao's death was carried in every conceivable direction and by every available means in order to ensure that it was common knowledge across Jiangxia and most of western Jiangdong in less than a week, and Ling Tong would not take long to learn the identity of the mysterious defector from the western southlands. The rift that Sun Quan's administration feared was imminent, and it was, as usual, far from being their only problem.

＊＊＊＊＊＊＊＊＊＊＊＊

57

Sun Quan was quietly confident that he would have his clan's long-desired victory over Huang Zu within 2 years: few shared his view, but he was not the only one that felt anguish and frustration when more distractions arose.

"I thought those bandits in Wu were dealt with!" Sun Quan snapped as a messenger finished reading a request from Zhu Zhi.

"Nothing is ever truly 'dealt with'," Zhang Zhao said. "Men beget sons, ideas propagate in private as well as public, and–"

"Spare me the lectures!" Sun Quan said angrily. **"Don't tell me about the 'nature of men'! I *know*! But I also know that I am trying to move the capital and fight Huang Zu and am getting nowhere with either! Tell me how to deal with this!"**

"...We'll need to send an army back into Wu," Zhang Zhao replied. "We could do as we did in Po County and–"

"Leave this to me."

All eyes turned to Gongjin, who added, "I just need one good man to act as my second."

"Are you sure...?" Zhang Zhao asked. "Wouldn't it be better to–"

"Moving men from the east to the west is one thing: moving them from the west to the east is another," Gongjin replied. "Yuzhang must enjoy consistent 'overmanning' because of the threat posed by Huang Zu and also our future plans. If I am given a competent second and ten-thousand men, I can do this in a month."

Sun Quan hummed thoughtfully and said, "My cousin Yu is here while Uncle Sun Jing recovers from his illness. Will he suffice?"

"That's ideal," Gongjin said. "Zhongyi is very sensible and a perfect choice for what I have in mind. But will his father's illness be a distraction...?"

Sun Jing's second son, Sun Yu, bowed slightly and replied, "I am quite composed."

"Then we should set out at once," Gongjin said.

The new army of bandits in Wu Prefecture had established their bases in Ma and Bao, just as the Wu Hills Bandits had done many months before: Gongjin and Sun Yu camped to the west of Ma and sent scouts to survey the area.

"This army is smaller – much smaller – than the last," Gongjin said. "We shall need no help from Ling Tong."

"Will we attack one base at a time or both simultaneously, Chief Commander...?" Sun Yu asked.

"Call me 'Gongjin', please, Zhongyi," Gongjin replied. "I am thirty, you are nearly so, we're both family men with ties to the Sun clan – mine by marriage, yours by birth – and to Lady Wu we were sons, which makes us brothers."

"...Forgive my formality, Gongjin," Sun Yu said. "Forgive me for my dishonesty as well, because I... I lied. I do worry for Father."

"He'll recover," Gongjin replied. "Sun Jing is tough. And as for your question, Zhongyi: I intend to attack the bases one at a time, starting with Bao."

"Bao...?" Sun Yu exclaimed. "But we are–! ...Ah, I see."

"I'm glad you do; let us hope the bandits do *not*," Gongjin replied.

Sun Quan was elated by the news that emerged from Ma and Bao: Gongjin and Sun Yu feigned a full camp at Ma using the ruse of extra campfires and patrols while they moved their main force to the bandits' camp at Bao under cover of night and attacked it. When the camp at Ma learned the news, they divided their forces to try to relieve Bao, which left them understaffed: Gongjin left Sun Yu to guard Bao and marched an army of 5,000 'at double-time' to Ma to seize it while it was more vulnerable. The entire operation took 4 days and ended with the deaths of the bandit leaders and the capture of thousands of able men that could be imprisoned, conscripted into the army or put to work.

"Gongjin is Heaven-sent!" Sun Quan chuckled. "Once again we are ready to focus on Huang Zu!"

"*Ayah*... Lord Sun, you keep saying that, and it is most unwise!" Quan Rou protested. "Let's pray for no more distractions instead of repeatedly declaring that there won't be any!"

"...You're quite right," Sun Quan said. "I shall do as you suggest."

But 'distractions' could not be avoided by not inviting them with poorly-chosen words: within two months, a messenger brought devastating news from Yuzhang Prefecture that threatened to ruin the Sun clan's campaign schedule once again. Taishi Ci – the famous wandering mercenary from Donglai in Qing Province – had been showing signs of physical deterioration for some time, and had taken increasingly symbolic roles on campaigns around northern Yuzhang; but his condition worsened whilst defending fields against some bandits in Haihun County, and he was confined to his bed. Gongjin and Lü Fan rushed to Qu'e on hearing the news, and by the time that they arrived, the worst had been confirmed by yet another messenger from Haihun.

"General Taishi Ci... is gravely ill," the messenger said emotionally. "He... he is not expected to last the month!"

"**This cannot be!**" Sun Quan cried. "**He's a hero among men! He's barely over forty! What nonsense is this???**"

"Calm yourself, Lord Sun!" Gongjin said. "Messenger, please give me your written report and go and get some rest."

The messenger handed his report – a letter inside a sealed tube – to Gongjin and retreated from the audience hall.

"...This... ... ...this is terrible, and unbelievable," Gongjin said. "It's true, Lord Sun. Taishi Ci is... he is *dying*."

The courtiers gasped and mumbled at the news.

"I must hurry to him at once!" Sun Quan insisted. "He is one of the foundations on which this state is built! I will not stay here while he fades away needlessly!"

"This news will inspire Huang Zu," Cheng Pu suggested. "I will replace Taishi at Haihun; we should fortify the region in case of-"

"**Again the Heavens favour that bastard that murdered my father!**" Sun Quan screamed. "**But I will not have it! We've been blessed with too many new opportunities to-!**"

"**Say no more, Lord Sun!**" Gongjin pleaded.

Sun Quan realised that he had almost spoken of Gan Ning's presence in Jiangdong; he calmed slightly and said, "You... are right, Gongjin."

"I'll go to Haihun as well," Gongjin continued. "Bofu and I were Taishi's friends, and I cannot know that he's gone without first

thanking him for who he was to us."
"I must accompany you," Lü Fan said.
"...Father is ill... and now Taishi Ci is *dying*...?" Sun Yu bleated.
"Everyone is sick... everyone is dying... everyone is being killed,"
Sun Quan whimpered. "I am... weary of it."

Taishi Ci was glad of his visitors, who were shown into his
quarters-turned-infirmary by his wife and young son: Sun Quan
knelt by Taishi Ci and said, "You're stronger than this."
"Mother... passed away before I could hear her say that she was
satisfied with my efforts," Taishi Ci replied. "It's strange, but... I
owe her for my reputation."
Sun Quan smiled and said, "I owe my mother for mine."
"She... urged me to save my lord and... make that trip... to
Luoyang," Taishi Ci recalled. "She... urged me to... save Kong
Rong... and... before that, when... when I was in Liaodong... I knew
I had to... save Liu Zheng from Gongsun Du..."
"Save your strength, Ziyi," Gongjin implored.
"...No point," Taishi Ci replied. "No... hope."
"None...?" Sun Quan asked as he looked at Taishi Ci's physician.
"None," Taishi Ci replied. "Thank you... for giving me a home."
"...I cannot take the credit for that," Sun Quan insisted. "Bofu-"
"The same," Taishi Ci said. "Bofu... you... the Suns... thank you."
"I am ashamed!" Cheng Pu cried. "I doubted you, Taishi Ziyi, and
told Lord Sun Ce that you were untrustworthy! I'm a fool! I could
not see the hero that you are!"
"It's... fine," Taishi Ci said. "Y-you're protective... I see that."
Cheng Pu exhaled fiercely and lowered his head.
"This isn't right," Taishi Ci said. "I want to die in battle, as a hero...
not like this."
"Then live, Ziyi, and recover, and fight again!" Sun Quan pleaded.
"He must rest," the doctor insisted.
"*Why*...?" Taishi Ci chuckled quietly. "I'm... still dying..."
"...We shall leave you," Sun Quan said, "so that you might spend
your precious time with your family."
"Yes... go," Taishi Ci replied. "Go... don't remember me like this."
Sun Quan got to his feet, bowed slightly, and retreated; Lü Fan
and Gongjin bowed humbly and followed their lord.
"...Heaven bless you, Taishi Ziyi," Cheng Pu said.
Taishi Ci smiled feebly, and Cheng Pu departed after bowing low
as a sign of the great respect that he now had for the younger
hero. Taishi's wife and son knelt at his side, and his wife took his
hand gently.
"...In life," Taishi Ci said, "a great man should take up a sword... of
seven feet in length... and aspire to become the Son of Heaven. I
had dreams of my own... none of them achieved... and now...
powerless... I die. What can I say...?"

Within days, the legendary Taishi Ci was dead: he was just 41
years of age.

****

58

Taishi Ci's death was a crushing blow to morale across Jiangdong, as Taishi was one of Sun Ce's most powerful allies when he finally chose to serve; the news would shock people across the whole of the Han Empire, in fact, since Taishi had become something of a legend for his one-man exploits. One place where Taishi Ci would not be mourned was Jing Province, where his death was almost celebrated for what it meant; no man was happier than Jiangxia Prefecture Administrator Huang Zu, who had been repeatedly thwarted by him.

"They'll be vulnerable now," Huang Zu chuckled. "Wu Jing, Sun Yi, Sun Hè and now Taishi Ci: the Suns are losing their clansmen and their great champions, and the moment has come to exploit it. **Deng Long!**"

The officer Deng Long bowed silently.

"You will travel to Chaisang," Huang Zu ordered. "Xu Sheng is not there, Pan Zhang is not there... take four-thousand good troops and siege the city. It shall be our first foothold!"

"I shall not disappoint you, Lord Huang," Deng Long replied.

Sun Quan buried his head in his hands and groaned when word of Deng Long's attack on Chaisang reached his capital.

"You must not react like that," Zhang Zhao said.

"I have just got back here," Sun Quan complained. "I was just in Yuzhang, ensuring that Taishi Ci's family was properly cared for... why could he not have attacked when I was in Yuzhang with Gongjin, Ziheng, and a small army of elite guards...?"

"It is better that he did not attack at that point, Lord Sun," Zhang Zhao said. "You-"

"In fact, Mister Zhang... why does he attack at all...?" Sun Quan asked as he raised his head and stared at his court. "How can this old skeleton Huang Zu attack me with such painful ease...? Who is Deng Long...? Is he some great hero that wasn't known to me...?"

"Send Xu Sheng back to Chaisang," Zhang Zhao suggested. "He defended the place before, so-"

"I'll go."

All eyes turned to Gongjin once again.

"...And who will train the navy?" Zhang Zhao asked. "The lord's cousin Sun Ben, who once led the entire clan for three years, is Administrator of Yuzhang, and Elder Cheng Pu – a seasoned strategist and general that has served since the days of Sun Jian – is in Haihun! Surely they-!"

"I'm moving units to the Chaisang region anyway, Mister Zhang, since we're almost ready to act against that 'old skeleton'," Gongjin replied. "I shall again take the reliable Sun Yu as my-"

"This... 'readiness to act'... it wouldn't have anything to do with a cutthroat called *Gan Ning*, would it...?" Xu Kun asked irritably.

"*Aiee*... please don't say anymore," Gongjin replied.

"I don't need to," Xu Kun said. "Gan Ning's the one that murdered Ling Cao, so everyone is saying now, and Ling Tong isn't too pleased about it: he's on his way here."

The court was filled with anxious murmurs; Sun Quan looked at Gongjin, who looked at Lü Fan and asked, "Can I leave that with

you and go to Chaisang...?"
"Yours is the easier task, Gongjin," Lü Fan replied. "But yes... leave it with me."

Gongjin and Sun Yu hurried to Chaisang with 3,000 men to bolster the existing force of 1,000 that guarded the city; Ling Tong arrived in Qu'e a few days later with a small retinue of men and asked for an audience with Sun Quan.
"...As you requested, I am here," Sun Quan said. "As you requested, the court is in session: what did you want to say, Colonel Ling...?"
"I am... distressed, Lord Sun," Ling Tong said as he looked around the packed court. "I want to know if the man called 'Gan Ning' is here today."
"He is not," Zhang Zhao replied, "but-"
"Actually, I am."
Ling Tong scowled as he turned to face Gan Ning, who pushed his way through the rows of seated officials at the back of the court and said, "I'm here, Mister Ling, 'cause I know that we had to have this out sooner or later."
Ling Tong drew his sword and pointed it at Gan Ning, saying, "Is it true, what they're saying in every tavern, every barracks, every-? ...Were... were *you* the one that killed my father?"
"...I regret it," Gan Ning replied: the confession stunned the court and led to countless murmurs and muted chattering.
"If you regret it, Gan Ning, then surrender your head to my father's altar!" Ling Tong screamed. **"I'll take it from you here and now!"**
"I'm not quite ready t'part with it yet," Gan Ning chuckled.
"You dare *heckle me*, you bastard...?" Ling Tong growled.
"No, I'm not 'heckling you', I'm sayin' that I ain't ready yet," Gan Ning retorted. "Ask me another time, after I've helped Lord Sun: if you want me dead before that, then I have t'insist on fightin'."
"Fine by me!" Ling Tong said. **"And I'll show you a proper hero: you'll die by my sword, Gan, and not a sneaky arrow!"**
"*Aiee...* **by all means have your fight if you must, but not *here*!"** Zhang Zhao cried.
"There will be no fight!" Sun Quan ordered. **"Ling Tong, you will lower your sword at once!"**
Ling Tong – who now had bitter tears running down his face – turned to Sun Quan and said, "I only ask for *justice*, Lord Sun Quan, and if not that, death, for if I cannot avenge my father, as you intend to avenge yours, then I cannot live honourably."
The eyes of the court turned to Sun Quan, who now felt very uncomfortable; Quan turned to Lü Fan, who said, "I cannot answer such a straightforward plea with the personal answer that it deserves, my lord."
Sun Quan exhaled deeply, turned to Ling Tong and said, "If you truly serve me... then listen. Gan Ning is sorry... while Liu Biao and Huang Zu are not. It was not Huang Zu that fired the arrow that killed my father; it was a man like Gan Ning, a man following orders... Huang Zu's orders, and if that archer that killed Father were here now, offering an apology and offering to atone with aid that would lead to the death of Huang Zu, then I would forgive him and make use of him as I now make use of Gan Ning. It is a

case of 'punishing the sword for what the executioner did': is there any sense in it…?"

Ling Tong turned and glared at Gan Ning.

"You and I, we have the same enemy: Huang Zu," Sun Quan continued. "Huang Zu ordered the deaths of our fathers, both to save his own hide. If you want revenge, then it is Huang Zu – not Gan Ning – that you should want to destroy. Gan Ning wants to help us to destroy Huang Zu: let him do that."

"And after that…?" Ling Tong asked.

"…*Aiee*… Ling Tong, you must let it go!" Sun Quan insisted. "Gan Ning is an asset! Cao Cao takes counsel from Jia Xu; see it as the same, and let it go."

"I… I cannot!" Ling Tong said as he turned and stared at Sun Quan. "I cannot!"

"Then… I must order you to, as my subordinate," Sun Quan sighed. "Failure to comply is… well, you understand. I need Gan Ning's help as much as I need yours."

Ling Tong lowered and then closed his eyes.

"Huang Zu is our true enemy; Gan Ning now wants to be our friend," Sun Quan continued. "Taishi Ci, whom I have just had to bury, was an enemy, another 'executioner's sword' that became our very good friend… we must not allow our judgement to become clouded."

Ling Tong opened his eyes, looked at Sun Quan and asked, "If someone gave you the arrow that killed your father, Lord Sun, would you not want to destroy it or offer it to the altar as much as Huang Zu's head…? Could you *truly* look the assassin in the eye and say that you could work with him…?"

"…If Liu Biao and Huang Zu were sorry for what they did, I would be working with *them* to defeat common enemies," Sun Quan retorted. "That I vow to you."

"…Then I can say no more," Ling Tong declared. "I will not try to harm Gan Ning: I only ask that you do not torment me by ever forcing me to work directly with him."

"I cannot promise that," Sun Quan replied. "But I will avoid it where possible."

"I am truly sorry, Ling Tong," Gan Ning insisted. "Honest, I am."

Ling Tong ignored Gan Ning's words, choosing instead to bow to Sun Quan and leave the court without saying another word.

"Mister Gan, I will ensure that Ling Tong – and all of his allies – are aware that they will be punished if you are harmed," Sun Quan said.

"…Thanks, Your Lordship," Gan Ning replied miserably.

As soon as Gongjin reached Chaisang, he established a camp to the east of the besieged city and had scouts survey the area. Over the next four days, Sun Quan's cousin Sun Ben travelled northward to join Gongjin and provide support, and the adviser Qin Song departed Xi'an for the same purpose.

"…What are you doing…?" Sun Ben asked as he watched Gongjin studying a battle map.

"I want to begin a larger operation while I'm here," Gongjin replied. "You'll find out soon enough, Boyang: Gan Ning, a pirate that served Huang Zu, has joined us and provided important information about Jiangxia's infrastructure. Unfortunately for us,

Gan is the man that killed Ling Cao as well, and his presence has been unavoidably exposed. His role in Ling's death was spread around Jiangdong by Huang Zu's agents, and Ling Tong's been compromised by it: so I must act before Huang can change the way he does things too much and Ling Tong's bitterness makes him less reliable for what's to come."
"...That's a lot to take in," Sun Ben admitted.
"It's a case of 'now or never', though I don't expect that we'll be actually invading Jiangxia for another year or so, even if we have no more distractions," Gongjin continued. "I want Deng Long's attack to reward us with more opportunities."
"...Alright," Sun Ben said. "I'm the prefectural administrator, and so I need to be seen as being somehow of value during all this, so... can I help...?"
"Militarily, yes," Gongjin replied. "How many men did you bring?"
"Four hundred," Sun Ben said. "What can I do...?"
Gongjin smiled and replied, "Look there, at that river point on the map: well..."

Deng Long was alarmed when he learned that reinforcements had arrived, as it was expected that Taishi Ci's death would have resulted in chaos and further rebellions.
"How can they spare so many men...? Deng Long said desperately.
"We should request extra support," Deng's adviser suggested.
"...I can't," Deng Long replied. "I'd look like a fool: no, we press on and take the city quickly before the enemy can engage us!"
The adviser sighed and said, "As you command."
        Deng Long sent every man that he had against Chaisang City: the siege was violent and unrelenting, and both sides were taking heavy losses as defenders made futile attempts to drive the attackers away and the attackers fell from the walls amid showers of rocks, arrows and boiling liquids. Deng Long became ever more daring as his patience thinned, and he started to approach the walls to inspire his men: he was at the walls when Gongjin launched a sudden surprise attack on his camp.
"I should have known that they'd try that!" Deng Long cried. **"Back, back at once! We cannot afford to lose our supplies!"**
Deng Long's retreat allowed much needed relief to be sent into the city, but it was not intended as a temporary respite. When Deng Long reached the ruins of his camp, Gongjin was waiting with a force of 1,000 men: Deng growled angrily and ordered a full charge toward the smaller army. Once Deng Long's men were fully committed to the attack, two more forces – each comprised of 800 men – attacked from different directions, surrounding Deng and panicking his men.
"Here is Zhou Yu of Shu County!" Gongjin bellowed as he confronted Deng Long with spear in hand. **"Why not surrender now and die with dignity?"**
Deng Long turned his horse and fled southward; his army scattered in all directions, leaving Gongjin free to pursue.
        "...I can't die here!" Deng Long said as he urged his exhausted horse forward; he had less than 50 men – including his long-suffering adviser – and no supplies, so it was vitally important that they reach safe territory.
"We're going the wrong way!" the adviser protested. **"We**

should be going west!"

"I *know that*!" Deng Long snapped. "**But they've planned this, so they'll have men along the western roads, therefore I'm going south to go *around them*!**"

The adviser sighed, as remaining close to the river was a poor idea; he was proven correct when Sun Ben's militia attacked from the river itself by way of boats.

"**We must flee again!**" Deng Long cried.

"**Were we ever not fleeing???**" the adviser retorted as his horse struggled to keep up with his master's; Sun Yu's men had managed to ensnare the infantrymen, so Deng was now left with a dozen riders.

"**Ah, there you are!**" Gongjin taunted as he blocked Deng Long's path with 20 horsemen and 200 infantry. "**Will you surrender now, Deng Long...?**"

Deng Long turned his horse and fled for a fourth time; his adviser surrendered, as did all but Deng's three remaining bodyguards.

"**I'll end this personally!**" Gongjin said as he urged his horse: he and eight of his riders caught up to Deng Long, unseated the general and killed his guards.

"**You have isolated me!**" Deng Long said as he brandished his sword and moved in a circular motion to watch for the movements of his multiple opponents. "**I'll die a hero for my lord Huang Zu, and at least one of you will die with me!**"

"**Your lord isn't a hero,**" Gongjin said as he leapt from his horse and drew his *dao* sword. "**He's a cowardly old man whose time is almost up.**"

Gongjin and Deng Long fought a brief duel, but the outcome was never in doubt; Gongjin was the better man, and he disarmed Deng within a few minutes.

"**Kill me, Zhou Yu!**" Deng Long pleaded. "**Give me the honour of a death in battle!**"

"**You don't deserve it,**" Gongjin replied. "**You're going to my lord's capital – whole – so that he might decide what to do with you. Don't expect mercy.**"

"**BASTARD!**" Deng Long screamed as Gongjin's men bound him with rope. "**You, your greedy master and your families will die dog's deaths!**"

"...**Nice try,**" Gongjin chuckled. "**You're not going to rile me.**"

Deng Long kicked and screamed as he was led away; Gongjin smiled as he pondered how Huang Zu would react to the loss of another senior general, his underestimation of Jiangdong's stability and the series of military surprises that lay in store for him in the coming months.

"You'll suffer a lot more than we have, Huang Zu," Gongjin said. "I guarantee that."

✳✳✳✳✳✳✳✳✳✳✳✳

59

The defeated Jing general Deng Long began his journey to Qu'e at the same time as yet another piece of startling news was coming out of the northern part of the Han Empire: Cao Cao had been under pressure from two fronts in the wake of his victory over Yuan Tan at Nanpi, but he had somehow prevailed swiftly and definitively yet again.

"Perhaps I am not as astute as I should be, but… I need to hear this again," Sun Quan said to his court. "Mister Zhang, can you…?"

"The surviving Yuan brothers, Xi and Shang, had allied with Wuhuan tribal leaders in Yòu Province and started to force the people to relocate to the Wuhuan's lands beyond the Great Wall whilst simultaneously harassing the local administration and inspiring rebellions among their supporters," Zhang Zhao reported. "His Excellency Cao Cao was about to deal with the problems in Yòu Province when Gao Gan – the Governor of neighbouring Bing Province and a cousin to the Yuan brothers – reneged on his earlier promise to yield and cooperate and staged a province-wide rebellion."

"That part I understand," Sun Quan replied. "What I don't understand is how Cao Cao now looks at restored order in such a short time."

"'His Excellency Cao Cao' enjoys sound counsel from the likes of Jia Xu and Guo Jia, and it is the latter that we must 'thank' for this outcome," Lü Fan said. "The-"

"Your tone is demeaning!" Zhang Zhao barked.

"I'll apologise to him later," Lü Fan retorted. "May I continue…?"

"…Do as you please," Zhang Zhao grumbled.

Lü Fan smiled and turned to Sun Quan, saying, "Guo Jia is the master of actually reading the classic texts and acting on their sagely advice, my lord. He is a particular lover of 'Swiftness is the key in war': he believes in speed and proves yet again that it is as important as Sun Tzu professed."

"I also strive to act quickly," Sun Quan replied. "But Mister Guo Jia's talent is enviable: Bing Province is the home of the Southern Xiongnu confederacy and the Black Mountain Bandits, and Yòu Province is home to tens of thousands of Wuhuan tribesmen that Elder Cheng Demou – whose family was forced to flee the chaos in Yòubeiping and come to the south – speaks of as 'an unending scourge'. The reports suggest that Cao Cao has somehow chased the Wuhuan and the Yuan brothers out of the Empire, routed every agitator in Yòu Province and completely pacified Bing Province: *how*…?"

Lü Fan waited for the murmurings to cease before he said, "Speed and careful choice of pacification tools. My own, more detailed reports say this: Yuan Tan chased his usurper younger half-brother Yuan Shang into Yòu Province two years ago, after Yè City fell, and Shang sought sanctuary with his elder half-brother Xi, who had been awarded Yòu to govern in order to get him as far away from the seat of power as possible. Most expected Yuan Xi – who shared a mother as well as a father with Tan, and whose wife was a hostage in Yè – would refuse to support his younger half-brother Shang, whose mother had connived to deprive Tan of the clan chieftainship and caused a civil war, but Xi was angry at Tan for siding with Cao Cao to aid in the capture of the Yuans' capital, and Cao Cao's son has since married Xi's wife, Lady Zhen, so-"

"Wait a minute," Xu Kun chuckled. "Xi's still alive...?"

Lü Fan smirked and looked at Zhang Zhao.

"**Answer me, someone!**" Xu Kun shouted. "**Xi's still alive...?**"

"...He is," Zhang Zhao said uncomfortably. "But-!"

"**But *what*, old man...?**" Xu Kun heckled. "**Cao Cao's notorious for taking Zhang Ji's widow, Lady Zou, as his consort against her will, and that was bad enough, but at least Zhang Ji was *dead*!**"

The court was filled with murmurs and muted laughter: Zhang Zhao waited until the worst of it had subsided before he said, "There is an obvious amount of controversy surrounding His Excellency's son's decision to wed Lady Zhen, but it is old news to many here, General Xu, and-"

"I think that you try to understate a terrible concept, Zibu," Sun Quan interrupted. "Cao Pi has married a woman whose husband still lives, and Cao Cao has allowed it: that sends an ominous message to Yuan Xi, doesn't it...?"

"...What message, son-in-law...?" Xie Jiong asked.

"'You will not survive'," Sun Quan replied. "Some observers have suggested that Yuan Xi – who is always spoken of as the moderate, good-natured middle brother – was going to be a negotiated with so that the Yuans could be preserved and stability returned to the four north-eastern provinces with minimal bloodshed: would you allow your son to marry the man's wife as though he were already dead if you did not intend that to be the final outcome...? It is no wonder that Yuan Shang and Gao Gan did not soften their stances and look for peace before Cao could reach out to Xi, because Cao had no intention of doing so."

"...That is quite true," Xie Jiong realised.

"We must do more to understand the entire situation from all sides!" Zhang Zhao protested.

"Perhaps, but before we do that, Zibu, I should like to hear the rest of the explanation of how Cao Cao has pacified the north without being even remotely conciliatory," Sun Quan replied. "We've all been so busy with our own problems that getting the all-important 'full story' from the north has been near-impossible, and I must not neglect the detail. Ziheng: please continue."

"I shall," Lü Fan said. "To recap, Cao Cao took Yè with Yuan Tan's 'help' – or rather, he took Yè because Yuan Tan was drawing support and resources away from Yè by fighting Shang in another part of Ji Province while Shang wilfully ignored the greater threat that Cao posed to his capital. Shang was then chased into Yòu Province by Yuan Tan, where he then found an unlikely ally in Yuan Xi, and the two started to court local magnates that had benefitted from Yuan rule, some of them having risen from peasantry and owing the Yuans everything. Gao Gan feigned submission, and Cao Cao turned his attentions to Yuan Tan, who had basically betrayed the earlier alliance pact by building his own fortunes instead of coordinating with Cao Cao. Yuan Tan met his end in Nanpi, which brought an end to the problems that Cao Cao was facing in Tan's provincial seat, Qing: that province has since been under the jurisdiction of the former Mount Tai Bandits, led by

Zang Ba."

"And Cao has the cheek to heckle us for recruiting former pirates," Xu Kun grumbled. "Is Zang Ba any different...?"

"No, but that is obvious," Sun Quan replied. "Ziheng...?"

"I shall continue," Lü Fan said. "With Yuan Tan – who was, as the eldest brother, the rightful heir – gone, and Yè City, the Yuan clan's capital in the north, under Cao Cao's control, and the Yuans' ancestral seat, Ru County in Yu Province, under Han government control, the Yuan brothers now had Yòu Province's rebels, the Wuhuan and little else, since the Black Mountain Bandits were never going to aid the Yuans as they aided Gongsun Zan. Cao Cao turned northward and lent aid to the local administrators in Yòu, who rebelled against the Yuans, but the Wuhuan surged into the province and overwhelmed the regional defenders: Bing Governor Gao Gan had been waiting for an opportunity to support his cousins, and he rebelled as soon as the Wuhuan drew blood and the Administrator of Hedong – who resented Cao Cao's use of Qiang tribal armies from Liang Province to counter an earlier invasion attempt by Gao Gan – staged a rebellion of his own and joined the unofficial alliance against Cao Cao's regime."

"...So Cao Cao had to split his army and fight on two fronts, then...?" Sun Quan prompted.

"No," Lü Fan replied. "The-"

"Wait, wait," Xu Kun pleaded. "Gao Gan invaded Hedong, and Cao Cao employed the Qiang??? Cao Cao employed the *Qiang* to help the Han???"

"...Cousin Kun makes a valid point," Sun Quan admitted. "I was about to move onto something else, but it does have to be said that the government employing the Qiang as enforcers is quite unbelievable... Cao Cao is quite the negotiator."

Xu Kun shook his head and said, "Yeah, but that aside, let me get this straight in my head: Gao Gan invaded Hedong for the Yuans, right...? And Cao Cao got the Qiang to repel Gao Gan, right...? And then Hedong's Administrator rebelled against Cao Cao and joined the same side that... Gao Gan was on... right...?"

"Politics is *never straightforward*, Kun," Lü Fan replied dryly.

"...Look, just... just keep talking," Xu Kun said. "I'll never make sense of it."

Lü Fan laughed and replied, "I shall go on. We talk of Cao Cao facing two fronts, but he actually faced more than that: remnants of Yuan Tan's allies and local crime lords still caused trouble in Qing, and Hedong – which borders both Liang Province and Bing Province – is strategically critical, so Cao Cao had to deal with that too, and then there are the tribes... and neither the Southern Xiongnu nor the Qiang are willing servants.

"But Guo Jia and the other geniuses around Cao Cao dealt with it all with their usual efficiency: clever strategies pushed the Wuhuan – who formed close to the entirety of the Yuan brothers' army – out of the Empire, which allowed Yòu Province to be temporarily abandoned in order to throw everything at Bing Province; the Black Mountain Bandits actually provided support in Bing while the Southern Xiongnu Chanyu, Huchuquan, refused to involve his people in Gao Gan's schemes, and the Qiang warlords remained cautiously aloof; yet another clever ruse was employed to neutralise the leaders of the rebellion in Hedong; and Zang Ba's large army of reformed criminals restored order to Qing Province autonomously. That left Gao Gan isolated, and he was quickly surrounded and eliminated. Now Cao Cao is preparing to return to Yòu Province to finish what he started there, although the current intelligence indicates that the ruthless crushing of every single ally the Yuan brothers had save for Liu Biao – who gave no aid – has rattled the Yuans and the Wuhuan chieftains and compelled them to remain in the lands beyond the Great Wall."

"His Excellency is the antidote to the chaos of the last twenty years!" Zhang Zhao said. "The peace that we all seek is truly achievable at last!"

Sun Quan looked to Lu Su, who was visibly unnerved by the news: the sight of the architect of the 'Tripod Theorem' grimacing and averting his gaze was enough to tell Quan that the 'grand dream' might not now be realised.

"...Cao Cao is indeed too professional, too cunning, too militarily strong for *any* warlord, rebel or tribal king to challenge," Sun Quan declared.

"Why say that with such a tone, my lord?" Zhang Zhao asked. "Were we intending to challenge him, then, and if so, for what...?"

"...I meant that to be a surmising of my thoughts," Sun Quan retorted. "Such exploits require tribute, I think."

"A fine idea!" Zhang Zhao said.

"*Aiee*... don't grovel to Cao Cao, Zhongmou!" Xu Kun pleaded. "He might be responsible for-!"

"Cao Cao... is the Han's Excellency of Works, a relation by marriage, and an unparalleled statesman surrounded by capable minds that know no boundaries, and that makes him a man that must be *honoured*, not 'grovelled to', Cousin Kun," Sun Quan insisted. "What would make a fitting tribute...? Mister Gu Yong, you have been silent: what say you...?"

"Whatever is sent must be grand but not sending a message that unintentionally suggests things," Gu Yong replied. "We honour the Excellency of Works, my lord, not a feudal king. Send tribute to Cao Cao at the same time that we send tribute to the Son of Heaven, and ensure that whatever is sent to Cao Cao is dwarfed in value and magnitude by what is sent to His Majesty."

"...I am to empty the treasury now...?" Sun Quan chortled. "I wish that I had not thought of it now."

"No, no, Lord Sun... you will not need to ruin our venture to send proper tribute," Lü Fan insisted. "Cao Cao should be sent a symbol of strength – his and ours – as tribute for a military exploit, while the Son of Heaven should be sent a similar item but in greater numbers to remind the world – and Cao Cao – that there is still a hierarchy that is still topped by His Majesty the Son of Heaven. What about an elephant...?"

"...You want to send an *elephant* to Yè...?" Zhang Zhao heckled. "You want to send an elephant to Yè, which means sending at least *two* to Xuchang...?"

"The sight of magnificent southern warships bringing such incredible beasts into the heart of the north would certainly send a lot of messages," Quan Rou said. "Are those messages properly known and intended...?"

"I, for one, know what I mean and say," Lü Fan replied. "The Son

of Heaven will enjoy having two – or more – elephants in his royal zoo, in addition to some fine jewellery, gold, silk and utensils, and Cao Cao's family will enjoy having a pet for their own menagerie. Cao Cao might even find such an animal useful for scaring the Wuhuan... and the entire exercise will remind the north that the south has grown but has always been great in its own way. We pay tribute where appropriate and reinforce our might in one stroke: what is wrong with that...?"
The court looked to Sun Quan, who said, "I concur. Have suitably strong warships prepared and send the gifts as soon as possible."
"It shall be done," Zhang Zhao replied uneasily.

Sun Quan's gift to Cao Cao would provide an interesting problem for the academically curious Cao to solve: determining its weight. Cao's prodigious 10-year-old son Cao Chong would solve that relatively unimportant problem by way of what most know today as *Archimedes' Principle* of buoyancy; the elephant also served as a temporary resolution to a greater problem, namely the tension that had built between Sun Quan's independent regime and Cao Cao's obedience-demanding Imperial court. Cao Cao appreciated the gesture, since it meant that he could look northward, beyond the Great Wall, to his Wuhuan and Yuan clan enemies with some certainty that Sun Quan would not attack him when his back was turned; Sun Quan hoped that it would reduce the likelihood of the Han court reprimanding him for his upcoming invasion of Jiangxia, which was, in essence, a treasonous act that could lead to future conflicts between the Suns and the state.

****

60

More months passed: the Han court's famous Excellency of Works, Cao Cao, was completing his victory over his enemies with his usual efficiency, which unnerved many in the Jiangdong court.

"...He surely *killed* Zhang Xiu," Sun Quan suggested.

"It says that he 'died whilst on his way to Ji Province to aid His Excellency Cao Cao'," Zhang Zhao said.

"I heard it the first time, and I don't believe it," Sun Quan retorted. "That man was marked for death! He was the nephew of Zhang Ji, one of Dong Zhuo's senior henchmen and a key ally of Li Jue and Guo Si during the regency! He killed Cao Cao's heir and nephew, and his bodyguard Dian Wei too!"

"So he deserved it," Zhang Zhao said.

"What is 'it'...?" Lu Su asked.

"Death!" Zhang Zhao snapped. "Early death, no doubt from distress at all the wrongs he committed!"

"...Regardless of the cause, it gives Cao Cao control of Wan City and the surrounding Nan County, which is a crucial stepping stone to invading Jing Province," Lü Fan said. "If it was, as Mister Zhang clings to, a coincidence, then it could not have happened at a better time for Cao Cao. His destruction of the Yuans is almost complete, and Jing is almost certainly next."

"And after Jing, *Yang*...?" Yan Jun suggested.

"Nonsense," Zhang Zhao scoffed. "My brother lobbies for Lord Sun Quan to be made a general, and all indications are that he *will* be appointed as such!"

"...It might be an idea to withdraw Zhang Hong from the imperial capital," Lü Fan said. "We don't him getting hurt."

"Why would my brother be in danger?" Zhang Zhao heckled.

"...You really don't understand, do you...?" Lü Fan snickered.

The officials murmured uneasily; there was an obvious division forming between the men from noble backgrounds and those from humbler origins when it came to discussions about opposing the will of the Han court.

"We cannot afford to rile Cao Cao," Liu Ji suggested. "I am as impressed with what the Sun clan has done in this region as anyone else, but if His Majesty – or, indeed, His Excellency Cao Cao – demands that the Suns relinquish power, that isn't the same as when my father was ordered here by the 'regents' to block the ambitions of Yuan Shu. His Majesty is power absolute, and Cao Cao is His Majesty's sword; we *must obey them*."

"Son of Liu Yao, you speak naively," Lü Fan said. "Like the 'Ten', Hè Jin, Dong Zhuo, Li Jue and Guo Si before him, Cao Cao is the puppet master, and he has already cut the strings of Consort Dong and let her fall lifelessly to the ground against the will of his sovereign. Nothing coming out of Xuchang is His Majesty's will; it is Cao's will, and Cao's will alone."

"Defy the court and you can expect to lose a lot of support, Lord Sun Quan," Liu Ji protested. "I respect the Sun family, so I only say this to aid your survival: see *sense*!"

"...**I don't intend to defy His Majesty!**" Sun Quan snapped. "**This discussion is ridiculous!** ...Aren't there more pressing matters...? What news from Yuzhang?"

"Gongjin 'is ready'," Zhang Zhao sighed.

"Then all that's left is to hear the right words from the right people," Sun Quan said.

"Indeed, Lord Sun," Lü Fan said. "And when we hear those words, we will begin."

Over the following months, Cao Cao's campaign against the Yuan brothers in the north reached a logical conclusion: Yuan Shang, Yuan Xi and their Wuhuan allies were routed in an attack by Han forces that had advanced so quickly that they were completely unexpected. The majority of the Wuhuan tribes capitulated, and the Yuans fled eastward to seek refuge in Liaodong with the independent warlord Gongsun Kang, who almost immediately betrayed them, killed them and sent their heads to Cao Cao; Cao then turned his attentions to the reorganisation of the court, since his main counsel, Guo Jia, had finally succumbed to illness and died, and Cao did not want to proceed with an invasion of Jing Province until he had found a match for that prodigious mind.

In the meantime, Sun Quan had allowed his personal secretary Zhuge Jin to visit Longzhong in Jing Province, which was the location of the Zhuge family farm: Sun Quan was excited when Zhuge Jin returned, but his smile quickly faded when he learned that Jin had failed to convince his younger brother Liang of the Sun clan's worthiness.

"I did what I could," Zhuge Jin sighed. "He's so *stubborn...*"

"He still favours the wandering mat weaver," Sun Quan supposed.

"Indeed," Zhuge Jin replied. "He twists the events to suit his own ridiculous notion that the Han is salvageable! I am not so cold-hearted that I want to see the Han die needlessly, but Cao Cao has eroded what little of its lustre remained, and we must look to the future now! But Liang... he's so proud of his little idea that he and Liu Bei – who has, perhaps, three-thousand men *at the most* – are going to somehow 'rescue the Han Dynasty from Cao Cao and restore order'!"

Sun Quan laughed and said, "I don't hope for that, and I have seventy-thousand men. Such a strange idea: Zhuge Liang is very different to Zhuge Jin!"

"But he weaves a good argument," Zhuge Jin complained. "He's very persuasive: even if you realise that you've been misled later on, you start to doubt at first. When he started on about- ...Well, it doesn't matter, Lord Sun. He's not ready to be convinced yet, but we'll see: when Cao invades, and Liu Bei is swatted aside like the bug that he is, we'll see."

"...Such a shame," Sun Quan said. "I had hoped to recruit the 'Crouching Dragon' and perhaps Pang Tong as well, since Lu Ji speaks so highly of the 'Young Phoenix'... but as you say, we'll see. Your family there are all well...?"

"Yes," Zhuge Jin replied. "But northern Jing is a very tense place, Lord Sun: Cao looms large to the north, and the fear of the Suns is tangible. Many fear a collaborative pincer and a massacre."

"I'd never collaborate with Cao Cao," Sun Quan insisted. "He wanted to take my boy from me and plots all manner of things: he's stolen the trust that I had in Ben and Fu, and I still wonder if he was behind the deaths of Bofu, Shubi and Bohai, since taking my brothers and cousin from me isolates me."

"The people of Jing only know what they're told," Zhuge Jin said. "When you finally take the place, they'll see that you're a good and kind lord and forget the lies sown by Liu Biao."
Sun Quan smiled and said, "You're a good man, Zhuge Ziyu."

Months passed: Jiangdong continued to have problems, but they were smaller and less frequent, which allowed for the collection of enough food and other resources for a campaign to the west. And then, one day, Sun Quan's trusted inner circle of advisers and officials were summoned to the grand hall so that the defector Gan Ning – who had recently returned from a secret visit to Jiangxia – could make an announcement.
"Your Lordship, it really is 'now or never'," Gan Ning declared. "Old Huang Zu's obviously lost his sense: everything's stagnant. He's prob'ly only built half o' the boat an' ships you'd expect him to want, y'know, to replace what he's lost before, and he hasn't done much recruitin' o' new men, and his arrow stocks are low, and his men's weapons an' armour are tatty, and he's not done much in the way of defence beyond moving supplies into Jiangxia's capital. The people in the south are pretty miserable, and from what I heard, the capital's not what it was: Zhang Shuo and Chen Jiu are his main officers now, and they don't know how to treat people proper at all, always bullyin' blokes that serve under 'em an' makin' money when they're s'posed to be makin' ev'rythin' right. If Liu Biao gets tetchy and harasses Huang about it, then he might improve his game, so we should act before he does that."
"My lord, we should be careful," Zhang Zhao protested.
"Look, friend, I ain't one for messin' about," Gan Ning said. "I work for the Suns now, and if you don't believe me, send your own spies!"
"Forgive our caution, but we have already done so, and our own reports from the south match yours, so we have no reason to disbelieve your appraisal of the capital," Lü Fan replied. "Huang Zu's officers are said to be mediocrities that are always looking after themselves first, so I am not surprised."
"This is too risky!" Zhang Zhao cried. "This man is a former agent of Huang's and a notorious cutthroat; and we haven't pacified Wu yet, so such a campaign risks further chaos!"
Sun Quan hummed thoughtfully; Gan Ning turned to Zhang Zhao, sneered and said, "You're Zhang Zhao, aren't you...? I've heard about you. Lord Sun treats you like you're *Xiao Hè*, or somethin', but if you're going to poop your pants every time everyone goes on a campaign, how can you be compared to a man like that...?"
A number of men covered their mouths to hide their smiles; a number of the scholars were also quietly impressed that Gan Ning knew of the Han founder's adviser and started to view him as a man that was wiser than his poor articulation suggested.
"Xingba, I've decided that I'll give you authority over the planning of this campaign, just as I proffer this cup," Sun Quan said as he lifted his wine dish and tipped it toward Gan Ning. "Make a success of this and you needn't heed Mister Zhang's harsh words."
"...So we're going to begin the campaign, then," Zhang Zhao said with obvious unease.
"We are, Mister Zhang," Sun Quan replied. "And Huang Zu *must*

be defeated this time."

"Act now and he will be," Gan Ning promised. "I tell you, he's not with it at all."

"...Thank you, Mister Gan," Lü Fan said. "Your help has been invaluable, but..."

"...You need to talk without me bein' here!" Gan Ning chuckled. "I understand. Best o' luck, Your Lordship."

Gan Ning exchanged respectful bows with Sun Quan and his counsel and departed.

"...*Loathsome man*," Zhang Zhao muttered.

"We must begin the final move of personnel to Jiangxia," Lü Fan said. "My lord, Gongjin and I agree that we should use Ling Tong, Dong Xi and Lü Meng for the campaign."

"It was my own idea that we allow Ling Tong to be the vanguard, since it is personal for him," Sun Quan replied. "Gongjin will be the Chief Commander, of course; Dong Xi can lead the army, and Lü Meng can be in charge of the navy."

"Leave 'A'Meng' in Wu County, where Zhu Zhi can watch him!" Zhang Zhao cried. "And as for Ling Tong, how can he go to Jiangxia when the Shanyue of Wu are untamed and there is a risk of him meeting Gan Ning...?"

"Ling Tong and Lü Meng are fierce fighters," Lü Fan suggested. "And Huang Zu ordered Ling Cao's death: Ling Tong may not understand a lot of other things, Mister Zhang, but he understands that."

"...And when it's over... southern Jing will be ours," Sun Quan said as he turned to look at Lu Su. "And then, your plan will begin to be realised, at last."

Lu Su bowed humbly and replied, "It is a day that I dream of, my lord. The-"

"Southern Jing will be taken from a rebel," Zhang Zhao said. "It will not be 'ours', Lord Sun, not if His Excellency objects, which he most certainly will since-"

"Let us worry about Cao Cao's reaction when the deed is done," Lü Fan interrupted. "If anything he should be grateful that we've helped him to remove a 'rebel', as you rightly called Liu Biao, and reward us handsomely: only a hankerer would react differently."

Zhang Zhao sneered and said, "Be sure that you know what you are doing... we are on uncertain ground now."

Sun Quan hummed thoughtfully but said nothing.

Gan Ning left the Sun estate and travelled down the road that led to a popular tavern: he was intercepted by Ling Tong, who said, "I won't share the sky with you."

"...We were told that we weren't to fight, Colonel Ling," Gan Ning replied. "I'm not raisin' a sword to you."

"Fine," Ling Tong said as he pointed his own sword at Gan Ning. "That only makes it easier! I have no guilt about *how* I kill you after what you did, Gan Ning!"

"...Don't do this, Colonel Ling," Gan Ning replied. "I'm tryin' to help Lord Sun Quan."

"Help us all by giving your head to my father's temple, you bastard!" Ling Cao cried as he lunged at Gan Ning; Gan dodged the attack and fled.

"What are you doing, Gongji???" Xu Kun exclaimed as he ran toward Ling Tong – who had started to pursue Gan Ning – and restrained him. "You promised that you would not harm him! Lord Sun will have you exiled or worse if you kill Gan Ning!"

"**I don't care!**" Ling Tong screamed. "**My father is unavenged! I lay awake at night and cannot-!**"

"Come on, you're going to a tavern to sit for a while and calm down," Xu Kun said. "I'm not leaving you alone until Gan Ning's had time to flee the province."

Ling Tong sobbed pitifully as Xu Kun led him away.

"...I'm disappointed," Sun Quan admitted; news of Ling Tong's attempt on Gan Ning's life reached him within an hour, and it had left him with a dilemma.

"We knew that he might do this," Lü Fan replied. "Gan Ning has to go to Jiangxia to aid Gongjin's plans: we'll just have to ensure that Ling and Gan do not meet again."

"I will have to punish one or the other of them if another row erupts," Sun Quan said. "It would have to be Gan Ning, since we must appease Ling Tong... yet I don't want to lose Gan Ning. The only way is to be seen to station Gan in some faraway place for a time and then persuade Ling of his folly."

"...That would be one way," Lü Fan replied uneasily.

The Han's Excellency of Works, Cao Cao, summoned Zhang Hong to his chancellery office in Xuchang and said, "I have decided to allow you to return to Jiangdong permanently, Mister Zhang: please select a man to replace you here."

Zhang Hong bowed and replied, "I am grateful to you, Excellency, for this opportunity to return to my home region at this most difficult and tumultuous time."

"...But I have conditions, Mister Zhang, something which you surely guessed," Cao Cao prompted.

"...I do not honestly understand," Zhang Hong said.

"Your lord acts in what is best described as 'a most confusing manner'," Cao Cao explained. "I know from conversations that you are a Han loyalist, so I know that you would not tolerate behaviour that in any way threatened the Han."

"...Of course not," Zhang Hong replied.

"So I want you to go back to Jiangdong to 'keep an eye on Sun Quan for the Han', as it were," Cao Cao continued. "Can you do that, Mister Zhang...?"

"...I... I can, Excellency," Zhang Hong replied uneasily.

"Very good!" Cao Cao said. "Prepare to leave at once."

Lü Meng was anxious to end the feud between Ling Tong and Gan Ning, since he respected both of them. Lü Meng travelled to Qu'e and invited Ling and Gan to a banquet at his home in the city without telling each man that the other was coming; Lü Fan, Xu Kun, Sun Jiao and Sun Shao were among the other guests, and everybody groaned when Gan Ning arrived, caught sight of Ling Tong and cried, "**Is this a trap???**"

"**No, no, Gan Xingba!**" Lü Meng insisted. "Please, the-!"

"**Whose idea was it to invite me and him to the same banquet!?**" Ling Tong shrieked. "**Why would I want to share a jar of wine with that murderer???**"

"Look, I'm gone, alright...?" Gan Ning said passively. "I'm leaving."

"Oh, you can 'leave'," Ling Tong growled. **"You can leave your head for my father's altar!"**

"No, no, don't say that!" Lü Meng pleaded. **"Gentlemen, you must calm down!"**

"*Ayah*... this is your most stupid act yet, A'Meng!" Lü Fan heckled. "I want you to change your name! You disgrace the name 'Lü', and I will not admit to sharing ancestry with you any longer!"

Sun Jiao started to laugh uproariously; Gan Ning turned to leave, but Lü Meng said, "Please, Gan Xingba, stay and sit, and we can discuss the classics. And please, Ling Gongji, calm down."

Gan Ning sighed, briefly turned his glance toward the vengeful Ling Tong and said, "Sorry, Ziming... not a chance," before departing quickly.

"...We *must* learn to get along," Lü Meng protested. "We must 'meet turmoil with calm' and 'distance with closeness', or our enemy could exploit our division. We must, as Lord Sun's loyal officers, 'share a single will', and-"

"*Aiee*...! You are *worse* now that you are schooling yourself!" Lü Fan complained.

"And quoting Sun Tzu at me changes *nothing*," Ling Tong growled. "*Confucius* said that one must *honour his father*."

"...So he did," Lü Meng sighed.

Lü Fan glared at Lü Meng, sneered and asked, "So what *now*, 'Taigong Wang'...?"

"...We must try to make the best of things, so let's eat and drink and share stories!" Lü Meng suggested. "We're soon to rid the world of the villain Huang Zu and-!"

"*That'll do*," Lü Fan groaned. "We'll toast the campaign."

"I want to leave," Ling Tong announced.

"Oh, no you don't," Xu Kun said. "You want to chase after Gan: you stay where you are."

"...Alright," Ling Tong sighed.

"...I'm disappointed," Lü Fan admitted. "Colonel Ling, you're better than this: you vowed, promised, that you would put your feelings aside for the greater good."

"I will try harder," Ling Tong whimpered.

"And as for *you*, A'Meng... *aiee*," Lü Fan said. "What did you hope to achieve...?"

"I have already told you... I hoped that both men would come to an understanding," Lü Meng replied. "But I see that simply quoting words of wisdom is not enough when the passions of the recipients deafen them to reason. Sun Tzu did not truly account for men's vulnerabilities, perhaps..."

"*Aiee*... you scare me," Lü Fan groaned.

Lü Meng's attempts at reconciling Gan Ning and Ling Tong would not be his last, but they were his last for the time being: the focus returned to the campaign against Huang Zu, which would be partially masterminded from the shadows by the controversial Gan Ning and his remaining contacts in Jiangxia.

****

61

All was ready at last for the campaign against Huang Zu: Ling Tong, Lü Meng, Dong Xi travelled to the Chaisang region separately and made their preparations for the battle ahead, and Sun Quan made ready to do the same. As those preparations concluded, Cao Cao suddenly despatched an official to Jiangdong to award Sun Quan a Han title: there was a lot of excitement in Quan's court until the official arrived, at which point the gathering was forced, as part of the protocol, to show the same humility and deference to the official as they would show for his master, Emperor Xian. Even Sun Quan had to kowtow as the lofty herald unfurled a scroll and started to read from it.

"By the grace of His Majesty, and at the request of the Han's Excellency of Works, Sun Quan is hereby titled, 'General That Attacks Barbarians' for his work – past, present and future – taming the criminals and the wild and undisciplined creatures! General Sun's representative, Zhang Hong, will be returning to Jiangdong and will bring with him the seal of office! That is all: glory to His Majesty the Son of Heaven!"

The court echoed the cry of loyalty to the Han Dynasty, and the official departed.

"My lord, you are a sanctioned General of the Han!" Zhang Zhao said with delight. "My brother is coming home to proffer the seal! This is all wonderful!"

Lü Fan suspected that Cao Cao was up to something and muttered, "*Is it...?*"

It did not take long for the mood in Jiangdong to be dampened by a second official from Xuchang: the court assembled yet again so that they could be told of a career advancement that would change the fate of the Han Empire.

"In recent months, a series of great threats to the Empire have been eliminated," the official began. **"The Wuhuan tribes – long a nuisance and more besides – have been chased out of the northern provinces, humbled in their own territories and forced to capitulate fully, ending once and for all the trouble that have ceaselessly caused. In addition to that, the Yuan brothers of Ru County – once great heroes and seen as pillars of the state, but now little more than seditionists – have been dealt with, and their self-serving independent state – built in Ji, Bing, Qing and Yòu provinces by way of treachery and vile disobedience of the laws set out by Heaven and men – has been dismantled."**

Sun Quan shuddered at the barbed words; Yuan Shu's son Yuan Yao closed his eyes tightly as he thought of his cousins and their uncompromising fate.

"The Qiang tribes of the northwest have vowed that they will make no more trouble, and the Southern Xiongnu have reaffirmed their commitment to cooperation in exchange for the right to coexist peacefully," the official continued. **"The Mount Tai Bandits of Qing Province have pledged to serve the Han and atone for their past crimes; the Black Mountain**

Bandits of Bing Province have submitted to the Han and will be rehabilitated; the White Wave Bandits that tormented the Imperial capital Luoyang were irredeemable and have been purged; the Yellow Turbans that spread their wicked desire to ruin Heaven's plan for order have been routed at every turn and their ideology proven to even the most disaffected to be a deviant falsehood. But there are still those that seek to undermine the government and prolong the chaos, and there must, therefore, be a change in the way that the Empire is administrated if we are ever to know the peace that all good men strive for. Strong governance – rigid, uncompromising government that strikes fear into the wicked and gives hope to the pious – is the only way forward."

Many officials in Sun Quan's court frowned at the words and what they seemed to be leading to.

"It has been decided by the majority of the officials and by His Majesty the Son of Heaven that the reformed ducal system is unsuited to the current political and military situation throughout the Empire," the robed messenger declared. **"It has, therefore, been temporarily abandoned in favour of the older model: henceforth, Cao Cao will be known as the Prime Minister and the Chancellor of State!"**

There were some that could not contain their shock at the unexpected announcement: several hastily muted gasps and groans were heard as the messenger paused to allow the news to be properly understood.

"…All appointed Magistrates and Administrators will be informed of the change by Inspector Liu Fu," the messenger continued. **"Further announcements on administrative reform will be issued in due course. That is all: glory to His Majesty the Son of Heaven!"**

Sun Quan was unable to stop his lip and hands from quivering as he watched the Han official's departure from his dumbstruck courtroom: he waited until the man had gone before he turned to Lu Su and hissed, "This is a *disaster*!"

"…Or it is an indication that we must press ahead with our own vision," Lu Su replied quietly. "If Cao Cao now emulates Dong Zhuo, then we must build our own state with the greatest urgency, for there will soon be no Han, only Cao Cao. And remember additionally that Guo Jia is now *dead*, Lord Sun."

Sun Quan turned his thoughtful gaze back to his court: there was obvious division, and Quan knew that he had to handle that division carefully.

"…I did not like the use of language in the closing sentences," Quan Rou admitted.

"We're about to branded as rebels," Sun Quan supposed.

"We won't be if we abandon the idea of invading Jing Province!" Liu Ji suggested.

"I agree," Yuan Yao said. "My late father, traitor that he sadly was, began his journey toward madness and heresy in Jing Province, my lord and brother-in-law. Perhaps we should rethink that campaign."

"No," Sun Quan replied. "My quest is for a strong, united south that is not forced to wait for the north to throw us scraps: I will not abandon that plan now, and certainly not at the instruction of a man that now announces that he is 'Chancellor of State'! You speak of madness, brother-in-law, but what madness is it that possesses Cao Cao now...? What next for that ambitious man, whose tastes for stealing women from enemies – be they dead or alive – and boasts of 'dismantling the Yuan clan's self-serving independent state' when he is, in fact, making Yè his own seat for some future power base...? What next, I ask again...? The Nine Dignitaries...? ...*Kingship*...?"

"*Ayah*...! Why would His Excellency Cao Cao – *Chancellor Cao Cao* – do all that he has done if all he sought was power...?" Zhang Zhao countered. "You listen too much to Lü Fan and Zhou Yu, and that wretch *Lu Su*, who is planting the seeds of sedition in your mind and attempting to justify it by slandering the Chancellor without proper foundation!"

Lu Su pointed at Zhang Zhao and cried, "You make a villain of me, Zhang Zhao, when all I seek is the proper course for the people of the south!"

"You want Lord Sun to challenge Chancellor Cao, to dash this fragile southern egg against a mighty northern mountainside, and you don't even know why you're doing it!" Zhang Zhao retorted.

"You have adjusted to calling Cao Cao 'Chancellor' very quickly, Zhang Zibu," Lü Fan heckled. "That's impressive, but can you also adapt your thinking to supporting your lord through this newly turbulent situation instead of talking about eggs and mountains and desperately trying to convince us all that Cao Cao's behaviour is reasonable...?"

"Chancellor Cao has appointed our lord as 'General That Attacks Barbarians'!" Zhang Zhao retorted. "Our lord is a Han-appointed general of the Imperial army, tasked with fighting the Shanyue and the other tribes and criminals that plague us here in the south, just as His Excellency has pacified the Qiang, humbled the Wuhuan and reminded the Southern Xiongnu of the debt that they owe the Son of Heaven! If we do as we are asked, Mister Lü, then can we not expect further rewards...? Does the appointment not suggest that there is a plan to stabilise the south...? Is Inspector Liu Fu 'keeping the south in its place' with his fine work in Lujiang and Jiujiang...?"

"Lujiang and Jiujiang Prefectures are north of the Great River, and so they are very much part of the north, and so I imagine that Cao Cao will say that they should be made part of Yu, Yan or Xu Province in the long term," Lü Fan countered. "Cao Cao obviously has Jing in his sights as his next conquest, and I don't see any instructions to his 'General That Attacks Barbarians' that imply that he wants a pincer attack on Jiangxia, which would make the invasion that he has planned much easier, would it not...?"

Zhang Zhao was silent.

"A general can only do as he is instructed or compelled," Lü Fan continued. "When Cao Cao attacks Liu Biao – and I believe that he will do it soon, and so does Liu Biao – then Huang Zu will act as well. Will Huang Zu fortify Jiangxia and prepare for Liu Biao's arrival after Cao Cao's four-hundred-thousand troops that he has stolen from Yuan Shao descend on Xiangyang and crush everything in their path...? Or will Huang Zu seek an alliance with Liu Zhang of Yi Province, or with us...? Or will he push eastward to secure territory from us to replace Northern Jing and give Liu Biao somewhere else to govern...?"

"How can I know any of that...?" Zhang Zhao asked snidely.

"We must ascertain the answers," Gu Yong said. "Cao Cao's proclamation was very confrontational, with all of its talk of crushing independent ventures and 'Liu Fu informing the appointed officials of changes'... so we must review our options, answer all of the necessary questions and make choices."

Sun Quan looked to Lü Fan, who said, "The attack on Jiangxia is, as Gan Ning noted, 'A case of now or never'. He said that before Cao Cao's unexpected and, I have to say, potentially seditious self-elevation, and-"

"The change was made with the backing of the majority of the Han court and the Son of Heaven!" Zhang Zhao protested.

"...Xuchang's court is made up almost entirely of Cao Cao's long-time supporters, since most of the 'old guard' courtiers died on the long march from Chang'an to Luoyang," Lü Fan noted. "And the Son of Heaven's actual will is debatable, as the 'Girdle Edict Crisis' made painfully clear. You'll get your turn to speak, Zibu, so please don't interrupt me again."

Zhang Zhao grunted angrily.

"Lord Sun, we're once again at a fork in the road," Lü Fan continued. "As Han-appointed 'General That Attacks Barbarians', you can await orders and not move, watch Cao Cao march on Xiangyang and wonder what comes next; alternatively, Lord Sun, you can do as you intended and attack Jiangxia, weakening Huang Zu – or even destroying him – and making Liu Biao's destruction certain. If Liu Biao is a mutual enemy of the Suns and the state, then your actions – which are best described as reactionary – will facilitate a swifter conclusion to the Han army's attack on Liu Biao's capital, which would surely be appreciated... a sensible Chancellor of State would then reward such a move by allocating Jiangxia to Yang Province in exchange for annexing Lujiang and Jiujiang into some northern province, granting higher rank to you, Lord Sun, for 'sharing a burden', and looking for some sort of peaceful accord."

"And if Chancellor Cao reacts by branding Lord Sun – General Sun – as a traitor that has disobeyed military law and acted seditiously by invading a Han province without proper instruction...?" Zhang Zhao asked. "It will then, as Yuan Yao has said, be seen as Lord Sun's own attempt to build an independent state, a 'reborn Chu': an act of madness that will be met with universal condemnation and unforgiving military force! Zhou Yu and Dong Xi have both made pretty speeches about 'the Great River as a natural defence and our army of happy, well-fed, competent men' and so forth, but fifty-thousand pirates and farmers cannot fight an army of two-to-four-hundred thousand professional soldiers!"

"If Chancellor Cao objects to our actions in Jiangxia, Mister Zhang, then we will withdraw to our own borders and allow the Han to regain control of territory that is already illegally governed by Liu Biao and Huang Zu," Quan Rou said. "Is that not so, Lord Sun...?"

Sun Quan hesitated before he replied, "It is so, Mister Quan."

"So we will proceed as we were," Lü Fan declared. "Gongjin will continue his work in Yuzhang and Huang Zu will know the righteous wrath of the Suns at last: after that, gentlemen, the rest is up to Heaven."

Zhang Zhao glared at Lu Su, who looked at Sun Quan in turn; the lord of Jiangdong smiled as he contemplated the idea of revenging his father, building a state called 'Wu' and ruling the south.

Zhang Zhao approached Sun Quan in his private study as soon as the meeting had concluded; Lü Fan and Quan's trusted servant Gu Li were the only others present.

"Turn away from this idea," Zhang Zhao pleaded. "That poor excuse for a schemer Lu Su is leading you toward destruction! And you, Lü Fan, are little better: why do you steer Lord Sun towards unnecessary conflict with Chancellor Cao?"

Sun Quan looked at Lü Fan and awaited the answer.

"...I did not want to reveal this in the court, but... something new has come to light," Lü Fan retorted. "Answer me this, Zhang Zibu: why would Cao Cao be training a navy in a specially-constructed training lake, and building a large fleet of ships...?"

Sun Quan frowned at the news, which was as new to him as it was to Zhang Zhao; he then looked at Zhang and awaited the answer.

"...For invading Jing Province!" Zhang Zhao snapped. "For transporting supplies southward quickly, for-!"

"He will be invading northern Jing by *land*, Zibu, through Yu Province and Nan County, and you do not build warships and train legions of sailors to transport supplies," Lü Fan retorted. "That navy is for invading Jiangdong... which, at such an early stage of negotiations, is not something that you do if you might have other options in mind, not when resources must be carefully managed."

Zhang Zhao shuddered involuntarily.

"So what we do is as an act of self-defence," Lü Fan continued. "Cao is playing chess with us; I am moving to counter an obvious attempt to end the game quickly."

"...I shall say no more," Zhang Zhao replied. "But you had better be reliably informed, Ziheng... or we're condemning ourselves."

Zhang Zhao retreated; Sun Quan turned to Lü Fan and said, "Is it true, about the training lake, and the navy...?"

Lü Fan nodded silently.

"...Then I must capitulate or defy, for he leaves us with no other choice," Sun Quan realised. "Either way, Ziheng, I must attack Huang Zu and seize Jiangxia, to avenge my father."

"And seize it you shall, Lord Sun," Lü Fan promised. "The rest is, as I have already said, in Heaven's hands."

Sun Ben had returned to his office in Yuzhang's prefectural capital in order to gather belongings and prepare for the upcoming conflict with Huang Zu: his brother Fu approached him and asked, "Are you alright with the latest developments...?"

"...By 'the latest developments', I assume that you refer to this attack now being tacitly discouraged by my daughter's father-in-law the Chancellor, dear brother...?" Sun Ben chuckled miserably.

"We're risking being branded as traitors if we invade Jiangxia, aren't we...?" Sun Fu prompted.

"*Lord Sun Quan* is risking being accused of *treason*, dear brother... we are tools, just as we were when we served Yuan Shu," Sun Ben replied insistently. "But I do of course hope that the words that were relayed to us were misunderstood, and that the official stance – that Mengde will thank us for crippling Huang Zu and reward us for making his pacification of Jing Province easier – is what comes to pass."

"And if it doesn't...?" Sun Fu prompted.

Sun Ben sighed desperately and stopped his frantic packing.

"...You must know what you – we – are going to do if Quan pits us against the Han government by doing this or anything else in the future, so please, tell me, what would we do...?" Sun Fu asked.

Sun Ben turned to face his brother and replied, "We would do the right thing, of course."

"...But that would be betrayal of a different kind," Sun Fu fretted.

"Either choice is betrayal, dear brother," Sun Ben retorted. "Which would you prefer to betray when pondering your ultimate fate: our divisive clan chieftain or the Han Empire...?"

"...I hope that we aren't forced to choose between the state and our family," Sun Fu admitted.

"So do I, of course, but that isn't up to us, is it...?" Sun Ben grumbled as he resumed his packing. "It's up to 'Gongjin', 'Ziheng', and that new man, Lu Su, who all fill Zhongmou's head with nonsense about becoming the ruler of a feudal state."

"You've not called him 'Zhongmou' in a long time," Sun Fu noted.

"...I don't want to confront him, Heaven knows I don't, but if I must, I will, directly or by more... by more 'indirect means', shall we say," Sun Ben replied. "But I have always prided myself as a vassal of the Han and do not intend to repeat a bad mistake by serving another pretender to the throne. And you said that I was forcing us to choose 'between family and state', dear brother, whereas I clearly said that this would be between *clan chieftain* and state: Quan does not embody and has never been the embodiment of the clan... he is, in fact, about as close as you come to the antithesis of it. A drunk, a womaniser, a thief, a liar and a hegemon: were Uncle Wentai, Cousin Bofu or Cousin Shubi describable in any of those terms...? Are we, or is any other high-ranking member of our clan...?"

"...But is Quan really a hegemon...?" Sun Fu asked.

"That's what we're about to find out, isn't it...?" Sun Ben sighed.

"...I'm with you every step of the way, no matter what you do," Sun Fu promised.

"Thank you," Sun Ben replied. "I... imagine that I'll need the support. Too many people here in Jiangdong have been blinded to what's right by what they've been told is necessary, and so I have a battle on my hands if I am forced to confront Quan and call him a traitor: Heaven surely wants the Han to endure, so... if we do what's right, then... then all will be well. But perhaps Quan – Zhongmou – will do the right thing and act only as he is instructed. Perhaps this will end well."

Sun Fu smiled encouragingly, but he was as inwardly certain of the outcome as his brother: there would be treason and betrayal and war in that order, and there would be few that would survive it unscathed.

∗∗∗∗∗∗∗∗∗∗∗∗

62

Jiangxia's Administrator, Huang Zu, was alarmed when news from the southern part of his prefecture told of supply depots being sabotaged and roads being blocked by men that claimed to support his hated neighbour Sun Quan.

"Are those men turning against me because of Deng Long...?" Huang Zu asked of his loyal court.

"I doubt it," the adviser Kuai Yue replied. "It's more likely that we have been compromised by a defector: the depots, supply roads, timber sources... all of them are either blockaded or vandalised in some way."

Huang Zu turned to his subordinate Su Fei and growled, "This is *Gan Ning*... this is *your friend, Gan Ning*...!"

"He and I are no longer friends!" Su Fei protested. "I haven't seen or spoken to the man in over two years! Ask around!"

"And we can't be sure that this is Gan Ning," Kuai Yue suggested.

"Of *course* it's Gan Ning!" Huang Zu retorted. "We've all heard rumours that he is in Jiangdong, and you even came to me to convince me of the possibility, Mister Kuai, and argued vehemently about it: this proves it!"

"Yes, but that was over a year ago now," Kuai Yue protested. "We've made changes, altered-"

"We've done what was financially and logistically possible, and that might not have been – no, it obviously outright *wasn't* – near enough!" Huang Zu barked.

"*Aiee*... Gan Ning was a good fighter," the officer Zhang Shuo said.

"Whine about the loss of the man at your own risk, Zhang Shuo!" Huang Zu bellowed. **"All along, gentlemen, you've tried to convince me that the wretched man could be trusted, and now look at what he's done! He's learned all of my military secrets from you gullible fools and then told it all to Sun Quan!"**

"They don't know everything," Kuai Yue insisted.

"The northern works are unaffected, Lord Huang," Zhang Shuo said. "The-"

"But I'm going to lose control of the south of my prefecture because of Gan Ning!" Huang Zu continued. **"Didn't I say that he'd be the cause of my ruin?"**

"You mistreated Gan Ning," Su Fei said. "He saved you, Lord Huang, and-"

"Why are you still defending him...?" Huang Zu heckled.

"...I am merely stating that his last words to me were disappointment that you failed to trust him," Su Fei replied. "If he has gone to Sun Quan, that is why."

"So I am to blame for this am I...?" Huang Zu said derisively. "You... are an imbecile at best, if not a *traitor* for tricking me into making him 'Magistrate of Zhu County'! But I cannot deal with you now! **Pan Jun! Zhang Shuo! Chen Jiu! Make preparations for defence of the region! Chen Jiu, you are the admiral, and you will ready the fleet for an advance downriver at once to blockade it! Zhang Shuo, you will carry out preliminary investigations of their movements and report your findings to Chen Jiu! Pan Jun and I will remain in the capital and**

oversee the preparation of the defences around it! Kuai Yue, we-!"

"I... can't remain here," Kuai Yue interrupted. "Cao Cao has moved troops into Nan County, and Lord Liu wants my assistance to-"

"Is this not as important, if not more so???" Huang Zu screamed. **"He has bushels of men like you, but he cannot spare _one_ to serve me...? If I lose Jiangxia, won't Liu Biao have nobody to cover his spineless back???"**

"...Please choose your words more carefully, Mister Huang Zu," Kuai Yue retorted. "I have been ordered to go, and that is that... I wish you luck."

The court was close to silent as Kuai Yue departed.

"...He is but one man, and we are thousands!" Huang Zu cried. **"As we were: every man to their posts! We must repel the Suns from Jiangxia at once!"**

The fighting began: Naval Commandant Lü Meng led the bulk of Sun Quan's navy against Huang Zu's larger fleet, which was led by Admiral Chen Jiu, while smaller units of each force played strategic games that they hoped would yield less costly victories. Huang Zu tried, unsuccessfully, to carry out attacks against Chaisang, Xi'an, Haihun and Luling, but Jiang Qin, Pan Zhang, Cheng Pu, Sun Ben and Sun Fu were able to foil him at every turn. The Jiangdong forces would have to navigate the Miankou River in order to reach Huang Zu's capital, but the relatively thin waterway was beneath a high cliff and therefore treacherous; Huang Zu knew this and sent Vice-Admiral Zhang Shuo to the area in a medium-sized ship to secure the cliff as an assault position, block the river and discover the size of the enemy fleet. Zhang Shuo had only half completed his task when he encountered a smaller craft piloted by Ling Tong; Zhang ordered two of his support boats to pursue Ling, who had been on his own scouting mission with a dozen followers and had no nearby reinforcements to call upon.

"The Jing men were scouting the area as well," Zhang Shuo realised. "We'll continue as we were and notify Lord Huang that their reconnaissance this far north is incomplete."

Ling Tong halted his craft once its pursuers had briefly lost sight of them and said, "We can't let that ship continue with its work unmolested: even if it succeeds, we'll do some damage."

"We shouldn't, Colonel," Ling Tong's mission deputy pleaded. "Attacking a much larger ship would surely lead to our deaths. We're scouts, not saboteurs!"

"There's always time to change a mission's remit," Ling Tong insisted. "We're behind enemy lines, so we're in danger already! We're going to take that ship, and we're going to do it now."

Zhang Shuo was glad when his first support boat returned, but he was alarmed to learn that the second had continued pursuit and disappeared.

"Why did you not continue your own chase...?" Zhang Shuo asked of the boat captain. "What if the enemy got the better of them?"

"Look!" a sailor cried. **"A boat approaches!"**

All eyes turned to look at what was, in fact, the second support boat, which was slowly moving toward the ship; the light was fading, but it was clearly the same vessel that had pursued Ling Tong's boat.

"…It would have been a mad fool that tried to attack us with such a small craft, so it could only have been our own!" Zhang Shuo chuckled. "Let them board: I want to know what they discovered." The ship's crew allowed the support boat to approach and lowered climbing ladders for the occupants to board; it was only when the men reached the deck that anyone realised that the boat's crew were Ling Tong and his followers in disguise.

"**You're brave, but stupid!**" Zhang Shuo said as Ling Tong's men began a battle with his; Ling charged at the older, slower Zhang and engaged him in a sword duel.

"**We must alert Lord Huang of this!**" the first support boat's captain said; he and his crew abandoned the ship and sped away in their boat while the battle on the deck continued.

Zhang Shuo was surprised at the skill that Ling Tong possessed and realised that he was not an ordinary scout commander: Zhang's curiosity got the better of him, and he asked, "**Who do I face this day…?**"

"**You face Ling Tong of Yuhang!**" Ling Tong retorted as he pushed Zhang Shuo backward and tried to run him through.

"**I shall give your name to Lord Huang along with your head!**" Zhang Shuo said as he dodged Ling Tong's lunge and made an attack of his own; Ling narrowly avoided the slash and counter with a kick to Zhang's leg that caused him to stumble. Zhang Shuo corrected himself, swiftly put distance between him and Ling Tong, and readied himself for the next attack; Ling Tong scowled, ran at the older officer and made strike after strike that finally wore Zhang down and caused him to make a mistake. Zhang Shuo cried out in pain as Ling Tong finally pierced his defences and drove his sword into Zhang's side; Zhang fell to his knees, and Ling ended the duel with a fatal blow to Zhang's head.

"**Surrender or die like Zhang Shuo!**" Ling Tong bellowed; the news of Zhang's death robbed many of the ship's crew of their courage or their will to fight.

"**We surrender!**" one of Zhang's sailors said.

"**Don't be ridiculous!**" one of Zhang's junior officers said. "**We outnumber them! We must fight to the end!**"

One of Ling Tong's men attacked and killed the defiant officer; the rest of the crew surrendered, despite their numerical advantage.

"…**Back to the camp!**" Ling Tong ordered. "**We'll take this ship for Lord Sun!**"

"…So Zhang Shuo is lost," Huang Zu said soberly; his court – which had shrunk as some of his less loyal supporters abandoned him – was almost silent.

"What do we do…?" Pan Jun asked.

"…The Miankou River must be held," Huang Zu replied. "Zhang was able to secure the cliff before it was taken: that was his last great service to me. **I want men on that cliff with rocks and arrows. We'll destroy them all as we once destroyed Sun Jian: by raining Hell down upon them from the Heavens!**"

✳✳✳✳✳✳✳✳✳✳✳✳

63

Gongjin ordered the main fleet to advance toward Jiangxia City, but the Miankou River was blocked by two multi-storied warships – *mengchongs* – that had been coated in ox-hide for extra resistance. The small boats that served as the vanguard were shot to pieces and their crews killed by the elite crossbowmen on the *mengchongs*, and those that survived were pursued and killed by the crews of the smaller support vessels. Ling Tong had to order a full retreat and inform Gongjin of the encounter.

"It's worse than expected!" Ling Tong said. "Our intelligence didn't include his possession of two mengchongs of such sound construction! And their bowmen, in addition to being competent, have plentiful ammunition! We must retreat and plan a strategy, else we'll be annihilated!"

"We'll have to smash our way through regardless!" Gongjin said. "I apologise for overriding you yet again, but I cannot delay any further! I will have our own large ships attack the mengchongs and destroy them!"

"What about the cliff?" Ling Tong asked.

"I've sent Dong Xi to secure the cliff by land," Gongjin replied. "But our intelligence stated that Huang's not stockpiled enough to harm us that badly!"

"It didn't tell us about the mengchongs!" Ling Tong protested.

"...I'm aware of that, but part of it has to have been right," Gongjin replied.

But Gongjin was quickly proven to be as wrong as the intelligence: Huang Zu's men were able to rain rocks, larger stones and flaming arrows on the advancing ships from the low cliff and do catastrophic damage to them. The demoralised Jiangdong navy did what it could to pass the gauntlet of projectiles and approach the *mengchongs*, but the two ships were connected by several ropes to steady them, and Huang Zu had additionally ordered a thick palm-fibre rope to be pulled across the width of the waterway and weighted at each end with heavy stones; no large ships would be able to get close to the enemy battleships while that rope barred their way, and smaller ships were at the mercy of small boats and crossbows. The captains of the forward ships noticed the rope too late: they then became trapped between that rope and the ships that were behind them, and the projectiles sank the near-motionless targets with painful ease. The attempts to secure the cliff also ended in failure: Dong Xi was forced to retreat amid a hail of arrow fire, and the infantry division that supported the archers was very professional. Gongjin called an emergency meeting in the command room of his flagship: the mood was sombre.

"This is *Gan Ning*... **he lured us into a trap!**" Ling Tong cried.

"Our own intelligence was flawed!" Gongjin insisted. "His betrayal might have been countered by others in the time since his flight from Zhu County, but this was more likely implemented even earlier by smarter minds that knew that Huang Zu was throwing away the region through his moping and procrastinating and acted on his behalf! The Kuais and Pangs are still guiding the old mobster from the shadows, and there are other clever minds besides them!"

"Sorry, but I'm not convinced," Ling Tong retorted. "This is Gan Ning's treachery."

"I don't care who's to blame," Dong Xi said.

"Neither do I, but I simply wanted to make the point clear so that we don't trust that vicious pirate anymore," Ling Tong retorted. "The main point now is that we must somehow cut that rope: it obstructs any proper attempt to defeat the mengchongs."

"...There's only one thing for it, then," Gongjin said. "If you two colonels are prepared to risk your lives in what many would call a reckless gambit..."

"I would gladly do whatever it takes to destroy Huang Zu," Ling Tong declared. "Even if it ends in my death, as it did my father, I will do what must be done."

"And I, Xi, am not afraid of my fate," Dong Xi said. "What are your orders, Chef Commander...?"

"...Select a hundred of the bravest, smartest, most skilful men that you have, and two-hundred sets of armour," Gongjin explained. "And then... well, the rest is very simple..."

The *mengchong* commanders reacted to the news that 100 men were assaulting their position with amusement: they ordered their crossbowmen to fire at will, and the commander of the ambush force on the cliff did the same. The small sabotage force came under heavy fire that was normally reserved for entire navies: Dong Xi looked at Ling Tong and shouted, **"I'LL CUT THE ROPE! YOU DIVIDE THE SHIPS!"**

Ling Tong advanced toward the *mengchongs*: his men were continually struck by arrows that mostly lodged harmlessly in their outer armour, but some were unlucky enough to be struck fatally as some arrows found weak points. Dong Xi's men bravely surrounded him while he set to work cutting the thick rope that barred the way: Dong flinched when a man screamed and fell into the cold waters, as he knew that the defensive circle had thinned and his own life – and mission – had been placed in greater danger. But luck was on Dong Xi's side, and he managed to cut the rope before he lost too many men; Ling Tong was equally fortunate, and the *mengchongs* were separated by his elite team.

"NOTIFY THE CHIEF COMMANDER!" Dong Xi ordered; one of Dong's men retreated to serve as a messenger and notify Gongjin that the way was clear.

"Maintain stability!" the 'left *menghong*' commander screamed. **"Don't cease firing! Don't let them board!"**

But the waters were rough, and the *mengchongs* were heavy vessels that started to rock from side to side when their connecting ropes were cut; the chaos of having the enemy within their midst had led to the support vessels attacking each other and being fired upon by their own crossbowmen, so there was a chance, however slim, of the ships being compromised by their tiny opponent. There would be no need for the remnants of the 100 men to work alone, however: Gongjin's larger ships arrived and attacked the *mengchongs* with flaming arrows and crossbows while their small support vessels routed what was left of the *mengchongs*' escort. Ling Tong and Dong Xi boarded and commandeered the two barrier craft simultaneously, ending the blockade of the Miankou River once and for all.

"**ONWARD TO JIANGXIA!**" Ling Tong cried. "**HUANG ZU'S HEAD IS MINE!**"

"**They've cleared the way???**" Huang Zu exclaimed; the messenger that brought the news shrank back in fear as Huang added, "**That's... that's *impossible*!**"

"**The most important thing is getting reinforcements!**" an official shouted.

"That's quite right, Lord Huang," Pan Jun said.

"...Pan Jun: you will hurry to Jiangling and request support from Kuai Yue," Huang Zu ordered. "Don't dally: we may have weeks or even days. **Hurry!**"

Pan Jun hurried from Huang Zu's silent court.

"**You: hurry and tell Chen Jiu that we need more men to fortify Miankou!**" Huang Zu said to the messenger that had brought the news from Miankou. "**This city MUST NOT FALL!**"

The exhausted messenger retreated.

"...We should consider surrender," a politician said.

"Don't be ridiculous!" Huang Zu chortled. "The Suns want us all dead as reparation for Sun Jian! They want Jing as well, to rebuild the Chu state of old and challenge the Han for the Imperial throne! The-!"

"**REPORT!**"

All eyes turned to another messenger, who added, "**A 'Ling Tong' sieges the city! There has been a failed attempt to take the east gate!**"

"**They're here already???**" Huang Zu exclaimed. "**All men to their posts! Defend this place with your lives!**"

One of the defenders of Jiangxia's capital was Gan Ning's friend and advocate Su Fei; his task was to keep Ling Tong's men away from the eastern gates, but his heart was not in the battle at all, and his officers could sense it.

"**Are we going to fight to the death or submit...?**" one major asked suddenly.

Su Fei smirked and said, "**I dunno. It's over, that's all that's certain: question is whether we want deaths as loyal servants of Lord Huang or if we should chance Sun Quan needing to show a bit of mercy.**"

"...**They're approaching again!**" a scout reported; Ling Tong's commander at the eastern gates was leading his men in person, and they were fearlessly preparing to try to scale the wall.

"**What do we do...?**" a captain asked.

"**I'll think about it as we fight!**" Su Fei joked.

That fighting would be costly and yet restrained; Su Fei was now seriously contemplating surrender and using his connection to the defector Gan Ning to secure clemency for himself and his men.

✱✱✱✱✱✱✱✱✱✱✱✱

Within an hour, Naval Commandant Lü Meng received word that the Miankou River was clear and said, "**Ling Tong and Dong Xi are set to grab all of the glory! I will look like a fool if I have not done something here!**"

"*Aiee...* **don't do something stupid!**" Lü Meng's deputy, Sun Jiao, pleaded as Meng started to shed some of his heavier armour.

"**Dong and Ling just cleared the Miankou River with a hundred men!**" Lü Meng retorted. "**Now I shall show them that they are not the only heroes!**"

Lü Meng left his command ship and boarded a small boat: the boat's captain was puzzled and asked, "**Where are we going, Commandant Lü?**"

"**Advance on their flagship!**" Lü Meng cried. "**I will slay Chen Jiu for Lord Sun!**"

"...**Forward!**" the captain replied excitedly.

Admiral Chen Jiu was frantically trying to give orders to his vast but disorderly fleet as word of Miankou's vulnerability caused morale to plummet: he was therefore unprepared when Lü Meng – at the head of a small collection of boats – cut his way through the carpet of enemy vessels and started to board Chen's command ship. Lü Meng was already on the deck by the time that his crew realised that there was a problem: Chen Jiu raised his sword and said, "**How nice: I actually get a chance to fight like a real warrior. I shall relish it!**"

Chen Jiu engaged Lü Meng while Meng's allies fought the crew and secured routes for other men to board; Meng was at the peak of his physical potential, and Chen Jiu quickly realised it as he struggled to land strikes and narrowly avoided fatal lunges.

"**You're a... worthy match!**" Chen Jiu wheezed. "**Sun Quan has good men!**"

"**Lord Sun Quan wants your head, Chen Jiu!**" Lü Meng retorted. "**Yield it now!**"

Chen Jiu laughed at Lü Meng's melodramatic response and forgot that he was fighting a younger, more dextrous opponent; Meng got the better of the admiral and cut him down moments later, ending the effectiveness of Huang Zu's navy in an instant.

"**Make sure they all know that Chen Jiu is dead!**" Lü Meng ordered. "**And then we'll hurry to Jiangxia City: let's get some glory for ourselves!**"

Lü Meng's followers cheered wildly.

****

"...How did this happen...?" Huang Zu said as he finished reading a report that had been delivered by a sobbing messenger; Miankou River was now blockaded by Jiangdong ships, Chen Jiu's men had surrendered by the thousands, Dong Xi had routed the cliff defenders, Ling Tong had the city surrounded and Huang Zu's military support had now dwindled to whoever remained within his fortified capital. Lü Meng was only being delayed in his advance by one last vestige of Huang Zu's loyalists that blocked his way, but Ling Tong's ferocity had rattled the city defenders and increased the chances that the city could fall within hours if Huang did not receive reinforcements.

"...Is this really all because I was rude to Gan Ning...?" Huang Zu wondered. "Is this really because I ordered the death of Sun Jian and showed contempt to his corpse...?"

Huang Zu's thoughts were interrupted by an official that entered his study and said, "The southern gates have been breached, Lord Huang. We cannot hold them."

"...**Then I must flee!**" Huang Zu cried.

Ling Tong's forces divided into multiple militias so that the defenders could be overwhelmed and other gates thrown open to the Jiangdong army; Ling personally advanced toward the eastern gates, where he found Su Fei awaiting him with his sword proffered as a sign of submission and all other signs of resistance eliminated or discontinued.

"...**Major Tian: open the gates,**" Ling Tong ordered cautiously.

"**I already gave that order to my own men,**" Su Fei bellowed.

"...You're surrendering...?" Ling Tong prompted.

"Could I be doing anything else...?" Su Fei retorted. "I've had enough: me and my men will submit and serve Sun Quan if we're allowed."

"Why should Lord Sun Quan want any of Huang Zu's men...?" Ling Tong challenged.

"Word is that he partly owes this victory to 'one of Huang Zu's men'," Su Fei retorted. "That man is a friend of mine, Gan Ning, and he'll vouch for me since it was me that told him to leave Huang Zu's service."

Ling Tong's expression hardened as he said, "You... are... one of Gan's friends...?"

"I am," Su Fei replied obliviously. "My name is Su Fei: get Gan to vouch for me, as I've always vouched for him."

"...*Su Fei*... and I am *Ling Tong*, son of *Ling Cao*, the man that nearly killed your master but was stopped – forever – by Gan Ning's arrow," Ling Tong announced. "Why would I want a friend of that man, a man that 'vouched for him', to keep his head...?"

Su Fei's men exchanged nervous glances.

"...I recommended Gan to Huang Zu," Su Fei replied fearlessly. "So perhaps I'm the executioner, then: what a shame that I picked you of all men to submit to. So Gan's dead, then, as thanks for what he did for your lord...?"

Ling Tong's expression softened; he turned to Major Tian and said, "This man... will be bound and taken into custody. It- ...It is not my place to decide what happens to him, it is Lord Sun's... and he may spare this man as he spared Gan Ning."

"Gan Xingba's alive...?" Su Fei exclaimed. "Lord Sun Quan is magnanimous, and-!"

"Gan's alive *for now*, and *only for now* if *I* have any say in it," Ling Tong retorted. "And don't go saying 'Lord Sun' too soon, either; he might not want to spare you."

"He spared Xingba, who deserves a second chance!" Su Fei replied as he was led away by two of Major Tian's men. **"He was not thanked for what he did and regretted it immediately; don't hate him, Mister Ling Tong! Hate Huang Zu, who laughed while Gan Ning sighed and went away thanklessly! Gan gave you revenge, Mister Ling: he's atoned as he wanted to! Kill me if you want, but understand *that*!"**

Ling Tong was shaken by Su Fei's words and left motionless and silent as he pondered them.

"...Colonel Ling...?" Major Tian prompted. "Colonel, what are your orders...?"

"...We will secure the east gates and then move on to the north gates so that we can rendezvous with Sun Jiao as planned," Ling Tong declared as his composure started to return. "And we shall do as that man asked, and have Gan Ning informed of his capture: perhaps it will flush the rat out and deliver him to me. **Let's go!"**

Huang Zu was rushed to the western gates of the city and given the best horse that could be found: the ageing Administrator galloped out of the gates with a small team of bodyguard riders while the remaining loyalists prepared for a final battle with Ling Tong, who had secured horses so that he and his men could move about at speed.

The battle for the heart of the city was brief: Ling Tong was angry and desperate for revenge against Huang Zu, and his lack of fear gave him an overwhelming advantage over the demoralised and terrified defenders of Jiangxia. But when Ling Tong reached Huang Zu's last stronghold in the centre of the vast city, it quickly became obvious that Huang was not going to be found there.

"He's fled!" Ling Tong realised. **"I will go westward, and Major Tian, you go northward! He could not have gotten far!"**

Huang Zu and his small group of riders had to navigate some familiar but nonetheless treacherous terrain as they tried to reach safety in Nan Prefecture: it did not take long for some of Ling Tong's cavalrymen to catch up to the fugitives, and the subsequent battle was notably violent.

"I MUSTN'T DIE HERE!" Huang Zu screeched. **"I AM THE LORD OF JIANGXIA PREFECTURE! I AM LIU BIAO'S SWORD AND SHIELD! I AM-!"**

"FOR MY LORD!" one man cried as he raised his sword and brought it down with all of his might, cleaving Huang Zu's back and knocking the Administrator from his startled horse; Ling Tong arrived minutes later, but Huang Zu had already expired.

"...So he's dead, then," Ling Tong sighed.

"I got carried away," the assassin protested. "Please forgive me,

Colonel Ling!"

"You did what was necessary, Feng Ze," Ling Tong replied. "It's better that he didn't escape again. Let us scoop him up and take his head to Lord Sun Quan."

Sun Quan was anxious as he sat in his study in Chaisang City's governor's mansion and awaited news of his navy and his grand plan: his servant Gu Li sensed the mood and said, "This time will be different."

"I hope so, Li," Sun Quan replied. "I... I can't withstand another defeat. I am tarnished by years of perceived ineptitude and lack of charisma. If I cannot defeat Huang Zu this time, then I might have to step aside and... ... ...well, I suppose that there's only Cousin Boyang now, or maybe Cousin Zhongyi, who gains ever-greater favour with Zhou Gongjin for his military ability."

"That won't be necessary," Gu Li insisted. "Your army is-"

"**REPORT!**"

Sun Quan turned to the cheerful, excited messenger that had stumbled into his study and said, "Speak at once, man! Is it good news that you bring...?"

"**Yes, Lord Sun!**" the messenger replied. "**Command-in-Chief Zhou Yu has defeated the Jiangxia navy; Ling Tong's men have taken the capital and Huang Zu's head! Jiangxia is yours, Lord Sun!**"

Gu Li smiled gratefully; Sun Quan could barely contain his excitement and laughed for almost a minute before he got to his feet, grasped the arms of his overjoyed messenger and said, "This is a great day! You... you go and rest, man, you've earned it! I shall hurry to Jiangxia... I shall hurry there and see Huang Zu's head and sit at his host seat and review what is now my domain! Jiangxia... Jiangxia is taken, and my father avenged! I – we – have waited so very long...!"

Sun Quan released the messenger, who immediately bowed low and retreated with a grin on his face: Quan then turned to Gu Li and said, "Li, you-! ...No, no, I won't send you, you're not an errand boy; find the fastest lad and have him bring Zhuge Jin to me so that I can speak with him and have the grandest entrance into Jiangxia... I must relish this, capitalise upon this...!"

"I shall do as you ask at once," Gu Li replied before he hurried to the servants' quarters.

"...Brother, I have completed your work: I have done what you failed to do before Heaven claimed you," Sun Quan murmured. "Father... your murderer is dead and you are avenged. Perhaps now... perhaps now, I will be deemed... worthy."

****

66

Sun Quan left Chaisang and arrived in Jiangxia City on the following morning: the streets were lined with nervous townsfolk and cheering soldiers. Sun Quan travelled to the governor's mansion – which had, until the day before, been the home of his clan's enemy, Huang Zu – and after taking the host seat, he said, "I requested the head of my old foe in a container made for that very purpose: where is it...?"

Feng Ze presented a box containing the head of Huang Zu to Sun Quan, who grinned and laughed as he took pleasure in viewing the grisly trophy.

"His face is twisted with fear!" Sun Quan cackled. "Oh, how this warms my heart, gentlemen, to know that he suffered to the very last! There will be a magnificent banquet for each of the heroes that made this day possible: for my elder brother, Zhou Gongjin, whose plan this was; for Ling Tong, who took the city; for Lü Meng, who toppled the navy; and last, by no means least, for Dong Xi of Yuyao, who stopped the rocks and cut the rope!"

The officials cheered and said as one, "**All hail Lord Sun Quan!**"

"Lord Sun, there is now the matter of how we deal with captured and surrendered officers," Gongjin declared. "Most of Huang Zu's higher-ranking officers died in battle, and the mid-ranking men were mostly taken by force or killed in action: the few that were captured and the one that submitted will now be brought to you."

"...The one that submitted...?" Sun Quan exclaimed.

"He... his name is Su Fei," Ling Tong reported. "He claims that he a friend of Gan Ning and that he encouraged Gan to defect."

"Oh...? Is that so...?" Sun Quan said. "Bring him to me first then!"

"You spared him...?" Gongjin noted as he stared at Ling Tong.

"It was not my place to kill a surrendered officer," Ling Tong replied. "I will not lie: I wanted to gut him just for knowing Gan Ning, but my heart must not rule my head, or I am unworthy of my rank as colonel."

"You... made the right choice, Colonel Ling," Sun Quan said as two men led Su Fei into the hall; Quan looked the bound Su Fei up and down and said, "So this is Su Fei."

"That's me," Su Fei retorted.

"I have a second box that was made especially for your head, to thank you for being the villain Huang Zu's last line of defence," Sun Quan announced. "What have you to say to that...?"

"I am a scruffy and untalented man all in all," Su Fei replied, "but I know right and wrong when I see it; Sun Jian was a great man that saved Wan from the Yellow Turbans during the rebellion and deserved better than being put in a plain wooden box and laughed at. Huang Zu never did know how to treat good men right; he had it coming, what happened to him, and if I have to die too, fine."

Sun Quan hummed thoughtfully and said, "Aren't you just saying what you think I want to hear in order to save your life...?"

"I know that Gan Xingba would have told you about me, Lord Sun, because he is as good when he's your friend as he is vicious when he's your enemy," Su Fei retorted. "Huang Zu always laughed when I tried to tell him that Gan was a changed man, a man that was trying to learn the classics and better himself, become a smarter man that doesn't just kill, but he was trying to do just that, Lord Sun, and he'll be an asset to you: I know that your man Ling Tong needs to pay homage to his father, but Gan was no more responsible than his arrow was, and I beg you not to let him be wasted like that. I'm no loss to the world, but Gan's a good fellow, and so are my men that followed me, so please spare them as well, even if you don't spare me."

Sun Quan turned his eyes to look at Gongjin, who said, "It is your decision to make, Lord Sun, but Gan Ning has spoken highly of this man and pleaded with us to spare him if it is possible."

Sun Quan then turned his eyes to look at Ling Tong, who sighed forlornly and said, "His fate is in your hands, as is right, which is why I spared him to be brought here today."

Sun Quan nodded soberly and replied, "You have done the right thing as my subordinate, Colonel Ling, which must have been difficult at such a heated moment, in the middle of battle... when it was easy to 'act according to the moment'..."

"I do not deny that it was difficult... *very difficult*," Ling Tong said.

"...Whereas I have the last word, and I am not one to waste a good box," Sun Quan chuckled; Ling Tong smiled slightly.

"As I've said, fine," Su Fei replied as calmly as he could.

"**You hide your fear well,**" Sun Quan said. "**GUARDS: DE-!**"

"**WAIT!!!**"

All eyes turned to Gan Ning, who ran into the hall and wheezed, "You... can't kill Su Fei, your lordship, it... wouldn't be right."

"Is it any less right than what you did to my father, you faithless bastard?" Ling Tong heckled.

"No... and p'raps that's what we should think about," Gan Ning said. "I can't stay alive if Su Fei's killed."

Sun Quan smirked and replied, "But I have a box prepared especially for his head, Xingba, and he did insist upon holding the city for longer than was necessary."

"He was always stubbornly loyal, even to a dog like me an' a worthless lord like Huang Zu," Gan Ning retorted. "He risked his own head to save mine from Huang, though, so I owe him for still bein' alive: I beg you, your lordship, to let him go."

"...I would only release him if he then served me," Sun Quan said. "What if I released him and he fled...?"

"I wouldn't, Lord Sun," Su Fei insisted. "I-!"

"I want Xingba's answer, not yours," Sun Quan said. "Xingba...?"

"I don't believe that Fei'd run," Gan Ning replied. "Look, if you really can't spare him because you have to have a head in that box, then you can 'ave mine instead."

"*Ayah*...! **No, you idiot!**" Su Fei protested. "**Let me die!**"

Ling Tong grinned at the thought of Gan Ning's demise and turned to look at Sun Quan, who was moving his eyes back and forth between Gan and Su Fei.

"...If I have to beg, I'll beg," Gan Ning said as he fell to his knees. "I'll not have you kill Su Fei, your lordship: he's my friend!"

Sun Quan reached out and gasped as Gan Ning started to kowtow violently, striking his head against the floor and drawing blood.

"**Stop it, Xingba!**" Su Fei cried.

"**Yes, Xingba, stop!**" Sun Quan ordered. "**Stop at once! My word is final, and you will stop at once and hear me out if you are truly my vassal now!**"

Gan Ning stopped his self-harming protest and sat up slowly.

"...Su Fei, you also made good decisions that led, unintentionally or otherwise, to this moment, and I promised Gan Ning that I would spare you, and I am a man of my word," Sun Quan said as he turned his eyes to look at Su Fei. "You will be unbound, and then you will serve me. **GUARDS!**"

"Then you're taking Gan's head...?" Ling Tong asked excitedly.

"...No," Sun Quan replied sternly. "They are both free men."

Su Fei fell to his knees as soon as he was freed; he kowtowed and declared, "**I am your loyal servant from this moment on, Lord Sun! If I can help you even half as much as Gan Ning then I will die a happy man!**"

Ling Tong grunted irritably but said nothing.

"Very good," Sun Quan replied. "You are henceforth made a major, tasked with bringing others to my cause: go back to your men and tell them that they are also free to do as they please."

Su Fei bowed humbly, cried, "**Thank you, Lord Sun Quan!**" and left the hall.

"I have a headache," Gan Ning joked as he wiped blood from his forehead. "Can I go now...?"

"...Yes, yes, of course," Sun Quan replied. "You'll relocate to Dangkou now: and *thank you*, Xingba, for ensuring that I made the right decision... again."

Gan Ning got to his feet and bowed respectfully; he then turned, nodded toward the despondent Ling Tong and began a retreat.

"The mid-ranking officers that were caught will be spared as well, I think," Sun Quan continued. "I see no sense in killing tools; one might as well order every arrow to be snapped and every sword bent at the middle."

"I agree completely, Lord Sun," Gongjin said.

Sun Quan laughed as he looked at Huang Zu's lifeless head.

"Jiangxia is yours, Lord Sun," Gongjin prompted.

Sun Quan laughed again and said, "Jiangxia is *ours*... and that's just the beginning! My father and Ling Cao are both appeased by Huang Zu's demise, but Liu Biao – the master of all the wicked men in Jing – still lives! But he will be next!"

After so many years of trying, the Sun clan had finally achieved their long-term goal of slaying Jiangxia Administrator Huang Zu: Jing Province's governor, Liu Biao was irreversibly harmed by the news, and his health started to fail. To some, it was the Sun clan's finest hour: total revenge for the death of Sun Jian was within Sun Quan's grasp, the Han Dynasty had finally recognised the young chieftain's potential and appointed him as a general – which silenced a lot of his opponents – and the prosperous south that so many envisaged was looking to become a reality. But the plan that many of Sun Quan's followers – and Sun Quan himself – were following was to forge an independent southern state, all but defying the will of the Han government in the north: that was about to lead to one of the most famous battles in the history of the nation.

****

ACT VI: TO YIELD OR FIGHT

67

The Sun clan of Fuchun County had finally had their desired revenge on Huang Zu, the lord of Jiangxia Prefecture in southeastern Jing Province, for his part in the death of the clan chieftain Sun Quan's father, Sun Jian; the governor of Jing Province, Liu Biao, was now considered to be the next logical target. But matters were complicated; the attack on Jing was not authorised by Sun Quan's master, the Han Emperor Xian, and as a newly-appointed officer of the Han – 'General that Attacks Barbarians' – Quan was potentially guilty of several crimes against the state by attacking what was clearly a part of the Han Empire in order to annex it into his own autonomous territory south of the Yangtze River – territory which was, in fact, another part of that same Han Empire. The future of Jiangdong – 'East of the River' – as an independent state or as part of a loyal Han province was now the most important and potentially divisive question that was put to Sun Quan's main court in Qu'e City, and most looked to Sun Quan's Commander-in-Chief and brother-in-law, Zhou Yu – known familiarly as 'Gongjin' – to answer it from afar as the Jing campaign progressed further into enemy territory.

"Here is the situation as I see it," Gongjin said to Sun Quan's temporary court in Xiakou City in Jiangxia Prefecture. "Cao Cao's marching westward, toward Nan County, where he will then begin a push southward toward Liu Biao's northern capital Xiangyang. Nan County is now friendly territory for him, so half the work is done: Liu Biao will doubtless be reeling from our destroying his 'right arm', and if he falls gravely ill – which is likely, so I'm told – then we're talking succession conflicts and asking whether Cao Cao will be contested or submitted to."
The adviser and politician Zhang Zhao – who was in Xiakou to demand answers for the court – sneered and said, "You...! 'Whether Cao Cao will be contested or submitted to'...? The-!"
Sun Quan gestured that Zhang Zhao should stop talking, and Zhang reluctantly complied; Quan then turned to Gongjin and asked, "If Liu Biao *were* to fall ill... or even *die*... and the matter of a successor arose... what should I do...?"
"That depends on whom we deal with," Gongjin replied. "If we're fighting Liu Qi – Liu Biao's eldest son – then we're fighting a sickly idiot that sees Liu Biao's tenant Liu Bei as a 'worthy uncle' and will join forces with Bei to fight Cao Cao *and* us if he has to or, if he can, find a way to keep us placated and focus on Cao, who is Liu Bei's mortal enemy. That could enable us to keep hold of Jiangxia and expand to Liu Biao's southern capital, Jiangling, at the very least, forming a 'Jiangnan region' that covers most of the territory between the Great River and the remote Jiaozhi Province."
"And if we're fighting Liu Cong, Liu Biao's younger son...?" the veteran general Cheng Pu asked.
"...If we're fighting Liu Cong then matters are that much more complicated," Gongjin admitted. "Liu Cong is, as I understand it, favoured by Liu Biao's current principal wife, Lady Cai, who raised him as though he were her own son despite there being no blood ties: Cong is now married to Lady Cai's niece to strengthen the

connection. Lady Cai's brother, Admiral Cai Mao – with whom we're all familiar – is Liu Biao's left arm as Huang Zu was once his right, and now that Huang is dead Cai Mao must wield Biao's sword as both hands, which amplifies his influence and also his sister's; Biao's advisers and politicians prefer the more cautious Liu Cong to the vice-prone Qi, more so now that Liu Bei – whom they rightly despise – has got Qi's ear, and those men have long pushed for an end to hostility between the Han court and Jing Province. Liu Qi would guarantee war with the Han army and more influence for Liu Bei, who covets Jing Province to replace the twice-gained and twice-lost Xu Province; Liu Cong would prepare the way for peace with Han court – most likely via surrender – and a focus on expelling Liu Bei before Bei seizes the governor's seal and repelling us before we can advance any further north."

"I concur," Cheng Pu said. "Liu Qi or Liu Cong: neither is good, but which is worse...? And then, if it is Liu Cong, he can either retain the governor's seal whilst making peace with the government at our expense or he can yield altogether, handing control of Jing directly to Cao Cao; again, which is worse...?"

"Of the three scenarios, Cao Cao taking Jing is the worst by far," Gongjin replied. "It opens the Great River as a battle front and – if Cao does not then want to deal with Zhang Lu's cultist state or the Qiang tribes in the northwest, which would be the more sensible and patriotic option – it then turns every eye and ear in our direction... and every condemnatory pen and ready sword as well."

"And readier *warships*...?" Cheng Pu suggested.

"...Yes," Gongjin replied. "I insist that we had to do this in order to block key land routes, but yes, he has a vast navy that will be the next great obstacle."

"If Cao Cao does take Xiangyang, what will we do next...?" Sun Quan asked.

"We would have to see how he reacted to our own advance," Gongjin replied. "If he is indifferent then we would take Jiangling and the four 'independent counties' to the immediate west of us; if he were to be overly aggressive then we would retreat to Jiangxia and maintain a border."

"...And if Cao Cao advanced southward with the intention of taking Jiangxia...?" Sun Quan asked. "It's obviously a thought of yours, Gongjin, else I'd still be in the prefectural capital and not loitering here – as per your suggestion – in a commercial port city with swift access to transport."

Gongjin smiled uneasily and replied, "Well, we-"

"We would leave Jiangxia and return to Jiangdong," Zhang Zhao interrupted before Gongjin could answer properly. "There can be no other proper response to the demands of the Han's Chancellor of State."

"...Which was my intended answer, Zhang Zibu," Gongjin insisted. "I have no plan to oppose the Han government, only to defend against its 'Chancellor of State' should he go beyond his remit and start planning a military invasion of Jiangdong."

"Does the Chancellor of State have any such 'remit', or can he not just act in the best interests of the Son of Heaven as he sees fit...?" Zhang Zhao countered. "We must yield whatever we are asked to yield, Zhou Yu, even if he starts asking for our heads! To do otherwise would be *treason*!"

"He's another Dong Zhuo," Gongjin retorted. "You'll get that through your smart but stubborn head eventually, Zibu, and then, maybe, we'll be able to work together for the good of the people." Zhang Zhao harrumphed irritably.

"Why, then, was my daughter given to the man's son, and my cousin wed to his niece...?" Yuzhang Prefecture Administrator Sun Ben asked irritably. "If he is 'another Dong Zhuo', then why-?"

"His intentions were not clear at that time," Gongjin retorted. "His subsequent demands for hostages, links to Sheng Xian's court and prior links to Xu Gong were all 'the unknown and the undisclosed' when those marriage alliances were proposed. Don't let Cao Cao's affable demeanour fool you, Boyang, or it will cost you."

Sun Ben glared at Gongjin and said, "Thank you for your kind advice, Zhou Gongjin. But Mister Zhang Zhao nonetheless makes a valid point. Lord Sun Quan must not be seen to oppose the Son of Heaven: I for one will not be a party to any such defiance."

"You need not worry, Cousin," Sun Quan said. "I don't want to fight the Son of Heaven: I am a loyal subject, an appointed general, and I have a nephew with Cao blood in his veins, so if I can avoid fighting the Chancellor of State then I will do so."

"You speak of Mèn-! ...of *Chancellor Cao* as though he were a separate entity from the Han court, but he *embodies it*!" Sun Ben challenged. "Stop listening to the likes of 'Gongjin', Lu Su and Zhuge Jin, who twist you against the Han court for no reason that Heaven will tolerate!"

Gongjin smiled coldly and said, "Please calm down, Boyang... we're not looking for war with anyone."

Sun Ben exhaled angrily and replied, "I hope so, Zhou Yu... I really hope so."

Gongjin frowned at Sun Ben's use of his full name – rather than his courtesy name – in his response but he did not react to it.

"...So we are to proceed with advancing on Jiangling, then," Sun Quan prompted.

"We must finish what we have started," Gongjin insisted.

"The people of Jiangxia are divided," Zhang Zhao noted. "The astute have realised that we mean them no harm and welcome us cautiously, but there are many that owe the Huangs a great deal and do not want us here at all. We will find the same across Jing: is this not a case of 'putting our hand in the tiger's mouth' at a time when we can ill afford to, and for *why*...? Are we following Lu Su's absurd scheme to deliberately partition the Empire here, and if so, to what end other than be labelled as traitors...?"

The scrawny, visually unthreatening Lu Su scowled at Zhang Zhao's verbal attack.

"We have had our victory over the man that directly ordered the deaths of Lord Sun Quan's father and General Ling Cao: have we not already 'finished what we have started'...?" Zhang Zhao continued. "What good is there to be had from turning our exposed backs to the Shanyue, the pirates, the bandits and other undesirables that still threaten the stability of Jiangdong...? I came here from Qu'e to ask those important questions and take back answers that the court will be happy with: most importantly, Lord Sun, there are many that are fearful that we are about to confront the Han itself, and they cannot – and *will not* – do that."

"Have I not just said that I will not fight the Han...?" Sun Quan

despaired. "Go back and tell them all that their lord Sun Quan is not a traitor, Mister Zhang; we will advance northward as a Han army in order to unseat Liu Biao's actually-treasonous regime until or unless we are instructed otherwise by the Han court."
Zhang Zhao bowed respectfully and then retreated.
"Pedant and *fool*," Cheng Pu muttered.
"Zhang Zhao will see the truth eventually, Demou," Gongjin replied quietly. "He's a pedant, yes, but he's not a fool."
"I shall return to Nanchang if I'm not needed here," Sun Ben said.
"If your support is needed, Cousin Boyang, then I shall certainly ask it of you in person," Sun Quan replied. "You may take your leave, and please give my best regards to everyone."
Sun Ben glared at Gongjin and Lu Su as he bowed to Sun Quan and began his retreat.
"...We can't rely on him," Cheng Pu muttered.
"No, we can't," Gongjin agreed.
"But to what extent is he a problem...?" Lu Su asked.
Cheng Pu hummed thoughtfully; Sun Quan noticed the private discussion and said, "What are you three mumbling about?"
"We are 'mumbling' about the problems that we face, Lord Sun Quan," Cheng Pu replied. "I will briefly go back to Haihun and ensure that the region is stable: we don't need Huang Zu's acolytes deciding to cause trouble there and harming our supply and communications route."
"You do that, Elder Cheng," Sun Quan said, and Cheng Pu retreated. "...An ugly thought occurs to me," Sun Quan added suddenly. "What if Huang Zu's 'acolytes' are lurking in shadows as Xu Gong and Sheng Xian's did...? Might they try to harm me or those closest to me...? I have no desire to lose anyone else, particularly not to unseen blades!"
"Security is as tight as it can be, my lord," Sun Quan's bodyguard commander, Chen Wu, replied insistently. "If there are no risks taken then there can be no losses."
"And I've not found a dangerous man in Xiakou that hates you, Lord Sun; they all left here or were dealt with already," the defected officer Su Fei said. "If there were any new dangers found then I'd make sure and tell you."
"...Thank you, Mister Su," Sun Quan murmured; he then turned to his Chief Commander and asked, "Is that all, Gongjin...?"
"As far as I'm concerned, my lord, yes," Gongjin replied. "I'll begin a general march to Jiangling at once, seizing Changsha and Wuling on the way if needs be."
Sun Quan nodded slowly and said, "Very... very good."
Lu Su exchanged tense glances with Gongjin; the two were about to undertake the next phases of their plans – identical in goals, yet very different in terms of execution – and put the Sun clan on a direct collision course with Cao Cao in one way or another.
"...What will happen...?" Lu Su wondered.
Sun Quan heard the words but did not react to them; Gongjin settled for smiling encouragingly, but the smile was forced.

****

68

Gongjin was approached after the meeting by the newly-promoted General Lü Meng, who said, "Can I discuss some concerns that I have with you, Chief Commander...?"

"I'm reliably told that you're starting to actually out-think the scholars, Ziming," Gongjin replied. "By all means share your thoughts with me."

"I doubt that I'm 'out-thinking' them, Chief Commander," Lü Meng said humbly. "I'm not a bright man, as much as I'd like to be: I think that I just surprised them with the questions that I was asking about the classic texts. Anyhow, I'll get to the point and leave you be: I've not got anything in the way of 'military intelligence', in any sense of the words, but... I'm looking at what's going on and I see an outcome that worries me, and hope that your superior understanding of the situation will put me at ease and enable me to placate others."

"...Go on," Gongjin prompted.

"By all means stop me if what I say is a load of rubbish," Lü Meng continued. "Anyhow: I see it this way. Guo Jia's died, but not before allowing Cao Cao to recover all of the losses to men and morale that he suffered at Wan, at Xu, and so on, and conquer the whole of the northeast, even defeating the Wuhuan... leaving three opponents – Zhang Lu of Han'ning, Ma Chao of Xiliang and Chao's father's rival, Han Sui – in the northwest as threats that Cao may or may not eliminate before moving southward... I know that I'd want them out of the way before I moved south but that's me."

Gongjin hummed ambiguously and said, "Go on."

"...Well, anyhow... if Cao Cao has no willing enemies in the northwest, and now he advances on Jing, I can see only one way that this can end, if you don't mind me saying," Lü Meng continued. "Liu Biao needed Huang Zu, so I believe that the stress of the loss will weaken him and very quickly kill him. I listened to what what said earlier, and I am certain that Cai Mao and Lady Cai will already have the secret support of Liu Biao's court, and now Liu Qi is on his way here to 'attempt to take Jiangxia back', which can only be to put him as far from the seat of power as possible 'until the time comes'... so we're looking at Liu Cong as the new Governor of Jing, and that almost certainly means that Cao Cao has as good as taken the seal before fighting has even begun; I don't actually think that there will be any real fighting at all, to be honest, because there's only Cai Mao, Zhang Yun and Wen Ping to speak of, and only one of them has a reputation – to my knowledge – for wanting to fight without yielding."

Gongjin smiled and said, "Go on."

"That being said, it leads to Liu Bei being isolated, and he'll almost certainly try to seize control of Jing from Liu Cong or retreat southward in the hope that he can find refuge in one of the four semi-autonomous counties, Jiaozhi or – if all else fails – with us," Lü Meng continued. "He's said to be a wily sort, willing to forge alliances that most men would balk at, especially when it strengthens his faction for wars with his Heaven-appointed rival Cao Cao but sometimes just to save his own neck: he allied with the morally-questionable Gongsun Zan against the loyalist Yuan

Shao; he rushed to Tao Qian's aid and somehow got Xu's provincial seal as a reward; he then allowed Lü Bu refuge from Cao Cao in Xu when most men would have sent Bu's head to the capital, though that led to disaster; he then forged ties with Cao of all men to uproot Lü Bu, but then he betrayed Cao and took Xu Province back, though that again ended in disaster; he sought an alliance with Yuan Shao against the Han and willingly led an army of Yellow Turbans to attack Xuchang; now he's in Jing, ingratiating himself with the ailing Liu Qi as he once befriended Tao Qian."

"...Please, go on," Gongjin insisted.

"I paused because you're looking at me as though I am somehow unnerving or amusing you," Lü Meng replied. "But alright, I'll go on: I believe that Liu Bei will try to convince Liu Qi to seek peace with Lord Sun Quan if Jing Province falls into Cao Cao's hands. Whether he can, I don't know, but try he most certainly will, and we might actually have to consider such a ridiculous alliance, because Cao Cao is obviously going to attack us once Jing falls, no matter how amiable we are: his words to our envoy – shortly before having the acclaimed poet and social commentator Kong Rong dragged out of his court and beheaded – and the rumours of a training lake and warship construction leave little doubt in my mind about it."

Gongjin nodded agreeably and said, "Go on, Ziming... go on...!"

"...So anyhow, I believe that war is inevitable," Lü Meng continued. "Jing will surrender, Liu Bei will retreat southward looking for allies, and he will meet Liu Qi – if, indeed, his small militia can escape Cao Cao's army – and try to hold firm. At that point, Chief Commander, we might need to reach out to them without waiting to see what they do, for Cao Cao is the greatest threat that we face right now, not the Lius of Jing... although Liu Bei is a much greater threat in the long term, of course."

"...By all means elaborate," Gongjin said excitedly.

"Liu Bei – an unlucky descendant of a disinherited prince – is an eternal hankerer that is locked in a perpetual war with Cao Cao that can only end with the death of one of them," Lü Meng replied. "At the moment, Liu Bei is small and insignificant, but he can and will grow if not kept underfoot, and he must be for the sake of our lord: I don't believe that the Han Dynasty can sustain, because it has needed propping up like a sickly calf for the past twenty years and has been saved at least twice from passing away by ambitious warlords, and that means that its mandate must be taken by another, and only Lord Sun is a fitting candidate, though Liu Bei will entertain the notion that he can revive the Han with himself at the helm."

"...So what will happen, in your view...?" Gongjin asked.

"I know that Lu Su has an idea about 'tripods' – three warlords rising to equal strength and prominence and competing for the remnants of the empire, but we must avoid such a scenario if we can," Lü Meng continued. "By all means use Liu Bei as a buffer, a way of diverting Cao Cao's attention from us, but we must not let him grow: he'd draw Han sympathisers to his base at our expense when Cao Cao inevitably succumbs to hubris and neurosis and starts to promote himself beyond his already-treasonous role as Chancellor of State. It is as it has been so many times before: our lord and Cao Cao – or Cao Pi if Cao Cao dies - will vie for the empire, leaving it divided, and a sneaky opportunist like Liu Bei would surely want a 'tripod scenario' so that he could use us to divert Cao away from him while he seizes Yi, Hanzhong, Liang... and then contests Cao himself once we've worn ourselves out wearing Cao out, at which point Bei becomes another decadent Han emperor that will ruin everything that has been achieved. No: Lord Sun must be the one to inherit the mandate and ascend to the Heavenly throne, and Cao Cao *and* Liu Bei must be confronted and destroyed in order for that to happen."

"...You have seen everything, Ziming," Gongjin said. "I was told by someone that you were a great mind yet to manifest, and I laughed... and when I saw reports of your attack on Chen Jiu's flagship I believed that you were a proven idiot."

"That was me being reckless, I admit," Lü Meng replied sheepishly. "I'm a front-line officer, Chief Commander, and I must act within the limitations of my role: I might have found some great strategy or sent some other man, maybe, if I was a general or a strategist, but as it was I acted in the way that I felt would yield the best outcome."

"*Ayah...* you're almost fully fledged, Ziming, that much is clear," Gongjin sighed. "Perhaps you're a brighter star than me; you're certainly shining brighter than poor Lu Zijing, who clings to that 'tripod' idea with suicidal affection. I shall be open: if that was not some great speech that you have overheard and memorised – and I know that to be impossible – then you have just shown to me your potential as my successor in the future."

"Don't speak that way, Chief Commander," Lü Meng pleaded. "My ascension would require your demise, and nobody wants that."

"You're the future, Ziming," Gongjin insisted. "I have an allotted span, though I am yet to know its magnitude: you're the man that will replace me when that day comes."

Gongjin met with Lu Su a short time later and said, "I've just had the most extraordinary conversation with Lü Meng."

"He wanted to know where babies come from," Lu Su snickered.

"...You really need to speak to the man, I think," Gongjin retorted. "I know that Ziheng really cannot stand him and makes constant demands for him to change his family name, but he is, in actuality, an unseen genius."

"Like Zhuge Kongming...?" Lu Su prompted.

"...That man is not as deserving of the Taoist name 'Crouching Dragon' as Lü Meng of Fupo," Gongjin retorted. "Zhuge Liang has done no crouching to avoid being seen: he's done nothing but postulate and brag about his 'worldly knowledge', and he gave himself that name, which makes it somewhat ironic."

"Old 'Master Still Water', Sima Decao, gave him that name, I heard," Lu Su said.

"Alright, yes, he was probably given the name," Gongjin replied dismissively. "But where has he been...? He's been on a farm in Longzhong since his family fled the fighting in Langya fifteen years ago, making the occasional visit to Xinye to debate with traders and compose poetry with the biased local literati: Lü Ziming has made the transition from brave but stupid field officer to skilled debater and deep thinker. Zhuge is overrated."

"You're hostile because he's joined Liu Bei," Lu Su supposed.

"I'm 'hostile' because Zhuge Liang's wife is Lady Cai's niece, and because *yes*, he joined Liu Bei, and furthermore I'm 'hostile' because he denounced our lord to his brother Jin when the latter paid a friendly visit," Gongjin replied.

"...But Ziyu visited Kongming to ask if he'd join us, didn't he...?" Lu Su prompted.

"...Alright, yes, it was a 'recruitment visit', and he instead chose the wandering land thief," Gongjin grumbled. "Liu Bei is a determined-yet-bumbling career criminal: no baubles interest him though, only governor's seals! 'Zhuge Kongming' chose a pathetic lord to follow and yet he is still hailed as some great genius; his friend Pang Tong the 'Young Phoenix' has the sense to hide in Jiangling and await a better man."

"...I thought that you feared Liu Bei as a future threat, though," Lu Su prompted. "How can a 'pathetic' man be a threat...?"

"Liu Bei doesn't have to be weak to be pathetic," Gongjin retorted. "Yuan Shao had four-hundred-thousand men, four conquered provinces at his disposal in addition to his ancestral territory in Runan and vast wealth to draw upon, not to mention his famous name, and yet he was pathetic, as was his brother, who – his crimes against us aside – laid claim to the throne based on a string of defeats, an imaginary Imperial Seal and some 'signs' that were fanciful interpretations of events at best; Both died pathetic deaths, Shu on a road as a beggar-fugitive with not a penny to his name and Shao surrounded by opulence while his very necessary reputation was in tatters.

"Liu Bei is a pathetic man: his entire mission in life is to become a great man when all of the powers of the fates repeatedly beat him down and try to emphasise to him that he is not worthy. He truly believes that he is chosen for great things, even to this day! He was created 'Magistrate of Anxi County' after the Yellow Turban Rebellion but lost it very quickly, while his peers were given military promotions and posts as prefectural administrators and provincial inspectors and kept them; he twice obtained Xu Province – once by deceit, again by violence – and twice lost it when he was militarily outclassed; he ended his first period as Xu's governor by being forced to retreat to Haixi City, where he spent a year under siege, eating human flesh to stay alive, before being made to pledge allegiance to Lü Bu; he ended his second tenure as a fugitive in Yu Province commanding armies of cultists and bandits for his new lord, Yuan Shao; in-between that he was a guest of Cao Cao, whose courtesy was repaid with theft when Liu Bei borrowed an army to chase Yuan Shu and didn't return it; and yet look at him now. He has, at the most, three-thousand men at his command... that's it after two terms as Governor of Xu and all that time in Qing Province serving under Gongsun Zan, and how many of that three-thousand are former Yellow Turbans and bandits...?

"Liu Bei is pathetic, Lu Zijing, because he has no dignity, no ethical boundaries, no respect for others' talents whilst possessing no talents of his own, no understanding of others' right to their own property and no end to his scheming and greed, yet he considers himself to be above good men instead of his true place, which is beneath them: he'd therefore make a perfect Han emperor, admittedly, but that's why that corrupted bloodline so sorely needs replacing."

"…You're angry and frightened, aren't you…?" Lu Su suggested. "That's why you ranted like that."

"Of course I am," Gongjin replied. "The defeat of Huang Zu is not at all, as Zhang Zhao suggested, 'the end of it'. Huang Zu's nothing: he was as pathetic as Yuan Shao if not more so, a grizzled old bandit that was gifted a prefecture and lost it by making bad decisions and placing faith in the wrong people, and so his death was inevitable and unsurprising, if a little late in coming. Now we must fight Liu Biao, Liu Bei, Liu Qi, Liu Cong and Cao Cao: even those that I dub 'pathetic' – every one of those four Lius – are still very, very dangerous, and we might suffer heavy losses against them. Cao Cao is not pathetic at all… he is, in fact, a magnificent if troubled man, and so he terrifies me."

"…You *respect Cao Cao*…?" Lu Su exclaimed. "You respect Cao Cao, but not Liu Bei…?"

"That sounds strange to you, I know," Gongjin replied. "But Cao is a gifted poet, a composer of songs, a man that genuinely respects the arts and science and medicine, even though he is now more well known for his executing Kong Rong and Hua Tuo than his saving the works of Cai Yong or defending the intelligentsia during the 'Partisan Crisis': many of my father's mentors, friends and peers were persecuted during that awful time in our history and Cao was, like it or not, a hero in his youth that preserved many valuable lives at the risk of his own."

Lu Su nodded seriously.

"Liu Bei, on the other hand, is a staunch Legalist that poses as a moderate Confucian," Gongjin continued. "He favours harsh and often disproportionate punishment for crimes, forced labour to reduce the cost of development projects and with the – perhaps sole – exception of his 'friend of the underworld', Guan Yu, he believes that men are irredeemable and would have put Jiang Qin, Zhou Tai, Zu Lang and the like to death if he had been in Bofu's place… not that he would have fought to build the south, believing it to be 'rightly underfoot' for being the birthplace of Chu."

"But he worked with Liu Pi and Gong Du!" Lu Su protested.

"Because he was *ordered to*, by Yuan Shao," Gongjin retorted. "Look at him when he is autonomous, Zijing: he put hundreds of redeemable or expellable White Wave Bandits to death when he was stationed in Xiaopei, and he was infamous further north, when he was serving under Gongsun Zan, for showing less mercy to bandits than he showed to corrupt officials, choosing to execute the former and rebuke the latter unless otherwise instructed."

"…So he cannot be our friend, then," Lu Su said involuntarily.

"So you entertain the notion that Liu and Sun can be allies, then…?" Gongjin chuckled.

"I-I-I-uh… well… … …I have misspoken!" Lu Su lamented.

Gongjin smiled and said, "You spoke as every wise man must learn to speak, Zijing: of a time beyond 'the old feud' when past differences are put aside and mutual enemies are acknowledged and united against. If Liu Biao – or, if he dies, one of his sons – loses Jing Province, then there will be no reparation: the Lius of Jing will be displaced, those that choose to fight on, and we have two choices at that point, namely leave them to fight their own battles with Cao Cao or negotiate a truce, combine our armies and oppose Cao Cao together. Liu Bei will almost certainly try for such an alliance if Jing falls, as Liu Zhang will be unreceptive and the rulers of the four independent counties unwelcoming, and Jiaozhi is too far away to reach safely if he is being relentlessly pursued. I don't want the man as a friend, but I am a pragmatist: we might need to form a temporary alliance in order to survive, but that does not mean that we blindly trust him, especially now that he has 'Crouching Dragon' Zhuge Liang at his side concocting plots that could harm us as well as Cao Cao."

"…How worried are you about Sun Ben…?" Lu Su asked.

"Very," Gongjin admitted. "He's still resentful at being passed over as chieftain; I will never rule out the idea that he was in some way involved in Bofu's assassination, the sudden illnesses and deaths of Jizuo, Lady Wu and Wu Jing, or Shubi and Bohai's murders…"

"But I thought that they were all considered to be 'unfortunate and separate matters'," Lu Su said.

"…And they probably are, Zijing, but a strategist must never rule out a possibility, else they might be proved wrong and then wrong-footed later on," Gongjin replied. "Bofu's death left the way open for Sun Ben, but Lady Wu insisted that Lord Sun Quan be the heir; Jizuo then died and Lady Wu expired not long thereafter, and Wu Jing's grief claimed him months later; that left Shubi – the preferred choice of the military – exposed, and then Bohai…"

"Yes, but as we've discussed before, everything you say points to Lord Sun Quan as much as it might point to Sun Ben," Lu Su said frankly. "But we both know that it's more likely down to Cao Cao, and his recent actions only serve to reinforce that-"

"But he has to have 'a man inside'," Gongjin interrupted. "Jizuo is dead and his widow, Lady Cao, is kept under careful watch and told nothing; Sun Ben, on the other hand, is still privy to important logistics and serves as Administrator of Yuzhang Prefecture, which, if Cao were to be allowed to seize the four counties and Jiangxia, would make Ben – Cao Cao's son's father-in-law – the gatekeeper of our most vulnerable border."

"…I do see your point," Lu Su confessed.

"He's always protesting that he's a Han loyalist and insinuating that he'd choose to betray the clan before he'd fight a Han army," Gongjin continued. "He's got a personal grudge against Lord Sun Quan, ambitions that being a Prefectural Administrator do not satisfy, and strong family ties to a man that could make his wishes come true if he is willing to undertake certain missions 'for the state'. Even if he has never betrayed us before, he has excuses and a newfound urgency to justify it now, so he will have to be watched carefully… and secretly."

"It's so sad," Lu Su sighed. "They were such a close family…"

"Yes, but that's how it's turned out," Gongjin replied. "We must do what we can to get the outcome that we want now and be satisfied with that. I will be advancing soon; you will remain at Lord Sun Quan's side until I suggest otherwise."

"As you wish, Gongjin," Lu Su said humbly.

****

69

Gongjin led an army out of northern Xiakou and moved westward toward Jiangling City; news that Liu Qi had reached the city and sent a force to secure Huarong County did little to dampen spirits.

"Liu Qi is inept, and it is who is *not here* that is important," Gongjin said to the assembled officers in his Mian County command tent. "When I heard that an army marched eastward to intercept us, I expected to hear that it was led either by Liu Qi himself or by his 'worthy uncle' Liu Bei… but the latter has obviously chosen to remain in the north of the province, most likely in his base in Xinye."

"…Why is that important…?" Commandant Ling Tong asked.

"If Liu Biao had sent Liu Bei here, it would make Liu Bei our next opponent, which is… well, suffice to say that it means that Bei is avoiding a confrontation with us, which is telling of the political situation in Xiangyang," Gongjin replied. "Word filters through that Liu Biao is gravely ill and entrusts more and more of his duties to his vassals and sons; Liu Cong is in the capital and Liu Qi is here, which should be telling for anyone that knows their classics or remembers other, more recent examples of 'succession issues'."

"…Interesting," General Dong Xi said. "Where is Cao Cao now…?"

Gongjin pointed at his battle map and replied, "The last reports placed him in Nan County, preparing to march… but this situation will be fluid in nature, and messages and gossip have a long way to travel, so we can expect updates to surprise us or force us to act quickly."

"Are we to engage Liu Qi's vanguard force at Huarong or will we show restraint…?" Lü Meng asked.

"…'Show restraint'…?" General Han Dang said with a laugh. "*You*…? My goodness, you *have* changed, A'Meng… s'about bloody time 'n'all."

"We will show caution until we know whether Liu Qi fights as governor or exile," Gongjin shouted over laughter that quickly died down. "We will do as he doubtless does: we will await more reports from the north and be prepared to advance double-time or, if necessary, retreat at speed if-"

"*Retreat*…?" Sun Jiao scoffed. "Chief Commander, we-!"

"If we face Liu Biao or one of his sons, then we advance, but if we face Cao Cao then we retreat," Gongjin insisted. "I don't like it any more than you do, but that's the plan and we must adhere to it for the sake of our great enterprise."

There were muted grumbles at the words, but every man present knew that Gongjin spoke rightly and did not challenge him further.

Liu Qi's army in Huarong made no effort to advance further; Gongjin camped close to the county capital and began plans for a field battle.

"I don't like what's being said in these reports now," Gongjin admitted as he sat in the command tent with Sun Yu. "It's looking more and more like our old enemy Liu Biao has died."

"…So Liu Cong is now the Governor of Jing," Sun Yu supposed.

"Liu Qi is still in this region as a gate guard: he would not be doing that if he were the governor," Gongjin replied. "Cai Mao and his sister must have staged a coup of sorts with the help of the court; the first question now is what Liu Qi will do."

"Will he march north to challenge his brother or accept the decision…?" Sun Yu mused. "This is the same situation that Yuan Tan found himself in six years ago."

"Indeed it is," Gongjin replied.

"And the stakes are the same, as is the clan's opponent," Sun Yu noted. "Will Liu Qi show us his back and risk running right into a trap or stay here and… and achieve *what*, exactly…?"

"Precisely," Gongjin said. "The second question is what Liu Cong will do… if he has not already done it, given that the speed at which this situation will evolve will likely be beyond the fastest of messenger's feet. Yuan Tan was the one that forged an alliance with Cao Cao to take that which had been seized and denied; in this case it is Liu Cong that will forge an alliance with Cao in order to yield that which has been gifted, so the similarities are few when examining the detail."

"You believe that Liu Cong will yield…?" Sun Yu prompted.

"Oh, certainly," Gongjin replied. "That was never in doubt; he can't fight Cao Cao. Liu Cong is neither Yuan Shang nor Yuan Tan: he is more like Yuan Xi, the middle Yuan brother that did nothing except capitulate to the other two and follow their orders. Cong will be told that he must submit to Cao Cao and he will heed the advice… some of which will be coming from our treacherous friend Huan Jie. If so, how fitting! Huan negotiated a poor deal for the return of our dead sixteen years ago, and then he defected to Jing's court so that he could later destroy it from within, ironically doing our work for us whilst feverishly working against us: Heaven's will indeed! What a pity it is that that miserable excuse for a politician does it to serve himself and places Jing in Cao's hands; but never mind, for Jing will become ours eventually, even if I don't live to see it."

"I'm sure that you will," Sun Yu insisted. "But to keep to the point, Gongjin, we are probably about to learn that Jing Province has fallen into the hands of the Han's Chancellor of State, which means that to continue our campaign would be treason if I understand the situation correctly."

"And you do," Gongjin replied. "We might receive an Imperial messenger that orders us to withdraw before more neutral reports inform us of it… or we might not. Either way, we're probably going back soon, not forward, and I'd advise you to ready your men for that without being too obvious."

"I shall," Sun Yu said. "A shame, but… there wasn't likely to be any other outcome, was there…?"

"As I have said before, we had to advance and secure as much territory as possible," Gongjin replied. "And for a myriad of reasons: we've proved to the people of Jing that we don't intend to massacre them, which will make them ready for later attempts to take the region back again; we've scared Liu Biao into a coffin and divided his army, which will leave some feeling that Cao owes us a favour, which will make his subsequent campaign against us look that bit more unfair; and we've shown how impressive we are, which will hopefully make Cao Cao cautious about engaging us too quickly and give us more time to organise… or even compel him to broker a peace, although his expensive warship-building and naval training projects make a mockery of that idea."

"But we are at war with the state now, aren't we...?" Sun Yu said.

"...We're at war with Cao Cao, who ostensibly acts for the state," Gongjin replied. "It's up to us to repel him and expose him for the ambitious hegemon that he is. I want to see my family returned to the capital and in the service of the Son of Heaven so that my father can be truly proud of me; I want to see the chaos end and stability restored; I want to see the south keep its new lustre and continue to grow. The villain Cao Cao stands in the way of all that, so we have to oppose him... we're the only ones left that can."

The news was ever-changing and startling in its nature, just as Gongjin predicted: it was reported within days that Liu Biao was definitely dead and that his second son Liu Cong had ceded the governor's seal – and as a result, Jing Province – to Cao Cao as his very first act. Cao Cao was now marching southward to receive the seal in person, seize the northern capital Xiangyang, pursue the fleeing Liu Bei and stabilise the province; Gongjin convened a meeting in his command tent to update his officials and issue new and unwanted orders.

"Now we must retreat," Gongjin said to his agitated subordinate officers. "Cao Cao has managed to obtain a 'bloodless submission': save for a few skirmishes at the northern and eastern borders, Jing is his without a serious fight. He's sent the surrendered Jing general Wen Ping southward to take Jiangxia from whoever holds it, and so we must withdraw and leave this as a battle between Liu Qi and Cao Cao."

"But we've sent men ahead to go around Huarong and attack Jiangling!" Ling Tong protested.

"They've been recalled, Commandant Ling, and I'm sure that no harm will come to them," Gongjin replied. "Liu Qi will attack nobody that brings a third party into this unless it is strategically beneficial to him."

"How far will we be withdrawing...?" Dong Xi asked.

"We'll not likely keep anything west of the River Xiang," Gongjin replied. "We'll retreat to Xiakou and let Wen Ping take this region, and then we'll see what Liu Qi does: my current estimates are that he has a loyalist army of twenty-thousand at his command – some men from the north, some from the remnants of Huang Zu's army – so we must be ready for an attempt to take Xiakou as a base for a future fight with Cao Cao for his father's lost province."

"This is ridiculous," Sun Jiao complained. "We've come all this way, and we're going back...? What about our reasons for being here...? Doesn't avenging Uncle Jian matter anymore...?"

"War is often complex and the reasons for fighting are at times prone to becoming ephemeral, Shulang," Gongjin retorted. "It is as Sun Tzu has said: you do not fight battles that you cannot win. Sometimes such battles are battles of the mind or for the hearts of the people, or simply a case of right and wrong rather than a matter of numbers: in this case it is the last of those alternatives – a case of right and wrong – that prevents us from proceeding."

"We're here because of 'right and wrong'!" Sun Jiao protested. "Uncle Jian was killed by Liu Biao and Huang Zu, and-!"

"Liu Biao is dead, and the Liu clan no longer have jurisdiction in Jing Province, so our personal reasons for being here are as dust in the wind," Gongjin retorted. "We must not oppose the Han Imperial army that our Lord Sun Quan now serves as a general. We *must* make do with Huang Zu's head and eastern Jiangxia, Shulang. We *must retreat*."

"Will Zhongmou – Lord Sun Quan – thank you for this decision...?" Sun Jiao asked pointedly. "Uncle Jian was just that, my uncle... he was Lord Sun's father, and he was like a second father to me!"

"And he was like a second father to *me*, Shulang," Gongjin insisted. "But Cao Cao did not kill Sun Jian, and Cao Cao is the lord of Jing now, him or one of his subordinates, and the Lius that we feuded with are now an irrelevance here. If the Lius are not the lords of Jing, then we now have no reason to be here; Cao Cao did not let Liu Cong keep the seal for that precise reason, Shulang, if for no other."

"Be fair to Gongjin, Brother," Sun Yu pleaded.

"...I am just angry," Sun Jiao grumbled.

"Can we not cite that 'Girdle Edict' and Cao's past crimes against the people as reasons for opposing him...?" Jiang Qin asked.

"Later, maybe, but not now," Gongjin replied. "He's got to chase Liu Bei, and it looks like Bei's got half the population of northern Jing following him: there's plenty of opportunity for Cao Cao to repeat his past crimes and give us reasons to fight him, and I'm sure that he won't disappoint."

A short, uncomfortable silence followed that was broken by Lü Meng, who said, "We should hurry if we don't want any unwanted confrontations with Cao Cao or Liu Qi."

"Indeed we should," Gongjin replied. "I am dawdling: *hurry*, gentlemen, and pass the order to retreat!"

Jing General Liu Qi watched from the walls of Huarong City as the Jiangdong infiltration unit began its withdrawal from their camp and sighed angrily, saying, "I am the eldest son of Liu Biao, and I have an army of twenty-to-thirty-thousand men, yet I am forced to watch the enemy of our clan as he saunters away, and-!"

"You do not know who will remain loyal to you, my lord," Liu Qi's campaign adviser suggested. "I was assigned to you by Kuai Yue, who is right now kowtowing to Chancellor Cao Cao after persuading your foolish, selfish brother to yield the province; I find Kuai Yue's behaviour disgusting, especially after everything that his elder brother Liang did to grow this province, and I will serve you until my death as you are the rightful governor... others are not so loyal and sensible."

"I thank you for your loyalty, Mister Che," the pale, wasted Liu Qi replied as he touched his white turban instinctively. "I can only hope that my worthy uncle escapes from Cao Cao and joins me here, and that men defect to him if they must defect to someone."

"It would be better for you to place less faith in Liu Bei, my lord," Mister Che warned. "While I do not agree with any of the decisions taken by the likes of Huan Jie, Cai Mao, Wang Can, the Pangs and the Kuais, I agree with their belief that Liu Bei is-"

"He is like a kindly uncle to me!" Liu Qi protested. "He has tried to ensure that I became the governor but could not fight my evil, vicious stepmother and her treacherous, ungrateful brother Cai Mao! If not for him, Mister Che, I would be in Xiangyang, or at least part of me would be, with the rest scattered about the province, impaled on spikes! I owe my life to the ingenuity of his adviser Zhuge Liang, who helped me understand why I must lose a battle to win a war!"

"...Let us hope that Mister Zhuge Liang's advice is part of a sound strategy for *you*, my lord, and not Liu Bei," Mister Che retorted. "Your departing Xiangyang, as I have hinted before, is perhaps a way of sparing your army for another's use, not to save you from Liu Cong. If the army is loyal – and I must admit that initial signs are positive – then what makes more sense: staying in the capital and fighting Cai Mao for the seal and the right to protect Jing from the tyrant chancellor Cao Cao, or fleeing here to provide reinforcements for Liu Bei and risk upsetting said army by forging an alliance with the Suns of Jiangdong...?"

"There will be no alliance with the Suns of Jiangdong!" Liu Qi insisted angrily. "I don't want to share the sky with them, never mind a cause! We will coalesce here, we men of Jing and Uncle Liu Bei's men, and we will resist Cao Cao and take back what is rightly ours!"

"...If that is an option, my lord, then yes, and I would support you every step of the way," Mister Che replied. "But there is talk of truces, and the Suns' army has withdrawn without fighting, so-"

"There can be no peace," Liu Qi growled. "They seized Jiangxia and murdered Huang Zu! They hounded my father to his grave! Peace is *impossible*!"

"...Perhaps," Mister Che replied.

The Inspector of Yang Province, Liu Fu, was also observing the situation in Jing Province: Hefei Fortress was now externally complete, and he wondered if it would soon be put to the test.

"Chancellor Cao Cao is worrying me with his overzealousness," Liu Fu admitted as he sat in his private study with his aide Jiang Ji. "Lujiang's capital is now Hefei in all but name: scholars now come here on their way to teach in the schools and universities, and men that once lived by the sword now live by the pen. Hefei could be a centre of learning, a beacon of hope for a peaceful future, Zitong, and yet I sense that I am about to see the beginnings of another era of senseless violence."

"But we've had this conversation so many times, Inspector, and it's always been fine in the end, and yet you visibly make yourself ill worrying about it all," Jiang Ji suggested. "I started work as a newly-graduated twelve-year-old, naïve and unprepared for all of the intrigue, and greatly overburdened and given far too much responsibility for my age because of a shortage of experienced personnel, and now, at just twenty, I feel like I have lived an age. Why would the latest developments bring war to Hefei if Sun Yi's death didn't, or Li Shu's rebellion, or-?"

"That's up to Chancellor Cao," Liu Fu replied. "He must win in order to prevent the worst of it, but... I've had Chen Lan here, expressing concern that some of his men don't want to see the government fighting the Suns. Some of the Qian Hill bandits are former associates of the Suns from their days serving Yuan Shu together, and they respect the likes of Cheng Pu, Huang Gai, Zhou Tai and Jiang Qin; the family of Zhou Yu, Sun Quan's Chief Commander, lived in the small city of Shu for a time and became popular philanthropists."

"But the bandits did not go southward and join the Suns, which suggests a limit to their respect, and Zhou Yu has made more enemies since those times by attacking Liu Xun and indirectly allowing river pirates to thrive," Jiang Ji countered. "Inspector, you worry too much at this moment: Chancellor Cao has brought an entire army down from the north after defeating the Wuhuan – the *Wuhuan* – *and* pacifying the Northern and Southern Xiongnu *and* the Qiang *and* the Yuans of Ru County! Liu Biao of Jing has died, and his son has apparently ceded the province without a fight; the Suns have ended their invasion of Jiangxia and retreated; and a small army has moved into this region in order to support the efforts of Chancellor Cao's main army in Northern Jing as they prepare to... ... ...well, it looks like they're preparing to invade Jiangdong, and-"

"Precisely, and that is not the right course," Liu Fu interrupted. "Some of the Qian Hill Bandits have family in Jiangdong, being Yang Province men; the Suns, when cornered, may push northward to seize greater control of Lujiang and Jiujiang, and Guangling's Administrator Chen Deng is ill, meaning that there could be a change of personnel in that contested region at a very inauspicious time. I'm not a well man, Zitong, and I wonder if I might not have to politely ask the chancellor if I can retire now that I have overseen the completion of-"

"You-! ...You cannot retire!" Jiang Ji exclaimed. "Inspector, there are some criminals and rebels that submitted solely because they trusted *you*!"

"I'm not immortal, Zitong," Liu Fu replied. "Sooner or later I must retire or die: the government must do more to earn the trust of the people of Northern Yang, and this nonsense standoff with Sun Quan will do little to help. Before Chancellor Cao started to move warships onto the Great River he should have considered clemency, negotiations, a *peace*: if he can make peace with the Qiang, Zhang Xiu and *Jia Xu*, of all men, then why not Sun Quan...? If he can ignore Zhang Lu's heretical 'Theocratic State of Han'ning' then why can he not ignore Sun Quan's progressive, economically strong state of Jiangdong – or 'Eastern Wu', as some folks now seem to call it...? I worry that Guo Jia's absence has left us with the Cao Cao that went to Wan City with an heir, a nephew and a bodyguard that stayed there as corpses while he came back a disgrace."

Jiang Ji hummed thoughtfully and said, "I see your point, Inspector. But Cao Cao has other advisers, and the warships might just be a way – an expensive way, admittedly – of intimidating Sun Quan, forcing him to submit without a fight."

"...I really, really hope so, but then there will be a fleet of useless warships sitting on the Great River with nowhere to go, a forest wasted on a bluff," Liu Fu replied. "I pray that Chancellor Cao still has his reason, his sanity, and that he doesn't repeat mistakes of the past... or Hefei will have the men of 'Eastern Wu' at its walls before next year has ended... or, perhaps, the disgruntled men of Liujiang tearing it down from the inside."

****

70

Sun Quan was quietly distressed when Gongjin returned to his audience hall in Xiakou and said, "It is best that you return to Chaisang, Lord Sun, and maybe go on to Qu'e from there and explain what will be a very clear situation by that time."
The officials exchanged nervous glances.
"...Is there any way that you might make it clear for me *now*, Gongjin...?" Sun Quan asked.
"In short, Cao Cao has denounced us," Gongjin replied. "He has sent a man ahead to inform us that our presence in Jiangxia is unwanted and that we should withdraw at once to avoid 'unfortunate incidents'. We've been given some time to leave the east of the prefecture – he's obviously had scouts down this way already – but we must not stay here."
The officials mumbled anxiously and looked to Sun Quan, who said, "We will leave at once, then. I will advance to Chaisang and then to- ...Wait, why am I going to Qu'e...?"
"This is the beginnings of a larger matter," Gongjin replied. "You must first defend yourself from your critics within Jiangdong before you can defend against your enemies without, my lord."
"I ask again, Gongjin, why 'I', rather than 'we', go to Qu'e," Sun Quan said. "As my Chief Commander and senior strategist, you must surely accompany me."
"I must first remain here to oversee the evacuation, and then I must go to Ba Qiu and make preparations," Gongjin replied. "You have Lu Su, Lü Fan and a host of other supporters, regardless of what happens."
"...'Regardless of what happens'...?" Cheng Pu said. "What exactly is it that you expect to happen...?"
"This is the Chancellor of *State*, Demou," Gongjin retorted. "Need I elaborate...?"
"...No," Cheng Pu replied. "I will follow Lord Sun to Qu'e once the evacuation is complete and Haihun is secured... and I expect that Zhu Junli will want to be there as well."
"I agree, Demou," Gongjin said. "I doubt that you will need to write to him."
"*Aiee*...! We were so close to... well, *something*, and now we must endure this isolation!" Sun Quan complained. "Were we fools to come this far...?"
"We had to do what we did," Gongjin insisted. "We've bought time... time we'll need. Now we must make best use of it."
Gongjin turned his gaze toward Lu Su as he spoke; Lu frowned and said, "Why the glare...?"
"Yours will be the most important task of all," Gongjin explained. "You will not be accompanying Lord Sun to Qu'e either: you will-"
"*Ayah*! **This was *your* scheme, you two, and yet you're both abandoning me???**" Sun Quan snapped as he pushed Lu Su away slightly. "**Who can explain and defend this insanity better than the two of you, mm...? Who will *want to*...?**"
"Please remain calm, Lord Sun," Gongjin replied. "I am your brother, as I was Bofu's brother... I would do nothing to cause you harm. You must *trust me*."
Sun Quan did not remain angry for long: he looked into Gongjin's

eyes, remembered the bond between their clans and smiled, saying, "I don't need to be forced to trust you, Gongjin... I apologise for my outburst. Whatever needs to be done, both of you, just do it and pay no heed to my mood. I'm just sad that- ...I'm sad, disappointed – not just for me but for us all – that we must now abandon this place after having fought so hard for it."

"We will be back here soon enough," Gongjin promised. "Cao Cao will have his initial triumph and believe that he is an uncrowned king; we will be the ones that laugh last."

Liu Qi was initially delighted when he received word that Sun Quan's forces were withdrawing and General Wen Ping was advancing; that delight was quickly replaced by more distress when he realised that General Wen was now working for Cao Cao and was planning on seizing Jiangxia for the Chancellor.

"Damn Wen Ping!" Liu Qi cried. "That faithless, wretched...!"

"...We'll need to move to some other place, my lord," the adviser Mister Che insisted. "If you remain here you risk capture or-"

"Wen Ping wouldn't dare lay a finger or blade upon me if he truly valued the trust placed in him by Father!" Liu Qi retorted. "If he has a shred of dignity, a sliver of the moral character that Father sensed when he placed General Wen in charge of troops, then he'll return to my side when he gets here and-!"

"General Wen has rebuked our messenger," Mister Che said.

"...But what you suggest, it... it cannot be so...!" Liu Qi replied.

"It is so," Mister Che said. "Pan Jun now appears to be working for Liu Bei, and that's also disturbing. Furthermore-"

"Not at all," Liu Qi retorted. "Mister Pan 'serves' Uncle Liu because he cannot be here to serve me directly: when he reaches Jiangxia he will reaffirm his allegiance to me."

"...Hopefully," Mister Che replied. "As I was saying, my lord, there is more: the prefectural administrators – Jin Xuan, Liu Du, Han Xuan and Zhao Fan – have resisted calls to pledge allegiance to you, and are at best neutral if not serving Cao Cao, who, it is confirmed, has taken the seal of office from your brother and effectively serves as Acting Governor of Jing."

"...This is a nightmare," Liu Qi groaned.

"Liu Bei is fleeing, but Cao Cao is almost certainly pursuing him, and our own decision to support Liu Bei might affect our ability to liaise with Cao Cao should we wish to later on," Mister Che suggested. "If I may, Lord Liu, we-"

"There will be no peace with Cao Cao," Liu Qi insisted. "I will save Uncle Liu as he saved me, and together we will oppose Cao Cao and his wicked band of-!"

"Oppose the Chancellor of State...?" Mister Che chortled. "He has four-hundred-thousand men, Lord Liu, and control of the Imperial court, while you now have twenty-to-thirty thousand men at the most and part of Jiangxia to call a base! We *must* consider a peaceful solution to this!"

"I would do a deal with the netherworld – as Cao has apparently done – to see Jing restored to me," Liu Qi replied. "There will be no peace... there *cannot be*."

The Chancellor of State, Cao Cao, had advanced to Xiangyang once Liu Bei's forces had fled the region with their vast civilian following; he sat in the main audience hall with his heir Cao Pi, his giant bodyguard Xu Chu and his senior advisers, Cheng Yu, Xun Yòu and Jia Xu, while he decided what he should do next. Cao Cao was pretending that he did not understand the meaning behind the sudden disappearance of 100,000 of Northern Jing's population: he laughed falsely as he examined reports on the advance southward.

"Very good…!" Cao Cao said.

"…I am glad that you are pleased with the situation, Excellency," Cao Cao's Registrar, Liu Yè – the same Liu Yè that had served Liu Xun in Lujiang 9 years earlier – said as a prompt.

"Liu Bei's destruction is only a matter of time, and I've waited long enough for that day!" Cao Cao declared. "Liu Biao… maintained this place well."

"Those two statements are both in need of a response, I think, but which response should come first, Excellency…?" the middle-aged Cheng Yu asked.

"Neither needs a response, Mister Cheng," Cao Cao insisted. "They're observations, not invitations for discussion. The only discussion that I'm interested in is how we should deal with the next target on our list…"

"…Zhang Lu…?" Cheng Yu said with false ignorance.

"…Don't pretend that you don't know who we're going after next, Old Cheng, we've discussed it often enough," Cao Cao replied. "Sun Quan *must* be toppled before I go westward in search of more demented cultists: I've had my fair share with the Yellow Turbans, and we all know that no matter how quick the battle on the field, the war with their warped minds takes far too long to be starting with that when the likes of the Qiang and the Suns are still around."

"That's not the popular view," Xun Yòu noted.

"No, but it is *mine*, and it is based on *experience*," Cao Cao retorted. "Zhang Lu is a long-term project, and he requires total isolation first."

Cheng Yu and Xun Yòu exchanged weary glances.

"…I pray that this pain in my head doesn't worsen," Cao Cao continued. "I can well do without one of my 'afflictions' in the middle of a campaign of this magnitude."

"So can we all," Cheng Yu muttered.

"I heard that," Cao Cao chuckled. "Don't worry… I won't make any mistakes. I have a piece on this chess board that will end the game very quickly: it will do so without warning, for it is of the opponent's colour."

"I presume," Cao Pi said, "that you mean S-"

"I mean who I mean," Cao Cao interrupted. "Even in this place that seems safe, my son, you should say nothing that does not need to be said."

"…He might be compromised," Cheng Yu suggested.

"Only if he's parted ways with his wits," Cao Cao insisted. "Our communications are not suspicious, his loyalties are well known, and he needs no outside help to bring this sorry matter to a conclusion: all of that is what makes it so delicious! I shall ensure that the Suns are aware of my dissatisfaction with their conduct by sending many, many denunciations, and by deploying my fleet… and then we can simply sit back and await the return of the south to the control of the Han, just as we enjoyed a near-bloodless victory here in Jing."

"And if the 'man on the inside' cannot do as you ask of him, Excellency...?" Cheng Yu asked.

"...Then we will crush Sun Quan as we crushed the Yuans, and as we crush Liu Bei right now, as we speak," Cao Cao replied. "I will win: in the end, despite any setbacks... I always do."

Many eventful days passed. Liu Bei barely escaped Cao Cao's wrath after a series of encounters that became known to history as 'The Battle of Steep-slope', but the cost to Bei's faction was high: his two adult daughters were seized during the retreat, as were dozens of trusted officials, part of his 3,000-strong militia and most of the 100,000 civilians that had placed their lives in his hands. Liu Bei finally reunited with Liu Qi in eastern Jiangxia, after which discussions began concerning what sort of fightback – if any – could take place. One of the main contributors to those discussions was the adviser Zhuge Liang, who predicted that there could be an alliance with the Sun clan if the Suns made the first move: the suggestion was generally dismissed as nonsense, but he was soon proven to be correct as hasty, improvised plans formed in the minds of the defenders of Jiangdong and one man – Gongjin's friend and former benefactor, Lu Su – prepared to be the bridge between two old enemies as they prepared to face the ambitious Han Chancellor.

****

71

Sun Quan's court was silent as he entered his Qu'e audience hall; he could sense that there were many that intended to question, rebuke or even denounce him as he sat down and looked to Zhang Zhao to start proceedings.

"Chancellor Cao Cao has, in effect, denounced the government of Jiangdong for our recent activity in Jiangxia and other parts of Southern Jing Province," Zhang Zhao reported. "Furthermore, he has stated that Lord Sun Quan's remit as 'General that Attacks Barbarians' does not, and I quote, 'include annexing neighbouring territories into Yang Province, which is itself not his to govern'. The Chancellor is willing to consider Lord Sun Quan as 'Administrator of Kuaiji', but-"

"This is outrageous!" Sun Quan complained. "I have done nothing to deserve such rebukes from the Chancellor! My forces withdrew from Jiangxia, and-!"

"They still loiter in Xiaxou and other cities in the east of that prefecture, Lord Sun Quan, and Jiangxia only tells half the story," Liu Ji suggested. "His Excellency the Chancellor is also stating clearly that all this... *all of it...* is unsanctioned."

Liu Ji's statement was met with anxious murmurs.

"...I thought we had an accord, you and I," Sun Quan retorted. "My clan did not want to harm yours. My brother-"

"The majority of the 'accords' that you have had with your vassals has been due to an ambiguity that has now disappeared," Liu Ji interrupted. "I serve here in Qu'e as a Han subject, as my father did when he was the court-appointed governor: that's not now the case if you are *defying* the court, *General Sun*."

Zhang Zhao and Zhang Hong looked at one-another nervously before turning to their lord Sun Quan, who was shaking angrily.

"...As hypocritical as it may seem, I share Liu Ji's reservations," Yuan Yao announced. "My father was a famous traitor, and I say what I have said before: I do not want to repeat the crime. My sister is your consort, and I accept that I therefore no longer have the right to speak of her, but I cannot be your vassal if you oppose the Han: my family have a long-standing reputation as Han loyalists that my father near-ruined and my uncle and his sons didn't much help either, and so I'd like to make sure that I serve a better example. If you are defying the Han – defying the Son of Heaven – by holding court here, General Sun, then please, for your own good, heed the warnings that Chancellor Cao has sent and relinquish that which is not yours before it is taken."

Sun Quan looked to his father-in-law, Xie Jiong, for support.

"...I am divided," Xie Jiong admitted. "You are my son-in-law, and I understand all of the arguments regarding Cao Cao being 'another Dong Zhuo, another Liang Ji, another Wang Mang', but... but if these denunciations come from the Imperial court, and if there is no way to unequivocally prove that this rebuke is *not* the Son of Heaven's will, then... then I cannot truly stand at your side on the battlefield."

"Nor me," Xu Sheng said. "I've come down from Wuhu to tender my Magistrate's seal, retire from service and remain in my home: I'll not serve a lord that defies the Son of Heaven, and until I know differently, I cannot serve you."

Xu Sheng handed his Magistrate's seal to one of Lü Fan's aides and left the hall.

"I can't serve either, not completely," the adviser Bu Zhi declared. "I am a Han subject also, Lord Sun Quan, and if I am asked to fight I must respectfully remain neutral and ask that I be given leave to travel."

Sun Quan looked to Lu Xun, who said, "I am unsure, Lord Sun Quan, of how to proceed: my uncle's last wishes included my serving the Han devotedly, but he also praised Lord Sun Ce's virtue at such an hour, and as well as understanding the criticism of Chancellor Cao Cao and sharing concerns about his true intent, I have much to thank you and your clan for in recent years."

"As do I," Lu Ji declared. "Cousin Xun speaks for us both: we are conflicted in our devotion to His Majesty and our loyalty to you, and must decide how best to honour both. My father would want us to do the right thing, as would my elder brother in Xuchang."

Lü Fan hummed thoughtfully.

"...And you, Mister Gu Yong...?" Sun Quan pleaded as he looked to the unreadable adviser.

"I will not confront the Han, only its enemies," Gu Yong replied. "I do not believe that you are an enemy of the Han, but I cannot state unequivocally that Cao Cao presents a threat to the court that he claims to serve, so I must ask that I be given civil administrative duties and-"

"**What's the matter with you all???**" Cheng Pu raged. "Actually, why do I ask...? **You're slimy, toadying bastards, the lot of you, eating Lord Sun's food and living the good life off of his clan's efforts to invigorate the south, and now-!**"

"*Elder Cheng*... that is not *constructive*," Lü Fan suggested.

"Listen to what they're saying! They-!"

"**Cao Cao is an obvious villain!**" Cheng Pu retorted. "**He had a pregnant Imperial consort strangled, murdered loyal friends, forced himself on grieving widows and massacred a hundred-thousand in Xu – and it looks like he's repeating that last crime at Steep-slope as we speak!**"

"There's no proof that His Excellency Cao Cao's pursuit of Liu Bei at Steep-slope bears any resemblance to his supposed actions in Xu Province," Zhang Zhao insisted.

"Hark at the worst of the crawlers," Cheng Pu heckled. "**Why are you even here, you and your brother...? You belong in Xuchang, like Huan Jie!**"

"**How dare you compare me to that dog!**" Zhang Zhao cried. "**I want what's best for the south, I always have: I only suggest that we should be conciliatory because it might spare lives and lead to a better outcome than violent confrontation!**"

"*Aiee... **enough**, both of you!*" Sun Quan pleaded. "**This is not constructive, as Lü Ziheng has rightly said!** ...If I am to yield this region – if, indeed, it is mine to yield – to Cao Cao, or, as Cao claims, to the Han, then so be it! I am here to debate the matter properly and explore options! I am here to *listen*, not proclaim!"

"Well put," Lü Fan murmured.

"...Lü Ziheng, I should like to hear more from you," Sun Quan said as he turned to Lü Fan. "What say you, as one of my late brother's oldest friends and counsel...?"

"As you tacitly state, this is Bofu's – Lord Sun Ce's – legacy that we debate as much as it is yours," Lü Fan replied. "When he began his campaign, Jiangdong was a poor and wretched place, cruelly neglected by the Han government and mostly ruled by bandits and unruly tribes. Lord Sun Ce began that campaign – including the unfortunate destruction of Liu Ji's father, Governor Liu Yao – as a vassal of Yuan Yao's father, Yuan Shu, but when Lord Sun Ce finally broke free of the traitor's grip he did not seek kingship, he sought the approval of the Han government and received it... and it is that recognition – now apparently forgotten by Cao Cao – that Lord Sun Quan inherited, not – as modern propaganda conceived by the villain Xu Gong and perpetuated by Cao Cao's allies proclaims – a conquered kingdom."

"That is true," Liu Ji admitted. "Even my father – who was, in a sense, hounded to his death by Sun Ce – spoke of Sun Ce's sincerity and lamented the Han government's attitude toward this region. Sun Ce was made a general, like Lord Sun Quan, and I believe that was an appointment approved by His Majesty, as Cao Cao was the Excellency of Works then, surrounded by enemies, rather than the 'power absolute' that he is now."

"...You insinuate that Cao Cao is now a hegemon!" Zhang Zhao said angrily.

"His benevolence is debatable," Liu Ji replied. "I must concede that or I am not a proper statesman. Tao Qian was a complex man, as you well know, Mister Zhang, but he was not a criminal as Cao Cao suggests, merely flawed, and in any case his people did not deserve what Cao's soldiers inflicted upon them... and it did happen, for many here – Mister Yan Jun, for one – know relatives and friends of the deceased and saw the corpse-dammed river with their own eyes."

Zhang Zhao's expression softened as he turned to look at Yan Jun, who said, "I have no reason to lie, Zhang Zibu: even Cao Cao himself admits to it, anyway."

"But you said that you could not serve here, Liu Ji," Zhang Zhao's brother Hong noted. "You contradict yourself!"

"Not so," Liu Ji insisted. "I will not directly oppose a Han army; I will not serve in a seceded southern government that has been denounced by His Majesty; I will, however, serve in a seceded government that has not yet been recognised by His Majesty so long as the role that I play is administrative and in no way connected to the military campaign."

"That is my thought also," Yuan Yao said. "Yes, Father was a traitor, but Cao Cao's opposing him does not make Cao a hero: the 'Girdle Edict' was dismissed by the majority, but it has never been proven to be false, and can the Son of Heaven really admit to its authenticity when surrounded by the men that it decried, men that killed his pregnant consort without a second thought...?"

Zhang Zhao exhaled fiercely.

"What about you and your brother, uh, Sun Fu...?" Xu Kun asked as he glared at his cousin.

"I came here from Yuzhang to... to assess what the mood was, discover Lord Sun Quan's intentions," Sun Fu replied. "I am unchanged in my views, Cousin Kun, as is Boyang."

"...And old man Zhu...?" Xu Kun asked as he looked at Wu

Administrator Zhu Zhi. "If you're here, who's watching our half of Guangling... or are you leaving the door open for Chen Deng and White Tiger...?"

"Don't question Junli's loyalty!" Cheng Pu snapped. **"He-!"**

"I can answer for myself, Demou," Zhu Zhi insisted. "Kun, I am as devoted to the Suns as I have always been: their faith in me has given me purpose, and I will not abandon them now. Lü Dai is managing Southern Guangling; White Tiger – or whoever inherited his kingship of the Wu Shanyue – will not aid Cao Cao after seeing what happened to the Wuhuan, and Chen Deng is either sick or dead, which has left Northern Guangling's administration at the mercy of rebels, tribes and bandits."

"...I shouldn't have doubted you, Junli," Xu Kun sighed. "Sorry."

"This is a troubled time," Zhu Zhi said as he glanced at Sun Fu. "Men are right to be cautious."

"We 'four old men' that have served since the days of Lord Sun Jian are as devoted to the clan as we ever were," Han Dang promised. "Isn't that right, Gongfu?"

Huang Gai was rubbing his beard thoughtfully; he hesitated before he replied, "That is right, Yigong... quite right."

Cheng Pu noticed Huang Gai's hesitation and apparently unenthusiastic tone and frowned disapprovingly.

"...Where are Zhou Gongjin and Lu Zijing...?" Sun Quan asked miserably; he knew where the two men might be and where they would not be, so the question was more of a lament that they were not present.

"A good question," Zhang Zhao grumbled. "Where *are* the 'great thinkers' that got us into this mess...?"

"Zhou Gongjin is at Ba Qiu, readying our navy for the upcoming defence; Lu Zijing is making preparations to cross the river," Lü Fan replied. "He-"

"To 'cross the river'...? ...*Why*...?" Zhang Zhao asked snidely.

"We must explore every option open to us," Lü Fan explained. "Zhou Gongjin has tasked him with opening a dialogue with Liu Qi and Liu Bei, so-"

The court was immediately filled with heckles and panicked questions; some of the officials flicked their sleeves in contempt and left the hall.

"Quiet, please!" Lü Fan shouted. **"How can I explain if you shout like this?"**

The deafening noise was replaced by discontented murmurs.

"...*Thank you*," Lü Fan sighed.

"I must admit that I am unhappy with this course of action, no matter how much I trust Gongjin, whose idea it is," Sun Quan said. "Liu Qi is the eldest son of Liu Biao, lord of Jing and murderer of my father, and I am told constantly that Liu Bei is a 'crafty old owl' and 'lofty schemer'; why would we want to work with such men, and why would they want to work with us...?"

"If we are to effectively oppose Cao Cao, Lord Sun, then we must do so as part of an alliance with the only men that are militarily capable of such a thing," Lü Fan replied. "They will want an alliance for the same reason that we would want one: *desperation*. Liu Biao and Liu Qi are men, one dead and one alive, kin and yet distinct in their minds and actions: Liu Qi might not necessarily desire the continuation of the feud, and he may, in fact, be truly sorry for his father's crimes, as Yuan Yao is for Yuan Shu's, and you yourself have said that such remorse might be enough to bury the matter, especially now that Liu Qi has nothing but his head to give in reparation now that Cao has stolen his province from him."

Sun Quan nodded soberly.

"Liu Qi and Liu Bei may, of course, refuse to cooperate, in which case they will die," Lü Fan continued. "But if they do want to work with us, then we can negotiate more readily with them than we can with Cao Cao, who has done nothing since seizing Jing but issue threats."

"...But I am losing support!" Sun Quan pleaded; it seemed that an official was getting to his feet and leaving the hall at the end of every sentence, and only half of Quan's court remained.

"This is a difficult time, but we must, as Zhang Zibu said, do what's best for the south, which will, in turn, be what's best for the state, for the Empire," Lü Fan suggested. "I am gathering intelligence so that we can make a proper decision, but I urge you as I have urged Elder Cheng: *listen to what is being said*! The majority of the men that refuse to serve you are refusing to leave Jiangdong as well! Even Xu Sheng, whose words verged on condemnation, noted that he would remain here in Jiangdong! Mister Bu Zhi is not asking to leave in order to join Cao Cao: he is asking to remain *neutral*! They are not abandoning you to join Cao Cao: they are refusing to serve either side until the facts are better known!"

Sun Quan looked at his reduced court; many men refused to make eye contact, but some bowed slightly as a sign of their loyalty.

"We must await the man sent by Liu Qi and Liu Bei, who will be their best spokesman," Lü Fan continued. "We'll ascertain their motives and learn of the extent of the harm done to civilians during the retreat at Steep-slope. If Cao Cao butchered them, then we must assume the worst of him and expect no different from him if we resist... or, perhaps, if we capitulated. He hasn't the best record for managing surrendered warlords, and nor does his eldest son."

Sun Quan looked to the Zhang brothers: Zhang Zhao grunted irritably and said, "We must not act until we know everything: I concede that. But don't expect me to fawn on Liu Qi's envoy, Lü Fan! I still favour submission to the Han!"

"You've made that very clear, Zibu," Lü Fan replied.

"...Very well," Sun Quan said. "We'll await the outcome of the Lius' retreat, hear them out if they want an alliance and then have one last discussion about the proper course of action."

The court session ended on a sombre and awkward note: over half of the initial attendees had already left, and Sun Quan could tell that the desertions would continue as Cao Cao's rhetoric became increasingly threatening.

✳✳✳✳✳✳✳✳✳✳✳✳

72

Sun Quan left the audience hall, retired to his study, dismissed his assistant Zhuge Jin and asked his servant Gu Li to sit with him as though he were a guest.

"That would not be proper, Lord Sun," Gu Li insisted. "I am an indentured servant, not a free vassal: would it not have been more appropriate to keep Mister Zhuge here…?"

"Indentured servant, 'free vassal'… are the roles that different…?" Sun Quan asked. "And besides, Li, you will soon pay off your family's debts and be free, will you not, with the increase in salary that I have given you…?"

"I will, Lord Sun," Gu Li replied. "But you did not answer my second question, Lord Sun: why did you want to speak with me and not Mister Zhuge…?"

"Mister Zhuge… has family among my rivals, and might not be lacking in bias when giving his answers," Sun Quan said.

"Then my ear is ready, Lord Sun, for your concerns to be voiced," Gu Li replied. "I only hope that I can help you."

"…They're a lot of them turning on me, Li," Sun Quan explained. "Pan Wengui's on his way here, and so is Zhu Yifeng, and as my closest friends and supporters I value their presence at such a horrible time. Liu Ji, Lu Xun, Lu Ji, Yuan Yao… them, they were expected. But even Gu Yong, Bu Zhi, Yan Jun…! …Even Xie Jiong, whose daughter is still my principal wife despite my innermost desires, has threatened to abandon me!"

"I have, of course, seen it all and know what's going on," Gu Li replied. "They're frightened, but as Mister Lü Fan said, they are frightened not of Cao Cao but of His Majesty the Son of Heaven, for whom Cao Cao supposedly speaks and acts."

"Cao Cao… probably murdered half my family, Li, and I *hate him*," Sun Quan said. "He was talking to Xu Gong, tried to save Sheng Xian, and demanded my boy as a hostage… and in every case, a death occurred, if not more than one. My son, my elder brother, two of my younger brothers, my mother, my uncle, and Cousin Bohai… all dead under suspicious circumstances and Cao can be linked to it all. But at the same time I'm being asked to consider an alliance with *Liu Qi*!"

"…Ling Tong will have to stomach working with Gan Ning, will he not, now that you have lost so many personnel to 'neutrality'," Gu Li suggested.

"You're right, of course," Sun Quan chuckled.

"Right, or perhaps pragmatic," Gu Li said.

"And I too must be 'pragmatic' for the sake of the state," Sun Quan replied. "If Liu Qi is truly sorry, then I must 'let it go', as I demand of Ling Tong. And if I'm honest, I can't hate Liu Qi as I hated his father; I look at Lu Ji, Lu Xun and Liu Ji and finally understand how they can work for me after my brother took their patriarchs from them so violently. But I'm scared too, to be honest, and I find Gongjin's decision to go to Ba Qiu and not come here to argue his approach somewhat odd…"

"He leaves the matter with Mister Lü Fan, who argued the case well enough," Gu Li suggested. "But your fear, that's a more problematic thing: if you, the lord of Jiangdong, cannot fight with your whole being, then the cause is already lost."

"...I feel exactly as I felt after Bofu died," Sun Quan said. "I didn't want to wear armour and inspect the troops... I wanted to crawl into a hole. And just like then, I must be seen to be strong, but... I don't want to show that kind of strength and then be forced to back down, and we might have to if the arguments for resisting are not strong enough... and I don't know what that 'show of strength' should be."

"The main point will be to assert your authority over your subjects, the second to prove your manliness in the face of a great threat," Gu Li suggested. "The 'show of strength' must refer to the problems and address them."

"...My thanks, Li," Sun Quan replied. "One day you'll be better placed to sit here with me as you do now, and I for one hope that the day will come soon."

Cheng Pu went to Huang Gai's quarters and confronted him angrily, saying, "Have you lost your nerve or something?"

"I had a thought, that's all," Huang Gai replied. "You don't have to doubt that I'm with the boy any more than you can doubt your own loyalty."

Cheng Pu's anger subsided and was replaced by obvious guilt.

"...Except that you do have your own reservations, don't you...?" Huang Gai said with a smile.

"Lord Sun Quan... doesn't command the respect that Lord Sun Jian and Lord Sun Ce commanded, because... because he doesn't deserve to," Cheng Pu replied. "There, I said it: I don't like him. But I will still serve him!"

"And so will I," Huang Gai promised. "My thought was whether the obvious rifts will be exploitable strategically."

"...Strategically...?" Cheng Pu exclaimed.

"They're either going to be a public and irrefutable sign that Lord Sun Quan's regime is crumbling – in which case the dream is over – or they'll be cleverly obscured, or in some way used to our advantage if they cannot be obscured," Huang Gai suggested. "Which will it be...? That was my thought."

"...I was thinking the same, and I'm sure that Junli'll agree as well," Cheng Pu said. "This isn't like the old days: Lord Sun Quan is a letch, a drunk, a... ... ...well, he's flawed, seriously flawed, just like Cao Cao, and that means there's little to choose between them in the end."

"Except, perhaps, that Lord Sun Quan would hesitate before forcing himself on the wives and daughters of the southern court, whereas the Caos would not," Huang Gai countered. "They none of them trust Cao Cao: that's why they've all 'retired' and 'taken leave' instead of colluding and staging an open rebellion. I half-expected that court to issue a near-unanimous demand for Sun Quan to step down, perhaps a call for Sun Ben to take over, if not outright submission... but instead – and Sun Fu, for one, was obviously unhappy about it – they all chose to voice concerns and melt away."

"I don't think that the Zhang brothers liked it much either," Cheng Pu grumbled. "Your 'demand' was still made by those two in the form of a feeble 'plea to reason' when they realised that they lacked support for something more forceful, and they won't stop trying to convince him either, they said as much."

"They're… complicated," Huang Gai replied diplomatically. "The Zhangs want what's best for the south, their home, but don't actually know what's best and aren't much better at guessing. They want a bloodless solution, and so they advocate surrendering, and they make lots of suggestions about 'Chancellor Cao' being a great statesman, but you can see that they know that Cao Cao is a monster – Hong saw it for himself before he left Xuchang, and I'm sure that his successor's reports make for uncomfortable reading."

"But if they know he's a monster, why advocate submitting to him…?" Cheng Pu despaired.

"You know why as well as I do," Huang Gai replied. "They don't really see that they can oppose 'a million men' or do anything about Cao's puppet court, so it's best to submit and have no power to do anything. 'No power' means 'No responsibility', so how is the fall of their Han in any way within their power to prevent…? …Or, to be more precise, how is the rise of the Cao clan avoidable when the Suns will not have the strength to change history if they submit…?"

"…Wretches!" Cheng Pu growled. "This is fate! How dare they take an easy road that leads to such a dark place!"

"They can't win the argument, even if the Lius send a fool to negotiate," Huang Gai insisted. "The vast majority of the men that would have argued for peace have shown that they don't trust Cao and remained neutral, which has left the sides equal: Zhou Yu, Lü Fan and Lu Su advocate fighting, as does Zhuge Jin, who has a brother in Liu Bei's employ that he worries for."

"But that is in itself worrying," Cheng Pu suggested. "Zhuge Jin's brother Liang is widely lauded in Jing as an orator, a debater… a debater that wins unwinnable arguments. In the one single case – convincing our lord to fight – I am happy to have the man here… but after that, his loyalty to Liu Bei makes him a threat."

"Worry about the threat that he 'might pose later on' later on," Huang Gai retorted. "For now, Demou, our greatest worry is Cao Cao, and after him, Sun Ben and Sun Fu, and after them, the Zhangs and their misguided advice."

"…Agreed," Cheng Pu said.

Sun Quan decided to visit his father's consort Lady Chen, who was still known to the court as State Mother Wu despite her never having attended a single court session.

"…Lord Sun Quan," Lady Chen hailed.

"No need for formalities, Second Mother," Sun Quan insisted. "I have brought no guards or aides, and am not dressed formally. I just… wanted to talk."

"I hope that I can be of help, Quan," Lady Chen prompted.

"…I don't know how much you're aware of," Sun Quan said.

"As per your instruction, a serving maid brings me news so that I could make an appearance at court and speak with some understanding of the situation," Lady Chen explained. "But there is little point, Quan: I am not a clever woman like Lady Wu, and can offer nothing beyond encouraging smiles and best wishes."

"…But… but if Mother *were* here… what would she tell me to do…?" Sun Quan pleaded.

"She would tell you to decide what to do for yourself, I think," Lady Chen replied honestly. "Cao Cao demanded your son as a hostage, as I recall, and Lady Wu complained and cursed Cao for it relentlessly; she would probably dislike the idea of yielding to a man like that, but at the same time she knew that we all of us have our limits..."

"...And that I must act within my own limits," Sun Quan sighed.

"...Basically, yes," Lady Chen replied. "But that's guessed advice from a woman that is not here to speak for the moment."

"What's your own thought...?" Sun Quan asked.

"...I would like to see Lord Sun Jian's children and grandchildren continue to thrive here in Jiangdong," Lady Chen replied. "Your half-brothers and sisters are there for you as well, hoping that you do what's best for our family."

"...I don't really involve them enough," Sun Quan realised. "Now that so many are gone – Jizuo, Shubi, and Bohai, who was like a brother – I have all the more reason to invite them to be at my side. Thank you, Second Mother, for reminding me of the large and wonderful family I have."

"And don't forget Lady Qiao, your elder brother's widow," Lady Chen added. "She visits with her little one from time to time, and she does ask after you..."

"I spend so much time scheming and leading armies that I don't get to see my family," Sun Quan lamented.

"Lady Wu did more than I do to keep us together, so I must take the blame," Lady Chen suggested.

"You're not at all to blame," Sun Quan insisted. "We're all scattered about now, since our domain is so large, and so getting together for family dinners is next to impossible; even Mother couldn't keep us all together at the end, when our reach got so large. Perhaps that's why we've... well... drifted apart, spiritually, as a family. Or perhaps not. Losing Bofu and Shubi changed things a lot too, and Ben never was nice to have around..."

"You've inherited a great burden," Lady Chen sighed.

"...Yes: now we'll see if I deserved it," Sun Quan replied miserably.

Zhuge Jin visited Lu Su's home and said, "I hope you don't mind me coming here without an invitation, what with you packing for your trip and everything."

"Nonsense," Lu Su replied as he gestured for Zhuge Jin to be seated as a guest. "I have time to speak with you, Ziyu. Tea...?"

"It is not convenient," Zhuge Jin replied humbly.

"*Ayah*... you really are the most miserable-looking man!" Lu Su said as he gestured to a servant as a request for a tea kettle.

"For once, Mister Lu, I am actually as miserable as you assume," Zhuge Jin sighed.

"What's happened...?" Lu Su asked. "Have you been dismissed...?"

"Yes... not 'from service', but I am obviously not trusted, Mister Lu," Zhuge Jin replied. "There is every chance that you will be inviting my brother back here with you, Mister Lu, and–"

"Please stop calling me 'Mister Lu'," Lu Su insisted. "I have a courtesy name that is known to you, Ziyu, as I know yours."

"...Sorry, Zijing," Zhuge Jin sighed.

"And stop being sorry! You're worse than me!" Lu Su chortled. "And yes, I might be bringing Kongming back here with me; I'm excited about meeting him, actually. But Liu Qi might have his own man to send, and it's really Liu Qi that-"

"Liu Bei's the lord of the house now," Zhuge Jin suggested. "Liu Qi is little more than a stable keeper now."

"...That's my belief also," Lu Su admitted. "But Liu Bei has other men to send, such as Jian Yong, or one of the Mi brothers that supported him in Xu Province, or his official envoy Sun Qian, who might be seen as a stronger 'bridge between lords' because his family name is homophonous to the family name of the lord that Liu Bei wants to manipulate."

Zhuge Jin smiled – which was itself a curious sight – as he asked, "Is that appraisal of Liu Bei yours or Zhou Yu's...?"

"I don't see Liu Bei as Gongjin does," Lu Su replied. "But Gongjin is a genius and I am not, so... maybe he's right, and maybe Liu Bei really is a 'crafty owl'."

"...Liu Bei might send Sun Qian, but that's unlikely, and the rest are very unlikely," Zhuge Jin said. "Sun Qian is apparently a mediocrity, and Jian Yong a crude, carefree and mischievous sort, and the Mi brothers are too closely linked to Tao Qian, who once imprisoned Zhang Zhao and Lü Fan."

"Ah, yes, that's right," Lu Su realised. "So Kongming is really the best choice...?"

"It will be Kongming that talked Liu Qi into leaving the capital as ordered and going to Jiangxia," Zhuge Jin suggested.

"Why do you say that...?" Lu Su asked. "Wouldn't asking him to stay and be there when Liu Biao died have made more sense...?"

"Liu Qi did not have the support of the officials in Jing; I could see that for myself," Zhuge Jin explained. "And Liu Bei was nothing short of hated and mistrusted. Liu Qi's loyal army – an army that Liu Bei might later lend or inherit – would remain intact and not rebel or surrender if it was not in Xiangyang when Liu Cong yielded the region. Kongming hinted as much as I was leaving."

"But that visit was over a year ago, wasn't it...?" Lu Su noted. "Kongming plans quite far in advance, then...!"

"...You'll probably find a 'kindred spirit' in Kongming as far as strategies and methods go," Zhuge Jin replied knowingly. "Just don't let him talk you into defecting to Liu Bei, mm...?"

"That could never happen," Lu Su insisted. "I owe the Suns – and Zhou Gongjin – for my life's purpose; I saw the good they did in Lujiang and Jiujiang first-hand, and I have seen their work here in the south. Yes, Lord Sun Ce did not like me, just as he did not think much of you, and we both had to wait a long time before we were given worthy roles, but I would never turn to Liu Bei, same as you."

"...If only we could sway Kongming, but it can't be done," Zhuge Jin lamented. "If he served Lord Sun, then Liu Bei would be finished and our lord guaranteed as the victor in any battle with that vile criminal Cao Cao, whose work *I* have seen first-hand; Cao Cao *mustn't win*, Zijing. He mustn't, or there will be no peace, not ever."

"I will make the necessary peace between Liu and Sun," Lu Su promised. "We will stand together against Cao Cao, and Cao Cao will lose. I've been given permission to offer condolences for Liu Biao's death... which is utterly ridiculous, but it shows that Gongjin and Lord Sun both understand the urgency of the hour."

"And on that note, I should leave," Zhuge Jin suggested.

"B-but I have requested a tea kettle!" Lu Su cried.

"It is not the time for tea," Zhuge Jin insisted as he got to his feet, bowed tersely and started a retreat from the house. "Get back to your preparations, Zijing, and get across that river: we'll have plenty of time to talk later."

Lu Su nodded soberly and bowed, and Zhuge Jin departed.

Pan Zhang arrived in Qu'e before Zhu Ran; Sun Quan had him brought to the Sun clan estate by Song Qian's trusted men and said, "Your presence is appreciated, Wengui."

"...Word's flying around that half your court's deserted you," Pan Zhang replied. "What did you do...? You haven't taken all of their women as consorts, have you...?"

Sun Quan smirked and said, "You're either oblivious or you're trying to lighten the mood."

"Of course I'm trying to 'lighten the mood'!" Pan Zhang chuckled. "Look, you lost a few toadies: better they spoke out now rather than go 'lead the way' and then run off or stab you when your back was turned. Sounds like they just don't want to take a risk with you but know that Cao's a guaranteed bad bet."

"...You put it in your own unique way, but that's what Ziheng and my servant Li have said," Sun Quan noted. "I can rely on *you*, though, can't I...?"

"You know me well enough to know that I'd have already emptied the coffers and ran, Lord Sun, if I wasn't with you," Pan Zhang replied. "Cao Cao's going to have to deal with me if he comes for you, don't worry about that: who would I be if not for you...? You're the only man that ever placed any faith in me, whether I deserve it or not, so I've got your back, your front or whatever needs covering."

Sun Quan laughed and said, "You know exactly what I needed to hear, Wengui! Yes, the hard work's yet to do, but... but with you and Zhu Yifeng on my side I feel better already."

"Is he here yet, your friend...?" Pan Zhang asked.

"Tomorrow, so he reckons," Sun Quan replied. "I'll feel better when I know I have so many trustworthy friends around me... especially when I even have family that I can't completely trust."

"Sun Ben...?" Pan Zhang guessed; Sun Quan nodded silently, and Pan added, "That's a shame. But as you say, Lord Sun, you have your friends... and we won't let you down."

****

73

Sun Fu hurried to Yuzhang Prefecture, unaware that he was being pursued: he went to Nanchang and urgently requested a private audience with his brother Ben. Sun Fu relayed the Qu'e court discussions in great detail, and as he spoke, Sun Ben became increasingly agitated and frightened.

"They...? ...**Fools!**" Sun Ben cried as soon as Sun Fu had concluded his report. "They should have surrendered straight away! ...Neutral??? How can there be 'neutrality' when the proposed enemy is the Son of Heaven???"

"What do we do, Brother?" Sun Fu fretted.

"I... ... ...well, if it's as you say, then there's no point marching on Qu'e and demanding that Quan step down, not if our only allies would be the ineffectual and unpopular Zhang brothers," Sun Ben conceded. "We're two of a very small number of isolated voices of reason, voices of *sanity* as the rest scurry off to hide and hope that His Majesty's wrath does not find them later on, or Lord Sun's in the case of the ridiculous outcome wherein he actually *wins*... but does one win against a Son of Heaven...? Did Liang Ji, the 'Ten', Dong Zhuo or the Regents 'win'...? Did Wang Mang, truly, in the end, or Xiang Yu of Chu, who tried to 'prevent the birth'...?"

"...I suppose that we have to see Quan that way, don't we," Sun Fu said hesitantly.

"What other way is there?" Sun Ben retorted. "Even if Lord Sun somehow vanquished the million-man army that Mengde has assembled, what would happen next...? Would His Majesty simply 'roll over' and allow Sun Quan of Fuchun, a low-born son of a lesser Marquis, to take control of everything south of the Great River and rule it all as a king...? ...Or would His Majesty order a second expedition, and then a third, a fourth... in fact, if any other man were to lead such a subsequent expedition but Mengde, then it would be clear that it was His Majesty's will that the south be yielded, and so Lord Sun's head would be on its way to Xuchang before the denunciation reading was complete! Quan *cannot win*! Quan *must not win*!"

"But we're alone in our thinking, or near enough!" Sun Fu protested. "There's tavern talk across Yang Province that even gives a name to Quan's 'kingdom', calling it 'Eastern Wu'! How can we help this madness to end...?"

"...I must yield Yuzhang at the proper moment," Sun Ben replied. "The Han army has already taken control of western Jiangxia and begun the establishment of small, covert bases in Changsha and Wuling... Guiyang will certainly follow."

"I hadn't heard that... how do you know that...?" Sun Fu asked.

"Isn't it obvious...?" Sun Ben scoffed. "Look how I know isn't important, it's that the situation is as such, and we have to act sensibly. You're the 'General Who Pacifies the South', which is fitting, I think: when the time is right we'll both submit to the Han and hand over our land and armies in order to facilitate a smooth takeover, just as Liu Cong has done in Jing. Without Yuzhang as a buffer, Danyang and Kuaiji's western borders are exposed, and that will be the end of Quan's little kingdom, regardless of the names that fools want to give it. We'll have restored the reputation of the Suns as loyal Han vassals and that will be that. Even if we're not rewarded, we'll have done the right thing."

"...Submission, right, to... to the Han," Sun Fu rambled. "The... the right thing, to... submit, and... rewards... right."

"Did you listen to me properly...?" Sun Ben asked. "Don't panic now at the critical moment! Let that be what the other fools do!"

"I heard you, I heard you!" Sun Fu insisted. "I... I have to submit."

"Right, at the *proper moment*," Sun Ben reiterated. "Mengde will secure us clemency... it will be alright."

Sun Fu nodded slowly as he got to his feet and left the study.

"**Remember, Fu: the *proper moment*!**" Sun Ben shouted after his confused and disoriented brother. "**We must coordinate: do not mess this up!**"

Sun Fu travelled to his barracks in Nanchang and sat at his study desk: his two eldest sons, Xing and Zhao, looked on as he picked up a pen and stared at the blank piece of paper that would soon bear a declaration of surrender to the Han government.

"...Can I do this...?" Sun Fu whined. "To... to *betray Zhongmou*...?"

"What's wrong with Father...?" Sun Zhao wondered.

"**Father...?**" Sun Xing prompted. "Father, what are you-?"

"**Leave me, please!**" Sun Fu barked. "**Go and do something, both of you, and leave me in peace!**"

Sun Xing recoiled at his father's unexpected outburst and had to be steadied by Zhao: the two young men then retreated without another word.

"...You'll forgive me later, both of you," Sun Fu whimpered as he lowered the pen into the ink post with his shaking hand. "You'll... you'll forgive me...!"

Three days passed.

A messenger hurried from Nanchang to Sun Quan's mansion in Chaisang City: Sun Quan had relocated there to better receive the man that would soon accompany Lu Su from Liu Qi and Liu Bei's temporary headquarters in Jiangxia, and he wrongly expected the messenger to be announcing their imminent arrival. Sun Quan had Lü Fan, Zhuge Jin, Zhang Zhao, Zhang Hong, Gu Yong and Zhu Ran join him in his private study, where the visibly awkward and anxious messenger would be heard.

"...Speak, man," Sun Quan ordered. "Time is against us!"

"...Report!" the messenger began at a conspicuously low volume. "I have come from Nanchang on the orders of Mister Zhu Zhi!"

"*Zhu Zhi*...?" Sun Quan exclaimed.

"Father...?" Zhu Ran murmured. "What's he doing in Nanchang...?"

"Speak, Messenger," Lü Fan said. "What has Zhu Zhi to report...?"

The messenger hesitated before he said, "M-Mister Zhu Zhi insisted that the report be read only in the most secure environment, Lord Sun Quan, in the company of the most trusted and no other!"

Sun Quan closed his eyes tightly and fought the urge to scream.

"Every man here is trusted highly," Lü Fan said. "Please continue."

"Mister Zhu Zhi... has intercepted correspondence between 'General Who Pacifies the South' Sun Fu and Cao Cao, Chancellor of State!" the messenger sobbed. "General Sun... had

communicated his intention to surrender!"
Every man groaned or gasped at the news.
"*Wretch*... **he commands thousands of my men!**" Sun Quan cried. "**He-!**"
"Lower your voice, Lord Sun, or this good messenger's efforts to help us to smother this incident are undone!" Lü Fan pleaded.
"...I... am sorry," Sun Quan sighed. "Please, messenger, go on."
"Mister Zhu Zhi has told me to stress that General Sun's letter did not leave Yuzhang," the messenger said. "He is now ensuring that Yuzhang Prefecture Administrator Sun Ben, the brother of General Sun Fu, is notified."
"I'm sure that he is," Sun Quan chuckled ominously.
"Thank you, young man," Zhuge Jin said. "You may go with Zhu Ran to receive refreshment."
Zhu Ran led the messenger out of the room.
"...Lord Sun, you must not act irrationally," Lü Fan pleaded.
"So how should he react, then...?" Zhang Zhao heckled.
"That's a grand thing coming from you!" Zhuge Jin said. "You were trying to get the entire court to do what Sun Fu has just done!"
"I was doing what I did *openly*, Zhuge Jin, publicly, and using viable arguments to present my case, not skulking off in a cowardly fashion and betraying our borders to the enemy as Sun Fu has just attempted to do!" Zhang Zhao retorted.
"At least you call Cao 'the enemy'," Sun Quan sighed.
"...In this case, Lord Sun, that is technically the correct word, although I still doubt that the Chancellor is a villain," Zhang Zhao replied. "There is every likelihood that Sun Ben and Sun Fu are acting without provocation or suggestion!"
"In a way, I hope you're right," Sun Quan muttered.

Sun Ben sat at the host seat of his Nanchang mansion's private study and stared at Zhu Zhi, who sat as a guest but had the authority of a ruler as he spoke.
"This is very difficult for me, Boyang," Zhu Zhi insisted. "I do not want to be the bearer of such terrible news..."
"I... I know that, Elder Zhu Junli," Sun Ben replied.
"But the fact is that your brother was caught with a letter that leaves the matter clear and without a shred of ambiguity," Zhu Zhi continued. "He was writing to Cao Cao to surrender."
"You... you already told me that," Sun Ben said.
"I want to make sure that you understand," Zhu Zhi replied. "There has been no slander, no entrapment... he did this terrible thing, there is no doubt about that."
"I... I acknowledge that, Junli," Sun Ben said. "What I must now ask is under what circumstances you now come here to inform me, precisely."
"...This is so very, very difficult for me, Boyang," Zhu Zhi promised. "I... I come here to urge you not to do the same."
Sun Ben nodded silently and turned his gaze away from the older Zhu Zhi; he looked to his left and realised that his eldest son Sun Lin was watching the exchange.
"This is a private meeting, son," Sun Ben said. "Please leave."
Sun Lin glared at his father as he bowed with mock humility and retreated; Zhu Zhi had turned to look at Lin, so he noticed the irreverence and was forced to say, "I did not intend to create a rift

between father and son."

"Lin is devoutly loyal to the Sun clan, so his uncle's actions will hurt, and the idea that I could have been intending to do the same would certainly divide us," Sun Ben replied.

"So you have another reason not to contemplate following your brother's path," Zhu Zhi suggested.

"...I can see that there's no fooling you, Junli," Sun Ben sighed.

"No, there isn't," Zhu Zhi replied. "You've long been disaffected: you do not do a very good job of hiding it."

"...It isn't what you might think," Sun Ben insisted. "I know what they'll all be saying, and-!"

"Who is 'they'...?" Zhu Zhi asked.

"Zhou Yu, Lü Fan, Xu Kun, to name three – but there are others!" Sun Ben replied. "They all think that I hanker for the chieftainship, like some sort of half-measure Yuan Shu! They think that I want Quan to step aside, or that I'd actually collude with my daughter's father-in-law to have it happen some other way, but I swear to you that such things are beneath me!"

"I am a long-standing supporter of the Sun clan, serving since the days of Sun Wentai, so I was there when you became acting chieftain and I was there when you stood aside for Lord Sun Ce," Zhu Zhi said calmly. "You did so with humility and dignity, so I find it very difficult to believe that you are a 'hankerer'; I doubt that 'they' think such things either. But you must nonetheless explain now that you have tacitly promised to."

Sun Ben exhaled angrily and replied, "I... I have to confess that I find Quan to be uncharismatic, uninspiring, a poor judge of character and a poor choice of successor to the chieftainship, based not on myself but on Bofu and on Uncle. There have been many reasons over the years – the drinking, the stealing, the fraternising with wasters like Pan Zhang – but there are others that are new and very much his own doing, like the rest."

"...Go on," Zhu Zhi prompted.

Sun Ben shrugged and said, "He has failed to win the respect of the army; his bungling cost us Ling Cao; his insistence on recruiting Gan Ning – Ling Cao's murderer – will probably cost us Ling Tong and perhaps more; he promotes his friends to high posts regardless of their ability – and *no*, I don't mean your son Ran, I mean Pan Zhang; and, worst of all, he now takes us on a path to direct confrontation with the Son of Heaven."

"...So you definitely intended surrender, then," Zhu Zhi supposed.

"I am a Han subject before all else, even my clan, Junli," Sun Ben retorted. "There is an unhealthy notion being peddled that suggests that we are preparing for war with 'the hegemon Cao Cao', but the decrees and condemnations come not from my daughter's father-in-law but from the Imperial court that he presides over. Yes, the demands might be unreasonable to some, but since when have the Suns been rebels...? I seem to remember a campaign to subjugate the Yellow Turbans, and another to fight Dong Zhuo!"

"Yes, and it is another Dong Zhuo that we face, Boyang," Zhu Zhi insisted. "Cao Cao is a violent, ambitious tyrant that adopts the guise of a loyal vassal in order to avoid meeting the same fate as Dong Zhuo, but what else is he...? Does a righteous man slaughter a hundred-thousand civilians in not one but two trips to Xu

Province...? Does a loyal Han subject have a pregnant Imperial consort strangled for her father's crimes when marriage changes the relationship between father and daughter and makes the daughter part of the clan that she has joined...?"
Sun Ben laughed ominously and said, "A clever move, Junli! So I am to forget my daughter – who is now a 'Cao' – and wage war on Cao Cao regardless...?"
"Lord Sun Ce's late brother Kuang was married to Cao Cao's niece," Zhu Zhi retorted. "She is now a 'Sun' and lives among us as a loyal member of the Sun clan, so I am not being unreasonable or hypocritical."
Sun Ben lowered his gaze and said, "I... I know you're not."
"Do you at least acknowledge that Cao Cao is obviously a villain...?" Zhu Zhi asked.
"...This isn't just because I have given my daughter to his clan," Sun Ben insisted. "I have seen his family, and... and I did not see the 'villain' that others have seen. He explained his past errors and transgressions quite eloquently."
"I would expect no less from a man that was educated by the very best tutors and is the son of a magnate that was adopted by a court eunuch – who was, some say, a member of the 'Ten' – and elevated to the greatest heights," Zhu Zhi retorted. "I urge you to rethink your position with regard to Cao Cao, Boyang, or you will end up on a path that will bring you into direct conflict with your own clan, and that will harm you more than fighting a tyrant Chancellor of State."
Sun Ben sat and thought for several minutes.
"...What will you do – or, more appropriately, what will you not do...?" Zhu Zhi prompted.
"...I won't submit," Sun Ben replied. "I... I know that Cao Cao is a complex man that cannot be easily fathomed, but that isn't the main point. I must choose between standing by my clan and best serving the Son of Heaven, and the latter is a difficult situation to fathom. I only ask that my brother-"
"The decision is made," Zhu Zhi said. "He is stripped of rank and will be exiled to some far-off village to live out his days in disgrace; his sons agree with the decision wholeheartedly, and so should you."
Sun Ben nodded slowly and silently.
"...I'm going now," Zhu Zhi continued. "I don't see any reason why you need to be removed from your position: you are an honest man, Boyang, and so I know that I can take you at your word."
"I- ...Yes, Junli, you can take me at my word," Sun Ben replied. "I will not write a letter of submission, and any draft letters will be destroyed. There will be no further communications leaving here and going to Cao Cao, and any letters that I receive will be ignored and destroyed."
Zhu Zhi smiled and said, "You will be proven correct in the end, Boyang; and who knows? Perhaps Cao Zhang will turn out to be a staunch Han loyalist and turn against his father, and then you and your daughter can know each other again."
Sun Ben smiled falsely and nodded.
"...I will remain in the region for a few days because I have to oversee Fu's removal and some other matters," Zhu Zhi continued as he got to his feet; Sun Ben stood up as well and prepared to

guide the elder out of the room. "I regret this, Boyang, I really do," Zhu Zhi added, "but the law is the law, and Fu has erred. If he had only made his feelings known and tried to reach a different, more amicable conclusion...!"

"Indeed," Sun Ben replied. "Now I must see Sun Fu as a brother no longer, but it was entirely his own doing. His sons shall remain as my nephews, of course, and I shall do what I can to support them at this difficult time."

"I know you will," Zhu Zhi said. "Goodbye for now, Boyang."

Sun Ben and Zhu Zhi exchanged polite bows, and Zhu left the study; Sun Lin entered the room as his father turned away and slowly returned to his seat.

"Forgive my brother, Mengde, for his haste," Sun Ben murmured. "Forgive me, too, Mengde... for how badly I've failed you. How many will die now so that Quan can play at being a king, and-?"

"Father...?" Sun Lin exclaimed. "Father, did you just-?"

"N-nothing," Sun Ben replied. "I said *nothing*."

"...Nothing."

Cao Cao drummed his fingers on the edge of his writing table as he glared at his tall, thin adviser Cheng Yu; the two were alone – save for Cao's hulking bodyguard, Xu Chu – in the command tent of a newly-established camp in the west of Wulin County, and Cao was visibly agitated.

"He's probably been discovered," Cheng Yu replied, "or perhaps he has delayed his response until such time that-"

"If Sun Ben and Sun Fu are no longer useable pawns, that... that complicates things," Cao Cao complained. "I had truly hoped that I would take Jiangdong by subterfuge, not by a prolonged campaign; I have too many enemies in the capital to be risking-!"

"Such as...?" Cheng Yu scoffed as he stroked his long greying beard. "Wenruo manages the court, and the only disagreeable men left are petty hecklers."

"...Not necessarily," Cao Cao said. "I often wonder if are a few 'Girdle Edict' plotters that I didn't catch."

"They're *hecklers*, Excellency," Cheng Yu insisted. "All of the dangerous men are dead."

"All except Liu Bei and Sun Quan," Cao Cao said. "Now I must face the prospect of both of them opposing me."

"Yes: *together*!" Cheng Yu retorted. "I know that I am continually laughed at and shouted down for saying it, Excellency, but-!"

"You are indeed 'shouted down', Elder Cheng, and with good reason!" Cao Cao said. "Those two clans have been fighting for years: how can they now forget that and fight together...?"

"Liu Bei is a deep thinker, a schemer, that has no army of his own, and Sun Quan is desperate despite his resources," Cheng Yu replied. "And remember that Lius serve in the Sun clan court, and that the feud was between one Liu – Liu Biao – and the Suns, and Liu Biao is dead. They'll join forces, Excellency: they'll join forces."

"...*Nonsense*," Cao Cao muttered.

Registrar Liu Yè entered the tent with the adviser Xun Yòu; the two bowed humbly, and Liu Yè said, "Your latest envoy has reached Chaisang safely, Excellency."

"That's something, I suppose," Cao Cao grumbled. "Perhaps Sun Quan will submit anyway when he hears of the vast army that I intend to throw at him... but I admit that I am saddened by the apparent loss of our contacts in Yuzhang."

"The letter is *a little late*, Excellency," Xun Yòu replied. "There might still be some chance of a reply... an idea of who might defect, who has left Sun Quan's court..."

"...Has that fellow that knew Sun Quan's Chief Commander been found yet...?" Cao Cao asked.

"We're still looking," Liu Yè replied. "It seems that he went travelling not long ago, but he'll be found."

"...Have him brought here as soon as he's found," Cao Cao said. "If I cannot get at the Suns, gentlemen, then I shall try their closest allies: if there is a scrap of decency left in the heart of Zhou Yu of Shu, then it can perhaps be brought to the fore and his dignity restored. Any word on either of the missing geniuses...?"

"Jia Xu's found Pang Tong: he's in Jiangling, but all the strange, ugly little man does is grin at you with those nasty little mismatched teeth and say something placatory before tottering off, or so I understand," Cheng Yu grumbled. "And as for the 'great hermit', Lou Gui, well... he's still being evasive... and rude."

"Which, coming from you, means that he's rude to the point of being impossible to work with," Xun Yòu said. "We should leave both of them be, Excellency: you have a lot of advisers, and if we needed more we can call upon Sima Yi, Xue Ti-"

"I know who they all are, Gongda," Cao Cao interrupted. "I... I wanted Lou Gui and Pang Tong, the 'Young Phoenix'... for they truly sounded like men that could perhaps match Guo Fengxiao... and not just speak to me, but *guide me*."

Cheng Yu stared at Xun Yòu, who grimaced as he recalled an earlier conversation with Cheng regarding Cao Cao's obsession with the 'unparalleled genius' of his deceased adviser Guo Jia.

"But I shall have to 'make do' with whatever Heaven places before me, won't I...?" Cao Cao chortled. "I shall have to 'make do'... and rely on my own wits a little more."

Cheng Yu was not the only man that shuddered.

❋❋❋❋❋❋❋❋❋❋❋❋

74

Sun Quan retired to his private study after another exhausting debate with his diminished court; his servant Gu Li handed him a letter and said, "Mister Zhu Zhi had this sent here while you were busy, Lord Sun."

"...He is unapologetic," Sun Quan groaned as he finished reading the short report from Yuzhang Prefecture. "My cousin Fu, who... who I once saw as a *brother*... has not a shred of guilt!"

"What will you do...?" Gu Li asked as Zhuge Jin entered the room.

"...I will do as I have already decided," Sun Quan replied coldly. "This changes *nothing*, Li. Mister Zhuge, we must be completely ready for our visitor."

"My lord, it... it will almost certainly be my brother," Zhuge Jin said. "I worry, though, because Zhang Zhao makes preparations of his own, and-"

"And with good reason," Sun Quan interrupted. "Cao Cao has sent an 'envoy' here."

"...An 'envoy'...?" Zhuge Jin exclaimed.

"A man that has been sent to politely demand our surrender," Sun Quan replied. "First appraisals of Cao Cao's military might indicate an overwhelming advantage, and I even have relatives turning against me. I am now at a 'fork in the road', Zhuge Ziyu: I must honestly consider surrender, and I honestly do, so whoever is sent here from the north must be very, very convincing."

"...And if he is *not*...?" Zhuge Jin prompted worriedly.

"I... I wouldn't hurt the man, but I would send him back to his master, and they would face Cao Cao without our support, and that would almost certainly mean death," Sun Quan replied.

"That's... quite true," Zhuge Jin realised.

"And we must be convincing as well," Sun Quan suggested. "I can't greet this man and have him see a half-empty court or hear of my divided clan... unless he already knows...?"

"I would never divulge such things to Kongming," Zhuge Jin insisted. "And Lu Zijing wouldn't either, Lord Sun: we might both desire a friendship with Kongming but we are well aware that he is Liu Bei's adviser."

Sun Quan nodded seriously and said, "Very good: go and continue your work in your new capacity as a senior minister, Ziyu."

Zhuge Jin bowed humbly and retreated.

"...And the sooner that we get you out of indenture and into my service as an official, the better," Sun Quan added as he turned to look at Gu Li. "Do you require another increase in salary?"

"I am careful, Lord Sun, and put every coin toward freedom," Gu Li replied. "You will have my help as an official very soon."

"...I'm almost tempted to force your 'owners' to cancel your clan's debt, or buy that debt from them, for the good of the south," Sun Quan admitted.

"A man without honour can never feel at peace," Gu Li insisted. "I must earn my own freedom, else I have achieved nothing."

"As the son and brother of two wrongly-indentured warlords, I will respect your desire to free yourself," Sun Quan replied wearily. "I know how you feel: I want to free myself... from this ridiculous situation that I now find myself in. My greatest opponent is my

own court... but can I beat them, even with the help of Zhuge Liang, who is sent here to rescue his lord at my expense...?"
"I cannot say," Gu Li said.

Sun Quan suddenly felt compelled to visit the "women's training camp" that his sister Shangxiang had established; they had followed him to Chaisang due to Shangxiang's desire to meet the Jing envoy and protect her brother from harm, but Quan was keen to avoid embarrassing scenes. Sun Quan was overwhelmed at the sight that greeted him as he arrived at the camp with his bodyguards: the dilapidated temple that housed the "training camp" was musty and devoid of many of the feminine contributions that he had been expecting, and the women were steely-eyed as they practiced their martial arts under his sister's watchful gaze.
"...*Ayah*... these women are formidable," Chen Wu sighed.
"I will *never* find her a husband," Sun Quan lamented. "What man would want to marry a woman that might break his neck by accident...?"
Two of Sun Quan's bodyguards stifled laughter.
"...And she is here to make trouble, and I can't have that," Sun Quan decided. "I must confront her and secure a guarantee that she will not do anything unwanted."
"That would be best, Lord Sun," Song Qian said with a poorly-hidden smile.
"...*Aiee*... even now, I am intimidated by her," Sun Quan admitted. "All of you stay back: I don't want a fight, and these women are- ...I don't believe that I'm saying this... these women believe that they are here to *protect me*, so-"
One of Sun Quan's bodyguards was unable to stop a gasped cackle; he covered his mouth, but he had made an unmistakable noise that none could ignore or fail to understand.
"...You need not fear discipline for your laughter, Gan," Sun Quan promised. "This *is* laughable."
Song Qian glared at Gan, but his own disapproving frown was cracking and giving way to a smile; the other bodyguards lowered their heads to hide their expressions as Sun Quan advanced to meet his sister.
"**Quan!**" Shangxiang exclaimed.
Sun Quan winced and said, "Yes... yes, Shangxiang, it's me. I can't stay long, but-"
"Your arms are bigger," Shangxiang noted. "Been training...?"
"...I have," Sun Quan replied. "Not as much as you, I see, but-"
"**Look at how good they all are!**" Shangxiang interrupted excitedly. "**No Jing man will be laying a finger on *these* women, or on me! Cao Cao won't be molesting me the way he molested Lady Zou! We'll *smash them*!**"
Sun Quan looked at the rows of disciplined young women in matching trousers and monk's shirts and groaned involuntarily.
"What's that mean...?" Shangxiang asked. "Why did you groan...?"
"I...! ...Look, Bofu would be glad to see that you've got what you wanted," Sun Quan replied. "It's all a bit too much for me to take in, though; my serving maids are quite 'feminine', for want of a better way of putting it, and-"
"Yeah, but what use are they?" Shangxiang asked. "If they could

all fight, like these women, then-"

"Wait a minute: that's…! …**That girl there, she's one of my serving maids!**" Sun Quan cried as he pointed at one of the women, who lowered her head in shame. "**Ren, you-!**"

"**Why are you angry???**" Shangxiang asked. "Why do you call me by my given name like that…? Why would you be angry that even your serving maids could defend you if something happened, or that we women can defend ourselves during an invasion without waiting for the help of men that might have something else to do…?"

Sun Quan pondered the point as he slowly lowered his arm.

"We've lost Ce, Kuang, Yi and Hè," Shangxiang continued. "Three of them were taken by surprise and murdered… I can't face the same happening to you."

Sun Quan smiled and said, "Thank you."

"For what?" Shangxiang asked. "I'm your sister… you're my brother… I love you, Quan, and I want to keep you alive. I won't let Cao Cao or this man from Jing cause you harm, not like-"

"About- …About that, the 'man from Jing'," Sun Quan interrupted. "I have to give the right impression. The northerners, they won't understand you: they'll see what I'm letting you do as 'weak', as a sign that I 'need women to protect me because the men are feeble', or that 'I am so feeble a ruler that I cannot even control the women', and they'll laugh."

"Let them: we'll be the last to laugh," Shangxiang retorted. "But I'm guessing that you want me to stay away from this man from Jing Province…?"

"Yes, please," Sun Quan replied desperately. "By all means continue to train these women, but don't try to intimidate this envoy; it won't help me."

"I cannot promise that I won't approach him, but I will not harm him," Shangxiang said. "I would just warn him, show him that the south has tigers *and* tigresses."

"*Aiee*… well, I can see that I must trust you to do the right thing, and that you will not heed orders or requests," Sun Quan replied. "I shall leave now… and prepare for this visitor."

"Good luck, Quan," Shangxiang said cheerfully. "You'll impress them, I know you will: you're a tiger, like every other Sun!"

"…Apparently," Sun Quan sighed as he turned and advanced toward his bemused and cynical bodyguards.

"Some of those women are very beautiful, Lord Sun," Song Qian noted. "There is something almost… attractive about their movements as they train."

"I had noticed," Sun Quan admitted. "I had, but… … …look, uh… can we go…?"

"That's your choice, Lord Sun," Chen Wu replied.

"So it is… alright, let's go," Sun Quan ordered; he clutched his forehead as he walked and muttered, "Just *please*, Shangxiang… don't make this any *worse*…!"

****

75

Sun Quan's court gathered for the historical meeting between their lord and an envoy of the Lius of Jing that had been a hated enemy for years. Cheng Pu, Huang Gai, Han Dang and Zhu Zhi were present as the last of Sun Jian's famous followers and sat close to the host seat as a sign of their respected status; Lü Fan, Zhang Hong, Zhuge Jin, Gu Yong, Yu Fan, Lu Ji, Lu Xun and Yan Jun were the most prominent of the officials that sat along the left side of the hall, although many of their number were junior administrators and student scholars that had been invited to hide the absence of the many that had deserted their lord; Dong Xi, Pan Zhang, Hè Qi, Ling Tong, Lü Meng, Jiang Qin, Zhou Tai, Xu Kun, Sun Yu and Sun Jiao were the senior representatives of the military that lined the right side of the hall, and they were noticeably less diminished than the civilian side, though Xu Sheng – who was known as a hero in Chaisang for his repulsion of Huang Zu's forces some years earlier – was notably absent.

"I hear that it's Zhuge Jin's brother that was sent," Yu Fan whispered to Gu Yong.

"Yes," Gu Yong replied. "You've heard about him...?"

Yu Fan nodded, smiled and said, "I won't challenge him."

Sun Quan entered the court: some officials gasped when they realised that their lord had selected robes emblazoned with dragons that made him look like a vassal king.

"...Lord Sun," Zhang Zhao mumbled uneasily.

"I should like food brought," Sun Quan ordered.

"...As you wish," Zhang Zhao replied.

The courtiers were perplexed and amused as they watched servants bring trays of food and jugs of wine for their lord; a group of musicians were now preparing their instruments to Sun Quan's right, and two serving maids were fanning him despite it being seasonally chilly.

"He's overdoing it," Cheng Pu muttered.

"Perhaps," Zhu Zhi replied.

"Is Lu Su here...?" Sun Quan asked.

"...He is, Lord Sun," Zhang Zhao replied. "He's brought-"

"Please have Mister Lu brought before me, Mister Zhang," Sun Quan interrupted.

Zhang Zhao was about to carry out his orders when he spotted Assistant Zhuge Jin among the senior officials; he turned, crouched close to Sun Quan and hissed, "Why is *he* sat there!? Have we promoted that donkey-faced idiot because-!?"

"Please go and fetch Mister Lu Su, or order him brought," Sun Quan replied coldly. "You'll have plenty of opportunities to have your say when he is here."

Zhang Zhao glared at Zhuge Jin as he got to his feet and shouted, **"Lord Sun Quan demands the presence of Mister Lu Su!"**

A junior official retreated from the hall to fetch Lu Su, who entered the hall moments later with a nervous expression on his face; Sun Quan noticed Lu's demeanour and feigned excitement, saying, "Zijing, you have returned safely!"

"...My lord," Lu Su said as he bowed low. "As requested, I have brought back with me Zhuge Liang, the brother of Zhuge Jin."

"'Requested'…?" Zhang Hong muttered as he turned and looked at the unreadable Lü Fan, who did not respond or meet his gaze; Hong then turned to look at his brother Zhao, who nodded seriously as a sign that he would act.

"Very good!" Sun Quan chuckled.

Zhang Zhao did not allow Sun Quan or Lu Su to continue: he stepped forward and said, "My lord! This man 'Zhuge Liang' has come to talk nonsense to you!"

The irritated Lu Su sneered and retorted, "As always, you make trouble before it is necessary, Zhang Zhao. The man is not even here with us yet."

Sun Quan had assumed that Zhuge Liang was waiting outside: the revelation that Zhuge was elsewhere puzzled and concerned Quan, who said, "Indeed, he is not with you now… why not…?"

Lu Su grinned sheepishly and replied, "I know, my lord, that you asked me to bring him here immediately, but…"

Zhang Zhao scoffed quietly.

"…I needed to be sure that things had not changed," Lu Su concluded as he glared at Zhang Zhao.

"My lord, we are wasting valuable time," Zhang Zhao said. "Cao Cao's envoy cannot be delayed forever: a decision must be made, and quickly."

"…Envoy…?" Lu Su exclaimed. "…I knew it. Zhang Zhao wants us to surrender."

"He does," Sun Quan replied uneasily; his generals voiced their disgust at the idea and at their young lord's apparent willingness to consider it.

"We can't surrender, Demou!" Han Dang whispered. "After everything that we-!"

"Hush," Cheng Pu retorted. "I think we will fight."

"Damn that Zhang Zhao!" Xu Kun hissed.

"We should have purged the court of men like him years ago," Hè Qi replied.

"But Lord Sun considers it!" Ling Tong despaired.

"He considers it… and that's all," Dong Xi insisted.

"…It was my desire to see the options that were open to us before I made a decision," Sun Quan said, "and now, Zhuge Liang of Longzhong has come to speak with us."

"…And who *is* this 'Zhuge Liang'…?" Zhang Zhao asked snidely.

Yan Jun scoffed and hissed, "He knows who-!"

Zhuge Jin silenced Yan Jun with a gesture and got to his feet, saying, "My brother. He is a genius of the age, and cannot be taken lightly."

Zhang Zhao snickered and said, "Oh…? Tell me, Ziyu, what merits this man has got, what achievements he has made, that we should call him a genius…?"

Zhuge Jin hid his dislike of the smirking Zhang Zhao with immense difficulty and replied, "He is a man of brilliant insight, and excellent at debate."

"…And this is enough to call him a genius…?" Zhang Zhao heckled. "Well, then, are not all the men in this line a genius… except maybe *you*…?"

Many of the newer members of the line of officials were students or admirers of Zhang Zhao; they laughed derisively as Zhuge Jin struggled to keep his composure.

"...Here we go," Lü Fan sighed. "This will be one of Zhang's usual put-downs. He enjoys them so, but do they help us at all...?"
Yu Fan looked to Sun Quan, who was visibly uncomfortable as Zhang Zhao began a long, scathing denunciation that had his own supporters howling with laughter and left most others feeling irritated or angry; Fan shook his head sadly.

"Did you watch the proceedings from the shadows...?" Sun Quan asked of his servant Gu Li after returning to his private study after the meeting.
"I did," Gu Li replied, "and I have to say that I didn't much like what Mister Zhang Zhao had to say or how he said it."
"But every point made was valid," Sun Quan suggested. "Zhang Zhao is spiteful, I confess, and he obviously takes pleasure from humiliating people that he deems 'deserving of denunciation', but he ultimately does it for the state, which is why I tolerate that spite. He countered the claim that Zhuge Liang is some great debater or persuader with such relevant counterpoints, Li... I had hoped that Ziyu would follow me back here to defend him, but Ziyu fled the hall, no doubt to warn his brother that he might not be warmly received tomorrow, perhaps even persuade him to quietly creep away during the night."
"If Zhuge Liang had persuaded Liu Bei to ask for – demand – a stake in Jing, then Bei would have been branded as a hankerer by Liu Biao and forcibly ejected from Xinye," Gu Li replied. "If Zhuge Liang had been able to convince Liu Cong to withstand Cao's advance, then Liu Biao's advisers would have had him silenced and taken control of the court anyway, as surrender was their obvious desire."
"...That's probably true," Sun Quan admitted. "But the flight from Xinye... Steep-slope..."
"That was an unfair portrayal," Gu Li suggested. "If the populace travelled with Liu Bei then they were more prepared to risk homelessness, poverty, sickness, famine and pursuit by Cao Cao's men than they were prepared to risk staying after what Cao Cao did to the people of Xu Province; Bei would have been unavoidably slowed by such a burden, as would any man, no matter how much of a genius he was. Zhang Zhao said that he could not do better: some small truth amid the criticism."
Sun Quan nodded slowly and said, "That's right... I remember Bofu's worries when he was forced to aid the evacuation of tens of thousands from Lujiang after he defeated Liu Xun, and that was the same, I suppose. But the battle...!"
"Numbers are only part of the equation of war, Lord Sun," Gu Li retorted. "I know little, I admit, but I listen to others speak, and that battle was never going to be won: Cao Cao was on the offensive with men that were at the peak of their morale and better trained, while Bei's men were demoralised, displaced in hostile territory, reeling from the abandonment of Xinye, and with their backs to marshlands and rivers. That Liu Bei didn't lose *all* of his men is the wonder, not that he lost half."
"But that last heckle makes sense," Sun Quan said. "Zhang said that Zhuge Liang is either a genius that is ignored or a fool that is always heeded: what other thing is there...?"
"...A man bound by circumstance," Gu Li replied.

Sun Quan nodded, smiled and said, "Like me... you're right, Li. I should not abandon the hope that this man Zhuge Liang can convince my court – and me – that we should fight Cao Cao. I will try to be open-minded... and hope that Zhang Zhao is wrong. I do not want to yield the south to Cao Cao. I want to keep it... I want to fight to keep it if that's what must be done."

Gongjin remained at his Ba Qiu residence and naval training facility while the political situation evolved in Chaisang; his wife Xiaoqiao would often sit and watch as he played self-composed melodies on his *qin* and pondered various strategies.
"...Lord Sun sent another man to ask for your presence in Chaisang," Xiaoqiao noted.
"I know," Gongjin replied as he continued to play.
"...But yet you're ignoring him," Xiaoqiao prompted.
"I am ignoring his requests for my presence because it is not necessary right now," Gongjin replied. "He has Ziheng and Zijing, and now he has Zhuge Jin as well."
"...But you're his Chief Commander," Xiaoqiao said.
"This isn't a military decision, as much as it might seem so at face value," Gongjin replied. "This is entirely political: we must enter into an alliance with the Lius of Jing or submit to Cao Cao."
"...Cao Cao is a famous womaniser that has taken advantage of the widows of his enemies," Xiaoqiao said. "I worry for my sister."
"His eldest son is a famous womaniser that takes the wives of living enemies that quickly become dead enemies," Gongjin chuckled. "I worry for you and for myself!"
"...So you do not want to submit to Cao Cao, then...?" Xiaoqiao asked hopefully.
"No, my lady, I do not, and I will do everything possible to dissuade Lord Sun," Gongjin replied as he finally stopped playing. "I did not do everything that I have done so that I could now surrender to that monster. There will be a war with Cao Cao, and whether the Lius of Jing support our efforts or not, there will be a victory for us, after which we will continue to forge our own destiny, our own state, where the Han Dynasty will have no jurisdiction until and unless it is cured of its usual malady – widespread, all-encompassing corruption that is currently embodied by Chancellor Cao Cao. And not to worry: I do intend to go, but I will do so quietly and suddenly... and very soon."
Gongjin waited for a moment to see if Xiaoqiao had anything else to say; she smiled warmly, so he resumed playing and returned to his musings.

Cao Cao was becoming increasingly impatient as he started to consider the finer points of his campaign against Sun Quan, Liu Bei and Liu Qi; he was lost in thought when Registrar Liu Yè entered the command tent, nodded respectfully toward Cao's bodyguard Xu Chu, coughed deliberately and said, "We have the latest reports, Excellency."
"...So what is there to say that's new after such a short time...?" Cao Cao asked.
"Sun Quan is confirmed as being in Chaisang," Liu Yè replied. "His entire court has moved there. His security is impressive: he obviously has a lot of very protective underlings."

"A surprise given his unpopularity," Cao Cao admitted. "And Zhou Yu... where is he...?"

"He's in Ba Qiu in Yuzhang, supposedly, where a supposedly very impressive naval training facility is located," Liu Yè replied.

"...I hear nothing of the south but 'supposedly' and 'impressive', and it vexes me, because it is too vague!" Cao Cao said. "Is there any more about the 'supposed' drain of officials from his court...?"

Liu Yè sighed miserably.

"I'm assuming that the 'mass walkouts' were a piece of disinformation," Cao Cao prompted.

"No, they are widely suggested to have happened, but... well, nobody is crossing the border," Liu Yè replied. "It seems that any walking out was not to come over to us, but to go into semi-retirement and avoid the conflict altogether."

Cao Cao grunted irritably and scowled; that scowl was slowly replaced by a smile as he said, "On the other hand, it does show that he has lost support, even if I have not gained from it, and that will do! We might not need Sun Ben and Sun Fu after all, so if the sudden lack of passion in the replies to my letters is, as I suspect, a sign that they have been put under scrutiny at the very least, it matters not. If Sun Quan's courtiers are walking away, he has an undermanned administration... and that will harm his little kingdom even if his military might is impressive. That will do! What about the other two...?"

"Liu Bei and Liu Qi are just... sitting there," Liu Yè replied uneasily.

"What else can they do...?" Cao Cao chuckled.

"They could flee southward, into the independent counties and perhaps beyond," Liu Yè suggested. "Or..."

Cao Cao frowned and said, "You haven't started to entertain Old Cheng's nonsense idea about Sun-Liu alliances...?"

"It's... not impossible," Liu Yè replied. "Liu Bei is sneaky and desperate, and Sun Quan is just desperate; Jing is lost, and with it, the 'reparation' that the Suns sought from Liu Qi's clan; yes, it seems unlikely, but we cannot dismiss the idea, not when there are schemers that can make such ideas a reality."

"...I will admit that I have always entertained the idea, mainly because Guo Fengxiao suggested it as a possibility and he was nearly never wrong," Cao Cao said. "If that alliance occurs, Ziyang, then it only grows the reputation of that magnificent man: yes, Old Cheng thought of it too, but doubtlessly after discussing the matter broadly."

Liu Yè nodded silently.

"...Watch Liu Bei and Liu Qi carefully," Cao Cao continued. "And if there's any chance of an alliance, we must adapt our plans accordingly: have Gongda and Old Cheng report to me so that I might discuss it further."

"I shall do so at once, my lord," Liu Yè replied as he bowed and began a swift retreat.

"...Liu Bei and Sun Quan, *allies*," Cao Cao chortled. "Only *I* could bring such a thing upon myself."

****

76

Sun Quan arrived at his court before his followers had fully assembled; he was once again dressed in elaborate dragon robes, and he once again requested food and drink so that he could give his visitor the impression that he was a carefree, wealthy and powerful warlord. The officials and military officers lined the sides of the halls, and Lu Su brought the Jing envoy, Zhuge Liang, into the court.

Many of the courtiers gasped and stifled curses and snickers at the sight of the 27-year-old Zhuge Liang, courtesy name 'Kongming', whose Taoist name was 'Crouching Dragon': he wore white Taoist robes, had a soft, well-kept beard, had his hair bound with a white silk turban, and carried a large, white feather fan that he waved back and forth at a slow, rhythmic pace. Sun Quan was immediately struck and quietly impressed by the apparent calmness of his visitor, despite the obvious distaste, distrust and danger that he might be facing; Lü Fan, Gu Yong, Lu Ji, Lu Xun and Yu Fan were compelled to nod slowly as they observed the young scholar-turned-adviser, and Lü Meng hummed thoughtfully and rubbed his chin.

"Whom does he mourn with his white attire: himself...?" Zhang Hong whispered.

"Let's hear him speak," Gu Yong replied.

Sun Quan was almost forced to shuffle backwards when Zhuge Liang made eye contact and smiled: there was a power accompanying the calmness that Sun Quan had not been expecting, and he suddenly felt that the visitor had won the debate before it had even started.

"...Master Zhuge Liang, my lord," Lu Su said.

"So this is the fabled 'Crouching Dragon'," Zhang Zhao heckled.

Zhuge Liang bowed slightly and said, "Lord Sun Quan."

"...You have travelled a long way," Sun Quan replied. "You must be very tired."

"I will never tire of fulfilling my lord's will," Zhuge Liang retorted.

Zhang Zhao sneered at the visitor and scoffed as his response.

"You are here to represent your lord, Liu Bei," Sun Quan said. "I should like to hear your appraisal of the situation."

Zhang Zhao smirked, took two steps forward and laughed, saying, "Perhaps we should first hear another recital of the situation of the lord of young master 'Crouching Dragon'!"

Zhuge Liang smiled ever-so-slightly, moved his gaze from Sun Quan to Zhang Zhao and replied, "Perhaps not. I expect their ears are still ringing with the sound of yesterday's session of self-indulgent cruelty at my lord's expense."

Zhang Zhao pointed at Zhuge Liang and gasped, "You...!"

"You stand there, old man, talking about me as though you know me," Zhuge Liang continued. "Would you like me to tell you what I know of you...?"

Cheng Pu smirked and snorted a laugh as he admired the visitor's frankness and unexpected retort; Huang Gai, Zhu Zhi, Lü Fan and Yu Fan shared Cheng Pu's delight, while Lu Su and Zhuge Jin were quietly worried that Zhuge Liang had only invited further cruelty upon himself and potentially jeopardised the mission.

"...I have nothing to hide!" Zhang Zhao insisted.

"No...?" Zhuge Liang replied. "...And neither do I."

Zhuge Jin turned to look at Zhang Hong, who was obviously restraining an urge to rush to his brother's defence.

"I know all about your appraisal yesterday," Zhuge Liang continued. "...And before we continue with urgent matters, it saddens me to say that we must first refute your childish claims that my lord and I are both incompetent, else there is no point in my being here."

Zhuge Liang then turned to look at Sun Quan, who said, "Go on."

"I have been in Lord Liu's service for a year and a half... that is all," Zhuge Liang explained. "In that time, Lord Liu has been the guest of Liu Biao, who gave him shelter after he was defeated by Cao Cao. For eight years, Lord Liu has served Liu Biao diligently, and defended the region from both large and small enemies. In fact – as Mister Zhang failed to note – he successfully repelled Xiahou Dun at Bowang, destroying that force and seizing Xiahou Lan as a captive... that man now works within Lord Liu Bei's service as a civil administrator. Such is Lord Liu's good nature that a member of Cao Cao's extended family now willingly works against him."

"Interesting," Cheng Pu murmured.

The majority of the officers and the more experienced officials quietly voiced respect for Liu Bei's ability to turn Cao Cao's followers against him with sound arguments; Lü Fan, Cheng Pu, the Zhang brothers and Sun Quan, however, were equally concerned that their own vassals might be swayed by Liu Bei or his cunning adviser in the future.

"...It was around that time that I first met Lord Liu," Zhuge Liang continued, "and I found him to be of good character, though perhaps too prone to trusting others."

Zhang Zhao shorted a laugh; Zhuge Liang turned to face Zhang, who then said, "Your lord is a cunning owl, whose history of defections and double-crosses is renowned."

Zhuge Liang frowned bemusedly and replied, "Really...? Relay this history to me."

"...No," Zhang Zhao replied as he stared into Zhuge Liang's eyes and found no fear or weakness to exploit. "You tell me your own interpretation."

"Very well, although it wastes time," Zhuge Liang said with apparent indifference. "Lord Liu has served Gongsun Zan – who he left without malice. He then served Tian Kai and Tao Qian in succession – each bore him no malice at the end of his service, in fact Tao Qian bequeathed his province to my lord on his deathbed. The 'famous defection' you speak of is, no doubt, my lord capitulating to Yuan Shao, which was to spare Xu Province another ravaging by Cao Cao. Had it not suffered enough...?"

Zhuge Liang paused to await an answer; Zhang Zhao scowled and growled, *"Go on."*

"From there, Lord Liu worked tirelessly against the traitor Yuan Shu, and there is not a warlord in the land that could have dealt with Lü Bu any better, especially in a disadvantaged situation," Zhuge Liang continued. "Cao Cao then took Lord Liu to Xuchang, where he learned the extent of Cao's evil... hence his next 'famous defection', spurred by an Imperial decree to execute Cao for

treason. Is there a better reason to turn on a man…?"
Zhang Zhao could sense that the officers were enjoying his suffering; he forced himself to maintain eye contact with Zhuge Liang and again growled, "*Go on.*"
Zhuge Liang smiled, slowed the speed of his self-fanning slightly and said, "From there, my lord fled the capital, was allied temporarily with Yuan Shao until he too proved his lack of true character… that is when my lord settled in Jing."
Zhang Zhao briefly turned his gaze to his brother Hong, who wanted to rise and join him in heckling the visitor; Zhao shook his head slightly and turned to face Zhuge Liang once again, although Zhuge was now looking in all directions as he spoke.
"But Jing was truly ruled by the Huang clan in Jiangxia, and the Cai clan in Xiangyang," Zhuge Liang explained. "The Cais despised Lord Liu, and sought a way to turn him over to Cao Cao in exchange for rewards… something Liu Biao objected to, but when he died, and the puppet Liu Cong took his place, fate was already written. He did not even tell Lord Liu of the plan to surrender to Cao Cao, leaving Lord Liu with no time to make plans: the people followed because they did not respect Liu Cong and the Cais, and they feared Cao Cao, whose reputation for violence is known to all. I advised my lord to seize Xiangyang: he refused, and in doing so, gained the trust of Liu Qi… so he is wise in his own right."
Zhang Zhao seized what seemed to be a mistakenly-gifted opportunity and pointed at Zhuge Liang, saying, "But then you have made a fool of yourself! If the decisions are made by Liu Bei alone, where then does your 'wise counsel' come into things…? …*Steep-slope*…?"
The room was silent as the assembly awaited Zhuge Liang's answer: Liang's brother Jin believed that a mistake had been made, but Liang suddenly looked his way and smiled slightly.
"…What are you up to…?" Zhuge Jin whispered.
Zhuge Liang turned to look at Zhang Zhao, sighed theatrically and said, "Steep-slope was a disaster. Burdened – if that is the right word – by a horde of a hundred-thousand refugees, we were caught between the dual duties of protecting the weak and fighting our enemies. Topographically, we were at a disadvantage, hemmed in by the River Han to the north and east, most flammable foliage that was as much a danger to us as our foes and therefore of no value with regard to an ambush; we had no allies in proximity, the only supplies being what we had with us, and they had to be shared with the common people. Our total force in that battle was about three-thousand, not double the size of his force, as you claim."
Zhang Zhao took one reflexive step backwards.
"…Three-thousand infantry – tired, from days of ceaseless marching – and only a couple of good generals, against five-thousand of Cao Cao's elite cavalry, on open ground in alien territory, while protecting a hundred-thousand *unarmed people*," Zhuge Liang said as he took a small step forward. "I dare say, Zhang Zhao, that you can tell me how you would have dealt with such a situation."
Zhang Hong stared at his brother, whining quietly, "*Answer…!*"
Zhang Zhao was trying to think of a clever retort, but Zhuge Liang had no intention of letting him speak; he leant forward slightly

and said, "I suspect that your answer would be the same as it is when facing Cao Cao with *thirty-thousand* soldiers, *dozens* of brave and marvellous generals, *dozens* of wise officials, the *Great River* as a barrier, *hundreds* of warships, the best navy in the land, and an ally that would stand tall if Cao Cao sent a **demon from the underworld against them.**"

Zhang Zhao was alarmed by Zhuge Liang's suddenly-raised voice and took a second step backwards.

"...Marvellous," Lü Fan whispered uneasily.

Zhuge Liang looked at every man in turn before he settled on the humbled Zhang Zhao and said in a tone that implied utter contempt, *"Surrender."*

The officers quietly voiced their approval of a man that had spoken so highly of them, even after their recent destruction of an ally of his lord Liu Bei; Zhang Zhao's supporters lowered their heads as the more experienced officials murmured respectfully; Lu Su and Zhuge Jin exchanged grateful smiles and looked to their lord Sun Quan, who was obviously happy to see a successful advocate of war with Cao Cao; but to the surprise of all, the visitor was far from finished.

"For my lord, surrender is not an option," Zhuge Liang continued. "Not just because he is noble and righteous... but because he has now been implicated in a plot to kill Cao Cao, a plot that has claimed the lives of his co-conspirators within Xuchang. That may never be forgiven... while Cao Cao lives, Lord Liu can never visit the Son of Heaven and pay His Majesty the respect he wishes to, and that breaks his heart."

The room was once again silent.

"What must be decided now in Jiangdong," Zhuge Liang concluded as he turned to face Sun Quan, "is whether surrender is an option for *you*, Lord Sun... and that, I am glad to say at last, is what I am ready to discuss."

The more astute of Sun Quan's courtiers could sense that their lord had not been as immediately impressed by a man since he first met the hustler-turned-official Pan Zhang; Quan studied Zhuge Liang intently while the stunned audience looked on in near-total silence.

"...Well...?" Zhu Zhi whispered.

"Another Gongjin," Cheng Pu replied quietly. "That frightens me."

Zhu Zhi and Huang Gai nodded agreeably.

"...What is our lord going to do...?" Zhang Hong fretted.

Lü Fan was about to answer, but Sun Quan suddenly slammed his hand onto the table in front of him, got to his feet and said, "Very good... **very good!**"

"...But my *lord*...!" Zhang Zhao bleated.

"I should like to hear your thoughts in private, Mister Zhuge Kongming," Sun Quan announced as he walked to Zhuge Liang and extended his hand; Zhuge took Quan's hand and followed Quan to his private study for further discussions.

"...*Ayah*! This is a disaster!" Zhang Zhao muttered as he retreated to the line of officials and sat down amid taunting stares and whispered comments.

Sun Quan nodded toward his servant Gu Li upon entering his study; Gu Li retreated but remained hidden so that he could listen to the conversation. Sun Quan then gestured that Zhuge Liang should sit as a guest as he said, "I was very impressed by the way you dealt with Zhang Zibu."

Zhuge Liang smiled humbly as Sun Quan took his own host seat and replied, "I did not mean to rebuke him so harshly."

Sun Quan laughed dismissively and said, "He brought it on himself. He is always lofty and confrontational... but enough. You can obviously speak for a long time and fight a good debate: now all I ask from you is a simple summary of where you think I should go from here."

Zhuge Liang laughed and replied, "Well then, in that case, this will be quickly said. You have but two choices: resist, and surrender.

"Fight, and you will have the assistance of Liu Qi of Jing, and Lord Liu Xuande. They will fight Cao north of the Great River, while you confront him on the water. With the right scheme, he can be defeated: but even if he cannot, you will have at least tried to maintain your dignity, and you can improvise a plan for peace. If we win, then we can destroy him once and for all, restore the Han, and bring peace to the entire land.

"Surrender, and you will be forced to send your son to the capital to serve as a hostage: you will later be summoned to court yourself, and be labelled a dissenter and a traitor if you refuse, justifying a punitive expedition against you that you will face alone. You will lose your land, and be at the beck and call of Cao Cao, who will command you to send gifts and pay respects, and supply him with anything he demands: if you do not believe me, you need only look at Liu Zhang of Yi, who is now nothing more than a supply warehouse for Cao Cao. You will no longer be a master of your own domain: you will be a vassal to another lord...

"That is all there is to say... it is your choice."

Sun Quan was silent for a short time as he considered Zhuge Liang's words; he eventually replied by saying, "My father lived - and died - a vassal to Yuan Shu. My brother despaired at his lack of ambition: all I have is earned, by me or by my brother. I would be a ruler, free of others, and fairly govern all below the Great River. ...But Cao Cao boasts of *eight-hundred-thousand men*..."

"...A boast, nothing more," Zhuge Liang insisted. "Forgive my frankness, but only fool pedants who know nothing of the world would believe it."

Sun Quan smiled warmly and said, "Your lord is lucky to have a man such as you in his service... your brother spoke highly of you, and it is deserved."

"I simply do what I can," Zhuge Liang replied with humility.

Hours passed in which Sun Quan and Zhuge Liang discussed many matters; Zhang Zhao and Zhang Hong were openly distressed at the apparent ease with which the envoy from Jing had won their lord's confidence and confronted Lu Su and Zhuge Jin about it in Lu Su's office.

"This is worse than when he was taken in by Pan Zhang!" Zhang Zhao complained. "At least Pan is one lone wretch; this man brings with him three-thousand hankerers, liars and fools that will want Jiangdong as their base now that Cao Cao has denied them Jing Province!"

"You were outmatched and dislike it," Lu Su retorted. "But face facts, Zibu: Cao Cao is a villain, and we'll have to fight him sooner or later."

"...Your donkey face wears smiles uneasily, and rightly so!" Zhang Zhao said as he turned his wrath on Zhuge Jin. "This brother of yours condemns us to three, four, who knows how many years of bitter warfare with the Han government, war that will cost us everything, and all because his lord Liu Bei is-!"

"I won't lie to you, Zibu: I don't trust Liu Bei any more than you do," Zhuge Jin interrupted. "But we must find allies somewhere, and they are often men that we would sooner pass by without acknowledging; the point here is not our choice of allies but our choice of enemies. Liu Bei has no mass murder on his conscience, while Cao Cao harmed Xu Province not once but twice, damming rivers with the corpses: that is an irrefutable fact. Kongming's account of the chase at Steep-slope evokes memories of the violence in our home province that forced us to move to Jing, and that was Lü Bu and Cao Cao fighting over neighbouring Yan Province, so Cao's not learned a thing."

Zhang Zhao hesitated.

"And Kongming deliberately refrained from mentioning that Liu Bei's co-conspirators were not the only casualties of that coup being thwarted: remember that a pregnant Imperial consort died too and be glad that he didn't raise that and use it to full effect," Zhuge Jin continued. "Kongming is trying to be conciliatory."

"...I can see that," Zhang Zhao admitted. "But what he proposes is military suicide! Cao Cao's envoy boasts-!"

"I know the numbers boasted," Zhuge Jin interrupted. "'Eight-hundred-thousand'... Kongming insists that Cao Cao does not have such numbers and I believe him, mainly because he's a student of the Art of War that knows that you do not fight unwinnable battles unless they are completely unavoidable, and even then you do so as a fighting retreat."

"And this battle *is* completely unavoidable, Zhuge Jin, by submitting to the Son of Heaven and ending this fool's dream of a reborn state of Chu!" Zhang Hong protested. "They're all calling the late lord Sun Ce 'The Little Conqueror' in Xuchang, implying that he is Xiang Yu reborn, and adding that Lord Sun Quan wants to build on that, defying the Han: is that what we want, mm...?"

Zhuge Jin remained silent and looked to Lu Su.

"...No, but times are changing, and we must accept those changes," Lu Su said. "I have spoken at length to Kongming, and he has – completely separately, I might add – come to the same conclusion as I have, namely that Liu, Sun and Cao will each control a piece of the fractured Empire until such time as one of them outwits the others and restores order. He, of course, favours maintenance of the Han through the incumbent or through his lord Liu Bei; I see a different outcome, as does Zhou Gongjin. Admit it, both of you: the Han has lost all of its lustre and teeters on destruction. You, Zigang, have seen it with your own eyes as our envoy to Xuchang, so you know it."

Zhang Hong harrumphed irritably, but his failure to respond properly was telling.

"In ten years' time it will be a Cao on the Imperial throne, and will the south prosper then...?" Lu Su asked. "Will *anywhere* thrive, I wonder, with an afflicted, lecherous, ill-tempered, genocidal tyrant on the throne...?"

"...My resistance to Cao Cao is, I admit, based principally upon the threat that he poses to the people and the state that we have built here," Zhang Zhao replied. "Of course I wonder if the 'Girdle Edict' – another thing that 'Kongming' only alluded to – was legitimate, but with no way of knowing it must be spoken of as false! We cannot do what Yuan Shao did when he opposed Dong Zhuo, for unlike that occasion there is no regicide to avenge! A pregnant consort is not the same as a murdered prince! Accusations of puppetry are no substitute for forced abdication!"

"The unborn prince – or princess, perhaps – in Consort Dong's belly is as dead as the Prince of Hongnong, so there is a murder of royalty, therefore a regicide," Zhuge Jin suggested. "Kongming tries to avoid discussing that matter because it makes him weep with anger, but discuss it with me he did, and he's right; he's also right to say that the 'accusations of puppetry' *are* at least parts of the same problem as forced abdication because one tends to eventually lead to the other in a cycle of control, and Cao Cao obviously controls His Majesty, else it would have been Cao, not Consort Dong, that died that day, for the crime of high treason."

"...And your brother will no doubt be telling Lord Sun that very thing as we speak," Zhang Zhao said bitterly. "All of it is conjecture, supposition: he asks that we act without *certainty*!"

"So do you," Lu Su countered. "You admit that yourself."

Zhang Zhao turned to leave, saying, "If our lord is convinced that we should fight, then so be it; it will be because that's the right thing to do. But he must then convince the officials and, more importantly, the officers of his ability to lead such a campaign. This is not another petty criminal like Huang Zu that harmed the lord and the people of the south and deserved retribution, and whose army matched ours in size and strength, which gave any of the Suns the ability to lead and be followed with passion; this is the Han Chancellor, who commands an army and navy of a far greater magnitude, has an Imperial mandate to march and who, despite his 'reputation', has no bad personal connection to the southern people. None of the people – not even the generals – can be expected follow such a path blindly... they will only follow the strong."

Zhuge Jin waited until Zhang Zhao and Zhang Hong had departed before he turned to Lu Su and said, "He's right, you know. How will Lord Sun show his ability to lead the army – the people – to where we'd have him go...?"

"That's up to Lord Sun," Lu Su replied miserably. "At least Kongming is making it easier, but Gongjin will have to help as well... and he will be here soon..."

"He's on his way?" Zhuge Jin exclaimed. "When will he arrive...?"

Lu Su smiled and said, "Very soon."

＊＊＊＊＊＊＊＊＊＊＊

77

Lu Su was visited by a messenger with a letter from Gongjin on the very next morning; he hurried to Zhuge Jin's home and said, "Gongjin will be here tomorrow!"

"*Tomorrow...*?" Zhuge Jin exclaimed. "When you said, 'Very soon', I thought-!"

"He wanted to keep his movements a secret in case of spies, I presume," Lu Su said. "He has not bringing much with him, just his wife, his qin, and some books."

Zhuge Jin frowned thoughtfully.

"He won't be here to oppose Kongming," Lu Su insisted. "He wants this war as much as the rest of us."

"I worry less about his objections to war and more about his objections to my brother, who will doubtless worry him," Zhuge Jin said.

"Gongjin is a pragmatist, yes, but he also has immense respect for intelligent men such as Kongming: he even respects *Cao Cao*, solely for the man's creative accomplishments," Lu Su replied. "Kongming is quite safe. Anyhow, I have been invited to speak with Lord Sun as well, so... I'd best be off."

"...Good luck," Zhuge Jin murmured.

Sun Quan smiled as Lu Su walked into his private audience room. "Please, sit!" Sun Quan prompted.

Lu Su sat as a guest facing Sun Quan and awaited his words.

"...Zhuge Kongming is a great talent," Sun Quan began. "It is a pity that he has chosen to serve a future rival of mine."

"You do not need to fear Kongming," Lu Su insisted. "He is trustworthy, as is his lord. Both have been given a bad reputation by people like Zhang Zhao... they are doing their best in difficult circumstances."

"Zhuge Kongming has suggested that I can only fight or surrender, which is obvious enough," Sun Quan said. "He has pointed out that I will be reduced to a worthless nobody were I to surrender... but still, to fight... what do you think...?"

"I hear that Gongjin is on his way here to discuss this matter with you in person," Lu Su replied. "But you know what I think...? ...I think that it's easy for Zhang Zhao and the others to surrender... you can't."

"How so...?" Sun Quan prompted.

"It's very much as Kongming has already said," Lu Su replied. "You may be called to court... you may be exiled... you certainly wouldn't live as you do now. You would have to live as a vassal of the court... you might even be eliminated."

"...True," Sun Quan supposed.

"While your officials – yes, like Zhang Zhao – may keep their positions, or even be rewarded by Cao Cao for convincing you to surrender," Lu Su suggested further.

"...Again, you are right," Sun Quan murmured. "It's just that... it is a big decision to make, one that could result in a massive loss, death... suffering to my people..."

"Talk to Gongjin," Lu Su urged. "He'll be here soon enough."

Sun Quan nodded slowly.

"…I'll go and see Kongming again in a few days, but for now I've let him be at Gongjin's suggestion," Lu Su continued.

"Why is he still in a hotel…?" Sun Quan asked.

"For the same reason that he was put there in the first place: it is seen as inappropriate for him to stay with his brother, given his role as a 'foreign envoy'," Lu Su replied. "Kongming is very comfortable, and his brother visits him daily."

"…Very good," Sun Quan said. "But I say again, I want that man to serve in my court one day: he is wasted on Liu Bei!"

"We can only hope," Lu Su replied. "Is that all, my lord…?"

"You should go now, Zijing, and await more correspondence from Gongjin, since he is avoiding direct contact with me for now," Sun Quan ordered. "If I need you, I'll call for you."

Lu Su got to his feet, bowed humbly and departed.

"…**Li**," Sun Quan bellowed.

"I heard everything, but what is there to say…?" Gu Li replied as he entered the room from a hallway.

"I… I want Gongjin to persuade me now," Sun Quan said. "This decision, it is so important, that… that I need to know that I have Gongjin's full support, that he has no doubts, that… that we can definitely win."

"Nothing in life is certain," Gu Li suggested. "Did Cao Cao think that he could lose at Wan City…? Did Liu Bei think that he could win at Bowang Slope…?"

"…You really are a keen mind, Li," Sun Quan said. "But all the same, I must hear from Gongjin. *He* must be certain, or *I* cannot be certain."

Lü Fan visited Gongjin as soon as the latter was installed in his Chaisang mansion; Gongjin welcomed his old friend and colleague, had him sit as a guest and asked, "Before we get down to pleasantries and business, I must ask: why do you not demand that you play a greater role…?"

Lü Fan smiled dryly and replied, "This is your moment, Gongjin. I have my own role to play, but we must keep our 'friends' and enemies guessing. They are both convinced that Cheng Pu and Zhou Yu are their main military concerns, and that's how it should be, and besides, I'm Chief Treasurer now, amongst other things, and I was always more comfortable with administrative matters, pedant that I am. I'll be there, but in the shadows, as you'd prefer, in case of the worst occurring… am I right…?"

"…Yes," Gongjin said. "In the future, I see Lü Meng and Lü Fan being the men that will contest the enemies of the south."

Lü Fan laughed and replied, "A year ago – or even a few months ago – I'd have insisted that you were joking! But Ziming has turned into a magnificent genius… who'd have thought it…?"

Gongjin smiled.

"But then I should scold you for talking about the years beyond your span," Lü Fan continued. "Why are you so obsessed that you will not see the end of the road…?"

"Cao Cao is vindictive, and his son is the same if not worse; Liu Bei is sneaky and ruthless, and his followers will do whatever it takes to get him the throne that he secretly covets," Gongjin explained. "The main obstacle to the ambitions of either faction is the south, and that obstacle is currently embodied not by Lord

Sun Quan but by Zhou Yu of Shu, sworn brother of Sun Ce the 'Little Conqueror', architect of 'Eastern Wu, the reborn kingdom of Chu', as some now say. You've probably done more than me to make this all happen, Ziheng, but it is only *my* name that is uttered in shadowy corners, though only Heaven knows why."

"...It's not escaped me, though I don't really care one way or the other," Lü Fan replied. "As you say, it means that Lord Sun has a 'Crouching Dragon' of his own that actually remains hidden."

Gongjin smirked and said, "You weren't impressed with Zhuge Liang, then...?"

"I was extremely impressed," Lü Fan replied. "That's the problem: he's obviously very talented, though he mostly relied on bluff, dramatics and wrong-footing his opponents by drawing them in with false unguarded statements, which isn't really that difficult, especially when your opponent is Zhang Zhao. He's possessed of that usual northern attitude that we somehow don't know anything that happens in the north unless it directly affects us, as evidenced by his referral to famous events as though he felt we'd be ignorant of it all... though that might have been a ruse to have us think that *he* knew nothing of *us*, I suppose."

Gongjin rubbed his chin and hummed thoughtfully.

"He plays the qin and composes poetry, as you know: that was not a false fact," Lü Fan continued. "His wife, though reputed to be ugly and uninteresting, is actually said by some to be quite the opposite, though not perhaps a match in beauty for Lady Qiao."

"Mm, yes... I know the tale of how he chose his wife for her wits, caring nothing for her looks, and that she had her family falsely report her as unattractive to deter men that only cared for such things," Gongjin replied. "It's all very romantic. Perhaps I should feel shallow for not seeking the same, but I enjoy beauty, whether it be music, art, or the woman I have at my side, and I have peers with which to converse, so my lady's inability to discuss military matters with me is actually refreshing; it means that I actually rest when I go home."

"...You've thought about that quite a bit," Lü Fan noted.

"A man like Zhuge Liang – 'Kongming' – is critical of others, and he will no doubt criticise me for not putting brains before beauty when I chose Lady Qiao," Gongjin replied. "He's bound to think it even if he doesn't ever say it. But he's not perfect: choosing Liu Bei as a lord aside, he doesn't, as you say, live up to Master Still Water's Taoist name for him at all. 'Crouching Dragon'...? ...He's done nothing but advertise his existence, to the point that people actually started to doubt whether he was really that clever at all. And yet he's actually very clever indeed; a little arrogant, maybe, though he doesn't realise it, but clever – not unlike me when I was his age. He obviously worried that he would be missed and die an unknown: how Jing's reputation for valuing talents is overrated, then, and how little he thought for Liu Bei's ability to see talented men underneath that devoted exterior!"

"...There's less than ten years between you," Lü Fan noted.

"We'll both die young!" Gongjin chuckled. "Now then: is there anything else I should know before I meet with him ahead of speaking with Lord Sun...?"

"You're going to meet with him before...?" Lü Fan prompted.

"It's going to be a bit difficult to have this alliance without working closely with Liu Bei's chief strategist," Gongjin retorted. "Honestly, Ziheng, you've been spending too long in the treasury with-"

"I knew you'd meet him later on, but not before you met with Lord Sun," Lü Fan explained. "Why would you want to do that...?"

"Liu Bei has one of two plans in mind, but Zhuge Liang will have at least three, and I have ideas of my own," Gongjin replied. "The alliance will be announced at some point by our actions: I need to know what form the alliance will take and when its existence will be made known, for it affects our overall strategy. Does Bei want to cross into Jiangdong, or does he want to try and stay in Jing for the sake of his 'nephew' Liu Qi and the army that belongs to that sickly mediocrity...? If he chooses to stay where he is, does he then expect military aid from Jiangdong that will drain resources from our own defensive efforts, or will he stand alone, and if so, why...? I will then have to answer sternly in order to ensure that the actions taken benefit us at all times."

"So we're in agreement, then," Lü Fan said with relief. "Oh, and on the subject of awkward rivalry... Lord Sun has asked me whether Gan Ning should be retrieved from his place of exile."

"Has he not been retrieved already...?" Gongjin exclaimed. "We need every capable man we can get! Ling Tong must understand and accept that!"

"...Again, we agree," Lü Fan said. "I'll have Gan brought to Chaisang at once and politely warn Ling Tong that he should put personal feelings aside, just as Lord Sun does by making peace with Liu Qi."

"And I shall prepare for my meeting with 'Kongming'," Gongjin replied. "In a way, I look forward to meeting a like mind, and in another, I am apprehensive, for I might well see in him the man that will be the undoing of everything that we are trying to achieve... a man that I might one day need to kill or, out of necessity, be killed by. Heaven has a cruel sense of humour."

Lü Fan sighed and said, "I won't argue with that."

Two days passed: Lu Su visited Gongjin to report recent events.

"*Ayah... ayah...!* Gongjin, she...! *...Ayah!*" Lu Su whined as the smirking Gongjin led him to his guest seat and had him sit down.

"...'She' is Lady Sun," Gongjin guessed.

"She...! *...Ayah!*" Lu Su replied. "Can Lord Sun not...?"

"...Not *what*, Zijing...?" Gongjin chuckled. "Better yet, instead of telling me what Lord Sun should do, why don't you tell me what *she* has done? Has she caused a ruckus in the market again...?"

"Worse!" Lu Su replied. "She... she *threatened Kongming*!"

Gongjin's smile disappeared.

"She came to the hotel while we were talking and *threatened him*, said, 'Don't cause trouble' or something like that!" Lu Su continued. "She walked around him, glaring at him, looking him up and down, and she had a *sword*, Gongjin: a *sword*!"

"... ... ...*Ayah*...! ...Is she mad...?" Gongjin groaned as he put a hand to his face; he then looked up and saw that Xiaoqiao was standing in a doorway with her mouth covered to hide her laughter. Gongjin shook his head disapprovingly, and Xiaoqiao retreated.

"She didn't attack him, but... but...! *...Ayah!*" Lu Su said miserably. "He says he's alright about it, that his wife is a handful, or maybe I used that word and he used some other phrase, but... but what if we need to have *Liu Bei* over here at some point...? He's a Legalist, Gongjin, that thinks that women are- ... ...What's he supposed to have said...?"

"...That 'brothers are like arms, and women like shirts'," Gongjin replied as he lowered his hand from his face. "No, that's a problem: Shangxiang cannot threaten envoys with swords... I'll speak to Lord Sun about it. But he's alright...?"

"Kongming...? Yes, yes, he seemed to be more bemused than anything," Lu Su said. "He quickly returned the conversation to meeting you and Lady Qiao."

"He specifically said *both of us*...?" Gongjin exclaimed; he then glanced at the doorway and saw that Xiaoqiao had returned and was now smiling warmly, her urge to laugh having subsided.

"Yes," Lu Su replied. "Is that a problem...?"

"No... it's just unusual," Gongjin said. "But at the same time, it fits with my plans. Perhaps he hopes to persuade me to fight by reminding me of Cao Cao's lecherous ways while my lady is nearby... but don't I already know about them...?"

"He said as much," Lu Su replied. "He knows that you're a smart man, maybe as smart as or smarter than him. I think he said something about wanting to see your 'togetherness'..."

"...Unusual," Gongjin murmured. "He's... quite unique, or at least rare, in his thinking; in some ways stubborn to the point of painful predictability, and yet so broad in thinking that he has the ability to surprise. I shall have to be extremely cautious, for he might actually outthink me at some point."

"...You get all that out of him asking to meet your wife...?" Lu Su exclaimed. "How...?"

"It's... look, never mind that," Gongjin replied. "Bring him here tomorrow afternoon and monitor him until then, in case Lady Sun's irrational behaviour has caused him concern and led him to ponder fleeing in the night or something."

"Y-yes, alright," Lu Su said. "Really, Gongjin, she...! ...*Ayah*."

Lu Su got to his feet, bowed and retreated at speed; Gongjin then gestured that Xiaoqiao should enter the room and sit at his side.

"Will I be present for your meeting...?" Xiaoqiao asked.

"...I don't know what he has in mind," Gongjin replied. "Is he spiteful...? Will he try and humiliate us by showing that you do not match his wife's supposed ability to debate important matters...?"

"Why would he do that...?" Xiaoqiao asked. "If he's as clever as you and Mister Lu Su suppose him to be, then wouldn't he want to befriend you, not antagonise you...?"

Gongjin hummed thoughtfully, smiled, patted Xiaoqiao's hand gently and said, "I'm supposed to be the smart one, but you are correct and I am wrong in this instance, my lady. I am allowing my own self-doubt to cloud my judgement; perhaps that is what he intended, or perhaps I am too neurotic for my own good. No, my lady, we shall meet him tomorrow and behave normally as the loving couple as we are. Whatever his intent, we shall be honest and welcoming."

Xiaoqiao smiled and said, "I look forward to it."

★★★★★★★★★★★★

78

The next afternoon arrived more quickly than some would have preferred: Lu Su brought Zhuge Liang to Gongjin's mansion as arranged. One of Xiaoqiao's serving maids reported the approach of the two men, at which point Gongjin smiled, pulled his qin closer to his legs and started to play.

"...Are you not going to greet them in person...?" Xiaoqiao asked as she took a seat by her husband's side.

"A game of chess has begun," Gongjin replied as he strummed. "We might shift the battlefield to a lively debate, or a real chess board, as Lü Fan did when he recruited himself to Bofu's cause... or perhaps he will see an opportunity to find accord."

Gongjin nodded toward a low table on one side of the room; a second, older qin was placed atop it.

"...I think that I understand," Xiaoqiao said. "But I'll leave the thinking to you."

Gongjin smiled and replied, "Hopefully, my lady, Lu Su will as well... and, if I am very lucky, so will Zhuge Liang."

Gongjin continued to play; he was still playing when Lu Su led Zhuge Liang into the room. Zhuge Liang was calmly fanning himself and smiling as he entered, but he was visibly stunned by Xiaoqiao's beauty: he gasped and halted sharply at the sight of her. Lu Su smirked knowingly but said nothing.

"...My apologies," Gongjin said as he finally finished playing and sat upright: Xiaoqiao smiled warmly, and Zhuge Liang smiled awkwardly in response.

"...Shall I leave you to speak, my lord...?" Xiaoqiao asked.

Gongjin smiled and nodded, replying, "We shall be discussing banal things... yes, why not retire...?"

"I shall fetch some tea first," Xiaoqiao said: she got to her feet and retreated, and Gongjin turned his gaze to his guests. Zhuge Liang was watching Xiaoqiao as she left the room; Gongjin was as amused as his visitor's unguarded behaviour as Lu Su was.

"...So, Zhuge Kongming," Gongjin hailed with a slight bow, "it is good to meet you at last. Was your journey pleasant, and how do you find our land of Jiangdong...?"

"...Beautiful," Zhuge Liang replied with a tone that implied that he was awestruck.

"...The journey, or the land...?" Gongjin asked pointedly.

"...Uh... the land," Zhuge Liang replied as he finally regained his senses. "I was surprised by the humidity... it has been some years since I visited the land with my brother... some years ago. ...Oh, and the journey was fine, thank you... the Great River was calm, thank goodness...!"

"Unlike the times we live in," Gongjin said wistfully. "Please, friends, do not just stand there... be seated."

Zhuge Liang and Lu Su took guest seats opposite each other; Gongjin studied Zhuge with interest, as his behaviour now matched the calm, unreadable man that he had heard about. Once both men were seated, Gongjin sighed and said, "I understand that your lord Liu Bei is taking refuge in Jiangxia at the moment, after an unfortunate loss in the Steep-slope region of Dangyang County. Cao Cao is a force to be reckoned with... after so many successful victories against so many opponents whose strength vastly exceeded his, one might wonder who could stop him."

"...I think the answer lies in numbers," Zhuge Liang replied; his eyes were obviously turned to Gongjin's expensive qin as he spoke. "Not just soldiers, but also the number of heroes willing to face him together."

"But what heroes do you speak of...?" Gongjin asked as Xiaoqiao returned with a tea kettle. "Once, there was not just my own lord and yours, but Yuan Shu, Yuan Shao, Liu Biao, Liu Yan, Han Sui, Ma Teng, Gongsun Zan... now, Ma Teng is a willing lackey of the court, and the rest are dead, and their sons are either dead as well or willingly bent at the knee, grovelling to Cao Cao and ceding their territories."

"Liu Qi, eldest son of Liu Biao, will fight to regain what is rightfully his," Zhuge Liang replied. "...The question, then, since my lord Liu has no choice but to fight... is what your lord Sun will do."

Gongjin was silent: he realised that Zhuge Liang – who was fanning himself slowly with his large white feather fan – was now staring at the qin in order to avoid looking at Xiaoqiao.

"Do you play...?" Xiaoqiao asked as she stared at Zhuge Liang, who reluctantly raised his eyes to meet hers as she started to pour tea.

"...I do, my lady," Zhuge Liang replied awkwardly, "though not as beautifully, I regret, as Zhou Gongjin."

"Sometimes, it is not the beauty of the playing, but the content, and the intent," Gongjin suggested. "Would you like to play a tune now...? I have another qin... we can harmonise... or at least, we can try to."

Zhuge Liang obviously understood Gongjin's words to be a challenge: he smiled, nodded, and put his fan to one side. Gongjin got to his feet, walked to the table where the second qin was placed and took it in his hands, saying purposefully, "This qin was my first... but then I acquired another. The new one is more elaborate in design yet less hardy, but then, it is still a qin, and only as good as the notes one chooses to play. Each has its own qualities, like the lords I have served."

Xiaoqiao moved the tea tray so that Gongjin could set the second qin down in front of Zhuge Liang's legs: he then returned to his own seat, readied his own qin and said, "Well, then, shall we...?"

Zhuge Liang nodded, and the two started to play as Xiaoqiao took her place next to Gongjin once again, despite having said that she would retire.

The two musicians quickly harmonised, finding a common thread in their work that married calmness, dedication, tumultuous strides, rousing crescendos, and short, continuous rhythmic strums that evoked the march of thousands to battles unknown. Lu Su and Xiaoqiao sat and watched, awestruck at the power in the music being played: Gongjin studied his rival as he played, smiling at the grace with which the younger man met and matched his work and added his own touches that brought more to the piece and enlivened it. Gongjin was determined that he should be in control of the music, and Zhuge Liang was obviously aware of it: Zhuge made no move to conclude the work in any way, choosing to keep the pace and await Gongjin's signal that they should start to wind it down. Gongjin waited until he had heard what he had wanted to hear, at which point he began to strum notes that implied an imminent end; Zhuge Liang followed his lead, and the piece came to a graceful halt, having allowed the two strategists to learn more about each other than any debate would have managed.

"Magnificent," Lu Su said. "...Simply magnificent...!"

"...You are very good," Gongjin said to Zhuge Liang with absolute sincerity. "Your mind and mine are, I think, in accord on what must be done. My thanks for your visit, both of you: it has been most productive."

"...Wait, what...?" Lu Su exclaimed. "But... what about-!"

"I will speak with Lord Sun," Gongjin added, "and I will enthuse – in the strongest possible terms – the need for our cooperation – Sun, and two Lius – in facing down the tyrant Cao Cao."

Zhuge Liang nodded silently and picked up his fan.

"Now," Gongjin said, "let us discuss some of our shared learning!"

Zhuge Liang fanned himself and laughed.

Lu Su escorted Zhuge Liang to his hotel after the small banquet that followed the initial meeting; Gongjin sat with Xiaoqiao and stared at his qin, prompting Xiaoqiao to ask, "Why do you not play, husband...?"

"I am robbed of inspiration," Gongjin admitted. "Zhuge near outplayed me a few times there... I must improve still further."

"...He seemed nice enough, but very shy," Xiaoqiao said.

"He was annoying me at first with his inability to look at you without bordering on lechery, but he's young, and you robbed *me* of my wits when we first met," Gongjin recalled. "I was surprised, actually, at his ineptness; can it be that the 'Crouching Dragon of Longzhong' can have his guard so easily lowered by a beautiful woman after all that is said of him...?"

Xiaoqiao giggled awkwardly.

"I am embarrassing you," Gongjin continued. "Zhuge did not come here to play music and talk about whimsical nonsense, as nice as it was to have such a break from the daily urgencies: he came here to debate and prove his and his lord's absolute dedication to this endeavour. I have the information that I needed to know: Liu Bei will not turn Cao's attention toward us and then flee, nor will he ask for asylum and then expect us to protect him. We will fight separately at first, only coordinating when it will have the most impact; we will feign division where there is unity and unity where there is division, and do the same for strength and weakness, as Sun Tzu has taught. The south will dictate the strategy, just as I dictated the music we played, and Liu Bei will follow; with that assurance, my lady, I can go to Lord Sun and tell him to fight with absolute certainty."

"...And then you will leave," Xiaoqiao prompted.

"I will... though hopefully not for long," Gongjin replied. "If Cao Cao is as impatient and stubborn as I sense, he'll insist that his navy attacks us in winter, and that means that the w- ...Well, anyway, it means that we will have certain advantages, and I'll say no more for fear of jinxing us. No, my lady, there will be no long, drawn-out war on the Great River... nor will there be a victory for Cao Cao. It will all begin soon: all that is left to do is reassure the army that we have a tiger lord in Lord Sun Quan, and

I'm sure that he can find the strength to convince them once I have shown him my own resolve. It all begins soon..."

When Sun Quan heard that Gongjin had not only returned without the proper announcements but spoken with Zhuge Liang before either the court or Quan himself, his reaction was discomfort.

"Has Gongjin lost the will to fight...?" Sun Quan asked of his servant Gu Li. "Has his resolve faded, and he now needs others to convince him to fight...? If so, then how will he convince me, and I the court...?"

"I wouldn't worry, my lord," Gu Li replied as he tidied Sun Quan's writing desk.

"*Sit down*, Li!" Sun Quan pleaded. "I can't talk to your back!"

Gu Li turned and said, "I am not your counsel, Lord Sun. I don't mind being a ready ear, but I haven't the right to be giving advice, and I doubt that your actual counsel – including Zhou Yu – would take kindly to finding that I was doing so."

"...I suppose so," Sun Quan sighed. "Perhaps I should summon Lü Ziheng... but he suddenly seems to be reluctant to serve me wholly again, as he did when I first became the lord of this region, when he thought that I-! ...That... well, you may already know from overhearing things, but... I stole treasury money once, when I was young, and Lü Ziheng reported me to my brother."

Gu Li hummed ambiguously.

"It was the making of me, what he did," Sun Quan continued. "Any other man would have allowed me to get away with it and allowed my moral character to deteriorate as a result, but he had the courage to do the right thing... which is why his reticence scares me. Does he believe that I should surrender...?"

Gu Li pondered the question for a moment and then smiled, saying, "I'll answer *that*, Lord Sun: if he is the man that you assume him to be, then he would have come here and told you as much, not remained silent."

Sun Quan nodded slowly and said, "You're right. He-!"

"A letter from Chief Commander Zhou, Lord Sun!"

Sun Quan winced at the bellowing voice of the messenger that had suddenly arrived: Quan nodded toward Gu Li, who took the letter and passed it to him before dismissing the messenger with a nod and a polite smile.

"... ... ...He will come to the court tomorrow!" Sun Quan said excitedly. "He will come to the court and...! ...But he makes no mention of his decision."

"Security, no doubt," Gu Li replied.

"...No doubt," Sun Quan muttered. "If the likes of my cousin – who ate at my table and slept on a bed no further from me than you are now – could betray me, then he is right to show caution. But what will he say...?"

Gu Li shook his head and replied, "I cannot know."

"...*Please*, Gongjin," Sun Quan whispered, "save what we have built together, you and my clan; save *it*, and save *me*."

* * * * * * * * * * * *

79

Gongjin visited the Sun mansion audience hall on the following day: there were many officials and officers assembled, and the atmosphere was tense.

"**Gongjin!**" Sun Quan cried.

"...So he is here after all," Cheng Pu murmured.

"Yes, but what will he say...?" Han Dang retorted.

Gongjin's eyes briefly met Zhang Zhao's scathing gaze before he looked at Sun Quan and asked, "May we speak privately...?"

Zhuge Jin lowered his head and sighed quietly.

"...Yes," Sun Quan replied.

"Why can he not speak before us...?" Ling Tong wondered.

"...Because he must be sure that the response fits the occasion," Lü Meng replied.

Sun Quan gestured sternly, and the courtiers silently departed. Once the court was empty save for servants and guards, Sun Quan turned to Gongjin and said, "Shall we go to the private audience room...?"

Gongjin nodded and followed his lord; Lu Su – who was one of the last to leave the hall – hurried to the hotel that Zhuge Liang was residing in to warn him that the moment of truth had arrived.

"He must not tell our lord to fight!" Zhang Zhao whined as he reached the courtyard.

"We may have no choice," Zhang Hong admitted at last. "Cao Cao... is *mad*."

Zhang Zhao shuddered.

"Cao Cao asked me to return here to *spy* on Lord Sun, citing my 'loyalty to the Han' as the reason for me being the best choice, though my trusted status here has more to do with it, I think," Zhang Hong revealed. "He called Lord Sun's behaviour 'confusing' and tacitly asked – ordered – that I work to undo Lord Sun's court from within, 'for the Han'. I agreed, but only because I truly wondered whether I would see Jiangdong – or, indeed, another day – if I refused."

Zhang Zhao's eyes wandered.

"I'd say it to other but you," Zhang Hong continued. "He's mad: he had Kong Rong – one of the last descendants of Confucius, and a fine scholar in his own right – dragged away and beheaded for a barbed comment to our envoy, and then killed Kong's family as well. He had Hua Tuo beaten to a pulp and then executed for refusing to become his personal physician. You know the rest."

"...And my response, brother, is equally said to no other but you," Zhang Zhao retorted. "I know what we're up against, and I maintain that we should not fight for that very reason! Lord Sun Quan will not be able to command the respect and discipline that would be required to mount such a defence, and if we lose the consequences will be beyond what one wants to think about!"

"I... see that, which is why I have stood by you," Zhang Hong said. "But we must be aware that we are isolated and that Zhou Yu will probably advise fighting. Will you walk away as others have done if that is the case...?"

"No," Zhang Zhao replied without hesitation. "If that is what is

best for the south, then I will fight loyally and without reserve."
Zhang Hong smiled and said, "As will I."

Cheng Pu, Huang Gai, Han Dang and Zhu Zhi were gathered in another part of the courtyard; Cheng frowned and said, "Zhou Gongjin is one of the finest men in the south, and so I don't doubt that his decision will be the right one."
"I never thought I'd ever hear you say that Zhou Yu was anything but a pedant or worse," Han Dang chuckled.
"...It's as I've said before," Cheng Pu replied. "He's like a fine wine that is hard to take to initially but grows in its appeal; I feared that he was a typical northern snob that came to the south out of necessity and yet secretly pines for the north and its ways; but I come from the north, brought here by necessity, and I sometimes think of home, and yet you will never find a more southern man than me. He's the same: this is his home, the Suns are lord and family, and he'll do whatever it takes to keep this place safe. Even if he advocates surrender, I'll abide by his decision."
Huang Gai hummed thoughtfully.
"But he won't, though," Han Dang protested.
"No, I don't believe that he will," Cheng Pu replied.
"He won't," Zhu Zhi insisted. "The south can only survive if it fights, and he knows that. We will fight."

Ling Tong, Dong Xi, Lü Meng, Jiang Qin, Zhou Tai, Yu Fan and Hè Qi gathered together in yet another part of the courtyard; they were as concerned about the legacy of their previous lord, Sun Ce, as the older men were for the work done by Ce's father.
"My father can't have died for nothing!" Ling Tong complained.
"He didn't," Zhou Tai insisted. "Lord Sun is not going to yield to Cao Cao."
"...There's word that Gan Ning is on his way here, that he's meeting his friend Su Fei outside Chaisang and then coming here," Jiang Qin said. "Are you alright with that, Gongji...?"
Ling Tong was silent for a moment before he sighed and replied, "It means that we're going to fight, so I must see the greater good beyond the obvious negatives."
"You won't try and kill him again, will you...?" Yu Fan asked.
"...I will try to stay away from him, and I will try to avoid becoming angry if I am forced to be near him or speak with him," Ling Tong replied. "That's the best that I can do, Mister Yu."
Hè Qi glared at Zhang Zhao and Zhang Hong – who were isolated save for a few of the younger scholars – and said, "Would those two accept us fighting...?"
"At worst, they'll 'retire', as the likes of Bu Zhi, Xu Sheng, Liu Ji and Yuan Yao have done, and that's no big loss," Dong Xi replied.
Hè Qi turned his gaze toward Lü Fan, Gu Yong, Lu Xun, Lu Ji and Yan Jun, who were gathered together nearby with some other members of the civilian administration; Qi frowned and said, "I wonder what they think. They don't stand with the Zhangs, but they don't say much either..."
"I am 'one of them', if you will, and I can assure you that they want to avoid Cao Cao seizing power here," Yu Fan replied. "They'll fight."
"...But if Lord Sun is seen to be weak, don't we risk another

rebellion in the ranks, another 'Li Shu Incident'...?" Ling Tong asked. "Father was upset at what happened, but he admitted that he understood Li Shu's 'confusion', as Lord Sun Quan was... well... not the popular choice."
Hè Qi and Yu Fan hummed ambiguously.
"...He will need to show strength," Lü Meng said. "That said, most will fight because they want to protect the things that they hold dear, not because they were impressed at some small show of strength by Lord Sun."
"Zu Lang's here," Dong Xi noted; the group turned as one to watch as the former bandit leader entered the courtyard with two scowling subordinates.
"That's something, provided that Lord Sun impresses him," Lü Meng suggested. "That leaves Fei Zhan's 'Danyang Bandits' as a major concern, maybe Peng Hu's followers in Po County... but a sign of strength, coupled perhaps with incentives to remain neutral, will ensure that we will suffer no 'internal issues' while we fight Cao Cao, except perhaps the on-going 'epidemic management' in the southeast, and Zhu Huan's dealing with that well enough."
Dong Xi smiled and said, "You are certainly considering everything, Ziming."
"I'm trying to," Lü Meng replied humbly.
"I'd not thought of that," Ling Tong exclaimed. "Cao Cao might bribe the bandits to cause trouble for us!"
"If we're not submitting then I'll be going to Danyang as soon as this meeting's over, and Zu Lang can join me," Hè Qi replied.
"And if needs be, I'll go back to Yuzhang or down to Kuaiji," Dong Xi replied. "In the end, though, it is Lord Sun's posture and decision that matter now... and they, in turn, are down to the Chief Commander."

Pan Zhang was generally as isolated as the Zhang brothers, though for entirely different reasons; Zhu Ran approached him and said, "Ready for the madness to begin...?"
Pan Zhang laughed and replied, "I think so, Yifeng. It... is alright to call you 'Yifeng', isn't it...?"
"Of course it is, Wengui," Zhu Ran said. "You're the lord's trusted friend, same as I."
Pan Zhang bowed slightly and replied, "Thank you."
"Do you think he'll find the right way to show he's capable of leading us...?" Zhu Ran asked.
"...I honestly don't know," Pan Zhang admitted. "He has to though... I do see that, and he does as well. But what do you do...? How do you best show strength...?"
"I've been wondering that myself," Zhu Ran said. "Let's hope that he thinks of something that works..."

The officials that were also family members – who included Xu Kun, Sun Jing and his three eldest sons, Sun Quan's half-brother Lang and Wu Jing's sons, Wu Fen and Wu Qi – were all stood together by the outer gates of the mansion.
"He does not consult us," Xu Kun complained.
"He doesn't need to, Kun, and it is better that he decides alone," Sun Jing replied.

"But he doesn't decide alone, he asks *Zhou Yu*!" Xu Kun protested.

"...You're quiet, brother," Wu Qi said to Wu Fen.

"What is there to say?" Wu Fen retorted. "We were only invited here to know what Cousin Zhongmou – Lord Sun – intends to do, and then we have to go back to Danyang."

"...I thought you'd at least wonder what Father or Auntie would say if they were here," Wu Qi sighed.

"Nothing's been the same since 'State Mother Wu' died," Xu Kun grumbled. "If Auntie were alive, she'd *never* have let Quan marry my-! ...Forget I spoke."

The frail Sun Jing exhaled weakly and said, "My nephew is as divisive as ever, I see... but we *have* to rally behind him for the sake of the entire region."

"I know that, Uncle," Xu Kun retorted. "It doesn't mean that I have to like it."

"Where's Ben...?" Wu Fen asked. "I thought that loudmouth'd want to be here, supporting the Zhangs and saying nice things about Cao Cao."

"Oh, right, you don't know, do you," Sun Jing replied miserably. "Ben and Fu... let us down, shall we say. Ben was narrowly talked out of surrendering; Fu actually wrote something that was intercepted, and so he's been exiled."

"They were colluding with Cao Cao," Xu Kun said angrily.

"*Aiee*... no wonder we're out in the cold!" Wu Qi exclaimed. "Ben was like a brother to Zhongmou, trusted to run the household when Uncle Jian was-!"

"Why should he stop trusting his entire blood family because of Ben and Fu?" Xu Kun asked bluntly. "That's nonsense!"

"He still trusts us," Sun Jing insisted.

"But Uncle, I'm Quan's actual brother, and it looks like I'm not trusted, and I didn't do anything to deserve it," Sun Lang complained. "I get nothing to do; I just live here and do nothing."

"That will change now," Sun Jing replied. "That's why you're here at this meeting: he trusts and relies on us more than ever, but he cannot look to us for advice on how to respond to Cao Cao. Zhou Gongjin will advise him rationally... and properly. We will do what is right."

Sun Quan had Gongjin sit as a guest and sighed, saying, "It is good of you to travel here, brother-in-law. I rely on you even more than my brother did for guidance in all things beyond my domain..."

Gongjin could sense that Sun Quan was speaking as he did because he was nervous, so he smiled and said, "My lord, I've come here to discuss the matter of Cao Cao."

Sun Quan sighed for a second time and replied, "A worrisome matter, indeed. Speaking frankly, Gongjin... I am scared. Cao Cao boasts nearly a million men in his letter, where he calls for us to submit graciously, promising no...!"

Sun Quan became upset and could not continue.

"Cao Cao is a liar," Gongjin insisted. "He lies while promising to be honest! ...A *million men*, indeed. My lord, I have been sending spies to learn of the true situation, and the estimations are, I understand, less than a quarter of a million... and seventy thousand or so of that are former Jing forces that will not fight with heart, especially if their first opponent is the son of their former governor. Cao's men are unaccustomed to the south, and will fall victim to disease… many are not veterans of sea battle, and will suffer sea-sickness. Cao's forces will fall apart, and then it is a matter of sweeping them away."

"You make the challenge sound almost too trivial," Sun Quan suggested.

Gongjin shook his head and said, "My lord, Cao comes here only because he feels that the north is pacified. Is it…?"

Sun Quan was silent.

"Ma Chao of Xiliang still lives, and he would go against Cao at the first opportunity," Gongjin continued. "Liu Zhang of Yi might bow to Cao Cao, but his former vassal Zhang Lu refuses, so where is the peace in the north or the west…? …And Cao Cao speaks of his mighty cavalry… what use will they be, in a land of high mountains and wide rivers…?"

Sun Quan nodded in agreement but remained silent.

"My lord," Gongjin continued, "give me the word, and I will march thirty-thousand troops into battle, and give you not only victory over Cao, but dominion over Jing Province as well!"

Sun Quan searched Gongjin's face for signs of bravado or doubt, but found none: Quan shook his fist and cried, "**Very good!**"

Gu Li watched from the doorway to the servant's quarters as Sun Quan got to his feet and momentarily pondered his next move; Quan recalled every conversation with family members, advisers, servants and officers, and then he thought of the past, turned his gaze to the empty pedestal that would house his 'Sword of Authority' – which was still on its pedestal in the main hall – and came to a decision.

"Yes…!" Sun Quan whispered; he turned, moved toward the corridor that led to his main audience hall and shouted, **"SUMMON THE COURT!"**

****

Sun Quan would have to wait for an hour before his entire court was assembled; he ordered his desk to be cleared of all objects, which puzzled all but Gu Li, who sensed that it would somehow be part of a much-needed demonstration of strength.

"Here's where we learn our lord's true worth," Cheng Pu murmured as he took his seat.

"And the true worth of every man in Jiangdong," Zhu Zhi replied.

"...He's here already," Dong Xi gasped as he looked to the main entrance and saw the brawny, scruffy Gan Ning, who was discussing his placement with Su Fei and a wary Lü Fan.

"...I'm alright," Ling Tong insisted.

Gongjin sat to Sun Quan's right; Zhang Zhao sensed the significance and sighed, "It is down to Lord Sun's strength, then."

"So be it," Zhang Hong replied miserably.

Zhuge Jin was obviously distracted; he was looking toward the entrance, quietly hoping that somebody would not be there.

"He will stay at the hotel," Lu Su insisted. "Kongming's no fool... and he gave me his word."

"...Perhaps he should go home," Zhuge Jin whined.

"Look at where Gongjin sits!" Lu Su retorted. "Stop worrying!"

Sun Quan waited until every man was seated and he had silence before he said, "I am glad to see you all here."

There was then a painful pause; some worried that their lord had suddenly changed his mind, but they were quickly put at ease.

"...We are now at a turning point," Sun Quan continued. "When my father lived, he fought for justice and honour, battling the likes of Dong Zhuo in a quest to rid the land of suffering and build a land of peace. When he died, my brother took it upon himself to pacify the region. He won the hearts of the people, and earned the respect of men like Taishi Ci, who sadly passed away only a few years ago... and, of course, Zhou Gongjin, whose genius is unparalleled in all the realm.

"Before my brother died, he did all he could to serve the realm, but he was felled before he could achieve his greatest dream: to smite Cao Cao, and liberate the land from his tyranny. He would have allied with the indecisive Yuan Shao to battle Cao, and perhaps he might have won some glory... perhaps not. That, sadly, we will never know.

"From him I inherited a vast realm, but also work unfinished: to settle our lands, I opted, reluctantly, for peace with Cao Cao, and left Yuan Shao to fight - and die - alone. While some may question my loyalty to the throne, I question the chance of our success with such an ally, whose superior numbers meant nothing when his slander-prone ear and truth-blind eyes prevented him from following sound advice and having good judgement. Instead, I focussed on ridding us of Liu Biao and his henchman Huang Zu... our forces took Huang Zu, and victory was ours: but then, not unexpectedly, the heavens took Liu Biao, and his unambitious son and heir-by-usurpation drove the true heir from his lands and then conceded to Cao Cao without a fight."

"And received from him the title of Inspector of Qing Province," Zhang Zhao proposed as Sun Quan paused momentarily.

"...That is correct," Sun Quan replied. "He was granted modest rank, and lives quite comfortably... as I could, no doubt, in some far-off place, if I too surrendered to Cao Cao. Then I, too, could be a **laughing stock, a target for the world's scorn and disdain, and watch from a safe distance as Cao Cao makes my homeland his playground, my people his slaves, while I live a carefree life of luxury!**"

The relief that many felt was almost tangible; the fear felt by the rest was equally clear but supressed by other fears.

"**...I will not, and cannot!**" Sun Quan cried: he then leapt to his feet, turned to the pedestal that held his 'Sword of Authority' and took up the blade with his archery-tempered right hand.

"My lord...!" Zhang Zhao protested. "Cao Cao commands near a million men!"

"Let him *bring* a **million men!**" Sun Quan boomed. "Let him bring **one, two, or TEN MILLION MEN! I'll drown them all in the Great River! I will fight him to the last man, and the next person that speaks to me of surrender will be answered as I tell this table!**"

Sun Quan slashed at his table with the expensive, heavy sword, shearing off one corner, and then he glared in all directions, seeking signs of dissent: the sight was enough to convince the officers that their lord was serious, and they grinned and bowed respectfully; the officials that still entertained ideas of surrendering shuddered, reflexively touched their necks, and indicated that they would protest no further.

"...We will discuss roles as soon as the Chancellor of State's envoy is informed of my decision," Sun Quan concluded. "For now, that is all: you are all dismissed."

The courtiers filed out of the hall; Lu Su and Zhuge Jin hurried to inform Zhuge Liang of the decision while the remaining doubters pondered the best way to withdraw from the court and avoid upcoming chaos. Zhu Ran halted to smile at his lord and friend; Quan returned the gesture before turning and leaving the hall.

"With his strength born of discipline, Lord Sun has proved his worth!" Cheng Pu said as left the meeting with his old friends.

"He has, Demou," Huang Gai replied. "The officials won't make any more trouble."

"But when Cao's politely rebuked envoy reaches Wulin, we'll see a response almost immediately," Zhu Zhi suggested. "Cao Cao will probably lay siege to Liu Qi's base, and then begin drills on the river; this will escalate quickly."

"Good," Han Dang replied. "The sooner he brings his sorry arse here is the sooner that we can kick it into his throat and send him back to Xuchang."

"...You're haunted," Cheng Pu said as he stared at Huang Gai.

"I... am just thinking, Demou," Huang Gai replied. "This is a battle for everything that we've built here, and the enormity of it has struck me very hard."

"...Yes," Cheng Pu murmured. "It... it is as you say."

Gongjin and Lü Fan left the meeting together; Fan frowned and said, "He did not want to discuss 'next steps' with you...?"

"He has just sent us on a collision course with a quarter-of-a-

million men from Jing, Yu, Qing, Xu, Yòu, Bing and Yan Provinces, and tens of thousands of boats and ships, and worst of all an angry, humiliated Cao Cao that has failed to cow us with bluff," Gongjin replied. "Lord Sun might just want to get drunk, but I imagine that he at least wants to *think*."
"...That was brave," Lü Fan said. "Bofu would be proud, I think."
Gongjin smiled and replied, "Very, Ziheng... very."

Sun Quan withdrew to his private study and fell to his knees, saying, "I... I have done it."
Gu Li had followed Sun Quan from the hall and stopped in the doorway; he nodded slowly and replied, "You have, my lord."
"...Am I mad...?" Sun Quan asked as his eyes searched the room for a wine jug. "Now that I think about it again, I really do have to- ...No. No, I had no choice... I have to do this."
Gu Li remained silent.
"...Now I must act like the lord of a third of the Empire," Sun Quan continued. "I will take a short amount of time to gather my thoughts, and I will not find them in the bottom of a wine jug... that's the mistake that Yuan Shao made, and I'll not end up like him. Cao Cao will not find me as easy to defeat as he thinks."

Cao Cao's envoy was crying as he shuffled into Cao's command tent to deliver the news that there would be no southern submission; the officials – including the advisers Cheng Yu and Xun Yòu – were nervous as they awaited the announcement and their lord's reaction.
"...Need I ask...?" Cao Cao said with a smirk.
"P-Prime Minister... Prime Minister, forgive me!" the envoy pleaded. "General That Attacks Barbarians Sun Quan has refused to submit! He... he states that he must politely decline your request and says that he will meet you on the battlefield!"
"Oh great," the one-eyed general Xiahou Dun said. "Months of rotting here in this sodden, muddy place, waiting for 'more auspicious weather'."
"...Not necessarily, Cousin," Cao Cao replied.
"Please show mercy!" the envoy cried. "I-!"
"I'm not going to harm you," Cao Cao interrupted. "You're going to rest, eat and get ready to go back to Xuchang."
"...Th-thank you, Prime Minister!" the envoy sobbed. "Thank you!"
Cao Cao nodded toward Xun Yòu, who guided the distressed envoy out of the tent.
"Shall I craft a response, Excellency?" Registrar Liu Yè asked.
"And say what?" Cao Cao retorted. "It's his funeral: let him resist if he absolutely must. And no, gentlemen, I will not be sitting here for months. This will be over in weeks as far as I'm concerned."
Cheng Yu cleared his throat and said, "Excellency, we cannot risk combat in winter. The conditions are not favourable: the water is fatally cold and the winds-"
"I will not wait, Elder Cheng," Cao Cao insisted. "We'll sweep Liu Bei away at once, and then we'll give Liu Qi one last chance to submit. If Sun Quan lends them aid, then his destruction is guaranteed; if he sensibly keeps to his borders, then perhaps he can be negotiated with again."
Cheng Yu exhaled heavily and said, "Excellency, you did not let

me finish: the winds are not favourable in winter, and the men that we brought here are yet to become acclimatised to the region, which leaves us dependent upon Jing's navy, which might be fine when we come to fighting Sun Quan – *perhaps* – but not when we confront the son of their former governor, and-"

"Elder Cheng, I shall be blunt, as you usually are," Cao Cao interrupted. "If we have a thousand men with dysentery now, we'll have *twenty-thousand men* come down with it by the spring."

"Yes," Cheng Yu replied, "but-"

"And there are more than a thousand men sick with it now, aren't there, and many more with other illnesses, am I right...?" Cao Cao continued. "Is it not the case that there are many things that will simply get worse as time goes on...?"

"...Yes," Cheng Yu replied, "but if we fight now, Excellency, then the vulnerable men will be getting sick as we fight, and the men that are destined to stay well will be poorly trained for naval combat, and only add to-"

"I don't have time to wait," Cao Cao insisted. "I'll hear no more talk of waiting. First thing's first: we march against Liu Bei and grind him into the mud."

"I'm for that," Xiahou Dun said enthusiastically. "I owe that pig butcher Zhang Fei some pain for humiliating us at Steep-slope."

"Go easy, Cousin," the stocky Xiahou Yuan pleaded. "He's my son-in-law, like it or not, and he has not mistreated my daughter."

"You can't know that, not after we captured Bei's daughters at Steep-slope," Xiahou Dun protested. "It's not nice to say, Miaocai, but I'll say it anyway: forget her, assume the worst and-"

"You'll say no more, Yuanrang," Cao Cao ordered. "I will agree, however, Miaocai, that daughters and nieces and sisters must be forgotten once married to enemies: don't let 'Zhang Fei of Yan' become a reason for hesitation or undue mercy."

"...I won't, Mengde," Xiahou Yuan promised. "But what if Sun Quan supports Liu Bei and Liu Qi...?"

"I have a quarter-of-a-million men, and Sun Quan must still wonder whether I really do have nearly four times that number, else his refusal to submit would have been at the cost of my envoy's life," Cao Cao retorted. "As I have said, we'll see... but I will not allow this admittedly unwanted – but *minor* – setback to demoralise me."

"Who will lead the vanguard against Liu Bei...?" Cao Pi asked.

"I have no desire to lose you in battle, my son, and particularly not against the likes of *Liu Bei*," Cao Cao replied. "I have decided that you will return to Xuchang within the next two days."

"But... *Father*...!" Cao Pi gasped.

"Leave this one to the seasoned generals," Cao Cao insisted. "You'll have your moment soon enough."

"...As you wish, Father," Cao Pi replied calmly.

"Forward, then," Cao Cao said. "Liu Bei dies *now*."

The time for words was over: the Battle of Red Cliffs had begun.

****

ACT VII: THE BATTLE OF RED CLIFFS

81

Attempts by the Han Dynasty's Chancellor of State, Cao Cao, to end the rule of the Sun clan in their native region of Jiangdong – or 'East of the River' – by way of 'rough diplomacy' had failed: the head of that clan, Sun Quan, had defied all of his critics and shown strength in the face of an enemy that vastly outnumbered him and had the word of Emperor Xian – coerced or otherwise – as justification for an attack on the south.

Sun Quan's defiance had not been without cost: many courtiers deserted him for fear of being seen to go against the will of their sovereign, and others simply walked away because they believed that Quan – who had inherited a vast domain that amounted to a quarter of Han China from his charismatic elder brother Sun Ce – was not capable. Older vassals had their reservations, not least because their first lord – Sun Quan's father, the 'Tiger of Jiangdong' Sun Jian – had been a loyal Han vassal that would never have dared to take up arms against a sovereign, but they were forced to concede that he had battled a previous Chancellor of State, Dong Zhuo, who was guilty of a multitude of crimes against nation and throne, and that Cao Cao was now being likened to that famous tyrant. Vassals that had joined the cause when Sun Ce was the lord were more divided, and had always been so: Sun Quan's reputation was a mixed one, and he was a very different personality. Some vassals had hoped that one of Sun Quan's younger brothers, Sun Yi, might have one day been allowed to take over when Sun Ce was assassinated, but Quan was chosen by Sun Jian's widow, State Mother Wu, and that immediately led to a civil war between Quan and a disgruntled general that had the support of half of the Jiangdong army; Quan was victorious, but the evident disaffection led to more insurrections, attacks by tribes and incursions by the Sun clan's long-term nemesis Liu Biao, the Governor of Jing Province, whose right-hand man, Jiangxia Administrator Huang Zu, had been directly responsible for Sun Jian's death when the latter was forced to attack Jing by his lord Yuan Shu.

Sun Ce had repeatedly tried to avenge his father's death after assuming the role of clan chieftain, but he was repeatedly forced to attend to other matters, while Sun Quan had, after one disastrous first attempt, finally overseen a successful invasion of Jiangxia and the death of Huang Zu, which drove the ageing Liu Biao to his sickbed and convinced some critics that the young lord might have potential after all; the victory was immediately soured, however, by Cao Cao's invasion of Northern Jing, the appointment of Liu Biao's malleable second son Cong after the former's death and the subsequent surrender of the Jing Governor's seal to Cao Cao, which ended the dream of seizing Southern Jing and creating a new state of 'Jiangnan' – or 'South of the River' – that could enjoy near-autonomy. But Cao Cao did not allow the Suns to retreat without incident: he publicly issued harsh condemnations and demanded that the Suns relinquish not only Jiangxia but also Jiangdong, implying that the Sun clan were hegemons and enemies of the Han.

Relations with Cao Cao had been difficult: there were high-level marriage alliances between the Suns and Caos, but some blamed Cao Cao – directly or indirectly – for the untimely deaths of Sun Ce, State Mother Wu and her brother Wu Jing, two of Quan's younger brothers, Quan's much-trusted cousin Sun Hè and Quan's infant son. To make matters worse, Quan's cousin Ben – who had once been a trusted friend and had even briefly led the clan immediately after Sun Jian's death – had been caught liaising with Cao Cao, who was now his daughter's father-in-law; the fact that Cao was apparently hoping that Ben would either submit – opening Jiangdong's western land border in the process – or attempt a coup before negotiations had ended did little to improve the chances of a peaceful outcome.

Sun Quan's brother-in-law and Chief Commander, Zhou Yu – whose courtesy name was 'Gongjin' – determined that the route to victory required an alliance with Liu Qi, the elder son of Liu Biao, and Qi's distant relative and ally Liu Bei, who had both fled Jing as Cao advanced. To the surprise of all, Sun Quan agreed to it, and to even greater surprise, Liu Qi also accepted the idea of a truce with his father's enemies and allowed Liu Bei to send his chief strategist, Zhuge Liang, to Jiangdong to make the case for a united stand: that extra voice, in conjunction with Gongjin's, gave Sun Quan the momentum to silence those that advocated submission and rebuke Cao Cao's envoy. Cao Cao's response was unnervingly calm: he readied his forces for a decisive attack on Liu Bei and Liu Qi – who were still on the northern side of the Yangtze River – and continued to amass boats, warships and personnel along the northern bank in preparation for a full-scale invasion of Jiangdong.

"My lord: a messenger has apparently arrived," Sun Quan's senior servant Gu Li announced as he entered Quan's private study.
"...So I should attend a private court session, then," Sun Quan murmured. "Have Mister Zhuge summon the most trusted, Li, and have them come to my private audience hall..."
"It shall be done, Lord Sun," Gu Li replied.
Sun Quan watched Gu Li's retreat and hummed thoughtfully, muttering, "Here is where our 'allies' reveal their intentions... and where my 'loyal vassals' reveal theirs."
Sun Quan then turned and looked at his bodyguards: he looked at one in particular – a tall, charismatic man with a benign expression – and murmured, "And *I* must think of the *state*."

Sun Quan's decision to fight the Han's Chancellor of State had robbed the south of a large number of civil administrators, but the army was relatively unaffected and Quan still had a reasonable number of reliable advisers and state officials.

Aside from Gongjin, Sun Quan had his late brother's chief adviser Lü Fan, although Fan seemed to be content to act as a subordinate to Gongjin for reasons that were unclear; there was the quick-speaking Lu Su, who had once saved Gongjin's militia from financial ruin and enjoyed the Chief Commander's friendship and confidence as a result; there was the loyal but acerbic Zhang Zhao, who advocated submission until Sun Quan's dramatic 'slicing of the table' silenced all dissenters; there was Zhao's brother Hong, who had served as Jiangdong's envoy to the Imperial court and shared Zhao's desire for a peaceful solution; there was the melancholic Zhuge Jin, whose brother, Zhuge Liang, was the main diplomatic bridge between the Lius and Suns; there was the quiet, pedantic Gu Yong and the politician Quan Rou, who would administrate the state during the crisis; Yan Jun, Yu Fan and Qin Song would administrate and supply advice to the various prefectural defenders; and there was Zhu Zhi, who was a veteran of the days of Sun Jian and Sun Ce and the adoptive father of Quan's closest friend Zhu Ran.

The officers included many men that were relations: Sun Quan's uncle Sun Jing would remain in the background due to age and ill health, but his eldest sons – Hao, Yu and Jiao – would serve as mid-ranking officers; Quan's cousin Xu Kun – who had fought as a senior officer since the days of Sun Ce – would serve as a defender of the capital despite some friction between the two after Quan married Kun's sister with the intention of elevating her to his principal spouse; the late Sun Hè's sons and nephew would guard various counties and prefectures; and despite their fathers' attempts at submitting to Cao Cao, the sons of siblings Sun Ben and Sun Fu – who were now under close watch and exiled, respectively – remained loyal and were fortifying the western border that their fathers had been entrusted with.

The remaining officers were not blood family, but they were as trusted as any brother or uncle: there was the gruff, intolerant Cheng Pu, who was a general and adviser to Sun Jian in the early days of fighting Yellow Turban cultists and was now the longest-serving man in the Sun army, having been the first man to join Sun Jian's militia 24 years previously; there was the quiet, observant Huang Gai, who was the second man to join Sun Jian; there was the affable, plain-speaking Han Dang, who was the third man to join Sun Jian; there was the controversial former gambler Pan Zhang, who had impressed a teenaged Sun Quan with style rather than substance but grown into a formidable – if morally ambiguous – civil administrator and officer in the 9 years that followed; there was the honest but ostentatious Hè Qi, who would be entrusted with guarding Danyang Prefecture against bandits and tribal raids; there was the fearsome but intelligent Dong Xi, who would maintain stability in the innermost parts of Yuzhang Prefecture and neighbouring Kuaiji Prefecture during the campaign; there was the brave, compassionate Ling Tong, who inherited the defence of Wu Prefecture from his reckless father Ling Cao, but whose place on the campaign would be as a front-line Commandant; there was the ill-mannered, straightforward Gan Ning, a pirate-turned-officer whose previous service under Huang Zu included killing Ling Cao; there was Lü Dai, who would serve as the guardian of Wu Prefecture and Southern Guangling Prefecture during the campaign; there was Lü Meng, who had evolved from reckless idiot to enlightened genius in recent months; there was the humble, frugal ex-pirate Jiang Qin, who would serve as a defender of Danyang and Yuzhang during the campaign; there was the fearless, loyal ex-pirate Zhou Tai, whose actions always disregarded self-preservation; and then there was Chen Wu, who – along with the reliable Song Qian – was currently acting as a leader of Sun Quan's bodyguard force, though that would not be the case for much longer.

"*Zilie*," Sun Quan hailed.

"...Lord Sun...?" the tall bodyguard – Chen Wu – replied uneasily.

"Chen Zilie, your presence here is my selfish folly," Sun Quan continued. "I will certainly invite you back here when this matter is at an end, but right now you're needed where you've always made the most impact, namely on the front lines, inspiring acts of heroism and bringing us new friends by swaying our enemies. You will leave at once and join Chief Commander Zhou: I have Song Qian to protect me, so you need not worry."

"As you command, Lord Sun," Chen Wu replied as he started an immediate withdrawal from the study.

"And to think that instead of sending Zilie off to fight, I almost demanded that Zhou Youping be sent here!" Sun Quan said guiltily. "What good are a million palace guards if the state is lost...? I'd send you too, Colonel Song, but I do still need protection from my enemies."

Song Qian bowed slightly and said, "I gladly remain at your side, Lord Sun."

"You have my thanks for saying that, Colonel, even if it isn't true," Sun Quan replied. "Now I must go and learn of our allies' fates... and what it might mean for our own."

****

82

Chancellor Cao Cao's advance would be swift and unforgiving: he had brought most of his most formidable officers with him on his campaign to pacify the south, but had, in contrast, a conspicuously low number of advisers.

The officers included many men of the related Cao and Xiahou clans: there was Xiahou Dun, who was also known as 'One-eyed Xiahou' after an encounter with one of the infamous Lü Bu's generals while supporting Liu Bei in Xu Province; there was the thoughtful, affable Supply Coordinator Xiahou Yuan, who was seen as one of Cao Cao's most trusted allies yet whose daughter was now, by way of strange fate, wed to Liu Bei's famous general Zhang Fei; there was Cao Xiu, a cousin and close friend to Cao's eldest living son Cao Pi that would one day lead a famous attack against the Suns; there was the overweight, deep-thinking Cao Zhen, whose destiny as Commander-in-Chief of all of the Imperial forces was barely conceivable as he embarked on the first real campaign of his career; there was Cao Hong, who had a reputation for loutish, idiotic and childish behaviour despite being a trusted general that had saved Cao Cao's life at least once; and there was Cao Ren, whose reputation as an able defender would be put to the test in the following years.

But Cao Cao, like Sun Quan, was not a proponent of out-and-out nepotism when it came to appointments: his family were only used when they were deemed competent, and many of the most famous officers occupied those roles with good reason and had no initial ties to the Caos. There was the cautious, cunning Yu Jin, who had come to Cao from the ambitious courtier Wang Lang and now served as Cao's most trusted vanguard general; there was Zhang Liao, who was formerly Lü Bu's right-hand man and known in his own right for fearsomeness, though his reputation still had one historic leap to make; there was the cautious yet fearsome Zhang Hè, who was one of Yuan Shao's most valiant generals until slander forced him to surrender and defect during the climaxing stages of the Battle of Guandu; there was the quiet, studious Li Dian, whose devotion to the cause always outweighed his disinterest in holding a military post; there was the former White Wave Bandit Xu Huang, who was, like Jiang Qin of Jiangdong, known for his humility; there was Zhu Ling, who had been 'loaned' to Cao Cao by Yuan Shao many years before but opted to stay with Cao; and then there were Feng Kai and Lu Zhao, two officers that had so impressed Cao during the first campaign against Liu Biao that they had been promoted to senior generals for the battle against the Suns. Another general – the short, courageous but ill-tempered and competitive Yue Jin – had asked if he might contribute to the entire campaign and add to his already-impressive list of victories against Cao Cao's enemies, but Cao would ultimately have him return to Xiangyang and act as a reluctant defender when the army's attention turned from the Lius to the Suns: that was a telling sign for those that knew what to look for.

The officials, though few in number, were notable: there was the tall, middle-aged Cheng Yu – though many called him

'Elder Cheng' in light of his age, just as many did for Cheng Pu in Jiangdong – whose early advice was controversial and yet incontrovertibly effective; there was the adviser Xun Yòu, who – along with his more famous uncle Xun Yu – had served Cao Cao for over a decade; there was the Legalism proponent and prominent consultant Cui Yan, who had served the Yuan clan prior to Cao's conquest of the northeast; there was Cao's Registrar Liu Yè, who had served as Liu Xun's adviser during the latter's time as Yuan Shu's Administrator of Lujiang and fled to Cao when Sun Ce had defeated Liu Xun 9 years before; there was Zhao Yan, Cao Cao's chosen 'Commandant-Protector of the Army' whose role it was to supervise 7 of the vanguard generals; and then there was Jia Xu, the most controversial of Cao's advisers – having served Dong Zhuo, Li Jue, Guo Si and Zhang Xiu in prior years – but whose contribution to the campaign would be uncharacteristically small, namely as the guardian of Jiangling while his colleagues marched at the Chancellor's side.

The first real battle of the campaign would be between Cao Cao and Liu Bei: it would take place on the plains of Northern Wulin County, and it would define the mood for the rest of the campaign on both sides.

Lu Su accompanied Liu Bei's envoy, Zhuge Liang, on his return trip to Bei's camp on the north side of the Yangtze River; Sun Quan patiently awaited the outcome of the first encounter of the campaign, and the result made for uncomfortable listening when it arrived by way of a messenger from Lu Su.

"The battle between Liu Bei and Cao Cao ended with a resounding defeat for Liu Bei," the messenger explained to a small audience in Sun Quan's private audience hall. "Liu Qi remained at a distance, leaving Liu Bei with only five-thousand men to resist Cao Cao's thirty-thousand-strong vanguard at Wulin."

"...I see," Sun Quan said calmly.

"You *see*...?" Zhang Zhao exclaimed. "My lord, the-!"

"Please do go on, messenger," Sun Quan ordered.

"Cao Cao's forces were apparently stunned, momentarily, by the use of an advanced array formation, but numbers ultimately dictated the outcome," the messenger said. "Liu Bei retreated, losing perhaps a thousand to fifteen-hundred men."

"...Is that everything...?" Sun Quan prompted.

"Mister Lu Su and Mister Zhuge Liang are on their way back to Chaisang," the messenger concluded. "Mister Lu Su said that he would report any other important matters in person to you or the Chief Commander."

"...Very good," Sun Quan said. "You may go and rest now."

Zhang Zhao watched the messenger leave and then turned to Sun Quan, saying, "I am your loyal vassal, Lord Sun: you know that."

Sun Quan smiled dryly and replied, "I know, Zibu, else you'd have left after I sliced the table. What do you want to say...?"

"What is 'very good' about that report...?" Zhang Zhao asked.

"The ruse has begun," Lü Fan explained. "Cao Cao now wonders whether there is any unity at all, even between the two Lius."

"...I see," Zhang Zhao said. "You need explain no more of that part of it all to me, Ziheng: I understand the plan fully. What, though, is the scheme to snare Cao once he is fooled...?"

"We have a number of options," Lü Fan replied.
"Such as…?" Xu Kun asked.
"Ruses are many in shape, form and guise," Lü Fan replied. "We must first see what Cao does and react appropriately."
"Why is Zhuge Liang coming back here?" Zhang Hong asked. "Does his presence not risk exposing the alliance?"
"The answer to the second question is 'Not at all'," Lü Fan replied. "The defeat at Wulin ensures that Zhuge has a good excuse to be here – unpopularity – should anyone find out, but it's unlikely that anyone will. As for 'Why is he coming back here', I counter with 'Why do you have to ask?'"
"…I see," Zhang Hong said. "He is our liaison… I understand."
"And we shall try appealing to him," Zhuge Jin proposed. "If my brother sees what a fine nation we are, he must surely start to change his mind about serving that mediocrity Liu Bei."
"It is certainly worth a try," Sun Quan said. "We'll need many great minds if we are to survive… even if we win."

Cao Cao was quietly succumbing to hubris as he watched his latest military camp take shape on the northern bank of the Yangtze River; he smiled, turned to his only company – Registrar Liu Yè – and asked, "Any word from Miaocai…?"
"Supply Coordinator Xiahou has reported that he has completed the establishment of the supply route through Jing Province and awaits further instructions," Liu Yè replied. "Mister Jia Xu also reports that he has finally managed to secure a neutral conversation with Appraiser Pang."
"…Pang Tong, the 'Young Phoenix'…?" Cao Cao exclaimed. "If Mister Jia and Mister Cui could sway that young prodigy to our cause, Ziyang, then how could his friend Zhuge Liang fight for Liu Bei with any enthusiasm…? That might lead to the peaceful conclusion that we all seek!"
"Mister Jia is not optimistic, but he will treat Appraiser Pang carefully – as instructed – and report the outcome of the meeting at once," Liu Yè concluded.
"And Jing is completely secure…?" Cao Cao prompted.
Liu Yè nodded and said, "General Li Tong has secured the northernmost regions; Mister Man Chong has reached Xiangyang, met with General Yue Jin and liaises with Wang Can, Huan Jie and Kuai Yue; General Cao Ren, Colonel Niu Jin, Mister Cui Yan and Mister Jia Xu have pacified and fortified Jiangling; General Wen Ping has secured western Jiangxia; officials have been despatched to Yi and the four 'independent counties' in order to reassure the administrations and request support."
"Very good…!" Cao Cao chuckled. "With Liu Bei routed and Liu Qi in hiding, Sun Quan is isolated: now it is just a matter of time…!"

****

83

Jia Xu and Cui Yan were characteristically apprehensive as they prepared for their meeting with Pang Tong; they were both surprised when a short, scrawny man with disorderly teeth, a crooked nose and coarse hair entered Jia Xu's office and bowed slightly, saying, "It is a pleasure, gentlemen."

"...Likewise," Cui Yan replied uneasily; Pang Tong had made no presentational effort, and his brown robes looked well-worn.

"So," Pang Tong said with mischief, "are you both here for character appraisals...?"

"Uh, no!" Jia Xu chuckled. "I fear that my record makes for poor reading and an even poorer appraisal, Mister Pang."

"You may call me 'Shiyuan'," Pang Tong replied. "And I am known for my fairness, Mister Jia: some have even accused me of toadyism, but I simply think – unlike better-known appraisers such as the late Xu Shao – that being too harsh or too frank can sometimes make poor achievers or even monsters out of men that might have been quite different with a little encouragement."

Jia Xu and Cui Yan exchanged nervous glances.

"Oh, yes, and congratulations, 'Senior Clerk in the East and West Bureaus Cui Yan'!" Pang Tong continued. "That is quite the accolade to be receiving from Chancellor Cao... or should I call him 'Prime Minister'...?"

"*Either will do*," Cui Yan retorted.

"...You appear to have taken unnecessary offence," Pang Tong said. "Why would you be offended by my congratulating you for a promotion by the Chancellor of State...?"

"Because... because His Excellency Cao is controversial here in Jing and in some other places, Appraiser Pang, and because you are a well-known associate – or, perhaps, a better term would be 'close friend' – of Liu Bei's new chief strategist, Zhuge Liang," Cui Yan replied.

"And I therefore, in your opinion, intended spite," Pang Tong sighed. "How little you understand men, Senior Clerk Cui, which flies in the face of your reputation."

Cui Yan's eyes wandered.

"...Then you do not support Liu Bei's cause, Pang Shiyuan...?" Jia Xu prompted.

"If I did support him, Mister Jia Wenhe, then I would be with him in Wulin, supporting him," Pang Tong replied. "I am here in Jiangling, continuing my work as an appraiser and trying to maintain stability."

"...Would you then support His Excellency more directly...?" Cui Yan asked.

"I do not see how I can serve the Chancellor of State more directly than by maintaining the stability of the state, Senior Clerk Cui," Pang Tong replied.

"...You are known to be a genius, Appraiser Pang, comparable with Zhang Liang and Wei Zi of ancient times," Jia Xu suggested.

"...Wei Zi...?" Pang Tong chuckled. "He famously defected to King Wen of Zhou and worked tirelessly to draw others away from his former master, King Zhou of Shang, thus weakening the Shang Dynasty; if the Han Dynasty is benevolent and to be preserved,

why would I want to be like Wei Zi...?"
Jia Xu exhaled miserably and said, "You misunderstand me... and yes, that was perhaps a poor choice of comparison."
"And so, in a way, is Zhang Liang," Pang Tong retorted. "He aided the founding of a new dynasty – the Han – but that was at the expense of the incumbent: if the Han is not corrupt and in need of replacing, then why would I want to be like Zhang Liang...?"
"*Aiee*... I mean, uh... Mister Pang, Pang Shiyuan... your words are true," Jia Xu said. "It is particularly uncomfortable for me to realise that I made such poor comparisons, given that I have a past that includes serving – advising – Dong Zhuo, who did such harm to the throne. I now serve Chancellor Cao because he means to restore the Han's lustre, and we are here to ask if you would lend your considerable talent – I shall let you choose your own comparisons – to the Han more directly, serving as an adviser to the Chancellor as I now do."
Pang Tong hummed thoughtfully and replied, "I have to say that I am flattered, of course, but unlike Kongming, I do not see what good I can do: I am not that travelled, knowing only the roads in men's minds to some degree, and I lack the physical qualities that ensure that a man is heard... or were you going to pretend that you did not notice that I am quite ugly...?"
"N-no, Appraiser Pang, you... are not a handsome man, that is true," Cui Yan said as Pang Tong grinned in his direction. "But His Excellency Cao is not a man that judges men by their appearance! He truly values your ability and desires your help to restore order to the Empire."
"But how can I do that...?" Pang Tong asked. "I am not another Guo Jia: I am a character appraiser. Why not ask Lou Gui, styled 'Zibo', who lives in the mountains of Northern Jing...? He would surely be of more use than I."
"We... have already approached that famously outspoken genius, and he has honestly rebuked us," Jia Xu replied. "Shiyuan, the Prime Minister, His Excellency Chancellor Cao, needs every able mind in the land if he is to bring stability and peace to the land and put down the likes of Sun Quan, Zhang Lu and Liu Bei!"
"And I say again, gentlemen, that I am no Guo Jia," Pang Tong retorted. "A guide is no use if he will not be followed; I must respectfully decline, purely because of a modest, honest belief that I am not the man that His Excellency seeks."
"...Alright," Cui Yan conceded.
"...Yes... yes, yes, I see that you are best left where you are, serving the state in the way that you know to be best," Jia Xu said. "Thank you for your time, Appraiser Pang Shiyuan."
"You're welcome," Pang Tong replied. "I shall, as a gesture of goodwill, give free appraisals to you both before I go."
"I need no appraisal," Cui Yan said coldly. "I received an appraisal years ago, from the famous Xu Shao."
"And I know my own faults," Jia Xu protested.
"...Mister Cui, you are a good man, bound to your Legalist beliefs, and you have brought much stability to the north, which has much to thank you for," Pang Tong declared. "You are loyal to your friends and do all that you can for them, which is very commendable: may they always deserve your support."
Cui Yan laughed awkwardly and replied, "I said that I had no need

of an appraisal, but... thank you, Mister Pang."

Pang Tong smirked and turned to Jia Xu, saying, "And you, Mister Jia, are a man of great talent – the talent that Chancellor Cao is looking for, in fact, if only he'll look past old matters and fully trust you, and I believe that one day he will. You truly seek a role as the adviser to a man that will restore order to the land, but you are held back by your guilt and a prevailing fear of mistakenly serving another tyrant; overcome those fears and you will one day bring the stability that you seek, serving a Son of Heaven that will have their mandate affirmed in the eyes of all."

"...You are, as you say, very kind in your appraisals, Shiyuan," Jia Xu replied. "It was a pleasure speaking with you: Heaven willing, Shiyuan, I might do so again one day."

"We'll doubtless cross paths again, Mister Jia, unless I stumble or fall along the way," Pang Tong said. "Good day to you both!"

Jia Xu and Cui Yan exchanged bows with Appraiser Pang Tong, who then departed.

"*Aiee...* he might look like some sort of strange ape, but those *eyes*...!" Cui Yan said honestly. "They pierce your soul...!"

"His words cut deeper still," Jia Xu sighed. "But then, did he say anything really, or is it my own estimation of myself...?"

"Best not to think about it," Cui Yan decided. "I'll forward the bad news to His Excellency... and hope that he does not harm Mister Pang as he harmed Hua Tuo or, less directly, Mi Heng."

Jia Xu hummed thoughtfully and said, "Or, more directly, Kong Rong, though he, like Mi Heng, was rude and brought it upon himself: yes, that... that would be a sad end for such a clever man, but I am sure that His Excellency will not harm him, for... for no good would come of that."

Jia Xu and Cui Yan were both haunted by Pang Tong's words; Pang returned to his work as an appraiser in and around Jiangling, and Cao Cao reluctantly accepted that he would not have the service of the 'Young Phoenix' in the immediate future. Another man would try to recruit Pang Tong in the wake of the encounter at Red Cliffs although, in the end, Pang Tong would seek out the lord that he would go on to serve; that, however, was in the future, and for Cao Cao, nothing mattered more than the present as his conflict with Sun Quan continued.

✳✳✳✳✳✳✳✳✳✳✳✳

84

Gongjin and Cheng Pu had relocated to Red Cliffs County – a region that sat along the southern bank of the Yangtze, opposite Cao Cao's bases at Wulin – and established a headquarters in the capital city; the Jiangdong navy was deployed along the riverbank in response to the swift build-up of Cao Cao's forces.

"So Zhuge Liang is on his way back and on his way here," Cheng Pu said as he stood on the city wall with Gongjin, Huang Gai and Ling Tong.

"He is, with Lu Zijing," Gongjin replied. "Or, rather, Lu *Su*, since we must now avoid courtesy names and speak in as professional a way as is possible; how do you want to communicate with our visitor, General Cheng…?"

Cheng Pu smirked and said, "I'm gathering that you'd like for me to be the 'gruff old man', no great mind, hateful of the north, displeased with my rank and locked into an infamous battle of wits with you."

"I'm glad that I don't have to explain," Gongjin replied.

"So what are *we* doing?" Ling Tong asked.

"Cao Cao will attack us soon, lightly, as a test," Gongjin replied. "We'll respond appropriately, namely by testing him first: that will be your job, gentlemen."

"…I understand," Huang Gai said tonelessly.

A messenger approached and said, "**Mister Lu Su and Mister Zhuge Liang are here, Chief Commander!**"

"We'll go and meet them at the docks, 'Veteran General Cheng'," Gongjin suggested. "Commandant Ling, General Huang, you may go back to your preparations."

The four men exchanged respectful bows and left the wall to carry out their assignments.

Lu Su and Zhuge Liang had just left the pier when Gongjin and Cheng Pu reached them and began a charade of inspecting the ships.

"Zhuge Liang's demeanour is as calm as before," Cheng Pu noted.

"A ruse… I think," Gongjin replied. "Regardless, he is-"

"**Chief Commander Zhou, General Cheng!**"

Lu Su's cry ended the conversation; Gongjin bowed to Lu and Zhuge Liang in turn, saying, "Zijing, Master Zhuge."

Cheng Pu bowed – making the gesture as slight as possible – and sneered disapprovingly.

"We have done our part," Zhuge Liang confirmed. "The rest is up to you."

"You will be staying, Kongming…?" Gongjin asked.

"I really shouldn't," Zhuge Liang said uneasily. "My lord has full faith in me, but his vassals…"

Gongjin laughed and replied, "Yes, I imagine that Zhang Fei and Guan Yu are not much fun to work with. I hear that both men are arrogant and imprudent."

"That would be a fine description of Guan Yu, despite his bravery," Lu Su said confidently. "Zhang Fei, I would say, is more belligerent and irrational. Would you not agree, Kongming…?"

Zhuge Liang paused before replying, "I would not. Guan Yunchang is lofty but principled, while Zhang Yide is passionate and honest.

Had they been allowed to fight Cao Cao, the casualties would have numbered in the tens of hundreds: sadly, we only scratched Cao without them, since the point was to make Cao overconfident. Their doubts stem from my brother being here, and I can understand that... so really, I should take my leave once-"
Gongjin laughed with mock embarrassment and said, "Forgive me, but I just realised that it probably won't be possible now; what part of the north bank will be safe now that Cao Cao has arrayed his fleet along it...? We could risk it, but-"
"Uh, Gongjin," Lu Su interrupted. "Trapping him here..."
"...Is no fault of mine," Gongjin insisted. "Surely, Zijing, you did not bring him here without realising that the way back would be blocked...?"
Zhuge Liang smiled knowingly and started to fan himself slowly as Gongjin turned to him and feigned sadness and disappointment in anticipation of some form of comment that Zhuge never proffered.
"...My apologies, Kongming," Gongjin prompted.
"...Perhaps I can be of service here," Zhuge Liang replied cordially. "Maybe you, Zijing and I can discuss how to repel such a large force with this – it has to be said – impressive yet inadequate naval fleet you have."
"...**You miserable little pedant!**" Cheng Pu barked. "**I should-!**"
"Please, control yourself, General," Gongjin said. "Master Zhuge was correctly pointing out the numerical disparity, and I confess, it concerns me. I shall be sending a force to test Cao's forces, see how we do... after that, we'll look at the options, shall we...?"
Cheng Pu grunted quietly, bowed and withdrew; Zhuge Liang nodded silently; Lu Su looked at Gongjin and wondered whether he was being kept informed at all.

"...You look irritated," Huang Gai said as Cheng Pu neared him.
"Partly an act, partly due to speaking with that smug, self-righteous Zhuge Liang," Cheng Pu replied. "Everything ready...?"
"As it'll ever be," Huang Gai said.
"...Is that *Chen Wu*...?" Cheng Pu exclaimed as he spotted a familiar face among the officers.
"Lord Sun sent him to bolster our ranks, since we don't have Hè Qi and Dong Xi," Huang Gai replied. "Uh, Demou- ...I mean 'General Cheng'... I have something that I wanted to discuss with you and the Chief Commander. When would be a good time...?"
"...Are you having doubts...?" Cheng Pu prompted.
"That's not it, I assure you," Huang Gai replied. "I... wanted to discuss an idea of mine, although perhaps it might be better to wait and see if it's even needed at all."
"...Alright," Cheng Pu said. "You let me know when you want to speak with us and I'll arrange it."
Huang Gai bowed silently.

****

85

Gongjin, Lu Su and Zhuge Liang journeyed to a nearby watchtower so that they could overlook the Jiangdong fleet and, more relevantly, the task force as it prepared to sail.

"Impressive," Zhuge Liang declared.

"We'll send a small contingent to initiate a battle," Gongjin explained. "If what you said was true of the men you fought, Kongming, we're dealing with the signs I hoped for... now is the time to know it for certain."

"...Uh...?" Lu Su grunted unintelligently.

"Cao's vanguard did not number the full thirty-thousand that he had with him initially," Zhuge Liang explained. "In addition, his soldiers were slow, unsteady; there were a lot of men stumbling as they charged, their reflexes were poor..."

"...They're sick," Lu Su murmured. "...They're *sick*...!"

Zhuge Liang sighed and said, "While I should not wish such a thing on a man, this is war. I think that yes, Zijing, the men were sick and tired. So that long trip sailing down the Great River, with no real option to stop anywhere due to the marshlands..."

"His men are seasick at best, or riddled with disease, and good as dead," Gongjin supposed. "...Or, at least, this is my hope: now, we shall see."

Zhou Tai led part of the small harassment force toward Cao Cao's larger navy while making as much noise as possible: the attack was reported to Cao Cao, who said, "With such a small force, they are just testing our resolve."

"They'll be gladdened by what they find," Cheng Yu suggested irritably. "Your Excellency, the men are in a state, and-!"

"So what do you propose, then, Elder Cheng, that we sit here and let them attack us?" Cao Cao barked. **"The men will fight; perhaps they will understand the urgency of the hour and overcome their sickness as they did when we travelled northward to pacify the Wuhuan!"**

"The illness suffered on that campaign was nothing compared to this!" Cheng Yu protested. "Their men are-!"

"Enough!" Cao Cao ordered. **"General Feng Kai!"**

Feng Kai bowed humbly.

"You have fought on the water before, General," Cao Cao noted.

Cheng Yu groaned miserably and said, "So has General Li Dian, when together we thwarted-!"

"Have I in some way failed to win your respect, Elder Cheng...?" Feng Kai asked as he stared upward at the considerably taller adviser. "What have I done that you have no faith in my-?"

"Enough!" Cao Cao cried. **"I am *weary of it*! How did Yuan Shao tolerate the bickering year after year...? And do we have *time* for this? Mister Cheng Yu: stop whining! General Feng: you will take General Lu Zhao as your second, go, and foil this attack before they get to my command tent!"**

Feng Kai hurried out of the tent.

"Xu Huang and Li Dian will provide support," Cao Cao added. "Xun Yòu, you will act as their adviser and observe the enemy, see if you can learn anything."

Xun Yòu bowed humbly and retreated.

"...This is *ridiculous*," Cheng Yu muttered.

"Your lack of insight cost us men in that last battle, Old Cheng," Cao Hong suggested. "When you've made up for that, then maybe Mengde will-"

"Don't say anymore, Cousin," Cao Cao grumbled. "Just... *aiee*."

Han Generals Feng Kai and Lu Zhao led a small reactionary force comprised of attack boats that were staffed by lancers, swordsmen and archers; Xun Yòu and Generals Li Dian and Xu Huang followed in some larger ships in case of an ambush.

"General Yue insulted me again before he departed for Xiangyang, General Xu," Li Dian complained as he watched Feng Kai's advance from the deck of the lead ship. "Years, now, I've been putting up with his irrational hostility, his constant questioning of my rank and my achievements: what did I do, I ask...? Do I truly deserve it?"

"I... don't know whether I should comment, but I will," Xu Huang replied as he quickly glanced at Xun Yòu and saw no signs of disapproval. "General Yue is becoming increasingly confrontational and obsessed with his ability in comparison with his peers, and I worry that it will affect us in later years."

"...Well put," Li Dian said. "He resents His Excellency's decision to send him elsewhere, and he'll take it out on us... me most of all."

Xu Huang nodded silently.

Zhou Tai attacked Feng Kai and Lu Zhao before they could rally their men; the Han sailors were obviously too giddy and sick to perform at their best, and their inability quickly started to cost lives despite their numerical advantage.

"**Damn... it... all...!**" Lu Zhao cried as he tried to stay upright; his men were vomiting, stumbling and falling all around him, destabilising the boats further and leaving them exposed.

"**We'll have... to retreat!**" Feng Kai suggested.

"**But the Chancellor will rebuke us!**" Lu Zhao retorted. "**We... we can't... retreat! We must prove our worth or face obscurity! Get these men out of my way so I can fight!**"

Lu Zhao pushed a nauseous Han sailor to one side, repelled two enemy sailors and engaged a Jiangdong boat captain in a sword duel; Zhao matched the southern man move for move but was forced to withdraw when Zhou Tai's archers started to fire.

"**Damn it!**" Feng Kai whined. "**Where are *our* archers???**"

Some of the Jiangdong men were laughing and taunting the Han forces as their archers repeatedly misfired, spearmen's lunges hurled them into the water and swordsmen flailed after waving their swords; Zhou Tai was smiling as well until a second enemy force arrived that passed Li Dian and Xu Huang's reinforcements and started toward the Jiangdong men at speed.

"**...That's Jing ships!**" Zhou Tai realised as he spotted the different uniforms that the crewmen wore. "**They're better trained, men, so show some care!**"

The Jiangdong forces briefly engaged the Jing men, who were led by Admiral Cai Mao's nephew Zhang Yun; Gongjin quickly realised the new danger and signalled for a retreat.

"**Run, southern dogs!**" Feng Kai shouted as he finally found his footing. "**Next time... will be a different story!**"

"**Should we pursue?**" a Jing captain asked of Zhang Yun.

"The Chancellor's orders were to chase them off and nothing more," Zhang Yun replied. **"We'll withdraw now."**
The confrontation ended on an embarrassing note; Feng Kai and Lu Zhao retreated to their camp to report the farce to Commandant-Protector Zhao Yan.

Lü Meng, Ling Tong, Chen Wu, Su Fei and Gan Ning watched as their allies returned from their sortie; Ling Tong frowned and asked, "What are they all laughing about?"
"The northerners are all sick," Su Fei replied. "The news from friends in Jiangxia is true, then: Cao's men haven't had barely any, uh… what's the word I'm looking for…"
"'Acclimatising'," Gan Ning grunted.
"…Yeah," Su Fei chuckled. "No training, nothing."
"…Cao Cao has not prepared for his invasion of Jiangdong very well, then," Ling Tong said. "That's good for us."
Gongjin and Cheng Pu approached the group of officers.
"Looks like it was a success, Chief Commander," Chen Wu said.
"…It does indeed," Gongjin replied.
Cheng Pu looked to the east, grunted irritably and said, "Zhuge's wandered off with Lu Su."
"We should see what they're discussing," Gongjin replied.
Cheng Pu and Gongjin passed a group of sailors as they approached Lu Su and Zhuge Liang; the group captain laughed, shouting, "I *said*, 'What idiots'!"
"For being sick…?" a sailor asked.
"For coming here to the south to die!" the captain retorted. "If that's the best that they can do, then this battle's over before it even started!"
"Some are prematurely overconfident," Cheng Pu suggested.
"I think that our visitor agrees," Gongjin replied as he stared at Zhuge Liang's disapproving expression. "But let's see if he'll share his thoughts."
"…Which is all fair and fine, but it still leaves us with the problem you have noted several times," Lu Su said in response to a statement by Zhuge Liang. "…Even with all that, he outnumbers us greatly, so how can we defeat them…?"
"Have heart," Gongjin said as he reached Lu Su. "We now know that Cao cannot fight an effective battle on the water… that is, I think, a start."
"Do we have a strategic battle map…?" Zhuge Liang asked.
Cheng Pu scoffed and replied, "Of course. It is not just you northerners that know how to enact strategy, Zhuge Liang."
"…I was speaking obviously, as a friendly prompt, General Cheng," Zhuge Liang said with evident desperation. "Can we not put our regional prejudices aside for a moment…?"
"…Indeed, General Cheng," Gongjin scolded. "Come, friends, we should go to the war room and look at the plans."
Lu Su shivered and muttered, "Good… we can get away from this biting cold."

Gongjin led the way to the war room, which was located on the top floor of the well-furnished, near-palatial governor's mansion in Red Cliffs City.
"It is not to scale," Gongjin joked as he walked to the large model

of the area that stood on a table in the middle of the room; a burning lamp was placed at each corner of the room to light the area, and the fires were dancing as the wind intensified.

The model depicted the region: small wooden ships – each representing multiple ships in reality – and small boats representing the strike attack vessels lined the northern shore of the Yangtze River, with small figures representing Cao Cao's ground forces placed in and around a model city that represented Wulin. Gongjin's obviously smaller force was arrayed neatly on the southern bank, and to the east, units representing Liu Qi and Liu Bei's forces were positioned close to the port city of Xiakou.

"...To have had such toys as a child," Zhuge Liang sighed.

"You think war is a game...?" Cheng Pu asked irritably.

"...To some, I think it is," Zhuge Liang replied. "It depends on how it affects you, I think, Veteran General. ...I see it is placed such that north is north... very good."

"So what are the options...?" Lu Su asked.

Gongjin frowned worriedly and replied, "Well, we can take them down bit by bit with small skirmishes... but that relies entirely on Cao Cao being a fool. If his problem is the condition of his men due to naval engagements, he'll eventually facilitate a crossing and pincer us from the northeast. We don't have enough troops to help the Liu forces hold the riverbank while simultaneously engaging in continuous, costly naval battles."

"Fortunately, he wouldn't dare risk crossing further north or to the southwest, due to the marshlands and hostile resistance forces, so that limits his possible points of surprise attack," Cheng Pu suggested. "But yes, we have to be concerned about the region north of here, where there are dry plains, suitable for a safe cavalry and infantry march. We have watchtowers, but getting significant ground forces or naval interception there in time, that's another matter altogether."

"Well then," Zhuge Liang said, "a fast, decisive engagement is required."

"Yes," Gongjin agreed. "But... *how*...?"

"He won't be expecting a second battle straight away," Lu Su supposed. "What if we capitalise on our victory and go to him now...?"

"Not so," Gongjin replied. "He will have archery towers and ground-based archers along the river bank and piers, and the Jing force's attack boats are a threat as well."

"But how do we goad him into coming to us...?" Lu Su asked. "Surely, after that last battle, he'll no longer believe he can win a naval engagement and go for the land crossing, at which point we'll be...!"

As Lu Su's voice faded away, Gongjin turned and stared at the map; Cheng Pu grunted with frustration; Zhuge Liang lowered his fan and sighed. After a short pause for thought, Gongjin said, "Retire for now. We have plenty of time to wonder about this tomorrow, I think..."

Lu Su and Zhuge Liang exchanged polite bows with Gongjin and Cheng Pu and retreated silently.

"Are things desperate...?" Cheng Pu asked.

"...Yes," Gongjin admitted. "I worry that we might have to risk going to Cao, accepting the losses we'll inevitably suffer... I see no

other way."
Cheng Pu nodded and left Gongjin to ponder the matter alone.
"...What will you do, Cao Cao...?" Gongjin whispered. "What will you do...?"

"What will you do, Excellency...?"
Commandant-Protector Zhao Yan's question was obviously unwanted; Cao Cao drummed his fingers on the edge of his writing desk and glared at the gathering of officials and officers that had invaded his command tent to press him on the issue of river-sickness and the army's general inability to fight effectively.
"If we leave things as they are, disaster will befall us," Cheng Yu insisted. "Excellency, you must find a way to-!"
"I... have got a suggestion," Cao Cao said at last; the command tent gradually quietened in response. "I have thought about it at length, and I think that we must resort to something that might sound or even look ridiculous, but will nonetheless solve the problem instantaneously."
"...What do you propose, Excellency...?" Li Dian asked.
"You are the very man that I hoped would ask," Cao Cao said. "We must procure many large chains and fixing bolts at once."
The announcement was met by bemused murmuring.
"...*Chains*...?" Xun Yòu exclaimed.
"Yes, Mister Xun, *chains*," Cao Cao replied.
"...You don't mean to...!" Cheng Yu exclaimed. "Excellency, the risks that such a thing would pose would be-!"
"It is better than our men being worthless!" Cao Cao barked.
"What's the plan?" Xiahou Dun asked. "Mengde, what's the plan, and why does Old Cheng think it's stupid...?"
"*Something* is stupid," Cheng Yu heckled. "The chains are for linking the ships together, like a giant child's training pool!"
"...I can see the merits," Zhao Yan said. "It would make them into a stable floating platform... we could even put cavalry aboard...!"
"It might work," Jing Admiral Cai Mao admitted. "We use linked ships for early training exercises; it's unorthodox, but with such a large, intimidating fleet the enemy would be overwhelmed."
"Initially, *perhaps*, when they are taken by surprise by the move, but not later on!" Cheng Yu retorted. "Later on they'll see that the ships cannot be quickly separated and-!"
"Enough!" Cao Cao barked. **"I must give my men stability in order for them to be able to fight: what ideas do *you* have?"**
"...*Fine*," Cheng Yu grumbled. "I'll say no more."
"...They made fools of us because our men could not fight, but when the ships and boats are linked, that will change," Cao Cao replied. "We will then have eight times the number of men that they do again, if not twenty, thirty, a hundred times the men, for our men are each worth ten of theirs! Victory is assured!"
The officers applauded Cao Cao's words; Cheng Yu glared at Xun Yòu, who was visibly resigned.

****

86

Days passed.

"I don't like it," Gongjin said to Cheng Pu as they waited for Lu Su and Zhuge Liang to return to the war room for another morning of deliberating.

"Me neither," Cheng Pu admitted. "Such a large amount of activity can only mean that Cao is retreating or he's up to something…"

"…Yes, and I don't think he's retreating," Gongjin said. "But what could he have come up with to turn his fortunes around…?"

"*Heaven only knows,*" Cheng Pu muttered as Lu Su and Zhuge Liang entered the room.

"Anything new…?" Lu Su asked.

"I'm awaiting a new report," Gongjin replied. "Hopefully, we should have someone here in the next hour or so."

Zhuge Liang fanned himself slowly and smiled.

Over thirty minutes passed before a messenger was announced; Gongjin admitted the youth and said, "Speak."

"Their soldiers have been ordered to acquire large amounts of giant, wrought iron chains, fixing bolts, and wooden linking bridges!" the messenger explained. **"Cao Cao has moved the hospital further back from the river bank, and has moved the bulk of his troops, including his infantry, next to the ships! Large supplies of medicine are arriving from Jiangling to cure the minor illnesses!"**

Cheng Pu dismissed the messenger with a polite gesture.

"*Chains…?*" Lu Su murmured. "…What is he up to…?"

"A land invasion, it has to be," Gongjin said worriedly.

"Yes, but the *chains…?*" Lu Su reiterated.

Zhuge Liang smiled; Gongjin noticed it and said, "Something has occurred to you, Kongming. It has occurred to me too, yet I see nothing to smile about."

"I smile only at the ingenuity, Gongjin," Zhuge Liang replied sadly. "What will you do to confirm this new and unexpected turn of events…?"

"Test him again," Gongjin replied. "What else can I do…?"

"What's going on…?" Lu Su asked obliviously. "What would he need chains f- … …wait a minute: chains, bolts, bridges… what, he isn't going to…!"

"Ingenious," Zhuge Liang conceded. "It will solve the 'river-sickness' issue, and allow him to have cavalry and stable archery lines aboard his ships."

"But it will leave us helpless!" Lu Su cried. "Linking the ships to stabilise them…? …He has the will of Heaven supporting his-!"

"Zijing, *please,*" Gongjin sighed as he walked to his war model and reviewed it.

"…Interlocking ships…" Zhuge Liang pondered. "That will not be easy to counter."

"I know, I know," Gongjin fretted.

"Can you not, between the two of you, think of *something*???" Lu Su cried. "Can't we send men to sabotage the ships…?"

Gongjin sighed and replied, "Not likely. This plan… so, he intends to sail directly across to us, not at all passing us by… he intends to attack us head on."

"…Which is what we wanted… though not quite like this," Zhuge Liang said.

"We might need to smuggle you back to Lord Liu to change the plan, suggest that they sail from Xiakou and pincer Cao's ships while they are in the water," Gongjin suggested. "We'll lose a lot of lives… particularly with Cao's superior numbers and archery support… but it would take a miracle now to avoid that."

"Such a battle could result in mutual destruction," Zhuge Liang said plainly. "Would that have a point to it, all of our men drowning at sea…? …And Cao has more men that he could send… we'd lose all of ours, and lose in the end anyway."

"No!" Lu Su gasped. "Zhang Zhao… will laugh at us!"

"I doubt that he will *laugh*, Zijing," Gongjin retorted. "He hates capitulation as much as any of us: he just accepts the necessity of it in dire circumstances more readily than we do."

"…Some of the ships must be linked by now," Zhuge Liang said. "We should do as you say, Gongjin, and test his mettle."

"I intend to, this very evening," Gongjin replied.

Zhuge Liang and Lu Su left Cheng Pu and Gongjin to plan the evening's attack on Cao Cao's linked fleet; Gongjin stared at the battle map and said, "I wonder if there's any point, Demou."

"Aren't we supposed to avoid courtesy names…?" Cheng Pu joked.

Gongjin smiled and said, "I am forgetting myself: my mind is flooded with ideas. Have *you* any thoughts…?"

"Not really, but Gong- I mean, General Huang Gai has been pestering me for an audience, more so since the rumours about the chains started to circulate," Cheng Pu replied. "He'd like to speak with you, but about what, I don't know."

"By all means," Gongjin said. "Fetch him at once if at all possible!"

Cheng Pu left the room to find a man to summon Huang Gai.

"…Perhaps Heaven has sent him," Gongjin murmured.

Huang Gai entered the war room with Cheng Pu and bowed humbly, saying, "Thank you for agreeing to see me, Chief Commander Zhou."

"You're welcome, General Huang," Gongjin replied. "I understand that you have a proposal."

"I do, though… though it might seem to be unworkable, though I'll leave that for you to decide," Huang Gai said. "I am no fool: Cao Cao's ordered chains to be brought in order to link his ships together. I realised it almost straight away, but now there are signs that his work is already half done."

"…Indeed," Gongjin replied. "Go on."

"Such a ploy will doubtlessly ruin our own plans, since a linked network of ships and boats will make a floating battle platform that – provided no serious mishaps occur – gives him back full control of his fighting force and leaves us at a numerical disadvantage," Huang Gai continued. "The most obvious 'mishap' is fire, though the current northwest wind makes such an attack option unavailable to us."

"In fact, it raises the possibility that *Cao* might decide to use fire against *us*," Gongjin replied. "The combination of linked ships and fire is certain defeat."

"It is… for *him*," Huang Gai said with a smile. "You've done some farming in the south, Chief Commander… and fought in a fair few river battles. You've seen all of the seasons… so you must know what I'm thinking."

Gongjin laughed and replied, "I am very worried, General Huang, and worry often robs a man of his full wits: I'm afraid that I might not know what you mean."

"This is the mid-winter," Huang Gai said, "and mid-winter is a time for dramatic fluctuations in the weather; it is not unusual for the wind direction to not only change, but to *reverse*."

Gongjin's smiled; Cheng Pu smiled almost simultaneously as he realised what Huang Gai was suggesting.

"That being the case, we need a ploy to get such a large amount of kindling close enough to their flagships at the right moment," Huang Gai continued. "The smarter advisers will notice the change in wind direction and order vigilance, even as Cao Cao acts as recklessly as ever; we must somehow convince them to let us sail toward them in such conditions without fear of attack…"

"…A surrender," Gongjin said.

"Precisely," Huang Gai replied. "That's the uncomfortable part of it, Chief Commander: I propose that I be the man to offer to submit and carry the flames to Cao Cao's fleet."

"*You*…?" Cheng Pu exclaimed.

"We will be humiliated in the next encounter… I think that we all know that," Huang Gai replied. "After that, and with all of the other men leaving Lord Sun's service and writing letters of submission – including the lord's own trusted cousins – I believe that my surrender – that of a long-serving general, frustrated with a 'feeble, unpopular and worthless third lord' and 'pining for a swift end to a futile endeavour' – would be taken as genuine."

"…I agree, sad to say," Gongjin murmured.

Cheng Pu frowned; Huang Gai noticed his old friend's expression and said, "You must trust me, Demou."

"I… I *do*," Cheng Pu replied hesitantly.

"Not entirely," Huang Gai said sadly. "You have seen my own concern and mistake it for a desire to submit as Sun Ben and Sun Fu have done, but I assure you that such treachery could not be further from my mind."

"…Lord Sun is divisive, gentlemen, and has almost led to many a man walking away, saying everything that General Huang has said and meaning it," Gongjin said suddenly; the older men turned and stared at him with obvious incredulity. "We're all here now because we have chosen to stay, regardless of Lord Sun Quan's faults, because we care very much about the south and want to honour Lord Sun Jian and Lord Sun Ce – Bofu – if nothing else."

"…Yes," Cheng Pu admitted. "Wentai gave this old fool from Yòubeiping a reason to be alive: young Lord Sun Ce inspired this same old fool to go on after my friend – his father – died, and even though Lord Sun Quan does not really inspire me at all, the south is about more than its lord… it is my home."

"And that's why you can trust me to do this without suddenly making a false surrender genuine," Huang Gai insisted. "I cannot pretend that Lord Sun Quan has my full faith, but he does have my full support, and the south is my life… I won't let it die. I implore you, Chief Commander, to let me do this! Please, Chief

Commander, allow me to feign betrayal and then destroy the villain's fleet!"

"...This must not go beyond this room," Gongjin replied. "Our guest Zhuge Liang cannot know of it, so Lu Su must not know of it, for the cunning Zhuge reads him too easily; even Lord Sun Quan must not know of it if at all possible, and if he must, then it must be kept to the smallest number of people possible. I will send a trusted man to Chaisang to inform Lü Fan of our idea so that he can manage things."

"I shall now return to my preparations for the battle if it pleases you, Chief Commander," Huang Gai said.

"Yes, you... you do that, General," Gongjin replied as he started to sink into deep thought; the three men exchanged low bows, and Huang Gai retreated.

"...We can trust him, Chief Commander," Cheng Pu insisted.

"Mm...? ...Oh, I don't doubt that," Gongjin replied. "Heaven has sent him to lend credence to a plan that needed just such a man!"

"Oh...?" Cheng Pu exclaimed. "You had your own 'surrender ruse' in mind...?"

"Yes, but I didn't think that I'd have a volunteer," Gongjin chuckled. "I also had no idea who to approach... Gongfu is ideal."

Cheng Pu hummed thoughtfully and said, "I didn't much like his estimation of our chances against Cao's fleet in that next battle, though; will we really be 'humiliated'...?"

"We'll lose, but honourably," Gongjin replied.

Cheng Pu started to pace as he asked, "But if the plan doesn't work, what then...?"

"I don't know," Gongjin admitted. "I suppose we'll have to hope that Lü Ziheng has an idea or our genius guest comes up with something, won't we, if we were that unlucky."

"...I'll go and oversee the preparations, I think," Cheng Pu decided. "You'll be alright watching proceedings with Lu Su and 'Zhuge the Crouching Dragon'...?"

Gongjin laughed half-heartedly and said, "Yes, Demou... go on."

"You used my courtesy name again, Gongjin," Cheng Pu joked as he bowed and retreated.

"...It begins," Gongjin murmured.

****

87

Dusk arrived: Cheng Pu stood in front of the assembled officers and said, "You're all about to go and fight Cao Cao's fleet... which is now chained together. *Don't* – I repeat, *don't* – underestimate the danger."

"But it's a trick for helping children!" one captain suggested.

"Maybe, Captain Hu, maybe," Cheng Pu retorted, "but the stability that the chains bring to his ships as platforms will restore their ability to fight using all weapons... so again I say 'do not be reckless'. Remember above all that this is just a sortie to test his lines: don't start thinking that we're going after another Huang Zu and making heroic one-man dashes for the flagship... and when I say that, I mean *you*, Lü Meng and Ling Tong."

"There's no direct line of attack to exploit when boats and ships are connected together by chains instead of ropes, Veteran General," Lü Meng said. "I will remain at the rear to provide emergency support as instructed."

"...I can put it no better!" Ling Tong chuckled.

"...**Alright, then,**" Cheng Pu concluded. "Good luck to all: let us see just what sort of advantage these chains give to our enemies! Perhaps we might link our own ships if it works! **Dismissed...!**"

The officials laughed and started to disperse; Huang Gai – who had volunteered to serve as mission commander in battle – looked at Cheng Pu, nodded purposefully and had his subordinates follow his slow retreat.

Gongjin, Lu Su and Zhuge Liang journeyed to a watchtower to view the battle from a high vantage point; Cheng Pu remained on the ground and watched as two groups of vessels left the piers.

The 'vanguard' component of the assault – comprising smaller ships and boats – was led by Huang Gai and Zhou Tai, who would be supported by numerous subordinate officers as they dispersed to attack different parts of Cao Cao's front lines; the second component – which served as a buffer between the southern piers and the enemy and as a relief force in case of the worst occurring – was led by Han Dang, Chen Wu, Ling Tong, Lü Meng, Su Fei and Gan Ning. Third and fourth forces that, for fear of inviting disaster, nobody spoke of – which were the remainder of the Jiangdong fleet and an entirely land-based defence army – were on full alert in case of a sudden exploitation of opportunities on Cao Cao's part.

"...Heaven favour us," Cheng Pu muttered.

"**They're back again, Excellency!**" Xun Yòu cried as he ran into Cao Cao's command tent; Cao was sitting quietly and reading a bamboo book that he immediately – but casually – set down on his table.

"Why am I needed, Gongda...?" Cao Cao retorted. "Can my advisers not respond without authorisation from me...?"

"I... thought that you should know, Excellency," Xun Yòu replied.

"My forces are dealing with them, though...?" Cao Cao asked.

"...They have been deployed as five units as instructed," Xun Yòu replied. "But should Cai Mao be asked to send reserve forces in

case of-?"
"There will be no need for Cai Mao this time, Gongda," Cao Cao said dismissively. "The southerners will shortly learn that have met their match in Mengde: they'll wish that they had submitted!"

The five Han 'linked fleets' were commanded by Generals Yu Jin, Zhang Liao, Xu Huang, Zhang Hè and Cao Hong; Li Dian, Cao Xiu, Zhu Ling, Lu Zhao and Feng Kai had been relegated to seconds for this encounter, although Zhao Yan stressed to Lu and Feng that their roles were in no way because of their earlier 'humiliation'. There would be no defeat this time, since the connected ships and boats provided the stable platforms that the northern soldiers required in order to combat the worst of the sickness and balancing issues that came with travelling on the water.
"**Show no mercy,**" Lu Zhao said to his subordinate officers. "**The river will run red, coated with the bodies of southerners.**"
"**You shouldn't allow the last encounter to anger you, General,**" Lu Zhao's colleague Zhang Hè suggested. "**We might want to parley with them later.**"
"**They'll 'parley', General Zhang, from a position of weakness that we shall inflict here today!**" Lu Zhao retorted. "**We'll smash them!**"

Even the resigned Huang Gai was stunned by the battle that followed; the Han forces outnumbered the Jiangdong forces by four-to-one, had surprisingly high morale despite their ailments and an obvious yearning to exact as much damage as possible. Han archers pummelled the rear of the Jiangdong fleet with arrows while the Jiangdong vanguard suffered attacks by lunging spearmen and swordsmen that had no difficulty fighting when the boats beneath their feet barely moved.
"**We'll be routed!**" Huang Gai cried. "**We must withdraw!**"
Zhou Tai looked about him and grunted angrily, saying, "**Agreed!**"
"…Bollocks to *this*," Gan Ning grumbled as he left his post and started to leap from boat to boat on a path that would take him toward the front line.
"**Come back, Xingba!**" Su Fei pleaded.
When Gan Ning reached the front he quickly realised that the Han forces were not stepping off of their stable platforms to engage the Jiangdong men on their own boats; he hopped toward the nearest Han position and yanked a spearman over to his own unsteady craft, saying, "**Let's even this up, shall we?**"
The Han spearman screamed with fear as his feet touched the bobbing craft; Gan Ning ran the man through and then took up his bow, shouting, "**Firing arrows at a distance, uh…? A real man is here!**"
Two Han archers fell to Gan Ning's precise shots, but the effort was ultimately futile and Gan knew it; he ducked the return fire and retreated while laughing falsely to hide his frustration.
"**RETREAT!**" Huang Gai ordered. "**Preserve yourselves!**"
Zhou Tai signalled to the ships at the rear; Lü Meng turned to his subordinate major and said, "**Get us moved, and send word across the other ships to move aside and allow our men to flee: *quickly*, before they're all killed!**"
The Jiangdong force started to move backwards, boat by boat, as

the ships at the rear parted and started to provide more effective covering fire from the decks; Cao Hong laughed and said, "**We'll pursue them!**"
"**We can't!**" Zhu Ling protested. "**Being chained together slows our craft and–!**"
"**What harm has it done us so far?**" Cao Hong retorted.
"**We'll be isolated and risk traps if we get too close to their side of the river!**" Zhu Ling said. "**We should do as we have been ordered, General Cao, and chase them away! We've had our revenge!**"
Cao Hong glared at the retreating boats and grunted, saying, "We have... this will do. ...**HOLD POSITION!**"

Huang Gai sighed miserably as he started to see the cost of the 'test'; there were corpses floating on the river in every direction.
"What a waste," Zhou Tai sighed.
"...**Pardon...?**" Huang Gai prompted; he was now distracted by the nearby sight of Captain Hu, who was lying on his back and staring at his partially-severed right leg, while his three remaining subordinates were sobbing as they realised that their many colleagues had been lost as part of the first wave.
"**I said that it's a waste!**" Zhou Tai shouted over the enemy's heckles and their own men's sobbing and grumbling.
"**That's one way of putting it,**" Huang Gai replied.
"**Chief Commander Zhou's signalling that we should go back, so we won't be criticised, which is something,**" a captain suggested.
"**Who'd dare criticise?**" Huang Gai retorted. "*Look at us*! **This has *harmed us*! The enemy will feel that it is already over, and so will a lot of our men!**"
Zhou Tai looked about and said, "*Yes*... **but we knew it that it would cost us, though, didn't we, General...?**"
"...**I must see this for what it is,**" Huang Gai replied. "**It was... it was necessary.**"

Cao Cao welcomed his returning officers with jars of wine and meat and a great deal of satisfied laughter.
"Very good...!" Cao Cao said. "This is all very good...!"
"Generals Yu Jin, Zhang Liao and Cao Hong were most ferocious, slaying the enemy by the dozens," General Lu Zhao reported. "I only wish that I had matched their prowess, Excellency, and compensated for my earlier efforts."
"You all performed well," Cao Cao insisted. "The enemy came here again to test us, see if they could repeat their spiteful humiliation of His Majesty's army and navy, but Heaven has spoken, and justice is served! You will all dine well tonight, gentlemen, courtesy of my purse, on the deck of the flagship for all to see! We have nothing to fear from these southern men now: let us banquet and laugh at them as they laughed at us!"
"*Ayah*... don't do that!" Cheng Yu protested. "Excellency, we must be careful! We must be vigilant! Remember that Sun Tzu has taught 'Show strength where there is weakness, and weakness where there is strength'! This might have been a ruse!"
"They lost hundreds of their best men," Cao Hong scoffed. "What sort of ruse is that?"

"Sometimes loss is used, impractical though it may seem, to give a false impression of weakness!" Cheng Yu retorted. "You should know that, General! 'The Art of War' and other military texts clearly state that deceptions, ruses, can take many forms and our enemies may understand that more than they are-!"
"You said that before we destroyed Liu Bei at Wulin, *and* when we marched against the Wuhuan, who couldn't even *read*, never mind read 'The Art of War'," Xiahou Dun heckled. "You're in danger of losing my respect, Old Cheng: stop making our enemies sound so clever and powerful! **They're eggs and we're smashing them!**"
"I quite agree, Cousin Yuanrang," Cao Cao chuckled.
"You *shouldn't*, Excellency," Cheng Yu insisted. "Don't-!"
"Stop making a great tiger out of Sun Quan, Elder Cheng: he is a *mouse*, a silly little pirate king with delusions of grandeur, and his motley bunch are unable to match our wits *or* our might," Cao Cao said calmly. "We will show our contempt for our weak enemy: we will banquet loudly and fearlessly until the day that they finally realise that their little game is over!"
The generals cheered; Cheng Yu scowled bitterly and muttered, "This is *idiocy*."

The Jiangdong war room was tense as Gongjin and Cheng Pu tried to find the words to console an assembly of officials – mainly officers that had freshly returned from the battle with Cao Cao's 'linked fleet' – while Lu Su and Zhuge Liang looked on.
"...We'll find a way to turn this around: you have my word," Gongjin declared. "For now, please, all of you, retire... *rest*. Leave this to me."
Many of the officers were grumbling as they retreated; Huang Gai refused to leave and said, "I want some more reassurance, *Chief Commander*, and will not leave until I get it."
Gongjin nodded seriously and replied, "Fine: stay."
        "...Veteran General Huang is right to want more reassurance: what is it exactly that Zhou Yu can come up with...?" Sun Jiao asked as the officers filed out of the governor's mansion and started toward the gates. "General Dong Xi defeated Huang Zu's navy when he cut the rope, but we can't cut chains!"
Lü Meng hummed thoughtfully and replied, "It isn't the chains that we should aim to destroy, I think: chains can't be cut, but wood can burn."
"There's a *northwest wind*, A'Meng," Han Dang heckled.
Lü Meng was going to reply but thought better of it; he smiled humbly and said, "So there is, General Han... so there is."

****

88

Three days passed.

"...It can't end like this," Gongjin insisted as he surveyed his battlefield model. "There has to be a way... there *has to be*."
Cheng Pu, Lu Su, Huang Gai and Zhuge Liang looked on silently: the night was cold, and the lamp fires were dancing in the wind.
"They're going to go out," Lu Su murmured as he watched one of the lamps.
"We cannot stay here all night," Cheng Pu said.
"We... we have no choice," Gongjin retorted.
"Chief Commander," Huang Gai said with anger, "there is no point to this! I won't lose any more men to these futile stick-poking actions! We know his strength, so let's just have it out with him!"
"Brave, but suicidal," Gongin retorted. "There... there must be something we can do... maybe... maybe a surprise march through the marshes... he won't expect that, will he...? If we sailed to Ba Qiu in Changsha, crossed the Great River there, took a straight route northward to Wulin..."
"That is desperate and futile," Cheng Pu said. "Trudging through the mud to fight a vast force that specialises in land battles... once their inevitable signal towers spotted us, we'd be finished. Even Cao's forces located in other regions could be sent to intercept us while he sailed south and hit Red Cliffs."
Gongjin sighed and said, "You're right, you're right. There *must* be some way to destroy his fleet... there must be."
"It would help if you could see," Lu Su chuckled as he took a lamp from its stand and walked to the model. "Here, I'll hold it for you."
"...My thanks," Gongjin said. "Now... we're back to the pincer idea again. If Liu Bei attacks from the north..."
Gongin pointed at the model of Xiakou; Lu Su lowered the lamp slightly to get greater focus, but as he did so a gust of wind carried the lamp fire southward, setting fire to one of the sails of the model southern fleet that sat directly south of it.
"...Sorry...!" Lu Su said with embarrassment.
"It matters little, since it is just a model," Gongjin replied before he picked the model up and blew the flames out. "But in reality such a northwest wind is lethal for us..."
"...Ah," Lu Su exclaimed. "Such a wind can rush their ships to our shores with the sails hoisted, and rout us without warning. And if they used *fire*..."
"...Then such a wind is most inconvenient," Zhuge Liang said tonelessly; Gongjin frowned instinctively before he wiped the expression from his face, turned to the smiling Zhuge and stared at him expectantly.
"B-but... if Cao Cao knows this... and he must... then...!" Lu Su fretted.
"Calm yourself, Zijing," Gongjin pleaded. "Sometimes, war seems as though it has an inevitable conclusion... what we must not do is lose heart. Master Zhuge, I think it best for you to return to your lord and prepare for the land battle; this matter of the wind should not be broached, lest it cause panic. I promise, all of you... this will have the positive outcome we seek."

Gongjin looked at his veteran generals and smiled encouragingly; Cheng Pu nodded silently, but Huang Gai was unflinching.

"...I shall take my leave, then," Zhuge Liang said as he bowed to each of the other four men in turn; Lu Su bowed uneasily and led Zhuge from the room while Gongjin followed the guest from Jing Province with his eyes.

"...He's insightful," Cheng Pu said knowingly.

"Indeed he is," Gongjin replied. "He's figured it all out; whether that is because of his farming background or a latent strategic genius is another matter, but... yes, he sees it all. Let us hope that Cao Cao does not have such a man in his employ... and that Zhuge's insight extends no further while he serves a rival."

"So am I clear to proceed, Chief Commander...?" Huang Gai asked.

"...Yes, General, at once," Gongjin replied; once Huang Gai had departed, Gongjin said, "Demou, you must watch the other officers closely: if anyone – anyone – starts to suspect that Gongfu 'is going to defect', then-"

"Then I should take that man aside and reassure or inform where appropriate," Cheng Pu interrupted. "I understand, Gongjin. But we'll be preparing everyone for an all-out attack, won't we...? How will we disguise the true nature of it and not risk genuine desertions and defections...?"

"We can't," Gongjin replied. "You know that, else you wouldn't ask: we are asking our men to show faith, blind faith, and to follow orders no matter how suicidal they might seem, but is that not normality now...?"

Cheng Pu laughed dryly, turned to leave and said, "True enough..."

"...The fire ships *must be ready*," Gongjin muttered. "Perhaps I should assign more men to them..."

Cao Cao insisted on holding banquets to taunt his enemies: Cheng Yu and Xun Yòu were becoming increasingly concerned about their lord's apparent flippancy with regard to the enemy, but Cao Cao and the majority of his officers were not to be swayed.

"...**This is not the way that we should be behaving!**" Cheng Yu scolded as he looked about him: he was one of dozens of guests at a banquet on the Han flagship, but his presence was at best reluctant.

"All you do is *whinge*, Old Cheng!" Cao Hong said as he bit into a piece of cooked pork. "What is there to fear from Sun Quan and his army of river rats...?"

"Cousin Zilian's right: you're always moaning, but when was the last time that you were right...?" Xiahou Dun heckled drunkenly. "We should have left you in Jiangling with that other bastard!"

"*Please* don't call Mister Jia that, Yuanrang," Cao Cao sighed.

"He's... a *bastard*, Mengde," Xiahou Dun retorted. "I know you've decided that you like him, an' I nearly did, an' even if it *is* 'cause I'm *drunk*, he killed Ang, an' Anmin, and-!"

"**Drunk or not, don't repeat that same old nonsense!**" Cao Cao ordered. "**Mister Jia has made up for his past mistakes!**"

"...Alright, *fine*," Xiahou Dun grumbled.

"Is there any word of Cousin Zihe...?" Cao Zhen asked.

"...No, Zidan," Cao Cao replied miserably; the 'Zihe' that Cao Zhen referred to was Cao Chun, the charismatic former leader and founder of Cao Cao's 'Tiger and Leopard Cavalry', and his grave injury during the climax of the 'Battle of Steep-slope', less than an hour after his men had captured the bulk of Liu Bei's baggage train – including Bei's daughters, who were then gifted to Chun as a reward – weighed heavy on Cao Cao's mind. "Nothing *yet*," Cao Cao added, "but he'll be *fine*."

"S'right, he will, so stop asking, Tubby, or you'll curse him," Cao Hong heckled.

"**What???**" Cao Cao exclaimed.

"Alright, alright," Cao Hong said. "Sorry, Zhen."

"Mock my girth all you want, Cousin Zilian: I've got a commission now, and it will not be long before I'll *outrank you*, you ignoramus," Cao Zhen retorted.

"...So you keep saying, but the worst you'll ever do is *outweigh me*," Cao Hong retorted; Xiahou Dun laughed so hard that he spat the food from his mouth and narrowly missed Cao Cao's bodyguard Xu Chu and Cao's cousin Cao Xiu, who sighed irritably and wiped slobber from his sleeve.

"**Sorry, Wenlie,**" Xiahou Dun said as he cackled uncontrollably.

"...It's fine," Cao Xiu insisted.

"...Look, let's have a truce," Cao Hong said as he stared at the irritated faces of Cao Zhen and Cao Cao in turn. "I don't want a fight, particularly not if-"

"**Shut up, Zilian,**" Cao Cao growled.

"Alright, *alright*," Cao Hong muttered.

"*Aiee...* my extended family really is a burden sometimes," Cao Cao complained. "Can we somehow raise the intellectual standard of this gathering before it sinks any lower?"

"We shouldn't be up here at *all*, Excellency, not at night, not while there are enemies within striking distance!" Cheng Yu protested.

"The 'linked fleets' have made cornered rodents and corpses out of them," Cao Cao replied dismissively. "They'll take days to think, but what is there for them to do...?"

"As I have tried to say time and again before, they'll only be stunned for a short while!" Cheng Yu retorted. "After that, Excellency, they'll see the impediment to movement that chains introduce and-!"

"And *what*...?" Cao Cao heckled.

"And employ *fire*," Cheng Yu warned.

Cao Cao smirked, sniggered derisively and pointed at a flickering brazier; the flame was moving toward the southeast.

"...Yes, *now*, but winds change direction!" Cheng Yu retorted.

"Am I missing something...?" Xiahou Dun asked.

"The flames are licking in a south-easterly direction, Cousin," Cao Zhen explained. "The wind is a north-westerly wind; if they tried to use fire it would blow back on them."

"...Ah, right!" Xiahou Dun said. "So Old Cheng's worried for nothing, then!"

"No, *fool*, 'Old Cheng' is not 'worried for nothing'!" Cheng Yu protested. "*Winds change direction*! If they sense an opportunity, they might-"

"'They' are *ignorant bumpkins*, Elder Cheng, with no understanding of the changes!" Cao Cao said dismissively. "If they knew such things, gentlemen, then would they now be at such a sudden disadvantage...?"

"*Disadvantage*...?" Cheng Yu exclaimed. "The-!"

"What would it take, I wonder, for you to enjoy a certain victory...?" Cao Cao asked derisively. "They have nowhere to run, except perhaps to Shi Xie, who will make humble Buddhist monks of them all! They cannot fight, because they are hopelessly outnumbered and outclassed! All that's left to them is submission to His Excellency Cao Cao, Chancellor of State and Prime Minister of the Han, and there will be no leniency for Sun Quan or Zhou Yu now: they'll lose *everything* for wasting my time here!"

"...So when do you intend to deliver your 'killing blow', then, *Prime Minister*...?" Cheng Yu asked snidely.

"They have ten days in which to propose something that will save them, after which I will do to them what I did to the Wuhuan and the Yuans," Cao Cao replied nonchalantly. "Until then I intend to enjoy a respite from the pressures of recent years: we have all worked very hard – including you, Elder Cheng – and deserve a straightforward campaign after years of slogging! So why don't you relax for once and stop looking for miracles for the enemy, mm...? Let them chase those futile dreams themselves."

"Don't you have anything to say...?" Cheng Yu pleaded as he stared at General Li Dian, Xun Yòu, Commandant-Protector Zhao Yan and Registrar Liu Yè in turn. "Mister Xun: you're an adviser as well, and must be able to see that this is reckless."

Xun Yòu smiled slightly and said, "Sometimes reckless behaviour has benefits: that is the *commonly-held view*."

"...You know the risks as well as I do, Gongda, so why do you keep your silence...?" Cheng Yu despaired. "If Jia Xu, your uncle Wenruo or Guo Jia were here, they-"

"If *Guo Jia* were here, Old Cheng, I wouldn't need others," Cao Cao barked. **"I'd be certain of everything, and none would question! If Guo Jia were here, the southern men would already be under my heel! Instead of *that*, Old Cheng, I must tolerate whiners and ditherers that force me to look to the Art of War; and as Guo Jia said, it's all in there if one only looks, so why do I need advisers if all I have to do is *read*...?"**

Cheng Yu shrank back and said no more.

"...**Music,**" Cao Cao ordered, "**to taunt the southern rats!**"

Cheng Yu glared at Xun Yòu, who smiled apologetically; the banquet continued as the demoralised southerners looked on at a distance and wondered if Cao Cao was right to be so jubilant.

✳✳✳✳✳✳✳✳✳✳✳✳

89

Days passed.

"Prime Minister!"
Cao Cao stopped reading the book that he was holding – a text on the principles of good governance – and looked at the messenger that had entered his personal tent without warning: his bodyguard Xu Chu was poised to strike, but Cao gestured that Xu should back down and returned to his reading.
"Urgent!" the messenger cried. **"Veteran General Huang Gai of the southland wishes to surrender to you!"**
Cao Cao had expected the report to be about some mundane matter; he looked up and replied, "Mm...? ...*What did you say...?*"
Cheng Yu neared the tent at that moment and prepared to enter in order to apologise for not intercepting the messenger, but he halted when the messenger shouted, **"Prime Minister! Urgent! Veteran General Huang Gai of the southland wishes to surrender to you!"**
Cheng Yu hummed thoughtfully and entered the tent as the brief report was ending.
"...Has he presented a letter of submission...?" Cao Cao asked.
The messenger got to his feet, pulled a letter from his sleeve and presented it to Cao Cao, who snatched it and started to read; the messenger stepped back and knelt in penitence once again.
"...I wonder if this is to be believed," Cheng Yu said. "...Messenger, you may retire for now."
The messenger got to his feet and left the tent.
"... ... ...He speaks of humiliation in our last battle, and the inevitability of defeat," Cao Cao said as he finished reading; he then passed the letter to Cheng Yu, who read the letter carefully; Cao waited impatiently for a few moments before asking, "What do you think...?"
"... ... ...Things we want to hear are said," Cheng Yu replied. "He accounts for sending his family later as a point of avoiding suspicion... understandable, if he is so close to Sun Quan and Zhou Yu; he speaks of futile schemes, disorganisation, putting men at risk; he speaks well, indeed. He is obviously disgruntled, since he talks of glory under Sun Jian and Sun Ce that is not reflected in this new ruler... he speaks of general discontent among the veteran generals regarding the new Chief Commander, Zhou Yu... it is very likely that this is genuine."
"Are you sure...?" Cao Cao asked cautiously. "Can we be sure that there is no scheme in this...?"
"How can one be *sure*...?" Cheng Yu replied as he handed the letter back to Cao Cao, who started to read it again. "This man is known for his fiery disposition, and probably finds the style of leadership and military disposition unbearable. He speaks of other generals that would also defect once the right amount of damage was done to Zhou Yu... of senior advisers that advocated surrender... I would say that is quite possible."
"...Still... it is too good to be true," Cao Cao decided. "We should... ... ...but then, what if it really *is* true...? It is entirely and logically right that this old soldier should fear me, I think..."

"My lord, you know my thoughts," Cheng Yu said.

Cao Cao wanted to believe that the surrender was timely and genuine: he glared at Cheng Yu and growled, "Again, you sow doubt. Jia Xu now holds Jiangling because I cannot rely on his counsel to inspire... and since we arrived, you have veered between fawning and floundering."

Cheng Yu was exasperated at Cao Cao's description of his contribution, but he could not think of the words to retort.

"But I can see I will have no peace while you are silent," Cao Cao grumbled. "...Speak."

"It is as I have said before," Cheng Yu insisted. "Firstly, something about Liu Bei's feeble resistance makes no sense, especially since they have now disappeared, yet the courtiers of Liu and Sun have been in strong diplomatic contact."

Cao Cao sneered; the 'strong diplomatic contact' consisted of assumptions about seemingly innocent fishing boats that had reportedly travelled back and forth across the Yangtze River.

"Secondly, as Jia Xu correctly predicted, disease is rampant, and we have lost many men to it... and even with the boat-connecting plan in place to combat 'river-sickness', we still have many sick soldiers," Cheng Yu continued. "Thirdly-"

"*Thirdly...?*" Cao Cao scoffed. "How many objections do you have???"

"...*Thirdly*," Cheng Yu continued, "I am worried about the weather in these parts... the *winds*..."

Cao Cao was weary of Cheng Yu's repeated protestations about the weather; he scowled and replied, "The winds are *north-westerly*." Cheng Yu was about to interject, but Cao Cao did not give him a chance to do so, adding, "Yes, I am aware that the direction of the winds can sometimes change in these parts... but what do these southern fools know of it, mm...? Can they predict the exact days that this phenomenon occurs, and work with it...?"

"Is it worth risking...?" Cheng Yu protested. "My lord, you hold lavish parties and drink heartily, singing songs and reciting your own poetry that mocks the south for their stupidity. We have connected boats... a fire attack assisted by a southeast wind would wipe out our fleet."

"Nonsense!" Cao Cao retorted. "I know of all that you say, and it is all too chancy for them to exploit! They cannot even *pray* for such miniscule odds to be in their favour!"

Cheng Yu lowered his gaze and frowned silently.

"...Now, I think that this man, on second reading, surrenders sincerely," Cao Cao continued. "The only bitter wind that blows, blows for Zhou Yu; let this old general come here. We will interrogate him carefully, ascertain his honesty, and if he is genuine – another Zhang Hè, or Zhang Liao – we will have him be the vanguard! Get the messenger back! We will reply immediately!"

"Very well, *Prime Minister*," Cheng Yu said before he retreated to locate the messenger.

Cao Cao took up a piece of writing material to compose a response and smiled, whispering, "I might have lost Sun Ben, but I have gained Huang Gai! Heaven truly favours me!"

Cheng Yu crossed paths with Xun Yòu and Registrar Liu Yè as he made his way to the barracks; Xun Yòu frowned and asked, "What's the hurry...?"

"A messenger has brought word that 'Veteran General Huang Gai' wishes to surrender," Cheng Yu replied wearily. "I'll leave you ponder that and decide whether you will proffer any advice while I go and fetch the messenger back."

Liu Yè watched Cheng Yu walk away at speed and muttered, *"Huang Gai...?"*

"You've had more contact with the enemy than Elder Cheng or me," Xun Yòu noted. "Do you consider this to be genuine...?"

"...Possibly, Gongda," Liu Yè replied. "My dealings were with a Jiangdong army led by Sun Ce, who was a charismatic hero to his followers; Sun Quan's an entirely different man. Remember that the trusted general Li Shu that Sun Ce left to safeguard Lujiang – after defeating my previous lord, Liu Xun – was the first to rebel and take half of the Jiangdong army with him when Sun Quan inherited the region."

"...Yes, Ziyang, and since then we've heard about a whole list of self-inflicted disasters, and, of course, Sun Ben's attempts to come over to us," Xun Yòu said. "Huang Gai is, like Sun Ben, a veteran of the days of Sun Jian and Sun Ce; perhaps it is not ridiculous to assume that- … … …But nonetheless, Ziyang, we must show caution."

"Sun Ce fooled Liu Xun with obviously false pandering, and my warnings were ignored," Liu Yè recalled. "Before that, Zhou Yu – the same Zhou Yu that now serves Sun Quan as Chief Commander – fooled Yuan Yin with a ruse and held Danyang for Sun Ce, and before that Ce himself – widely regarded as a dumb thug – feigned death at Zhou Yu's suggestion to lure out and defeat Ze Rong. Ruses are not beyond these enemies of ours, and they're certainly not beyond Zhou Yu."

"...But Jia Xu and Cheng Yu have protested in vain, and I can't say that I believe that I would do any better," Xun Yòu admitted. "His Excellency Cao Cao, the Chancellor of State and Prime Minister of the Han, has decided that we are not worth listening to, so we must hope that Huang Gai submits genuinely and that Elder Cheng really *is* wrong..."

Later that night, Huang Gai and a small group of loyal followers waited by the riverbank for a response from Cao Cao; they did not have long to wait before a messenger – disguised as a fisherman – sailed to the riverbank, produced a letter from his sleeve and handed it to Huang Gai before retreating quickly.

"...What does it say...?" an old soldier asked.

Huang Gai read the letter carefully; his expression changed from a frown to a smile as he realised that his ploy had worked.

"...In three days," Huang Gai said, "we go to Cao Cao."

Huang Gai's men smiled and nodded agreeably.

****

90

Cao Cao summoned his officers to his tent on the morning after receiving Huang Gai's letter; he laughed and said, "I had intended a series of harassment engagements, gentlemen, but I don't think that they will be necessary now."

"But Prime Minister, we have all but defeated them!" Feng Kai protested. "Glory is ours for the taking if only you'll let us-!"

"There will be glory, General Feng," Cao Cao promised. "You're usually a very patient man: months of frustrating stalemates on the Jing-Yu border never once elicited such a reaction from you."

"Forgive my bluntness, Prime Minister, but we weren't facing mass deaths due to disease when we were on the Jing-Yu border," Lu Zhao said. "The southerners might have feigned defeat in order to have us sit here and slowly waste away!"

"Not so," Cao Cao retorted. "Without saying too much, I can confidently suggest that there will be the beginnings of an end to this campaign in three days and an outright end to it in ten days beyond that."

"...*Another* ten days...?" Xiahou Dun exclaimed. "That gives them more time than you wished, and yet you're happy: what has happened, Mengde?"

"I'll explain after the meeting, Cousin Yuanrang," Cao Cao chuckled. "Suffice to say that this will soon be over!"

"...And we'll have destroyed Liu Bei...?" Xiahou Dun asked.

"His end will swiftly follow the submission of the south," Cao Cao replied. "But I shall say no more: we'll banquet on land from now on and await our inevitable victory!"

Some of the more cynical officers turned to look at Cheng Yu and Xun Yòu, who were both unreadable; but orders were orders, and no objections were heard.

Sun Quan was glad when a report arrived from Red Cliffs: the messenger fell to one knee and said, **"REPORT! Chief Commander Zhou has ascertained that since the battle with the 'linked fleets', Cao Cao's forces have remained moored and his men do nothing but partake in loud, well-lit banquets to taunt our forces!"**

Lü Fan, Zhang Zhao, Zhang Hong, Zhuge Jin, Gu Yong, Pan Zhang and Zhu Ran looked on silently.

"...I see," Sun Quan replied. "Is that all...?"

"Chief Commander Zhou has given me this secret report that is 'for highly trusted eyes and ears alone'!" the messenger said as he reached into his sleeve and produced a small wooden tube that had been sealed shut by wax that had etched patterns stamped into it to prevent easy tampering.

"...Mister Zhang, would you...?" Sun Quan prompted; Zhang Zhao stepped forward, took the tube from the messenger and passed it to Quan.

"That is all!" the messenger said.

"...Then you may go and rest: Mister Pan, please escort him to the city barracks," Sun Quan replied as he studied the wooden tube.

The messenger retreated from the private audience hall with Pan Zhang; Zhang Zhao turned to Sun Quan and asked, "Why do you not open it, my lord...?"

"I... fear that I will not like its contents," Sun Quan admitted. "It might contain some 'ray of hope', but it might also contain instructions to flee to Jiaozhi as well..."

"...Or, perhaps, to take Chancellor Cao's last offer of 'Administrator of Kuaiji' and tender submission...?" Zhang Zhao asked.

"He'd not say that, not after what has already been said," Sun Quan retorted. "Zhou Gongjin will speak of victory or defeat... nothing else."

"Like it or not, Lord Sun, it must be opened," Zhang Hong urged.

"...Then so be it!" Sun Quan said as he tore the wax and took the letter from the tube; Quan then read the letter slowly and carefully, and smiled as he neared the end.

"We are saved...?" Zhu Ran prompted.

"...Cao Cao laughs, banquets his men and ignores the obvious dangers, as I once did at Xuan City, for which I was rightly humiliated and for which I am humbled to this very day," Sun Quan replied. "And like me, he will deserve what comes next. Yuzhang and Guangling are secured, and Cao's fleet at Wulin will soon be no more: we are to prepare for an imminent attack on Hefei at once in order to capitalise on what will occur and begin the reclamation of Lujiang and Jiujiang Prefectures from Liu Fu. This, gentlemen, is Gongjin's assessment: victory will be ours in less than ten days!"

"...*Attack Hefei*...? ...*Victory* in *less than ten days*???" Zhang Zhao exclaimed. "Has Zhou Yu lost his mind?!"

Sun Quan passed the letter to Zhang Zhao and said, "Ten days or less, Zibu."

"...And my brother has returned to Liu Bei...?" Zhuge Jin asked.

"He has, Zhuge Ziyu, so that our allies can coordinate their own actions with ours," Sun Quan replied.

"... ... ...If *this* is what happens, then it is *Heaven's will*, along with 'Jiangnan' and perhaps *more*," Zhang Zhao declared as he finished reading. "If this is the outcome, Lord Sun, then there is no height to which you cannot aspire!"

"Northern Yang will do for now!" Sun Quan replied. "We will make ready at once!"

Events were now set in motion that would make history: deadly fire ships neared readiness and false defectors prepared themselves for the final stage of the ruse while their optimistic opponents relaxed and looked forward to the end of a costly and wearying campaign; and all the while, the unseen participant in the conflict – the winter winds – continued to blow from the northwest to the southeast without giving any indication of what was to come.

****

91

The night of Huang Gai's planned departure from the south was in no way unusual to most, but for those few men that knew the truth it was a tense and exciting time; Huang surveyed the small ship that would take him to Cao Cao and smiled with satisfaction.

The innocuous 'fire ship' was one of many that would be making the journey across the Yangtze River; each was packed with kindling, reeds and jars of oil, and the hulls were treated with oils and fats.

"I really wouldn't like to be on the receiving end of this," Han Dang murmured.

"This is going to a man that richly deserve it," Huang Gai replied. "Cao Cao deserves to burn in the lowest depths of the netherworld; we're just giving him a taste of what Heaven has in store for him in the afterlife."

"You be careful, Gongfu," Han Dang insisted. "Don't go up with this lot like Zu Mao would've: make sure that you jump clear and live to see another day."

"Yes, Father, you must survive!" Huang Yi pleaded.

"...That's not up to me," Huang Gai replied as he stared upward at a hoisted flag; the winds had been dying down over the last hours, but they were now picking up again.

"...What way is it going to blow...?" Han Dang wondered.

"I haven't the time to ask or answer!" Huang Gai said. "Wish us all luck... and be ready to follow."

Han Dang smiled slightly and bowed; Huang Gai bowed to his friend and son before he turned and boarded his floating incendiary device and prepared to set off.

The area around the Han military camp was fully lit with lamps ahead of the meeting. Cao Cao dressed in his full military regalia, left his command tent with Xu Chu and travelled to the docks to greet Huang Gai in person; Cheng Yu met him and bowed silently.

"In ten days," Cao Cao said, "I will destroy these southern rats, and finally reunite the lands above and below the Great River."

"It will be a great day indeed, Prime Minister," Cheng Yu replied tonelessly.

Cao Cao surveyed the area with a satisfied smile: lines of infantry and cavalry were assembled in case of an ambush, so Cao believed that there could be no unwanted outcome to the encounter with the approaching enemy general.

"...It's cold!" Cao Cao chuckled. "Oh well, at least we won't need to be here for much longer."

Cheng Yu hummed almost inaudibly.

"...It's almost time, isn't it...?" Cao Cao prompted.

"It is," Cheng Yu replied.

Cao Cao sensed Cheng Yu's unease and suddenly felt worried; he put a hand to the side of his head and said, "Well, I... I shall retire and read, since this cold does my condition no good. Let me know when this fellow arrives."

"Very good, my lord," Cheng Yu replied.

Cao Cao turned and started back toward his command tent.

"...Gongfu should be leaving right about now," Cheng Pu said as he turned from a viewing window and looked at Gongjin, who was studying his battle model.

"We'll need to be going ourselves soon, then," Gongjin replied.

"The winds are changing as we wanted," Cheng Pu said as he walked across the war room and stood by the model with Gongijn. "They've even waited until the last possible moment! Heaven's with us."

"Heaven's against Cao Cao, which is something else entirely," Gongjin retorted. "If it is also with us and not Liu Bei, then-"

"**Chief Commander! ...Terrible news...!**" Lu Su cried as he ran into the room.

"Oh...?" Gongjin prompted. "What terrible news, Zijing...?"

"Veteran General Huang Gai... has defected to Cao Cao!" Lu Su sobbed.

"Ah," Zhou Yu said with a smile. "So he has departed as expected."

"As *expected*...?" Lu Su exclaimed. "You... you knew he was...?"

"Come here, Lu Su," Gongjin said as he beckoned Lu Su toward the war model.

"...Nothing is different, is it...?" Lu Su asked as he examined the model.

Gongjin smirked and replied, "Not at first glance... or perhaps it's dark. Bring a torch, will you...?"

"*Aiee*... you want me to set fire to our ships again?" Lu Su complained.

"Just get a torch," Gongjin ordered.

Lu Su collected a torch from the nearest stand and returned to the model: Gongjin then gestured that he should examine the map more closely. Lu Su reluctantly lowered the torch, at which point the wind picked up the flames.

"*Ayah*! Why are you making me do this...?" Lu Su whined as he reflexively pulled his arm back. "I...!"

But Lu Su's reactions were too slow: the flames blew toward the sail of one of the model ships that represented Cao Cao's fleet.

"...Do you see...?" Gongjin whispered.

"See what...?" Lu Su asked awkwardly.

Gongjin hid his disappointment and slowly reached out to pick up the affected model.

"...Put it out!" Lu Su implored.

"...Watch," Gongjin said tonelessly: he then returned the model ship to the table and slowly pushed it toward the other models that represented Cao Cao's fleet.

"What are you doing...?" Lu Su fretted: he was about to protest further when another gust of wind carried the flames to the other models and set them alight.

"What are you...!" Lu Su cried as he started forward, but then he suddenly understood; he smiled and said, "A southeast wind...! ...Blowing from our position, directly to *his*...!"

"A fire attack," Cheng Pu said. "It's perfect: and Cao has even chained his ships together to make it easier for the fire to spread. We've won."

"We *have*...?" Lu Su asked bemusedly. "But... but how to get the fire ships close enough to his ships to start this 'chain reaction'...? We cannot simply sail toward him with attacking boats full of

kindling!"
"Can't we…?" Gongjin chuckled.
"…*Huang Gai*…!" Lu Su realised. "But… why was I excluded…?"
Gongjin sighed, replying, "Some things are best left unsaid. I was hoping you'd understand, as Zhuge Kongming obviously did. With his knowledge of seeing the signs and predicting the weather, he knew exactly what I had in mind. Now, let's prepare: Cao Cao is about to be destroyed!"

Cao Cao's adviser Cheng Yu was haunted; he remained at the docks, staring outward toward the expanse of the Yangtze River. Generals Yu Jin, Li Dian and General Zhu Ling were close by; Li frowned as he watched Cheng Yu but did not approach him.
"…The old man's usually right," Zhu Ling suggested. "I don't like to admit it, but I do wonder if we're being careless."
"I'll get closer to him, see if he wants to share his concerns," Li Dian replied.
"I shall accompany you," Yu Jin said.
Cheng Yu gazed to the left and right as if searching for something; he did not acknowledge Li Dian or Yu Jin, who opted to wait until they were spoken to.

Huang Gai's men rowed the 'fire ships' toward Cao Cao's tightly-connected fleet; Huang was waiting until the last possible moment before he gave the orders that would begin the attack.
"…Shouldn't we raise the sails now…?" a captain asked.
"Not yet," Huang Gai retorted. "Not yet…"

Cheng Yu looked at the flags and lamps that surrounded him; the winds were finally starting to strengthen, and to his horror, they were south-easterly.
"…The… the wind…!" Cheng Yu whispered.
Li Dian noticed the look of horror on Cheng Yu's face and neared him, asking, "What's the matter…?"
"The wind," Cheng Yu fretted. "If… if they have come with fire…!"

Huang Gai saw that the moment had arrived: he raised his arm and bellowed, "**Hoist sails and prepare!**"

"…They're in sight," Yu Jin as he pointed to a large number of approaching ships bearing Huang Gai's standard.
"**No!**" Cheng Yu exclaimed. "They must not be allowed to…!"
"What…?" Li Dian prompted.

Huang Gai's men threw lit sticks of kindling into the ships and began to abandon their positions as the wind rushed the craft toward the northern docks; Huang was one of the last to jump into the freezing waters and swim toward a waiting raft, smiling at the thought of what awaited his enemies.

"…No… **NO!**" Cheng Yu exclaimed. "**We have to STOP THEM!**"
But it was already too late: the engulfed 'fire ships' rammed into the 'linked fleet' and – aided by the winds – spread the fire to the coated hulls of the warships in a matter of seconds. The fires caught the attention of the main barracks, where most of the

officers were stationed with their men.

"**Where are the enemy???**" Cao Hong screeched as he dashed out of the barracks with his sword drawn. "**How did they sneak up and do this???**"

Zhao Yan covered his mouth and gasped quietly.

"**We must notify Mengde!**" Cao Xiu said.

"**We must *save him*!**" Cao Hong replied.

"**Yu Jin and Li Dian are with Old Cheng!**" Xiahou Dun said. "**I'll go to them and help them get Mengde out!**"

"**Where are General Feng and General Lu?**" Zhang Liao asked as his eyes scanned the burning ships. "**They're not... still...!**"

Zhao Yan groaned desperately and said, "**They are.**"

Generals Feng Kai and Lu Zhao were aboard two of the large command vessels and stood no chance of surviving; the screams of the victims were being drowned out by the cries of their comrades as they panicked and tried to decide what they would do next. The vast fleet was still mostly intact on either side, although the fires were quickly changing that: some men were trying to prise the bolts that held the chains in place from their rooting in the hulls of the ships and boats, while others were trying to move their craft forward at speed to break the connections, but the wind was against them, and Huang Gai's naval reinforcements were now approaching at speed.

"**Bastards!**" Cao Hong cried. "**I'll gut every southern-!**"

"**REPORT!**"

Cao Xiu turned to the anxious messenger, who added, "**An attack from the north: banners, reading 'Liu Bei', and... 'Liu Qi'...!**"

"This was... a *trap*...!" Cao Xiu whined.

Xun Yòu approached with a small militia; Cao Hong turned to him and said, "**Mister Xun! Mengde's in danger and-!**"

"**Generals Cao Xiu and Cao Zhen will get His Excellency out of here, General!**" Zhao Yan interrupted. "**The rest must limit the damage and stage an orderly fighting retreat!**"

"**Commandant-Protector Zhao is right, General Cao!**" Xun Yòu said. "**We must delay their advance!**"

Cao Hong turned, looked at the ships and scowled angrily.

"**General Zhang Liao: we will fetch General Zhu Ling and engage the enemy at the river!**" Zhao Yan bellowed. "**General Cao Hong, Mister Xun Yòu: locate General Zhang Hè and engage Liu Bei and Liu Qi! May the Heavens forgive my worthlessness on this campaign and give us a chance to at least escape destruction with some dignity!**"

"**Don't berate yourself, Commandant,**" Xun Yòu replied. "***This... horror... was no fault of *yours*.**"

Zhao Yan nodded respectfully and gestured to General Zhang Liao, who followed at once with Zhu Ling.

"**Let's get moving, Zilian!**" Cao Xiu urged.

"**...They had better pray that Mengde survives this, or that I do not!**" Cao Hong replied.

Cao Xiu nodded and turned to Cao Zhen, saying, "**Let's hurry!**"

"**I wish that I could fight!**" Cao Zhen lamented; he and Cao Xiu then retreated as the camp's defences started to crumble.

"No... this...!" Jing Vice-Admiral Zhang Yun gasped as he watched the fires spread to the Jing contingent of the Han fleet.

"**We've got some smaller craft that weren't chained to the rest!**" Jing Admiral Cai Mao noted.

"**But our large ships _were_ chained together for this _bloody stupid plan_...!**" Zhang Yun cried. "**Cao Cao's not just destroyed his own navy, Uncle: he's destroyed _ours_ as well! How will we defend against the Suns now???**"

"**I-! ...I don't know, but we must start now!**" Cai Mao retorted. "**We must get onto the river with whatever moves freely and block their advance!**"

Zhang Yun sighed, nodded obediently and prepared for battle.

Han General Feng Kai stood and watched as the fires swallowed up the command ship that was to the left of his; he sighed, mourned the loss of his colleague Lu Zhao and turned his attentions back to the battle in the waters below. Feng Kai's archers were firing at the Jiangdong boats that were darting about, desperate to kill as many of the enemy as possible before they were consumed by the fires. Huang Gai laughed as arrows whizzed past his men and struck the waters harmlessly; some Han troops had leapt from the burning ships, and they were proving to be easy targets as they flailed about in the tumultuous waters.

"**This is for all your victims, Cao Cao!**" Huang Gai declared. "**This time it is _your_ people that will dam the river!**"

"**General Huang, they've put free-moving boats in the water that are headed in our direction!**" a captain reported.

"**That'll be Cai Mao!**" Huang Gai decided. "**Caution, everyone!**"

A mixture of better-trained Han sailors and Jing sailors approached on small craft; Huang Gai's men met them at the same time that Chen Wu, Zhou Tai, Ling Tong, Lü Meng, Su Fei and Gan Ning brought contingents of men northward. Han Dang wanted to take part in the attack, but his ship had to remain at the rear until it was deemed safe to proceed.

"**I'll be there soon, Gongfu!**" Han Dang bellowed.

"He can't hear you from over here, Father," Han Zong said.

"I know that," Han Dang retorted. "I- ...Never mind."

Cao Cao had left his tent to discover the cause of the frenzied screams and hastily-issued orders; he was dumbstruck at the sight of the fires, and his simple-minded bodyguard Xu Chu was nervous as he awaited orders.

"**WE HAVE TO GET OUT OF HERE!**" Li Dian screamed as he approached Cao Cao with Xiahou Dun and Cheng Yu; Cao slowly and shakily raised an arm and silently screamed as he pointed at the wall of fire.

"...**PRIME MINISTER!**" Xiahou Dun shouted. "**PLEASE, PRIME MINISTER, WE HAVE TO FLEE!**"

"I... I...!" Cao Cao croaked.

Xu Chu finally decided to act: he took hold of Cao Cao and hoisted him onto his shoulder so that he could carry him to safety.

"**With me...!**" Cheng Yu ordered.

The Han army fled the camp and the neighbouring city of Wulin, ignoring the pleading screams of their sick comrades in the infirmary and the men that were trapped on the ships or floating helplessly in the water.

Huang Gai's small militia was separated from their reinforcements by corpses, flaming debris and enemy craft; the Jing sailors were skilled enough to resort to archery, so some of them maintained distance and began firing on the two distinct Jiangdong forces that were trying to reach the shore. Huang Gai raised his arm to order an advance, but as he did so, an arrow found its mark; Huang groaned with pain as he clutched his punctured armpit and staggered backwards, falling into the river. The fighting was too intense for a rescue to be feasible; Huang's men fought on leaderless, but their isolation led to their being decimated before Chen Wu and Zhou Tai could force their way through the obstacles and come to their aid.

"**Where is General Huang???**" Chen Wu asked.

"**He was hit!**" a young sailor replied. "**He**... he...!"

"...**We must keep fighting!**" Chen Wu said. "**You'll join my men, and we'll avenge Veteran General Huang!**"

Chen Wu led the renewed attack on the demoralised Han forces, leaving behind a mess of floating bodies – dead and alive – that included Veteran General Huang Gai.

Lu Su and Gongjin had left the safety of the war room and moved to the deck of the flagship of the Jiangdong navy; the two observed the raging blaze with satisfaction and excitement.

"We did it!" Lu Su said. "I... I don't believe it...! We defeated him...!"

Gongjin shook his head and replied, "Arrogance: *arrogance* defeated Cao Cao, not us. But there's time enough for praise later; **let us pursue!**"

The flagship advanced with the rest of the navy, intent on ending the threat of Cao Cao's armed forces once and for all.

Veteran General Han Dang's second wave of reinforcements reached Chen Wu's position just as the Jing sailors were in retreat; he saw that some of Huang Gai's men were among Chen's and asked, "**Where is he? Where's Gongfu...?**"

Chen Wu sighed miserably.

"...**Don't you dare!**" Han Dang barked. "**He didn't do *this* to end up as fish bait!**"

"**I can't answer you any other way!**" Chen Wu replied desperately. "**All we can do is keep going!**"

"...Yeah," Han Dang said miserably. "Yeah..."

The last of the Han forces abandoned the Wulin camp as the Liu-Sun 'alliance' started to seize the grounds around the city and the camp itself; the Battle of Red Cliffs was more or less over, but the fighting would continue as Cao Cao's fragmented army fled Jiangxia Prefecture and coalesced around Jing Province's southern capital, Jiangling City, where the next phase of the battle between Cao and the Suns would be partly fought.

****

92

The battle between the Imperial armies and the Jiangdong navy had ended with a seemingly impossible outcome, but the mood was souring generally as the news of in-fighting among Liu Bei and Liu Qi's reinforcements, Cao Cao's escape and the presumed death of the hero of the hour, Veteran General Huang Gai, started to circulate.

"**Bloody *fools*...!**" Gongjin cried as he threw his decorated Chief Commander's helmet to the floor of his flagship command room. "**I trusted Liu Bei, Liu Qi and Zhuge Liang with one tiny element of this scheme and they've made a mess of it! Fighting over *boats*; they've given Cao an easy escape!**"

Lu Su hummed ambiguously.

"...And Gongfu... deserved better, *if* he has perished, which is not necessarily the case," Gongjin continued. "I am having the waters dredged in order to recover as many wounded men and corpses – of all sides – as possible. I want Gongfu identified properly: I will not have him interred in a plain wooden box, not after he's just made history."

Lu Su nodded silently.

"...And as a 'gesture of goodwill' – since our enemy Cao Cao has apparently lived to tell the tale and bear grudges – we will ensure that any enemies of note are properly treated, even if it just because it would be hypocritical at the very least to make the same mistake as Liu Biao and Huang Zu," Gongjin continued. "I have sent word to Lord Sun that he can begin his campaign to seize Northern Yang, but I have omitted the preliminary casualty reports since they do not make for encouraging reading; Demou is advancing to seize Xiakou before Liu Qi can do so, and we will now press on to Jiangling, where we might hopefully catch up to Cao Cao and do what Liu Bei – incompetent cretin that he is – obviously could not, even when Cao's survival risks his own."

"...Yes," Lu Su sighed. "But I-"

"Or perhaps I underestimate him," Gongjin interrupted. "Perhaps Bei has stationed men at some critical place, such as Huarong."

"I imagine so," Lu Su said. "Kongming will-"

"You'd think that Liu Bei would have been eager to end the cycle of hatred!" Gongjin chortled. "You'd think that Liu Bei would be the best choice for the task! *I* certainly did, else I'd never have ignored his hitherto-terrible reputation for *bungling things* and-!"

Gongjin suddenly stopped talking and stared vacantly.

"...And what...?" Lu Su prompted.

"...He-! ...No... no, that couldn't be it, surely," Gongjin murmured.

"That what couldn't be what...?" Lu Su prompted.

"...That Zhuge Liang... perhaps 'misadvised' Liu Bei," Gongjin said numbly. "Could it be that... that this show of incompetence is...!"

"...Is *what*???" Lu Su whined.

"...I will know for sure if he did not ensure that there were men sent to Huarong or some other place to intercept Cao Cao," Gongjin said. "I will know for certain then."

"Know *what* for certain???" Lu Su protested.

"...That Zhuge Liang is either a buffoon or a menace," Gongjin replied. "But if he really *has* allowed Cao to escape, then it is

because he *understands*... and that is not good at all."
"Good for him that he 'understands' if he does, because I don't!"
Lu Su complained. "All I know is that I maybe could see why he'd
mess us about if he has done, because we've betrayed their trust,
haven't we...? We promised a pincer to eliminate Cao Cao once
and for all, and instead we've burned the fleet, seized Xiakou –
which means most of Jiangxia – and we're about to begin an
attack on Liu Qi's southern capital to take it from Cao Cao!"
"It isn't Liu Qi's capital, Zijing, it's the capital of 'Han-controlled'
Jing Province, and is no more Qi's than it's ours, though it soon
will be ours, I assure you," Gongjin retorted. "And yes, you – with
your idealistic view of 'Kongming' and his master that will change
as you wise up to them – see *my* efforts as the treacherous ones,
but I'm doing this to give the Empire a Son of Heaven that has a
mandate and keep Cao Cao's bloodied hands from taking any
more from the people! What is Liu Bei's ultimate intent...? What
then, by design, is Zhuge Liang's...?"
"...To preserve the Han," Lu Su said.
"Aha, but in what form...?" Gongjin asked. "You know as well as I
do what the answer is to that, else you wouldn't still be touting
your 'tripod theorem' at every opportunity. Zhuge Liang cannot
revive a mummified relic, nor can Liu Bei govern wisely. There's
only our lord Sun Quan left to credibly oppose Cao Cao now, and
Heaven has spoken: that wind was not just timely, it was a
statement. The Han is a living corpse, a puppet controlled by the
Cao clan that will one day be cast aside so that the Caos can rule
directly. The Suns of Fuchun are blessed by more than a
southeast wind, Zijing: they're blessed by fate, by destiny, by the
will of Heaven, and I will exhaust all of my remaining energies to
put them where they belong."
"...I suppose what's just happened means that it's safe to talk that
way, doesn't it...?" Lu Su mumbled. "...I suppose that Lord Sun
might really be... be chosen by the fates to succeed the Han...!"
"I believe it," Gongjin said. "I believe it enough to fight and if
needs be die for it."

Cao Cao's entourage reached Jiangling City, where they were
welcomed at the gates by a shocked and horrified Cao Ren.
"Cousin Mengde...!" Cao Ren gasped.
"...Enough," Cao Cao retorted. "We've little time, Zixiao: the
enemy will be here soon!"
Cao Ren looked to the adviser Cheng Yu, who was scowling.
"...Inside, then, at once," Cao Ren said.
        Cao Cao was settled into the governor's mansion; he
looked about him and sighed, saying, "Liu Biao once sat here...
sometimes, when he was not in Xiangyang."
"You said we've not much time," Cao Ren prompted.
"...No, we haven't," Cao Cao replied. "As you know, the enemy
army based at Red Cliffs dealt us a 'surprise defeat'..."
Cao Cao paused and looked to Cheng Yu, who remained silent.
"...Perhaps it was avoidable, perhaps not," Cao Cao continued.
"The point is this: we were routed. *Completely.* We are now in a
position of weakness not unlike Yuan Shao's in the wake of the
Battle of Guandu."
Jia Xu frowned and said, "I was aware that the cost was high,

Your Excellency, but can it be compared to Guandu...?"
Cao Cao smiled and replied, "Perhaps, perhaps not, Wenhe: I am alive and well, thanks to their feeble attempts to capture me, and I still have a large army and many capable generals, despite the considerable losses."
"...What *were* the losses, exactly, Mengde...?" Cao Ren asked.
"... ... ...As much as a hundred-thousand men, and most if not all of the fleet," Cao Cao replied; the small Jiangling court was filled with gasps from the men that had not been at Wulin to witness it.
"I... cannot find words," Xiahou Yuan admitted.
"And Zhou Yu pursues you, Excellency...?" Jia Xu asked.
"They will try to seize Jiangling, and perhaps Lujiang and Jiujiang Prefectures as well," Cao Cao replied. "My cousin Zilian – who thankfully survived – has forwarded correspondence from Xun Yòu, stating that the pursuit was stymied by in-fighting between Liu Bei and Liu Qi's troops."
"And Commandant Zhao Yan...?" Xiahou Yuan asked.
"...I know not," Cao Cao admitted. "Ask me about some matters, Miaocai, by all means, but not who lived and who died: Li Dian recalls Feng Kai and Lu Zhao being stationed on vulnerable ships at the time the fires struck, so they are likely dead, and the Jing navy was partly linked to ours, so Cai Mao might well be a casualty, but Zhao Yan was alive when last I heard, although that was too long ago to be sure of anything."
"...As many as a *hundred-thousand*...?" Cao Ren exclaimed.
"Yes, Zixiao: a *hundred-thousand men*, and *all of the ships as well*!" Cao Cao barked. **"I have outdone Yuan Shao in every respect now, it seems: I seized more land, built a larger army, amassed a larger collection of useless, bickering advisers, wrote more pompous denunciations, made more enemies and saw my great navy burn in a greater conflagration than that seen at Wuchao!"**
Cheng Yu exhaled loudly and fiercely.
"...Advisers that are not heeded are worthless," Cao Cao added defensively as he glared at Cheng Yu. **"Speakers that cannot make themselves heard must bear some of the blame for their inability to convince!"**
"...I shall go and inspect the troops," Cheng Yu replied.
"...Do that," Cao Cao grunted.
Jia Xu waited until Cheng Yu had withdrawn from the hall before saying, "My lord, we must do all that we can to fortify Jiangling."
"We – that is, you and I – will not be staying here," Cao Cao replied. "I must return to Xuchang and deal with the political aftermath of this defeat: I will insist – as all of those that are truly loyal to me shall – that we were beset by disease and forced to burn the fleet and withdraw. To be forced to admit that I was taken in by a 'surrender ruse'... would be too humiliating."
"So Generals Yu Jin, Zhang Hè, Zhang Liao and so on are ready to face the enemy when they arrive...?" Cao Ren prompted.
"...No," Cao Cao replied. "I will have Yue Jin remain at Xiangyang and Li Tong move southward, and ask Wen Ping to do whatever he can do to hold onto western Jiangxia, but Yu Jin, Zhang Hè, 'and so on', as you put it, will be needed to deal with the military aftermath in the north: this will embolden the Suns, who will try to expand their already vast domain further, and it will give the

Qiang ideas as well. I have no guarantee that Ma Chao might not try to rescue his father and such from Yè, or perhaps stage a rebellion and hope that I don't execute his entire family for it."
"So who will fortify Jiangling...?" Cao Ren asked.
"...I have asked many things of you over the years, Zixiao, but this is perhaps the most difficult," Cao Cao replied. "I am entrusting this place to you, Generals Xu Huang and Niu Jin, and Chen Jiao, who worked with Chen Deng in Guangling, as Chief Clerk."
"Just the four of us...?" Cao Ren exclaimed.
"If I could spare more, I would, but I cannot," Cao Cao insisted. "You will liaise with Man Chong, who will ensure that you have a supply line and reinforcements where they are feasible."
The hitherto-silent Cui Yan coughed deliberately and said, "What about the four so-called 'independent counties'...?"
"Their rulers are self-serving in addition to being self-ruling," Cao Cao replied. "Changsha ignored our requests for support, and I doubt that we'll hear from Wuling unless they're attacked. Now, then: I must begin my journey to Xuchang."
"Mengde, you're needed here!" Cao Ren protested.
"Zixiao, I can spend no more time on the Suns of Fuchun," Cao Cao retorted. "It was, perhaps, folly to expend energy on them at all: perhaps I should have left this campaign to somebody else."
Cao Ren shook his head and said, "But a sign of strength, you-!"
"'Perhaps', 'perhaps', 'perhaps'... is all I am reduced to," Cao Cao continued. "I embarked upon this, and the result is the result: now I must face the Son of Heaven, who will doubtless demand my resignation. No, if I stay here, Zixiao, it will not be perceived as strength: it will be perceived as the opposite! It will be seen that I have no capable men to hold Jiangling, which is why I must entrust it to others, and why it must then be *held*!"
Cao Ren sighed and said, "I understand, Mengde."
"...Xiahou Yuan: you will go at once to Qing Province to oversee matters there and in Xu Province," Cao Cao ordered. "Jia Xu: you will prepare for departure at once. Cui Yan: you will go to Yè as quickly as possible and report the outcome to my court there, and then you will journey to Xuchang."
Each man bowed and accepted their instructions.
"...I doubt that I'll have many more direct dealings with the Suns, if any at all," Cao Cao continued. "Such a shame: I had hoped that Sun Ben would inspire insurrection, that veteran loyalists would see that Sun Quan is a Wang Mang, that the end would be swift and- ...But the result is the result. Vexed as I am, I must not linger: I must return to Xuchang and answer for that result."
"I'm sorry, Mengde," Cao Ren said.
"Don't be sorry, be resolute," Cao Cao retorted. "Hold this place, Zixiao: don't let the Suns take Southern Jing!"

****

93

Veteran General Han Dang wandered around the infirmary and stared at each wounded man with a pained expression; some of the older faces that stared back at him had joined Sun Jian's pro-Han, Yellow Turban-quelling militia and served the Sun clan for as long as Dang. But there was a more specific reason for Han Dang's visit: something told him that he should not give up on his old friend Huang Gai, who had not been seen since being shot in the armpit and falling from his boat during the last battle.

"Veteran General," a physician hailed.

"…A lot o' these men look like they might be alright with a bit o' rest," Han Dang said optimistically.

"Admittedly, Veteran General, a siege produces worse injuries than we're seeing here," the physician replied as he returned to his examination of a screaming sailor with two broken legs. "But there are still a lot of men that were exposed to long periods of time in freezing water, most inhaled a lot of smoke from the fires, quite a few were burned or at the least had their facial hair burned off… you get the idea."

"Yeah, I get the idea," Han Dang sighed.

"And we can't house everyone with those kinds of ailments," the physician continued. "We're overwhelmed with arrow wounds, serious stab and cut wounds, broken limbs… you get the idea."

Han Dang nodded slowly and said, "I know that you probably consider every man here to be the same, and that's probably the right way o' lookin' at it, doc, but… have you seen Veteran General Huang Gai…?"

The physician frowned and asked, "Was he hurt…?"

"That's what I heard," Han Dang replied. "I… I already had one o' your colleagues suggest that I check the… the…"

"…Corpses…?" the physician prompted.

"He *can't* be dead, doc!" Han Dang whined. "He just…!"

"…A lot of men here are practically unrecognisable, what with all the soot and blood on their faces, burnt hair, broken noses, cut skin, swollen bruising… all I can suggest to you is a very thorough search," the physician replied as he moved to another man – who was staring vacantly and shivering – and started to check for signs of hidden injuries under his shirt.

"I *have* been searchin' thoroughly, doc, and I'll keep doin' so," Han Dang said. "But… … …there are so *many*…"

The size of the infirmary – which was basically a series of connected tents and rows of open-air wards due to the number of casualties – had suddenly struck Han Dang.

"…Yes, there are a lot of injured men," the physician replied as he turned his attentions to yet another man.

Han Dang patted the physician's arm and said, "You're a good bloke, lookin' after all these men… Heaven bless you. I'll leave to you to get on… I shouldn't be takin' you away from your work."

The physician smiled sadly and moved to another patient as Han Dang resumed his search; his son Zong ran to him and said, "Here you are, Father! We-"

"I'm not doin' anything until I've searched this whole place," Han Dang insisted. "I know I have work to do, but I can't face Demou

or Junli – or Wentai's altar – until I find Gongfu. You run along and fill in for me."
Han Zong nodded and retreated.
"...Where are you...?" Han Dang whispered.

Lü Fan and Lu Xun had left Sun Quan and travelled to Red Cliffs City to replace Gongjin; the two were immediately approached by Sun Jiao, who asked, "Is Lord Sun well...? How is Father?"
"Lord Sun Quan is well, and Sun Jing is well," Lü Fan replied. "How do things proceed...?"
"Gongjin- I mean 'Chief Commander Zhou', and Colonel Lu Su, Commandant Ling Tong and General Lü Meng have advanced to Jiangling, and Gan Ning – sorry, but I don't know his rank – has gone to Yiling," Sun Jiao reported. "Veteran General Cheng Pu has advanced to seize Xiakou and pacify Jiangxia, while Veteran General Han Dang, he... remains here; Liu Bei and Liu Qi are camped close to Xiakou at the moment but they seem to be accepting the way it is."
"And so they should," Lü Fan chortled.
"I should like to go to Jiangling," Lu Xun announced.
"...I hadn't really intended that, Boyan, but perhaps we're not both of us needed here," Lü Fan replied. "By all means join the- ...Wait a minute. Shulang, I notice that you've not mentioned Veteran General Huang Gai."
Sun Jiao lowered his head and groaned.
"*Aiee*...! He's not *dead*...?" Lü Fan exclaimed.
"He... is 'missing in action'," Sun Jiao replied miserably. "Veteran General Han Dang refuses to advance until...!"
"...The two are friends, so I am not at all surprised," Lü Fan said with a sigh. "Junli and Demou... will be heartbroken if the worst is confirmed. I can see why Gongjin didn't pass that news on, but it must be known sooner or later: where is Veteran General Han Dang now...?"
"The infirmary, I think," Sun Jiao replied.
"...I don't have the time to deal with that right now, as much as I want to," Lü Fan decided. "I'm here to ensure that the Lius don't try anything now that Cao's gone, and to manage the camps at Wulin and Red Cliffs."
"Will Lord Sun be coming to the site of the victory as he did when Huang Zu was beaten...?" Sun Jiao asked.
"No, Shulang, he has a campaign of his own to fight, in order to show that he can do more than slice tables," Lü Fan replied. "He's on his way to Hefei."
"*Hefei*?" Sun Jiao exclaimed. "But won't he need you?"
"He has the Zhang brothers, who are capable enough," Lü Fan insisted. "Hefei is sparsely defended: it is Jiangling that serves as the great challenge now."
"Well then you should be in Jiangling, then!" Sun Jiao said.
"Not so," Lü Fan replied. "Gongjin and Zijing can manage, and as I have already said, we must worry about the Lius now, what they intend to do... when they learn that the main army has gone westward they might exploit the situation and try to retake Jiangxia, and that is why I must be here, as must Veteran Generals Cheng Pu and Han Dang."
"...I see," Sun Jiao said. "What about Cousin Ben...?"

"He will advance to Jiangling," Lü Fan replied. "Fu is another matter - Lord Sun never wants to see that wretch again, and with good reason – but Ben has done nothing proven, and his presence at Jiangling – even if it's just a banner in the end – will send a clear message to Cao Cao."

"...Fu is... he's a *dog*," Sun Jiao muttered. "If he has any dignity at all, he'll kill himself."

"I cannot disagree," Lü Fan replied. "But enough about him: let us stabilise this place while others do their work. Mister Lu Boyan, I wish you luck as you advance to offer your considerable talent to the efforts taking place at Jiangling: I might advance there myself later if I am sorely needed, though Heaven willing, I won't be."

"I shall go and prepare myself an escort," Lu Xun said.

Han Dang's search for Huang Gai had moved him to tears that were blurring his vision; he continued to wander along the rows of wounded men, but his morale had all but gone and so had his hope of finding his friend alive.

"Gongfu, I should have gone in your place...!" Han Dang croaked. "*I'm* the stupid one out of all of us now that Zu Mao's gone: the world can do without a fool like me, but can it do without *you*...?"

Han Dang's melancholy had, without him realising it, caused him to continue his search without actually examining the men that he passed; he walked by one man that immediately stared to reach out and gasp with what little strength he had, but Dang did not immediately notice amid the chorus of howls and laments.

"Maybe... maybe I *should* search the corpses," Han Dang whimpered. "P'raps I need something white t'wear, something-"

"**Yigong...!**"

Han Dang froze: the cracking voice that had shouted his courtesy name could only belong to one man, but there was a part of Dang's mind that dismissed it as a hallucination.

"**Yi... gong...!**"

The second cry was enough to tell Han Dang that he had not imagined it; Dang looked about him, desperate to figure out the direction that the laboured cries were coming from.

"**Yi**... gong...!"

The voice was starting to weaken; Han Dang intensified his search, but it took him a moment to realise that he was walking further from the path that he has been taking and that the voice could only have come from someone that he had already passed. It would then not take long for Han Dang to find the source of the cries: he ran to the battered, bandaged Huang Gai – whose face was almost lost amid his unbound hair – and knelt by his side, laughing and grinning appreciatively.

"Did... we beat them...?" Huang Gai asked weakly.

Han Dang laughed desperately and replied, "Oh, for-! O' *course we did*, you silly beggar, else-!"

"That's... good," Huang Gai said. "Where's... Yi...?"

"Yi was lookin' as well, but he had work t'do so I said I'd-
...Couldn't they at least have bound your hair...?" Han Dang complained. "Me or your son'd have found you a bit sooner if-"

"I want to get out of here and... fight," Huang Gai pleaded. "I'll be alright, if... if I can just get out of here."

"You've been badly injured!" Han Dang exclaimed. "You've

obviously hit your head, for one thing: 'fight', indeed!"
"...I can't just lie here," Huang Gai pleaded.
"No, no, you can't," Han Dang replied. "No offence to all these lads, but you need to be somewhere else, recovering in better conditions than this."
"Help me up," Huang Gai said. "Take me to my son."
Han Dang reluctantly hoisted Huang Gai off of his stretcher-bed and onto his feet; a nearby soldier – who was bringing a colleague in for treatment – recognised the wounded general at that moment and cried, "**Veteran General Huang!**"
The infirmary gradually quietened; staff and patients alike did what they could to show respect to a visibly embarrassed and humbled Huang Gai as he limped along the path to the outdoors.
"Don't look so awkward," Han Dang said. "Enjoy the praise: you earned it."
Huang Gai lowered his head and hummed.

Sun Ben's court in Nanchang welcomed a robed official from Red Cliffs that said, "Sun Ben, the Administrator of Yuzhang, is hereby promoted to 'General Who Attacks Barbarians' for his enduring loyalty and invited to join the emerging front at Jiangling at the earliest possible opportunity!"
"I shall prepare for departure at once," Sun Ben promised.
"You are forgiven for wavering, Father," Sun Lin said as the messenger withdrew.
"I must now do my utmost to follow the proper path," Sun Ben replied. "You and I will go together: your brothers will remain here with their cousins and defend the region."
Zhu Zhi observed the exchanges and hummed thoughtfully.
"This is a pivotal moment for the nation, gentlemen," Sun Ben declared. "I am privileged to be witness to it."
Zhu Zhi turned to a loyal subordinate and said, "You must use his absence to investigate thoroughly, Mister Zou: miss *nothing*."

As far as the majority of the people of the Jiangdong region were concerned, Huang Gai's survival ended the Battle of Red Cliffs on an even more palatable note: the infamous Cao Cao had been humiliated, his army decimated and the southeast of the Han Empire saved from a costly invasion. What would happen next was a genuine unknown: the defeat of the Han's Chancellor of State changed everything across the entire empire, and the ultimate outcome could truly be almost anything, even the beginnings of a new empire – an empire led by the Sun clan – in the south, and perhaps beyond. Gongjin, Lu Su and Lü Fan were adamant that they would be the sole architects of that indeterminable future, but one man – Liu Bei's adviser, Zhuge Liang – would ensure that nothing would be simple for the Suns in the years to come.

****

ACT VIII: A WAR ON TWO FRONTS

94

Although there had been no grand conflict between two large armies, the so-called 'Battle of Red Cliffs' – which consisted of some river-based skirmishes, a submission ruse, a large-scale, fire-based sabotage operation aided by the weather and a subsequent rout of the confused survivors – was one of, if not the most important events of the era. The Chancellor of State, Cao Cao – who had, to that point, enjoyed a decade of seemingly-impossible victories against foes that greatly outclassed him in terms of numbers and resources – had himself been routed by a smaller army led by Sun Quan, the second member of the Sun clan of Fuchun to enjoy independent rule in the southeast Jiangdong region of Han Dynasty China.

None would have placed faith in Sun Quan if they had met him years before: the younger brother of the 'Little Conqueror' Sun Ce was not physically imposing, charismatic, disciplined or popular with the military as Ce was, and his inheritance of Ce's legacy – a previously ungovernable region that was now an emerging second power in the empire – was met with much distress and outrage. But Sun Quan had built his strength with extensive archery training and used that strength to slice a table with his Sword of Authority, silencing his critics and declaring that he would defy Cao's calls for him to yield control of Jiangdong to Cao's government forces: half of the administration walked away, but the other half fought without reservation and won. A false surrender by a veteran general, Huang Gai, had left the overconfident Cao Cao's fleet – which was linked by chains to reduce 'river-sickness' amongst his poorly acclimatised northern troops – open to a fire attack, and a fortuitous – some said 'Heaven-sent' – change in wind direction allowed General Huang to sail a small fleet of kindling-laden 'fire ships' toward the Han navy and destroy it completely. Cao Cao had limped away as the loser, fortifying the southern capital of neighbouring Jing Province, Jiangling, as he went; Sun Quan's Chief Commander, Zhou Yu – known as 'Gongjin' – would now siege Jiangling while Quan went northward to attack the undermanned fortress city of Hefei in Lujiang Prefecture.

But the battle was not simply between the Suns and the Caos: in addition to the undeniable fact that Cao Cao was, regardless of circumstance, the Han's Chancellor of State, the Suns had been forced to ally with two former enemies, Liu Qi and Liu Bei, in order to have their victory.

Liu Qi was the eldest son of the recently-deceased Governor of Jing Province, Liu Biao, and although some claimed that a long-standing feud between the Suns and Lius – begun when Sun Quan's father, the then-indentured 'Tiger of Jiangdong' Sun Jian, was killed by Liu Biao's agents while reluctantly invading Jing for his master, Yuan Shu – effectively ended when Biao died, there was still a great deal of enmity, since Liu Biao had 'died of distress' after the Suns had killed Biao's main ally Huang Zu and seized Jiangxia Prefecture in the southeast of Jing in the name of reparation, and the sudden death gave certain officials in Biao's court the opportunity to betray Liu Qi and hand the governor's seal to his younger brother Cong, who then yielded the province to Cao Cao on the advice of those same officials.

Liu Qi hated the idea of joining forces with his father's enemies, but Qi's 'distant uncle', Liu Bei – who was the descendant of a disinherited Han prince and 'wandering warlord' that insisted that he was a misrepresented loyalist – convinced the governor's son that he should bury old grudges and face 'the real enemy of all good men', namely Bei's own nemesis Cao Cao, and Qi reluctantly agreed. But the outcome at Red Cliffs had allowed the Suns to recapture Jiangxia Prefecture and advance to Jiangling, which meant that southern Jing was now likely to become part of Sun Quan's territory: that went against the plans conceived by Liu Bei's strategist, Zhuge Liang the 'Crouching Dragon', who wanted Bei – who had only a few thousand under his command – to become a 'third great warlord' that could oppose not only Cao Cao but Sun Quan in the years to come, and it was that unpredictable ally that would be concerning Gongjin most as he prepared to engage the defenders of Jiangling, Han Generals Cao Ren and Xu Huang.

"...Can I help at all...?"
Gongjin's concentration was broken by his friend Lu Su's question: he smiled half-heartedly and replied, "Not really, Zijing, not with this specific thing."
"Are you sure...?" Lu Su asked. "I-"
"REPORT FROM WULIN!"
Gongjin and Lu Su turned to face the messenger that had dashed into the command tent and bowed humbly; Gongjin grimaced and said, "Don't recite the report, messenger, if there is a written version. Give it to me, go, and get some rest."
Gongjin took the report, read it and scowled.
"What is it...?" Lu Su asked as soon as the messenger had gone.
"*Aiee*... a clever move, Zhuge Kongming," Gongjin said angrily.
"What do you mean?" Lu Su prompted. "Come on, Gongjin! I feel like I am in the dark again, as I was at Red Cliffs!"
Gongjin passed the report to Lu Su, who read it with concern; Lü Meng entered the tent and asked, "You summoned me, Chief Commander Zhou...?"
"Sit, Ziming, and listen well," Gongjin replied.
"... ... ...So Cao Cao escaped because...?" Lu Su murmured.
"*Yes*," Gongjin chortled. "It is there in that report, the truth of it, as I suspected: nobody was sent to intercept him!"
"You suspect that it was deliberate," Lü Meng suggested.
"Oh, *undoubtedly*!" Gongjin replied. "Cao Cao is not merely another Dong Zhuo or Wang Mang; no, no, he is more than that. He is a great schemer, capable of greatly profound thought! While he lives, I am blocked from fulfilling all of my lord's wishes!"
"...But *why*...?" Lu Su wondered.
"Zijing, my future plans were completely reliant on the death of Cao Cao!" Gongjin explained desperately. "With him dead, the Han court would be in sudden disarray – perhaps the eunuchs would seize power again if there are any left, or some other opportunist would, like the house-hostage Ma Teng, or Cao Cao's son Cao Pi, or one of the advisers, like Jia Xu or Cheng Yu!

Regardless of who it was, they would be untried, untested, unable to keep the army together, many of Cao's vassals would be disconsolate and unwilling to fight without their master, and we could seize Jiangling, advance into northern Jing, and cut a path to the capital while the name 'Zhou Yu of Lujiang' still made northern men's souls tremble! We would have marched on the capital, met the Son of Heaven, and ensured that our lord was king of 'Eastern Wu', an independent state respected by one and all! We would have repaired the damage of years of corruption, and perhaps, by way of marriages, paved the way for the progeny of our lord Sun to one day govern with a mandate! And thanks to Zhuge Liang... my plan is **ruined**!"

Gongjin slammed his writing desk with his right hand and screamed with frustration.

"... ... ...I really don't see how this works," Lu Su admitted. "I'm beginning to think that I'm some sort of fool."

Lü Meng smiled and said, "Intrigue often appears senseless."

"But so well played...!" Gongjin chortled. "Now Cao lives... the memory of Red Cliffs burned irrevocably into his head, like the branding given as part of the Five Pains... he'll never forget, and he'll never forgive, and more than any man of the north, he knows what he faces, and will never underestimate us as others would. Others would be arrogant, and say 'Cao Cao ignored good advice!', 'Cao Cao should have known about the wind!' and 'I would never be so foolish!' Such thoughts would lead them like animals to the slaughter... but Cao Cao will make no mistakes. No, he'll be eternally cautious, and never let us set foot in his domains, nor tread carelessly into ours... ensuring a tiresome, resource-sapping standoff that can only end in one way... by way of a *pincer*."

Lu Su frowned.

"The little sneak, that farmhouse bumpkin, that self-serving...! ...He's *forced* me to use that stupid plan!" Gongjin continued. "Oh, I *shall* use it, of *course* I will, I *have* to... but never, *never* will it involve Liu Bei. Liu Bei will *rot*."

"Liu Bei has no troops," Lu Su noted.

"He obviously thinks that he'll get some at some point... from *Yi*, perhaps...?" Gongjin snickered. "Perhaps Liu Bei does not understand this anymore than you do; perhaps Zhuge Liang is the only man that really understands this... this *nonsense*."

"So we will not attack Jiangling now, then...?" Lu Su prompted.

"We have no choice," Gongjin replied numbly. "We're here now: a pity that Zhuge saw fit to do this thing, since Cao Cao will have Yi reinforce its border and provide support to Jiangling while he throws everything he can from his two-hundred-thousand strong horde at us... and, of course, at Lord Sun's force at Hefei. We haven't the resources to conduct a pincer alone... yet he did it all the same, he did it despite knowing that his lord is weak, unable to help us... so *why*...? There were other ways to do what he wanted to do, now that I come to think about it... ways that removed his lord's sworn enemy, Cao Cao and still gave him opportunities... what else is he-? ... ...*Ah*... I see."

"...You suspect that Liu Bei wants to try and take the counties," Lü Meng guessed.

"It can be only two things, and the other is beyond his reach right now," Gongjin replied. "It can only be the counties... but he must not acquire them. It will give him too much bargaining power."

"Forgive me, Gongjin, but do you *really* believe Zhuge Kongming deliberately allowed Cao Cao to escape?" Lu Su asked plainly.

"*You* do *not*," Gongjin said with a smile. "I can see *why not*, of course... but Zijing, this is a long-term plan of his, a variant of your own fanciful 'Tripod'."

"I really wish that you'd see the merits of it," Lu Su complained.

"Zijing, the original plan relied upon our sworn enemy *Liu Biao*, the man that killed our lord's beloved father, being the third power; surely that was an *insult*!" Gongjin chuckled. "But Liu Bei or Liu Qi...? That is less an insult than a *joke*."

Lu Su lowered his head.

"The plan favours the weak yet shifty, as all plans of that nature do," Gongjin continued. "Zhuge favours it for his wily yet weak lord for the same reason that I might have done in our early days: it splits our enemy and gives them two focal points, leaving them open to destruction by the first, 'true' arm of the pincer while they expend resources on the second, 'decoy' arm. That plan is fine when you are the 'true'; are *we* the 'true' when seen through the eyes of Zhuge Liang?"

Lü Meng nodded slowly and silently to indicate that he understood Gongjin's point, while Lu Su remained dejected and kept his head hung low.

"Cao Cao may hate Liu Bei, but he hates being utterly humiliated a lot more, I think," Gongjin suggested. "Cao Ren has been placed in charge of Jiangling, with Xu Huang as a second: two truly fearsome and durable men. If we cannot get around the city and cut off their supplies, we'll still be here when the Son of Heaven finally decides to change his reign title, and it will no doubt be changed to 'Sun Remains Confounded'. All the while, Liu Bei can do what he does best: plant himself somewhere in Southern Jing, like a tree, and slowly grow by cultivating the local populace with acts of false benevolence, like he did in Xu Province in order to 'inherit' it from Tao Qian, and like he tried to do in Northern Jing to seize the province from Liu Biao. He'll use us, like he's using Liu Qi, and while we grow weaker fighting Cao Ren and Xu Huang, he'll grow stronger, ready for his next move... seizing Yi Province from the worthless Liu Zhang."

"...Can we not then use his meagre forces to attack Cao Ren, and exhaust them before our own?" Lu Su countered.

Gongjin shook his head and said, "His advisers – or rather, 'Zhuge Kongming' – will suggest that he evade that fate, I think. Did they not do that to spare his forces from annihilation at Xiakou, fighting for Liu Biao...?"

"He refused to aid Liu Biao at Xiakou in order to pave the way for our current alliance!" Lu Su pleaded. "Can you not-?"

"He'll squirm out of it: *I* would," Gongjin insisted. "All the same, however, I... I cannot really hate Zhuge Liang for this. He is serving his lord, and after all... and does he not now see it as retribution for *us* foiling *his* plan...?"

"I assume that you mean your having Veteran General Cheng Pu secure Jiangxia," Lü Meng supposed.

"Exactly," Gongjin said. "Zhuge no doubt intended to send a small force of troops – Liu Bei's, of course, not Governor Liu Qi's – to take Jiangxia once our forces left the city to pursue Cao Cao. Once he saw that we were going to leave them to do it alone, he realised that we were intending to hold Jiangxia, and opted for releasing the old villain to fight another day. He realised that I'd thought of everything, including any attempt by either Liu to take Jiangxia from us... but yet he still found a perverse way to outfox me. But I have another plan... he'll not have his way."

Lu Su shook his head, and said, "I refuse to believe that Zhuge Kongming would be so deceitful, so underhanded, so... *so*...!"

"...Then you are going to *suffer*, Zijing, for your groundless faith," Gongjin promised sadly. "The alliance is all but superficially over now: we're rivals seeking the same prize, and that will mean a lot of little actions such as this – even if they will knowingly harm us – because now it is about *power*, not survival."

Lu Su was morbidly silent.

"...Perhaps having Huang Gai here as a 'mascot' isn't such a bad idea after all," Gongjin replied. "Perhaps it would speed things up... but no: he's hurt. He must stay away and recuperate."

"But having 'The Hero of Red Cliffs' here *would* demoralise the enemy further," Lu Su said.

"Not if he dies of his injuries!" Gongjin retorted desperately. "The man was shot in the armpit, Zijing, and spent hours in the water, near freezing to death, and then-!"

"And then 'a lot longer in an infirmary, unrecognised and ignored'," Lu Su interrupted. "I think that we've done this conversation already, Gongjin."

"Have we...?" Gongjin sighed. "A thousand curses on Liu Bei and Zhuge: it's their fault that I can't think straight!"

"It's a good thing that General Cheng is leaving his son to guard Jiangxia and coming here to join us, I think," Lu Su suggested. "You could use the help, because I'm certainly of no use at all."

"...Veteran General Huang Gai is truly a loyal, considerate man... a hero of the era," Gongjin said suddenly. "Not a care for his own health, he worries only about the cause; had Cao known his character, that ploy would never have worked!"

Lü Meng nodded agreeably and asked, "What next...?"

"Gan Ning will take Yiling for us, that's a given," Gongjin replied. "We'll lay siege to Jiangling and see what happens: if Cao Cao has remained in Jing it will be more troublesome, but I doubt that he can afford to while his courts in Yè and Xuchang crumble."

"And the Lius...?" Lu Su prompted.

"...They'll try to take Xiakou once General Cheng leaves the city or they'll follow us to Jiangling in order to see what they can steal for themselves, as we've just discussed," Gongjin said with contempt. "Either is fine by me: they can't aid our enemies and they can't serve as anything but subordinates to us. We can maybe pit Jing troops against Jing troops and maybe inspire some defections to our cause, but I doubt that Cao Cao would be fool enough to leave Jing soldiers here now that Liu Biao's 'true heir', Liu Qi, might be on his way here. We'll see what happens and react... *as usual*."

****

95

Han Dang was making preparations for his role in the siege of Jiangling City when he was visited by Huang Gai, who was visibly far from recovered.
"You're mad," Han Dang suggested. "Go and rest!"
"No, Huang Gai retorted. "There's still work to be done. Chief Commander Zhou will need us as advisers here at Jiangling, if nothing else."
"*Ayah...* he *has* advisers! He *is* one!" Han Dang chortled. "Enjoy being a living legend, Gongfu, and go back to bed, before you end up as a dead one."
"*No*," Huang Gai insisted. "I'm desperate to do something useful."
Han Dang's eyes glazed.
"...I mean 'again', do something useful *again*," Huang Gai bumbled. "Is it enough to burn a few boats?"
"No, I won't have this conversation," Han Dang chuckled. "Go back to your tent and go back to bed, you mad idiot, or you'll be fit for nothing later on."
"If I am unfit to be here, then I am unfit to travel back," Huang Gai suggested.
"*Aiee...* well, don't blame me, Gongfu, if you die," Han Dang muttered. "You shouldn't even be in Jiangling, never mind-"
"*Huang Gongfu...?*"
Han Dang and Huang Gai turned to face Gongjin.
"Chief Commander," Huang Gai said humbly.
"*Ayah, ayah*! No, *no*!" Gongjin whined. "You are a lucky charm, Gongfu; you should be at home, *resting*! *Aiee...* what fool let you travel here???"
"I am my own master, and hence my own fool," Huang Gai retorted. "I think that General Cheng has been injured many more times than I, and yet he kept travelling alongside his lord; I knew that I might be of use in this siege, knowing the counties as well as I do."
Gongjin looked at Han Dang, who said, "I really cannot be more annoyed, but he's here now. He wants to be an adviser; I s'pose we should be lucky that he doesn't want to fight in the vanguard."
Gongjin turned his despairing gaze back to Huang Gai and said, "Don't you *dare* die here, Huang Gongfu."
"Only if I might ask the same of you, Chief Commander," Huang Gai replied.
"...*Ayah*!" Gongjin exclaimed as he turned and retreated.
"You've distressed him," Han Dang suggested.
"I will distress Cao Ren far more," Huang Gai retorted. "Anyhow, there is no need for my presence here to be unknown any longer: I shall attend meetings and appear at the walls of the city to intimidate the defenders."
"...You're *mad*," Han Dang chuckled miserably.

Gan Ning's small militia reached the walls of Yiling City after a long journey along the Yangtze River: the city's defender, Xi Su, peered over the walls, reviewed the enemy banners and grimaced, saying, "Of all the men to send here...!"
"What's wrong...?" a captain asked.

"That's Gan Ning of Linjiang!" Xi Su explained. "He staged a rebellion in the south of Yi after Governor Liu Yan died, and we had a terrible time chasing him out of the province! He's a notorious mercenary! Have you never heard of the pirates that wear bells to announce their arrival...?"

"...*That's him*...?" the captain exclaimed.

"We only have three-hundred men here!" Xi Su fretted. "We can't fight him if he decides to siege this city!"

"...But we have to hold the city for Chancellor of State Cao Cao," the captain noted.

"I'll do nothing for that evil man," Xi Su retorted. "I've heard about what he did in Xu Province fifteen years ago, and I've heard about what he did to civilians at Steep-slope just a few months ago: he's no better than Gan Ning, if not *worse*! If I insist on refusing to yield the city, Captain, it's for the people, not-"

"**OY!**"

Xi Su stopped talking and peered over the wall; Gan Ning was standing on the ground below with two of his subordinates.

"...*WHAT...?*" Xi Su asked.

"**YOU THE BOSS HERE...?**" Gan Ning asked.

"...**YES,**" Xi Su replied uneasily.

"**I DON'T WANT TO KILL NO ONE IF THAT'S POSSIBLE!**" Gan Ning explained. "**SURRENDER AND I PROMISE THAT MY MEN WON'T HARM A HAIR ON NO ONE'S HEAD!**"

"**IF YOU'RE THE SAME GAN NING THAT FLED YI PROVINCE FOURTEEN YEARS AGO, THEN YOU'RE A FAMOUS LIAR, KILLER AND PIRATE!**" Xi Su retorted. "**I AM XI SU, AND I WAS IN GUANGHAN!**"

"*Guanghan*...?" Gan Ning exclaimed. "This bloke's from Yi: the Chief Commander was prob'ly right, then, when he said Liu Zhang'd start sendin' help through to Jiangling. We've got to take this place and block the supply route off."

"So what do you want to do...?" one man asked.

"...I meant what I said," Gan Ning insisted; he then turned to the wall for a second time and bellowed, "**YEAH, ALRIGHT, I WAS A TROUBLEMAKER IN YI: BUT THIS IS JING! WE'RE BOTH OF US HERE 'CAUSE O' THAT BASTARD CAO CAO ONE WAY OR THE OTHER: IS HE WORTH DYING FOR...?**"

Xi Su grunted angrily and said, "No, he *isn't*."

"Don't tell me, tell Gan Ning!" the captain protested.

"...**ALRIGHT, WE'LL SUBMIT!**" Xi Su declared. "**WE'LL THROW OPEN THE GATES!**"

"That was pretty easy," Gan Ning chuckled. "Maybe I should become a diplomat!"

Xi Su met Gan Ning at the gates of Yiling, tendered the city administrator's seal to Gan and said, "I can't give you the County Magistrate's seal since I'm actually the Administrator of Guanghan... although Peng Yang's probably stolen that job from me now, the opportunist."

"I don't care much about seals," Gan Ning replied. "I was the Magistrate of Zhu County in Jiangxia a few years back; can't remember using mine much."

Xi Su laughed and said, "You seem to be a very amiable fellow, General Gan."

"I'm not a general," Gan Ning replied. "Leastways I don't think so, anyhow... I must ask someone about that at some point. Can we go and talk somewhere...?"

"The governor's mansion," Xi Su suggested. "Follow me!"

Xi Su had Gan Ning sit as the host in the audience hall of the Yiling governor's mansion and said, "What will you do now...?"

"I dunno," Gan Ning admitted. "My orders were to take Yiling, which I've done, and really quick, thanks to you lettin' me in. Why did you give up, if you don't mind me askin'...?"

"I was sent here by my lord Liu Zhang, Governor of Yi Province," Xi Su replied. "I was given three-hundred men and told to fortify Yiling on Cao Cao's orders."

"You don't like Cao then...?" Gan Ning guessed.

"He's 'another Dong Zhuo', if that isn't becoming a tired phrase," Xi Su replied. "We got a lot of refugees from Jing when he invaded the first time, five years ago; a lot of them were formerly refugees from Xu and Qing that fled his atrocities there, and... well, the stories were awful."

"What, worse than what's said about me in Guanghan...?" Gan Ning prompted.

"...You were as famous for generous acts as you were for bad ones," Xi Su admitted. "I'm not blind: my lord's late father, Governor Li Yan, colluded with Zhang Lu – a cultist – to seize Hanzhong, and he also parleyed with crime families to minimise threats to his rule, but that made the local governments prone to corruption, and when that happens it's often the case that criminals are living more honest lives than the appointed officials."

Gan Ning laughed and said, "I was an official's assistant for a while myself, lousy though me attempts at learnin' were: got the job on someone's word, but I quit after a few weeks and took to the rivers wi' me mates. Mum was disappointed: it's a family tradition to go on about us bein' descended from Gan Mao, an' we weren't completely poor, but all that's not for me, not when it's all crooked, as you say."

"...*Gan Mao*...?" Xi Su exclaimed. "Do you mean *Chancellor* Gan Mao of the Qin state...?"

"Apparently, yeah," Gan Ning replied. "Didn't do us much good, did it...?"

"...But then I hear stories of men misused, underused or unused wherever you go," Xi Su said. "Zang Ba, leader of the Mount Tai Bandits, was the honest son of a prison warder that had to seek the aid of a crime lord to free his father, who had been imprisoned by a corrupt official for speaking out."

"I wouldn't go so far as to say that I'm 'another Zang Ba'," Gan Ning chuckled. "Horrible bastard I was, flashing wealth about an' makin' friends with lots of officials that were prob'ly as crooked as anything, but I didn't care: if they were polite and seemed to be treatin' people alright then I was their mate, but if they took the piss wi' me or anyone I knew then I robbed 'em, beat 'em up, killed 'em in one or two cases. I killed people for money a few times 'n' all, and that I ain't proud of."

"...That shame indicates that you want to be a better man than you were," Xi Su prompted.

"Too right I do," Gan Ning replied. "When Li Yan died, a few blokes – men that you prob'ly knew, come t'think of it – they

came to me, said that a men under Liu Biao had come to Yi lookin'
to stir things up, put things right, and did I want to help them, an'
I said 'Yeah', an' we all caused a big fuss, but Liu Zhang got the
better of us, hard as that is to believe, and we all had to run off to
Jing... that's how I started under Liu Biao, really, though it was Su
Fei that got me the post with Huang Zu."
"You were probably 'bested' by Wu Yi or some other general," Xi
Su suggested. "Governor Liu isn't really up to 'besting' people."
Gan Ning smirked.
"Are they still with you, those officials...?" Xi Su asked.
"Nah," Gan Ning replied. "None o' them was pirate material."
"And now you work for Sun Quan...?" Xi Su prompted.
"I know he gets a lot o' bad words said about him, but his setup is
really honest," Gan Ning insisted. "Never a more honest bunch o'
men, in that way that yeah, a lot o' pirates about, but they're the
way they are and that's that, you know...? You do wrong, they
give you a chance to do better: I met Zu Lang, Jiang Qin and
Zhou Tai – all pirates or bandits at some point – an' they're all
workin' for the Suns as bodyguards, generals an' all that! And
apart from Ling Tong, I get along with everyone, but that's 'cause
I shot an' killed Ling's dad a few years back, an' I don't reckon
he'll ever let that go no matter how many times that Lord Sun
tells him to 'Drop it', not that I blame 'im."
"...And Cao Cao...?" Xi Su prompted.
"Nasty piece o' work," Gan Ning replied. "All I heard when I was in
Jing was how he was findin' excuses to invade; all I heard in
Jiangdong was stories about people dying s'spiciously, y'know,
sudden like, an' assassinations. A lot o' blokes reckon that Cao
Cao was behind Sun Ce being shot; man dammed a river wi'
bodies an' had a pregnant woman strangled, an' even *I* never did
that sort o' thing at me worst."
Xi Su hummed thoughtfully and said, "I was right to submit: you,
Gan Xingba, are a good man, and I would've been serving Cao
Cao – the worst thing to happen to the Empire – if I'd held out
and waited for support. Consider my men as your own, and you
can trust me when I say that I will not try to signal for help from
Cao Cao *or* Liu Zhang, nor will I answer any begging letters from
either of them."
"That's just what I wanted to hear!" Gan Ning replied. "Now... any
chance of some wine...?"

The Jiangdong forces rejoiced at the news that Yiling was theirs;
Yi Province Governor Liu Zhang, meanwhile, was distressed when
he received word that Xi Su had yielded without a fight, but he
could do little more than apologise to Cao Cao for his poor choice
of defenders. Now there could be no workable supply route from
Yi Province to Jiangling City unless Yiling returned to Han control:
that would be yet another problem that the beleaguered Cao Ren
would have to solve.

✱✱✱✱✱✱✱✱✱✱✱✱

96

While Gongjin and the bulk of the Jiangdong army began its siege of Jiangling City in Jing Province, Sun Quan's army had reached Hefei County in Northern Yang Province and camped close to the fortress, which loomed large. Sun Quan had his servant Gu Li make his personal tent ready while he invited his main campaign adviser, Zhang Hong, to the command tent for discussions.

"We have men enough to take this place quickly, then...?" Sun Quan prompted.

"We have ten-thousand, Lord Sun, while the enemy have less than a thousand to call upon, according to our reconnaissance," Zhang Hong replied.

"And what about the various armies of bandits...?" Sun Quan asked. "They're known to like Liu Fu a great deal, I understand, for the improvements to conditions that he has introduced to this region; might they help him...?"

"They might like the man, but would they die for him...?" Zhang Hong retorted. "We're getting reports that one of the leaders, Lei Xu, has actually risen up in rebellion against Cao Cao, ignoring his beloved Liu Fu's demands to stand down and forcing Cao to send the former 'Bandit King of Kaiyang', Zang Ba, to the border to intimidate him. If anything, my lord, the rebels in Lujiang are actually helping *us*."

"...How long will it take your brother to seize Dangtu, do you think...?" Sun Quan asked.

"I cannot say," Zhang Hong replied. "He would not have gone to Dangtu without being very sure that he could take the place, Lord Sun, so my answer will have to be 'in good time'."

"...Liu Fu is, as I have already said, a good man," Sun Quan continued. "My main concern here is 'history repeating itself', as it were: Bofu was popular here until he besieged and destroyed Lu Kang, and now I am here to besiege and destroy Liu Fu."

"Heaven is on your side, Lord Sun," Zhang Hong replied. "The southeast wind told us that."

Sun Quan smiled and said, "Yes, that's very true."

"And we don't know whether this man had anything to do with what happened to your younger brother Yi," the bodyguard leader Song Qian suggested. "He was certainly in correspondence with the two murderers, and he's Cao Cao's man in Yang."

Sun Quan's smile disappeared.

"Song Qian is quite right," Zhang Hong said. "Don't feel too sorry for Liu Fu: as Inspector of Yang Province at Cao Cao's decree, he's the man that liaised with Li Shu's rebels, facilitated any communications between Xu Gong and the capital, passed Cao Cao's bribes to the likes of Fei Zhan and Pan Lin, and promised shelter to Sheng Xian's cronies!"

"...That's all of it true," Sun Quan replied angrily. "No more mercy for this man: we shall begin, then, and reclaim northern Yang!"

Yang Province Inspector Liu Fu resisted calls to stay away from the walls of Hefei: he peered downwards at the siege preparations and groaned painfully.

"Inspector Liu, you must go and rest or your condition will

deteriorate further!" Attendant Officer Jiang Ji pleaded.

"You and I… have been here years now, Zitong, and for every day that we've been here, we've… we've dreaded this moment and prayed it would never come," Liu Fu said as he allowed two soldiers to aid his retreat from the wall. "Now that they are here at last, my wits have left me! The people of this city, must… must they suffer the horrors of a siege…?"

"We must write to Xuchang at once, Inspector, requesting aid," Jiang Ji suggested.

"That rout on the Great River has stripped the Chancellor of his navy, half the army and most of his credibility!" Liu Fu retorted. "All the good done since Wan, undone in a single foolish moment – the Chancellor has wrong-footed himself *again*! Every traveller that came here in the last two weeks speaks of nothing but lavish parties on the decks of linked ships, and every traveller in the last two days speaks of fire, a southeast wind and a cheap trick! After all my best efforts, Chen Lan, Mei Qian and Lei Xu will be *uncontrollable now*, and…!"

Liu Fu winced with pain and was forced to stop speaking.

"Don't strain yourself, Inspector," Jiang Ji pleaded. "Hefei needs your leadership."

"I am an academic, yes, and a civil administrator, yes, and a fairly competent negotiator, yes, but in no way am I a general, which is what this city needs right now that the young wolf Sun Quan is at the door," Liu Fu retorted. "No, he's no Sun Ce, but might that young man make me 'his Lu Kang' in order to prove himself…?"

"Our enemies can be beaten by way of ruses too, Inspector," Jiang Ji insisted. "If we can just think of a scheme, then-"

"I… should not have gone to the wall," Liu Fu croaked. "Let us return to my study, Zitong, and… and discuss this matter further."

Jiang Ji turned to an archery captain and said, "Do what you can: I know I ask a lot, but…"

"…We're all dead if we don't try our best," the captain replied. "That, alone, will serve as an incentive."

"…I must write to Xuchang," Jiang Ji murmured as he left the wall and followed Liu Fu's laboured retreat.

A messenger would leave the fortress city of Hefei before the siege was properly begun: that siege would be merciless and costly, as most sieges were, and it would test the humiliated Chancellor of State as he struggled to find the soldiers and officers to deal with the rapid spread of chaos throughout the Han Empire.

****

97

The siege of Jiangling was fully underway when Liu Bei arrived in the region and established his own camp; Gongjin immediately left the walls and retired to his command tent with Lu Su.
"Liu Qi is lagging behind, if he is even travelling here at all: Veteran General Cheng has slowed his advance in order to ensure that the Lius aren't up to something," Gongjin explained. "This confirms my worst fears, I believe: Zhuge Liang wants Liu Bei to have Jing, starting with the independent counties."
"They might just want to help!" Lu Su protested.
"...Zijing... *no*," Gongjin retorted. "*No*, they are not a friendly lot that offer their swords to struggling armies in exchange for heavenly praise. Liu Bei needs a base."
"He also needs an army," Lu Su chuckled.
"Bei's been gathering men to replace those that he lost at Steepslope and Wulin," Gongjin replied. "And more men have come to Liu Qi, so their combined strength at present is *twenty-thousand*, give or take a thousand."
Lu Su was silent.
"Twenty-thousand men with no base: what a predicament!" Gongjin said with theatrical humour. "But rest assured, Zijing, that Zhuge will be eyeing the counties for his lord, and when we all meet for the first time the counties will be mentioned."
"But how can they *not* be mentioned...?" Lu Su asked.
"Of course they must be mentioned, but in what terms...?" Gongjin retorted. "You'll see, Zijing: then, perhaps, you'll understand."

The wandering warlord Liu Bei brought several of his most trusted officials to Gongjin's main camp in order to discuss coordinated manoeuvres: Gongjin welcomed them and had them sit as guests opposite Lu Su and Lü Meng.

The first person that Gongjin noted – even before Liu Bei himself – was Bei's intimidating bodyguard Chen Dao, who opted to remain outside the tent with his elite cavalrymen; he then looked at Liu Bei, who was a quiet, approachable middle-aged man with long earlobes – seen as a sign of great promise – and a regal air despite his weathered robes and armour. Gongjin was then distracted by Liu Bei's mischievous friend and adviser Jian Yong, who was smirking as he observed Lu Su; he then looked at the tall, imposing Guan Yu, who was stroking his long beard and glaring at Gongjin with contempt; that stare was nothing, however, when compared to the beady eyes of the swarthy, thick-whiskered Zhang Fei, who gave the impression that he should like to kill the Jiangdong men if given the chance; Gongjin quickly turned his gaze toward the last of the generals – the fearless, charismatic Zhao Yun – who was less aggressive but no more approving; Gongjin quickly turned to the remaining advisers.

Liu Bei's middle-aged envoy, Mister Sun Qian, was timid and unimpressive; that made Gongjin smile as he moved onto Xiang Lang, who was a former adviser to Liu Biao and visibly uncomfortable; the smile faded slightly when he settled on Zhuge Liang, who was fanning himself and smiling casually.
"...Welcome, allies, welcome," Gongjin hailed.

Liu Bei bowed slightly and said, "Our congratulations to you."

"...It was our joint victory," Gongjin replied carefully.

Lu Su turned to Zhuge Liang and said, "So tell me: how is the young governor Liu Qi...?"

"He is fine, Zijing: just fine," Zhuge Liang replied tonelessly.

"We are making good progress," Gongjin said as warmly as he could. "As you are no doubt aware, Xi Su of Yiling surrendered without conflict, so General Gan Ning is now in control of that city. Our lord is at this moment besieging Hefei in the east. We're now in the middle of carrying out some preliminary military manoeuvres against Cao Ren and of course, if you have any helpful advice to give, we would like to hear it, since you probably know more about this region than we do, as former residents."

Liu Bei was obviously hiding irritation as he replied, "My thanks for your gracious words regarding the outcome at Wulin. I only wish I had been more help militarily. ...But that is why we are here now, is it not...?"

"It is, Lord Liu," Gongjin said. "But most of the assistance we need is actually best managed from Jiangxia, so once we have spoken, you really should return there, Lord Liu, and-"

"And go back to our *tents*...?" Zhang Fei barked.

"...*Tents*...?" Zhou Yu said with surprise. "Why are you in tents...?"

Zhang Fei leant forward and cried, "**Don't give me-!**"

Liu Bei gestured to Guan Yu, who – along with Zhao Yun – escorted Zhang Fei from the tent; Gongjin briefly turned his gaze toward Lü Meng, who immediately followed Liu Bei's generals.

"...My apologies, Chief Commander," Liu Bei chuckled. "I am afraid that age has not mellowed my friend and brother at all."

"If you are all in tents, then his anger is understandable," Lu Su said worriedly. "Has General Cheng thrown you all out of your homes in Xiakou...?"

"...Not as such," Liu Bei replied carefully. "We preferred, since the city appears, like Yiling, to have been occupied in the name of your lord Sun Quan, that we-"

"...'Occupied'...?" Gongjin said irritably. "Lord Liu, you misrepresent the situation. Cao Cao successfully annexed Nan Prefecture after he defeated you at Steep-slope, so all of our current actions are not an attempt at 'occupation' in the way you seem to indirectly imply, but 'liberation', by adding Nan Prefecture to the territories that are liberally and fairly governed by my lord Sun Quan."

"And Jiangxia...?" Mister Sun asked snidely. "What of that blatant occupation...?"

"I do not so far see any resistance, which you would expect from an occupation: why, have you seen some...?" Gongjin countered. "Besides, you speak of the region as though you want it... but could you defend it...? Both Steep-slope and Wulin suggest that not to be the case."

"We lost at Wulin intentionally," Mister Sun retorted.

"...As part of our joint plan to rout Cao Cao, I concede that point in part," Gongjin replied. "But if you had not had our help, would that rout not have been a genuine one, however, and resulted in your total annihilation...?"

"That, we will never know," Zhuge Liang said calmly. "The matter now, Gongjin, is whether we will share the burden of liberating Jing, so that it is seen as just that by the world... or if you will monopolize the retaking of Jing against the wishes of its former governor and also its people, turn down the help of the allies that fought alongside you and shared your suffering at Red Cliffs, and be held up by the world as a seditious conqueror in the months and years to come."

"...I dislike that accusation, Mister Zhuge," Gongjin retorted.

"I make no accusation," Zhuge Liang insisted. "I simply point out that when you have an army of twenty-thousand men, led by a popular lord and the son of the beloved former governor, who are ready, willing and able to assist you in stabilising the region, and you turn them down, thereby making your lone task a harder one to achieve, well... tell me, what other conclusion will historians draw...?"

Gongjin was too angry to respond immediately; Zhuge Liang started to fan himself slowly and fearlessly.

"We want no quarrel," Liu Bei protested. "We just want to help you. Say, for example, with regard to the matter of the four counties of Changsha, Lingling, Wuling and Guiyang: why not allow us to take control of those territories, use them as our base, so that Jiangxia is no longer a point of contention...?"

Lu Su was startled: Gongjin's prediction had come to pass.

"...Those counties are also on a border with Jiangdong," Gongjin replied calmly. "I do not think it would be wise to let them fall into weak hands, as it were, lest they give an enemy easy passage into our domains... no disrespect intended."

A long pause followed as Liu Bei silently fumed; Zhuge Liang smiled and said, "None assumed. But I think that we can genuinely be of service in that endeavour, since young governor Liu Qi is popular in those counties, and peaceful surrender in all four cases is guaranteed, whereas otherwise... especially since those counties know of his current plight... that may not necessarily be quite so guaranteed."

Another pause – shorter, but no less significant – followed Zhuge Liang's thinly-veiled threat: Gongjin nodded and said, "I see; okay, perhaps you can assist me in that 'endeavour', after all, and act in our name... but once I am done with Jiangling, I expect them to be given over to Lord Sun for collective governance."

"You demand another's territory...?" Jian Yong scoffed.

"Is it Liu Qi's now, or Lord Liu's...? ...No, it is Cao Cao's, surrendered to him by Liu Cong," Gongjin retorted. "By all means, if you think you can defeat Cao Ren in Jiangling, best Man Chong in Dangyang, rout Yue Jin in Xiangyang, and hold Yiling, and liberate the counties, and then hold off the inevitable reprisals by Cao Cao on your own, well, then we will leave..."

"And you'd return Jiangxia...?" Mister Sun prompted.

"We took Jiangxia from Huang Zu before Cao Cao invaded the region," Gongjin replied. "We were forced to remove our military presence and reallocate it to Red Cliffs because of that invasion: Jiangxia was already ours when you fled there from the rout at Steep-slope. All that Veteran General Cheng Pu has done, Mister Sun, is ensure that there is no more lack of clarity on the matter."

Liu Bei, Mister Sun and Jian Yong were all looking to Zhuge Liang, as though they hoped that he would say something: Zhuge continued to fan himself slowly and silently.

"...You think that I am unfair," Gongjin continued. "This is war...

and in war, one can only be sure of oneself, and even then, that is a luxury. You are probably very sincere and righteous, but militarily, you have done nothing but fail at every turn, and therefore, you are unfit to hold the land. If you were strong as well as just, like Lord Sun, then of course I would give more credence to the idea... but you are a weak partner, and I cannot trust a weak partner with key strategic locations. Even if you were my friends, I would not trust you with such responsibility."

Liu Bei lowered his gaze, but more from anger than hurt.

"By all means, if you can take the counties without a fight... go, take them!" Gongjin chuckled. "But now, I would like to discuss the matter I invited you here for. I wonder, perhaps your marvellous general Guan Yu can do us a service, as he has done in the past for you and for Cao Cao."

Liu Bei raised his head and glared at Gongjin.

"If I could borrow Guan Yu's might... he could sail down the River Han to Xiangyang and attack there: a pincer would not only cut supplies from the north, it would surely terrify Cao Ren into an early retreat," Gongjin continued. "The city is guarded, as I said, by Yue Jin, with support from General Wen Ping, and who knows what advisory assistance... but Guan Yunchang is a champion, and with his record for crossing hostile territory and besting the likes of Yuan Shao's fearsome general Yan Liang, he is probably the only man for the job."

"That's a dangerous mission, but I am sure Yunchang would jump at the chance for such an adventure," Liu Bei replied passively.

"My thanks," Gongjin said. "I will, of course, give him troops and a second to support him... because I believe that if we find the right ways to work together... we can genuinely achieve great things."

"Very well then," Liu Bei conceded.

"Excellent!" Gongjin said. "Now, you must all be tired from such a long journey; please, go and get some rest and refreshments: our home is your home."

Liu Bei bowed respectfully and gestured to his subordinates; a brief exchange of respectful bows followed that obviously lacked sincerity. Zhuge Liang was the last to leave: he glared at Lu Su before departing.

"...*Aiee*...! If looks could kill, Gongjin, we would both of us have died a thousand times in those few minutes," Lu Su complained. "That last look that Kongming gave me, it-!"

"Leave them for now, but... I think you should pay 'Kongming' a visit tomorrow morning and gauge his mood, and from that, his intent," Gongjin suggested.

"...Why do you want Guan Yu to attack Xiangyang...?" Lu Su asked. "He's no sailor: wouldn't we want Jiang Qin, Dong Xi, Ling Tong, or some other-?"

"Su Fei will second him," Gongjin interrupted. "Must I explain...?"

"...You hope to coerce Guan Yu into joining us," Lu Su realised.

"...It's worth a try," Gongjin suggested. "I mean it *is*, isn't it...?"

Lu Su was absolutely convinced that attempting to recruit Guan Yu was a waste of time, but he nodded agreeably anyway.

Gongjin was examining his battle maps when Lu Su returned from visiting Zhuge Liang's tent 'office' on the following day; Lu groaned miserably and said, "Gongjin, he... he...!"

"...'He' what...?" Gongjin prompted indifferently.

"Kongming, he... he said something terrible!" Lu Su replied. "He... he was with the Ma brothers and Yi Ji: Yi Ji accused us of theft, saying that-"

"I don't care about what Yi Ji said," Gongjin interrupted. "Yi Ji is a worthless former lackey of Liu Biao. What did *Zhuge* say...?"

"...I brought it upon myself," Lu Su decided.

"Unlikely," Gongjin scoffed. "Just *tell me*, for the love of the gods!"

"I suggested, after Yi Ji provoked me, that Liu Cong might have ceded Jiangxia to Lord Sun if Cao Cao had not invaded Jing when he did," Lu Su admitted.

"That... is nonsense, Zijing, and you should have known that," Gongjin said. "But please, go on."

"...Well... Kongming said that Cong would have been able to send Liu Bei to aid Liu Qi's reclamation of Jiangxia if Cao hadn't invaded, and then Qi could've wrested control back from Cong," Lu Su reported. "I retorted that it was supposition, and Yi Ji called me 'insufferable', and then Kongming said, after sarcastically berating Yi Ji, that we only 'fled Jiangxia' out of fear of the Huang clan and Liu Biao, 'who still lived then', and that... that...!"

"...Would you just *tell me*...?" Gongjin pleaded.

"...He asked if, 'once this obvious ruse of contention ends', he... he asked if we intended to send Cao Cao tribute to 'thank him for his assistance'!" Lu Su whined.

Gongjin laughed and said, "I'm sure that Zhuge Liang was joking."

Lu Su was silent.

"I doubt he'd dare say such things and mean it," Gongjin insisted. "His lord is in a very weak position right now, and Zhuge Liang is no suicidal fool."

Lu Su laughed awkwardly and said, "Yes, yes; they're irritated at their predicament, no doubt."

"I feel for Kongming, actually," Gongjin admitted. "I really, genuinely respect him, Zijing: his intellect equals or perhaps exceeds mine, for he knows as much as me, yet is several years my junior. It is a real, genuine pity that he chose to serve Liu Bei, a real shame."

"...But 'war is war'...?" Lu Su prompted.

"Yes," Gongjin replied. "And to that end, I cannot afford to show pity, as he cannot show weakness. We both have difficult jobs: such is life."

"So what will happen now...?" Lu Su asked.

Gongjin sighed and replied, "The situation in Hefei is not ideal, but could be worse: I spoke to Zhang Zhao and Zhang Hong before I left Chaisang, and as my lord's seconds on that mission, their job is to contain his newfound valour, and prevent him making critical errors of judgement. Zhang Zhao is attempting to take nearby Jiujiang, since that divides Cao Cao's forces even further; but we must still be cautious. Cao Cao still has enough men to outnumber both of us simultaneously, even after Red Cliffs."

"We must act quickly, then," Lu Su said.

"Yes," Gongjin replied. "This siege must end, and end quickly."

∗∗∗∗∗∗∗∗∗∗∗∗

98

Gongjin remained in his command tent over the next few days, poring over a map of Southern Jing; Lu Su visited him after one particularly costly attempt at scaling the walls of Jiangling and silently awaited some sort of response.

"Liu Bei is holding his position," Gongjin said without turning to face Lu Su. "They're even considering withdrawing to Jiangxia."

"...Why...?" Lu Su asked.

"They want to fetch Liu Qi, they say," Gongjin scoffed.

"But Guan Yu will still take part in the raid on Xiangyang...?" Lu Su prompted.

"Yes," Gongjin replied tonelessly. "As an officer of Liu Bei... yes."

"...Ah," Lu Su murmured.

"Why, Lu Zijing, does this faithless sandal weaver command such loyalty...?" Gongjin asked as he turned to face Lu Su at last. "Why do such wise, courageous men follow such a whining, treacherous old owl...?"

"...There are some that may say that we are fools for serving Lord Sun," Lu Su suggested. "Opinions, Gongjin, are opinions: theirs are high with respect to Liu Bei, and remember that Guan travelled across treacherous terrain to flee Cao Cao and return to Liu Bei, forsaking all manner of gifts bestowed on him. If Cao Cao could not buy the man with Imperial titles, what is there to say...?"

"...*Sometimes*, you are wise," Gongjin chuckled as he returned to his map.

"...Something else concerns you," Lu Su prompted.

Gongjin laughed ironically and said, "And *sometimes*, you are insightful, too. I have had word that Cao Cao has significant forces near the city of An Feng."

"...*An Feng*...?" Lu Su exclaimed. "That... that could seriously threaten our lord...!"

"Let us hope not," Gongjin said.

"...To change the subject, how go things in Jiangdong...?" Lu Su asked. "Sometimes it's easy to forget that we have a whole region that we call home that has problems of its own."

"You really are excelling today," Gongjin praised. "Hè Qi and Dong Xi alternate their time between Danyang, Yuzhang and Kuaiji, and Lü Dai maintains the peace in Guangling, which stabilises Wu in turn; Lu Xun is here, but that doesn't mean that he's ignoring his responsibilities: he's assigned men to distribute supplies to the needy, had water rerouted to serve isolated villages, recruited militias to fight the bandits, and even found the time to draw up a list of tax evaders! There's another man that can follow us when our allotted spans are at an end, Zijing."

"*Ayah*...! I wish you'd stop talking about being *dead*, Gongjin!" Lu Su complained. "And worse yet, you're killing *me* as well, now!"

"See it as a compliment," Gongjin joked.

"...Wait... wait, you... you see *me* as your successor as Chief Commander, then...?" Lu Su realised.

"And not just because you saved me," Gongjin said as he turned to face Lu Su for a second time. "Zijing, I have no time whatsoever for your 'Tripod Theorem', but you're shrewd enough to properly deal with Liu Bei, because deep down, under that optimisitic façade, there beats the heart of a pragmatic man. I'll give you an example: you coaxed the name of 'Wu Ju', Administrator of Cangwu, from that wily owl, and you passed it on to me, which shows that you know what must be done."

"…I do, much as it pains me," Lu Su admitted. "But if Kongming can be spared…"

"If he can be spared, he will be," Gongjin promised. "But Liu Bei… must be dealt with. For our lord to take flight… that old dragon must be felled, and *soon*."

The commander in charge of Jiangling City's defence, General Cao Ren, left the walls after an hour of watching the usual horrors of oil-pouring, rock-dropping and dodging arrows in order to have a much-needed rest. The ground around the city was scarred by trenches, palisades, earth mounds, the remains of campsites and a number of active, abandoned or damaged archery towers; the advantage was currently with the Jiangdong forces, and Cao Ren's men were all but trapped within the city itself.

"…Zhou Yu must not break us," Cao Ren said to his chief clerk, Chen Jiao. "We have a constant flow of resources coming down to us through Northern Jing, so we can hold: Zhou Yu will have to withdraw eventually, for he cannot – or surely *does not* – have the supplies to stay here indefinitely."

"But we're not simply going to endure this day after day…?" Chen Jiao protested. "You must have some plan to speed the process?"

"There is, of course, a way to confound them, for there is always *something*," Cao Ren replied. "I am looking at the possibility of attacking Yiling and forcing them to either rush to its aid – thus giving us time to reorganise – or face the reestablishment of our supply route from Yi Province."

"Can't Yi's governor, Liu Zhang, do more…?" Chen Jiao suggested.

"He's an ineffectual coward," Cao Ren sighed. "Mengde – Chancellor Cao – should replace Liu Zhang when this is over, if not before, or Yi is at risk of falling into another's hands."

"…There's reports of suspicious vessels on the Han River," Chen Jiao said suddenly. "They move *northward*."

"Oh…? But then they might be…!" Cao Ren exclaimed. "If it *were*, then they-! …But I cannot worry about that! That's Man Chong's problem, Wen Ping's problem, or Yue Jin's problem! I cannot deal with *everything*! …What news from Lujiang…?"

"None," Chen Jiao sighed.

"…Zhou Yu *cannot beat us*," Cao Ren grumbled. "Zhou Yu is a rebel: we fight for the *Han*…!"

The boats that travelled down the Han River were, as Cao Ren feared, carrying men under the command of Liu Bei's general Guan Yu and Huang Zu's former subordinate Su Fei; the infiltrating force passed Jiangling, routed the small defensive positions and began a siege on Jing's northern capital, Xiangyang City, which isolated Cao Ren and Yue Jin from each other and severely weakened the supply routes that Ren depended upon. Cao Cao's other notable man in the region – the adviser Man Chong – was based between the two capitals and now had the unenviable task of proffering advice to two desperate, proud generals as they did their best to repel their attackers.

500

At the same time, Liu Bei – who had been deliberately underused by Gongjin – finally received permission to take Linju, a strategic position to the west of Steep-slope and north of Yiling: that was yet another mission that took the attackers behind the front line with a view to isolating the city completely.

"…Truly a god among men," Gongjin said upon hearing a report from Xiangyang: Guan Yu had routed most of the opposition and was now sieging the city despite it being guarded by the formidable Yue Jin.

"This is marvellous news," Lu Su said excitedly. "We will surely win, with so many attack fronts! Liu Bei's forces have taken Linju City already!"

"It seems that Heaven may be on our side," Gongjin replied. "However, it pays to avoid complacency. We shall press Cao Ren, and hope for the best."

But while the western front was progressing nicely, the eastern front was faltering despite the odds: Sun Quan was disturbed and angered when Zhang Zhao returned to his camp at Hefei with tears in his eyes and said, "I have failed you, Lord Sun… Dangtu would not fall!"

"…Could you not have stayed, tried to press the place for longer…?" Sun Quan despaired.

"My brother is not one for needlessly retreating before a task is completed," Zhang Hong protested. "If Zibu could not stay there, then only the likes of Zhang Liang or Jiang Ziya of old times might stand a chance."

"We'll need to tell Gongjin that Jiujiang Prefecture could not be taken," Sun Quan said as he glared at Zhang Zhao. "His plan relied on our securing these two prefectures quickly… but we'll have to do it one at a time, then."

"I truly don't understand," Zhang Zhao admitted. "We were met with such *hostility* at Dangtu; how has our reputation here in the north of our own province been so badly tarnished…?"

"…Perhaps Cao Cao has done there as he has obviously done here, and moved large numbers of his own people into the region to ensure loyalty," Zhang Hong replied. "Come what may, though, that's the situation: we'll concentrate on taking Hefei for now, and then we'll move northward and seize Shouchun, which will give us Jiujiang by another means. And with both of us here, my lord, Hefei will fall all the faster."

Sun Quan looked to his servant Gu Li, who nodded once as a sign that he believed that Quan should let the matter rest.

"…Very well," Sun Quan sighed.

"My lord, allow me to play a greater role in this siege," Song Qian pleaded. "I have been a bodyguard to you for so long, though gratefully so, but at a moment like this, when there are no direct threats to you from the enemy, I am not needed: let me lead men to the wall and bring this siege to an end for you!"

"…It's true that you don't get to do much, and I did allow Chen Wu to take part in the Red Cliffs campaign," Sun Quan replied. "Alright: pick three men to guard me in your stead and take to the field. But preserve your life, Song Qian! I will have need of you again soon enough!"

"Thank you, Lord Sun!" Song Qian cried. "I will fight like a hundred men to reduce the walls of Hefei to dust!"

And so the siege of Hefei continued: Sun Quan rallied his men from his command tent, since the Zhang brothers were adamant that he should remain out of harm's way. Hefei Fortress was sturdy enough, but the winter had brought rains that were damaging the integrity of the soil and the rice-paste mortar that had been used to build some of the walls; the frail Liu Fu knew that time was against the defenders as well as the weather, and there had not been a response from Xuchang that had made it through the chaos further north.

"…Bandits are everywhere, and Lei Xu's mob is the worst," Liu Fu grumbled as he returned to his office after a day of issuing orders to the defenders on the walls. "How an Imperial messenger is supposed to get here amid all this… is beyond me. Hefei is *isolated*, and…!"

"Don't allow despair to harm your recovery, Inspector," Attendant Officer Jiang Ji said. "We won't be abandoned: help will come."

"But will Hefei be more than rubble by then…?" Liu Fu asked. "You've seen the damage to the south wall…?"

"…It will take weeks if not months for that damage to become severe enough to worry about," Jiang Ji insisted.

"But we might *have* to wait for weeks or months!" Liu Fu retorted.

"…Help will come," Jiang Ji insisted. "We must have faith."

"I do have faith, Zitong, but I am also a pragmatist," Liu Fu said as he rotated his shoulder to relieve some pain. "We're always stuck when it is dark, and at the moment we have little daylight: we need to do something to stop them being able to move about out there without us knowing what they're up to."

"Sun Quan is not at all like his famous father, and none of the men the he has brought here are great generals," Jiang Ji noted. "We needn't worry about them trying to scale the walls in the dark, and this city is already proofed against sappers."

"I worry more about the walls being further damaged, not scaled or dug under," Liu Fu retorted. "I know that the interior has some maze-like qualities with certain paths blocked, but that won't do more than buy us time. We must keep them from breaching the outer defences, and being unable to move about freely at night will lengthen the time that it will take for them to do the necessary damage."

"I see your point, Inspector," Jiang Ji said.

"…When they leave the walls at the end of each night, we must light the area around the city somehow," Liu Fu insisted. "We can watch them then, and they won't be able to approach the walls without casting shadows or extinguishing the fires, which will both serve as alarms. We should plan and implement that as soon as possible, Zitong."

"I will do whatever is necessary," Jiang Ji promised.

Days passed.

To the west, Cao Ren was equally despondent when he learned of the progress being made against his own defences in and around Jiangling County.

"**This is impossible!**" Cao Ren cried as he stared at Man Chong's reports. "Linju??? *Xiangyang*??? Will Zhou Yu's men appear at the gates of *Xuchang* next???"

"There's no sense in being so desperate," Xu Huang suggested.

"...No... no, you're right," Cao Ren realised. "We have to turn this around: have our scouts finished their reconnaissance...?"

"Linju is best left for now," Chief Clerk Chen Jiao reported. "Liu Bei's men and Zhou Yu's men are obviously not working together that well and, perhaps, have conflicting agendas, so-"

"So Linju should be left: *fine*," Cao Ren said impatiently. "And Yiling...?"

Chen Jiao nodded and replied, "Gan Ning and Xi Su have, between them, maybe a thousand men to call upon, and a third of them are men from Yi Province that might come back to us if the circumstances were correct."

"They can die if that's what they want, for all I care, but Yiling *must be retaken*!" Cao Ren said. "We'll attack the place with our cavalry, since they're of no use here right now."

"Yiling is a night's ride away at least, and if we go at speed the horses will arrive exhausted, and the men will be tired as well," Xu Huang suggested.

"Then we send six-thousand!" Cao Ren retorted. "Six times the men – lucky in all respects, but only for us! We'll cause a distraction at nightfall and have them ride out of the west gate and straight to Yiling!"

"Who will command them...?" General Niu Jin asked.

"I cannot spare you or Xu Huang, mainly because your absence would be obvious," Cao Ren replied. "We'll need to trust the cavalry captains: they are – *were* – men that were hand-picked by my brother, so..."

Cao Ren's mood suddenly worsened: his brother – the founder of Cao Cao's elite 'Tiger and Leopard Cavalry', Cao Chun – had not recovered from the serious wounds that he sustained at the end of the Battle of Steep-slope, and it was quite possible that Chun was already dead.

"We must keep our spirits high," Xu Huang suggested.

"...Quite right," Cao Ren said. "Zihe would – *will* – be proud of what his cavalry will now do for the state! The plan will be executed immediately: we proceed at nightfall!"

When night came, Cao Ren had a large group of soldiers feign an incompetent attempt at charging out of the east gate: Gongjin ordered his forces to contain them, but the fracas allowed Cao Ren to exploit the poor light and speed his elite cavalry out of the western gates to meet up with other contingents scattered about the region and form a 6,000-string assault force. The deception would not be known until its purpose – a counter-siege of Yiling – was known as well.

****

99

"Blimey... that's a lot to deal with," Gan Ning said as he stared over the eastern wall of Yiling City; a ring of enemy cavalrymen were circling the city and chasing away the infantrymen that guarded the exterior, and there was a much larger contingent of cavalrymen in the near distance.
"**How many are there???**" Xi Su cried.
"...I ain't never been much of a one for countin', but I'd say there's a few thousands, all horsemen, and I doubt we can see all of what's here, so you can maybe double that," Gan Ning replied. "I don't reckon that I can scare 'em off, and they're settin' a camp up already: we have to send for help."
"To Linju...?" Xi Su supposed. "That's quite close."
"What, to Liu Bei's lot...?" Gan Ning chortled. "No way: he'd prob'ly send his men here t'take Yiling for himself. We'll write to Chief Commander Zhou."

Gongjin was starting to feel the pressure of being the Chief Commander of a newly-emerging independent state at war; he convened daily meetings with his leading officers and officials, who became increasingly worried about him.
"The Chief Commander should delegate some of his work to others," Cheng Pu said as he walked toward the command tent with Huang Gai and Han Dang.
"He'll be fine," Han Dang replied. "Besides, I thought you hated him, Demou... or is it that you want him to give you more to do because-?"
"It's only because I know that you're being mischievous, Yigong, that I don't break your front teeth," Cheng Pu retorted. "I am content with my role if that's what Lord Sun Quan wants, just as Lü Fan – who did more for Lord Sun Ce's military advancements than Zhou Gongjin – is content with civil administrative positions."
"Yeah, I know, and like you said, I was messin' about," Han Dang replied. "He's a strong bloke: anyone that can go up against Cao Cao as the man that – if it all went wrong – is the one that gets the Five Pains an' all that, is a very, *very* strong bloke."
"But things do not go well," Cheng Pu suggested. "Yiling is, as far as we know, secure, but Gan Ning's untested, and this 'Xi Su' might have feigned submission; Cao Cao's movements in Lujiang are hard to fathom, with sightings of soldiers one minute and then nothing the next, so Lord Sun could be endangered at any moment; and here in Jiangling, the usual 'siege matters' strip away the essence of what we are, as they always do."
"We'll win, though," Han Dang insisted. "Right, Gongfu...?"
"*Aiee*... don't even remind me that he's here!" Cheng Pu complained. "He-!"
"I say to you as I said to the Chief Commander: you, Demou, fought on after serious injury countless times in the old days," Huang Gai retorted.
"Yes, but I was a lot younger!" Cheng Pu protested. "We're going grey! We're *old*! *You're* old! You were shot, fell in the-!"
"I'm fine," Huang Gai insisted. "I'm won't die by being here."
"...Alright," Cheng Pu grumbled. "I shall content myself with

worrying about Zhou Gongjin, then."

"Not again!" Han Dang cried. "He'll be fine!"

The meeting was attended by Gongjin, Lu Su, Cheng Pu, Huang Gai, Han Dang, Lü Meng, Ling Tong, Chen Wu, Zhou Tai, Sun Hao, Sun Yu, Sun Jiao, Sun Ben, Lu Xun and Pan Zhang, who had newly arrived after entrusting Chaisang to Xu Kun; Gongjin sighed angrily and said, "I wish that we were here to talk cheerfully about our multitude of successes, gentlemen, but this siege is filling the infirmary with familiar faces and making it very difficult to maintain morale."

"That's the nature of sieges," Cheng Pu suggested.

"...All the same, it is unpleasant," Gongjin replied. "And I must admit that I am unhappy with Liu Bei's man holding Linju for us... and Guan Yu being so dominant in Xiangyang."

"They're our allies," Lu Su said. "And they have twenty thousand-"

"I am entitled to whinge about being forced to rely on them, Zijing," Gongjin chortled.

"We'll commandeer Linju as soon as possible," Cheng Pu said. "Oh, and Liu Qi's not threatening Xiakou anymore, so you can stop worrying about that."

Gongjin smiled as he replied, "Good! I am just about-!"

A sudden din outside the command tent ended the sentence: Gongjin's face fell as a dirty, exhausted messenger staggered into the tent.

"...Speak," Gongjin said weakly.

"...**Re... REPORT!**" the messenger began. "**Cha... Zhang Zhao... has... has failed to take Jujiang, and has withdrawn!**"

"What, *already*...?" Gongjin complained. "...We *needed* Jujiang... ... ...okay, okay. Anything else to report from that region...?"

"**No... no more news,**" the messenger panted. "**No... further news known at this time... c-commander.**"

"Okay... get some rest," Gongjin said warmly.

"Thank you, commander," the messenger wheezed.

"**REPORT!**" another messenger bellowed as he dashed into the tent; the first messenger slowly passed the second and shook his head sadly.

"D'aaagh... **what NOW???**" Gongjin cried.

"Gongjin, please remain calm," Lu Su said quietly.

"**Gan Ning and Xi Su are besieged at Yiling by six thousand cavalry sent covertly by Cao Ren to rescue the city!**" the second messenger reported.

"**How???**" Gongjin exclaimed.

"...That explains those disturbances at the east gate," Lü Meng proposed.

"They were distractions, to allow these men out of the west gate," Lu Xun said.

"Quite so, Lu Boyan," Lü Meng replied. "You suspected as much."

"I agree with you both," Gongjin said. "I overlooked it... I was tired, but that is no excuse... it was obvious, that was foolish."

"General Gan Ning only has a thousand men," Cheng Pu noted.

"And three hundred of those are Xi Su's men," Han Dang recalled.

"...He might perish," Ling Tong said with a smile.

"This isn't the time for personal feuds!" Huang Gai scolded.

"We will have to rescue him," Lu Su supposed.

"No!" Ling Tong cried. "Forgive me, but feuds aside, that would be foolish: to break the siege of Yiling, we would need to send everything we have there, and Cao Ren has enough men left here to destroy us if we divide our forces to rescue one scabby little pirate!"

"I regret that I agree, for different reasons entirely than hating the man," Cheng Pu lamented. "I agree that we cannot divide our forces; it is worth losing Yiling to gain Jiangling. We are better off using Cao Ren's reduced retinue to our advantage and taking Jiangling now."

"I feel the same way," Huang Gai admitted: Ling Tong's did nothing to hide his elation.

"As do I," Han Dang said. "I admire Gan Ning's bravery, but would not risk a greater cause for him."

"It's regrettable, but it's the situation," Sun Ben suggested.

Zhou Tai grunted ambiguously; Pan Zhang sighed and said, "S'a pity, but we can't let Jiangling go, can we…?"

Lu Xun said nothing; Lü Meng shook his head disappointedly and said, "Regrettable."

"…You have an opinion, A'Meng…?" Lu Su teased.

"Zijing," Gongjin scolded, "this man is-"

"I know his talent," Lu Su insisted. "My apologies: please, Ziming, tell us your plan."

The ensemble turned as one to Lü Meng, who said, "We can turn this around, and with the greatest of ease. I have a plan, but… it requires courage."

"The men here are made of courage," Cheng Pu declared. "Speak."

"We can all go and rescue Gan Ning, leaving one general to hold the camp," Lü Meng suggested: the words were met with anxious murmurs, but Meng continued by saying, "General Ling Tong, would you be prepared to hold the camp for ten days, with aid from Lu Xun…?"

"Yes," Ling Tong replied, "but no more than that."

"Excellent!" Lü Meng said. "Now that's settled-"

"Ziming," Lu Su interrupted, "I don't-"

"I will need three hundred men to cut logs," Lü Meng said.

Gongjin smiled and replied, "Uh… fine…! I might sound like a child saying this, but… I'm almost excited to see what you're up to."

"…Hopefully, we shall keep Yiling and lose Gan Ning," Ling Tong muttered. "Heaven, please make it so."

Cao Cao received Liu Fu's request for reinforcements at Hefei and complied, although the exact numbers that he had sent would soon be a matter of debate among Sun Quan's observers and advisers: confirmation of the actual number – 1,000 men under the command of the lesser-known general Zhang Xi – was met with horror by Inspector Liu Fu and his small band of defenders.

"We couldn't defend a *village* with those numbers!" Liu Fu exclaimed. "And they'll *never* break through all that chaos that Lei Xu is creating! The Chancellor has *condemned us*…!"

"We must place faith in Zang Ba, who even now negotiates with Lei Xu and tries to clear the way for Zhang Xi to assist us," another official implored. "Who knows…? Perhaps Lei Xu and Chen Lan will realise that the Suns mean this region no good and will lend us their own swords: that would be maybe twenty-thousand men, and that would end the siege in hours!"

"That won't happen," Liu Fu retorted.

"Sad to say, I agree," Jiang Ji said. "The situation is, as His Excellency has stated, dire, and we must accept that. There's only one option open to us: we must adopt Sun Tzu's stratagem of 'appearing strong where we are weak'."

"...*How*...?" a second official whimpered.

"I admit that I'm not seeing a way to achieve such a deception either, Zitong," Liu Fu sighed.

"Illness has sapped not only your physical strength, Inspector, but your spirit, else this idea would be yours, for all of my small measure of wits was nurtured by you," Jiang Ji replied. "We will write urgently to General Zhang Xi as he marches, and..."

Cao Ren's 6,000 cavalry had set up a camp to the west of Yiling's capital and entertained themselves with regular attacks on the walls and those that came out to defend them: Xi Su watched from the wall as Gan Ning personally repelled one such attack and sighed, saying, **"Gan's impressive, but he can't do anything about this. How many days has this gone on for...?"**

"Only a few," an archery captain replied. **"Are you that distressed that you have lost all sense of time, Commander...?"**

"...It seems like an age, and I suppose that I include Gan's own occupation of Yiling, which I shouldn't do," Xi Su admitted. **"I don't know: will we be forced to surrender to yet another man...?"**

"I don't think so, Commander," the captain replied. **"I think we're being relieved!"**

The archery captain pointed westward, and Xi Su followed his gaze: Gongjin, Sun Hao, Sun Yu, Chen Wu and Pan Zhang were riding at the helm of a 10,000-strong force that had taken Cao Ren's cavalry by surprise.

"...By the gods...!" Xi Su exclaimed. **"Zhou Yu has such an army at his disposal???"**

"Look! To the south!" an archer cried.

A second force – again numbering around 10,000 – was closing in from the south and west, led by Cheng Pu, Han Dang, Zhou Tai, Sun Jiao, Sun Ben and Lu Su: the Han cavalry were now hopelessly outnumbered, and they fled by way of the deliberate gap that had been left between the two main flanks of his forces.

"...Heaven has spoken," Xi Su sighed. "The Suns of Fuchun will have the south."

The Han cavalry commander involuntarily cursed when he and his demoralised riders reached an enormous roadblock comprised of dozens of logs; more logs had been randomly scattered along the road beyond that barricade in order to make it impossible for the horses to build or maintain speed.

"What now?" one rider complained.

"We must pass this!" the cavalry commander replied.

"There's half a wood there!" a captain retorted. **"It must stretch for...!"**

"...We'll have to abandon the horses!" the commander declared. **"Dismount, and-"**

"And flee on *foot*???" the captain exclaimed. **"Our supplies,**

our-!"
"**We've no choice!**" the commander barked. "**They'll be here soon: abandon everything and retreat!**"
Cao Ren's horsemen abandoned their well-trained steeds and fled from Yiling on foot; Gongjin's pursuit force arrived a short time later and took great pleasure in gathering the horses and supplies.
"**Ziming is a genius!**" Gongjin said. "**A *genius*...! Lord Sun's future is assured!**"

When Gongjin returned to his main camp at Jiangling, he was greeted by Ling Tong and Lu Xun, who were obviously enjoying a victory of their own.
"Everything went well at Yiling...?" Ling Tong asked.
"Gan Ning is alive, and Yiling is still ours," Lü Meng replied.
"...That's... good," Ling Tong said numbly.
"And we repelled an attack by Cao Ren himself," Lu Xun reported.
"Tell me everything!" Gongjin said as he ushered Ling Tong and Lu Xun toward the command tent.
        "It was as we expected, Chief Commander," Lu Xun began once Gongjin and the officers were seated in the command tent. "Cao Ren's spies obviously reported the change in activity and Ren sensed that the army had probably moved to rescue Yiling: they attacked the camp, and we feigned abandonment in order to lower their guard."
"We attacked as soon as they started to relax, killing dozens," Ling Tong said. "They fled in fear, and have remained hidden in the city ever since!"
"And General Lü Meng's plan was, I take it, a success as well...?" Lu Xun prompted.
"I want no more flattery!" Lü Meng pleaded. "It wasn't that incredible a plan! It just seemed to me to be a good idea!"
"And it was," Gongjin said. "I'll say it again, Ziming: you're a genius. I'd have wasted time trying to figure out ways to ambush them, but your use of logs to impede their retreat forced them to abandon everything – *everything* – and go back to their master humiliated! Poor Cao Ren: he hoped to retake Yiling and relieve Jiangling in a single stroke, but lost six-thousand horses and a hundred men instead!"
The officials laughed and revelled in their enemies' failures.
"...This is all wonderful," Gongjin continued. "We've held Jiangling and Yiling despite risking both with our manoeuvres: it's unfortunate that we've lost an opportunity to take control of Jiujiang, but there will be others! Xiangyang is besieged, Dangyang is isolated, Linju is compromised, Hefei is slowly crumbling... we might not claim every prize that we seek, but we can only end this campaign with more than we started it with."

But there was about to be yet another change in fortunes as weeks became months: Guan Yu and Su Fei's siege of Xiangyang was about to come to a sudden and generally unexpected end.

****

100

Sun Quan was becoming increasingly frustrated and impatient as the siege of Hefei continued: the walls were, as Inspector Liu Fu had feared, starting to crumble as the rains and continuous pummelling by catapulted stones took their toll, but the defenders' repairs – using simple materials such as large leaves and straw – were maintaining the integrity of the fortress' outer defences, and Liu Fu's deployment of torches to light the ground around the fortress at night had slowed the besiegers further still. Sun Quan's desperation-driven attempts at charging the walls had almost cost him his life on two occasions, and his suggestion that he should advance once again was met with understandable distress.

"**Do not risk it, Lord Sun!**" Song Qian implored.

"**...But I am as much of a tiger as Bofu!**" Sun Quan cried angrily. "**Have I not achieved what even he could not...? Haven't Huang Zu, Liu Biao and Cao Cao been humbled by me...? Why, then, does this little man Liu Fu pose so much of a threat???**"

"With all due respect, Lord Sun, your late brother *did* charge at swords and arrows... and if Xu Gong's cowardly assassins hadn't got to him, one of those swords and arrows would have, eventually, taken his life instead; you are usually known for your caution, Lord Sun, and that is why your noted successes, all of them gained by your remaining in your palace or command tent, can be known as such," Zhang Zhao suggested. "Song Qian has already volunteered to fight in your stead, and-"

"But that has led to the enemy becoming bold and sending out mediocrities to challenge us, and their restoration of their walls, accompanied by this rain, is turning this campaign into a farce!" Sun Quan protested. "If I lead one effective charge with light cavalry, repel their defenders, show my strength...!"

"Yes, that can sometimes work, but it can also be counter-productive," Zhang Hong said diplomatically. "Morale is high, despite the conditions, but if we were to suddenly launch a fierce attack and it lacked the desired outcome, then the troops will be disappointed and morale might drop."

Sun Quan exhaled fiercely.

"Your efforts might lead to the destruction of their captains and majors – or even a general, if there is one – and yes, we might capture their flags and fill them with fear as a result, but is that a job for the Chief Commander...?" Zhang Hong continued. "I say nay: this is a mission for a general, not you, Lord Sun. Why send a dragon to fight a lizard when you have bears like Song Qian for such things...? I hope you can temper your zeal and save your courage for a more appropriate time, thereby showing that you possess the strategic mind of a conqueror-*king*."

Sun Quan was silent as he pondered the words: he then looked at his servant Gu Li, who nodded to indicate that he agreed with Zhang Hong's words. Sun Quan smiled and said, "You know what to say to me, Zhang Zigang! Alright, I will refrain from undertaking further charges: but what about the reports of enemy reinforcements...?"

"Nothing has been seen so far save perhaps a thousand men, mostly on foot, led by some mediocrity," Zhang Zhao said dismissively. "And they – like our scouts – are being impeded by Lei Xu's rebellion."

"And has there been any progress with regard to liaising with Lei Xu…?" Sun Quan asked.

"He is resistant," Zhang Hong replied. "It seems that he rebels against Cao Cao, not Liu Fu: he'll cause harm to Cao, but not Liu."

"*Aiee*… but he cannot do one without doing the other!" Sun Quan said desperately. "Is he some sort of simpleton?"

"He has a bandit's principles," Zhang Zhao suggested. "They're hard to fathom."

"And Chen Lan won't aid us either," Sun Quan sighed. "Fine: we'll proceed as we are, and hope that we have some success before Cao Cao can find the men to relieve this place."

"REPORT!"

Gongjin's packed command tent awaited the words of the messenger from Xiangyang, but none were in any doubt that the news was bad.

"Acting General Su Fei and General Guan Yu were deceived by false communications and tricked into abandoning their positions!" the messenger continued. **"Han General Li Tong has joined Generals Yue Jin and Wen Ping, who have repelled our forces and begun a counterattack! Xinyang and Linju are lost! Yue Jin continues to move southward while Wen Ping and Li Tong move to counter any attempts at-!"**

"That's enough," Gongjin said sombrely. "You can leave the written report and withdraw."

"*Aiee*…! Well, that's what happens when you rely on Liu Bei and his band of useless idiots," Sun Jiao said as the messenger retreated. "What now…?"

Gongjin stared at the written report and struggled to find the words to respond to it or to Sun Jiao's question.

"Our main concern is Yue Jin, surely," Ling Tong said. "I've heard stories about him: didn't he scale the walls of Nanpi and-?"

"His ability is known to me, General," Gongjin said tonelessly. "He will be dealt with, preferably by Liu Bei since it is Liu Bei and the incompetence of his generals that brought this man down here from Xiangyang to attack us with such confidence."

"…Such a shame," Cheng Pu sighed.

Gongjin was silent for several moments before he said, "Well, they say that war is a constantly changing thing, like nature; we have lost – quite significantly, in fact – at Xiangyang… but we have won at Yiling, and dealt a blow to Cao Ren that will make him think again about blindly charging at Yiling or at us. We've shown him that we have thinkers: a pity Guan Yu had none."

"What now, though…?" Huang Gai asked. "It is all well and good throwing words at Guan Yu: with Xiangyang restored, Linju and Xinyang lost, and the River Han fortified against repeat attacks, does that not mean that Cao Ren has unlimited supplies from the capital now…?"

The anxious murmurs that followed frustrated Gongjin, who replied, "Veteran General, do not, for the sake of morale, say such things! There is no such thing as 'unlimited supplies'! Food and wood has to be grown, and men born and raised! Cao Cao still has the eastern front to occupy his mind, and our lord's actions in Hefei are so far brave and commendable! If we are courageous, tenacious, and continue to thwart the efforts of the enemy, then we can defeat them! *You*, Veteran General, were the one that ignited the flames that destroyed the 'unbeatable' fleet at Red Cliffs not a few months ago, and yet now you speak as though the situation is desperate...?"

Gongjin's words were met with an uneasy silence.

Lu Su waited until the meeting was at an end and all but Cheng Pu and Lü Meng had departed before he turned to Gongjin and said, "Is Xiangyang really lost...? Have we really lost Linju, and Xinyang, and-"

Gongjin's hummed as confirmation.

"...So Guan Yu's entirely to blame for the failure...?" Lu Su prompted.

"...Su Fei's role was minor," Gongjin retorted. "Guan Yu's hubris caused him to underestimate the enemy, and his adviser, Ma Liang, might has well have been mute."

"Ma Liang...?" Lu Su exclaimed. "You said that Guan 'had no thinkers': 'White-browed Liang' is Kongming's best friend and a smart man that-!"

"I know," Gongjin interrupted. "I was being unfair to Ma Liang, I know that, but it really doesn't matter: if Zhuge himself had been there, the outcome would have been the same, because Guan Yu is stubborn and ignorant. The only consolation that we can draw from this is obvious: if Guan is ever an adversary, then inflating his ego in order to make him deaf to advice is a painfully easy way to defeat him."

Lü Meng hummed thoughtfully; Cheng Pu grunted angrily and said, "We *need* Xiangyang to be unsafe for them...!"

"It's safe all the same," Gongjin said. "Now we must improvise."

As the days wore on, the sieges of Jiangling and Hefei continued: a conclusion of the latter was inevitable, but one man would not see that conclusion.

"*Why*, Inspector...?" Jiang Ji asked as he sat by Liu Fu's deathbed.

"I... cannot help being ill, Zitong," Liu Fu replied.

Jiang Ji sighed and said, "I know that, Inspector, but so far from comfort and peace, after all that you've done...!"

"Heaven's will... is hard to fathom," Liu Fu replied painfully. "Zitong, you must... not let Chen... and Lei... know."

Jiang Ji exhaled wearily and said, "I will try and hide word of your d- ...of your *condition*, Inspector, but they will learn the truth eventually, which is why you must fight this malady and recover!"

"I am a man... no m-more than that," Liu Fu replied miserably. "I... had other plans, you know. I wanted... to b-build... more...!"

"Rest," Jiang Ji insisted. "I know that food is scarcer, but I'll give you some of mine, help you get some strength-"

"*Don't*... waste," Liu Fu said with a smile. "But... *thank you*."

Jiang Ji released Liu Fu's hand and got to his feet, saying, "We have a siege to repel, so I shall leave you with your family."

"You're... a good man," Liu Fu replied.

Jiang Ji said no more: he left the wizened, gaunt Liu Fu to spend his last hours with his family and returned to the walls of Hefei in order to oversee the defences.

"…Something's changed," Zhang Hong said as he stared at the walls of Hefei.
"There's been no sign of Liu Fu for a couple of days, and he was slow on his feet when last seen," Zhang Zhao noted.
"…He's ill," Sun Quan said with a smile. "That vicious, conniving wretch has been punished by Heaven! His collusion with my brother's killers has finally caught up to him! Hefei – and the rest of Northern Yang – can only be ours soon!"
"…We've caught another messenger, and the signs are not good," Zhang Hong reported. "We're only seeing about a thousand men on the road, but the letter speaks of *forty-thousand*."
"…A bluff, surely," Sun Quan said uneasily.
"Perhaps, but Cao Cao cannot afford to lose Hefei, and so he might have decided to throw a massive army at the city in the hope of scaring us off," Zhang Hong replied. "It's the strategy that Chief Commander Zhou has recently employed to relieve Yiling, and it worked, so…"
"…So there might really be an army of that size on its way here…?" Sun Quan fretted. "We've only got ten-thousand, and no generals save for Song Qian! Won't we be in serious danger?"
"We'll persist, and hope that it's a bluff," Zhang Hong replied.

Liu Fu died a few days later, leaving Jiang Ji as Acting Inspector of Yang Province while word was sent to the Imperial capital Xuchang: Sun Quan's men intercepted one of the messengers and ensured that everybody knew that Liu Fu was gone, hoping that it would encourage rebellion. The bandit kings of Lujiang – Chen Lan, and Mei Qian– and a self-made magnate called Mei Cheng were certain that Liu Fu would not be succeeded by a man of such agreeable character, so they quickly agreed that they would rebel against Chancellor Cao Cao together, and Lei Xu – who had only just agreed to Zang Ba's demands for talks – added his considerable army to Chen Lan's: news was rushed to Gongjin, who called Lu Su, Cheng Pu and Han Dang into the command tent and said, "This mass uprising is a golden opportunity for us."
"Hefei's as good as ours," Cheng Pu suggested. "If Lujiang and Jiujiang are beset by enemies of Cao Cao in every direction, then how can we lose the place now…?"
"If the rebels don't like us either…?" Han Dang proposed.
"…That's a fair point, Yigong," Cheng Pu admitted.
"Which is why we must ingratiate ourselves," Gongjin said. "We must send a high-ranking general to Lujiang to offer military support to Chen Lan and Mei Qian: they'll leave Hefei alone then, and we'll take it without difficulty."
"I take it that *I'm* here for that task," Han Dang chuckled. "I did kind of wonder why anyone would invite a stupid old fool like me to a strategy meeting."
"You berate yourself unfairly, Yigong," Gongjin insisted. "But yes, I did ask for you for that purpose: will you do it…?"
"You're the Chief Commander, so how can I refuse…?" Han Dang replied. "Do you want some sort of pledge that I'll surrender my head if I fail, or something…?"
"This may go wrong, so no," Gongjin said. "There's no need for

formalities: take whoever you want as a second from the second-tier officers and head for Lujiang at once."

"Consider me gone," Han Dang replied as he bowed and departed.

"...And let's try and keep this from Liu Bei," Gongjin suggested.

"We might just turn this around!" Lu Su said with optimism.

But it was not to be: Han Dang's army had not even got beyond Jiangling's borders when one last gamble by Jiang Ji forced Sun Quan to make a decision about the siege of Hefei Fortress.

"Explain it to me again," Sun Quan said as he glared at the timid Zhang brothers.

"They sent out an official to welcome Zhang Xi 'and his forty-thousand'," Zhang Hong began. "Then three junior officers left the city to travel to Yulou, where the main army is apparently stationed: the thousand that we've seen is just the vanguard, advanced to provide more immediate support."

"But are we *sure*...?" Sun Quan pleaded.

"...There were three officers despatched," Zhang Zhao replied. "We intercepted two of the three as they returned, and they carried letters that spoke of 'possibly waiting until the rest of the army arrived instead of forwarding the vanguard' and 'planning a dash out of the city, timed to coincide with their arrival'. There are also suspicious communications passing back and forth between Zhang Xi's 'vanguard' and some other, as-yet-unseen party."

"Then there *is* a great army on its way here," Sun Quan decided. "We must leave before it arrives!"

Song Qian groaned disappointedly and said, "But my *lord*...!"

"I like this no more than you, Song Qian, but I must not take unnecessary risks!" Sun Quan retorted. "What if the supposed death of Liu Fu is a part of this attempted ruse, and he charges out of the city with his army? What will that do to morale?"

"What are your orders, Lord Sun...?" Zhang Hong asked.

"We... we will retreat, burning our camps as we go, leaving nothing for them, not even a tent," Sun Quan declared. "We will return to Chaisang, leaving an obvious presence at the riverbank to dissuade this forty-thousand from chasing us into Jiangdong. I will then maintain regular communications with Gongjin and await his signal to attempt another campaign."

"...That is best," Zhang Zhao replied numbly.

Jiang Ji watched as Sun Quan's forces began their hasty retreat and smiled sadly; it was a bittersweet victory, as the city was crumbling and Ji's mentor and lord – Yang Province Inspector Liu Fu – was gone, and with him the stability that had been so hard-fought and hard-won. Sun Quan might have failed to take Lujiang or Jiujiang, but he had brought disorganisation and rebellion to both prefectures that would require costly and time-consuming solutions. Hefei would continue to be isolated as Mei Qian and Chen Lan's bandit armies tore Lujiang apart; Zhang Xi's 1,000 men could do little more than settle outside the walls and assist with restoring order to the immediate area.

****

101

Han Dang's militia – which numbered only 3,000 – reached Lujiang Prefecture and settled close to the prefectural capital Huancheng; Han then sent word to Chen Lan, who summoned Lei Xu and said, "Sun Quan's trying to lend us support."

"What will you say...?" Lei Xu asked.

"...I don't know," Chen Lan admitted. "Sun Ce was a real hero that I almost joined a few times: when Cao and Yuan Shao were fighting, I prob'ly would have gone to Sun Ce if he hadn't've gone an' died. But Sun Quan...?"

"He put Liu Fu in a coffin, which I don't much like," Lei Xu said. "I hate Cao Cao, but Cao put Liu Fu here, and things were really gettin' better."

"We could use the help," Chen Lan sighed.

"...Is it really *Zhang Liao* that's coming here...?" Lei Xu asked.

"He's already here," Chen Lan replied. "And Zang Ba never left after you told him what you thought of him, so now we're dealing with both of them."

Lei Xu nodded soberly and asked, "What do you want to do?"

"...I reckon we'll have to agree to this help from 'Han Dang'," Chen Lan said. "I'll write back and ask him to move north and join up with us here in Liujiang City: but I'll make it clear that we don't like him, and that we're doing our own thing, not joining up with the Suns or helping them get Lujiang back."

"Agreed," Lei Xu replied.

The Han General Zhang Liao travelled to Zang Ba's main camp near Lujiang City and asked for a private audience in Zang's command tent.

"Seems like an age since we last met," the swarthy Zang Ba chuckled once the two were alone.

"I hope that the past will have no impact on our ability to cooperate, Governor Zang," Zhang Liao retorted.

"I'm not one for grudges," Zang Ba insisted.

"You misunderstand me," Zhang Liao replied politely. "I hoped that you would forgive my own troubled past as the most trusted of Lü Bu's generals and my subsequent persecution of your forces as an agent of the Han."

"I brought it on meself," Zang Ba said. "But why the apologies...? Have I ever acted like I care when we've met since then?"

"...I am haunted since Red Cliffs, and every day involves some sort of 're-evaluating' on my part," Zhang Liao replied. "But that's my problem, Governor, not yours: I shall get to the point. We have a number of rebellions to deal with, but I understand that Sun Quan is adding his own mischief to it."

"He's pretty much why we have the rebellions in the first place!" Zang Ba chuckled.

"...True enough," Zhang Liao conceded. "But how do we keep Sun Quan from aiding the rebels and bringing them to his side...?"

"Simple, and also my orders," Zang Ba replied. "We stop Sun Quan's men from getting here: if we keep them separated then they'll not have any kind of alliance, will they...? It worked against my lot in the old days, so it'll work against Chen Lan's lot."

Zhang Liao smiled and said, "I imagine that my old colleague Gao Shun, the 'Camp Smasher', would have suggested the same. So you will intercept Sun Quan's army for while I attack Chen Lan...?"
"That's the plan," Zang Ba replied. "I'll go south at once."

Han Dang was concerned when his scouts reported the approach of Zang Ba's 'Qing Militia'.
"You look like a corpse, Father," Han Zong prompted.
"Son, I... I think I need to be honest," Han Dang replied. "S'just the two of us here in the command tent, so I can talk frankly; Zang Ba's a hero to a lot of the men, so fightin' him is not goin' t'go down well."
Han Zong frowned and said, "But Zang is an agent of Cao Cao, who is himself an agent of the netherworld!"
"Perhaps, son, but Zang's served worse and still liked," Han Dang explained. "His lot were some of the first to come out against the Han and actually fight the army; and even though that was the case, he did the right thing and signed up to fight the Yellow Turbans even before me and the other lads joined Lord Sun Jian."
"I know enough about Zang Ba," Han Zong insisted. "His 'Mount Tai Bandits' were running Qing Province years ago, pretty much."
"Yeah, but you'll notice that never once did Taishi Ci – who was committed to fighting 'corruption and evil' – go up against Zang Ba," Han Dang continued. "Zang was well liked then an' he's well liked now: yeah, he joined up with Lü Bu, but he fought Bu before that and was one of the few men to survive being sieged by Bu."
"...So he's quite formidable," Han Zong supposed.
"Hell, yeah," Han Dang replied. "This man's been active for thirty years now, and he's still as scary as he was on that first day: he united the bandit gangs of Mount Tai under his banner and built a million-man army before any of the others – the White Waves, the Black Mountains, the Qing Hill lot, and so on – were even thought of. He's fought and beaten the Han army and the Yellow Turbans, and he lasted against Lü Bu and Cao Cao when they were not only powerful but *unrestrained*. He's scary enough that Cao accepted a surrender and even took hostages but still made him Governor of Xu, and Xu – which has never been stable, 'specially not since Cao torched the western half of it and Ze Rong looted the rest – is now a very, very calm place that gives Cao no grief."
Han Zong hummed thoughtfully and said, "He's going to give us a tough time."
"He's here to kick our arses, son, not 'give us a tough time'," Han Dang scolded. "He outnumbers us, and our men will be awestruck and frightened: but we have to proceed somehow, 'cause I can't go back and tell the Chief Commander that I failed."
"We'll fight to the best of our ability," Han Zong said, "and hope for the best."

Zang Ba's forces intercepted Han Dang with even greater speed than Han Dang had anticipated: the two armies formed lines and prepared to do battle.
"I sent men to go around 'em," Han Dang explained to his son. **"Hopefully he's not done much about training to deal with-"**
A sudden mass of raised voices ended Han Dang's explanation; Zang Ba had ordered his infantry forces to charge, and the

thought of being attacked by the legendary 'Bandit King of Kaiyang' had caused dozens of the Jiangdong men to panic and scatter. Han Dang shouted frantically in an effort to reorganise his lines and stage some sort of counterattack, but a second mass of shouts – from his own men this time – told him that something bad had happened.

"**They've attacked our supply train!**" a major cried.

"**…I'll hold the rear: Zong'er, you go and defend the supplies!**" Han Dang ordered. "**Even if I have to fight Zang Ba in a duel, I won't let him beat us!**"

Han Zong took his personal force and retreated to protect the supply train; Han Dang turned to the infantry major, who said, "**What are your orders, General?**"

"**Our own trap's being sprung, which must count for something!**" Han Dang replied; Zang Ba's forces were now reacting to the futile attempts to attack their flanks, but it was enough to slow their charge and cause Zang to think again.

"**So what are we doing, Boss?**" Zang Ba's second, Wu Dun, asked anxiously.

"**…This 'Han Dang' is an old veteran of Sun Jian's days,**" Zang Ba noted. "**We shouldn't kill him if we can avoid it! Send word out to the men: try and capture Han Dang!**"

Zang Ba's force was winning the battle, and there was no way to turn it around; Han Dang's divided forces scattered in all directions, and the humiliated Jiangdong general fled along the road that he had travelled down from the Jing-Yang border.

"**We made a fool of him!**" Wu Dun cackled.

"**He'll be back,**" Zang Ba said tonelessly. "**He's an old tiger: he'll be back. And then we'll beat him again.**"

Han Dang returned to a border-based camp that had been built and then abandoned as he advanced; he entered an infirmary tent – one of the few structures that remained standing – and threw down his helmet, screaming, "**I feel *useless*!**"

"…Don't, Father," Han Zong pleaded.

Han Dang turned and looked at his son with tears in his eyes as he replied, "Cheng Pu is a warrior *and* a genius; Huang Gai *tricked Cao Cao* and *burned his fleet*; Zhu Zhi's kept Wu safe from everything that's been thrown at the place; even *Zu Mao*, reckless idiot that he was, saved Wentai at least twice and died a hero's death at his side! But what will people say about Han Dang, mm…? **What have *I* done???**"

"You helped those men and a lot of other men to do all of those things, Father," Han Zong said. "Why are you suddenly so upset…? Being defeated by Zang Ba was always a possibility: it was *you* that said so."

"…I did," Han Dang sighed. "I… am getting old, and *weak*."

"You're not that old, firstly, and secondly, you held the rear as we retreated: a lot of men would have left their son to do that and gone to protect the supplies or just fled altogether, and Cao Cao, very famously, is one of them," Han Zong retorted. "You're a hero, Father: not one of the most famous, perhaps, but you *are*."

"…Thank you, Zong'er," Han Dang replied. "I'm… I'm not that weak, o' course, I… I'm just angry. I wanted to be like Huang Gongfu and surprise everyone by beating Zang Ba, but that was never gonna happen. I have to accept that and get back on the road before Chen Lan starts to think that we're not coming."

"I'll go and ready my men," Han Zong said.

But for all of his best efforts, Han Dang would not defeat Zang Ba: the two met for a second time and the outcome was the same. Han Dang's forces turned, began a second, ignominious retreat to the Jing-Yang border and sent word to Gongjin and to Sun Quan, who had just returned to Chaisang after his own humiliating defeat in Lujiang Prefecture.

"Should I be angry or empathetic...?" Sun Quan asked once Zhang Zhao had finished reading Han Dang's report.

"You should be pragmatic," Zhang Zhao replied. "Han Dang failed: perhaps he is not the right man to send back there, but who else is there to send...?"

"It is less a matter of 'who to send' but 'what to send', Brother," Zhang Hong suggested. "Zang Ba is a legendary brigand that commanded hundreds of thousands when he was at his peak: a lot of the men that follow Lord Sun are in awe of Zang, and he is a master of adapting to situations."

"...When you say 'what', Zigang, I take it that you speak of numbers," Sun Quan prompted. "But should I also be recalling Lü Fan from Red Cliffs to lead the army that we send...?"

"Lü Fan is already on his way back here, but will not be needed for this venture," Zhang Zhao said dismissively. "The man's quite happy to sit in the treasury and keep a careful watch on the bags of money, so let him do that: Zang Ba is best met by a vast horde, so send thirty-thousand to Lujiang to overwhelm him!"

"Yes, Zibu, I will, if that's what it takes to reclaim Lujiang, but led by *whom*...?" Sun Quan demanded. "A tiger without a head is a fangless lump! ...Perhaps I should await Zhou Gongjin's analysis."

"...Han Dang should be given another chance," Zhang Hong replied. "He's camped at the border. Inform him that there is a fresh army crossing the Great River and have him meet them and lead them northward. Zang Ba will not have the troops to deal with such a force."

"Are we sure about that...?" Sun Quan heckled.

"We now know with near-certainty that the 'forty-thousand relief troops' were a 'phantom army' and that there was no need to retreat from Hefei," Zhang Hong said with regret. "That being the case, Zang Ba will not have such numbers either, my lord, else he'd have used them to destroy Han Dang."

"...Send the troops, then," Sun Quan ordered half-heartedly. "But do not let this be my 'Red Cliffs', Zhang Hong! A lot depends on our success!"

But once again, it was not to be. Zang Ba's second, Wu Dun, saw to it that Han Dang's forces were prevented from meeting the reinforcement army as it arrived at the northern riverbank by way of large ships, and so the first men to meet the advancing reinforcements were Zang Ba's: the relatively inexperienced officers were unable to control their men, who panicked when they saw Zang Ba's banners approaching: there was a mass scrabble for the boats that would return the men to their ships, and the resulting chaos led to upturned boats and mass drowning while

Zang's men dealt severe damage to the part of the army that chose to stand and fight. Hundreds of Sun Quan's men were injured, drowned or killed in battle, and hundreds more fled or surrendered; the disaster was reported to Sun and to his Chief Commander, Gongjin, who was left numb. Zang Ba's greatest success was not his repeated routs of the Sun forces, but rather the direct consequence of them: the third and final victory left Chen Lan and Mei Qian to face Zang and his campaign partner Zhang Liao without any military assistance.

"**They *lied to us*!**" Chen Lan cried as he paced back and forth across the audience hall of Lujiang City's governor's mansion. "That bastard Sun Quan... he *lied*...!"

"But what about the rumours of their armies trying to get here...?" Lei Xu asked.

"**That's all they are: rumours!**" Chen Lan retorted. "**They just burned Cao's fleet to ashes and routed his ground forces, or so they keep boasting: what, so they can't get an army to Lujiang now after all that???**"

"We didn't want their help anyway!" Lei Xu said. "And besides, do we need it?"

"...Mei Qian's hemmed in and can't get here... so he might not last," Chen Lan replied. "I'm going to risk a charge against Zhang Liao before he gets any more settled in."

"Is that wise...?" Lei Xu asked.

"I was one of Yuan Shu's front-line generals not so long ago," Chen Lan retorted. "I still train, and I've also trained the men well enough to fight as professionals, or we'd not have lasted a day: to me, Zhang Liao's just another general!"

"No offence, but... he's survived duels with *Lü Bu*, who considered Zhang to be a near-equal," Lei Xu noted. "You're good, but..."

Chen Lan reluctantly agreed; he exhaled through his nose and said, "I have to try, since we're not getting help that... that yeah, we need it. If I don't make it back, or if I die at any other point, you're in charge. What will you do?"

"...I don't know," Lei Xu admitted.

"Well then *think about it*," Chen Lan said. "But I don't want our lot giving Cao another twenty-thousand men, so whatever you think of, don't dare make it *that*."

"I'd rather die than surrender to Cao Cao," Lei Xu promised.

"...I thought I'd last longer," Chen Lan said suddenly. "Perhaps I should have gone south and joined the Suns after all: bit late now, though. Wish us luck..."

Chen Lan would meet his end in battle against the forces of Zhang Liao and Zang Ba, and Mei Qian would suffer a similar fate within days. The Lujiang Rebellion was all but over, and now Lei Xu had the unenviable task of fighting his way out of Lujiang City and taking his upwards of 20,000 followers to the only man – to the exasperation of most – that Lei saw as fit to receive them: that man was the self-proclaimed mortal enemy of Chancellor Cao Cao and homeless fugitive warlord, Liu Bei.

****

102

Han Dang was welcomed back to the Jiangling camp by Cheng Pu and Huang Gai, but the mood was understandably sombre.

"I feel so *useless*," Han Dang groaned.

"Stop saying that, Father!" Han Zong pleaded. "It wasn't your fault that we failed!"

"Your son is right, Yigong," Cheng Pu insisted. "You did what you could with your resources, and-"

"*Zang Ba*... of all the men that I get sent to fight, it's bloody *Zang Ba*!" Han Dang complained. "That was...!"

"...But there's no other man that could have done it," Cheng Pu suggested. "Xu Sheng, if he hadn't deserted us, might have been able to rally support among his high-class, high-priced elite men, or Ling Tong, perhaps, if he were more experienced, but the bulk of our forces and the officers that lead them are former pirates and bandits, and they all revere Zang Ba: it couldn't be helped."

Han Dang shook his head and said, "But the reinforcements: what happened to them was-!"

"It's all said and done now," Huang Gai insisted. "Cao might want to see it as revenge for Red Cliffs, but there's no comparison."

"Lei Xu's pledged allegiance to Liu Bei, which only makes it worse," Han Dang said. "His lot had to pass my men, and the way they addressed us was...!"

"...I won't lie, Yigong: the Chief Commander and Lord Sun are bitterly disappointed," Cheng Pu replied. "But it wasn't your fault and they know that. Hefei ended badly, and that was down to the Zhang brothers 'misreading the signs'; Zang Ba's a veteran saboteur, Zhang Liao a veteran siege breaker, and Chen Lan and Mei Qian were arrogant, neurotic and outclassed. Forget about it now and focus on the siege of Jiangling, which proceeds well enough despite the knock to our confidence."

Han Dang nodded silently and followed his old friends to the barracks while his son Zong managed the remnants of the militia.

Gongjin, meanwhile, was struggling to find anything positive to say as he looked at the maps of Jing and Yang Provinces; Lu Su looked on helplessly as usual.

"The famines and droughts in Kuaiji and eastern Yuzhang are worsening," Gongjin said. "There's going to come a point where the people will start to ask why – and, indeed, *how* – I am sustaining a supply route from Jiangdong to attack this place while they starve and succumb to disease."

"Because you have to chase Cao Cao out of the south and build a 'Jiangnan' that is self-sustaining, protected on all sides from its enemies and ready to embrace a future beyond the span of the Han," Lu Su replied.

"...So you are in one of your more ambitious and clear-thinking moods, then, Zijing," Gongjin said. "But what to do...? Do I send Lu Xun back to manage this now, or do I place faith in Zhu Huan, Chunyu Shi and all of the other men that-?"

"Lu Xun is tasked with all of that, and he will decide what to do for the best, for he knows what you know," Lu Su replied. "You have enough to worry about, I think."

"…Lei Xu's men are starting to bleed into the region," Gongjin said bitterly. "They… they go to… to…! **How can this be???**"

"But surely it is better that these men go to an ally than the enemy," Lu Su suggested. "And… well… do you think that you need to speak to Han Dang?"

"I will, I promise," Gongjin replied. "I'm not angry at him; I'm not even angry at the Zhang brothers for sending an army of over twenty-thousand men that worship and-or fear Zang Ba to Lujiang without proper leaders when Zang Ba was their likely first opponent. I'm angry at me for mismanaging this."

"In what way…?" Lu Su asked. "And shouldn't *Lü Fan* share the blame if-"

"Ziheng is right to remain in the background as the 'unseen piece on the board' for the foreseeable future," Gongjin insisted. "Cao Cao is a man that bides his time and eliminates his enemies and rivals when they least expect it: ignoring our own casualties, one can still see that when they look at the cases of Kong Rong, Yuan Tan, Yuan Shang and Yuan Xi, Zhang Xiu and Xu Yòu. I will be a target, but Ziheng will survive: let others think that he is 'pushed into obscurity' and 'reduced to a coin-counter in the treasury' because he exposed Lord Sun's financial impropriety, for it only lends him greater strength."

"But 'being in the background' is no excuse for failing to proffer advice, Gongjin," Lu Su suggested. "The Lujiang forces needed proper counsel."

"…I know," Gongjin admitted. "But what's done is done: I must make plans to take the four 'counties' of Wuling, Changsha, Lingling and Guiyang so that I can harvest supplies from them and ease the burden on Jiangdong. But the problem is obvious: can I – a 'rebel' that took Jiangxia from Liu Biao and burned Cao Cao's fleet – march into any of those places and take them without great cost?"

"You know the answer to that," Lu Su replied. "You must ask L-"

"*Not*-! …Not *now*, not *yet*, not until I have exhausted every other possibility, no matter how ridiculous," Gongjin insisted. "For Lord Sun, for our great cause, I *must* find another way."

Moments later, a robed official entered the tent and bowed humbly: Gongjin frowned and asked, "What is it…?"

"I am here from Yuzhang," the official replied. "I am Zou Pu, the-"

"The man that was tasked with looking into 'matters' by Mister Zhu Zhi," Gongjin said carefully. "What have you found…?"

"A letter," Zou Pu replied. "It is… delicate."

"You can speak in front of Lu Su," Gongjin insisted.

"…It is better if you read this for yourself," Zou Pu suggested as he took a wooden tube from his sleeve and passed it to Gongjin, who immediately extracted the letter and started to read it.

"…Well…?" Lu Su asked impatiently.

"That… *that*…!" Gongjin fumed. "He must be dismissed from here at once, before he ruins us! And Zhuge must not learn of this!"

"*Aiee*… that bad…?" Lu Su asked.

"Mister Zou, you may go and get some refreshments," Gongjin said. "I will deal with this personally."

Sun Ben was enjoying a kettle of tea with his son Lin when Gongjin, Lu Su, Cheng Pu and four guards entered his tent and

said, "We need to talk, Ben; whether your son stays is up to you."
Sun Lin frowned and looked at his father.
"I am undone," Sun Ben chuckled. "So what has been contrived?"
"*Contrived*...?" Gongjin exclaimed. "You actually try to deny it?"
"Deny *what*...?" Sun Ben asked coldly.
"That you were offered rank – Imperial court rank – by Cao Cao in correspondence that is recent enough to suggest that you did not 'waver' until you were cornered, and even then your 'change of heart' is likely false," Gongjin replied. "Or do you have some other version of events that you want to suggest...?"
"...Father...?" Sun Lin prompted.
Sun Ben's eyes filled with tears as he said, "You slander me unfairly, Zhou Yu! Mengde – Cao Cao – is my daughter's father-in-law! Why would he not offer me rank when we are related by marriage and I am proven to be a competent statesman?"
"We were in a state of war," Gongjin retorted. "You were being offered rank at a time when communications were severed between the Sun and Cao clans: Lady Cao was being left in the cold by her father, who is Cao Cao's *brother*! At moments like this, casual offers of promotion to the Imperial court constitute bribes... bribes to defect, to submit, and to betray your clan!"
"**And I *didn't*, did I...?**" Sun Ben bellowed defensively.
"Only because you were denied the chance by your brother's self-confessed 'haste'," Gongjin said. "You lied to Zhu Zhi and chose to wait until another opportunity arose... but you will find no opportunities here. Your son will continue to fly your banner for the sake of keeping our enemies and rivals unaware of our internal problems, but you will be going to Qu'e, where you will stay under careful watch while we decide what to do with you."
"...I have done nothing!" Sun Ben pleaded. "You-! ...Son, Lin'er, you know that I would not betray the clan."
"I... I wish that I could believe you," Sun Lin replied angrily. "It all makes sense now, and... and I have nothing to say."
"You will leave tonight, Ben," Gongjin ordered. "Your being here is a security risk that I dare not allow at such a critical moment."
Sun Ben nodded slowly and got to his feet to pack his belongings.
"I can't stay here," Sun Lin said. "I... will stay with Cousin Jiao."
"I understand," Sun Ben replied tonelessly; Sun Lin harrumphed, flicked his sleeve and left the tent.
"Should we pursue...?" one guard asked.
"No need, no need... Lin is a good man," Gongjin sighed.
"...I will stay and watch Sun Ben now," Cheng Pu said. "Go and rest, Gongjin: you look exhausted."
"I... will be *fine*," Gongjin replied. "Everything will be *fine*."

But weeks passed, and no opportunity to take the four semi-autonomous regions presented itself to Gongjin, who started to despair. Cao Cao, on the other hand, was starting to see an opportunity to turn Sun Quan's forces away from Jiangling: he found and sent a man to the city that, he hoped, would bring an end to the siege one way or another.

****

103

Han Dang, Ling Tong and Lü Meng stood close to the main gates of the camp and glared at their latest visitor, a man named Jiang Gan: he wore expensive blue robes and an elaborate hat that were obviously chosen to give the man an air of authority, wealth and wisdom.

"What's this idiot here for?" Han Dang growled.

"He made it clear enough, Veteran General," Lü Meng replied tonelessly. "He's an 'old friend of the Chief Commander', sent here by Cao Cao: what, though, will the Chief Commander do...? That's the question."

"What *should* the Chief Commander do...?" Ling Tong wondered.

"It's what the Chief Commander *does*, not what he *should do*, that concerns me," Lü Meng said as he turned and walked toward the command tent.

"Hark at A'Meng," Han Dang chuckled. "One little trick with logs that worked, and now he's suddenly acting like he's Zhang Liang."

"I'm worried, Veteran General," Ling Tong admitted. "Why has Cao Cao sent this man here...? Can he affect the Chief Commander and harm our cause...?"

"I wouldn't worry," Han Dang insisted. "The Chief Commander's a very smart man: he'll know exactly what to do."

"...I am at a loss, Zijing."

Gongjin made the confession as he sat in his personal tent and shared tea with Lu Su.

"Months... *months...* and still, there is no sign of Cao Ren's defences cracking," Gongjin continued. "And now, Yue Jin is behind our lines, harassing us from all directions. We have killed so many men, yet they still hold on: what to do...?"

Lu Su smiled awkwardly and said, "Well..."

Gongjin pointed at Lu Su and cried, "**No!** Not... not Liu Bei. I don't want to hear about Liu Bei."

"He has the men of Lujiang now," Lu Su said. "Liu Bei's forces now equal our own; he does not even need Liu Qi anymore."

"You think I don't see that...?" Gongjin replied weakly. "But... we *cannot* ask his help!"

"We haven't a choice," Lu Su insisted. "Gongjin... if we made a fierce push on the city... our own men with their bolstered forces..."

"They're moving as though they intend to take the four counties!" Gongjin said desperately. "After all we have expended here... will they just...!"

Lu Su sighed and said, "I... I don't know what to-"

"**REPORT!**" a messenger hailed from outside the tent.

"...Is there anywhere else left to fall...?" Gongjin asked dryly as he turned to look at the entrance to his tent. "Never mind; **COME IN AND REPORT!**"

The messenger entered the tent and said, "**Jiang Gan of Jiujiang is here to see the Chief Commander!**"

"...*Who*...?" Lu Su murmured.

"...Thank you; where is he...?" Gongjin asked.

"He is currently waiting in a visitor tent near the entrance

to our camp!" the messenger replied.

"...Fine," Gongjin said. "I'll speak to him privately in here. Go and tell him that, please."

"**Yes sir!**" the messenger replied as he turned and retreated.

Lu Su frowned bemusedly and asked, "Who is Jiang Gan...?"

"An old acquaintance of mine, though certainly no friend," Gongjin explained. "He is handsome, charismatic, has a good way with words... but he is shallow, and he serves Cao Cao as an adviser, though perhaps he does not know that I am aware of that. Or perhaps he *does*...!"

"...And you're going to have a private chat with this man...?" Lu Su fretted. "Gongjin, you-!"

"He's no assassin," Gongjin chuckled. "More a persuader, I imagine. Cao Cao has sent this smooth-talking snake here to induce me to leave or defect."

"Why now...?" Lu Su wondered.

"The siege of Hefei is broken; Lujiang, my hometown, has fallen; the Xiangyang infiltration plot failed; Yiling barely holds; why *not* now...?" Gongjin asked.

"...Surely this meeting should be held publicly," Lu Su suggested. "A private chat with an agent of Cao at such a critical moment... what if others suspect your loyalty to Lord Sun...?"

"*Dare they*...?" Gongjin scoffed.

Lu Su remained silent.

"Now go, Zijing," Gongjin ordered. "This is a private discussion between me and this man from Xuchang..."

Lu Su got to his feet and left the tent; Gongjin hummed thoughtfully and muttered, "What will you say, Jiang Ziyi: what will you say...?"

Lu Su had walked straight into an anxious Lü Meng as he left the tent: Lu Su laughed condescendingly and said, "Don't bother: he's going to talk to him."

"...Even he's a spy from Xuchang...?" Lü Meng exclaimed. "I wonder..."

Lu Su guided Lü Meng away from the guards around the command tent and asked, "You cannot suspect his loyalty, surely...?"

"No," Lü Meng replied. "He's the sworn brother of our lord's late brother: he sees Lord Sun as his younger brother. No, I wonder why he would not just turn this man away: perhaps he feels this man should be allowed to put his case and have it firmly rejected... but I hear that Jiang Gan is matchless in debate in the region he hails from."

"That's worrying," Lu Su replied as he turned and watched the enigmatic and charismatic Jiang Gan being escorted toward Gongjin's tent.

Lü Meng sighed and said, "We have to hope that the Chief Commander can outwit this arrogant pedant and send him crying back to Cao Cao. But what if he's come here to offer an alliance, or surrender terms, or withdrawal terms...?"

"We'll accept none of it," Lu Su insisted. "Even if all Cao wanted was for us to withdraw, we won't do it, even just to prevent giving Liu Bei a shot at Jiangling."

Lü Meng chuckled softly and said, "Ah, yes: I see that Liu Bei has acquired himself quite a force now... near to thirty thousand men he has now, some say. My friend Zijing, does it not worry the Chief Commander that they are mostly stationed in and around key positions in *Jiangxia*...?"

"What...!" Lu Su exclaimed.

Lü Meng snickered and said, "I wonder if their strategists have something planned. I wonder... should we not encourage Liu Bei to move them into Nan Prefecture, in preparation for action against the southern county governors, and away from our newly acquired prefecture...?"

"I'll talk to Gongjin as soon as this 'visitor' is gone," Lu Su insisted; his faith in Zhuge Liang was being tested, and his concern for Gongjin's mental state was growing by the minute.

Gongjin finished the traditional exchange of greetings, gestured that Jiang Gan should sit down and asked, "So what can I do for you, Ziyi, after all these years...?"

Jiang Gan smiled and said, "Gongjin, you cannot be ignorant of that. I will not deceive you, mislead you, or patronise you. I will be concise, and to the point."

Gongjin smiled and replied, "My thanks."

"You are a hero of the age, but now you have a dilemma," Jiang Gan continued. "I shall explain: your family has long served the imperial court, and has earned respect and favour for it. But one day, you met a man called Sun Ce, and together, you decided to break away from the bonds of your allegiance to the house of Han, and seek fame and glory in the south.

"You both married beautiful women, and conquered vast regions, quelling bandits and even subjugating lords and governors appointed by the imperial court: a romantic adventure, but not entirely filial, so far as serving your family name goes, nor loyal, so far as serving the Son of Heaven goes.

"There was, however, still hope: when Yuan Shao, the treacherous conqueror of the north, asked your lord and sworn brother Sun Ce to aid him, he was reticent, and his successor, Sun Quan, refused him outright, and paid proper tribute to the Imperial court, leaving Yuan to his fate. But then the Prime Minister requested your lord's help in bringing true stability to the south by officially swearing loyalty to the court, and ceding all territories unlawfully seized by Sun Ce... and your lord, supposedly on the advice of yourself and others, refused and declared war.

"The Prime Minister gave you many chances to reconsider, but you entered into a doomed alliance with Liu Bei and Liu Qi, who were rightfully dispossessed when the righteous Inspector of Qing Province, Liu Cong, surrendered his inherited land of Jing to His Majesty. Those two rebels were chased into Jiangxia and routed, and at that moment, if not for your 'advice', peace would now be ours.

"Instead, you still hungered for those heady days of wine, women and adventure, and you opposed the Prime Minister at Red Cliffs, winning only because the Prime Minister's forces – in strange and foreign territory, with no medical supplies or adequate immunity – fell victim to rampant disease, and the Prime Minister was forced to burn his fleet to contain the disease, and retreat.

"Now, you capitalise on a stroke of good luck, and you

524

pursue this folly of facing down the Prime Minister to the Han, attempting to seize Imperial lands from our majestic forces despite being under-resourced and outnumbered! But Heaven is obviously against you, Gongjin. Your sieges at Xiangyang and Hefei have failed; the rebellion in your home region, come to nothing; all you have to hope for now is a relatively graceful conclusion to this debacle here in Jiangling. Back home, we were acquaintances... nay, *friends*, and I do not want to see you come to harm. Please... see *sense*, Gongjin, and do the right thing...!"

Gongjin smiled politely as Jiang Gan gave his speech: as soon as that speech was at an end Gongjin coughed deliberately and asked, "What's the 'right thing'?"

"The 'right thing' is to lay down arms here in Nan Prefecture, return to Jiangdong, allow the Prime Minister to apprehend the felon Liu Bei, and see if he can placate the disgruntled elder son of Liu Biao and find him some territory as compensation for his loss, as he did for the younger brother," Jiang Gan replied. "Further to that, tender your services to the Prime Min- no, to *His Majesty*, and show loyalty, as your ancestors did! Turn away from this false king Sun Quan! He can only come to a bad end! Or do you wish to come to a bad end also...?"

Gongjin feigned calmness and said, "So I should order a withdrawal, and join Cao Cao...?"

"Yes," Jiang Gan replied. "You *must*, to save yourself from ruin."

"...I would *die* for my lord Sun Quan," Gongjin insisted. "He and I are brothers, as his brother and I were sworn brothers. That is that."

The dumbstruck Jiang Gan smiled awkwardly and lowered his head to hide the shame that he felt at being rebuked.

Gongjin got to his feet, urged Jiang Gan to do the same and laughed, saying, "Sorry, but you wasted your time. I have no quarrel with you, Ziyi: we serve different masters, our fates cast in different directions. I hope we never have to match wits on the battlefield; I would rather we keep to exchanges of words. Please, ensure you get some rest and refreshment before you go... and please, my friend, take care."

Jiang Gan was escorted to a visitor's tent within the camp and treated like an envoy for the rest of his demoralising visit: he was then escorted to the gates and shown out by a captain while Gongjin and Lu Su looked on at a distance.

"...You are sad that he serves another master, Gongjin...?" Lu Su enquired.

Gongjin smiled slightly and said, "No: I wonder how such an inflated ego, such a worthless excuse for a grovelling pedant, could ever have been an acquaintance of mine. 'Concise'...? I would hate to hear his idea of 'detailed': it may be enough to bore me to death. But still, I heard him out for a reason: he was anxious to portray himself in a strong position, which betrays Cao Cao's true position."

"Cao Cao is *weak*...?" Lu Su exclaimed.

"Not at all, but this campaign is draining his resources," Gongjin replied. "If we persist, he will eventually break... that, I now know for sure. It may take weeks – it may even take months – but he will eventually break, and Jing will be ours."

Lu Su smiled and said, "Uh, I, uh… I should say, now that meeting's over, that-"
"That Liu Bei's military manoeuvres in Jiangxia are suspicious," Gongjin said. "I know it: Lü Meng is not the only one with eyes. I'm going to approach Liu Bei and request his devoted cooperation to subjugating Nan Prefecture: we may be forced to wrangle for it afterwards, but it's better than the crafty old devil stealing Jiangxia while we're stuck here, under the dishonest pretext of 'helping Liu Qi'. Further to that, he can keep Yue Jin busy for us."
Lu Su nodded and said, "I'll go and talk to them for you."
"Thank you," Gongjin replied; he watched Lu Su walk away and murmured, "I wonder what will surprise you first, Zijing…"

Lu Su returned from his visit to Liu Bei's camp with a haunted expression on his face: he visited the command tent and said, "That's not the same Liu Bei."
"He shows his true self to you, at last," Gongjin chuckled.
"They even have a small navy, Gongjin, and a fine cavalry led by Zhao Yun!" Lu Su explained. "They're getting money from somewhere, and-!"
"I've heard enough," Gongjin ordered. "Did they agree to relocate to Jiangling and assist us…?"
"Mm…? Uh, yes, yes, they did," Lu Su replied.
"Then I must be satisfied with that most undesirable – but far from the worst – of outcomes," Gongjin said. "We must swallow our pride and work with the 'crafty owl': at least, as I have said, we now know that this is not in vain. We will take southern Jing, and after that, we- …and after that, we'll see."
"I'm sensing that you're worried that you're being baited somehow," Lu Su prompted.
"Of *course I am*!" Gongjin despaired. "Zhuge's obviously one of those types that has a knack of always benefitting from a position of weakness: he's used my concern – our concern – about Liu Bei's conspicuous activity in Jiangxia to force us to invite Bei here and effectively hand him a victory! They probably have no chance of seizing Jiangxia, but Zhuge knows that I can't take the risk and…! …*Aiee*."
"…Well at least we'll keep the counties from Cao Cao, who is the real threat here," Lu Su suggested.
Gongjin hummed ambiguously in response: he saw a future where Liu Bei was the greater threat and was annoyed at the way that he was probably being manipulated into giving Bei the power that he needed in order to become that threat.

✳✳✳✳✳✳✳✳✳✳✳✳

104

Gongjin's expression betrayed his distress as he awaited the arrival of Liu Bei; the command tent was uncomfortably silent. A Jiangdong soldier entered the tent and saluted silently by touching his fist to his chest; Gongjin smiled falsely and asked, "Have the guests arrived?"

"Liu Bei has been admitted to the camp by Colonel Lu Su, Chief Commander," the soldier replied.

"...Where are they now...?" Gongjin asked quietly.

"They are awaiting admission to the command tent, Chief Commander," the soldier replied.

"...Very good: you may go and fetch them," Gongjin sighed; the soldier then saluted and retreated, and Gongjin got to his feet to welcome his unwanted guests as protocol demanded.

"...Such a shame," Huang Gai said.

"This... is *my fault*!" Han Dang whimpered.

"It can't be helped," Huang Gai replied.

Gongjin brought Liu Bei into the command tent and has him sit as an honoured guest: Bei was accompanied by Zhuge Liang, the envoy Sun Qian, Liu Bei's financier-turned-adviser Mi Zhu and Bei's old friend Jian Yong, and their countenance betrayed their satisfaction at their improved fortunes.

"...Welcome once again," Gongjin croaked; he then coughed to strengthen his involuntarily weaken voice and added, "You are most welcome."

"I doubt that," Jian Yong snickered quietly.

"We have been here now for so long that I worry I might take root," Gongjin said with false joviality as he sat in his host's seat. "This has to end soon for all our sakes. Even though our losses have been minimal, the toll it is taking on grain supplies is ridiculous... I can only imagine what it is doing to the north."

Liu Bei smiled slightly and asked, "Do you have a proposal for us, Chief Commander...?"

"I do, Lord Liu," Gongjin replied with reluctant humility. "Your now considerable might is needed to bolster us; forgive my remarks about your weakness at our last encounter, but even you have to admit that at the time, the point was sound, if not so much now."

Liu Bei nodded and said, "It was: now, as you say, not so much."

"...Quite," Gongjin sighed. "So: have you any suggestions as to how you would prefer to deploy your forces...?"

Sun Jiao's face was contorted with anger; his brother Yu grunted quietly to prevent him from speaking out as he obviously wanted to. Others were equally angry and distressed, but they knew that they would have to endure the alliance and kept their silence; a small number wanted to shout out as much as Sun Jiao, but Gongjin silenced them with a stare.

"I have no suggestions at this point beyond those already made," Liu Bei replied. "If you are still happy with the idea, Chief Commander, I would like to confront Yue Jin's saboteurs, and try and seize the four counties now, so that Cao Cao cannot rely on those for support. I have, despite the risk to his health, asked Liu Qi to join us in Nan Prefecture, so..."

Liu Bei paused deliberately.

"...Fine," Gongjin said after an uncomfortable pause.

"We shall set out immediately," Liu Bei declared. "Now that our numbers are considerable, we can march on and secure all four in a stroke, and then return to you and see how we can support you further."

Gongjin started to nod, but his distress caused him to continue nodding beyond what was usual, which obviously amused Jian Yong and Zhuge Liang.

"...We shall depart," Liu Bei prompted.

Lu Su realised that Gongjin was lost in his thoughts and got to his feet to see Liu Bei's group out of the command tent; Cheng Pu urged the officials to rise and extend their own insincere greetings to Bei as he departed. The officials turned as one and looked at their despondent Chief Commander after the guests had gone: he was staring vacantly and muttering inaudibly as he struggled to come to terms with the idea of employing Liu Bei and losing territory to him.

"...Chief Commander...?" Lü Meng prompted.

Gongjin's face contorted as his rage grew: he bared his teeth at the last, slammed his fist onto his knee and cried out helplessly.

"This is *my fault*," Han Dang said once again.

"If you must blame someone, Yigong, blame Liu Bei or his schemer Zhuge Liang," Huang Gai suggested. "If they had caught Cao Cao after we burned the ships..."

Lu Su knelt by Gongjin and said, "Compose yourself!"

"*If*... if there... is *any way*... to turn this around... I *must find it*," Gongjin replied. "I *cannot*... not after *everything*... that we... to... to allow... Liu *Bei*...!"

"*Aiee*... this is unfair," Sun Yu said.

"We can attack their camp when they leave," Sun Jiao suggested.

"I doubt that they'll leave it vulnerable," Lü Meng said.

"But they're going to try and take four places and hold them, aren't they???" Sun Jiao protested. "They-!"

"They will secure their camp," Lü Meng insisted. "No, we are destined to lose today... but there's always 'tomorrow'."

Liu Bei's forces departed for Wuling, Changsha, Lingling and Guiyang with such speed and efficiency – on the very next morning, in fact – that the Jiangdong officials were left stunned.

"Kongming tells me that the forces have set out to take the counties," Lu Su said to a subdued Gongjin. "They departed together this morning."

Gongjin looked around his command tent as though searching for something as he asked, "Which one are they taking first...?"

"They've gone in four directions to seize all four counties at once, rather than one at a time," Lu Su explained. "Each group has one emissary, one significant general from Liu Bei's four best field generals – Guan Yu, Zhang Fei, Zhao Yun and Wei Yan – and several well-trained archers, cavalrymen and infantry."

"Mm; and 'Lord Liu' is where...?" Gongjin prompted.

Lu Su smiled cynically and replied, "Accompanied, 'as always', by his bodyguard force of *over a dozen expert swordsmen, archers and cavalrymen, led by Chen Dao* – as you can tell, that was emphasised – Lord Liu will be going to Lingling, since it is governed by Liu Du, a possible relation. Liu Qi is on his way to

Changsha."

Gongjin laughed ironically and asked, "What can I say...? ...You say that Zhuge Liang told you this... so where is *he*...?"

"Camped in a position where he can send forces in any one of the five directions: to assist the four raids, or us," Lu Su replied. "He has almost a dozen well-organised crack forces led by individual generals or officials of respectable merit, and says that they are ready, *always*, to go into action. Messenger units are placed along all key routes to 'give advance warnings' and 'detect incursions'."

"...Which means that in addition to aiding us, he can also defend himself from us," Gongjin said sombrely. "What can I say...?"

Lu Su smiled encouragingly and said, "General Lü Meng wants to know if we are going to intensify our attacks on the city now that we have rear support from Lord Liu."

Gongjin's morale was now at its lowest ebb for some time, and his sanity was starting to fracture; he sighed and replied, "We should... we should."

"... ... ...Don't act like this!" Lu Su pleaded. "This isn't Yuan Shu, Liu Biao, Ze Rong or Liu Xun that we're forging an alliance with!"

"No, it isn't," Gongjin retorted. "We could outwit and defeat *them*... but can I outwit and defeat Liu Bei and Zhuge Liang...?"

"We shouldn't be trying to destroy them," Lu Su said.

"I am not contemplating such things because I am some sort of fanatical schemer!" Gongjin replied angrily. "Our lord will one day have to contend for the throne with Liu Bei if I do not find some way to stifle the man now!"

"He might fail to take the counties," Lu Su suggested.

"You know that he'll succeed, Zijing," Gongjin scoffed. "He has a secret weapon: the sick, easily-manipulated Liu Qi. Those four administrators, they're formerly nominal vassals of Liu Biao as Huang Zu was: the sight of their late lord's heir will melt hearts, just as memories of our incursions would have hardened them. We would, at the most, have taken Changsha with ease because Sun Jian was their Administrator and saved them from Ou Xing twenty years ago, and that makes Bofu – the late Lord Sun Ce – the rightful heir to the seal of office and Lord Sun Quan the rightful heir after him, but Jin Xuan is a Han loyalist that would probably resist us and force us to harm his people."

"...I know it," Lu Su admitted.

Gongjin smiled icily and said, "Wuling will not like us seizing neighbouring Yiling and unleashing Yue Jin upon them, and its ruler, Han Xuan, is an idealist that will probably see Liu Bei as a hero; Lingling is governed by Liu Du – an imperial relative – and Guiyang by Zhao Fan, who is a coward that feared our presence in neighbouring Yuzhang. Liu Qi and Liu Bei will easily take the places that they visit: the other two will have heroes sent to intimidate them until they submit or until one of the Lius can reach them later on."

"...I know it," Lu Su sighed.

"Our only hope is that seizing Lingling and Guiyang will take them longer – even if it is just because of their distance from here – and delay their return until I have taken Jiangling from Cao Ren," Gongjin continued. "I could then demand Changsha's return, and maybe send Ling Tong to Guiyang so that Bei only claims the other two. I want – *need* – Wuling as well if my plan to take Sun

Yu as my second and seize Yi is ever to come to fruition, but-"

"Seize Yi?" Lu Su exclaimed.

"...Your tripod idea relies upon there being *three great warlords*, each with a third of the land or thereabouts," Gongjin replied dryly. "Unless you now think that Liu Zhang would make a good third man – I, for one, would have no problem with that simply because he is a *joke* – then I imagine that you understand that Liu Bei, Cao Cao or Lord Sun Quan must have Yi and then Hanzhong. Which would you prefer?"

"Liu Bei doesn't have a base," Lu Su noted.

"Ah, Zijing, but if he has the 'four counties', then he *will* have a base, will he not...?" Gongjin retorted. "Wuling will give him a place to launch an attack on Yi Province from, just as I could use Yiling! Do you not see that I must secure *both* and blunt the old owl's claws before he can take flight...?"

Lu Su sighed and said, "Yes, of course, but-!"

"He's *forced my hand*!" Gongjin chortled. "You think that I don't know what you were going to say...? 'Why intrigue against them while we still fight Cao Cao?' *I* could ask the same of your friend *Zhuge Liang*! Or have you forgotten that he allowed Cao Cao's escape so that his master could thrive at our expense...?"

Lu Su lowered his head.

"I have to prevent them from exploiting our being distracted and ensure that the way is clear for Lord Sun to grow as Heaven obviously intended when he gave us our victory over Cao Cao at Red Cliffs!" Gongjin continued. "Can you imagine what would happen if Liu Bei had Yi...? The west and north of that region form a natural fortress, a complex sea of hills and mountains that make invasion near-impossible: that's the reason that Liu Yan wanted the place and asked for it all those years ago, and that's why Liu Zhang has kept the governor's seal when every other inept man has been ousted by Cao Cao already, and that's why Bei wants the place, especially now that he has an army of thirty-thousand men, two-thirds of which are former bandits that are most comfortable operating out of *hills and mountains*!"

Lu Su rubbed the back of his neck and said, "I understand."

"I must accelerate the siege to completion, regardless of the cost," Gongjin decided. "I must go to the front, and-"

"*Ayah*! No, you mustn't, not until you calm down!" Lu Su said. "Han Dang is eager to 'atone for losing Lujiang' there at least ten men besides – of which the most suitable are Ling Tong, who wants his record to equal his rival Gan Ning's, and Su Fei, who still regrets being unable to sway Guan Yu over to us – that should be given the role of agitators! If you were hurt, the-!"

"**Alright, alright, you've made your point!**" Gongjin barked. "I will allow others to take the lead, and watch from afar... *for now*."

Lu Su could sense that one more setback would push Gongjin onto the front line and towards certain danger, but he could only nod agreeably and hope against hope that no such setbacks occurred.

The Administrator of Yuzhang Prefecture and 'General Who Attacks Barbarians', Sun Ben, shuddered as Zhu Zhi 'welcomed' him at the gates of Nanchang City and said, "I have already taken the Administrator's seal into my custody, so you will not need to stay here for long. Follow me, please."

Sun Ben's eyes wandered momentarily before he replied, "I suppose I must."

"...This sorry affair ends your role as Administrator," Zhu Zhi said once he, Sun Ben and a group of officials and guards had reached the governor's mansion. "I should also like to note that my search for documents has been completed without further finds, although our main find was incriminating enough."

Sun Ben whined involuntarily.

"I must say that 'Mengde' was intending to be quite generous!" Zhu Zhi said. "You were looking to gain a very nice role in the capital... very nice indeed... and one can only wonder what you might have done to earn it."

Sun Ben lowered his head and sighed.

"You have, however, done nothing to earn the role that you are about to lose," Zhu Zhi continued. "You were *trusted*, Ben: did that ever mean *anything*...?"

"Just get it over with!" Sun Ben retorted.

"I have nothing more to 'get over with'," Zhu Zhi replied. "There's nothing more to say, really, other than that you'll get some sort of role, of course, because you'll need to be kept at court in order to keep an eye on you and your correspondence, but you'll do little more than shuffle unimportant papers and receive the occasional visit by relatives that may, for some reason, take pity upon you, although that's unlikely."

"Don't lie to me, Junli!" Sun Ben chortled. "Quan's just going to let me off that easy, give me a little desk job and that's that...?"

Zhu Zhi smirked and said, "So you think that you deserve a larger punishment, then, for fraternising with an enemy that probably assassinated half of your family and brought a fleet here to flatten every town and village in Jiangdong...?"

Sun Ben looked away.

"Or do you think that tacitly agreeing to betray Lord Sun and bring the rule of a tyrant to this region deserves no punishment...?" Zhu Zhi continued. "You wanted to shoot down a dragon in flight and let a wolf into the chicken coop, but it has gotten you absolutely nowhere. What is there left for you now, I wonder...?"

Sun Ben remained silent.

"...These men will help you gather your belongings, since your sons do not want to assist you," Zhu Zhi concluded. "Hurry, please, if you can."

Sun Ben smiled strangely and said, "Don't worry, Junli... I won't be here for long now."

Sun Ben's health would take a turn for the worse and continue to deteriorate as his worsening situation increased his distress; he would eat less, refuse the few visitors that he had, gradually become bedridden and finally die within months without ever being forgiven. Though his banner would fly for the remainder of the Jiangling campaign, Sun Ben's name would rarely be uttered again: he was, in a sense, deliberately forgotten by his heartbroken family.

****

105

The news that reached the defenders and besiegers at Jiangling was expected and, with the exception of those that resided within Liu Bei's camp, unwanted: Bei's forces had taken Wuling and Changsha from their Administrator-governors with relatively little effort, and the marches to Lingling and Guiyang were unimpeded. Gongjin summoned his senior officials to the command tent and said, "I wish that Lu Xun had been able to remain here, or that Lü Fan could offer more assistance, but our home needs to be secured, so… so I must continue to be the 'brain trust' here and hope that I am adequate for the task."

"Your efforts have delivered victory so far, Chief Commander," Huang Gai volunteered. "Red Cliffs was-"

"You should not be here, Gongfu," Gongjin retorted. "You were the hero of Red Cliffs, not I, and you were injured: why do you insist on endangering your life by not returning to Jiangdong to convalesce…?"

"My answer is the same as before," Huang Gai replied.

"…We are heroes, one and all, and yet we struggle with this little man Cao Ren!" Gongjin complained. "It was his brother that excelled: Ren is a nobody! If not for Xu Huang's aid in the city and Yue Jin's infiltration of Wuling…"

"Guan Yu is checking Yue Jin's actions to atone for his ineptness during the Xiangyang operation," Su Fei suggested. "Allow me the chance to atone for my own failure, Chief Commander, and-"

"A mediocre former subordinate of Huang Zu is not the right man for this," Ling Tong interrupted. "I, Tong, beg permission to issue a challenge to Xu Huang, so that I might prove my worth after spending so long on the back ranks and never really offering any service after the liberation of Jiangxia!"

"No offence, Commandant Ling, but you lack the experience to beat Xu Huang in a duel," Gongjin replied. "I know from Guan Yu and Zhang Fei that Xu was an even match for them, and they locked blades with the likes of Zhang Liao and Lü Bu."

"So have I, years ago, when I helped the lord's father to liberate Luoyang from Dong Zhuo, and Xu'll know that 'cause he was likely there as a low-level officer serving under Li Jue or Guo Si," Han Dang announced. "I, Dang, will challenge Xu Huang to atone for *my* incompetence in Lujiang and prove that Zang Ba would have been a dead man if he'd been a visible one!"

"…Is *everyone* out to atone for some incompetence or poor performance of some other sort…?" Lu Su asked. "Is everyone really so lacking in self-worth…?"

"That's irrelevant, Zijing," Gongjin replied enthusiastically. "What matters is the eagerness to serve, and I will ensure that every man has his moment. Veteran General Han: you will issue your challenge to Xu Huang; Ling Tong, Su Fei: you will form part of the trap that will await Xu Huang when he emerges!"

Han Dang, Ling Tong and Su Fei touched their fists to their chests and nodded obediently.

"Lü Meng, Sun Yu, Sun Jiao, Pan Zhang, Zhou Tai: you will also ready your men!" Gongjin continued. "Xu Huang will be trapped on all sides! Xu Huang will die by Han Dang's blade or a hail of

arrows: it's his choice! That's our plan: go to it!"
The officers started to retreat from the command tent.
"…'When Guan beats Yue and Han beats Xu, what will poor little Cao Ren do?'" Gongjin cackled. "And *then*, Liu Bei, when I have Jiangling and no more need of your self-serving 'help'… what will *you* do, mm…? What will *you* do…?"
Lü Meng noted Gongjin's hysterical expression and saw the desperation that lay beneath; he looked at Lu Su, who shook his head sadly.

Han Dang rode to the front and stared at the walls of Jiangling City: the area around the walled settlement was a mess of trenches, earth mounds, wooden towers, discarded siege ladders and corpses, and the smell was enough to turn the stomach.
"Here is Han Dang of Lingzhi!" Han Dang cried. **"Where is Xu Huang of Yang?"**
There was a noticeable amount of commotion on the battlements above as the duty captain ordered archers to take aim and sent a messenger to Cao Ren's command room to report the challenge; Cheng Pu watched from afar with understandable concern for his isolated friend.
"I am tiring of waiting!" Han Dang bellowed. **"I ask again: here is Han Dang of Lingzhi, so where is Xu Huang of Yang… or is he *afraid*…?"**
"It isn't as though Han Dang is some great duellist," Lu Su said as he and Gongjin watched the drama unfold from a watch tower in the main camp.
"No, he isn't," Gongjin replied. "I imagine that Xu Huang would tear Yigong apart, actually, since he regularly sparred with Guan Yu and earned that arrogant man's *respect*; that's why Yigong tacitly agreed to do little more, in truth, than lead that superior warrior into this cowardly and disrespectful trap that I have laid."
"…Your assessment of your own plan is disconcerting," Lu Su said.
"I respect great men," Gongjin replied. "What I do now, it… it reeks of what was done to Bofu. But like Xu Gong's son and like Dai and Gui that killed Shubi in so despicable a fashion, I have no choice if I am to succeed *quickly*: this must be done for the sake of Lord Sun. I would rather chase this man away or have him join us, but I am pressed for time: if you must blame someone, blame Zhuge for yet again forcing my hand."
Lu Su shook his head and exhaled noisily.
The mood was tense as the besiegers awaited the response to Han Dang's confident challenge.
"Do I have to sit on this horse all day, shouting at myself?" Han Dang heckled. **"Here is Han Dang! Where is Xu Huang?"**

A considerable number of minutes passed before the drawbridge was lowered; the disappointment was almost tangible when it became clear that the officer that emerged from the city on horseback with 300 volunteer cavalrymen was announced by banners that read "General Niu Jin".
"Who is this nobody???" Han Dang exclaimed.
"Here is Niu Jin of Nan County!" Niu Jin retorted. **"Are you the old general Han Dang from Lingzhi that wanted a duel?"**
"Go away, you unimportant bastard!" Han Dang heckled. "I

want to fight Xu Huang, not his standard-bearer!"

"*Aiee*...! Even I am too far away to read those banners, they are *not* Xu Huang's, else the reaction would not be as it is!" Gongjin complained. "What game is Cao Ren playing?"
A messenger ran to the base of the tower and shouted, "**Cao Ren has sent out a 'General Niu Jin' to challenge Veteran General Han Dang!**"
Lu Su gestured politely, and the messenger retreated; Gongjin punched the air in front of him and cried, "**We asked Cao Ren for a tiger and he sends us a *mouse*! What's the use of trapping something so worthless???**"
"He insults us to lower our morale," Lu Su supposed.
"...Well then we must trap this 'Niu Jin' anyway and hope that it forces Xu Huang to rescue him," Gongjin replied tensely. "Perhaps a prolonged torture of this man in full view of the walls will draw Xu out anyway... **MESSENGER!**"

Gongjin's orders quickly passed to the front: Niu Jin was drawn into a brief duel by the reluctant Han Dang, who saw Niu as hardly being worth his time. Han Dang feigned weakness and fled as he had intended to do, with far better reason, against Xu Huang; Niu Jin succumbed to the excitement of battle and pursued with his 300 riders, whereupon he was surrounded by Jiangdong officers and men that taunted him loudly in order to provoke another response from Cao Ren.
"**Where is Xu Huang?**" Han Dang cackled. "**We've had fun with this cub that you sent out here to insult us, but we're bored now: where is Xu Huang?**"

Cao Ren was livid when Niu Jin's capture and subsequent torment was reported to him by a distressed messenger; Ren's Chief Clerk, Chen Jiao, sighed and said, "I did say it was a bad idea."
Cao Ren did not respond: he continued to pace back and forth and bite his hand as he wondered what his next move should be.
"This is going to be exceptionally bad for morale," Xu Huang suggested.
Chen Jiao gestured frantically and said, "It may even cause us to lose the siege, especially since we no longer have our northwest side covered by Yiling."
Cao Ren took several moments to respond: he hummed tersely and said, "I'll have to rescue them."
Xu Huang shook his head and replied, "Commander, if someone must go, let me! You are the commander of the defence of Jiangling!"
"I'm also the reason that man is surrounded and near death!" Cao Ren said. "How can I expect others to atone for my mistakes???"
"...This is extremely unwise," Chen Jiao insisted. "You do not correct one mistake by making another, larger one! If you die, this place is lost! The indigenous population will open the gates, and-"
"**Be SILENT!**" Cao Ren screamed. "I shall get my armour, and I shall save my comrade... and his men also... and then we will do something about Yiling."

What happened next was scarcely believable: Cao Ren gathered his elite cavalry – many of whom were veterans of the earlier rout at Yiling and therefore eager for revenge – and charged out of the city toward the complacent besiegers. Even the older generals, such as Cheng Pu and Han Dang, were taken aback and unable to respond to the swift and savage advance; the fact that the assault was led by a man whose banners read 'Commander Cao Ren' led to even greater confusion and fear, since Cao Ren had no reputation and immediately became enigmatic.

Cheng Pu was in the front line barracks with Huang Gai and Han Dang's son Zong when the rescue began: the first he knew of it was the screams of the men that were falling victim to Cao Ren's cavalrymen.

"What's going on out there…?" Cheng Pu exclaimed.

"We'd better see," Huang Gai replied.

"You stay here, you madman!" Cheng Pu retorted. "You're hurt, and…! Look, just *stay here!*"

"…Alright," Huang Gai sighed.

But Cheng Pu would arrive too late: Cao Ren's cavalry had divided and scattered the Jiangdong forces, rescued Niu Jin and fought their way back to the city by the time that the Chief Commander joined his humiliated generals at the front.

"…This is *ridiculous!*" Cheng Pu heckled. "I-!"

"THE DEMON COMES AGAIN!"

A simple soldier's cry was enough to throw the Jiangdong army into a panic for a second time: Cao Ren had returned to the field to rescue a group of Niu Jin's cavalrymen that had strayed during his first rescue. Cheng Pu was forced to watch as Cao Ren's horsemen dashed this way and that while Ren himself sought out the trapped men and brought them to the city gates; the defenders on the walls were cheering and hollering Cao Ren's name when the gates finally closed behind him, while the besiegers were eerily silent as they wandered about to check on the injured and dead.

"…I… must report this to the Chief Commander," Cheng Pu sighed.

"I… I failed *again!*" Han Dang cried. "This was *my* task, *my-!*"

"Just… don't," Cheng Pu ordered. "We *all* of us succumbed to panic, Yigong, and let them make fools of us *all*. The responsibility is collective: look around you."

Han Dang looked at the faces of Ling Tong, Pan Zhang, Sun Jiao, Lü Meng and Su Fei; morale had plummeted, even amongst the generals, and the situation was dire.

"…I need to find a man to send to the command tent," Cheng Pu said. "I can't go myself… I can't face him."

Gongjin and Lu Su had retired to the command tent before Cao Ren's first foray out of Jiangling, and had missed the entire rescue; they were therefore surprised and distressed when a man ran into the tent, fell to one knee and cried, **"Message from Veteran General Cheng Pu! Cao Ren has twice left the city to rescue Niu Jin's forces, and-!"**

"*Cao Ren…?*" Gongjin exclaimed. "*Cao Ren* charged out…? Then he is trapped…? He is *dead…?*"

The messenger trembled as he replied, "No, Chief Commander: Cao Ren twice defeated our forces and rescued the-"

"D'AAAAAAAGH! My cause is *ruined!*" Gongjin screamed.

Lu Su walked to the terrified messenger and took a written report from him before dismissing him.

"Give me that," Gongjin ordered. "I don't want it read to me."

Lu Su passed the report to Gongjin, who snatched it, read it and laughed strangely.

"…I don't understand," Lu Su said. "Cao Ren beat *everyone*…?"

"He did no such thing, but he might as well have done!" Gongjin replied. "He led a mad, fearless charge on our men as they heckled and laughed, and the shock of suddenly being attacked by cornered tigers, it…"

A second messenger entered the tent and said, "**Message from Veteran General Cheng Pu! The enemy are taunting our forces and firing arrows from the walls, and the men are unable to effectively respond! Veteran General Cheng requests permission to move the front line back to-!**"

"I'll… I'll deal with it," Gongjin replied. "Is that it?"

The messenger nodded slowly.

"…**Fools!**" Gongjin cried. "**Fools, and cowards!**"

"Calm down, Gongjin," Lu Su pleaded.

"You're… you're right," Gongjin said. "Thank you, Zijing… I should remain calm. But… this is terrible. The men are completely confused and scared: they think Cao Ren is some sort of super-man now. We cannot… we cannot leave things as they are. But… but what to do…?"

"…The generals are suggesting bringing the forward positions back a bit to avoid any more rushing strikes, since they seem to be severely hurting morale," Lu Su replied softly. "I don't know, if-"

"Do it," Gongjin ordered. "Just… just get the lines pulled back, out of range… and we'll rethink things… go."

Lu Su was about to leave, but he noticed that Gongjin was staring vacantly and wondered if some sort of encouraging statement might help; Lu quickly thought better of it and departed to carry out his orders.

"…*Damn you*… Cao Ren!" Gongjin croaked. "*Damn you*… Sun Ben! *Damn you*… Liu Bei! *Damn you*… Zhuge Liang…!"

The demoralised Jiangdong army moved their attacking positions away from the ground around the walls of Jiangling in order to avoid the arrows, stones and, most damagingly, the insults that the defenders were pelting them with; Cao Ren was able to send men out of the city to claim that ground for his own defensive purposes. That would have harmed the besiegers enough, but as the days passed, word reached them that Liu Bei had suffered no such setbacks and had taken Lingling and Guiyang counties with minimal effort. New and terrifying scenarios were starting to form in the minds of some: the thought that Cao Ren would triumph was most common, but Gongjin was starting to think that there was a possibility, no matter how slight, that Liu Bei would be the eventual master of southern Jing if he did not defeat Cao Ren in short order, and that would drive him to take more and more risks in the days to come.

****

106

As the days passed, Cao Ren capitalised on the morale-crushing effect that his twin rescues of Niu Jin's stranded cavalry had inflicted and continued to push the besiegers further and further away from the walls of Jiangling: more and more defensive works were constructed, and when they were deemed sufficient, Cao Ren ordered the deployment of wheeled siege towers to advance and rain arrows down on the Jiangdong forces. One definitive attack forced Cheng Pu, Han Dang and Huang Gai to go to the command tent and request advice from the weary Gongjin, who was alone save for one attendant.

"**Chief Commander!**" Cheng Pu said as he ran into the tent. "They're moving their defensive positions forward again!"

"I know," Gongjin replied. "We need to push them back."

"What are your orders...?" Cheng Pu asked humbly.

"...I will personally lead the troops forward to strike their positions and stop this gradual advance," Gongjin said as he got to his feet. "Let's force them backwards, force them back into the city."

Gongjin's toneless response unnerved Cheng Pu, who asked, "Are you alright, Chief Commander...?"

"Would my answer change anything, Demou...?" Gongjin retorted. "Return to the front, General Cheng and General Han; General Huang, you... will do as you please, I expect."

The three veteran officers were startled; Huang Gai bowed slightly and said, "I... shall return to my tent, Chief Commander, to spare you the need to be concerned for my welfare."

"That is much appreciated," Gongjin replied. "Dismissed."

The sight of Gongjin in his shining golden armour was enough to lift the spirits of some of the Jiangdong men as he approached them on his white steed: he raised his sword of authority and shouted, "**Why do we allow Cao Ren to enfeeble us so...? He surprised us because he feared the loss of one of the only two men that he can rely upon, and he fought like a cornered tiger, but that should not make you afraid: it should make you see how weak he is!**"

"Well said, Gongjin," Cheng Pu murmured.

"**We're scared of a few rocks...?**" Gongjin continued. "**Lü Meng: your loggers will find us the timber and build us catapults to start returning those rocks to their owners!**"

Lü Meng – who was frustrated that being demoralised had somehow robbed him of his wits – saluted and nodded obediently.

"**And his siege towers will fall!**" Gongjin insisted. "**Ling Tong, Sun Jiao, Su Fei: you will work toward their destruction!**"

The 3 officers saluted silently.

"**And Cao Ren's men are nothing special when robbed of their undeserved advantage!**" Gongjin continued. "**Veteran General Cheng, Veteran General Han, Sun Yu, Chen Wu: you will lead the infantry and cavalry in flash strikes against them and push them back!**"

Those 4 officers saluted in response.

"**And we will push *them* back as they pushed *us* back!**" Gongjin concluded. "**Sun Hao, Pan Zhang, Zhou Tai: you will**

oversee the archery divisions and have the best of them target the enemy saboteurs, siege tower and hill-based archers and the men that rush to the defence of the hills!"
The 3 officers responded respectfully.
"**Go to it!**" Gongjin urged. "**In four days or less, we will be back at the walls, and if that false tiger Cao Ren ventures out here again he will face this true tiger's sword of authority and he will die by it!**"
The soldiers cheered loudly and chanted; Cao Ren was watching Gongjin's address from atop the battlements of the city, and the sight of an enemy with restored morale unnerved him greatly.

Gongjin was true to his word: he remained at the front, giving words of support that belied the fears and concerns that plagued him, and the combined resolve of some of the greatest military talents that Jiangdong had to offer pushed the Han forces back in a matter of days, eliminating the siege towers and toppling the artificial hills that Cao Ren's men had used to launch their archery attacks. The reversal was completed to Gongjin's schedule: Jiangling was surrounded once again, and the morale of besiegers and defenders switched accordingly.
"It is a hollow victory," Gongjin said to Lu Su once he had returned from giving a rousing speech to the officers at the front.
"How so...?" Lu Su asked.
"Liu Bei has the counties," Gongjin replied. "Zhuge Liang has made a show of leaving their camp and going southward to 'meet with each of the victorious heroes in turn'. He knows that I cannot attack their camp no matter how sparsely defended it is, and he knows that his lord now has vast expanses of land to draw upon for men and resources while I have done little more than take back a scrap of land between here and the walls of Jiangling!"
"You reversed a situation that had humbled the likes of *Cheng Pu*, Han Dang, *Chen Wu*, *Zhou Tai* and Ling Tong, and showed that Lü Meng's intelligence might be overrated after all," Lu Su suggested.
"Others might have said that we needed to call upon Jiang Qin, Dong Xi and Hè Qi for military reinforcement and Lü Fan to add some more brains to our effort, but you proved that you could rise to the occasion as Cao Ren did and do even better than he did!"
"...I suppose so," Gongjin sighed.
"Don't suppose, comprehend," Lu Su insisted. "You proved that you are a hero: Cao Ren could have come out of the city to challenge you, but where was he...?"
Gongjin smiled and said, "You're right: he left everything to Xu Huang and Niu Jin, and they were unable to build any momentum. Cao Ren's one desperate attack on us was, as I myself said, done to save Niu Jin because he needed him: a real 'super-man' would have charged out and prevented this reversal. I have proved that I am a true hero while he is a false one, and-"
"And *that*, Gongjin, should be that," Lu Su insisted. "You turned it around: now you must either stop dressing like a gilded dragon when you go to the front or you must leave matters to the others now that their confidence is restored."
"Can I afford to...?" Gongjin scoffed. "I must end this siege quickly: when I left it to others – even heroes like Chen Wu and Zhou Tai that I believed to be incapable of succumbing to fear or

confusion – I was left disappointed. Even if I must fall here at Jiangling, we-"

"Don't talk like that!" Lu Su pleaded. "You will curse yourself!"

"I did that already when I defeated the 'Crafty Villain' and burned his fleet," Gongjin replied. "If Heaven had been kinder to us, then it would be *Bofu* at the front, rallying men that joined him to build a fairer nation: now *I* must ride to the front and lead from the front where my new lord cannot."

"...I can see that there will be no swaying you," Lu Su sighed. "Just... just be cautious, will you...? You obviously understand how precious you are to our cause, so... preserve yourself."

Gongjin exhaled fiercely and said, "I shall do what must be done, and no less. Now then: we must rebuild the camp and expand it. Can you oversee that while I plan manoeuvres with Cheng Pu...?"

"...Yes, I can," Lu Su replied.

"And... I will seek an audience with our fair-weather ally at the earliest possible opportunity," Gongjin decided. "Like it or not, we... we *need* their assistance."

More days went by where little changed, though some in the Jiangdong camp saw the stagnation as better than another reversal; Liu Bei's triumphant forces returned to the region, whereupon Gongjin sent a man to politely request an audience. The reply was cordial and restrained: Gongjin met Liu Bei at the entrance to the command tent within days and said, "My thanks to you for coming, Lord Liu, and congratulations on securing the four counties so quickly and easily."

"Not worth mentioning...!" Liu Bei replied as he took his seat as an honoured guest.

Gongjin sighed miserably and said, "We have been going back and forth with Cao Ren now for far too long: this... 'stalemate'... has got to end soon."

"Perhaps we should try raiding his supply routes again," Liu Bei suggested.

"...Did you have a stratagem in mind...?" Gongjin asked.

"The enemy can transfer goods by river if they please," Liu Bei explained, "but they must still get them to Jiangling by road: perhaps if I deploy forces under Guan Yunchang and Zhang Yide, simultaneously striking the supply roads from the north and west, it might be enough to break Cao Ren's spirit."

Gongjin and Lu Su exchanged glances as Gongjin replied, "Perhaps: it is a sound idea, but the-"

"Excellent!" Liu Bei said. "Together, there's nothing that Yunchang and Yide cannot accomplish!"

"...You seem committed to the endeavour," Gongjin replied. "Very well... we'll launch a simultaneous attack on all sides of Jiangling, in order to prevent Cao Ren sending aid. Good luck, then: I suppose that's all there is to say about that. Now, there are some other matters..."

"...Such as, *Gongjin*...?" Zhuge Liang asked.

"General matters, such as supply distribution," Gongjin retorted. "We have combined forces numbering over eighty-thousand now, *Kongming*: we must ensure that they are properly fed, clothed, armed, and suchlike for the foreseeable future."

"...And what is the 'foreseeable future'...?" Zhuge Liang asked.

"…That's down to Cao Ren, not me," Gongjin replied irritably. "Shall we proceed?"

The meeting continued, but the atmosphere was tense, and the majority of the Jiangdong officials were, like Gongjin, starting to not only dislike Liu Bei but fear him and his plans for the future.

Liu Bei's self-assured generals, Guan Yu and Zhang Fei, set out on their mission to sabotage Cao Ren's supply lines while Gongjin ensured that Jiangling was attacked on all sides: the result, however, did more harm than good.

"Bloody fools!" Gongjin cried as he slammed his hand on his writing desk and sent an empty wine dish flying. **"They are lucky that I consider this to be unintended incompetence and not a deliberate ploy to weaken my grip on the city!"**

The command tent was silent: Lu Su, Cheng Pu, Lü Meng, Han Dang and Sun Yu were visibly concerned as they watched the beleaguered Chief Commander's attempts to find some good in the reports that Liu Bei had sent to him.

"I mean, he actually tries to *defend* those two brainless thugs!" Gongjin said as he waved one of the cloth reports back and forth like a rag. "Why I wanted Guan to join us, I will never know! All that they had to do was isolate Yue Jin – which, since they now control Wuling, should have been easy enough – and carry out simultaneous raids on the roads into Jiangling. They had *thousands* of men – *thousands* – where they have been lucky to command *hundreds* in past times, and *still* they were humiliated by *Li Tong* – a *nobody* like *Li Tong* – a pedant like *Man Chong*, and *Wen Ping*! I am starting to think that the legends of their matching the likes of Lü Bu, slaying Yuan Shao's best officers in seconds and 'putting Cao Cao's army to flight with shouts' were little more than baseless propaganda! Guan and Zhang can't even take a couple of roads off of a couple of mediocrities!"

"Perhaps they have not aged well," Cheng Pu suggested dryly.

"I empathise," Han Dang muttered.

"If they are past their prime, then Bei should not have sent them," Gongjin said. "I suspect that it was not their strength but their egos and intellects that failed them, but that is not my main concern: their loss has given Cao Ren renewed vigour, and now we are being pushed away from the walls *again*!"

"With allies like *them*, I wonder whether we need enemies," Han Dang growled.

"We must try and restore order," Gongjin said. "We must not let their failures cause our own morale to plummet!"

But as the days continued to wear on, successive attempts to break Cao Ren's supply lines ended in failure and the defenders' confidence grew once again. The besiegers' battle lines were pushed further and further away from the walls of Jiangling, the soil mounds and siege towers returned and the Jiangdong men started to succumb to despair.

****

107

Gongjin spent the days studying his maps and trying to find a way to change the situation, preferably without the support of Liu Bei.

"We need to do something to fight back against this decisively," Gongjin said as he addressed his senior officers in the command tent. "Tomorrow, I will go out again and rally the men personally."

"You shouldn't keep doing that," Lü Meng suggested. "At least change your horse, if you insist, and wear duller armour: you're too obvious a target."

Gongjin grunted irritably, walked to the pedestal that held the 'sword of authority' and said, "Fair enough... but this has to end."

Gongjin donned a less impressive collection of armour and travelled to the front lines on the following morning: the men were conspicuously excited when he arrived, despite their commanding officers' best efforts to tell them not to alert the enemy to his presence.

"We'll try to take his external camps and get ourselves back to the area around the walls," Gongjin announced. "If we can just undo the damage done by 'The misadventures of Yunchang and Yide', we'll prove that we're the better men to anyone that hasn't already figured it out."

The officers laughed loudly; Cheng Pu scowled and said, "**Why do I have to keep telling you all? Don't start chanting!**"

"Sorry, Veteran General," Sun Jiao chuckled.

The laughter subsided, and Gongjin said, "Save your laughter for the result of our efforts: we'll get them back inside that city, and then we'll show Liu Bei how to conduct a sabotage operation since he obviously does not know. We have held Yiling and maintained our siege of this city despite all odds: next we will take and keep Linju, and after that, friends, we will cut Cao Ren's supplies ourselves. **Go to it!**"

The officials dispersed, and the operation began: Xu Huang and Chen Jiao were watching events unfold from the top of the city wall, but Cao Ren was nowhere to be seen.

"...They can see that we're rallying," Lü Meng said. "They are conspicuously quiet."

"I agree," Cheng Pu replied. "Chief Commander, you should-"

"I should do as my role demands and have a public presence, showing my men that, like Cao Ren, I have no fear, so that they are forced to ignore theirs," Gongjin interrupted. "I am aware of the risks, Demou, but the cost of failure matters more."

Cheng Pu nodded silently; Gongjin smiled and said, "To the front, then, to restore order!"

Cao Ren joined Xu Huang and Chen Jiao on the battlements of Jiangling City and smirked as he observed the activity below; Xu and Chen bowed respectfully and awaited Cao Ren's words.

"Today," Cao Ren said, "Zhou Yu dies."

Xu Huang and Chen Jiao exchanged glances: Cao Ren then raised a small flag as a signal, and his trap was sprung. The archers on the wall raised their bows and nocked their arrows, and on the ground below, scores of archers appeared from concealed places and began firing on Gongjin's position. The result was immediate chaos: the Jiangdong infantry darted about in a desperate effort to avoid being shot, and even the guards around Gongjin were struggling to control their horses as men screamed and arrows whizzed past them.

"**Stay calm!**" Gongjin protested. "**Place our own archers in a line at the rear! Infantry, pull back to the-!** ...*The...!*"

An arrow had found its mark; Gongjin stared at the arrow that was protruding from the area below his ribcage and groaned as he guessed the consequences of it.

"...Why...?" Gongjin whispered as he slumped forward; he fell from his horse moments later and landed on his back, his eyes staring vacantly at the sky above him.

"**CHIEF COMMANDER!**" Cheng Pu screamed: Gongjin's frenzied bodyguards were being struck as they tried to defend their master from further harm, so Cheng ordered more men to brave the arrows and protect the most important man on the battlefield.

"We got him!" Cao Ren exclaimed. "Xu Huang: finish them off!"

"As you command," Xu Huang replied.

"...We got him...!" Cao Ren cackled. "Sun Quan, Liu Qi, Liu Bei: you will be next!"

"**Morale has collapsed: we'll have to retreat!**" Cheng Pu said as he met with Lü Meng and Han Dang.

"**But we'll be shot down as we flee!**" Han Dang protested.

"**We don't have a choice!**" Cheng Pu insisted. "**They'll follow this up with-!**"

A soldier looked toward Jiangling and shrieked, "**THE CITY GATES ARE OPENING!**"

"**Xu Huang,**" Lü Meng guessed. "**We must get the Chief Commander to safety! We can't let them have him!**"

"**They'll have to make do with me!**" Han Dang replied. "**I'll take the rear: get everyone back to the camp!**"

Gongjin, meanwhile, had been lifted onto another horse – his own having been shot to death – and was being led away from the front line by the remnants of his bodyguard force; the arrow had been left in his body for fear of worsening matters by pulling it out, but the sight of it was driving some men to tears.

"We... must... orderly... must... *regroup*...!" Gongjin pleaded, but the day was Cao Ren's: the retreat continued regardless.

∗∗∗∗∗∗∗∗∗∗∗∗

108

In the wake of the ambush, Lu Su, Cheng Pu, Huang Gai and Lü Meng watched as a physician did his best to save Gongjin's life: the command tent was close to silent until Huang Gai asked, "What do the men know…?"

"They know," Cheng Pu replied. "Chen Wu is working to keep the men's spirits up; we do this here, because… because…!"

"…Because we must be able to explain matters at leisure, without the panic that accompanies immediacy," Lu Su said. "In other words, we… we will have time to plan our response if… *if*…!"

Cheng Pu snorted guiltily and said, "Our incompetence pushed you to this, Gongjin: now we must live with it, but so must you!"

"He'll live," Lü Meng insisted. "He won't be as he was, but that doctor has saved men in a worse state than that."

"But a badly wounded tiger will still harm morale!" Cheng Pu retorted. "He was harmed while trying to push the front line back to the city walls, which will never happen now: how long will the enemy wait before they camp outside our gates in order to taunt him to death?"

"When the Chief Commander can speak again, we will ask him how to proceed," Lu Meng replied. "Until then-"

"The outcome is in Lord Sun's hands now," Lu Su said. "Word has been sped to him, so that he might decide."

"…Lord Sun will order a retreat if Zhang Zhao has *his* way," Cheng Pu supposed. "Zhang recommended a retreat from Hefei for less than this: after that, he'll likely suggest another truce with Cao Cao, and-!"

"Things have changed," Lu Su said. "The Zhang brothers are as committed to a 'Jiangnan' or an 'Eastern Wu' as the rest of us now, so… so have faith."

Sun Quan read the report from Jiangling and shuddered: his Chaisang court was already aware of the incident and divided on how to react to it.

"Send Ziheng to replace Gongjin, and send Gongjin to Wu to convalesce," Xu Kun suggested. "Auntie always said that the two of them were both of them geniuses, and-"

"Lü Fan must stay and manage the chaos in Jiangdong!" Zhang Zhao interrupted. "One does not lose a house to take a hill!"

"I agree," Zhang Hong said. "Lü Fan, Lu Xun, Yu Fan and Qin Song are needed here in Jiangdong, as are Dong Xi, Jiang Qin and Hè Qi: Zhou Yu himself said that."

"…But Lu Xun was in Jiangling and left to return to Kuaiji," Sun Quan noted. "He is familiar with the situation, so could he not go back there…?"

"No," Zhang Hong insisted. "Kuaiji is at breaking point, and the bandit lords of Danyang and Yuzhang are threatening insurrection, no doubt at Cao Cao's prompting. We cannot ignore tax evasion, rebels and raids at any time without being wrong, but to do so now in a time of crisis would be both stupid and catastrophic."

"But what is to be done, then…?" Sun Quan asked. "Ziyu, you are quiet: have you no thoughts…?"

Zhuge Jin was about to respond, but Zhang Zhao sneered and

said, "Of course he is quiet: that donkey-faced fool is well aware that the main reason for this disaster is the continual disruption caused by his brother, the 'Crouching Dragon'!"

"Is that a correct assessment, Ziyu...?" Sun Quan asked as he stared at Zhuge Jin.

"...My brother is only able to do his best," Zhuge Jin protested. "I know that he is blamed for Cao Cao's escape, but-!"

"It's either a perverse scheme or unforgivable *incompetence*," Zhang Zhao heckled.

"Can I finish?" Zhuge Jin retorted. "Yes, it was one of those two, but I believe it to be the latter, and Kongming stressed that it was a 'tactical mistake' in his letter to me. The Lius are not entirely united: Liu Qi's advisers fear Liu Bei as much as we do, and they are perhaps right to. I have read the despatches: yes, Liu Bei has seized the four counties, ostensibly for the purpose of preventing them falling into Cao's hands but probably for the purpose of making them his base, which was his dream long before my brother joined him! And the failures reported – the attempts to take control of Xiangyang, Linju, and the supply roads – are no worse a setback than nearly losing Yiling and Cao Ren's repeated pushing out of the city. The Chief Commander has been the greatest victim of the circumstances, but the aim now should be to undo as much of the damage as possible, not look for those to blame! And if we *must* apportion blame, then whose arrow was it anyway: was it Liu Bei's or Cao Ren's...?"

"...The whys and wherefores can wait," Zhang Zhao replied bitterly. "If there is no capable man to send, then we have two choices: we entrust the campaign to those that remain – men that are usually very capable and must find their lost prowess, like Cheng Pu, Zhou Tai, Han Dang and Chen Wu – or we must order a retreat and leave Cao Cao and the Lius to fight over Jiangling."

"*Ayah*... but doesn't a retreat mean we must yield Yiling as well, and accept that we might end up with eastern Jiangxia and not much else...?" Sun Quan asked. "Wouldn't we probably have to yield Jiangxia in the end, and end the campaign with less than we started it with while Liu Bei grows and Cao Cao recovers...?"

"But to stay means that we risk losing half of our army to slow erosion, and that, in the end, will lose us Jiangdong," Zhang Hong suggested. "Yes, a way might be found to turn the situation around, but-"

"I'll go!" Xu Kun declared. "Let me go, Cousin Zhongmou, and-!"

"I might need to attack Hefei again, in which case I must rely upon you to lead the vanguard or guard Chaisang," Sun Quan replied. "No, we must either persevere or flee: my heart tells me to persevere, but I am at a loss."

"Well then we should await Lü Fan's suggestion," Zhang Zhao said. "We must write to Qu'e and demand his appraisal."

"...I already have his appraisal, which arrived mere hours after the report from Jiangling," Sun Quan admitted.

"Why didn't you say so before...?" Xu Kun asked. "What did he say, then?"

"Ziheng advocates waiting for Gongjin's opinion," Sun Quan replied. "I said nothing because... because I didn't know what to say. He says that I must wait: if Gongjin- ...if Gongjin *dies*, then Ziheng will 'provide support', but if Gongjin survives, then it must be *his* decision."

"Well then that's it," Xu Kun said. "We'll do as Ziheng says: he's always been right before."

"...Then I shall await Gongjin's decision," Sun Quan decided. "Heaven would not give me Red Cliffs and then rob me of the mastermind: he will live, and our dreams will be realised."

Gongjin survived the operation to remove the arrow from his body: there was no serious organ damage, but a rib had been shattered and he was in excruciating pain. Cao Ren exploited the disintegration of morale in in Jiangdong ranks and pushed the besiegers back as far as their main camp, after which he set up a bivouac camp of his own to the north of the fenced base and led daily excursions to the main gates with a force of men: they would bring a large drum, jars of wine, tea, food and bedding in order to taunt their foes with a show of relaxation and hours of heckling that was mostly aimed at Gongjin himself. The favourite chant was devoid of any subtlety:

**"YOUR LIFE IS AT ITS END, ZHOU YU!
GO TO YOUR GRAVE, AS HEAVEN DEMANDS!"**

"...*Scum*," Sun Yu muttered as he sat with Gongjin in the latter's personal tent.

"I'm just... trying to ignore them," Gongjin replied. "They can't hurt me anywhere near as much as... this wound."

"But your *wound* was down to *them*!" Sun Yu groaned.

"...I have meant to ask, and... now that I am bedridden I can... ask without feeling that I waste my time or... offend," Gongjin said. "What is the matter with you all, Zhongyi...? The reason that... that I'm stuck here like this is... that I had to nursemaid you all through a reversal of fortune: didn't I earn a reputation for undue caution, weakness, floundering and... and indecision because I didn't always charge madly and fight recklessly...? Why do the men that... are heralded as heroes... now hesitate, flounder and weep like... children... at the sight of a few horsemen or a... a couple of rocks...?"

"I can't say," Sun Yu admitted. "I don't know, I... I suppose that I was so busy watching the others heckling Niu Jin's men and enjoying a respite from the siege that I dropped my guard: we none of us expected them to launch such a concerted attack on us when they had reacted so sluggishly to that point."

Gongjin smiled and hummed thoughtfully despite the pain that he was enduring; an important idea had come to him.

"Generally, I think that we're losing our minds," Sun Yu continued. "I can't speak for Cheng Pu, Lü Meng, Zhou Tai and so on: I suppose that they reacted to sudden surprise at seeing a silly little man like Cao Ren leading cavalry like that, and knowing what a clever, talented man his brother was, and that they were his cavalry, it... I don't know. I suppose that it's because everything changed after that fire. Being honest, I suppose it is that... that we set out to fight *Liu Biao* and *Cao Cao*, but we defeated the *Han army*... we burned the *Han fleet*."

"...We are in... uncharted territory, where every day threatens... the *unknown*," Gongjin said.

"Precisely," Sun Yu replied. "Under Uncle Jian and Cousin Bofu, our task was taming the tribes, thrashing bandits, bringing stability and fighting wicked lords that broke the law and harmed the people. Now, after that fire, I wonder what Heaven's will is: the fires were brought to us by whom or by what…? Is the Han's mandate expired, or are we working to some other end without knowing…? Nothing is clear."

Gongjin was going to respond, but the pain had worsened and the chanting was becoming louder; he winced and groaned but spoke no words.

"…*Wretches*!" Sun Yu exclaimed. "Give the word, Gongjin, and-!"

"*No… response*…!" Gongjin insisted. "Not… not *yet*."

Days turned to weeks: frustration reached boiling point, and there were regular shouting matches and scuffles between Jiangdong soldiers and even the lower-ranking officers as their inability to attack the hecklers turned them on each other. A sign stating that the occupants would refuse all challenges had been placed on the gates at Lu Su's instruction, and that only served to intensify the taunts and the anger that they generated. The trapped men from Jiangdong waited for they knew not what, and all the while, familiar words ate at them:

**"YOUR LIFE IS AT ITS END, ZHOU YU!
GO TO YOUR GRAVE, AS HEAVEN DEMANDS!"**

"For the love of the gods!" Sun Jiao exclaimed one morning. **"For how long d'we have to endure this?"**

A small group of officers were stood at a distance from the gates: they were supposed to contain any outbursts by the regular troops, but they were having difficulty restraining themselves.

"We'll endure for as long as the Chief Commander insists that we do not retaliate," Sun Yu replied.

"…Hark at you, Older Brother," Sun Jiao retorted. "The Chief Commander's *pet*! He always crows about what a *great officer you are*, but where's your *spine*, Brother? Why aren't you insistin' that we go fight 'im, mm…?"

"If you weren't *drunk*, Brother, I'd scold you for your words, but I know what an idiot you become under the influence of drink and must ignore you," Sun Yu said calmly. "Instead of asking me what I'm doing, ask why you're drunk at dawn: what if we *were* ordered to charge? What use would you be?"

"I'm not drunk," Sun Jiao grumbled. "I jus' had a couple of cups."

"A couple of cups of *what*…?" Su Fei joked. "That stuff they use to coat ships with to make them waterproof…?"

"Shut up, you pirate," Sun Jiao retorted. "You worked for *Huang Zu*, you-!"

"*Don't remind me*," Ling Tong pleaded. "We're here to *keep* the peace, not wreck it."

Ling Tong's words were met with silence that lasted for a full minute before Sun Yu said, "Colonel Lu Su approaches."

"…*Toady*," Sun Jiao muttered.

Lu Su stopped in front of the officers and asked, "Any problems?"

"They haven't even pissed on your sign, 'Colonel'," Sun Jiao replied icily. "It's just the usual-"

"Brother!" Sun Yu cried. "Colonel Lu might – *might* – rank below us militarily during normal times, but he is the trusted aide of the Chief Commander, and at present he is the Acting Chief Commander, and he could have you at the very least reprimanded for insubordination for speaking so rudely!"

"I wouldn't," Lu Su insisted. "I know how angry everyone is, and I know that the stance that I have taken is not popular, but we are awaiting responses from Lord Sun and others, and the Chief Commander must recuperate! Let them throw words... we'll throw something worse back at them when the time is right."

Sun Jiao grunted irritably; Lu Su ignored the gesture, bowed respectfully and retreated to Gongjin's personal tent.

"...*Stupid little man*," Sun Jiao grumbled. "Why isn't Old Cheng in charge? He'd have ordered an attack on the bastards long ago!"

"That's probably why he isn't in charge," Sun Yu replied dryly.

Lu Su entered Gongjin's tent and said, "Is there no way that I can do something else...?"

"It was your... suggestion that... we put the sign up, Zijing," Gongjin replied as he tried to resist the pain and read an old book on warfare.

"Not for *weeks*!" Lu Su retorted. "What are we doing?"

"...I don't... know," Gongjin admitted. "I... I can't just... leave. If I leave... Liu Bei will...!"

"If it helps at all, Kongming doesn't think that we should leave," Lu Su said.

Gongjin looked up and asked, "When did... he say that...?"

"A while ago," Lu Su replied. "He obviously doubts that Liu Bei can take our place, especially after that last mess that led to this."

"Or... or he wants me to remain and... *expire*," Gongjin suggested. "But I will *recover*, Zijing... you hear...? I will *recover*... and *win*...!"

Lu Su shook his head and said, "I haven't the words. Shall I go?"

"What is there... to stay for...?" Gongjin retorted; Lu Su bowed slightly, turned and left, after which Gongjin muttered, "Jiangling... and Jing... will be *ours*, Liu Bei... not *yours*."

More days passed.

The majority of the Han soldiers became increasingly relaxed and often arrived at the Jiangdong army's camp without armour, singing, play-fighting and even, to Xu Huang's growing distress, a state of intoxication; Cao Ren did nothing to end that conduct, as he was becoming as self-assured and complacent as his men.

"...What are we waiting for?" Ling Tong asked as he watched the enemy's heckling and partying through the wooden fence.

"I'm not sure anymore," Sun Hao replied. "I wondered if we wanted them to start acting like this so we could surprise them, but they've been like that for days and days now, and still the order is 'sit quietly'. What about supplies...?"

"We have ample supplies," Sun Yu replied.

"Perhaps there are reinforcements coming," Sun Jiao suggested.

"Unlikely," Lü Meng replied. "After we lost the chance to take Hefei, Cao Cao's been building support in Lujiang and Jiujiang through population changes and additional barracks. If we moved too many men here now we'd be risking an invasion from the north when he saw that we were undermanned."

"...So the dream is over, then," Sun Jiao sighed.

"Not at all," Sun Yu insisted. "There is a way to turn this around: I do not know what the Chief Commander is waiting for, but I have my suspicions."

Lü Meng smiled sadly and replied, "So do I."

"Whatever or whoever it is that we wait for, I hope that the wait ends before the patience of the men does," Ling Tong said. "All it takes is for one ambitious captain or major to remember Li Shu and we'll be in serious danger."

"There will be no such man," Sun Yu insisted. "We-"

"DEATH TO ZHOU YU, YOU SOUTHERN DOGS!"

The assembled officers were startled by the Han infantry captain that had approached the gates of the camp at Cao Ren's instruction: the inebriated captain tore the battle-refusal sign from the gate, broke it across his knee and tossed it onto the dusty ground at his feet. The response was immediate: the soldiers that witnessed the offence began shouting and demanding that the gate guards open the way so that they could fight.

"**That's it!**" Sun Jiao shrieked. "**I'm with the men! We-!**"

"**We will do *nothing*!**" Sun Yu insisted. "**The Acting Chief Commander made it quite clear that-!**"

"**His sign is smashed!**" Sun Jiao retorted. "**Are we going to ignore a challenge like that?**"

The Han captain was slowly moving backwards and making offensive gestures as a handful of his subordinates ran to his aid in the event of a retaliatory attack: the Han camp was slowly rousing as Xu Huang dashed about in an effort to be ready for whatever might happen while Cao Ren laughed and continued to sip from his tea dish.

"**We have to ignore it!**" Sun Yu protested. "**Heaven only knows, Brother, that I don't *want to*, but we *must*!**"

Chen Wu and Zhou Tai arrived to quell the anger of the soldiers that were now massing by the gates and loudly demanding a military reaction; Ling Tong exhaled angrily and said, "**My blood is boiling, but... Zhongyi is right. We have to calm the men.**"

Cheng Pu and Han Dang approached moments later; Sun Jiao nodded and replied, "Alright... **alright.**"

The demoralised officers did as they had been ordered to do, and a potentially serious incident was averted; Lu Su watched at a distance but refrained from approaching the men and becoming the focus of their anger.

****

109

The next week passed without any change in stance: but just as the patience of even the most loyal men was starting to run out, Gongjin summoned Lu Su, Lü Meng, Cheng Pu, Huang Gai, Ling Tong and Han Dang to his personal tent for a meeting. The Chief Commander was an alarming sight for those that expected to see strength: he was wincing uncomfortably after even the slightest movement, and his entire upper body was swathed in thick bandages that were visible under his silk pyjamas.

"Day after day, all I hear is their wishing for my death," Gongjin declared. "This cannot go on."

Cheng Pu sighed and said, "Chief Commander, we would gladly go out and fight, but 'Acting Chief Commander Lu Su' insisted we put up a sign of battle-refusal, and remain in the camp... stating that any who disobeyed would be *executed*."

The frustrated Lu Su huffed and replied, "You tattle on me like a whining child. What else can I do? The men are demoralised, and we do not know what other schemes Cao Ren may have in mind, do we...?"

"If we leave him be," Cheng Pu retorted, "he'll build mounds and towers right outside the camp, and rain arrows down on us."

Lu Su scowled and said, "We have archer towers. Letting him chant and pontificate is one thing: of course, if he started building assault points, we'd retaliate! I'm not *that* stupid!"

Cheng Pu was about to answer Lu Su when Gongjin raised his hand and said, "*Please*... stop arguing. They are convinced that I am dying... else he would not be doing this. There is only one way this is going to end besides my death..."

Gongjin started to turn his body so that he could get up: his face betrayed the agony that he was enduring, and that added to the guilt and distress that his officers were feeling.

"Chief Commander!" Cheng Pu exclaimed.

Lu Su clutched at the empty air in front of him and said, "Gongjin, you mustn't...!"

"This is... the only... way," Gongjin replied insistently. "Someone... get my armour ready. Someone... help me up."

"*Gongjin*...!" Lu Su sighed.

Gongjin turned his head, looked upward at Lu Su and said, "You... gave me, and hence my lord... your entire fortune, Zijing, for... the sake of peace... so what's my life...?"

"Your life is worth more than some granaries!" Lu Su retorted. "Don't be reckless! You do not need to do this!"

Gongjin looked at the assembled officials – who wore expressions that reminded him of herd animals that required guidance – and laughed, saying, "Yes I do."

Cao Ren had brought his small army of hecklers to the Jiangdong camp as usual: he sat in front of his tent – dressed, to Xu Huang's irritation, in an expensive robe instead of armour – and had a servant pour heated wine from a kettle while Xu Huang – who was dressed in full armour – reluctantly sat opposite Cao with a half-filled dish of cooled wine in his hand. Cao Ren would occasionally rouse his men to start shouting abuse, but he was mostly content with drinking and discussing various topics with his anxious subordinate general.

"...My brother would be *proud*," Cao Ren insisted. "He would... he'd be proud."

Xu Huang was silent.

"This is a turning point," Cao Ren continued. "We'll break them here, Xu Gongming, and then we'll chase them back to their swamps and smash them! Our loss at Wulin will be avenged!"

Xu Huang could contain his concern no longer: he exhaled fiercely and said, "This is dangerous."

Cao Ren grinned and replied, "Every day, every single day, you say that, General, and what has happened...? ...*Nothing*. Zhou Yu is good as dead. ...**Men, shout some more! Shout some more!**"

A group of young soldiers laughed and chanted repeatedly, **"YOUR LIFE IS AT ITS END, ZHOU YU! GO TO YOUR GRAVE, AS HEAVEN DEMANDS!"**

"Drums, drums!" Cao Ren cackled. **"DRUMS!"**

The drummers synchronised their work with the chanting.

"Your life is at its end, Zhou Yu...!" Cao Ren said with as much musical timing as he could muster: he then laughed and took a sip from his wine dish.

Xu Huang shook his head and started to look about him: his eyes found the Jiangdong camp, and he suddenly realised that the area around the gates had been cleared of angry onlookers. Xu Huang pondered the possible meanings, but one possibility became the most worrisome: he said, "Something's going to happen," and got to his feet to fetch his long-handled war axe.

"Coward!" Cao Ren retorted. "You're afraid of a dead ma-"

A sudden yelp ended Cao Ren's heckling, along with the realisation that one drum had fallen silent: a drummer collapsed and fell from his raised platform moments later. The Han men were stunned and confused despite there obviously being some danger, but it was only when another drummer was shot and killed – and then, moments later, a third and a fourth – that panic started to spread.

"ARCHERS!" one man shouted.

Weeks of complacency had robbed the hecklers of their basic ability to react to danger, and that was about to have serious consequences: the camp gates opened, and the occupants – infantry and cavalry – rushed toward their unprepared enemies.

"QUICKLY...!" Xu Huang cried. **"WE MUST ORGANISE!"**

Cao Ren frowned and asked, "What the...? What's going on...?"

Xu Huang turned and glared at Cao Ren, who finally realised the situation and started to look about him for his armour.

"WE HAVE TO RETALIATE!" Xu Huang ordered. **"RALLY AT ONCE!"**

But there would be no effective response: the Jiangdong men were angry and consumed by bloodlust after weeks of enduring torment, and they possessed nothing but hate for the men from the north. Cao Ren was trying to equip his armour without assistance as he watched the carnage around him: he grimaced and said, "This can't be happening...!"

The Jiangdong forces were inexplicably organised and efficient: Cao Ren started to wonder how that could be possible, and his questions were answered when a charismatic general rode out of the camp on a white horse with a decorated saddle. The shining armour that the general wore and the expensive sword that he carried were instantly recognisable to Cao Ren, who was robbed of the ability to speak.

"**See Chief Commander Zhou Yu here!**" Gongjin shouted as he charged toward the enemy commander's tent. "**Do you come to deliver yourself into my trap, Cao Ren?**"

Cao Ren was, at that moment, unable to think rationally: he entertained the idea that the pale, wild-eyed general that fearlessly charged toward him might be a ghost or a demon, and so he turned and fled before he was forced to find out. The sight of Cao Ren stumbling away from his own camp on foot with pieces of his armour hanging from his body was enough to rouse many men to laughter: Gongjin pointed his 'sword of authority' and laughed loudly to further empower his men and ensure that they completed the rout.

Xu Huang was eager to find some way to prevent the Jiangdong men from chasing the Han forces back to the city and resuming their costly siege, so he found a ready horse and prepared to lead a resistance, but Lü Meng, Ling Tong and Han Dang surrounded him and forced him to withdraw.

"**Next time, Xu Huang, it'll just be me that you'll face, but you'll still run!**" Han Dang declared.

Lu Su was stood by Gongjin's horse as the last of the Han forces fled from their camp: he smiled and said, "We won! Gongjin, we…!"

Lu Su paused; Gongjin was slowly lowering his sword, and the smile was slowly disappearing from his face. The sword of authority hung from Gongjin's arm as the last of the adrenalin left him, at which point his grip failed and the heavy sword fell from his hand, landing on the hard ground and making a clanging noise that somehow distressed those who heard it. Sun Yu, Sun Jiao, Cheng Pu, Zhou Tai and Pan Zhang cried, "**Chief Commander!**" simultaneously as they rushed to Gongjin's side: he was staring vacantly in the direction of the city of Jiangling, where the next, familiar phase of the campaign would begin within hours.

"…Gongjin…?" Lu Su whispered.

Gongjin was in indescribable pain, but he found the strength to ask, "They're… they're gone…?"

Lu Su fought tears of guilt as he replied, "Yes. They're gone."

"**Chief Commander!**" the generals cried.

"Get… me inside," Gongjin pleaded.

"**Quickly: get the Chief Commander to his tent at once!**" Sun Yu ordered: a number of worried soldiers and officers assisted Gongjin's bodyguard force despite their being no need.

"What are your orders, 'Acting Chief Commander'…?" Cheng Pu asked as he turned his horse and glared at Lu Su.

"Now that the threat has passed, Veteran General, we can return to the city walls and end this once and for all," Lu Su replied wearily. "I know less about such things, so the Chief Commander has said that you can oversee that next crucial phase."

Cheng Pu turned and stared at the sword of authority, which was still on the ground where it had fallen; Cheng Pu dismounted, walked to the sword and picked it up with obvious reluctance.

"I will go to the Chief Commander," Lu Su announced. "The rest is up to you, Veteran General Cheng."

"...I did not want to hold this sword," Cheng Pu retorted. "I have failed to earn it!"

"All the same, you'll have to wield that sword for the rest of the campaign," Lu Su said with a smile. "I can barely lift the thing."

Cheng Pu stared at the sword of authority as Lu Su retreated into the camp; Han Dang returned from chasing the enemy away moments later and rode to Cheng's side, saying, "They're going back into the city: we should allocate more men and keep them trapped in there."

"...Agreed," Cheng Pu replied. "Let's not make what might be Gongjin's last great effort a wasted one. Throw everything we have at that city: Cao Ren won't be coming out again!"

Gongjin was settled into his bed after the process of removing his armour and battle robes was finally completed: he somehow resisted the urge to scream or cry despite the pain, and his sacrifice moved every one of his subordinates and left many of them feeling ashamed. Gongjin ordered the officials to withdraw with the exception of Lu Su, who was noticeably uneasy.

"Now... it is over," Gongjin said at last.

"...Do you really think so...?" Lu Su asked.

"He- ...*Aiee*.... he won't... come out of the city again," Gongjin replied. "We... can siege until... Cao Cao... orders..."

"...A full withdrawal...?" Lu Su supposed.

Gongjin nodded tersely.

"And then Jiangling will be ours," Lu Su said. "Nan Prefecture will be ours: and then we can liaise with Liu Bei for-"

Gongjin tried to laugh, but it was too painful.

"...You really think that he'll double-cross us," Lu Su sighed.

"Don't 'think'... *know*," Gongjin replied. "Next is... finding real allies for... next-"

"Don't talk," Lu Su pleaded. "Save your strength."

Gongjin nodded compliantly; he was quite aware that some of the most taxing battles were yet to come and that they were likely to be 'battles of the mind' that he might not necessarily win.

****

110

Cao Ren could not face the men that guarded the walls of Jiangling: he remained aloof in the weeks that followed his farcical retreat from the Jiangdong camp and left Chief Clerk Chen Jiao and General Xu Huang with the responsibility of maintaining a defensive posture and very little else. Cao Cao's Admininstrator of Runan and Acting Administrator of Dangyang, Man Chong, ensured that there was a steady flow of supplies into the region, but it was clear that there was no plan: many were unsurprised when a miserable and demoralised official from Xuchang brought a letter from the Chancellor of State, Cao Cao, that Cao Ren was forced to explain to his officials.

"...We have been ordered to withdraw," Cao Ren announced.

"*Withdraw*...?" Chen Jiao exclaimed. "Who will replace us?"

"That's up to the enemy," Cao Ren replied dryly.

"...You mean that we are to abandon Jiangling – Nan Prefecture – to the Suns...?" Chen Jiao prompted.

"Mengde makes it clear that this is a desperate action," Cao Ren replied. "Yes, we could throw more men and food at this place, but after a year, we have nothing to show for our efforts, really."

"Their Chief Commander was shot and badly wounded!" Niu Jin protested. "They try to hide it, but he was harmed! Yes, he – or some other man of a similar build and countenance – charged out of their camp and chased you away, but where has he been since? Yes, I know that there are reports of his conducting troop inspections inside their main camp, but has he *once* come to the walls in the last few weeks...?"

"His standards are always seen at a distance, and the morale of the enemy has remained high," Cao Ren countered. "Even if the man is dead, General Niu, it has changed nothing: that mocking letter that they sent us spoke of 'bushels of capable men' and made it clear that there will always be someone to face. I reluctantly agree with and abide by this decree: we will send word to Yue Jin and Wen Ping and withdraw all of our forces from southern Jing."

"Jiangxia too...?" Chen Jiao exclaimed.

"Jiangxia too," Cao Ren confirmed. "Mengde – the Prime Minister – has placed an army in Huancheng and makes greater effort to pacify Lujiang and neighbouring Jiujiang, but everything below the Great River is theirs... for now."

"So where are we relocating to...?" Xu Huang asked.

"You and I will be stationed in Xiangyang and Fan, on opposite sides of the River Han, to administrate northern Jing, which is still very much ours," Cao Ren explained. "Man Chong, Niu Jin, Wen Ping and Chen Jiao will remain to support us in that endeavour, at least for now; Yue Jin is to travel to Hefei to reinforce that important place against the inevitable incursions to come."

"...I cannot believe this," Niu Jin said. "First Wulin, and now this!"

"Say no more," Cao Ren ordered. "None can know Heaven's will: we can only react to the situations in which we are placed and do what we believe to be right. I will withdraw to Xiangyang gladly: perhaps I can now visit my poor brother and aid his recovery."

The defenders of Jiangling were upset and frustrated, but there was no escaping the truth of the matter: they had failed, and the Suns had claimed the south of Jing Province.

"Our dream of a 'Jiangnan' is realised!" Sun Quan said to his Chaisang court. "Gongjin, even while injured, is a genius and a tiger of the battlefield: none can compare to him! The mighty Cao Cao has for a second time been forced to yield, and after years – *years* – of wasteful bloodshed, half of Liu Biao's province is ours, and the rest will surely follow!"
The courtiers murmured agreeably; Lujiang and Jiujiang Prefectures were now under the control of the Han government in all but a few areas, and Cao Cao had never lost his grip on northern Guangling, so there had been as much gained as lost over the last year.
"I can now return to Qu'e and personally oversee the last stages of the move to Wucheng," Sun Quan continued. "A great reorganisation will be needed: there are so many places to govern and only the same number of great minds to govern them, so I will need more, many more!"
"They will be found," Zhang Zhao promised.
"And after that, we must look ahead," Sun Quan said. "Lujiang and Jiujiang, Guangling and the 'four independent counties', they all need to be properly stabilised, and Jiaozhi, our southern neighbour, must pay proper tribute and understand that there must be a new relationship with us that ignores the decrees of the puppet Han government."
"...The Suns are now masters of a realm that recalls the Chu state of former times," Zhang Hong noted. "A mighty fleet burned to ashes, and now the corrupted Chancellor of State leaves Nan and Jiangxia to us: it can only be the will of Heaven!"
"I am increasingly convinced of it," Sun Quan replied. "And by Heaven's will our state shall have a name: my father was 'Marquis of Wucheng, and my brother 'Marquis of Wu'... and more and more, gentlemen, we hear the people of this region referred to by external parties as 'the men of Wu'. So as our new capital will be Wucheng, let our state be known to all as 'Eastern Wu'! We shall march onward to bring new prosperity and peace to all!"

The reaction was far from universally praising, but the majority agreed to it: less would be said of 'Southern Yang', 'Jiangdong' or 'Jiangnan' in the future, and more would be said of 'Eastern Wu', a state that was, in effect, opposing the ailing Han Dynasty for control of the south of the empire if not the entirety of it. That would not sit well with some of Sun Quan's officials, but for many of them – and for the population of the south as a whole – it was a necessary move if the south was to continue to enjoy the relative prosperity that it now enjoyed. But none could ignore one sure consequence: a long and costly war with the Han government and the vengeful Chancellor Cao Cao.

∗∗∗∗∗∗∗∗∗∗∗∗

ACT IX: PLANNING FOR THE FUTURE

111

A pivotal moment had passed: the Sun clan, long-time rulers of the southern Yang Province region that was better known as Jiangdong – or 'East of the River' – had now defeated the Han Dynasty's Chancellor of State, Cao Cao, on two separate occasions despite the odds being against them, and most of southern Jing Province – which spanned the central south of the Han Empire – was now under their control, creating a 'Jiangnan' – 'South of the River' – that in many ways evoked the ancient Chu State that had become a model for all states and empires that followed. The Sun clan chieftain, Sun Quan, had previously defeated Huang Zu, the semi-autonomous ruler of southern Jing and nominal subordinate of the Governor of Jing Province, Liu Biao: that victory avenged the death of his hero father, Sun Jian, at Huang Zu's hands and put an old matter to rest after close to two decades, but it had allowed Cao Cao – who was uniting the north of the Empire by eliminating all of the 'rebellious' warlords, bandit armies and tribal confederacies that ruled the various regions – to invade northern Jing and challenge the Suns for their perceived 'sedition'.

The Battle of Red Cliffs became the first of the two great victories that were overseen by Sun Quan's prodigious Chief Commander, Zhou Yu: the second – the siege of Jiangling – ended after a year of draining stalemates, although it was offset by the complete loss of northern Yang Province – Lujiang and Jiujiang Prefectures – to Han forces. The outcome was, nonetheless, a crushing blow to the already-weakened Han, a dual humiliation for Cao Cao – who had, until Red Cliffs, seemed to be indestructible – and it allowed Sun Quan to ponder names for his growing state: 'Eastern Wu' became the popular choice, as it evoked titles awarded to Sun Quan's father and elder brother – the infamous Sun Ce – by the Han and made Wu Prefecture – site of the Sun's home town of Fuchun – a capital within a defined independent region that would dictate its own destiny. Zhou Yu – whose courtesy name was 'Gongjin' – was far from done, however: he was duty-bound to honour his late friend and brother-in-law Sun Ce – whose courtesy name in life was 'Bofu' – and, like many others, Zhou felt that 'Heaven had spoken' when Cao Cao was humbled, but his grander plans for his lord Sun Quan meant that the worst of the fighting was yet to be seen.

"...I wonder why Heaven favoured me and not them," Sun Quan said to his senior servant Gu Li. "I am not the hero that Father was; I'm not the great warrior that my brother Bofu was. Why has Heaven chosen me to bear this great burden? Is it because they failed to see that the Han government was corrupt and chose to serve it, and I have chosen differently...?"
Gu Li was silent: he was assisting his lord with preparations for a meeting in the grand audience hall, and time was against him.
"...I suppose that it's unfair to ask you such things, Li," Sun Quan chuckled. "How long now until you are free...?"
"Not long, Lord Sun," Gu Li replied.
"...Good," Sun Quan said. "When you are no longer indentured, I will gladly bring you back with immediate effect as my Senior

Attendant, and Zhuge Jin can be permanently reallocated: you will enjoy the trust that you have now, but not the wearisome, servile duties. They can be another's of your choosing, since you know my other servants so well."

"I will choose appropriately, Lord Sun," Gu Li replied.

"...I wonder who I should send to take Huancheng," Sun Quan said. "I know that Gongjin will ultimately choose, but I should like to guess correctly, so that- ...so that I might impress him... *reassure him*."

Gu Li hummed in response.

"...He'll be fine, I know that," Sun Quan continued. "He'll be fine, and we'll take Lujiang and Jiujiang; after that, we can choose whether we go west, south or north. There is so much to do..."

"Indeed there is, Lord Sun," Gu Li replied; he knew that Sun Quan was actually thinking about the life-changing – and potentially life-shortening – wound that Gongjin had sustained toward the end of the siege of Jiangling.

"...In times gone by, my brother Bofu relied not just on Gongjin, but on Ziheng... Lü Fan, I mean," Sun Quan said. "I wonder whether I can do the same."

"He has served you well as treasurer," Gu Li noted.

"But his first role was as an adviser!" Sun Quan retorted. "Bofu was dependent upon the advice of both men, and Ziheng – Lü Fan – was, more often than not, the one that made the grandest plans! Does he still fear or loath me and deliberately fail to provide advice...?"

"I can answer that no more knowledgably than when you last asked, my lord," Gu Li replied. "Perhaps he should be asked."

"...Or perhaps I should turn to Zhu Zhi, who served my father and uncovered my cousin's plot to betray me to Cao Cao," Sun Quan said. "I realise that I cannot put the entire burden of fate on Gongjin's shoulders now that he is weak: he *must* be given a chance to recover so that he can finish what we have started."

"...I thought that Mister Lu Su was Acting Chief Commander," Gu Li prompted.

"Your observation is correct, but Gongjin worries that Lu Zijing's idea of a 'power tripod' – where Sun, Cao and Liu temporarily contend for the empire as near-equals is... 'potentially harmful', and so Gongjin prefers that I don't take too much advice from the man," Sun Quan explained. "*I* dislike the idea of Liu Qi – or Liu Bei – having the power to match me, but if it is only *temporary*... mind you, I dislike the obvious hesitation that Liu Bei is showing when it comes to yielding the 'four counties' to their rightful owner. I am the lord of Jiangling, therefore I am the lord of all of the lands that form part of Jing below the Great River: am I not then the lord of those counties...? ...And the notion that we are being diplomatic because their 'true governor', *Liu Qi* – the son of Liu Biao – must be appeased is sickening. Why should I appease the son of my father's murderer?"

"You offered condolences to him prior to the truce that saw Sun and Liu fight Cao Cao together," Gu Li replied. "I had thought that the diplomacy was in order to avoid accusations of faithlessness."

Sun Quan pondered the point for a moment, laughed and said, "You really are a clever man, Li! I should probably entrust more to you when you are free!"

"I am not worthy," Gu Li replied.

"Ah, but I imagine that you will become worthy, as I have," Sun Quan said. "Yes, it is Heaven's will: the south is the birthplace of a great upheaval. Cao Cao thinks that Red Cliffs was the worst of his losses and humiliations: the worst is yet to come!"

Sun Quan entered his Chaisang City audience hall and observed his changed court: there were a number of faces that had not been seen since the 'Red Cliffs Dilemma' began, so he was compelled to say, "Before we talk about the situation in each place, Chief Clerk Zhang, might I be acquainted and reacquainted with my court...?"

Zhang Zhao coughed deliberately and replied, "Yuan Yao returned only this morning; Liu Ji has been here for several days but was waiting for the right moment to appear."

"...Very good," Sun Quan said as he stared at the humble face of Liu Ji. "It is good to see you again, of course, Mister Liu."

"Heaven has spoken: it is only right that I should be here to show my allegiance, Lord Sun," Liu Ji replied. "My father fought with your brother's lord for control of this region, the latter citing that the Han's day was over: though I ache at the thought of our clan being stripped of the Mandate of Heaven, it is the Cao clan – and before them, Dong Zhuo – that harm the Son of Heaven, and they can only do so because he lacks the protection of Heaven. The fleet burned and Cao fled: the Suns must now act accordingly."

Sun Quan smiled and turned to Yuan Yao, who said, "Brother-in-law, I am here once again to offer my support, and I will not abandon you again. My father allowed jealousy and madness to make a cruel liege lord and seditious villain of him, and I must confess that I did, for a time, fear that the same had happened to you: that was a foolish thought, for you obviously have Heaven on your side."

"...You are both a most welcome sight," Sun Quan said as his eyes scanned the room for more returning faces; he caught sight of one man that was lurking at the rear of the line of officials and asked, "Is that Xu Sheng that I see...?"

Xu Sheng nodded meekly and said, "It is I, Sheng, returned to beg forgiveness for my faithlessness and request that I be allowed to atone with good service in the years to come."

"You cannot expect to receive a colonel's rank again, Xu Sheng," Zhang Zhao heckled. "Even I, Zhao, had doubts, but I remained loyal! Men like Yuan Yao and Liu Ji walked away for a time but insisted that they knew Lord Sun to be a good man! You came here and tendered your seal, pontificated as though you were an Appraiser and sauntered out of here with your head held high! Now you slither back and hide in the back ranks, simpering and-!"

"That's enough," Sun Quan ordered. "I agree, though, that you were quite pompous, Xu Sheng, when you resigned your civil and military posts: you will have to earn them again."

"I will, Lord Sun Quan!" Xu Sheng promised.

"...You shall be a captain, serving under other officers," Sun Quan declared. "I hope that the experience will teach you true humility."

Xu Sheng bowed penitently.

"...And I see new faces," Sun Quan prompted.

"From Wushang in Kuaiji, we have Luo Tong, styled 'Gongxu'," Lü

Fan reported. "He is the son of Luo Jun, the late Chancellor of Chen County City in Runan, and stepson of-"

"Luo Jun...?" Zhang Zhao interrupted. "If I am not mistaken, young Mister Luo, Yuan Shu killed the administration during his last campaign against the Han government: my condolences."

The 16-year-old Luo Tong bowed humbly and said, "It is no fault of yours, Mister Zhang, nor is it the fault of Lord Sun Quan."

"I extend my own sorrow at your loss," Yuan Yao declared. "It was my father that killed yours, and that is a painful thought."

"We do not have any reason to quarrel, Mister Yuan," Luo Tong replied. "As Mister Lü Fan was about to say, I am, by cruel fortune, the stepson of the Sun clan's enemy Hua Xin: I opted to distance myself from my mother when she married that villain out of pure necessity and later moved to Ji Province with him."

"Oh...? You can't have been more than thirteen when Hua Xin fled Yuzhang," Sun Quan said. "You are quite resourceful and independent, then, Mister Luo. What role do you currently hold...?"

"I am a fully qualified official, so I hold a position in my hometown as a clerk," Luo Tong replied.

"...You lack the experience necessary for the highest offices in the state, but I shall ensure that your superiors promote you properly and keep me informed of your progress," Sun Quan said carefully. "In a few years, Mister Luo, we will speak again and we can see what you should be doing."

Luo Tong bowed humbly and replied, "Thank you, Lord Sun."

"...And that fellow there," Sun Quan prompted as he looked at a thin, timid man in plain robes. "Who is he...?"

"That is Kan Ze, styled 'Derun', from Shanyin, which is also in Kuaiji, of course," Lü Fan reported. "He is also a fully qualified official with a particular interest in calendars."

"...*Calendars*...?" Zhang Zhao chuckled. "The-!"

"Stop being petty," Lü Fan said. "Are calendars useless...?"

"No, but I wonder why you should feel the need to mention it," Zhang Zhao retorted; he then turned to Kan Ze and asked, "From which 'Kan' clan do you hail...?"

"I am 'low-born'," Kan Ze replied. "It is therefore unlikely that you will know my clan well, Mister Zhang."

Sun Quan's close friend Zhu Ran frowned, turned to Quan and said, "Zhongmou, he's a *peasant*: how can he be 'fully qualified' if he hasn't-?"

"That's unfair, son," the elder statesmen Zhu Zhi said angrily. "Many of our greatest contributors are 'peasants'."

"In the army, perhaps, but in the *court*...?" Zhu Ran protested. "Even if there are a few men that have 'risen from nothing' here today, we are about to emerge as a state to rival or even-!"

"I think that you should say no more," Sun Quan said. "Mister Kan Derun, you are most welcome here in my court: what is your current position...?"

"Having recently joined the civil service, I am a clerk," Kan Ze replied. "I am also, for the record, nominated as a *xiaolian*."

"...Only the most honest men, the most loyal men, the most diligent men are considered for such an honour," Sun Quan said. "You shall henceforth be 'Assistant to the Magistrate of Qiantang', since that position is open, and when I have completed my reorganisation of Wu Prefecture's administration you shall be the

Magistrate outright."

Kan Ze bowed humbly and said, "Thank you, Lord Sun."

"Now I must move on to other matters," Sun Quan decided. "Mister Zhang, please briefly explain the state-wide situation."

Zhang Zhao coughed deliberately and said, "I shall begin in the northeast: in Guangling, Lü Dai maintains order effectively, and neither Cao Cao's appointed Administrator or the Shanyue cause trouble. In Wu Prefecture, work continues on the new palace in Wucheng and the Shanyue are once again making no trouble."

"After years of their mischief, that is a welcome relief," Sun Quan said. "Do go on."

"Danyang is also experiencing little trouble from the Shanyue, but rebels and bandits are another matter," Zhang Zhao continued. "Lu Xun and Hè Qi are the main operatives there, and Commandant Sun Shao does his part, but Lu Xun has indicated that Fei Zhan – our long-time problem in that place – will have to be dealt with sooner rather than later. Lu Xun also operates in Yuzhang, where he has identified the newly-returned Yòu Tu as planning the raids in Po County, and in Kuaiji, where he reports that Pan Lin is the main source of trouble, although…"

"…'Although' what…?" Sun Quan prompted.

"…The Administrator of Kuaiji, Chunyu Shi, has said that he feels that Lu Xun is 'cruel and oppressive', my lord, and doing little to help matters," Zhang Zhao replied. "I think that he refers to the 'aggressive' tactics that Mister Lu uses to force tax evaders to pay their dues and other such things."

"Nobody should be defending tax dodgers," Lü Fan suggested. "Every coin that they fail to pay leads to rises for the rest and diminished resources that harm the state."

"…Thank you, *Chief Treasurer*," Zhang Zhao retorted snidely. "All that I do is report what I am made aware of! When, exactly, did I 'defend' anybody…?"

"You didn't, but Chunyu Shi did," Lü Fan replied. "Perhaps it is he that needs investigating… although we *must* take his complaint seriously, Lord Sun, much as it pains me to say."

Sun Quan turned to the official Gu Yong and said, "You are most diligent, Gu Yuantan: please look into this 'complaint'… and also the complainant."

Gu Yong bowed and replied, "I shall."

"I shall continue," Zhang Zhao said. "Dong Xi and Jiang Qin are, as before, dividing their time between Kuaiji, Danyang and Yuzhang, depending on where they are most needed; Zhu Huan is managing the civil situation in Kuaiji, but sad to say, my lord, the plague has not yet fully subsided and the famine is far from over."

"I will go back to Kuaiji now that the whole 'Red Cliffs' thing is over, Zhongmou," Zhu Ran suggested. "I'll leave as soon as the meeting is over."

Sun Quan nodded slowly and said, "This is still a most troubled place, is it not."

"But the problems are now manageable," Zhang Hong promised. "With the threat of Cao Cao gone, we can manage well enough… provided, of course, that we do not overstretch ourselves."

"…There are very few officers here, Mister Zhang, else I think that remark might have solicited a bad reaction," Lü Fan said. "By 'overstretch' I presume that you mean our ambitions in the west and north...?"

"And *elsewhere*, truth be told," Zhang Hong retorted. "No conqueror-king ever built a nation by reaching out in all directions at the same time, Mister Lü. Can we really hope to demand tribute from Jiaozhi, annex Yi, contend with Liu Bei for the four counties and reclaim Lujiang *and* Jiujiang *and* the northern part of my native Guangling *all at the same time*...?"

"We do no such thing," Lü Fan insisted. "Guangling must wait, but Lujiang and Jiujiang are indeed reclaimable, and they are our priority now that Jiangling is secured: I detest the idea of Liu Bei seizing the counties – in fact I detest Liu Bei in general – but that's why I'm not venturing too many opinions at the moment. That's all left to Chief Commander Zhou Yu and his temporary replacement, Lu Su..."

Sun Quan sighed and said, "Indeed."

After the meeting, Zhuge Jin followed Sun Quan to his private study at Quan's request; once the two were seated, Jin asked, "Is there some concern...?"

"...Two," Sun Quan replied. "I am becoming increasingly worried about the suggestions that your brother and his lord are determined to hold onto the four counties, even if Liu Qi – the only man with any sort of right to them – passes away from his self-inflicted illness."

"I understand you worry and share it, but what can I do...?" Zhuge Jin asked. "I cannot come between lord and vassal, even when the lord in question is Liu Bei."

Sun Quan laughed and said, "I suppose so."

"...You had a second concern," Zhuge Jin prompted.

"I am noting a lot of whispers about deals with Ma Chao and Zhang Lu," Sun Quan said.

"I know nothing of that," Zhuge Jin insisted. "My brother would never work with the founder of the 'Theocratic State of Han'ning'. In fact, he was quick to decry not only Zhang Lu but also his 'creator', Liu Yan."

"Liu Zhang's father and predecessor as Governor of Yi Province," Sun Quan said needlessly. "Yes, I... I have heard many denunciations of that complex man as well."

Liu Yan's main legacies were convincing Emperor Ling to upgrade certain provincial Inspectors to Governors – which increased their autonomy and paved the way for the divisive 'super-warlord era' that followed – and employing the cult leader Zhang Lu for the purpose of seizing power in neighbouring Hanzhong Province without being directly blamed for it; Zhang effectively betrayed Liu and turned Hanzhong into the theocratic state of Han'ning, run according to the teachings of his family's cult, the 'Way of the Five Pecks of Rice', but Liu Yan maintained some control of Zhang by way of hostages that Yan's son executed within a year of taking power, losing his only leverage and allowing Zhang Lu to become completely autonomous. The Han despised Zhang Lu: he ruled the birthplace and namesake of the dynasty as an antithesis of everything that the empire represented, which was both an insult and an ill omen. But Zhang Lu's state – which had done away with coins in favour of a bartering, 'fair distribution' and reward system that used food, primarily rice, as its currency – was actually quite stable, and Zhang's following were fanatically devout, so there would be no easy solution.

"...I should not like to form an alliance with a cultist any time soon," Sun Quan continued. "It is not only abhorrent to me but also too similar to the actions taken by Yuan Shu in times past, and I will do nothing that likens me to that wretch."
"As I said, I know nothing of it," Zhuge Jin replied. "Perhaps it is some idea of the Chief Commander's...?"
"...Gongjin is, I confess, rumoured to be the architect of this plan, although no one dares to broach the subject properly so far," Sun Quan said. "It is just whispers... but whispers can develop into ideas, and I must know what path my new state takes else how can I truly be its ruler...?"
"I am sure that the Chief Commander intends to inform you of any actual actions taken," Zhuge Jin replied.
"I should hope so!" Sun Quan chortled. "Ill or not, I would reprimand him for reaching out to Zhang Lu *or* Ma Chao without consulting me first! We've spoken of Zhang Lu, but is Ma Chao – a violent savage whose father fought mine – any better...? Are the Qiang any less a worry than the Shanyue of Jiangdong...?"
"History suggests not," Zhuge Jin replied.

The Qiang tribes of Liang Province – which made up most of the northwest of the empire – were one of the indigenous peoples of the region, but internecine warfare had hollowed them repeatedly over the generations and enabled the Han Chinese to settle and build around them. The forced coexistence was far from peaceful: the Qiang would often raid Han villages and take people as slaves or consorts, and the Han would continuously encroach on the lands that the Qiang still held in an effort to integrate and assimilate them. But at the same time, there were compromises: some Han people actually left their own civilisation and joined the Qiang, although that was often because of the poverty and famines that struck the poorly-supported settlements that they came from, and Qiang men joined the Han army. As such, Liang was a 'melting pot': the Qiang, the Hu and the Di – who were the larger ethnic groups – existed alongside each other and the Han people, and that was the way that it was.
     The widespread corruption caused by the 'Ten Attendants' during the reigns of Emperors Huan and Ling brought the divisions and tensions to a point of no return: the Governor of Liang committed one offence too many and the region was beset by rebellion just a year after the Yellow Turbans had been successfully quelled. The leaders of this new uprising – a joint effort by disaffected Han Chinese peasants and the Qiang tribes – changed over time, but by the time that the crisis ended, three men had emerged as great warlords: the former Han officials Ma Teng, Han Sui and Song Jian. None of the three identified as Han men any longer, however: they were married to Qiang women, raised their children as Qiang and ruled large confederacies of Qiang tribes. The rebellion had ended with a stalemate: the rebels were on the verge of being defeated by a Han force that was led by Commander-in-Chief Huangfu Song and the treacherous

General Dong Zhuo, but Emperor Ling died at the critical moment, forcing the Han army to withdraw and leave the provincial leaders to fend for themselves while proper funeral proceedings and succession debates dominated the imperial capital.

Song Jian retreated into a primarily defensive state to the north of Liang, while Ma Teng and Han Sui contended for power with each other and with Dong Zhuo, who quickly ingratiated himself and bought their allegiance when he became Chancellor of State. When Dong Zhuo was assassinated by his foster son, Lü Bu, a power struggle ensued in the designated capital, Chang'an, that ended with the rise of the 'co-regents' Li Jue and Guo Si, who were Dong Zhuo loyalists: the Qiang warlords then allied with the Governor of Yi Province, Liu Yan, and attacked Chang'an, ostensibly to rescue Emperor Xian from his ambitious regents but possibly with a view to putting Han scion Liu Yan on the throne. Liu Yan's true motives would never be known: his assault failed, and he died a year later from illness, leaving Yi to his little-respected fourth son Liu Zhang, who immediately pledged allegiance to the Han and made it clear that he was not an ambitious man at all. Ma Teng and Han Sui turned on each other and fought continuously, and they were near-irreconcilable until Cao Cao, as the new head of the government, approached them and brokered peace: the Qiang served as government militias at first, but Cao eventually demanded that Ma Teng hand himself over as a hostage and move to Cao's capital, which placed Teng's short-tempered son Ma Chao in charge of his father's tribes.

"Ma Chao is said, by some, to be as strong and talented as Lü Bu, but there are just as many that fear that he might also share Bu's capricious nature and lack of filial devotion, and his elevation to acting chieftain of his father's tribal confederacy only adds to the danger," Zhuge Jin continued.
"Yes," Sun Quan said. "Ma Chao would only be the lesser of two very controversial choices of ally because Zhang Lu's ethos is so radically different to anything that anyone else – including me – wants to follow. I know that Gongjin fears your brother's lord – I worry since he took the counties – but we cannot look to creatures in order to avoid doing business with villains."
"If I am ever given the opportunity to discuss that matter with the Chief Commander, I will stress that to him," Zhuge Jin promised.
"It will likely fall to me to do so," Sun Quan said with a sigh. "It must be discussed, come what may: the future of our entire endeavour might depend on such choices."

****

112

Cao Cao's abandonment of southern Jing meant that Sun Quan now controlled every major city along the path between the southeast coast of Han China and Yi Province's southeast border, while Liu Qi and Liu Bei had shared jurisdiction over Wuling, Changsha, Lingling and Guiyang that both Sun Quan and Gongjin were keen to bring an end to: the responsibility for all of the necessary advancements was Gongjin's, but his health was now in irreversible decline, so his thoughts turned to resolving as much as he could in as short a time as possible and leaving a legacy that could not be easily undone.

"I must ensure… that Zijing doesn't give *anything* to… to *Liu Bei*," Gongjin said as he tried to play a tune of his own devising on his seven-stringed qin; he was wincing at regular intervals, sometimes because of the pain and sometimes because that pain – which would drive other men to tears – was causing him to make mistakes and play badly. Gongjin's beautiful wife, Xiaoqiao, was watching and listening quietly despite wanting to beg her husband to stop overexerting himself and rest; Gongjin could sense her distress and said, "This is how I relax."

"I know you well enough, Husband," Xiaoqiao retorted. "You are said to frown disapprovingly if another musician makes a mistake, and have earned an unfair reputation for pedantry for it in the past: you cannot tolerate musical imperfection from anyone, not even *yourself*, so every time the pain makes you-!"

"I… I must learn to… *accept it*," Gongjin replied. "I am at war with… myself, my lady. I have made… mistakes, *serious mistakes*, that… have done damage, and I must learn to… to *live with them*."

Xiaoqiao exhaled softly and lowered her head.

"I must… face my imperfections," Gongjin continued. "Lu Su… must overcome his. Lü Meng… is not ready yet; Lu Xun is too busy, and… and Lü Fan is… unable to step to the front. I am still Chief Commander."

Xiaoqiao raised her head and asked, "Is there really no other man to take the pressure away from you…?"

Gongjin smiled and said, "People say I am a pedant for… for judging music. In all things, my lady, I am a pedant, obsessed with perfection; sometimes I… can allow for less than the best, and sometimes I… I cannot. For the state I demand… I demand only the best that… that even *I* cannot deliver."

Xiaoqiao nodded silently.

"I must stay here… in Chaisang… and oversee… the next phase," Gongjin continued. "Lü Meng, Ling Tong and… Gan Ning will… go to Huancheng and take it from the new city adm-m-ministrator, Xie… *Xie Qi*. I…! …Heaven forgive me, I can do no more."

Gongjin finally gave up on his attempt to play his *qin* and gestured to two concerned servants that immediately started to help him back to his sickbed.

"Will you now stay in bed…?" Xiaoqiao pleaded.

"Regrettably, my lady, the… the answer is 'yes'," Gongjin replied. "I… am truly spent. I… must leave it… to others… *for now*."

Xiaoqiao closed her eyes and lowered her head once again.

"…Zhang Lu… and Ma Chao… for a *pincer*," Gongjin mumbled as

he tried to use his plans as a distraction to take his mind off of the pain. "*Zhang Lu... Ma Chao...*"
Gongjin's plans involved seeking alliances with two of the most controversial figures in Han Dynasty China, but he was insistent: in the interests of employing a pincer that only the men of the northwest could assist him with, and with the uppermost thought in his mind being 'Anyone but Liu Bei', Sun Quan's Chief Commander proceeded to take initial steps toward a formal alliance with men that were not only enemies of Cao Cao and the Han Dynaty but, some felt, of civilisation itself.
"*Zhang Lu...* and *Ma Chao*," Gongjin wheezed. "Them... or a mongrel dog in Yòubeiping, if I must... but *never Liu Bei...!*"

Sun Quan had not had the time to visit his sister Shangxiang and ensure that she was making no mischief: he went to her temple 'training grounds' and waited for her to finish her routine.
"I was beginning to forget what you looked like!" Shangxiang joked as she approached her weary older brother.
"I am hard to forget, I think," Sun Quan grumbled. "My arms and body are unusually long, my legs unusually short, and my beard-"
"You're *just fine*," Shangxiang insisted. "Why are you here?"
"I want nothing other than to see you," Sun Quan promised.
"You defeated old Cao Cao," Shangxiang noted. "That's good: one less reason for us to be training, though!"
Sun Quan shuddered and said, "You'll not be stopping, though."
"Not a chance," Shangxiang replied. "There's still the Shanyue, and the bandits, and Cao Cao might come back. How's Gongjin?"
"He, uh... he'll be alright if he gets rest," Sun Quan said.
"Some say it was Liu Bei's fault," Shangxiang prompted.
"Cao's men shot Gongjin; I must be *fair*," Sun Quan replied.
"I asked about Liu Bei, and I was told that he's seen as a hero," Shangxiang said. "Is he really a famous hero...?"
"Why speak of him...?" Sun Quan asked cautiously.
"I just wondered," Shangxiang replied. "He's our ally, so-"
"He's more of an *acquaintance*," Sun Quan insisted. "And you shouldn't be worrying yourself with the politics of the day."
"Mother did," Shangxiang retorted. "Mother sat in on meetings."
"...That's true," Sun Quan sighed.
"We never get together anymore," Shangxiang continued. "Back then, we were like a family, and we always had dinners together, and... ... ...what happened...?"
"I'm not sure," Sun Quan replied.
"Lang says it's because of power struggles," Shangxiang said. "Maybe he's right: when Dad and Bofu were just soldiers, it-"
"Even if it is, dear sister, we must be grateful for the opportunity to become great," Sun Quan interrupted. "What good is family solidarity when it could be snatched away at a moment's notice by our masters...? As much as I care for our half-brother Lang, he talks nonsense: we lost Father when we were indentured to Yuan Shu, and we lost Bofu, Jizuo and Shubi when we were blindly loyal to the Han. We also lost Cousin Bohai, Uncle and Mother, and I lost my *son*; what power is it that we were struggling for then...?"
Shangxiang frowned and said, "I... I suppose so. But Boyang-"
"Don't speak of him by that name," Sun Quan ordered. "Don't speak of that traitor to our clan at all if you can avoid it."

"I'll do as I please," Shangxiang retorted. "We're all equals when it's about family: that hasn't changed, has it? I want to talk about him, and about Fu. They grew up with us, Quan: they were there, all the time. They were more like older brothers than cousins: sometimes I really thought that Dad had adopted them, and that they *were* our brothers. Don't you ever wonder how-?"

"Of *course I do*!" Sun Quan snapped. "And things *have* changed, Shangxiang: I'm the lord of a state, not a vassal warlord, and-"

"So I must bow and scrape to you, then...?" Shangxiang heckled.

"...No," Sun Quan said as he stared into his sister's fearless eyes. "I... it hurts to talk about Ben and Fu, because they betrayed me."

"Betrayed *us*, you mean," Shangxiang prompted.

"No, they betrayed *me*," Sun Quan admitted. "Elder Zhu spoke with them, and they both believed that they were working towards ousting me as chieftain for the good of the clan."

"They betrayed *us*," Shangxiang insisted. "Mother made you the chieftain, and we all agreed: Ben and Fu betrayed *all of us*."

"...Thank you," Sun Quan murmured.

"I want to know why," Shangxiang continued. "Dad treated them like his own sons and trusted them, Ben especially. Ben gladly stepped aside for Bofu to become chieftain; what changed...? It can't be your fault: something changed Ben, made him different, because even Mother started to dislike him, and she really, really didn't want Ben as chieftain again. Was it his daughter marrying Cao Cao's son...? Did Cao Cao turn him against us...?"

"I don't know," Sun Quan replied.

"And what some people are saying... *you* sort of said it just now," Shangxiang continued. "What if all the deaths – Mother, Uncle, and our brothers – what if they were *Cao Cao*... or Ben and Fu doing it all for Cao Cao, or themselves...?"

"That's... always a possibility," Sun Quan replied uncomfortably. "But *please*, Shangxiang, do we have to discuss this...? I came here to see you and have a nice chat about ordinary things! I've just fought a costly war with the Han government and avenged Father's death by seizing Jing! I don't now want to darken the mood by discussing Ben and Fu: Ben's dead, Fu's in exile, and their sons – our cousins – have disowned their fathers and pledged allegiance to me. Let's leave it at that."

"Alright," Shangxiang said. "So have you seen little Shao...?"

"...No," Sun Quan replied. "He's been in Danyang, fighting-"

"Not Cousin Shao!" Shangxiang giggled. "I said 'little Shao': I meant our *nephew*!"

"Oh, yes, right," Sun Quan said uneasily. "Yes, I visited Daqiao very briefly before I went to Hefei, and the children were-"

"That was *months ago*," Shangxiang scolded. "Don't you *want* to see your nephews and nieces grow up? I bet you haven't seen Lady Cao's boy either, or given any time to Lady Xū and Yi's-"

"I... am very busy," Sun Quan insisted. "I barely have the time to see my own family. I will try to find the time for a banquet soon."

"That'd be great!" Shangxiang said excitedly. "Little Shao, though, he's just like Bofu and Yi were! Throwing punches everywhere, and that grin...! When he grows up he'll be just like them, I think!"

Sun Quan shuddered and replied, "That... would be nice."

"He's only nine now, but one day we'll have another tiger!" Shangxiang continued. "He'll be another hero, like Bofu and Yi!"

"...That's right," Sun Quan mumbled.

"And a banquet will be fun anyway," Shangxiang rambled. "I haven't seen Hao, Yu, Jiao or Huan in a while; and Cousin Shao could come here from Danyang, and-!"

"I'll arrange something," Sun Quan interrupted. "I... have to go."

"Already...?" Shangxiang exclaimed. "Alright, well... we'll talk again soon, won't we...?"

"We will," Sun Quan promised. "We most certainly will."

Shangxiang lunged at Sun Quan and hugged him tightly; Quan lightly tapped her arm as a sign of affection and retreated toward his bodyguards.

"Let's go," Sun Quan ordered. "She's fine: that's all that matters."

"As you command, Lord Sun," Song Qian replied.

Cheng Pu had returned to Jiangxia after the end of the Jiangling siege so that he could defend the capital city against any possible attacks by Cao Cao, Liu Bei, Liu Qi or any disaffected Huang Zu loyalists that might be lurking; Huang Gai joined Cheng briefly so that the two could enjoy a meeting over tea before Huang began his journey back to Danyang.

"You'll be looking after yourself...?" Cheng Pu asked.

"Yes," Huang Gai replied. "I must be ready to fight at all times."

"*Ayah*...! Don't think for a moment that you'll be called upon!" Cheng Pu said. "You've done your part for the cause now, so-"

"Have I...?" Huang Gai retorted. "I am not ninety, and even if I was I'd still want to do more. I wrote a deceitful letter and guided some boats: is that all that I want to be remembered for...?"

"...Is that really how you see it, Gongfu, or are you being falsely and irritatingly modest...?" Cheng Pu asked.

"I cannot see Red Cliffs as being my 'greatest moment'," Huang Gai protested. "The Chief Commander agreed with my plan, but he had the same idea: if I had not aided the ruse then another – Yigong, perhaps, or *you* – might have been the one to bask in glory. I believe that I can do more: I don't want to be like Taishi Ci and die an ignominious death in a sickbed after so many-"

"Please... don't continue," Cheng Pu said emotionally. "What you say, it is true not just of Taishi but of Zhou, Zhou Gongjin, who after years of heroism is now condemned to end his career in a sickbed or at a desk!"

"...I wasn't thinking," Huang Gai sighed.

"You worry for your reputation: I say to you what I would say to Gongjin," Cheng Pu continued. "You might never take up another sword or ride into another battle on a horse, but the actions that you took ensured that others will do so in times to come, and your place in history is assured. To a hero, nothing is ever enough, but what they achieved, to the rest, is more than enough."

"...You really do respect him now," Huang Gai said.

"Gongjin...? He is a friend to me, even if he does not reciprocate the thought," Cheng Pu replied. "In all my years, Gongfu, I never thought that I would ever find a friend in a man like that: son of a high-born Han lackey, pedantic to the point of frustration, handsome and cultured yet content to befriend a wild tiger of the south and fight at the tiger's side like a brother against the state that reared him for 'better things'. Gongjin has forsaken a life of complicit contentment in favour of fighting for a principle: the

south has in him one of its greatest men. I have said it before, and I will say it again: yes, I once despised him, but now, he is a man that I would happily take orders from, knowing that he has the people's well-being foremost in his heart. Gongjin is like a fine wine: bitter to taste at first, but appreciated in time and all the more intoxicating for it. I am not even jealous of his great fortune in marrying Lady Qiao: he *deserves* that peerless beauty!"
Huang Gai smiled.
"I even have a greater appreciation for music and poetry, thanks to that man," Cheng Pu continued. "I can even see some of the flaws in my musicians' work for myself. And now he has given us a chance to build a great state, but it has been at the expense of his health; he wanted – wants – to do so much more..."
"Yes, and I want to do more as well," Huang Gai protested.
"Gongfu, I already respected you and saw you as a friend: I did not need to spend years re-educating myself to see that you are a hero and a good man as I did with Zhou Gongjin," Cheng Pu retorted. "We've fought together for years, first under Wentai's flag and then under Bofu's: both were an honour to serve. Now we serve Lord Sun Quan: he will build a state to rival the Han and hopefully surpass it, and it will be joint effort, because he is not the hero that his father and brother were, and he knows that. Many men will contribute to that state, and it will take years: neither of us will probably live to see it take its final shape. We must both be content with whatever Heaven deemed to be our contribution: yours is the stuff of history, and so you must smile and say, 'Enough'."
Huang Gai lowered his head and exhaled loudly.
"There is only one thing worse than a slow decline, and that's a surprise reversal of fortune," Cheng Pu continued. "Poor Yigong is confused and scared: his losses against Zang Ba and being deprived of a duel with Xu Huang have left him thinking that he'll die a 'nobody'. Why risk it...? Why fight again and see your career end with a surprise defeat when you can retire a hero and be remembered for the victory...?"
"...Your point is noted," Huang Gai said. "I was shot in the armpit: I am not as badly hurt as the Chief Commander, but I have lost the full use of the arm and suffer pain every day. You're right, Demou, I... I cannot and will not fight in the vanguard again."
"No, but you can be an inspiration to the heroes of the future," Cheng Pu replied. "Don't err and get back in the saddle, Gongfu, and end your career with a lame dog's whimper: end it with the tiger's roar that burned and sunk a fleet."
"...I shall miss our meetings," Huang Gai said.
"There will be others," Cheng Pu insisted. "There are always lulls between conflicts; you, me, Yigong and Junli will meet again soon enough to talk of old times. And this meeting is not yet over!"
The two men drank and talked for a while longer, and then they parted: Huang Gai returned to his civil work in Danyang, and Cheng Pu remained in Jiangxia. The two would meet again in a matter of months, but under the oddest of circumstances.

✱✱✱✱✱✱✱✱✱✱✱✱

113

The city of Jiangling was now under the control of Acting Chief Commander Lu Su and Acting Deputy Chief Commander Lü Meng; Lu Su was unhappy with the idea of working with a 'famous idiot', despite Meng proving to be a future genius during the relief of Yiling City.

"You do little to hide your contempt for me, Acting Chief Commander Lu," Lü Meng prompted.

"I don't have contempt for you, General: you're a fine soldier," Lu Su replied. "And I don't want to waste time on how we all get on: we have a lot to deal with. In-keeping with Gongjin's desire to have more fine minds in our stable, I have tried to secure an audience with the famous 'Young Phoenix' Pang Tong, but he is claiming to be busy."

"He probably desires an audience with Liu Bei over our lord Sun Quan, since his friend Zhuge Liang is with Bei already," Lü Meng said. "Forget him."

"…You know who Pang Tong *is*, at least," Lu Su sighed.

"There are five main concerns," Lü Meng continued. "The first is the pacification of Jiangling: that does not require both of us. The second is the reclamation of Lujiang and Jiujiang: I am going to be leaving soon in order to build a fortified position at Ruxu and seize Huancheng, which will give us a road to Hefei."

"Gongjin's suggestions, of course," Lu Su said dryly.

"…The third concern, Mister Lu, is the acquisition of Yi Province, which is a priority after the toadying support that Liu Zhang offered to Cao Cao during the siege of Jiangling," Lü Meng continued. "That will require a large military campaign that the Chief Commander is insistent on leading personally with the lord's cousin Sun Yu as his second, so-"

"If he *must*, A'Meng, he can entrust such matters to you, because you are a great field general and Liu Zhang will require no subtlety, although there are others that might get the chance first," Lu Su interrupted. "What is the fourth concern…?"

"…I really wish that you wouldn't call me by that offensive name, Acting Chief Commander," Lü Meng retorted. "Yes, I was a fool, but when you see a man that you have not seen for three days, you should view him again, with a new eye."

"I've seen you often enough over the last three *years*, Acting Deputy Chief Commander, and view you accordingly," Lu Su said. "What is the fourth concern…?"

"…The fourth concern is Jiaozhi," Lü Meng replied sadly. "Shi Xie is an upright man, devout to his peaceful Buddhist faith, but-"

"There is no 'but'!" Lu Su chortled. "Honestly, A'Meng, you ask me to 'view you with a new eye' and then suggest thoughtless violence against a place and a man that are of no threat to our lord! …*Honestly*."

"It is a concern that the Chief Commander has, and Lord Sun agrees," Lu Meng said. "And I believe that they also agree on the fifth concern… *Liu Bei*."

Lu Su frowned condescendingly and shook his head.

"Those four southern counties that Liu Bei took with such ease while we shed blood in the siege of Jiangling should now be returned to us," Lü Meng continued.

"No," Lu Su replied. "I am aware that there is a lot of mistrust, but we also have to consider the size of Liu Bei's army here; Lord Sun has written to express concern at the possible threat Liu Bei now poses to our future enterprise, and wonders what we can do to placate him and maintain the alliance."

Lü Meng sighed sadly and said, "A regrettable but understandable stance: perhaps we need to consult the Chief Commander."

"Let poor Zhou Gongjin rest," Lu Su retorted. "I'm in charge, and I think that Lord Sun is correct. Liu Bei has helped us to get rid of Cao Cao, the least we can do is help him establish a temporary base for himself and his followers."

"But we must get from Liu Bei an assurance that he understands exactly who it is that now governs Nan Prefecture," Lü Meng protested. "He cannot stay in Jing as a warlord king: he'll have to remain here as a guest-subject, or go elsewhere."

"Yi Province," Lu Su said. "My lord supposes Yi to be the next target, as does Gongjin, and why should Liu Bei not take that?"

"The Chief Commander does not want Liu Bei to have Yi either," Lü Meng retorted. "He has already said that he sees Zhang Lu and Ma Chao as allies, sharing Yi with our Lord Sun."

"...So where does Liu Bei go...?" Lu Su asked.

"That isn't my concern," Lü Meng replied coldly. "So long as he isn't in Jing, or Yi, I do not care where Liu Bei goes."

Lu Su sighed and said, "I'm going to go to Gong'an and speak with Liu Bei. Perhaps we can resolve this without incident."

"Do not be fooled by Zhuge Liang," Lü Meng insisted. "Your shared 'dream' of 'Tripods of Power' should not take precedence here."

"...It won't," Lu Su promised. "But I argue again that Zhuge Kongming is an ally; he will help me find accord, I'm sure of it."

Lu Su turned and walked away; Lü Meng shook his head and muttered, "And he thinks that *I* am a fool."

Lü Meng led his army out of Jiangling, had them board ships and sailed past Jiangxia and across the Jiangxia-Lujiang border; he halted at Ruxukou, a port settlement in Ruxu County, and had the army camp around the city. Ling Tong and Gan Ning were being forced to work together on the campaign, and many subordinate officers – and Ling and Gan themselves – could see that it might be a bad idea.

"You don't seriously intend that we fight together in the vanguard, do you, Commander...?" Ling Tong asked of Lü Meng; the command tent was uncomfortably silent.

"...The state comes first, Commandant Ling," Lü Meng replied.

"Look, I know that Ling Tong won't like me agreeing with him, but I do," Gan Ning said. "We're never going to get on; can't one of us get another assignment so's we're not forced to-?"

"Lord Sun values both of you highly," Lü Meng replied. "Can you not repay his faith and strive for further merit...?"

The lower-ranking officers exchanged cynical glances.

"...Chen Wu; Han Dang; Zhou Tai; Pan Zhang; need I go on...?" Ling Tong said. "There are a number of men that could be here instead of either of us: I could be in Wu, taming the Shanyue, or that scabby pirate could be finding us some more faithless cutthroats in Jiangxia or some other place!"

Gan Ning exhaled angrily.

"You don't like my appraisal...?" Ling Tong heckled. "**Let us have it out here, then, Gan: you can either give your head to my father's altar or add mine to your vast collection!**"

"Really, I can go someplace else," Gan Ning protested.

"**You will both stop arguing and do Lord Sun's bidding!**" Lü Meng barked. "**I might not have the sword of authority, but my own sword is sharp enough!**"

Ling Tong and Gan Ning bowed slightly and lowered their heads.

"...I am 'Acting Deputy Chief Commander'," Lü Meng continued. "I expect obedience. We have a lot to do and speed is, as Sun Tzu has said, the key to victory: Cao Cao's adviser Guo Jia proved that many times before his death. We'll establish a proper base here at Ruxu, and then we'll go east to Huancheng, where we'll meet upon Magistrate Xie Qi, a mediocrity that Cao Cao has been forced to use because of the losses that we have inflicted upon him. Let us defeat this 'Xie Qi' and make Huancheng ours so that we can advance to Hefei!"

The officers responded enthusiastically; Ling Tong glared at Gan Ning, but Gan refused to meet his gaze and engaged in meaningless conversation with his subordinates.

Sun Quan was elated when Pan Zhang returned from Jiangling and asked for an audience that was immediately granted.

"It is good to see you, Wengui," Sun Quan said, "As you may or may not know, Zhu Yifeng has gone back to his capital, and I am once again surrounded only by men that only want to speak of ledgers and schemes."

"Such is the price of power," Pan Zhang quipped. "I can't stay long either: I have to go back to Xi'an in my capacity as Magistrate. There's another rebellion there, you know, and Dong Xi could use the help: I at least owe him for when-"

"Am I so despised...?" Sun Quan asked suddenly.

"...You're having doubts *again*...?" Pan Zhang exclaimed. "I hoped that winning Jiangling might help you understand that you're a great man, but-"

"I know that recent events point to my being favoured by Heaven, and even men like the Zhang brothers, who were raised to worship the Han, are becoming increasingly convinced of it, but I still have to wonder," Sun Quan said. "I might be an instrument, a tool, whose purpose is to clear the way for another, perhaps-as-yet unseen, hero of the age that will ultimately receive the Mandate of Heaven: what if that is my only role, and the signs are misunderstood...? What if my loss at Hefei, and Veteran General Han Dang's subsequent humiliating defeats at the hands of Zang Ba are also signs that I must heed...? What if Liu Bei-?"

"Liu Bei's a whining, grey-haired sandal weaver that dreams of great things but can't keep what he receives or steals: he won't keep those counties that he took while we were sweating blood, just as he didn't keep Xu Province on either of the two occasions when he stole *that*," Pan Zhang insisted. "You're hearing that from Pan Zhang, a gambler and a drunk that amounted to nothing until you placed faith in him; you know that Pan Zhang knows an opportunist and a loser when he sees one. That man is no emperor, no more than Yuan Shu was. And Cao Cao won't take

the throne either. If the Han are destined to fall, Lord Sun, then the throne will go to a *better man*: it will go to *you*."
Sun Quan smiled and said, "You always know what I need to hear... always. You are an asset, Pan Wengui."
"There are always rebellions because there's always someone that's unhappy with their lot," Pan Zhang continued. "The lot in Xi'an might be hungry, but I did open the grain bins for them so that can't be it. It might be Cao Cao, paying men to cause trouble: Liu Biao used to do that."
"...Even when Bofu was chieftain, there was constant trouble," Sun Quan recalled.
"Yeah, and he's who you're trying to do as well or better than, for some reason, instead of just being you," Pan Zhang said. "He spent his whole short life going backwards and forwards, up and down, here and there, trying to pacify everyone, and he never dealt with it all: you *inherited* most of this chaos."
"...But I will deal with it as I dealt with Liu Biao and Huang Zu, and with Cao Cao," Sun Quan decided. "Keep me informed of your work, Wengui: if you need more support, ask and I shall do my very best to provide it."
"I shall," Pan Zhang replied. "But no more worrying about whether you're worthy! And no more worrying about Liu Bei and his motley lot either; you'll get your four counties off of him sooner or later."
"I'd prefer 'sooner', but getting them will do!" Sun Quan said.

Lü Fan visited Gongjin without informing anyone of it; he sat by his peer's sickbed and asked, "Must I now take the reins before the carriage goes over the cliff...?"
"...No," Gongjin replied. "The unfit... are still better suited than... the disinclined."
"But as much as I am, as you put it, 'disinclined' – I prefer 'lacking the proper opinion' – we are now at a precipice, are we not...?" Lü Fan said.
"What is... your opinion...?" Gongjin asked.
"Liu Bei – a middle-aged disinherited scion of the imperial ruling family and self-styled 'sworn enemy of Cao Cao' – has exploited the rebellions in Lujiang and Gongjin's preoccupation with Jiangling and managed to gain an army of thirty-thousand and the four 'autonomous counties' to the south of Jiangling, all by deception," Lü Fan replied. "He gained the counties by promoting his ties to Liu Biao's exiled eldest son Liu Qi; he gained his new army by fawning on its former leaders without ever actually supporting them. Such a man is dangerous and should not be tolerated at all."
"He *is* dangerous," Gongjin agreed. "So dangerous that... we cannot risk open... confrontation... not *yet*."
"I cannot concur with that," Lü Fan said. "We've fought men that are as dangerous as Liu Bei before, and our victories came by just having the battle."
"You... like chess," Gongjin replied. "Take a week, an hour, a minute or... a year to move your piece... a move is a move."
"Pieces in a game of chess do not grow more powerful when left idle," Lü Fan retorted. "Liu Bei has the peculiar ability to become exponentially more powerful every time that he is defeated – provided that he is then underestimated and left alone – and the

more common ability to become more powerful when he is left alone in the first place. Don't leave him in Gong'an or he will outgrow our ability to control him."

"No choice," Gongjin said. "My... hands are tied, as it were."

"By your being injured," Lü Fan supposed. "I ask that I take the reins, then, and steer us to safety before Liu Bei somehow ends up with Jing Province."

"Not because... I'm injured," Gongjin replied. "I'm... waiting."

"For *what*, in Heaven's name...?" Lü Fan asked.

"...Zhang Lu... Ma Chao... and *Zhuge Liang*," Gongjin replied.

"Zhang Lu and Ma Chao?" Lü Fan exclaimed. "Have you written to them already?"

Gongjin shook his head and said, "Making... *enquiries*."

"I'd hope so," Lü Fan replied. "Those two are really a case of 'digging around at the bottom of the barrel', I must say, even though I understand why we consider it at all. But what are you waiting for from Zhuge Liang?"

"...What he plans for," Gongjin said. "What he plans... for Liu Bei: *he* is the danger, not... not Bei. Before he had... Zhuge, Liu Bei was... a joke."

"Well, you know best, since you've had the displeasure of speaking at length with both of them," Lü Fan sighed.

"Zhuge is... very clever, very cunning," Gongjin continued. "Until I can get... a true measure of his worth... I daren't risk a fight. Neither should you if... I cannot come back to court."

"That's a very euphemistic way of putting it," Lü Fan replied miserably. "Gongjin, I genuinely wonder if the state can last without your presence. I know that it isn't fair to you, placing such a burden on your soul, but I cannot lie to you: Lord Sun Quan is still hugely unpopular among some at court. The treasury is still mostly opposed to his appointment, even after eight years where not one coin has been misappropriated by our lord; Xuan City still has vigils for those who died due to his arrogance; and his decision to fight Cao Cao – and, by proxy, the Han – has done irreparable damage, for just as many failed to return as did."

"Xu Sheng... came back, I hear," Gongjin prompted.

"Yes, although he will rightly have to work to rebuild Lord Sun's faith in him," Lü Fan replied. "Bu Zhi has also expressed a desire to return."

Gongjin smiled and said, "Bu Zhi: that is the man... that I am glad to hear of...!"

"He's quite the, uh... 'professional', I suppose you'd say," Lü Fan replied. "Far from simply touring at random, he's been southward, to the Jiaozhi region, and learned more about Cangwu's Administrator, Wu Ju, and the Governor of Jiaozhi, Shi Xie. That, I imagine, is music to your ears."

"Very much so," Gongjin said. "Wu Ju... is a friend of Liu Bei. That's a man that we do not... not want... running Cangwu."

"*Aiee*... you're in pain that I don't want to imagine, and yet you insist on thinking constantly and talking when others would be screaming," Lü Fan noted. "What drives you, Gongjin...?"

"My duty... to Bofu," Gongjin replied. "And yes... I know that Lord Sun Quan... is still unpopular with some. I don't know what... to do about that. Perhaps... that is his problem alone, and not mine."

"...You might as well know," Lü Fan said. "Some of the lesser military minds increasingly look to Sun Jing's second and third sons, Sun Yu and Sun Jiao, as possible replacements, and there's the usual notions of Bofu's son being given the chieftainship when he is old enough to-"

"*No*," Gongjin insisted. "That will... cost us lives, and fracture the state. Tell them to stop."

"I cannot influence them, but I can refuse to entertain their ideas if they present them," Lü Fan replied. "Anyhow: Lü Meng has proceeded to Ruxu as planned, and I presume that Lu Su is going to Gong'an to speak with Liu Bei, since Quan Rou is going to Jiangling in some sort of 'temporary replacement capacity'."

"Correct," Gongjin said. "Soon, we... will know. Then, if I can just... recover... we can contact... Ma Chao, and-"

"You'll recover more quickly if men don't keep coming here and causing you to waste your breath talking," Lü Fan said as he got to his feet. "I am one of them: I shall therefore leave you and get back to work. Get better, Gongjin: get better and come back to us. We need you."

Gongjin smiled gratefully; Lü Fan bowed low as a sign of the great respect that he had for his friend and fellow adviser before he turned and departed.

Liu Bei's adviser, Zhuge Liang, was brother to Sun Quan's trusted attendant Zhuge Jin and a pivotal figure in the decision to unite against Cao Cao at Red Cliffs, but he was now, in the aftermath of that encounter, working toward building a state for his lord, even if it was at the expense of Sun Quan. It was Zhuge Liang that Lu Su visited when he travelled to Liu Bei's capital, Gong'an: days later, an ashen-faced Lu sent a messenger to Ruxu to inform Lü Meng that he was going to Chaisang to speak with Gongjin.

"So do you have to delay your departure and return to Jiangling now, Acting Deputy Chief Commander?" the official Qin Song asked of Lü Meng.

"Not at all," Lü Meng replied casually. "Jiangling can do without Lu Su and Lü Meng for a few days: my concern is what Liu Bei has said to cause Lu Su to go running to the Chief Commander when he was telling me to 'let him be' only a few days before."

"...He probably spoke to Ziyu's brother again," Qin Song said. "Zhuge Liang seems to be Liu Bei's primary diplomat as well as his main schemer; he lacks tact, and so does Lu Su, so arguments are inevitable."

"Zhuge – or whoever Lu Su spoke to – said something that caused concern," Lü Meng suggested. "But it matters little to me right now: I have a mission to undertake. Please inform Lord Sun, upon your return to Chaisang, that I have fortified Ruxu and begun the preparations for taking Huancheng in short order."

"I shall," Qin Song promised. "Good luck to you."

****

114

Gongjin learned of Lu Su's arrival from a servant and frowned; Xiaoqiao sensed that Lu had come to say something distressing, so she said, "Please don't have this audience, Husband! You had a bad night, and-!"

"I... suffer every night and every... *day*, my lady, even when I... have your beauty to gaze upon," Gongjin replied. "Zijing's my... *replacement*, and he wouldn't visit without... good reason, and Lord Sun... frets, so... so I must see him."

Xiaoqiao said no more: she retreated to a doorway and watched powerlessly as the servant that had brought the news of Lu Su's arrival scurried away to fetch him. The servant returned with Lu Su moments later; Lu smiled sheepishly and said, "Chief Commander... Gongjin..."

Gongjin turned to face Lu Su and replied, "Zijing... welcome..."

"You... ... ...are you better...?" Lu Su prompted.

Gongjin laughed momentarily and said, "You have... come here to talk. It must be important... for you to come all this way, Zijing. ...Speak."

"I only come here to see if you are well," Lu Su insisted.

Gongjin laughed once again – despite the pain that it caused – and said, "Lying was never... something you were good at. I insist... that you tell me... what Liu Bei said to you."

"What...!" Lu Su gasped.

"Lord Sun... has asked me about it," Gongjin continued. "It can only be that... Zijing... so out with it! Is it... about Yi...?"

"No," Lu Su replied.

Gongjin sighed and said, "Jing, then. Liu Bei... pleads to be allowed... to remain in Jing...?"

"...Not exactly," Lu Su replied.

"...Then... what...?" Gongjin prompted.

Lu Su lowered his head and replied, "He... uh..."

"Just *tell me*...!" Gongjin demanded.

"He has refused to cede the county seals," Lu Su admitted. "He threw me out of Gong'an."

"Faithless rogue...!" Gongin cried. "We should...!"

Pain halted Gongjin before he could say more: Xiaoqiao rushed to his side and glared at Lu Su, who said, "Rest yourself. There will be time to deal with them later."

"Please, listen to Mister Lu Su's advice," Xiaoqiao said.

It took several moments before Gongjin could speak again: he then said, "You haven't finished, have you...? What else... did *Zhuge Bumpkin* say to you...?"

"Nothing," Lu Su replied unconvincingly.

Gongjin smiled icily, chortled and said, "You're not fooling me. Zijing, we are friends: what did he say...?"

"...He accused us of being the ones to break faith, not Liu Bei," Lu Su reported. "He called Sun Quan the 'meritless son of a feudal vassal', and..."

"...*And*...?" Gongjin prompted.

"He... he said you were shallow, and vain, a 'beautiful song without true content or good intention'," Lu Su said. "He... he...!"

Gongjin grimaced at the words: his eyes wandered for a moment

before he said, "He...? ... ...**AAAUGH...!**"
Gongjin was wracked with pain and could not move: Lu Su gestured as an indication that he would say no more, but as soon as the pain became more manageable Gongjin retorted with a gesture that made it clear that Lu Su should go on.
"He... he cited your family's service to the Han," Lu Su continued. "He said you had betrayed your ancestors for personal ambition... he said that... that... that you were... ... ...'disgusting'... and... no better than Cao Cao..."
"...**BUMPKIN!**" Gongjin cried as he momentarily felt more anger than pain: Xiaoqiao tried to calm him, but her efforts were in vain. Gongjin was livid: his eyes bulged as he shouted, "**Wretch! ...Bare-footed cow-herder!**"
"...I refuse to continue," Lu Su mumbled.
"...He dared say *more*...?" Gongjin realised. "You... you *continue*, Lu Su...!"
"...I daren't!" Lu Su pleaded.
"You *must*!" Gongjin insisted. "Just... just *tell me*!"
Lu Su sighed and said, "He's deduced your scheme to ally with Zhang Lu and Ma Chao."
Gongjin's eyes wandered, and he silently mouthed, "How...?" That bewilderment was quickly replaced by fear and anger, as the lack of secrecy could have any number of consequences.
"He said that, with your 'unholy design' to put Jing in the hands of our 'two-faced master'," Lu Su continued, "and Yi in the hands of 'cultists and barbarians', he..."
Lu Su could see that Gongjin was shaking violently and that he was on the verge of a violent and potentially self-harming outburst: Lu shook his head as a sign that he would not go on, but Gongjin grunted angrily as an insistent prompt.
"...He jeered me," Lu Su continued, "asked me if we intended to make peasants or eunuchs out of them in our master's imperial palace; that we had always had 'sinister intention' to usurp the imperial throne and belittle the Liu house; that we were treacherous, and that we had played a sleight of hand against them, and that you... that... that you were a 'would-be kingmaker' for a 'shameless thief'."
Gongjin was gripped by rage and agony that stripped him of the ability to speak for a few moments: when he could answer, he said, "I... *swear*... that I will personally *gut* that fan-waving pedant... and Liu Bei...? No simple castration or... or servitude for *him*! I'll... dismember them *both*...!"
Gongjin succumbed to pain yet again; Lu Su lowered his head and mumbled something inaudible.
"Wha... *what*...?" Gongjin exclaimed. "There... is *more*...?"
Xiaoqiao glared at Lu Su, who deliberately ignored her and replied, "Kongming told me to return here and think about what he had said."
"*Please*, Mister Lu Su!" Xiaoqiao cried. "*Don't*-!"
"My lady," Gongjin said, "this... this is business. Please... let him speak."
Xiaoqiao covered her mouth, turned, and walked away.
"...He asked me to reconsider the Sun-Liu alliance, implied that we should be keeping to his and my plan of a tripartite state. He... that was all he said," Lu Su insisted.

"No, it... *wasn't*," Gongjin said. "Your... plan... is not to my liking... you know that, and... *he* knows... that... and as the lord's... c-confidante, it will never be so, Lu Su, n-not s-so long as I... ... ...that's it, isn't it...? ...He... told you to... think about it... f-for... *future*...!"

Lu Su wept and replied, "Gongjin...! I... do you see why I did not want to-?"

"Soulless **cow herder...!**" Gongjin screamed. "**Deviant r-rice p-picker...! ...Heartless, w-wicked pedant...!**"

Lu Su grasped at thin air and whined miserably.

"He... wishes *death* on me...?" Gongjin exclaimed. "He will... *he* will die... for this... Lu... *Su*...!"

Gongjin's convulsions became too disturbing to ignore: Lu Su turned to a servant and shouted, "A doctor... **GET A DOCTOR!**"

The servants gave in to panic and scattered in all directions as one level-headed youth left the house to fetch a physician; Lu Su touched Gongjin's arm, but he immediately drew his hand back as though some of the pain had been transferred to him.

"Zhuge... *Liang*...!" Gongjin croaked.

"**You should not have come here!**" Xiaoqiao shrieked.

"*No*, m-my... lady!" Gongjin replied. "He...!"

Gongjin passed out; Xiaoqiao rushed to his side once again, and Lu Su moved away and said, "I am sorry; I... I will leave."

"No... no, Mister Lu," Xiaoqiao replied. "Please... stay."

Lu Su remained at Gongjin's bedside until the latter finally regained consciousness; the two spoke briefly before Lu departed and Xiaoqiao took Lu's place at Gongjin's side.

"I frightened you," Gongjin whispered.

"You frightened us all," Xiaoqiao replied. "Your children-"

"I... am sorry," Gongjin said. "Lu Su is gone?"

"I believe so," Xiaoqiao replied.

"...I have had to yield my... authority to him, for my own sake," Gongjin revealed. "Heaven knows, it... it pains me more than my wound to do so, but... I will never recover while... I am burdened so greatly."

Xiaoqiao smiled and said, "So you are relieved of duty...?"

"By my own... hand," Gongjin replied. "I can't endure... such abuse... in such a weak state."

"...I *hate* Zhuge Liang," Xiaoqiao admitted. "Those things that he said, he-!"

"He was right," Gongjin said.

"He called you a traitor!" Xiaoqiao exclaimed. "He called you 'disgusting'!"

"...That part was unfair," Gongjin replied.

"What part of it was 'fair'...?" Xiaoqiao asked.

"...That I am plotting against the Han, and m-making... making use of 'barbarians' and 'c-cultists' to achieve my goals... that was true," Gongjin replied. "But to call my master 'two-faced' is hyp-po-pocracy... in the... ex-extreme."

"Say no more," Xiaoqiao pleaded. "I should not have-"

"I'm alright," Gongjin lied. "You're right... that none of the rest... was fair. But that is Zhuge's gift: he can b-bury one fact inside a ball of... of *distortions*, throw it and... and 'bring down the tower'. Zhuge uses my intention to... to ally with Zhang Lu and Ma Chao to… to brand all of my actions as unjust, so that… he can aggrandise that sandal-weaving whiner that… he has incredulously placed… his hopes for the rescue of the Han upon. Zhuge must… lay waste to other men's r-reputations in-in order to make Liu Bei sound… e-even *halfway* a *man*… so he must *know* Bei is no *hero*… so *why*…?"

"Do not try to make sense of it," Xiaoqiao insisted. "I'll leave you for now."

Xiaoqiao got to her feet and walked away; Gongjin stared at the ceiling and said, "*Why*, Zhuge…? …*Why*…?"

Lu Su met with Zhuge Jin as dawn broke on the following morning; Lu shook his head and said, "I am in charge of strategic matters now in all respects: you can thank your brother for that."

"…What has Kongming said…?" Zhuge Jin asked.

"I will not relay it again," Lu Su replied coldly. "Suffice to say that it nearly killed Gongjin last night: I have probably taken months off of his lifespan."

"*Aiee*…! So Sun and Liu are enemies now?" Zhuge Jin said.

"We are still allies, though reluctantly so," Lu Su replied. "Gongjin has conceded that the plans that he had regarding Yi, pincer attacks and the like must be put on hold: I intend to propose that we maintain our ties with Liu Bei – and Liu Qi, of course – and, perhaps, strengthen them."

"So Gongjin does not want revenge for the harsh words…?" Zhuge Jin prompted.

"Is that not what I just said, Ziyu…?" Lu Su retorted. "We must both speak with Lord Sun, and I must put a most unpalatable set of suggestions forward: if I am allowed to live and explain, then maybe – *maybe* – we might be able to avert a greater disaster."

Zhuge Jin was confused, but he nodded compliantly and followed Lu Su to Sun Quan's mansion.

****

115

The morning's court session began in Sun Quan's Chaisang audience hall: the mood was so relaxed that none could have expected the drama that was about to unfold.

"Welcome, all!" Sun Quan said to gathering of civil officials and military officers. "I am sorry that Veteran Generals Huang Gai and Cheng Pu cannot be here, but Veteran General Han Dang is a sight for sore eyes."

"You are too kind, Lord Sun," Han Dang replied humbly.

"I am aware that our operations to the north are proceeding well enough, so I should like to move onto other business straight away," Sun Quan continued. "Mister Zhang Zhao, if you would...?"

Zhang Zhao smiled and said, "I am happy to report that no situations have worsened: that, in this age, is a blessing. Kuaiji, Yuzhang, Danyang, Wu and Guangling are all being managed well enough. But before I continue with banal matters, I understand that 'Acting Chief Commander Lu' is here to propose something."

"You manage to make every word drip with venom, Zhang Zhao," Lu Su retorted. "Can you not be more cordial when-?"

"*Zijing*," Sun Quan said. "Mister Zhang Zibu is a familiar figure to you now: what is it that you have come here to 'propose'...?"

"My unease is tangible," Lu Su replied. "I... I am here to say that I am now authorised to make decisions at Chief Commander Zhou Yu's suggestion, provided that Lord Sun agrees, and-"

"He does!" Sun Quan snickered. "I have the utmost respect for you, Zijing, so why would I not be quite satisfied with your taking decisions if Gongjin – with whom I would entrust anything – has suggested it...?"

Lu Su looked at Lü Fan as he replied, "My first proposal will not be popular... but I plead that I be heard in full before I am judged."

"*Aiee*...! This timid little man is no Chief Commander!" Han Zong whispered; the lower-ranking officers to immediate left and right nodded in agreement.

"...What is so unpalatable that you don't just come out and say it, 'Acting Chief Commander Lu'...?" Zhang Hong asked.

"...I am here to propose that... that...!" Lu Su said weakly.

"*Zijing*," Sun Qian prompted sternly.

"...That Jing should be lent, *temporarily*, to Liu Bei, just until the numerous other problems that we have are dealt with," Lu Su declared; he was gradually drowned out by more and more heckles as he added, "**I... I only propose this... I only... I-!**"

"**SILENCE!**" Sun Quan barked: the heckling stopped.

"...This is terrible, even for *you*, Lu Su," Zhang Zhao said with theatrical regret. "Gongjin must be ill if he entrusted the fate of Jiangnan – Eastern Wu – to another, given his undeniable passion; he must be greatly mentally affected by the pain, methinks, to entrust it to *you*!"

"Don't start your usual antics, Zibu," Lü Fan interjected. "I, for one, want to hear this idea in full and as quickly as possible, as much as it sickens me."

"He's shared it already!" Zhang Zhao retorted. "And 'sicken' is right, Ziheng; of all the ideas this fool could proffer, *that* is the *worst*! To suggest, after all the blood shed, and all the coin spent...

that we must cede Nan Prefecture to Liu Bei???"

"No, no, ridiculous," Zhang Hong agreed. "That would never do."

"...I said 'lend', not 'cede'," Lu Su retorted: he then turned to face Sun Quan and said, "My lord, Gongjin is seriously injured: he will take a long time to recover, and that means he is no fit state to keep the wolves from the door. This plan pits the wolves and tigers against each other."

Sun Quan turned and looked at Zhang Zhao, who was suddenly lost in thought; after several moments Zhang smiled and said, "Mm... perhaps... perhaps, seen like that, my lord... ... ...Shall we retire to the private chamber to discuss it further...?"

"...Very well," Sun Quan replied as he turned to look at Lü Fan, who shook his head purposefully; he then turned to look at Zhuge Jin, who was obviously concerned at what Lu Su and Zhang Zhao were about to plan together.

"...It should be as small and closed a meeting as possible," Zhang Zhao suggested.

"...Yourself and Zijing, then," Sun Quan said.

"That would be proper," Zhang Zhao replied. "Others can be consulted if the need arises."

Lü Fan watched as Sun Quan, Lu Su and Zhang Zhao left the court and sighed, saying, "This... is *bad*."

Zhang Hong frowned and hummed thoughtfully.

"...But not, I trust, irrecoverable," Gu Yong said.

"No cause is 'irrecoverable'," Lü Fan replied.

Zhang Zhao waited until he, Lu Su and Sun Quan were all seated and said, "I understand your reasoning now, Zijing. It really could have marvellous benefits if played correctly."

"Really, Zibu, I am not a fool," Lu Su replied. "Remember that my original plan saw only a temporary tripartite situation, until we could isolate Cao by setting him against enemies from barbarian states, and then we would annex Jing and fight Cao as the stronger of two parties. I only placate Liu Bei and Zhuge Liang with my other rhetoric."

Sun Quan smiled and nodded; Zhang Zhao hummed thoughtfully and said, "So then Liu Bei would become an unwitting shield...?"

"Exactly so," Lu Su replied as he turned to face Sun Quan. "My suggestion is not, as Zibu obviously thought, an act of folly; if we put Liu Bei in Nan Prefecture he will then be seen as the intended beneficiary all along. That will placate the people – who are afraid that, due to the previous enmity between you and Liu Biao, you may mean them harm – and it will also direct any retaliatory action at Liu Bei, not us.

"It will be Liu Bei's troops, not ours, that will be pitched against Cao Cao... weakening him so that he will not be a threat in the future. It is a case of 'pitting two tigers against each other'... where only we will benefit in the long run. Once we are strong again, fully recovered from Red Cliffs and the sieges at Jiangling and Hefei, and Gongjin is back to full health... if we really want to, we can take it back."

"But still, Liu Bei is very strong now," Sun Quan said. "His troops now number close to forty-thousand: he has acquired strong generals, and able advisors."

"...What is your concern...?" Lu Su prompted.

Sun Quan frowned and replied, "With that much borrowed territory, he may try for Yi himself, jeopardising our own plans for managing that province."

Zhang Zhao smirked and said, "Well then, in addition to loaning him part of Nan Prefecture, I think we should enter into a marriage alliance with him."

"...*What*...?" Lu Su gasped.

"Your sister, Lady Sun, is not yet married, my lord," Zhang Zhao said. "Now-"

"No, no! That won't do!" Sun Quan insisted. "He is an old man, near sixty, my sister in the flower of her youth!"

Zhang Zhao waved his hand and said, "My lord, she has often spoken of wanting for her husband a true hero: why not the 'hero' Liu Bei...?"

Sun Quan groaned and retorted, "I expected an idea like this from *Zhuge Jin*, but not *you*! If I am to lend him Jing and my sister, why not let him borrow all of Jiangdong, and the clothes on my back...?"

Lu Su was silently pondering Zhang Zhao's suggestion: he smiled as he finally grasped his peer's intent and laughed icily, saying, "Ah, I see...! Very good, Zibu, very good."

Sun Quan raised both hands and cried, "*No*! No, no, why do you venture to *ruin me*...?"

"This has three advantages to you, and no disadvantages," Lu Su replied. "The first advantage – while it is the least meaningful in our grand plan – is obvious to all, and will obscure the other two from even the likes of Zhuge Liang."

"...Explain," Sun Quan demanded.

"First, you will be married into the Liu family: he currently lacks a wife, Ladies Gan and Mi having both passed away in recent times, which will ensure Lady Sun – who is young and beautiful – is of high status and priority," Lu Su replied. "Therefore, producing more children will be uppermost in Liu Bei's mind, and any children born of the marriage will be distant – yet significant – heirs to the imperial house."

"...So even if Liu Bei won out at first, we would still win in the end," Sun Quan said. "...Very good... very good...! ...What are the other two advantages...?"

Lu Su smirked and replied, "Secondly, Lady Sun's loyalty to you exceeds all else: even if, by some unwanted miracle, she actually came to love Liu Bei, she would still hold the interests of the Sun family foremost... making her an ideal contact that will provide us not only with general information, but perhaps also court proceedings and pillow talk that could have us knowing what Liu Bei intends to do even before his most trusted vassals find out."

"...Marvellous... marvellous...!" Sun Quan said. "I am convinced already; but still, what is the third advantage...?"

"In addition to being loyal, Lady Sun has the courage of a tigress, the spirit of a warrior... almost matching any man," Lu Su replied carefully.

"...It is true," Sun Quan said with regret. "Her antics are sometimes embarrassing."

Zhang Zhao leant forward and laughed cruelly, saying, "Think, then, what havoc she will cause for Liu Bei...!"

Sun Quan laughed with similar cruelty and said, "Indeed...! Oh, we

must make these things happen as soon as possible...! ...Zibu,
Zijing, your plans are wonderful, and accord well with my own
thinking. Go, quickly, and begin negotiations...!"
Lu Su and Zhang Zhao rose, bowed and retreated; Sun Quan
continued to laugh for a few moments until a thought entered his
mind that robbed him of his cheer and left him feeling distressed.
"...What will *she* say...?" Sun Quan murmured. "I...!"
Sun Quan's servant Gu Li entered the room and asked, "Is there
anything that I can do, Lord Sun...?"
"Your timing is perfect, Li," Sun Quan replied. "I have a problem."
"My ears are open," Gu Li prompted.
"...I have just agreed to a ruse that will see my sister Ren –
Shangxiang – married to Liu Bei, and my lands in Jing becoming
his by way of a loan," Sun Quan explained.
"I imagine that you forgot to ensure that Lady Sun Ren will
actually agree to the plan as well," Gu Li said knowingly.
"Yes: in my excitement, Li, I forgot that very thing," Sun Quan
replied. "She is, as you know, quite feisty, and intolerant of
discipline and protocol; what if she refuses outright, or feigns
agreement and ruins the plan further down the line...?"
"You must speak with her, Lord Sun, and be as honest as
possible," Gu Li suggested. "Perhaps you can convince her that
she will be performing a service."
"...It's worth a try," Sun Quan sighed. "I must go to her at once,
before some other fool alerts her to it; no, wait, such a discussion
in public...? She must come here to me."
"I know the very person to send to Lady Sun with this request,"
Gu Li replied. "I will fetch her at once."

Lu Su, meanwhile, returned to Gongjin's home and asked for
permission to sit by his sickbed once again: Xiaoqiao fled the
room, and Gongjin – who expected the worst – sighed and said, "I
entrusted matters to... to you as a way of sparing myself grief, but
I see that was... another bad decision: *speak*, Zijing, and finish
what your friend 'Kongming' started."
Lu Su was about to reply when a servant entered the bedroom
and said, "Mister Lü Fan has requested an urgent audience!"
"...What have you done...?" Gongjin asked as he glared at Lu Su.
"I... I simply proffered my original suggestion about letting Bei
have Jing for now," Lu Su replied. "But then Zhang Zhao started
talking, and he-!"
"**So he's here trying to justify it then,**" Lü Fan barked as he
forced his way into the room; several servants were trying to
quietly plead with Fan, but Gongjin dismissed them with a weary
wave of his hand.
"...It was not my idea, as I am sure that Zhang Zhao has made
clear, but you must see the merits of it!" Lu Su protested.
"Ceding Jing to Liu Bei...?" Lü Fan chortled. "Since when was that
Zhang Zhao's idea...?"
"...I thought you meant the other thing," Lu Su mumbled.
"What-! ...What 'other thing'...?" Lü Fan demanded.
"Before either of you continue, might I... ask whether I should...
know this 'other thing', for the sake of my health...?" Gongjin said.
"...You don't really have a choice," Lu Su replied. "I'll come right
out with it: Zhang's convinced Lord Sun – with my help, I confess

– to wed Liu Bei to Lady Sun."

Lü Fan covered his face with his sleeve and exhaled loudly; Gongjin tried to supress laughter – if only because of the pain that it caused – as he said, "Please, Zijing, tell me... tell me that... you mean one of Lord Sun's... *nieces*, *cousins*, or, at worst, his *half-sisters*, and not...!"

"...I wish I could, Gongjin," Lu Su replied.

"So... what does 'Lady Sun'... have to say...?" Gongjin asked dryly. "Do we... know yet...? Am I to... expect *her* here next, with... her armed women, blaming *me* for this...?"

"I will, of course, accept responsibility for it, and so will Zhang Zhao," Lu Su promised.

Lü Fan lowered his arm from his face and cried, **"You're damn right you will! What kind of naïve simpleton *are* you?!"**

"Leave him, Ziheng," Gongjin said. "This... is Zhang Zhao's poor attempt at intrigue that Zijing had little choice but... to be an accomplice to. We must now... improvise accordingly, once we... know that Shangxiang... will agree to it."

"And if she doesn't...?" Lü Fan asked.

"Then Zhang will be forced to forget it," Lu Su insisted. "I won't be pushing the idea anymore."

"Have you even been our lead mastermind for a *day*, Lu Su...? And *this* is what happens...?" Lü Fan said disbelievingly. "I've half a mind to-!"

"You'll... remain in the shadows," Gongjin interrupted. "You want to... fight Liu Bei, and... we discussed that already. Let this story tell itself, and... plan accordingly. Now please... both of you... I need to *rest*."

Lu Su and Lü Fan glared at one-another as they left the room and then the house; Xiaoqiao returned to the bedchamber once they had departed and asked, "Are you alright, Husband...?"

"I *must* recover soon," Gongjin replied. "No one can do this except me: I *have* to recover."

Xiaoqiao did not ask what Gongjin meant; she returned to his side, held his hand and sighed miserably as he muttered to himself and shook his head.

****

116

Sun Quan sent a trusted maid to his sister Shangxiang's 'training ground' with orders to summon her to his study; Shangxiang grinned as she entered the study and said, "What did you want then, 'Lord Sun Quan'...?"

"This... is serious," Sun Quan replied. "Sit down, please."

Shangxiang's smile disappeared: she sat facing her brother and asked, "Is someone else ill...?"

"No... no, that's not it," Sun Quan replied. "I... I have something that I must ask of you, and if needs be *demand* of you."

"...This is about me getting married, isn't it," Shangxiang guessed. "Quan, you *promised*! You promised me that-!"

"This isn't just any marriage," Sun Quan interrupted. "I... I would ask that you marry *Liu Bei*."

Shangxiang grinned for a second time and said, "You're joking... you're joking! I thought that-!"

"No, I'm not joking," Sun Quan replied.

Shangxiang's smile disappeared again.

"You're my sister, and I love you very much," Sun Quan continued. "I have done my very best to allow to live as you please, but there must come a time when all of the people of the south must do what is necessary to preserve what our father and older brother fought and died for, and for you, dear sister, that time is now."

Shangxiang's eyes wandered.

"You're upset and angry, I imagine, and I assure you that I am generally unhappy with this now that I have given it more thought," Sun Quan continued. "But before you tell me that you don't want to marry someone that you don't know and that Mother would never have forced such a thing on you, remember that I was betrothed to Lady Xie, whom I had never met, at half your age, by that same mother that you don't consider to be capable of such things, and I really didn't like Lady Xie. I still don't. But I did what I was expected to do and had children with her. I did what was expected of me."

Shangxiang turned her gaze toward her brother.

"I will, however, explain my reasoning, since I owe you that at least," Sun Quan continued. "Liu Bei is, as I have said before, twice your age, and far from the hero that you expected to marry, though there are some that might suggest that he is underrated. He once fought the Yellow Turbans, as Father did, and became a Magistrate for it; he later fought on the side of Gongsun Zan – against the government – and by doing so he indirectly fought on the side of Tao Qian and Yuan Shu. When Cao Cao attacked Xu Province, Tao Qian invited Liu Bei to the province to repel Cao, but when Cao's genocidal rampages distressed Tao and sent him to his deathbed, Liu Bei and his smooth-talking allies found a way to take the provincial seal of office, and Bei became Xu's Governor. He later gave shelter to that enemy of our father's, Lü Bu, after Bu fought Cao Cao; but Bu made a secret pact with our former master, Yuan Shu, and stole the province from Bei, and Bei was forced, in the end, to go to Cao Cao for help."

Shangxiang frowned and said, "That makes no sense!"

"No, it doesn't," Sun Quan replied. "But I am not finished, and so I shall continue. Liu Bei and Cao Cao joined forces and routed Lü Bu, after which Cao Cao appointed his own man as Xu's new governor, not Liu Bei; when our former master's brother, Yuan Shao, finally declared war on his old friend Cao Cao – after Cao Cao had sent Liu Bei to kill Yuan Shu, who, at the last, Shao decided to protect and rescue as he fled from-"

"Wait, wait, wait," Shangxiang pleaded. "But I thought that Yuan Shu and Yuan Shao hated each other and fought over their clan chieftainship, like... like..."

"...Like Sun Ben and me...?" Sun Quan said with a smile.

"...But in the end, Yuan Shao tried to help his brother...?" Shangxiang prompted. "Even after everything, all that hate, all that blood...?"

"He did, though there are many reasons offered as to why, and none of them are anything to do with fraternal love," Sun Quan replied. "But I am not done: yes, Yuan Shao tried to save Shu at the last and failed; Liu Bei chased Shu down, and Shu later died a pauper on the road to Shouchun, as you know from 'listening from around corners'. Liu Bei then refused to return to the capital with the army that he'd borrowed from Cao Cao, and when Yuan Shao turned on Cao Cao and declared war on him – citing the unverifiable 'Girdle Edict' as his excuse, but really because he wanted the Son of Heaven for a hostage so that he could control the government, just like Cao Cao, and just like the regents and Dong Zhuo before them – Liu Bei pledged allegiance to Yuan Shao and seized Xu Province for a second time, murdering Cao's appointed governor in the process."

Shangxiang's expression betrayed her alarm.

"Cao Cao was then forced to go back into Xu for a fourth time: he routed Bei, who fled to Yuan Shao, borrowed yet another army, and fought Cao Cao again," Sun Quan explained. "Bei lost again, so he went to Liu Biao, our clan's nemesis, to seek shelter. Bei was in Jing for six years, or thereabouts, aiding Liu Biao's defence of his northern borders; Bei never once travelled southward to help Huang Zu, which, some say, is because he always entertained the idea of a truce with us after Liu Biao's death. Some also say that he coveted Jing's provincial seal, having lost Xu twice; that would not be difficult to envision."

"...I don't understand," Shangxiang said.

"Ah, but I am still not done!" Sun Quan replied. "As you know, I avenged our father and defeated Huang Zu, and Liu Biao died later of distress. Liu Bei fled when Liu Biao died, having made a pact with Liu Qi, Liu Biao's eldest son and heir, who was unceremoniously ousted by his stepmother, Lady Cai, and his younger brother Cong. In fact, Liu Qi and Liu Bei fled together, more or less, when Liu Cong submitted to Cao Cao, who then took northern Jing; Bei then used his deliberately hazy relationship with us as the foundations for a truce and an alliance, and I accepted, sensing that Cao Cao – who might, yes, have been behind our clan's misfortune – would bring the full wrath of his puppet emperor's armies down upon us, and I was right. We won, but Liu Bei's role was minor: he gave Cao the impression that we were weak so that ruses could deceive Cao later on."

"...But I don't understand," Shangxiang pleaded. "The-!"

"I'm almost done," Sun Quan promised. "Cao Cao insisted on trying to hold onto Lujiang, Jiujiang and Jing Province after that catastrophic loss that we inflicted upon him; I could not take Hefei, but Zhou Gongjin took Jiangling. But while Gongjin and our other brave men faced arrows and rocks at Jiangling, Liu Bei cheerfully strolled through the 'four counties' – Wuling, Changsha, Lingling and Guiyang – and used Liu Qi as a totem with which to seize them bloodlessly. My inability to send support to the Lujiang Rebels led them to pledge allegiance to Liu Bei instead in the aftermath, which has made him strong. Now Liu Bei sits in Gong'an with his borrowed armies and insists that he is the lord of those counties, even though Changsha should at the very least be ours: it was Father's prefecture until Yuan Shu indentured him and stripped him of his court-appointed roles."

"I know about Changsha," Shangxiang replied. "But-"

"I am almost finished," Sun Quan said. "Now I am forced to do one of two things: allow Liu Bei to borrow them as he has borrowed so many other things, or fight and risk his turning to Cao Cao for help again, as he did when he lost Xu to Lü Bu. Cao Cao blames his defeat at Red Cliffs on *me*, not Bei, and his losing Jiangling can be no other man's fault: it is *me*, and *me alone*, that Cao Cao wants to slow-slice for being made to look a fool."

Shangxiang was silent and unreadable.

"...Our half-sisters are too young: it would be distasteful, and besides, they are our half-sisters, and if I am honest, they are none too bright and totally unsuited to this scheme, which is what this is in truth, else – I swear it – I would have approached them and not you," Sun Quan protested. "You are smart, resourceful, and I know that you will not be swayed by Liu Bei's honeyed words and forget your family; you will remain a tigress and always act in our interests."

"...So I will be a spy...?" Shangxiang prompted.

"I need someone to be close to him, 'listening from around corners', as you are so very good at doing," Sun Quan replied. "I need someone trustworthy to hear his true thoughts, see his hidden actions and report them to me. If you were his principal wife, you would be tasked with raising his heir, which would be beneficial. If our houses were to come to blows you would return, the marriage would be dissolved and you would return to your life as you want to live it, but... but if our houses remained allied, and you were to have children with him, then they would be Han princes – contenders for the *Imperial throne*, potentially – which-"

"If – *if* – I do this for you, Quan – and if I did, I would do it for our clan – then he'll have to make do with looking at me," Shangxiang interrupted. "He'll not lay a finger on me, not unless-"

"*Alright*, *alright*, that will be up to you," Sun Quan replied. "But... you agree to it then...?"

"You have already said that you'd use your position as clan chieftain to force me if I didn't agree," Shangxiang said calmly. "My choices are 'agree' and 'take poison'."

"Don't say things like that," Sun Quan pleaded.

"...One more thing," Shangxiang said. "If I do this, it's as an agent of our clan, as a role. I will act as I please when I get to Jing, and if he complains you will tell him to accept my behaviour or release me. And if it doesn't work out, then you must keep your word that

I am never – *never* – 'asked' to do anything else."

"That's two things, but I agree, and to both," Sun Quan replied.

"Do… do you forgive me for asking this of you…?"

"Mother forced you to marry Lady Xie… and she forced Kuang to marry Lady Cao as well, which is actually worse when I think about it," Shangxiang said. "I don't know… maybe Ben didn't like being told that he should marry his daughter to Cao Cao's son, and that's why he…?"

"…I doubt it, but maybe," Sun Quan sighed.

"I… I don't know why I was never forced to marry, but I can see that I have been allowed to live in my own way for a long time," Shangxiang continued. "I was always scared that I'd be forced to marry one of Yuan Shu's men when we were hostages in Shouchun, especially when they were always visiting the house, always… … …I'm rambling. When will I marry Liu Bei…?"

"If he agrees – and he will – then it will be within the year, possibly as soon as a couple of months," Sun Quan explained. "I'll remain in constant contact, I promise, and if he in any way mistreats you, then-"

"Then I'll cut his throat," Shangxiang said.

"…Yes, yes, you probably would," Sun Quan mumbled. "What have I been talked into…?"

Shangxiang smiled slightly and asked, "So you will marry one of Liu Bei's daughters? I'm presuming that he has daughters and that they're very pretty…"

"He has two adult daughters, both very agreeable… or rather *had*, because Cao Cao's men abducted them both during the rout he suffered at Steep-slope," Sun Quan replied. "What happened to them, I don't know… but *I* won't be marrying either of them, that much is certain."

"Oh, I see," Shangxiang said. "That's awful for them. So you'll be marrying a niece of his, or something, then…?

Sun Quan rubbed his beard and replied, "There will be no reciprocal marriage."

"That's not right, is it?" Shangxiang said.

Sun Quan laughed and replied, "I did say that this was not to my liking generally. I can only hope that Gongjin recovers soon and comes up with something more agreeable."

Sun Quan sent word to Gongjin as soon as Shangxiang had left his study; Gongjin read the short letter, sighed and said, "So it is to be, then."

"What is…?" Xiaoqiao asked.

"…*Shangxiang*… marrying *Liu Bei*," Gongjin replied.

Xiaoqiao laughed involuntarily and said, "Forgive me, Husband, but even before you said the name of her future husband, just the *notion* of her marrying is… unbelievable. Did you say *Liu Bei*…?"

"I am speechless," Gongjin replied. "And I am also… *helpless*: *please*, Lü Ziming, take Huancheng… without incident, and… give me some small shred of *hope*…!"

****

117

Lü Meng and his army marched on Lujiang's formal capital Huancheng and surrounded it before Cao Cao's scouts could report the extent of the military build-up in Ruxu: Lü then had a letter demanding the city's surrender fired over the wall by Gan Ning.
"Fine marksmanship, General Gan," Lü Meng praised.
"Yes, Gan: a very impressive display indeed!" Ling Tong heckled. "You could shoot an arrow any distance and find your mark."
"*Aiee*...! Look, I can't undo what I did!" Gan Ning retorted. "I-!"
"Enough from both of you," Lü Meng ordered. "The message is delivered: now we must wait and see what the response is. Follow me, please, both of you."
Ling Tong and Gan Ning exchanged hateful stares as they followed Lü Meng to the command tent of their fenced camp.

The guardian of Huancheng, Xie Qi, reviewed the Jiangdong army's banners, turned to his aide Song Hao and said, "This man that comes here demanding my surrender, this 'Lü Meng'... what do we know of him...?"
"He's a 'rising star' of the south," Song Hao replied. "I knew that he was ferocious, Lord Xie, but his banners read 'Deputy Chief Commander', so he must be more than a soldier."
Xie Qi hummed thoughtfully and said, "We must either fight or submit, then: what should I do...?"
A second man gestured that he would like to speak and said, "You might have to submit, Lord Xie, since the other banners read 'Commandant Ling Tong' – who is a valiant officer and son of Ling Cao, who is well known in Lujiang as a hero – and 'General Gan Ning', who-"
"Gan Ning needs no introduction, Sun Zicai," Song Hao said anxiously. "His Excellency almost sent me to Yi Province once, and I learned of Gan's activities there... it makes me shudder to think that such a man is here now."
Xie Qi looked at each of his followers in turn and silently pleaded for them to find a way to resist, but his gestures went unheeded.
"Submit, my lord, and we might be rewarded," Sun Zicai suggested. "Fight, my lord, and we face three very capable heroes when we have nobody of that calibre here to match them."
"...But that's easy for you to say!" Xie Qi retorted. "You're a 'Sun' that can claim distant shared ancestry with Sun Quan!"
"Isn't there a 'Xie Jiong' that's Sun Quan's father-in-law?" Sun Zicai said. "I don't recommend this for any selfish reason, or I'd be in Jiangdong already!"
"...But if I submit, how can I then show my face in Xuchang?" Xie Qi asked. "I am a Han loyalist! I would be surrendering and then going back to the capital, and how would I be received...? Would His Excellency Cao Cao make an example of me for failing him...?"
"So you intend to resist, then," Song Hao prompted.
"I have more to lose by submitting!" Xie Qi suggested. "I would leave this place a broken man if I surrendered, but if I send for help and resist – as Liu Fu and Jiang Ji did at Hefei – then I might do the Han a proper service! Are we any less equipped for a siege than Hefei...? Has Huancheng not held out against Sun Ce before?"

"Not for long," Sun Zicai replied. "But you are the lord of Huancheng: if you say 'fight', then we fight."

"And I *do* say 'fight'!" Xie Qi retorted. "Have a message returned to this 'Lü Meng' at once, and leave him under no illusions: he faces *real men* here today!"

"...And your other proposal, Lord Xie, regarding a request for reinforcements...?" Sun Zicai asked. "Do we do that first, before replying to the enemy...?"

"Of *course* you will do that *first*!" Xie Qi snapped. "But our enemy has insisted that we answer quickly, so we *must* do *that*!"

Lü Meng read Xie Qi's response and sighed, saying, "So be it."

"We're not looking to kill ev'ryone, right?" Gan Ning prompted.

"Don't be so sure of that," Ling Tong replied. "Why bring the likes of you if wanton murder is not a considered option...?"

Gan Ning rolled his eyes and turned away; Lü Meng shook his head and said, "General Gan is here because he is an expert at breaking sieges, and also because he is credited with securing a bloodless surrender from Xi Su at Yiling. Xie Qi is not Xi Su, however, and so we must think again: we will attack the walls with unbridled ferocity and scare the occupants into giving this man up to us."

"But I don't understand: if Huancheng is a former holding of Lord Sun's, why is it so resistant...?" Ling Tong admitted. "Yes, I know that many people moved to Jiangdong, and that the upheaval changed the population, but those that remained were not mistreated by Li Shu or Lord Sun Ce; why are they so hostile...?"

"It is best described as 'social engineering'," Lü Meng replied. "Cao Cao is slowly – but surely, and definitively – relocating the people that lived in Lujiang and replacing them with military families from the north. He'll be doing the same in Jiujiang. The inhabitants of that city are probably from Yan, or Yu, or possibly northern Jing, since that would ensure enmity."

"...So attacking Huancheng is no different to attacking Jiangling, then," Ling Tong said. "We will only be met by enemies. But a siege is not the way to make friends of them, and I had supposed that we intended that. Why wasn't Chen Wu – who encouraged many of the people of Lujiang to join the Suns on two occasions – invited here instead of-?"

"Chen Zilie is needed elsewhere," Lü Meng interrupted. "Pacifying southern Jing and restoring order to Jiangdong are considered to be better uses for him at present."

"...So we are to show no mercy," Ling Tong said as he glared at Gan Ning.

"We are to show no mercy to the *walls*, Ling Gongji, and the earth around them," Lü Meng replied. "What the men inside the walls do is up to them. They have certainly requested help, so begin at once, in case Cao Cao actually sends help. Rumours state that not only is *Zhang Liao* in Hefei, but that *Zang Ba* is still in Lujiang somewhere, and after the effect that he had on Veteran General Han Dang's men – and the thirty-thousand that followed them – I have no desire to confront the 'Bandit King of Kaiyang' myself if we can avoid it, and certainly not *before* we have the city."

"Consider it done," Gan Ning said as he bowed slightly, turned and left the tent.

"**Rude creature!**" Ling Tong cried. "He didn't even bow!"

"He *did*, but he understood the urgency and did so *briefly*," Lü Meng retorted. "Now could you please go and assist him with taking Huancheng…? I have a letter to compose, and then I will join you both."

Ling Tong bowed low, turned and retreated.

"…I yearn for simpler days," Lü Meng sighed as he took up a pen.

Ling Tong and Gan Ning led the assault on the walls of Huancheng; both had frustrations to vent that could not be aimed at their cause, and so the city made for a good alternative target. Xie Qi watched with horror as the usual elements of siege warfare sprung up all around him: his composure failed him, and he shrieked, "**I will not sit here and be pecked at by these carrion birds! I will charge out of the city and face them!**"

"**That's Gan Ning and Ling Tong, not two mediocrities!**" Song Hao protested. "**What do you hope to achieve?**"

"**Either aid me or leave my service!**" Xie Qi barked.

Song Hao and Sun Zicai exchanged weary glances and hoped that they would get an opportunity to decide their own fates.

Xie Qi was good to his word and charged out of the gates of Huancheng with his 200 infantrymen and 50 cavalry, but Gan Ning's elite gang of 'brigands' were there to meet him: they only numbered 200 men, but they were riding horses that were many of them foreign steeds that had been stolen from Cao Ren's "Tiger and Leopard Cavalry" after their repulsion from Yiling, and the men's tactic of wearing small bells that continually jangled and pealed as they circled their opponents was enough to confuse Xie Qi's infantry and cause many of them to drop their weapons and flee. The Huancheng cavalry's horsemen were exclusively riding smaller 'native' horses that were slower and poorly trained; Xie Qi's charge collapsed, and Ling Tong's subsequent, retaliatory charge forced Xie Qi to flee northward, leaving Song Hao and Sun Zicai as the defenders of the city. Ling Tong forced Gan Ning to take a secondary role as he moved to the wall and urged taunts to be shouted at the remaining defenders; Song Hao and Sun Zicai returned to the battlements and – after calming the terrified and angry soldiers on those battlements – prepared to make their next collective move.

"…**What shall we do…?**" Song Hao shouted.

"**You need to ask…?**" Sun Zicai replied.

Lü Meng was glad to receive word of Huancheng's surrender; he summoned Ling Tong and Gan Ning to the command tent and said, "Magnificent: Lord Sun will be pleased as well, since this victory is less costly and more swiftly earned. I doubt that Zang Ba or Zhang Liao will bother to send aid when Xie Qi reports to them: we can instead expect a larger response, but that will not be for a long while, and by then, gentlemen, we might have taken Hefei as well!"

"So what are we doing now…?" Gan Ning asked.

"For now, General, we will occupy Huancheng and properly fortify it, just in case Cao Cao does send men to recapture it," Lü Meng replied. "We will have a banquet tonight to celebrate our victory!"

"Fine," Ling Tong said. "Just ensure that I do not have to sit anywhere near Gan, unless you-"

"I'll place the two of you wherever I choose," Lü Meng retorted. "You're both of you officers under my command, Commandant Ling, and you will end this pointless feud with General Gan!"

Ling Tong exhaled angrily and said, "As you *command*."

"...Let us not sour this victory," Lü Meng continued. "We'll banquet tonight, and we will invite Song Hao and Sun Zicai as guests in order to thank them for submitting and saving lives."

Lü Meng's banquet was, initially, a civil affair. Song Hao and Sun Zicai were allowed to sit with the senior officials, and the official Qin Song – who had been on his way back from reporting to Sun Quan in Chaisang anyway – arrived in time to join the guests as well; Gan Ning and Ling Tong sat away from each other, with Gan designated as an officer and Ling as an official.

"This is splendid!" Qin Song said. "You have again proven your evolution as an officer and strategist, Deputy Chief Commander!"

"Not so," Lü Meng replied humbly. "I am afraid that the plan was nothing more than 'ask them to submit and attack if they refuse': Sun Tzu would be unlikely to heap praise upon me for it."

"Others might have resorted to convoluted schemes that wasted time and achieved nothing," Qin Song insisted. "Don't berate yourself when victory was the outcome."

Lü Meng gestured toward Song Hao and Sun Zicai and said, "These two men have submitted and brought their families: it is they that should be thanked before I am thanked, I think."

Qin Song bowed toward the two surrendered officials, who reciprocated silently.

"...And Ling Tong and Gan Ning were the heroes that chased Xie Qi away," Lü Meng continued. "I didn't do much, all in all."

Qin Song looked at Ling Tong and said, "Has there been much...?"

"...They are manageable," Lü Meng replied.

But as the banquet progressed, drink flowed freely and inhibitions were eroded: Ling Tong glared at Gan Ning as the latter laughed and joked with his subordinates, and his hatred for the man that had killed his father started to surface. Lü Meng had twice stared at Ling Tong as a warning that he should control his temper, but the alcohol had done its work: Ling Tong glared at Gan Ning and smiled slightly as a thought suddenly entered his mind. Ling Tong waited until the gathering was lost in a series of harmless conversations and then announced, **"I shall do a traditional sword dance for entertainment!"**

"*Ayah*! **This is a 'Hongmen'!** Gan Ning cried as Ling Tong jumped to his feet, drew his sword and began his ceremonial dance, turning this way and that and thrusting the sword outward.

"Hongmen...?" Sun Zicai exclaimed.

"For *who*...?" Song Hao asked. "*Us*...?"

"We *surrendered*!" Sun Zicai protested.

"So now I am of no more use to you, Ziming, and you allow Ling Tong to have his 'Hongmen'!" Gan Ning protested.

"Not so!" Lü Meng protested. **"Ling Gongji: sit down at once!"**

"I am just performing a sword dance!" Ling Tong insisted. "You read too much into an honest gesture!"

"*For the love of the gods*," Qin Song muttered.

Ling Tong was inching closer to Gan Ning, who sensed danger and leapt to his feet, produced two short swords from their concealment behind his back and declared, "**I can dance too!**"

Gan Ning and Ling Tong were now doing their own separate performances while the others looked on with increasing desperation: Lü Meng sensed that he would have to intervene and leapt up, took a sword and shield from a decorative display to his right and said, "**I shall show my own ability!**"

Lü Meng placed himself between the feuding dancers while performing a routine of his own; Qin Song groaned desperately and said, "This is a *farce*! **Stop it at once, all of you!**"

"...**I demand reparation!**" Ling Tong screamed. "**He killed my father! I-!**"

"**Get out of here, Gan Ning!**" Qin Song barked; Song Hao and Sun Zicai looked at each other and frowned bemusedly.

"...Yes, you'd better go, General Gan," Lü Meng realised.

Gan Ning left without saying a word; Qin Song then turned to Ling Tong and said, "You *can't kill him*."

"...To do this at a victory banquet... is actually as sign of *contempt*, Commandant Ling," Lü Meng suggested. "Our guests might have suspected ill will."

"We are fine," Song Hao insisted. "We had no idea that..."

"You should *never have*, either," Qin Song sighed.

"...So what will my punishment be, Deputy Chief Commander Lü...?" Ling Tong asked.

"I... must consult others," Lü Meng replied. "This is too complex a matter for me alone to adjudicate. Remain and be seated, Ling Tong: we still have banquet to conclude."

Ling Tong nodded apologetically and returned to his seat; the matter was not spoken of again, and the guests did their best to enjoy the food, drink and music for the rest of the evening.

Sun Quan received a visit from Gu Yong, Zhuge Jin and Quan Rou when Lü Meng's report arrived via Lu Su, who had returned to Jiangling: Quan frowned and said, "You three together implies some serious issue: what has happened...?"

"Huancheng is ours, but Ling Tong has, it seems, attempted a 'Hongmen'," Quan Rou reported. "Gan was his target, of course."

"...*Ayah*...! So they are irreconcilable, then!" Sun Quan lamented. "I cannot afford to lose either of them, so what must I do...?"

"Acting Chief Commander Lu has suggested that we must try some sort of 'technical punishment', and we agree," Gu Yong said. "Banish Gan: send his family to some place away from here, as a sign to Ling that you value him, and if problems occur after that, well... we'll act accordingly."

"Do I have a choice...?" Sun Quan sighed.

Sun Quan reluctantly 'exiled' Gan Ning to Banzhou, which was a place that would offer few distractions; Ling Tong was temporarily appeased, which – Sun Quan hoped – would ensure that he served to the best of his ability. Gongjin heard of the incident and once again hoped that he would be able to recover quickly.

✶✶✶✶✶✶✶✶✶✶✶

118

Liu Bei received the proposal of a Sun-Liu marriage alliance and replied enthusiastically, despite his vassals showing a considerable amount of unease. The communications between the soon-to-be-joined houses of Sun Quan and Liu Bei were subsequently cordial over the weeks that followed; preparations were underway for Bei to travel to Jiangdong for the wedding – which was seen by some as yet another oddity – when Liu Qi, the eldest son of Liu Biao, suddenly suffered a deterioration of his health and died. Sun Quan immediately summoned Lu Su to his private study, rambled at him and then sent him to speak with Gongjin; Quan hoped, when Su returned, that he had brought an elaborate scheme with him, but he was quickly disappointed.

"Gongjin is still very poorly," Lu Su reported. "He… he has no scheme to change our management of this matter."

"But that's *ridiculous*!" Sun Quan said. "If Liu Qi is dead, and Qi was Liu Bei's 'magic totem' that allowed him to take the counties with ease, then-!"

"We have no such 'magic totem', and Liu Bei has ingratiated himself with the people of those counties in the months that he has been touring them," Lu Su explained. "We, sad to say, are still viewed as enemies of peace, even in Changsha, which is where Bei placed Liu Qi for maximum effect."

"…So even in *Changsha*, where my father governed justly and fought bandits for the people, we have no influence…?" Sun Quan exclaimed. "*Aiee*…! So we can only obtain those counties by violence or by cunning that Gongjin is unwilling or unable to supply! And if Liu Qi's death does not rob Bei of the counties, then I can't release my sister from that awful union that I have agreed to, and…! …*Aiee*."

"I wish that I were a more capable schemer," Lu Su said. "We must make do with what I have proposed: Bei will have Jing and bear the brunt of Cao's wrath."

"And I must hope that Cao makes a widow of my sister," Sun Quan replied. "The thought of her married to that old owl…"

"I will continue to ponder it," Lu Su promised. "If there is anything at all, Lord Sun, I will make use of it – and who knows what the next few weeks might bring…?"

But those weeks went by quickly, and there were no visible opportunities to annul the agreements with Liu Bei. The day fast approached when Liu Bei would be leaving Gong'an and beginning the journey to Chaisang; Lu Su visited Gongjin once again and sat by his bedside to relay reports from across the region.

"…Anyhow, so that's what Lu Xun has to say about Kuaiji," Lu Su concluded. "I think that's everything: naturally I will-"

"So Liu Bei will soon be in Jiangdong," Gongjin prompted.

"He will be bringing Kongming, Mister Sun Qian, and Mister Jian Yong," Lu Su replied tonelessly. "We have agreed to the suggestion that Liu Bei should be made Governor of Jing…"

"I disagree strongly, Zijing," Gongjin said. "You cannot lend a man the signs of kingship and then complain when he calls himself a king. By appointing him Governor, you make him Liu Biao's legitimate successor, something Bei himself was not prepared to do for Liu Qi when he only recommended him as an Inspector. Why do we do this for a man we only loan the province to…?"

"We are going to make him the target for Cao Cao's wrath," Lu Su explained.

"You're opening the way for him to take Yi as well, Zijing," Gongjin said. "I am fearful of the man *now*: if he also had Yi… he would become a true king, with domains greater than ours, and *then* what…?"

"Kongming insists that he has no intention of taking Yi," Lu Su replied.

Gongjin started to laugh, but the pain quickly reduced him to a writhing, wriggling mess; he glared and Lu Su and said, "You… *idiot*…! You *believe*… him…?"

Lu Su lowered his head guiltily.

"He is… danger… *danger*…!" Gongjin continued. "*Zijing*…!"

"I will do what I can to keep them from becoming a threat to us," Lu Su insisted.

Gongjin tried to say more, but the agony was too much to bear; Xiaoqiao entered the room and stared at Lu Su, who shook his head, got to his feet and left. Gongjin watched his replacement leave and sighed; Xiaoqiao knelt at his side, took his hand and whispered, "Please don't let him come here again."

"I… must write to Lord Sun," Gongjin decided. "I… can see that I have no choice."

The day of Liu Bei's arrival was a tense one: Sun Quan paced back and forth across his study and said, "Am I to have the countenance of a governor or a king when I meet this man, Li…?"

Gu Li smiled and replied, "I would imagine that others would say that you should avoid looking like a king in front of a scion of the Imperial house; others might say that vassal kings are commonplace in an empire."

Sun Quan laughed and said, "An interesting way of evading a proper answer! I will dress as a wealthy, influential governor would when I meet my future brother-in-law… although he is old enough to be my *father*…"

"Will State Mother Wu attend this meeting…?" Gu Li asked.

"No," Sun Quan replied. "Bei is, I understand, 'Confucian in appearance but Legalist in principle' and balks at the idea of women attending court; few men like the idea of it, but he apparently cites 'countless manipulative and destructive Empress Dowagers and the harm that they caused to his clan from behind their silk curtains' for his specific prejudice."

"…This will be an unusual match, then," Gu Li suggested dryly.

"Don't remind me," Sun Quan replied. "Gongjin makes matters worse: at first he suggested nothing, but now that Liu Bei is here, he has sent me *this*."

Sun Quan took a letter from his belt and passed it to Gu Li, who immediately started to read it.

> "My lord Sun Quan,
>
> Now comes a critical moment. Liu Bei arrives in Jiangdong, and we are committed to an alliance

with him by circumstance, but we must seize the moment and do otherwise: this goes against my ideals, but against certain foes we are forced to do what is necessary – that was the case with Cao Cao, and it is so in this instance as well.

Liu Bei has the bearing of a strong and ambitious hero of the age: he has in his employ generals such as Guan Yu and Zhang Fei, who are like bears and tigers on the battlefield and loyal to a fault. Though he may come here to seek peace from a weak position, he is not a man that will show deference to another lord for long – he has shown that before and will do so again.

I have deliberated this while remaining silent so that there would be no evidence of schemes, but now that he is here I can speak: I suggest that we take this opportunity to move Liu Bei to Wu Prefecture, build him a palace and ply him with women and wealth in order to tame and placate him, for he has known great hardship and will be easily bought. We can then have him move his two great generals, Guan and Zhang, to different, distant places so as to lessen the threat that they pose: that done, we can, at the right moment, use Liu Bei as a hostage, capture Jing and force Bei's men to submit to us, thereby bolstering our own forces with yet more capable men.

At that stage, our dream will be fulfilled: some will agree while others will criticise, but how can the critics be judgemental when they suggest that we let Liu, Guan and Zhang exist together and carve out their own place from lands that are yours? It is a case of 'the dragon' – Liu – encountering 'clouds and rain' in Guan and Zhang: the dragon will not then be content to remain in a pond.

Please consider my words carefully.

Zhou Yu, Chief Commander of the armies of the state of Eastern Wu"

Gu Li turned his eyes upward from the letter to Sun Quan, who said, "Can I ignore this?"
"...What do others say...?" Gu Li asked.
"As Gongjin supposed, Zhang Zhao and Lu Su were dismissive while Lü Fan agreed completely," Sun Quan replied. "But I am torn: a part of me yearns for Jing to be mine at any cost, and I hate the idea of my sister marrying this man anyway; but Cao Cao looms large in the north – something that, as Zhang Zhao pointed out, Gongjin deliberately ignores – and means me and my people no good, and in Liu Bei I have a much-needed ally that cannot be easily reconciled with Cao. I... I want to agree, because Gongjin is

my most reliable vassal, and because he is my brother-in-law, and because he is a friend to my family… but at the same time I am the lord of a large domain, and I cannot afford to be reckless as Bofu was. And I want to be seen as sincere as well: can I hope to recruit Liu Bei's men, or anyone else's – and, in fact, could I retain my own men – if I now gain a reputation for luring rival lords to my capital with the promise of a beautiful wife and then taking them hostage…?"

Gu Li handed Gongjin's letter back to Sun Quan and said, "You have answered your own question, Lord Sun: you have already decided that you must endure the situation as it stands and show that you are magnanimous."

Sun Quan nodded slowly, smiled and replied, "You're right: I have. I will reply later, but for now I must prepare to welcome my future brother-in-law… sincerely."

Sun Quan's court convened later that day: Liu Bei and a small entourage – Zhuge Liang, Bei's friend Jian Yong and the middle-aged envoy Mister Sun – strode into the court with obvious confidence while Bei's elite bodyguards waited outside the hall – and under the watchful eye of Zhou Tai – at Sun Quan's request. Zhang Zhao and Zhang Hong made no secret of their dislike of Liu Bei, despite the marriage alliance being Zhang Zhao's idea; Lü Fan watched silently but gave no indication of his feelings.

"Greetings, Governor of Jing Province," Sun Quan said.

Liu Bei smiled, bowed slightly – as a sign of respect but not of deference – and replied, "And greetings to you, Governor of Jiangdong and founder of Eastern Wu. I am glad to see that you are well, and take the opportunity to wish a speedy recovery to Chief Commander Zhou Yu."

Sun Quan smiled coldly, bowed even more slightly and said, "Please, be seated, Governor." Liu Bei and his three subordinates sat along the officials' side of the hall; Sun Quan then leant forward slightly and added, "I am glad that the situation in Jing is finally starting to stabilise…"

Liu Bei nodded and said, "The last of Cao's puppet governors is removed, and the region is now safe; I only wish that… that Inspector Liu Qi, my nephew, could have lived a little longer to enjoy the moment."

Liu Bei wiped a tear from his eye; Sun Quan did nothing to hide his lack of sadness over the death of his hated enemy's son as he replied, "My condolences to you and to the people of Jing for the loss. It is regrettable that the feud between our families prevented peace in the land; I appreciate Liu Qi's desire to see that feud ended, and can now say that it has. But Jing Province is still divided, Governor, and that cannot change while things remain as they are."

Liu Bei nodded and said, "I concur. Feuds between men are a poison: if only every man showed such high-mindedness, and realised that the needs of the many outweigh the needs of the few."

Sun Quan sensed that Liu Bei was trying to avoid properly answering a prompt that he fully understood the meaning of, so Quan leant forward even further and said, "But you do agree that things cannot remain as they are in Jing Province."

"Quite," Liu Bei replied tersely.

"...Chief Commander Zhou Gongjin retains his position as Administrator of Nan Prefecture, and controls Jiangling and Yiling," Sun Quan continued. "You, Governor, are the *figurehead* governor, while a more permanent solution is sought. I hope that the proposal of a union of our families will solidify your position, build our trust, and inspire you to succeed in your own ambitions..."

Liu Bei's face briefly betrayed a need to plan his answer carefully; he hesitated before he replied, "My only ambition is to destroy Cao Cao and rescue the Son of Heaven."

"The *audacity* of the man," Lü Fan muttered; others were quietly snickering at what they also believed to be a complete dishonesty.

"Jing is governed by me in the name of His Majesty: I see no ambiguity, no lack of clarity, and no need to speak of solidifying positions," Liu Bei continued. "I am solid as a rock in those parts of Jing that I now control, and it suits me well as a base from which to carry out Heaven's will."

"What did he say...?" Zhang Hong whispered.

Zhang Zhao calmed his anxious brother with a silent gesture; other men had now stopped laughing and were murmuring and coughing instead.

"...I understand that our officials have been discussing ideas such as lending you the use of the rest of Nan Prefecture," Sun Quan said. "Tell me, Governor Liu, what ideas you have concerning the fate of Yi Province...?"

"I have no ideas, Governor Sun, besides making Provinicial Governor Liu Zhang of Yi turn away from the darkness," Liu Bei insisted. "What are your own thoughts...?"

Sun Quan looked at the disapproving face of Lü Fan as he sighed and said, "We have considered attacking Liu Zhang, I confess. Our main reservation is his kinship to you, Governor Liu; and, it goes without saying, his kinship, however distant, to our sovereign. I wonder, would you object to his being removed as a threat to Jing Province and the land as a whole...?"

"Before I would ever seize Yi Province, I would rather unbind my hair, become a recluse, and retire to the mountains!" Liu Bei insisted. "I make that vow to all the land and men under Heaven, and I'll never break that vow!"

Sun Quan took Liu Bei's words to be a sincere vow and a thinly veiled threat: he sighed sadly and said, "Your benevolence is known throughout the land, and today, it is known to me. Very well: I shall speak with Chief Commander Zhou, and consider alternative ways of resolving the crisis in Yi."

Liu Bei bowed slightly and replied, "My thanks, Governor Sun."

"Now let us speak of more pleasant matters," Sun Quan continued. "Let us have music and food and wine, Governor Liu, for soon we shall be family!"

The announcement was followed by the court's best attempts at joviality, but the atmosphere was tense: Zhuge Liang was quietly fanning himself and apparently enjoying the hate that Sun Quan's vassals had for him while his brother, Zhuge Jin, wondered what would come of it all.

The banquet ended on a positive note; Liu Bei and his followers retired to the accommodation that Sun Quan had provided, and Quan invited Lu Su, Lü Fan, Zhang Zhao, Zhang Hong and Zhuge Jin to his private audience chamber for further discussions.

"You seem pleased, Lord Sun," Lu Su prompted.

"I must say that Liu Bei seemed very upright: an outstanding man," Sun Quan replied. "Is there no way we can find accord with this man, since I see in him none of the 'crafty owl' I've heard so much about...?"

Zhang Zhao was about to say something when Zhuge Jin pre-empted him and said, "Well, I have talked at great length with my brother Kongming, and he assures me that Liu Bei has no desire to contend with you: he simply wants the land to be at peace, and for all men to have the land that should be theirs."

"*Nonsense*," Zhang Zhao heckled. "While I may not always agree with Gongjin, I do agree with one thing: Liu Bei should be left out of any long-term plans that we have for Jing or for anywhere else."

"Then why do you want to marry Lady Sun to the man...?" Zhuge Jin asked irritably. "Is this some farcical attempt at a 'Beauty Trap' then...?"

Zhang Zhao took a moment to think – and calm down – before he said, "You are not thinking about the lord! Why should he not have Jing...? The marriage is a means to several ends: it ties our families together, so that any act of Liu Bei that is not in our mutual interest will earn him the scorn of future historians; it ensures that any aforementioned act of ill-will is known to us before it can harm us; it ensures that Bei can be Governor, since he will then be related by marriage to the true ruler of the province... our own Lord Sun."

"Petty, nonsensical subterfuge: unprovoked, needless backstabbing!" Zhuge Jin said. "You are a schemer for scheming's sake, Zhang Zhao, and you plot against a good man that has done nothing but help us!"

Zhang Zhao laughed icily and replied, "You should cross the river now, brother of Zhuge Liang: you obviously have no desire to serve here any longer."

Sun Quan looked at Zhuge Jin, who scoffed and said, "Oh, I'm going nowhere: someone has to keep your snake's tongue closely watched."

"Can we... have some calm...?" Lu Su implored. "Zhang Zibu, Zhuge Ziyu, I see both of your arguments... but my heart is with accord between the families of Sun and Liu. Let us see this marriage not as petty subterfuge, but as a way to set things right, and also as a means of reducing risk if we are wronged."

"And if Liu Bei is content to remain in Jing, building trust and respect amongst his leased vassals, until he is one day ready to seize it...?" Zhang Zhao countered.

"Liu Bei will invade Yi, Brother," Zhang Hong insisted. "He yearns for that land of prosperity; how could he resist snatching it from feeble hands and claiming it to be 'the righteous passing of lands from Liu to Liu' when he's challenged, like he is doing in our own Jing Province...?"

"If Liu Bei says he will not invade Yi, then I believe him," Lu Su said sternly. "He defends Jing as an uncle to the late Liu Qi, not as a thief."

Lü Fan laughed disbelievingly and said, "And so, Zijing, now *we* are thieves...?"

"You...!" Lu Su replied; he was obviously angry, but he was also upset that Lü Fan now appeared to view him as an opponent.

"Ziheng makes a fair point," Sun Quan said. "You imply that we are thieves when you state that Liu Bei is not."

Lu Su sighed, shook his head, and replied, "Jing was fairly rescued from Cao Cao."

Zhang Zhao smirked and said, "The matter of who belongs on a piece of land is a matter of opinion. The truth is that there are none with an eternal right to land: the strongest, most able, wisest and most productive will always win out, because it is the will of Heaven.

"Once, parts of Yi belonged to the barbarian Nan tribes: did they build roads, reap the silk, till the fields, and build bridges to cross into other lands, and share the bounties of their land...? No, they fought us and each other, and enacted pagan ceremonies, and disrespected the law of the land. When the Han people took those lands, they took them rightly, to make proper use of them, where the ignorant Nan 'masters' of the land could not! Man's purpose is to grow, and to do that, we must use all things as best we can... not live like animals!"

"What have the Nan tribes got to do with Jing...?" Zhuge Jin asked irritably.

"Righteous governance," Zhang Zhao replied. "We now rule Jing because we are righteous: once, Jiangdong was unfit for purpose, now it is a thriving nation in its own right. What we have done is take a piece of worthless clay, and make a valuable pot from it. Jiangdong was stagnant, so is Yi: we'll help them find their true worth, in ways that the imperial court has never tried to do!"

Zhuge Jin frowned and asked, "Are you saying that...?"

Lu Su laughed nervously and said, "Uh... let's end the discussion there...! Jing is ours, Liu Bei is the governor in name only, at our discretion; if he will not seize Yi, then we must do it, else we must find someone who can, or Liu Zhang will continue to act in Cao Cao's name and aid attempts to take Jing back from us."

Sun Quan glared at Lu Su and said, "Agreed... so for now, let's retire; is Liu Bei in good accommodation...?"

"Since he is marrying Lady Sun," Lu Su replied, "he has been placed in the best hotel in Chaisang... pending a better solution, should one exist."

Sun Quan smiled half-heartedly and said, "Very good. Tomorrow, I am going to visit Gongjin, and see if he is well; Lu Su, please feel free to attend."

"I shall," Lu Su replied.

Lu Su, Lü Fan and the Zhang brothers bowed and retreated together, although Lü Fan deliberately avoided having anything to say to Lu Su; Zhuge Jin remained, which prompted Sun Quan to ask, "Was there something else, Ziyu...?"

"N-no, Lord Sun," Zhuge Jin decided. "I... I shall leave you."

Gu Li entered the room once Zhuge Jin had left; Sun Quan sighed and said, "You heard them, Li. What will happen, do you think...?"

"I don't know what to make of any of it," Gu Li admitted. "Liu Bei is as obviously shifty as he is compellingly convincing; your advisers are divided, I think, because they are as unsure as everyone else. But then I am a servant, Lord Sun, and know little of intrigue."

"...How long now...?" Sun Quan asked.

"I make my last payments in the next few months, and then my family is no longer indebted, Lord Sun, and I am no longer indentured," Gu Li replied.

"...Very good," Sun Quan said. "That story, at least, has a happy ending; I pray that this 'wedding tale' ends even half as well for my sister, and for me."

"Will you go to the wedding...?"

Xiaoqiao's question – asked after Sun Quan had paid his visit on the following day – made Gongjin smile: he turned and said, "I *must*, my lady, and so must you. I will be fine... and besides, I want to see 'Kongming', stare into his eyes and see what he does and says, so that I might plan accordingly."

"Will you be well enough...?" Xiaoqiao fretted.

"I have to be," Gongjin replied. "Lord Sun depends on me."

"But he rejected your suggestions," Xiaoqiao said.

"Lords often reject their advisers' advice: they must if they have a lot of advisers and they... don't agree with each other on all matters," Gongjin replied. "Lü Fan and I are in the minority, as we were before the battle with Cao Cao: the rest are... ... ...well, I hesitate to use the word 'cowards', but it does not amount to pragmatism, for no one would pragmatically hand their lord's land over to a habitual thief, much less advocate marrying his sister to them so that he is the one that has the hostage. I must accept, however, that Lord Sun will now be swayed by the 'weaker' arguments that involve less risk, primarily because he now has more to lose. I must wait, watch, and, as I have said, plan accordingly. When Liu Bei shows his true nature, I must be there to salvage victory, and I will be, if that is Heaven's will."

∗∗∗∗∗∗∗∗∗∗∗∗

119

The day of Liu Bei and Shangxiang's wedding was turned into a grand state occasion: red flags fluttered above every street in Chaisang, and Sun Quan's palatial mansion was decorated with red flags and tassels. The guest list numbered in the hundreds, and the additional well-wishers would take the number into the thousands: the Sun clan's veteran vassals, Cheng Pu, Huang Gai, Han Dang and Zhu Zhi, observed the affair with understandable cynicism as they met in Zhu Zhi's office.

"I say again: this makes no sense," Han Dang sighed.

"I just hope that Lu Su and Zhang Zhao know what they're doing," Zhu Zhi replied. "They think that they are competent schemers, but I see many ways for this to go wrong."

"Gongjin looks so pasty and frail," Cheng Pu said. "He obviously hates the idea, but he's too weak to oppose it: why, then, doesn't *Lü Fan* object more strongly...?"

"Because he'll be ignored, as we are, and with good reason," Zhu Zhi replied. "I've made my own quiet enquiries, and Bei is a formidable rival now. Liu Qi's death hasn't made him weaker at all: Qi's men have one and all shifted their allegiances to Bei, so now he has at least forty-thousand men at his command."

"...To change the subject, how does our occupation of Lujiang proceed...?" Huang Gai asked.

"Lü Meng doesn't feel that he can leave Huancheng unguarded for long, but he's on his way here," Cheng Pu replied. "We've fortified Ruxu, and Lord Sun is supposed to be going there soon to oversee the beginnings of an expansion plan that will see more docks for military use. Cao Cao's added more personnel to Hefei, but that's all he's done... *so far*."

"...We must hope that Chief Commander Zhou Yu recovers," Zhu Zhi said. "I am becoming increasingly convinced that Cao Cao's strategy will depend upon that man: we must wish him well so that the wolf remains at a distance."

Gongjin and Xiaoqiao entered the Sun mansion and met with the surviving members of the clan: Daqiao was being conspicuously protective of her confident and energetic 9-year-old son Shao in Sun Quan's presence, which unnerved Gongjin.

"Hello, my nephews and nieces by marriage," Gongjin said as he stooped to greet Sun Shao and his three sisters.

"You look ill, Uncle Yu," Sun Shao replied.

"I'll be fine," Gongjin insisted. "So, then, sister-in-law; is all well?"

"...All is well," Daqiao said. "I... sometimes find my son difficult to keep up with...!"

Xiaoqiao frowned; Gongjin coughed awkwardly, straightened up and said, "I see that Sun Lin is here, and his brothers... and Sun Xing and his brothers also."

The Qiao sisters turned to look at the 4 sons of Sun Ben and 4 sons of Sun Fu; they were obviously grateful that they were being welcomed as kin and not chastised for the actions of their fathers.

"...This is a strange day indeed," Gongjin said. "The Sun clan has seen so much tragedy in the last ten years... and it is happy occasions like this that sometimes highlight it most strongly."

Sun Yi's widow, Lady Xū, was talking to the 'State Mother Wu', Lady Chen, and Sun Hè's widow; Sun Kuang's widow, Lady Cao, was stood close to them but was offering no contributions.
"Do I really look like my father?" Sun Shao asked suddenly.
"Yes," Gongjin said as he smiled, turned to the boy and touched his shoulder. "You remind me very much of Bofu... of my sworn brother, brother-in-law and friend. You remind me of what I must do... and I swear to Heaven that I shall do it."

The wedding began a few hours later: Sun Quan took his seat as the ruler of Jiangdong, Lady Chen sat to Sun Quan's left and the 'match-makers' – Lu Su for Shangxiang, and Mister Sun Qian for Liu Bei – took their own seats in front of Sun Quan.
Liu Bei and Shangxiang had to arrive at the mansion separately, so the latter had been taken to another location: they then met at the gates and walked to the podium together. Shangxiang was a sight to behold in her flowing red robes: even Sun Quan was struck by her femininity and grace as she approached. Liu Bei, on the other hand, was controversial: he was dressed in elaborate dragon-patterned robes and a black mortarboard hat topped with rows of beads, and a casual observer might have mistaken Bei for a king or an emperor.
"He looks magnificent!" Lady Chen exclaimed.
"...*Too magnificent*," Sun Quan muttered as anger started to overcome him.
A Taoist priest blessed the couple once they reached the podium, after which they sat opposite their designated matchmakers. Shangxiang and Liu Bei paid their respects to Lady Chen and gave thanks to the heavens before the priest led them through one last set of vows; and then, at last the two were officially married. Congratulations and cheers could then be heard throughout the mansion; Sun Quan forced a smile, but his gaze was fixed on the back of Lu Su's head as he started to wonder what he had been coerced into setting into motion.

Sun Quan left the celebratory banquet early and summoned Lu Su, Zhang Zhao, Zhang Hong and Zhuge Jin to his private audience hall; Gongjin pondered the idea of attending without invitation but decided to return home instead. The meeting began with an uncomfortable silence: none dared speak as Sun Quan glared at the four men and tried to decide what he should say. Eventually, he found the strength to speak and said, "I've just wed my sister to Liu Bei. I've just forced my sister to marry that-"
"My lord, nobody forces Lady Sun or State Mother Wu to endure anything," Lu Su protested. "Both were perfectly happy with the arrangement. State Mother Wu is shrewd and clever: she sees things as we do, and Lady Sun understands her role perfectly."
Zhang Zhao wanted to point out that the current 'State Mother Wu' was nothing like her predecessor, but he realised that it would harm his own cause, so he remained silent; Sun Quan, however, was determined to vent his rage, and he replied, "What, to sleep with Liu Bei and steal secrets...? I could have asked one of *you* to yield a daughter for that!"
The advisers remained silent.
"I have just married my tigress sister to an old snake, a lofty owl,"

Sun Quan continued. "He came dressed to *outshine me*, to portray a man whose destiny is to rule the land… even my mother said he looked like the next Emperor!"

Lu Su fidgeted as he said, "But then, is it so bad that you are now the brother-in-law of a possible future emperor…?"

"Is that supposed to be funny…?" Sun Quan cried. **"What of *my* ambitions??? Did I pit thirty-thousand men against Cao Cao at Red Cliffs, and did my brother lose his life building the state of Eastern Wu, all in order to put that sneaky old peasant Liu Bei on the throne???"**

Lu Su gestured meekly and said, "My lord, you must be assured that your tone matches your intent. Were you to say such things in front of the wrong people… those people might say that you had ideas about taking the throne yourself."

Zhang Zhao and Zhang Hong exchanged awkward glances; it took Sun Quan a few moments before he realised that his anger had led him to speak too frankly, and he tried to calm down.

"Liu Bei has the right, however indirect, to claim succession: you do not," Zhuge Jin said. "As Zijing said, the main reason that Cao Cao is reviled is the same reason that your father's lord, Yuan Shu, was so hated: for coveting the throne."

Sun Quan smiled humbly and replied, "You are both right: I risk damaging my reputation as a benevolent statesman by speaking of Liu Bei in that way. It is true that the mandate can legitimately pass to one of greater worth, but for that to be so, there has to be no worthy successor to the line of Liu. I shall choose my words and thoughts with greater care in future."

"We should now focus on keeping Liu Bei in comfort, my lord, to reassure him that we have no wicked intent, as Gongjin suggested," Zhang Zhao said eagerly.

It was now Zhuge Jin's turn to lose his temper: he pointed at Zhang Zhao and screamed, **"A supposed act of reassurance that is, of course, being done for entirely the opposite reason! You have nothing *but* ill intent! You want to trap Liu Bei, keep him here in Jiangdong!"**

Zhang Zhao smiled calmly and said, "If he does not want to stay, he can leave. Nobody will make him stay and enjoy the palace we will give him, or the magnificent treasures, or the beautiful serving maids, or the fine food and well-brewed wine…"

"…*Treachery*," Zhuge Jin heckled.

"If he ignores his vassals and his mission, and he stays, then he only proves that he is a greedy peasant that craved nothing more than fame and wealth, and that he never had a true heart," Zhang Hong said. "If such a thing were proved… then no more worthy Lius live… *do they…?*"

Zhuge Jin looked to Lu Su for support, but Lu smiled in response.

"Sometimes, subtlety is quite important," Zhang Hong said. "Of course my brother and I agreed with Gongjin's 'Luxury Trap' idea, but could we even risk open discussions at the point that Gongjin deemed proper…? You, Zhuge Jin, would have gone running to your brother."

"I would not," Zhuge Jin insisted. "I believe your schemes to be unnecessary, but I am aware that to alert Liu Bei to them would be treason, and I am loyal to the Suns."

"So we employ that 'dividing the dragon from its clouds and rain' scheme that Gongjin suggested after all...?" Sun Quan prompted.

"We do," Lu Su replied. "Moving Liu Bei to Wu Prefecture as soon as he got here was guaranteed to provoke Guan or Zhang, or possibly Zhuge Kongming, who would have sensed the truth of it at once, and I don't in fact believe that Gongjin really meant 'at once': if we keep him here and let him decide to move to Wu Prefecture of his own accord – which is, I think, what Gongjin really meant – then we tame, rather than break the spirit of, the dragon, and that is the best course."

"The other part of it – that involved dividing Guan and Zhang, invading Jing, Bei as a hostage and so forth – will need to be revised, Lord Sun, for it failed to take our enemies' wily strategists into account," Zhang Zhao suggested. "We may have to wait a while for results, but..."

Sun Quan smirked and said, "That will do: let's test Liu Bei, and see what happens..."

Weeks passed: Sun Quan visited Gongjin's home and found him playing his qin in the living quarters while Xiaoqiao looked on.

"Welcome once again, Lord Sun," Gongjin prompted; Xiaoqiao quietly retreated.

"You look better!" Sun Quan said.

"As much as I'd like to say that I *feel* a lot better, Lord Sun, I don't," Gongjin replied. "I am sat here because I could not bear to be stuck in that bed for... for any longer."

"But you wince less often from the pain," Sun Quan noted.

"I do," Gongjin replied. "It still hurts a great deal, though."

"...Liu Bei appears to be feeling very comfortable," Sun Quan sighed miserably.

Gongjin smiled and said, "Tell me: has Mister Bu Zhi returned from his wanderings...?"

Sun Quan smiled as he replied, "You know that he has, Gongjin: what are you up to now...?"

Gongjin continued to play the qin as he said, "I would ask you, my lord, to grant Bu Zhi with the title of a general of the field and give him special permission to act as he sees fit. Give him a special elite force of men, and send him southward... to collect tribute from the independent southern rulers."

"...Do we need to take such steps...?" Sun Quan asked.

Gongjin did not answer the question: he instead said, "Furthermore, give him permission to discipline – to any degree, as he sees fit – lower-to-middle-ranking officers."

"...Gongjin, that would give him the right to discipline the governors themselves, 'as he sees fit'," Sun Quan replied uneasily.

"It would," Gongjin said pointedly. "He could even *execute them*, if he saw fit."

"...I shall do it, although I do not know why," Sun Quan replied.

"My lord, these independent rulers cannot, like those in the four Jing counties, remain independent forever," Gongjin said. "Rulers whose allegiances may not be reliable... must be dealt with to ensure your safety and your authority. I like it no more than any man would; but for my lord, I will compromise any 'principle' to ensure his success."

Sun Quan smiled and said, "I am lucky to have you to rely upon."

Gongjin hummed thoughtfully and said, "I wonder, Lord Sun, if you might rely upon me to make another suggestion."

Sun Quan laughed and replied, "Speak, Gongjin: say whatever is on your mind."

"...Liu Bei is, at present, free to leave whenever he chooses," Gongjin noted.

"And that will remain so," Sun Quan insisted. "I... I appreciate your deep-rooted concerns about the man, for I have many of my own: but we cannot be seen to break faith. So far, he seems contented to stay... but when he wants to leave... let him."

"This is a golden opportunity to remove him as a threat," Gongjin said. "We could keep him where he is, living as he does... is that such a crime...?"

"His vassals would not stand for it," Sun Quan replied insistently. "Leave him be."

Gongjin conceded that his lord was right and nodded silently.

"And besides," Sun Quan continued, "I worry for Shangxiang."

"...It's my understanding that she barely lets Bei come near her," Gongjin said with amusement. "Why do you worry when dear Shangxiang is making such an obedient pet of the 'unbending Confucian Legalist'...?"

"*Aiee*...! That's *precisely why*!" Sun Quan replied. "She won't even let him 'claim his entitlements': how would he then react to being held hostage as well?"

"You were right, though: Zhuge would thwart us," Gongjin said. "He'll find a way to get Liu Bei to go home as well: that I know for certain. But I am able to travel now, so I intend to go to Jiangling City and become more acquainted with the place: Lu Su can come back here permanently and be my liaison."

"...I wonder when I can move to Wucheng," Sun Quan sighed.

"Everything in good time," Gongjin replied quietly. "Everything... in good time..."

Bu Zhi received his promotion from Sun Quan within a day, and he received a private letter from Gongjin within hours of that: he then began a journey to Cangwu County, which lay southwest of Jiangdong and south of Guiyang Prefecture. The population in those southernmost regions – which neighboured what was later known as North Vietnam – was relatively sparse, and the time taken to reach the distanced settlements was so long as to grant their rulers autonomy: the ruler of Cangwu, Wu Ju, therefore enjoyed living in a world of his own making. Wu Ju was an old friend of Liu Bei, and Cangwu's remoteness made him a useful friend to have: Gongjin had been planning to 'deal with him' since learning of his relationship with Liu Bei from an offhand remark to Lu Su prior to the Battle of Red Cliffs, and it was Bu Zhi's sole purpose as he demanded an audience.

"Who is this 'Bu Zhi'...?" the middle-aged Wu Ju grumbled as he prepared to enter his audience hall. "Who does Sun Quan suddenly think he is, for that matter...?"

"This man is cold, like stone," Wu Ju's senior adviser said. "I strongly advise caution: in fact, I strongly advise hiding men behind the curtains."

"I will not resort to a 'Hongmen'," Wu Ju retorted. "If Sun Quan wants tribute, he'll get it, but not for long if my friend Xuande continues to grow."

Wu Ju sat in his host's seat and gestured to the two guards at the end of the small audience hall: there were less than thirty officials in attendance – four of them visitors from neighbouring counties – and none of them were armed. Bu Zhi and four innocuous officials in plain robes were escorted into the hall moments later by two more guards: Bu wore a sword on his belt and kept his head held high. There were a number of servants stood on one side of the hall: they were holding trays of food in preparation for a banquet.

"Welcome to Cangwu, Mister Bu Zhi," Wu Ju hailed.

"My thanks, Governor Wu," Bu Zhi replied.

"…As you can see, Mister Bu, I intend to banquet you in lieu of your lord, and then I will ensure that you return to his court with sufficient tribute," Wu Ju continued.

"He will appreciate that, Governor Wu," Bu Zhi replied.

Wu Ju frowned and said, "Let's waste no more time, then: sit, Mister Bu, as my guest, and I shall have wine brought."

Bu Zhi and his allies complied: the banquet began, although the mood was tense.

"You are new to this region, Mister Bu, and perhaps unfamiliar with men that you will soon get to know very well!" Wu Ju said. "Mister Guan is the envoy from Jiaozhi; he is a friend of Cheng Bing, the noted scholar, who resides there now!"

"Is that so…?" Bu Zhi prompted.

Mister Guan bowed humbly and replied, "I am acquainted, Mister Bu: I dare not claim to be a friend of wise Master Cheng."

Wu Ju laughed and said, "Cheng Bing studied with Zheng Xuan, the famous scholar who was himself taught by-"

"Ma Rong," Bu Zhi interrupted. "Gu Yong, one of our leading lights, was taught by Cai Yong, the equally-famous scholar who knew Zheng Xuan well."

"…You are a smart man," Wu Ju said.

"I would like to think so," Bu Zhi replied. "Time will tell, though, Governor Wu."

"Again, Mister Bu, you refer to me as 'Governor Wu'!" Wu Ju chuckled. "I am surprised that your lord Sun Quan would suggest referring to a simple county chief as a 'governor'…!"

"You *act* like one," Bu Zhi retorted. "I speak as I find."

The mood suddenly soured; Wu Ju scowled and said, "Your tone implies dissatisfaction with my behaviour."

"Lord Sun Quan is now the ruler of Jiangdong and southern Jing – a third of the Empire – but he is yet to receive proper tribute," Bu Zhi explained. "I have been sent here to reprimand you for your insolence, Wu Ju, and-"

"Reprimand…?" Wu Ju chortled. "The idea of it! Sun Quan is not my master! He is an ambitious tiger that enjoys a large den at the Han's expense, but for how long…?"

Bu Zhi leapt to his feet, drew his sword and said, "That will be your last mistake."

"What are you doing…?" Wu Ju asked disbelievingly; Wu's head left his shoulders moments later, and the guests shrank back in horror. The guards finally reacted, but Bu Zhi's four aides were, in fact, part of his 1,000-strong team of elite soldiers, and they were quick to meet the guards' blades with their own, previously-hidden short swords.

"Let this be a lesson to you all," Bu Zhi declared. "Envoys: go back to your masters and make it known that Lord Sun will not tolerate your rudeness any longer. The south is ruled by Lord Sun Quan, and he expects tribute: ensure that it is paid or your lords will know the same fate as Wu Ju."

"My lord Shi Xie will know of it," Mister Guan promised.

"As will my lord, Mister Bu!" another man cried.

"...Then my work is more than done," Bu Zhi said with a smile.

Gongjin received Bu Zhi's report a week later: he had now relocated to Jiangling City, where he intended to stay for a short time to monitor Liu Bei's allies, receive local reports on Yi Province and assess the situation beyond the north-south border.

"This is ideal," Gongjin said to his colleague Sun Yu. "Wu Ju is dead, and the autonomous counties scrabble to be the first to yield and pay tribute; Liu Bei is in Chaisang enjoying the trappings that his life has hitherto denied him; Zhuge Liang and the rest of Bei's cohorts sit in Gong'an and despair; and Cao Cao flounders, doing nothing about Huancheng. You and I can freely plan for a careful invasion of Yi over the coming months, I think."

"Are you well enough to plot such a thing...?" Sun Yu asked.

"Oh yes," Gongjin insisted. "You and I, Zhongyi, are the heroes that our lord depends upon: you must be the new 'Bofu' and-"

"I'm not Bofu," Sun Yu said. "I wouldn't try to be."

Gongjin's face fell, and he replied, "Yes, I... I suppose that I shouldn't say such things. It is wrong of me to cling to... to the *past*. I must look *forward* now, to the *future*... Bofu is... is gone, and now I – we – strive for Lord Sun Quan."

"So what's the plan...?" Sun Yu asked.

"Everything can be planned here," Gongjin replied. "I-"

"I suppose that I should explain," Sun Yu said. "I understand that you want to ally with Zhang Lu and Ma Chao; I can just about grasp an alliance with Ma Chao, but *Zhang Lu...?*"

"Only temporarily," Gongjin promised. "I can see that I must go back to Lord Sun and present my idea publicly... but now I must plan another meeting... with Pang Tong, the 'Young Phoenix'."

"Zhuge Liang's best friend...?" Sun Yu exclaimed. "Why would you want him to join us? Wouldn't he be a spy for Liu Bei...?"

"I don't believe so," Gongjin replied. "Regardless of the outcome, I will present our case: we must always cling to *hope*."

Sun Quan was elated when Gu Li asked to speak with him and said, "I am now a free man, Lord Sun, and as my first act in that capacity, I should like to pledge my loyalty to you and ask for a place in your service."

"Of course, Li, of course!" Sun Quan cackled. "Oh, how the Heavens must favour me: Liu Bei is no longer a threat, Jing is mine, the villains fall one by one, and the right and good are freed from servitude! You are now my Senior Attendant, Gu Li, and on a salary that will see your family never falls victim to debt again!"

"I am grateful, Lord Sun," Gu Li replied.

"And Gongjin is getting better with every passing day," Sun Quan continued. "Our victory over Cao is assured...!"

Gongjin finally had his audience with Officer of Merit Pang Tong:

Pang entered the chancellery office and said, "You summoned me, Administrator Zhou…?"

Pang's strange appearance was initially discomforting, but Gongjin smiled and replied, "Yes, Master Pang… please, enter, sit down!"

Pang Tong bowed low as a sign of humility and deference before he took a seat as a guest; Gongjin was quietly rejoicing, as he supposed this to be a sign that Pang Tong was about to tender his service to Sun Quan.

"I would prostrate myself on the ground to welcome such a man as you, were I not still nursing a wound, Master," Gongjin insisted. "Please forgive my inability to show you the respect you deserve."

"Hardly," Pang Tong replied. "I am a mere pedant… not worthy of your time or such shows of respect."

Gongjin frowned and said, "You are 'Young Phoenix'… one of the talents of the age! Why do you work as an Officer of Merit, when you could hold high office, like your friend Zhuge Liang, the 'Crouching Dragon'…?"

Pang Tong grinned and replied, "Perhaps I take my Taoist name too literally: while all a crouching dragon must do is come out of the shadows, can a young phoenix really hope to fly…?"

Gongjin laughed nervously and said, "An interesting response. How would you rate yourself when compared with Zhuge Liang…?"

Pang Tong shrugged and replied, "Kongming and I are equals… or, perhaps, he exceeds me… or I exceed him… I do not truly know."

"Or is it that you don't want to find out…?" Zhou Yu asked. "Master, your skill and knowledge would be of immense value to the cause of Eastern Wu: would you condescend to helping us…?"

"I am content to remain in my current post," Pang Tong said. "Here, I appraise people, and harm not a hair on a person's head, in accordance with my wishes to live a peaceful, benevolent existence. Of course, I am aware that this may be more of a demand than a request…"

Gongjin shook his head and replied, "Not at all! I would not dare to harm a man such as you, Master… never."

Pang Tong laughed and said, "I am lucky. Now, Cao Cao's agents and yourself have spared me, despite my refusal to do service. Most who refuse Cao Cao, like the venerable Hua Tuo, meet an early death; yet here I am, alive to refuse another hero of the age… I wonder, then, what will become of me…?"

"Is it that you do not wish to contend with your friend, Crouching Dragon…?" Gongjin asked. "If so, please be aware that his lord and mine are allies: surely you have heard that they have now secured their everlasting friendship with a marriage between Governor Liu and Lady Sun."

"I have," Pang Tong replied. "A great boon for the people of Jing, indeed: there has been no peace here since the death of Liu Biao. To once again know that wonderful time when men of learning could go from county to county, town to town, debating and lyricizing, composing and pondering… alas, the times since Liu Biao's demise have been dark ones, indeed."

Gongjin wondered whether Pang Tong was making a point: he nodded soberly and said, "I hope the recent stability has brought those times back."

"It is too early to say," Pang Tong replied honestly. "The signs are good, however, as are the signs that good relations between the

houses of Sun and Liu at all levels, from the meek to the mandated, will be sound. Let us hope that those signs point to the truth, shall we...?"
Gongjin nodded repeatedly and mechanically.
"...I wonder, were you interested in hearing about the worthy men of the city, so as to know what great minds to employ?" Pang Tong continued. "What I do not already know, I can find out, Administrator Zhou."
"Uh... no, not for now, thank you," Gongjin replied. "In fact, I expect that you are very busy, as I am... I shan't keep you any longer, Master."
Pang Tong smiled cheerfully and said, "Feel free to call upon me anytime for advice on worthy men to serve your administration. Good day, Administrator Zhou."
Gongjin smiled and nodded sadly; Pang Tong got to his feet, bowed humbly and departed.
"...Such men are free spirits," Gongjin murmured. "...Who am I to trap him...?"

Gongjin's morale was further dampened when Liu Bei's imminent return to Gong'an was announced within weeks; he quickly learned that Zhuge Liang had feigned a crisis in order to lure his master away from the 'Luxury Trap' and bring him back to his senses, just as Gongjin had feared.
"So what now...?" Sun Yu asked.
"...I am confounded again," Gongjin replied. "But I must accept it, Zhongyi: it is the way of things. Yuan Shao knew Gongsun Zan, and so Yijing burned; Cao Cao knew Yuan Shao, and so Wuchao burned; I knew Cao Cao, and so the Han fleet burned at Red Cliffs. Now *Zhuge Liang* knows *me*, so... so I must become harder to know if we are to avoid future disasters."
"Yes, I understand that, but does Liu Bei's return mean that we are not going to invade Yi now...?" Sun Yu asked.
"I will let *no one impede me*," Gongjin replied. "Yi will be *ours*."

There would be no change of plan: Gongjin prepared to make the journey to Chaisang and properly explain his future plans to the court for the first – and, unbeknownst to him, last – time.

✳✳✳✳✳✳✳✳✳✳✳✳

120

Sun Quan asked Liu Bei to attend a banquet in order to see his reaction: Bei agreed to it, and a grand feast in Sun Quan's residence was prepared ahead of Bei's departure.

"So why do you suddenly hurry off, then, Xuande...?" Sun Quan asked after some time had passed and the other guests were suitably distracted by music and their own conversations.

"Please do not be offended, Zhongmou," Liu Bei replied. "I am alerted to some small internal matters that require my immediate attention, after which I might well return since you have been so courteous and welcoming."

"...Know that you are welcome here at all times," Sun Quan said as his eyes wandered and caught sight of Lü Fan, who was frowning thoughtfully.

The banquet continued for a few more hours, after which the guests started to leave: Sun Quan contrived it so that Liu Bei would remain as the last guest, after which he asked, "Why do you really leave here, Xuande...? It's just you and I that sit here now, so you can be honest. Are you afraid of something...?"

"Not at all," Liu Bei insisted. "And I am drunk, Zhongmou – though only slightly – and not really equipped for telling convincing lies."

Sun Quan laughed and said, "I, too, am far too honest when drunk! Some say it's a sign of a poor leader."

"Nonsense," Liu Bei retorted. "How did you get – or keep – all of this if you did not earn it...?"

Sun Quan smirked but did not respond.

"...I know that I should not say what I say next, Zhongmou, but I must," Liu Bei continued. "What you have is yours, earned by sound g-governance, and that's how it should be. But you rely too much on others."

"Doesn't every lord...?" Sun Quan asked. "Don't you rely a lot on Jian Yong, Sun Qian, Zhuge Liang, Guan Yu, Zhang Fei...?"

"I rely on them... a lot," Liu Bei admitted. "Why I rely on Jian Yong, I do not know, with all the trouble he causes me, and Zhang Fei can sometimes, with his temper, ruin my fortunes, and he has done! But they're friends as well, I suppose."

"I have 'friends' as vassals too," Sun Quan replied. "Pan Zhang, Zhu Ran, Zhou Yu–"

"Ah! Ah, yes, well, that's the very man," Liu Bei said. "Zhou Gongjin... he's a genius, but you shouldn't rely too much on him."

"...Oh...? Why not...?" Sun Quan asked.

"Don't misunderstand," Liu Bei protested. "He's a fine man, Zhongmou: his great genius won us our victory against Cao Cao. But men like that, they... they are not content to serve another forever. Men like him, they... they will want their own fief sooner or later, because–"

"The dragon won't be content in a pond...?" Sun Quan chuckled.

"Yes!" Liu Bei replied. "Yes, that's a very good way of putting it."

"...I'll ponder your words, Xuande, but he's my brother-in-law," Sun Quan said.

"That won't necessarily matter," Liu Bei replied without thinking: he realised his error moments later and added, "His loyalty was to

Bofu, with whom he went on great adventures: you and I, we-"
"Say no more," Sun Quan said. "I will ponder your words."
Liu Bei could sense that he had spoken too frankly: he laughed
uneasily and raised his wine dish, saying, "No more politics."
"I think that would be best!" Sun Quan replied.

The two rulers drank together for a few hours more and
discussed less controversial subjects, but Sun Quan was left
perturbed once Liu Bei had left his home and begun his journey
back to Gong'an.
"Are you alright, Lord Sun...?" Gu Li asked.
"...I don't know, Li," Sun Quan admitted. "One thing that great
power brings with it is an unwanted inability to know whom you
should really trust..."
Gu Li hummed thoughtfully but said nothing.

Time passed. Gongjin left Jiangling in the hands of capable and
reliable officials and travelled to Chaisang, where Sun Quan was
preparing to make the move to his new capital, Wucheng City,
after years of patient waiting; Quan immediately summoned the
court for a meeting at Gongjin's request.
"Welcome back, Gongjin," Sun Quan said. "Do you feel better...?"
Gongjin was obviously poorly; his face was gaunt, his skin pale
and his muscle wasted from a year of convalescence for the
wound that he had sustained while taking Jiangling. But Gongjin
had not come to Chaisang to discuss his own health: he smiled
and replied, "I will feel like a tiger that has grown wings if I can be
of proper service to you at this latest critical hour, Lord Sun."
"...Oh...? Has something happened...?" Sun Quan asked.
"Your new brother-in-law, Liu Bei, has returned to Gong'an,"
Gongjin replied. "Liu Zhang, Governor of Yi Province, faces new
hostility from his father's secret 'pet tiger', Zhang Lu, who now
demands vengeance for the destruction of his family at Liu
Zhang's hands; Ma Chao and Han Sui have made their peace, and
Ma now ponders a way to have his closest family – his father and
brothers – released from Cao Cao's custody; and Cao Cao himself
is plagued by rebellions, political pressure in the Imperial court
and tribal uprisings, so he cannot seek his unjust 'revenge' for his
loss at Red Cliffs right now – in fact he tells the Son of Heaven's
court that we did nothing, and that he burned his own boats to
curtail the spread of disease."
Some of the officials and officers laughed in response; other
officials frowned disapprovingly.
"So what do you propose...?" Sun Quan asked.
"Huancheng is ours, and nearby Ruxu is, as you will soon see, a
promising dock for the landing of ships," Gongjin replied. "That
opens the way for a second attack on Hefei and the subsequent
reclamation of my home region, Jiujiang: how I long to see Shu
again, but it is another Shu – the 'river-lands' of Yi Province' –
that will be my focus while Lü Meng leads men to the northeast."
"You are committed to an invasion of Yi Province, then," Zhang
Zhao prompted.
"I am, Zibu, with Lord Sun's cousin Sun Yu as my second, as he
has been on other campaigns where success has been quickly
achieved," Gongjin said. "I know that Liu Bei has been mooted as
a possible 'negotiator' with Liu Zhang, and that we have discussed

approaching the lord of Yi as an ally, but Liu Zhang is a coward and a toady that once reprimanded his own father at the Regency court's decree, and any man that can let Li Jue and Guo Si – men that made a hostage of the Son of Heaven – tell him to reprimand his own father and *actually did it* is not an ally that we want. He will betray us later on."

"But your proposal implies a military alliance with *Zhang Lu*, Chief Commander Zhou," the politician Quan Rou said. "Is that wise…?" Many of the officials started murmuring anxiously.

"Agreed," Officer of Merit Wei Teng said. "I stood here nigh-on ten years ago and decried our then-lord – your brother-in-law Lord Sun Ce – for his reckless actions, and I do the same today: how can we be seen as righteous if we will stand alongside cultists that openly call for the destruction of the Empire…?"

"Quite right," Liu Ji said. "Zhang Lu wants my clan to be eradicated, and a pseudo-theocratic dictatorship installed in their place that uses rice as money: I, for one, won't be seen to work with such a man."

"Do not let this be another 'Red Cliffs moment' for this court, Chief Commander," Yuan Yao pleaded. "Fighting a treasonous Chancellor of State was too much for some men to stomach; allying with an enemy of Heaven to seize another's province is-"

"**Might I explain?**" Gongjin protested.

"Yes, let the Chief Commander explain, gentlemen," Qin Song said. "There is plenty of time for heckling later, when we know what we actually heckle."

"*Thank you*, Mister Qin," Gongjin replied dryly. "Any 'alliance' with Zhang Lu is ostensible, circumstantial, and never actual. Zhang Lu's shared goal is the removal of Liu Zhang as Governor of Yi, and he will unintentionally aid us in achieving that goal, though our paths will then immediately diverge, for he seeks the expansion of his heretic state while we seek the maintenance of order. Once Yi is secured, Lord Sun, I will immediately wage war upon Zhang Lu, destroying his grip on Hanzhong and bringing it under *our* control."

That announcement was met with some disquiet among Han loyalists that had returned to the court: many had been placated by the suggestion that Cao Cao was an 'ambitious hegemon', but Gongjin's plan to secure Hanzhong – the 'birthplace of the Han' in many minds – for Sun Quan was closer to an act of treason than they would have liked.

"I would then, with Yi and Hanzhong pacified, leave Sun Yu to guard those territories against our enemies and form an alliance with Ma Chao of Xiliang, whose father, Ma Teng, is a court-appointed Han general and former rebel in Liang Province that fought against the corruption spread by the 'Ten'," Gongjin continued. "Ma Teng is now Cao Cao's hostage in *Cao's capital*, Yè, rather than the Imperial capital Xuchang, which should-!"

Gongjin was forced to stop speaking by a sudden and debilitating burst of pain in his chest; Sun Quan leant forward and grasped at the air, but Gongjin gestured that he would be alright.

"…But didn't the lord's father, Sun Jian, the 'Tiger of Jiangdong', once go to Liang to fight Ma Teng and his Qiang barbarian hordes…?" Quan Rou said. "I mention it only because others will if I do not."

"It might cause us problems," the official Yan Jun agreed.

"I… am aware that we will be criticised," Gongjin replied. "But we must bear the criticism: Cao Cao made militias of the Qiang without ever punishing them for their perceived crimes, and when one sees how Cao dealt with the Wuhuan one must draw the proper conclusions. If Cao can employ the Qiang for himself, then we can employ the Qiang for the good of the people."

Sun Quan looked to the politician Gu Yong, who said, "That answer will do."

"So you would defeat Liu Zhang to take possession of Yi and then defeat Zhang Lu to take possession of Hanzhong," Zhang Zhao prompted. "What then, Chief Commander…?"

"The aforementioned alliance with Ma Chao would give us the pincer that we need to defeat the old villain and bring order to the nation," Gongjin replied. "I would then advance to Xiangyang, where I would be met by a second army led by Lord Sun Quan, and together we would conquer the north in the name of the people and bring an end to this era of chaos."

Sun Quan looked to his officials for signs of accord or discontent: Lü Fan, Lu Su, Zhang Zhao, Zhang Hong, Gu Yong, Quan Rou, Qin Song, Yan Jun, Yu Fan, Lu Ji and the majority of the others were visibly happy with the suggestion – or at the very least neutral – while a lesser number including Liu Ji, Yuan Yao and Wei Teng were noticeably unenthusiastic but unwilling to say or do more.

Sun Quan then turned to look at his senior officers: those that were present – Sun Yu, Sun Jiao, Xu Kun, Han Dang and Zhou Tai – were obviously keen, and that was enough.

"Very good… very good!" Sun Quan declared. "My esteemed brother-in-law, Liu Bei, has said that he would rather live as a hermit than attack Liu Zhang, and so he will do nothing to deal with that obvious threat to peace in our land: I will be the 'tiger lord' that succeeds where others fail and does what is right when others forget their obligations! Proceed at once, Zhou Gongjin: show all that live in the world the courage and strength of the men of the south!"

Gongjin bowed humbly – despite the pain – and replied, "I will toil like a horse or dog in your name, Lord Sun Quan: I will work tirelessly to-"

"*Ayah*…! Don't do that!" Sun Quan pleaded. "By all means toil, but not tirelessly, and do not try to bow! There is a world beyond these wars that you must live to see!"

"…I shall endeavour to do so," Gongjin replied tonelessly. "I shall leave at once."

"…At once…?" Lu Su whimpered.

"Yes, at once," Gongjin retorted. "Time is against us."

"I… think that we should take a brief recess," Sun Quan announced. "Good luck, Gongjin, and… and we shall speak soon."

Gongjin nodded silently and clasped his hands together in salute.

"Good luck indeed, Chief Commander," Zhang Zhao said. "You take with you all of our best wishes, of course, but also our hopes for the future."

"I shall not fail," Gongjin promised. "I could not face Bofu in the afterlife if I did not finish what he started."

Lü Fan approached Gongjin as the courtiers started to file out of the hall and said, "We have to talk… I can't let you go to Jiangling

without knowing that you have planned for every eventuality."
Gongjin nodded and replied, "That would be the proper course. Shall we discuss this in your office in the treasury...?"
Lu Su watched as Gongjin and Lü Fan departed the hall together and sighed, saying, "What will happen next...? Gongjin, what do you intend...?"
Zhuge Jin – who was stood at Lu Su's side – frowned and said, "You fear that he will go beyond even your ideas about double-crossing Liu Bei...?"
"My dream, Ziyu, is that your brother sees sense and comes over to us, and Liu Bei serves us as the third leg of my tripod until the time is right for Lord Sun to reach his full potential," Lu Su replied. "Gongjin is impatient and seeks a quicker, more dangerous end to the crisis: I only pray that this ends well."

Sun Quan returned to his private study and turned to Gu Li, saying, "Now I willingly place all of my faith in Gongjin: he is truly a great man, and even if he is 'a dragon in a pond' under me, I know him to be loyal and honest and concerned for the south before his own well-being."
Gu Li was silent.
"No man would try to undertake such a stressful, exhaustive venture in his condition unless he was thinking of others before himself," Sun Quan continued. "I have in Gongjin a man without compare: he is a hero, and I would bestow upon him whatever he desired if he was to bring greatness to the south, for he would have earned it!"
Gu Li hummed quietly.
"The people of the south will rise above all others," Sun Quan continued. "It is quite obviously our divine *destiny* to rise above all others: that is why the Yuans lost their hold over us, why Liu Biao and Huang Zu withered and yielded half of their well-guarded province to us, and why Cao Cao watched his mighty fleet burn when he brought it here to crush us! We shall shake off the last of the oppressive shackles that the Han court has placed on us and ascend to the sky, all of us, out of the pond that the Han has made us live in, for we are all dragons! The state of Eastern Wu will one day be the greatest nation under Heaven... for Heaven wills it so!"
Sun Quan smiled: he knew that he could rely on Gongjin to fulfil the dream of an Eastern Wu that could, one day, cover the land and supplant the Han Dynasty.

Lü Fan and Gongjin had their conversation, after which the two left the Chaisang treasury office and approached the carriage that would take Zhou to the docks so that he could then travel by ship to Jiangling; Lü Fan smiled awkwardly and said, "Well, anyway, as I said earlier... good luck, Gongjin."
The two men then exchanged polite but slight bows; Lü had said his last words, but they were suddenly reluctant to end their conversation. Gongjin sighed and replied, "I know that you fear the worst, Ziheng: so do I, but is there any other man that I can entrust with this?"
"I suppose not," Lü Fan said. "But you are not fully recovered from your injury at Jiangling: you struggle with drinking tea, and

you wince periodically, and those are not signs of-"
"For my lord Sun Quan, and for his late brother, my friend Bofu, I would gladly risk my life," Gongjin insisted. "I have two guards and a physician as travelling companions until I reach Jiangling, whereupon I will have Sun Zhongyi with me, and he is as reliable and solid as a rock. Liu Bei will not get the better of us anymore than Liu Xun did: like Xun, Bei has an unexpected army from Lujiang, and like Xun he will flee to some far off place, where he will doubtless resume his former life as a sandal weaver."
Lü Fan laughed and said, "I'm reassured! Farewell, Gongjin."
Gongjin nodded, smiled and turned to board the carriage.
"...Wait," Lü Fan said suddenly.
"What now...?" Gongjin chuckled.
"You will not visit your home before you go...?" Lü Fan asked.
"My household is preparing to join me in Jiangling," Gongjin replied. "Why visit now when we will be together before long...?"
"...Of course, yes," Lü Fan said. "Yes... farewell again."
Gongjin shook his head bemusedly and continued on his way.
"...We cannot meet again soon, my friend," Lü Fan murmured as he watched the carriage move further and further away. "What... what a shame that is... what a shame."

Gongjin contented himself with reading a classic text as he travelled toward the Chaisang docks; the journey was endurable for the most part, but Gongjin was jolted violently as the carriage passed over a stone, and he felt something inside him stir.
"Are you alright, Chief Commander?" the physician asked.
"I...! ...I am fine," Gongjin insisted. "It... it's nothing."

But Gongjin was obviously in a great deal of discomfort as he boarded the small ship that would take him back to Jiangling: he stumbled twice, despite being a seasoned sailor, and that worried his companions.
"...I can see... the looks on your faces," Gongjin chortled. "To Jiangling at once: I'm fine!"
The physician could sense that the Chief Commander was not at all fine, but he did not argue.

The boat ride was, at first, quiet, although Gongjin repeatedly winced and clutched his chest for several moments before dismissing his physician's concerns: but as the ship neared the western edge of Changsha Prefecture, Gongjin's condition suddenly deteriorated, and he fell to his knees.
"**Chief Commander!**" one guard cried.
"**What is wrong with him?!**" the second guard exclaimed.
The crew of the ship were torn between halting the vessel and continuing with their work; the physician looked at the captain and asked, "Where is the nearest settlement where the Chief Commander can receive proper treatment?"
"...We could go to Ba Qiu," the captain replied.
"**Ba Qiu is back the way we came!**" the first guard said.
"Not *that* Ba Qiu," the captain retorted. "There's a 'Ba Qiu' port very close to here with hotels and-"
"If it is a proper settlement then that will do," the physician said. "Hurry, Captain, and take us there!"

"S-summon them all," Gongjin pleaded. "I... must be heard...!"

Gongjin was settled into the governor's mansion in Ba Qiu, Changsha Prefecture while someone sent word to Sun Quan: the court's reaction was understandable horror.
"Gongjin must be saved!" Sun Quan cried. "I will go myself, and take with me my personal physicians!"
"He is in Ba Qiu, Lord Sun, in territory controlled by *Liu Bei*!" Zhang Zhao said. "At such short notice we cannot-!"
"Who else is there that I can rely on?" Sun Quan retorted. "He must endure, or Cao will... no, Zhang Zhao, I must leave at once! Lu Su, Zhuge Jin, Song Qian, Zhou Tai: we will go together!"
Gu Yong coughed deliberately and said, "Shouldn't you also take Lady Qiao and Chief Commander Zhou's children, in case he... *cannot* endure...?"
Sun Quan was suddenly lost for words: he nodded silently in response and turned his gaze downward to hide his tears.

Xiaoqiao was silently resigned when Lu Su and Lü Fan entered her home together: she knew that two men that disagreed so strongly would only visit her together if something terrible had happened.
"...I... Lady Qiao... I...!" Lu Su whimpered.
"What... has happened, gentlemen...?" Xiaoqiao asked.
"He needs you," Lü Fan said as calmly as he could. "You must hurry to his side at once."
Xiaoqiao's eyes filled with tears as she smiled falsely and replied, "I understand, Mister Lü: I shall ready myself at once."
Lu Su exhaled forlornly as he watched Xiaoqiao's retreat from the living quarters: Lü Fan waited until she had gone before he turned to Lu Su and said, "Now it is our turn to discuss the future."
"...I suppose it is," Lu Su replied. "I- ...Never mind. Lead the way."

Gongjin did his best to fight the pain, but his physical health could not be recovered by positive thoughts: he managed to make one last statement – saying that he believed that his former benefactor Lu Su should succeed him as Chief Commander – before he lost the strength to do anything at all.
Zhou Yu of Shu City, Lujiang Prefecture finally lost consciousness and passed away before Sun Quan's boat was ready to leave Chaisang: he was just 35 years of age. Zhou Yu had outlasted his friend and brother-in-law Sun Ce by ten years, and he had died, just as Ce had, by a wound inflicted by an assassin's arrow; and, like Sun Ce, Zhou Yu would be remembered as a man that had changed the politics of Han Dynasty China in previously unimaginable ways. The formerly poverty-stricken region of Jiangdong was now the fledgling state of Eastern Wu with a standing army of close to 100,000 men and a healthy, growing economy: that was largely due to the efforts of Sun Ce and Zhou Yu, and few denied it. Sun Quan had often wondered what could not be achieved while Zhou Yu lived: the answer to that question would never be known.

****

EPILOGUE: A NEW DIRECTION

"...So here we are."

Chief Treasurer Lü Fan had his lord's adviser Lu Su sit as a guest in his living quarters; after taking his own seat as host, Fan added, "I am so upset that I am numb... which is a strange feeling, after all the loss that- ...I ramble."

"I feel the same, Ziheng," Lu Su replied. "Please, carry on."

"I shall, but with *business*," Lü Fan said. "You know what I think."

"...And as Acting Chief Commander, I must protest and ask that you change your mind, Ziheng!" Lu Su retorted. "With Gongjin... *gone*... you and I must work together more closely now, and-!"

"Chief Commander," Lü Fan said. "You are Chief Commander now. The 'acting' is somewhat over."

"...That has not been stated," Lu Su replied.

"No, but it will be," Lü Fan said. "Like it or not – and I do not – you are now the man that will take us forward, and I have only invited you here to ask of you one simple, achievable thing."

"...What do you ask...?" Lu Su prompted.

"Don't render our cause irrecoverable," Lü Fan replied.

"I thought that you believed that no cause was irrecoverable," Lu Su said.

"A bit of denial, perhaps, or placatory language for others," Lü Fan explained. "Of course there is a point where a cause is beyond achieving: all that I ask is that you do not do the things that will leave us in that terrible situation. I know that you know what those things are, Mister Lu, because you are not as stupid as you are gullible. You divide your enemies to win, not yourself."

Lu Su shook his head angrily and said, "Your binary approach to everything is too idealistic! Life is not a game of chess! There are always more than two sides, even within a single faction!"

"But any good strategist knows that you then treat each division as a separate game and win it before you approach the largest challenge," Lü Fan retorted. "Just as every situation is not binary, so every smaller situation can be analysed and one or more binary situations found that can be resolved, simplifying the situations that will be dealt with later on. You think that allowing Liu Bei to grow into a powerful 'third player' will work to our advantage...? Have you ever wondered what a game of chess with three equal and opposing sides might look like...?"

"Oh, for-! ...This is *not a game of chess*!" Lu Su protested.

"No, it isn't, not anymore, thanks to you," Lü Fan replied disappointedly. "It is a sprawling mess with no clear objectives."

"When was it ever binary...?" Lu Su asked snidely. "How do we have no objectives...?"

"...Twenty-six years ago, there was the Han," Lü Fan replied. "That was it, on the surface: but peel back the façade and there was division at varying levels that could not be resolved so long as men added more objectives and created further internal division... in the end, even the 'Ten' were divided into two because of their differing personal ambitions, and that destroyed them. We risk the same by dividing one faction – 'Those that oppose Cao Cao', if you will – into two factions with competing objectives, and that will, in the end, be our ruin if we continue down that path."

Lu Su was silent.

"After the victory at Red Cliffs – which was my dear, departed

friend Gongjin's greatest gift to us – we had two paths to take, and we chose wrongly," Lü Fan continued. "We should have reined in Liu Qi and Liu Bei, and-"
"And risk them turning to Cao Cao...?" Lu Su heckled.
"...That was not an option for either of them," Lü Fan insisted. "Qi faced amnesty and exile at best; Bei would only know suffering and death. They would have had to accept whatever was offered, and we should have annexed their forces, put Liu Bei somewhere so that he could not scheme, and given Zhuge Liang, Guan Yu and the rest an ultimatum: serve Lord Sun or achieve nothing for the rest of their miserable lives. Zhuge Liang would have retired at worst; Guan Yu would have yielded, as he did to Cao Cao years ago; Liu Bei would have lived a meaningless life of luxury in Wu, married not to Lady Sun but to some other woman, and the way would be open for the straightforward, 'binary' encounter that Heaven demanded. Instead of that, we have a mess of your and Zhang Zhao's invention, tolerated by Gongjin only because he was wounded at Jiangling."
"He 'tolerated' Liu Bei before the siege ended!" Lu Su snapped.
"Necessity," Lü Fan retorted.
"Yes, 'necessity', and that is what tolerating him now is: necessity!" Lu Su insisted. "Trust me, Ziheng, I beg you: I can turn this to our advantage!"
"...I will remain in the treasury and continue to guard the finances that our state requires," Lü Fan replied. "I will never endorse your plan, for it is idiocy, but I will accept Gongjin's decision to appoint you as his successor... if only because I believe that he knew that it would all come right in the end. But I warn you again, Lu Su: do not ruin everything. We have come too far."
"...You have my word, Ziheng," Lu Su said. "I will sweat blood for Lord Sun Quan and for Gongjin: our dream *will* be realised."
"*Eventually*," Lü Fan sighed. "It will... *eventually*."

The state of Eastern Wu would continue to grow in the years to come, but in the short term, Zhou Yu's death meant the threat of war with the Han's Chancellor of State, Cao Cao – who would have felt relief at the death of the man that orchestrated the Battle of Red Cliffs – and the threat of fearless action by Liu Bei, whose advisers saw Zhou as the main obstacle to their faction's plan to seize Jing Province and either ally with or annex Yi Province in the name of restoring the lustre of the Han Dynasty; but the Han would not survive. Within ten years of Zhou Yu's death, Cao Cao's son Cao Pi would sweep the Han aside and found the Cao Wei Dynasty, leading in turn to Liu Bei declaring the west to be the Empire of Shu Han with himself as its emperor; Sun Quan, chieftain of the Sun clan of Fuchun, then completed Lu Su and Zhuge Liang's prophesied 'tripod' and declared himself the king of Eastern Wu, bringing about the 'Three Kingdoms' era of 3rd Century Imperial China that is so well known today.

****

CHARACTER PROFILES AND NAME PRONUNCIATION GUIDE

It may or may not come as a surprise that the author of a novel about China cannot actually read, write or converse in Chinese (I know a few words for the purpose of research and that's it): that could be seen as an indication of how interesting this era can be regardless of knowing the language or culture well, but it severely reduces what you can find in the way of further reading or information. The Three Kingdoms era is very popular in Far East Asia, so there are a lot of works based on the period, although there are only a few that have been translated to English and other European languages. But even when you find the work in your own language, there is the pronunciation hurdle to jump; this is a (admittedly simplistic) guide for the completely uninitiated to at least get started, although I should note that I am not a professional historian, language teacher or linguist of any kind and that my guide is not meant to be a professional start of a Chinese language course. That said, here we go.

Pronunciation of Chinese names can be very awkward, since the spellings generated by the Hanyu-Pinyin system are sometimes misleading. Cao Cao, for example, is often thought to be 'Cow Cow' at first. The first attempt at translating *Three Kingdoms* by C. H. Brewitt-Taylor used a different method for pronunciation, known as the Wade-Giles system, wherein Cao Cao was spelt T'sao T'sao: the modern approach assumes awareness of 'C' never being used as a 'K' (as in, say, *continue*), but always as an 'Ts' (similar to its usage in *central*). The pronunciation guide below does not use either Wade-Giles or Pinyin, and might itself be open to interpretation: hopefully, it will serve as a rough guide for English speakers. The characters are ordered alphabetically rather than by order of appearance or affiliation. Place names are completely translated or partially translated depending on what I felt worked best.

In every case, the family name is first, the given name second: nobles often take on a 'style name' in addition, which is often used to differentiate the friend, focus of respect, or ally from a stranger or enemy in conversation, hence I say 'in familiar terms' after the style name. Some of the details have been rewritten or corrected where mistakes were found post-publishing the previous books (As I always stress: I'm only human).

Some of the information provided along with the name – intended as a refresher, as an explanation as to what happened to them after they disappeared from the narrative, or to elaborate where the person was only mentioned in some context – can sometimes spoil surprises for a first-time reader. **You have been warned.**

NB: 'ow' on its own or after an apostrophe in a compound should be pronounced as it is in 'cow', 'ay' as in 'pay' and 'eye' as is. 'X' is a tough one, as is 'J': I vary my approach to the latter quite a bit, since it is a soft 'ch' that's almost a 'j' (just as 'B' is a soft 'P' and 'G' is a soft 'k'), but 'X' can be seen as 'Sh' or 'Hs' (I use 'Sh' because it best reflected it so far as my research went).

Name [Pronunciation] – *brief refresher on who the person was.*
*Any other name they were known by, typically their style name.

PEOPLE

Bian Hong [P'ee-arn Hong] – *attendant official in Danyang that serves Sun Yi and becomes increasingly disaffected*

Bu Zhi [P'oo Ch'ee] – *official in Sun Quan's court that plays an increasingly greater role through the years*
*Known by the courtesy name Zishan [Tz'ee-s'arn].

Cai Mao [Ts'eye Mah-oh] – *Admiral of Jing Governor Liu Biao's navy and his brother-in-law; Cai became very powerful and influential, and when Liu Biao died he supported Liu Cong inheriting the governorship and submitted to Cao Cao. His historical fate is vague at best, but in popular fiction Cao Cao is tricked into executing him (and hence weakening Cao Cao's naval capability) by Zhou Yu (Gongjin) during the 'Battle of Red Cliffs'*
*Known by the courtesy name Degui [T'er-k'oo-ee].

Cai Yong [Ts'eye Yong] – *famous polymath and Han official that was responsible for saving the unaltered works of many classical literati by petitioning the court for the creation of the Xiping Stones; he later earned the ire of the 'Ten Attendants' and suffered a long period of exile in the north and east of the country. During his stay in the east, he educated Gu Yong. He is responsible for launching the careers of many other men, including Chang'an magistrate and calligrapher Zhong Yao and scholar-prodigy Wang Can, who was the author of the Cao Wei Empire's official histories and a vassal to Liu Biao in his younger days. Dong Zhuo invited Cai Yong back to the court during his usurpation of power, and he accepted after less-than-gentle prodding; this would have fatal consequences when Dong Zhuo was finally murdered and his allies scrutinised. Cai Yong was named as one of those that tolerated and even assisted Dong Zhuo, and he was executed for it. His prodigious daughter Cai Wenji [Ts'eye Wern-jee] – who had been abducted and forcibly married to a Xiongnu tribal chieftain – was later saved by Cao Cao, who felt personal grief at the fate of her famous father and wanted to right what he believed to be an unforgivable wrong. Cai Wenji is a possible mother to the founder of the Han Zhao state of the so-called 'Sixteen Kingdoms' era that followed the Jin Dynasty's brief reunification of China.*
*Known by the courtesy name Bojie [Boh-Jee-eh]

Cao Ang [Ts'ao Arng] – *Cao Cao's ill-fated eldest son that is dead – killed during his father's famous defeat at Wan City – at the start of this work, and is only referred to*

Cao Anmin [Ts'ao Arn-min] – *Cao Cao's ill-fated nephew that is dead – killed during his uncle's famous defeat at Wan City – at the start of this work, and is only referred to*

Cao Cao [Ts'ao Ts'ao] – *famous and significant figure of the era;*

he was Sun Jian's colleague during the Yellow Turban Campaign and Eastern Pass Coalition but became a rival to Sun Ce and Sun Jian thereafter. He was the son of a marquis, and adopted grandson of a favoured palace eunuch. Cao lived a relatively charmed life, suffering far less than his contemporaries for acts of mischief and outright defiance. He had many influential friends, served successfully against the Yellow Turban rebels and was appointed one of the colonels of the 'Army of the Western Garden' shortly before the death of Emperor Ling. He then served as a field general in the anti-Dong Zhuo coalition, and was appointed as Governor of Yan Province. He later rescued Emperor Xian from the ruins of the capital and kept him in his own capital, Xuchang and locked horns with Yuan Shu, the Sun clan's master when Shu declared as an alternative emperor. The act of bringing Emperor Xian to his own province prompted many to accuse Cao of sedition, and he was then forced to face former friend and ally Yuan Shao and defeat him. Cao Cao then waged war on all of the remaining warlords in China, and by the last quarter of the first decade of the 3rd Century, only the exiled and disinherited Jing heir Liu Qi, wandering warlord Liu Bei and Wu ruler Sun Quan were prepared to oppose him. The famous 'Battle of Red Cliffs' resulted in a famous victory for the rebel warlords that forced Cao Cao on the defensive and lost him southern Jing. By the time of Cao Cao's death at the end of the second decade of the 3rd Century, he was Prime Minister of the Han, King of Wei, and perfectly placed to seize the imperial mandate, but it would be his son, Cao Pi, that would actually depose the Han Emperor and begin the era known as 'Three Kingdoms'.
*Known by the courtesy name Mengde [Mung-der].
*Also known as A'Man [Ah-Marn] as a child and for varying reasons in adulthood, from affectionate to derisive.
*Once labelled a *jianxiong* [jee-arn-shee-ong] (which the author translates at various point as 'Crafty Villain' and 'Hero of Chaos', as either might apply) by the appraiser Xu Shao.

Cao Cao's younger brother [Ts'ao] – *he is only referred to during this work; his daughter married Sun Kuang*

Cao Chong [Ts'ao T'ong] – *Cao Cao's prodigious son that once implemented Archimedes' Principle to weigh an elephant; he died young from an unspecified illness, not long, ironically, after Cao Cao had executed the famous physician Hua Tuo. He is only referred to in this work*

Cao Chun [Ts'ao T'oon] – *Cao Cao's cousin, Cao Ren's brother; he created Cao Cao's 'Tiger and Leopard Cavalry' that inflicted many defeats on Cao's enemies over the years. He was injured during the Battle of Steep-slope and died around the same time as Zhou Yu; he is only referred to in this work*
*Known by the courtesy name Zihe [Tz'ee-her].

Cao Hong [Ts'ao Hong] – *Cao Cao's cousin; the author portrays him as childish and idiotic, despite his being in his forties, because that appears to be his actual character. He is highly favoured because he once risked his life to save Cao Cao, and he is fiercely*

loyal, but his antics strain his relationship with his family, particularly Cao Zhen and future Cao Wei founder Cao Pi
*Known by the courtesy name Zilian [Tz'ee-lee-arn].

Cao Pi [Ts'ao Pee] – *Cao Cao's eldest living son; he only appears briefly in this work, but he eventually usurped the Han Dynasty, founded the first of the 'Three Kingdoms', Cao Wei, and became the Sun clan's greatest enemy for the 6 years that he reigned*
*Known by the courtesy name Zihuan [Tz'ee-hoo-arn].

Cao Ren [Ts'ao Rern] – *Cao Cao's cousin; he quickly gained a reputation as a fierce defender after guarding Jiangling for a year in the wake of the Battle of Red Cliffs and, a decade later, guarding Fan City against Guan Yu against all odds*
*Known by the courtesy name Zixiao [Tz'ee-shee-ow].

Cao Xiu [Ts'ao Shee-oo] – *Cao Cao's cousin and close friend of Cao Pi; he often fought at the front in his youth, but he became a prominent commander in later years. He was famously outwitted and defeated by Sun Quan's forces at the Battle of Stone Town during the Three Kingdoms era*
*Known by the courtesy name Wenlie [Wern-lee-er].

Cao Zhang [Ts'ao Ch'arng] – *Cao Cao's second eldest living son; he had a warrior's outlook on life and had little time for academia, much to his father's disappointment. He married Sun Ben's daughter as part of a marriage alliance*
*Known by the courtesy name Ziwen [Tz'ee-wern].
*Known by the nickname 'Yellow-beard'.

Cao Zhen [Ts'ao Ch'ern] – *Cao Cao's cousin; he was said to be obese through no fault of his own, likely a medical condition, but he was shrewd and intelligent. He often suffered bullying by his cousin Cao Hong in his youth, but he later rose to the position of Imperial Chief Commander under Cao Cao's grandson Cao Rui and fought primarily against Shu Han's Prime Minister Zhuge Liang*
*Known by the courtesy name Zidan [Tz'ee-t'arn].

Cao Zhi [Ts'ao Ch'ee] – *Cao Cao's third eldest living son; he was Cao Cao's preferred choice as crown prince when Cao founded the Kingdom of Wei, primarily due to his poetic talent*
*Known by the courtesy name Zijian [Tz'ee-jee-arn].

Captain Hu [Hoo] – *ADDED FOR NARRATIVE COHESION; junior officer during the Battle of Red Cliffs, non-fatal casualty of war*

"Chaisang Qin" [Chin] – *rebel leader in Yuzhang; historical full name was Qin Lang [Chin Larng]*

Che Zhou [T'er Ch'oh] – *Cao Cao's choice of Governor of Xu Province after wresting it from Lü Bu at the Battle of Xiapi; he was later murdered by Guan Yu when Liu Bei briefly recaptured the province prior to the Battle of Guandu*

Chen Dao [T'ern Da-oh] – *Liu Bei's trusted bodyguard and last line of defence; he is often excised and his role merged with Zhao Yun's in fiction*

Chen Deng [T'ern Derng] – *Cao Cao's appointed Administrator of Guangling; he is the son of Xu Province magnate Chen Gui and a minor 'antagonist' at the start of the work*
*Known by the courtesy name Yuanlong [Yoo-arn-long].

Chen Gong [T'ern K'ong] – *career adviser that initially served Cao Cao – who was, at that time, Governor of Yan Province – until Cao ravaged Xu Province; the disgusted Gong then allied with Cao's friend Zhang Miao and invited Lü Bu to invade Yan Province. Cao Cao killed Zhang Miao and chased Lü Bu and Chen Gong into Xu Province, where they then sheltered under the then-Governor Liu Bei; Lü and Chen then seized Xu, made a subordinate of Liu Bei and resisted for close to 4 years by way of an ever-more-complicated series of alliances. Lü Bu was defeated and captured at the Battle of Xiapi, and Chen chose to die alongside his lord*

Chen Gui [T'ern K'oo-ee] – *Xu Province magnate and father of Chen Deng; he was one of the men that conspired to rid Xu of Liu Bei and Lü Bu in succession, after which he served Cao Cao*

Chen Jiao [T'ern Ch'ee-ow] – *Han official that serves in Guangling (under Chen Deng) and then Jiangling (under Cao Ren) during the course of the work*

Chen Jiu [T'ern Ch'ee-oo] – *officer under Huang Zu that participates in a number of battles against the Sun clan's navy*

Chen Lan [T'ern Larn] – *Qian Hills Bandit that once served as an officer under Yuan Shu; later a leader of the Lujiang Rebellion*

Chen Qin [T'ern Chin] – *an unprofessional local official in Wu that is abusive when drunk and fatally provokes Ling Tong*

Chen Qun [T'ern Choon] – *son of the respected scholar Chen Ji [T'ern Chee], who was a victim of the 'Partisan Crisis' created by the 'Ten Attendants' during Emperor Huan's reign; Qun became a vassal of Liu Bei by circumstance, but came to disrespect Bei and defected to Lü Bu and then Cao Cao. Qun served the Han and Cao Wei Empires as a politician and adviser for many years*

Chen Wu [T'ern Woo] – *early ally of Sun Ce that became a formidable vanguard officer; he was supposedly very popular due to his good nature. He later served as a bodyguard to Sun Quan as well as continuing to serve as a field officer*
*Known by the courtesy name Zilie [Tz'ee-lee-er]

Chen Ying [T'ern Ying] – *younger brother of Chen Deng*

Cheng Bing [T'erng P'ing] – *a respected scholar that resides in Jiaozhi; he later served Sun Quan as Grand Tutor, but he is only referred to in this work during a banquet in Cangwu*

Cheng Pu [T'erng Poo] – *a well-known ally and close friend of Sun Jian from his first days as a military officer: he may have known Sun Jian before that, but the author has them meeting prior to volunteering to fight the Yellow Turbans. Cheng Pu went on to serve Sun Jian's eldest sons in turn: he served Sun Ce until the latter's death as a senior adviser and officer and then became an elder statesman during the early years of Sun Quan's reign*
*Known by the courtesy name Demou [T'er-moh]

Cheng Yu [T'erng Yoo] – *a respected scholar that became Cao Cao's adviser. He joined Cao Cao at around 50 years of age, and he was known for being cantankerous, frank and devoid of conscience when matters required it but prone to bouts of melancholy; he advised – with little success – his lord Cao Cao during his ill-fated campaign against Sun Quan*
*Known by the courtesy name Zhongde [Ch'ong-der]

Cheng Zi [Ch'erng Tz'ee] – *Cheng Pu's son: he is only referred to as being the guardian of Jiangxia when Cheng Pu moves to Jiangling to support the siege force*

Chief Ji [Ch'ee] – *ADDED FOR NARRATIVE COHESION; bandit chieftain in Yangxian that is humbled by Pan Zhang*

Chunyu Shi [T'oon-yoo S'ee] – *Sun clan's appointed Administrator of Kuaiji; the author has him in the role early into Sun Quan's rule. He once criticised Lu Xun's handling of local justice*

Colonel (later General) Yin [Yin] – *ADDED FOR NARRATIVE COHESION; an officer in Wanling that decides to support Dai Yuan and Gui Lan's plot to seize control of Danyang Prefecture*

Consort Dong [T'ong] – *daughter of Dong Cheng and concubine of Emperor Xian; she was strangled to death at Cao Cao's instruction after the 'Girdle Edict' plot (as the author refers to it) was exposed, despite being pregnant at the time*

Cui Yan [Ts'oo-ee Yarn] – *a Legalist scholar and official that served the Yuan clan until they were defeated by Cao Cao; he then served in the Han court in various important roles*
*Known by the courtesy name Jigui [Ch'ee-k'oo-ee]

Dai Yuan [T'eye Yoo-arn] – *a subordinate of ousted Wu Administrator Sheng Xian; he went on to plot against the Suns as revenge for Sheng Xian's assassination by Sun Quan*

Daqiao [T'ah-chee-ow] – *also known as the older Lady Qiao [Chee-ow], she is one of two beautiful sisters; she married Sun Ce after he broke away from Yuan Shu's regime. Sun Ce died young, but he had at least 3-4 children (a son and 2-3 daughters) in the year (or less) that he was married to Daqiao: Daqiao may have been the mother of them all, and the author assumes this to avoid controversy (Sun Ce and Daqiao are popularly portrayed as a devout loving couple, and the polygamy practiced by most influential Chinese men of the time – including Sun Ce's father –*

tends to debunk the sentiment in modern times).

"Demon Lü" [L'] – *rebel leader in Yuzhang; historical full name was Lü Hè [L'Her]*

Deng Dang [T'erng T'arng] – *the brother-in-law of the famous Sun family vassal Lü Meng; Meng followed him into Sun Ce's service.*

Deng Long [T'erng Long] – *officer under Huang Zu that once fought and lost to Zhou Yu at Chaisang*

Dian Wei [Tee'arn Way] – *Cao Cao's fearsome bodyguard; he was killed during an ambush at Wan City, and is only referred to*

Ding Yuan [T'ing Yoo-arn] – *a Han official and Inspector of Bing Province at the time of the Liang Province Rebellion and the Black Mountain Bandit attacks in the north; he later discovered and recruited the warrior Lü Bu. He was murdered by Bu, who then joined Dong Zhuo*

Dong Cheng [T'ong Ch'erng] – *former vassal of Dong Zhuo, Li Jue and Guo Si that asked Cao Cao to support the rescue of Emperor Xian; he later decided to plot against Cao and used a document – referred to by the author as the 'Girdle Edict' in reference to a famous version of the story – to rally men against Cao in, according to said document, the emperor's name. The plot was exposed, and Dong's family – including his daughter, who was a pregnant imperial consort – were put to death; his efforts lived on, however, and gave many men, including Liu Bei and Yuan Shao, justification for opposing Cao Cao later on*

Dong Xi [T'ong Shee] – *officer that joined Sun Ce during the latter's pacification of Kuaiji Prefecture: he went on to become a senior figure in the regimes of Sun Ce and Sun Quan, and played an important part in Quan's appointment as clan chieftain*
*Known by the courtesy name Yuanshi [Yoo-arn-shee]

Dong Zhuo [T'ong Ch'oo-oh] – *The infamous tyrant that seized the capital after the deaths of Emperor Ling, Commander Hè Jin and the 'Ten Attendants' and ruled villainously, protected by his foster son Lü Bu. Sun Jian encountered Dong Zhuo twice during his career – once in Liang, during the rebellion there, and again after Dong Zhuo seized power – and can be considered as one of his fiercest rivals and enemies. Dong Zhuo deposed the eldest son of Emperor Ling and placed his younger brother on the throne as Emperor Xian, an act that led to the majority of the warlords in the east of the country forming a coalition against him; that coalition later collapsed, but not before Sun Jian had forced Dong Zhuo to abandon the capital Luoyang and flee westward, toward the former Han capital Chang'an. Dong Zhuo remained in Chang'an with the young emperor as a hostage and enjoyed a life of vice and luxury while the warlords fought amongst themselves; eventually, a small group of officials managed to convince an ever-more frustrated Lü Bu to betray and kill Dong Zhuo*

Emperor Ling of the Han [Ling] – *the successor to Emperor Huan [Hoo-arn], who had no issue; some blame his misrule for the decline of the Han. He was Emperor during one of the most famous events in 'pre-Three Kingdoms era' history and folklore, the 'Yellow Turban Rebellion'. His death was followed by the rise of Dong Zhuo and the fission that resulted from that*
*Also known as (Han) Lingdi [(Harn) Ling-t'ee] (lit. Han Emperor Ling) when Lingdi is a better option for conciseness.

Emperor Shao of Han [S'ah-oh] – *Emperor Ling's eldest son, born to Empress Hè; he became Emperor shortly after the death of his father, but when Dong Zhuo came to power in the capital the young emperor was deposed, created the Prince of Hongnong and replaced by his younger brother Liu Xie, who became Emperor Xian, the last Emperor of the Han Dynasty. Bian was murdered by Dong Zhuo's agents during the crisis that followed his deposition*
*Known as Liu Bian [Lee-oo P'ee-arn], Prince of Hongnong [Hong-nong] after being deposed by Dong Zhuo.

Emperor Xian of Han [Shee-an] – *Emperor Ling's second son, Liu Xie [Shee-er] was born to Consort Wang [Warng] rather than Empress Hè: the jealous empress then poisoned his mother. He was first created the Prince of Bohai and then the Prince of Chenliu after the 'adoption' period ended, but despite being a second son by a consort, he would later become Emperor Xian after a series of extraordinary events in the court. It is no secret or 'plot spoiler' that the Han Dynasty was finally eradicated in the early 3rd Century; Xiandi was the last Han Emperor and had the 'privilege' of overseeing the final years of the decline. He is said to have lived for over a decade after abdicating as the Duke of Shanyang; his given date of death is unusually close to – as in not long after – the death of Zhuge Liang, Chancellor/Prime Minister of the independent state of Shu Han, whose mission it was to restore the Han in some form*
*Also known as (Han) Xiandi [(Harn) Shee-an-t'ee] (lit. Han Emperor Xian) when Xiandi is a better option for conciseness.

Empress Dowager Hè [Her] – *the second empress taken by Emperor Ling; her brother, Hè Jin, would go on to become Commander-in-Chief. She was the mother of Liu Bian, later Emperor Shao and Prince of Hongnong. She was later murdered by Dong Zhuo's agents, along with her son*
*Known as Empress Hè before the death of Emperor Ling.

Fei Zhan [Fay Ch'arn] – *powerful bandit chieftain in Danyang that is often mentioned but never seen*

Feng Kai [Ferng K'eye] – *a general in the Han army that serves at the Battle of Red Cliffs; the author makes him one of the estimated 100,000 casualties due to a lack of a historical fate*

Feng Ze [Ferng Tz'er] – *the man named as Huang Zu's killer during the Battle of Jiangxia; what happens to him after that is not known to this author at present*

Fu Xun [Foo Shoon] – *a politician in Liu Biao's court that later submitted to and served Cao Cao*
*Known by the courtesy name Gongti [K'ong-tee]

Fu Ying [Foo Ying] – *a subordinate of Sun Yi*

"Gan Ji" [K'arn Ch'ee] – *the author will either relish or regret the addition of this character! The stories surrounding Sun Ce's death are many and vivid, and one of the most famous is the one that partially or entirely blames his untimely end on the Taoist 'saint', Gan/Yu Ji. The historical Gan Ji gave his teachings to a mid-2nd Century Han Emperor, so by the time that he is supposed to have appeared in Jiangdong – 2 years before the dawn of the 3rd Century – he would have to have been very old indeed. Folk tales state that Sun Ce had this popular healer and philosopher put to death for heresy and that his spirit then exacted a revenge of sorts by hounding Ce while he was recovering from an assassination attempt: the author plays with this myth and the popular debunking by having the text's Gan Ji be an almost certain fraud but showing that Sun Ce's decision haunts him and earned him critics and, perhaps, dangerous enemies.*
*Known as Yu Ji [Yoo Ch'ee] in some works.

Gan Ning [Garn Ning] – *pirate leader and mercenary that actually began his career in Yi Province; he fled the region after a failed rebellion against the recently-installed governor, Liu Zhang, and sought shelter with Liu Biao, who was probably supporting the rebellion in some way (or even planning it). Gan did not remain in Liu Biao's court for long: he went south and joined Huang Zu, who never trusted him and ultimately drove him to the side of the Sun clan despite his killing Ling Cao during a failed attack on Xiakou*
*Known by the courtesy name Xingba [Shing-p'ah]

Gao Gan [K'ao K'arn] – *a relation of Yuan Shao; he served as the Yuans' appointed Governor of Bing Province. Gao tried to aid Yuan Shang's attempts to defeat Cao Cao, but he was ultimately defeated and killed; his fate is referred to in discussions*

Gao Shou [K'ao S'oh] – *a subordinate of Sun Shao (1)*

Gao Shun [K'ao S'oon] – *a subordinate of Lü Bu; he remained with Bu until his death, but the two men had a difficult working relationship. Gao Shun was known for his honesty and his skill as a field commander; he was nicknamed 'The Camp Smasher' for his very successful tactics against bandit armies*

Gong Du [K'ong T'oo] – *a bandit leader in Runan that aided Liu Bei's forces during the Battle of Guandu*

Gongsun Du [K'ong-soon T'oo] – *warlord-governor of the Liaodong Peninsula at the time of Taishi Ci's self-imposed exile that reputedly respected Taishi very much: Taishi rescued a man from Du's wrath, however, leading to Taishi becoming a fugitive from Gongsun as well*

Gongsun Kang [K'ong-soon Karng] – *warlord-governor of the Liaodong Peninsula that inherited the role from Gongsun Du; he turned the Yuan brothers over to Cao Cao after the White Wolf Mountain campaign*

Gongsun Zan [K'ong-soon Tz'arn] – *a warlord during the last two decades of the 2nd Century; he was a friend of Liu Bei, and was known for his tumultuous relationship with the Ru County Yuan clan. He collaborated with Yuan Shu from time to time and briefly worked with Yuan Shao, but he later became fiercely antagonistic toward the latter for a number of reasons. He then fought Yuan Shao for control of Ji, Qing and Yòu provinces. He once sent his nephew to aid Sun Jian. Gongsun Zan was defeated and killed by Yuan Shao, and his ill-gotten holdings became Shao's*
*Known by the courtesy name Bogui [P'oh-goo-ee]

Gu Li [K'oo Lee] – *an indentured servant in Sun Quan's household that eventually earned his freedom and became one of Quan's most trusted subordinates at home and in battle*

Gu Yong [K'oo Yong] – *a student of the famed scholar Cai Yong while the latter was in exile in Yang Province; Gu joined Sun Ce and became one of the men that helped Ce and his brother Quan to build the state of Eastern Wu*
*Known by the courtesy name Yuantan [Yoo-arn-tarn]

Guan Yu [K'oo-arn Yoo] – *an early ally of Liu Bei who is famous in his own right; he is known for his long beard, his green robes, his learnedness, his lofty demeanour, his 'Green Dragon' weapon (which the author has retained despite its being a possible fiction), his fictional inheritance of the equally-fictional 'Red Hare' warhorse from Lü Bu, and his similarly fictional unmatched skill in battle, although his historical skill is still quite impressive. He is revered by the lawful and the lawless alike, since he is seen as a man that applied morals where appropriate to achieve an ultimate end*
*Known by the courtesy name Yunchang [Yoon-charng]

Gui Lan [K'oo-ee Larn] – *loyal vassal of ousted Wu Prefecture Administrator Sheng Xian; he plotted against the Suns as revenge for Sheng Xian's assassination by Sun Quan*

Guo Jia [K'oo-oh Ch'ee-ah] – *perhaps the most famous of Cao Cao's advisers, and one of the most capable; he guided Cao towards historic victories against Yuan Shu, Yuan Shao, Yuan Tan, Yuan Shang and the Wuhuan tribal confederacy. He was, however, not a well man – the author follows the notion that he was vice-afflicted in order to deliberately shorten his life and 'relieve the boredom – and he died aged 37, just after the White Wolf Mountain campaign against the Wuhuan. Cao Cao lamented for years thereafter that Guo was the only man that he could rely on: he famously blamed his defeat at Red Cliffs on Guo's absence*
*Known by the courtesy name Fengxiao [Fung-shee-ow]

Guo Si [K'oo-oh See] – *a general serving Dong Zhuo; he later cooperated with fellow Liang Province general Li Jue and became co-regent after Dong Zhuo's death. He later fought with Li Jue after external provocations by unwitting agents of the emperor's loyalists that included Guo Si's own wife: Emperor Xian fled the capital and the regents – minus their vital hostage – quickly lost power and were killed by their own vassals. Guo Si died first.*

"Haixi Chen" [H'eye-shee T'ern] – *bandit king from the Haixi region of Xu Province that was defeated by the Sun clan forces: his full name was Chen Yu [T'ern Yoo]*

Han Dang [Harn T'arng] – *one of the first men to join Sun Jian when he began his military career: he is not as prominent a figure as Zhu Zhi, Cheng Pu and Huang Gai, but his contributions were considerable, even if he was not always successful. His son went on, regrettably, to be less of an asset to the Sun regime*
*Known by the courtesy name Yigong [Yee-k'ong]

Han Hao [Harn hah-oh] – *a Han officer serving Cao Cao*

Han Song [Harn Song] – *adviser and politician in Liu Biao's court that later submitted to and served Cao Cao*
*Known by the courtesy name Degao [T'er-k'ow]

Han Sui [Harn Soo-ee] – *a Liang Province official that became one of the three Qiang tribal kings in the region*

Han Xi [Harn Shee] – *an officer serving Huang Zu*

Han Xian [Harn Shee-arn] – *Liu Biao's chosen ruler of Changsha*

Han Yin [Harn Yin] – *adviser to the warlord Yuan Shu; he met his end when acting as a go-between for a marriage alliance between Yuan Shu and Lü Bu, when Bu made one of his famous political turnarounds and sent Han Yin to Cao Cao for disposal.*

Han Zong [Harn Tz'ong] – *son of Han Dang that appears in this work as Dang's oft-used second on campaigns (in lieu of knowing who might serve Han Dang in that capacity historically); he became famous in Eastern Wu for entirely the wrong reasons immediately after his father's death*

Hè Jin [Her Jin] – *the brother of Empress Hè; the Hè family were not nobles or magnates, but Lady Hè's beauty elevated Hè Jin from a butcher to the head of the Imperial army within a few years. After the Yellow Turban Rebellion, Hè Jin tried to change the structure of the court, and in particular to reduce the influence of the eunuch faction known as the 'Ten Attendants'; his feud with the eunuchs had a number of unforeseen consequences. Hè Jin invited Dong Zhuo to the capital Luoyang and began a plan to slaughter the 'Ten', but they learned of his intentions and were able to strike first, slaying him in the palace gardens while he was unarmed, alone and vulnerable. Hè Jin's ally Yuan Shao avenged his death by leading a purge of the palace eunuchs, but it was too late to undo the political damage: when Dong Zhuo arrived, he saw the chaos that had resulted from Hè Jin's death and exploited*

it, taking over the imperial court and beginning the next dynastic crisis. His grandson Yan was adopted by Cao Cao when Cao controversially took Yan's widowed mother as a consort
*Known by the courtesy name Suigao [Soo-ee-gah-oh]

Hè Qi [Her Chee] – *a Kuaiji official that defected to Sun Ce during the latter's Kuaiji campaign against the Administrator Wang Lang. He was adept at pacifying the ethnic tribes and famous for his ostentatious lifestyle, generosity and careful budgeting*
*Known by the courtesy name Gongmiao [K'ong-mee-ow]

Hè Yan [Her Yarn] – *the/a grandson of the famous Han Commander-in-Chief Hè Jin, who was murdered by the 'Ten Attendants' during the succession crisis that followed the death of Emperor Ling; Yan's father also died unexpectedly, and his mother was taken by the Han's Excellency of Works, Cao Cao, as a consort. Cao Cao adopted Yan, but Yan kept his father's family name – so that his clan would survive - with Cao's blessing*
*Known by the courtesy name Pingshu [Ping-s'oo]

"Heng" [Herng] – *ADDED FOR NARRATIVE COHESION; a loyal subordinate of the agitator Xu Gong that is shown avenging Gong by taking part in an assassination attempt on Sun Ce*

Hua Tuo [Hoo-ah Too-oh] – *famous physician, acupuncturist, spiritualist and scholar; he travelled Han China in an endless quest for knowledge and the advancement of medical science. The Han Chancellor, Cao Cao, suffered violent migraines and wanted Hua to not only cure them but serve as his personal physician in the capital thereafter; Hua resisted the idea of being permanently stationed in Xuchang – and therefore unable to do vital research – and repeatedly found excuses to escape, whereupon Cao – in a fit of rage and fuelled by mistrust – ordered Hua to be imprisoned, tortured and finally executed for disobeying orders. Hua Tuo was said to be a pioneer in a number of disciplines, so his loss – along with his extensive book of research – is often said to be one of Cao Cao's worst missteps. Hua is usually given an extended lifespan in fiction, dying over a decade after he was historically executed, and he is often given Guan Yu and Zhou Tai as other famous patients; he is only referred to in this work*

Hua Xin [Hoo'ah Shin] – *appointed Administrator of Yuzhang; he was initially allied to Liu Yao but went on to serve Sun Ce, Sun Quan and then Cao Cao*
*Known by the courtesy name Ziyu [Tz'ee-yoo]

Huan Jie [Hoo'arn Ch'ee-er] – *a politician and diplomat that served Sun Jian until the latter's death in Jing Province, whereupon he negotiated the return of Sun Jian's body to the Sun family and then defected to Jing Governor Liu Biao. He later served Cao Cao and may, according to some sources, have been a vocal proponent of the last Han Emperor's abdication in favour of Cao Cao's heir Cao Pi*
*Known by the courtesy name Boxu [P'oh-shoo]

Huang Bing [Hoo-arng P'ing] – *eldest son of Huang Gai*

Huang Gai [Hoo-arng K'eye] - *an early ally of Sun Jian and veteran officer to Sun Ce and Sun Quan: he is most famous for his key role in the Battle of Red Cliffs, where he feigned defection to Cao Cao's forces and guided several boats containing flammable articles toward Cao's fleet, destroying it. He was injured in that battle, but he continued to serve Wu until his death*
*Known by the courtesy name Gongfu [K'ong-foo]

Huang Longluo [Hoo-arng Long-loo-oh] – *a bandit chieftain in Kuaiji Prefecture; he rose up against Sun Ce with his ally Zhou Ba, but both were killed by Dong Xi, giving Dong a legendary status that he capitalises upon during this work on multiple occasions*

Huang Shè [Hoo-arng S'er] – *son of Huang Zu and an officer in Zu's army: his father repeatedly deploys him against the Suns*

Huang Yi [Hoo-arng Yi] – *son of Huang Zu and an officer in Zu's army: his father repeatedly deploys him against the Suns*

Huang Zu [Hoo-arng Tz'oo] – *Administrator of Jiangxia Prefecture in southeast Jing Province and the head of a powerful family in its own right; he effectively ruled Jiangxia, despite being in the service of Jing governor Liu Biao. He is considered to be the man that orchestrated the death of Sun Jian. He was eventually defeated by Sun Quan prior to the famous 'Battle of Red Cliffs' in a series of battles that are recounted in this work*

Huangfu Song [Hoo-arng-foo Song] – *a prominent general of the Han Dynasty army; he was extremely effective against the Yellow Turbans, and he was renowned for his upstanding moral values and generous nature. He challenged the 'Ten Attendants' and therefore suffered a temporary downturn in his career, but he had one last significant victory against the Qiang rebels that was then impacted by concurrent events in the capital. He died in relative obscurity during the Li Jue/Guo Si regency period.*

Huchuquan [Hoo-t'oo-choo-arn] – *the 'Chanyu' – chieftain of chieftains – of the Southern Xiongnu tribes that live in Bing Province and supply the Han with cavalrymen. He is the brother of the famous rebel Yufuluo and uncle of Liu Bao, whose progeny would one day rule part of China. Huchuquan is passively serving the Han during the timeframe of this work and is only referred to*

Hui Qu [Hoo-ee Choo] – *a vassal of Yuan Shu that was later appointed as 'Inspector of Yang Province' to rival the court's appointee Liu Yao; he is briefly referred to but his fate is unknown*

Ji Ling [Jee Ling] – *a high-ranking officer serving Yuan Shu; he was one of Shu's best officers, but he died defending Shu's domains and is only referred to in this work*

Jia Xu [Jee-ah Shoo] – *an adviser and politician; Jia Xu served the tyrant Dong Zhuo until the latter's death, at which point he aided*

Dong's generals Li Jue and Guo Si when they tried to govern as co-regents to Emperor Xian. He is probably one of the most divisive and decisive figures of the period, and is, it might be argued, one of the greatest strategists of the time, an equal or perhaps superior to more famous figures such as Zhuge Liang, Pang Tong, Zhou Yu, Lü Meng, Lu Xun, Sima Yi and Guo Jia. He is serving Cao Cao's clan at the beginning of this work, and does so for over twenty years, dying during the reign of Cao Pi, whose place as Emperor of Cao Wei was due, in part, to Jia
*Known by the courtesy name Wenhe [Wern-her]

Jian Shuo [Jee-arn S'oo-oh] and his uncle – *Jian Shuo was one of the 'Ten Attendants', the eunuch faction that held immense power during the reigns of Emperors Huan and Ling; his uncle was arrested for insubordination and whipped until near-death by the then District Captain of Luoyang, Cao Cao, who was looking for a way to harm the 'Ten'. Cao Cao was exiled to Ji'nan for his 'mischief'; Jian Shuo later became the Commander of the 'Army of the Western Garden', a coalition of private militias that was created to rival the standing army and its Commander-in-Chief, Hè Jin, but Jian was a victim of in-fighting between the eunuchs and was betrayed and executed for plotting. Jian and his uncle are both referred to in discussions during this work*

Jian Yong [Jee-arn Yong] – *an ally of imperial scion Liu Bei who is said, in some accounts, to have travelled with Bei from the earliest days of his career; he was said to be vulgar and direct, so the author tends to use Jian Yong as a means for lightening the mood. He does not appear prominently in this work*
*Known by the courtesy name Xianhe [Shee-an-her]

Jiang Gan [Jee-arng K'arn] – *a Han official that knew Zhou Yu as a youth; they were likely schooled together. Jiang is employed by Cao Cao during the siege of Jiangling in an unsuccessful effort to convince Zhou Yu to retreat, defect or submit; in many fictional works Jiang is employed even sooner, approaching Zhou during the Battle of Red Cliffs and becoming an oblivious pawn Zhou's very successful scheme to remove the threat posed by Admiral Cai Mao (and Cai's nephew Zhang Yun) and thus weaken Cao's navy*
*Known by the courtesy name Ziyi [Tz'ee-yee]

Jiang Ji [Jee-arng Jee] – *a young assistant to Yang Province Inspector Liu Fu that went on to become an adviser to Cao Cao in later life; he jointly masterminded the schemes that prevented Sun Quan from taking Hefei Fortress on his first visit, and he later assisted Cao Xiu's defence of Stone Town with less success*
*Known by the courtesy name Zitong [Tz'ee-tong]

Jiang Qin [Jee-arng Chin] – *a reformed pirate that initially served as a bodyguard to Sun Ce and eventually became a renowned officer to Ce and his brother Quan; he was renowned for his frugal ways and his scholarly pursuits, but he did not enjoy a good relationship with the elitist Xu Sheng*
*Known by the courtesy name Gongyi [K'ong-yee]

Jiang Yi [Jee-arng Yee] – *son of Jiang Qin*

Jin Xuan [Jin Shoo-arn] – *Liu Biao's appointed ruler of Wuling*

Kan Ze [Karn Tz'er] – *a young official that joined Sun Quan at some point in the first of second decade of the 3rd Century; he is more well known for his fictional involvement in the Battle of Red Cliffs, where he saw through Huang Gai's 'self-torture ruse' and was subsequently employed to ensure that it succeeded. In history, Kan was renowned for his honesty and shrewdness*
*Known by the courtesy name Derun [T'er-roon]

Kong Rong [Kong Rong] – *a descendant of the famous philosopher Confucius; he assumed many respectable roles and was an acquaintance of men such as Cai Yong, Sheng Xian, Wang Lang, Liu Bei and Yuan Shao. At some point after Emperor Xian escaped his regents and settled in Xuchang, Kong Rong was forced out of his role in Qing Province by Yuan Tan and given a role in the Han court. He became an outspoken critic, and one of his targets was Cao Cao, who eventually found an excuse to be rid of him*
*Known by the courtesy name Wenju [Wern-joo]

Kuai Liang [Koo-eye Lee-arng] – *Liu Biao's senior adviser that is already 'fading into the backgound' at the start of this work; he is cited as a likely contributor to the plan that led to Sun Jian's death*

Kuai Yue [Koo-eye Yoo-er] – *brother of the adviser Kuai Liang; the author uses him as an adviser to Huang Zu in lieu of any named figures. He eventually joins Cao Cao.*
*Known by the courtesy name Yidu [Yee-t'oo]

Lady Bian [P'ee-arn] – *mother of Cao Cao's eldest living sons, Cao Pi, Cao Zhang and Cao Zhi*

Lady Cai [Ts'eye] – *wife of Liu Biao, stepmother to Liu Qi and Liu Cong, sister of Admiral Cai Mao; she conspired to have her niece marry Liu Cong and successfully lobbied for Cong to inherit the clan chieftainship and the governorship of Jing*

Lady Cao [Ts'ao] – *niece of Cao Cao that married Sun Kuang*

Lady Chen [T'ern] – *Sun Jian's consort and mother to some of Sun Jian's younger children. In 'Crouching Dragon', a 'State Mother Wu' is present during Sun Shangxiang's marriage to Liu Bei, but this could not be Shangxiang's mother Lady Wu since she was already dead: the author has taken the liberty of modifying the mythical version (that has State Mother Wu as Lady Wu's sister) to have Lady Chen elevated to a 'Second Mother' by Sun Quan and to 'State Mother Wu' at Lady Wu's request.*

Lady Ding [T'ing] – *Cao Cao's second principal wife; she raised his eldest children as if they were her own but never bore him sons. She was angered by the deaths of Cao Ang and Cao Shuo (one died at Wan City, the other from illness) and effectively divorced Cao Cao; she then lived in a separate house on his estate and*

Lady Du [T'oo] – *beautiful widow of Lü Bu's general Qin Yilu and mother of Qin Lang; she became Cao Cao's consort*

Lady Huang [Hoo-arng] – *niece of Liu Biao's spouse Lady Cai that married the famous strategist Zhuge Liang; she is known in some stories by the name Yueying [Yoo-er-ying], and she is often said to have been a gifted astrologer and inventor. She is a protagonist in 'Crouching Dragon: the Journey of Zhuge Liang', but her only presence in this work is when the tale of her spreading word of her ugliness to deter unfit suitors is relayed during a discussion*

Lady Liu [Lee-oo] – *Yuan Shao's second principal wife after the death of the mother of his eldest sons, Yuan Tan and Yuan Xi; she conspired to have her own son, Yuan Shang, appointed as clan chieftain after Shao's death, which led to a war between Shang and his embittered older half-brother Yuan Tan. Cao Cao made use of the division and managed to defeat the powerful Yuan brothers as a result*

Lady Sun – *daughter of Sun Ben that married Cao Zhang*

Lady Wu [Woo] – *Sun Jian's wife and mother of Sun Ce, Sun Quan, Sun Yi, Sun Kuang and Sun Shangxiang; she later becomes a strong voice in the administration of the region and was known as 'State Mother Wu' after the establishment of a more tangible southern state, although this is more of a posthumous honour since Lady Wu died before the 'Battle of Xiakou' and 'Battle of Red Cliffs' that allowed Sun Quan to establish Wu. Lady Wu was a strong-willed woman that had even been forced to support her brother, Wu Jing, when he was in dire straits. She raised Sun Jian's children to be courageous and wilful, and that is most evident in Lady Sun (known as Shangxiang in this work), the famous tomboy that later married the warlord Liu Bei. Lady Wu died shortly after Sun Quan assumed the role of head of the clan; in 'Crouching Dragon: The Journey of Zhuge Liang', a 'State Mother Wu' is seen at Lady Sun's wedding to Liu Bei a decade later, but it is explained here as Lady Chen, Sun Jian's consort, having been given that status for the purpose of continuity.*

Lady Xie [Shee-er] – *daughter of Han official Xie Jiong that married Sun Quan; he did not favour her and eventually elevated his second cousin Lady Xu to the status of principal wife. Lady Xie is portrayed as the mother of Sun Quan's ill-fated young son in this work, but that may not be correct*

Lady Xu [Shoo] – *daughter of Sun Quan's cousin, Xu Kun; Quan took her as a consort and later elevated her to his principal wife*

Lady Xū [Shoo] – *wife of Sun Yi that was said to be a diviner and astrologer; use of 'ū' in her name is to differentiate her from Xu Kun's daughter. Her remarkable actions are recounted in this work*

Lady Yuan [Yoo-arn] – *Yuan Shu's daughter; she later became a consort to Sun Quan*

Lady Zhen [Ch'ern] – beautiful, intelligent heiress that became a philanthropist in Ji Province; she was initially married to Yuan Shao's second son Yuan Xi, but the two spent no time together due to Xi's stepmother, Lady Liu, conspiring to have him posted to the frontier while Lady Zhen remained in Ji's capital, Ye, as a hostage to ensure that Xi did not contest Shang being made clan chieftain. When Cao Cao conquered Ji Province, his heir Cao Pi took an immediate liking to Lady Zhen and had his father contrive a divorce from Yuan Xi, who was still alive and on the frontier at the time; Cao Pi then married Lady Zhen, and Yuan Xi was later killed by Gongsun Kang. Stories concerning the paternal lineage of Lady Zhen's son Cao Rui persisted over the years, with many suggesting that Yuan Xi had somehow approached her in captivity and conceived the child before Cao Pi married her; it led to Cao Pi becoming estranged from her in later years, but Cao Rui was allowed to become the next emperor of Cao Wei regardless

Lady Zou [Tz'oh] – the beautiful wife of Dong Zhuo's general Zhang Ji; Cao Cao's taking her as a consort (whether this was voluntary or not is disputable) triggered the 'Battle of Wan City'

Lei Bo [Lay P'oh] – Qian Hills Bandit that once served as an officer under Yuan Shu alongside his former colleague Chen Lan; he disappears from the narrative and is 'replaced' by Lei Xu, who may or may not be a relation

Lei Xu [Lay Shoo] – Qian Hills Bandit and subordinate of the chieftain Chen Lan; he 'replaces' Lei Bo, who may or may not be a relation. Lei Xu submitted to Liu Bei after the failure of his and Chen's rebellion in Lujiang Prefecture, giving Bei his first proper army, but his fate after that is unknown

Li Dian [Lee T'ee-arn] – officer serving Cao Cao; he only plays a small role in the narrative, but he went on to be one of the defenders of Hefei Fortress alongside Zhang Liao and Yue Jin
*Known by the courtesy name Mancheng [Marn-t'erng]

Li Jue [Lee Joo-er] – former officer under Dong Zhuo that took charge of Chang'an with Jian Xu and fellow officer Guo Si after Dong Zhuo's death, becoming a 'co-regent'. He later clashed with Guo Si and lost control of the emperor when he was tricked into allowing the court to return to Luoyang under escort. Once Li Jue had lost his valuable hostage his power disappeared, and he was later killed by a subordinate

Li Shu [Lee S'oo] – an officer serving Sun Ce; this relatively unexplored man opposed Sun Quan's rule, causing one of the more important early crises for Quan's government

Li Tong [Lee Tong] – an officer serving Cao Cao; he played an important background role during the siege of Jiangling

Liang Ji [Lee-arng Jee] – Emperor Huan's father-in-law and a controversial figure; he was liked by the literati for his support of the arts, but others accused him of being a moral deviant and having designs on the imperial throne. Liang was eventually ousted by Emperor Huan himself, who enlisted his eunuch attendants in his efforts; the grateful emperor then rewarded the eunuchs handsomely, allowing them to form the power clique that became known as the 'Ten Attendants'

Ling Cao [Ling Ts'ao] – *an early volunteer in Sun Ce's army; he later became known for his bold charges and general heroism. He was succeeded by his more famous son, Ling Tong, after he was famously killed on campaign by the pirate Gan Ning*

Ling Tong [Ling Tong] – *son of the valiant vanguard officer Ling Cao; Tong inherited his father's role and became fanatically dedicated to avenging his father's killing by the pirate Gan Ning, who later came to serve Sun Quan as well. Ling's feud with Gan Ning is a recurring subplot in the last acts of this work*
*Known by the courtesy name Gongji [K'ong-jee]

Liu Bao [Lee-oo P'ow] – *briefly-mentioned son of Yufuluo and heir to the Southern Xiongnu chieftainship; his progeny ruled part of China after the collapse of the Jin Dynasty*

Liu Bei [Lee-oo P'ay] – *a member of the Liu family that ruled China as the Han Dynasty; his ancestors were disinherited after committing an offence, so Bei was forced into a life of weaving straw shoes and mats. He was later pitied and advanced by a wealthier relative, and quickly made friends in high places. He gained initial notoriety for his victories against the Yellow Turbans, and made many acquaintances that would become famous in their own right. He was said to have had imperial ambitions as a youth and eventually became one of the three dynastic founders of the 'Three Kingdoms' era. He joined forces with the young Sun Quan to fight Cao Cao at the 'Battle of Red Cliffs', and then had an uneasy alliance with the Sun family for over a decade: Sun Quan and Liu Bei eventually came to blows over Jing Province. He later marched against Sun Quan's state of Eastern Wu to avenge a personal matter and was defeated by Commander-in-Chief Lu Xun in the so-called 'Battle of Xiaoting'; he died shortly thereafter, leaving his mission to reunify the country to his trusted Prime Minister, Zhuge Liang. Liu Bei appears only briefly in this work, 'aiding' Zhou Yu's siege of Jiangling and marrying Sun Shangxiang*
*Known by the courtesy name Xuande [Shoo-arn-der]

Liu Biao [Lee-oo P'ee-ow] – *Governor of the 'artery region' of Jing Province at the start of this work; Biao is a major antagonist for the Sun family due to his role in Sun Jian's early death*
*Known by the courtesy name Jingsheng [Ch'ing-s'erng]

Liu Cong [Lee-oo Ts'ong] – *second son of Liu Biao*

Liu Dai [Lee-oo T'eye] – *the Governor of Yan Province at the time of the Eastern Pass Coalition against Dong Zhuo; Dai's vassal Cao Cao was given control of the province by Yuan Shao after Dai was killed by Yellow Turban rebels. His younger brother, Liu Yao, fought against Sun Ce as Governor of Yang Province*

Liu Du [Lee-oo T'oo] – *Liu Biao's appointed ruler of Lingling*

Liu Fu [Lee-oo Foo] – *official in Lujiang that was employed as Inspector of Yang Province by Cao Cao; his dedication to improving living standards earned him the respect of almost everybody, but he was, due to his role, and enemy of the Suns. He oversaw the construction and first defence of Hefei Fortress*
*Known by the courtesy name Yuanying [Yoo-arn-ying]

Liu Hu [Lee-oo Hoo] – *nephew of Liu Biao's nephew that aids Huang Zu in Jiangxia as an officer and official*

Liu Ji [Lee-oo Ch'ee] – *son of the court-appointed Governor of Yang Province, Liu Yao: he serves the Sun clan despite his father being at odds with Sun Ce and dying in disgrace after losing the provincial capital to the young warlord*

Liu Pan [Lee-oo Parn] – *nephew of Liu Biao's nephew that aids Huang Zu in Jiangxia as an officer and official*

Liu Pi [Lee-oo Pee] – *a Yellow Turban leader in Yu Province that once fought against Sun Jian; he is only referred to in this work for his alliance with Liu Bei during the Battle of Guandu*

Liu Qi [Lee-oo Chee] – *Liu Biao's eldest son that was passed over in favour of his younger brother Liu Cong; he allied with Liu Bei and, to the surprise of all, Sun Quan to fight Cao Cao*

Liu Xun [Lee-oo Shoon] - *a vassal of Yuan Shu that became Administrator of Lujiang Prefecture after Sun Ce had defeated the incumbent Lu Kang. Liu Xun is the first antagonist in this work, taking Sun Ce away from a campaign against Huang Zu by seizing Lujiang after Yuan Shu's death. Liu Xun served Cao Cao as an official after being defeated by Sun Ce; his prevailing arrogance eventually angered his 'old friend' Cao and ended his career*
*Known by the courtesy name Zitai [Tz'ee-T'eye]

Liu Yan [Lee-oo Yarn] – *a scion of the ruling Liu family; he convinced Emperor Ling that the Provincial Inspectorate system was inadequate for dealing with the nationwide rebellions, and he was then installed as Governor of Yi Province in the far west, where he exercised near-total autonomy and immediately had the cultist Zhang Lu carry out a takeover of neighbouring Hanzhong. Yan later challenged Li Jue and Guo Si but was humiliated, losing two of his four sons in battle. He then lost a third to illness and became ill himself: he died a miserable man, and his legacy was inherited by his timid fourth son Liu Zhang*

Liu Yao [Lee-oo Ya-oh] – *the brother of Liu Dai; he was promoted to Governor of Yang Province by the Han Regency court and ordered to confront Yuan Shu. Liu Yao fought unsuccessfully against Yuan Shu's vassal Sun Ce: Ce emerged as the victor after*

Liu Yao repeatedly ignored sound advice and made poor use of his followers, who included prodigy and friend Taishi Ci. Liu Yao died in technical exile, and his son Liu Ji submitted to Sun Ce

Liu Yè [Lee-oo Yer] – *Liu Xun's oft-ignored senior adviser and later an adviser to Cao Cao*
*Known by the courtesy name Ziyang [Tz'ee-yarng]

Liu Ying [Lee-oo Ying] – *scholar friend of Zhuge Jin and Yan Jun that resisted calls to serve the Sun clan*

Liu Zhang [Lee-oo Ch'arng] – *Liu Yan's fourth and only surviving son after a series of misfortunes; he inherited the governorship of Yi Province. Liu Zhang is not seen but is often referred to when discussing the future of the nation: he is viewed as obsequious, incompetent and cowardly by his contemporaries, and he is usually seen as a weak ruler that is destined to be usurped. Zhou Yu's last proposal was an invasion of Yi to unseat Liu Zhang*

Liu Zheng [Lee-oo Ch'erng] - *a respected intellectual in Liaodong Peninsula that angered the ruler Gongsun Du somehow; he was then rescued by Taishi Ci and taken to the mainland*

Lou Gui [Loh K'oo-ee] – *a hermit in Jing Province that proffered advice to Liu Biao occasionally; he later advised Cao Cao during the Battle of Tong Pass but eventually angered Cao with his tactlessness and was executed for insubordination*
*Known by the courtesy name Zibo [Tz'ee-p'oh]

Lu Ji [Loo Ch'ee] – *the younger son of Lu Kang, cousin to Sun Quan's famous fourth Chief Commander Lu Xun, a long-serving vassal of the Sun clan in his own right and one of the '24 Filial Exemplars' in Chinese history; he is not a major character in this work but he does deliver an early remonstration against Sun Ce's plan to combat the tribes*
*Known by the courtesy name Gongji [K'ong-jee]

Lu Jun [Loo Ch'oon] – *the elder son of Lu Kang that is referred to but never seen: he was supposedly rewarded with rank by the Han court for his late father's loyalty in the face of Yuan Shu's siege, but his fate is unknown at the time of writing*

Lu Kang [Loo Karng] – *a long-serving vassal of the Han Dynasty; his grandfather and father were poorly treated by the eunuch-led government and fell victim to slander. Kang was principled, honest and a good negotiator, which enabled him to pacify at least two troubled regions that others had given up as lost. He opposed the 'Ten Attendants' and was arrested: Liu Dai led calls for his release and reinstatement, wherein he took the role of 'Administrator of Lujiang Prefecture'. When Dong Zhuo seized power, ousted Emperor Shao and installed Emperor Xian, Lu Kang opted to recognise Xian, refused to join the Eastern Pass Coalition against Dong Zhuo and braved the chaos to take tributes to the capital. When the coalition dissolved and siblings Yuan Shao and Yuan Shu began their 8-year-long feud, Lu Kang refused to serve either, citing loyalty to the Han: Yuan Shu refused to accept his stance and attacked him. Lu Kang – who was in his late sixties at this point – held out until Sun Ce was deployed to siege his capital Huancheng; the defenders were overwhelmed, Lu Kang died and Lujiang submitted to Sun Ce, who was then forced to cede it to Liu Xun. Lu Kang's younger son Lu Ji would go on to serve the Sun clan, while Lu Kang's great nephew Lu Xun would go on to be one of Sun Quan's Chief Commanders and his Prime Minister*

Lu Su [Loo Soo] – *a vassal of the Sun clan; he befriended Zhou Yu in Jiujiang and travelled to Jiangdong with him. Su did not achieve high rank under Sun Ce, despite famously donating an entire granary to Zhou Yu, but Sun Quan eagerly employed him and gave great importance to Su's 'Tripod Theorem', which suggested that the Han empire would be briefly divided between three powerful warlords – Cao Cao, Sun Quan and a member of the ruling Liu clan – before it reunited under one of them (Liu Bei's strategist Zhuge Liang had the same idea but envisioned his own lord being the eventual victor)*
*Known by the courtesy name Zijing [Tz'ee-jing]

Lu Xun [Loo Shoon] – *a long-serving vassal of the Sun clan that started his career proper under Sun Quan; he was initially deployed as a tax collector and disciplinarian, but he eventually became Chief Commander and defeated the vengeful – and careless – Shu Han Emperor, Liu Bei, at the Battle of Xiaoting. Lu Xun initially enjoyed favour in later years as well, marrying one of Sun Ce's daughters and becoming Prime Minister of Eastern Wu; he disagreed with Sun Quan in later years, however, and he and his clan paid a heavy price for it*
*Known by the courtesy name Boyan [P'oh-yarn]

Lu Zhao [Loo Ch'ah-oh] – *a general in the Han army that serves at the Battle of Red Cliffs; the author makes him one of the estimated 100,000 casualties due to a lack of a historical fate*

Lü Bu [L' Boo] – *one of the most infamous men of the era; he is known particularly for his disloyalty, inconstancy, and inevitable downfall. In fiction, he is portrayed as a near-invincible warrior – a 'Man among men' – that rides the unparalleled horse, 'Red Hare' (one popular adage is 'Among horses, Red Hare; among men, Lü Bu); he is dead by the time that this work begins, but his actions are still a talking point due to their lasting impact. He murdered his foster father Ding Yuan and empowered the tyrant Dong Zhuo; he then murdered Dong Zhuo but fled when his former colleagues Li Jue and Guo Si seized power afterwards; he invaded Yan Province at Chen Gong's invitation and fought Cao Cao for the provincial seal; he fled Yan and sought refuge in neighbouring Xu, but he quickly seized power from Governor Liu Bei at Chen Gong's suggestion; he then made a series of deals with Cao Cao and Yuan Shu but reneged or was betrayed at every turn. Bu was eventually isolated after betraying Yuan Shu once too often, and Cao Cao – who had tired of his duplicity – surrounded him in his capital Xiapi and besieged the city until it submitted. Bu contradicted his reputation for fearlessness at the last and begged for his life; Cao*

Cao had him strangled with a cord – an execution method usually reserved for women – as a sign of his contempt

Lü Dai [L' T'eye] – *a long-serving vassal of the Sun clan; while he is relatively unimportant in this work – he spends most of the narrative in Guangling as a 'gate guard' – he is a high-ranking official in later years and actually outlived Sun Quan by 4 years, dying at the age of 95/96.*
*Known by the courtesy name Dinggong [T'ing-k'ong]

Lü Fan [L' Farn] – *a long-serving vassal of the Sun clan and personal friend of Sun Ce: the author almost contemplated referring to him by his style name 'Ziheng' as a result, but refrained from doing so to highlight the importance of Sun Ce and Zhou Yu's closer relationship. The author chose to include a variant on the popular story that he gained his important role by demonstrating his skill through a game of weiqi ('Chinese chess'), although he is depicted as already knowing Sun Ce well at that point. In fiction, Zhou Yu often replaces Fan as the main strategist: historically, Fan seems to take a background role during the Battle of Red Cliffs and never assumes the role of Chief Commander, allowing the position to be taken by Lu Su, Lü Meng and Lu Xun; the reason for this is not clear, so the author makes some suggestions through dialogue with his peers*
*Known by the courtesy name Ziheng [Tz'ee-hung]

Lü Meng [L' Mung] – *a long-serving vassal of the Sun clan; he is reckless, impulsive and apparently slow-witted in his earlier years, but he starts to mature into a calculating genius and formidable general over time. His greatest achievement was during his brief tenure as Chief Commander, when he outwitted Guan Yu and took full control of southern Jing from Liu Bei's forces; he died within weeks – if not days – of that victory, however, and folklore often attributes his demise to Guan's vengeful spirit*
*Known by the courtesy name Ziming [Tz'ee-ming]
*Ridiculed in his early career as A'Meng [Ah Mung]

Luo Jun [Loo-oh Joon] – *Han official that served as Magistrate of Chen County in Yu Province; he was murdered by Yuan Shu, and his wife and his son Luo Tong fled to Yuzhang, whereupon his widow married Administrator Hua Xin*

Luo Tong [Loo-oh Tong] – *adopted son of Hua Xin and Sun clan vassal that gains prominence in later years; he is only a young junior official during his brief appearance in this work*
*Known by the courtesy name Gongxu [K'ong-shoo]

Ma Chao [Mah T'ah-oh] – *eldest son and heir to the Qiang warlord Ma Teng; he is acting chieftain for the latter part of the work after Cao Cao takes Ma Teng as a passive house-hostage in order to control the tribes of Liang Province. Chao's actions in this work are of no strategic importance to the Suns and are not mentioned, although Zhou Yu controversially considers an alliance with him instead of Liu Bei after the siege of Jiangling; Chao later starts a series of rebellions that are put down by Cao Cao's forces, after which he seeks refuge with Zhang Lu and then Liu Bei*

Ma Liang [Mah Lee-arng] – *friend of Zhuge Liang and future envoy to Sun Quan's court; he only plays a minor role in this work*

Ma Rong [Mah Rong] – *respected (but long-dead) scholar that tutored other renowned figures, including Zheng Xuan*

Ma Su [Mah Lee-arng] – *brother of Ma Liang and student of Zhuge Liang that later causes Zhuge to lose an important battle against Cao Wei's forces in the north; he is only mentioned in this work*

Ma Teng [Mah Tung] – *a mid-ranking officer in the Han imperial army that defected to the Liang Province rebels; he later married a Qiang woman and became the father of the famous Qiang warlord Ma Chao. He was forced to seek refuge with Cao Cao after a feud with fellow warlord Han Sui, whereupon he was put under house arrest by the Han Prime Minister; when his son rebelled against the Han in the wake of the 'Battle of Red Cliffs', Ma Teng and all of the family that he had brought with him to the capital were executed. In fiction that is biased toward Liu Bei (or against Cao Cao), Teng's execution occurs before Ma Chao's uprising so that Chao is not responsible for the death of his own family*

Magistrate Teng [Tung] – *NAMED FOR NARRATIVE COHESION: the Magistrate of Yan that refuses to support Hè Qi's efforts to quell the rebellions in the region and is killed for it*

Man Chong [Marn T'ong] – *Han official that was tasked with supporting Cao Ren's defence of Jiangling after the Battle of Red Cliffs; he is also said to have proposed building Hefei Fortress*
Known by the courtesy name P'oning [P'oh-ning]

Mei Cheng [May T'erng] – *bandit/rebel leader in Lujiang and Jiujiang Prefectures; he may or may not be the same man as (or is related to) Mei Qian, but the author makes them individuals*

Mei Qian [May Chee-arn] – *magnate/rebel leader in Lujiang Prefecture; he may or may not be the same man as (or is related to) Mei Qian, but the author makes them individuals*

Mi Fang [Mee Farng] – *younger brother of the magnate Mi Zhu*

Mi Heng [Mee Herng] – *recently-deceased scholar that is only referred to; Kong Rong recommended him for a court role but he was so disruptive and rude that Cao Cao sent him to Liu Biao, who quickly sent him to Huang Zu, who quickly killed him*

Mi Zhu [Mee Ch'oo] – *an influential magnate in Xu Province that gravitated toward Liu Bei when the latter arrived to aid Governor Tao Qian; Mi financed Bei and supported his becoming governor after Tao Qian's death. Mi's sister married Bei, and his brother joined the cause as a vassal (mainly to Guan Yu); when the Mi clan fortune was exhausted by hardship, Zhu served as an official*

Mister Bi [P'ee], Mister Gan [K'arn] and Mister Teng [Tung] – *NAMED FOR NARRATIVE COHESION: officials in Shicheng County that Huang Gai is forced to 'deal with'*

Mister Che [T'er] – *ADDED FOR NARRATIVE COHESION: adviser to Liu Qi when he is in Jiangxia*

Mister Shen [S'ern] – *ADDED FOR NARRATIVE COHESION: Li Shu's senior adviser*

Mister Sun [Soon] – *Liu Bei's envoy and politician; his full name was Sun Qian [Soon Chee-arn], but is usually referred to as 'Mister Sun' to minimise confusion with the Jiangdong Suns*

Mister Wang [Warng] – *ADDED FOR NARRATIVE COHESION: official in Wanling County that becomes embroiled in Dai Yuan and Gui Lan's plot to kill Sun Yi*

Niu Jin [Nee-oo Jin] – *Han officer that aided Cao Ren's defence of Jiangling; he served the Han and Cao Wei for many years*

"Old Yin" [Yin] – *ADDED FOR NARRATIVE COHESION: stable-keeper in Qu'e that prepares suitable horses for Sun Ce and Sun Quan so that they can go hunting*

Ou Xing [Oh Shing] – *bandit and-or rebel leader in Changsha County that Sun Jian was sent to the region to quell*

Pan Jun [Parn Joon] – *Liu Biao vassal that aids Huang Zu; he later defected to Liu Bei and then to Sun Quan*

Pan Lin [Parn Lin] – *powerful bandit chieftain in Jiangdong*

Pan Zhang [Parn Ch'arng] – *a Sun clan vassal; portrayed as a 'hustler' that impressed Sun Quan with his charisma and became a trusted vassal. Pan understands the 'way of the world' and can often negotiate with criminal elements to great effect. In fiction he kept Guan Yu's 'Green Dragon' glaive after the latter's death and was eventually murdered by one of Guan's vengeful sons*
*Known by the courtesy name Wengui [Wern-k'oo-ee]

Pang brothers [Parng] – *advisers to Liu Biao*

Pang Tong [Parng Tong] – *an Officer of Merit in Jiangling and friend of Liu Bei's strategist Zhuge Liang; he is considered to be the intellectual equal of Zhuge, but he tries to avoid serving a warlord. He is only shown occasionally in this work (avoiding service), but he went on to join Zhuge in serving Liu Bei after attending Zhou Yu's funeral and deciding not to aid Sun Quan; he was killed while leading Bei's forces on a campaign in Yi Province*
*Known by the courtesy name Shiyuan [S'ee-yoo-arn]
*Known by the Taoist name 'Young/Fledgling Phoenix'

Peng Hu [Perng Hoo] – *rebel leader in Yuzhang*

Peng Yang [Perng Yarng] – *official serving Liu Zhang*

Qi Ji [Chee Jee] – *an officer in Yuan Shu's army that defected to Cao Cao after being won over by Liu Fu*

Qin Lang [Chin Larng] – *adopted son of Cao Cao that is the biological son of Lü Bu's general Qin Yilu*

Qin Song [Chin Song] – *adviser to Sun Ce and later Sun Quan*
*Known by the courtesy name Wenbiao [Wern-p'ee-ow]

Qin Yi [Chin Yee] – *an officer in Yuan Shu's army that defected to Cao Cao after being won over by Liu Fu*

Qin Yilu [Chin Yee-loo] – *officer serving Lu Bu that defected to Yuan Shu when sent to Shouchun as an envoy; he abandoned his beautiful wife Lady Du and his son Qin Lang by doing so. Qin later tried to return to Bu but disappeared during the Battle of Xiapi; he was assumed dead after Bu was defeated, and Cao Cao took Lady Du as a consort, which angered Guan Yu, to whom she had already been promised by Cao. Qin Yilu then reappeared and unashamedly tried to join Liu Bei; he was then killed, and Cao Cao kept Lady Du thereafter and adopted Qin Lang as well*

Quan Rou [Choo-arn Roh] – *adviser to Sun Ce and his successor Sun Quan; his son Quan Cong [Choo-arn Ts'ong] – who is yet to reach adulthood in this work – went on to marry Sun Quan's daughter and fight for Eastern Wu as a senior officer.*

Sheng Xian [S'ung Shee-arn] – *the Administrator of Wu Prefecture during the reigns of Emperors Shao and Xian: he was ousted by the agitator Xu Gong and forced to seek refuge with the retired general Xu Zhao. Sheng Xian was trapped in Xu Zhao's estate for many years; his final fate is a subject of this work*
*Known by the courtesy name Xiaozhang [Shee-ow-ch'arng]

Shi Xie [S'ee Shee-er] – *the Governor of Jiaozhi, the region to the south of Yang Province (which includes part of Northern Vietnam); he plays no important part in this work, but he and his descendants have a lot of dealings with the Sun clan in the future*

Sima Hui [Ss'mah Hoo-ee] – *an eccentric scholar in Jing that is a vocal proponent of Zhuge Liang and Pang Tong*
*Known by the courtesy name Decao [T'er-ts'ao]
*Known by the Taoist name 'Master Still Water'

Sima Yi [Ss'mah Yee] – *an adviser to Cao Cao that also happens to be the grandfather of the founder of the Jin Dynasty*
*Known by the courtesy name Zhongda [Ch'ong-t'ah]

Song Hao [Song Hah-oh] – *a subordinate of Magistrate Xie Qi*

Song Jian [Song Jee'arn] – *a Liang Province rebel leader that formed his own independent state that endured for 4 decades*

644

Song Qian [Song Chee-arn] – *a vassal of Sun Ce and Sun Quan that served as an officer and bodyguard*

Su Fei [Soo Fay] – *an officer serving Huang Zu; he was an associate of Gan Ning. The author takes the liberty of combining this Su Fei with a Su Fei that supposedly tried to convince Guan Yu to defect to Sun Quan (they were probably the same man)*

Sun Ben [Soon P'ern] – *the eldest son of Sun Jian's twin brother, who died suddenly; Sun Jian took Ben and his younger brother Fu into his own home and cared for them as though they were his sons. Sun Ben accompanied Jian on campaigns and became acting head of the clan when Jian died during the Jing Province campaign: he also inherited Jian's appointments from Yuan Shu, although their actual value is debatable. Sun Ben yielded to Sun Ce and continued to follow him as he consolidated southern Yang Prefecture. His relationship with Sun Quan was not as good, and forms a major part of this work*
*Known by the courtesy name Boyang [P'oh-yarng]

Sun Ce [Soon Ts'er] – *referred to as 'Bofu' in the narrative until his death; Sun Ce is the first protagonist of this novel, and he was a great hero of the era. Sun Ce's death is another great mystery, like that of his father: historically, Ce was attacked whilst out hunting with inadequate security (how long he lived after the attempt on his life is unknown exactly); he survives that assassination attempt in fiction, but is then persecuted to the grave by the spirit of a Taoist saint that he had executed earlier. The author highlights various possibilities throughout the work*
*Known by the courtesy name Bofu [P'oh-foo]
*Known later by the epithet 'Little Conqueror' (mainly by enemies)

Sun Fu [Soon Foo] – *the younger son of Sun Jian's twin brother, who died suddenly; Sun Jian took Fu and his older brother Ben into his own home and cared for them as though they were his sons. Sun Fu's fate is recounted in this work*
*Known by the courtesy name Guoyi [K'oo-oh-yee]

Sun Gao [Soon K'ah-oh] – *an officer serving Sun Yi*

Sun Hao [Soon Hah-oh] – *the eldest son of Sun Jing; he is relatively unimportant to the narrative. Two of Sun Hao's grandchildren – Sun Chen [Soon T'ern] and Sun Jun [Soon Ch'oon] – individually became regents during the later years of the Sun Wu Empire and were highly controversial.*

Sun Hè [Soon Her] – *a cousin from the related Yu clan, he came to live in the Sun household and was made an honorary member of the clan, going so far as to take the Sun name. Sun Hè served Sun Ce as a bodyguard throughout the latter's life, but he fatefully missed an opportunity to save Sun Ce from an assassination attempt by followers of Xu Gong. Sun Hè served Sun Quan as an official; his unexpected fate is recounted in this work*
*Known by the courtesy name Bohai [P'oh-h'eye]

Sun Hè's sons – *mentioned briefly in the narrative; at the time of his death he had four sons, Sun Zhu [Soon Ch'oo], Sun Yi [Soon Yee], Sun Huan [Soon Hoo-arn] and Sun Jun [Soon Joon], but Zhu is the only one mentioned by name in this work*

Sun Huan [Soon Hoo-arn] – *Sun Jing's fourth son*

Sun Jian [Soon Jee-arn] – *a southern man whose well-known military career began during the Yellow Turban Rebellion and continued with a sizeable role in the Liang Province pacification campaign, Changsha pacification campaign and the campaign against Dong Zhuo. His progeny –beginning with his eldest son Sun Ce – would found the state of Eastern Wu (and later the Sun Wu Empire) and improve the fortunes of the beleaguered south of China, but Jian himself died an ignominious death in Jing Province; the circumstances surrounding his deathled to a feud between Liu Biao and the Suns that went on for two decades*
*Known by the courtesy name Wentai [Wern-tigh]

Sun Jian's (two) younger daughters – *neither of the two are named in history, and little is known about them*

Sun Jiao [Soon J'ee-ow] – *Sun Jing's third son; he was known for his professionalism when sober, but he could be dangerously tactless when drunk*
*Known by the courtesy name Shulang [S'oo-larng]

Sun Jing [Soon Ch'ing] – *the younger brother of Sun Jian; he aided his nephew Sun Ce on campaigns.*
*Known by the courtesy name Youtai [Yoh-tigh]

Sun Kuang [Soon Koo-arng] – *a younger son of Sun Jian by his wife Lady Wu; when Jian died, Kuang was given his father's marquisate as an act of generosity by Sun Ce. He died young after marrying into the Cao clan; his fate is recounted in this work*
*Known by the courtesy name Jizuo [Ch'ee-tz'oo-oh]

Sun Lang [Soon Larng] – *a younger son of Sun Jian; his mother's identity is not known at the time of writing, but it is likely to be Lady Chen or Sun Jian's possible second consort. He is a youth during the timeline of this novel: he later has a disaster-prone career whilst serving his brother Quan*
*Known by the courtesy name Zao'an [Tz'ah-oh Arn]

Sun Lin [Soon Lin] – *Sun Ben's eldest son; his 3 younger brothers are never mentioned by name*

Sun Qian [Soon Chee-arn] – *Sun Jing's fifth son*

Sun Quan [Soon Choo-arn] – *Sun Jian's second son; he inherited the clan chieftainship after Sun Ce's death, and he is the second Sun clan protagonist of this work (Zhou Yu is the true second protagonist). Sun Quan would rule Jiangdong – later expanded to the state of Eastern Wu – for 50 years and have a significant role in some of the most important events of the time, such as the*

'Battle of Red Cliffs' (as the main opponent of Cao Cao), the 'Battle of Xiaoting' (as the target of Liu Bei's wrath) and the creation of the 'Three Kingdoms' era itself (as one of the three rulers). He was made a king by the Cao Wei emperor Cao Pi (as a placatory gesture), but he later became First Emperor of the Sun Wu Empire. As he aged, his sanity appears to have eroded: he became increasingly unstable, turning against early allies and even having some of them executed. He left the management of Sun Wu and the welfare of his heir to Regent Zhuge Ke upon his death, which did not turn out to be a sound decision
*Known by the courtesy name Zhongmou [Ch'ong-moh]

Sun Shangxiang [Soon S'arng-shee-arng] – *the eldest daughter of the Han Dynasty officer Sun Jian; she is famous (although this might just be embellishment by scholars or folklore) for being a tomboy that surrounded herself with weapons and an elite force of female bodyguards, one of whom married her brother Sun Quan. She later married the warlord Liu Bei but they were forced to separate when her husband's ambitions conflicted with those of her family. In fiction, she is sometimes called Shangxiang since, like most women in ancient China, her given name is unknown (the name 'Shangxiang' seemingly originates from folklore, and she is simply known (like her sisters) as 'Lady Sun' when mentioned in historical texts); the author has used this name in order to allow family members to refer to her as something other than 'Lady Sun'. Sun Shangxiang's marriage to Liu Bei is one of the last events in this novel*
*Known occasionally as (Lady) Sun Ren [Soon Rern]

Sun Shao (1) [Soon S'ah-oh] – *Sun Hè's nephew; he served as an official and officer and was highly valued by Sun Quan*
*Known by the courtesy name Gongli [K'ong-lee]

Sun Shao (2) [Soon S'ah-oh] – *Sun Ce's posthumously-born son; he was said to resemble his father but never knew success*

Sun Xing [Soon Shing] and Sun Zhao [Soon Ch'ah-oh] – *Sun Fu's eldest sons; his 2 younger sons are never mentioned by name*

Sun Yi [Soon Yee] – *Sun Jian's third son; he was said to be similar in appearance and nature to his older brother Sun Ce, and many considered him a preferable heir to Ce's legacy. Sun Yi served Quan as an official, but his easy-going nature was his undoing. His fate is part of a major subplot in this work*
*Known by the courtesy name Shubi [S'oo-bee]

Sun Yu [Soon Yoo] – *Sun Jing's second son; he served as an official and officer and was greatly respected by Zhou Yu*
*Known by the courtesy name Zhongyi [Ch'ong-yee]

Sun Zicai [Soon Tz'ee-ts'eye] – *subordinate of Magistrate Xie Qi*

Taishi Ci [Tigh-sher Ts'eh] – *a famous 'lone wolf' that had a mixed career; Taishi Ci died 6 years after his lord Sun Ce, but popular fiction would award him another decade of incredible service and a*

more fitting end in battle.
*Known by the courtesy name Ziyi [Tz'ee-yee]

Tao Qian [T'ow Chee-arn] – *a Governor of Xu Province; Tao Qian is revered in some fiction as a righteous man, but historical accounts suggest a wily, jealous man that hankered for talented subordinates and reacted badly to any that rejected his work offers. He once employed the official Wang Lang, who advised him to avoid fighting Dong Zhuo or the 'co-regents' and instead focus on defending his borders. Tao Qian is famous for being held responsible for the robbing and death of Cao Cao's father, Cao Song; Cao Cao took a force into Xu Province and massacred 100,000 of its inhabitants in reaction to the affront, and Tao Qian died shortly thereafter of an illness*

Tian Kai [Tee-arn K'eye] – *officer and trusted offical serving Gongsun Zan; Gongsun made him Inspector of Qing Province.*

Wang Can [Warng Ts'arn] – *a Han Dynasty official that served Liu Biao and then Cao Cao; his family were prestigious enough for his grandfather and great-grandfather to be Excellences alongside the Yuan clan. He was said to possess an eidetic memory and have a fascination with donkeys, among other things, and the famed polymath Cai Yong was a vocal sponsor. Wang Can wrote a historical work, 'Record of Heroes', that serves as an alternative biographical compendium to the more famous 'Record of the Three Kingdoms', though it might be seen as biased toward Cao Cao's faction. It includes alternate fates (or even dates of death) for some notable figures, such as Sun Jian.*
*Known by the courtesy name Zhongxuan [Ch'ong-shoo-arn]

Wang Lang [Warng Larng] – *official that served the Han Dynasty; he was a friend of Kong Rong. He was appointed as Administrator of Kuaiji by the court, and he allied himself to Governor Liu Yao, although he was not averse to forging alliance with bandits, anti-Han rebels and hostile tribes as well. He served as a major antagonist to Sun Ce during the latter's Kuaiji Campaign; he fled to the north after his defeat and was brought into Cao Cao's court by Kong Rong. Wang Lang served Cao's administration and received many promotions. He was (allegedly) a proponent of Han Emperor Xian's abdication in favour of Cao Cao's son Cao Pi: he served the Cao Wei Empire until death. He had an influence on the next political transition through his progeny: his granddaughter Wang Yuanji [Warng Yoo-arn-jee] was the mother of the first Jin Dynasty Emperor, Sima Yan [Ss'mah Yarn].*
*Known by the courtesy name Jingxing [Jing-shing]

Wang Yun [Warng Yoon] – *a Han Dynasty official; when Dong Zhuo seized the court and relocated the capital to Chang'an, Wang Yun decided to plot against the tyrant. Wang managed to convince Lü Bu to betray Dong Zhuo, and once Dong was dead, Wang Yun took charge in Chang'an, condemning most of Dong's former aides as traitors and executing the renowned scholar Cai Yong for collaboration. Wang Yun was eventually isolated and murdered by some of Dong Zhuo's former vassals when they realised that they would not receive amnesty from him; they then seized control and formed their own regency government led by Li Jue and Guo Si*

Wei Teng [Way Terng] – *an Officer of Merit in Sun Ce's court; he angered Sun Ce with his criticisms and was only saved from death when Lady Wu, Sun Ce's mother, intervened. This (supposedly historical) event is referred to at the start of this work and was the last dramatic scene in 'East of the River'*

Wen Ping [Wern Ping] – *an officer under Liu Biao that submitted to Cao Cao and became a trusted guardian of Jing Province*

"White Tiger" Yan [Yarn] – *a 'khan' of the Shanyue tribes in Wu Prefecture; he is referred to in many texts as 'Yan Baihu' [Yarn P'eye-hoo], where 'Baihu' translates to 'White Tiger': the author used the translated form to make him stand out. He is a major antagonist to Sun Ce at the start of the novel; he and his tribal allies repeatedly rise up in revolt, sometimes alone and sometimes in alliance with others. He was repeatedly defeated, and he eventually contented himself with fuelling unrest from the shadows: in fiction he is often killed by Sun Ce or one of Sun Ce's generals, but he probably outlived Ce by many years*

Wu Can [Woo Ts'arn] – *a trusted Sun clan vassal that is a victim of court in-fighting in his later years*
*Known by the courtesy name Kongxiu [Kong-shee-oo]

Wu Dun [Woo T'oon] – *ally of the former bandit king Zang Ba*

Wu Fen [Woo Fern] – *the elder son of Wu Jing*

Wu Jing [Woo Ch'ing] – *Sun Jian's brother-in-law; he served Jian and then his sons as an officer and official until his death.*

Wu Ju [Woo Ch'oo] – *the autonomous ruler of Cangwu County in the south of Han China; he was a friend and possible military ally of Liu Bei, so Zhou Yu sent Bu Zhi to 'deal with him' and ensure that the other rulers paid proper homage to Sun Quan*

Wu Qi [Woo Chee] – *the younger son of Wu Jing*

Wu Yi [Woo Yee] – *Yi Province Governor Liu Zhang's brother-in-law and trusted general; he is briefly mentioned by Xi Su*

Xi Su [Shee Soo] – *Yi Province Governor Liu Zhang's choice for defender of Yiling after the Battle of Red Cliffs; it was a bad choice, as Xi hated Cao Cao (for whom he defended Yiling) and was unwilling to risk his life when Gan Ning – who he knew from Gan's notorious rebel activities in Yi – sieged the city*

Xiahou Dun [Shee-ah-hoh T'oon] – *famous 'cousin' of Cao Cao that became a trusted general in command of tens of thousands of men despite his most well-known military 'exploits' being his losing an eye to Gao Shun's snipers during an ill-timed cavalry charge (during Cao's attempts to uproot Lü Bu from Xu Province)*

and walking into an obvious ambush at Bowang Valley (in Jing Province) and losing hundreds (at least) of his men to Liu Bei's subsequent fire attack
*Known by the courtesy name Yuanrang [Yoo-arn-rang]

Xiahou Yuan [Shee-ah-hoh Yoo-arn] – *famous 'cousin' of Cao Cao that was considered to be Cao's most trusted ally; he was placed in charge of supplies at various points and tasked with leading attacks and defending key positions. He had no real direct dealings with the Suns; he fought against the Qiang and Liu Bei many times and died fighting the latter's forces in Hanzhong*
*Known by the courtesy name Miaocai [Mee-ow-Ts'eye]

Xiang Lang [Shee-arng Larng] – *Liu Biao official that defected to Liu Bei and served him thereafter*

Xiaoqiao [Shee-ow-chee-ow] – *also known as the younger Lady Qiao [Chee-ow], she is one of two beautiful sisters. She married Zhou Yu, while her older sister Daqiao married Sun Ce. At the time of the 'Battle of Red Cliffs', Xiaoqiao is happily married to Zhou Yu while her sister is an early widow: the two women are the subject of various tales, and one well-known element of the Red Cliffs fictional narrative is Cao Cao's supposed obsession with them. Cao Cao was renowned for lechery, and he coincidentally orders the construction of a 'Bronze Bird Tower' with two 'qiao' (bridges) linking the structure: some interpret the 'two qiao' to be 'the two Qiaos', and Zhuge Liang employs this rumour to anger Zhou Yu is many popular retellings. Whether Cao actually commissioned the tower before he declared war on Sun Quan is for historians to ponder, as is what Cao actually meant by 'two qiao': that story cemented the Qiao sisters in history and gave rise to the many romantic depictions of the two couples. Zhou Yu may have had consorts, but the author has not given him any, opting instead to portray Zhou Yu as having Xiaoqiao as his sole muse and being completely infatuated with her.*

Xie Jiong [Shee-er Ch'ee-ong] – *Han official that was respected by Lady Wu; his daughter became Sun Quan's first principal wife*

Xie Qi [Shee-er Chee] – *Han official tasked with guarding Huancheng after the siege of Jiangling*

Xu Chu [Shoo T'oo] – *Cao Cao's second famous bodyguard*

Xu Gong [Shoo K'ong] – *an official in Wu Prefecture; his contribution to the story was pivotal but difficult to present because the information is so unhelpful at times. The author pieced it together as follows: Sheng Xian was the court-appointed Administrator of Wu Prefecture; Xu Gong overthrew Sheng Xian (by, it is implied, popular demand), but was then recognised by the regency court led by Li Jue and Guo Si; Xu Gong then lent his support to the regency court's appointed Governor of Yang Province, Liu Yao; both Liu Yao and Xu Gong were then defeated by Sun Ce; Xu Gong went into exile (the author has him shelter with the same Xu Zhao that is sheltering Sheng Xian, for better or worse); Xu Gong is then recognised again, this time by Sun Ce (the author states that this is because Sheng Xian will not cooperate); Xu Gong plots secretly against Sun Ce, is discovered and then killed by Sun Ce's agents. Xu Gong's followers then assassinated Sun Ce, but they did not live to enjoy their victory.*

Xu Huang [Shoo Hoo-arng] – *Han officer and former White Wave Bandit (and former Dong Zhuo subordinate, most likely – the author assumes as much) that submitted to Cao Cao and became one of his most reliable generals; he defended Jiangling from Zhou Yu alongside Cao Ren and later supported Ren again when Guan Yu attacked Fan City*
*Known by the courtesy name Gongming [K'ong-ming]

Xu Kun [Shoo Koon] – *Sun Jian's nephew (his sister's son); he appears sporadically throughout the novel as a field officer and trusted clan member. His daughter married his Sun Quan*

Xu Lang [Shoo Larng] – *NAMED FOR NARRATIVE COHESION; Xu Gong's son that successfully avenges his assassination*

Xu Shao [Shoo S'ah-oh] – *a famous appraiser who was known for fearless frankness; it was said that men feared his judgement and would try to curry favour with him in the hope that it would result in a career-boosting response. He is famous for having supposedly judged Cao Cao to be 'An able statesman in times of peace, and a 'jianxiong' (meaning a 'crafty villain', more or less) in chaotic times'. He later travelled to Yang Province and served the court-appointed governor Liu Yao, who was fighting Yuan Shu and the indentured Sun clan; Shao fled with Liu Yao after the latter's resounding defeat and died whilst in exile in Yuzhang*

Xu Sheng [Shoo S'erng] – *nobleman-official that joined the Sun clan as an officer and quickly proved that he was a great military mind despite being obnoxiously vain and elitist; he had a feud with Jiang Qin and looked down on the likes of Zhou Tai. He appears to have been a staunch Han loyalist, as he refused to aid Sun Quan during the Battle of Red Cliffs and suffered a temporary career setback as a result*
*Known by the courtesy name Wenxiang [Wern-shee-arng]

Xu Yòu [Shoo Yoh] – *a friend of Cao Cao and Yuan Shao that joined Shao as an adviser but betrayed him during the Battle of Guandu to escape imprisonment for financial impropriety; Xu then served Cao Cao, who tolerated the overly familiar and tactless Xu until he had seized the Yuan's capital. Cao gathered his followers to show respect to Yuan Shao's temple; Xu Yòu was killed during the ceremony by Cao's bodyguard, Xu Chu, for 'showing gross disrespect' (it is suspected that he had outlived his usefulness)*

Xu Zhao [Shoo Ch'ah-oh] – *a retired Han general that gave sanctuary to any officials that were down on their luck. His motivations are hard to fathom, and the list of figures that he did supposedly shelter is strange (perhaps it is even nonsensical)*

Xue Ti [Shoo-er Tee] – *Han official that served Cao Cao; he was an adviser to the defenders of Hefei Fortress during the Sun clan's more famous efforts to attack it and gain control of Lujiang*

Xue Zhou [Shoo-er Ch'oh] – *a pirate king that was active along Guangling Prefecture's waterways*

Xun Yòu [Shoon Yoh] – *a Han official with noble lineage; he served Cao Cao as an adviser alongside his uncle Xun Yu*
*Known by the courtesy name Gongda [K'ong-t'ah]

Xun Yu [Shoon Yoo] – *a Han official with noble lineage; he was an early supporter of Cao Cao and brought many others – including his nephew Xun Yòu and Guo Jia – into Cao's court. He later advocated Cao Cao bringing the isolated Emperor Xian to Yan Province, and he remained Cao's staunch supporter for many years; he was a staunch – some might say 'obsessive' – Han loyalist, however, and it was that loyalty that finally ended his career under the ambitious Cao Cao*
*Known by the courtesy name Wenruo [Wern-roo-oh]

"Yan" [Yarng] – *ADDED FOR NARRATIVE COHESION; a loyal subordinate of the agitator Xu Gong that is shown avenging Gong by taking part in an assassination attempt on Sun Ce*

Yan Jun [Yarn Ch'oon] – *a friend of Bu Zhi and Zhuge Jin that joined Sun Quan; he was a candidate for Chief Commander after Lu Su's death, but the role went to Lü Meng instead*
*Known by the courtesy name Mancai [Marn-ts'eye]

Yan Liang [Yarn Lee-arng] – *a famous general that served Yuan Shao; he was said to be fearsome, but he was famously killed with ease by Guan Yu in the early stages of the Battle of Guandu (historically it was an ambush of sorts; in fiction, a duel)*

Yan Xiang [Yarn Shee-arng] – *an adviser to Yuan Shu whose fate is unclear; a 'Yan Xiang' was appointed as Inspector of Yang Province' by Cao Cao, and this author took the liberty of assuming them to be the same man and 'ressurecting' Yan from his M.I.A. status at the end of 'East of the River' at the start of this work*

Yan Yu [Yarn Yoo] – *the brother of 'White Tiger Yan'; he supposedly died fighting Sun Ce (this novel assumes so).*

Yang Hong [Yarng Hong] – *an adviser to Yuan Shu that outlived his lord; he was captured by Liu Xun (along with his lord's coffin and family), and what happened next is dramatized in this work*

Yang Si [Yarng See] – *a respected elder statesman and mentor to Wang Lang; Wang served as his assistant and briefly retired when Yang Si died.*

Yi Ji [Yee Ch'ee] – *Liu Biao official that defected to Liu Bei and served him thereafter; also a friend of Zhuge Liang*

Yòu Tu [Yoh Too] – *a rebel leader in Yuzhang*

Yu Fan [Yoo Farn] – *an 'Officer of Merit' in Kuaiji that initially served Wang Lang; he surrendered to Sun Ce after Wang Lang's first defeat and joined the Sun clan's court*
*Known by the courtesy name Zhongxiang [Ch'ong-shee-arng]

Yu Jin [Yoo Ch'in] – *a famous general that served Cao Cao; he defended Xiangyang against Guan Yu during the siege of Jiangling and was one of the three famous defenders of Hefei Fortress in later years*

Yuan Huan [Yoo-arn Hoo-arn] – *a vassal of Yuan Shu that defected to Cao Cao and served him as an adviser*
*Known by the courtesy name Yaoqing [Yah-oh-ching]

Yuan Shang [Yoo-arn S'arng] – *third son of Yuan Shao that was elevated to clan chieftain after Shao's death; he had the support of the majority of the officials and officers but was opposed by his eldest half-brother Tan. Cao Cao successfully divided the Yuan brothers and – after killing Yuan Tan – isolated Shang and his brother Xi, chased them into the lands beyond the Great Wall and then pursued, subjugating their Wuhuan tribal allies as he went; Shang and Xi fled into Liaodong, where they sought refuge with Governor Gongsun Kang, but Kang rightly distrusted them and turned Shang and Xi's severed heads over to Cao Cao*

Yuan Shao [Yoo-arn S'ah-oh] – *one of the most important figures of the later years of the Han Dynasty: he was the descendant of generations of trusted court officials and, by adoption, heir apparent to a vast fortune that then made him one of the most influential men in China. Shao was, initially, a force for good: the 'Ten Attendants' – a clique of court eunuchs – were so powerful that they could select key government figures and have anyone slandered and-or killed, but Yuan Shao defied them and protected many officials and scholars that were persecuted during the 'Partisan Crisis'. Shao became the closest ally of Commander-in-Chief Hè Jin, whose nephew was heir to the Han throne. Jin was murdered by the 'Ten' after a failed attempt to purge them: Yuan Shao was the man that avenged Jin, slaughtering many allies of the 'Ten'. Dong Zhuo then seized power, and Yuan Shao opposed his plan to depose Emperor Shao and replace him with Emperor Xian. Shao formed the 'Eastern Pass Coalition' to blockade the capital and force Dong to reinstate Emperor Shao. Dong's response was to kill the deposed emperor and then torture and execute the families of the coalition leaders, including Yuan's. The coalition imploded, and Dong Zhuo fled east with Emperor Xian: Yuan Shao's brother Shu had declared that he should be clan chieftain, and Shao and Shu began a military feud that engulfed the east of China for the next eight years. By the time of Yuan Shu's death, Yuan Shao was ruler of the northeast of China: he then declared war on his childhood friend Cao Cao, who, by then, had Emperor Xian in his protective custody and a petition labelling him as a seditionist hanging over his head. Yuan and Cao fought a series of military encounters known collectively as the 'Battle of*

Guandu': Yuan lost to Cao and died shortly thereafter of illness

Yuan Shu [Yoo-arn S'oo] – *the eldest legitimate son of the brother of the heir to the Yuan clan chieftainship, and the Sun clan's master after Sun Jian mistakenly pledged lifelong service to him; his older half-brother, Yuan Shao, was born to a maidservant but was adopted by their heirless uncle - the clan chieftain – and made the heir as a result. Shao's adoption ended Shu's dreams of being the heir, and it caused deep resentment that never eased; he eventually challenged his brother, causing 8 years of civil war. Shu's mental health deteriorated, and he then decided that he was worthy of the imperial mandate, but he lost most of his vassals – including the indentured Suns – and died homeless and penniless*

Yuan Tan [Yoo-arn Tarn] – *the eldest son of Yuan Shao; most of his father's vassals disliked his aggressive and unintelligent approach to government, so they conspired to have his younger brother Shang elevated to clan chieftain after Shao's death. Tan opposed Shang politically and then militarily; he even went so far as to ally with Cao Cao to unseat Shang, but Cao turned on Tan after seizing the Yuan's capital and eventually killed him in battle*

Yuan Xi [Yoo-arn Shee] – *the second son of Yuan Shao; he was forced to stay in Yòu Province during the clan's succession crisis because his stepmother, Lady Liu, had taken his wife Lady Zhen as a hostage. When Cao Cao seized the Yuan capital, Cao's son Pi decided that he wanted Lady Zhen for a wife and had his father divorce her from Xi. Yuan Xi allied with his younger brother Shang and tried to resist Cao, but they were chased into Liaodong and killed by Liaodong's governor, Gongsun Kang. Xi would live on, however: theories have persisted that Cao Pi's heir, Cao Rui, was actually Yuan Xi's son (because he was born too soon after Pi's marriage to the divorced Lady Zhen).*

Yuan Xiong [Yoo-arn Shee-ong] – *officer in Wu serving the Suns*

Yuan Yao [Yoo-arn Yah-oh] – *the eldest son of Yuan Shu; he is captured by Liu Xun at the start of this work*

Yuan Yin [Yoo-arn Yin] – *a cousin of Yuan Shu that served him as an adviser; he is captured by Liu Xun at the start of this work*

Yue Jin [Yoo-er Ch'in] – *a famous officer that served Cao Cao for many years; he was 'gifted' to Cao by Wang Lang. Jin was not initially trusted but became Cao's choice of vanguard general as the years went by; he undid his record of good service in later years by surrendering 'too readily' to Guan Yu during the siege of Fan City, and Cao Pi ensured that he was humiliated for it*

Yufuluo [Yoo-foo-loo-oh] – *the chieftain of a rebel faction of Southern Xiongnu; he had been selected as the Chanyu (king) of his people by a meddling Han court, but instead of accepting Yufuluo the Southern Xiongnu exiled him and his followers (although his brother Huchuquan stayed and was actually elected as the next Chanyu by the Xiongnu themselves). Yufuluo then* became a 'wildcard' that supported or opposed the Han until he was finally defeated by Cao Cao. He was the father of future Southern Xiongnu Chanyu Liu Bao, whose progeny would enjoy great power in northern China

Zang Ba [Tz'arng P'ah] – prison warder's son-turned-bandit king that fought the corrupt Han government but briefly had a truce to fight the Yellow Turbans; he then returned to his old ways but was finally forced to submit by Cao Cao, who turned his 'Mount Tai Bandits' into a pacification force in Qing Province. Zang became one of the Han's most fearsome enforcers; he confounds Han Dang during the siege of Jiangling, and he later fought Sun Quan's forces in the Ruxu and Hefei regions of Lujiang
*Known by the courtesy name Xuangao [Shoo-arng-k'ao]

Ze Rong [Tz'er Rong] – a Buddhist cultist in Xu Province that established a 'utopia' for his acolytes with funds misappropriated from the provincial treasury; he later fled to Yang Province and established a second 'utopia' there before being defeated by Sun Ce. He left a trail of murders and looting wherever he went, but he was eventually killed by irreverent tribesmen in Yuzhang

Zhang Fei [Ch'arng Fay] – an early ally and sponsor of Liu Bei, and frequently paired with Guan Yu as one of Bei's most fearsome front-line generals, though his temperament is an impediment
*Known by the courtesy name Yide [Yee-der]

Zhang Hè [Ch'arng Her] – a famous general that once served Yuan Shao but submitted to Cao Cao during the Battle of Guandu; he had few dealings with the Sun clan, but he became a recurring nemesis to Liu Bei and Zhuge Liang over the years

Zhang Hong [Ch'arng Hong] – one of the 'Two Zhangs' (the other was his brother Zhang Zhao) and an adviser/envoy/politician that served Sun Ce and Sun Quan in succession; he spent a lot of time in the Han capital as Sun Quan's envoy but he returned to the south prior to the outbreak of hostilities (the 'Battle of Red Cliffs') and remained there afterward. He died four years after Red Cliffs, but his descendants continued to serve the Sun clan
*Known by the courtesy name Zigang [Tz'ee-k'arng]

Zhang Ji [Ch'arng Jee] – a general serving Dong Zhuo; he was envied for his beautiful wife, Lady Zou. He later served Li Jue and Guo Ji and was part of the Emperor's escort to Luoyang: the escort was defeated by Han loyalists and Zhang fled to nearby Nan County, Jing Province. Ji died taking Nan County from Liu Biao's forces; his nephew, Zhang Xiu, 'inherited' the county.

Zhang Jue [Ch'arng J'oo-er] – The founder of the Taoist sect 'The Way of Peace' (his name is sometimes Romanised to Zhang Jiao [Ch'arng J'ee-ah-oh], but the author has chosen the older, more traditional version); he also instigated the first Yellow Turban Rebellion but died before it ended

Zhang Liao [Ch'arng Lee-ow] – a subordinate of Lü Bu; he went

on to serve Cao Cao and earn greater fame as dangerous enemy of the Sun clan in eastern China. His most famous exploit is his defence of the Hefei fortress in Lujiang Prefecture: he almost succeeded in killing Sun Quan (and, in fiction, he is partially responsible for the death of Taishi Ci in the same encounter) and earned a fearsome reputation in the south (and was used as a bogeyman to scare naughty children)
*Known by the courtesy name Wenyuan [Wern-yoo-arn]

Zhang Lu [Ch'arng Loo] – *leader of the 'Way of Five Pecks' (a Taoist cult founded by his clan) that was asked to invade Hanzhong by Yi Province's newly-installed governor Liu Yan; Zhang decided to turn Hanzhong into a theocratic state and rule it himself, and is still doing so at the start of this work. Zhou Yu is said to have contemplated an alliance with him, which would have been highly controversial*

Zhang Miao [Ch'arng Mee-ow] – *a trusted and valued friend of Cao Cao and Yuan Shao; he became Administrator of Chenliu Prefecture and supported Cao Cao's rise to power in Yan Province. Zhang criticised Yuan Shao's leadership of the Eastern Pass Coalition and unintentionally made an enemy of him; he then opposed Cao Cao's 'revenge massacres' in Xu Province and allied with Lü Bu and Chen Gong to seize control of Yan. Zhang was eventually isolated and killed by Cao's forces, and his fellow conspirators fled to Xu Province*

Zhang Shuo [Ch'arng S'oo-oh] – *vassal of Huang Zu that serves in the Jiangxia navy and fights the Sun clan many times*

Zhang Xi [Ch'arng Shee] – *Han general that was given 1,000 men and tasked with relieving Hefei during the siege of Jiangling*

Zhang Xiu [Ch'arng Shee-oo] – *nephew of Zhang Ji; he later received Jia Xu's service after occupying Nan County in Jing Province. Cao Cao made 'pacifying' Jing Governor Liu Biao his next major project after defeating Yufuluo and the Yellow Turbans in Yu Province, and he started the Jing campaign by attacking Nan County's capital, Wan City. Jia Xu advised surrender, and Zhang Xiu complied: Cao Cao then behaved unprofessionally, going so far as to take Zhang's widowed aunt, Lady Zou, as his consort. The enraged Zhang Xiu vented his feelings privately, but Cao's spies reported it to Cao, who then plotted to kill Zhang: Jia Xu's spies reported that, and Jia Xu launched a pre-emptive attack that robbed Cao of his eldest son, nephew and bodyguard. Zhang Xiu later submitted to Cao Cao again: Jia Xu joined Cao on that occasion, and Zhang enjoyed a short career as a Han official before dying (cause unknown, probably illness)*

Zhang Xun [Ch'arng Shoon] – *a former senior officer under Yuan Shu; he remains loyal to Shu even after Shu's disgrace and death. He is a friend of Sun Ce and respects him greatly, but his obsessive loyalty to Yuan Shu – likely due to Shu elevating his family from poverty – prevented him from joining the Suns. He reluctantly joined Liu Xun and went northward with Liu when Sun*

Ce captured Lujiang; Zhang Xun's fate after that is unknown

Zhang Yi [Ch'arng Yee] – *junior officer serving the Sun clan*

Zhang Yun [Ch'arng Yoon] – *an officer serving Jing Governor Liu Biao; he was the nephew of Cai Mao.*

Zhang Zhao [Ch'arng Ch'ah-oh] – *one of the 'Two Zhangs' (the other was his less famous brother Zhang Hong) and an adviser/politician that served Sun Ce and Sun Quan in succession; he was a highly-talented debater and could destroy a man's reputation with ease if allowed to. He was one of the most vocal supporters of surrendering to Cao Cao during the political tension leading up to the 'Battle of Red Cliffs', and many – including Zhou Yu, Cheng Pu, Lu Su and Liu Bei's adviser Zhuge Liang – were forced to debate with him on the issue. He later plotted against Liu Bei, Cao Cao and whoever else was considered to be a threat to Eastern Wu: he is often portrayed as a spiteful antagonist of sorts in popular fiction (this author tends to as well) but, in his defence, he had Eastern Wu's best interests at heart*
*Known by the courtesy name Zibu [Tz'ee-p'oo]

Zhao Fan [Ch'ah-oh Fan] – *Liu Biao's appointed ruler of Guiyang*

Zhao Yan [Ch'ah-oh Fan] – *Cao Cao's appointed 'Commandant-Protector of the Army' during the Red Cliffs campaign; the author could not find much information about him and settles for a vague portrayal and an ambiguous fate for him after the battle (the death count was estimated at 100,000 and he might well be one of the dead or the thousands more that were 'retired by injury')*

Zhao Yun [Ch'ah-oh Yoon] – *one of Liu Bei's most famous generals after Guan Yu; he served Gongsun Zan originally but decided to serve Bei and did so until his death. He is said to have done many great things, but none of them are relevant to this work save for, perhaps, one: he rescued Liu Bei's infant son, Liu Shan [Lee-oo S'arn] at the Battle of Steep-slope (this is not mentioned in the novel itself) and ensured that Bei had an heir to his eventual legacy – the Shu Han Empire in western China*
*Known by the courtesy name Zilong [Tz'eh-long]

Zhen Bao [Ch'ern P'ah-oh] – *a rebellious general in Huainan that Liu Yè defeated through a ruse; Zhen's troops then ceased to be a threat to Liu Xun and became Xun's to command. The story is mentioned in passing when Liu Xun is rebuking Liu Yè for failing to recognise his disputable evolution from vassal lord to state ruler*

Zheng Xuan [Ch'erng Shoo-arn] – *a famous scholar that tutored other respected figures such as Cai Yong*

Zhou Bo [Ch'oh P'oh] – *a powerful bandit leader in Shanyin that was defeated by Dong Xi; the victory gave Dong Xi a reputation that he exploits several times in his battles with other bandits*

Zhou Tai [Ch'oh Tigh] – *a former pirate that joined Sun Ce and*

served as an officer and bodyguard; he later became Sun Quan's personal bodyguard and almost lost his life defending Quan during a Shanyue attack on Xuan City. When Zhou Tai recovered he became an official and vanguard general that participated in many of Sun Ce's final campaigns. He became Sun Quan's bodyguard yet again after Sun Ce's death, and he almost died saving him yet again when a campaign to take Hefei Fortress went horribly wrong. Sun Quan valued him and did not allow anyone to treat him disrespectfully, despite his poor background
*Known by the courtesy name Youping [Yoh-ping]

Zhou Yi [Ch'oh Yee] – *the father of Zhou Yu; he was Magistrate of Luoyang around the time of Emperor Ling's death and fled the capital when Dong Zhuo took power, settling in Shu City in Lujiang Prefecture. He had Sun Jian's family stay in his vast home during Sun Jian's time in the Eastern Pass Coalition, and his son Zhou Yu went on to become Sun Ce's closest friend and ally. He is only referred to in this work and assumed to be recently deceasad*

Zhou Yu [Ch'oh Yoo] – *referred to as 'Gongjin' in the main narrative; he is a major protagonist throughout, and everything that needs to be said is said during the course of the novel*
*Known by the courtesy name Gongjin [K'ong-jin]

Zhu Huan [Ch'oo Hoo-arn] – *a long-serving Sun clan official; he does not play a large role in this novel, as he was tasked with stabilising remote regions during the timeframe covered*
*Known by the courtesy name Xiumu [Shee-oo-moo]

Zhu Ling [Ch'oo Ling] – *a Han officer that once served Yuan Shao; Shao 'gifted' him to Cao Cao, and despite being treated poorly he stayed and served Cao as one of his most reliable men*

Zhu Ran [Ch'oo Rarn] – *born 'Shi Ran'; he was adopted by Sun Jian's chief strategist Zhu Zhi. Zhu Ran was a close friend of Sun Quan, and when Quan inherited the state from Sun Ce, Ran became a very important official and officer. He is most famous for his role in the 'Battle of Xiaoting', where his fire attack decimated Liu Bei's poorly-organised forces while they camped, rather foolishly, in a forest at the height of summer*
*Known by the courtesy name Yifeng [Yee-fung]

Zhu Zhi [Ch'oo Ch'ee] – *a Han official that joined Sun Jian during his middle career; he was a capable administrator and strategist, and his adopted son Zhu Ran would be a pivotal figure in future times. He spends most of this work thanklessly defending Wu Prefecture from various enemies, but he gains late notability for how he deals with Sun Ben and Sun Fu during the Battle of Red Cliffs and the siege of Jiangling*
*Known by the courtesy name Junli [Ch'oon-lee]

Zhuge Jin [Ch'oo-ker Jin] – *the eldest of three brothers that were descendants of prominent Han officials; his family fled the troubles in Qing, Yan and Xu Provinces to the east and settled in Jing Province. Jin then travelled to Yang Province to find work and*

eventually found reasonable employment under Sun Ce and Sun Quan, despite the political suspicions surrounding the family (Jing was governed by an enemy of the Sun clan, and Jin's sisters were married to prominent politicians in the Jing regime). Zhuge Jin was eventually trusted by Sun Quan, who gave him ever-higher ranks, and he tried, repeatedly, to get his talented brother Liang – known as 'Crouching Dragon' – to join him. Zhuge Liang chose to serve the wandering warlord Liu Bei, which often placed Liang and Jin on opposite sides of a feud, but the two remained close. When a lasting peace was established between Liu Bei's son and Sun Quan, Jin allowed the childless Liang to adopt his younger son, but that young man died within a few years of the adoption. Jin's eldest son, Zhuge Ke [Ch'oo-ker Ker], was eventually trusted as a regent to Sun Quan's young son, despite many – including Zhuge Liang and Jin himself – questioning Ke's character, and the worst suspicions were proved correct
*Known by the courtesy name Ziyu [Tz'ee-yoo]

Zhuge Liang [Ch'oo-ker Lee-arng] – *Zhuge Jin's younger brother and a genius inventor and strategist; he is the protagonist of this author's first work, 'Crouching Dragon: the Journey of Zhuge Liang'. He serves as an ally and rival to the Sun clan, just as his chosen lord, Liu Bei, does. Liang shared a vision with Lu Su of a 'tripartite empire' ruled by Cao Cao, Sun Quan and one other, with Liang envisioning the relatively weak Liu Bei as that other; he managed, by utilising various schemes, to grow Bei's 3,000-strong militia into a 100,000-strong army that was well-trained and loyal, and he also ensured that the homeless Bei received control of southern Jing Province (from Sun Quan) and then Yi Province (by taking it from its governor Liu Zhang before Sun Quan could). Liu Bei then gained Hanzhong (from Cao Cao) but lost Jing (when Sun Quan's Chief Commander, Lü Meng, defeated and killed Guan Yu and occupied the region); Liang opposed Bei's plan to avenge Guan Yu before he fought the recently-enthroned Cao Pi (to avenge the extinguished Han Dynasty), but Bei ignored him and marched the army to utter defeat and decimation at the hands of Sun Quan's new Chief Commander, Lu Xun. Liu Bei died a broken man, leaving Zhuge Liang to be co-regent of his Shu Han Empire; Liang miraculously restored cordial relations with Sun Quan and turned his attentions toward the new Emperor of Cao Wei, Cao Rui, who was not universally popular. Zhuge Liang launched 5 successive campaigns against Cao Wei, but he was thwarted by supply problems, prodigious generals, treachery, in-fighting and incompetence at every turn: despite inventing 'wooden oxen' to resolve supply issues, 'mantou' buns to improve the army's food, signalling lanterns and a number of new military tactics, he could not outwit the Cao Wei Commander-in-Chief Sima Yi and died without fulfilling his dream to restore the Han. The state that Zhuge had helped to build – Shu Han – was invaded by Sima Yi's 'student of war' Deng Ai and extinguished 3 decades later.*

Zu Lang [Tz'oo Larng] – *a bandit leader in southern Yang Province that was defeated by Sun Ce; he assists the Suns in later years*

Zu Mao [Tz'oo Mah-oh] – *an early ally of Sun Jian; he seems to have been a bodyguard of sorts. Little was known of him at the time of writing; he was mentioned as having acted as a decoy when Sun Jian suffered a critical loss against forces led by Dong Zhuo's best generals; some fictional accounts kill him there, but the author chose to let him survive until Sun Jian's death in northern Jing, perishing 'off-stage' alongside his master*

UNNAMED YU PROVINCE MERCENARY – *unnamed sword-for-hire that aids the fugitive Yan Xiang at the start of the novel*

HISTORICAL CHINESE FIGURES

Confucius (Romanisation of Kong Fusha/Fuzi, lit. Master Kong) – *a famous scholar and philosopher whose beliefs and teachings became a philosophy in their own right, with many noted figures throughout Chinese history adopting 'Confucianism' as a way of life. Confucius' 'analects' were seen as the model for a morally correct way of living: their teachings usually sat alongside any other moral or spiritual beliefs that the practitioner had.*

Gan Mao [K'arn Mah-oh] – *a Chancellor to Qin Shi Huangdi, First Emperor of the Qin Dynasty, that is suggested to be a direct ancestor of the pirate Gan Ning.*

Guan Yiwu [K'oo-arn Yee-woo] – *an adviser to Duke Huan of Qi that proposed applying benevolent methods of 'pacification' (or assimilation) when dealing with native tribes; Lu Ji uses his approach to recommend a softer attitude toward the Shanyue.*

Jiang Ziya [Ch'ee-arng Tz'ee-yah], also known as Taigong Wang [Tigh-k'ong Warng] – *an adviser to King Wen of Zhou that helped to bring down the tyrannical King Zhou of Shang; this 11th Century BCE figure is often referred to as one of the greatest sages.*

Lao Tzu [Lao Tz'oo] (sometimes Romanised to Laozi [Lao-tz-er], but the author has opted for the older form) – *famous philosopher and founder of Taoism (again, this can be Romanised to Daoism, but the author has opted for one over the other)*

Liu Bang [Lee-oo P'arng] – *the founder of the Han Dynasty; his region of influence, Hanzhong, gave his dynasty its name. One of his descendants was eventually overthrown by the chancellor Wang Mang; Wang was defeated in turn by a popular uprising led by Liu clan members, and the Han Dynasty was restored. The second of the new line of Han Emperors, Liu Xiu/Emperor Guangwu, moved the capital to the eastern city of Luoyang to create distance between his government and the foreign tribes that threatened to devour the western provinces. As such, some historians tend refer to a Western Han (pre-Wang Mang) and an Eastern Han (post-Wang Mang).*

Sun Tzu [Soon Tz'oo] (sometimes Romanised to Sunzi [Soon-tz'er], but the author has opted for the older form) – *a legendary scholar, famed for his work 'The Art of War'; while new* technologies outdated some strategies and forced later scholars such as Zhuge Liang to annotate the work, his understanding of the psychological aspects of warfare were used to great effect, and unlike technology, those references remained relevant since people, unlike their inventions, did not and do not change. The 2nd Century warlord Sun Jian and his progeny claimed descent from Sun Tzu, though this was never completely proven or disputed.

Wang Mang [Warng Marng] – the regent and Chancellor to the last Chang'an-based Han Emperor and founder of his own short-lived Xin Dynasty. He was eventually overthrown by members of Liu clan, who revived the Han Dynasty. Wang Mang is treated as a villain by Han loyalists and subsequent imperial regimes, while some historians argue that his government was not entirely malevolent. His name was typically used in Han times as a slander to imply that a person was seditious – or, more typically, make a specific accusation of evil ambition

Wei Zi [Way Tz'eh] – an adviser to the tyrant King Zhou of Shang that defected to King Wen of Zhou and did all he could to bring down his former master; this 11th Century BCE figure is referred to by Jia Xu and Pang Tong at one point.

Xiang Yu [Shee-arng Yoo] – a powerful figure in the Chu State that seized control after the collapse of the Qin Dynasty; he eliminated the Chu king and declared himself to be 'Hegemon-king (or Conqueror-king) of Chu', and then he tried to establish a new empire by conquering the other liberated kingdoms and states. His main opponent was Liu Bang, founder of the Han Dynasty; Xiang ultimately lost despite massive advantages and Liu reunited the land. Sun Ce is likened to Xiang Yu by Xu Gong, and one interpretation/translation is 'Little Conqueror'

Xiao Hè [Shee-ow Her] – one of the advisers that helped to bring about the birth of the Han Dynasty; he is referred to by Gan Ning when Gan is rebuking Zhang Zhao (for Zhang being timid in comparison to the risk-taking 'king maker' Xiao that Zhang is supposedly being compared to by Sun Quan)

Zhang Liang [Ch'arng Lee-arng] – one of the advisers that helped to bring about the fall of the Qin Dynasty and the birth of the Han Dynasty; he is used in complimentary terms or to suggest that a situation could only be resolved by a man of his calibre

PLACES

In this book, land locations are sorted by their provincial-level location and other landmarks – rivers and such – trail the list. Most of the novel takes place in Yang and Jing Provinces, but other places (such as Xuchang) are mentioned or visited.

Luoyang [Loo-oh-yarng] – the eastern and current capital, used by Han Emperor Guangwu (Liu Xiu) onwards during the second phase of the Han Dynasty; the capital is the scene of many *dramas, including the Partisan Crisis, a series of attempted coups (including one by the 'Way of Peace'), and a war between the court eunuchs and followers of assassinated Commander-in-Chief Hè Jin before it is finally pillaged and burned to the ground by Dong Zhuo and his allies, prior to their move to the former capital Chang'an. Luoyang does not enjoy a revival until the early 3rd Century, when it becomes the seat of a new dynasty, Cao Wei*

Chang'an [T'arng Arn] – *the western and former capital, designated so by the Han Dynasty founder Liu Bang and used until the usurper Wang Mang temporarily ended the Han Dynasty and founded his own Xin [Shin] Dynasty. It was still considered to be the capital for a very short time after the restoration of the Han, but for a number of reasons (primarily that the Qiang and other tribes in the west were a constant threat, and Emperor Guangwu had an established power base in the east), a new capital – Luoyang – was created. Dong Zhuo moves the court back to Chang'an during his time as Chancellor of State, and the regency court maintained Chang'an as their capital despite a new threat from the Qiang tribes of Liang Province (this is because the east is more hostile and Luoyang had been looted and gutted by Dong Zhuo during his move to the west) At the start of the text, Cao Cao has already moved Emperor Xian to Xuchang (see below)*

Xuchang [Shoo-t'arng] – *located in northwest Yan Province; Cao Cao's chosen imperial capital while Luoyang was being rebuilt (sometimes known as Xu [Shoo] but that leads to confusion with Xu Province). Cao Cao was Governor of Yan, so the vast majority of the officials in Xuchang were Cao Cao's loyalists (even more so after the purge of men that followed Zhang Miao and Chen Gong's rebellion, and in addition, many of Emperor Xian's loyalists were killed by the regents or died on route to Luoyang): this would later lead to accusations of plotting sedition (the 'Girdle Edict Crisis' of 200CE that eventually led to the 'Battle of Guandu')*

Yang [Yarng] Province – *located in the southeast of China, east of southern Jing and south of everything else; it is quite a large province, and can be divided into two as the Yangtze/Great River bisects the province. The southern part is also considered to be east of the Great River, and is sometimes known as Jiangdong [Jee-arng-t'ong] (lit. river-east, or 'east of the river'). Lujiang and Jiujiang Prefectures comprise the majority of the northern part, although Guangling and Danyang could be partially included (and were often considered as annexed into Xu Province as well). It is mentioned during discussion that Lu Kang was appointed as Magistrate of Gaocheng [K'ah-oh-t'erng], a 'remote and troubled place' in Yang Province, and pacified it, earning him great respect. The vast Lake Chao [T'ow] in northern Yang is mentioned at one point for its strategic importance (it flows into the Yangtze and could therefore be used for training and deploying navies).*

Wu [Woo] Prefecture – *located in the east of Yang Province, south of Guangling and west of Wu Prefecture, 'below' the Yangtze/Great River; the Sun clan hailed from this region, and the scholar Cai Yong hid here for 12 years. NOTE: Wu and Danyang tend to overlap and the boundaries change a few times.*

Wu County City is used as a prefectural capital by Zhu Zhi during most of the text; Qu'e [Choo-er] becomes the capital after boundary changes; Wucheng is the proposed capital of Jiangdong when Sun Quan takes power (although he never actually gets there due to various distractions), and Sun Jian was made 'Marquis of Wucheng' during his life. Fuchun [Foo-t'oon] County – located in the south of Wu Prefecture – was the ancestral home of the famous Sun clan that founded Eastern Wu. Xuan [Shoo-arn] City was the site of one of Sun Quan's early tactical blunders and the setting of a major battle between Sun Ce and the Shanyue; Sun Quan was made Magistrate of Yangxian [Yarng-shee-arn] County as his first proper appointment, and Kan Ze is given a role in Qiantang [Chee-arn-tarng] at one point. Ling Tong's clan hail from Yuhang [Yoo-harng] County in the south. Major battles against bandit/rebel armies take place in Bao [P'ah-oh] and Ma [Mah]. Dantu [T'arn-too] is the site of a base and of the assassination attempt that claimed Sun Ce's life

Lujiang [Loo-jiang] Prefecture – *located in the northwest of Yang, 'above' the Great River; there are land borders with Jing, Yu and Yan Provinces. Zhou Yu (Gongjin) hailed from Lujiang. The capital, Huancheng [Hoo-arn-t'eng], was the site of several sieges. The Qian [Chee-arn] Hills served as a base for bandits and deserters from Yuan Shu's army (such as Chen Lan and Lei Bo), and Mount Xisai [Shee-sigh], to the west, is the site of a major battle between Liu Xun and Sun Ce after the former flees there; the Qiao sisters that married Sun Ce and Zhou Yu hail from Wan [Wahn] County, where the capital is based.*

Hefei [Her-fay] is located in the south of Lujiang Prefecture; this strategically useful area was eventually fortified by Liu Fu (supposedly at Man Chong's suggestion). The resultant fortress was a major obstacle to the Sun clan's plans to reclaim northern Yang Province. Lu [Loo County] County is to the northwest of Hefei; Yuan Shu camped here during the campaign against Dong Zhuo. Shu [S'oo] City was the home of Zhou Yu's family after fleeing Luoyang, and Sun Jian settled his family here while he went to fight Dong Zhuo. Cao Cao's vassals feign a massing of troops in Yulou [Yoo-loh] to the north, which fools Sun Quan and causes him to abandon his first attack on Hefei.

Jiujiang [Jee-oo-jee-arng] Prefecture – *located in the northeast of Yang Province, 'above' the Great River; the provincial capital Shouchun [S'oh-t'oon] is based here (Shouchun was also Yuan Shu's 'Imperial capital' when he proclaimed that he was 'First Emperor of the Zhong Dynasty'. There are land borders with Yan and Xu Provinces to the north. Liyang [Lee-yarng] County is used as a temporary capital by Yan Xiang at one point. Zhang Zhao tries (and fails) to seize the strategic region of Dangtu [T'arng-too] at one point during the twin sieges of Jiangling and Hefei.*

The Huai [Hoo-eye] River runs to the north of the prefecture: Shouchun County is part of Huainan [Hoo-eye-narn]. Lu Su's home region, Dongcheng [T'ong-t'erng], is to the east.

Danyang [T'arn-yarng] Prefecture – *located in the centre of Yang*

Province, south of Jiujiang and 'below' the Yangtze/Great River; the region was famous for producing good cavalrymen. Its capital varied: Qu'e [Choo-er] was used until it became part of Wu, and after that, Wanling [Wahn-ling] seems to be the capital (Sun Yi is based there after becoming Administrator). Wuhu [Woo-hoo] – once the location of a hilltop base for Taishi Ci when he was waging a guerrilla war against Sun Ce – is once again a problem for Sun Quan, and Xu Sheng and Jiang Qin are sent to deal with bandits. Shicheng [S'ee-t'erng] County is deemed so unstable at one point that Cheng Pu and Huang Gai spend considerable time there as pacifiers.

Guangling [K'oo-arng-ling] Prefecture – *located in the east of Yang Province, on the coast, north of Wu Prefecture and south of Xiapi in eastern Xu Province; it appears to be controlled by various warlords most of the time; it is divided between Xu Province (under Administrator Chen Deng) and Yang Province (ruled by the Sun clan) for the duration of the work, and it is a battle over Guangling that lures Sun Ce eastward and leaves him open to an assassination attempt by Xu Gong's loyalists.*

Yuzhang [Yoo-ch'arng] Prefecture – *located in the southwest of Yang Province, west of Danyang and Kuaiji and on the border with Jiangxia in southern Jing Province; Nanchang [Narn-t'arng] is the capital. Sun Ben was 'given' the remote Luling County [Loo-ling] (to the far southwest) by Yuan Shu (with the probable intention of a pincer attack on the capital Nanchang), but he did not go there (his brother Fu went instead); Zhou Yu established his naval training facility in Ba Qiu [P'ah Chee-oo] in Luling. Po [Poh] County and Xi'an [Shee Arn] are located to the northwest (they are harassed by bandits and Huang Zu; Pan Zhang is made Magistrate of Xi'an at one point). Haihun (High-hoon) County is the site of a supply depot and appears to be important to food production; an attack on this place by Liu Xun is one of the first major events in this work, and it is later guarded by Taishi Ci and Cheng Pu. The attack is thwarted by trapping Liu Xun's forces in a pincer at Shangliao [S'arng-lee-ow], a strategically important region that Sun Ce tricks Liu Xun into marching upon.*

Kuaiji [Koo-eye-jee] Prefecture – *located in the southeast of Yang Province, on the coast, south of Wu Prefecture; Wang Lang was Administrator of this prefecture when Yuan Shu sent Sun Ce to seize it. Shanyin [S'arn-yin] County was the capital (and the site of a sizeable rebellion). Other notable locations include Yuyao [Yoo-yow] County (Zhu Ran is sent here to manage unrest), Wushang [Woo-s'arng] (Luo Tong hails from here and later has a government role here) and Yan [Yarn] County (Hè Qi was recruited by Sun Ce in Yan, and Qi is forced to argue with his successor as Magistrate at one point in this novel).*

Jing [Jing] Province – *a province located in the centre of Han China; it has borders with Yi, Hanzhong, Yu, Yan and Central provinces, which makes it strategically desirable to a would-be conqueror. A number of important events occur here throughout the novel, ranging from battles to political upheavals. Longzhong*

[Long-ch'ong] County in the north of the province is the site of the Zhuge family farm: the eldest brother, Zhuge Jin, serves Sun Quan, and the famous second brother, Zhuge Liang, becomes a strategist to the warlord Liu Bei. Gan Ning is, at one point, ceremonially 'banished' to the 'remote' Banzhou [P'arn-ch'oh] region in order to appease Ling Tong.

Nan [Narn] County – *a county located in the far north of Jing; it borders Yan Province, Yu Province and Central Province, making it strategically invaluable. The Yellow Turbans almost took the county during their first rebellion; Sun Jian saved it during that campaign and later seized it for his then-master Yuan Shu, and Zhang Xiu later governed with surprising popularity.*

The capital, Wan [Wahn] City, has its own story; it is strategically important, so it suffered repeated seizure attempts over the years. Dong Zhuo's former vassal Zhang Ji seized the city after leaving Chang'an, but died and left the place in the hands of his nephew Zhang Xiu and the adviser Jia Xu; the two fugitives were then forced to fight Cao Cao's army, and that event is famous for its outcome and numerous consequences.

Xiangyang [Shee-arng-yarng] – *a county (and city named for the county) located in the lower north of Jing Province; it serves as Jing Governor Liu Biao's northern capital.*

Xinye [Shin-yer] – *a county located in the north of Jing Province; it served as the fugitive warlord Liu Bei's base when he was taking refuge under Liu Biao (after the Battle of Guandu).*

Fan [Farn] – *a county (and city named for the county) located in the lower north of Jing Province; it straddles the north bank of the River Han, directly opposite Xiangyang.*

Nan [Narn] Prefecture – *located in southern Jing Province; Jiangling [Jee-arng-ling] was the capital of Nan Prefecture and southern capital of Jing Province, and the siege battle for control of Nan is fought here after the Battle of Red Cliffs. Gan Ning seizes Yiling [Yee-ling] to the west (close to the border with Yi Province) during the siege of Jiangling, and Liu Bei's forces vie for Linju [Lin-ch'oo] County twice and fail to hold onto it. Liu Bei makes Gong'an [K'ong Arn] his first base after acquiring the four counties (and before Sun Quan cedes the whole of Nan Prefecture to him).*

Jiangxia [Jee-arng-shee-ah] Prefecture – *located in southeast Jing Province; this is Huang Zu's power base, and is the site of many battles between Huang Zu and the Sun clan: Xiakou [Shee-ah-koh] seems to serve as a capital, but there is a Jiangxia City, where the final battle with Huang Zu takes place. Three Rivers is a port region in eastern Jiangxia; Shaxian [S'ah-shee-arn] serves as an important base; Wulin [Woo-lin] is the site of battles prior to the fateful ones at Red Cliffs, which is also in Jiangxia. Chaisang [T'eye-sarng] is a strategically important fortified city close to Po County Lake that serves as a capital of sorts when Sun Quan is vying for Jing Province; Xu Sheng and Zhou Yu defend the region from Jing's army at various times. Gan Ning is briefly made the*

Magistrate of Zhu [Ch'oo] County in the south by Huang Zu; Gan was stationed in Dangkou [T'arng-koh] by Sun Quan after Huang Zu's death. A major battle takes place at Mian [Mee-arn] County in the north. Huarong [Hoo-ah-rong] County in the north is not only a site of battles between Liu Biao and the Suns: it serves as part of Cao Cao's escape route after being routed at Red Cliffs.

Dangyang [T'arng-yarng] County – located in central Jing Province; Liu Bei famously retreated through here with 100,000 refugees and 3,000 soldiers after Cao Cao took control of Jing. The main 'confrontation' took place at Steep-slope: Liu Bei's forces were crushed and Bei fled into Jiangxia thereafter.

Changsha [T'arng-s'ah] "County" – located south of Jing Province and considered part of Jing; Changsha is more a prefecture, but is often referred to as a county, perhaps because it is sparsely inhabited. Changsha was administrated by Sun Jian after the Yellow Turban Rebellion; it is later occupied by Liu Bei's faction with Sun Quan's 'blessing' (after Red Cliffs). Zhou Yu spends his last hours in Ba Qiu [P'ah Chee-oo], a port city that shares a name with Zhou's training facility in Yuzhang.

Wuling [Woo-ling] "County", Lingling [Ling-ling] "County" and Guiyang [K'oo-ee-yarng] "County" – located south of Jing Province and technically part of Jing; they are all better described in terms of size as commanderies/prefectures, but are often referred to as counties, perhaps because they are sparsely inhabited and therefore have county-sized populations. Huang Gai hails from Lingling; they all become targets for Zhou Yu and Liu Bei during the siege of Jiangling, but Liu Bei ultimately claims them all.

Yan [Yarn] Province – located in central China, to the east of Central and Jing Provinces, west of Xu Province and south of Ji Province; it was entrusted to Cao Cao by Yuan Shao, but Cao quickly became autonomous and brought the imperial court here after it escaped the regents. Xuchang, the third capital that Emperor Xian 'ruled' from, is here, but is detailed at the start of the 'PLACES' section. Cao Cao has a base at Anmin [Arn-min] to the north of the province during his 'Guandu campaign' against Yuan Shao, where he is shown to be in one scene; he later fights Yuan Shao's forces one last time at Cangting [Ts'arng-ting] in the northeast of the province.

Guandu [K'oo-arn-t'oo] County – located in northern Yan Province; key roads run through here, and a fortified city is its capital. This is the place that gives a name to the greatest battle between Yuan Shao and Cao Cao and, in fact, one of the most important battles of the era: Cao placed a large part of his army here to block the route to Xuchang, and a siege took place that was not, in truth, the main part of the campaign. Yuan Shao retreated when he lost his supply depot; he lost a great deal of his army to defections and desertion, and never recovered militarily.

Central Province – known at the time as 'Sili' [See-lee], but the author chose to refer to the province by its political purpose and geographical location. Luoyang is to the east of the region, and Chang'an is to the west, bordering (and also inhabiting, technically) Liang Province. Notable places are White Wave Gorge (once the base of operations of the White Wave Bandits, who were named for the place) and Hedong [Her-t'ong] Prefecture, where an unsuccessful rebellion takes place during Cao Cao's attempts to seize control of the northeast.

Xu [Shoo] Province – located in the centre-east of China, south of Qing Province and east of Yan Province; it was governed by Tao Qian, Liu Bei and Lü Bu for varying times, but it is under Han government control at the start of the work. The novel's second 'antagonist', Cao Cao, hails from Pei [Pay] County in the west of Xu (he famously employed 'scorched earth' tactics when he invaded Xu, but one can presume that he spared Pei entirely). The capital is Xiapi [Shee-ah-pee]: the previous capital, Peng [Perng] was abandoned when Cao Cao began his campaigns against Tao Qian (Yan Jun and Zhuge Jin discuss Peng's fate briefly). The adviser Bu Zhi hails from Huaiyin [Hoo-eye-yin] in the south.

Haixi [High-ee-shee] County – located in the north of Xu Province; a local bandit king, Chen Yu (known as 'Haixi Chen' in this work) once moved into Yang Province to cause trouble for the Suns. Liu Bei also endured a year-long siege here before tendering the provincial seal to Lü Bu (who stood by while Yuan Shu's forces attacked Bei, despite Bei giving Bu refuge from Cao Cao).

Kaiyang [K-eye-yarng] County – located in the northeast of Xu Province; the warlord Zang Ba occupied this place for a time.

Xiaopei [Shee-ow-pay] County – located in the southwest, on a border with Yan and Yang Provinces; Liu Bei was posted here by Lü Bu as a 'gate guard' against Yuan Shu and Cao Cao.

Liang [Lee-arng] Province – located in the far northwest of China; the region is home to the Qiang and Yuezhi peoples, who rose up (alongside the disaffected Han Chinese populace) against the Han government in rebellion. The conflict ended with the Qiang controlling most of the province. Longxi [Long-shee] Prefecture in western Liang was under Qiang control; Zhu Ran casually refers to this place in derogatory terms.

Yu [Yoo] Province – located south and east of Central Province; the Yuan clan's ancestral home, Ru [Roo] County, is here. Yang [Yarng] City in the west of the province was the site of the first battle between the forces of the feuding Yuan brothers (Sun Jian was attacked without warning by Yuan Shao's vassals). Lu [Loo] County is briefly mentioned as being one of Xu Sheng's choices for family relocation during the upheaval in his native Langya. An Feng [Arn Fung] is at one point thought to be the base for a massive Han army, giving Zhou Yu cause for concern.

Runan [Roo-narn] Prefecture – the capital prefecture of Yu Province, located in its centre; the Yuan clan's ancestral home, Ru [Roo] County, is located here, Lü Meng's family originates in Fupo

[Foo-poh], Lü Fan's family originates in Xi [Shee] County and Luo Tong's father was Magistrate of Chen [T'ern] County before he was murdered by Yuan Shu's forces.

Ji [Jee] Province – *located in the northeast of China, south of Yòu Province, east of Bing Province and west of Qing Province; this became the Yuan clan's power base after losing their home region of Runan. Its capital is Yè City [Yer]: Cao Cao captures it during an important 'off-stage' battle against the Yuan clan. The city of Nanpi [Narn-pee] to the northeast is briefly mentioned; Yuan Tan fought his last battle here after Cao Cao ended their truce in the wake of the capture of Yè. Gongsun Zan's battle with Yuan Shao at Jie [Ch'ee-er] Bridge is also mentioned; he was routed by Yuan Shao's leading general, Qu Yi [Choo Yee].*

Qing [Ching] Province – *located in the northeast of China, east of Ji Province and south of Yòu Province; the region seems to suffer from high crime and corruption, despite several principalities. Linzi [Lin-tz'eh] – located in the centre-north of Qing Province – served as the provincial capital*

Donglai [T'ong-l'eye] Prefecture – *located to the east, this is Taishi Ci's home region (he refers to it at one point).*

Ji'nan [Jee Narn] Prefecture – *located in the west of Qing Province, near the Ji River; Cao Cao was sent here by the court, but he could not cope with the pressure and retired*

Mount Tai [Tigh] Prefecture – *located in the northwest of Qing Province, near the actual Mount Tai, and the home region of minor warlord Zang Ba: prior to the Yellow Turban Rebellion, Zang Ba's father was arrested after criticising the corrupt administrator, leading to his son becoming a criminal to free him.*

Langya [Larng-yah] Prefecture – *located in the centre of Qing Province; Yangdu [Yarng-t'oo], located in the southwest of Langya Prefecture, was the famous Zhuge clan's ancestral home.*

Yi [Yee] Province – *a province located in the centre-west of Han China, south of Hanzhong and west of Jing; it is a relatively harsh and unforgiving place at this point (now it is Szechuan), but Liu Yan craved the governorship precisely because it was isolated enough for him to have complete autonomy. Liu Bei later set his sights on making Yi his first base (after the loaned piece of Jing that he has obtained by that point) and seized it from Liu Yan's son Zhang after a long campaign. The capital is Chengdu [T'erng-doo], in the south of Yi Province; that place was protected by a complex natural defensive barrier of rivers, hills and mountains. Yi is never visited during the work, but Zhou Yu's acquisition of Nan Prefecture facilitated an invasion that he died whilst planning. Gan Ning is said to have been part of a failed rebellion in the northwest Guanghan [K'oo-arng-harn] region after Liu Zhang took power, and he hailed from Linjiang [Lin-ch'ee-arng] in the southeast.*

Yòu [Yoh] Province – *located in the northeast of China, on the* *frontier; it is therefore prone to frequent attacks by Northern Xiongnu, Wuhuan and other tribes. The famous warlord Gongsun Zan was based here. Its capital is Fanyang [Farn-yarng]. Cheng Pu hails from (Yòu)Beiping [Yoh-p'ei-ping] in the far northeast, and Han Dang hails from nearby Lingzhi [Ling-ch'ee] in Liaoxi [Lee-ow-shee] County. A major battle between Cao Cao and the Yuan-Wuhuan alliance takes place 'off-stage' here during the course of the novel; it is also briefly mentioned that Gongsun Zan's final battle (versus Yuan Shao) takes place in the northern fortress city of Yijing [Yee-ch'ing]. Liu Bei's home region, Zhuo [Ch'oh] Prefecture, is in the far north (he was briefly the Magistrate of Anxi [Arn-shee] County in Zhuo Prefecture after the Yellow Turban Rebellion; Gongsun Zan was Zhuo's Administrator).*

Bing [P'ing] Province – *located in the centre-north of China, north of Central Province; it is relatively unimportant to the narrative. The Southern Xiongnu mainly live in Bing, and the Black Mountain Bandits are very active here; it is under Yuan clan control for the first half of the work and government – or Cao Cao's – control in the latter half after Cao defeats the Yuans.*

Hanzhong [Harn-ch'ong] Province – *also known at the time as (The Taoist State of) Han'ning [Harn Ning]; this region was the fief of sorts of Liu Bang, founder of the Han Dynasty, and he named his dynasty for this region. When Zhang Lu occupied Hanzhong, he renamed it: if Hanzhong is read as meaning 'Amidst/In Han', Han'ning could, when taking individual characters, mean 'Tranqil Han' or, possibly, 'Rather than Han/Preferable to Han', which fits perfectly with Zhang Lu's beliefs. The region is only mentioned in this text, but it becomes a battleground for Cao Cao and Liu Bei in later years.*

Jiaozhi [Ch'ee-ow-ch'ee] (Province) – *a region to the south of Kuaiji Prefecture (in Yang Province) that includes part of Northern Vietnam: the Sun clan later stake a claim on the region as part of the expansion of the state of Eastern Wu.*

Liaodong [Lee-ow-t'ong] Peninsula – *a region to the northeast of Qing Province: Taishi Ci lived here when in exile. The defeated Yuan brothers, Shang and Xi, sought sanctuary here after the Battle of White Wolf Mountain.*

Cangwu [Ts'arng-woo] – *a region to the south of Jing Province that may be seen as part of Jiaozhi, Yang or Jing: its ruler, Wu Ju, was fully autonomous and deemed a threat by Zhou Yu.*

Great Wall [a.k.a. 'The Endless Wall'] – *commissioned by various rulers throughout history to repel the Xiongnu and other tribal invaders; it spans the entire northern border. Cao Cao actually passed the wall and went into Xianbei and Wuhuan territories in order to fight the latter and pacify them once and for all: he took the Wuhuan by surprise at White Wolf Mountain (they were not expecting Cao to arrive so quickly) and killed their lead chieftain, and the tribes submitted to the Han thereafter.*

Han [Harn] River – *runs through Hanzhong and Jing Provinces at the very least; it was a major waterway in central Han China.*

Xiang [Shee-arng] River – *runs down northern Jing Province and into the Han River*

Huai [Hoo-eye] River – *runs through Yu, Xu and Yang Provinces from west to east; part of the north of Jiujiang Prefecture is named Huainan, lit. 'Huai (River) south'*

Si [See] River – *located in Qing and Xu Provinces; it flows south and east toward the east coast. Xiapi is east of its banks. Cao Cao famously dammed the river with corpses during his revenge campaigns against Xu Province Governor Tao Qian.*

Mian [Mee-arn] River – *runs through part of northern Jiangxia*

Yangtze [Yarng-tz'ee] River – *spoken of in the text as the Great River, it runs from the west of China to the east, separating the land naturally into north and south. The Sun clan's home region is Jiangdong, which roughly translates to 'East of the (Great) River'.*

Yellow River – *located in the centre-north of China; this vibrant river – which literally runs yellow with sand – runs south and west from the northeast coast to the lands east of Luoyang, whereupon it turns west and runs north of Luoyang as far as the lands east of Chang'an, whereupon it splits and runs north and west.*

MISCELLANEOUS

Di [Dee] – *a northern, non-Han Chinese race, broken down further into tribes; they were indigenous to the mountains of Hanzhong.*

Qiang [Chee-arng] – *non-Chinese ethnic tribes that lived in the northwest on either side of the Great Wall. The various tribes were typically enemies of the Han Dynasty. Ma Teng and Han Sui famously joined the tribes, and the eldest son of the former, Ma Chao, became a notorious warrior king.*

Shanyue [S'arn-yoo-er] – *non-Chinese tribes that lived in and around various regions: they lived in Yang Province in large numbers. They resented Han rule, but their allegiances shifted dramatically through the eras.*

The 'Ten Attendants' – *a clique of eunuchs in the imperial capital Luoyang; they began life as loyalists that helped Emperor Huan to purge Liang Ji and Empress Dowager Liang's influence, but over time they formed a power base of their own. By the year 166, they were almost untouchable, and anyone that crossed them, deliberately or otherwise, was dealt with in the harshest fashion: hundreds of non-compliant intelligentsia were labelled as traitors and persecuted, an event known as the 'Partisan Crisis'. They were finally purged after thwarted political action by Commander-in-Chief Hè Jin and decisive military action by his ally Yuan Shao.*

'The Way of Five Pecks' – *a religious cult that was led by Zhang Lu, the ruler of Han'ning; their doctrine was based around a non-monetary system where rice was the currency and community was paramount, although many decried the way that potentially troublesome elements were kept loyal by providing them with whatever they needed at the expense of others.*

'The Way of Peace' – *the religious group that started the Yellow Turban Rebellion; although it can probably be said that many of those that fought were not followers of this Taoist cult, they had a 16-character mantra that was a simple, inspirational way to gather followers and rally other forms of support.*

Wuhuan [Woo-hoo-arn] – *non-Chinese tribes that lived across China and the surrounding territories; this work only refers to them, but their activities in Yòu and Ji Provinces, their alliance with the powerful Yuan clan and their eventual pacification in the aftermathof the Battle of White Wolf Mountain are an important 'off-stage' struggle that is covered in the sister work '"Intention": War for the Han Frontier'.*

Xiongnu [Shee-ong-noo] – *non-Chinese ethnic tribes that lived in the north on either side of the Great Wall; the various tribes were enemies, economic trading partners or allies of the Han Dynasty. The Southern Xiongnu provided troops to the Han army.*

Xianbei [Shee-an-p'ay] – *a confederacy of mostly Xiongnu tribes that became a powerful force in the lands north of the Great Wall.*

Yellow Turbans – *a 'common army' that earned their name from the yellow scarves that they used to cover their hair. They were mostly made up of peasants that were tired of heavy taxation and poor treatment by the state. The founder was a Taoist cultist, Zhang Jue. The rebellion was eventually crushed by a combination of government forces and local militias, but they reappeared many times over the next decade before they were finally suppressed by the Han government.*

Nan(man) [Narn(-marn)] – *a southern, non-Chinese race, broken down further into tribes; they were indigenous to Nanzhong, which once included Yi Province until the Han Chinese expanded into their territory. They play no role in this book, but they are mentioned by Lu Su and Zhou Yu.*

＊＊＊＊＊＊＊＊＊＊＊＊